Palm South
UNIVERSITY

BOOKS 1-7

Palm South UNIVERSITY

BOOKS 1-7

Kandi Steiner

Table of CONTENTS

Published by Kandi Steiner
Cover Design by Alli, https://www.instagram.com/artsiidaisy/
Formatting by Elaine York/Allusion Publishing, www.allusionpublishing.com

Palm South
UNIVERSITY

RUSH

BOOK 1

EPISODE 1

Welcome to PALM SOUTH

Cassie

Palm South University. A small, private college tucked away in a shady haven right near the beach just south of Miami. When Mom and I took the tour around campus, I knew without a doubt this is where I wanted to be. The longboarding opportunities alone made me giddy, and the Bio-Med program sealed the deal. But now, standing next to my high school best friend staring up at a large house with Greek letters that mean absolutely nothing to me, I'm wondering if this was the right choice.

This campus is crawling with walking, talking Barbies.

"Are you sure we should do this?" I ask Paris, twirling a strand of my fiery red hair around my finger as she runs a small brush through hers. It isn't even noon yet and we've already been getting curious looks from the other new members in our breakout group. Redheads are like unicorns, and seeing two of them attached at the hip like Paris and I are is always a mystical sight to anyone who's not us. We've spent the past four years in high school trying to convince people that no, we aren't sisters, and I had a feeling we'd be having that same conversation here. At this point, it might be easier to just nod and go along with it.

"Um, duh," Paris says, rolling her eyes. "Why else did we come to college if not to live it up in a sorority? Hello," she draws out the word and starts counting on her fingers. "Parties, boys, lavish events, boys, study groups, boys. Need I say more?" She pulls her long red locks over one shoulder, showing off her delicate collar bone. She's always been extravagant, which aligns with her name perfectly. Her parents must have known what they were doing when they named their baby girl after the most fashion-savvy city in the world. Even now while most of the girls are in shorts and nice shirts trying to beat the Florida heat, she's in a designer sun dress that's only knee-length but I know is heavy enough to make her sweat. Yet somehow, she's not.

I laugh at her comment, but shift uneasily. I was excited to rush, but judging by the girls we've met so far, I'm not sure the sorority life is for me. We've already visited the Zeta Pi Alphas and Delta Beta Gammas. To be honest, I can't really recall anything specific about either because they were so much alike that they're blurred together in my brain. Both of them were stocked with beautiful blondes and brunettes with exactly the same body build and no interest whatsoever in anything that doesn't involve booze or boys. And don't get me wrong – I like both – but college is more than just parties and dates to me. I'm going to be a doctor, and this is where my journey starts.

I open my mouth to voice my uncertainty, but before I have the chance I'm cut off by our group leader clapping her hands together.

"Okay!" she squeaks, her rosy cheeks and big green eyes bouncing along with the dark chocolate curls in her hair. "Kappa Kappa Beta is almost ready for us. After this, we'll take a lunch break and meet up with the other new members before visiting the last two houses this afternoon. Any questions so far?" Silence. "Are you enjoying Spirit Day?!" Cheers. From everyone but me, that is. I just tuck my hair behind my ear.

Just as the screams die down, a cheer erupts from inside the house. All the potential new members, sans me, cheer back. After a few rounds of the cheering back and forth, a tall, long-legged girl steps outside. She's beautiful – smooth, creamy skin and exotic features, almost like she stepped out of a tequila ad. Her smile reveals perfect teeth as she clasps her hands in front of her hips.

"Good afternoon, ladies," she says, her voice polished and polite. "My name is Siomara and I'm the president of KKB. I know you've already been to two other houses today and you're probably feeling pretty overwhelmed." Some girls nod and Siomara smiles in return. "I hope you can relax a bit with us before lunch and just enjoy the conversation. Each of you is different. I know some of you will end up running home to other houses on this block, but some of you will soon be my sister. Regardless of which side of the coin you land on, I'm looking forward to getting to know you. And," she adds, smiling wider. "I have forty-two other sisters who feel the same."

Siomara steps to the side as the double doors open and reveal a group of equally beautiful girls dressed in various shades of teal and orange, Palm South's school colors. Every girl is smiling, cheering, and clapping along with an upbeat pop song as we walk through the doors. A perky blonde steps up to me as I enter, smiling as she laces her arm around mine and leads me through the house to a room that I assume is normally a family room. There's a large flat screen TV on the wall opposite a beige leather sectional and photos hung up all around the room. They're all of sisters in various settings ranging from community events to the beach. The first thing I notice is that the girls in the photos all look different from one another – a stark contrast to the girls in the other houses we've been to this morning. It's refreshing, and I feel myself relax a bit as the bouncy blonde guides me to have a seat at one end of the sectional.

"Hi," she says loudly, trying to speak over the rest of the noise as she takes the seat next to me. With their forty-two sisters and the twenty-seven girls in my potential new member group shoved in one house trying to speak to each other, it's a little loud, to say the least. "My name's Erin Xander." She holds out her hand and I take it in mine, shaking it firmly but not too hard.

"Cassie McBee."

"Pretty name!" She smiles wider. She has a classic face – rounded, but with well-defined cheek bones. Her large mocha eyes shine and I feel like I've known her forever even though we just met. "Welcome to the KKB house. How has your morning been so far?"

Erin seems friendly, but I know any minute now the shoe will drop and she'll start talking my ear off about things that probably don't matter to me. "Not too bad, I guess."

She frowns a little. "Well, hopefully by the time you leave here you'll have a different answer to that question." She crosses her legs, leaning in. "So, tell me a little about yourself, Cassie."

Wow. This is the first girl who's asked about me instead of just rambling on about how great her sorority is. "Well," I cross my legs to mimic hers. "I'm from Phoenix, I just moved here two days ago with my best friend, Paris." I point to Paris across the room.

Erin follows my finger and then turns back, smile still in place. "Awesome! It must be so fun rushing with your best friend."

"Yeah," I nod. "It really is. Although, she's a lot better at this than I am."

Erin cocks her head a little. "What do you mean by that?"

"I don't know, she's just more into the sorority stuff than I am, I guess. All the girls have loved her so far."

"Well," Erin says, leaning back a little. "It may just be that you two are growing up a little already, and maybe not in the same direction. Would you be okay if you ended up in a different sorority than she does?"

That thought makes my stomach lurch. "I don't know. We moved here together, we're rooming together , we're best friends – it only makes sense that we'd be in the same sorority."

Erin nods. "Yeah, it might make sense now, but don't let her make this decision for you. It's true what they say, you know." She pauses. "You end up where you belong. So, follow your heart and don't worry about what Paris is doing. If she's your best friend now, she'll still be your best friend after rush week – no matter where you end up." She smiles and I return the gesture, hoping like hell that she's right. "So anyway, what's your major?"

I cringe. "Um, Biology. I want to go pre-med."

Her eyes grow wide and I wait for it, I wait for the loss of interest, the *"Oh no, she's not here to party? That simply won't do."*

"That is amazing!" I blanch, but her smile remains intact. "I'm hoping to go to law school when I finish here at Palm South. We can be study buddies together!" She giggles and I can't help but join her, the shock dissipating. “Oh!” she claps her hands together. “You have to meet my two best friends. You'll love them. Come on.”

Erin grabs my hand and pulls me through the house, weaving between groups of girls until we reach a large kitchen, complete with granite countertops that remind me of home.

“Jess! Lei!” Erin drops my hand as we reach two other beautiful blondes. Uh oh, here we go. Here comes the we-all-look-alike-and-like-the-same-things. “Meet Cassie. She just moved here from Arizona and she's a Bio major.”

“I'm Ashlei,” one of them says, reaching her hand out for mine. She's slightly shorter than Erin and Jess, but I can tell just from the dress she's wearing that she must be really into fitness. Her legs are toned, her arms cut – she's gorgeous, but I can tell she works hard for it. “My grandma lives in Arizona. I love it there! Looks like you won't have to worry about giving up the weather. It's hot here, too.” She winks.

“Yeah, but no one told me about this humidity.” I point to my hair, which was frizzing out before I even left the apartment this morning. I'm sure it's a complete mess by now.

Jess extends her hand to me next. “Girl, that's one of the biggest problems living in Florida. Don't worry, we all go through it.” She grins, running her fingers through her long, pin-straight blonde hair. Hers is a little darker than Ashlei's and Erin's is the darkest, but they're all blonde bombshells. I can imagine them turning heads when they go out in public together. “So what are your hobbies, Cassie?”

Again, not one of them has told me anything about the sorority. It sounds odd, but I actually love it. It's nice to know they're interested in me as a person, not just in selling themselves. “I'm really into school,” I offer kind of sheepishly. “As nerdy as that sounds. And I longboard, so I'm looking forward to coasting around this campus.”

“I just started longboarding!” Jess yells excitedly. “You'll have to help me when classes start. I'm a complete mess, but I really liked it.”

“Yeah, it's not as easy as it looks, but it's definitely not as bad as skateboarding. I'll help you!” The loud music starts playing again, signaling that our time in the house is up. Even though I know I could potentially be back tomorrow, I'm kind of disappointed it's over already.

“Oh!” Erin laces her arm through mine again. “Looks like it's that time. Let's head toward the front so you don't get in trouble for being in here too long.” She winks and I wave to the other girls as we start for the door. Just before we reach the foyer, Siomara waves to us.

“Thanks for visiting us today!”

I wave in return and Erin leans in to yell over the music, “That's my Grand Big Sister. Basically, she's my Big's Big.” She chuckles at my confused expression. “Don't worry, you'll catch on. Anyway, she's brilliant. I'll have to introduce you next time!”

I smile, hoping there will be a next time. After the day is over, the sororities select who they want to come back another day as do the potential new members. It's all a secret, how the selection process works, but I know there's a chance I could get my list of houses to visit tomorrow and Kappa Kappa Beta could not be on it. “I would love that.”

Erin offers me one last smile and a slight wave as we reach the door and I file back out into the suffocating August heat. South Florida is beautiful, there's no denying that, but it. Is. Hot.

I shield my eyes and make my way back to Paris. I'm so excited to tell her about my conversation with Erin, but before I can open my mouth she rolls her eyes and cuts me short. “Thank God that's over,” she mumbles. “Those girls were so boring. And did you see their house? Not even half the size of the Zeta house. Yawn.”

I frown, my mouth pulling to one side. Since when does Paris care about the size of a house? “I thought they were cool,” I say softly. “Nice. Different.”

“I guess,” she says, sighing a little, like she's too bored to argue. “Anyway, I'm excited for the Tri Phis after lunch. They have a swimming pool!” She jumps excitedly and we fall in line behind the rest of the girls marching towards the cafeteria. As we walk, I can't help but think back to what Erin had said about us maybe ending up in different places at the end of this week. My heart aches at the thought and I wonder if I'll even have the strength to write down a different choice than Paris when the time comes.

She smiles over at me and nudges me playfully and I smile back. College is about change, my parents have always told me. My sister said the same thing when she gave me my graduation gift.

It's about growing, finding who you are and who you're not. It's about daring to live differently than you ever have before.

I wonder if part of that means friendships change, too.

Bear

"Please promise me you'll have beer available when this week is over," Skyler whines into the phone and I chuckle, dropping the Xbox controller and moving back through the Omega Chi Beta house toward my room. It's the week before classes start, but already the house is filling up with brothers. It's loud as fuck and no matter how clean our housekeeper kept it over summer, we've somehow already found a way to make it dirty and smelly in here.

"Well hi to you, too."

"I'm serious," she says, but laughs a little this time. "I need alcohol. And also to not wear high heels for like, a year."

I close my bedroom door and fall back on the small bed, staring up at the ceiling. "You know we always have a rager on Bid Day. Too much freshman tail to pass up that opportunity."

"If I were there, I'd smack you."

"Whatever. You know your sisters do the same when we have rush week in the spring."

"Can't argue that," she says, sighing in defeat.

"How was the rest of your summer?"

"Busy. I had a tournament practically every week. It's weird," she adds, pausing. "People are starting to notice me. Like, they know who I am when I enter tournaments and stuff."

I lift my brows. "Yeah? That's awesome, Sky." Skyler Thorne is a sophomore, a year younger than me, but she's one of my best friends. We met last year on the annual Kappa Kappa Beta and Omega Chi Beta spring break trip and I recognized her from a poker tournament I watched on TV a few weeks before that. She was shocked that I realized who she was, but I follow poker pretty closely. Well, I follow *all* sports pretty closely. We started hanging out more and more after break and over summer until I went home to visit before the school year started. My face hardens at the thought of home, but I shake it off and focus on Skyler. "You know it's only going to get worse. You're too good not to get noticed, Sky. You're a winner. Winners don't get to stay in the background for long."

"Yeah, well, if I ever get that good, I'll have to enter tournaments with bigger prizes. I had to work all summer to pay for this year and I still couldn't give as much to my family as I wanted to. But I'm not ready for the big tournaments yet."

"Why do you say that? You know you could win them. You're skilled, Skyler. You know your shit."

"I'm not that good, Bear." She sighs. "I still have a lot to learn before I belly up to play with the big boys."

I shake my head. "Whatever you say. You know I'm in your corner when you do decide to go pro."

"I know, and you know I love ya for it." I hear a loud voice yell in the background and Skyler huffs. "Gotta go, practice time. Apparently we aren't cheering loud enough."

I bark out a loud laugh. "Good luck with that. I'm going to go drink a beer."

"Hate you."

"Love you, too."

I go to end the call, but just as I'm about to push the large red button, my Mom's face pops up on the screen. I frown, but click the button to end the call with Skyler and answer hers.

"Hey, Mom."

"Clinton Pennington, why haven't you answered my phone calls? I've called at least ten times since you left last Saturday!"

I groan inwardly at the use of my full name. No one at Palm South has called me Clinton since my freshman year. I gained the nickname Bear after flag football season due to my tall, fit build and aggressive technique – in other words, I tackled people a lot. Skyler always says I'm more like a teddy bear, but that's really only with her. I don't show my soft side to many people.

"Because I'm busy. Why? You all out of drug money? Need me to break into my savings and send you more?"

"Don't get smart with me, young man. I'll drive down there and slap your ass so hard my grand-kids will feel it."

I sigh. "What do you want, Mom?"

"I wanted to check in and see how my son was doing, but apparently there's a crime against that in your book."

"I'm fine. Class starts next week. How are you?" I say the words flatly, not hiding the lack of respect I have for her. I know I shouldn't talk to her the way that I do – or at least, if she were a normal mother, I shouldn't – but she never earned the respect she demanded from me. And I'm finally getting to the point where I'm tired of giving it for no reason. I love the woman, I do – but I have no respect for someone who uses and abuses everyone in their life the way she does.

"Well that's good, sweetie," she says, her voice softening. "I miss you. Wish you would have just stayed up here for school." She pauses, waiting for me to say something but I don't. "Anyway, your brother is bringing the kids out this weekend. I'm sure he'll want to call and talk to you."

"Can't wait."

She huffs, but doesn't press me on it. My older brother and I are far from close and she knows it. The only person in that whole family who I genuinely care about is Clayton, my baby brother. He's only twelve, but already he's being exposed to the things I had to fight to get away from in Pittsburgh. He's the only reason I even visit during breaks. I'm the only positive role model he has, and I have every intention of reminding him what he can accomplish if he gets out of that house.

"Well I guess I'll talk to you then. Have a good night, Clinton."

"You too."

I end the call and toss my phone to the other end of the bed, letting out a long exhale. I don't have the chance to think about my fucked up family long before I hear my brothers yelling for me from the living room. I smile, leaving my phone and heading back toward the group.

I fall down in a large bean bag as my Little, Josh, hands me a cold Bud Light. I pop the top and throw it back, letting the sting of the ice cold liquid burn away the phone call with my mom. Looking around, I can't help but feel excited about the new school year. I'm a junior now and our fraternity is the top on campus. We're going to have a fucking blast this semester and I'm anxious to get started.

Thank God I have my fraternity brothers.

Real families are a disappointment.

I know Siomara will have my ass if she finds out I snuck out to go to a bar tonight, but I'll take my chances. I'm going stir crazy being stuck in that house with all forty-one of my sisters. I love them, don't get me wrong, but damn – a girl needs a break.

And a penis.

Just saying.

I'm all about sisterhood and I truly do care about the new girls coming into our organization this year, but tomorrow is a late day – we don't have to be at the sorority house until eleven – so tonight, I'm getting drunk.

And hopefully laid.

I pull into a small beach bar and check my makeup once more before strolling inside. It's casual, not too many people, but it's a slightly older crowd which is exactly what I want. Fraternity boys are immature and stupid and I'm over their shit. I've spent the last two years wrapped up in their drama and I know that other than fulfilling my desire to not want to masturbate, they're not good for much. This bar is crawling with men in their mid to upper twenties – dress shirts, ties hanging loose around their necks – they're looking for a good time and I'm about to deliver them one on a silver platter.

My phone pings with another warning text from my Big Sister, Stacy. I sigh and type out a quick *don't worry, Mom* text to her before tucking my phone away again. Stacy and I are really close, but she graduated early last spring. Even though she continues to Mom me even after she graduated, she's still a bad ass mentor and one of the closest friends I have. I just wish I could say the same about my Little.

But that's a worry for another time.

Sauntering up to the bar, I take a seat on a bar stool facing the majority of the bar and scope out the possibilities. The bar is half inside, half outside and the breeze rolling in from the beach blows my long blonde hair out of my face, allowing me full view of the prospects. Just as I'm zeroing in on a group of guys at the pool table, the bartender strolls up to me and throws a small white towel over his shoulder, placing both hands on the bar in front of me before leaning over a bit. "What's your poison tonight, princess?"

I wrinkle my nose and pull my attention from the pool table to stare up at the man the voice came from. Instantly, the wrinkles leave and I swallow. Holy hell, this guy is hot. And he's bald? I have never in my life found a man without hair even slightly attractive. I guess there's a first time for everything, right? My eyes fall slowly down his body, lingering on the muscles in his chest stretching against the dark red fabric of his work t-shirt. His tan skin is covered in tattoos, though I can't quite make them out in the dim lighting of the bar. My lips part slightly as my eyes drift back up to his face. He cocks a brow in amusement and I swallow again, sitting up straighter.

"Really? *What's your poison?* Could you be any more cliché?"

His other brow shoots up to join the first and his head cocks back, as if my words smacked him across that beautiful, chiseled jaw of his. "Wow. My bad. Is *what can I get you* any better?"

"Same thing, pretty much. But, regardless of how predictably you ask me, I'm still going to want the tallest glass you have filled to the top with a fruity rum and juice. You figure out the rest. Just make it strong."

He smirks, pushing off the bar and reaching down for a large glass. "Well okay then. You on vacation?"

"I wish. But, I can still drink like I'm on vacation, right?" I give him a wink and he smiles, shaking his head a bit.

"I'm Jarrett." He slides me my drink and I tilt it to him in a *cheers* before taking the first sip. It's strong. And delicious.

Score.

"Jess. And this is scrumptious."

He chuckles. "Glad I could brew up your poison, princess." I glare at him, but he just winks and walks to the other end of the bar.

After I finish my first drink and order another, I wander up to the group of guys at the pool table. We play for a little over an hour, drawing an even larger crowd because – clearly – we're the most fun this joint has seen in a while. I'm cozied up and working on one of the hottest guys in the group when he informs me he has a fiancé.

Wow.

Buzz Killington, ladies and gentlemen.

I hang out with the group a little longer, hoping to move on to a new prospect, but they all head out before I have a chance to seal the deal with any of Mr. I'm-Engaged-But-You-Don't-Need-To-Know-That-Until-It's-Clear-You-Expect-To-Sleep-With-Me's friends. Sighing, I take my place in the same barstool as before and Jarrett slides a fifth drink my way.

I hold up my hands. "I should probably say no this time. It's almost closing time and I need to drive."

"Not necessarily," he offers. I eye him curiously and the corner of his mouth pulls up mischievously. He finishes wiping down a glass and hangs it above his head before leaning across the bar, his minty breath tickling my drunken senses. "You've been trying all night to get with that douchebag when I could have told you from the beginning that he wasn't available. And now, you're left with an ache between your legs that you don't want to take care of on your own. So yes, you could drive home, get up and go to work tomorrow and just try again another night. Or," he pauses, licking his bottom lip and dragging his teeth across the top as his eyes fall to my mouth. "You could give me your keys, jump in my truck, and let me take you back to my place so I can cure you of your current situation."

Oh hell to the fucking yes.

Keeping my eyes locked on his, I fish my keys from my purse and drop them on the counter, cocking a brow. Jarrett bites his lip as he grabs the keys and shoves them in his pocket.

"Give me five."

Four and a half minutes later, we're tangled up in the back seat of his truck. I run my hands down his incredibly cut abdomen and lift his shirt up and over his head as he pulls the straps of my dress down over my shoulders. His lips are hard on mine and his hands run the length of my body until they grip my hips so hard I'm not sure if I should cry out in pain or pleasure.

"Are you sure you don't want to go back to my place?" he pants, kissing down my neck. My eyes roll back and a moan escapes my lips.

"I think I'd rather see how all that talk holds up in the back of a truck."

Jarrett growls against my neck before biting down and lifting me from his lap. It's then I realize he's wearing dark gray board shorts. He quickly unties them and pulls them to his knees, followed by his boxers. And there he is in all his thick, perfect glory. I bite my lip and stare up into his dark eyes. They're hooded with desire and I feel the want spread through my entire body as he grips my hips again and lifts me up from the seat, rotating me to face away from him. His rough hands slide my dress up and over my thighs and ass, exposing me to the heat radiating from his body behind mine. There's a rip of a condom wrapper and seconds later, Jarrett leans flush against me and grips my hair in one hand, pulling my head back so he can whisper in my ear.

"Is this what you want, Jess?" He thrusts against me and I feel his hard cock against the curve of my ass. I inhale deep, need coursing through every vein.

"Yes," I breathe, biting my lip in ecstasy.

"Then take it," he hisses into my ear, running his tongue up my neck before sucking my lobe in his mouth. The feel of him against me combined with his breath hot in my ear evokes a loud moan from my throat. "Take my cock inside you."

He pulls my hair harder and I groan, maneuvering my body until I feel him at my entrance. Slowly, I push back against him and feel as every inch of him sinks deep inside me. I don't even try to be quiet anymore. Loud moans and screams rip through me as he moves his other hand up to grip my hair, too, pulling it back each time he pounds into me. He fills me over and over, our hot breath steaming up the windows in his Ford truck.

I push my hand against the back passenger window and it slips down, leaving my fingerprints marked on the glass. "Harder," I moan and Jarrett delivers, hammering into me with more force before smacking my ass. It stings, but I can't deny that I love it. I've never been spanked before, but now I'm tempted to beg for it again.

"Oh," I cry out and he runs his hands back up into my hair before trailing them down my back and over my ass. He holds me firmly in his grip before rearing back and smacking my skin again, this time with enough force to send me spiraling over the edge of desire. I climax hard, maybe harder than I ever have before and Jarrett quickens his pace before driving into me with slow, hard precision. I ride out my orgasm like a California wave, completely spent by the time it crashes on the shore.

But Jarrett isn't done.

Quickly, he flips me over to straddle him. My legs are Jell-O, I have no idea how I'm going to ride him after what he just did to me, but he pulls my legs up to prop my feet on the seat and then leans my back against the console, lifting his hips to meet mine. In this position he feels even bigger than before and he hits places I never even knew existed.

Jarrett slowly drags the palm of his hand through my hair and then over my face, the pad of his thumb catching my bottom lip before he trails it down my neck, my chest, my abdomen, and rests it between my hips. His thumb finds my clit and he begins a torturous circle against the already tender spot. I arch my back in response and he groans, plowing into me with the same rhythm.

"You didn't wait for me last time. That's fine. But you're going to come again. *With me*, this time." I moan as he pumps harder, his breath growing shallow. Just as his body starts to shake inside mine, I reach another climax and tremble with him, our bodies moving together in a sweet and passionate harmony as we cry out into the foggy air of the truck. Every touch is amplified and I feel every last thrust. When we finally slow to a stop, Jarrett remains inside me, the sweat from our efforts making our bodies stick together in every place our skin touches. I'm not complaining.

He pulls me forward slowly, my back aching from being pushed back against the console. Licking his lips, he brings my mouth to his and kisses me hard, branding me with a passion I've never experienced. And I don't care what time it is or how much sleep I lost by sneaking out to this hole in the wall beach bar tonight. I'd do it all again. This is the best sex I've had in a long, long time.

And I can't wait for round two.

Bear

I'm drunk. And it's hot as balls in South Florida. Therefore, I'm also sweating. But I don't give a shit because I'm drunk.

Almost all my brothers are back on campus now. It's the night before sorority Bid Day and we know we'll be raging all day and night tomorrow, but that didn't stop us from getting a head start tonight. My Little, Josh, is currently doing a keg stand that I know will land him on his ass but I can't help but hoot in encouragement.

"You better not let me down, Little Bro! I'll kick your ass!" I smack him hard on the back and he sputters a bit, but keeps going. Josh is kind of a douche. Okay, he's a really, *really* big douche. But I'm doing my best to mentor him into being a half-decent guy. I'll never understand his obsession with fake tanning, but no one can keep up with me in the gym like he can and I respect him for that. I wanted him to be my Little from the start of his rushing process last spring. A Little is someone you can bond with, but more importantly someone you can guide. Although, I'm not sure I'm much of a mentor.

Suddenly, I'm picked up on a few of my brothers' shoulders and carried to the other keg. I grab it with my hands just in time to avoid smacking my chin against the metal and my legs are lifted up into the air. Then the nozzle is in my mouth and I have a two second warning before the beer starts flowing.

Challenge accepted.

After forty-seven seconds counted out loud, I kick my feet a little and they drop me to the floor with a roar of approval. I almost spit out the last swig of beer when the room settles and I'm face to face with Skyler.

"Not bad, Bear." She grins. "Although I'm pretty sure you've done better."

I shake my head. "How the hell are you here right now? Tomorrow's Bid Day."

"What Siomara doesn't know won't hurt her. I figured I could trust you and your brothers to keep it quiet."

I frown, unsure if I trust them as much as she does. I scan the room for our president and drag Skyler with me when I finally find him. After whispering the situation in his ear, Matt whistles loud enough to quiet the entire house.

"Listen up!" he shouts above the music. "See this girl right here?" He gestures to Skyler and her face flushes a bit, but she stands straighter and gives a wink. Always so sassy, that one. "No, you don't. You don't see her at all. She isn't here. She never was. Got it?" There's a cheer of understanding and Matt nods once. "Carry on."

He smiles back at us and throws his arms around Skyler's shoulder. "There. Problem solved. If anyone finds out you were here, let me know and I'll haze the shit out of these fuckers. I don't care if they are brothers."

Skyler giggles a little. "Why thank you. And what do I have to do to pay off that favor?" She quirks a brow and tilts her head a little.

A sly grin creeps over Matt's face. "I can probably think of a few things."

"Alright," I throw my hands up and back away from them. "I'm leaving the two of you to settle your debts. Find me when you're ready for shots, Sky."

She gives me a wink and Matt's eyes scan the length of her toned body in the tiny shorts she's paired with a loose t-shirt. I know without a doubt that she dressed herself tonight. Usually, her sisters were dressing her up – *sororitizing* her or whatever. She's far from a dress and pearls type of girl. But tonight, in her natural form, I think she's prettier than she ever is when they doll her up in all that makeup and shit.

I get asked all the time if I'm into Skyler. Some of my brothers have steered clear of her even after I assure them we're just friends. For a while, I wondered if maybe there was something between us that we just weren't seeing – something we were giving off that made other people look at us the way they did. But, at the end of the day, Skyler is more like the baby sister I never had than anything else. I just care about her. And, surprisingly, she cares about me.

Plus, that girl can play some poker. And that is something I'll always respect.

"I'm sloshed." Josh grins and lifts the red plastic cup in his hand to his mouth once more. "What's up with Skyler being here?"

"She snuck out. Keep your mouth shut about it, Little. I mean it."

"I'm not saying anything," he says, his hands up in mock surrender. "She single?"

I nod toward her and Matt, who are now cozied up on the back couch, her legs in his lap and his fingers playing in her hair as they talk over their drinks. "Technically, yes. Not sure if that's going to matter much tonight, though. Matt moved in right after his little announcement."

Josh's shoulders deflate. "I want to bang her so fucking bad, dude."

I smack him hard across the back of his head and he curses, spilling some of his beer. "The fuck, man?"

"You know better than to talk about her like that around me. Show some fucking respect, douchebag, before I make you."

"Whatever," he mumbles, still rubbing his head as he stumbles off toward the beer pong tables.

My phone vibrates in my pocket and I pull it out to yet another call from my older brother. Great.

He's been calling me all day, but until now I hadn't been drunk enough to answer. I almost always have to be intoxicated to deal with his shit. Who knows what kind of state he'll be in tonight.

"Hey," I answer simply, maneuvering through the house to find a semi-quiet spot. I settle on the back hallway that leads to the bathrooms.

"'Bout fucking time you answered your phone. What the hell are you doing?" His voice is high-pitched and springy and I know without even asking that he's high off pills.

Doubly great.

"I'm partying. Sounds like that makes two of us tonight."

There's a grunt on the other end. "You implying that I'm high, little bro?"

"Depends. Are you?"

He pauses, then sighs. "Listen, I didn't call to fight with you. I need your help."

Here we go.

"Let me guess, you need money?"

Another pause.

"The fuel pump went out on the car and I had to use the last of my check to pay for it to get fixed. I found a guy to do it for less than the shop was asking, but it still wasn't cheap. And now the boys don't have food." His voice trembles just a little when he says that last part, but I'm not sure if it's because of his high or the content he's spewing. "I just need a little bit, Clinton. A hundred bucks for gas and food. Please."

I curse under my breath and glance across the room where Skyler is watching me intently, her brows furrowed. "You can't keep doing this shit, Carleton."

"What shit? It's not my fault the fucking car went to shit." I wait for him to just admit the truth, but instead he grows more frustrated. "You know what? Whatever. My bad for thinking you would want to help your fucking nephews."

"Stop." I sigh, pinching the bridge of my nose. It's not even worth arguing with him over where his money really went. Regardless, his sons don't deserve to starve because of their father's piss poor decisions. "Give me twenty minutes to get to the store. I'll wire you what I can."

"Thank you, little brother. I love you. I'm so proud of you, you know."

I roll my eyes as he continues, his words falling on deaf ears. When I'm sending money, I'm a great little brother chasing my dreams in college. When I'm not sending money, I'm a stuck up brat who thinks I'm better than everyone else.

I startle a bit when Skyler's hand touches my arm. I lift my eyes to hers and when I see the worry in them, my face hardens. The last thing I need is anyone at Palm South knowing about my fucking family drama.

"Yeah. I'll call you with the confirmation number." I hang up before he has the chance to respond. Skyler is still staring at me, her hand gentle on my forearm. I think I'm shaking, but I can't tell.

"Bear, what's going on?"

For a moment I just stare at her. I blink. I breathe. Then I shrug her off and turn for my room. "Nothing. I have to run an errand. Don't stay out too late, you know Siomara will throw a fit."

She chases after me. "Wait. What happened? Where are you going?"

I whip around too quickly to face her and her eyes grow wide. Sighing, I run a hand over my short, coarse hair and calm myself. "I just have to handle something, Sky. I'm fine, I promise. Just go back to Matt and have a good time tonight. I'll see you at the Bid Day Bash tomorrow. Cool?"

Skyler hesitates, chewing the inside of her cheek, but finally nods with a small smile. I try to return it, but it dies halfway and I turn back toward my room instead.

She doesn't follow this time.

Cassie

The night air is still hot and sticky as I sit on one of the benches facing the campus fountain. I stare at the blank card in my hand with three lines that I've yet to fill. I'm supposed to pick my top three choices for the sorority I'll be in for the next four years of my life and hope that one of them chooses me back. Most of the girls in my small group filled theirs out right away.

Paris was one of them.

She told me last night that she was choosing Zeta Pi Alpha. "Suiciding" them is specifically how she put it, which means she only wrote them down on her sheet – not even allowing for a second or third option. If they don't choose her back, she won't have a home to run to tomorrow.

Which is kind of where I am right now. Without a home.

My group leader told me I could walk campus if I wanted to. To "clear my head". So here I am, staring at the way the light jumps off the water of the fountain each time it spews into the air and wishing it could somehow spout up the answer to what decision I should make.

There are a few houses that I actually like. Delta Beta Gamma has grown on me throughout the week and the Kappa Kappa Beta girls were super nice. But Paris went Zeta. And she expects me to do the same. Meanwhile I can't help but wonder if I should write down any of them at all.

"I love this pond at night."

I startle at the interruption of my thoughts just as a slender brunette plops down on the bench next to me. Her long, loosely curled hair falls over her shoulder slightly as she turns to me with wide blue eyes. They're slightly glazed, like she may be buzzed, but her smile is genuine and warm. "It's a great place to think."

I hold up the card in my hand slightly. "Well, I could use all the thinking power this pond can offer."

She glances at the card. "Ah, rushing a sorority?"

"At this point, I'm not sure."

"Well what are you thinking? Talk it out to a stranger. Might help." She smiles again and for reasons unknown to me, I feel like I can trust her. At the very least, I don't know her, which means she can't really judge me. And if she does, it doesn't really matter, I guess.

"I'm thinking that I'm not sure any of these places are for me. My best friend from high school is going Zeta but I know *for sure* that I don't fit in there. I'm worried about going somewhere else. We did this together. We were supposed to end up in the same house and have the next four years just like we had the last."

The girl thinks for a moment, her hair blowing in the breeze slightly. "Just because you don't rush the same sorority doesn't mean you can't still be great friends. You'll just have her plus your sisters. It doesn't have to be one or the other," she offers. "You said before you weren't sure any of the sororities were for you. You really think that?"

I sigh. "I don't know. There is one house that I really liked. All the girls seemed nice and actually interested in me as a person. But even still, I'm not sure I want to be Greek. I only did this because of my best friend."

She smirks, but pauses a second, as if she's looking for the right words. "You know, I felt the same way you did when I rushed." My eyes grow wide. I didn't think she was a sorority girl. "I came from a small town and, well, let's just say my life there was a lot different than I wanted it to be." She shrugs. "But here, I knew I could be anyone. On the last night of rush when I had to make my choice, a girl in the last house I visited told me that the best part of being in a sorority is always knowing you have a group of sisters who have your back no matter what. Through the good times and the bad, you've got someone there to fight through college with you. To me, that was the best thing someone could promise me." She nudges me lightly. "What about you? Do you want a group of friends who will be by your side for the next four years?"

I think about Paris and our group of friends back home. They were my sisters then, but already I can feel that bond breaking. Paris has changed so much just over the summer, I can't imagine what she'll be like over the next four years. I lift my head to meet the stranger girl's eyes and smile. "Yeah. Yeah, I really do."

"Well," she says, returning my smile and lifting herself from the bench. "Then think about who you've met this week and who you think would be great to have in your corner. I know you will fit in wherever you end up. And they'll be lucky to have you."

She turns to leave but I stop her. "Wait!" She's still smiling. "What sorority are you in?"

She laughs a little. "Well, I can't tell you, actually. That would be dirty rushing. But, just follow your heart. You'll end up where you belong." She adjusts her bag on her shoulder and my eyes fall to the embroidered letters on the side.

KKB.

I grin and look back up at her, but she never looks back as she retreats. And once again, it's just me, the fountain, and a decision waiting to be made.

But now, *finally*, I know how to make it.

***

They make us sit on our bids in the gym for ten minutes before we can open them and find out what sorority we're running home to. Our group leader is trying to talk to us and distract us from the wait, but I feel like this card is burning a hole into my shorts right now.

I suicided Kappa Kappa Beta last night and I have no idea what's about to happen.

"Can you believe it? We're going to be *sisters*!" Paris squeals, squeezing my arm and bouncing a little. I smile back at her nervously and watch the clock on the far wall. Time has never passed so slow.

"Alright, ladies," our leader says after an eternity. "Open your bids!"

The gym fills with a combination of rustling and envelope tearing followed by screaming, laughing, and crying. I slowly, calmly rip the top of my envelope and stare at the card when I pull it free. And then, I exhale.

Kappa Kappa Beta.

"AH! OH MY GOD OH MY GOD I'M FREAKING OUT!" Paris grabs my card and suddenly her smile fades. "Oh no..."

I'm still smiling. "No it's okay, Paris. It's what I wanted."

She screws her face up. "What? What do you mean, *it's what you wanted*? We were supposed to both go Zeta, Cass."

"I know, but I just don't fit in there, Paris. And that's okay. You do, and I know they're going to absolutely love you."

She shakes her head, but doesn't press me further. "Well, I'm sure you'll like KKB, I just really thought we were in this together." She hands my bid back. "I guess I'll see you at the dorm tonight?"

"Yeah, for sure." I pull her in for a hug, though she seems stiff. "I love you. Congratulations. We're sorority girls!"

That seems to bring back a little of her pep and she squeezes me tight before squealing again. "I know, right?!"

"Just wait a second, why is everyone celebrating?" our group leader interjects. "You're not home yet, ladies. Now... RUN!"

Everything turns to chaos. There are bags being tossed and girls tripping over their own feet as they clamor toward the doors and out onto the main campus road. I wait a little, but make sure I'm not last as we run toward Greek row.

Paris veers off at the Zeta house, looking back at me one last time with a sad smile. I blow her a kiss and keep running. Kappa Kappa Beta is the last house on the street. When I finally reach it, I'm completely out of breath. There are fraternity boys everywhere handing me flowers and teddy bears and giving me kisses on the cheek. I scour the crowd trying to figure out what to do next and notice all the KKB sisters are holding anchor-shaped signs with names on them. One of them says mine in all capital letters.

Making my way through the crowd, I smile when I see the hand attached to the sign. It's the girl from last night. Her long hair is pulled up into a high pony with strands falling around her face and her makeup is immaculately done. She looks so different from last night, but her smile is still the same.

"Looks like that pond has a little magic in it, after all," she says.

"Looks like it."

"I'm Skyler," she offers her hand. "Skyler Thorne."

I reach out to shake her hand but she pulls me in for a gripping hug, instead. When we pull back, I say what I wanted to say last night but forgot. "Thank you."

She winks. "We're just getting started."

Skyler takes me around the yard and inside the house, introducing me to other sisters and new members. We take so many pictures my face feels numb from smiling by the time we finish, but it's fun. Everyone is so welcoming.

"Okay, it's time to drink. Let's hit the back yard!" Jess, one of the girls I met earlier this week, pops up beside Skyler, waggling her eyebrows.

"No arguments here. What do you say, Cassie?" Skyler asks.

And at first, I'm not sure what to say. This week has been all about figuring out where I belong. But now, the decision has been made and school doesn't start until Monday.

I think it's time to enjoy myself.

"Hell yeah!"

They both cheer and we make our way through the house and up to the rooms. Apparently they room together, because as soon as we walk into the large, two-bed room, they each cross to a different dresser and begin rummaging through it. Skyler tosses a skimpy bathing suit back to me.

"Here, I think this one should fit you. You can change in the bathroom right here." She points to an open door leading into a large, white-tiled bathroom and I can see another bedroom on through the opposite door. I duck in, change quickly, and meet them back in their room. They each have sundresses on, Skyler in a cute yellow maxi dress and Jess in a short red number with no straps.

Jess tosses me a cute lavender sundress and I pull it on over my suit. They both appraise me, smile, and then we head back downstairs and out to the back yard. When Jess swings the door open and gallivants off, I have a hard time closing my mouth.

The yard is covered with people – guys, girls – all in letters. There's a blow up slip-n-slide on one side of the yard and a pit full of bubbles in the other. A few people are already in their swim suits, either laying out in the yard or wandering around. More and more people join them as I stare.

"We kind of have to sneak the drinks," Skyler says, sliding me a flask and watching over my back for someone. Who, I'm not sure. "Technically we're not supposed to drink on KKB property."

"Really?" I take a swig from the flask and my face twists, but I stomach it. Rum.

She nods. "Yeah. The guys can drink all they want at the frat houses, but our council is pretty strict about not allowing sororities to drink in or around their houses. I guess it's unladylike or something." She shrugs, taking the flask from me and throwing it back. "Whatever. We have our ways." She grins just as someone bumps me from behind.

"Whoa!" I feel strong hands grip me around my middle and steady me. "Sorry about that." I turn to tell whoever it is that it's fine but when I come face to face with a lean, dark-haired guy with a heart-stopping smile, I forget how to speak. Or breathe. "You okay?"

I nod, which I'm surprised I can even remember how to do. He smiles wider, revealing perfect, blazing white teeth and one dimple on the left side of his beautiful face. His eyes are dark – almost as dark as his jet-black hair – and in nothing but floral-print board shorts and a white fraternity tank top, his lean muscles are on full display.

I swallow.

The guy's eyes move from me to Skyler and back again as he removes his hands. I feel a slight sting on my skin where he was touching me when he does. "I'm Adam Brooks, Alpha Sigma." He reaches his hand out to me first and I shake it numbly before he moves to Skyler. He eyes us both carefully, grin still intact.

"Skyler Thorne. And this is one of our new members, Cassie McBee."

"Nice to meet you both. Although we have a problem."

Skyler cocks a brow. "Oh?"

"Yeah. You see, you've got a flask. I've been here at least two minutes now and you have yet to offer me a drink."

Skyler giggles. "Why, whatever were we thinking, Cassie?"

I find my voice and try to keep up with the banter. "We're not being very ladylike, at all!" Taking the flask from Skyler, I hand it to Adam, shaking slightly and hoping he won't notice.

His grin intensifies and his eyes assess me, falling down my body slowly before meeting my eyes again. "I knew you two would be good hostesses." He tips the flask to us before downing back a shot. Then, he reaches behind him and grips his shirt just behind his neck, pulling it up and over his head. My eyes immediately fall to his chiseled abdomen and toned chest and my throat is dry again.

Holy hell.

"Are you a freshman, Cassie McBee?" he asks and again I can only nod in response. He chuckles, tossing me his shirt and tipping back the flask once more before handing it back to me. "Welcome to Palm South!"

He takes off running and dives headfirst down the inflatable slip-n-slide, leaving me holding fast to the cool metal of the flask and staring like an idiot. Slowly, I look over at Skyler, my mouth still wide. She laughs, shrugs, then pulls her sundress up and over her head, too.

"What he said." She grins and then takes off running in the same direction.

And I realize this is it. This is the first day of the next four years of my life. I'm here to get a degree, and that's more important to me than anything else. But at the same time, I'm here to have fun. And right now, standing in a yard full of shirtless fraternity boys and sisters who will be by my side through all the shit college will throw at me, I know without a doubt there will be no shortage of fun in my life.

This is Palm South. This is Kappa Kappa Beta.

And I am *so* excited for both.

EPISODE 2

"You look like you could USE A DISTRACTION."

Jess

The first week of class is my favorite. It's syllabus week, which means we only go over the hell we're about to endure instead of actually getting any of it assigned to us just yet. As I take a seat near the back of my last Wednesday class, Scope and Methods of Political Science, I chug down the rest of the iced coffee I picked up on the way over and sink down into the chair. I'm still hungover from post-rush weekend and I can't wait to get back to the sorority house. I need a freaking nap.

I'm one of the last ones in and less than a minute later, the professor claps her hands together. "Alright, let's get the logistics out of the way, shall we?" She's a middle-aged woman with dark brown hair and a smile too cheerful for me at the moment. She's dressed modestly in an all-navy dress suit and dark red lipstick covers her bird lips. Yep, definitely fits the part of a political science professor. "I'm Dr. Louise Maynard and hopefully you all already know that this is Scope and Methods. If you're here, I'm also safely assuming that you're Poli Sci majors. So, show of hands, how many of you are pre-law?"

I raise my hand along with a dozen others and we all look around the room at each other. If Erin were in this class, she would raise her hand, too. Of course, she already took this course last year when we were sophomores.

Show off.

"I see, I see," she appraises as our hands slowly fall back down. "Well great. As you know, this course is required for the major. Let's jump into what the semester will look like." She leans back against the desk and crosses her ankles, pulling the syllabus out from a notebook behind her. "My Graduate Assistant will be here soon to pass out your copies. Take notes until then."

She starts going over class policies and grading. I groan when she says attendance is required and worth ten percent of our grade. I hate classes that count attendance. I'm paying for this class. I should be able to decide if I want to attend or not. But whatever, I don't really have a say in it. My parents let me do whatever I want as long as I keep B's or better, so that's that. Looks like my Wednesday evenings will get off to a late start. This class is from 5:30 – 7:50p.m.

Dr. Maynard is just wrapping up the breakdown of test scores versus presentation scores when the large wooden doors open, causing her to pause. I'm still jotting down notes as she claps her hands together again. "Ah! There he is. Class, this is my GA. He'll be helping out throughout the semester with grading and tutoring along with various other tasks." I finish my notes and lift my eyes to the front. When I do, I drop my pencil along with my jaw. "Jarrett, would you like to introduce yourself to the class? Tell us a little about your graduate program and career goals?"

Jarrett, AKA the guy who had his hands weaved into my hair last week, is standing tall at the front of the room with Dr. Maynard. He's dressed in black slacks and a teal Palm South button up that accentuates his tan but covers the tattoos I know are lining his arms. Definitely a huge change from the boy in board shorts I jumped in the back of a pickup truck.

He casually runs a hand over his smooth head before tucking both hands in his pockets and appraising the room with a small grin and a glimmer in his dark eyes. "Hey everyone," he says, clearing his throat. *Is he nervous?* "I'm Jarrett Locke. I graduated with my undergrad from PSU last spring and decided to stick around for grad school. I have a particular interest in government relations for non-profits, so I hope to one day have a career where I can explore that passion daily." A few of the girls around me sigh and I fight against the urge to join them. Holy swoon. Please, someone wake me up. Someone tell me I don't want to bone my professor's graduate assistant.

Or that I already did.

"And I have nothing but faith that you will do just that," Dr. Maynard says, beaming at Jarrett. "Okay class, that's all for today. Jarrett's going to call attendance and then you're free to leave."

I repeatedly try to swallow as Jarrett goes down the list of names and one by one, students get up to leave. *Why did my German ancestors have to leave me with a name close to the end of the alphabet?*

"Jess Vonnegut," he says, my last name rolling off his lips slowly.

I stand and quickly throw my messenger bag over my shoulder. "Here," I chirp and bolt for the door. He checks me off and glances up quickly before his eyes fall back to the clipboard in his hand. When he realizes what he just saw, his eyes snap back up to mine.

Crap.

I cringe and try to duck away from his glare as I make my way up to the front of the room toward the door. It feels like it takes me ages to walk there, and his eyes never leave me. I feel them burning into my skin every step of the way. When I reach the front of the room and cross right in front of him, I chance meeting his gaze. And instantly regret it.

His eyes are smoldering, dark, hungry – and they automatically ignite the same animalistic fever he inflicted on me last week. I gulp and he closes his mouth, opens it again like he might say something, but then snaps it shut.

"Fuck," I mumble under my breath, pulling my eyes away and breaking through the door. I hold my breath until I reach the end of the hallway and burst out of the glass doors to the outside world. Panting, I pull out my phone and send a text to the girls.

- Emergency meeting. My room. Ten minutes. -

When I make it back to the sorority house, Erin, Ashlei, and Skyler are all waiting in mine and Skyler's room. "Oh my God," I say immediately, tossing my bag down on my bed. "You are never going to believe who the graduate assistant is in my Scope and Methods class."

"Oh! Are you taking Dr. Maynard?" Erin interjects. "I love her. Whoever her GA is, they're lucky. She's the best professor in the department."

"Yes, I am. And he may be lucky, Ex, but I'm definitely not."

Ashlei checks her phone for the second time since I've arrived. "Spill, Jess. You're not making sense."

"It's Jarrett." I wait, but they all just stare back at me so I sigh and toss my hands in the air. "The guy? From last week? Hot bartender, *super* hot truck?"

"Oh shit!" Skyler says at the same time Erin gasps, "No!" Ashlei just laughs. I toss a pillow and smack her square in the head with it.

"I'm sorry," she says through her laughter. "It's just, only you, Jess. Only you."

I groan, plopping my ass down on my bed and covering my face with my hands. "I know, right? Motherfucking fuck, dude. I really wanted to bang him again!" This time they all crack up and I toss pillows until I run out of ammo.

"Well, you win some you lose some, J-Love," Erin says, wiping a tear from the corner of her eye. I grin at the ironic use of my nickname. They gave that to me freshman year when I said I was "in love" with every single guy I dated. Luckily, heartbreak got me out of that phase. Now I just have fun with boys – and it's a lot less stressful that way.

"Shit," Ashlei murmurs, typing out a text on her phone before hopping off Skyler's bed. It's then that I realize she's got a gym bag packed and thrown over her shoulder. "I have to go. I'll see you later."

"Where are you going?" I ask, appraising the bag.

Her eyes dart around the room but she smiles confidently. "Just the gym. Then maybe out for a while."

"Hell yes, I could use a drink," I say. "Where you going? Ralph's?"

"Um." She hesitates, shifting. "I'm not sure yet. I'll text you after the gym. Love you!" Then she's gone.

Skyler and Erin eye me curiously. "Don't ask me, she's been weird since we got back. Did either of you talk to her over the summer?"

"I called and spoke to her a few times and we chatted on Facebook," Erin says, taking her spot on Skyler's bed. "But other than that, not really."

"Yeah, I saw her during Shark Week but that's it," Skyler adds. Since we're the Palm South Sharks, there are always huge parties and events during Shark Week on campus. I was on a cruise with my family this past summer and missed it.

"Hm..." I kick off my wedges and fall back against the cool sheets of my bed. "I don't know, maybe I'm thinking too much into it. She's probably just busy with the first week of classes. What are you two doing tonight?"

Skyler looks at Erin and they both shrug. "I was going to see if Cassie wants to hang out, but other than that, no plans," Skyler says.

"Girly movie night? I've got a bottle of wine stashed under my bed." I waggle my eyebrows.

"Done and done. I'm already stressed from classes this semester," Erin says. "I'm going to change into yoga pants. Be right back!" She trots out of the room just as Skyler types out a text on her phone.

"I invited Cassie," she says, dropping her phone to the bed. "I really think I want her as my Little, Jess. Do you like her?"

"Yeah, she's cool. But if you want her as your Little you better put in work. Jamie Dapreese has been hanging out with her a lot since Friday, too."

Her eyes widen. "Really?"

I nod, grabbing the remote to our TV off my bedside table and powering it on. "Yep. I saw them having lunch today between my two earlier classes."

"Well," Skyler replies, kicking back and letting her shoes fall to the floor, too. "I'm Skyler Fucking Thorne. I love Jamie, but she doesn't have shit on me. I'm going to show Cassie a kick ass time in the next few weeks and she'll realize our group is the best place to be in this sorority."

"Well, duh," Jess says, winking. "Just beware. You know Jamie, she likes to buy everything she wants – even if what she wants is a person and not an actual thing." Skyler nods and I know she's thinking back to Jamie's past boyfriends and all the shiny toys she's bought them. She's clever, that girl.

"Noted. Alright, what are we watching?"

"Something with lots of smut," I say, flipping through the channels. "I need a sexual distraction." Skyler giggles and I smirk, still looking for something that fits that description.

When I find a channel with a Rom Com on, I drop the remote and grab the wine bottle from underneath my bed. After a few swigs, I start to relax. So what if the bartender I hooked up with is one of my teachers now? At least he's just the GA and not the actual professor. *That* would be awkward. Still, I was sort of hoping for a repeat of that magic he gave me in the truck. I had so many scenarios imagined already. The shower, the bed, a public dressing room, his kitchen...

Sighing, I take one last pull of the wine before passing it to Skyler. Oh well, no use dwelling on it now. He's off limits.

Right?

Skyler

I can still remember the first moment I knew I wanted Erin as my Big Sister. I met her during rush week and I knew she was smart, I knew she was driven, and I knew she wanted to do big things in the sorority. But that wasn't what won me over. It was two weeks after I rushed that I realized she would be the perfect Big for me.

We snuck a bottle of whiskey into her room in the sorority house and played truth or dare, just the two of us. By the time we finished half the bottle, we were drunk, crying, and had each been tasked with at least a dozen dares that made for a lot of great stories that semester. Seeing her let loose that night and opening up to her about my past was what sold me on wanting her as my mentor. She didn't pity me for the poor circumstances I came from or my loser high school days. Instead, she promised she'd help me reinvent myself at Palm South. She was the first one who told me I could convince anyone I wanted that I was the shit. And I believed her.

So far, it's paid off.

And now, I want to be that same choice for Cassie. She reminds me a little of myself when I was a freshman last year, except I'm pretty sure she was just as popular in high school as I know she'll be here. Me, on the other hand? I didn't have a single real friend in high school. My family was dirt poor. We played poker to pass our time. Little did I know then how much that would play into my future.

"So are you hanging out with her again tonight?" Ashlei asks. She ties her hair up into a high ponytail and starts packing up the rest of her stuff spread out on the bed. She's been listening to me worry over Cassie choosing me as her Big for the past hour.

"She's supposed to text me after her last class. I know Jamie already asked her to go to some fancy steak place for dinner tonight too, though, so I guess we'll see."

"You think she'll bail to hang out with you instead?"

"I don't know. She doesn't strike me as the kind of person to bail on anyone, but I guess I'm hoping she does."

Ashlei smiles. "You're so cute. She's going to pick you as her Big, Sky. I see the way she looks at you. She admires you already."

"I hope you're right, Lei. It's just..." I trail off. "Erin and I were always hanging out last year, but I can already tell she's going to be busier this semester. And then she wants to run for a position for next year. And then she wants president. When is she going to have time for us?"

"You know she'll make time," Ashlei says pointedly.

"I guess, but I still want an awesome Little to add to our family. Someone I can depend on, someone I want to hang out with. I haven't really connected with any of the other new members like I have with her."

"It'll work itself out," Ashlei says again, reassuring me. Suddenly, her door flies open and Jess and Erin waltz in.

"Dudes. We're drinking tonight," Jess says, pointing at each of us. "Put on your party panties and let's go."

"I can't," Ashlei says, zipping up her bag and throwing it over her shoulder. Standing next to Jess, their similar features are on prominent display. Long blonde hair, tan skin, lean figures with curves in all the right places. Ashlei is just a bit more toned than Jess, but their body types are almost identical. Where Ashlei has playful chocolate eyes, Jess has more of a hazel hue, but in low lighting they're pretty much the same. They're like twins. Except they're polar opposites.

"Where are you going now?" Jess asks, her hands outstretched toward the bag Ashlei just slung on. "Are you in some sort of gang we don't know about? A roller derby squad? A porn star league?"

"I'm meeting a friend at the gym and then we're supposed to work on a project together."

"A project? Already? It's the second week of school, Lei." Then her eyes grow wide. "Wait a second. Who's this *friend*? Oh my God, are you keeping a guy from us?!"

Ashlei blushes and looks a bit uncomfortable, but just shrugs in response. "We're juniors now, Jess. It's not all fluff in our classes anymore. I'm going to the gym and then working on this project. That's it, nothing more to tell."

Jess still seems skeptical, but she sighs in defeat. "True story. I already have a paper due for Scope and Methods next Wednesday."

"See?" Ashlei kisses Jess' cheek. "I'll see you at breakfast tomorrow." With that, she's gone and Jess turns to us.

"So, you two in?"

Erin declines and starts telling Jess about some sorority council sleepover she's going to so she can rub elbows with other sorority officers on campus just as my phone pings with a text. It's Cassie. She's going to dinner with Jamie. I sigh.

"Okay, you've got to come drink with me, Sky. You're the most fun anyway."

"Hey!" Erin says, smacking Jess playfully.

"What? You know it's true!" She grins, turning back to me. "What do you say?"

"Yeah, I'm in," I reply, sighing again.

"Speaking of fun," Erin says. "Omega Chi Beta is having their first social on September twenty-second. And," she pauses for effect. "It's an ABC theme! We're going, right?!"

ABC. Anything But Clothes. It's one of the most cherished social themes because the outfits are, well, endless. Anything but clothes, goes.

"Oh hell to the yes," Jess says without hesitating.

"Ugh," I groan. "I can't."

"What are you talking about? Why?"

"I have a poker tournament that night."

Erin and Jess exchange awkward glances. "Oh," Jess says. "Well, can't you just do a different one or something?"

"It doesn't work like that. I already paid the entry fee and it's the best payout they're having at the casino downtown for a while."

Erin's eyes soften and I know she knows. She's the only one who understands my parents' financial situation. "Are you sure you can't make it? Not even after the tournament?"

I shake my head. "It'll go all night."

"I don't understand why you play anyway," Jess says. Her words sting a little, but I try not to let them affect me. "It's a total boys' game." I don't respond and she sighs. "Sorry, but seriously, it is. Anyway, let's go drink."

"Actually, I think I'm going to pass," I say, standing from where I'd been sitting on Ashlei's bed. "I'll see you guys at breakfast."

Jess throws her hands in the air. "Are you serious? What does a girl have to do to find a drinking partner around here?"

Erin laughs and I give an apologetic smile as I slip through Ashlei's door and out into the hall. Pulling out my phone, I text Clinton.

- I'm coming over. Need to talk. -

He's been short with me since the party during rush week and I can't figure out why, but two seconds later he texts me back.

- I'm here. See you soon. -

I smile. Clinton and I met during Spring Break last year and he's the only one at PSU who got excited when he realized I play poker. I just wish he could transfer that excitement to my sisters.

When I get to the O Chi house and make my way back to his room, the music is already thumping through the house and brothers are lining up shots in the kitchen. Most of them look like they just woke up to start their days and it's already seven. Gotta love college.

"Your brothers are reckless," I say when I reach his room. He smiles, not even trying to argue. The Omega Chi boys are known for their partying. It's one of their best selling points during rush.

Clinton pats the spot on his bed next to him. "I taught them well. Come here." I sit down and he pulls me into his large chest. "Bear hugs fix everything."

I giggle before pulling back. "I can't argue that."

"What's going on?" he asks. He almost seems back to normal, but his eyes keep drifting to his phone on the bedside table and I know there's something going on that he isn't telling me. But, it's not my business to pry. I know Clinton. He'll tell me when he's ready.

"It's my sisters," I confess, sighing. "I can't go to our first social because I have a poker tournament, and they just don't understand. Erin still thinks I can just bail on them and Jess looks at me like a nasty bug on the ground every time I bring it up."

"What about Ashlei?"

"She hasn't been around much, but she's sort of in the same boat as Erin. I know they don't mean to hurt my feelings but... it just sucks. I want them to get that it's more than just a stupid hobby to me."

He leans back against his headboard, thinking. Clinton's room is one of the best in the house, design wise. He's got a thing for interior design, and I've never known another guy to keep his room as clean as Clinton does. It's themed in beiges, dark greens and mints with décor strategically placed to make the room appear bigger than it really is. His bedspread is a dark forest color that pulls out the slight hint of green in his hazel eyes. "You're right – I know for a fact they're not trying to hurt your feelings. But, Skyler, you have to understand their perspective, too. These are girls who were born into money – good money. They don't know what it's like to work for it yet. And poker? Please. Other than the blackjack we play at fundraisers, these girls are clueless when it comes to the game."

"So why don't they ask me more about it then? It's not like I couldn't teach them."

"Probably for the same reasons you don't ask them to show you how to do your makeup or how to shop for the dresses that will make you look skinnier or whatever. It's not their thing, Sky. And, to be honest, that's what makes you so special – because it's not something you share with many other people."

I smile at that and chew on his words, digesting his point of view. "Yeah, I guess you're right." Thinking back to high school, my smile fades. "But... what if I don't want to stand out? What if I'd rather... blend."

"I think the key is finding a balance. You can fit in without becoming someone you're not."

"Such wise words, Bear," I joke, cocking a brow. Feeling more at ease about my situation, I turn the conversation to him. "So, you going to tell me what that phone call was about at the party last week?"

His jaw tenses. "It was nothing."

"Bear..."

"Don't," he says, jumping to his feet. He runs his hands through his short hair and inhales a deep breath before expelling it from his chest. "Sorry, I'm just not in the mood to talk about it. I'm fine, though."

I study his features, and without even a minute passing I know he's lying. Clinton's poker face is weak, at best. He wears his emotions on his sleeves, whether he wants to or not. But, again, I know he'll tell me when he's ready.

"Okay. I need a drink. Let's go take shots with your brothers."

He laughs, but his eyes still wear a coat of worry. "Yeah, enough of this girly talking shit. I need tequila."

With that, we make our way into the kitchen and join in on the drinking games. Slowly, all the stress I had when I walked through the door starts to fade. After my third shot, Matt, the Omega Chi Beta president, slides up behind me and starts nibbling on my earlobe.

"Come to my room," he whispers and tiny goose bumps flow from where his lips graze my skin all the way down to my toes. I follow him back and throw Clinton a devious smile on the way. He just shakes his head and chuckles.

"You look like you could use a distraction," Matt says when we reach his room, closing the door behind us.

"You have no idea." I slam my mouth on his and before long, poker is the last thing on my mind.

Bear

Last night got out of hand. What started as just a few innocent drinking games with brothers turned into a rager that lasted until just before the sun came up this morning. It's just after three in the afternoon now, but I'm just finding the energy to pull myself out of bed.

When I sit up, I immediately regret it. A sharp pang shoots through my head and I squint against it, grabbing my phone off the bedside table.

No missed calls or texts.

Cursing, I unlock the screen and type out another text to Carleton. When I finish, it pops up into our conversation along with the seven other unanswered messages from me. Typical. I send him money and he disappears from the face of the earth. I can't stop thinking about my nephews. He knows I worry, which is exactly why he doesn't answer. It makes it easier for him to ask for money when he knows I care.

A girl's groan breaks the silence and I startle, whipping around to find another body in my bed. *The fuck? Was I really that drunk last night?* All I can see is one tan leg outstretched from beneath the covers. The rest of the body, including the head, is still buried beneath them.

"Well that was an interesting Tuesday night," Skyler mumbles, throwing the covers off.

"Why are you in my bed, Sky?"

"Come on," she remarks with a look that implies the answer is obvious. "You know I don't sex and sleep. I sex and leave. Only, I was too tired to do the second part of that mantra last night, so I settled for leaving his room. If it's under the same roof but not within the same walls, it doesn't count as sleeping with them, right?"

"You're ridiculous."

"You cuddled with me last night." I blanch and she barks out a laugh. "Kidding, Bear, kidding. You do snore though."

I grin, but slowly reach for my pillow and then tackle her, holding it playfully over her head while she squirms beneath me. I tickle her sides and she shrieks hysterically, kicking at me to no avail. Suddenly, my bedroom door flies open.

"Uh..." my Little trails off, standing at the door with wide eyes. "Should I come back later?"

Skyler is still giggling as she smooths out her hair and jumps up from the bed. She's in nothing but a tiny tank top and boy shorts, but she's not the least bit ashamed. She starts shimmying into her jeans like it's a normal everyday occurrence for us. "Hey Josh. He's all yours," she says, nodding toward me. "I was just on my way out. Class in twenty. See you!"

And with that, she pats Josh on the shoulder and happily skips out of the room. I smirk as Josh watches her walk all the way down the hall before turning back to me, eyes still wide. "Holy shit. Did you fuck Skyler Thorne?"

"Bro," I deadpan.

He throws his hands up. "I won't say a word, I swear. But come on, you *have* to give me details."

I roll my eyes, standing and pulling on my sweat pants. No wonder it looks like we slept together. We were both in our underwear. "She's like a sister to me, dude. Don't act like you don't know that."

"Yeah. A seriously hot sister you don't mind going incestual for." I punch him hard on the arm and he winces. "All right, all right, I get it. You didn't sleep together. You just *slept* together." He winks. "Your secret's safe with me."

"I give up."

"Hey," he says, changing the subject and following me down the hall to the kitchen. "Check this out." He shoves a small pink piece of paper into my hands and I squint to read the cursive writing beneath the bold letters: NOTICE.

"Is this a sound violation?"

"Yeah. Last night was epic," he answers with a goofy smile.

"We need to watch that shit," I say, crumpling up the notice and tossing it in the trash. I reach into the fridge for the orange juice with my name on it and chug it straight from the jug. "We're already on thin ice after Spring Break last year."

"Whatever. What are they going to do?"

"They could suspend us, Josh."

"Nah." He waves me off. "They won't. We're too fun. By the way, I'm throwing an unofficial social tonight. First one of the year. Stoplight theme."

"Seriously? Did you not just hand me a sound violation notice? Maybe we should lay low until the weekend." It pains me to say it, seeing as how a stoplight social is one of my favorites. You wear red if you're taken, yellow if it's complicated, and green if you're single. I always love hooking up with the chicks dressed in yellow. Those girls are working through some screwed up shit and they love having revenge sex. And me? Well, I'm the first one to volunteer.

"Bro, relax," he says, clapping me on the shoulder. "It'll be fine. See you later, I'm going to actually make an appearance in my chemistry class today."

I'm still glaring at him disapprovingly when he bounces out of the kitchen. He's *way* too energetic for me right now. Sighing, I place the OJ back in the fridge and resolve to let it go. He's right – we'll probably be fine. And, truthfully, anything to get my mind off home is welcome right now.

I guess I better clean up the yellow Jordans.

Jess

"Wait, What?" I ask my Little incredulously, standing from where I'd been sitting next to her on the couch in our sorority house living room. She cringes a little, but repeats what I thought I heard the first time.

"I don't want to take a Little."

I groan, pinching the bridge of my nose between my fingers. "What are you talking about? You've been in a year, it's time to take a Little. This is how it works, Bo." I look to my petite Little pleadingly, but she doesn't budge.

"I'm not ready, Jess. I thought I would be, but I'm not. I want to take a Little, just not right now. I need another year."

The front door swings open, letting in the fading rays of sunshine from the evening light as Ashlei walks through the frame.

"Oh thank God," I say. "Please, help me talk some sense into my Little, Lei. I'm at a loss for words."

Ashlei eyes us both hesitantly before dropping her gym bag to the floor. Her hair is high in a ponytail and she looks like she's been sweating. I really need to get on her level if I'm going to be taking pictures next to her this semester.

"What's going on?"

"Bo doesn't want to take a Little," I let out the words in one exasperated sigh. "Selfish little brat."

Bo throws me a look, but her mouth actually curls up into a small smile. My Little is part Asian, with long, straight dark hair and kind eyes that make you feel like you can tell her anything. And with Bo, you really can – she's loyal and steadfast.

"Okay, well... if she doesn't want to take a Little, is that really the end of the world?"

My jaw drops. "Are you kidding me? It's an honor to get a Little and you know that! Sisters who don't get Littles are devastated until they finally do. And I know for a fact that there are at least two new members who want Bo as their Big."

"Is that true?" Ashlei asks Bo. She only nods in response. "Oh... well why don't you want to take one?"

Bo opens her mouth to answer but I cut her off. "There is no logical answer. She's been in a year, she's been a Little for a year, now it's her turn to be a Big."

"But that's just it," Bo says loudly, standing and tossing the pillow that was on her lap to the side. Her brows pull together and her long, sleek black hair slides behind her back as she stands. "I've been a Little, but I don't feel like I've had a Big."

My mouth snaps shut and I blink, not sure what to say. Ashlei shifts uncomfortably.

"I'm sorry, but it's true. You and Stacy are so close. I thought we would be the same way, especially after she graduated, but we've barely hung out since I became your Little. It's like you hung out with me nonstop to get me to choose you as my Big and then just stopped trying. I mean when is the last time we did something together just the two of us?"

I scoff and turn to Ashlei, looking for help. I don't find it.

"I can't argue with that one, Jess," Ashlei says apologetically. "Maybe she's got a point here."

"We hang out all the time!" I shout a little louder than I intend to. "We just hung out the other night."

"Yeah. At sisterhood movie night. But when is the last time we did something just the two of us? Something not sorority related?"

I chew my lip, but can't come up with an answer. She's right. I know she's right. Hell, I was just talking to the girls about how I wish I were closer with Bo. But right now, I don't want her to be right. I don't want this to be about us. I want her to take a damn Little and not let our family line die.

"Whatever." I snatch my Lilly Pulitzer bag off the couch and throw it over my shoulder. "Do what you want, Little. I'm late for class."

"Jess..." Ashlei tries to stop me, reaching out for my arm but I shrug her off and jet for the door, letting it slam behind me. I'm fuming. Bo should want to take a Little, she shouldn't be so fixated on what our relationship is like. I'm her mentor. That's what I'm supposed to be. Not every Big/Little pair is best friends. It's a special relationship, just like a big and little sister in real life. Yes, sometimes friendships bloom out of that sisterhood, and yes Stacy and I are an example of that. But, Bo shouldn't be holding back because she's searching for that with me, too.

I frown at myself as I speed walk into the Political Science building. *God, I'm being such a bitch.* Here my Little is basically saying she just wants to be better friends with me and I'm yelling at her telling her to go find new friends.

Yeah. I suck.

I snatch a packet of papers from someone as I storm in the classroom and up to a seat near the back. It's only when I sit down and unload my textbook that I realize I snatched those papers from Jarrett. He's watching me intently, his dark eyes narrowing as his brows pull in. I grit my teeth and start scribbling in my notepad as hard as I can with my black ink pen, trying to work out the tension that I know only has one true release.

A release I'd really like to get from my professor's assistant right now.

By the end of class, all the muscles in my body are growing sore and I know I can't take it any longer. I ignore Ashlei's text asking if I'm okay along with Jarrett's concerned glare asking pretty much the same thing and head straight to Ralph's after attendance is called and Dr. Maynard excuses us. What a fucking Wednesday.

Ralph's is a small, shitty bar but it's the closest one to campus and therefore always packed. It's something between a biker bar and a club and it's pretty much my home. As soon as I sink down into the barstool, I feel a little better.

"You need a drink," a deep voice says from behind me. I quickly glance back and fight the urge to roll my eyes. It's Matt, the president of Omega Chi Beta. He's always been a huge flirt, which is kind of a lame turn-off to me, but I can't deny that he's hot. Bleach blonde hair, hazel eyes, cute grin and tall frame? Yeah. He'll do.

"I have one," I point out, lifting my fruity rum drink in his direction before taking a sip.

"Let me buy the next one?"

"I've never been one to turn down free booze." Eying him, I take another sip. "I'm surprised you and your brothers aren't throwing another rager tonight."

"Yeah well, we're trying to lay a little low after last week's stoplight party. Cops were called, tickets issued, alumni freaked out. You should have seen Bear ripping into Josh. I've never seen him so pissed off."

"Skyler said he's been acting weird lately."

Matt frowns. "Yeah, he kind of has. But I think it's just school shit. And his Little is a dick, so there's that."

I laugh. "Yeah, there's that."

Matt's eyes fall to my lips. "You have a beautiful laugh."

Rolling my eyes, I drain the rest of my drink and nod toward the perky bartender at the other side of the bar. She slides me a refill and I nod to Matt. "It's on his tab."

"Ruthless," he says, whistling.

"Hey, you offered."

"Indeed I did," he agrees. "But you were supposed to fall for my stupid pick-up lines."

"Do you want to have sex tonight?" I ask bluntly.

He chokes on his beer, wiping at the corner of his mouth quickly. "Um..."

"Let's cut to the chase here, Matt. You're a horn dog. You're buying me drinks. It's clear where you want this night to go, and luckily for you I've got some tension to work out and I'm more than happy to take it in that direction, too. So," I pause, slamming back the fresh drink he just bought me and licking the last of it from my lips. "Where to?"

He leans in quickly and presses his lips to mine, running his hand back through my hair and gripping it lightly. I'm a little bored, but I let him kiss me anyway and we make out like high schoolers until I feel him dragging me toward the door.

"Wait." I pull away from him, breathless. "My bag is behind the bar. One sec." I rush back to our bartender and she retrieves my bag from the back. When I sling it over my shoulder and turn back to find Matt, I find dark brown eyes, instead.

Jarrett is staring at me from the other side of the bar. His head is low, his elbows propped on the bar as he sips on a dark liquor. He swallows and his jaw tenses as his eyes flick to the door where Matt's waiting for me. I swallow, too, but lift my bag higher on my shoulder and make my way to Matt. He kisses my neck and runs his hands down my backside when I reach him, growling in my ear about what he can't wait to do to me.

As he tugs me out the door, I look back over my shoulder, expecting to see Jarrett still watching me. But he's gone. I frown, more disappointed than I care to admit, but force a smile when Matt pulls me the rest of the way through the door.

Matt's fun. I like the way he peppers me with kisses as we move between the sheets of his bed and I can't say I'm not surprised to see he's packing more than just a wallet in those frat shorts of his. But, I know I should feel guilty right now.

I should feel guilty because it's Matt's hands touching me, it's his mouth on mine, it's his cock driving into me, but it's not him who's responsible for my moans right now. It's not him that's making me scream as I orgasm in his bed.

No. It's Jarrett. Because all I can think of is him and those dark brown eyes.

And that mother fucking truck.

Skyler

I can't stop smiling in the limo ride to Ralph's. Somehow, I landed Cassie as my Little. I've known all week – found out on Tuesday and have been showering her with gifts and clues ever since – but tonight was the night *she* found out, and it was priceless.

"Did you really not have a clue that it was me?"

"Well, I hoped it was, but all your clues threw me off!" she says, giggling. "You said you had blonde hair and you were a Poli Sci major. I thought it was Jess at one point."

"Well I wanted it to be a surprise!"

"It definitely was," she says, still smiling. Our limo is packed with ten other girls. It's tradition after Big/Little reveal that all KKB sisters convene at Ralph's, a dirty, old bar just off campus that's been around longer than the library. Most of the new Big/Little pairs take limos just for fun. It's cheesy and kind of lame, but it's tradition.

"Hey," I say, touching Cassie's shoulder when I notice her smile slip. "What's wrong?"

"Nothing," she tries, shaking her head. I give her a pointed look and she sighs. "I don't know. I'm so happy, Skyler. I am. I was freaking out thinking you weren't my Big but you are and now we're going out and it's going to be so much fun. But..."

"You're thinking about Paris, aren't you?"

Cassie frowns. "She's changed so much already, Skyler. She's always been a little... refined, I guess. But now she's getting snobby. And mean. And it's like now that we're not in the same sorority, she doesn't think it's fit for us to hang out. Like, ever. I don't understand it."

I really want to punch this Paris chick right in the left tit, but for now, I need to make Cassie feel better, so I put on my happy face. "Listen, she's just going through the growing pains. College changes people in a lot of ways. I know sisters who have plenty of friends outside of the sorority and friends in other sororities, too. If Paris is saying that's why she can't be friends with you, she's using it as an excuse for something she's been thinking for a while now."

Cassie's frown deepens and I realize that probably didn't make her feel better at all. *Cool. Great job, Skyler.*

"But do you remember what I said when we first met? By the fountain?" I ask and Cassie nods. "Well, it's still true. Your time in KKB is just beginning, but just know you've got an army of sisters on your side and we all want to get to know you better and form a lifelong friendship with you."

She smiles at that. "I know. I'm excited. And you're my Big!"

I squeeze her in a tight hug. "Hey." I pull back, assessing her. "Did I ever tell you the stories behind some of the girls' nicknames?" Cassie shakes her head no. "Well, I just realized we probably sound completely crazy to you, huh?"

She giggles. "Sometimes. It's kind of hard to follow."

"Well, let me clear it up. So, Ex is short for Erin Xander. Also, it's kind of an inside joke between the other girls and I that she's always someone's ex, never someone's girlfriend. We're still not sure how that happens." Cassie laughs and I join her a bit before continuing. "Lei's is easy, it's just the second half of her name. Everyone has always called her Ash and she bitches about it, so we call her Lei to get her to shut up."

Cassie chuckles again and I see the worry start to truly fade. "I like that. Kind of like how they call you Sky."

"Right," I agree. "It's just a shorter version of our names. J-Love's is the most fun, I think. It's kind of like J-Lo, but J-Love. It started because she used to say she was in love with every guy she hooked up with. Now, it's just because she's a heartbreaker. That girl is always hooking up with all kinds of hotties on campus and making them fall in love with her. Man eater, that one is." I smile, shaking my head. "I try to keep up with her and give her a run for her money, but it's tough."

"What does Bo stand for?"

"Oh, that's her actual name. It's Chinese for precious, I think."

"Neat." She pauses. "What do you think my nickname will be?"

I look up toward the neon ceiling of the limo, contemplating. "Well, you'll be Little Nug to me. That's all I really know right now. But who knows, maybe you'll get a nickname from the girls, too."

"I like Little Nug."

I smile just as the limo pulls to a stop in front of Ralph's. "Me too. Now let your new Big buy you a drink!"

"Um," she stammers, wrapping her fingers in her wild red hair. "I'm not twenty-one."

"Neither am I," I say with a wink. "Not yet. But, according to these..." I trail off, pulling two fake IDs from my purse. "I'm twenty-two and you just turned twenty-one last week. Happy birthday!"

We both laugh together as we file out of the limo and into Ralph's. The bouncer checks our IDs with a smirk and I'm pretty sure he knows they're fake, but he lets us in anyway and slaps neon green wristbands on our arms. Perks of being in a college town.

We meet up with Jess, Bo, Ashlei, and Erin at the bar. Jess is still a little sour about Bo not taking a Little, but she apologized to her earlier this week and they're trying to work on building their relationship before adding another sister to their line. I actually kind of think it's smart. Erin and I are pretty close, and Cassie seems like the perfect addition to the family. They haven't had much one-on-one time yet, but that's mostly because Erin is insanely busy. With the way Cassie is showing interest in school already, I have a feeling they'll have that in common, soon.

Jess and I exchange glances and devious smiles when Matt shows up with Clinton and a few more of their brothers. We found out earlier today that we're officially eskimo sisters – meaning we shacked up with the same guy. Although, luckily, neither of us have any hard feelings. He was a distraction for me and he figured that out when I showed up wearing green to their stoplight party. Jess feels the same way – though she did mention he may be distracting her again in the near future.

Adam Brooks slides up to the bar right between Cassie and I just as we finish our fifth game of flip cup. His dark eyes are hooded from his buzz and he grins goofily at each of us. "Well if it isn't the slip-n-slide sisters."

"Wow," I turn to face him completely, bringing my drink with me. "I like our reputation already, Little."

Adam's brows shoot up. "Little?" He looks from me to Cassie and back again. "Well hot damn. Congrats, ladies."

"I guess that means you should buy us a shot, right?" I ask as Cassie blushes and tucks her hair behind her ear. She's so innocent and cute. *Dear Lord, help her with being my Little.*

"You know what," he says, leaning up with a grin. "You are absolutely right."

He orders us three lemon drops and we throw them back and talk between more games of flip cup. My buzz is pretty strong now and the more I see his little dimple, the closer I lean in.

"You girls should come to the A-Sig concert next month."

I cock a brow. "Oh yeah? No offense, but Alpha Sigma events are usually pretty lame."

"Yeah well," he says, tilting his drink back. "I'm going to change all that this year." He throws a wink at Cassie and I can't help but smile. This kid is cute.

"What do you think, Little Nug? Should we go?"

Cassie's grin grows wider. "Well it wouldn't be a party without the slip-n-slide sisters, would it?"

Adam points two fingers in her direction. "She's got a point."

"I guess it's settled then. But, I do have one condition."

"Oh?" Adam asks, amused.

"Dance with me." I don't give him the chance to reply before I pull him out onto the packed dance floor, sticky with spilt liquor. Throwing my arms around his neck, I move my body against his in time with the heavy bass of the music.

After a few songs, I lean in and speak over the music. "So, you're changing Alpha Sigma's reputation, huh?"

"That's the plan. As long as my douchebag president stays out of the way."

I smile, my lips grazing his neck just a fraction. "Better be careful messing with the man in charge."

He shrugs, pulling back to catch my eyes with his. "What can I say? I like a challenge."

I return his grin and just like that, there's a new player at the table.

I wake up to a loud banging on the front door Sunday morning. I know it's loud because I never hear a knock from my bedroom but this one sounds like it's thumping on my head. Groaning, I swing my legs over the edge of my bed and make my way down the hall. Whoever it is continues to bang until I quickly pull the door open.

"About fucking time," the guy on the other end of the knock says, pushing past me into the living room. I bow up to him and he rolls his eyes. "I'm Alec. I was president of Omega Chi Beta six years ago and I'm here to save your ass."

"What the fuck did you just say to me?"

"Did I stutter?" he asks. *Dick.* "My name is Alec Carriker. Are you Matthew Dishman?"

I shake my head. "He's down the hall. What are you doing here?"

"I'd rather talk to Matt about that."

I cross my arms over my chest. "Well he's asleep and insanely hungover and I'm probably the only brother you're going to get a sober conversation out of right now. So if you don't want to wait around for several hours to get whatever has your panties in a wad off your chest, you can start talking now."

Alec steps up to me, his chest puffing out as his eyes level with mine. He's just as tall as I am, which I'm not really used to, but his frame is lean where mine is stout. "I don't know where you get off talking to an alumni that way, *boy*, but I'm about five seconds away from reminding you why you shouldn't."

"*Boy*?" My nose flares and I beg myself to calm down, but I'm not sure it's going to work.

He rolls his eyes. "Oh please, don't start with the race card. I didn't mean boy like that, I meant it as in you *are* a boy. You are young, you're naive, and you have no respect for your older brothers."

"I don't give my respect. You have to earn it. And you're doing a piss poor job right now."

Alec appraises me for a moment before exhaling a long breath. "Look, I didn't come here to fight. But, I'm pissed off and so are a lot of other alum. We got a call from nationals and they're assigning me and two other brothers to mentor the chapter for the rest of the year due to the copious amount of shit you've been getting yourself into."

I gulp, but don't respond. I know exactly what he's talking about. After last semester, the crazy parties over summer, and the now four times we've had the cops called on us this semester – it doesn't surprise me nationals has stepped in. But it worries me.

"So what does this mean?"

"It means you're in a pretty precarious situation and if you don't listen to me and get your shit together, you're going to get suspended. Or worse." He gives me a pointed look and my jaw tightens.

"I'll go wake Matt."

"Don't bother." He sighs, looking around the house. It's disgusting. Empty cups and beer bottles litter the tables and the floor and it smells like ass. He turns his nose up. "Just let him sleep, I'll come back later." He pauses. "I didn't catch your name."

"You didn't bother to ask. I guess *boy* will suffice for now."

He smirks. "Look, I'm sorry. I'm just... I'm really tied to this fraternity. I don't want to see it go down in flames. What's your name?"

I frown, but extend my hand anyway. "Clinton Pennington. Everyone calls me Bear."

"Bear," he tries my name and I know he's wondering why anyone would call me that. Or maybe he's figured part of it out by now. "Well, Bear, I'm sorry we got off on the wrong foot. I'll be back later with the other brothers." His eyes flit around the room again. "Might consider cleaning up a bit before then. Believe it or not, I'm the most forgiving of the lot."

After Alec leaves, I shut the door and curse under my breath. I type out a quick text to Josh and just as I hit send, my phone starts ringing.

Mom.

Fuck. I am not in the mood for this. Hell, I'm still half asleep. But I answer anyway.

"Hey Mom."

"Clinton, baby?" she asks, sniffling.

"Mom?" My heart races in my throat. She's crying. "What's going on? Is Clayton okay?" She cries harder and I sink down onto the couch, my breath caught in my chest. "Mom?"

"He's fine, honey. I," she chokes out over a sob. "I need you to send me a little money, baby. I was stupid. I did some stupid shit and now I don't have money for Clayton's school fieldtrip and he doesn't have any lunch money and I barely have an ounce of food in the house. I know I was stupid, Clinton. Please don't penalize me. Please, baby, just help me out. Just this once."

As if the anger I had after Alec's morning visit wasn't enough, I feel it double in an instant. Heat rushes to my cheeks and I have to grip the arm of the couch to keep from punching something. "How much?"

"Just a little, baby."

"How. Much?"

She pauses, her voice growing smaller. "A hundred, maybe two."

I don't argue. I don't fight her. I don't have the energy to do either. "I'll text you with the confirmation." With that, I end the call, grab my keys, and head for the store. I'm gripping the wheel and driving too fast the entire way, but I can't calm myself down. I try texting Carleton, but he doesn't answer. Still. Letting out a frustrated growl, I throw my phone against the passenger side window and it bounces back into the seat.

I send her two hundred. I can't afford it, but I do it anyway. The thought of Clayton suffering at all makes me hate myself for leaving him behind. He should be here with me. Being only twelve, he's got a long time to go before he can leave on his own. Too long.

When I get back to the house, I change clothes and take off walking across campus toward the gym. I call Clayton when I'm halfway there and he answers on the second ring.

"Big bro!" he exclaims, his grin carrying through his voice. "What's up? How's Florida life?"

"Hot," I say with a chuckle, the sweat already beading on my forehead. "How's Pennsylvania life?"

"Boring. But you already know how that goes."

I smile. "How's school? You feel any different being a seventh grader?"

"Well, the schoolwork still sucks. But the girls are filling out, if you know what I mean." He laughs through the receiver and I can't help but join him. That's my brother.

"Attaboy." My smile fades as I think about him not having food to eat. "Is everything okay at home, Clayton?"

There's a pause on the other end, but he answers after a beat. "Yeah. I mean, you know how she is. How everyone here is."

"Yeah. I know." Silence. "You know I love you, right? I'm always here for you. No matter what time of day."

"I know. I'm okay, bro."

"I know you are. You're tough."

"I learn from the best! But I have to go. I'm at Mac's and we're about to jump on Xbox. Call you later?"

"Sure thing, little bro. Kick his ass."

"Always!"

We end the call just in time for me to open the gym door. I feel broken. All I want is for Clayton to get the hell out of there and then we can both be done with our shitty family. But really, I know that's not true, either. Because there's still the boys. And even when Carleton and Mom pull their stupid stunts, they're still family. And blood runs thick.

I'm just not sure how much more I can give anymore.

***

By the time I limp my way back to the fraternity house, the sun is already setting. I didn't intend to stay at the gym all day but I wanted to numb myself. It worked, but I'm paying for it now and it'll be even worse tomorrow.

When I push my way through the front door, I'm met with thumping music and a packed house.

What the fuck.

"Josh!" I growl, catching sight of him first. I grab him by his shirt and yank him back toward the hallway where there are less people. "What the hell are you doing? Did you not get my voicemail earlier about the alumni?"

"Oh fuck them," he spits out. "They came by earlier, ripped us a new asshole, and then left. They said they're moving our chapter meeting to tomorrow night, so we're getting in one last rage fest before the party police move in."

I sigh, but just like with Mom, I don't have the energy to argue. "Whatever." Releasing his shirt, I limp back to my room and jump in the shower, letting the hot water and steam melt away some of the tension from today. Then, against my better judgement, I join the party.

And I make it my mission to get hammered.

Before midnight even hits, I'm pinballing down the hallway with Lacy's mouth on mine. Lacy is a Zeta. She's small, almost doll-size, and her caramel skin against the bright white dress she's wearing are too much for me to handle. You would think with her wearing white to a frat party that she was trying to be innocent tonight. But with one hand under my basketball shorts, I know that's far from the truth.

"Fuck," she curses as I slam her back against my bedroom door. "Easy, Bear."

I suck and bite down her neck and toss her onto my bed with ease, pulling my shirt up and over my head at the same time. "I'm not doing easy tonight, babe. You either get me hard and rough or you don't get me at all. Your choice."

She swallows, but her lips part slightly and I can feel the want radiating off of her. When she doesn't answer, I fall down on top of her and slam my mouth on hers, hiking her leg up in the process. I know she's only a temporary numbing, just like the gym was earlier, but she's what I need. Sweat, alcohol, and sex. That's the distraction I'm looking for, and Palm South is the perfect place to find it.

I don't even bother taking off her dress or even the lacy thong I feel underneath it. I just quickly maneuver it to the side, roll on the condom I pulled from my top drawer, and thrust inside her in one fluid motion. She moans loud in my ear and it sends chills down my back. Thank God Josh likes the music loud.

"Oh God," Lacy screams, gripping my headboard as I slam into her over and over again. Her breasts are nearly tumbling out of her dress and her head hits against the board a little each time I thrust in.

"Nope, just me, babe."

I make sure she gets her release and as soon as she finishes, I lift both of her ankles up onto my shoulders and push deeper inside her pussy. She screams even louder and it doesn't take long for me to find my release, too. It completely numbs me and awakens every nerve at the same time. Finally, even if just for that moment, I don't think about anything else but the way it feels to come inside her.

When we finish, I make my way to the bathroom to flush the condom and then I fall back into bed, turning on my fan on my way over. I pull a pillow over my head to drown out the music and let my temporary euphoria drag me toward sleep. I don't know if Lacy stays and I honestly don't care. She can stay and sleep or she can leave. Right now, I'm not talking. Or cuddling. Or doing anything other than reveling in the fact that coming feels fucking amazing.

Before my thoughts have the time to sneak their way back in, I pass out.

Skyler

"You don't need to send that much home to us, Skyler," my mom says softly and I can hear her tearing up a little.

"Mom. I want to. Please, just take it. It's not even that much."

"A thousand dollars is a lot of money."

"Well, it's not as much as I wish I could send."

Mom's silent, probably crying, so Dad takes his cue. They always talk to me on speaker phone. "We are so, so proud of you, honey."

I shrug. "It was just a little tournament, nothing to get too proud over."

"It is to us," he says. "And it may just be a small tournament now, but I know without a doubt that one day, you'll win tournaments so big you can't even imagine them right now."

"Whatever you say, Dad. Any word on that promotion?"

He pauses. "Not yet. I'm still holding out though."

I nod, but my gut tells me I should be worried. Mom and Dad both work in retail. Dad has been up for promotion to manager at least four times that I can remember, but his boss always screws him over. They do what they have to to make ends meet, but since neither of them finished high school, they don't have much to work with. But they work hard. *Damn* hard. And I'm determined to help them and maybe, one day, make it where they don't have to worry about working, at all.

"You'll get it, Dad. I know you will." I smile just as I key in the door code to the sorority house. "I just got home, I'm going to turn in. Love you guys."

"We love you too, sweetie," Mom replies through what are now clear sobs. I chuckle a little and end the call, stepping into the foyer. When I do, I nearly crash into Ashlei.

"Whoa!"

"Oh my God," she whisper-yells, clutching her chest. "You scared the shit out of me!"

"What are you doing? It's after three in the morning, Lei." I note her eccentric makeup and eye her curiously. She's dressed in what looks like pajamas, but clearly she wasn't sleeping. She, Jess, and Erin helped me get ready for the tournament earlier, much to my surprise, before Jess and Erin headed off to the social. But Ashlei said she couldn't go, so why was she covered in neon makeup?

Ashlei shifts under my gaze, adjusting the gym bag on her shoulder. "Um, I went out. To a club downtown."

I cock a brow. "Really? With who? I thought you couldn't go out tonight."

She bites her lip, curses, and pulls me to the couch. "Listen, please don't say anything to Jess or Erin, okay? I had other plans tonight. That's why I couldn't go to the social."

"What other plans?" My brows rise higher.

"I can't tell you..."

"And why is that?"

She sighs. "Just, please, Skyler. Don't tell them and don't make a big deal about it. I was out with a few friends. That's all."

I study her for a moment more, but nod. "Okay, Lei. I won't say anything." She lets out a breath of relief. "Should I be worried, though?"

"No. I'm fine. Trust me."

"Okay." I nod again. "Well, I won the tournament tonight but I am exhausted. I'll see you in the morning?"

"Yeah," she says, smiling. "And congrats, Skyler. I may not understand the whole poker thing, but I know it's important to you. And I know what it's like to be worried about what others might think of the things that make you happy. So just know I'm proud of you."

I smile, but can't help but wonder how she knows what I feel like. Ashlei fits this sorority and all our friends like a glove. I'm not sure what she knows about worrying what others think of her. "Thanks, Lei. Love you."

She blows me a kiss and I scamper up the stairs to mine and Jess' room, quietly letting myself in and stripping down to my underwear before crawling into bed. Before I plug in my phone, I type out a quick text to Clinton. When no answer comes in after five minutes, I sigh and roll over toward the wall, pulling the covers up to my shoulders.

Something weird is going on with Clinton, and now Ashlei is acting strange, too. I know Jess is hiding something from all of us – something boy-related, if I had to guess. And Erin has barely spent more than ten minutes with me since classes started. I hate not knowing what's going on with my friends, and it hits me that maybe I need to stop focusing on distracting myself and start paying attention to the people around me, instead.

There are way too many secrets floating around PSU right now, and I'm determined to start uncovering them. It's time to hone in on my friends and reveal their truths.

Starting with Clinton.

EPISODE 3

"But it could be FUN, RIGHT?"

Ashlei

Pulling my tight spandex shorts out of my ass, I wipe down the pole and pat my hands together around a pinch of chalk. I don't usually chalk my hands before I work out – especially after seeing so many of my teammates start to rely on that method – but today, I need it. My palms are sweaty as hell.

There's a nervous pit in my stomach and I'm not sure if it's because the competition is less than a week away or if it's because I know what Hayden is doing behind the studio right now. Regardless, even with the chalk, I'm straining more than usual when I grip the pole and climb my way up, warming up with basic climbs and spins to keep my mind off everything else.

Skyler caught me sneaking in the house the other night and I know she's getting more and more curious about my whereabouts, which means I have to be extra careful. Pole dancing fitness isn't something you can easily explain to just anyone. Hell, I was a judgmental bitch when I first started learning about it. But then I met Hayden. Once he and Leslie started training me, I felt myself become addicted. Over the summer, I trained hard and used everything I learned from dancing my entire life to transfer into the moves on the pole. My flexibility made some of the moves almost natural for me, but building the body strength took time and patience. I'm proud of everything I've accomplished, but there's no way I can ever tell the girls about my hobby.

I'm pretty sure Erin would faint.

Jess would be pissed and say it's slutty.

Skyler would probably laugh and broadcast it across campus.

And my parents? Jesus... I can't even imagine.

No, I can't tell anyone. Sometimes, it's just better to keep certain parts of your life separate from others.

"Damn girl," Hayden smacks my ass playfully just as I transition into my Russian splits.

I giggle and drop back down to my feet. "Way to break my focus."

Hayden pulls me into him for a long, sensual kiss that I feel all the way down between my thighs. "All part of the training, I swear." As much as I love the way his hands feel on me, I can tell he's high, and it turns me off as much as his tongue turns me on.

"Mm hmm. I'm sure." I push him away and climb back up. Leslie and Kya enter through the door he came through just moments ago and Leslie immediately starts warming up while Kya changes her shirt. Both of them are gorgeous, but Leslie is just downright hot. When I first met her, I was more attracted to her than I knew how to handle. I've always known I have a bisexual mindset, but I'd never really considered trying to openly hit on a girl until Leslie. That was, until Hayden stole my attention.

"Just us today?" I ask just before performing a simple drop.

"Only the ones who want to win, it looks like," Leslie answers. Her long, jet-black hair spins around her tight body as she warms up and I can't help but be temporarily mesmerized. The chick is still insanely hot, whether I'm with Hayden or not.

And I'm not even sure what we really are, anyway.

The South Florida Pole Dance Event is this Saturday and everyone in our troupe is entered in the competition. Leslie is the owner of Kitty Heels, our small-but-talented dance company, and she tells me every day that she could all but kiss Hayden for bringing me to them this summer. She sees potential in me, and this will be my first time to prove her right.

"You ready for your first competition, Ashlei?" Kya asks, her eyes shining in the flattering lighting of the studio. Kya is another star student of Leslie's. She's been dancing with Leslie since the beginning. Standing just shy of six feet and breaking that point in heels, she's the tallest girl in our troupe. But, she's also the strongest, and her moves are perfected to a point that I'm envious of. I'm not easily intimidated, but I'm threatened by her, for sure.

"Getting there." I answer, trying to feign confidence.

"You're going to be amazing," Hayden says, stretching on the floor by his pole. They brought Hayden in a little over a year ago, but he seems to fit in perfectly. He's one of only two males in our entire studio and when he's on the pole, he's absolutely hypnotizing. His strength is out of this world. "When you bring home better awards than the rest of us, I expect a kiss of appreciation."

"And just where do you want this kiss, Hayden?" Leslie teases.

Hayden flashes his model grin. "I have a few ideas."

The girls chuckle and I drop to the floor long enough to toss my sweaty towel at him. Hayden Rivers is trouble walking. He's covered in beautiful tattoos, has a pierced eyebrow, and wears his shoulder-length hair back in a man bun that I swore I would never find attractive but did after the third time we hung out. He's lean, ripped in every muscle group from his neck to his ankles, and has just the slightest bit of facial hair. His piercing blue eyes top off his look and I swear he's the most exotic creature I've ever come in contact with. He's just as handsome as he is strange – and I love it.

He's also into hard drugs that Leslie doesn't know about, which makes me worry more often than I care to admit. But, he's a big boy – he makes his own decisions.

We run through our routines until we can barely stand anymore. By the time we finish, it's past midnight and I know I'll have to figure out a way to sneak back into the house again. Luckily, I room with Erin this year and she's always passed out by this time. With all her campus and sorority activities, she's exhausted by the time night rolls around and she sleeps heavier than anyone I know.

"Stay with me tonight," Hayden whispers into the back of my neck just as I pull a loose white t-shirt over my sports bra. He wraps his arms around my middle and pulls me back into him, pressing his hard on against my ass and forcing me to exhale a long, needy breath.

"I can't," I turn toward him, wrapping my arms around his neck. "I have class early in the morning and a sisterhood event tomorrow night. I have to get some sleep or I'm not going to make it."

"Sleep is overrated." He holds me tighter and nips up my neck to my earlobe, pulling it between his teeth. Hissing, I place my hands on his chest and try to put distance between us.

"You're killing me."

"I could be pleasuring you if you'd come home with me."

I push him off and grab my gym bag. "Goodnight, Hayden."

"Temptress," he teases, but he lets me go and I silently thank him for not trying again. Lord knows I can only say no to that kind of offer so many times.

When I climb into my little white Lexus SC convertible, my phone rings and I'm surprised to see Erin's name on the screen.

"Hello?"

"Where are you?! It's after midnight!" she yells into the receiver. At first I think she's scorning me, but then I realize it's exceptionally loud wherever she is and she has to yell over the noise.

Shit. The O Chi party.

"I... uh," I stammer, trying to figure out how to save my ass. I promised the girls I would go out to the Omega Chi Beta party tonight since I'd bailed on so much this semester. "I'm on my way. I got caught up working on this group project thing."

"Listen, if I'm up past my bedtime on a school night, you can blow off a group project," she jokes. "Get your ass here!"

"See you soon!"

I end the call and curse. All I want is a hot shower and my bed, but it looks like I'll have to settle for a quick shower and a frat party. I guess there are worse things I could be complaining about.

Running to the sorority house just long enough to rinse off and change, I make it to Omega Chi just after one. Erin and Jess find me as soon as I get through the door.

"About fucking time!" Jess yells. "Here, drink this." She shoves a red plastic cup full of beer into my hand and tips it up to my lips. Before she has the chance to spill any on me, I meet the lip of it with my mouth and drink. She's not satisfied until it's drained. "You have some catching up to do."

"I see that," I laugh the words, wiping beer from my lips. "Sorry I'm late."

"Whatever," Jess cuts me off. "Let's get hammered!"

Erin leans in to whisper to me. "I think someone already is."

We both giggle and start to follow Jess toward a game of flip cup in the next room when Clinton's booming voice carries from down the hallway.

"Just fucking drop it, Skyler!"

He emerges from the hallway just as Skyler tries grabbing his arm. He rips it away and turns to face her. Seething, he yells so loud it silences everyone else.

"It's none of your fucking business. If I wanted to talk to you about it, I would. But I don't, so leave me the fuck alone. Stop being so goddamn nosey!" With that, he storms through the front door and slams it hard behind him.

Everyone is staring at Skyler, including us, but like a pro she doesn't miss a beat. Smiling, she shrugs. "Well damn. Anyone got a shot ready?"

The crowd laughs, although a little uneasily, and then the games resume and everything is back to normal. Skyler's eyes find ours and she makes her way across the room.

"What was that about?" Erin asks.

"It's nothing. He's fine, just stressed."

"He shouldn't talk to you like that, Skyler," Jess points out. "That's fucked up. Whatever has his panties in a wad, he didn't need to go all douchebag captain on you."

"It's all good. I'm fine." She turns to me and smiles. "And Lei is here! Let's drink!"

And we do. All night long. By the time we stumble our way into the house, I only have two hours to sleep before I have to be up for class. So much for sleep.

Tomorrow is going to be rough.

Adam

"So I'll see you there, right?" I ask the three freshmen girls standing in front of me. They all giggle and nod, their eyes flitting from the flier to me before they turn and walk away. I throw Jeremy a cocky grin and he just shakes his head.

"Only you could pull this off, you know that right?"

"Anyone could have before me," I say, handing a few fliers out to groups of students walking past our booth. "It's just that no one made the effort."

"That's because no one cared."

"And that's exactly why we're the lamest fraternity on campus," I deadpan.

"Touché." Jeremy chugs half of the water bottle in his hand and wipes his forehead. "Damn it's hot. Florida sucks."

"What's wrong, Michigan? Can't hang?"

He glowers at me before grabbing another stack of fliers. "Shut up or I'll make you do this shit by yourself."

"You'll make me flirt with every girl on campus to convince them to come to our concert? Wow. What a dick."

He flips me the middle finger before walking up to a group of Zetas. I laugh, but it's cut short when I spot our president making his way toward the tent.

Shit.

I'm not in the mood to put up with Clay, but I don't really have a choice. Out of all the brothers, he's the most resistant to the changes I want to make to our organization. In my opinion, he should have been doing all this a long time ago.

"So do we have a packed house for the concert yet?" he asks mockingly, eying our booth. I want nothing more than to smack that smug look off his face but I smile instead.

"Getting there. You want to help us pass out some fliers?"

"Nah, I'm on my way to the gym. Just wanted to see this shit show for myself." He snickers. "I can't wait to see this thing fail. Then maybe the alumni will realize why I didn't listen to you the first time you suggested it."

"Why are you against me on this?" I finally ask him, perturbed. "We're brothers, Clay. If we pack this concert, we'll put Alpha Sigma on the map again."

"We're on the map now."

I scoff. "You really are stupid if you honestly believe that."

His face drops and he steps forward, bowing up his chest to mine. "Maybe you should watch the way you speak to your president if you want to keep those letters."

I bite down on the inside of my cheek hard to keep from opening my mouth. Shaking my head, I don't give him another word before taking off toward a group of Omega Chi Betas. As much as we're rivals with them, we need their support just as much as the girls' at this event.

I'm still steaming over the conversation with Clay two hours later when Jeremy and I start breaking down the tent. It pisses me off that he can't stand to see me try to better our fraternity.

Part of me thinks he's jealous or worried I'll overshadow him, and part of me knows he's just a miserable human being.

"Looks like I missed the party," a soft voice says behind me just as Jeremy and I pack the large navy tent into its cover. When I turn and come face to face with Cassie McBee, I smile.

"We can always take the party somewhere else."

"Oh yeah?" She grins. "Where to?"

Cassie is cute, I can't deny that, and part of me wants to tell her we can move whatever party she wants to my bedroom. But there's something about her that's innocent – too innocent for me to screw up. "Ralph's?"

Her face falls a bit, but she snaps out of it quickly. "Wish I could. I'm actually on my way to class."

"Let me walk you?"

"Uh," she falters, holding up the longboard I didn't realize she had tucked under her arm before.

"I didn't know you longboarded," I say, genuinely surprised. "Can't say I've met a sorority girl who rides before."

Cassie blushes. "Yeah well, I'm not initiated yet. Maybe the sorority girl life will wipe away my longboarding habits eventually."

"I hope not. But, can you ditch it long enough to let me walk you the rest of the way to class?"

"Sure."

I toss a glance at Jeremy to make sure he's cool with taking our equipment back. He nods and I grab a flier from our bag and hand it to Cassie as we turn away from the Student Union.

"Oh yeah, the concert," she assesses. "I already told you I'd be there."

"Just making sure you didn't forget. You bringing your slip-n-slide sister?"

She scrunches her nose in a way that makes her look even more innocent than before. "I don't like that nickname. But yes, she'll be there, too."

"What's wrong with that nickname?"

"I think it sends the wrong message." She waits for me to catch on and when I do, I blanch.

"I'm sorry, but that's hilarious. I like it even more now."

Cassie punches my arm lightly and I grin. Her bright scarlet hair is braided over her right shoulder, accenting the natural pink blush of her cheeks. I've never really been into red heads, but there's something about her that intrigues me.

The problem is, I feel the same way about her Big.

Skyler Thorne has always been a gorgeous girl, but getting to talk to her more this semester has piqued my interest. She's a spitfire and her confidence is unparalleled by any girl I know. Funny – it's like she and Cassie are almost polar opposites. One is innocent and light, one is mysterious and dark. They're like two sexy little devils perched on each one of my shoulders.

"This is me," Cassie says as we reach the Sciences Building. "Will I see you before the concert?"

Her hazel eyes assess me and I throw her a sideways grin. "I'd be disappointed if you didn't."

When her cheeks flush red, I'm not sure how to feel about it, but I don't have time to analyze it before she turns and disappears behind the large wooden doors. Pulling out my cell, I type out a text to a few brothers to meet at the house. We have a lot to get done before next weekend and I'm determined to do it right.

Alpha Sigma may be in the back of everyone's minds now, but if I have anything to do with it, we'll be all the campus can talk about by the end of the semester.

Erin

"I can't believe this will be your last initiation," I say to Siomara, hugging one of her chevron square pillows close to my chest. "You're graduating, G-Big. That's insane."

Siomara smiles, her white teeth blazing against her dark Spanish skin. "I still have a couple of months."

"It's just crazy," I whisper, shaking my head. "And then you'll be president, Big." I turn to Kelsey. Her soft grin spreads into a full-blown smile and she looks to Siomara.

"If I get voted in."

"Like it's even a question." Kelsey has been training for this moment since she became a KKB sister. Regardless of the fact that everyone in our Greek family line for the past seven years has been president, Kelsey is literally the only candidate for the position. She's incredibly driven, smart, and talented. If anyone can lead our sorority and make it even better than it is now, it's her.

"Speaking of which, how do you feel about our newest family addition, Ex?" Siomara asks.

"She's really sweet. Quiet, kind of shy, but when she's around Skyler she seems to open up."

"Have you had the chance to connect with her one on one?"

My mouth pulls to the side. "Honestly, I've been so busy I really haven't."

"Erin," Kelsey scolds me. "She's your Grand Little. Don't you want to have the same relationship with her that you have with Siomara?"

"Ugh, I suck," I groan. "Sometimes I get so wrapped up in all the event planning that I forget to be a good friend. Or in this case, a good Grand Big."

Siomara pats my back sympathetically. "Don't let yourself drown in the logistics of it all. At the end of the day, this is still college and these four years are supposed to be full of amazing fun. Don't let friendship fall second to leadership."

"Wow, so deep, Big," Kelsey teases. Siomara sticks her tongue out and continues making notes in our initiation guidebook.

"Just make some time for her, okay? She's new to all this. Once we initiate her, she'll be a sister for life. Help her understand what an awesome thing that is," Siomara adds. I nod and we get back to work, prepping everything for the ceremony and the celebration after.

Maybe it's the Greek family line I was brought into or maybe it's just my inherent nature to always be a super nerd, but our sorority ceremonies have always been close to my heart. I love planning them, and I love seeing new sisters experience them even more. There's something magical when we're all singing or reciting principles that were founded more than one-hundred years ago that gives me chills. So many people judge Greek life and claim it's "buying friends". If only they were open-minded enough to see what it's really about.

Friendship.

Family.

Scholarship.

Community.

And so much more.

Taking Siomara's advice, I text the girls and ask them all to meet me at Ralph's when we finish initiation practice. I'm applying the last bit of liner to my button-shaped brown eyes when my phone rings.

"Hey Mom," I answer, putting her on speaker phone so I can finish up my makeup. My medium-length blonde hair is a tangled mess so I pull it up into a high pony and let a few strands hang, framing my face.

"Erin, dear, how are you?" My mom's voice is like a mixture of milk and honey – smooth, with a thick southern drawl.

"I'm well. I'm actually about to head out with the girls, can I give you a call tomorrow?"

"Please tell me you're behaving in a lady-like manner, Erin Xander," she warns. "You don't want to get yourself a reputation."

Fighting the urge to roll my eyes, I suck my lips between my teeth and think before responding. "I have a great reputation on campus, Mom. Don't worry."

"I hope so. For how much your father and I donate to the school, you know you have eyes on you at all times. And let's not forget you'll be a senior next year." Her voice trails off, but she doesn't need to finish the sentence for me to pick up what she's implying. My parents expect me to find a "suitable man" to date by next year so I can be engaged right after I graduate. I want law school, they want an MRS degree – Mrs. Rich Ass Doctor.

"Mom, you know I'm going to be president, which means I'll be here an extra semester. And regardless of how you and Dad try to ignore me when I say it, I want to go to law school."

"Oh Erin," she says with a sad sigh. "You're much too pretty to be a lawyer."

I don't even try to argue. "I have to go, Mom. Talk soon."

"Okay, darling. Kisses."

Suddenly, my need for a drink escalates from an eight to an eleven.

My parents are from what I've always known as "old money". They both come from rich parents who also come from rich parents. None of the women in my family have ever worked a day in their life, unless you count fitness and party-hosting as work. My mom was hesitant to even entertain my idea of getting a degree at all, but conceded only when she realized I'd probably need to go to college if I wanted to meet a doctor or an entrepreneur.

I may be the only girl in the country whose parents would be disappointed if I passed the BAR.

When I get to Ralph's, Skyler, Cassie, Bo, and Jess are already waiting at a back table. It's happy hour, so I slide up to the bar and grab a cheap plastic cup filled with beer before heading back to them.

Mother would be so proud.

"Let me guess," I say, chugging half my beer before taking a seat next to Bo. "Lei was busy again?"

"We shouldn't be worried, right?" Skyler asks, her brows furrowed.

"Why would we be?" Jess challenges. We all turn to Skyler, waiting. She looks uneasy, like maybe she said something she shouldn't have.

Shrugging us off, she grabs her drink and lifts it to her lips. "I don't know. No reason. I'm just being weird."

No one pushes the subject, but when I see Jess sketchily glaring at some bald guy across the room, I decide it's the perfect time to call her out. "Speaking of weird, what's going on with you and teacher guy?" I waggle my brows and Jess groans.

"He's annoying."

"Oh?" Bo chimes in. "So you're not into him anymore?"

"Oh I'm still *very* into him."

We all exchange blank stares.

"He's annoying because he won't go the fuck away." She groans. "I'm not allowed to have him, yet he has to look sexy as hell in class every day and then he somehow happens to party at the same bars, too. I mean really," she dramatically gestures toward where the bald guy she was just staring at is seated at the bar. I guess that's Jarrett. "How unfair is it that he looks that good right now and I'm three drinks past buzzed?"

"Just go talk to him," Skyler urges, being her normal, confident self. "I mean seriously, he probably wants to bone, too."

"No way," Jess argues, shaking her head. "You should see the pained looks he gives me in class. Like I'm the biggest regret he has and he's just waiting for my ticking time bomb to go off and expose his shit."

We all fall silent, unsure of how to argue that. If I were Jarrett, I'd be worried about Jess blabbing, too. He has more to lose. He has *everything* to lose.

Suddenly, a wide grin breaks out on Bo's face. "Well look who decided to show."

Ashlei gives her a pointed look. "Talking shit about me, girls?"

"Always," Skyler jokes, cheersing Ashlei's fresh cup of beer. "Looks like you have some catching up to do again."

"Well," she concedes, lifting her cup as we all do the same. "I guess it's a good thing I like a challenge."

Ashlei

Sitting at the sorority house is driving me insane. I don't feel prepared for the competition tomorrow, but there's nothing more I can do. I practiced all day and if I do any more, I'm going to be too sore and worn out to compete. This is the time when I'm supposed to rest and prep my body, but all I feel is anxiety.

Ever since I can remember, I've always been competitive. And not just a little bit, but to a fault. I blame my need to win for all my failures in dance throughout the years. I would constantly push myself too hard and then punish myself if I didn't win. I even went through a cutting phase, which I knew was wrong and hurtful and stupid but I did it anyway. Now, I'm older. I'm more mature and I've learned from my past.

But I still feel that same need to win overpowering every other sense right now.

"What I would give to get inside that pretty head of yours," a sweet voice says in the darkness. I jump, but relax when Bo's smiling face comes into focus. She joins me on the small white porch swing set up in the back courtyard of our house and I return her smile.

"Trust me, you don't want to know everything going on in my head right now."

"Actually, I do. And I'm not the only one." Her brows pull together. "Everyone is talking about you, you know. The way you're always dodging events, the weird makeup, the late nights." She shrugs. "Some of us are worried."

The way she says that last part does something to my stomach that I know isn't good. Bo is stunning, and more than that – she's unlike anyone I've ever known. It's not just her culture, which is night and day different from the one I grew up in, but the way she carries herself, the easy, open-hearted way she sees the world.

"You guys don't need to worry about me."

"Well," she says, chewing her cheek. "Maybe if you tell me what you're up to, I can help ease the tension in the group."

Her dark brown eyes are almost black in the low lighting of the courtyard. With her hair pulled over one shoulder and her kind smile, she radiates beauty in the simplest way imaginable.

"I can't tell you, Bo. I can't tell anyone."

Bo frowns. "Are you in trouble?"

"No," I answer honestly. "Promise."

"Tell me anything," she tries again. "Whatever you feel like you *can* tell me."

I sigh, struggling with my inner voice telling me I need to keep my mouth shut and my inner anxiety fighting to tell someone – anyone – about the competition.

"Let's just say... I have a unique hobby. I love it, I'm good at it, and tomorrow I'm going to be..." My voice trails off as I struggle for the right words. "Tested on it."

Bo looks confused, but she doesn't press for more. "Well, whatever it is, I can tell you're stressed about it." I nod, but then she places her soft hand over mine on the edge of the swing. My breath catches and her eyes flick to mine. Swallowing, she pulls her hand back. "But you shouldn't be, Lei. You're amazing. At everything you do. And whatever this thing is that you can't tell us about, I can tell it's important to you. I know you're going to pass whatever test it is that you have tomorrow because that's the kind of person you are. You're a winner."

For a moment, I don't respond. The air around us feels different from when she first joined me on the swing and I can't figure out how to comprehend the change. "Thank you," I finally manage just above a whisper.

Bo nods, then she lifts herself from the swing. "I'm going to make some tea. You want some?"

"Yeah, actually that sounds great."

"Come on." She notions inside and I follow, possibly watching her a little more closely than I should. Before this semester, Bo Hán was just my best friend's Little.

But now, I have a troubling feeling that I might want her to be more.

***

"Oh my fucking fuck!" Leslie screams when we all pile back into our private dressing room. The entire troupe is jumping up and down, trophies and medals in hand. The energy is uncontrollable.

"I seriously can't believe this," I chime in, shaking my head. "We won. First place. In four categories!"

"Well believe it," Hayden says, picking me up and twirling me in his arms. "And I think we can all agree that we have you to thank." He plants a long kiss on my lips.

"It was all of us. We're a team."

"True," Kya says, unfastening her bra. I used to be shocked by how comfortable she was stripping in front of anyone and everyone, but I'm used to it now. "But we've all competed before and we've never done this well. You kicked ass today, Ashlei." She winks and strips off her spandex, quickly replacing it with a pair of fitted sweats.

"To Ashlei," Leslie says, pulling a flask from her Kitty Heels gym bag. We all chuckle as she takes a swig and begins to pass it around. Various members of the troupe clap me on the back in congratulations after they take their swigs. Then, everyone starts getting dressed, energy still buzzing around us.

"Hey," Hayden says, grabbing my hand. "Come with me. I have a better way to celebrate." He winks and a roaring fire instantly lights in my stomach.

Pulling me through the dressing room to a back bathroom, he locks the door behind us and props me up on the counter, pressing himself between my thighs in one quick motion. Slowly, he kisses down my neck, his strong hands gripping my hips as he does. He's still in the tight, barely-there shorts from our final routine and nothing else. I drag my fingernails down over his chest and abs before tucking them beneath the thin fabric. Even though I just barely graze him, I can feel how hard he is and I bite my lip in anticipation.

"Wait," he breathes, pecking my lips once more before backing up slightly. When he pulls a small plastic bag filled with white powder out of one of the bathroom cabinets, I immediately shake my head.

"No, Hayden. No way. You know I'm not into that stuff."

"Come on," he says sexily, his voice low and his eyes bright. "We just won in four categories. We qualified for semi-finals in January. Celebrate with me. Just one line. I promise, I'll take care of you. I won't let anything happen. It's just going to make you feel even more alive than you already do."

I bite my lip, feeling my heartrate accelerating. I know I shouldn't, but the way Hayden is looking at me makes me want to. I'm already on a high, I *do* want to celebrate, and I do trust Hayden. I know he won't let anything bad happen to me.

But I know cocaine is no joke.

But it could be fun, right?

But I shouldn't do it...

Sensing my inner battle, Hayden moves toward me and slowly shakes some of the white powder onto my cleavage. Using a small blue plastic card, he situates it into a clean line and then looks up at me with heated eyes. He shoots the line, then takes my mouth with his in a frenzy, igniting the desire in my body again.

When he pulls back, he gently empties out a small amount of powder onto his strong trapezius muscle and situates it in a clean line. Then, he hands me the small metal pipe. "Just a little bit,

Ashlei. Come up with me," he pleads. I just sit there with the pipe in my hand, staring at the line and telling myself I should hand the pipe back to him. But something inside me is curious.

Hayden bites his lower lip, letting his teeth drag across the flesh before trailing his hand down my abdomen to land between my thighs. When his fingers snake their way through the fabric and plunge inside of me, I let out a sharp cry of pleasure and let myself fall back against the mirror.

"Come up with me, Ashlei," he says again, working his magical fingers inside me. The ecstasy is already too much, I can't imagine it any more heightened. But with Hayden's hooded eyes devouring me right along with his hands, I can't find the energy to argue anymore. Leaning up, I take a deep breath, plug one nostril, and shoot the line off his bare flesh.

It stings like hell and my eyes water as I wipe my nose, but Hayden is looking at me like I'm the sexiest thing he's ever seen. He steals the pipe from my hand and tosses it on the counter before pulling my mouth to his. While his other hand still works beneath my outfit, the other grips the back of my neck, pulsing a need straight through me.

Suddenly, Hayden pulls my spandex off and rips his to the floor, leaving us both exposed. He teases me at my entrance with his head, nipping playfully at my bottom lip. "You're so fucking sexy, Ashlei. This is going to feel amazing. Trust me."

With that, he plunges into me and I let out a loud moan. At first, I don't feel any different, but after a few minutes, everything changes. I feel incredibly alert, my senses extra-sensitive, and the pleasure I normally feel when Hayden touches me is amplified to a level I've never experienced before. Each time he thrusts into me, every time his thumb brushes my nipple, each flick of his tongue on my skin sends me spiraling toward a dangerous cliff of ecstasy.

"This feels amazing," I moan into Hayden's lips. "*Everything* feels so amazing."

"Like this?" he asks, palming each of my breasts. I nod and grind my pelvis against his as he works in and out. "And this?" he asks again, this time letting his fingertips fall to circle my clit. My moans grow louder and it's my only response before I tumble over the edge and experience an orgasm I never knew existed. It takes over my entire body, my entire soul, my entire being. And when I finish, I'm spent. Completely, totally spent. Crashing, fading, falling.

Hayden comes moments later and then he pulls me into one of the showers with him, planting small kisses down the back of my neck as he runs his hands through my wet hair. Even as the high fades, every touch sparks my sensitive skin and I feel alive. But slowly, the guilt starts to creep in along with the realization of what just happened. Before today, alcohol and the occasional joint were the only drugs I'd ever messed with. Now, I've jumped over the fence into hard drug territory. It was electrifying, it was terrifying, but what scares me most is...

It was fun.

Adam

There's nothing quite like the feeling of seeing something you've worked hard for pay off. You bust your ass for weeks, months, or maybe even years and then it all comes together and you finally feel like you can breathe again.

That's how I feel right now as I stare up at the big stage while a local band kills their set and the crowd goes crazy. Crowd. Yeah, there's actually a big turnout at an Alpha Sigma event. I shake my head, still shocked I somehow pulled it off, and glance down at my clipboard.

"Okay, Filthy Innocents are wrapping up. Give our headliner the five minute warning," I say into the mouthpiece wrapped around my head.

"Ten four," Jeremy answers and I roll my eyes.

"You don't have to talk like a fucking trucker, Jeremy."

"Ten four."

As I make my way across the crowded lawn to the stage, I spot Skyler, Cassie, and a group of their sorority sisters close to the front row. It's Cassie I notice first, her scarlet hair standing out in the crowd of brunettes and blondes. She's dressed in a tight little green dress that takes my eyes down her body whether I try to fight it or not. Which I don't, by the way. She looks great tonight, and she's definitely the one I noticed first.

But it's Skyler who keeps my attention.

A stark contrast from her sisters, she's in distressed jeans and her sorority jersey. Her hair is pulled up into a messy bun and even though I can tell she has makeup on, it doesn't look like she tried as hard as her sisters to look as amazing as she does.

Fucking Christ, the girl is gorgeous.

"Well if it isn't the –"

"Don't even say it," Cassie cuts me off, shoving me playfully as Skyler and the rest of the girls turn around. The three blondes, one I know to be Erin Xander and the other two I'm not familiar with, give me a onceover before turning back toward the stage. Skyler's eyes, however, stay fixed on mine.

"You know, I can honestly say you surprised me tonight."

I cock a brow. "Oh?"

"Yep," she nods. "I did not think A Sigs could get down like this. I'm impressed."

"Me too," Cassie chimes in, her cheeks flushing a bit with the words. It's not lost on me, and I can't say it doesn't give me a thrill to know that blush is because of me.

"Let's get a drink before the headliners go on," one of the blondes says, grabbing Skyler's arm before turning to Cassie.

"I'll save our spot," she says. The girls all nod and squeeze their way past me toward the Alpha Sigma house where the open bar is. It's an illegal open bar, one the campus coordinators wouldn't approve as part of the concert, but I knew without booze this show would go down in flames. So, our basement was transformed into a speakeasy.

"I'll stay with you." Cassie turns to me wide-eyed and I flash a smile. "It's the least I can do, since I'm assuming it was probably you who got all your sisters here."

She flushes a deeper red. "It didn't take much to convince them. Music. Food. Booze. And boys."

"Which of those did you come for?"

She gulps. "The first one... mostly."

I grin. "How's your first semester going?"

"It's good." I can tell by her hesitance there's something she's not saying. "Lots of parties and sorority events. I'm having fun."

"But?"

"But what?" She looks at me confused.

"You're upset about something."

"Why do you say that?"

I shrug. "I can just tell."

Sighing, she looks down and picks at her nail polish. "It's nothing, really. I just... I moved here with my best friend. We both rushed together, but she went Zeta. Ever since rush, she's been a mega bitch and it's just getting worse every day. She doesn't understand why I went KKB and she thinks Zetas are better. She keeps pulling away from me and I feel like I'm going to lose her this semester if I haven't already."

"Is she really that great of a friend if she's treating you like this?"

"She used to be. I don't know, maybe this is just the whole growing up thing. I just miss the girl I knew a few months ago."

I lean in closer, speaking over the sound of instrument tuning and mic checks. "People change, Cassie. You're going to notice in the next few years and probably for the rest of your life that some friends stay and some friends go. The trick is learning that real friendships don't have to be fought for."

She smiles, looking up at me through her lashes. In the bright blue and green lights of the concert, she looks sort of angelic. And I know she kind of is – she's innocent in a way I've never seen a girl before.

Suddenly, there's a surge in the crowd as the lights go down and Cassie is knocked forward hard. When she smacks into me, she apologizes, but I just grab her arms to steady her. "You okay?" She nods, but then suddenly the air around us is thicker than before. Her body is pressed against mine and I can feel the slightest hint of shaking as I hold her. Before I know what I'm doing, I lower my mouth to hers, our lips touching just as the first notes of the new set play.

She sighs into my mouth and I pull her closer, parting her lips with my tongue and moving my hands up to cup her face. Her hands fist my shirt and a soft, almost inaudible moan escapes when I dip my tongue in again. It's then that I realize what I'm doing.

I pull back, pressing my forehead to Cassie's. Then I laugh. What the hell am I doing?

"Man, I'm so sorry. That was weird, huh?"

Cassie pulls all the way back.

"I don't know why I did that. I guess I'm just caught up in all the excitement tonight. I hope this won't make anything weird between us." I rub the back of my neck with one hand and shove the other in my pocket. This chick is one of the coolest I've met at Palm South and of course I let my penis talk me into fucking up that friendship.

Cassie bites her lip, her brows pulled together. I can't tell if I really wigged her out or if she's still trying to register what happened. "No, uh, no. Not weird at all."

I let out a breath I didn't know I was holding. "Good. I really like hanging out with you, Cassie. I didn't mean to take it there."

"It's not, you didn't," she stammers, shaking her head. "It's all good. You were just excited. Zero weirdness, I promise."

I pull her in for a hug just as the girls join us again. "Thanks. I have to run backstage. See you after the show?"

"Yeah. See you."

I turn to leave, still shaking my head at how idiotic I am when Skyler grabs my arm.

"Hey, do you have a thing for my Little?"

I glance at Cassie behind her, but her eyes are fixed on the stage. "No. She's cool, though. I like her, but as a friend."

Skyler nods. "Okay."

Once more, she grabs my arm as I try to leave.

"I just had to clear that up before I did this."

"Did what?"

She runs her soft hand down my arm, her blue eyes dazzling in the rave lights as she tucks something into my front pocket. I swallow when she does, her hand falling way too close to a part of my body she awakened earlier tonight.

"My number," she answers the question I haven't even asked yet. "Call me tonight." With that, she winks and rejoins the girls, not even giving me a second look.

I jog backstage with a shit-eating grin on my face, but it's knocked off almost immediately.

"This concert sucks," Clay says, draining the rest of the dark liquid in his water bottle. From his breath, I assume it's whiskey.

"Don't be a prick, Clay." I shove past him, ordering a few of our brothers to get everything ready for the finale.

"It does. These bands are all local. No one gives a shit."

"Well, there's about a thousand people out there that say you're wrong."

"Whatever. I'm embarrassed that our name is associated with this mess."

Clenching my jaw, I whip around to face him again. "What the fuck is your problem? Are you worried, Clay?" I know I'm crossing a line I shouldn't, but I don't care, even with Jeremy grabbing my shoulder in warning. "Afraid someone might notice what a shit president you are and vote someone else in who actually gives a fuck?"

"And what?" he challenges. "You think that someone is you?"

"Maybe." I stand tall, and Jeremy finally drops his hand, giving up.

Clay stares at me for a moment, then he lets out a guttural laugh, leaning over and bracing his hands on his knees. Clenching my teeth, I surge toward Clay but Jeremy holds me back.

"It's not worth it, man," he mutters.

"I'd listen to him, Brooks," Clay says through his laughter. "You may not want me to be, but I'm still your president. And I can have you kicked out of this fraternity faster than you come in bed. And that's saying something."

I rush forward again, but this time more hands join Jeremy's and they all hold me back. Clay chuckles once more before turning and disappearing into the crowd.

"Don't let him ruin your night, man," Jeremy says. "He's just being a dick. He's mad he didn't think of this first and he's even more upset that you actually pulled it off."

I know he's right, I know it's jealousy – but he's still a fucking prick who deserves to have his jaw broken. Shaking Jeremy off, I nod and check the set list. One song away from the finale. "Let's do this."

In the middle of the last song, just as the music builds, two cannons shoot neon confetti over the black light crowd and the lights strobe in time with the beat. The crowd goes crazy, fog machines mixing with the confetti and the lights. It's exactly the ending I wanted, everyone's going nuts, but I can't even fucking enjoy it.

Then, through the fog, I spot Cassie. She's looking up at the confetti falling, a wide-eyed look on her face. She looks happy, and that makes me feel like maybe it's okay for me, too. I may not be innocent like she is, but I've worked my ass off for this moment.

Grabbing one of the bottles of champagne lined up backstage, I run out into the crowd with Jeremy and several other brothers following. I shake the bottle and open it quickly, spewing the liquid everywhere as more people scream and jump in time with the music. The feeling coming from the crowd is electrifying and the band feeds off of it, making the show even better than I could have imagined.

Clay may have power over me now, but something tells me it won't be that way for much longer.

Erin

My heart is full. I don't know how else to describe it.

I thought initiation as a Big was special, but seeing Skyler pin Cassie during our initiation brought an entirely new kind of pride to my heart. I watched as each of the new girls listened to our founding principles, committing them to memory and swearing to keep them secret for life. Their eyes were wide, their expressions eager – it was an amazing sight to behold.

For me, it always seems too short. We've been preparing for weeks, but already the ceremonial clothing is packed away, along with the candles and ritual books, and sisters are scattered around the hotel venue taking photos with their lines. Spotting my line, I pull my phone from my Kate Spade purse.

"Cheese!" I snap the photo before any of them have the chance to realize what I'm doing and they all groan in unison.

"Not fair!" Kelsey shrieks.

"Seriously this time," I say, grouping them together. I find another sister to take our photo and jump in right behind Skyler. We make a long line, starting with Siomara at the top standing on a chair and ending with Cassie on her knees. Our family tree is one of the biggest in the sorority, since Siomara stays an extra semester to be president. I love the feeling of being the largest and, in my opinion, the best.

After a dozen photos at the fountain and around the hotel garden, I steal Cassie away from the group.

"So, you're officially a sister," I say, grinning. "Do you feel different?"

Her smile is just as big as mine and I have a feeling she'll be more like me than Skyler. She seems to have that same passion for history that I do. "Honestly, yes. I really do. And I wasn't expecting that."

"It's amazing, isn't it?"

She nods. "I have to admit, I was a little creeped out at the beginning. The dark room... candles... weird clothing."

I laugh, nudging her. "Trust me, I was freaked out too. But you have to think, that ceremony was created in the late eighteen hundreds."

"That gives me chills. How awesome to think how many sisters we have across the states."

"Across the world," I correct her. Cassie smiles wider and we walk the grounds of the hotel, talking about her roommate, classes, and a little about my family. I don't go into full detail, but I give her a little sneak into my parents and their craziness. Her family seems to be the polar opposite of mine – loving, supportive, kind.

It makes me envy my Grand Little.

When we make our way back to the lobby where all the sisters are waiting for our charter bus, I notice Skyler is missing.

"Where'd Sky go?" I ask Siomara.

"She said she had some errands to run but that she'd see us at Ralph's later."

"Oh. Want to grab dinner, Cassie? We can go back to the house and get ready for Ralph's afterward."

"Yes!" she answers excitedly. "I'm starved."

Siomara and Kelsey join us for dinner at the sushi restaurant on campus. Glancing around the table at my sisters, I feel an overwhelming warmth envelop me. In high school, I was lost. I went through so much that no one ever knew about – not even my parents. It was the summer before my senior year when I found myself, and ever since then, I've thrown myself into everything I love – this sorority being one of those things.

Some people go to college for the education, some for the parties, some to find love. Me? Well, I guess I want all of those things, too – but more than anything, I want memories. I want friendship. And I know without a doubt that I've found both in Kappa Kappa Beta.

***

We're still laughing as we pile into the sorority house, Kelsey and Siomara heading up to the President Bedroom while Cassie and I made our way to my room.

"Do you need to borrow clothes or did you bring some?"

Cassie's mouth pulls to the side. "I didn't bring any. Would you mind letting me borrow something?"

"Of course not! Come on," I lead her up the stairs. "I have the perfect outfit for you."

I help Cassie dress in tight, dark jeans and a slinky black top with an open back before pulling out a simple red dress for me. I can tell Cassie is new to the dressing up thing – almost as new as Skyler was last year when she rushed. But, at least Cassie has some grasp on makeup and what to pair with an outfit. Skyler is clueless. She'd much rather be in ratty jeans and a t-shirt and, more often than I care to see, she does end up in that. But, when it comes to something important, she lets us dress her.

Thank God.

"I feel like it's missing something," Cassie says, staring at her reflection in the full-length mirror.

"Hmm... Oh! We need a pop of color. Skyler has some killer red heels she wore for some poker thing last semester. Let's go steal them from her. Pair those with some red lipstick and you're set!"

Giggling as we rush down the hallway to her room, we burst through the door and flick on the lights.

"Shit!" A voice says from beneath the covers on Skyler's bed. Her head pops out and she's completely flushed, her hair a mess and her makeup smeared. There's someone else in the bed with her, but they won't reveal themselves.

"Are you fucking serious, Skyler?!" I yell, but quickly close the door behind Cassie. Lowering my voice, I storm to the bed and rip the covers back, revealing the guy from the Alpha Sigma concert. "You have got to be kidding me. I know you did not bail early on initiation to bring a BOY back to the sorority house. Mom Cindy will literally skin you alive if she finds out!"

"Well, she doesn't have to if you stop screaming!" Skyler whispers, giggling. The man in her bed is attractive, I'll give her that. His dark hair is messy, but his even darker eyes are hooded with lust. Pair all that with his charming grin and I can see why she brought him back.

"Okay, you have two minutes to get him dressed and out of here."

"Um," she pauses, looking to the guy. "Could we maybe get like five?"

"Oh my God just get him out!" I throw the covers over both of them, grab her red heels from the bottom of her closet, and lead Cassie back to my room. I'm chuckling a little as we reach my door.

"Your Big," I start, tossing her the heels. "She's something else, that one."

Cassie's face is sheet white. "Yeah."

"Are you okay?" I rush to her side. "Oh crap, did you eat bad sushi?"

"I'm fine." Cassie slips on the heels as she hops into the bathroom. "Just let me put on some lipstick and I'll be ready."

"Perfect. I don't know about you, but I'm ready for a drink. You have your fake, right?"

"Yeah," she says, finishing the last coat of red on her lips. She packs the lipstick in her clutch and turns back to me, a new determination on her face. "And I don't just need *a* drink. I need ten."

"Now you're talking like a KKB!"

I throw my arm around her shoulder, steering her out the door. Just as we reach the bottom of the stairs, the front door flies open and Ashlei stumbles through.

She's still in her initiation dress, but the white fabric is wrinkled and stained in several places now. Her skin is covered in a light sheen of sweat and I can tell without a second glance that she's been crying.

"Oh my God. Ashlei, what happened?"

Ashlei's eyes are empty as they meet mine. She gazes around the foyer for a moment before closing the front door behind her and stumbling toward the stairs. "I'm fine. I'm skipping Ralph's."

She starts making her way up and Cassie and I exchange worried glances. "Ashlei," I call out, following her. Cassie is on my heels. "You're clearly not fine. What's going on?"

"I said I'm fine!" she screams, turning on me. "God, Erin, you're not my mother. Back off!" With that, she runs the last few stairs and a few seconds later I hear the door to our room slam shut. Swallowing, I turn back to Cassie.

"Do you want to stay with her?" she offers.

"No, no. She won't talk to anyone when she's like that. Let's just go. I'll talk to her in the morning."

Cassie offers a soft smile and nods.

Regardless of the tension at the house, Cassie and I loosen up once we get to Ralph's. Jess and Bo are already there and Skyler joins us not too long after, looking satisfied and ready to party. Jess high fives her when she finds out what happened and Bo buys her a shot. I can only shake my head.

Initiation is over. The semester is halfway over, too. Looking around the bar at my sisters, I feel the heaviness of that settle in on me. Something is going on with Ashlei, Skyler's hiding something with Bear, Jess is skating on thin ice with a teacher and my parents are on my ass more than ever. Sighing, I sip on my shitty college-bar martini. I don't have much time to think on all the drama, though, because Jess and Skyler jump up on the bar and start pouring shots straight out of the bottle into the mouths of students lining the barstools. I let out a laugh and raise my glass.

The KKB girls may be kind of crazy, but I wouldn't have it any other way.

EPISODE 4

"I didn't peg you for A GOOD GIRL."

Cassie

It's strange how some memories are fleeting, almost gone the moment they happen, and others are burned into our brains and locked on replay. The kiss I shared with Adam just a little over a week ago is one of the latter. Lying in the hot South Florida sun right now only seems to sear the impression of his mouth onto mine even more. I'm not sure I'll ever be able to lick my lips again without tasting his.

"Seriously, why would anyone want to live anywhere other than Florida?" Jess asks with a sigh, leaning back into her beach chair further. "It's a Tuesday. In late October. And we're on the beach."

"One of the many perks of Palm South," Erin adds, sipping on the vodka water mix she has in her Kappa Kappa Beta tumbler cup. Jess, Erin, and Ashlei are still tan from the summer and each little bit of sun they've managed to catch since fall hit. My skin, on the other hand, never seems to stray too far from a pale white. Sometimes I get tan lines, but usually they're more like *peach* lines. I don't ever get truly tan.

"Where's your Big, Cassie?" Jess asks. I steal a glance at Ashlei through my shades. She's been quiet all day, barely saying more than a few words. She just keeps steadily sipping on her own tumbler and staring out at the waves.

"Skyler had to practice for that tournament she's in this weekend. I've barely seen her since initiation." I gulp, remembering exactly the way I saw her that night – tangled up in the sheets with Adam.

"Boo," Jess resolves. "I don't think I'll ever understand her obsession with that game."

"I think there's more to it than she tells us." I notice Erin avoiding the conversation when I hint to Skyler holding something back and it only confirms it. There's something she's not telling us.

Seems to be a lot of that going on around here.

"I'm going in the water." Ashlei doesn't wait for anyone to respond before she's up out of her chair and halfway to where the gentle waves are rolling in.

"Is she okay?" I ask, not really pointing the question to anyone directly.

"She hasn't really talked to me since we ran into her before Ralph's on Saturday," Erin answers, her mouth pulled to the side. "Ashlei is really private, though. She'll tell us what's on her mind when she's ready." Erin turns to me. "How's the situation with your roommate, G-Little?"

I groan. "Awful. I can't wait to move into the sorority house next semester. I don't want to lose my relationship with Paris but I swear she couldn't care less if I was eaten by a shark."

"What's her deal, anyway? Weren't you best friends in high school?" Jess asks, reapplying lotion to her shoulders.

"That's what makes it so difficult. She's completely different and we've only been here two months. I don't understand it." I frown and sip on my own drink, enjoying the buzz of day drinking in the sunshine. It's an entirely different kind of tipsy than a bar at night.

"Oh my God." Jess fumbles with her drink, trying to pull her large, floppy beach hat over her face. "Shit. Shit shit shit."

"What?" Erin and I ask in unison.

"It's Jarrett. Fuck! How is it that this guy is everywhere I am?! I know our campus is small but Jesus Christ."

Just as she says the words, I spot Jarrett down the beach. His bald head is covered with a baseball cap pulled on backward and his eyes are shielded behind thick black sunglasses. Even from this distance I can see a plethora of tattoos sprawling up both of his arms.

"Damn, Jess," Erin says, shaking her head. "I have no idea how you're resisting that hotness. I kind of want to pour my drink on him and lick it off."

Jess pegs Erin with the bottle of tanning lotion she was just using and Erin laughs, the sound echoing off the waves. Jarrett turns toward us and we all snap our mouths shut and face the water again.

"Tell me he did not just see us," Jess whispers. "Oh my God, he's coming over here."

Erin and I are giggling when Jarrett reaches us.

"Jess, can I talk to you?" He frowns, tucking his hands into the pockets of his forest green board shorts. "Please?"

"Is it Wednesday night?"

Jarrett looks confused. "What?"

"If it's not Wednesday night, then I'm not in my Scope and Methods class," Jess asserts, lifting herself from her chair. Even with sunglasses on it's hard for Jarrett to hide the way his eyes are taking in Jess's body now that she's standing. "Therefore, we have nothing to talk about."

"I beg to differ," he starts, but Jess is already halfway to the water.

"See you in class!" she calls out behind her before joining Ashlei. Jarrett sighs, gives Erin and I a slight nod of his head, and then makes his way back up the beach.

"Poor guy," Erin says. Jess and Ashlei are wading waist-deep in the water, but neither of them say a word. They just stare out at the boats passing by in the distance and let the ocean breeze roll through their hair. As Erin drifts off in her chair, I fall into the comfortable silence and my thoughts settle on the one person who seems to haunt them most nowadays.

Adam.

My stomach twinges and I shift in my chair. No matter how much I tell myself I need to stop, I can't quit thinking about our kiss. More specifically – what the kiss was to him as opposed to what it was to me. When his lips met mine, I felt a spark – an electricity I've never experienced before. It caught at the point of contact and spread like wildfire through my entire body within seconds.

But then he pulled back and brushed it off like it was nothing to him.

And maybe it wasn't.

That's what kills me most.

Friends. That's what he wants to be. And now that I know Skyler is interested in him, too, I'm doubly screwed. Is there a protocol for Big/Littles liking the same guy? Do I tell her I like him? Would that be selfish since he essentially said kissing me was weird?

Sighing, I fall deeper into my chair and pull my psychology textbook from my beach bag. Our chapters this week cover the signs and psychology of social acceptance and unrequited love. Though I know what I'm feeling is far from love, the coincidence isn't lost on me.

We stay on the beach until the sun sets and then pack up our bags and head back to campus. The girls drop me at my dorm on their way to the house and Paris is home when I arrive.

She looks up at me, assesses the beach gear I'm still holding, and then looks back down at the fingernail she's painting. She doesn't even acknowledge me and I can't decide if it pisses me off or just feels like a punch to the gut.

"Hey, Paris."

"Hey."

"Going out tonight?"

"I have a sorority event at the house in an hour."

"Oh," I say softly. "Okay. Well do you maybe want to hang out tomorrow night after your late class?"

"Sorry, can't."

"What about Thursday?"

"Busy."

"Friday?"

She sighs, tightening the lid on the bright pink polish and blowing on her fresh coat. "Honestly, Cassie? I really don't want to hang out. No offense, but I've got a lot going on with Zeta right now and I know you probably do with KKB, too." She wrinkles her nose a bit as she says my letters and I clench my teeth.

"I'm not too busy to hang out with my best friend. Or has that changed and I'm just unaware?"

"We're in college now, Cassie," Paris says, resigned. "Aren't we a little old for the best friends thing?"

Shaking my head, I don't even answer her question before storming back to my room, silently thanking my parents for getting me a dorm with separate bedrooms. I slam the door and toss my beach bag in the corner before falling face first onto my bed. I want to cry, or scream, or anything that will help get the emotion out of me but nothing comes. When my phone's beachy ringtone fills the silence, I reach for it and answer before even checking caller ID.

"Hello?"

"What are you doing?"

I bolt upright when I recognize Adam's voice on the other end of the line. "Just got home from the beach."

"Are you hungry? My class just ended and I'm starved and could use a beer. Want to hit The Plaza with me?"

I swallow. "Uh, sure. What time do you want to meet?"

"I'm heading there now. Just come to Pie Heaven when you're ready."

"Okay. See you in a minute."

I don't even bother changing and within fifteen minutes I'm walking into the pizza place. The Plaza is a casual little shopping center with a few restaurants, two bars, and a dozen little Mom and Pop shops ranging from a nail salon to a custom t-shirt shop. When I walk into Pie Heaven, Adam is already there. He waves at me from a booth in the very back.

"I ordered us a large pepperoni. You're not a vegetarian, are you?"

"Nope. Total meat lover here." My eyes grow wide as the words leave my lips and I realize the implication behind them. *Could I be any more of a spazz?*

Adam smirks. "Good to know. How was the beach?" As his eyes scan my bathing suit and small cover-up I suddenly wish I would have taken the time to change. I can only imagine how my hair looks after being in salt water and wind all day.

"Fun. Coming home, on the other hand..."

"What happened? Roommate drama still?"

"Unfortunately."

Adam crosses his arms across his chest and leans back. "Whatever. Her loss. Zetas are bitches, anyway."

I laugh at that just as the waitress drops off our pizza. Adam immediately digs in, draining the rest of his beer to wash down the first slice which I'm almost positive he just inhaled. There was no chewing going on.

"You going to Ralph's next week for Halloween?"

"I heard that I really don't have a choice," I reply. "Sounds like that's what everyone does."

"It's a huge block party. There are other bars hosting events, but Ralph's is the place to be. It always has been."

"Well, then I guess I'll be there."

"Cool. Me too. Is Skyler going?"

My heart sinks along with my smile. "I'm not sure. She's been really busy training lately."

"Training? For what?"

"She has a poker tournament this weekend."

"Oh shit, I didn't know she played. That girl is full of surprises."

"Yeah."

Adam watches me carefully for a moment before speaking again. "Well, regardless, I'll be there. Do you know what you're dressing up as yet?"

"I'm deciding between Ariel from *The Little Mermaid* and a zombie bride."

Adam quirks a brow. "Those are two very different directions."

"Yeah, well, I haven't decided if I want to be cute and innocent or scary as hell."

He smirks, wiping his mouth with a napkin and finishing his second beer. “Well, my vote is for Ariel.”

“Yeah? It’s not too cliché?” I twirl a strand of my frizzy, beach-blown hair around my index finger. “You know, red hair and all?”

“Nah,” he asserts, watching me with a sideways grin. “Besides, I think you’d be cute in a little purple shell bra.”

My cheeks flush, but I don’t know if Adam notices as he calls the waitress over for the check. He pays and then walks me back to my dorm, chatting about the concert almost the entire way. Once I’m back in my room, I strip down and run a cold shower. Even with the icey water raining down, my skin is still red hot.

And something tells me it’s not a sunburn.

I've never really loved school, but class feels especially long tonight. It could have something to do with the fact that Jarrett's eyes haven't left me for more than thirty seconds. Every time I glance over at him, he's staring at me – and not in a creepy way, but in the way that makes me feel like he's weighing all the options he has for how to take my clothes off.

It's so strange, seeing him dressed in sharp black slacks and a gray button up shirt with a black vest to match. I'll always see him in board shorts and a t-shirt, just like that first night. Just like yesterday on the beach when I avoided him. That man belongs on a beach – or at least somewhere where he's not restricted by clothes.

When Dr. Maynard releases us and Jarrett finishes calling attendance, I pack up my bag and keep my eyes fixed on the door as I walk past him. When a strong hand wraps around my wrist just as I reach the door, I close my eyes and exhale through my nose.

"We need to talk."

"No, we don't," I say softly, watching the other students pass. None of them notice us, but I'm still paranoid. When the last person leaves and we're the only ones left in the room, Jarrett curses.

"It's been almost two months. Why are you avoiding me?"

I scoff. "Really? If you have to ask, you're seriously stupid."

"It doesn't have to be like this, Jess." His dark eyes are sheltered beneath furrowed brows. "I don't... I didn't want what happened to be a one time thing."

"Yeah, well, it was."

Jarrett blinks. "Is that all you wanted?"

No.

"Obviously. You knew that when you took me in the back of your truck." Saying the words out loud, even though we're alone, makes me blush. And I *never* blush.

Jarrett's mouth thins out into a flat line. "Don't act like you're not still attracted to me. Don't act like you don't watch me every class. Don't act like you don't have the same things going through your mind that I do right now." He steps closer to me, reaching his hand up to grasp behind my neck. My eyelids flutter at the contact but I keep my cool. "You want me. And I want you."

Fuck.

Like seriously, FUCK.

Pulling away, my eyes fall to the floor and I notice his bag is packed with a change of clothes – board shorts included. I need to kill this – whatever *this* is – between us, and I think I know exactly how to do it.

"You're my professor's assistant," I state firmly, though my voice sounds shaky. "The only thing I want from you is the answer key to our next test."

With that, I turn on my heel and push through the heavy wooden door of the classroom.

Then, I set my plan into motion.

***

My vagina is trying to talk me out of my plan the entire drive to the beach.

What is wrong with you? Fuck him, you idiot!

But it's not that simple. Do I want to keep hooking up with Jarrett? Obviously. The way he pulled my hair and grabbed my neck in the back of that truck has me more than curious about what he could do with an entire bed at his disposal. The sad truth is that he *is* my professor's assistant. He could get fired, I could get expelled, we could both damage our reputations – both professionally and socially.

So tonight, I'll get my point across.

My light cotton spaghetti strap dress sticks to my skin as I walk through the sand to the beach bar. I could blame the still-hot-even-though-it's-October Florida air, but the truth is that I'm nervous. I don't know if what I'm doing is even what I really want. All I know is that it has to happen.

Jarrett's eyes find mine as soon as I walk through the entryway. His hand that was just wiping down the left end of the bar halts and he stares. Swallowing, I walk purposefully up to him and order a beer. As soon as he slides it into my hand, I drop cash on the bar and strut over to a group of guys I recognize from school.

Game time.

One of the guys is Josh, Clinton's little, and he just so happens to be the easiest guy I've ever known. I'm pretty sure he'd hit on a plastic bag if the wind blew it in a way that made it resemble tits. As soon as he sees me, he jumps out of his chair.

"Oh shit! J-Love has graced us with her presence!"

"And you're damn lucky, too."

He swoops me up into a hug and I giggle, though only for show. I am not into Josh in any way, shape, or form. Josh has an amazing upper body, but he's missed one too many leg days and his skin is constantly a burnt orange from the self-tanner he applies daily. His hair is a light brown, but I swear he dyes it. There is no way this kid isn't a ginger. If his freckles aren't a dead giveaway, the brownish-red beard he's sporting right now certainly is.

Josh's brothers order the first round of shots and I make sure to lean into Josh more than necessary, letting his hands rest on my hips and ass. I don't even have to look Jarrett's way to know he's watching. I can practically feel my skin burning.

"Where's Bear tonight?"

"No idea. Probably changing his tampon." My brows shoot up. Josh has always been very respectful to Bear. "He's been a pussy lately. He keeps raggin' on us for partying, saying shit about how we're going to get us in trouble. Plus he's been moody as hell for no damn reason. Don't you remember him freaking out on Skyler at our party a few weeks ago?"

"Oh yeah. That was awkward."

"Yeah. Whatever." He grins with a smile too big for his face and pulls me in closer. "The real question is, what do you want to drink next?"

Ick. Typical Josh. He always has to get a girl wasted before he can get laid, which only makes my skin crawl more at the fact that I have to use him of all guys to get Jarrett off my ass. But he's easy, and he's working. I saunter up to the bar pretending like I'm still giggling about something Josh said and order another round of shots.

Jarrett fills the order silently, slamming glasses around more than necessary. After he pours the blue liquid in a straight line over the shot glasses, he snatches the cash from my hand but holds my gaze.

"What are you doing?"

"Paying for shots," I deadpan. "Should I be doing something else?"

With that, I gather up the shots and make my way back to the table, casting a glance back at Jarrett just to confirm that he's watching my ass.

And he so is.

As the night progresses, Josh pushes his luck more and Jarrett watches every minute of it. I feel kind of shitty using Josh, but I need to piss Jarrett off. I need him to see that I'm not interested, he was just a one night stand, nothing more and nothing less.

Even if it is a lie.

The truth is, I would love nothing more than to take him in his truck again and feel his strong hands splayed on my lower back as I ride his massive cock. But he's my teacher – or, pretty close to it – and he could get fired. For some reason, I care about him enough to not want that.

Which is also weird.

"You're so damn sexy," Josh whispers into the nape of my neck before kissing his way up to my earlobe. He bites it seductively, but I don't feel the slightest bit turned on.

"Can you walk me to my car?" I flirt, biting my lip. I made sure to stop after the first two shots, fake drinking my beer and refilling the guys' drinks as necessary. I fully intend to drive my happy ass home tonight.

Josh groans. "Gladly."

As we stumble toward the door, Josh cups my ass in his hands and I swat at him playfully, letting him kiss up and down my neck. When we reach the entryway, I cast one last glance at Jarrett. His dark eyes are haunting, his jaw tense beneath the skin stretched over it. His nose flares with every breath as he watches Josh push me the last bit out the door, and then he's out of view.

And I'm off the hook.

I keep Josh occupied for a half hour, kissing him feverishly in the back of my BMW. When I think it's been long enough for him to walk back into the bar and raise eyebrows, I peel him off me and open the door.

"Thanks, Josh. See you around."

"Wait, what?" The look on his face almost makes me feel bad.

Almost.

"Yeah, not happening, Josh," I say, crawling into the front seat. The engine purrs to life and Josh slowly crawls out of the back seat, his face still twisted in confusion.

"What the fuck was all that?"

I shrug. "Just having a little fun. Like I said, see you around." I flash him a smile and then pull away, leaving him stroking his ego and maybe something else in the parking lot.

The farther I get away from the bar, the more I feel like I can breathe. I blast Eric Church as loud as I can to drown out whatever thoughts of Jarrett are still stuck in my head, but it only helps momentarily.

It was luck running into Josh tonight. I figured I'd have to work hard for some business suit to walk out the door with me, but I lucked into him and his brothers breaking away from the normal college bars. Jarrett saw everything, he saw that he wasn't anything special, and now I don't have to worry about him trying to seduce me.

Mission accomplished.

Skyler

A hard knock on my bedroom door wakes me from my nap and I groan. "Go away."

"Sky? It's me..."

My eyes fly open at the sound of Clinton's voice. Snatching my phone from the table, I sigh when I see I haven't even been asleep for twenty minutes. With the news I got from my parents last week coupled with practicing for my upcoming tournament, I haven't been sleeping at night. Afternoon naps are my only savior, and this one just got interrupted.

But Clinton hasn't talked to me since the O Chi party when he blew up on me. I've tried texting him, calling him, showing up at his room – but he's avoided me every time. So, as much as I really want to hit snooze and tell him to go away again, I refrain.

"Come in."

I sit up in my tiny bed and attempt to fix my disheveled hair as he peeks in. Seeing that I'm decent, he lets the door close behind him and stands awkwardly in front if it with his hands in his pockets. "Hey."

"Hi."

I don't know what else to say. Clinton and I have never been in an argument, but I pushed him too hard at the party and he let me know that I needed to back off. It's hard for me to do. Clinton is one of my best friends and I don't know how to help him if he won't tell me what's going on.

Of course, the past week and a half I've been more occupied with my own shit. Dad didn't get the promotion he'd been promised, which means the money he and Mom spent on fixing up the house thinking he'd have the paycheck to pay it off set them back. By a lot. I have a gut feeling there's more they aren't telling me because they don't want me to worry, but it just makes me even more anxious.

I'm entered in a fairly large tournament at the casino downtown on Tuesday. If I win, I could pay off the credit card debt they racked up and finish paying off my tuition from this semester. It's the biggest tournament I've played in a long time. With stakes this high, I've been practicing every night – and it's definitely catching up to me.

Clinton lets out a heavy exhale, breaking me from my thoughts. It's then that I notice how rough he looks. His dark skin is even darker under his eyes and his shoes don't match his hat, which is saying a lot for Clinton. "Look, Skyler. I'm sorry. I'm bad at this shit but I'm sorry I blew up on you. You didn't deserve it, you were just trying to help and I was a dick."

I shrug, trying not to make a big deal about it. He hurt my feelings, but at the same time I meant what I said to the girls when I said he'd come around when he was ready. That's the way Clinton works. "It's all good, Bear. I'm just worried about you."

"I know you are." His eyebrows knit together as he assesses my appearance. "Shit, by the looks of you maybe it's me who should be worried."

I run my fingers through my tangled hair. "Yeah. Tournament this week."

"Yeah? Been at the casino every night getting in some practice?"

I nod, yawning. "Exactly."

Clinton sits down on the bed next to me and pulls me into his big chest, his arms enveloping me in a warm hug that almost puts me back to sleep. "You stress yourself out too much with this."

"Well, I have a lot to lose. And a lot to gain."

"Family stuff again?"

Clinton doesn't know the whole story with my family. He gets the gist of it – I grew up piss poor and I have to work for everything I want and need – but he doesn't know that I also have to provide for my family. Or, rather, I choose to.

"Dad didn't get the promotion like he thought he would. Mom said they racked up some credit card debt, but I think it might be more than that, Bear." I lean up to look at him. "I think there's something they're not telling me."

"So you're going to kick everyone's ass at this tournament and then send some money home?" I nod and Clinton smiles. "'Attagirl. Are you going to Ralph's for the annual Halloween rager?"

"I doubt it. That's the day after the tournament. I'll probably sleep through it."

"What?" Bear jumps up, making me instantly miss his warm embrace. "Oh hell no. You need to have some fun, Sky. You're prepared enough. Get some rest and enjoy your college experience."

"It's just one party."

"But it's the *Halloween* party," he points out.

I chuckle, but concede. "Well, when you put it like that." Clinton winks and sits back down on the bed. Without even asking, I lean into him again and let my eyes close.

"We have an intramural football game tomorrow. You should come."

I nod against his chest, but don't have the energy to say anything else. He chuckles and leans us back, holding me until I succumb to sleep.

***

I've never really been a sports person, other than poker – which is still kind of tough for me to see as a sport. In high school, I was too unpopular to be involved in any sporting events and in college I only go to support the guys. I can't name one professional team of any variety and I have no idea what the penalties mean, but I'm still geared up in green and black – Omega Chi Beta colors – with Cassie as we cheer on Clinton and his brothers against Alpha Sigma.

"I'm glad you came out tonight, Big," Cassie says, smiling. "I feel like you've been hidden away the past two weeks."

"I know, I'm sorry. It's just –"

"The tournament," she interrupts, still smiling. "I know, I know. I'm just glad you're finally hanging out with me."

I frown a little at that, but decide not to think too much about it. I'm here now. That's what matters.

Cassie and I jump off the bench every time O Chi scores, cheering like we should be carrying pompoms. Even though the leaves don't really turn colors in South Florida, being outside cheering on a football game gets me in the fall spirit. When the last whistle is blown, the score is twenty-one to seven – Omega Chi Beta.

Clinton throws me up and over his shoulder when he rushes off the field, spinning me around and cheering. I beat my tiny fists against his back to no avail and end up just giving in, celebrating with him. When he finally puts me down, the grin I'm so accustomed to seeing is plastered on his face. *This* is the Clinton I know, the Clinton I've missed.

"Fuck yeah! You saw me sack that wimpy ass Alpha Sig, right?" Clinton holds up his hand for a high five and I slap mine against it.

"You were awesome, Bear."

"Fuck yeah he was," Josh chimes in. I fight against the urge to roll my eyes as he throws his arm around my shoulder. "You coming out to celebrate with us, Sky?"

"She has to practice for her poker tournament," Cassie chimes in.

"Boo," Josh says, but I'm thankful that he pulls his arm off me and rushes toward his brothers. Clinton gives me one last hug and then joins them.

"Uh oh, I smell trouble," a voice says behind us. Cassie and I turn around at the same time to see Adam.

Shirtless.

"Are you sure that's trouble? Might be defeat."

Adam clutches his bare chest and stumbles back a bit, tossing his drenched red shirt over his shoulder. The view of his insanely cut arms and chest is definitely a nice sight. "Ouch, Skyler. Why don't you just kick a guy while he's down?"

I giggle and bite my lip. Adam is cute. No, he's *hot* – and seeing his dark hair mussed on top of his head right now only makes me think of the last time I saw him that way, after rolling around in my bed for half the afternoon.

"What'd you think of the game?" he asks Cassie. She blushes and I shake my head. My Little is so damn innocent. Just talking to a boy makes her nervous. How the hell did she end up with me as a Big?

"It was good. You were good."

He grins. "Does that mean you'll give me a loser hug?"

Cassie's eyes bulge as she takes in his sweaty body, but he doesn't give her a chance to run before he wraps her in his arms and spins her around. She squeals and flails her legs until he finally puts her down.

"Thanks for the help, Big!"

"Hey, I'm not trying to get up in that sweaty mess."

Adam turns his attention to me. "Oh yeah?" I take off sprinting in the opposite direction but he catches me easily and smothers me against his slick chest. I have to say, I don't really mind it.

"You going to Ralph's Wednesday?" he asks, finally letting me free.

"I'm thinking about it."

"You should go."

"Oh yeah? Why's that?"

"Because I'll be there."

I bite my lower lip and assess him. I can't say for sure, but I think I just might like Adam Brooks. "Well I have a tournament tomorrow night, so I might be too tired to go."

"Oh yeah," he muses. "I heard about you and your kick ass poker skills. Can I come watch?"

"Um, absolutely not."

He blanches. "Why not?"

"I don't really mix business with... pleasure," I say, quirking a brow on the last word. Adam smiles at me devilishly, but doesn't press the subject. Suddenly, his eyes flick behind me and his face hardens. When I turn to see what he's staring at, Cassie is blushing talking to one of Adam's brothers.

"Isn't that your president?"

"Yeah."

Adam is still focused on the scene behind me when I turn back around, his mouth flattened into a thin line. "I take it you don't exactly care for him?"

"That's putting it lightly," he scoffs. "The guy's a dick." He shakes his head and turns his attention back to me. "Let me come to the tournament with you."

"Not a chance."

Adam narrows his eyes. "Fine. Well, at least tell me what you'll be dressed as at Ralph's so I can find you. Because let's be honest, you'll be there. Everyone will be there."

I roll my eyes, but can't really argue with him. "Are you going to dress as the other half of my costume if I tell you what it is?"

"Maybe."

"Well then, I'll either be Sandy from Grease, the black swan, or a princess. Choose your costume wisely."

With that, I throw him a wink and saunter back over to Cassie before linking my arm in hers and pulling her away from Adam's president, who she informs me is named Clay. When I cast a glance back, Adam is still staring, shaking his head with his arms crossed over his chest.

Maybe this party won't be so bad after all.

Cassie

I learn quickly that Halloween in a sorority house is an explosion of glitter, spandex, and make-up.

Adjusting my boobs in the too-small purple shell top the girls talked me into, I look around at all the costumes. Bo is a sexy ninja and Ashlei is a go-go dancer. They're both giggling in the corner of Skyler and Jess's room as they apply the last of their fake eyelashes in the full length mirror. Bo's outfit is a two-piece and hugs her tight body, accentuating the lean muscle that stretches all the way from her collarbone to her ankles. Ashlei's neon green dress cuts off just below her ass, but it pairs well with the white go-go boots that end at the top of her knee caps. It feels good to see Ashlei laughing again. She's been distant the past two weeks and I know I'm not the only one who's been worried.

"Are you sure I look okay?" I ask, picking at the sequin green skirt hugging my waistline. "I feel a little cliché going as the only redheaded princess."

"You look fucking hot," Jess says, smacking my ass as she saunters over to her closet. She's dressed as a sexy cowgirl, complete with a tight, short jean skirt and plaid top that ties off right beneath her chest. Her cleavage is accentuated by the open buttons at the top of the shirt and she tops it all off with a straw cowgirl hat and matching brown boots.

"She's right, Little. Just watch out for nip slips." Skyler winks and pops her lips after applying a final coat of lip gloss. Of all the costumes, I love Skyler's the most. She's the only one of us who didn't openly go for sexy but landed there anyway. Dressed as the black swan complete with black spandex one-piece and tutu, she's not just sexy – she's intriguing. In fact, she's almost scary – especially with the contacts she's wearing that color her eyes red just like Natalie Portman's in the movie.

When Erin blows the whistle that came with her bedroom referee costume, we all jump. "Let's get the hell out of here. I need a drink!"

We all cheer before following her through the house and out into the yard. Several cabs are lined up and down Greek row waiting to pick up fares, so we climb in the first van we see and the cabbie takes off without even asking where to.

"You look great tonight," Ashlei says to Bo quietly. The three of us are sandwiched in the very back of the van and I adjust our air conditioning vents, trying to keep my hair from frizzing out in the hot October air. I swear it never gets cold in South Florida.

"Thanks," Bo replies, offering Jess a glittering smile. Her hand reaches out for Ashlei's knee and she squeezes it lightly. "Although, I think we both know I look a little more than just great."

She says the last part as a whisper, but I still hear her, and I can't help but notice she doesn't move her hand from Ashlei's leg. I don't have time to overthink it as Skyler thrusts a flask into my hand. "Drink up, Little Nug."

Ralph's is always packed, being that it's the closest bar to campus, but tonight it's on an entirely new level. The entire parking lot is sealed off by a makeshift fence for the block party and there are laser lights bouncing in time with the music thumping from the large speakers by the entrance to the main bar. Fog machines, cobwebs, mechanical monsters and mummies bring the Halloween theme to life and I finally understand what all the fuss is about.

Jess, Ashlei and Bo immediately sprint to the makeshift dance floor and start grinding on each other and every guy around them while Erin scampers off to find the rest of our family. Skyler and I just make a beeline for the bar.

Priorities.

Just as we down a lemon drop shot and chase it with our fresh drinks, large hands wrap around my waist. “I was right.” The butterflies that have been lying dormant in my stomach since the IM football game Monday night suddenly burst to life and flutter around manically. Adam sidles up beside me, one of his hands still lingering on my hip as he throws me a wide smile. “You do look cute in a little purple shell bra.”

He looks absolutely delicious. His dark hair is gelled in a 50s style twist and black-framed Ray Bans hide his eyes but accentuate his strong jaw. The white shirt he’s wearing blazes against his tan skin and stretches across his hard chest muscles. Paired with a black leather jacket and tight dark jeans, he’s the entire Danny Zuko package and I imagine him giving young John Travolta a run for his money.

“Almost as cute as you in your little leather jacket,” I retort, cringing once the words leave my lips. *Really? Did I really just call him cute?*

Adam just grins wider.

Suddenly, Skyler bursts into a fit of laughter and both of our heads snap in her direction. “I’m sorry,” she says, trying to control herself.

I’m still confused but Adam seems to catch on to the joke because he lets out a loud spurt of laughter, too. “Well shit. I guess I picked the wrong costume, huh?”

Skyler nods. “Yeah. I mean, unless we’re doing a really terrifying mashup of Black Swan and Grease.”

Adam grabs his chin between his finger and thumb and looks up at the ceiling. “You know, that might not be half bad.”

Clearly, I missed out on the joke.

“Dance with me?” Skyler asks, but it doesn’t really sound like much of a question as she grabs Adam’s hand and leads him toward where Jess and Bo are still dancing wildly. As soon as they reach the floor, Skyler runs her hands up through Adam’s hair and grinds her body against his. He bites his lip and pushes his sunglasses up onto the top of his head so he has a better view and my stomach flutters again, but in a completely different way.

Quickly, I drain the rest of my drink and order another one.

“Hey you.” Clay appears right behind me and wraps his arms around my middle, pulling me flush against his chest. It’s a bold move for having only met me a couple of days ago. “I can’t find room at this damn bar. Order me a drink?” he whispers.

I peek over my shoulder at him. “What’s your drink of choice?”

“Hmm...” he thinks, still holding me tight. “How about whiskey on the rocks. That always gets me in the mood.” I gulp at his suggestion, but he just chuckles in my ear. “To party, that is.”

I smile nervously and order his drink before turning to face him. His hands stay on my hips as I swivel around. When I notice he’s dressed as a lifeguard, I swallow. His abs are on full display. Every single freaking *ripple* of his body is on display, actually, in the tiny red board shorts he’s donning. His dirty blonde hair is wavy and messy and the bright blue hues of his eyes contrast with the bronzer he’s clearly applied to pull off the beachy look. I didn’t realize how tall he was on the field Monday, but the way he’s towering over me now makes me feel six inches tall.

The corners of his mouth curl into a devilish grin as my eyes wander across his skin. “You think a mermaid could dance with a lifeguard?” he asks, quirking a brow.

“Well, I did pass over the part where I have a tail and skipped straight to the legs.”

“And what incredible legs they are,” he husks, allowing his own eyes to devour my body now. Clay grabs my hand and pulls me out onto the dance floor before I have the chance to say anything further. As I turn away from him and we grind our bodies to the beat, I catch Adam staring at me from where Skyler and the girls are gathered. His brows are furrowed, his mouth pursed, and he looks like he wants to either kill me or save me.

Suddenly, the butterflies are back.

"I have to pee," I slur, finishing my drink before slamming the plastic cup on the bar. "Be right back."

"Want me to go with you?" Ashlei asks, her eyes wide at the thought of me going to the bathroom by myself.

I giggle. "I'm fine, Lei. Keep my Little company and order me a shot. Be back in a sec."

Ashlei's eyes find Bo's and she smiles. "I can do that."

The bathroom is packed with girls just as drunk as me waiting to pee. I pull a bitch move and tell them I'm just going to use the mirror as I pass until I duck inside the first empty stall that opens up. After I relieve myself, I really do check my reflection and thank sweet baby Jesus for the waterproof makeup Ashlei let me use. My eyes still look awesome and after a quick touch up of gloss, I'm ready to go.

Another text message from Josh comes through my phone as I make my way back to the bar and I sigh. The kid just can*not* take a hint.

Suddenly, I'm ripped backward and my phone flies out of my hand and crashes to the floor, splintering in three different directions. I panic as a hand is crushed over my mouth and I'm yanked back into a dark, confined closet.

"I would tell you not to scream, but that defeats the purpose of this," a deep voice growls in my ear. I recognize it immediately.

Jarrett.

He removes his hand from my mouth and I gasp, my heart still beating rapidly in my chest. His hands move to my hips and he pulls my back against his chest, his breath hot in my ear. "You think those little boys you're toying with can give you what you want?" His voice is husky, dark, and laced with desire. Instantly, my panties grow wet and I moan as he nips at the skin on my neck. "I think you've forgotten what I can do to you, Jess – what I can make you *feel*. I'm here to remind you."

With that, he whips me around and his mouth crashes down on mine. His kiss is passionate and needy. He discards my cowgirl hat before fisting his hands in my hair as my nails rake his back. I know I should push him away, I should remind *him* that he could get fired for this. But right now, the alcohol swimming in my system paired with the intense way Jarrett's tongue is moving against mine is crippling my desire to make him stop.

I *definitely* do not want him to stop.

Jarrett grabs both of my thighs in his hands and lifts me, crashing us back against a shelf. I still can't see anything but I feel product crash all around us as I wrap my legs tight around his waist, using the leather from my cowgirl boots to gain traction and hold my ankles together.

"You walk into class every Wednesday night," he pants against my skin, letting his hand trail down my neck. I moan when his fingertips dip inside the low-cut v-line of my shirt and graze my nipple. "Looking sexy as fuck," he continues, his hand sliding up under my jean skirt. "And you just ignore me." His fingers rub slow circles on the fabric of my lace panties and I buck against his touch. "You *torture* me." He slips one finger inside the lace and rubs my opening. "Christ, you're so wet, Jess. You're so ready for me. Why do you pretend like you don't want me?"

"I do want you," I whisper, kissing him again. The music from the bar is muffled inside the closet and every breath shared between us is amplified.

"Are you sure?" he teases, sliding the tips of his two fingers against my core as his other hand works to hold me pinned against the wall. I squirm, rotating my hips to try to get his fingers where I really want them.

"It's dangerous."

"Maybe," he agrees, his fingers stilling. He pauses for a moment and I think maybe he might be realizing what could happen if we get caught. Then suddenly, he slides his fingers inside me in one smooth thrust and kisses me hard, pulling my bottom lip between his teeth. "But it's also really fucking fun."

My moans turn to screams as his fingers work inside me. My skirt is now completely bunched at my waist and my hands slide down Jarrett's abdomen until I feel him through his shorts. He's just as ready for me as I was for him and I grip him tightly through the fabric.

"Fuck," he growls, removing his fingers and making quick work of the tie on his shorts. He doesn't wait for me to ask, he just drops my feet to the ground, spins me around so my hands are on the wall, moves my panties to the side and thrusts into me from behind, making me cry out in a mix of pleasure and pain.

His hands move around to palm my breasts as he pumps into me. Each thrust makes me moan more as I feel him growing harder inside me. When he wraps one hand around my neck and uses the other to push me flush against the wall, I let out another cry.

"Do your frat boyfriends fuck you like this?" he husks in my ear, sliding one hand down and around my hips until he finds my clit. My face is pushed hard against the concrete wall and Jarrett uses his free hand to pin mine above my head. "Do they?"

"No," I pant.

"What was that?"

"No!" I scream louder.

"Does anyone fuck you the way I do?"

"No," I whisper again.

Jarrett pounds into me hard, reaching me deeper than ever before. I bite my lip and gasp against the shocking pain mixed with the pleasure still rocking my entire body.

"I'm sorry?"

"No! No one fucks me the way you do!" I scream, not caring if anyone hears at this point. He growls and begins circling my clit wildly, still holding my wrists above my head with his other hand. "I love the way you fuck me, Jarrett," I pant against the concrete. He bites and sucks at the back of my neck in response. "Don't stop, Jarrett. Don't you fucking stop."

"Quitting isn't in my vocabulary, princess."

The combination of his words, his finger working my clit, and his cock thrusting into the deepest parts of my core are too much. The pressure builds until I'm sure I'll combust before I finally tumble over the edge, screaming and moaning Jarrett's name as each wave of pleasure rocks through me. Jarrett curses as he releases too, his entire body convulsing behind me. Our breathing slows and Jarrett moves his hands to grip my hips firmly as he plants kisses down the back of my neck and across my shoulder.

After a moment, as our breathing is still steadying, Jarrett releases me and quickly pulls his shorts back on. My eyes are finally adjusted to the dark, but even so I can barely make out his form. He pushes me back against the wall once more after he dresses, his tongue demanding my own.

"Don't ever fuck around with another guy in front of me," he commands. "It doesn't piss me off, it doesn't make me hate you – it only makes me want you more."

With that, his lips leave mine and he slips out of the closet, leaving me alone in the darkness. My breaths are still ragged, my thong soaked, and my hair a tangled mess as I try to make sense of what just happened.

Holy. Shit.

Cassie

My mermaid braid is sticking to my neck as I fan myself at the bar waiting for my order to be filled. The night has surprisingly cooled down, but dancing with Clay has done nothing but heat me up.

Clay is definitely good looking, but I've come to realize that there aren't many guys at Palm South who aren't. Besides his looks, I haven't really connected with him on anything, but he's a good time. Tonight, he's a good distraction from other people... people I need to stop thinking about.

"Water?" Adam asks, sliding up beside me at the bar. The way his skin is glistening lets me know he's been dancing just as hard as me.

"It feels like I'm out there doing cardio. I need rehydration."

"Nah, just take another shot. You'll feel better." He smirks, but it fades quickly. "What are you doing with Clay?"

"What do you mean?"

"I mean, are you here with him?"

My stomach twinges at his question, or rather, what the underlying implications of it might be. "No. I don't know. We met the other day at your game and he showed up tonight, so we've been dancing."

"Cassie," he breathes my name, shaking his head slightly. "Don't get caught up with him. He's a dick."

I gulp. "I think he seems nice."

"That's just the thing. He *seems* nice, but I know who he is. He's bad news."

Suddenly, I realize what's going on. Adam is clearly into Skyler, he's shoved me in the friend zone, yet for whatever twisted reason, he doesn't want to see me with someone else. What, does he think I should just wait around long enough for him to have his fun with Skyler and then move on to me?

Yeah. Not happening.

"Well, I think I'm a pretty good judge of character," I state matter-of-factly, trading my water for the fruity cocktail just placed in front of me. "And I can take care of myself. But thanks."

Adam grabs my hand and his brows pull together, worry evident in his features. "Please, Cassie. Just be careful."

"Hey Brooks," Clay says, appearing seemingly out of nowhere and clapping Adam hard on the back. Adam drops my hand and glares at Clay. "Having fun?"

"Yep." The word pops at the end, but his eyes soften as they turn to me once more. "See you around, Cassie."

"Yeah. See you."

Adam rejoins Skyler on the dance floor and they're back to grinding without missing a beat. Clay pulls me in closer, his lips falling to my ear. "Want to get out of here?"

I gulp. I didn't plan on leaving with anyone other than the girls tonight, but part of me wants to prove a point to Adam. He's not going to play me or my Big. If he wants her, which clearly he does, then he needs to focus on her. He needs to know that if we're just friends, the way he declared we were, then he would have to see me with other guys.

I can't believe I'm being so bold. This is definitely a far reach from who I was just a few short months ago. Smiling, I nod to Clay and his grin widens. He laces his fingers with mine and tugs me through the crowd.

As we reach the exit, I glance over my shoulder and find Adam watching me, too. He's scowling and even though Skyler is still pressing her body in all the right places against him, his stare doesn't leave me. I think this is the way a man looks when he realizes he doesn't have it all figured out the way he thought he did.

And that's the thing about Halloween. Everyone feels like they can hide behind a mask or a costume, but in the morning, they still wake up as the person *beneath* the mask. I didn't think Adam was the kind of guy to want to play the game between two sisters, but maybe I don't know him as well as I thought.

With that realization and with his eyes still locked on mine, I smile, wave, and walk through the door.

Skyler

Jess is unusually quiet as we strip off our sweaty costumes and throw them on our bedroom floor. She keeps alternating between a goofy smile and a twisted look of confusion.

"Are you going to tell me what's going on in that blonde head of yours?"

Jess startles at my words as if I'm pulling her back to reality. "What?"

I quirk a brow. "Care to explain why you're blushing with only me in the room?"

Jess's cheeks shade deeper but she just jumps up into her bed, pulling the sheets up high. "I'm not blushing. I'm still hot from dancing."

I eye her warily, but don't push it. "And yet you're climbing into your clean bed?"

"I'll shower in the morning."

"Okay," I say, chuckling. My phone buzzes and I'm surprised when I see my dad's picture light up the screen. Excusing myself to the bathroom, I answer.

"Hey Pops. A little past your bedtime isn't it?"

"You're on the news!"

My stomach drops. "What?"

"Well, okay, not exactly the news – but a big blog wrote an article and you're featured in it!"

"What are you talking about?"

"Check your email."

Just as he says the words, my phone pings in my ear and I pull it away long enough to pull up the new email from Dad. Sure enough, it links to an article from a large poker blog about the top five hottest women in poker.

And I'm number three.

"Whoa," is all I can say as I read through the small amount of verbiage under my picture. It talks briefly about the tournaments I've won in the past before complimenting me for my most recent win – the tournament Tuesday night. The rest talks about how "smoking hot" I look even in a hoodie and glasses, which makes me roll my eyes.

"Can you believe it?" Dad asks, still excited.

"I mean, it's just an article talking about how attractive I am. I don't know how to feel about it."

Dad scoffs. "Look past that, Sky. The fact that they even know who you are is huge." He pauses and I can almost feel him smiling through the phone. "You're really doing it, girl. You're making it."

I read over the article again. "It is kind of cool, isn't it?"

"Hell yes!" Dad beams. "That's my girl. I'm so proud of you. And just wait, they won't be talking about your looks for long once they realize just how good you are at the game."

"We'll see, Dad."

There's another pause before he speaks again. "Thank you, Skyler. Thank you for sending that money… and for always looking out for us." I feel the worry radiate off him and permeate through the phone. "We should be the ones taking care of you."

"Stop," I say, not allowing him to continue. "You always *have* taken care of me. It's okay to let me help out a little now." I smile, thinking of how my parents were the only real friends I had up until Palm South. "Besides, you're going to get that promotion soon and then you can take me out to dinner."

"It's a date, baby girl."

"I love you, Dad. Night."

"Night."

I thumb through the article once more, sizing up the other girls mentioned. I've heard of every single one of them and the fact that my name is even in the same list as them floors me. Suddenly, my phone buzzes again.

Adam.

"Miss me already?" I ask playfully.

"Actually, yes. Plus, I realized we need to celebrate you winning that tournament Tuesday night."

"Um, didn't we kind of already do that tonight?"

"I suppose, but the night is still young, right?"

I glance at the clock and laugh when I see it's just past three in the morning. "Uh..."

"Just go with it. Come downstairs."

With that, the line goes dead and I'm left shaking my head. Adam Brooks is something else.

I pull on a pair of gym shorts and a PSU tank top before sneaking down the stairs and outside. Adam has changed out of his costume and into a relaxed pair of basketball shorts and t-shirt, yet he still looks just as yummy as he did earlier. Leaning against the pillar of our house, his bright smile is illuminated by the moon and his eyes sparkle as he watches me approach.

"Ever gone banner diving before?" he asks.

"Uh... can't say that I have."

"Well, there's a first for everything."

Every house on Greek row has at least two posts where "banners", AKA bed sheets with text and images on them, hang. Usually, the banners advertise an upcoming event or wish a sister or brother a happy birthday. When Adam explains to me that we're going to be diving into them and tearing them down, I pull back.

"What? We can't do that!" I whisper, as if anyone on the completely empty street would hear me. "That's... vandalism. Or something."

He chuckles, his dark eyes still shining in the moonlight. "I didn't peg you for a good girl."

I purse my lips. "I'm just saying. It's rude."

"Kind of. But wouldn't you love to see the look on the Zetas' faces when they see their precious banner shredded in half?" He's got a point there, I really don't like the Zetas. And what the hell? It's just sheets, not like we're throwing bricks at car windows or anything.

"Screw it," I say and then I take off running down the street and dive straight into one of the Zeta banners proclaiming that their sister should be the Alpha Sig Sweetheart. Adam tries to quiet his laughter as I bounce back off the sheet instead of tearing through it like I'd imagined. My laughter, on the other hand, is incredibly loud and awkward.

When a light flickers on downstairs in the Zeta house, Adam and I both snap our necks in that direction.

"Oh shit," I say, scrambling to pull myself up. Adam pokes fun at me trying to hobble away before he scoops me up in his arms and conceals us behind tall scrub bushes near the edge of their yard.

The Zeta house mom appears on the front porch, straining her neck to look both ways before shrugging and retreating back inside the house. Adam and I both die in a fit of laughter and then I realize how close we are. His arms are still wrapped around me, our mouths are just inches apart.

Adam lifts his fingers to cradle my chin before pulling me in for a long, soft kiss. It's the kind of kiss that doesn't make me want to go jump in the sack, but rather cuddle up to watch a movie. It's sweet.

It's nice.

We spend the rest of the night doing absolutely nothing yet talking about everything. We walk all around campus, get into places we're not supposed to, and even play ding-dong-ditch at a few of the dorm rooms. When the sun starts rising, he drops me back off at the house with another long kiss and then I fall into bed completely exhausted, but happy nonetheless.

Maybe Adam Brooks *isn't* just a fun hookup.

Maybe.

EPISODE 5

"Whats with all the fucking SECRETS AROUND HERE?"

Jess

"See! You've got it," Cassie encourages right as I lean back too far and bust my ass. The longboard jets out from under my feet and races down the sidewalk as Cassie cringes. "Well, you're getting there."

"I don't think falling eight times within one hour means I'm getting there," I volley, wincing as I lift my sore ass off the concrete. I chase down my board as Cassie rides smoothly beside me, like it's the easiest thing in the world.

"It just takes time. You'll get it." She hops off her board and stomps her foot on the back end, popping it up and tucking it under her arm. As we walk, I continue rubbing my ass. I was serious during rush when I told Cassie I wanted her to teach me how to ride, but I didn't think it would be this difficult. Then again, I've never really been active in any capacity other than catching cycling and Zumba classes at the gym, so it doesn't really make sense that I thought I'd be a natural. I guess I just thought my experience riding other people – er, *things* – would come in handy.

"So, you excited about your first semi-formal?" I ask Cassie as we walk. The sun is fading over the campus, casting it in a soft orange glow. Her hair looks even redder in this kind of light and my appreciation for it grows with every passing minute. I feel like there are too many blondes in the world. I'd love to be a redhead – to stand out the way she does.

"Yeah, but I don't really know what to wear."

"It's kind of like high school. Remember how you got kind of dressed up for homecoming, but *really* decked out for prom? Well, semi-formal is homecoming, formal is prom. Just get a short, sexy dress and do something nice with your hair and makeup."

Cassie sighs. "I need to go shopping."

"Oh! I want in. Let's get the girls to go later this week."

"Deal. Speaking of which, who are you bringing with you?"

My stomach drops at her question, which doesn't make any sense because it's an easy enough one that I already have the answer to, but for some reason my mind immediately snaps to Jarrett. "I think I'm taking Matt."

"The O Chi president?" I nod. "Well, looks like we can be twinzies."

"Wait." I halt, grabbing Cassie's arm. "Are you taking Clay? Holy shit. You like him, don't you?"

Cassie's face screws up. "I don't know. Maybe. He's nice."

"Nice enough to take you home and bang the shit out of you on Halloween?" I waggle my brows and Cassie's face turns crimson red.

"Uh, no. I mean, I went home with him for a while but... we didn't... do... *it*."

"Oh? What *did* you do?"

Cassie covers her face with her hands and starts walking again.

"Oh my God! Spill!" I jog to catch up with her and she mumbles something into her hands, but I can't make it out. "What was that?"

"He went down on me." She says the words just above a whisper even though we're the only ones on this path.

"He ate you out?" I say louder. "Well damn, get it, Cassie!" She shushes me and I just laugh. "You should be proud. Why are you acting like it's a bad thing?"

"I didn't really like it, to be honest. And I think he expected... more."

"Ugh," I groan. "I hate when they don't know what they're doing down there. It's like, why even make the effort if you're just going to slobber and make a mess without getting me off?" Cassie blushes and looks down at the ground, which makes me laugh. "Sorry. I'm kind of crass, aren't I?"

"I'm just not very experienced in this kind of stuff."

I pat her shoulder with sympathy, leaning in a bit. "It just takes time. You'll get there," I tease, repeating her encouragement about me on the longboard. She smacks at my arm but misses as I drop my board and hop on it, speeding down the sidewalk.

"How's my carving?" I call out behind me, my eyes on my feet as I shift my balance from my toes to my heels. Cassie yells something back at me but I don't hear it. My speed is picking up faster than I anticipated and I realize I'm on a hill. Before I have the chance to jump off or correct it, I slam hard into what feels like a brick wall and bounce back off the board, crashing to the ground.

I groan, squeezing my eyes shut against the pain already throbbing in my skull. When I finally lean up on the heels of my hands and squint to see what I hit, I immediately regret it.

"Well, fuck."

Jarrett reaches down and helps me to my feet, steadying me as I try to gain my balance again. Just having his hands on my arms sends flashbacks of Halloween parading through my memory and suddenly it's not just the fall that's making me feel disoriented.

"Are you okay?"

"Peachy," I remark, snatching my board from the ground. The quick motion of bending over and standing upright again sends me spinning and Jarrett's hands find my waist to steady me again. "My phone on the other hand, not so much."

At that, Jarrett's lips twitch into a devilish smirk. "It was a necessary casualty."

My heartbeat quickens and my mouth feels like I swallowed cotton. I know Jarrett can sense it. He feels my nerves. He can feel me trembling. I know, because he's smirking wider now, his dark eyes hooded in a mixture of lust and amusement. When he bites his lower lip and drags his teeth along the tender flesh, my eyes flutter closed before I realize what I'm doing.

"I can buy you a replacement, if you'd like," he adds, but he says it huskily and I know it's on purpose. "We could go to the mobile store on campus after class Wednesday."

"It's fine," I say, snapping out of my trance. "It's already being fixed." Why is my voice shaking? Why am I staring at him like he's stark ass naked instead of fully clothed in a tight gray t-shirt and basketball shorts? *Wait... he's wearing basketball shorts?* My eyes fall lower and I can clearly see the outline of him straining beneath them.

Oh, for fuck's sake.

Really? Like *really*?

Jarrett coughs and my eyes snap to his. He's clearly entertained by my squirming, one brow quirked as he nonverbally calls me out on my crotch staring.

Clearing my throat, I salute him. "Okay. See you in class." When I turn around and race back toward where Cassie stands watching, I cringe and shake my head. *Did I just salute him? Like a fucking skipper or a sergeant?* Good God, I'm a fucking idiot.

"Was that – "

"Yep. Let's go." I grab Cassie by the crook of her arm and drag her in the opposite direction, regardless of if it was where we were originally heading. When I glance over my shoulder, Jarrett is still watching, his arms crossed over his chest and a smug look cemented on his face. He knows he has the upper hand now. He knows he affects me in a way I can't control.

Fuck me.

Ashlei

I feel better today than I have in weeks. It's been rough at the studio, but today I feel strong – focused – and as I spin fast around the pole, the smile on my face is irreplaceable. The moves I've been working on since July are starting to come effortlessly to me and I know if I stay on track, I have a chance of taking the title in January.

That's my sole focus now.

Sometimes it takes getting to a low place, maybe even falling to the bottom, before you realize that it's time to start climbing up again. For me, I didn't know I was falling until I came face to face with the dirt. *Literally*. In a way, I'm glad it happened quickly. At least now I can save myself before it's too late.

A stream of sunlight interrupts the darkness of Kitty Heels as Hayden and Kya enter through the front door. When Hayden's eyes find mine, he offers me a forced smile, but I just drop to the floor and walk in the opposite direction toward the water fountain.

"Hey," he says softly, sliding up next to me as I continue to drink. I wipe my mouth with my wrist when I stand to face him, but the pit in my stomach almost makes me spew the liquid out.

"What do you want, Hayden?"

"Listen, I'm sorry about what happened." He can't even say it out loud, which just makes it hurt more. "We got a little carried away, it happens sometimes when you're high. But it won't happen again."

"Damn right it won't because I'm never touching that shit again. Ever. Do you hear me?" I turn on my heel and retreat back to my pole, but Hayden follows.

"Christ, Ashlei, just wait a second." His long hair is disheveled and stringy, his eyes surrounded by dark circles. Hayden is insanely sexy to me – or at least, he always has been before now – but today he just looks sad. And broken. And pathetic.

He nervously plays with his eyebrow ring as he tries to find the words to say next. "You weren't hurt, right? I mean, everything is okay, right?"

My mouth drops open. "Are you fucking serious?" When he doesn't blanch, I snap my mouth shut. "Wow. You are." Hayden snatches my arm as I try to turn away from him again, but I rip it free.

"Why are you acting so crazy?"

"Crazy?!" I scream louder than I intended. "You shoved me out of a moving vehicle, you vapid asshole. You could have *killed* me."

"We weren't even going thirty miles an hour, Ashlei. It was a joke."

"Yeah, well I'm not laughing."

"We were high."

"Exactly!" I cut him off just as he says the word. "We were being stupid. And you? You're *always* being stupid. You mess around with that stuff like it's not going to catch up with you. Well, I'm done. I've sat on it for weeks now, trying to figure out how I felt about all of it, and now I know. I'm staying to dance, to work for Leslie, but I want no part of what you and Kya are mixed up in. Do you hear me? None."

"Ashlei."

"Eat a wiener, Hayden."

I don't give him the opportunity to answer before I climb back up my pole and start working on my advanced moves, the adrenaline still pumping hard through my veins. There's an achingly heavy pressure on my chest at the thought of not having Hayden in my life anymore, but I know this is the right move. I was crazy to let him talk me into trying cocaine in the first place. I should have known it would blow up in my face.

The night after initiation, I blew off my sisters to hang out with him and Kya. It was only my third time getting high with him, but apparently the third time is a charm. What started as a fun evening letting loose ended up with me limping on the backroads back to campus. Since then, I haven't been myself. I've been lost. The only night I felt even semi-normal was on Halloween with Bo.

I bite my lip at the thought of her and slip a little in my transition, making me fall into a Nose Breaker Drop without meaning to. I catch myself just in time, my face inches from the ground. Circling the pole a few times to gain my composure again, I swing my way back up and do a few rounds, trying to ignore the voice in the back of my mind that wants to talk more about what Bo means to me.

"You okay?" Leslie's voice is kind and soft, but it startles me nonetheless and I drop back to the ground, panting.

"I'm good."

She assesses me for a moment before nodding. "Okay then. I need you sharp for January. I know the holidays are coming up and you're probably stressed with school, but I need your focus here as much as it can be. Can you do that?" I nod. "Great." Her eyes soften and she glances up at Hayden before addressing me again. "I'm always here if you need help, Ashlei." She levels her eyes and I have a feeling she means more than just pole practice, but I just give a curt nod again and climb back on the pole.

I need to work out this adrenaline – and fast. When I go back to the house, it's shopping and semi-formal preparation. How I ended up in two vastly different worlds, I'll never know – but balancing them is getting to be more of a challenge than what I thought I signed up for.

Adam

"God, you taste to good," I moan into Skyler's neck, trailing my tongue across her skin. She moans and I grind between her legs harder, pulling the sheets up and over our heads. The movie we put on almost two hours ago is now playing the credits, but it doesn't matter because we haven't seen a single minute of it.

"Best Friday night ever," she whispers before leaning up to press her mouth to mine. She bites my bottom lip between her teeth and holds it there as I continue building the friction between us. If we don't actually fuck soon, I might bust in my basketball shorts.

Lifting one of her legs to rest on my shoulder, I slide her wet panties to the side and thrust my fingers inside. Each time I've fingered her tonight, I've brought her just to the edge of pleasure before pulling out and teasing her more. She's been doing the same to me, working us both up to the point where I don't think we'll last more than two minutes once we actually take our clothes off.

"Fuck," Skyler groans. "I can't take this anymore. Take your shorts off."

"Wait," I demand, still teasing her. Her eyes pop open and she glares at me.

"Don't make me ask you again." She smirks, but the undertone of her voice lets me know she's serious. Her delicate fingers shove my shorts down over my ass and she grips me tight, pumping as she maneuvers out of her underwear. When I finally rip open a condom and slide inside her, I know my theory about time is correct.

"Oh God," she moans after just a few thrusts. "I can't hold out, Adam."

"Don't," is all I manage before we both come, our bodies trembling together at the release we've been working toward for hours. When we're finally spent, I roll over to lie beside her, panting. She giggles and curls into my chest and I tuck my arm under her shoulder, pulling her closer.

"Seriously though, best way to spend Friday night."

"No arguments here," I say, kissing her hair. Gently, I run my fingertips up and down her arm, lulling her into a post-orgasm trance. As the music from the movie credits fills the room along with our steady breathing, I pull Skyler in closer and nuzzle my nose into her neck. She sighs contently and holds me in response.

Ever since Halloween, Skyler and I have been pretty much inseparable. Whenever I'm not tied up with fraternity events and she's not playing poker, we're together. She turns me on no matter what she's doing, and apparently she feels the same about me because we hardly spend time outside of the bedroom. I'm not complaining about it, either – not even a little bit. I haven't had a steady hookup in over a year. It's kind of nice to know I can call her at pretty much anytime and she'll be here.

"Hey," I say softly, still trailing my fingertips across her skin. "How's the other half of the slip-n-slide sisters doing?"

"Mmm?" Skyler asks, still dazed.

"Your Little?"

"She's good," Skyler responds sleepily. "Her roommate is a bitch, but nothing new there."

"They're still having problems?"

Skyler nods against my chest. "Yeah. Cassie has been pretty down about it lately. Apparently Paris said some hurtful things to her last weekend." Skyler leans up, kissing me quickly. "I hate to say this, but I have to go."

"You should stay," I try, pulling her back down to the bed. She giggles, but evades my grip and hops out of bed, jumping into her tight jeans. The view is quite nice.

"I don't sex and stay, Adam Brooks."

I frown. "Ouch. I figured we were a little different than your... usual."

At that, she smiles and leans in for another long kiss. "We are. I think. But I can't be sure yet."

"Fair enough." God knows I can't expect her to commit when I know I'm not ready for that, either. "Text me tomorrow."

"You got it, stud." Skyler throws me a wink before climbing out of my bedroom window. She could have gone through the house to the front door, but odds are there are still guys partying in the living room, and I'm betting Skyler doesn't want to answer to all that.

When I hear Clay's annoying ass laugh filter back through the hallway, I roll my eyes, but then my thoughts instantly land on Cassie. Snagging my phone off the bedside table, I type out a quick text.

- You busy tomorrow? -

It's the first thing I've said to Cassie since our confrontation on Halloween, if that's even what that was. I'm not sure. I feel like maybe I should be apologizing to her, but I can't really figure out what for. I meant what I said when I told her Clay was bad news. From what I've heard, she's still been hanging out with him. As much as I want to support whatever choice she makes in regards to who she hooks up with, I can't co-sign anything that has to do with Clay.

I'm a little surprised when she answers a minute later.

- Going shopping with the girls for semi-formal. -

- Breakfast with me first? -

A few minutes pass before she responds.

- Sure. Café? -

- See you at 10. -

I set an alarm on my phone and fall back against my bed, stretching out and working my muscles still sore from the tension of tonight's festivities. When I roll over on my stomach and shove my arm under the pillow, I feel a piece of paper crumble beneath the weight of my hand. Retrieving it, I smile at the note from Skyler with a silly face and an inside joke.

Skyler Thorne is not a one-guy kind of gal. I didn't know that when I met her, but I've figured it out along the way. I'm not saying I'm ready to be in a relationship, either – but at the same time, I really like Skyler. She's fun, feisty, and different. We spend all of our free time together and, to my knowledge at least, she's not hooking up with anyone else and neither am I.

Deciding not to think too much into it tonight, I tuck the note into my bedside table drawer and close my eyes, letting sleep pull me under.

***

The café at Palm South is small, but it's a chill place to eat. Usually, it's crawling with freshmen because their parents get sucked into buying the meal plan at orientation. By the time students get to their second year, they realize they'd rather get that two grand in an allowance from their parents so they can use three-hundred dollars of it to eat and the other seventeen-hundred to get shit-faced at Ralph's.

Filling my plate with an omelet, four pieces of toast, two pancakes, four slices of bacon and a tall glass of orange juice, I find the back corner booth and slide in. I used to sit here when I was a freshman and I chuckle thinking of the food fights I started from this spot, not to mention the girls I picked up.

"Thanks for slumming it," Cassie says as she slides into the booth across from me. Her bright hair is pulled into a low braid over her right shoulder and she plays with it absentmindedly as she organizes her tray. "My parents insisted on getting this stupid meal plan and now that I eat at the sorority house most of the time, I don't even use it."

"Hey, feel free to get me free food whenever you feel like it. I won't argue."

She blanches at the pile of food on my plate. "Yeah, I see that. Is someone else joining us or is that all for you?"

"Hey! A guy's gotta eat if he wants to make gains in the gym, Red."

Cassie freezes, her eyes snapping to mine. "Do *not* call me Red. Ever."

"Whoa. Did I hit a nerve?"

"It's just stupid. I have red hair, we all get it, no need to point it out with a nickname." She shoves a big bite of pancake into her mouth and licks the syrup off her bottom lip, wiping whatever smartass remark I planned on saying from my mind.

"I heard your roommate is being especially bitchy lately," I comment, changing the subject.

"How'd you hear about that?"

"Skyler told me."

She stills for a moment, her fork hovering over her plate, but almost quick enough for me not to notice before she takes another bite. "Oh. Yeah. I don't know, I guess I shouldn't really care anymore."

"Of course you should care," I interject. "She was your best friend. No one's faulting you for caring about what happens to your friendship, Cassie."

Her pained eyes find mine. "I feel stupid for caring about her when she clearly couldn't care less about me."

"Hey." I reach across the table and grab her hand in mine. "It's her loss. She's a fucking moron if she doesn't see what a good friend you are. She'll regret burning this bridge when she's standing alone on that Zeta island, I can tell you that much."

Cassie chuckles, which makes me smile. That's the way I like to see her.

"You're silly."

"I'm also serious." I rub my thumb against hers and she glances up at me through her lashes. Realizing I'm probably holding on to the point of making it awkward, I pull back, cutting another bite off my pancake with my fork. "Just keep trying to make it work with her. If she doesn't try on her end by the time the semester is up, let her go and move into the KKB house. At that point, you know you did all you could to save the friendship and it was her decision to end it."

"Yeah, I think that's a good plan." She smiles. "Thanks, Adam."

"Anytime, Red." Cassie purses her lips and I bark out a loud laugh. "Kidding. So anyway, you going to semi-formal?"

"Of course I'm going. Why would I miss my own semi-formal?"

I shrug. "I don't know. I know some girls are weird about the whole going stag thing." Cassie shifts uncomfortably and I pause mid-bite. "Or do you have a date?"

"Uh, yeah. I'm going with someone."

"Who?" When she doesn't answer and her eyes skirt mine, I drop my fork completely and shove my plate forward. "Cassie. Please tell me you're not taking Clay."

"Why does it matter?"

"Because," I say exasperated, but can't figure out what to say next. "I told you. He's a dick."

"Well, he's really nice to me. And I assume you're going with Skyler, so why do you care?"

I scoff. "Yeah, I am going with Skyler. What does that have to do with anything?"

"Nothing." She sighs, gathering her leftover food items and piling them on her tray. "I have to go meet the girls. Thanks for breakfast."

I don't get the chance to say anything further before she's across the cafeteria and out the door.

Bear

"This is bullshit!" Josh yells and a few brothers join in with his assessment. I just cross my arms harder over my chest and kick back in my chair, shaking my head. This cannot be happening.

"No," Alec, the fuckhead alum who's ruining our lives interjects. "What's bullshit is that you asshats can't pull your own dick out of your ass long enough to realize worse will happen if you don't reign it in."

"We're in college," Josh argues. "Partying is part of that package."

"Maybe, but getting multiple sound violations, police calls, and write ups from the council aren't. If you want to still have letters to wear next year, you'll heed this warning and play ball our way for a while." The rest of the alumni brothers behind Alec all nod in unison, agreeing with this stupidity.

"Whatever. No parties for the rest of the semester. Got it. Are we through here?" I know I sound like an ungrateful dick, but on the inside I'm just as pissed off as my brothers. I get where the alumni brothers are coming from. Hell, I've been warning my Little all semester to get his shit together, but at the same time I'm not ready to give up parties completely. The fact that we're doing so without even being on suspension or probation is absolutely idiotic. The alumni want to teach us a lesson and also get our names off the radar. Whatever their reason, it sucks.

"If we're all at an understanding, then yes," Alec concedes. "Chapter is over."

"Great."

I stand before everyone else and jet out the door, shoving it a little harder than necessary when I exit. It bounces off the brick of our house before I slam it closed again and start off across campus toward the gym.

This is total, complete, utter bullshit. Horse shit. Fucking cow manure. I understand that we have to be careful and not do anything crazy enough to get our asses in the news, but throwing a few ragers and having too much fun shouldn't be a fucking crime. And Alec seems all too pleased to tell us we were on temporary probation. It's already November, so not throwing any parties for the next month doesn't seem like a big deal, but for us it's like asking us to cut our dicks off. Partying is what Omega Chi Beta does. It's who we are.

Fuck!

I punch a tall plastic sign advertising an event on campus and someone laughs. Spinning on my heels with a glare I know is murderous, I find Erin Xander sitting on one of the benches that line the main sidewalk leading to the gym.

"Whoa," she says, wide eyed. "Sorry. I've just never seen you so pissed." She puts her hands up in mock surrender. "Everything okay?"

Exhaling, I toss my gym bag to the ground and fall onto the bench next to her. "We just got put on temporary probation. No parties for the rest of the semester."

"Are you serious?" Erin runs her delicate hand through her dark blonde hair. "Wow. What are you guys going to do with yourselves? Isn't that like... all you do?"

"Exactly."

Erin Xander and I are nowhere near close. Really, I never talked to her much before I met Skyler. She's a cool chick, but she's way too spunky and involved for me. I've always been freaked out by women who like to juggle a thousand activities on top of school. Any girl who has to have control over that many things in life doesn't sound like a good time to me.

"Well, at least you can still *go* to parties. It's not total lockdown."

I scoff. "Who's going to throw parties like us? Mu Beta Chi? Alpha Sigma?" That last option makes me roll my eyes. "Let's be real."

Erin giggles, but then stops abruptly and snaps her fingers. "Hey! I have a temporary fix. Come to semi-formal with me this weekend." I'm pretty sure I look at her as if she just sprouted a dick on her face because she instantly clarifies. "As *friends*, Bear. I've been too busy to even slightly worry about getting a date and I know all the other girls will have one. Come with me so I'm not stag. There will be plenty of booze and you know the Kappa Kappa Beta girls are a good time."

"Can't argue that," I concede, considering the option. The KKB semi-formal is always rumored to be a pretty decent party. I've never been before, and the thought of going with Erin kind of makes me want to shove my head into an ant pile, but then again Skyler will be there along with a bunch of my brothers. Kind of like moving the party, I guess. "Okay, I'm in."

Erin lifts her brows. "Yeah?"

"Why not? Free booze, sexy women all dressed up – sounds like a good time to me."

"Come to the house at six-thirty. We'll be taking a few buses over." She smiles, revealing her perfectly straight teeth that I'm sure her parents paid good money for. "And I'm wearing white."

I nod, snatching my bag off the ground and throwing it over my shoulder as I stand. "It's a date, Erin Xander." I wink and she shakes her head as I continue in the direction toward the gym.

Semi-formal isn't exactly what I have in mind when I think about partying, but it'll be fun, and anything is better than nothing. Pulling my phone from my pocket, I sigh when I see there's no missed calls or texts. Ever since I sent money home to both Carleton and my mom, I haven't heard a word. Not a peep. I must have ATM stamped on my forehead instead of SON and BROTHER.

As much as it irks me that I haven't heard from them, it's kind of a relief at the same time. Maybe that was it. Maybe they'll leave me alone now and I can focus on school and Omega Chi. Temporary probation is going to suck, but in a way, Alec is right – I can't imagine being on actual probation. Maybe we do need to take a step back and stay off the radar for a while. There's not much time left in the semester anyway. It can't be that bad, right?

Right?

Ashlei

I'm going to be sick.

I'm literally going to vomit.

Holding the phone tight to my ear, the only thing keeping me from passing out is focusing hard on the breaths I'm taking. *In and out. Inhale and exhale.* Half of my brain is screaming that this can't be happening while the other half is scolding me for getting myself in this situation.

I fucked up.

Royally.

"Are you there?"

I swallow, but it feels like dry wood scraping my throat rather than saliva. "I'm here." I manage, raking my hands through my greasy hair. I need to shower. Ten minutes ago I was about to start getting ready for my semi-formal. Now, the thought of that seems so trivial.

"Do you understand what I'm saying to you?"

"Kya," I squeak her name, trying to reason. "You can't ask me for that kind of money. This isn't my fault and you know it. Hayden is the reason you lost that stash, not me. I had nothing to do with it."

"According to him, you did have something to do with it."

I groan, realizing that in a way, I did. "Listen, yeah, I fucked up and let him talk me into going up with him a few times but I swear I didn't know it was yours. I didn't know anything. I don't even know why I did it at all!" I scream. I'm panicking, I can't help it. "I told him to go fuck himself, Kya. I'm done with him and with that shit. You know me. You *know* this has never been my thing."

She sighs, and I can picture her pinching the bridge of her nose in frustration like she does when she's watching competition. "I love you, Ashlei. You're the best girl on our team right now – better than me, even. I'm not too proud to admit that. I wish I didn't have to do this, but now it's my ass on the line. You need to get me that money. I'm sorry."

"I don't have it, Kya!"

"Well, you've got rich ass parents and a sorority full of daddy's girls. I'm sure you can figure it out. I have to go."

"But what if I can't figure it out?"

The silence between us steals the breath from my chest as I wait for her to answer.

"You don't want the answer to that, Ashlei."

"Kya, wait. Seriously. We have to talk about this."

The line goes dead and I curse, throwing my cell across the yard. Tears sting the back of my eyes but I fight against them. In a way, I feel more numb than anything – like I'm living in a dream or someone else's life. This is *me*, Ashlei Daniels. I don't do drugs. I definitely don't do *stolen* drugs. I don't owe money to a drug dealer who owes her distributer. This isn't my life. It can't be.

"Gah," I hear a soft voice exclaim behind me. Bo plops down on the bench swing beside me and tucks her legs up, hugging them with her arms. "It's so cold!"

It's the first cold front of the season, if you can even call winter in Florida an actual season, and even with the sun still high in the sky it's just barely over fifty degrees. I was a little chilly when I answered the phone and stepped outside, but now my skin feels boiling hot.

I try to smile at Bo, but fail miserably and end up choking on a sob I should have seen coming. Bo's face immediately drops along with her legs and she quickly wraps me in a hug, her long dark hair falling all around me. "Oh my God, Lei. What happened?"

For a moment all I can do is cry, but I don't really even shed a tear. I'm sobbing, my face is twisted in pain, but no wetness pools in my eyes. I think I'm still in denial.

"I'm in trouble, Bo." I sniffle, pulling back from her grasp to align my eyes with hers. "Please, don't tell anyone. Not a soul. Not Jess, not anyone."

Bo shakes her head feverishly, her dark eyes wide. "I won't, I promise. What's going on?"

I chew my cheek, debating if I should even tell Bo. Up until now, these two sectors of my life have been kept completely separate. There's Palm South sorority girl Ashlei and there's pole dancing vixen Ashlei. Those two don't belong in the same world. They don't mix. They damn sure don't match.

"What would you say if I told you there's something about me that no one knows, not even my family?"

Bo smirks. "Honestly? I think we all know there's something you keep from us. It's just that no one pushes you on it."

I swallow. Am I really that obvious? I always felt like I did a decent job covering my tracks. "Okay, well, what if I told you that something that I've been hiding got me mixed up in something I always swore I would never do and now it's blown up in my face?"

"Lei," Bo stops me, reaching out to grab both of my hands in hers. Her long fingers are delicate, her hands soft and small, but she grips onto me firmly like she'll never let go. "Stop skirting around the issue and just tell me what happened. I'm not going to judge you. I love you." Her eyes grow wide at that and she quickly follows it with, "You're my sister."

"Okay," I say, expelling a long breath and letting my eyes fall to where our fingers are interlaced. "I'm just going to say this all really quickly and I'm not going to stop to look at you because if I do, I'll cry or scream or break down or something." I pause, waiting, and Bo just gives me a gentle squeeze. So I take one last breath and then put all my shit on the table.

"I started doing pole dance fitness over the summer and I'm really good at it and I've been sneaking off to practice and we won first in almost every category at a competition last month and now we're in the semi-finals in January and everything seems fine, right? Except that after I won I let this guy, Hayden, who I'm kind of sleeping with but not anymore talk me into doing cocaine which he does all the time and I swore I would never do but I did and I liked it and then I did it two more times with him but he pushed me out of a moving car because he was high and all of our friends thought it was hilarious because they were high, too, so I'm done with all of them but now Kya is saying that cocaine was actually her stash that she was supposed to be selling and Hayden stole it and now she owes her supplier money and I have to pay for half of the missing stash even though I only did it three times and I'm freaking out because I don't have that kind of money and I hate Hayden for making me do this but it's my own damn fault and fuck!" I can't say anything else after that last part, because in reality I know it is my fault that I'm in this situation. I screwed myself. I gave into peer pressure like a fucking thirteen-year-old.

I wait for Bo to gasp or pull back or shake her head, especially after I just expelled all that shit in one long exhausted breath. I wait for *any* kind of reaction. After a moment, she only squeezes my hands tighter and ducks her head a little low, urging me to look at her. When I do lift my eyes to hers, all I see is compassion and understanding.

"How much do you owe her?"

"A lot." I sigh. "Ten-thousand, to be exact."

Bo whistles under her breath. "I'm assuming parents are out of the question?" I nod. She pulls her hands from mine and runs them through her hair, thinking. "Well, I have to say I was not expecting to hear any of that from you." I cross my arms over my chest defensively, wishing I could crawl into a hole. "But you know what? You'll figure this out. We can do a fundraiser or sell some of your designer clothes and bags. You probably have ten grand in shoes alone."

I chuckle at that. "That's pretty accurate, I think."

"See!" Bo smiles, placing her hand gently on my knee. I shiver, but something tells me it's not from the cool breeze. "I know it feels like a lot right now, and to be honest – it is. It's not something you can ignore or take lightly. But at the same time, there's nothing you can do about it right at this moment. You'll need some time to get your thoughts figured out and your plan together."

"I just don't even know where to start."

"Start by going to formal with me," she whispers. She gazes up at me through her dark lashes and blushes slightly. My stomach knots instantly. "I'm going stag and I know you are, too, so let's just go together. Take the night off and don't think about all this shit. What's this Kya girl going to do anyway?"

"She told me I didn't want the answer to that question."

Bo scoffs. "I'm sure she's just trying to save her own ass, Lei." Another cool gust of wind brushes both of our hair back and off our shoulders and Bo curses. "Damn, it's getting colder." Her soft dark eyes find mine and she rubs her arms through her long sleeve shirt. "Come inside with me. Let's put on pretty dresses and dance the night away. Then tomorrow, I'll help you figure out where to start. Sound like a plan?"

Just a few minutes ago, it felt like my entire world was crashing down around me. How did Bo make something that felt so heavy suddenly feel like nothing at all?

"I don't know how much fun I'll be," I admit, but I stand nonetheless.

Bo smiles mischievously. "Just break out your stripper moves. I bet that'll get the party started." She smacks my ass playfully and skips inside while my mouth hangs open. Quickly, I retrieve my phone from where it landed in the yard and trot off after her.

The last thing I want to do is get dressed up and pretend like I'm not in deep shit, but the way Bo was looking at me has my curiosity running wild. I could dwell on my misfortune or I could dive deeper into what unsaid words lay behind her soft chocolate irises.

Yeah.

Option two sounds a *lot* more fun.

Adam

The Kappa Kappa Beta girls are fucking crazy.

After pre-gaming for an hour, we all piled into the charter buses and continued partying the entire drive to the hotel where the dance is being held. It's not even eight yet but one of the Omega Chi brothers already threw up in his date's purse trying to keep up with the shenanigans. I, on the other hand, am just trying to figure out how to hide my boner as we make our way inside the large venue. Skyler was rubbing up against me and kissing my neck the entire ride here.

To say I'm a little worked up would be an understatement.

"God, it's freezing," Cassie says, crossing her arms tightly and shivering. "Leave it to Florida to give us our first cold night when we're all in dresses."

Skyler laughs. "I don't know, I'm actually kind of warm after that bus ride." She winks at me with that last line and I shake my head. The girl has no shame.

And it's so hot.

Skyler's soft brown hair cascades down past her shoulders, curling just a bit at the ends. Her makeup is dark and intense, making her icy blue eyes stand out even more than usual. She's wearing a skin tight crimson dress that matches the lipstick she was smearing all over my skin on the bus and her heels make her almost as tall as me. I don't give a shit, though, because her legs look fucking incredible.

Cassie, on the other hand, has her hair tied up into a soft up-do with tiny tendrils framing her face. She's dressed in a floor-length white dress that accents her slender frame along with the innocence she seems to wear like an accessory everywhere she goes. Where Skyler's makeup is fierce and sexy, Cassie's is minimal and simplistic.

One is in red, one is in white.

The devil and the angel.

When Clay doesn't offer Cassie his coat, I roll my eyes and fight back the words I'd like to say to him, shrugging off my own jacket instead. "Here," I say, hanging it over her shoulders. "Better?"

Cassie pulls the front of my coat tight around her and visibly sighs at the warmth. "Much." She turns to me, a curious look in her green eyes. "Thank you."

It doesn't take long for us to reach the front of the hotel and as soon as we're inside the large glass doors, we're immediately shielded from the brisk air. The hotel is lavish with gold and navy accents, giving the atmosphere a regal feel. We're ushered into the main ballroom and one of the waiters shows us where the bathrooms are as well as the bars. I follow Skyler and some of her sisters to claim a table before we head for the closest one.

No time to waste.

"I kind of want to skip all of this and fast forward to the part where we're in your bed. Is that bad of me?" Skyler asks, her voice just above a whisper as she kisses right behind my ear. I grip her small waist firmly in my hands and meet her lips with mine.

"Kind of. But I like you better when you're bad."

She smiles against my lips before kissing me swiftly and turning just as the bartender asks her order. "Vodka tonic, please."

"Captain and Coke for me," I chime in, propping my elbows up and leaning back on the edge of the bar. Scanning the room and taking in the scenery, I spot Clay and Cassie at our table. He peels my jacket off her shoulders and tosses it over a chair haphazardly, smirking when her cleavage is more visible. She's barely showing any skin at all, but it's enough to drive a guy crazy, that's for sure. I can tell she's still shivering slightly, but she doesn't reach for my coat again. She just links her arm through his and follows him to the back of the line at the small bar across from where ours is.

I shake my head. I shouldn't be watching Cassie so closely, but I fucking hate Clay and I know there's only one thing he could want from her. The thought that he might actually get it literally makes me sick. She's too good for him. How does she not see that?

"Let's dance," Skyler yells over the music the DJ just started, throwing back a shot before handing another to me. I follow her lead, swallowing what I'm pretty sure is vodka and letting it burn the entire way down before following her back to our table. We take a couple of pulls from our mixed drinks before leaving them on the table and moving to the dance floor.

Skyler places her hand in mine and I twirl her out and back into me before wrapping my arms around her waist. Slowly, she winds her body, turning to face away from me and pressing her ass into me. My hands roam her body before gripping her hips and I move in time with the music and the tempo she's setting.

Damn. Now I kind of want to skip this shit, too.

After a few songs, we're already working up a sweat and I'm ready to finish my rum. Just as we leave the dance floor and make our way back to the table, Clay leads Cassie past us and out onto the space we just left open. My eyes find hers just as Clay grips her ass hard, pulling her close and grinding against her. I clench my jaw and quickly look away, reaching for my drink and draining the rest of it in one pull.

"Round two?" Skyler asks, eying my now empty glass. She chugs the rest of her drink and I do my damndest to keep my eyes on her and off the situation on the dance floor.

"Let's do another shot."

Skyler thrusts her hands into the air. "That's what I'm talking about!" Laughing, she grabs my hand and leads me through the crowd and back to the bar. I don't let myself look at Clay and Cassie again. I'm here with Skyler. Cassie and I are just friends. She can do whatever the hell she wants with whoever the hell she wants. It's none of my business.

But then why does it feel like it is?

Jess

"This blows," I say, sucking down the last of my rum punch. I signal to the bartender for another and Erin laughs.

"It's not that bad, Jess. At least you have Matt here."

I cringe and immediately drink half of my new drink. "Don't remind me. He's been pawing at my chest like a middle schooler all damn night."

"Hey, you're getting action tonight. Be thankful. Some of us came with friends," she reminds me, nodding her head toward where Clinton is chatting with a few of his brothers. He looks absolutely delicious in the simple black and white tuxedo he's donning and I shake my head.

"How you're sticking to that friends-only rule with him looking like that is beyond me."

"Jess!" Erin squeals, her blonde curls bouncing. "It's *Bear*, for God's sake."

"And? Bear's hot!"

"He's practically like Skyler's brother."

"Again, and? That doesn't mean he's your brother."

Erin seems to chew on that along with her straw as she sips on her drink, still staring across the room at Clinton and his brothers. Suddenly, Matt slides up and wraps his arms around my waist. Even though he's a decent lay, I still inwardly groan and roll my eyes.

Because all I can think about is how he's *not* Jarrett.

Bastard.

"Let's dance."

"I'd rather not," I say bluntly.

Erin chuckles and I subtly flick her the bird.

"Wanna sneak off and find a closet somewhere then?" Matt smirks and bites his lip but the second the word *closet* leaves his lips my ovaries react. I'd like to find one, alright, but only if Jarrett is inside it.

Fuck!

"Sorry, I need to go..." I consider telling him I need to fix my hair or powder my nose but decide against it. "Piss."

At that, he grimaces and I offer a sweet smile, pulling away from his grasp and making my way across the room. I drain the rest of my drink and leave the empty glass on a table as I pass.

When I reach the bathroom, I splash my face with cold water and lean against the counter, shaking my head. *This is impossible.* As much as I try to deny it, Jarrett has invaded my every thought. He's right – none of these little boys can fuck me the way he does. God, just thinking about it makes me squirm. If there weren't several other stalls occupied in here I'd probably just rub one out and be done with it.

The uncomfortable ache that I usually have no issue handling is building even more as I exit the bathroom. I notice Skyler and Bear talking outside the tall glass doors in front of the hotel and I smile. It's about time they worked out whatever the hell has been going on between them. I can't decide if they act like an old married couple or siblings or both.

I'm just rounding the corner to the hallway that leads back to the main room when I hear a breathy giggle. Halting, I back up a few steps to peer down the opposite hall that leads away from the bathrooms. I smile, happy at least someone is getting their kicks tonight.

Slowly, and as quietly as I can, I tiptoe a little further down the hall and peek around the corner where I heard the noise. I'm still hidden behind the wall, but I just barely make out the hem of Ashlei's long, glittery coral dress. *Damn, Lei! Get it!* I fight back laughter as I spy more, leaning my head out further so I can get a glimpse of whoever's date she stole. I know she came here stag, so who's the mystery man?

I bite my lips between my teeth and cringe as the beads of my dress just barely scrape against the wall, making a soft scratching noise. Ashlei and her man friend don't even blanch, though, so I lean out even further.

And then I gasp.

Slamming my hand hard over my mouth, I tuck myself back around the corner and press my back against the wall.

"What was that?" Ashlei asks and I slowly skirt the wall down the hall, desperately trying to keep my cool. When I reach the end of the hall I give up trying to be quiet and quickly cut across the lobby, flying out the door where Bear and Skyler are still talking.

"J-Love?" Skyler asks but I don't turn. "Where are you going?"

I don't answer, I just jump in one of the waiting cabs in the car-pool area and tell him to drive. I spout off the name of the beach bar before I even realize what I'm doing, but I don't take it back. My breath is labored, my heart beating rapidly out of my chest. No way did I just see that. No fucking way did I just see Ashlei making out with... with...

Oh, God, what's the point?!

I know exactly what I saw. Ashlei was getting action, alright. She had her tongue down someone's throat and she had her hands on their body.

But it wasn't any guy I know.

It wasn't any guy at all.

It was my Little.

Bear

I'm glad I let Erin coax me into going to semi-formal with her. More than half of my brothers are here and my theory about the girls looking hot as fuck turned out to be extremely accurate. I'm not a fan of putting on a tuxedo by any means, but for a non-Omega Chi party, this shit's not bad.

Matt excuses himself from our group, murmuring something about bagging Jess as he cuts toward the bar just as my phone pings. Frowning at the all-caps text from my mom, I quickly call her.

"I'm outside."

"What?" I yell against the noise, plugging the ear opposite my phone.

"I'm outside, Clinton."

Scanning the room, I find the opening that leads out into the lobby and across to the large glass doors at the front of the hotel. Sure as shit, my mom is standing just beyond them. Her slight frame looks even smaller under the grand doors with gold trim, her over-sized t-shirt hanging nearly down to her knees.

Ending the call, I shove my phone back in my pocket and briskly cross the room. I'm trying to calm down, but I'm pissed. Why the fuck is my mom showing up to the KKB semi-formal? Why is she in Florida, period?

The chilly air immediately hits me as I push through the outer doors, cooling my hot skin. "What are you doing here?"

"That's the first thing you have to say to me?" she asks, her face falling a little. She looks strung out, her skin ashen and her hair a mess. I have no doubt she's been using and the first thing I think of is my little brother.

"Where's Clayton?"

She sighs, shaking her head. "Your brother is fine. Well, your younger one, anyway. He's staying with some friends in Pittsburgh."

"Which brings me back to my first question."

My mom waits for sympathy to show on my face, but it's nowhere in sight. I can't feel sorry for her anymore. That passed after I turned sixteen.

"Clinton, I need some money. Carleton is in the car." She turns, pointing back to an idling, beat up piece of shit Cadillac. "We're in some trouble and we need a way out. Now I know what you're thinking," she says before I have the chance to cut her off. "And I'm telling you, we're getting clean after this. Carleton wants his baby boys to have a father they can look up to and I'm tired of this shit ruining my life. But we aren't going to have the chance to get clean if you don't help us, you understand?" Her eyes hit me hard with that last line and I understand all too well.

"What the fuck, Mom?!" I run my hands over my head, frustrated. "What the hell did you do?!"

"I'm not getting into that with you. You don't care, anyway."

"Oh? And what, you don't owe me an explanation for having to ask for money from me... *again*? Or how about for the fact that you haven't talked to me one fucking time since I sent you money last time?"

"We've never been close, Clinton. Stop acting like I'm the big bad mom in this situation."

"The big? The?" I laugh, my hysterics reaching an all-time high as I try to repeat what she just said but fail. "Do you hear yourself?"

"Please, Clinton," she begs just as the doors open behind me.

"Bear?" It's Skyler, and now I'm even more pissed. My life at Palm South is not my life back home. In fact, the person I was before college doesn't exist anymore. I don't want anyone – especially not Skyler – seeing where I came from. Or *who* I came from.

"You need to go," I say firmly, my jaw hard.

Mom nods, at least having enough common sense to not push the subject now that Skyler is present. "Just please, help your family, Clinton. Consider what will happen if you don't." She swallows and I shake my head in warning. "We're staying at the Motel 8 down the road."

With that, she turns and jumps back in the car and I'm left with Skyler. I know she wants to ask what happened, but she doesn't – she just walks up and leans her head on my arm. After a moment, she asks, "That your mom?"

I nod.

"You don't look anything like her."

I don't know why, but for some reason, hearing her say those words makes me smile. Skyler shivers a bit against me and I pull her into me, wrapping my arms around her shoulder and burying my nose in her hair. She smells like nothing I've ever smelled before, something too clean and put together for my life.

"You can talk to me, Bear. I know it may seem like I won't understand, but I might surprise you."

Sighing, I don't even try to fight it anymore. I spill everything. I trust Skyler more than anyone else at this school and she's done nothing but prove time and time again that she's a great friend. So, I tell her about my shitty past – about my mom, my brother, the drugs, the money, my little brother caught in the middle of it – everything. When I finish, she pulls back, crossing her arms over her chest.

"They need money again?"

"Yeah. Who knows how much this time."

Skyler chews her bottom lip so hard I think she might draw blood and then quickly reaches for her clutch. Pulling out a slender wallet and a pen, Skyler scribbles out something and tears the small sheet of paper away, handing it out for me to take. "Here."

When I pull it under the light shining from inside the hotel, I realize it's a check.

For two-thousand dollars.

"What the fuck, Skyler?" I shake my head, thrusting it back to her. "No. Hell no."

"Bear, hear me out."

"No! First of all, who even has checks anymore?"

Skyler laughs. "I send money home to my family all the time. Checks are the easiest and safest way to do that."

At that, my hand drops to my side, the check still firmly grasped between my fingers. "What? How often?"

"At least once a month." She shrugs. "They don't ask me for it, but I send it anyway."

I don't have words for that little nugget of information. I knew Skyler had a strange family situation at home, I knew she entered poker tournaments all the time for a reason, but I had no idea she was sending money home that frequently.

"Give that to your mom, Bear. Tell her that's it, that's all she's ever getting from you again, and call it done. They'll get themselves out of whatever trouble they're in and you can breathe easy knowing you don't have to drain your savings."

"This is too much," I say, shaking my head and staring down at her neat handwriting.

"Psh," she says, waving her hands. "I can make that back in a weekend at the downtown casino. No sweat." She winks and I know she's lying, but she's trying her best to make me feel okay with this situation.

"Why Skyler?"

"Why am I helping you?" I nod. "Are you kidding, Bear? Your family may be fucked up, but what you don't realize is that you're *my* family now, too. And families help each other – always.

That's why you have always helped your mom and your brother, and that's why I'm helping you now."

"I don't know what to say."

"Don't say anything. Call your mom, have her come back to pick up this check, and then get back in there and drink with me."

Still staring at her like everything she's saying to me is completely ludicrous, I pull her in for a crushing hug. She laughs against my chest and wraps her small arms around me, too. "I love you, Bear."

"I love you, Sky."

"Hey," she says, pulling back. "What are you doing for Thanksgiving?"

I shrug. "Probably staying on campus with some of my brothers."

"Will you come home with me? Meet my parents and my older brother? Please?"

"What is this, Bear Charity Case Night?"

She chuckles. "No, I just want them to meet my new brother." At that, I return her smile and kiss her forehead.

"You have a knack for making a big guy feel really small, you know that?"

Skyler opens her mouth to respond just as the doors beside us fly open and Jess tears across the parking lot. Skyler calls out after her but Jess doesn't stop. She hops into one of the waiting cabs and before we have the chance to digest it, she's gone.

"Well shit," Skyler says. "Wonder what that's about."

I sigh. "Omega Chi parties never have this much drama."

Skyler barks out a laugh and punches my arm. "Yeah, yeah, whatever. Call your mom and come back inside."

After Skyler leaves, I do call my mom back. I make Carleton get out of the car with her and I stare both of them in the eyes when I hand them the check and threaten that this is the last time they better ever contact me for money. They both seem insanely grateful, but I know it's just temporary. As much as I want to believe they won't ask me for money again, I know they will.

But tonight, I don't let that thought hold me down. After their car leaves, I make my way back inside and Erin slides me a new drink as soon as I reach our table.

"I've been looking for you."

I cock a brow. "Yeah?"

She smiles, her light brown eyes shimmering in the soft light of the ballroom. Her dark blonde hair that's usually hanging to her shoulders is pinned up in an organized mess of curls and it accents her slender face. She always looks classic and traditional, but tonight she looks royal. "Yeah. I want to dance."

"Well, it is your ball, princess." I wink and chug down the rest of my Hennessey before letting her drag me to the floor. And then I dance and drink and laugh until I forget everything else.

Everything except Skyler.

I'll never forget that girl.

Adam

Skyler has been outside with Bear for almost half an hour now, and that means I'm finding it harder and harder to ignore Clay's douchebag ways. Pair that with the fact that I'm two shots past drunk and you could say I'm not exactly in the best state of mind right now.

Clay spots me watching him and Cassie dancing and he whispers something in her ear, making her giggle and me growl before excusing himself. Moments later, he slides up next to me at the bar, but I don't even turn to acknowledge him. Even without looking directly at him, I can see his douchey Ken doll smirk.

"Having fun, Brooks?"

"Yep." I let the end of the word pop as I take a large drink from my glass. "You?"

"Oh yeah. But I guess you already know that since you've been watching me all night, huh?"

I shake my head, finally turning to face him. The cocky grin plastered on his face makes me snarl my next sentence. "I don't fucking like you being around Cassie."

"Oh, I'm sorry – did I ask for your permission?"

"She's a good girl, Clay. I'm serious. Don't fuck her around."

"Didn't plan on it," he says, sipping from the shot glass the bartender just slid him. He props his elbows up on the bar and scans the room until he finds Cassie. "Now fuck her up and down every inch of my room tonight? Definitely."

"Goddamnit, Clay!" I growl, slamming my glass down hard on the bar. He just cackles and I grit my teeth before storming across the room. Cassie's eyes widen as I approach her but I don't say a word, I just hook her by the inside of her elbow and drag her out to the hallway near the bathrooms.

"What the hell, Adam?"

"You can't leave with Clay tonight."

Her mouth pops open. "Oh my God, are you serious right now?" Her green eyes take on a more hazel look under the low light of the hotel and she crosses her arms, popping one hip to the side. It's the sassiest I've ever seen her.

"Yes, I'm dead serious. He just wants to get in your pants, Cassie."

"Well, I guess it's lucky for him that I'm not wearing any pants tonight, huh?" She rolls her eyes and tries to stride past me but I pull her back.

"Damnit, this isn't a game!"

"And you're not my boyfriend!"

I blanch. "That's not what this is about."

"Oh?" she asks, stepping closer. "It's not?"

Swallowing, I search her eyes for the hundreds of questions that lay hidden behind that one she posed. The air between us feels thicker, charged with an energy I can't quite determine. "I'm just looking out for you. Can't you just trust me when I say he's bad news?"

"He's been nothing but nice to me," she murmurs softly, still not stepping out of my space. Reaching out, I let my hands just barely rest on her arms.

"He knows what he's doing, Cassie. He's good at it."

Her brows pull together, and for a moment I think she might listen to me, but then she shakes her head and pulls back just as Clay emerges from the ballroom. "I can handle myself, Adam."

"Everything okay?" Clay asks, faking a concern I know he doesn't have.

"Yeah. You ready to get out of here?" Cassie asks.

"Absolutely." Clay tosses his jacket over his shoulder and throws his other arm around hers. Cassie glances at me once more before turning toward the door, and then it's Clay who looks at me. With a smirk, he winks, pulls Cassie closer, whispers in her ear and bites her earlobe. She leans into him, giggling, and I curse, punching the padded wall outside the main room just as he tosses back his head with a laugh and walks her through the large glass doors.

I'm still frustrated when I snap for the bartender's attention back at the bar. Skyler reappears, looking just as gorgeous as ever, and wraps her arms around my neck. Desperate, I pull her in for a long, hard kiss, tangling my hands in her hair as she moans against my mouth.

Cassie is my friend and I do care about her, but I can't make her decisions for her. I can't make her *mistakes* for her either. I may have lost my cool, but there's nothing I can do to take any of it back now. Instead, I'm just going to focus on the beautiful girl wrapped around me and the sounds she'll be making in my bed later tonight.

Cassie McBee is on her own.

Jess

It's a longer cab ride from the hotel to the beach than from campus, but it gives me time to think. No matter how hard I try, I can't get the image of what I saw earlier out of my head. Maybe I should have called them both out on it right then and there, but I didn't have the balls. I mean, how often do you see your best friend and your Little making out in the back of semi-formal?

It's not even the kissing that bothers me. At least, I don't think so. I mean, I'm not exactly cool with it, but then again, whatever – who am I to judge, right? But why did they have to lie to me? Bo's been making me feel like shit about how we never hang out and Ashlei has been sneaking around at all hours of the night. Is that where she's been going? To be with Bo?

God, just thinking about it makes my blood boil.

What's with all the fucking secrets around here?!

I let everyone in on my dirty laundry. Hell, not only do I hang it up to dry in front of all my sisters but I practically ask them to take pictures and post them on social media. I couldn't give two shits what they think about my scandals. Maybe that's where I'm doing it wrong. I missed the memo about not sharing shit with your fucking sisters.

When the cab finally pulls up to the bar, I toss two twenties over the seat and bolt for the door. Jarrett sees me before I even make it to the entrance. I'm not sure if it's because he knows me or just because he knows my body but as soon as his eyes meet mine, he drops the glass he's cleaning. Planting one hand hard on the bar, he balances himself and jumps up and over the bar. He strides toward me purposefully and tosses the small white bar towel behind him just in time to catch me as I jump into his arms and wrap my legs around him, crashing my mouth down on his.

"Are you finally done with those little boys?" His voice is low, husky, needy.

I kiss him harder, fisting his shirt in my hands and not giving two fucks if anyone is watching us. "I'm done with everyone."

Jarrett doesn't ask questions. He doesn't poke and prod to get me to talk to him. He doesn't tell anyone inside the bar that he's leaving or that he'll be right back. He just carries me back out the door, across the parking lot, and out to the beach. Dropping me down onto one of the cushioned beach chairs owned by the bar, he rips his board shorts down to his ankles and pushes my short, mint green dress up to my hips. He wastes no time, tearing a condom wrapper open with his teeth and rolling it down over his massive cock before burying himself inside me.

And then, everything else is lost. Jarrett's hands and mouth completely own me. They take me down, pull me under, push me deep into the earth until there's nothing and no one left but me and him.

Just the way I like it.

EPISODE 6

"I don't want this TO BE COMPLICATED."

Erin

I can't remember the last time I had a hangover, but my eyes aren't even open yet and my head is hammering away in my skull. It's safe to say I have one now. Groaning, I squeeze my eyes shut tighter and pull the fluffy, light blue covers up and over my head. When they're jerked back, I bolt upright.

What the hell?

Slowly craning my neck to the side, I squeak and scurry from the bed, taking the covers with me and quickly wrapping them around my chest.

"Fuck, Josh, stop messing around!" Clinton sprawls out, naked as the day he was born, stretching his legs and wiggling his toes. I swallow as the tight muscles of his abdomen ebb and flow with the movement. His dark skin is a vast contrast against my cream sheets and my eyes can't help but fall to the cut V that leads right down to another part of his body coming to attention this morning. When his eyes open and he finds me cowering in the corner and staring at him wide-eyed, he blanches. "Erin?"

"Bear."

We just stare at each other for a moment in disbelief. Slowly, our eyes scan my room, surveying his clothes in a pile on the floor and my dress thrown over the back of my desk chair. Ashlei's bed is still made from the day before, which means she probably didn't come home at all.

Which also means I was alone with Bear all night.

As if I just emerged from beneath a salty wave, my eyes clear and I remember in blurry, yet surprisingly vivid details what happened after semi-formal last night.

I snuck Clinton inside. We made out. He ripped my dress off. There was some sort of talk about stopping that neither of us listened to. And we had sex.

We totally, *totally* had sex.

"Did we?"

I nod. "Uh, yep."

Clinton's brows furrow and he pinches the bridge of his nose. "Well, shit."

All at once, I spring into action, gathering his clothes off the floor and shoving them toward him before pulling on a pair of shorts and sleep shirt to cover my still-naked body. "You have to get out of here. Mom Cindy is going freak out if she finds you here." I shake my head, cracking my door open just enough to peek down the hall before turning back to Clinton. "Oh my God. I can't believe this happened."

"Relax," he says groggily, pulling on his last dress shoe. He left the belt off his slacks and his white dress shirt is unbuttoned at the top. With his tie and jacket in one hand, he moves toward the door where I'm still standing. "It's fine. We had a few drinks and then had a little fun. No harm, no foul, right?"

My heart is beating rapidly against my rib cage and I can't seem to find enough breath even though I know I'm inhaling and exhaling over and over again. Skyler would probably kill me if she found out this happened. And the other girls would totally judge. It's *Clinton* we're talking about here. Plus, I'm trying to move up in the sorority – I can't do that if word gets out that I'm sneaking boys into the house.

"Bear… we can't…"

"I know. I won't say anything."

"Like, *no one* can find out."

"Erin, it's fine," he assures me again. Holding up two fingers, he cocks a brow. "No one hears a peep about it. Scout's honor. Okay?"

I nod. "Okay. I won't tell anyone either."

At that, Clinton smirks. "Obviously."

Placing his free hand on the door handle, Clinton glances back at the bed and it's as if he remembers what happened, too, because he smiles a little broader and throws me a wink before disappearing down the hall. Forcing the door shut behind him, I press my back against it and let out a mixture of a moan and a sigh, shaking my head.

That did *not* just happen.

I can feel myself hyperventilating. I don't have control of this situation. I *clearly* didn't have control of anything last night. I need something I can exercise power over and fast. Right now I'm spinning, losing balance, and this is not me. This is not Erin Xander.

The last time I let myself lose control of my emotions and actions was the summer before my senior year of high school. It was the summer I visited my grandparents in Kansas and in a way, I found myself in those short two months – but I also lost myself, too. I shiver, the blue eyes of a boy I haven't thought about in a long time sneaking up on me out of nowhere. I vowed after that shit show that I would always have a plan and more than that – I would always stick to said plan.

Hooking up with Clinton was *not* in my plan.

Quickly, I cross the room and rip my laptop from its power cord before falling back onto my bed. Before I can process it, I'm feverishly typing out my essay for my Recruitment Chair application. I was hesitant about applying, since usually executive positions are reserved for seniors, but I'm too impatient to wait around for the presidency and I don't want a small chair position. I want to lead. I want authority.

More than that, I need it.

As if my morning couldn't get any worse, my phone rings and my mom's picturesque face fills the screen. Though her hair is dark unlike my own, I definitely inherited my high cheek bones and chocolate eyes from her. I pray every day that I don't inherit anything else – especially characteristically.

She's ensuring my arrival for Thanksgiving, no doubt, especially since they're hosting their annual dinner at the country club. Just the thought of making small talk with my parents' friends and listening to Mom and Dad's incessant pleas for me to find a suitable man make me want to crawl under my bed and die. *If only they knew about last night…*

I laugh out loud at that and silence my phone at the same time. I can call her back later, and she will definitely *never* know about last night. I can't even imagine the lecture I'd get if she ever did find out.

What *is* Bear's major? Football? Beer? Mind-blowing Sex?

Shit. Did I really just think that?

Typing faster, I set my focus back to the task at hand – on something I have control over. I can't help what my parents feel about me or take back my actions from last night, but I can take over what will happen when I get back from Thanksgiving.

I'll be elected Recruitment Chair, ace my finals, party with my sisters and then take off for a European Christmas trip with Kelsey. I had a little too much fun last night, but now it's back to business.

And, this time, no straying from the plan.

Skyler

Thanksgiving is by far my favorite holiday. For most families, it means turkey dinner, football, and Black Friday shopping. For mine, it means homemade pizza, craft beer, and poker.

Absolute perfection.

Having Clinton with me this year makes it even more special. I was slightly terrified on our drive up, realizing he was going to be walking into a completely different atmosphere than the one at Palm South, but then I realized it's Clinton – he's the last one I have to worry about judging me. If anything, it seems like Clinton came from a similar situation – if not a worse one.

I may have never had money or nice things growing up, but I always knew my family loved me.

I'm not sure Clinton can say the same.

That thought wrecks me as I watch him working in the kitchen with my mom. I can tell it's his first time making a homemade pizza because he's having trouble with the dough just like I did the first time I made it. I can't help but chuckle at his determined scowl as his large fingers work against the sticky concoction, not really making any progress at all until Mom jumps in to help. He just grunts and takes a long swig of his IPA.

My parents' house is small but homey, and I think I love it even more for that. There are family photos on every wall and not one shelf or coffee table is clear of clutter. Mail, magazines, and other odds and ends cover the dining room table and car keys and wallets sit alongside vases and knickknacks on the mantel. The forest green and cream white colored accents in the living room don't really match any of the furniture and the kitchen is an explosion of tonight's dinner ingredients and dishes. The fridge is hidden by mismatched magnets and takeout menus and not one plate matches another in the cabinet. I love my home, and I love Clinton being in it even more.

"He seems like a great guy," Dad says, placing his rough hands on my shoulders and squeezing. He's a tall, lean man with light blonde hair slowly graying at the ends. The wrinkles on his face tell the world that he's had to work hard in his life but the smile he always has plastered on says he's enjoyed every last minute. He gave me my favorite feature – my ocean blue eyes. "I can tell he cares about you."

"It's not like that, Dad," I clarify, patting his hand with my own. "We're just friends. But he is really special to me."

"I see that." Dad plants a kiss on the top of my head and adjusts his glasses just as Clinton removes his hands where he's just kneaded out the dough. He curses as it folds back in on itself and Dad chuckles. "Let's go help them or we're never going to eat."

After dinner, Mom and my older brother, Skott, start setting the table up for our poker game. Skott is seven years older than me and lives in Alaska. He works for a wildlife preservation society and the fact that he even got the time to come home for the holiday is amazing. With his long, disheveled brown hair and newly sprouted beard, he looks nothing like what I remember. Then again, I haven't seen him other than the occasional video chat in almost two years. His blue eyes are still the same, though – they match mine and Dad's. When he ruffles my hair as I pull the last dirty dish from the table, I smile and stick out my tongue at him before brushing past.

"Your family is amazing," Clinton says as he dries another dish. I start scrubbing the one I just retrieved and smile.

"Yeah, they are. Definitely far from the other families of Palm South though, huh?"

Clinton shares my smile, shaking his head. "That's an understatement. I can definitely say I'd rather be here playing poker with your family than playing golf with one of my brothers'."

"Or drinking tea."

"Or browsing the newest BMW line."

I hand him the last dish to dry and whip out my best attempt at a rich southern accent, which kind of sounds more like a hick because I have no idea what I'm doing. "Or sitting around talking about how perfect our houses are."

Clinton laughs, but mimics me, his accent more European. "Or comparing trust funds like dicks."

My mom walks in just as he finished the sentence and she blushes, her dark chocolate hair falling in her face a bit as she hands us a dish I must have missed. "It's okay, Bear. No need to prove to us how big your... *trust fund* is."

Dad and Skott crack up at that and I can't help but join them. Even though his dark skin doesn't show it, I swear Clinton is blushing as he apologizes to my mom. She pats him on the arm and then we all gather around the table as Dad divvies out the chips and explains the blinds. Clinton watches poker and plays at the casino with me sometimes, so luckily we don't have to teach him how to play the game itself.

"Ready for me to take all your money, sis?" Skott asks as Dad deals the first hand.

"Keep dreaming," I tease.

The rest of the night is a mixture of laughter and good conversation, both of which I appreciate. It's been so long since I've been able to let loose without thinking about what guys are around or what my sisters might be thinking. I can tell Clinton is enjoying himself, too, and I know he needs the break from life just as much as I do. Neither of us have even really been on our phones, other than me responding to Adam's texts and Clinton following up with his mom – who still hasn't reached out to him since semi-formal.

I take everyone's money by the end of the evening. Dad and Mom aren't surprised in the slightest but Skott fought me until the end. He's still a little bitter when he knuckles my head and slinks down the hall to his old bedroom. Clinton and I opt to sit on my front porch for a while, talking a bit but mostly just enjoying the nice November weather and listening to the soft buzz of insects.

When we go back to campus, it'll be finals and elections and then we'll all disperse for Christmas break. It's kind of nice to just take a moment to enjoy life without all the rush that goes along with being in college.

Too bad it's short lived.

***

I'm quiet on the ride home Sunday, though my thoughts are loud in my head. After the first hour passes, Clinton finally breaks the silence.

"Are you going to tell me what you're thinking so hard about?" When I don't answer immediately, he sighs. "Skyler, what's going on? Did Adam say something? Everything was fine, we were having a great weekend. What changed?"

"Shit," I groan, sliding my hands down to the bottom of the steering wheel and stretching my back out against the scratchy seat. Since everything is so close to campus at Palm South, I always leave my car at home and take cabs or buses around the university, so I rented a car for the drive home and back. The small economic car isn't nearly as comfortable as my old beat up Pontiac, though. "My parents are in trouble, Bear."

"What do you mean? They seemed fine to me."

"I found a letter from the bank in the stack of mail my mom gave me. She must have gotten theirs mixed in with mine. It was a warning letter." I sigh. "They're about to lose the house."

Clinton blanches. "Holy shit."

"Yeah."

He looks out the window for a short moment before shaking his head. "Damn it, Skyler. You shouldn't have given me that money. Your family needs it just as much as mine does. And at least yours isn't using it for fucking pills."

"Don't, Bear," I warn. "I gave you that because I care about you and I wanted that situation to be squashed. I wouldn't take it back now even if you tried, and you know it." Sighing, I brace myself for what I'm about to say next. "I just need to figure out a new plan."

Clinton cocks a brow, curious. "You say that like you already have one."

"I do. Well, kind of."

"What do you mean?"

I sigh again. "There's a huge tournament over Christmas break in Atlantic City. It's not like what I usually play, Bear." I pause, shaking my head at the audacity I have for even thinking I have a chance at this. "The pros will be there. There's a lot of money at stake and I'll be lucky if I can even hang on until the final table."

"Skyler, you sell yourself too short." Clinton reaches his large, rough hand across the console and squeezes my knee. "You're good at this. *Really* fucking good. You don't enter larger tournaments because you get in the way of yourself." He lifts his hand to tap the side of my head. "It's all up here. You psych yourself out."

"But this isn't just a tournament. It'll be on television. People will be watching. People have been practicing all year for this."

Clinton smiles. "Well, then I guess you better not get used to no one knowing your name because after you win this thing, everyone will."

I have no idea why, but my eyes fill with water that I don't blink away. I don't want the tears. I just let them sit there, blurring my vision a bit as I glance at Clinton. "You really think I can do this?"

"I know you can." I let out a large breath and he continues. "In fact, when we get back to campus, we're going straight to my room and signing you up."

"Maybe I should sleep on it."

Clinton shakes his head. "No chance. We're signing you up and then we're booking our flights."

"Our?"

He nods. "Yep. Our. I'm going to be there the first time the poker world wakes up and realizes who Skyler Fucking Thorne is."

At that, I laugh and blink, granting my tears access to roll down my cheeks in two symmetrical rivers. After a few moments of silence, my heart surges and I reach across to grab his hand. "Thank you."

He just squeezes it in response and then reaches forward, raising the volume on the radio. We goof around, sing, and joke about absolutely nothing that makes sense the rest of the way home.

And I silently thank whatever God is listening for sending me Clinton Pennington.

Jess

Ah, I love breakfast in bed.

Or should I say, Jarrett loves breakfast in bed. I just love serving it.

"Oh, fuck," I moan, arching my back and grinding my pelvis against his god-like tongue. "Right there. Yes." I drag out the word, my breaths ragged and intense.

Jarrett just smiles against my tender flesh and continues moving his magical fingers inside me, hitting the spot I need him to touch most. The rough stubble on his face provides just enough friction to drive me mad, and combined with his skilled alternating motions somewhere between sucking and licking, I'm ready to combust any second.

"Come here," I pant, grabbing at the bare skin of his shoulders to coax him up to me. I'm ready for him to be inside me. I need it. Now.

"You come first."

"I want you to fuck me."

He moves his fingers faster and sucks my clit, causing me to cry out his name. "And I will. But first, you're going to come just like this."

Realizing there's no use in arguing, I relax against the sheets and move my hands to cover his gripping my hips. He squeezes harder, his tongue flicking up some sort of magical combination I'm pretty sure they don't even teach at Hogwarts before he sends me flying into ecstasy.

I ride out the orgasm, bucking my hips up to meet his mouth with each wave until I'm spent. When I finish, Jarrett kisses and bites his way up every inch of my body until he meets my mouth, letting me taste myself on his tongue. "You'd do well to listen to me and not argue when I'm trying to pleasure you."

"Oh shut up and fuck me," I moan. He's all too happy to oblige. Flipping me over and pressing my face into his soft goose down comforter, he takes all of six seconds to fill me from behind. My entire body is flat against the bed and my legs are still squeezed tight together as he straddles my ass and pounds into me hard. In this position, I swear I feel him all the way up to my ribcage.

He doesn't come in this position though.

Or the next one. Or the next one after that. No, Jarrett takes his time fucking me all morning, switching positions when I know he's close just so he can ride out another ten minutes. When we're both slick with sweat, our legs aching, our mounting climaxes ridiculously uncomfortable – that's when he lets me come again and releases with me.

"Goddamn, Jess," he whispers, dropping his forehead against mine. I wait for him to continue, to say something else, but apparently those two words are all he needed to convey what he meant – just my name and the most offensive curse word in the English language.

Oddly, I'm flattered.

He removes himself gently, kissing my lips once more before peeling off the condom and retreating to the bathroom. For a moment I just watch his tight ass waltz away, trailing my eyes along the lines of the tattoos covering both his arms. He rubs his hand over his bald head and half closes the door, blocking my view. Sighing, I spread out in the sheets and flex my muscles, wincing as they ache in protest. Jarrett chuckles from the doorframe a moment later.

"You need a banana and some water."

I quirk my brow at the phallic fruit reference, but decide not to comment on it. "I'm thinking more along the lines of bacon and a mimosa."

"You have class in a half hour."

I shrug. "And? I'll sober up before our test tonight, professor. Promise." I wink and he shakes his head. It's the week after Thanksgiving and already finals have kicked in. Dr. Maynard decided to give us our last test tonight before finals week officially starts next week so we don't feel overwhelmed. It doesn't matter, though. We're college kids – we wait until the last minute and then overdose on Adderall and Red Bull until we get the job done. It's what we do.

"So," Jarrett muses, taking a seat at the edge of the bed and pulling my left foot into his hand. When he gently starts massaging it, I lean my head back and moan. "Are we going to talk about what this is."

"What *what* is?" I ask, my head still against the pillow, eyes closed.

"Don't be naïve," he warns. "After tonight, I won't be your professor's GA anymore."

I lean up on my elbows, but don't pull my foot from his hands. "Are you trying to be my boyfriend, Jarrett Locke?"

"I'm not necessarily trying to title it like that, no."

I frown, but not really because I'm disappointed – more because I'm confused. I mean, I'm not looking for anything serious, either. But then again, what else is there?

Oh. Right.

"So, fuck buddies, then?"

"I'm not necessarily trying to title it like that, either."

I huff, yanking my foot back this time. "So then what exactly *are* you trying to say?"

He shrugs. "I'm just saying I don't want to fuck anyone else. And I don't want *you* to fuck anyone else."

"So, like I said..."

"But I also want to hang out with you."

"But we can't be seen in public because you're a GA for next semester, too – even if I won't be in the class again."

He nods, but for once, he looks sheepish, his normally lusting eyes taking on a childish glow.

I consider it for all of two seconds before abruptly moving from the bed and pulling on my clothes. "Yeah, I don't know about that."

"What don't you know about? What's there to question?" I just give him a pointed look, my long blonde locks falling in my face a bit as I do. My hair is usually shiny and radiant, but since I've been in his bed for two straight days, it's taken on a greasy appearance instead. Hastily, I tie it in a messy bun and let it sit on my head.

"What if I just see you when I see you?"

Jarrett stands, towering over me as he moves his hands to my waist and pulls me into him. "We've already established that no one on that campus can fuck you into oblivion like I can. So what are you going to do? Buy a new vibrator? Name it after me and pretend it's half as good?"

I scoff. "Cocky bastard." I try to peel myself away from him but his grip remains firm.

"You and I both know when I'm being cocky and this is not one of those times." He pauses, his intense dark eyes searching mine. "I'm being serious. And honest. You should try it."

"I don't want this to be complicated."

"Me either."

Sighing, I pull my tank top over my head but it stops where his hands are still firmly planted. Jarrett does make a good point. I've never met a man who can give me pleasure the way he does. And I know when I leave here all I'm going to think about is the next time I can come back.

So I cave.

"Okay." Jarrett smirks but I poke my finger hard into his chest. "But if shit gets complicated or dramatic, we end it. I'm serious."

"Deal."

I eye him cautiously. "Okay."

"Okay."

***

After my test in Scope and Methods, I meet the girls at Ralph's for drinks. Finals week is about to really kick in and we know we won't see each other much until the celebratory parties next weekend. They're all chatting animatedly, but I can't stop staring at Ashlei and Bo. They're sitting right next to each other, laughing and talking to us like nothing happened at semi-formal.

And it's really irking me.

I never called them out on their shit. In fact, I haven't talked to either of them since semi, but they haven't questioned it because it was Thanksgiving and now we're all in finals mode. Ashlei is always sneaking off anyway. Now, anytime she disappears when Bo isn't around, I can't help but wonder if that's where she's going.

But, then again, staring at them now, I can't help but wonder if maybe it was just a drunken kiss. Hell, I've kissed a few girls in my drunken state of shenanigans – it's not like it doesn't happen. Still... something feels off.

"Ready to be roomies next semester, Cassie?" Bo asks, cheersing our little red head from across the table. I have to admit, I was a little skeptical about Cassie when I first met her. I wasn't sure how she'd fit in with us. I'm not that close with her yet, but she has easily melded into our group and I love the color she brings to it.

"I'm ready to be out of the hellish situation I'm in right now, that's for sure," she says, clinking Bo's glass before taking a sip. "Paris will be in the Zeta house next semester, too. I guess it was only a matter of time."

Ashlei shakes her head. "I have plenty of girlfriends in other sororities. If Paris ended your friendship, it's because that was her choice." I kind of blanch at the term girlfriends, wondering if there's more to that than she lets on, but I decide not to press it.

"I'm going to miss her," Cassie mumbles, trailing the condensation on her glass.

Skyler gently pats her back. "And there's nothing wrong with that."

"Except that you're not allowed to miss her anymore because you're clearly in better company now," Erin adds, winking at her Grand Little.

"I'm more curious about how your night went after semi-formal," I add. We made jokes about how we both went with frat presidents that night. The difference is I left without mine. She didn't.

Cassie's cheeks blush a furious shade of red that almost competes with her hair and she immediately sucks down half her drink. "It was fine."

My eyes scan the other girls and they're all looking around the table, too, before we burst into a fit of laughter. Cassie covers her face with her hands and tosses a napkin in my direction.

"You guys are the worst."

"Hey," I say, throwing my hands up. "Ain't no shame in getting some penis action. Clearly I'm not going to judge."

Everyone laughs harder at that before the topic of conversation changes to Erin and her application for Recruitment Chair. It's a ballsy move, especially since there are at least three other senior girls going for the same position. They've been waiting over three years to get their shot at that chair, but something tells me it's going to go to Erin anyway. She always has everything under control and the entire chapter knows that no one can run recruitment and bring us a better pledge class next fall than she can.

"So, since we're not going to be together for New Year's Eve, I want to hear everyone's resolutions right now," Erin says and we all groan in unison. She's all about the sharing/sisterhood shit and even though we all secretly love it, too, we pretend like it's annoying. Mostly because it's fun to tease Erin.

She gives us all a pointed look, but lifts her glass. "Oh, stop. Little, you go first."

Skyler blows out a long breath before lifting her glass to join Erin's. "I resolve to stop being afraid of what might happen if I take risks. Starting with this tournament." We all smile at that, even if we don't fully understand it. I certainly have no interest in poker or her obsession with it, but I can tell from how she's been talking that this Atlantic City tournament is a big deal. So, obviously, I'm going to support her.

Cassie raises her cup next. "I'm going to ace my classes and get a head start on my pre-med program."Ashlei and I give her pointed looks and she concedes. "Okay fine, I'll have a little more fun, too."

It's not quite good enough for me, but again, I let it go. Little Miss Innocent can stay our little angel for a while longer.

Bo toasts to new beginnings and Ashlei ditto's her as they lift their glasses in unison. The soft and knowing look they exchange isn't lost on me and I frown, thrusting my drink up next. "Well, other than changing my major because clearly political science is not for me, I resolve to be honest. I just think honesty is an important virtue and I'm making it a priority."

Nearly everyone at the table seems uncomfortable at my toast, but I hold my glass high along with my head and smile.

"I resolve to bring us the best pledge class yet when I'm elected Recruitment Chair," Erin finishes us off. None of us even comment on the fact that she didn't say *if*. We all know she'll get the job.

We clink our glasses together and say "Happy New Year" in unison before throwing back the liquid. Bo hugs me, which is surprising, and asks me to study for finals with her this weekend. I agree, because I really do need to get closer to her – especially if I expect her to grow our family tree next year. I consider telling them about my recent romps with Jarrett and what we agreed to at his apartment this morning, but as I open my mouth I think better of it.

For once, I'm going to keep my little private affair to myself.

"Drink up, ladies," Skyler says, signaling for the bartender to return to us. "We survived another semester at Palm South University."

Scanning the faces of my beautiful sisters, I can't help but wonder how many secrets survived right along with us.

Adam

This has to be a joke.

That's all I can think as I stare at Clay. His blue eyes are hard, like he's pissed the words are coming from his mouth just as much as I'm surprised by them. Running his hands back through his dirty blonde hair, he repeats them again, but I still don't understand.

So this time, I say it out loud.

"This has to be a joke."

Clay purses his lips, but then takes a deep breath and crosses his arms hard over his chest. "It's not. Tommy is transferring and that leaves Social Chair open. Since you practically did his job this semester anyway, it only makes sense that you step into the position officially." He shifts and I can tell he hates admitting any of this.

"Is this some sort of peace offering?"

"In a way, I guess," he admits. "But honestly, I still think you're a little punk who has no respect for older brothers. That aside, you did get us recognized a lot this semester. You're the best brother for the job. That's a fact I can't ignore as president."

If I weren't focusing so hard on clamping my jaw shut, my mouth would be hanging wide open. Is this really Clay right now? Where's the colossal asshat I'm so used to dealing with?

"So, are you in?"

Shaking my thoughts, I nod. "Yeah. Of course. I, uh, thank you. Thanks for this." I sound like an idiot, but this is the most cordial conversation I've ever had with Clay. It's fucking weird.

Clay nods and extends his hand to me. We shake firmly and then walk side by side back into our fraternity house. For once, it's quiet – mostly because our Academic Chair has deemed the house a study zone for finals.

Before I can stop myself, I clear my throat and ask Clay the question that's been burning in the back of my mind for weeks now. "So, how is Cassie?"

Clay smirks, and it's like the douchebag I've always known emerged out of him to overpower the professional stand-in. "Oh, she's *amazing*." He cocks a brow in a sideways glance at me in a way that suggests he means that in every sense of the word. "Something about the little innocent ones, isn't there? It's almost like you get to play the role of teacher."

I grind my teeth together. "Clay, don't be a fucking dick. She deserves your respect and you know it."

"Oh, of course," he agrees. "And she got it. All night long after semi-formal." His slimy grin grows wider and I shove him hard against his chest. He stumbles back, his legs hitting the arm of our couch and he just falls down to sit in it, laughing hysterically. I consider rushing him again but he stands, wiping the corners of his eyes. "Ah, man, next semester's going to be fun." He claps me hard on the back. "Welcome to the Executive Board, Brooks."

With that, he turns and practically struts down the hall to the President's Room, still chuckling to himself. I growl, frustrated, and make my way into the kitchen to grab a beer. Cracking back the top and sucking down half of the can, I let the icy liquid cool my temper and inhale a deep breath. When my phone pings in and I see a text from Skyler, I smile.

- I need a study break. Come to your window. ;) -

I throw back the rest of my beer and jog down the hall to my room, locking the door behind me. When I yank down on the string to lift my blinds, Skyler's aqua eyes meet mine. She smiles seductively and bites her lip and I just shake my head, lifting the window and immediately covering her mouth with mine.

"What happened to not seeing each other until after finals?"

"I lied," she says simply, breaking from my kiss long enough to crawl through the window. She's dressed casually in a tiny pair of dark jean shorts and a light purple Kappa Kappa Beta tank top. It was freezing just a couple of weeks ago but, in typical Florida fashion, it feels almost like summer again today.

I'm about to offer Skyler a drink when she presses her lips to mine again and slides her hand down to grip me through my basketball shorts, effectively silencing my words. My cock immediately responds to her touch and I back her up to my bed, pulling her down into the sheets. She bites my neck and I hiss through the slight shock of pain as her long brown hair falls all around us.

Flipping her head back and still straddling me, Skyler smiles down at me with hooded eyes as she grinds her hips against mine.

"You look a little stressed," she whispers, slowly winding. "Let me help."

Maneuvering herself to sit between my legs, she fists my shorts and boxers together in her hands and pulls them down over my thighs. I kick them the rest of the way off and she grips my cock firmly, stroking from the tip down to the bottom of my shaft and back. I bite my lip and let my eyes roll back at the feel of her hands, groaning.

"Hey," she whispers and I open my eyes just enough to peer down at her. Still grinning, she twists her long locks up and piles them in a mess on top of her head. "I forgot a hair tie." She grabs my hand and moves it to replace where hers was holding her hair up. "Keep it out of my way."

With that she licks her lips, her blue eyes dazzling in the low light of the afternoon sun streaming in through my window, and then her mouth is on me.

Holy. Mother. Fucking. Fuck.

Skyler swirls her tongue around my tip before pressing her lips firmly against my skin and pushing lower. She takes me in completely with a slight gag and I curse under my breath, fisting her hair tightly. When she moans, I feel the vibrations through her throat and with her slick, hot mouth it's a deadly combination.

She alternates teasing my head with deep throating, every move pushing me closer to climax. Every time I get close, though, she removes her mouth and flattens her tongue, running it from the base to the tip and back down with just enough pressure to tease me but take away the mounting pressure. She's good – *so* fucking good. I've had plenty of blow jobs over the years but nothing could compare to how she's making me feel right now.

When she twists her hands over my shaft to fill the space her mouth isn't covering and works them in combination, I stop breathing and the fiery numbness starts to consume me.

"Fuck, Skyler," I growl. "I'm coming."

I try to pull out of her mouth to finish but she doesn't budge, digging her nails into my thighs in protest. When her devilish eyes gaze up into mine through her lashes while her mouth is still wrapped around me, the visual is too much and I throw my head back against the bed and explode. She doesn't stop working as I bust inside her mouth, my entire body consumed with the intense pleasure she's inflicting. I still as I finish, my body falling limp, and Skyler just pulls back, swallows, and smiles.

Goddamn.

She crawls back up to lay on my chest and I numbly run my fingers through her hair. When I catch my breath and try to roll her over to repay the favor, she stops me, wrapping her arms around me and snuggling back into my chest.

"Today was for you."

"What?" I ask, leaning up slightly. She peers up at me and smiles contently.

"I wanted to please my boyfriend. What's so surprising about that?" She's still smiling but when she sees my face, she realizes what she said and her smile drops. I wait for her to recant, but she doesn't.

"Boyfriend?"

She swallows, but again, doesn't take it back.

I consider it for a moment, wondering if either of us is ready to be in any kind of steady relationship. We're about to break for Christmas and next semester we'll both be busy, as usual. Then again, I don't have any interest in fucking around with any other girls, and Skyler doesn't seem like the overbearing type of girlfriend. She's beautiful, funny, and talented – *in many ways*. What's holding me back?

"Well, I guess I'll allow it. As long as I can pay you back next time."

Skyler looks visibly relieved and she smiles again, leaning in to kiss me. "Looking forward to it."

She rests on my chest again and I continue gently trailing my fingers over her shoulder and up into her hair. "Clay made me Social Chair."

"Yeah?" Skyler asks lazily, her eyes closed. "Not surprising to me. You practically do it all already, right?"

I nod. "Yeah. I guess now it's just titled and official."

She smiles and squeezes me tighter. "I've never slept with a man of such power."

I scoff. "What, Omega Chi presidents don't count?"

Skyler nails me hard in the stomach and I double over but laugh and pull her into me. She squeals and fakes like she's trying to get away before giving up.

"You're an ass."

"And you have a nice ass. Look! We're perfect together."

She rolls her eyes but settles back into my chest with a smile. "I'm so tired," she says, yawning. "Can I nap here for a while? It's so much quieter than our house."

I kiss her forehead in response and in less than a minute, her breathing steadies out and I know she's asleep.

I try to think of the last time I had a girlfriend. I was hooking up with several girls last year, and I think Jazmine might have put a title on us at one point – though I didn't really abide by said title. Still, Skyler doesn't strike me as the type of girl to get hung up on titles. I wonder if it almost slipped as an accident but she was just afraid to take it back and hurt my feelings. Regardless, I like her – a lot – and now at least I have some reassurance that no other guys will be touching her the way I do. Relaxing against Skyler, I let my exhaustion from the day take me under and decide not to overthink it.

But just before I drift off, my mind wanders to a shy redhead with soft green eyes.

Bear

I'm a little nervous as I stride into the Kappa Kappa Beta house and back to their chapter room where all the girls are seated. It's the last chapter of the year and election night, which means they've already had a long meeting and are probably dying to get out of the room. Skyler just texted me less than ten minutes ago to let me know Erin was elected Recruitment Chair. When I find Erin at the front of the room, she looks insanely happy – maybe more so than I've ever seen, but her face falls when she sees me.

I still can't fucking believe I hooked up with Erin Xander. Even more hilarious, she thought *I* would go around telling people. Is she crazy? There's a reason that chick is known around Greek world as Ex. The girl has gone through boyfriends like designer shoes the past three years. No way am I in any way interested in being added to that list – especially since she has the reputation to not know how to let shit go.

Yeah, fuck all that.

I just smile at her briefly to show her she doesn't need to worry before I turn with my brothers to face the rest of the room.

"Good evening, beautiful ladies of KKB. The brothers of Omega Chi Beta wish you all a fun and safe winter break and look forward to next semester. We brought you all chocolate to celebrate the end of finals," I add with a smile. The girls all cheer and clap and the guys laugh. Girls fucking love chocolate.

"I also wanted to take a minute to share something else with you ladies," I say, swallowing back the nerves. I have no idea why I even have them. "I'm not good with words, so I won't make this too long, but some of you may have noticed that Skyler Thorne is a pretty amazing girl." All the sisters smile and turn to stare at Skyler, who's seated near the back. She just smiles at me and suddenly I'm not the least bit nervous anymore. "She and I met last year during Spring Break and we've become closer every day since then. I can't think of anyone else in the world who I care about more than I do her. There are some people who help you through tough times, but then there are some who help you hold on when you think you have nothing else left to grip. Skyler, you are the best friend I have ever had and I could never thank you enough for always being there for me." Even from across the room, I see her eyes gloss over. I shake my head. "Okay, fuck this sappy shit." The room bursts into laughter and I make my way up the makeshift aisle between where the chairs are set and hold out a bouquet of flowers to Skyler. "Sky, I want to officially ask you to be my Little Sister."

The room explodes with a deafening cheer and Skyler laughs, eyes still laminated in a film of unshed tears. She nods and jumps up to throw her tiny arms around my thick neck. I squeeze her in return and she takes the flowers, slugging me on the arm and wiping at her face. "Damn you for making me all emotional."

I throw her a wink and toss my arm around her shoulder before addressing the rest of the room again. "Now all of you go change and get your cute asses down to the O Chi house. Our alumni told us not to party for the rest of the semester and technically finals are over. So, fuck it! Let's rage!"

The cheers ring out even louder and Skyler throws her fist into the air. Quickly, she plants a kiss on my cheek and then jogs off to join her sisters as they filter out of the room. My brothers clap me on the back and we exit the house, joking and singing our obnoxious fraternity drinking songs the entire way back to the house. My Little, Josh, starts the party as soon as we make it back inside, blasting the stereo and breaking out our liquor bottle stash while some of the younger brothers call about getting last minute kegs. Even on short notice, there's no party better than an Omega Chi party.

I haven't heard a single word from anyone other than my younger brother since I gave my mom that check. And, for once, I'm actually happy about it. I feel like a weight has been lifted and Skyler has made me realize that I have a new family here at Palm South. I'm spending Christmas break with her and her family so we can prep her for the big tournament in Atlantic City and I can't imagine a better way to end the semester. It's been a rough and crazy ride, but right now I feel at peace.

And I am beyond ready to rage.

Cassie

I made it through my first semester at Palm South University.

Red Solo cup in hand, I snake my way in-between other Greek students stuffed into the Omega Chi house and make my way back over to Skyler and Jess. Now that finals are over and all that's left to do is celebrate, everyone is in a better mood. Jess has been distant and bitchy lately, but she has a huge smile plastered on her face tonight. Ashlei, Bo, and Erin are playing flip cup against Clinton and two of his brothers across the room. Skyler looks relaxed, and for once I don't see the impending tournament weighing on her. It's like we're all filled with a sense of accomplishment and joy tonight.

Nothing can bring us down.

I'm well on my way to a nice buzz when Skyler and Adam challenge me and Jess to a game of beer pong. We claim one of the empty tables and Adam and I grab beer while Jess and Skyler set up the water cups. We haven't talked since the night of semi-formal, and I feel an awkward tension set in between us as we reach the kegs.

"I heard you're going to be the new Social Chair," I say after filling the third cup. I move it to rest on a small table with the others and grab the next.

Adam smiles. "I'm sorry, Cassie."

"For moving into a leadership position?"

He chuckles and it does something to my stomach that makes me falter the keg nozzle a bit. "No, for being a douche to you. I know you're too nice to call me out on my shit, but I'm not too proud to admit I was wrong. I shouldn't have been in your business that night."

My cheeks burn and I shrug, topping off the last cup. "It's whatever. I haven't even thought about it. Really," I lie with a forced smile. We both balance our cups, gripping them by the lips three in each hand as we make our way back to the table.

"Well, good. I've missed my friend. Let's get breakfast tomorrow morning before everyone heads out."

His dark hair has grown out over the semester and as it falls into his eyes a bit, I can't help the grin that curls on my lips. "Okay."

Adam and Skyler win the first game but Jess and I win the second. I learn that the more intoxicated I get, the easier it seems to be to land that little white pong ball in the cups across the table. We're halfway through the tie-breaker game when I spot Clay sitting on the couch behind where Adam is standing.

And Paris is sitting on his lap.

Handing my ball to Jess without taking my eyes off them, I cross to where they sit and nervously fold my hands together. They don't seem to notice as Clay's hand moves further up where it's resting on Paris' bare thigh. "Hey, Clay."

He's mid-laughter, his mouth close to Paris' neck when I interrupt. They both turn in unison to face me and Paris tucks a long strand of her crimson hair behind her ear, smiling sweetly at me though I feel her intentions are laced with poison. We barely talk anymore, but she knows I've been with Clay since Halloween, which is why this scenario doesn't make any sense to me.

"Oh, hey Cass. What's up?"

I shift. "Uh, what are you doing?" God, I suck at this. How do I confront him? He never said we were boyfriend and girlfriend but still, there were things said. There were things... done.

"Actually, Paris was just telling me that you two are roomies." He turns back to her with a devilish smirk. "My imagination is running wild with that thought."

Paris giggles, and it's as if it breaks the fragile band that was holding me together. "What the hell is wrong with you?" I snap.

Clay's smile falls as he looks back up at me and I realize I called attention to us, which was definitely not what I intended. Clay doesn't seem fazed in the least. "Oh, Cassie," he says, speaking to me like a child. "You didn't think that because we hooked up we were..." he trails off, his hand covering his mouth a bit as he turns to face Paris momentarily before my eyes again. "Oh shit. You did, didn't you?"

"That's so adorable," Paris says, still smiling. I know I'm blushing furiously as I snap my attention to her and plead with my eyes for my best friend to emerge. Where is she? Where's the girl who was practically my sister just four short months ago? Have I lost her completely?

When she just smiles wider, revealing her perfect white teeth, I know I've found my answer.

I want to yell. I want to scream. I want to make them both feel small and insignificant but for some reason, tears prick the corners of my eyes instead. I whip around and storm toward the door. Adam tries to grab my arm and calls out for me but I shake him loose. When I push through the door out onto Greek row, Skyler follows closely behind me. I don't turn around as I all but sprint to the KKB house, but Skyler still trails me. When I finally make it, I punch in our door code and immediately fall onto the couch, letting the tears fall.

I swipe at them furiously, pissed that I'm letting those two assholes affect me this way, but the rivers of betrayal just keep streaming down my cheeks. Skyler doesn't speak a word when she enters through the door, but she sinks down next to me and pulls my head onto her shoulder. It's such a simple and comforting move, but for some reason it breaks me more and I sob harder.

"Shh," she coos, rubbing my back softly. "It's okay. Clay's a dick, Little Nug. He doesn't deserve your tears."

And I know that, but there's so much more to it than Skyler could understand. She continues consoling me, attempting to make me laugh by pointing out oddities in Paris' appearance and making fun of Clay's "Ken Smile". Eventually, I do stop crying, and I pull back from her embrace.

"Thanks, Big. You should get back," I say, nodding toward the direction of the O Chi house. "It's the last party of the semester. Don't miss it on my account."

"You don't want to come back? Prove to everyone that you couldn't care less about those two twat-lickers?"

I force a small smile, but it falls too quickly. "I just want to be alone. Can I sleep in your room for a while?"

"Of course," she says, pulling me in for another long hug.

After Skyler leaves, I crawl into her bed and curl up in the covers, facing the wall. I close my eyes, steady out my breathing, and clear my head, but still, sleep doesn't come. Instead, I feel an overwhelming emotion take hold that I've never experienced in my eighteen years of life. It's something I hoped I never would have to feel, especially not this intensely. But, here it is, washing through me and leaving a sticky residue behind.

Regret.

***

I wake later, my eyes puffy and my cheeks still hot as I lean up and check the clock on Jess' side of the room. She's absent and Skyler is in her bed. It's just after five in the morning.

Quietly, I slip out of Skyler's soft lavender sheets and tiptoe out of the room. After slipping on my Keds, I start walking down Greek Row. It's pitch black outside and cool, but there's a hint of dawn on the horizon and I let it comfort me as my feet numbly carry me to the Alpha Sigma house. When I'm finally standing outside his window, my stomach flips, but I softly rap on it with my knuckles anyway. It only takes a minute for two chocolate eyes to peer out at me through the blinds.

When the blinds shoot up, Adam stands in their place in nothing but green and blue plaid boxer shorts. His hair is disheveled, his eyes squinted from sleep, and his brows slightly furrowed as he takes me in. He lifts the window and holds out his hand, helping me climb inside. I kick off my shoes and crawl into his bed first, pulling the covers up and over my shoulders and facing the wall just like I did in Skyler's room. His sheets smell like him, a mixture of mint and his Burberry cologne, and I inhale deep as he slides in the sheets behind me.

Hesitantly, he snakes his arm under mine and pulls me into him, aligning his body with mine. Even though I can feel every muscle of his abdomen pressed against my back, it's still a friendly gesture, and I don't feel uncomfortable or like we're doing anything wrong. He holds me like a friend who knows he may be the only person who can keep my cracking pieces from splitting completely right now.

"You were right," I whisper.

He sighs and I feel the air softly blow the back of my neck. He holds me tighter around my middle and buries his head into my back, his lips just barely touching the skin left exposed from my tank top.

"I wish I wasn't."

For a moment he just holds me, neither of us saying anything else. I know I'm not falling asleep anytime soon and I feel like Adam isn't either, but we don't make any moves to get up and do anything else. When he does speak again, his voice is softer than before.

"Skyler and I made things official."

I swallow and he waits for me to respond, but I'm not sure how to. I know they're together. They've been together for a while now. Yet somehow, hearing that they're official hits me hard in the gut and I curl up into myself tighter. Adam doesn't release his grip on me though, which comforts and confuses me both.

I could comment on what he said, but what do I really say at this point? I'm happy for them, Adam knows that. He knows I would never say otherwise. At the same time, I feel like he's waiting for me to say the words I haven't even quite formed on my own yet.

In the end, I don't speak again. I just nod and smile, which Adam takes for what it's worth. His thumb lazily rubs against my lower stomach and I close my eyes tight, one lone tear escaping and falling to his pillow silently and without him noticing. Even though Skyler comforted me earlier, for some reason having Adam hold me makes me truly feel like everything will be okay. Even so, there's still something neither of them know that is the reason for most of my tears tonight.

I'm upset that Paris is no longer my best friend. I'm confused about my feelings for Adam. I'm hurt that Clay spoke words to me he didn't mean before laying me down in his room just a few feet down the hall from where I lie in Adam's right now. But, more than that, I regret that I didn't listen to Adam that night when he warned me. I hate myself for giving something so precious to someone who feels absolutely nothing for me. Clay wasn't just the first guy at Palm South I've had sex with.

He was the first.

Period.

Ashlei

"I'm going to miss you girls!" Erin pulls us each in for a hug, squeezing us a little too tightly.

"Oh yeah, I'm sure you'll be thinking of us every minute while you romp around Europe over break," Jess says sarcastically.

"Hush, you. I'm serious. Promise me you'll all call."

"We will," Skyler assures, throwing one arm around Cassie's shoulders. Cassie's eyes are dark, her face long. I don't talk to her much – hell, I guess I haven't really been around enough this semester to form much of a relationship with anyone – but even I can tell she's not okay right now. Hopefully winter break in Phoenix will help her get back on track.

Erin's town car pulls up just as she hoists her bag up onto her shoulder. She offers one last wave before climbing inside. Jess leaves next, blowing us all a kiss and then flipping us off as she climbs into her Beamer. Clinton pulls up not too long after in a cab and Cassie and Skyler climb in. They're hitting the airport for Cassie to catch her flight and Skyler to grab a rental car for the trip home. Bo and I wish her luck at the tournament and then it's just us.

"I'm going to miss you," I say honestly, tucking my pinkie into her front jean pocket. I consider asking her to go back in the house with me to properly say goodbye, but her parents will be here any minute.

"I know. It's only a few weeks, though."

She's so damn beautiful. Her dark hair is pin straight and shaping the thin features of her face as her inviting brown eyes appraise me. It's like she's trying to figure me out. Or maybe, how she feels when she's with me.

Lord knows it's not an easy feeling to digest.

Life has been a whirl since semi-formal. We took what we have – whatever that is – to the next level, for sure. Yet, at the same time, we still haven't really talked about what that means. Still, staring at her now, beautiful smile wide on her face, I don't really care what we are – as long as we're something.

"Uh, Lei?" she asks suddenly, her face falling. "Is that..."

I turn to where her eyes are focused and my heart stops before hammering in my chest. Kya is standing on the other side of our front yard, leaning against her black Jeep. She's dyed her hair a bright pink and streaked it with bleach blonde since the last time I've seen her. Even leaned up against her car, she's still as tall as Hayden and intimidating as hell. Her green eyes are fierce, yet turned down as she waits for me.

"Hang on," I murmur to Bo before crossing the yard. When I make it to Kya, she stands straighter, only making me feel worse.

"Sorry to interrupt your goodbyes," she says, casting a glance at Bo before landing her eyes back on mine.

"What do you want, Kya? There's no practice today."

She sighs. "You still owe me, Ashlei."

"What?" I blanch, then shake my head. "No, I paid you. I gave you the ten thousand." After semi-formal, I swallowed my pride and asked my parents for the cash to pay Kya and be done with the whole situation. I told them it was for a study abroad program this summer and they gave it without question. I felt awful lying to them and I'll have to figure out what the hell to do about my actual summer situation later, but for the time being, my problems were solved.

So what the hell is Kya talking about?

"Hayden stole a kilo from me, Ashlei," she says with a sigh. "My supplier threatened him with his life if he didn't pay. He lied about what happened and threw your name in the mix." I stiffen at her words, but she just continues. "He skipped town. It's on you now."

"What? But you told them it wasn't true, right?"

She nods. "I did, but it doesn't matter, Ashlei. You can't reason with these guys. You were a part of this and the ten thousand you paid barely covers any of what was stolen."

"Jesus," I murmur, pressing my clammy hand to my forehead. "A fucking kilo? What did he do with it?"

Kya shrugs. "I don't know. He probably snorted some of it himself and sold the rest or used it to party. You know Hayden."

But that's the thing. I thought I knew him, but clearly, I was wrong.

"Kya, we have to go talk to this guy you owe. I only did the shit three times and I've already paid for that plus some. We can talk him off of this."

She shifts. "I don't need to talk to him, Ashlei. He doesn't blame me, not since Hayden told him what happened."

"But Hayden lied!"

"I know," she says, holding up her hands to calm me. "I'm sorry, Ashlei. You have to pay them the rest. Just call your parents and ask for more."

"I can't do that, Kya. They're not a fucking ATM."

She looks at me like she doubts that, but then frowns. "There's only one other option for you to pay them and trust me, you don't want to take plan B. Just call your parents. Make up another lie."

"I'm not paying them. Fuck this. I didn't do shit."

"Ashlei, please," she begs. "You have to listen to me. They will come after you." Her voice grows quiet. "They'll find ways to make you pay." Her eyes shift to Bo and I swallow.

"How much more?"

"Thirty thousand."

I blanch. That's three times what I've already paid.

"There's no way my parents will just hand that over." I pinch the bridge of my nose and shake my head. "What's my other option?"

Kya cocks her head in warning but when she sees I'm serious, she sighs. "My supplier's name is Xavier Rojas. He owns a high-end club downtown. He said," she pauses, considering her words carefully. "He told me if you couldn't get the money, he would let you work to pay it off."

"Really?" I ask excitedly. "Well, that's no problem. I can work. What does he need? Bartenders and stuff?"

She swallows, and I take a moment to think about what else he could mean.

Then my stomach drops.

"He wants me to dance, doesn't he?"

She nods.

"Oh my God," I whisper, shaking my head. Pole dancing is an art to me – a sport, a release, a personal challenge. I would never dance for money. I would never *strip* for money. "I can't. I *won't* do that."

"What other choice do you have?" Kya asks, her eyes soft and sad. I hate her for telling me this, but I know she doesn't mean to hurt me. It's Hayden who fucked me over. It's him I should hate, and he's not even in the state – hell, he might not even be in the country. Kya is just covering her own ass, and if what she says about Xavier is true, can I really blame her for not shifting his focus back to her, even if she doesn't want to see me hurt?

Then again, maybe she couldn't give two shits what happens to me. We're not friends. We dance together, sure – but at the end of the day, the troupe isn't a family. It's not a sisterhood.

It's not Kappa Kappa Beta.

There's no way my parents will fork over that amount of cash, not unless I tell them what happened, which I definitely can't do. I could ask the girls, but that would involve telling them about my life outside of Palm South – another option I can't consider. I can't lose KKB. I can't lose my sisters.

Casting a sideways glance at Bo, I scan her face as she nonverbally asks me what's going on. How did I end up here? How did I land myself in this shithole? And what the hell do I do now? My palms sweat as I consider my options. I rack my brain for a way out, for a way to make this nightmare disappear, but I come up short.

"Well?" Kya interrupts my thoughts and I turn to face her again. My head is spinning, my mouth is dry, my heart is thundering against my rib cage and threatening to knock me down to the cold earth. When she speaks the next words, I almost can't hear them through the ringing in my ears.

"What are you going to do?"

Palm South
UNIVERSITY

ANCHOR

BOOK 2

EPISODE 1

"Well, so much FOR THAT PLAN."

Bear

"Happy twenty-first birthday, Bear!"

I smirk at the chorus of screams from Skyler and her sisters when I open the door of the Omega Chi house. Skyler leans up to kiss my cheek as the rest of the KKB girls filter around her, filling the already-packed living room.

"Thanks, ladies."

"I'm going to get you so wasted tonight," Skyler promises, throwing me a devilish grin. I have no doubt she'll deliver.

Skyler is my best friend on campus and, as of last semester, officially my Little Sister in Greek life. The way every guy in the room is eye-fucking her right now, I know they all think I'm crazy for not trying to score with her. But Skyler and I have always just had an unspoken connection — love, but in a family way.

Spring semester is already in full swing, even though classes just started this week. We already made it through spring rush, adding just shy of twenty new brothers to our fraternity, and now those pledges are finding out exactly what it means to be an Omega Chi Beta. It's Saturday night and our house is wall-to-wall with brothers and girls from every single sorority on campus. Our alumni brothers are supposedly leaving us alone since we held our act together last semester, but something tells me they won't exactly be pleased with us in the morning.

It's only eleven and we've already had two noise complaints.

Oops.

"Come on," Skyler says, grabbing my hand. "It's time for shots!"

I don't have time to argue because she's already tugging me through the crowd, brown locks swaying behind her. We brush past the two beer pong tables set up inside and jet around the living room where a make-shift dance floor has been set up. The entire house is dimly lit, a soft glow on the dark wood floors. As soon as we reach the island bar in the small house kitchen, she scores two shot glasses and fills them with tequila.

Fuck me.

"To finally being able to drink legally in a bar but still drinking here, anyway, because it's way more fun." Skyler holds up her shot glass to mine, her long, soft brown curls falling over her shoulder. Her bright blue eyes are radiating with an infectious energy, amping up my own excitement. Birthdays have never been a big deal to me, but I guess twenty-one is kind of worth celebrating.

"And to best friends who know exactly what alcohol to give you so you don't remember what happened the next day."

We clink our glasses together and throw the shots back, the tequila burning the entire way down. Our eyes water and we both reach for lime slices at the same time, laughing.

"Should I be getting your autograph? It's not every day I take shots with the hottest new poker player on the scene."

Skyler rolls her eyes, sucking her lime slice dry before snatching up two red Solo cups. Several brothers are watching her, drooling, my Little included — but Skyler doesn't even notice. "Hardly."

"You can't even deny that after the tournament over break, Sky."

She chews her cheek, filling our cups from the keg. She drinks half of hers as she hands me mine. "I know. It just feels weird. I don't want to think about it right now."

I chuckle. "Fine. Let's go numb our minds with drinking games."

"Now that's a plan I can get behind."

We make our way to the backyard where several tables are set up. It's January in Florida, so for once, I'm not sweating. In fact, a few of the girls are wearing light hoodies and everyone is in jeans. It's one of the maybe five cold days we'll have before spring shows up again, and all the windows to the house are open, taking advantage of the cool air.

"Any news from your family?" Skyler asks as we scan the tables. I stayed with her all break, so she's well aware of the fact that I haven't heard a peep from my mom or my older brother since I wrote them the check after semi-formal last semester.

"Just Clayton. He's starting back up at school and says he's been sleeping over at his friend Mac's house a lot lately. He sounds good."

"You okay?" She turns to face me when she asks, probably to make sure I don't lie to her. This time, I genuinely feel like I don't have to.

"I am. Not even thinking about them." And it's true. Maybe I'm finally sick of their shit enough to where I refuse to let it weigh on me, or maybe I'm being selfish for once. Either way, I'm just excited to be back at Palm South — especially since we're just a few short months away from Spring Break.

Skyler smiles. "Good. Oh! I think I see a table."

She points to a half-empty table and I nod, following her toward it. We start gathering a few of my brothers and her sisters to play chandelier with us when a girl I've never met before pops up in front of me.

"Hi!"

Her voice is loud and perky, and my eyes widen a fraction.

Taking a second look, I realize there's a very long, very sexy pair of legs attached to the too-spunky-for-me voice.

"Are you the birthday boy?"

Her question catches me off guard, almost as much as her unique appearance. Her hair is just past her shoulders, jet black at the roots and faded into a deep purple at the ends. It's curled, falling similar to the way Skyler's does naturally, and she's wearing a thick pair of black frames. She's dressed simply in a black v-neck t-shirt and bleach-washed jeans, though they hug her in all the right places. Her smile is bright, curious, and unapologetic.

I can't for the life of me figure out why, but I immediately want to nail her.

My eyes flick to her plump lips.

Okay maybe I do know why.

I hold one finger up. "Guilty."

Her smile widens. "Thank fuck." Without warning, she wraps her arms around my neck and pulls her mouth up to mine. Her lips are soft and wet, and even though I have no idea what the hell is happening, I grip her small waist tight in my hands and snake my tongue into her mouth. She moans, her hands fisting at the back of my neck. I bite her lower lip as she pulls back, releasing it with a pop.

"They dared me to give you your first birthday kiss of the night," she pants, her eyes still on my mouth. When she lifts them again, I realize they're a bright green. "It was really going to suck if you were unfortunate looking."

"Does that mean you think I'm hot?"

She smirks. "I mean, I wouldn't mind giving you your *last* birthday kiss of the night, too, if that answers your question."

I can't say I'm not shocked by her honesty. Most girls play hard to get, or not interested, or whatever other fucking games they think make them seem like they're not easy targets. This girl is standing tall, eyes on mine, confident and sure.

And it's so fucking sexy.

Grinning, I lean in closer, brushing her hair behind her ear so I have easier access. My dark hands are a stark contrast to her pale white skin. "And what if I want more than just a birthday kiss?" I whisper.

She inhales a stiff breath, just enough to let me know I'm affecting her the way I want to. Then, she licks her lip and pulls away from my grasp. "I guess you're going to have to hope my friends have your interests in mind the next time I pick dare." She winks, turns, and rejoins a small group of girls across the yard. They all giggle and keep their eyes on me, but I can't take mine off of her.

"What the shit was that?" Skyler asks, sliding up beside me with two freshly filled cups. She holds one out to me and lifts the others to her lips, her eyes following mine to the group of girls still watching us.

"No idea," I murmur, taking the cup.

"Come on, let's drink." Skyler starts setting up the game and more people gather around us, but I keep my eyes focused on the girl with the purple hair until she finally turns to sneak a peek at me again. I hold her gaze steady for just a moment before her friends drag her back inside the house.

I don't even know her name, but by the end of the night, I'm determined to know her bra size.

***

It's almost three in the morning.

Skyler took off about an hour ago to meet up with Adam, her boyfriend in Alpha Sigma, but not before completely following through on her promise. I'm drunk. And that's an understatement.

Lacy is hanging all over me, licking up my neck and whispering what she wants to do to me. Had this been last semester, I probably would have given her a second round in my bed. She's cute — caramel skin and carefully-styled natural hair. She wasn't a bad lay, per say, but she was just a distraction for me during a shitty time. My mom had just asked me for money and I needed a temporary escape. But tonight, I'm celebrating. I'm not looking for a distraction.

I'm looking for a really long, really hard, really incredible fuck.

And I know just who I want to get it from.

"Excuse me," I say softly, grabbing both of Lacy's wrists in my hands to peel them off me. She pouts as I let them drop into her lap and make my way across the living room where only a few Zetas are left lazily dancing. The girl from earlier is leaning against our pool table, talking to one of our new pledges. He's a cool guy, but judging by the look on her face, she's two seconds away from yawning or completely falling asleep.

As if on cue, she covers a yawn with her hand, still nodding along with his words to make it seem like it couldn't possibly be him who evoked that reaction.

"Hey, Caleb," I interrupt, clapping him on the back. "Having fun at your first O Chi party?"

He's clearly about as sober as I am, because a shit-eating grin spreads on his face. "Bro, this is the best night of my life."

I chuckle. Caleb is a freshman, and after that comment, I'm a little scared for his pledging process. He has no idea what he's in for.

"Glad to hear it. Unfortunately, I'm going to have to pull the birthday card and steal this beautiful girl away from you." My eyes cut to the girl with the purple hair and she fights back a smile.

Caleb's face falls. "Wait." I cock one brow, letting him know he really shouldn't argue, and his shoulders deflate a little. "Yeah... yeah, okay. Happy birthday, Bear." He offers a reluctant smile before taking a long drink from his cup, leaving me alone with the girl I can't wait to get back to my room.

"Kind of presumptuous, don't you think?" She asks, but her eyes are already undressing me.

"Depends."

"On?"

I shrug. "On whether you let me take you back to my room or not."

She stares at the hand I'm now holding out toward her, seemingly debating her options. She could easily walk away, find one of her girlfriends and leave the party without so much as another word. But the way she's chewing her lip tells me that's not exactly the plan she has in mind.

"I'm only going back with you on one condition."

I wait, hand still outstretched as she narrows her eyes.

"I want two orgasms tonight. And not the kind I fake, the kind I can't hold back with. The kind that make my legs sore in the morning."

My teeth find my bottom lip, fighting back a smile. *Who the hell is this girl and where has she been hiding?*

"I'll give you three."

The left side of her mouth lifts just slightly as she looks confidently up at me through her lashes. Then, she slides her small hand into mine.

Tugging her through the remaining crowd, I lift her as soon as we reach the hallway. Her back is pressed against the wall right next to our founding brothers' class photo, her legs wrapped around my waist. I suck the skin on her neck between my teeth and she hisses.

"What's your name?"

"Shawna," she answers, panting.

"I'm Bear."

"Nice to meet you."

"Likewise."

Gripping her ass in my hands, I shove us through my room and kick the door closed behind us. Shawna is already stripping her shirt off as I drop her feet to the floor at the end of my bed. I follow suit, tugging my jeans and boxers down in one fluid movement and kicking them to the side. Shawna is impatiently naked and pulling at my shirt. She lifts it over my head and I take it the rest of the way, tossing it to the side.

Then she's staring at me.

More specifically, at my cock.

"Holy shit," she breathes. She reaches out, trailing her fingertips down the middle of my abdomen, all the while still staring at my dick. When she reaches my waist line, she pulls her fingers to her mouth, her eyes flicking back to mine.

I smirk.

The only light in my room is streaming through the window from a street light, but it bathes Shawna in a soft blue light, hitting every curve. Dropping to my knees, I run my rough hand over the smooth skin of her neck, her breasts, her flat stomach.

Wait.

Are those nipple piercings?

Oh, fuck.

Definitely going to have to play with those later.

"Round one," I growl against the sensitive skin of her clit, one side of my mouth quirked in a cocky smile. She smiles back, but her face falls into a soft *O* when I close the distance.

She's moaning, bucking her hips forward with each flick of my tongue. I groan, too, because she tastes so fucking sweet. Sliding two fingers inside her, we both exhale together, her at the way my touch feels and me at how wet she is.

Snaking my free hand up her stomach, I palm her breast, massaging it in time with her rolling hips. Shawna cries out, fisting her hands in my barely-there hair and pulling me closer. When I suck her clit between my teeth, I pinch her piercing at the same time and roll it between my fingers.

She gasps.

Stiffens.

Holds her breath.

And then she comes.

I'm pretty sure she's waking up every single brother in my house right now but I don't give a single fuck. She's completely unfiltered, moaning my name like it's the last word she'll ever say. When she steadies out, her legs still shaking, I stand and put my mouth hard on hers. She tastes herself eagerly, panting as I slip my tongue between her lips.

Her hands wrap around my neck and she lies back on the bed, wriggling her way up to the pillows and tugging me with her. The purple ends of her dark hair are highlighted in the dim light of my room, sprawled out on my pillows, framing her bright eyes and swollen lips.

I spread her legs with my own, hitching one up at my waist as I position myself at her entrance. Her eyes are wide, and I have to steady my breathing and remind myself to go slow. Judging by her reaction earlier, I'm not exactly the size she's used to dealing with.

Kissing her lips, I bite the lower one before moving down her neck to her collarbone. Then, slowly, steadily, I flex my hips and bury my cock inside her.

And she is so. Fucking. Tight.

"Oh God," she cries, digging her nails into my back. With any other girl, I'd pull out my usual line — *Nope, just me, babe.* But with Shawna, I have no words. I literally can't say a fucking thing because I'm focusing too hard on not busting after being inside her for less than thirty seconds.

But I hold out, adjusting my rhythm to please her without granting myself the same gratification — not just yet. And then, I give her round two.

And three.

And just for the hell of it, four.

Cassie

"I'm just saying, you're not living if you've never tried a finger in the ass before," Jess says with a shrug, not the least bit ashamed, just as I reach the small table in the middle of our campus coffee shop.

I blink, dropping my bag into the only open chair. "Well, conversation at Joe's has certainly progressed."

Jess smirks, waggling her eyebrows at Ashlei who just shakes her head. I try to fight back my own smile, but give up when Jess starts fingering her donut.

"Gross, J-Love!" Erin tosses her napkin and it hits Jess square in the nose, but she just laughs and keeps violating her pastry.

Cup O' Joe's is a small coffee house, dimly lit and walls peppered with local student art. The open roof and piping paired with the wood and rustic furniture give it a modern, hip vibe. It's one of my favorite places on campus to study, and I talked the girls into meeting for coffee this morning before my second class. Spring semester has already kicked off and we had yet to all be together outside of sisterhood functions, so I wanted us to make time to catch up.

Jess demonstrating anal on a glazed donut wasn't exactly what I had in mind.

"I think I'm with Jess on this one," Skyler chimes in. "I mean, I'm not saying it needs to get crazy. Just a little boop, you know what I mean?" Skyler and Bo crack up laughing while Erin covers her face with her hands. Ashlei smiles, but it doesn't quite reach her soft brown eyes. She seems off.

"I'm grabbing coffee. Anyone need a refill?"

They all shake their heads, holding up full cups. Retrieving my wallet from my Vera Bradley messenger bag, I take my place in line, scanning the menu.

It feels kind of strange being back at Palm South, especially after how my first semester ended. I shift at the thought of Clay and Paris, but shake it off quickly. Winter Break was my time to regroup. I opened up to my older sister about what happened – everything from losing my best friend to losing my v-card to a complete douchebag. Surprisingly, she had some pretty great advice. The best piece being that, at least for freshman year, I should just avoid boys in general and focus on myself.

So that's exactly what I'm doing.

No boys, no drama — that's the way it works. And I am more than looking forward to being drama-free.

"Excuse me," a smooth voice says over my shoulder. I turn in place, swallowing when I see the exotic creature the voice belongs to. "Just going out on a limb here, but are you by chance a caramel latte girl?"

My mouth is so dry. *Why can't I swallow? Is it hot in here? Oh God, I hope I'm not sweating.*

I'm *totally* sweating.

Of course, this creature picks the semester I choose to be boy-free to waltz up behind me in line at the coffee shop. His long chestnut hair is pulled back into a messy bun, giving me full access to stare into his glorious blue eyes. They're peppered with flecks of gold, and I'm sure he's some sort of god. He's just standing there, crooked smile beneath his beard, tattoos lining the muscles of his right forearm like a warning sign to the mortals. The way the sun is streaming through the tinted windows of the coffee shop illuminate him in a way that lets me know I'd be cursed if I touched him.

Probably dead if he touched me.

He clears his throat, cocking one brow. "Is that a no, or did I forget to put pants on again?" He chuckles, but I squeeze my eyes tight.

Do NOT think about him without pants on, Cassie.

"Sorry. I, uh, no." I shake my head, nervously reaching for a strand of my fiery red hair to twirl. "I mean, yes, I like caramel lattes, but no, you can't buy me one."

"Good thing I didn't buy these." He holds up the two cups in his hands.

I'm confused.

"I work here," he says, gesturing to the small stage on the book store side of the shop. A lone guitar is propped up against a tall metal bar stool and I stare at it a moment, blink, and then find his eyes again.

Of *course* he plays guitar. Of course he does.

"They give me a free drink when I play, and they accidentally made two cups. So, I have this extra one, and I figured it'd be better served in the hands of a pretty girl than getting cold at my feet while I play." He smiles, this time showing a row of beautiful teeth that make me forget how to breathe.

"Well, I appreciate it, but I can't take your coffee."

He frowns. "Why not?"

"Because you're a boy."

"That is a fact," he says with a soft laugh. It's a soothing sound, the sort of laugh that makes me feel like I can trust him.

I blush just as the girl in front of me leaves the counter and it's my turn to order. "Exactly. So, thanks, but no thanks." I offer one last smile before turning to place my order. I still feel him behind me, his godliness just radiating off of him, but I don't dare turn around. He finally chuckles, and I feel him leave, which allows me to finally release the breath I didn't realize I was holding.

I quickly pay for my order and rejoin the girls at the table.

"So, Skyler became famous over break, Jess watched a lot of porn, Bo ate shit trying to figure out how to ski and I suffered through a stomach flu in Europe, which wasn't half as bad as suffering through my mother when I got back home," Erin summarizes, lazily dunking the tea bag in her large beige coffee cup. "Ashlei, Cassie, you're the only ones left. What'd you do over break?"

Ashlei's chewing her straw, avoiding all eye contact. She looks tired, and I notice dark circles under her eyes that weren't there before break. I'm not that close with Ashlei, but even I know there's something she's not telling us.

"I just worked."

"Worked?" Jess asks, pausing with her cup halfway lifted to her mouth. "What are you talking about? You don't have a job."

"Well I had one over break," Ashlei spits back. She's definitely sassy today.

"Doing what?" Jess challenges.

"Bartending."

"Bartending," Jess repeats flatly.

"Well, I swore off boys forever," I chime in, trying to take the heat off Ashlei. She gives me a *thank you* smile, but Jess is still eying her. "Or at least, for the rest of freshman year."

"I like that idea," Erin says with a smile. "Maybe I'll join you in that initiative, G-Little."

"Speaking of boys, how weird is it that I have a boyfriend?" Skyler asks, sucking the last of her iced coffee drink dry and shaking the ice in her cup.

"Super fucking weird," Jess replies quickly. Skyler laughs. My stomach turns.

"Sorry to interrupt, ladies." I hear the voice and I don't even have to turn around to know who's standing behind me again, especially when every jaw at the table drops. "I just had to come over because, well, because your friend here has completely shattered my confidence."

I turn slowly, my eyes trailing up his god-like body until I meet his own blue pools. He bends down on one knee, bringing us face to face.

"You see, I didn't actually get that coffee for free, I bought it when I saw you walk through that door over there." He points, but no one's eyes move from his face. Rubbing his hand over his beard, he shrugs. "I had no idea what kind of coffee you drank, but I figured it didn't matter – I just wanted to talk to you." Someone sighs. My money's on Erin. "But then you totally shot me down, and at first I was going to let it go, but my mom raised me to always go after what I want and never stop fighting for it. And what I want right now is your phone number."

This is not happening.

Pulling his phone from his pocket, he holds it out for me to take, his eyes still fixed on mine. "Well, your phone number and your name."

"Her name is Cassie," Skyler says quickly and he chuckles, that same smooth sound giving me chills.

"Cassie," he tries it on, testing how it feels on his lips. "What do you say? Make my mom proud and give me your number?"

"Oh my God, give me," Erin says, snatching his phone from his hands. She types out what I can only assume is my number and hands it back to him. "Thank me later, baby G."

I try not to laugh, but fail miserably. He smiles in triumph.

"Well, I guess you can live to be a momma's boy another day..." I trail off, waiting for him to tell me his name.

"Grayson," he says, holding the hand sans-phone out to me. My eyes trail the tattoos. "Grayson Anderson."

Yep, even his name is one of a god.

"Cassie McBee," I reply, tentatively taking his hand. He lifts it to his bearded mouth and kisses it softly.

I'm *really* trying not to swoon, I swear.

"See you around, Cassie McBee." He stands with a wink and a half-wave to the rest of the girls before making his way back to the stage. I stare long enough to watch him strap on his guitar before turning back around.

And everyone is staring at me with a shit-eating grin.

"I hate you all."

"I'm sorry," Jess offers through a laugh, throwing her hands up. "The no-boy rule doesn't apply to boys like *that*."

"Neither does the three-dates-before-he-scores rule," my Big adds.

"Little!" Erin chastises Skyler, but we all laugh regardless.

My eyes find Grayson across the room just as he begins strumming out a soft acoustic tune. He smiles, one strand of his hair falling from the bun he's haphazardly tied at the back of his head. Each strum of the guitar calls attention to the muscles in his arms and I allow myself to stare for just a moment longer before snapping my attention back to the girls.

They're all staring, too.

Well, so much for that plan.

Jess

I think I'm in heaven.

My feet are propped up on the dash of Jarrett's truck, Trey Songz is on the stereo, we've almost finished off a joint and I know in less than ten minutes, I'll have his glorious cock inside me.

Like I said, heaven.

Pinching what's left of the joint between my finger and thumb, I inhale long and hard, holding it in as I pass it back to Jarrett. His lids already low, he takes one last hit before extinguishing it in a half-empty bottle of Gatorade. I can't remember the last time I got high, but I know for a fact that it never felt this good. Maybe it's because Jarrett has better weed, or maybe it's just because Jarrett is involved – period.

With all the windows up, the smoke clouds around us, circling in new designs each time one of us breathes. Jarrett is watching me closely from the driver's seat, his eyes still hooded, his teeth just barely tugging on the flesh of his lower lip. Being away from him all break almost made me forget how fucking beautiful he is. Dark eyes, tattoos lining his arms, thick erection straining against his basketball shorts. I've never wanted him more.

"So now that you know about my boring ass Winter Break, what did you do?"

Jarrett smiles lazily. "Same old. Worked at the bar and surfed when the waves were big enough. I did spend some time with Spencer, too."

"Surfing buddy?"

"Kind of. She's trying to learn, but she's pretty new to Florida so it's like trying to teach a ten-year-old. She's getting better though."

I stiffen when I realize Spencer is a *she*, not a he. My mouth dry, I reach for my water bottle and try desperately to calm my racing heart. We're not exclusive, I told him I didn't want to title it, but he also said he didn't want to fuck anyone else. He didn't want *me* to fuck anyone else. And I haven't.

"Oh. Well, I'm sure she'll be just *fine* with you as her teacher." I try not to sound bitter, but I know I completely fail. I clear my throat, looking out my window at the soft waves crashing on the dark beach. When Jarrett's rough hand slides over my thigh and grips me gently at the knee, I chance a look in his direction.

One brow cocked, Jarrett looks amused – pleased, almost. *Asshole.*

"Are you jealous, Jess?"

I scoff. "No. Why would I be?"

He clicks his tongue, shaking that gorgeous head of his. "Shame. I was really hoping you were jealous."

"You're an ass!" I smack him across the chest but he grabs my wrist with his hand, pulling me over the console to straddle him. As soon as my knees settle on either side of him, he bucks his hips up, stealing my breath with the feel of him against me.

"She's the bar owner's daughter, and I'm not the least bit interested in her." Sliding both hands down my arms, he grips my ass firmly and rocks me against him, the friction making my eyes flutter. "You're the one I want, Jess. The *only* one I want."

My eyes are wide, my mouth just slightly open as I stare at him through the smoky darkness. I feel my heart tug, a sensation I'm far from used to. When Jarrett says shit like that, it makes me want to call him my boyfriend.

And I don't do boyfriends.

Not anymore.

"Good," I breathe. "Because I want you, too."

"Yeah?" Jarrett asks, tucking his hands into the back pockets of my jean shorts. He drags me up against the length of him, building the friction. "What do you want to do to me?"

Licking my lips, I lean in closer, biting his neck with more pressure than I intended. He hisses through his teeth as I softly kiss the same spot. "I want to ride you," I breathe against his skin, kissing his Adam's apple next. "I want to make you come with my name on your lips." Another bite on the other side of his neck. His hands move to my waist and he grips me hard. "And then," I whisper, dragging my tongue up his neck before pulling his earlobe between my teeth. "I want to take you to pizza."

Jarrett bursts out laughing as I sit back on his lap, waggling my eyebrows. The weed has settled in my blood, making me feel almost as high as Jarrett's touch makes me feel.

"God," he pants, still smiling. "That is the sexiest thing anyone has ever said to me."

"Did I mention there'd be... garlic knots?" I breathe the words in a sultry manner, biting my lower lip.

Jarrett groans. "Keep talking, baby."

I drag my hands down his chiseled abdomen before tucking one beneath the band of his shorts and palming his erection through the silky fabric with the other. "And," I continue, rolling my hips in time with my hand on him. "You can get whatever. Toppings. You. Want."

"Fuck," Jarrett growls. His hand flies to the side of his seat, reclining us back in an instant. He lifts me effortlessly, tossing me in the back and quickly following. Settling between my legs, he kisses me hard. "I think I just came."

"Better not have."

He smirks, but then his lips claim my own again and I no longer feel like joking. His hands are in my hair, pulling, tangling. His lips are on my neck, my collarbone, the swell of my breast. I arch my back and his hand finds the zipper of my shorts, tugging it down. His fingers snake beneath the harsh fabric of my jeans and he rubs me over the lace of my thong.

"Jesus Christ," he breathes, his forehead against mine. I can feel how wet my thong is and I know that's what he's noticing, too.

Pushing himself off the seat, he grips his shirt at the back of his neck and pulls it up and over his head. I follow suit, maneuvering out of my tank top and bra. Leaning up, I run my fingers down the middle ridge of his chest and abdomen before tucking my fingers in the band of his shorts. I push them down over his ass, his erection springing free. Taking him in my hand, I lift my eyes to his and lick my lips. His eyes are heavy, hooded with lust and a high I know I'm not experiencing alone. When I close my lips around his tip, he drops his head back, running his hands over the bald surface.

I grab his ass in my hands and pull him deeper into my mouth. He growls when he hits the back of my throat and I instantly grow wetter. Letting him take control, I reach up for his hands and move them to my hair, keeping my hands clasped over his. He's gentle at first, careful not to hurt me, but as his breathing shallows and his desperation grows, his hands fist in my hair. Opening my throat for him, he pulls me all the way down, my lips touching his base as I gag slightly.

"I fucking love that," he breathes, trying his best to slowly move in my mouth. When I gag again, he curses, pulling me back and grabbing my shorts at my hips. I lean back and arch up long enough for him to peel them off of me. A condom wrapper is ripped, he quickly rolls it over himself, and then he's between my legs, his tip at my entrance, his lips hard on mine.

Wrapping my legs around his waist, I use my heels to push into his backside, closing the distance between us. He fills me quickly and all at once. My breath catches and he groans as I drag my nails down his back.

Jarrett pumps slow and calculated, moving us in time with the slow R&B music crooning through the speakers of his truck. The closer we get, the faster we move. When he leans back on his heels, moving his thumb to circle my clit as he pounds into me, I moan in ecstasy. I'm close, so fucking close.

But then, Jarrett stops.

"Don't stop," I moan, wrapping my legs around him tighter.

"I need to hear you say it first."

I open my heavy lids, peeking at him through the smoky darkness of the truck. Or is that steam? Maybe both.

"I want you," I breathe, squirming beneath him.

"That's not what I meant."

I groan. "Then what?"

He smirks, his dark eyes ablaze. "You were jealous."

I'm panting so loud. "What?"

"You were jealous."

"No," I argue, but I'm quickly losing my resolve. "I wasn't. We're not exclusive."

"Oh?" he asks, pulling out until just his tip is still inside me before quickly slamming back into me. I cry out, an incredible sensation flowing through me. "Are you sure?"

"Oh God, Jarrett, just fuck me."

"I fully intend to. But first, I want to hear you say it." I lean up on my elbows, biting my lower lip as I gaze up at him. He simply cocks one brow, waiting. I still don't answer. He pulls out again, this time leaving me completely empty. I instantly crave him. "Say it."

"Fine," I mutter. "I was jealous."

"What was that?"

I purse my lips, trying to fight back a grin. "I was jealous, you ass hat. Now finish getting me off before I go find someone else for the job."

"We've already been through this, Jess," he says, shaking his head as he positions himself at my entrance. "No one can fuck you the way I do." As he slides back into me, filling me completely, his thumb mercilessly working my clit, I know he's right.

I come apart, crying out into the darkness of his truck just like I did the first night we met last semester. He follows shortly after, and then he collapses, his body deliciously heavy on mine. So much has changed since then, from me trying to fight him, to finally giving in, to now wondering if what we have is more serious than either of us are admitting. I shake my head, not wanting to think too much on it. We've having fun. That's what matters right now.

Our breaths still coming hard, Jarrett leans up, running one hand through my hair as his dark eyes devour my own. The way he looks at me completely immobilizes me. It's like he wants to lock me up in his room and never let me leave, like he wants to brand me, own me.

He smiles crookedly, biting his lower lip and planting one slow kiss on my mouth.

"Now about that pizza."

Bear

Reaching into my bag for my notebook, I let it drop on my desk with a slap and kick back in my chair. It's the second week of class, but since I decided to ditch the entire first week of class, being that it's syllabus week and all, I'm still trying to get in the swing of things. Omega Chi is a great fraternity to be in if you want to have fun. If you want to sleep, on the other hand, not so much.

The professor is already scribbling on the whiteboard as more students file in. She's odd — just as I would expect an art professor to be. She has wild curly hair and paint-stained overalls like she just came off the set of *She's All That*. I already know I'll struggle in this class, but it's a mandatory course for all Graphic Design majors, so here I am.

I'm debating sneaking in a quick five-minute nap session when Shawna walks through the door to the classroom.

Holy shit.

Sitting up straighter, I watch as her green eyes scan the room from beneath her black frames. Her hair is piled into a messy bun on top of her head and she looks like she just rolled out of bed in her yoga pants and tank top. Still, I feel an uncomfortable pressure in my jeans.

When she spots me, she blinks, almost as if she's unsure if I'm really there. Then, she smiles, and jogs up the stairs to my desk. I'm about to offer a *hello* when she throws herself into my lap, kissing me like we're alone. Her hands are on either side of my face, mine find her hips. If it were any other girl, I'd be weirded out or pissed or both, thinking she was under the impression we were dating just because we fucked. But, oddly enough, I'm completely fine with Shawna kissing me where everyone can see.

"Is this how you say *hi* where you're from?" I ask when she pulls back. She giggles and slides into the seat next to mine.

"I was just making sure you were still a good kisser. Sometimes when I'm drunk, I think guys are really great kissers and then they end up letting me down when I'm sober."

"Well?"

She scrunches her nose. "Yeah, you're still pretty good."

I can't help but smile at her. She's unlike any girl I've ever met before.

"You never called me."

"Well, you see, in order for me to call you, that would have required you actually leaving your phone number."

She blushes, but just slightly. "True. Tell you what — I'll give you my phone number, but you have to take me to dinner after class tonight first."

"Is that so?"

She grins wider and nods. "Mm hmm. I mean, I probably should have made that a requirement *before* I let you see my nipple piercings, but I'm not exactly a traditional type of girl."

"You don't say."

We're both smiling, eying each other, sizing the other one up.

I like this girl.

The professor calls the class' attention, so I lean over to whisper my response.

"Dinner it is. Where to?"

***

I've never watched a girl stuff a fat, chili and cheese covered hot dog into her mouth before, but it's oddly arousing. Maybe it's just because I'm stoked she ordered more than just a salad, but I'm just watching Shawna eat, grinning like an idiot.

"What?" she asks around a mouthful.

I shake my head, dunking a French fry into the ketchup on my plate. "Nothing. I'm just impressed."

"That I can eat a hot dog? What kind of weirdos do you usually take to dinner?"

"The wrong kind, apparently."

"So true."

Shawna winks, wiping her mouth with a napkin and taking a long pull from her soda before propping her elbows up on the table. "So, Clinton Pennington, AKA Bear, AKA birthday boy with a magical tongue — I never would have guessed you were an Art major."

I cock a brow at her tongue reference. "Graphic Design, actually. Are you an Art major?"

"For now." She smiles, her cheeks pushing her black frames up her face a bit. "Tell me more about you."

"There's not much to tell," I reply, feeling a bit uncomfortable. I don't really talk to anyone about myself other than Skyler, and that's just because she pries it out of me. Watching Shawna's lips press together, I have a feeling she and Skyler might have a bit more in common than I originally realized.

"Sure there is. What are your hobbies?"

"Sports, weight lifting, drinking, fucking."

"All the essentials."

"Exactly."

"What sports?"

"Football mostly, but I like basketball, too. What about you?" I ask, popping another fry in my mouth and leaning back. The small diner she picked only has five booths and they're a little too cramped for my liking, but I don't mind being closer to her.

"I love to draw and paint, and listen to live music."

"Favorite band?"

"Twenty One Pilots."

"Nice. I've heard a few of their songs."

"Careful," she warns me, sucking the fry salt off her fingertip. I'm momentarily distracted by her plump lips. "I'm a pusher. I'll talk your ear off until I convince you to listen to their album with me and then go to their concert."

"Hmm... dancing to good music with you all pressed up against me? Sounds terrible. Definitely don't do that."

She grins.

"Your turn. What's with the phoenix?"

Her face scrunches. "How do you know about the... oh." Shawna blushes a bit when she remembers exactly how I saw the phoenix tattoo on her lower back.

I just grin.

"It's my only tattoo, kind of a metaphor to live by, I guess. Rising from the ashes and all."

"How many times have you had to rise?"

She swallows, and I'm afraid I've maybe asked too much, but she still answers. "Enough times to know you never come back as the same person who went up in flames."

She keeps her eyes locked on mine a while longer before taking another drink of her soda. I'm studying her, noting the freckles on the apples of her cheeks, the chewed nails of the hand she's holding her cup with. Everything about her is so different than what I'm used to.

"So what's your family like?"

I stiffen, clearing my throat. "Shitty. Well, most of them. All of them, really, aside from my little brother."

Her mouth pulls to the side. "Shitty how?"

"Shitty like they're druggies, they use me for money, they told me I was worthless growing up and now they think I'm arrogant." I don't know why I just opened up about all that shit. I never tell people my family drama — Skyler is the only one who knows.

I wait for Shawna's mouth to drop open or her eyes to go wide, but she just offers a sad smile. "I'm no stranger to family drama, either."

"What do you mean?"

Shawna crosses her arms over her chest. "Definitely not first date conversation material."

"And mine was?" I ask, chuckling. She smiles, leaning forward over the table.

"I like that you opened up to me."

"I'm still trying to figure out why."

Her eyes fall to my lips. "Why don't we go back to my place?" She flicks her eyes back to mine. "Maybe you'll be able to hear yourself think better there."

"Good thinking," I reply, returning her smile. Calling the waitress over, I pay for our check and leave a cash tip on the table before grabbing Shawna's hand and leading her through the door. She's smiling wickedly at me, her green eyes curious yet challenging. And I know without a doubt that there will be absolutely no thinking going on once we make it to her place.

Cassie

It wouldn't be a new semester at Palm South without an Omega Chi party. At least, that's what everyone has been telling me all week. Since I bailed on Clinton's twenty-first birthday party last Saturday, Skyler is dragging me to their house tonight and I know trying to get out of it is pointless. But, I feel more prepared tonight, less in a funk than I was last week. Classes are picking up and so far, I've been drama-free.

Knowing who will be at this party, I just hope I can stay that way.

"So is it weird doing interviews for the blogs and stuff?" I ask Skyler as we walk toward the O Chi house. Kappa Kappa Beta and Omega Chi are on opposite ends of Greek Row, but it's a nice evening, cool without being too cold. The rest of the girls are already there waiting for us, but Skyler had a phone interview with one of the top poker blogs and couldn't reschedule, so I stayed back with her.

"A little." She shrugs. "Mostly I'm just annoyed by them."

"Really? Isn't it good exposure?"

"Sometimes. I mean, I like when they ask me about how I started playing or what my advice for new players is. But, most of the time, they'll ask me about shit that isn't relative — who I'm dating, what my diet is like, what lotions or hair products I use." She shakes her head, worrying her bottom lip between her teeth. "It just sucks. Because I'm a female player, they're less interested in my skills than they are in how I look."

"Wow. That is shitty."

She nods. "I mean, don't get me wrong. I know that looks can be used as a weapon. When I walk into a room of guys who don't know who I am, it's easy to fool them into thinking I'm a novice. I can flirt them into folding or hanging on when I have a good hand. But still, I just wish they'd stop publicizing it all over and start taking me seriously."

"They will one day, Big," I assure her, and I really know it to be true in my heart. Skyler is fierce, and even though I've never seen her play a game of poker, Clinton talks about how amazing she is all the time. "You'll see."

"I hope so, Little Nug." She winks at me just as we reach the Omega Chi house. We push through the front door without knocking and filter into the crammed house. It's insanely noisy, screams and music filling every room. I kind of miss the quietness of our walk.

Clinton scoops Skyler up in a crushing hug when we reach the kitchen, spinning her around as she pounds her baby fists on his chest. They're both laughing, and I can't help but notice how truly happy Clinton looks. I don't think I saw that big of a smile on his face at any point last semester.

"Skyler fucking Thorne! Keg stand. Right now."

Skyler laughs as he lets her drop back to the floor. "Done. Where's the keg?"

"Follow me," he says with a grin. Before we can exit, Skyler is scooped up in another hug.

"Damn, Bear. Not even going to let me kiss my girlfriend before you go stealing her away?"

Adam presses his lips to Skyler's as she giggles and I tuck my hair behind my ear, looking at Clinton instead. I am definitely not thinking about how good Adam's hair looks, or how his t-shirt is tight around his bicep muscles, or how his body wash smells the same as it did when I laid in his bed before Winter Break.

No, I'm not thinking about any of that.

"It's an O Chi party, Adam. Not Alpha Sig. My rules."

"Fair enough," Adam concedes, pecking Skyler one last time before smacking her butt as she scampers off. "Don't let me down."

"What? You're not going to hold my legs?" she asks, eyes wide and playful.

"Good point. I'll be right there." He turns to me as Clinton and Skyler make their way toward the keg near the kitchen. "Hey, Cassie."

I swallow a bit when he says my name, nothing but kindness shining in his chocolate eyes. He's looking at me like he's half-worried, half-expectant. Of what, I can't be sure. "Hey."

"Did you have a good break?"

"Yeah." I don't know why I'm making this so weird when it doesn't have to be. "I'm going to get a drink."

Without another word, I slip away and head in the same direction Skyler and Clinton had. Skyler's hands are already braced on the handles of the keg but I snake my cup in, quickly filling it before wishing her luck and heading off to find the other girls.

Jess and Erin are dancing in the living room, but I'm not quite on that level yet, so I wave at them before continuing to peruse the house. When I spot Ashlei and Bo in the hallway that leads back to the bedrooms, I make my way toward them.

"I told you I'm fine. Please stop worrying about me. I've got it under control, I promise." Ashlei's words catch in her throat when she sees me approaching, but Bo is still watching her carefully with a concerned look on her face.

"Hey girls," I say tentatively. "Am I interrupting?"

"No way, roomie," Bo replies with a smile. She cut her hair over Winter Break and I have to say it suits her. Her dark eyes and high bone structure are on prominent display. I didn't really get to spend much time with her last semester, but we're rooming together in the house this year, so I look forward to changing that.

"We were just talking about you, actually." Ashlei smiles and Bo waggles her eyebrows.

Oh no. This can't be good.

"Why do I feel like I should run in the other direction?"

They both laugh, and I notice Bo hooking her pinky in the jean pocket of Ashlei's shorts.

"The Kappa Kappa Beta date auction is coming up. We think you should be one of the girls we sell."

I blanch. "Um, absolutely not."

"Come on!" Bo pleads. "You're the only redhead we have and you're smoking hot. I know you could bring in some big bucks."

"Bo is Co-Community Chair this semester, so she really wants to try to outdo last year's results," Ashlei adds. "It'll be fun, Cassie. Promise."

I sigh. "Are you going to badger me until I give in?" They both nod, grinning, and I just shake my head. "Fine. But you two owe me."

Bo squeals. "Yay! Thank you, thank you, thank you!" She wraps her petite arms around me and I pat her back in return.

"Don't worry, we'll pay you back in the form of shots on your first Spring Break." Ashlei winks, lifting her cup before taking a sip.

"That doesn't sound like fair payment."

"That's because you haven't been on a Spring Break yet."

"Touché."

Bo hooks Ashlei by the crook of her elbow, dragging her toward the living room. "Speaking of Spring Break, we need to sweat off some pounds. Let's dance!"

Ashlei tries to grab my hand, but I pull back. "I'll be right there. Just going to get a refill," I say, wiggling my empty cup in the air. Bo blows me a kiss and then they disappear into the crowd and I lean back against the wall.

I'm not sure why I'm feeling so off. I haven't seen Clay or Paris since I got back from Winter Break, but the wounds they inflicted still feel so fresh. Thinking of the talk I had with my sister when I was home, I push myself off the wall and head for the kitchen.

Don't let anyone else have that much power over your emotions, Cassie. College is an amazing experience, but it's up to you to ignore the drama and focus on the good. Avoid silly boys, ignore spiteful girls, and don't be afraid to have fun.

I think it's time for a shot.

***

It only takes me an hour to get into the party spirit. I guess whiskey will do that to you.

I'm already sweating from dancing with the girls, so I squeeze my way through the crowd to the back porch to get some fresh air. When the cool January breeze hits my skin, I sigh with relief, leaning my forearms on the railing.

"Water?" He asks, and I know it's him before I even turn around. My heart picking up speed, I turn at the hips and take the water from Adam's hand, offering a small smile.

"Thank you."

"No problem. You girls are fun to watch."

"Creeper."

He smirks. "Can't help it."

"I'm surprised you're not out there dancing with Skyler." I don't know why the words sound so bitter when they leave my lips. I don't care that he's dating Skyler. I'm happy for them.

Truly, I am.

"Sometimes it's more fun to watch." His eyes light with an intensity at those words, his white teeth blazing against his tan skin as he smiles wider. I quickly take a drink of my water.

"Congratulations on your rush. I heard it was the best Alpha Sig has had in a long time. Stole a lot of guys Omega Chi wanted."

Adam beams. "Yeah, thank you. I'm pretty stoked about it. The pledges are all really excited to be here and to make a great name for our fraternity."

"Must be your infectious attitude," I tease. Adam smiles, but it fades after a moment and he just stares at me. I feel naked with his eyes on me that way.

"Why didn't you return my calls over the holiday?"

I drop my eyes to my hands, picking at the nail polish on the fingers gripping my cup. "I just needed a break from everyone."

"Even me?"

"Especially you," I murmur, my chest tightening.

"What?"

I sigh, lifting my eyes to his again, somewhat thankful he didn't hear me. "It's nothing personal. I was just homesick, so I tried to focus on my family while I had them close."

Adam's brows are still furrowed, but he relaxes a bit. "Understandable." For a moment he just watches me, and I really wish he'd stop. "I was just kind of worried about you, you know... after the way the semester ended." I really, *really* wish he'd stop looking at me the way he is. "Are you okay?"

"I'm fine." It's not a lie, not completely, anyway. I was far from fine over break, especially after Clay took my virginity and then embarrassed me in front of the entire school. But being home with my family really did help, and now that I'm swearing off boys, I know I'll be okay.

"You know I'm always here for you." His hand touches my arm just slightly with his words and I shudder.

"There you are!" Skyler bounds out the sliding glass door and throws her arms around Adam's neck. His eyes are still on me, but his hands wrap around her small waist. "Come dance with me."

Finally tearing his eyes from mine, he smiles down his nose at her, nodding. "Whatever you want, Poker Star."

Skyler's blue eyes dazzle in the low light of the night as she turns to me. "Coming, Little?"

"Yeah. Just give me a second."

Skyler drags Adam inside and I lean on the railing again, focusing on my breaths. My skin still feels hot, despite the water and the fresh air. Once I feel I have myself together, I pull out my phone to check the time.

And I have two missed texts.

Both from a number I don't have saved in my phone.

– Okay, so I waited a few days so I wouldn't seem so desperate, but I'm tired of playing the "I'm not interested" game. Can I take you out this week? –

– … Please say yes. –

I smile, biting my lower lip as I type out a response.

– Friday. Seven o'clock. Ralph's. –

If Grayson wants me to break my no boys, no drama rule, he's going to have to work for it. First test — saving me from the creeps at the auction.

Jess

Ugh. I'm fucking bored.

Buzzed.

But bored.

Refilling my cup at the keg, I watch as Ashlei and Bo dance in the living room. Ashlei's long blond hair is sticking to the back of her neck, but she somehow makes sweating look sexy. I swear she was born to dance. It still hasn't left her, even though she stopped dancing back in high school.

There are guys all around them, but they've turned every single one down enough tonight that they're staying away now. They only have eyes for each other. Ashlei's hand is on Bo's waist and they're giggling, hands lingering, eyes flirting.

It really doesn't bother me that they're together. Honestly. What really fucking pisses me off is that Ashlei is one of my best friends and Bo is my Little and yet neither of them have told me about their relationship. I tried talking myself out of it, thinking maybe it was just a drunken kiss, but ever since we got back from Winter Break they've been inseparable. I can just tell, the way they act around each other, the things they say, the things they *don't* say. In fact, I'm not sure how anyone else hasn't caught on yet.

I've been spending more time with Bo lately, making sure it's one-on-one attention and not just sister events. She made it clear last semester that she wasn't going to take a Little until she got the experience of being one herself, so I'm trying to be better. Still, every time we're hanging out and she skirts around questions about her dating life, I get a little more irked.

I swear I'm going to explode on the both of them if they don't fess up soon.

Sighing, I take a sip of my beer and whip out my phone, shooting a text to Jarrett.

– This party sucks. I'd rather be with you. –

– Ditto. This professor assistants game night is as about as exciting as tweezing out my eyelashes. Shocking, right? –

– Don't worry. I'll make sure you have a good time tomorrow night. ;) –

Smiling, I tuck my phone back in my pocket just as Skyler slides up next to me.

"Have you seen my Little? Or my Big?"

I shake my head. "Last time I saw Cassie she was dancing with you, and Erin said she had to pee but that was like thirty minutes ago."

"Weird. Oh well. Did Erin tell you what the Social Chairs have been thinking for Spring Break?"

"I thought they weren't telling us until chapter next week?"

Skyler's blue eyes gleam as she rakes her damp hair off her neck. "They aren't, but Erin has all the inside knowledge now that she's on the executive board. And she heard the girls talking to the O Chi boys about Key West!"

I squeal. "Fuck yes! Oh my God, I haven't been since my parents took me when I was in high school. I was too young to drink then. Oh my God, this is going to be amazing."

"The possibilities on Duval Street alone make me giddy."

Frowning, I eye the beer in my cup. "I should probably start drinking vodka waters like now."

Skyler laughs. "Spring Break diet here we come!"

My phone buzzes and when I check the message, my mouth goes dry.

– I'm not satisfied with just tomorrow. Go find an empty room. –

I smile, but can't deny the little flip in my stomach. I love when he goes into sexy Jarrett mode. It's like there's a switch — sometimes he's just hot, funny Jarrett in presentable PA clothing. But when the switch is flipped, he's unbearably sexy, demanding, fire-eyed Jarrett in nothing but a tight pair of boxer briefs.

I personally prefer the switch flipped.

– Are you asking me to sext you, Jarrett Locke? –

– Was there a question mark in that last text? Find a room. Now. –

I bite my lip, a little turned on at the thought. Dirty pics and words in the middle of a crowded party? I can dig it.

"Be right back," I tell Skyler, pushing myself off the wall we were leaned against and heading straight for the bathroom. There are several in the house, but the best one is in the upstairs loft. By *best,* I mean *cleanest*. Using the bathroom in a frat house is like hanging out the door of a speeding car. You're taking a risk. My Big used to always say, *"Shots and squats, my dear. Do not touch that seat."*

Making my way up the stairs, I type out a text to Jarrett asking him what he wants me to do to myself. The three little dots pop up letting me know he's texting me back and my stomach tightens in anticipation. When I push through the bathroom door and find Erin with her head in the toilet, my excitement fades.

"Shit, Ex, what the hell?"

She heaves, but it doesn't sound like much comes up. Cursing, I fall to the floor next to her and scoop her dark blonde hair up, fastening it at the top of her head with the spare hair tie on my wrist.

"You're such a freshman right now."

Erin groans, leaning back on her heels and lifting her eyes to mine. They're red, rimmed with tears, and her entire face is a sheet white. "I'm so fucked, Jess. I'm so, so fucked."

"What are you talking about?" I shake my head, ripping a few sheets of toilet paper off and offering them to her to clean her face. "You're fine. Just drunk. Let's get you out of here."

"Jess, you don't understand."

I groan when I see the dirty text from Jarrett, telling me, in *amazing* detail, what he wants me to do to myself. Then my phone pings again, and it's a photo of Jarrett palming himself. His abs take up most of the picture, but just the sight of his hand wrapped around his thick cock makes me whimper. It's clear he also snuck off to a bathroom, and all I want is to be bad with him.

But, sisters first.

Fuck me.

"I understand just fine. Do you not remember me on Spring Break last year?"

Erin huffs, grabbing my wrist with force. "Goddamnit, Jess, listen to me! I'm not drunk!"

"Clearly."

She levels her eyes. "I'm serious. I haven't had a single drink tonight... or this semester, period." She stares at me expectantly, like I'm supposed to understand. When the little lightbulb finally flashes on, I gasp.

"Holy shit. Do you think you're..."

"I don't know."

"Oh my God, Ex, how?!"

She sighs. "I've been throwing up and my body just feels weird. I'm freaking out, Jess. What do I do?"

"Have you missed a period yet?"

"I was supposed to have it this week, but nothing."

I curse, my hand flying to my forehead. No way. No fucking way is Erin Xander, the most angelic of all of us, pregnant. The girl doesn't party as much as we do, she hasn't had a boyfriend in I don't even know how long, and she's not exactly the hook-up kind of girl.

Actually, that's a great fucking point.

"Erin, who... um," I fade off, not sure how to phrase my question. "If there were, for argument's sake, a little bundle of joy in your belly — who would be responsible?"

She bites her lip just as the door swings open. Clinton startles when he sees us just as Erin yells something about them needing a new lock on the damn door.

"Whoa. You two okay?" Clinton asks. I ignore him, turning my eyes back to Erin.

But her eyes are still fixed on his.

And she's breathing really fucking hard.

When she looks at me once more, panic evident in her features, I know I don't need to repeat my question.

Well, shit.

Spring semester is off to an interesting start.

EPISODE 2

"Everything is CHANGING."

Adam

"Oh my God, give me that!"

Skyler flies through my bedroom door, kicking it closed behind her before snatching the large burrito I was just about to bite out of my hands. Her soft hair falls into her face a bit as she shoves nearly half of it in her mouth, her eyes rolling up. Moaning, she chews it slowly, like she's savoring every morsel.

I blink.

"Thank you," she says, handing me back what's left of the burrito and wiping the corners of her mouth.

"You sure you don't want to eat the tin foil, too?"

She swats at my arm before climbing into bed next to me. "Don't be an ass. This Spring Break diet is going to be the death of me, I swear."

I laugh. "Ah, it all makes sense now. Want the rest?" I offer her the burrito again but she pushes it back, shaking her head.

"I'm already going to have to do like fifty crunches and run a mile to get rid of that one bite. But seriously, who made kale a thing?" She grimaces. "I just want to eat cheese fries and lose ten pounds."

"You're beautiful," I whisper, kissing her nose. She scrunches it, so I kiss it again.

"Thank you," she murmurs, blushing a little. "Still, I'm going to be on the beach surrounded by a hundred tiny little things in thong bikinis. I need to be on my game."

Frowning, I take a bite of my burrito and chase it down with the soda on my night stand. "Don't remind me."

"Why are you all grumpy?"

I sigh. "I won't be with you that week. I'm kind of bummed about it."

"What are you talking about? Of course we'll be together."

"Did you forget what fraternity I'm in?"

Skyler's still frowning, but as recognition sets in, her brows pull inward and she chews her lip. The Kappa Kappa Betas always go on Spring Break with the Omega Chis, and being that I'm an Alpha Sigma, that pairing doesn't exactly do us any favors.

"Well, whatever. You can still come."

I chuckle around another bite. "Yeah, because that would go over well."

"I'm serious." Skyler sits up on her knees, making me look at her. She's dressed in nothing but a small Kappa Kappa Beta tank top and tiny little shorts. No make-up, hair natural and wavy. Stunning as usual. "I'm not giving you the option. You're my boyfriend and you're coming on Spring Break with me. Where's your laptop?"

"Why?"

She rolls her eyes at my question before hopping off the bed and retrieving my computer from the desk. Falling back into the covers, she flips it open without another word, clicking away at the keys.

"Done."

"What's done?"

"I just booked you for the all-day boat trip we're doing on the second day of Spring Break. And..." her voice trails off as she finishes typing off a text. Not a second goes by before her phone pings in her hand. "Perfect! You're set to go in the van we rented to take down there and you'll stay in our hotel room. All set!"

I shake my head, finishing off my burrito and chugging down half my drink. "Are you serious right now? You know the Omega Chis are going to flip their shit."

"They won't. Because if they do, I'll bitch at Bear, and he'll bitch at everyone else until they shut up. Trust me. It's all good." Smiling devilishly, she crawls up the covers and locks her lips on mine, grinding her hips against my own. My boxers, the comforter, and her tiny ass shorts are the only things separating us. I groan, tugging on her bottom lip.

"You're going to be the death of me, Skyler Thorne."

"At least it'll be a fun way to go," she whispers, nipping at the skin on my neck. Fastening my hands on her small waist, I flip her over, pinning her in the sheets.

"Can't argue that."

As I kiss my way down her neck, Skyler runs her fingers through my hair and gives it a small tug. "How are the pledges doing? You guys had a killer rush."

I move my lips to hers, snaking my tongue inside her mouth and stealing a moan before replying. "Good. We're getting ready for the camping trip before the bonfire next week."

"I always forget you do that," Skyler pants, bucking her hips up to meet mine. "Creepers. Kidnapping those poor kids."

Grinning against her skin, I slip my hands under her tank top and push it up and over her rib cage. "Trust me. It's the most fun they have in the pledge process."

"And what's the worst part?"

I pull her tank off the rest of the way, sucking the sensitive skin on the swell of her breast. "If I tell you, I'd have to kill you."

"Death by orgasm?"

"*Torturous* death by orgasm."

She smiles, biting her bottom lip as she peers down at me with heavy blue eyes. "Tell. Me. *Everything*."

***

Even though Skyler officially calls me her boyfriend, she never sticks around after we have sex. Sometimes she'll lie on my chest for a while or we'll talk, but sooner or later, she's out the door and it's just me alone in my bed.

And when I'm alone, I think.

About rush. About all the activities coming up. About the whispers I've been hearing around our fraternity concerning the presidency next semester.

I know I'm at the top of everyone's mind, and as fucking stoked as I am about that, I can't help but wonder if being with Skyler is going to pull me from what I need to do to make it actually happen.

I love being around her, we have fun together, but I can still tell it's not serious for either one of us. Couple that with the fact that planning events and taking on a presidency requires most if not all of my future time, it just feels like we're speeding fast toward an inevitable crash.

Sighing, I reach for my phone and type out a text to Cassie.

– Breakfast tomorrow – the usual spot? –

Letting my thoughts drift to that little redhead does absolutely nothing to soothe my stress. After what happened with Clay last semester, I knew she would need someone to lean on over break. Apparently, that someone wasn't me. It shouldn't bother me, but it does.

She came to my window that night.

I can still remember the way it felt to hold her, the way my chest ached when she told me I was right about Clay. It fucking killed me, because I didn't want to be right — not about knowing he would hurt her.

What she doesn't know — what no one knows — is that I laid that fucker out the next day. I stormed right into his bedroom while he was getting dressed, Paris having just left, and decked him hard across the jaw. I made sure he knew it was coming. Hell, I even told him to hit me back. But he didn't. He knew he was a piece of shit, even if he didn't admit it to anyone else.

But then, I didn't hear from Cassie all break, and when I finally saw her at the Omega Chi party last week, she made me feel like *I* was responsible for the hurt she endured — not him.

I can't figure this girl out.

After twenty minutes go by with no response, I sigh, plugging my phone into the charger and setting an alarm for class in the morning. Leaning back on my pillows, I tuck my hands under my head and stare up at the ceiling, brain still not getting the memo that it's time to turn off.

I'm excited Skyler wants me with her for Spring Break, but I can't shake the feeling that whatever is happening between us is going to be short lived. She's smart, funny, and gorgeous — but that's exactly it. She deserves to be with a guy who can give her all the time in his life, or at least to be able to have the freedom to do whatever she wants. I can't call her my girlfriend and then put other things before her — like the Alpha Sigma presidency.

Rolling over, I pull a pillow over my head and let out a large puff of air. There are too many "what ifs" and I don't have enough energy to figure them all out tonight. *One step at a time, Brooks.* Tomorrow starts the planning for the pledge retreat. I need to just focus on what I can control.

Except, I don't really feel in control of anything at all.

Erin

I am freaking out.

Erin Xander does not do well with freaking out.

I am in control of all things at all times. My planner is color coordinated and scheduled through the end of the year, with very few dates to spare. I'm already three weeks ahead in my classes, and even still I'm meeting up with Cassie in less than an hour to study. Because I need to be in control, and I'm running out of things I can hold onto.

It's only Sunday, the auction isn't until Saturday, and yet I've already handled every aspect of it — the food, the drinks, the paddles, the emergency kits, the girls we'll auction and the transferring of the donations. All done. Handled. As if that wasn't enough, I've also planned half of Spring Break and hand-crafted mason jars for the sorority council meeting at the Kappa Kappa Beta house this Wednesday.

And yet, I'm still freaking out.

Because no matter what I do, I can't control what will happen after I pee on this stupid stick in my hand. The stick that will tell me if I'm carrying Clinton's child.

Oh God.

Burying my face in my hands, I drop the stick onto my lap and focus on my breathing. I need Jess, since she's the only one who knows about my... situation, but she's not answering her phone and I've barely seen her since she walked in on me vomming my brains out at the O Chi party. I can't tell any of the other girls — especially not Skyler — and yet I can't wait any longer to take the test.

Chewing my lip and knowing there's slim to no chance in hell he'll answer, I thumb through the contacts in my phone and hover over his name. Just seeing it on the screen makes my heart jump and my breath accelerate — even after all these years. Before I can talk myself out of it, I let my thumb drop, dialing his number.

Ring.

Ring ring.

Ring motherfucking ring.

Hey, you've reached Kip Jackson. Sorry I—

"Gah!" Hearing his voice springs more memories on me than I'm equipped to handle at the moment. Why did I think it was a smart idea to call the blue-eyed boy who stole my heart so many years ago? Tucking my phone into my small purse, I lift myself from my bed and stare at the pregnancy test. Sighing, I slip it in next to my phone and give myself a once over in the mirror. My eyes are tired, my skin ashen, my hair greasy. I do not look put together. I do not look in control.

At this point, I have no choice.

I need to tell Clinton.

I don't want to stress him out with thinking about the possibility of a baby if there isn't one, but at the same time, I need him right now. If there's one thing Clinton Pennington is good at, it's being a friend. We both agreed that our little hook up was just us having too much fun that night at semi-formal, and something inside me just knows he'll be calm and collected through this. He'll be able to soothe me, tell me it's okay, and make me feel like whatever the test says — we can handle it. Together.

I walk slowly down Greek row to the Omega Chi house, focusing on my breaths with every step. I'm wearing my favorite Kate Spade high heels, trying to grasp the part of me I feel quickly fading away, and I listen to them click and clack on the pavement as I near the house.

The boys welcome me in, offering me a beer even though it's only eleven in the morning on a Sunday. I shake my head. "You boys need Jesus."

"Hey, Jesus liked red wine," one of the pledges retorts.

He's got a point.

My throat swells as I make my way down the hall to Clinton's room. I try to swallow, but there's nothing there to aid in the process. My mouth is dry, my heart hammering. How the hell do I have this conversation right now?

Loud music is spilling from his room, which brings me some relief because at least he's awake. I can't imagine having to stir him from a slumber to deliver this news. Steeling myself at the door, I tap on it lightly with my knuckles.

"Bear? It's Erin. Uh, can I come in?"

No answer.

The song blaring from inside his room is slow, rhythmic — a sultry R&B song with lyrics crooning how they could fuck the subject of their affection all the time. Growing anxious, I push through the door without another knock.

"Bear, this will only take a min—"

Clinton doesn't hear me, thank God, because he's currently buried beneath a pile of sheets and blankets. A girl is leaned against his headboard, her eyes downcast at the movement between her legs. One of her hands is locked on his headboard, the other is tangled in the purple ends of her hair, and if I had to guess, the moans drowning under the loud bass of the music are courtesy of whatever Clinton is doing beneath those sheets.

My cheeks burn as flashes of our night together hit me with rapid speed. Slamming the door closed as quickly as I can, I adjust my purse on my shoulder and storm toward the exit, desperate for fresh air. The girl didn't see me, even though I was standing right in the doorway. She was preoccupied. As was Clinton.

And I was just about to tell him I need him to be with me while I take a pregnancy test.

Smacking my forehead, I start the walk back to the KKB house, mumbling under my breath the entire time. How idiotic can I be? This is Clinton we're talking about. What happened between us was a mistake, an accident, a one-night thing. Did I really think he would hold my hand while I peed on a stick?

Throwing a quick wave in the direction of my sisters gathered on the couch, I quickly sprint up the stairs and back into my room, closing the door swiftly behind me. For once, I'm actually thankful that Ashlei isn't here.

I pull the test out of my purse and make my way to our bathroom, tossing it on the counter and planting my palms to steady myself. Telling Clinton would have been a dumb move, and now that I see it more clearly, I'm thankful he was preoccupied. This is just something I need to handle on my own, even if it feels impossible. After a few deep breaths, I lift my eyes to the mirror, trying to find the courage I need.

You can do this, Erin.

Everything will be okay.

I only half-believe myself, but it's all I need to make my next move. Grabbing the test, I rip open the package, pop off the clear plastic lid, and squat down on the toilet.

And then I pee on my hand.

A smart girl would have peed in a cup and dipped the stick in, but being that all of my intelligence is wasted in the classroom, my common sense is at exactly level zero.

Luckily, I do still manage to pee on the test strip, so I set it flat on the counter and walk away.

I try playing on my phone.

I try organizing my closet.

I try laying out my outfits for the next week.

Every time I look at my phone, no time has passed.

I open my planner.

I shut it again.

I make sure I have everything I need for my study session with Cassie.

Nothing distracts me, nothing stops my mind from racing with what the results of this test could mean, but enough time finally passes that I can check it.

Everything feels numb — my nose, my ears, my feet. The house is filled with girls, yet everything seems silent as I put one foot in front of the other, making my way toward the bathroom counter. My hand shaking, I take one last deep breath, and then I lift the stick and squeeze my eyes shut.

I open one, then the other, and the tiny screen comes into focus.

"Ready, G-Big?" Cassie pushes through my bedroom door without warning, causing me to curse and fumble the pregnancy test before quickly shoving it in my makeup bag.

"Hey baby G! Yes, all set. Just let me grab my bag."

"Can we hit Cup O' Joe's on the way? I need a pick-me-up," she says, thumbing through her phone as her bright red hair falls around her.

"Definitely." I toss my makeup bag, test still inside, into the messenger bag with my books and notes before slinging it over my shoulder. "Let's go."

Ashlei

My stomach rolls as I step out of my car and pop open my bright pink umbrella. It's one of those dreary days in Florida — the very few we have — where it's below sixty degrees and rainy. It rarely happens, but when it does, it seems to take a toll on all of us. We're usually bathed in sunlight and donning flip flops, so rain boots and big coats don't sit well with us.

The rain seems absolutely fitting for how I feel, though, so I revel in it. It takes so much effort to smile or even just exist around my sisters right now, knowing how different my reality is from theirs. When I'm alone, I finally get to think, to feel. So, on the way here, I let myself cry — just a little — enough to let a little of the pressure out.

Xavier Rojas' club makes me feel sick every time I step foot in it, and today is no exception. My feet splash in the puddles as I make my way toward the back entrance. There are a few hours until the club opens, so it should just be me and Xavier and a few of his guards, but that doesn't make me feel any more at ease. Hands shaking, I pull my coat tighter around my small frame.

The first time I met Xavier, I had tears streaming down my face, snot running from my nose, and a thousand dollars clutched in my hands.

I had danced for money.

And it had broken me.

I can still remember the men staring at me, their hands touching me when the bouncers weren't looking, their degrading remarks, their dirty money — it's all seared into my memory. It was almost a numbing experience, being on the stage. I don't quite remember taking off my clothes, but I can still feel the cold bar grinding against my bare skin. Rock bottom is an understatement when it comes to describing that night. When I handed Xavier that first payment, I knew I couldn't stomach it again.

So, I found another way.

I sold clothes, shoes, and electronics to give him the second payment. For some reason, Xavier seemed to take pity on me. He agreed to let me pay it over time, but it always feels like his patience is thin, his timeline relative. As I give my name to the outside guard and he quietly ushers me inside the bleak building, I fist the money in my purse, hoping it'll be enough to buy me more time.

Over break, I saved every penny of Christmas money and thought of small ways to get cash out of my parents. I'm disappointed with myself, but remembering how it felt that night in the club slowly made lying easier until it almost became second nature. I'll do whatever I have to do to never be in that position again, and once this money is paid, I'm wiping my slate clean for good. Hayden and Kya have ruined pole dancing for me. I never went back to Kitty Heels and I never plan to touch another pole or another line of coke for as long as I live.

"Ashlei, baby," Xavier greets, standing long enough to wrap me in a hug and kiss both of my cheeks. He's a short man, all muscles, clean-shaved face and short curly hair. His hugs always engulf me in a scent of cigarettes, ink, and sweat. "Nice to see you again. Come, sit."

He motions to one of the chairs facing his desk before taking a seat himself, leaning back and crossing his hands over his stomach. I sit lightly, back straight, ass on the edge of the seat. I don't plan to be here long. It's always pleasantries with Xavier, but I've heard of his darker side. I know Kya has seen it up close.

I never plan to.

"What do you have for me today, sweetheart?"

I shiver at his term of endearment, reaching into my purse for the cash I brought. It's folded neatly and wrapped in a rubber band. I slide it toward him, folding my clammy hands in my lap as he counts it out.

He sighs, just barely, almost low enough for me to question whether I heard it or not. Lifting his dark eyes to mine, he offers an apologetic smile.

"Ashlei, this isn't enough."

"It's two-thousand dollars," I croak, my throat dry. *It has to be enough.*

"You owed me thirty-thousand. You've only paid five, and this makes seven. You know it isn't enough."

"Please," I beg, my voice low. My eyes water, and I hate myself for being so weak. "I'm doing all that I can."

"No!" He screams the word, pounding his fist on the desk and I jump. My heartrate spikes as I wait for his next move. His dark irises are smaller now, his face red, but he pauses, steadying his breathing and unclenching his fist. "No, you're not." He levels his eyes and I know he's referring to dancing. Swallowing, I shake my head.

"I can't."

"You might not have a choice."

"There has to be another way."

Xavier watches me carefully. "I can't keep bending the rules for you, kid. If you were anyone else, I would have already killed that pretty girlfriend of yours while you watched."

I gulp. I've tried so hard to keep Bo out of this, not even telling her why Kya showed up at our sorority house at the end of last semester. She's too pure to be sucked into my black hole.

"I don't like giving you more time, Ashlei, because it sets a precedent. Other people who owe me are looking at you wondering what it is that makes you so special." His pudgy fingers pinch the bridge of his nose. "However, I don't really give two shits what any of those fuckers think about my business, and as it stands, I think we can make a deal."

My chest is still tight.

He leans back again, tapping the tips of his pointer fingers together as he thinks. "It's safe to assume you'll be going on Spring Break with your sisters, am I right?"

"If I can afford it," I whisper, still focusing on keeping the tears from falling down my cheeks. My stomach is in knots, my eyes tired. It still doesn't feel like reality. This can't be my life.

"Tell you what. You bring me at least another five-thousand by this time next week, I'll make that your last payment."

Wait, did I hear that right?

"Oh my God." The tears finally fall, but I'm smiling. Relief — that's what I feel. "Are you serious? One more payment?" I have no idea how I'm going to come up with another five grand, but it sounds a hell of a lot better than twenty-three thousand.

Just five-thousand.

Five-thousand dollars, and then I'm free.

My heart squeezes.

"Now hang on a second," he interrupts, holding one hand up. "That will be your last payment, but your debt is still far from paid."

Sniffling, I adjust my purse on my lap. "I don't understand."

A slow grin spreads on his face, and the relief I felt moments ago instantly fades.

"You're going to sell for me, pretty girl."

"Sell?"

He nods. "During Spring Break. Weed, coke, Molly. You're going to be a one-stop-shop, my dear. I'll give you enough stash to settle the rest of your debt and then we'll be even."

"No. Absolutely not." I stand, hands shaking, bile rising. "I'm not getting anyone else caught up in the shit that ruined my life."

"Don't be so dramatic," he snarls, rolling his eyes. "Besides, what other choice do you have? You either take me up on this offer, pay me in full by Friday, or dance four nights a week at my club for the next six months." His face is stone cold, his jaw set. "I don't make exceptions like this, Ashlei.

You should be fucking grateful. If you're not, we can take the route I usually take. Ask your friend Hayden how that worked out for him."

The mention of Hayden's name makes my jaw drop open. "What do you mean? Did he come back?"

Xavier's grin is menacing, his yellow teeth on full display. "He didn't have to, sweetheart. I have my ways of finding even those who try their damndest to stay lost."

I swallow. "What did you do to him?"

"Refuse my deal, and you'll find out."

Blinking, I let two more silent tears stain my cheeks.

And the helplessness sets in.

***

Jess is devouring her pizza like she hasn't eaten in seventeen years as I pour the dressing on my salad in Pie Heaven. Moaning, she licks extra sauce off her thumb and mumbles around the cheese in her mouth.

"Do not tell the other girls I'm eating this. Erin would kill me."

"Why? It's your love handles you're risking, not ours."

"Yeah but you know Erin. Sorority image and all that shit. She's serious about her Spring Break diets."

I laugh, shaking my head. "My lips are sealed." She throws me a *thumbs up* before folding her next slice in half and taking a huge bite. I blanch. "Even if yours aren't."

"Eat me."

I chuckle.

Pie Heaven is a small pizza joint across from campus, usually packed between the hours of midnight and 3 a.m. with drunk students. I've been holed up in my room most of the day, running over the conversation I had with Xavier on Monday, debating my options. It seems surreal, to sit here eating fast food with Jess, knowing that if I don't make a decision soon, I could get hurt. Even worse – Jess could get hurt. *Bo* could get hurt.

I feel like a weapon of destruction, harming anyone who touches me.

"So," she starts, chasing her last bite with a large drink of the extra-large Mountain Dew she ordered. "You never did tell me how your twenty-first birthday was."

Sighing, I take my first bite and grimace a little. Jess' pizza smells way better than this stupid salad tastes. "You know my birthday tends to get overlooked. Sadly this one was no different."

"Ugh, so shitty. You would think being born on the same day as Jesus would lend you some good birthday juju."

"Nope. All it lends you is a lot of combo gifts and no friends to party with. Plus it's not really the date that screws me over most."

"Let me guess. All the attention was on Abby and Amanda, as per usual?"

I offer a sour smile. "Abby was just accepted into med school and Amanda made the varsity softball team. So my twenty-first birthday wasn't exactly the most exciting thing going on."

I'm the middle child, and as much as it may be a stereotype, the whole "middle spawn is ignored eighty percent of the time" thing is pretty accurate when it comes to my family. My oldest sister is the smart one, destined to be the next family doctor, right behind my father. And Amanda, the youngest, is strikingly beautiful and incredibly talented in every sport she plays. I swear the girl could pick up a broom today and play Quidditch like Harry by the time I went to bed tonight.

And then there's me.

Crazy competitive and talented in all the things that don't matter to my parents.

Like event planning.

And pole dancing.

Funny enough, it almost feels like I'm the middle child with Jess and Erin, too. We all look so similar and hang out all the time that everyone groups us together. Except, Erin is known for running shit and Jess is the comedian. I'm just sort of there.

It's a curse.

Jess scrunches her nose. "That sucks, dude. Seriously. I wish I would have been there to take you out. Oh!" She snaps her fingers. "Let's go out this Friday before the auction. Ralph's. Break the place in before we glam it all up the next night."

"Deal."

We eat for a few moments in comfortable silence, which of course makes my mind drift to Bo. Valentine's Day is next week and I still have a few things to pick up for our date. With everything going on with Xavier, I haven't been showing her the attention she deserves, so I'm determined to make that night special.

I start to ask Jess what she's doing for the holiday but pause when I look up and see the furrow in her brow. Following her eyes, I find the sexy teacher she had a run in with last semester laughing in a booth with some hot brunette.

"Isn't that Jarrett?" I ask, turning back to Jess. She's worrying her bottom lip and staring blatantly at their booth.

"Mmhmm."

"Damn. I forgot how bangable he is."

"Ten-point-two on the bangable scale."

She makes the joke, but her eyes stay focused on Jarrett as her expression slips from confused to angry.

"Holy shit," I whisper, leaning in. "You're still messing around with him, aren't you?!"

"What?" Jess snaps her attention back to me. I waggle my eyebrows and she shakes her head, grabbing her soda and taking a big sip from the plastic straw. "I don't know what you're talking about."

"Oh come on! What's going on between you two?"

"I don't know," she snaps, her chocolate eyes hard on mine now as she crosses her arms. "What's going on with you and my Little?"

The air rushes from my chest in a whoosh.

Ears fuzzy, I swallow and force a smile.

"Bo? We've gotten a lot closer in the past few months. She's cool."

"Uh huh."

My smile falls. "Do you have something to say, Jess?"

"Do you have something to *tell me*, Lei?"

Jess is watching me carefully. I need to swallow, but I'm afraid if I do I'll give myself away. It's not that I don't trust Jess, but Bo is far from ready to tell anyone about us. Or about her, in general. And I'm the same.

"Oh thank God I found you." Erin slides into the booth next to me, planner in hand, highlighter at the ready. Jess is still eying me, but with Erin here, she knows the conversation is over for now, so she turns her attention back to Jarrett across the room. "I need you."

Finally allowing myself to swallow, I plaster on my best smile, pulling my long platinum hair over my left shoulder. "What's up, buttercup?"

"Are you busy the Monday after the auction?"

"I have class but that's it."

"Perfect. Can you please take the money we raise to the bank? I was going to after my morning classes but I have something that came up that I can't get out of."

I'm still a little too aware of Jess and her question about me and Bo, but I nod and smile wider. "Of course, no problem Ex."

Erin sighs with relief, and it's then I notice how tired she looks. Her dark blonde hair is pulled back into a tight bun and she's barely wearing any makeup, which is strange for her. "Thank you. Okay, I have to run." She stands, finally turning her attention to Jess. When she does, she frowns. "Uh, J-Love?"

"Hmm?" Jess' eyes are still on Jarrett.

"What are you eating?"

Erin points down at Jess' last slice of pizza and I cover my mouth, trying not to laugh. Jess glances at me, anger still evident in her features, but even she cracks a smile. "Um... well, it's totally *not* a five-hundred calorie slice of pizza, if that's what you're thinking. Because we're on the Spring Break diet. And pizza is not part of that diet. Therefore, that couldn't be what it is."

Erin rolls her eyes. "Whatever. I don't want to hear it when we go shopping for swim suits. See you girls later."

Jess and I wait for her to walk out the front door before bursting into a fit of laughter, which almost makes me forget that she's totally onto me and Bo. It almost makes me forget Xavier and the deal he proposed to me just two days ago. It almost makes me feel like I did last semester, before shit hit the fan and I fell into a hole too deep to climb out of alone.

Almost.

Adam

The Kappa Kappa Beta auction is one of the best events of the spring semester. It always kicks off Greek events, starting a string of fundraisers, socials, and everything in-between. Fraternity brothers and non-Greek guys alike clamor into the bar, cold cash in hand, ready to buy a date with a beautiful KKB girl.

My beautiful KKB girl is currently wrapped in my arms.

And luckily, she's not for sale tonight.

"I think my Little is about to pass out," Skyler says, chuckling a little. She finishes typing out a text and tucks her phone into her small purse before leaning in closer. We're in the back of a cab on our way to the auction and Skyler is all dolled up for the occasion. Tight black dress, gold high heels and jewelry to match, hair down and carefully curled. Red, red lipstick.

She doesn't ever have to try to look sexy, but when she does, it's enough to knock a full grown man on his ass.

"She texting you?"

"Yeah. She'll be fine. Some sex-on-a-stick piece of man candy is going to buy her and take her out. Then she'll thank us."

I shift, trying not to think about why hearing that scenario made my stomach uneasy. "Yeah, I'm sure. So, you still plan on ditching me for a tournament next week?"

"Don't say it like that." She frowns.

"What? It's true. It's Valentine's Day and my girlfriend would rather hang out in a smoky room full of smelly old men than let me take her out on a nice date."

Skyler pokes me hard in the rib and I double over, laughing. "Ass. You know this tournament is too big to miss. It's a qualifier for the one this summer."

"I know, I know," I relent, pulling her in for a kiss. I know her red lipstick will be smeared all over me, but I literally have no fucks to give when she's dressed like this. I'm not stupid enough to think she doesn't feel what I feel, like what we have has an expiration date quickly approaching, so I'm going to take full advantage while I still can. "We'll have our own Valentine's Day when you're done."

"Can it include Netflix?" she asks as the cab pulls into Ralph's. I pay the driver and step out first, extending my hand for hers.

"Of course."

"How about some under-the-covers action?" She licks her lips and lowers her eyes just enough to make me groan.

"*Definitely*."

The cab pulls away, but I tug Skyler's wrist back until she's flush against me in the dark parking lot of the bar. Grabbing her face in my hands, I press my lips to hers, tilting my hips so she feels exactly how excited I am for our date. She moans as I slip my tongue inside her mouth, letting one hand fall down the soft fabric of her dress, gripping her hip and pulling her closer.

And that's when the first flash assaults us.

Breaking the kiss, we both pull back confused, eyes trying to adjust to the darkness as we look for what caused the white burst of light. When three quick flashes follow, I pull Skyler against me, shielding her from whatever the fuck is happening.

"Skyler Thorne, is this how you're prepping for the qualifying tournament next week?"

Another flash.

"Who's this? Your boyfriend?"

Flash. Flash.

"Great dress. What do you plan on wearing to the tournament?"

Skyler's hand fists in my shirt and she buries her head into my chest. "Shit," she murmurs.

"Don't worry," I soothe, pushing through the small group of paparazzi as they try harder to talk over one another. I keep Skyler covered with my arms and she lets her hair fall in front of her face as I guide us toward Ralph's. When the bouncers notice us, they rush to help, fielding off the remaining reporters as their cameras continue flashing. When we finally break through the doors and are free from the questions, Skyler pulls back, eyes wide.

"Oh my God."

"That was insane."

Skyler nods, fingering the curls in her hair as she looks out the tinted windows of Ralph's where the bouncers are refusing to let any of the photographers in.

"You really are blowing up on the poker scene, aren't you?"

She just shakes her head. "This is unreal."

"Are you okay?"

Skyler nods, hard, for longer than necessary, her eyes still trained on the commotion outside. "Yeah. I just, I need a minute."

"Sky?" Clinton walks briskly toward us, engulfing Skyler in a crushing hug as soon as he reaches her. Her tiny hands grip his massive, dark arms and it's then that I see her shaking slightly. "Come on, follow me." He pulls her in closer. "Adam, can you go check on Cassie? She was freaking out waiting for Skyler to get here but I don't think she's going to calm anyone down like this."

I give him a curt nod, leaning in to kiss Skyler on the forehead. "Do you want me to come with you?"

She shakes her head slightly. "I'll be fine. Go help my Little. Please. I just need..." she trails off, trembling more. Clinton curses.

"Go, Brooks. I got her."

And I know he does, no one loves Skyler the way Clinton does. Still, I feel uneasy not being the one taking care of her right now. "Okay. I'll find you two in a minute."

Clinton tugs Skyler through the already packed bar and once they've disappeared, I make my way toward the stage where the KKB girls are setting up. Luckily, I run into Erin first, and she ushers me backstage to where Cassie is waiting after I tell her what happened with Skyler.

"Just don't be back here long. My Big doesn't like anyone seeing the girls before they go on stage."

"Sounds like a strip club."

Erin smacks my arm with a smile, though her face is pale, eyes watery. She doesn't look like the normal Erin Xander I'm used to seeing.

Cassie is pacing in a small space back near the bathroom, chewing her thumbnail with a contemplative look on her face. I can't help but take her in as I make my way toward her. She's not in a dress, but rather a tight, white pencil skirt and hot pink tank top with heels to match. Her bright red hair is pinned up, a few stray tendrils falling to frame her face, and her usually soft green eyes are glowing fierce against the dramatic makeup she's applied. Stuffing my hands in my pockets, I clear my throat when I reach her.

"I feel like I should save that freshly manicured nail from the wrath of your teeth."

Cassie chews for a second longer before stopping, her wide eyes finding me. She looks absolutely petrified.

And it's fucking adorable.

When she realizes it's me, I notice her face fall a bit, and I can't deny that it stings.

"Is Skyler here?"

"Yeah, but she needs a minute. We kind of got attacked by paparazzi on our way inside."

Cassie's mouth drops. "Oh my gosh. Is she okay?"

"A little shaken, but she'll be okay. Bear took her to get water and calm down."

She nods, but her eyes gloss over a bit and she goes back to chewing her thumb.

"Talk to me," I say softly, nudging her with my shoulder as I lean casually against the wall. She drops her hand from her mouth, her green irises roaming over me. I can't tell how I feel about it. She's either checking me out or questioning whether she can trust me.

Maybe both.

Sighing like I'm her last option, she leans back against the wall next to me, blowing air through her lips.

"I don't know why I let them talk me into this. I am literally the worst person for the job. I hate being the center of attention, I blush pretty much anytime someone looks at me, and on a scale of one to sexy I'm at a solid awkward turtle ninety percent of the time."

I chuckle, crossing one arm over my lower chest and bringing my opposite hand to cover my smile. Cassie glares at me, and I know she aims to intimidate me but it only breaks my resolve and makes me laugh. So, naturally, she smacks me across the chest.

"I'm serious, Adam."

"I know, I know," I say through my laughter. "It's just that all of those things are exactly why any guy out there would be lucky to win a date with you tonight."

Cassie's arms are crossed, a frown firmly in place, but she softens a bit at my words. "I beg to differ."

"Beg all you want, but I'd still never take those words back."

She chews her cheek, finally turning to face me. When I see the insecurity behind her eyes, I want to find every guy who ever put them there and kick them all straight in the teeth.

"I'm not desirable. At all. I'm going to get up there and make like twenty bucks and feel completely embarrassed."

"Listen to me." I grab her hands in mine, our shoulders still leaned against the wall, both of us hidden in our little corner of the room — of the world. "I have never, in my entire life, met another girl like you. And as much as you may think that's a bad thing, it is the exact opposite. You're intriguing, Cassie. You're light, innocent, sweet, kind, smart. I could go on and on."

"I don't think guys will buy me for my biology test scores."

Pulling her in a little closer, maybe a little too close, I bring my voice to a whisper. "It will be how fucking amazing you look in that tight little skirt that will make them want to buy you. It'll be everything else I just listed that will make them go crazy trying to keep you."

She swallows, and I watch with more curiosity than I should as her eyes flick to my mouth quickly before finding my gaze. "I should go touch up my makeup."

It's then that I realize how hard we're both breathing, how close we're standing. Dropping her hands, I shove my own back in my pockets and nod. "Okay. I'll see you out there."

Before I can think more about what the hell just happened, I turn on my heel and make my way toward the side stage exit.

"Adam?"

I pause, turning slowly, afraid she'll tell me I was over the line. Afraid I'll lose her, even though she's not really mine to keep.

"Thanks. Really." She smiles with just one side of her mouth, just for a moment, before backing into the bathroom and slowly closing the door.

"Anytime," I reply to no one. And I know even though she didn't hear it, she knows it's true as much as I do. I'd be there for her no matter what.

I just can't decide if that's a good thing.

Erin

There is nothing worse than throwing up.

I usually don't even let my thighs touch the toilet seats at Ralph's, yet here I am, backstage bathroom, face resting against the dirty, cool porcelain. My head is spinning, I have to go on stage in less than ten minutes, and I can't stop vomiting.

"Goddamn it, Erin." Jess closes the bathroom door behind her and locks it. The first wave of nausea hit me so hard I didn't even have time to close the door when I rushed in. "Get your shit together, dude. You have to go on stage and you look like hell. Come here."

She helps me stand, instantly going into caregiver sister mode, which is a rare form for Jess. She's the party girl, we all know it, but when she needs to be there for someone — she pulls out all the stops. She's one of the best friends anyone could ever have.

I watch her carefully as she uses a wet paper towel on the back of my neck, whipping out her makeup bag at the same time. "Thank you."

She smiles, but her usually playful brown eyes are sad. "You have to take a test. You can't keep avoiding it." Jess shakes her head, patting my face dry with a new paper towel before applying a little cover up under my eyes. "I know it's scary, but we can handle it together. You should have already taken a test by now. Hiding from the problem isn't going to make it go away."

She keeps talking, but my ears go fuzzy, along with my vision. I feel myself slipping into a sort of numbness, a dark hole, a place where I just need to be alone.

"It's fine." I cut her off mid-sentence, forcing a smile. "I took the test, Jess. I'm not pregnant. Must just be a stomach flu."

Jess' eyes are hard on mine, like she's searching for something, but then a sigh of relief leaves her lips. "Oh, thank fuck." She shakes her head, still working on my makeup. "A stomach flu we can handle. When did you take the test?"

"Sunday."

"Why didn't you tell me? I could have been there with you."

"I tried calling, you weren't answering." Jess swallows, her eyes flitting from mine to focus on her hand where she's reapplying my lipstick. Something tells me I'm not the only one who has something to hide.

"Sorry. I think I was with my study group, now that I think of it."

"Yeah."

"Erin?" My Big knocks on the bathroom door. "You're up. Are you okay?"

"Fine! Be right out."

Kelsey is absolutely slaying it in her new position as president, and I know I can't let her down. I'm next in line. Every KKB in our family line for the past several years has held the position of president. This is my year to prove myself, and I'm not letting anything get in my way.

Pulling my shoulders back, I turn from Jess to the mirror, giving myself a once over before pulling her in for a hug. "Thank you for your help."

"Anytime, Ex. Now go raise some money for charity, you fine piece of ass." She smacks my butt as I open the bathroom door and I laugh, throwing her a wink.

I don't have time to get nervous, because Kelsey immediately leads me to the stage, helping me walk up the back stairs before Siomara, My Grand Big and last semester's president, starts speaking into the mic to begin my auction. Even though her term ended last semester, she stuck around for one more so she could graduate in the spring. Then, she'll be headed to Antigua for medical school.

Everything is changing.

"Oh boys, you're in for a real treat with this one," Siomara begins and a few whistles ring out. I shake my head, but pull on my mask, the one that lets everyone in the room know that I can handle anything — everything. "Our new Recruitment Chair is classy, beautiful, and smart. There's a reason her nickname is Ex, boys, so beware." Laughter rings out and I flash a smile at the crowd, playing into it. "And, of course, she's the one in charge of choosing the hot group of freshmen ladies that will make up the next pledge class of Kappa Kappa Beta in the fall!" The crowd cheers, and I take a mini bow before laughing softly.

"We'll start the bidding at one-hundred dollars."

A paddle flies up in the back, but I can't see the hand attached to it. Siomara keeps raising the price, and paddle after paddle goes up in response. I should be happy, flattered, but I just feel so numb. I think I'm smiling, but I can't be sure. When the amount gets up to five-hundred, I focus enough to see who's still in the race.

The paddle that goes up for five-hundred is Clinton.

He smiles at me, that heart-stopping, white-teeth-blazing-against-dark-skin smile that had me more weak in the knees than I care to admit the night he took me to semi-formal. He winks, and a sharp pang shoots through my chest. I know he's just doing it as a friend, he's just being sweet, because that's the kind of man he is.

He would have made a great father.

He *will* make a great father. Someday.

But when Siomara raises the price to six hundred, a new paddle goes up. I recognize the face below it, perfectly symmetrical like a Ken doll, defined jaw, baby face, sandy blonde hair combed over and perfectly styled. Landon Turner is practically the definition of a frat daddy. Vice President of Mu Beta Chi, pre-med with a focus in plastic surgery, dressed in coral shorts cut just above his knee, a white polo, and Sperry's — when it comes to who my parents think I should marry, he's my mother's wet dream.

Landon is standing with some of his friends, elbowing them with a wide smile as he wins the auction. He makes his way through the crowd, helping me down from the stage as a few of my sisters take his cash donation. He has light, almost crystal-blue eyes, and he's not too shy to let me know he wants me with them.

"Looks like I get the privilege of taking you out on a date," he says with a slight southern drawl. Yep, my mom would have officially lost her mind.

"Looks that way." I smile, but it's still a mask. "What do you have in mind?"

"I want it to be perfect, so I need some time to think. Can I have your phone number, Erin Xander?"

This time I smile and it's somewhat genuine. Landon is cute, sweet — he could be fun. I just need to clear my head. Hopefully I can do that before he calls for our date.

I jot my number down in his phone and he gives me a soft kiss on the cheek before returning to his friends so I can join my sisters backstage. Kelsey hands me a clipboard immediately and puts me to work, organizing the rest of the sisters going up for auction and keeping a running tab on the funds raised. For the first time tonight, I feel in my element. Slipping into organizational mode, I push everything else out of my mind and focus on the tasks at hand.

It's the best kind of escape.

Adam

In the time I was backstage with Cassie and Skyler was behind the bar with Clinton, something changed. I'm not entirely sure what just yet, but something is different. Skyler has stopped trembling; she's smiling, talking to everyone in our group as we wait for the next sister to come up on stage. She's here, tucked under my arm, but she's not really *here*. Her mind is somewhere far away. She's thinking, and it's the kind of thinking that makes me uneasy.

I think we both feel it. We both feel something coming.

Excusing myself from the group, I slide up to the bar and get a refill on my Captain and Coke just as Cassie takes the stage.

I can tell she's still nervous, but she's much better than she was backstage. Her cheeks rosy, she's twisting her fingers together and smiling out at the crowd as Siomara talks into the mic about how great of a catch Cassie is. Paying for my drink and lifting it to my lips as I make my way back to the group, I catch just the tail end of the spiel.

"Plus, she's probably the cutest redhead Palm South University has ever seen, am I right?"

The room erupts into a mixture of cheers from her sisters and hoots from the guys crowding the bar. Cassie flushes a deep, crimson red, and I can't help but smile.

"We'll start the bidding at one-hundred dollars."

There's a lull in the noise, everyone waiting for that first paddle to go up. Only a few seconds pass, but I watch as Cassie's smile falls, worry appearing in the form of a small crease between her brows. Snatching the paddle out of my brother, Jeremy's, hand, I shoot it up into the air.

"One-hundred! Do I hear one-fifty?"

Cassie's green eyes sparkle when she sees it was me with the paddle. She mouths a *thank you*, and I just smile, handing the paddle back to Jeremy. Jeremy is one of my closest friends in the fraternity, the one brother who helped me with all the events last semester and believed in me when I said I could put our fraternity on the map. This semester, he's my right-hand man, and if we have anything to do with it, we'll be President and Vice President next year.

Skyler's arms wrap around my middle and she leans her head on my chest, looking up at me through her long lashes.

"You may officially be the best boyfriend ever. Thank you for doing that."

I shrug. "I just got the bets started."

And I did. A few more paddles go up before the bid levels out around three-hundred. Siomara is just about to call it when a last-minute paddle flies up.

"Five-hundred!"

Everyone cheers, and Cassie searches the crowd for the new bidder. When she finds him, recognition hits her eyes. She smiles, a bigger smile than I've seen on her face in some time. She knows the guy, and as he makes his way to the stage, panting slightly, like he rushed to get here and just barely made it, Cassie turns to Siomara.

"Sold!" she yells before Siomara has the chance to ask for a higher bid.

Siomara laughs, banging her make-shift gavel on the podium. "You heard the girl!"

A few laughs ring out and then everyone goes back to their conversations or to the bar, waiting for the next auction to start. My eyes, however, stay firmly on Cassie as she makes her way down the stairs. The mystery guy is waiting for her, but when she leaves the last stair, I lose sight of them just as he wraps her in a hug.

Who the hell is that?

"So, I hear you're joining us on Spring Break, Brooks. You think you can hang with a bunch of KKBs and O Chis?" Clinton clinks his class with mine and takes a drink. I sip mine and smile.

"I guess we'll find out. I am excited, though. I've never been to Key West."

"Me either," he says. "I heard Duval Street is crazy."

"I'm just ready for some sunshine and a break from classes. Homework is already killing me," Skyler adds.

"Yeah, I can't wait to see you in a bathing suit, either. Oh! I mean sunshine. Can't wait to be in the sunshine. *Totally* meant sunshine." I wink at Skyler and she elbows my side, but leans up to plant a swift kiss on my cheek.

"You two are so cute it's kind of disgusting," Jeremy says.

"Don't be jealous. I'm sure your hand looks very nice in a yellow bikini, too."

This time Jeremy slugs my arm and we all laugh just as Cassie joins our group. And she's not alone. There's a hand wrapped around her small waist, a hand attached to a long, tattooed arm.

"Hey guys, this is Grayson," Cassie introduces, looking up at the guy with a smile. He's tall, lanky but not too skinny. His hair and beard are dark, but his eyes are bright blue. He's not even remotely unfortunate looking, and for some reason, that irks me.

"Oh yeah, from the coffee shop, right?" Skyler asks, moving forward first. She gives him a hug before wrapping her arms around me again. "Thanks for donating to our cause tonight."

"Of course. I would have paid more if it meant getting Cassie to go on another date with me." He grins down at her and she flushes, just slightly, like she did the day I first met her.

"Another? I didn't know you two had already been on one," Skyler says, her arms still around my waist.

"We just went to dinner."

"She's playing hard to get," Grayson argues, but they're both smiling.

I'm highly annoyed.

"Well I guess she can't say no to a five-hundred dollar proposition," Clinton says, leaning forward to shake Grayson's hand. "I'm Bear."

"Nice to meet you, man."

"Oh! Yeah, this is my Big, Skyler, and Adam and Jeremy. They're in Alpha Sigma."

Grayson shakes Jeremy's hand first and mine last. His grip is strong, smile still in place.

"Hey, I know you. You're the one who threw that kick ass concert last semester, right?" he asks as we drop hands.

"Uh, yeah."

"Bro! That was so sick. Three of my favorite bands in the area were there. Are you doing another one next fall?"

"If I have anything to do with it, yeah." Cassie is smiling up at him as we talk a little more about the concert. He really knows his shit about local music, and before I can stop him, Jeremy is asking if he'll help scout talent next semester. The guy is nice, funny, not even a little douche-like.

I hate him.

My phone buzzes, and for the first time ever, I'm actually relieved to see a text from Clay demanding I get my ass to the house.

"Shit," I murmur. Skyler leans over to look at the text. "Clay just called an emergency meeting."

"Think it's about the retreat?" Jeremy asks.

"Not sure, but we should probably both go." I turn to Skyler, apologies at the ready.

"Don't," she says before I have the chance, holding up her hand. "It's completely fine. I'm exhausted anyway and need to call my parents about what happened tonight. I'll text you tomorrow?"

"Yeah, okay." I smile and she lifts on her toes to give me a kiss. She breaks away too soon for me, so I pull her back, running my hand up her arm to grip the back of her neck, holding her to me. She sighs a little, as if my kiss reassured her of something I didn't even know she was questioning.

"Have fun tonight."

"You too," she breathes when I break the kiss. "See you guys later. Nice to meet you, Grayson." I nod my head as he holds his whiskey up in a cheers to me.

My eyes flick to Cassie's, but just for a moment, not even long enough to read what lies behind them before I turn and make my way through the crowd with Jeremy.

Ashlei

There are times when our bodies warn us against the actions we choose. They make us sweat, turn our stomachs, cloud our vision, cause us to tremble. My body is sending me all the warning signs now as I clutch the donations raised Saturday night at the auction close to my chest. But I'm not walking up to the bank.

I'm walking into Xavier's office.

I know it's wrong, I'm ashamed that I'm doing it, but I don't have a choice. We raised just over five grand, just enough to buy me the time to Spring Break, just enough to move me closer to my freedom. It's selfish, it's against every value my sorority stands for, it's against everything that I am. But I know this isn't just some game I can quit and walk away from unscarred. My life is on the line.

Bo's life is on the line.

And if I want to make it out of this alive, I'm going to have to do some things I'm not proud of.

I already have.

Swallowing, I nod slightly at the body guard outside of Xavier's office as he lets me in the door. Xavier is seated at his desk, head down, looking through a folder with pictures of other men and documents I'm more than sure I don't want to know the details of.

"Have a seat, Ashlei. Just one moment."

I tuck my hair behind my ears, the ends of it sticking to my neck as I sit on the edge of the chair. Xavier shifts through a few more pages before closing the file and leaning back in his chair, steepling his fingers.

"I hope you're not here to beg for more time."

"I'm not," I say, shoving the large envelope toward him. He takes it hesitantly, his eyes on mine, before opening it and running his fingers over the money. "There's just over five-thousand in there."

He smiles, one that makes me even more uncomfortable than I was. "Does this mean you're taking me up on my offer?"

"I don't really have a choice," I squeak, my throat dry.

Xavier claps his hands together and I jump. "Beautiful! I love when it all comes together like this, kiddo." He pauses, noting my frown. "It'll be easy, I promise. You'll be on Spring Break. Everyone is looking for something."

I nod. "I just want it to be over."

He clears his throat, and I wonder if even he is uncomfortable at the position he's put me in. Then I think of how he's treated me in the past, how he's treated Kya, Hayden. There's no way this man can have a conscious.

But really, am I so different? Here I am agreeing to sell hard drugs to other students on campus. I could be starting an addiction. I could be ending a life.

"I'll call you when everything is ready for you to pick up," he says finally, dismissing me.

"Um, wait." I stand, wiping my palms on my shorts. "I, uh, I kind of need your help." Xavier cocks a brow and I close my eyes, ashamed of what I'm about to ask. I can't let anyone in Kappa Kappa Beta find out about this, which means I need an insurance policy.

"I have to convince my sisters I was mugged, that the money was stolen." I open my eyes again, hoping he'll understand without me having to explain more.

"What are you asking me, Ashlei?"

I feel it inside, a crack only I can hear as a piece of me breaks. "I need you to hit me."

Erin

I am empty.

I thought I knew what it felt like — emptiness.

The summer before my senior year of high school, I described myself as *empty*. I was searching for purpose, for something to make me feel like living, and luckily I found it in a blonde-haired, blue-eyed boy in the wheat fields of Kansas. Kip Jackson helped me find myself, and though we don't talk anymore, I still attribute a lot of who I am today to who he helped me become that summer.

But this emptiness I feel now, my hands wrapped hard around the steering wheel of Jess' BMW, white knuckles, dry eyes, tight skin, dry mouth — I've never felt anything like this before. My phone is ringing, but I can barely hear it. It's probably Landon. He's called twice today, but I'm not ready to answer. Hell, I can't even answer to myself right now.

Emptiness.

It's such a strange word.

A cup, half-empty or half-full?

I was brought up in a large, white house with light blue shutters. I went to church every Wednesday and twice on Sunday. My parents consistently donate to the Republican party, at all levels of government, and my political views are about as far right as you can go.

And yet here I am.

I wish I could cry. I wish I could feel the guilt, the shame, the pain I should feel at this moment in time. I'm angry that I'm numb, that I can't seem to wrap my mind around the word, around the act of horror I just committed.

Abortion.

Another strange word.

My right hand slides down the side of the steering wheel, dropping to my stomach, and I grip the soft cotton fabric of my t-shirt covering it. It's so flat, so hollow.

Empty.

Part of me wishes someone was here with me, but the larger part of me is thankful I didn't break down enough to ask anyone. I can barely face the facts of what I did, I'm almost sure I wouldn't be able to take the judgement from an outside party. No one knows what this feels like until they're here.

Erin Xander: College junior, pre-law, future president of her sorority, knocked up by the lovable jock in the fraternity house down the street.

That is not my story to tell.

Maybe, if I were stronger, if I were less selfish, we could have made it work. Maybe I could have given up my presidency to have the baby, put it up for adoption, still graduated and become a lawyer like I've always dreamed. Maybe Clinton would have wanted to keep it.

As it stands, Clinton will never know.

No one will ever know.

I sniff, but for no reason, because I'm not crying. I didn't cry when I read the all lowercase letters that spelled out *pregnant* on that little plastic tube in my bathroom. I didn't cry when I lied to Jess, or when I made the appointment. I didn't cry when I walked past the small group holding hand-painted signs outside of the clinic — *Choose Life*. And I know I'll never cry, because if ever there was a time, it would have been when they vacuumed my son or daughter out of my stomach like it was a mess made by an inconsiderate neighbor.

I am twenty-years-old, and yet I am a mother, to a baby I'll never have the fortune of meeting.

Except I am not a mother.

I am selfish.

I am a hypocrite.

I am empty.

Ashlei

Valentine's Day has never been a special holiday for me. In fact, the only true valentine I ever had was in second grade when Jordan Lewis bought me a stuffed white dog and small, heart-shaped box of chocolate. He ate half of the chocolates and pushed me off the merry-go-round later that afternoon.

Asshole.

After that, I either didn't have a boyfriend during Valentine's Day or the boyfriend I had didn't celebrate it. By the time I turned sixteen, I stopped caring, and that was a relief for the two boyfriends I had in high school. Neither of them had to worry about the holiday because it meant absolutely nothing to me.

But tonight, I'm wrapped in a massive pile of blankets and sheets with Bo tucked under my arm, her small hand resting on my hip, her fingers just barely under the hem of my t-shirt. It's Valentine's Day, and I'm determined to make it one we'll both remember.

It's barely over fifty degrees tonight, one of the last cold nights we'll have in South Florida for quite a while. It's mid-February now, which means sunshine and seventies are right around the corner. Spring Break is just a few weeks away, and while everyone else is focused on their diets, I'm focused on this moment — right here — lying under the stars with the only girl I've ever truly let myself be with.

It's not that I never found a girl attractive before Bo. I've known for quite some time that I'm bisexual. Still, I never let myself be with them. A kiss here and there, maybe some nights spent together where I wondered if they felt the same, but that's where it all ended. Bo is my first girlfriend, which is part of the reason I want tonight to be so special.

"This is nice," Bo whispers, snuggling in closer. I run my fingers through her short, silky locks and sigh in agreement. "How did you even think of this?"

I shrug. "I wanted to do something no one had ever done for you before."

"You succeeded," Bo says with a giggle.

Palm South University is undergoing a lot of construction this semester, and I heard they were tearing down this parking garage to make room for a new theatre. They stopped letting students park here a few weeks ago and construction is set to pick up in March. I wanted to be alone with Bo, somewhere where we could be ourselves without anyone watching. So, I bought an air mattress, stuffed two duffle bags full of sheets, blankets, and pillows, and set up our own private bedroom under the stars. I asked Bo to bring a few candles and two bottles of wine, and now here we are.

Paradise.

Leaning up on her elbow, Bo frowns down at me, the soft flicker of the candles illuminating her face just slightly. "Are you okay?"

Her hand leaves my hip and finds the side of my face as she runs her thumb across my cheek bone. I flinch a little, the bruise still tender, but force a smile. "I'm fine."

"I can't believe some asshole mugged you. On campus, nonetheless." She shivers. "Gives me the creeps."

"Me too. But I'm okay, and I just want to move on."

She nods, but her eyes are focused hard on mine. Bo knows about the trouble I got into last semester with Hayden and the drugs, but I never told her what Kya said when she came by the sorority house that last day of fall semester. How could I? Bo is the most special person in my life right now. I couldn't risk losing her because of a stupid decision I made.

I'm digging my way out of this hole on my own, and once I'm out, I'll stand in the sunshine with Bo.

I told Erin and the rest of my sorority that I was mugged on my way to the bank with our philanthropy money. Xavier came through with what I asked him to do, and with a smile on his face. He enjoyed it, I could tell.

"Do the campus police have any leads yet?"

I shake my head. "Not yet. But they'll find who did it. I'm not worried."

At least that's not a lie. The PSU police are the last item on my list of Shit to Worry About.

"You know you can talk to me, right?" Bo laces her fingers in mine, pulling my hand to her lips for a soft kiss. It's such an innocent touch, but my heart instantly accelerates.

"I know."

Bo seems so perfect on the outside — beautiful complexion, hair, body. She puts everyone else before herself. But over the last few weeks, I've gotten to know Bo on a deeper level. She opened up to me about her parents, the pressure they put on her to excel in life, the absolute horror she experiences at just the thought of telling them she's gay.

That I can relate to.

I've grown into my skin enough to know who I am. I like boys, but I also like girls. I just love to love, I guess. Regardless, my parents wouldn't understand — just like Bo's wouldn't. I've always thought that, maybe, they never really needed to know. After all, there's a chance I may end up marrying a guy, right? Still, I can't say I've never thought about telling them just to see their reaction. I wonder if I'd have their attention then?

But Bo doesn't have that same thought. She can't help who she loves, and she doesn't want who her parents think she should — who the bible says she should.

It's sad, and even though acceptance is spreading faster now than it ever did when my parents were my age, there are still so many who don't understand.

Our parents are at the top of that list.

"What are you thinking about?" Bo asks, sitting and pulling one of the blankets up with her to cover her shoulders. The candlelight is reflected onto the front of her face while the moon and stars shine bright behind her. It's absolutely stunning.

"Honestly?"

She nods.

I pause, leaning up to sit with her and nervously tucking my hair behind my ear. "I'm kind of scared."

Bo's face falls. "Of what?"

"Of what I want to do right now."

She swallows, pulling the blanket tighter around her petite frame. "What do you want to do?"

If I thought my heart was beating fast before, it's racing now — galloping — threatening to break my ribcage. "Kiss you."

She relaxes, just marginally. "You've kissed me before, silly." Bo leans forward, like she expects me to kiss her the way I always do, but I don't budge.

"That's not what I mean."

She halts, her midnight eyes snapping to mine. Recognition sets in and she exhales slowly, her breath just barely visible in the cool air of the night. With confidence, she drops the blanket from her shoulders as I open mine to her, instead. She crawls under, straddling me, her breath coming harder.

"Where do you want to kiss me?"

My hands shake as I frame her delicate neck in my hands, pulling her closer, our lips touching as I whisper.

"Everywhere."

Bo closes the distance, kissing me hard as we both let go of the breaths we were holding. Her hands find my hair and I trail mine down to her hips, holding her tight as I buck against her. She gasps, and the sound does something to me that I've never experienced before. Every nerve feels tight, but awake — alive.

It's suddenly no longer cold — not even close. It's scorching, too hot for blankets, too hot to touch, but we refuse to stop. Bo moves her hands to my waist, pushing my shirt up slowly, watching it roll over my curves before finally stripping it off over my head and letting it fall on the concrete. I pull her back into me, kissing her hard, my hands greedy as they roam her body for the first time. When I snake my right hand between her thighs, she tenses, moaning, grinding against the contact.

I'm breathing so hard yet I feel like I haven't inhaled once. Everything in my life is so wrong, but I only feel right in this moment. I'm scared, excited, unsure — and so fucking turned on.

Bo presses her forehead to mine, her breath labored as I find my way beneath the fabric of her yoga pants. When I find there's not another layer separating me from her, I swallow, my fingers circling her clit, my adrenaline pumping. She moans, her head falling, back arching, hips rolling. She bites her lip as her heavy eyes pin my mouth. It's like she can't wait another moment to taste me, like her life depends on our next kiss, and when she finally presses her mouth to mine I wonder if maybe it's true.

"Lay down," she whispers and I obey. Bo winds her hips to the soft music coming from my phone as she peels my sweatpants off, lining her face up with the hem, following the fabric from my hips all the way down to my toes. I can't stop shaking, even though I'm far from cold now. I will my heart to slow down but it won't listen. I am out of control — blissfully unsteady and wild.

When Bo kisses her way back up my legs, her lips trailing a fire from my ankles to my inner thighs, my shaking becomes visible. Her eyes find mine just as she places one, feather-light kiss over my lace panties.

"Lei?"

"Hmm?" I ask, sedated, squirming beneath her.

"Is this your first time?"

My eyes widen. "No."

She smiles, crawling up my body and settling between my legs. Using her knees to spread me open to her, she slides one hand beneath the hem of my panties and I inhale stiffly.

"I mean, is this your first time with a girl?"

Oh.

Her eyes pin my own, and all I can do is nod.

Her grin turns devilish, a dominance I've never seen in her before becoming more and more prominent. She breaks our stare just long enough to pull her sweater and sheer tank top up and over her head. Wrapping her hands around my wrists, she pulls them up over my head, pressing her lips to mine and rolling her hips into me. A jolt shoots through me at the point of contact and I moan, shaking hard, breathing harder.

With her shirt, Bo ties a soft knot around my wrists, pushing them into the mattress slightly before trailing her fingers down my arms to my face. "Keep your hands there. If you move, I punish you. Understand?"

Oh. My. *God.*

My mouth opens slightly as I nod and Bo smirks, kissing my lower lip. "Good girl." Kissing her way down my neck, her hands slide under me and pop my bra effortlessly. I pull my hands down, thinking she wants to take it completely off, but she pushes them back into the mattress.

"Stay."

I gulp.

Bo just smiles, blowing on my nipple before taking it in between her teeth. When her mouth closes over the sensitive skin, warmth spreads and I gasp. She moves to the other, giving it the same pleasure as chills break across my skin. I never knew Bo was the kind to take control, and with everything the way it is in my life, all I want is to give myself to her — completely. I want to submit. I want to let go.

Her lips graze my skin as she runs her tongue down my stomach, tracing the definition there. She tugs my panties off gently, slowly, her eyes devouring me. It feels forbidden, the way she makes me feel, and yet I'm only eager for more.

She barely kisses me first, her lips touching me just enough to drive me insane, but then her tongue drags against the sensitive flesh and I moan — loud, uninhibited. She smiles, sucking my clit between her teeth and sliding one small finger inside me.

Holy hell.

Arching my back, I buck my hips against her mouth and she sucks hard, adding another finger. Every pump sends me closer to the edge, every lash of her tongue makes me cry out her name. I'm rolling, reaching, trying to grasp the release just out of reach. It's like Bo knows my body better than I do. She knows where to touch, how to move, the exact pressure to give without me saying anything.

And suddenly, the benefit of hooking up with another girl comes into view.

My hands fly to her hair and I spread my legs wider, reveling in the ache that spreads from the point where her mouth is still on me.

"I told you not to move your hands," she says, breaking contact. She withdraws her fingers quickly, leaving me empty, and her eyes light me on fire. Gripping my hips, she flips me over with ease and before I can register what's happening, her hand pops my ass. I moan as the sting spreads, my mouth falling open. Bo falls down on top of me, her fingers stroking my opening before entering me from behind. I feel her everywhere — her hair on my shoulder, her lips on my skin, her fingers deep inside me as she curls them, stroking the spot I know will give me the release I'm chasing.

"Just let go, Lei," she whispers, thrusting her hips into her hand, forcing her fingers even deeper. Sliding her free hand down my back, she wraps it around my hip and presses her fingers hard into my clit, circling with just enough pressure to make me follow her command.

As I come, I let everything go. I scream her name, flex my hips, bite my lip, and with each wave I let a tiny piece of myself float away forever.

And though the release came slow, it crashed fast, and I collapse into the sheets, completely spent. Completely hers.

"Oh my God," I breathe, chest rising and falling with effort. Bo smiles, pulling the blankets over us as she wraps her arms around my waist and brings me flush against her. She kisses my neck, my jaw before finally claiming my mouth again, and I taste myself on her tongue.

"I think it's your turn." I pull back, eyes playful, but Bo shakes her head.

"Just relax."

I frown, but Bo just bites her lip with a smile.

"We've got all night," she says, kissing my nose. "How do you feel?"

I blow out a breath. "Incredible."

Bo grins, her eyes still heavy. "Happy Valentine's Day."

Happy Valentine's Day, indeed.

EPISODE 3

"*And we're just* GETTING STARTED."

Skyler

I watch as the water breaks around my paddle, the sun warm on my face, a slight sweat breaking on the back of my neck. Each stride pushes me farther from shore and I sigh at the instant relief I feel from being in my safe space.

I picked up paddleboarding after my freshman Spring Break trip, but I never would have guessed it would become such a constant in my life. When we got back to campus, I started renting boards every weekend, paddling out on my own, fighting against the familiar aches in my muscles until they weren't even affected anymore. After a few months, I bought my own board, and now I take solace in the time I have on the water, away from the world.

There's something about being on the ocean — the wind blowing through your hair, the smell of salt in the air, the sound of the waves on the shore — that sets you free. It reminds you how small you are while making you feel invincible all at once. It's fascinating.

I try not to take life too seriously, but my mind has been bogged down ever since the auction. It's been a little over a week now, yet I still can't shake the stampede of feelings that hit me out of nowhere that night. It was like with every flash of the camera from the reporter who ambushed me and Adam outside Ralph's, a new thought assaulted me. What am I doing with Adam? Is it more serious for him than it is for me? What does it mean that I have paparazzi following me now? Is this the new normal or a one-time thing? Am I holding Adam back from getting the presidency? Is he holding me back from chasing my dreams with poker?

Though I paddle for hours, none of the answers come, and by the time my feet touch sand again, my mind is still wound as tight as the sun-kissed skin stretched over my shoulders. A loud whistle brings me back down to earth and I smile when I see Jess and Cassie sprawled out in two low-sitting beach chairs just down the beach. Hiking up my board, I make my way toward them, trying not to laugh at Jess making lewd gestures the entire time.

"You're so sexy when you lug that board around, Sky," Jess says, and I note the nasally tone of her voice. "Your leg muscles are sick."

"Are we talking sick like impressive or sick like your red nose and dark eyes?"

Jess waves me off, flicking her sunglasses back down. "It's just allergies. I'll be fine."

Cassie scoffs and pulls her bright red hair off her neck, obviously annoyed, though that's way out of character for her. "She's been coughing all morning, but refuses to go to the doctor. And she hasn't eaten since yesterday."

"Jess!"

"What?" She sighs exasperatedly. "It's fine. Good for the Spring Break diet."

Cassie and I exchange knowing looks, but don't push further as I unpack the towels from my beach bag, spreading them out in the sand.

"You seem awfully sassy today, Little. What's with the permanent frown?"

Cassie shifts, her mouth pulling to one side. "Do you guys think I'm a good girl?"

Jess and I pause, unsure of what the right answer is. I opt for the truth. "I mean, I wouldn't say you're exactly a bad girl."

"You're like Snow White, is what she's trying to say," Jess adds.

"What's that supposed to mean?"

Jess shrugs. "You're pure, innocent. You focus on your schoolwork, never really get drunk, don't hook up with random guys. You're straight-laced."

"Which isn't a bad thing," I add, scolding Jess with my eyes.

"I'm not saying it is," Jess defends. "Why are you suddenly concerned, though?"

Cassie is chewing her cheek, eyes on the ocean. "I don't know. I overheard someone saying that I was too much of a 'good girl' for something, and it got under my skin."

"Who?" I ask.

She shakes her head. "Doesn't matter."

"Well, it's not a bad thing. It shouldn't be taken as an insult."

"I'm just trying to figure out if that's the way it was intended," she says, sighing.

"I say fuck whoever said it. And, if it were me in the situation, I'd take the opportunity to prove them wrong."

Cassie perks up a little. "What do you mean?"

She shrugs. "I'm just saying if someone called me Ms. Innocent like it was a racial slur, I'd show them just how not-innocent I can be."

"Jess Vonnegut – Life Advisor," I deadpan. She smirks, tossing a half-empty suntan lotion bottle at me. I catch it with ease and squeeze some in my hands, lathering my shoulders.

"Bitch."

"You love me."

"Also true."

I turn my attention back to my Little, who now has an intrigued look on her face. "Oh God, I think you might have actually given her an idea."

"Just let me know if you need to borrow some fishnets, boo." Jess makes a kissy noise to Cassie and we all giggle.

"Where are the other girls?" I ask, flipping over to rest on my stomach. I have to mold the sand beneath my towel a bit to make a comfortable spot for my chest. Boobs are inconvenient sometimes.

"Erin was supposed to meet up with the kid who bought her at the auction and I'm not sure where Ashlei and Bo are," Jess answers. "Have you guys noticed Ashlei being weird lately?"

"I mean, she was mugged," Cassie says softly, reminding us all of what the entire campus was trying to forget. "I'm not sure I'd be exactly normal after that, either."

"Even before that, though. She seems off, like she's hiding something."

"I could say the same about my Big," I add. Jess sniffs, avoiding my comment, and I lift a brow. "Wait, do you know something?"

"No," she says quickly. "I'm just thinking."

"Well, why don't we divide and conquer. You try to talk to Ashlei, I'll see if I can get my Big to open up."

"Deal."

"What about me?" Cassie asks.

"You just worry about adding some leather to your wardrobe," Jess says and we all laugh, but Jess' face falls quickly. "Wait. Is that guy taking pictures of us?"

My stomach drops and I sit up quickly, my eyes scanning the beach for what Jess is seeing. When I spot a tall man, dressed in khakis and a polo, large camera strapped around his neck and lens focused on the three of us, I curse.

"Oh my God, he is taking pictures of us." Cassie reaches for her sundress, hastily yanking it over her head just as Jess pops up, stomping toward the man.

"Jess! Don't!" I jump up, too, grabbing her elbow and spinning her back around just as she yells obscenities at the man, his camera still fixed on us. "He's probably a reporter for a sports network or blog. We need to get out of here."

"This is ridiculous. You're a poker player and a college student, for God's sake, don't they have better shit to do?"

"Apparently not."

We gather up our stuff quickly, making our way toward the small private beach parking lot. I check my board back into the surf shop I keep it at on our way and we all pile into Jess' car, the man following us the entire way.

"Is this going to happen all the time now, Big?" Cassie asks as Jess throws the car into drive, flipping the reporter off as we pull away.

"I don't know," I murmur, my mind racing.

"What are you going to do?"

I blow out a breath. "Wear cuter bathing suits, I guess."

I try for humor but fail, the heaviness of the situation settling around all of us. My Little offers a sad smile before turning back around and Jess clicks on the radio, volume up full blast. Thumbing through the contacts in my phone, I type out a text to my dad, hoping he'll know what to do.

Jess rolls our windows down, letting the warm breeze blow through our beach-tangled hair. I drop my hand out the window, riding the wind waves, eyes blurring as the scenery races by. Something tells me this is the last calm moment before everything in my life changes, and I try to hold onto it for as long as I can.

But just like the wind, the moment is fleeting, and I know any moment I'll wake up in my new normal.

I just hope I'm ready.

Cassie

There's something about watching Grayson play guitar that really gets to me. The way his hands strum the strings, each pluck so familiar to him, his rough voice rising just above the chords and combing through the warm air of Cup O' Joe's — it's enough to make a girl literally swoon. His bright blue eyes scan the coffee shop as he sings, dropping to his hands every once in a while, finding mine at the perfect times — when he wants me to really hear the words he's singing.

I just sip my coffee and smile at him, mesmerized, wondering why in the world he picked me for his muse. It's almost amusing how many girls fall over themselves trying to get him to notice them. They drop twenties in his tip jar, usually with their phone number, and sway their hips as they walk away. They cheer each time he finishes a song, they request Manchester Orchestra or other bands that they think might make him take them seriously, they compliment his beard or trace their fingers over one of his tattoos, pretending to be interested in the story behind them. Yet somehow, his eyes are fixed on mine, and I can't shake how lucky that makes me feel.

We've been a on a few dates, mostly dinners and movie nights, and each time I find myself falling a little more for him. We longboard for hours, talking about everything and nothing — laughing, existing. He took me to a local concert in the park downtown and we've even *studied* together, which usually involves less time studying our notes and more time studying each other. Not that I mind.

We're seemingly nothing alike — he's a tattooed musician with dreams of moving to New York City after graduation and I'm a freckle-faced Biology major who passes out at the mere thought of a needle going into my skin.

The stark contrast between us reminds me of the conversation I overheard between Adam and Jeremy the other night, and I frown.

They were walking toward the Student Union when I spotted them and I quickened my pace, thinking I could walk with them, but when I got close enough to hear their conversation, I slowed a little at the mention of my name. Jeremy was asking Adam which girls he thought would be good for their next philanthropy event — a B-list celebrity fight featuring two older fighters who happen to live in the Miami area. They need ring girls, and when Jeremy suggested me, Adam was quick to turn down the thought.

"She's too much of a good girl for that."

I tried not to take it personally, but how else is there to take it? He didn't say it like it was a characteristic I should be proud of, but rather like I would fail at the job. And though I've tried to strip Adam of the power he somehow holds over me, it still hurt to hear him say it. Add in the fact that my Big and Jess both agreed with him, and it's been practically impossible to let it go.

I snap my attention back to Grayson just as he finishes the last note of an X Ambassadors song, his bright smile revealing itself behind his beard, girls clapping and whistling when he blushes slightly.

"I'm going to take a quick break, and I'm taking requests when I return, so don't go anywhere," he says into the mic, tossing a wink at me that makes two girls at the table behind me nearly fall out of their chair. I just shake my head.

Grayson pulls his guitar strap over his head and props the instrument against the large metal bar stool he was seated on, hopping off the stage and making his way toward me. It's like slow motion as he walks, the muscles in his arms shifting as he shakes out his long, chestnut hair just to re-tie it in a haphazard bun again. I stand, smiling, and he pulls me in close, pressing his lips hard on mine to a symphony of groans from the rest of the girls in the shop. He knows they're here to flirt with him, yet he still makes it a point to show he's with me.

Yep, officially swooning.

"Come to the back with me? I need some water."

I nod, head still fuzzy as he grabs my hand in his and weaves us through the *STAFF ONLY* doors to a small back room. It has two faded purple couches and one long, dark, wooden coffee table along with an old stereo currently crooning out an old 90's alternative song I'm not familiar with. Grayson plops down onto one of the couches with a sigh, pulling me with him so that I straddle his hips.

"What happened to needing water?" I ask, giggling.

"I lied," he says with a grin, hands skating up my arms to frame my face and pull me into him. His beard tickles my skin as he presses his lips to mine and I fist my hands in his shirt, pulling, wanting him closer yet knowing I'm afraid of being too close at the same time.

So far, all we've done is kiss, and it's not that our make-out sessions aren't amazing — because that's an understatement — but I know Grayson wants more. Hell, *I* want more – but after Clay, I'm hesitant to take it too far too fast. I know Grayson would never push me, but I can only wonder how much longer he'll stick around if I keep holding out.

Breaking our kiss, I undo his bun and run my fingers through his long shaggy hair, massaging the scalp. His eyes close and he rests his head on the back of the couch, smiling. "That feels amazing."

"I love watching you play. You're really good, you know that?"

He chuckles, his hands gripping my hips. "Thank you. Let's hope the big wigs in New York feel the same way." He opens his eyes just enough to wink at me before letting them close again.

"They would be crazy not to."

We're quiet for a moment, my hands still running through his hair, his fingers playing with the hem of my blouse.

"Are you excited for Spring Break?"

I frown. "I'd be more excited if you were coming with me."

"Not really my thing," he says, pulling my hands to his lips. He kisses them with a smile and ties his hair back before letting his hands find my waist again. "You'll have all your sisters to keep you busy. Plus, I have to work."

"I know. Doesn't make me wish you were coming any less, though."

He smiles, blue eyes shining, the gold flecks in them playful. "You know, we could have our own Spring Break. Wear our bathing suits, grind on each other, get wasted."

"Oh?" I cock a brow as his grin widens. "And where exactly would we host this Spring Break?"

"In my dorm room, of course. I'll even put on some Skrillex for good measure."

"Well now you've thought of everything."

"Exactly. Can't turn down such a well-thought-out plan."

"Guess not," I agree, leaning in to kiss him. His hands tighten on my hips and he rocks me against him, causing my breath to hitch at the contact. Grayson deepens the kiss, wrapping his strong arms completely around me, surrounding me with his warmth. He sucks my bottom lip between his teeth and lets it go with a pop, fingers gliding just beneath the hem of my jeans, eyes hooded as he searches me for permission — permission I can't give him. Not yet.

"Can I ask you something?" I breathe and he nods, kissing me once before letting me continue. "Do you think I'm a good girl?"

His brows furrow at my question, his hand stilling. "I feel like I'm walking into a trap."

I laugh. "You're not, I promise. Just be honest."

He blows out a breath, releasing his grip around me and leaning back on the couch. "I don't know. I think you're kind and sweet, and I definitely wouldn't say you're any of the things I associate with a quote unquote *bad girl.*"

I sigh, but kiss him quickly to let him know it's not him I'm upset with. "Are you busy next weekend? There's a fraternity party Saturday night that everyone's going to, and I want you to come with me."

"You sure I'll be allowed? Frats aren't exactly inviting of non-brothers."

"It's an open invitation," I assure him. "And you'll be with me. Please?"

Grayson hums, thinking, thumbs still lightly circling the exposed skin above my jeans. "How can I say no to those pouty lips?"

Smiling, I lean down and press said lips to his, letting him pull me in closer for the few minutes we have left before his next set. And though having his hands and mouth on me are my main focus, my mind drifts to everything I need to do to get ready for next weekend. Everyone has it in their mind that I'm this innocent little girl, incapable of owning the vixen inside me. Well, maybe I don't always pull her out and throw her on display for everyone to see, but next weekend, that's exactly what I plan to do.

Time to show them a Cassie McBee they've never seen before.

One they'll never forget.

Jess

My head aches as I blow hard into a tissue, folding it in half and wiping at my raw nose again. "Gross," I murmur, dropping it into the light blue trash can in mine and Skyler's bathroom. Still sniffling, my dark eyes scan my appearance in the mirror. My skin is ashy white, nose like fucking Rudolph, hair greasy, eyes droopy. I look like complete shit, and regardless of how I try to act, I feel like it, too.

The most obvious thing to do in this situation is haul my happy ass to the campus health clinic, but just the thought of it makes me groan. I hate doctors — of all kinds. Dentists, nurses, vag docs — all of them. I hate the way it smells in a doctor's office, the way you have to weigh in every time, how long you have to sit before the grumpy old man waddles in to shove a thermometer in your throat and judge you for the amount of wax in your ears just to tell you you're fine and buy some over-the-counter meds. It's all an inconvenient circus and I'm over it before I even think of making the call for an appointment.

Throwing on a hoodie even though I know it's far from cold in the house, I pad down the hallway to Erin and Ashlei's room and let myself in without knocking. Erin is seated at her desk, head down, scribbling in her planner. Four highlighters are set up to the left of her hand and I sink into her sheets as she color codes her life.

"Don't bring your virus in here, J-Love," she barks without even looking up.

"Oh, shut it. I'm fine. What are you doing tonight?"

She sighs, shutting her planner and popping the caps back on her highlighters. "Landon is supposed to take me to dinner."

"Well don't seem so excited."

"I was hoping to go through my closet and make the agenda for the council meeting this Wednesday."

I eye her as I reach across her bed and rummage through her snack drawer. "You're kind of weird, Ex. Anyone ever tell you that?"

She shrugs. "I just like to throw myself into things I can control, that's all."

"Well, maybe you need to loosen up a little. You've been wound too tight since the semester started. I think this new position is putting a lot of pressure on you. Plus you had that stomach flu."

She blinks, crossing to her closet and flitting through the side with all her dresses. "Yeah. You're right. It'll be fun, I'm sure."

I shake my head, unrolling a bag of veggie chips and popping one into my mouth. Just chewing is so much effort and my appetite is nonexistent, so I huff and roll the bag back up, tossing it in her drawer again.

"Is it my turn to lecture you?" I know she's trying to joke about me being sick, but her eyes are so tired, so sad. There's something going on with her that she's not telling us.

"Erin, are you okay? Seriously. I know you had that pregnancy scare, and I'm sure even though the test was negative, it was probably pretty awful taking it on your own."

"I'm fine," she clips, stripping down to her underwear just to throw on a tight, lavender, knee-length dress. Ashlei flies through the door just as Erin bends to pull out her tall nude heels.

"Lei! What are you doing tonight? Hang out with me," I whine. That's one of my best qualities when I'm sick. I turn into the whiniest, neediest bitch ever. The problem is that what I want most right now is to either A, get drunk, or B, call Jarrett. And neither of those would be smart. Getting drunk would probably make me even sicker than I already am, and there's no way I could hook up with Jarrett with my snotty face and germy mouth, so what else could we really do? Nothing that would keep us in the safely non-defined zone we're in right now, that much I know.

"Uh, Bo and I are actually heading out to see the new Nicholas Sparks movie."

I groan. "Booooo. I don't want to go out. Can't we stay in? Sneak a bottle of wine and watch one of the other cry-inducing movies he has out already?" I don't even care that I just invited myself to crash their night. If she's lying to me about what her and Bo's relationship is, she should at least have to work to preserve that lie.

"We kind of already bought the tickets, J-Love." Ashlei frowns, tying her long blond hair up in a high pony. "I'm sorry. You can come, though. If you want. But I totally understand if you're not up for it."

As much as I want to crash what I'm *positive* is a date and make them sweat, I don't have the energy to. They'll both live to lie another day.

"Ugh. Where is Skyler? And Cassie?"

"Skyler's playing at a tournament downtown," Erin says, checking her makeup in the mirror.

Ashlei nods. "Yeah, and I'm pretty sure Cassie said she's hanging out with Grayson. They were going to check out some art festival that's in town."

I groan louder, exaggerating the noise, being as annoying as humanly possible. "Why is everyone happily living their lives tonight?"

Ashlei chuckles. "Just go to the doctor, Jess. Stop fighting it."

"I'm fine."

"Uh huh," she says, shaking her head.

"I'll *be* fine. It's just a cold."

"Whatever you say. Don't spread your germs to my side of the room."

"Oh don't worry, she's too busy rolling them around all over my pillow," Erin adds as she opens their bedroom door. "Make sure you Lysol before you leave." I toss a throw pillow at both of them just as they squeeze through the opening, laughing.

When they're gone and I'm alone, I sigh loudly, glancing at my phone and groaning again at the two missed texts from Jarrett. I've been avoiding him, which probably isn't a smart move, considering how that worked out for me last time. Although, I *really* wouldn't mind being fucked in a dark closet right about now. But ever since I saw him with that girl at Pie Heaven, I haven't answered his texts. Which is stupid. And petty.

Mrs. Stupid and Petty herself, ladies and gentlemen.

Huffing, I heave myself off Erin's bed and mope down the hallway to my own, burying myself in the covers. I tuck my phone under my pillow and will myself not to look at it again. Calling Jarrett and asking him to hang out with me while I'm sick would be crossing the line into boyfriend territory, and that's the last thing I want — the last thing *he* wants, obviously. We both understand what we are and what we are not, even if I am butt-hurt over him going to lunch with another girl, and sick cuddle buddies definitely falls on the what-we-are-not-list.

But the more time that passes, the more I want to text him — see him, be around him. The scary thing is that I don't even want to hook up, not really — not specifically, anyway. It would be a nice added feature to the package but really, I just want his company. I want to make him laugh, I want to hear him talk about his day, I want to put my feet in his lap and watch a movie. And the more that realization sets in, the harder it is to keep myself from picking up the phone — from giving into a feeling I haven't had in over a year.

I thought I could handle not putting a title on what we are, just doing what we want and going from there. But the truth of the matter is that I don't hook up with other people and when I'm not with him, he's all I think about. Toss in the fact that I get insanely jealous when I see him with any other woman, coworker or not, and the recipe for disaster thickens. I don't know who I thought I was fooling.

What have I gotten myself into?

Bear

"What's up, baby brother?"

"About time you answered your phone!" Clayton says as I toss my gym bag into the corner of my room. I'm taken aback by the deepness of his voice. He just turned thirteen, and already I can tell he's about to hit the glorious days of puberty. "I have a serious question."

"Uh oh. Do I need to sit down?" I joke, kicking off my basketball shoes. I push the speak-er-phone option on my phone and set it on the bathroom counter as I start the shower.

"Mac and I are stuck on this mission in Grand Theft Auto and can't figure it out. We've been here for hours, bro."

I laugh. "I can't believe I was playing basketball and missed your calls during this tragic time."

"I know. What a shitty big brother you are."

"Hey!" I scold as I peel my still-wet t-shirt over my head. "Since when do you curse?"

"It's not a big deal. Mac says shit all the time."

I frown. "You've been over at Mac's a lot lately."

There's a pause on Clayton's end and I still, wondering if there's something he's not telling me. "Sorry. I'll cool it on the cursing, Mom."

I laugh, asking him for more details on the mission he's on and walking him through it while the bathroom steams up. We chat for a while, mostly about school, not even a little bit about mom or Carlton. It feels good to catch up with Clayton and I can't help but feel like I should do it more often. Just because I'm not in the same state doesn't mean I shouldn't be there for him. I'm the closest thing he has to someone to look up to in his life.

That fact hits me hard. I haven't heard from mom or Carlton since I gave them enough money to get them out of whatever trouble they were in last semester, which gives me hope, at least, that they're doing okay. Still, just because I haven't heard from them doesn't mean I shouldn't pick up my phone and call Clayton more often.

"Hey," I say just as we're about to hang up. "Why don't you come down for family weekend? I'll book the flight. We can hit the beach and go go-karting."

"Really?" Clayton asks, excited.

"Yeah, really. I'll even let you get your ass kicked in Halo if you're lucky."

"Hey, what happened to no cursing?"

"I'm twenty-one. I'm allowed to curse."

He chuckles. "I really would like to. I feel like there's a lot we never get to talk about with all the distance, you know?"

I run my hand through my fade, catching my own eyes in the mirror. "Yeah I know. It'll be fun. I'll text you later with the flight details. If mom is upset or has questions, just have her call me," I add, jaw tensing at the mention of her.

"I doubt she will, but yeah, I'll tell her. Love you, big bro."

"You too."

We end the call and I thumb through my music, pressing play on a J Cole song and setting it to shuffle through my playlist. I take my time in the shower, letting the hot water soothe my aching muscles from playing hard at the courts. My knees are tight, arms sore, and I'm ready to collapse in bed and watch ESPN. But as I step out of the shower and wrap a towel around my waist, I see a completely different option presented.

"Your clothes smell, dude." Shawna says, her small frame leaning against the bathroom counter. "Like, bad."

"Hi to you, too."

"Hi," she says, kissing me swiftly before propping her ass on the bathroom counter, shamelessly watching me dry off. "There's an art festival in town. You should take me."

I chuckle. "You have absolutely zero fucks to give about the normal way people do things, huh?"

"Normal is boring."

"What do I get out of this deal?"

"My company, of course. Plus we can knock out that extra credit assignment for our art class. It's a win-win."

I brace my hands on either side of her legs on the counter, boxing her in, watching as her eyes follow the beads of water gliding down my chest. "Hmm... so what you're saying is you want me to do homework with you. Sounds like a favor of sorts."

She grins. "Okay, I'll bite. What do you want in exchange, Bear?"

"Come to Key West."

"No."

I laugh. "You're so exhausting. Just come with me. I want to bang you in at least four places on Duval Street."

"So romantic."

"It's your kind of romantic and you know it."

"Touché."

"So you'll come?" I ask, hopeful.

Shawna leans forward, her bright green eyes playful behind her black frames. "Nah."

I drop my forehead to hers. "You're impossible, woman." She just giggles, but the sound is cut short when I press my hips forward, meeting hers. She wraps her legs around my waist, pulling me closer. She's in a simple, strapless black dress, and with only my towel and her panties separating us, it suddenly feels a lot hotter in the bathroom.

"Well, if your persuasion tactics weren't so awful, maybe I wouldn't be so impossible." She bites her lip, rolling her hips just enough to stir up the friction between us.

"You're saying I'm not bringing enough to the table?" I ask, sucking her bottom lip between my teeth and reaching my hands into her jet black hair. When I reach the purple ends, I grip harder, tugging with just enough force to expose her neck to me. She gasps, arching her back.

"That's exactly what I'm saying," she breathes.

My hands still in her hair, I kiss across the swell of her breasts. "Well, let me sweeten the deal, then."

In one fluid motion, I drop my towel to the floor, push her panties to the side, and slide inside her, pulling her hair harder as she cries out. She's so wet, so ready, and I pull out before rocking back into her again, slowly this time, letting her feel every inch.

"Oh fuck," she breathes, letting her legs fall open wider as she takes me in. My hands snake up her thighs, bunching her dress just above her hips as I flex mine again. I grow harder with each thrust, hitting her deeper every time, and she rewards me with nails digging just as deep in my back.

I work her slow at first, watching her mouth hang slightly open, her eyes focused on where we meet. It's so hot that she loves to watch, and when she lifts her legs to rest on my shoulders, I find a new depth that makes us both moan. I know she loves when I work her clit, but this time I want her orgasm to come from the spot only I can reach inside.

Grabbing her ass in my hands, I lift her, just slightly, just enough to push deeper. Her head falls back, hair sticking to her back, and I take advantage of the access to her breasts. Using my teeth, I pull the top of her dress down and say a silent prayer that she's not wearing a bra. Sucking her nipple ring between my teeth, I pump harder, the steam circling around us, our breaths shallow.

Suddenly, Shawna bucks against me, pressing her hands into my chest until I stumble back a bit. She hops off the counter, spins around, and bends at the waist, pressing her chest to the cool counter, hooded eyes finding mine in the mirror. I take my cue, stroking myself as my free hand finds her center. Slipping two fingers inside, she moans, and the sound jolts straight through me as I place myself at her entrance. When I rock into her, my hands gripping her waist, she gasps.

I start slow again, savoring the feel of her warmth around me, but before long she's demanding harder, faster, more — and I deliver on all accounts. She comes first, her breath clouding the mirror, her eyes wide open and staring at me. It's the sexiest fucking thing I've ever seen to watch her fall apart so unabashedly. I follow right after, cursing under my breath at the electric release only she can bring.

For a moment I stay inside her, resting my chest against her back, my arms around her, our breaths leveling out. When I finally pull out, Shawna stands, shimmying her dress down and adjusting the top in the mirror.

Moving her hair off her neck, I press my lips to her salty skin. "So, Key West?"

She grins. "Valiant effort, but it's still a no." She spins in my arms, kissing me once before smacking my ass playfully. "Now get dressed and take me to this art festival."

I laugh, because what else is there to do? Shawna is unlike any other girl I've ever known, and even though she drives me mad, I wouldn't have her any other way.

Well, let me rephrase that: I wouldn't have her any other way *characteristically*.

There are countless ways I'd *have* her. Take her. Own her.

And we're just getting started.

Skyler

It's eight o'clock on Friday morning, and I have yet to sleep. The downtown casino has had back to back tournaments, and I'm raking up enough to pay off the rest of spring semester and hopefully to pay my entry fee for a larger tournament this summer. I'm on the leaderboard right now, but an opponent delivered a nice little blow to my mental stability this morning in the form of a printed out blog article.

Skyler Thorne: Poker's Hottest New Player

At first, it sounded flattering — and, some of it is — but most of it details my physical features, complete with a center photo of me in the small red bikini I was wearing on the beach with Jess and Cassie. Of the entire article, only one tiny paragraph mentions my skills at the table.

Entering the code for the Omega Chi house into the keypad, I let myself through the front door and make my way back to Clinton's bedroom.

"I brought bagels," I say, louder than I expected, as I kick his door closed behind me. "Coffee, too."

Clinton peeks at me through his heavy eyelids before reaching for his phone, noting the time. When he sees the look on my face, I sigh, setting the bag of bagels and coffee on his bedside table and retrieving the article from my pocket. I unfold it and drop it on his chest.

Squinting, he reads the headline, but his eyes widen at the slew of photos. I don't even think he reads more than the first paragraph. Sighing, he crumples it, tosses it across his room, and scoots over, lifting the covers. "Come here."

I crawl in, snuggling close to him as he tucks the covers around us. "They're such assholes."

"I know," he says, his voice groggy as he kisses my forehead. "Did you talk to President Whittington about the paparazzi on campus yet?"

"Yeah, but so far everything they've taken of me has been off campus, technically. He assured me that if they tried anything on school grounds, he would step in and take legal action against them. But off campus, I need to watch out for myself."

"I swear, if it ever happens when I'm around I'll pummel their asses."

I smile, resting my head on his chest. "Tell me about your life so I can stop thinking about mine for a while."

Clinton blows out a breath, his fingers lazily tracing circles on my shoulder. "Well, I've been steadily banging someone since my birthday."

"The random-birthday-kiss girl?"

"Indeed."

I nod. "Huh. That's kind of a big deal for you."

"Tell me about it." He reaches over me for the coffee I brought him. It's probably a good thing I don't drink coffee, otherwise I'd be even more wired than I am already. "She's cool, though. Different."

"Is she coming to Key West?"

He frowns. "No. I tried to convince her, but she's not having it."

I sigh. "Is it awful of me to feel like maybe I made a mistake inviting Adam?"

"Uh oh. Trouble in paradise?"

My stomach aches and I curl my legs into my body. "No, we're amazing — perfect, even. He's so sweet, funny, charming. We always have a great time when we're together."

"But?"

"But... I just feel like we maybe jumped into the whole boyfriend and girlfriend thing too fast. I never expected it to become as serious as it has. And I feel like Adam is really starting to feel things — real things. But he needs to be focusing on becoming president. Alpha Sigma needs him as president. And me, I feel like I'm on the precipice of something with my poker career — like there's something big coming. And every time I'm at a tournament, I feel bad for not spending time with him."

Clinton is quiet for a moment, sipping his coffee, his arm still around me. "I don't know, Skyler. Maybe the timing just isn't right for you guys right now. I think Adam is a cool guy, but — if I'm being honest — I've always felt like you two were meant to just hook up and hang out. It became more serious than a lot of us expected. And not that that's a bad thing or means anything, but if you feel it, too... well, maybe there's some truth to it."

Sighing, I sit up in the bed, pulling my knees to my chest. "I don't want to make any decisions right now. I think the reporter stuff is just getting to my head. I need to think for a while."

"Fair enough."

"Have you heard from your mom?"

Clinton clears his throat. "No. But I did talk to Clayton. I'm flying him down for family weekend."

"That's awesome, Bear! I can't wait to meet him!"

Clinton rolls his eyes. "Oh God, he's going to *love* you. I'm sorry in advance for the inappropriate comments he's guaranteed to make. Kid just started going through puberty and can't help himself."

I laugh. "So, don't hate me, but I won't be at the Fratalina Wine Mixer tomorrow."

"What?!"

I cringe. "I know, I'm sorry. This tournament isn't over until Sunday."

"Damnit, Skyler. It's the fucking Fratalina Wine Mixer!" he screams, exaggerating the words like the guys in Step Brothers where the event idea originated from. It's one of the best parties during spring semester and I'm more bummed than I admit to miss it.

"I'll make up for it. Promise. I'm not doing anything poker related at all during Spring Break."

"Fine. I'm making you do a beer bong as soon as we get there."

Laughing, I extend my hand and he shakes it firmly. "Deal."

My smile stays intact as I stare at my best friend who I can always count on — no matter the situation. There aren't many people in this world I can be completely honest with. Tugging the covers with me, I bury myself in his chest and squeeze him tight. He abandons his coffee on the table and wraps both arms around me, pulling me in as close as he can.

"Bear hugs really are the best," I say with a sigh.

"Good thing you have them available whenever you need them."

"Always?"

He smiles, giving me a noogie as I squirm against his firm grip.

"Always."

Cassie

It's times like these when I wish my life had a soundtrack.

I totally need a bad ass rock chick ballad playing right now as I strut up to the Omega Chi Beta house, bottle of Maker's in hand, looking completely unlike the normal me but in the best way possible.

When I was younger, I used to love to play dress up — it's part of the reason I enjoyed theatre so much when I did it in high school. For a while, you get to step out of your skin and be anyone you want to be. Tonight, I'm a too-hot-to-touch vixen with a mission to prove everyone wrong.

And there's something incredibly powerful about letting yourself be everything you're not.

My black, strappy heels click on the sidewalk as I take my last step before pushing my way through the door, but then it's too loud to hear my steps anymore. The house is packed, music blaring, students crammed in every open space. Hoisting the bottle of whiskey over my head, I snake my way through the crowd searching for the girls. The weird thing is, people don't ignore me this time. In fact, it's almost like the sea is parting as I maneuver through the crowd. Those who know who I am are staring, mouth open, while those who don't assess me with a mixture of curiosity and desire.

I smile.

When I spot Ashlei and Bo dancing, I adjust my path and clear my throat just as I reach them, popping a hip and holding out the bottle. "Who's up for a shot?"

It's Ashlei who reacts first — jaw dropping, eyes bulging. "Oh. My God."

Bo is still somewhat dancing, but she halts when she realizes it's me. "Holy shit. *Roomie*?!"

I give a little twirl, letting their eyes run over my exposed skin. I wasn't naïve enough to think I could pull this off with anything in my own closet, so I let Jess dress me before she finally gave in and went to the doctor. Even with a red, runny nose — the girl has style. I watch as Bo takes in my carefully teased hair and dramatic makeup, complete with smoky eye, winged eyeliner and bright red lips. Ashlei focuses more on the outfit — painted on black jeans ripped from the knee to the upper thigh, black sweetheart crop top and my personal favorite touch — sick black leather jacket. Black on black on black.

"Holy fuck. I kind of want to lick you. Can I lick you?" Bo asks and Ashlei smacks her arm, almost as if she wishes she was the one Bo wanted to lick. *Weird*. "What?! Look at her!"

"I am. Jesus, Cassie. What's the occasion?"

Confidence is not a virtue I possess, but it's almost like it came along with the heels and makeup tonight. I know it'll be gone again in the morning, but I'm rocking it tonight.

Cocking a brow, I smile wider. "It's the fucking Fratalina Wine Mixer, am I right?!"

They both throw their fists in the air and cheer.

"Fuck yeah it is!"

"Not sure if your intention was to make little boys cry tonight but if it was, you're spot on." Ashlei shakes her head. "You're going to be fighting them off all night."

I smirk. "My only goal right now is to finish this handle. You two want to help me get started?"

"You know this is a wine mixer... meaning you're supposed to get sloshed on wine," Ashlei points out.

Shrugging, I twist the top off the bottle and tilt it to my lips with a wink. "Whiskey works faster."

Bo and Ashlei exchange looks as I take three hits from the bottle without flinching, even though the shit burns like hell. It's not that I never drink, it's just that I usually stick to a few beers. Tipsy is about as far as I've ever gone, but that all changes tonight.

Realizing Grayson isn't anywhere near them as I wipe the corners of my mouth, careful not to smear my lipstick, I frown. "Did Grayson not show?"

Ashlei chews her cheek, her fingers twisting in her long blonde hair. "Sorry, Cassie. We waited an extra twenty minutes before leaving the house but we didn't hear from him."

My heart sinks a little. I set Grayson up to get here with Ashlei so I could finish getting ready and surprise him, too, tonight. Before the disappointment can wash in too much, I take another shot and offer the bottle to the girls, but they both decline and hold up their red plastic cups filled with white wine.

"Wine pong?" I ask, nodding toward the tables set up outside. This jacket is just as hot as it makes me look, and luckily it's chilly outside tonight. It's probably the last cold night we'll have until after fall, so we might as well enjoy it.

The girls agree and we set up quickly, reeling in some random Omega Chi pledge to be my partner against Bo and Ashlei. I sink the first cup without even hitting the rim and that's when I feel the whiskey settle in, the warmth spreading from my stomach to my toes.

I can feel it, tonight's going to be a good night.

***

Math and science have always been my strengths in school, which means I should have seen this coming.

Half a bottle of whiskey plus countless plastic cups of wine equals a very drunk, very smiley Cassie McBee.

Still, my makeup is holding up and I'm keeping myself together, heels and all, like a champ. The random Omega Chi pledge is actually a freshman like me. His name is Todd and we've been running the pong table ever since we stepped up to it. When we win our eighth straight game in a row, I climb onto the table on my knees and swing my hair around to the music, thumbing the strings of an air guitar like I'm Jimi Hendrix as the crowd gathered around us cheers.

The moment his skin touches mine, I freeze.

I don't even have to turn around. I don't even have to look down at the hand hooked around the crease of my elbow. I think I felt him before he even touched me, and that's even scarier.

Slowly, I climb off the table, fixing my hair as I come face to face with deep, chocolate brown eyes — eyes that are absolutely on fire.

"What the hell are you doing?" Adam asks, scowling, his hand still on my arm. I shake it off and hang a hand on my hip.

"Running the table. Want downs on the next ass-kicking?" I try my best not to slur my words, but I'm eighty-seven percent sure I fail.

His frown deepens. "You're drunk."

"And youuu are a buzz kill," I say sweetly, booping his nose with my pointer finger before prancing off to my spot behind the table.

Adam follows, hooking my arm again and pulling me away from the crowd as I protest.

"Hey!"

"You need water."

"I'm fine," I argue, ripping my arm from his grasp once more. This time I stand firm, crossing my arms over my chest, trying hard to focus on his slightly-blurry face. "And, once again, I need to remind you that you're not my boyfriend. Or my father, for that matter."

Adam sighs, pinching the bridge of his nose. "I didn't realize I had to be either of those to care about you."

I scoff, rolling my eyes as he lifts his to stare at me with more questions than I care to answer right now. "Whatever. Is this not enough, Adam? Am I not ring girl material yet? Want me to strip off this jacket and hold it over my head like a *round three* sign?"

"What are you talking about?"

"Hey, there you are." Grayson slides up beside me, wrapping an arm around my waist and pulling me into him for a panty-melting kiss. My brain fuzzy from the alcohol, I let the kiss sink in, feeling it weakening every limb.

"You came," I whisper against his lips.

Grayson pulls back, smiling, his blue eyes hot on mine. "I came." Adam clears his throat and Grayson turns to shake his hand, but his other arm stays fixed around me. "Hey man, nice to see you again."

"Likewise," Adam says, but his eyes don't move from where they've pinned me. "Cassie, please, drink some water. Just a little and I'll leave you alone. You don't need to be stumbling around in this with all these horny pledges around." He gestures toward my outfit, pain etched in his forehead for reasons unbeknownst to me.

"I think she looks hot," Grayson says, grip tightening on my hip. "And I'm pretty sure I can handle any asshole who even thinks about touching her. And I do mean *any* asshole." With that last line he glares pointedly at Adam. Adam's jaw tenses and Grayson stands taller.

And now we're in a pissing contest.

"Grayson, can you grab me a cup of water from the kitchen? I'll meet you in there." I say the words softly, but it does nothing to pull his icy stare from Adam. Framing his face in my hands, I press my lips to his and make him look at me, instead. "I'm right behind you. Promise."

With that he relaxes, kissing me back with purpose before finally letting me go and making his way inside. When my eyes find Adam again, a sharp, tiny pang shoots through my chest. *Why is it so hard to breathe?*

"I'll grab a water, and then I need to get back to the table."

I make to turn, but Adam stops me, gripping both my arms in his rough hands. "Cassie, look at me." I don't. Tucking my hair behind my ear, I look down at my freshly manicured toes, instead. "Look. At. *Me*," he demands again, but the moment I do, I wish I wouldn't have. I've never had eyes look straight through me before. Adam takes a breath, one that takes mine with it, and then he says what we both know to be true.

"This isn't you."

Swallowing, I stand as straight as I can. "Don't act like you know who I am."

"Oh, but he does?" he gestures to where Grayson just disappeared in the crowd without taking his eyes off mine. "I call bullshit."

"Well, he doesn't confuse me."

"And I do?"

My ears fuzzy, I answer only the way an intoxicated, uninhibited girl can.

"No one confuses me more."

Adam's hands drop from my arms, and I watch as the number of questions in his eyes multiplies at my words.

"Goodnight, Adam."

With that, I spin on my heels and walk with shaky ankles into the house, wondering if it was the leather jacket or the alcohol that gave me the balls to say what I just did. Maybe it was both.

Or maybe I had just lost the resolve to hold it back any longer.

***

It's just after four in the morning by the time Grayson and I crash through the door of his dorm room, all tangled arms and heavy breaths. The alcohol still buzzing through me intensifies every touch, every kiss, and I try as hard as I can but I can't seem to take a full breath.

Grayson pulls me back to his room, pushing me against his door to close it behind us before dragging his tongue along the skin of my neck. I moan, tiny alarms sounding in my head to no avail — his touch is too loud for me to hear anything else.

Breaking from our kiss, Grayson leans his forehead against mine. "You are so sexy in that outfit," he breathes and my confidence disappears, a blush breaking on my cheeks. "But I bet you can't wait to change."

I laugh. "These pants are the worst."

Smirking, Grayson pushes off the door and yanks open the first drawer on his tall dresser, tossing me a pair of boxers and a t-shirt. Rolling the fabric in my hands, I chew my bottom lip, trying to decipher my next move. My hands trembling, I drop the clothes on the edge of his bed and slip out of my jacket, letting it fall to the floor where my eyes are fixed. Slowly, button by button, I undo my pants, finally finding the nerve to flick my eyes to Grayson. His blue pools are on my fingertips, nostrils flaring. When my hands find the hem of my crop top and I pull it up and over my head, my hair falling against my naked back, he pushes a long breath from his lips and squeezes his eyes shut.

"God, why do I have to be a gentleman?"

I pause, my voice just above a whisper. "What do you mean?"

Grayson opens his eyes just enough to grab the shirt and boxers on the bed and press them into my hands, covering my chest, though his hands hover there for a moment while he tries to steady his breathing. "Cassie, I want nothing more than to take you right now. Right here. In my bed, on this floor, in that shower..." he trails off, releasing his grip on the clothes to run a hand through his hair. "But you're drunk. I'm drunk. And I don't want my first time with you to be tainted with alcohol."

My first instinct is to be upset, but the way he's looking at me, blue eyes pained, heart beating hard enough for me to hear it — I know it's as hard for him to say no as it is for me to hear it.

"My bathroom is right there," he says, gesturing to the door behind me. "Get changed and then come back in here so I can hold you."

My heart leaps and I smile, stepping up on my toes to kiss him quickly before escaping to the bathroom. I don't catch my breath as I change, so when I join him again, crawling into his sheets as he turns down the lights, I feel like I may explode if he doesn't touch me.

As if he can sense it, Grayson pulls me into him, my back against his chest, and a flash memory of being in Adam's bed assaults me in the darkness. Twisting in his arms to face him, I shake the thought, focusing on the man with his arms around me, instead. We lie with our eyes locked, his fingers lazily tracing the hem of his boxers on my hip bone.

"I think I might really like you, Grayson Anderson," I whisper in the darkness.

He swallows, taking his hand from my hip just long enough to run it back through my hair and pull me in for a kiss. "Likewise, Cassie McBee."

And just like that, another player is added to the game.

Bear

My first thought is that it's hot as balls in my room.

Kicking the covers off, I blindly reach for my phone and squint through the sunlight filling my small room to peek at the time.

Two o'clock.

PM.

Mouth dry, I pull a pillow over my head to block out the light, groaning. When a small, warm body snuggles up next to me, my eyes fly open. Peeking under the pillow, I spot bright purple tendrils sprawled on my chest and I sigh, smiling, pulling Shawna in closer.

"Morning," she says, her voice hoarse.

I chuckle. "Morning."

"I stayed the night."

"You stayed the night."

She pauses for a moment, thinking, then plants a kiss on my chest. "I'm hungry."

I laugh just as my door swings open and Skyler bounds through.

"Scoot over," she says, crawling into bed on the other side of me before I have the chance to say otherwise. When she notices the other girl in the bed, she smiles, blue eyes bright. "Oh my God, you must be Shawna! I'm Skyler, Bear's Little. I've heard so much about you!"

"Same here, chica!"

"I brought bagels again," Skyler says, tossing the bag in my lap. I'm still trying to process the fact that I have two girls in my bed right now.

"You da real MVP," Shawna says, rummaging through it like a raccoon, hair a mess, mascara smeared from having my dick rammed down her throat last night.

Again, still processing here.

"How was the tournament?" I ask Skyler, propping my pillow up behind me.

"Long, but I won." She waggles her eyebrows and I throw her a high five. "More importantly, how was the fucking Fratalina Wine Mixer?! Tell me everything."

"Well, let's see." I rub my chin, the pieces of last night slowly coming together. "We had slap the bag tournaments. Ashlei and Bo actually won, believe it or not."

"Those girls can drink some wine."

"Indeed. And your Little showed up with that dude who bought her at the auction. She was dressed way differently than she usually is — all black, leather jacket, crazy makeup. Turned a lot of heads."

"*My* Little?"

"Yep."

"Cassie."

"Cassie."

Skyler chews on that for a moment. "Interesting."

"Yeah. Your boyfriend was here, too," I add, shifting a bit.

"Really? That's awesome. I was afraid he wouldn't come since I didn't."

"I think he enjoyed himself."

She smiles. "That's good."

What I don't tell her is that I didn't just see Adam. In fact, I had a pretty drunken heart-to-heart with him after seeing the scene between him and Cassie unfold. I don't know where the kid's head is at, but I know for fucking sure that I'm not going to sit back and watch him dick Skyler or Cassie around — and I told him that. He assured me he would never hurt either of them, but I could see it on his face — confusion. Adam Brooks is caught up in a game I'm not even sure he knows he's playing. By the time he left, I know I had his wheels spinning. I just hope he takes the time to think about what he wants right now.

"What about Ex?" Skyler asks as Shawna passes her the bagel bag, licking cream cheese spread off her fingers.

Focus, Bear.

"Yeah she was here for a while. She mostly hung around that dude from the auction."

"She's been weird lately. Distant. More controlling than normal."

I laugh. "Is that possible?"

Skyler shakes her head. "I wish I was joking."

The girls start talking about how Skyler got into poker and I take my opportunity to relieve myself. When I'm behind the bathroom door, I remember the interaction between Erin and me last night. She practically avoided me all night, which isn't anything out of the normal, really, but when we did end up in the same place and I tried talking to her, she teared up, running out of the room without so much as a word.

And she was worried about *me* after we hooked up.

There's a reason everyone calls her Ex.

I wash my hands and make my way back into my room, casually picking up the random trash from the night before. Skyler and Shawna are cuddled up, staring at something on Shawna's phone and laughing.

"Are you cleaning?" Shawna asks.

"Just picking up a little."

"Oh, can you put on a little apron?" Shawna sits up in bed, excited.

"Maybe use one of those little feather dusters?" Skyler adds.

"Yes! And talk with a French accent."

They high five and I just stand there gaping.

"Shit," I murmur, scrubbing my hands down my face. "I'm in real trouble with you two, aren't I?"

They both giggle and settle back into the sheets, their direction fixed on the phone again. I shake my head just as a loud knock sounds at the front door.

"No making out while I'm gone." I say pointedly, mostly to Skyler.

"No promises." She winks and Shawna holds up two fingers, lewdly waving her tongue between them.

Lord help me.

I can't quite shake that image from my head as I walk down the hall, but when I wade through the brothers sleeping on the floor and the trash spread everywhere and find Alec on the other side of the peep hole, my stomach drops.

Squinting at the sun as I open the door just a fraction, hoping to hide the mess inside from the one alumni who's managed to shut us down for half a semester, I force a smile.

"Hey, Alec. What brings you by?"

His jaw is set, mouth in a thin line, and it dawns on me that I probably don't want to know the answer to my own question.

"We need to talk."

Jess

I'm dying.

Death by sinus infection.

Rest in peace. And mounds of tissues.

When I woke up yesterday morning with a stiff jaw and heavy head, I knew I couldn't push off going to the doctor any longer. If my voice wasn't an indication that there was way too much mucus happening in my head, my puffy cheeks definitely were. So, after I helped Cassie channel her inner Christina Aguilera circa 2002, I dragged my snotty ass down to the health clinic and faced my verdict.

Severe sinus infection.

And, because my luck is just the best, I made it to the campus pharmacy six minutes after they'd closed for a *mid-semester celebration*, whatever the fuck that means. So not only did I have to miss the Fratalina Wine Mixer because I felt like shit, but I also couldn't even get the meds started to make me feel better.

Perfect.

But, finally, here I am — in line to pay for my antibiotics and a can of condensed soup so I can start getting my life back on track. Spring Break is in a week, and I'll be damned if I'm going to be a snot head in a bikini come then.

"Jess?"

Shit.

Shit shit shit.

I don't even want to turn around, but at this point, I'm busted. Moving slowly as if I'm in the presence of a poisonous snake, I force a smile, cringing simultaneously at the thought of what I look like right now just as Jarrett's face comes into view.

Pissed is an understatement.

I wait for him to yell, scream, ask me why the hell I've been ignoring him — but instead, his eyes rake over my body, catching on the pharmacy bag clutched in my right hand.

"You're sick."

I chew my lip in response and he blows out a breath, closing his eyes for a short moment before springing into action. Snatching the soup from my hand, he walks it back to its place on the shelf with me trailing behind.

"What are you doing?"

"You don't need to eat that processed shit if you're sick."

"It's just a sinus infection."

Setting the can back on the shelf with more force than necessary, Jarrett takes a breath before turning to face me. "Don't argue with me right now, Jess."

I swallow.

"I'm sorry I've been avoiding you."

"Is this why?" he asks, his expression pained.

"Mostly, yes."

"Mostly?"

Ugh, this is the last thing I want to do right now. I was so close to soup and Netflix.

Jarrett runs a hand over his bald head before grabbing my hand. "Come on."

"Where are we going?" I ask, not really minding as long as I can have this view of Jarrett's tight ass in the basketball shorts he's wearing.

"We're paying for your script, going to a real grocery store, and then back to my place."

"Wait," I interrupt, tugging my hand out of his grip. "Jarrett, I'm sick. I don't want to..." I trail off. How do I say this lightly?

Hey Jarrett, can we lay off the fucking until I can breathe through my nose again? Kay thanks.

"We're not going to," he says as we reach the counter, taking my script from my hand and plopping it down in front of the cashier. She's a student, probably a senior, with dead eyes that light up just marginally when she sees Jarrett.

"I don't understand."

Jarrett pays for my script and then grabs my hand again, leading me out the door without another word.

***

I've been in Jarrett's apartment several times — hell, it's practically the only place we can hook up outside of his truck or my car or some random public place. I've slept over, we've made breakfast together — but no matter what, it always began or ended with fucking each other senseless.

So being wrapped in his goose down comforter on his couch, homemade soup in hand while he finds a movie on Netflix and pulls me close to him, I'm a little uncomfortable.

My appetite has been virtually nonexistent for weeks now, but when I take the first bite of Jarrett's homemade potato soup, I moan at the creamy deliciousness.

"This is amazing," I mumble around my next bite. "Thank you."

"It's my mom's recipe."

I pause, spoon halfway to my mouth. "Really?"

He nods. "She, uh," he pauses, sniffing. "She gave me the recipe before she passed."

The air in his apartment takes on a heavier weight and it's too much to even hold my spoon up. Letting it drop back into the soup, I reach out and gently touch his arm. "I didn't know. I'm so sorry."

Jarrett covers my hand with his own and squeezes. "It's all good, I was young. She had cancer. Classic kid-with-a-dead-parent sob story."

I frown. "Don't be like that."

"Sorry. I'm fine, really. Honestly, I came to peace with my mom's death a long time ago. What I can't understand in this moment is why you've been ignoring me." His dark eyes are hard on mine. "You said it's *mostly* because you're sick. What else?"

I take another bite, mainly to buy myself another minute to think. "Well, remember how you fucked me into admitting I was jealous over Spencer?" He nods. "I, uh, I saw you two together. At Pie Heaven."

Jarrett sighs, rubbing his face. "I told you she's just my boss' daughter. We surfed that morning and grabbed lunch after."

I shake my head. "Stop. You don't need to explain yourself to me. I know we're not together, and that's why I've been avoiding you, because I shouldn't feel jealous over who I see you with, Jarrett. Jealousy is dangerous. It leads to more intense feelings."

He watches me carefully, chewing the inside of his cheek. "Come here."

"Ew, I'm so gross right now."

Jarrett fights a smile. "Jess, come here."

I'm hesitant, but eventually comply, setting my bowl on the coffee table and maneuvering until we're both lying on the couch spooning. Jarrett wraps his arms around me, tight, pulling me into him and kissing my bare shoulder. "You are the most stubborn woman I have ever met."

I snicker, pulling the blanket up under my chin. "How long before I chase you away?"

He's quiet for a moment, his free hand running through my hair, lulling me into a sedative state. "You can't chase someone who's not running."

My heart accelerates at his words, but before I have the chance to call him out, he pushes play on the remote and we fall into a comfortable silence.

And that's how the rest of the afternoon and night go. We cuddle, watch movies, talk, eat when necessary, and eventually crawl into bed around midnight. Jarrett tends to my every need, making sure I'm comfortable, bringing me my medication with a fresh glass of water when the time comes and making sure I eat. When he flicks off his bedroom light and slides into the sheets next to me, pulling me until I'm resting on his chest, and kisses my forehead sweetly, I feel it all press in around me.

I thought I would feel the fall. I thought I would crash on the cold hard ground and look around wondering what the hell happened. But the truth is, I fell slowly, softly — like a feather floating down, down, down into an undiscovered world.

And now, I'm scared there isn't an option to go back to the person I was before.

EPISODE 4

"It's Spring Break BITCHES!"

Adam

It's one of those perfect South Florida nights.

Skyler's hand is in mine, the wind blowing through her hair as we cruise around campus. She rented a hot yellow Ford Mustang convertible for Spring Break but asked me to break it in with her tonight first, and with the moon bright in the sky and Skyler's short skirt, I should be ecstatic. I should be thinking of all the ways I'll have her tangled up in the backseat once we put this car in park.

Instead, I'm thinking of the right words to break up with her.

The thought brings on another surge of nausea and I shift in my seat, pulling my hand from Skyler's grasp to grip the steering wheel. She doesn't seem to notice, just pulls out her cell phone and clicks through a few messages while her right hand surfs the air waves out the window.

I watch her for a moment, taking a silent inventory of all the things I'll miss — her electric blue eyes, her almost-too plump bottom lip I love to bite, her contagious laugh and easy banter. The list is long — too long — but the list of reasons we should end things ran out of paper a long time ago.

The semester is flying by, spiraling me faster and faster toward elections. If I want the presidency, now is crunch time. I only have a little over a month to prove why I deserve the position and Clay seems hell-bent on finding anyone but me to move in. I've barely had time for Skyler this semester and it's only going to get worse. It's not fair to her, and to be honest — I know she feels the same when it comes to her tournaments. Whether she's ready to admit it or not, she's not a small-time poker player anymore. People know her, she has a strong reputation forming and more and more tournaments piling up, which means less and less time for me.

The fact of the matter is that we're both young and we both have more we want to accomplish before we can give ourselves to anyone else.

The timing isn't right.

I've tried to ignore it, but Clinton all but handed my ass to me at the Fratalina Wine Mixer, telling me I needed to make a decision that was best for the both of us. He's right, I just hate admitting it. Add in the hot mess of confusion that is my relationship with Cassie and it all points to Disasterville. Still, I can't help feeling like I'm about to do something I'll regret later.

Sighing, I roll the volume knob between my finger and thumb until the car is silent but for the light wind. Skyler turns to me, smiling, and I run a hand through my hair.

"Sky, we need to talk."

"Well that's not ominous or anything," she jokes, kicking off her sandals and propping her feet up on the dash. "Let me guess — you want to break up?" She giggles, sticking her pink tongue between her teeth in a teasing manner. When I just grip the steering wheel tighter in response, my eyes fixed on the road ahead, Skyler's smile fades in my peripheral. "Holy shit. You do, don't you?"

"Honestly, not really."

"But?"

I cut the wheel right, steering us toward the small road that circles the campus lake as the realization of what's happening settles in my stomach. "But I think we both know the timing isn't right."

Skyler wets her lips, turning to the windshield. "We've both been avoiding this moment, haven't we?"

"I'm still kind of wishing I'd stuck with that plan."

She sighs, wrapping her arms around her thighs and resting her chin on her knees. "Do you have some big speech planned?"

I shake my head. "I'll skip the stuff you probably already know because you've been thinking it, too — like how I'm in line to be president and you're blowing up on the poker scene — and tell you what I think you probably don't already know." Pulling the car into a parking spot in front of the lake dock, I cut the engine, reveling in the silence as I turn to face her. "I like you. A lot, Skyler. More than I've liked any other girl since I've been at PSU. And if I was a selfish asshole, I would stay with you as long as I could and let the pressure and the bad timing slowly tear us apart. I'd make you feel like shit for blowing me off on Valentine's Day for a tournament and I'd make you sound needy for being upset that I skipped out on the auction for a fraternity meeting. I'd hold onto you and what we could potentially be even though I know it'd hurt us both in the long run." I lean down in her line of vision, lifting her chin so that my eyes catch her blue irises. "But the truth is that I care about you too much as a person to become your enemy when I know I could be your friend."

Skyler smiles, her hand folding over where mine is on her face as she leans into the touch. "I really like you, too." Laughing a little, she shakes her head, pulling my hand into hers. "I almost broke up with you the night of the auction."

"Really?"

She nods. "Yeah. Everything you've said is right and I saw it then just as clearly as we both see it now. Things are only going to get busier for both of us, and as much as we have fun together, I think we're at the point where if we don't stop the train now, we could land at a much more serious station than we ever intended on reaching."

I can't help but feel a small sense of relief. Skyler isn't the kind of girl to lose her shit, but I had no idea how she would react to any of this. Knowing that she feels the same way about everything stings just as much as it soothes.

"I still want to be friends. And not in the cliché, asshole way. In the legit way."

"Me too. And you're coming to Spring Break. Don't think you can get out of the trip just by breaking my heart."

"Breaking your — "

She laughs, cutting off my mild panic attack. "Kidding! I'm kidding, Adam." Her smile is wide, genuine. "But seriously, you're coming."

"Don't you think it'll be weird?"

"Not if you don't make it that way," she sasses, still grinning. "Besides, the cars and hotels and activities are already booked. It's two days away. You're coming."

"Well, not yet, but we could change that," I throw back, waggling my eyebrows. Skyler smacks me across the chest and rolls her eyes, but then she pauses, her stare leveling, a fire lighting. She bites her lower lip just slightly.

"Actually, I really wasn't kidding about breaking this bad boy in."

"We have, haven't we? I can drive around a while longer," I say, starting the car and checking the time on the dash. Skyler just keeps her eyes on me, wicked smile in place. When the intention behind her words sinks in, I shake my head at my slowness. "Wow. Can we pretend like I didn't just miss that cue and you still want to bang?"

"Ex sex is the best sex, right?"

"That's what they say."

Skyler raises the volume on the stereo as loud as it can go before leaning over the console, her lips finding mine for what may be the last time as a strong electronic dance beat courses through the small space of the car.

"Let's prove them right."

Erin

"Come on, just one hit," Landon coaxes me, waving the joint in front of my face, eyes low. His goofy grin is on full display, Ken doll hair styled, teeth almost too white against his tan skin.

Giggling, I push his arm away and twist the top off my water bottle. "Not tonight. I still need to pack and I don't want to forget something because I'm high," I lie. The truth is that I packed this morning. I've never smoked before and I certainly don't plan on trying it now. When you're high, you don't have full control of yourself — and I'm not letting that happen again.

"It's Spring Break, Ex!" He takes another pull before passing to his brother on the other couch. The Mu Beta Chi house isn't the top party house on campus, since that title is firmly held by Omega Chi Beta, but it is a strong contender. The Mu boys are known for their involvement in student government mostly, though they do throw pretty solid ragers. "At least have a beer. Or a fruity cocktail. I'll even make you a vodka water so you don't break the diet."

"I think the Chinese food we ate earlier kind of ruined that already," I point out, pulling my legs up on the cushion to sit Indian style and dodging the drink offer. Again, alcohol equals stupid decisions. I've learned my lesson.

In probably the most excruciating way.

"You can't say you didn't thoroughly enjoy teaching me how to use chopsticks."

"You were pretty adorable."

"Almost as adorable as you in that sundress," he says sweetly, kissing my cheek.

Landon has been nothing but a gentleman since our first date. He took me to coffee first, but not in the morning. Instead, he picked me up at nearly midnight, driving us to a swanky coffee shop downtown that stays open until 2:00 a.m. with live acoustic music. We spent the night talking, and for the first time since I made the most horrific choice of my life, I smiled. And laughed. And had a good time.

Since then, we've been to the beach together, studied in Greek library, and he even went shopping with me to pick out my Spring Break swimsuits — not that he found that a particularly boring date. He's picked up the bill at every event, and though I haven't let him move even a hair past first base, he seems content with what we have. He reminds me a lot of the men my mom read about in her historical romances. He takes his time, he's patient.

Still, I'm not naïve enough to think Landon is anything but a numbing device, a distraction, a flimsy umbrella fighting against the storm inside me. When I'm by myself, the storm rages so hard I feel every gust of wind all the way to my core. But Landon is almost always available, and he's the storm shelter - at least for now.

The Mu house is buzzing, filled with brothers and sorority girls kicking off the first night of Spring Break. Landon pulls my legs into his lap and absentmindedly rubs my calves as he and his brothers chat over the music. Tomorrow, most of us will go our separate ways, including Landon and me. I'll be headed to Key West with the Omega Chis while he jets north to Panama City Beach with his brothers and the Zetas.

The realization that I'll be spending a week in close proximity to Clinton is one I've been trying to grasp unsuccessfully. I can't for the life of me figure out why he makes me feel so out of control. I keep trying to convince myself my head is just messed up from what happened, because what else could it be? It's not like I *like* him. I mean, this is *Clinton* we're talking about. I mean sure, I invited him to semi-formal with me, but only because his fraternity was on lockdown. I was being nice. And yeah, his sex appeal was comparable to Chris Hemsworth with his Thor hammer that night and we had a good time, but we were drunk — wild — and things just happened. Neither of us wanted them to. It's all just some sort of twisted fluke.

Still, every time I see him, my body does weird things — things it hasn't done in what feels like forever — and I can't get a grip.

The alarm on my phone sounds and I silence it quickly, pulling my feet from Landon's grasp and standing. "That's my cue. Time to finish packing and help my sisters decide on bathing suits."

"Tough job," Landon mocks, pushing to his feet. He grabs my hand in his and walks me out the front door, pulling me into his hard body as soon as the fresh night air hits our skin. "Are you sure you don't want to stay a while longer? Kick Spring Break off the right way..." He trails off, his lips just barely brushing the skin of my neck.

Uncomfortable, I shrug away from him and pretend to be teasing. "You'll have plenty of girls on the beach more than willing to take you up on that offer."

"I'd rather wait for you," he whispers, tucking a strand of hair behind my ear. His smile is so kind, glass-like eyes sincere, and for some reason I believe him when he says he'd wait. Part of me feels awful for even letting him think he has a chance, because I know in my heart I'm nowhere near ready to sleep with another man — I may never be.

Some girls my age see accidental pregnancy as a curse, a mistake, a run of "bad luck". I see it as a privilege, one that I threw away so carelessly for selfish reasons. If I can ever find it in me to forgive myself, I'd still have to push past my fear of landing in the same situation again.

Nope, control is my only option.

"Goodnight, Landon," I say softly, lifting up on my toes to kiss his slightly-chapped lips.

"Want me to walk you?"

"I'll be okay. I like the time to think." I smile through one of the only true sentences I've uttered all night.

"Have fun, but not too much," he adds, winking.

"You too." With one last wave, I adjust my purse strap on my shoulder and start down Greek row toward the Kappa Kappa Beta house.

It only takes a few steps for the loneliness to sink in. The front door opens and closes behind me, letting the laughter and cheers escape for just a short moment before the silence of campus on Spring Break blankets me completely.

I listen to my sandals clack against my heel with each step, trying my best to keep the dark thoughts at bay, but like monsters they creep in through the night and settle in around me. In the past weeks, I've trained myself to choose numbness over feeling, having yet to shed a single tear or scream or sigh over what happened. It's in the past, I tell myself, and the only thing to do now is move on.

The Kappa Kappa Beta house is alive with laughter and music as I make my way up the hardwood stairs to my room. All the doors are propped open, sisters bouncing from room to room with bathing suits and bottles of alcohol in hand. Mom Cindy doesn't even bother checking on us tonight because she knows she'd have to suspend the whole chapter if she did.

Ashlei is in Bo and Cassie's room when I get to ours and I take what's likely to be the only alone time I get in the next week and slip into our bathroom, shutting the door behind me. My palms braced on the pearl white sink, I close my eyes and inhale deeply through my nose, steeling myself for the challenges coming my way. Splashing water on my face, I dab my eyes and cheeks dry with a fluffy yellow hand towel and catch my dark eyes in the mirror.

For the next week, I'll have to be around the father of a child I never gave birth to.

A sharp pang rolls through my stomach and I double over, my palms finding the sink again as I grit my teeth through the ache. I'm so disappointed with myself, so disgusted. It seems utterly impossible to move on from who I am in this moment.

I'm hoping Spring Break will help me get past this, but inside my heart I know the chance is slim. The truth is, there are some challenges we face in our lives that completely change us. We step into a moment in time as one person and emerge in new skin, with a new, slightly-battered heart that doesn't beat the same. I'm still getting used to my new self, and the only way I know how to deal is to exert power over everything I can. I'm unsteady, trying to find balance at the edge of a cliff I've never been on before.

I just hope I don't fall in the process.

Cassie

Jess and Skyler are still shoving the last bags in the trunk of Skyler's bright yellow convertible rental as Grayson's thumbs run the hem of my tank top. Jess takes four steps backward before running full speed at the car and jumping on the bags, which only makes her fall flat to the ground and the rest of us die laughing. Her blonde hair is splayed out on the pavement as she curses. When one of my makeup bags tumbles out and hits her square in the gut, Skyler doubles over, laughing so hard she can't breathe.

Turning in Grayson's arms, I thread my fingers together behind his neck and squint against the sun's rays into his bright blue eyes. "Are you sure you don't want to come? Save me from my sisters?"

He chuckles, sweeping my red locks to the side long enough to kiss my forehead. The heat from the sun mixed with the warmth of his touch is just enough to make a film of sweat gather on my forehead. "You're going to have an amazing time."

"I would have a better time if you were coming, too."

"I know, Cass, I know," he says with a sigh. Running a rough hand over his beard, he glares at the space behind me. "I wish I could. You know I have to work," he explains again, his hand gripping the back of his neck. "I don't really fit in with this crowd, anyway."

"What?" I ask, shaking my head slightly at his assumption. "Everyone loves you."

"Not everyone."

I pause as his eyes harden right along with his jaw. Following his line of sight, I find Adam, and his eyes flick down to the ground as soon as I do.

"He's just protective over me," I say with a shake of my head, turning and forcing Grayson's gaze to me again. "We're friends."

"That's not what he thinks."

I scoff. "Trust me — Adam is *well* aware that we are friends." *He put the title there first*, I want to say, but I don't.

"If you honestly think that, then your pretty green eyes are more closed than I thought."

My mouth snaps shut, my mind suddenly racing with what he sees that I don't. The last thing I want is for Grayson to feel like he needs to compete with Adam. This semester was supposed to be about leaving all that drama in last semester — Adam, Clay, all of it.

So, I'll prove to him that I mean what I say.

"Is he looking at us?"

Grayson looks up and nods. "Of course he is."

Smiling, I slide my hands up into his hair and pull him down to me, pressing my lips to his, pushing my hips forward. He stiffens slightly, but when I moan softly and slide my tongue inside his mouth, he breathes a sigh of relief and tightens his grip on my waist.

When I finally pull back, panting just slightly, I smile. "Good. Now he knows I'm yours."

Grayson grins, breathless, his forehead to mine just as Skyler calls out after me.

"Come on, Little! Key West awaits!"

Jess does some sort of banshee call and Erin, Ashlei, and Bo join in from where they've already piled into one of the huge buses the Omega Chis rented out. I giggle, kissing Grayson once more.

"I think the time has come."

Grayson watches as Skyler slides behind the wheel of the Mustang and Jess finds her place in the passenger seat, leaving my only option right next to Adam in the small backseat.

"Ugh, I hate this," he breathes, his hands gripping at my shirt as he pulls me as close as he can. "But I trust you."

"It's less than a week."

"Barely."

I smile, pulling him in for a long, heated kiss before finally backing away. Grayson holds my hand until it pops out of his grip and I turn, jogging toward the car and hopping into the backseat. When I'm settled next to Adam, I blow a kiss back to Grayson and he catches it, tucking that hand into his pocket and using his free hand to push his shades back down. I watch him, still mesmerized by the tattoos on his arms as they flex beneath the hot Florida sun.

"I think you found a winner there, Little," Skyler says, eying me in the rearview mirror.

"Me too," I agree, and I know it's true. Grayson came when I least expected him, when I had sworn off boys completely, and every day with him since then has been amazing.

As we pull out of the Kappa Kappa Beta driveway, a string of cars, vans, and buses, horns blaring, voices cheering, I keep my eyes fixed on Grayson until we turn the corner out of campus and he fades from view. Flipping back around in my seat with a sigh and a smile, I type out a text to him on my phone, telling him once more how much I'll miss him.

"It's Spring Break, bitches!" Jess screams, blasting the music at the highest volume. Skyler lets her head fall back with a loud battle cry and Adam laughs, nudging me. When I don't move, partly from the unwanted shock of his skin on mine, he grabs my wrist and throws my hand into the air, waving it around with his own. My eyes are still trained on him, his dark eyes hidden behind black Ray Bans, hair disheveled and blowing in the wind, white t-shirt hot against his blazing tan arms. He joins in with the screaming, moving my arm more frantically, and I can't help it, I burst out laughing and thrust my other arm into the air with a yell, which makes all of them hoot louder.

It's Spring Break.

It's my *first* Spring Break.

And something tells me the KKB girls are about to take me on the ride of my life.

***

It's only about a five hour drive from Palm South University to Key West. The first little bit is highway, but then it turns into the two-lane US 1 that runs all the way down the Keys. Skyler and Jess traded spots with Adam and me in Key Largo and passed out soon after, the long night of packing finally getting the best of them. This was after copious amounts of Backstreet Boys, Spice Girls, and Britney Spears, of course. Still, sleep caught up with them in the end.

I, on the other hand, am wide awake — mesmerized by the bright blue and sea green water surrounding both sides of the highway as we drive. Adam is drumming his right thumb on the steering wheel while the left rests comfortably on the door, a wide grin on his face.

I've been to the beach plenty of times since my move to Florida for school, but this is the first time I've seen water this clear — this beautiful. It never gets old. Every clearing of trees exposes a new patch of bright water that I can't keep my eyes off or capture with my camera phone.

"So, how awkward is this? Be honest." Adam rolls the dial between his fingers until the music is only playing softly. I turn to the backseat, expecting it to be Skyler or Jess he's speaking to, but they're both passed out — Jess's head on Skyler's shoulder while Skyler leans hers back against the seat. Both of them have sunglasses on and headphones in, their music now louder than the tune coming from the Mustang speakers.

Is he really asking me to rate the awkwardness of being in the same car with him after what happened at the Fratalina Wine Mixer?

What's the correct number for somewhere between *conversation with old, distant relatives* and *waving back at someone who wasn't really waving at you in the first place*?

"What do you mean?" I ask, facing Adam again.

He shifts to hold the steering wheel with his left hand and drops the right to the console between us. "I don't know. I mean, she begged me to still come — swore it wouldn't be weird — and I guess I'm the only one making it that way. It's just like the closer we get to Key West, the more I wish I would have fought her on it."

Blinking, I push my sunglasses up into my wind-blown hair. "What are you talking about?"

"Me and Skyler?"

"What about you and Skyler?"

"She didn't tell you?"

My frustration climbs and I huff. "Tell me what?!"

Adam laughs a little, shaking his head. "Sorry, I just figured she would have by now." His smile fades. "We broke up the other night."

I try not to let the words slam into me. I try to run from them, brace for them, take them as a small wave — but they crash into me all at once. "Oh."

He runs his right hand through his hair, his shaded eyes still on the road ahead. "Yeah."

"I'm sorry."

"Don't be. We both agreed it was best."

I don't know why I have no idea what to say. There are millions of words out there, yet all I can do is face the windshield again and mutter the same one. "Oh."

Adam chews his cheek, silent for a moment. I almost reach for the radio dial when he speaks again. "Listen, I'm sorry about the party. I shouldn't have tried to tell you what to do. I learned my lesson on that last semester at semi-formal," he adds with a chuckle, and I blink at the thought of him warning me about Clay that night. I didn't listen to him then, and he ended up being right. "I don't know, I just saw how drunk you were and I've never seen you like that before. I was worried. And I know you're with Grayson and he can take care of you. I was out of line." He turns to me for just a moment and I scan his face, looking for a hint of jealousy, a molecule of dishonesty. I don't find either. "I was. I admit it. And I'm sorry."

"It's okay," I breathe, just barely over the music. I watch as he finally takes a breath.

"Can we just start over?"

I laugh. "You're so cliché."

"I'm serious." His hand finds mine and he gives it a firm squeeze — a friendly squeeze — but for some reason my heart still stammers. "I really do care about you, Cassie. I just want to be there for you, however you need me to be. And I'm sorry I ever... I'm sorry I confuse you." His tongue jets out to wet his lips just as one of the Omega Chi vans speeds around us. I let my eyes follow it just so I have somewhere — anywhere — to look other than at Adam. I almost forgot I admitted to Adam that he confuses me. *Stupid alcohol.* "I never intended to. For what it's worth."

"Gah," Jess yelps as she wakes, startling us all. "I need to piss and then we need to crack some roadies."

"Oh my God, J-Love," Skyler smacks her. "You scared the shit out of me!"

Adam drops my hand and I pull it into my lap, the skin still hot from his.

We pull into a gas station a few minutes later and as the girls climb out of the car and head inside, I stop Adam, holding him back.

"I agree."

"You agree?"

I nod, though I'm not entirely sure what I'm doing. "Let's start over."

He smiles, one of those dazzling smiles that makes it hard to breathe. "I think it's time for our first shot of Spring Break." Jumping out, Adam pops open the trunk and digs around before retrieving a small bottle of Jack. "If I remember right, you like whiskey." He winks and my cheeks heat, memories of the Fratalina Wine Mixer hitting me.

Adam rips open one of the packs of red plastic cups and pours us each a shot.

"What are we toasting to?"

He fixes his gaze on the console between us, tasting the words he's about to speak before lifting his eyes to mine. "To a second chance — for a boy who didn't deserve the first one." He offers a weak, half-smile. "And to the girl sweet enough to give it to him."

Our plastic cups click together as his eyes pin me, purpose in their gaze, and we lift the liquid to our lips. It burns on the way down, and I can't help but think it isn't the only thing.

"We come bearing snacks!" Skyler yells as she and Jess fly through the small gas station's doors, multiple white plastic bags swinging from their arms. We all pile back into the car as they pass around chips, candy, and drinks. Skyler and Jess both pop open Bud Lights but I pass, the whiskey is still settling in my stomach as Adam pulls back onto US 1.

He called me sweet.

But I think *stupid* might be the more accurate term.

Skyler

"Oh fuck yes, I see a pool!" Jess yells as we all pile through the door of the suites we booked, bags over our shoulders and sweat already gathering on the backs of our necks. She scoots past me and jogs up the stairs to where the two bedrooms are, no doubt taking claim to whichever room has the largest bed. I just smile, dropping my bags to the floor and immediately hooking up my iPhone speaker. Turning on my Avicii radio station, I pump up the volume and finally take in the surroundings.

Cassie and Adam are slowly making their way up the stairs where Jess is and I take the opportunity to check out the kitchen. It's full service — dishes and cooking utensils stocked — with a bar area and a dining room table set. The living room connects and everything is decorated just like a Key West suite should be — bright coral couches, light aqua-blue rugs and accents, beachy paintings hung on the wall, bamboo and light wood finishes. There's a sliding glass door that leads out to a back patio area, complete with a small hot tub that I'm sure will be occupied at the end of the night.

Slinging my bags back over my shoulders, I make my way upstairs and toss them into the room where Jess has set up camp.

"So, what's the sitch?" I ask, wiping the sheen from my forehead. Jess is spread out on the king size, pillow-top bed with a huge grin on her face. The bedrooms seem to embody the same beachy-vibe from downstairs, paintings and all. There's a huge mirror just above the master bedroom bed and I stare at my reflection. "Side note — I totally want to watch someone bang me in that mirror."

"Well, obviously you and I are in here. So I mean if you want to swing that way for a night, I'm totally down." She smirks and I cross my arms, rolling my eyes. "It's a king, so we can fit one more."

"Dibs!" Erin yells behind me and I jump. The Omega Chi bus must have arrived.

I chuckle. "Okay, well that's figured out."

"I'm calling the other room, then," Cassie says, propping herself against the doorframe and thumbing over her shoulder. Everyone's eyes fall to Adam standing behind her then.

"Uh, I can sleep on the couch." He rubs the back of his neck and offers a shy grin. I hate it, because I know he feels awkward, and as much as I swore it wouldn't be — I think everyone feels like it's a little weird that he's here.

"Actually, can we take the couch?" Ashlei asks, rounding the corner from the stairs, her wind-blown hair tossed into a messy bun. Bo is just behind her. "It folds out, so it would make sense that two people sleep there. And we don't mind."

"There we go. All settled. Adam, you can just crash in the other room with my Little." I smile, clapping my hands together as Adam and Cassie exchange glances. I know they go to breakfast sometimes and they seem to get along, so it shouldn't be too strange for them to sleep together. Definitely better her than me. "And now — we drink!"

Everyone cheers and we funnel down the stairs and into the kitchen, retrieving alcohol, cups, ice, and everything else we grabbed at the grocery store on our way to check in.

"Wait! I made us something," Erin says, heaving one of her bags onto the dining room table. It's a glass top, and whatever is inside her bag settles with a clink. When she unzips it and pulls out the first Bubba Keg, bedazzled with jewels and her name, I can't help but smile. My Big is one of the most thoughtful people I know, and any chance she has to make her sisters feel special, she takes.

"These ought to keep our drinks cold on the beach," she says, passing them around. Bubba Kegs are essentially giant mugs that keep cold beverages chilled and hot beverages warmed. For our purposes, they'll play home to our mixed drinks under the Key West sun. Each one is decorated with personal flair, including poker chips and dollar signs for me and glittery curse words for Jess. They're huge — holding about seventy-two ounces — and they're thermos-style with a silver middle and different colored tops and bottoms. Perfect for beach day drinking.

"Well shit, I made something, too. Hang on." Jess runs up the stairs while the rest of us fill our cups with our liquor of choice. When she rounds the corner again, she starts hurling neon balls of cloth at our heads. Cassie tries but fails to snatch hers out of the air, so it wraps around her face and falls to the floor as we all laugh. "Suit up, bitches!"

I catch the one she throws at me and unfold it, my eyes scanning the bold black letters on the neon yellow tank top.

OUTRAGEOUS? ALWAYS. OUT RAGE US? NEVER.

"Fucking right," Ashlei says. "We're wearing these tonight. All of us."

"Wait! Can't forget these," Bo adds, passing around the custom trucker-style snapbacks to match. They're all black with bright neon letters that read **KKB.**

"Hold on a second, did you two coordinate these?" I ask, adjusting the back of my hat and throwing it on backward.

Bo nods, smiling at Jess. "It was a Big/Little bonding sesh."

"The idea was hers," Jess adds, tossing her tank top over her shoulder. "Clearly. We all know I'm not that thoughtful."

Everyone laughs and once Jess and Bo finish filling up their cups, we cheers them together.

"Time to fuck Key West up, ladies." Jess turns to Adam. "And gentleman."

Chuckling, Adam shoves his free hand into his pocket and shakes his head. "I'm a little scared for my life."

"As you should be," I add with a wink. "Let's do this!" We clink our glasses together and throw back the first drink of Spring Break, dance music filling the room around us, our skin already sun kissed from the drive down.

And then, it begins.

***

I've never been to Key West before, but less than an hour on Duval Street and I already never want to leave. This place is *alive*. Every bar is packed, students from campuses all over the nation spilling out onto the streets, drinks in hand. The music is loud, the personalities colorful, the feeling — wild. These are the future business men and women, parents, doctors, lawyers, dropouts, travelers, teachers — but tonight, we're just young.

We started our night at Fat Tuesday, filling our Bubba Kegs with frozen deliciousness and an extra shot to kick off the night right. We managed to run into Clinton and some of his brothers there and now we're all cramming our way into the Coyote Ugly bar. Jess and Erin are hand in hand, arms swinging, voices carrying the tune of a popular country song as they head straight for the bathrooms. Breaking the seal, already.

"We're heading to Irish Kevin's right after this," Clinton says, pointing his finger in my face as he slides by. "Car bombs, baby!" We high-five as he continues down the bar with his brothers, nearly all of them dressed in the same white frat tank. **Omega Chi Wasted** is in bold letters like a dictionary entry, complete with the definition*: intoxication level – attempted by many, reached only by the elite.*

"You know what I love about these hats?" my Little asks me as we slide up to the bar. "They hide the effects of drinking in Florida." She lifts the snapback, revealing her crazy, slightly damp red hair underneath it. I laugh and tip mine up, showing the same hot mess beneath.

"And they're perfect for selfies," I add, pulling my phone from my pocket. I slide the camera icon up and flip the lens, my cheek touching Cassie's as I push the shutter button.

"Love it!"

"We need one with the whole group," I say, looking around for someone I could flirt into taking the photo for us.

"I can take that for you," a southern voice twangs from behind me. When I turn, ready to hand my phone to a stranger, I stop mid-pass. Key West is crawling with attractive men right now, especially fraternity brothers, but this one just might take the cake. His dark blonde hair is hidden beneath an orange University of Tennessee hat, his teal-green eyes bright even in the dark bar. The first thing I notice is how his smile is almost too big for his face, but in the most charming way. His jaw is wide-set, his face clean-shaven, his body thin but toned. I don't even care that he's watching as my eyes scan him from head to toe and back up again.

"Go Vols," I say, cocking a brow and finally handing him my phone. Then, I turn back to the bar and shout out, "Get together, everyone!"

We're all a little past drunk at this point, so it takes a minute to get everyone paying attention and lined up in a way that doesn't hide any faces. Hot Tennessee Guy takes several pictures, of which I'm sure only one is social media appropriate, before we all disperse and he slides the phone back into my hand.

"I'm Trevor," he says, holding the phone between our hands for a moment.

"Trevor from Tenneesee."

He nods, blushing slightly. I can't stop staring at his All-American features.

"Skyler, from Florida."

Trevor releases my hand and crosses his arms over his chest, his glorious arm muscles on full display. "You're a little far from home, huh?"

I chuckle. "A whole five hours."

"Well, I guess I'm lucky you decided to stay in your home state for Spring Break."

"Who said you're getting lucky?" I ask, crossing my arms to mirror him.

He shrugs. "The universe. When I happened to walk through that door over there as soon as you started scanning the room for trouble."

"I see. So, Trevor, the trouble from Tennessee, what now?"

"Now," he says, voice thick with a southern accent as he takes his place at the bar next to me. "I buy you a shot."

A smile finds my lips just as Ashlei hops up on the bar behind Trevor. I shout out her name, beating my fists on the bar, and everyone else joins in once they realize what's happening. The coyote girls are inviting other girls up on the bar to join them for a dance, but when *Pour Some Sugar On Me* starts playing and Ashlei whips out moves that put every single other girl to shame, all of our jaws drop. She's owning the hairography, dropping down to her knees on the bar and crawling across it, even going as far as kissing Bo for show. The guys, of course, go absolutely ape shit at that. When she bites her bottom lip, swollen from her kiss with Bo, and turns around to twerk, the entire bar erupts in a frenzy. All I can do is shake my head — that girl is full of surprises.

"Looks like you found the sexiest girls in Key West," a guy says to Trevor with a similar accent, clapping him on the back. I assume it's one of his brothers, especially as more of them filter in around us.

"You read my mind," Trevor agrees, holding out a liquid cocaine shot to me. I take it between my fingers with a wink before turning back to my sisters.

"Hey KKB! This handsome man just bought me a shot!"

All of my sisters in the bar cry out before starting a low, rumbling "Ohhh" that stretches out into the beginning of one of our chants.

Take a shot, take a shot, take a goddamn shot!
If you can't take a shot like a KKB can,
Then you shouldn't have a fucking shot in your hand!
Take a shot, take a shot, take a goddamn shot!

Everyone cheers and Trevor and I knock back the Jager and Bicardi 151 concoction. When we slam the glasses back on the bar, I use my thumb to wipe my bottom lip, my eyes finding his brothers all gaping behind him.

"Buckle up, boys."

Jess

I fucking love Spring Break.

As I guzzle down my second Flabongo in nothing but a cheeky, hot pink pair of bikini bottoms and black strapless top, I remember what all the dieting and gym time was for. In a way, I guess it's kind of a blessing that I've been sick the past couple of weeks. I feel completely back to my old self now, though, and I clear my bong well before the Omega Chi pledge opposite me. He's still struggling, holding the plastic Flamingo upside down trying to guzzle the beer inside it through the opening at the mouth while I'm passing mine off to the next contender. When his brothers start shoving him, teasing, I just wink and wipe my mouth with the back of my hand.

"Nice try, champ."

He grins, his dark eyes scanning me slowly. They remind me a little of Jarrett's, except this kid can't be much older than nineteen and therefore his eyes are missing that bit of confidence — the assurance of a good time. He's scrawny, cute, but just not Jarrett.

The sun is hot on my shoulders, no cloud cover to shield the rays, and I wiggle my toes in the hot sand as I make my way through the tents set up on Smathers Beach. There are students from all over the nation here for Spring Break and each tent has a university, fraternity, or sorority flag flying high. My eyes drift from the chaos to the bright blue, almost aqua water and I sigh, wishing more than before that Jarrett was here.

If this were any other Spring Break, I would have at least made out with five guys by now. There are so many eyes on me, so many easy targets, and yet I don't feel compelled to aim my dart at a single one. I almost want to take a frat daddy back to our suite just to prove to myself that I can, but then I think about Jarrett, and the truth comes to light — I can't.

Not now that I've had him.

"Hey sexy," Skyler says, words slurring slightly as she smacks my ass. Her all black sunglasses reflect my messy bun and the bright water backdrop behind me. I smile, eying her brand new, bright coral and rhinestoned bikini. She's catching a tan quickly, which makes it seem even more electric against her skin. "Tell me this isn't the best Spring Break ever."

"It's pretty epic so far," I agree, though I know something that would make it better. Or rather, some*one*.

"I'm hungry."

"Let's get some street meat," I say, hooking my arm in hers and steering us toward the hot dog stand set up on the other side of the boardwalk.

Skyler scrunches her nose, leaning her weight on me. "That sounds dangerous."

"There's only like a forty percent chance you'll get food poisoning."

"Well when you put it like that... YOLO!"

My eyes scan the beach where our crew set up camp, stopping abruptly when I find Ashlei and Bo cuddled up on a blanket together. They're sitting shoulder to shoulder, legs tangled, laughing. Ashlei occasionally plays with Bo's short hair and Bo lazily runs her fingers along Ashlei's freshly tan leg.

"I can't fucking hold this in anymore," I say suddenly, pulling Skyler to a halt just before the sand meets boardwalk. My hand flies up in the direction of Ashlei and Bo. "Sky. They're fucking. Look at them."

Skyler's eyes follow my hand and she blanches. "Cassie and Adam?"

I frown, noticing Adam and Cassie leaned over Adam's phone on the other side of the girls. Adam's hand is resting casually on Cassie's lower back and her cheeks are flushed, probably more from the heat and her day drinking buzz than him touching her. From what I can tell, it looks like they're laughing at a cat video or something else equally uneventful. Cassie is about as prude as they come and Adam is still up Skyler's ass as far as I'm concerned, no matter how he tries to deny it.

"Oh please," I say, rolling my eyes and grabbing Skyler's jaw in my hands. I squish her cheeks together and steer her eyesight toward Ashlei and Bo, who are now leaning so close I'm almost positive they're going to kiss. "Those two."

"Ashlei? And your Little?" Skyler's brows shoot up. "No... you think? I mean they hang out a lot, but wouldn't we know if they were... well... you know?"

"Skyler. *Look* at them."

She does, even taking the effort to lift her sunglasses over her wavy brown locks for a minute. She has drunk eyes to the max – slightly smeared mascara, glassy surface – but I know she still sees it.

"Shit," she murmurs, flicking her sunglasses back down.

"Yeah."

I grab her by the elbow and drag her toward the hot dog stand. "I saw them kiss at semi-formal."

"What?!"

I nod. "I didn't tell anyone because I thought it was a fluke – a drunken kiss or something. I mean, shit, you and I have shared a few of those."

"True. I saw Ashlei kiss her on the bar last night, but I thought it was just for show."

"Maybe. But I've been seeing them together all the time, always touching, always sneaking off," I add just as we reach the food stand. Skyler crosses her arms and eyes the menu. "I don't care. I mean seriously, I don't. But why won't they just fucking tell us?"

"I don't think it's that easy, J-Love," she says before leaning into the window of the food cart. "I'll just take a hot dog and French fries, please." She glances back at me. "Want anything?"

I shake my head.

"Anything to drink?" The man inside asks. He's short, balding, light blue t-shirt covered with grease. Every inch of his exposed skin is tan and leathery, but I guess you can't live in Key West and *not* be tan.

Skyler chuckles. "I think we've got the drinks covered."

The man eyes the rowdy scene behind us and nods, taking Skyler's wet cash. "Ain't that some true shit."

He ducks back inside and I chew my lip, still not wanting to let the subject go. "Look, Bo is my Little. She knows I'll understand. And Lei is one of my best friends! It just doesn't make sense."

"Do you know one other girl in our sorority who's a lesbian?"

I scoff. "I can think of at least three."

"*Openly*," Skyler adds, rolling her eyes. "Think about it. It's not something you see often in Greek life, especially not at Palm South. Maybe they're just taking their time. Or maybe they want to see if it's serious before they say anything." She shrugs just as too-tan man hands her a small cardboard box with her food. "Or, maybe, there's nothing to tell. They could just be friends, Jess."

"I highly doubt that," I grumble, snatching one of her French fries and popping it in my mouth.

She chuckles. "Just chill. If they are together, they'll tell us – when *they're* ready."

I'm still not satisfied, but I let out a long breath, conceding for the moment. "Fine."

Skyler looks proud. "Great. Now that we've got that out of the way..." she trails off, her tiny hand cupping the rather large hot dog out of her box. "Wanna suck my wiener?"

"I'd rather bite it."

"Oh, feisty!" Skyler waves the encased meat in my face. "Okay, fine. I'll let you eat my wiener."

"I bet you'd rather I eat something else, you cheeky bitch."

"Hey, don't post an offer you can't come through with." Skyler winks just as our feet reach sand again and someone chokes behind us. When we turn, two guys with pasty-white skin and University of Kansas tank tops on are staring wide-eyed right back at us.

Stealing Skyler's hot dog, I carefully take nearly half of it in my mouth and bite slowly, letting my eyes flutter back. "Mmmm... so tasty," I mumble around the mouthful.

The guys swallow, eyes shifting from me to each other before they scurry off.

Skyler bursts out laughing. "Oh my God, they're going to have nightmares."

"Or wet dreams," I combat, sucking ketchup off my index finger.

"You're such a bitch. I really am hungry," she pouts, inspecting what's left of her street meat.

"We can sixty-nine if you want?"

She shoves me just as we reach our spot on the beach and I fall easily into my lounge chair, still laughing and stealing another French fry on my way down.

"I love you," I coo, blowing drunken kissy faces at her.

Skyler eyes me, fighting back a smile. It's moments like these when I realize that maybe it doesn't matter who's hiding what. It's not about my future with or without Jarrett, my tests next week, or the career path I should probably be shaping. Sometimes it's just about living in the moment with your sisters. It's about being young, and silly, and wild and carefree.

With a content sigh, I lean back in my chair and let the sun rays soak in, lifting my freshly filled Bubba Keg cup to my lips and tasting the fruity cocktail inside.

It's good to be a KKB.

Bear

"Car bombs!" Matt, the president of Omega Chi, yells as we burst through the open doors of Irish Kevin's. Skyler and her sisters weave past us and make their way to the front of the stage where a small band is set up. They're doing covers of popular songs and taking requests in the form of cold hard cash, and Skyler is the first to pull out a twenty.

She waves it in the air and calls out, "*Sweet Caroline*!" The bar cheers and the tall, lanky guy behind the mic starts flirting with her as she drops it in the jar. When he takes note of all her sisters filing in around her, I just shake my head.

He has no idea what he's in for.

"I can't believe so many of us are still hanging in after day drinking at Smathers all day," I say to Matt as we slide up to the bar. The bartender is already pouring up our car bombs.

"Shit, you know how it is when Omega Chi and KKB get together."

"Fucking insanity?"

He waggles his eyebrows, handing me a car bomb and tipping his toward me. "Damn straight."

Matt's sporting a sunburn along with the rest of us, though his shows as lobster red and mine as dark chocolate. The tightness of my skin only reminds me what a kick ass day it was as we drop the shot of Bailey's into our mugs of Guinness and chug. Slamming them back down on the bar, Matt throws me a high five and wades through the crowd to where Skyler is. Poor guy, he's been trying since we got here to move in on her since she's not with Adam anymore. The thing is, I don't think she plans on giving Matt another round in her bed — especially not with literally thousands of other choices on Duval Street.

I whip out my phone to check for texts from Shawna, frowning when the screen is blank. We were writing back and forth all day today, but she stopped responding a few hours ago, making me realize just how much I wish I would have dragged her ass with me. Trying not to dwell on it, I tuck my phone back in my pocket and lean against the bar. When I notice Erin a few barstools down, eyes low as she watches the rest of her sisters in front of the stage, I pay the bartender for two beers and slide down next to her.

"You should go join them," I shout over the band singing *Wagon Wheel*. Erin's eyes flick to mine, her brows pinching together before she turns away again. Her makeup is flawless, her dark blonde hair pin straight beneath the snapback she and her sisters are all wearing. On the outside she seems put together and fine, but all it took was that one second of looking into her eyes for me to know she's not. I already feel like walking over to her was a mistake.

"I'm just hanging back for now," she says softly, forcing a smile. "How are you, Bear?"

"Fan-flipping-tastic. Here," I say, thrusting the beer I've yet to drink from toward her. "Special delivery."

She eyes the glass in my hand, readjusting to lean her opposite elbow back on the bar. It's then that I notice she's shaking slightly. I internally groan, cursing myself for thinking she would be able to keep it cool after our hook up last semester. I still don't even know how that shit happened, but Erin clearly can't let it go. It's like she thinks I'm going to jump on stage, steal the mic from the band and shout out to everyone that we fucked like porn stars in the KKB house.

"Thanks, but I'm not really… I don't want to drink." Her honey eyes find mine as she tucks a strand of hair behind her ear. "I tend to lose control when I do."

Pursing my lips together, I fight the urge to roll my eyes and shrug, instead. The girl is fucking ridiculous. "Whatever you say, peach. More for me." I tip back the glass I was holding out for her and drain it, popping it back onto the bar next to her.

"Bear!" Skyler bounds toward us, an infectious grin on her face. "I have a surprise for you." She drags out the last word, her buzz clearly still in effect.

"I feel like I should run."

She laughs, grabbing me by the wrist and dragging me through the bar back to Duval Street. "Trust me. You're going to *love* this surprise."

I follow her, my eyes on the neon KKB letters on the back of her hat as she steers us through the crowd. When she finally tugs me out into the warm night air, she drops my wrist and plants her hands on her hips, victorious smile still intact.

"Why are you grinning like you shit in my bed?"

Skyler just wrinkles her nose, but then her eyes jet to the space behind me. I barely have time to turn around before I'm tackled. I hold the offender tight as their legs wrap around me, and that's all it takes for me to realize who it is.

I'd know those legs anywhere.

"Surprise!" Skyler yells behind me as I grip Shawna tighter, inhaling the floral scent of her black and purple locks. She squeezes me tight in return until I drop her gently to her feet.

"What the hell are you doing here?"

She shrugs, tucking her hands into the pockets of her tiny ripped jean shorts. "I got tired of texting you, so I called Skyler and she told me where you're staying and helped me set this up. Hope you don't mind me crashing your bed."

She winks and I pull her under my arm, kissing her temple before whispering in her ear. "As long as you don't plan on getting any sleep, I think we'll be fine."

Shawna shivers under my touch and I grin against the skin of her neck.

"Uh, okay, looks like my job here is done. Have fun, you two!" Skyler quickly hugs Shawna and steps up on her toes long enough to kiss my cheek before skipping back inside, her beachy waves swinging behind her.

"Should we head in?" Shawna asks, thumb pointed toward the bar.

"I have a better idea."

***

Shawna is still blushing as we wander the empty streets of Key West, dawn just within reach. She's not exactly one who blushes lightly, but I kind of like the way the rosiness sets on her cheeks. I'm not sure if she's blushing from the heat we built up dancing or the fact that we just stripped down to our Birthday Suits and partied with a bunch of old naked men and women in the Garden of Eden.

Either way, I like that I put that blush there.

"I cannot believe we just did that," she breathes, still giggling. "I will never get helicockter guy out of my head."

"Hey! That's the best part about having a dick," I defend, swinging my hips to mimic the motion of the skinny sixty-year old biker from the bar. The Garden of Eden is a rooftop bar above a country bar on Duval Street and it's clothing optional. There are no phones or cameras allowed, but it still took three shots to get either one of us comfortable enough to take our clothes off. We were the hottest people there, and as soon as we lost our underwear, all the attention was on us. I expected Shawna to be shy or embarrassed, but she danced with me and flaunted her shit in front of everyone like she was the most confident woman on earth.

I'm starting to think she might actually be.

Shawna rolls her eyes and shoves me but I bounce back, pulling her under my arm. She sighs, content in my grasp. The night air has cooled down significantly, blanketing our hot skin in a relieving reprieve.

"What a wild place."

I nod, taking in the brightly colored houses on either side of the street. We're not really walking anywhere, just strolling, and we're the only ones left, it seems. Occasionally, a cab will blow buy, rowdy Spring Breakers hanging out the windows, but for the most part it's just us. "It's amazing." I kiss her temple, smiling down at her bright green eyes. "Even better now that you're here."

She's quiet for a moment, and we fall into a rhythm, her sandals and my Jordan's thumping the pavement with each step.

"You know, when we first started hooking up, I thought that's all you'd be to me," Shawna says, wrapping her arm around my waist and hooking her finger into my belt loop. "It made sense. You were hot, we had amazing sex, and it was fun." She shrugs. "But I didn't expect you to be a great listener. Or a protective friend. Or an amazing big brother. It's like everything I never thought I'd feel with you actually came easily — effortlessly, without even thinking about it." She smiles softly, biting her lower lip as her eyes stay fixed on her feet. "Somewhere along the way, I think I started falling for you."

My throat constricts at her words, the darkness of night just before dawn surrounding me. I swallow, wondering why I'm not laughing, or shaking my head, or planning my escape route. I never wanted anything serious with Shawna, and even now, it feels like a bad idea. But the truth is, I think I'm falling for her, too.

I halt, pulling Shawna into my arms. She wraps hers around my neck, eyes fierce as she stares up at me, not the least bit ashamed of what she just admitted out loud.

"Me too," I say simply.

She smiles, the black frames of her glasses lifting on her cheeks. "I really want you to nail me on the beach."

I choke out a laugh, snaking my hand up to brush one of her purple locks aside. "Hmm... I could possibly be persuaded to oblige."

Shawna's eyes sparkle as she lifts up on her toes, pressing her lips to mine. I pull her into me, hands gripping her shirt at the hem, slipping my tongue inside her mouth only to be rewarded with a moan.

We're all hands and lips as we stumble our way onto a private beach of a hotel, breaking contact just long enough to jump a fence or strip off clothing before collapsing into a beach cabana bed. The soft blue hue of morning battles with the dark night just as I sink inside her, her nails dragging down my sunburned back. I hiss at the sensation and she takes my mouth with hers. When she flips us over, her hips straddling mine, I watch with fascination as bright pinks and oranges light the sky behind her arching back.

By the time the sun breaks its kiss with the horizon, we're completely spent, skin slick, legs tangled. And for a while it's just the sound of our breathing and the waves on the shore that exist in the world. Shawna falls asleep on my chest and I let her rest for a while, knowing I'll have to wake her soon before we're caught. A strange emotion washes over me, one I've never felt but don't feel compelled to fight.

With my fingers in her hair and my heart on my sleeve, I let myself fall a little further.

Ashlei

I thought doing cocaine would be the highest high I would ever feel.

I still remember the first time, the night we won first place in four categories at the South Florida Pole Dance Event. Hayden pulled me into the bathroom, we got high, and then we had the best sex I'd had up until that point. I thought that was it. In my head, it couldn't get better than that feeling right there — the ultimate high.

But right now, stuffing the last bit of cash I needed into my small Vera Bradley backpack and handing off the final bag of Molly, a new kind of high sets in. It's the kind that can only be obtained when the optimum feeling passes over you.

Freedom.

The girl who bought the last bag from me is young, maybe a sophomore, from a small private college in New York. She's dressed in cut off, high-waisted jeans and a frayed top with a flower headband wrapped around her huge, bouncy blonde curls. She looks like she's ready for a music festival, and with her new possession courtesy of me, she might as well be.

"Thanks," she says sweetly, tucking the baggy in her pocket and skipping off to rejoin her friends standing outside of Sloppy Joe's. I pull my backpack over my shoulders again and tighten the straps, hiking it up to my upper back. Most of the money I've made this week is stashed back at our suite, but today's portion — the final portion — is finally resting right in the center of my back. Funny, it's the lightest my shoulders have felt in months.

It's only the third night of Spring Break.

I thought it would take so much longer.

Bo slides up beside me, her pinky hooking around one of my belt loops. Even though it's hot and humid tonight, her fingers are icy as they graze my skin. "Who was that?"

It's such a simple question, but her words chase away my momentary high of freedom. Because the truth is, I don't know who that girl is. I don't know if she's a druggie or if this is her first time. I don't know her apart from any of the other kids I've sold coke or Molly or marijuana to over the past few days. I knew going into this that I'd have to disconnect my personal feelings. I can't think about them and save myself, too. I had to make a choice.

I chose me.

Still, what if someone gets hurt because of me? Would I even know? Hundreds of kids get too stupid on Spring Break and hurt themselves. But until now, I never had to make peace with the fact that I could, potentially, be the one responsible for that.

But they would probably find a way to get the drugs with or without me, right? It's not like I'm the only one with a stash. And it's their choice to take the drug, not mine.

Sighing, a bit defeated, I realize it doesn't matter how I put it — I still did a shitty thing. But when I glance over at Bo's wide eyes sparkling in the bright lights of Duval Street, knowing she's safe from Xavier, knowing I'm free from his grip on my life, I don't feel sad. I don't feel guilty.

I feel relieved.

"No one. She just asked to borrow a hair tie," I reply. Sliding my hand up Bo's arm, I hook my fingers around the nape of her neck and pull her into me, pressing my lips hard on hers in the middle of the sea of Spring Breakers. For a moment, it feels like everything around us is muted — the harsh lights, the shrieks from tipsy girls, the bar chants from rowdy boys. Bo freezes, fighting the urge to moan, her hands gripping my waist before pushing me away.

"What are you doing?" she hisses, her eyes searching the busy street. "Someone could see us."

I grin, knowing she's right but not really caring at the moment. "Let's go fucking crazy tonight. I mean like let's take it to an entirely new level."

Bo's eyes light up and I feel my energy transfer to her. We're tied together like that — if she's low, I feel low. If I'm high, she feels high. We feed off each other.

"What do you have in mind, Ashlei Daniels?"

Grabbing her hand in mine and tugging her toward The Lazy Gecko, the excitement I felt building all day burns faster, consuming me inch by inch.

"Let's start with shots and go from there."

Bo giggles, bouncing with me. "Deal!"

***

A few hours later, Bo and I are closing our tabs at the fifth bar of the night. It's late, or should I say early, but Key West doesn't shut down until the patrons let it. Every bar stays open as long as they feel like it, and with the bass still thumping hard and bodies still pressed together on the dance floor behind us, I know they'll be here a while.

Bo is signing her check when I spot him.

I'm not the kind of person who finds attraction to a person slowly. I know from the first time I meet them whether I'll be into them or not. With Bo, the connection was instant, even if I didn't voice it out loud. And right now, staring at a tall, dark-haired, dark-eyed guy just down the bar, I feel it — that instant assault of flutters in my stomach.

"Bo, what if I told you I wanted to do something *really* crazy tonight?"

She eyes me, letting her pen drop to the bar. "What do you mean?"

I swallow, unsure of what her reaction will be when I pose my next question. But the adrenaline is coursing through my veins right along with the alcohol, my freedom from the hell that's been binding me for months making me feel more alive than ever. Taking her hands in mine, I kiss her knuckles and level my eyes with hers. "Have a threesome with me."

"What?" she balks, her mouth hanging open. "Ashlei, I don't... I just want you."

I swallow, nodding. "I know, and you know I want you, too. I love you," I say the words before thinking better of them, but I don't take them back. It's true. I do love her.

She closes her mouth, her brows pulling inward as her hands squeeze mine. "You do?"

I nod. "I do, Bo. You pulled me out of a darkness I didn't think I would ever survive. And now that I'm here, in a better place than I've been in months, with you — I want to celebrate by doing something wild. But only if it's with you. I want this with *you*." She frowns, but I pull her closer. "Please."

Bo studies me, chewing her slim bottom lip. "Have you ever done it before?"

I shake my head, and that seems to reassure her. "I just... I feel so alive right now, Bo. I feel spontaneous. It's Spring Break, I'm here with you, I'm free from all the shit that's been holding me back," I trail off, not wanting to get into details since Bo isn't aware of what I had to do to achieve said freedom. Tucking a strand of blonde hair behind my ear, I ask again. "Please. Let's experience this together."

For a moment longer, she keeps her bottom lip pinned between her teeth. But then, slowly, she nods, and when I smile, she does, too.

"Come with me."

I wrap my arms around her waist and walk her with me, straight up to Mystery Man, whose eyes are just as fiercely attached to mine as mine are his.

"Hi," I say softly, not even attempting to hide how my eyes are devouring every inch of him.

The corner of his lips tilts up in response, and he takes it as permission to do the same. "Hello, ladies," he replies, his gaze finding Bo next.

Bo swallows, flushing before she asks me, "Is he the one you want?"

I nod and she takes a deep breath, giving me a small smile that lets me know to make my next move. Excitement burns through me, its source at my core as I turn back to the guy.

"What's your name?"

"Alex," he answers smoothly.

"Alex..." I try it on, tasting it as my eyes skate over his muscular forearms. "Take us back to your place."

***

Bo's hand shakes in mine and I squeeze it gently, trying to soothe her nerves as the cab drops us at the large gate of a private home.

"I thought you said you were here with your fraternity brothers?" I ask, referencing Alex's conversation in the car ride over. It turns out, he's an Omega Chi. I have no fucking idea how I've never seen him before now.

He unlocks the large wooden door and gestures for us to walk in first. "I am."

I shoulder off my Vera Bradley bag and toss it into a small chair near the front door as Alex shuts it behind us, my eyes on the lavish surroundings and my hand still latched onto Bo's.

"A little high-end for a house full of fraternity brothers, don't you think?" I ask, glancing back at him. He runs a hand through his dark hair and grins, his eyes heavy from the alcohol. "It's my uncle's place. He rents it out most of the year, so when I found out this is where we were going for Spring Break, he blocked it out so I could have it."

"Wait, so you guys get to stay here for free?" Bo asks, now letting her own eyes wander the no-doubt expensive paintings lining the walls. Alex nods and I trail my fingers along the smooth, polished wood surface of the long dining room table before my eyes catch on something shiny in the next room.

"Oh my God, your uncle must be a bachelor." Dropping Bo's hand, I cross quickly into the other room, empty save for a few air mattresses blown up along the far wall and one, lone pole in the middle. One wall is made up completely of floor-to-ceiling mirrors and I note my wild blonde hair and dark, mascara smeared eyes.

Alex chuckles. "Yeah, I guess you could say that." He slides up next to Bo and watches me carefully as my hands find the pole. When the cool metal hits my palms, I exhale long and slow, a rush of emotions hitting me — fear, excitement, longing. I've missed being on the pole, and I'm just drunk enough to not let the dark thoughts creep in as I grip it hard and swing my legs, hoisting myself up into an easy spin and high kick hold. I drop back down to the ground gently, balancing on the balls of my feet as I circle the pole, one hand still attached, my eyes finding Bo's.

Suddenly, she doesn't seem so nervous.

She seems mesmerized.

Alex's eyes are on fire, one arm crossed over his chest while the opposite hand covers his mouth. They're both watching me, enamored, and the power of their stares sinks deep in my center.

There's no music in the room, but there's always been music in my heart, and I let the passion I feel move me. Climbing my way back up the pole, I start with a few more beginner moves, spinning and holding flexes before dropping back down to the floor each time, circling, arching my back, sinking low to the floor only to climb back up the pole again. I'm not sure how long I dance before Bo crosses the room to me, her chest rising and falling with heavy breaths as I press my back to the pole and wait for her. She steps closer and closer, dark eyes hard on mine. When she reaches the space in front of me, she bites her bottom lip.

"You are so fucking sexy."

I don't smile, I don't respond, I just slowly reach my hand out until I find her waist and then I pull her into me, pressing my lips to her neck and sucking her tender skin between my teeth, my back still flush against the cool surface of the pole. She hisses, letting her head fall back, and I kiss around the swell of her throat before finding her mouth. Her hands are in my hair, mine crawl her body as my tongue slides between her lips. When Alex steps into the space beside us, she stiffens, but I keep my touch calm and sure.

"It's okay," I whisper, my forehead to hers. She nods, concern still written in her features as I kiss her again. It's so strange seeing Bo this way, so nervous and unsure. She's the confident one in the bedroom — commanding, strong. As Alex's hand snakes its way into my hair and he pulls my mouth from Bo's to his own, I wonder if he'll be taking the captain's chair tonight.

My heart hammers beneath my ribcage as I taste him, new and exotic. Bo's lips trail down my neck to my cleavage as she palms the space between my thighs. Moaning into Alex's mouth at the touch, he pops the button on his jeans without breaking our kiss. I hear his zipper next, and then his shorts are on the floor. He kicks them away, just as Bo pulls me from him, her hand tugging at my tank top. I lift my arms and she rips it up and over, tossing it to the side before making quick work of my bra.

It's almost too much. We're all hands and mouths — stripping, kissing, touching, stripping more. Somewhere along the way we find the stairs, which lead up to a master bedroom Alex is clearly occupying. The four post bed is built with dark wood and lined with deep red accents that match the comforter Bo and I slide onto easily, feeling the cool fabric against our skin. Alex makes his way between us, propping himself up against the headboard and taking each of us by the waist as we kiss over him.

Bo's breaths are still shaky, her arms trembling as she holds herself steady on the bed. We're leaning over Alex, our tongues tangled, while he slowly strokes himself and watches. I massage her tongue with mine, each kiss an attempt to bring her energy back to mine. Just when I have her there, Alex's hand moves from my waist to behind my thigh. It hovers there for just a moment before I feel his fingers penetrate me, and from Bo's reaction, his other hand is doing the same to her.

"I don't know if I can do this," she whispers between our kisses. I pull back, panting at the feel of Alex's fingers inside me and how turned on I am by Bo's kisses.

"You don't have to do anything to him. Or vice versa. Just focus on me."

With that, I break contact from Alex and pull Bo with me, rolling over until I'm on my back and Bo's straddling me. I love the way the skin stretches across her petite hips as she rubs against me, building a friction that will drive her to the edge. Alex takes my cue, moving between my legs and spreading my thighs open to him as I maneuver Bo up my body. When her knees are on either side of my head, I slide my hands down her neck, her arms, until I lace my hands in hers. Placing them on the headboard above us, I curl her fingers, locking them in place.

"Hold on tight," I whisper, licking my lips. Bo's breaths are heavy, her eyes hooded as I grab her ass in my hands and invade the space between us, flicking my tongue out to stroke her clit. She moans, letting her head fall back as her knuckles whiten with her tightening grip.

Alex groans from somewhere behind Bo and then there's the sound of a condom package ripping. My view is blocked, my face completely owned by her, but I feel him. His hands — one on my hip, the other I can only assume palming himself as he places himself at my entrance. And then, with one, strong thrust, I'm filled.

I gasp against Bo, sucking her clit between my teeth to make her moan with me. My nails dig into the smooth skin of her thighs as she rocks her hips, her pelvis grinding against my mouth. Alex is so big, and it's been so long since I've felt a man between my legs that the sensation is overwhelming. Each time he pushes into me he reaches a new depth and I feel myself climbing, higher, higher.

My hands snake up Bo's frame to palm her breasts and she cries out as my fingers pinch her nipples. She's grinding harder now, and I know she's close. Wrapping my hands around her small waist, I flip her, her short hair blowing out in a whoosh against the sheets as it frames her face. Alex pulls out long enough for me to change positions, taking my place between Bo's legs, a grin on my face.

"Do you know how turned on I am by you?" I whisper against her neck before sinking my teeth into the flesh. "I have never wanted anyone more than I want you right now."

She moans, dragging her nails through my hair and pulling my mouth up to hers just as Alex sinks down over us. I'm sandwiched between them — Alex's hard chest and abs against my back, Bo's soft body below me. When Alex enters me from behind, I arch my back and Bo bucks her hips up to meet mine. One arm holding me steady, I glide the opposite hand down her navel, pausing at the small birth mark above her left hip before settling between her thighs. She's still shaking, but now I know it's because she's close. When I thrust two fingers inside her at once, moving them in time with Alex's pulses, her hands fly up to grip the headboard again.

"Oh God," she moans, sucking her lips between her teeth. She's fighting it. "Oh fuck!"

"Come," I demand, and she does, her wetness soaking my fingers as her moans echo off the walls. Alex moans, cursing under his breath. I'm so incredibly turned on, I can't imagine how he feels right now.

I lower myself for just a moment, kissing Bo softly, letting her ride the wave down. Her eyes flutter open to meet mine and she smiles. "You're amazing."

I just kiss her in response, but then Alex's hands grip my elbows, pulling them together behind me. He pins them at my middle back, forcing an arch in my back as he plows harder, deeper, his mouth on my neck. He's kissing, sucking, biting, and then he shares a look with Bo. They seem to agree on something not spoken aloud, because Bo leans up, taking my mouth with hers as her hand shoots between my legs. When she starts circling my clit, I break our kiss, crying out at the sensation. Her free hand grips my neck with just enough pressure to heighten my sensitivity.

Holy fuck.

Alex's hands are gripping me so hard, I know I'll be bruised in the morning, but I love it. Bo intensifies the pressure on my clit, biting my bottom lip, leaving my mouth open to scream as my orgasm shoots through me. Alex takes it as permission to come with me, and he flexes into me once, twice, deeper, three times, so fucking deep, his groans mixing with mine. It's the highest ecstasy I've ever known. Every touch is amplified, every movement too much yet never enough.

Bo's hands don't leave me until I collapse against her, Alex rolling off of us and sprawling out on the sheets beside us, his chest heaving. My head against Bo's chest, I watch him smile and shake his head before his dark eyes turn to us, flicking between the two.

"You girls are fucking wild."

Bo giggles, her fears shattered now that the experience is over. "I blame her."

Alex grins wider, baring his bright, beautiful teeth and I just shrug.

"I love Spring Break."

Cassie

After all the craziness of the first few days of Spring Break, it feels amazing to just lay on the top deck of a sail boat, sun rays hot on my skin, sea breeze blowing over me. We're all in a line — Bo, Ashlei, Jess, Skyler, Erin, and then me — our bright, matching beach towels beneath us. The few Omega Chi brothers who dragged their asses out of bed early enough to make our all-day excursion are on the bottom deck, getting boozy on the free drinks. For the girls, I think we're finally taking the time to soak in some silence.

It's already been a long day. I've applied sunscreen every hour on the hour just to be safe, and yet still I know I'll go back to our suite with a burn. It will eventually turn into a slight tan, but I never get as dark as the rest of the girls. Skyler always seems to catch the darkest tan, probably from paddleboarding all the time.

We started at eight this morning and we've already been snorkeling, parasailing and had lunch. Add that to the fact that I'm getting practically no sleep because I'm too self-aware of how close Adam and I are in our bed, and you could say I'm a little tired. Now, we're parked at a floating dock with plenty of activities at our disposal, but I'm not the only one who doesn't seem eager to jump on them. We're all catching our breath. Tonight, we'll be back on Duval Street, so for now, we're taking it easy.

Zack Brown Band croons from the speakers on the boat and I tap my toes to the beat, smiling as I recount all the memories we've already made this week. I was warned that my first Spring Break with Kappa Kappa Beta would be wild and crazy, but no one told me how amazing it would be, too. I've literally been having the time of my life, and we're only halfway through.

"Hey," a voice whisper-shouts right above me. My eyes fly open to a dark silhouette haloed by the sun. I shield my eyes with my hand and Adam's goofy grin comes into view, along with his abs and the hard V that leads right down to his dark red swim trunks. "Come ride the jet skis with me."

He looks like a little kid, grinning ear to ear, a small speck of sunscreen that hasn't been rubbed in resting on the bridge of his nose. His tan shoulders are starting to freckle, and a sheen of sweat has gathered across his pecs.

Scanning the rest of the girls, I realize he's talking to only me. Jess is snoring, mouth hanging open, while Bo and Ashlei lean together over a book. Skyler and Erin are both on their backs, eyes closed, and I assume since they're not stirring, they're probably sleeping, too.

I look back up at Adam, hand still over my eyes. "Yeah. Okay."

He smiles wider, holding out his hand to help me up. I take it, ignoring the dull buzz that always hums through me each time our skin touches. When I'm on my feet, Adam watches as I pull the straps of my light green top up and re-tie them at my neck.

"Um, they're parked over here. Come on." He leads the way down the stairs and over to the starboard side of the boat where ten wave runners are parked along the same dock as we are. We listen to one of the crew members go over safety and speed reminders before each climbing onto our own and pushing off the dock. We wade out a safe distance and then hit the gas, speeding off into the waves.

We ride side-by-side for a while, laughing as the waves spritz us with cool ocean water. Adam breaks off and goes wide left, jumping the wake of another boat and doing donuts. I just shake my head and speed off, pushing the jet ski as fast as it will go. The wind flies through my hair, my eyes shielded only by my sunglasses as I tear through the water. It's an amazing sound, an incredible rush, and I only slow down when I reach the distance the crew member warned was as far as we could go.

Releasing my thumb off the gas throttle, I let the engine hum and stare off into the distance, taking it all in. Adam rumbles up beside me and does the same and for a few moments, we just exist.

"My grandpa used to water ski," he says after a while. I turn, watching as he leans forward and crosses his arms on his handlebars, his eyes still off in the distance. "It was so amazing to watch. I was young, but I still remember it. He was one of those men who excelled at everything he did. It wasn't just on the water, either. He was like that in his job, as a friend, a parent, a grandparent. Everything."

I nod, smiling, getting the sense that maybe I'm just supposed to listen right now. Adam chuckles softly, as if he's recalling a memory as he leans back again.

"He raised me, you know?" he asks, turning to me with one eyebrow raised.

"Really?"

"Yeah. My mom and dad traveled a lot for work. They're both in sales for a technology company, so it's their job to schmooze the clients, keep them happy, and sell them on new products and services. They were gone at least ten months out of the year if you added it all up."

I blanch. "Wow. That's a lot, Adam."

A short laugh escapes his lips, the wind blowing his dark hair back. "I know. But I had my grandpa. I stayed with him most of the time or he would come sleep at our house. Either way, he was the one always there, teaching me the things I needed to know, helping me with homework, showing me how to throw a punch the first time I got bullied. He used to have this one, long patch of hair that he would comb over his bald head" He crosses his arms over his chest, still smiling, the waves rocking us gently. "I miss him every day."

A sadness washes over me. "He passed, didn't he?"

Adam gives one curt nod. "When I was a junior in high school. I had to stay with my aunt a lot after that, until college, anyway. But it wasn't the same." He blows out a long, slow breath. "He's the reason I do what I do, you know?" He turns to me, black sunglasses misted from the sea salt. "He never half-assed anything. So when I came to PSU, when I rushed Alpha Sigma, I knew I had the chance to take an organization that everyone underestimated and really make something of it — and maybe of myself, in the process."

My heart squeezes and I fight the urge to reach out to him. Adam and I have talked a lot since we met, especially when we were doing breakfast on a normal basis, but I never questioned why he cared so much about Alpha Sigma and the direction it was headed in. I always just assumed that was part of who he was, and I guess in a way it is — but it's not just a part of him, it's a part of his grandpa, too.

"That's really beautiful, Adam," I finally say, my voice low. He crooks a smile at me, his left dimple making an appearance as his hands find the handlebars again. But then he pauses, lifting his sunglasses, eyes wide.

"Cassie! Look!" I follow his finger and strain my eyes against the bright blue water.

"What?!"

"Do you see them? Dolphins!"

I scan the water, waiting, and then two fins break the surface followed by a third and fourth one.

"Oh my God!"

"It looks like an entire pod of them."

"Wow," I breathe, watching them as they come closer. "They're so close!"

"They're probably curious about us."

They're not alone there.

The dolphins play around us for a while and we just watch, pointing, laughing, talking. It's easy and relaxed, and for once, I don't feel awkward or afraid of my feelings around him. For once, it feels like maybe we really can have a real friendship.

As we ride back up to the dock, I think of Skyler and Clinton, how they are together. It's clear they love each other, but not in a way that crosses the friendship line. I wonder if maybe Adam could be that friend for me. The thought of it twists my stomach just as much as it makes me smile.

Adam helps me off my jet ski once we dock and I unzip my life jacket, tossing it to the crew member as Adam does the same. We both head straight to the bar on the first deck of the boat to grab water, taking our plastic cups to the back of the boat and leaning our arms against the railing.

"If I ask you something, do you promise to answer me honestly?" Adam asks, sipping from his cup. I nod, though something tells me I might regret it. For a moment he's quiet, but then he drains the rest of his water and turns to face me, one elbow still propped on the white railing. "What happened with you and Clay last semester?"

Yep. Instant regret.

I clear my throat. "You know what happened."

"No I don't."

I shift my weight to my other hip, chewing at the chapped skin on my top lip. "I don't know, Adam. I liked him. I thought he was nice. And honestly, I just wanted to have fun. We fooled around and stuff, and I didn't expect it to go as far as it did, but that night after semi-formal, I was just so upset with you and he was treating me so kindly, even though you told me he was an ass. And I don't know, I just trusted him for some reason. So we..." I trail off, shaking my head. "Well, I don't think I really need to say it."

Adam winces. "You slept with him because of me?"

My heart kicks in my chest. "Oh God, that didn't come out right." I know I'm blushing furiously, trying to save my ass but coming up with absolutely no words that help me achieve that. "I just mean that I was in a weird head space. I wasn't thinking. Normal me, in her right frame of mind, would have remembered that I have always wanted my first time to be special. I wouldn't have let some frat daddy take it after seeing each other for less than a month."

I chuckle, but when I lift my eyes to Adam, his fist is clutched around the empty plastic cup, crushing it, his other hand still gripping the bar. His nose flares, murderous eyes hard on mine. "He took your virginity?"

Oh God.

Now I'm *really* blushing.

Covering my face with my hands, I shake my head, peeking through my fingers. "This is so embarrassing."

"He took your virginity and then dumped you for your ex-best friend in front of everyone." It's not a question. His jaw is ticking beneath the strained skin. "Unfuckingbelievable."

Dropping my hands to my side again, I offer a sad smile, the scars from that night stinging a little. "It's okay, Adam. I mean, that's what college is all about, right?" I shrug. "Lessons learned and all that."

I force a smile, but Adam is still glaring at me like I took my own virginity. Finally, he sighs, blowing the breath out hard and loosening his grip on the cup in his hands. He doesn't say a word, just takes my cup, too, and walks them to the trash can nearby. I watch him, wondering if I should have lied about what happened. When he reaches me again, he doesn't stop in the space next to me. He pulls me into him completely, wrapping his arms all the way around me, his naked chest on mine, his abs pressed against my navel, his arms hard around my shoulders.

"I'm so sorry, Cassie," he whispers into my hair and chills race from the point of contact all the way to my toes. He doesn't break our hug, just holds me, and each second kills me and fills me with hope all at once. Hesitantly, I wrap my arms around him, too, and my eyes water.

When he pulls back, he sees, and he wipes at the corner of my eye with the pad of his thumb, catching the tear before it even had the chance to fall.

And it's in that moment I know for sure.

We will never be like Skyler and Clinton.

Skyler

My mom is a huge Ernest Hemingway fan. She has all of his books on her shelf at home and loves to quote him frequently. So, of course, I couldn't come to Key West without visiting his old-home-turned-museum for her.

"That was amazing!" mom squeals as I take a seat on one of the benches in the back yard area of the house, holding the phone so mom can still see my face on our video chat. I had her on video the entire tour, showing her every nook and cranny of the house. A cozy, black polydactyl cat is curled up on the bench next to me, and it doesn't stir in the slightest when I sit. Apparently, the six-toed Hemingway cats are pretty famous, and therefore, pretty immune to all the petting and picture-taking that happens to them every day.

"That was pretty cool. Hey, maybe I could be a writer," I joke, pulling my damp hair away from my neck. Still, the thought isn't too far off. I've been trying to figure out what I want to do after college, and the truth is, I was really fascinated by the tour. Ernest Hemingway was an interesting man. Oddly enough, even though he was one of the most prolific writers of his time, he was better known in Key West for his hunting, fishing, and fighting skills. And of course, his love for whiskey.

Sounds like my kind of lifestyle.

"You think so, baby?"

I scrunch my nose. "Nah, probably not. At least half the words in any book I write would be offensive."

Mom giggles, roping her dark hazelnut hair around her fingers and draping it over one shoulder. "Oh gee, I wonder who you get that from."

"Not me!" Dad calls out in the background and we both laugh.

"Well if it isn't Skyler from Florida," a voice twangs above me. Squinting against the rays of light streaming through the trees, I grin when I find exactly who I thought I would.

"Trevor, the trouble from Tennessee."

"Who's that?" Mom asks and I flip my phone, making Trevor blush and offer a half wave as my mom nearly falls out of her chair. "Oh my! Aren't you handsome."

"Thank you, ma'am."

Mom scoffs. "Did he just call me ma'am? What am I, eighty?"

I choke out a laugh and mouth a *sorry* to Trevor, turning my phone back to my own face. "Got to go, Mom. I'll call when we're back on campus."

"Don't get into any *trouble*!" she teases just as I blow a kiss and end the call, standing to join Trevor.

"Your mom is hot."

"Ew," I laugh the word, adjusting my purse strap across my chest.

He barks out a laugh, loud and strong. "You are the last person I expected to find here."

"What? I don't look like the literature loving type of gal?" *Did I just say gal?*

"I guess I shouldn't assume, huh?"

"Damn straight," I say, crossing my arms. "But I only came for my mom, so in this case, you were right." I wink and Trevor smiles. "You here alone?"

"Yeah, not exactly what my brothers had in mind for Spring Break."

"My sisters neither. They're at Smathers again."

"You heading there now?"

I shrug, reaching down to run my hand over the black cat's silky fur as she slumbers through our chat. If I remember right, the tour guide said this one is named Betty Grable. "I was, but I could be persuaded." Glancing up at him through my lashes, his tongue darts out to wet his lips and his eyes fall to his feet as he catches on.

He's so goddamn cute.

"I was going to be super touristy today. Want to join me?"

Betty mewls as my hand leaves her fur. "Sounds like Betty is on board, so I'm in, too."

He extends his arm, showing off those glorious bicep muscles I fell for our first night in Key West, turquoise eyes sparkling. "I'll guide the way."

***

I didn't realize when I agreed to being a tourist with Trevor all day that my feet would want to murder me for it. Luckily, that southern charm translates into some pretty stellar foot rubs.

"God, I don't know whether to scream or moan or pass out or cry," I spout, words running together as Trevor pushes his thumb into my heel. My feet are propped in his lap on the back porch of our suite and he just shakes his head, rubbing the arch next.

"I had a lot of fun today," he says and I nod in agreement, still watching as his hands move over my skin. "You're nothing like I thought you were, Skyler Thorne."

"Hey now," I warn, pointing my index finger at him. "Don't go falling in love on me. We go to different schools, remember?"

His eyes still on his hands, he just laughs. "I don't know. I'm not scared to fall in love. I think we should fall in love with as many things as we can."

"I think I read that on a pillow once."

"You're impossible," he says, squeezing my ankles once more before letting me drop my feet to the warm concrete. The sun is sinking lower, which means the girls will all be back soon, ready to start the nightly shower cycle and get ready for Duval Street.

"Tell me, Trevor," I say, leaning forward to rest my elbows on my knees. "Do you have any of those sexy country songs saved on your phone?"

He knows where I'm going with this, but he pretends he doesn't. "Indeed I do. I have an entire playlist, actually."

I nod, looking around the back porch, silent for a moment before meeting his eyes again. "How many times do you think we can get through the playlist before you make me come?"

He swallows, the Adam's apple in his throat bobbing with the action. Without another word, I grab his hand and pull him upstairs to my room, locking the door behind us. He turns on the playlist as promised, and when he kisses me for the first time, his hands framing my face, it's as if he's transported me to a wild field in the middle of nowhere.

He fucks me the way I thought he would — steady, strong and sure. His touches are gentle but firm and confident, and when we're done, I let him cuddle with me for a while, because I know he's the kind of guy who loves that sort of thing. But, before the sun sets, I walk him back downstairs and out the front door. Leaning against the frame, eyes heavy and limbs sedated, I offer him a soft smile.

"See you around, Trouble."

He grins, bringing my hand to his lips. He almost walks away, but thinks better of it, bringing me into him for one last kiss.

Click.

"Oh, who's this, Skyler?" *Click.* Trevor and I both turn, eyes wide, and the moment I take in a middle-aged woman with a tight bun, a camera, and *Star Poker Florida* badge slung around her neck, my stomach drops. "Latest flavor of the week?"

Well, shit.

Erin

I wish we were still on the beach.

When we're on the beach or out on the boat during the day, I have fun. I don't have to drink to soak up the sun or paddleboard or read or talk to the girls. But when the sun goes down and we all invade Duval Street, the intoxication levels increase as my patience decreases. Alcohol intensifies everything, so half of my sisters are loud and crazy and the others are blubbering messes. I was finally able to talk Skyler down after being ambushed by a stupid reporter earlier today, but now, Jess is the new patient in my office.

"You can't tell anyone," she slurs for the seventh time, her elbows propped on the bar at Sloppy Joe's as she lifts her rum and Coke to her lips. Her lips pucker a bit as she sips it down. "He could lose his job."

"I won't say anything. I promise. But I still don't understand why you're so upset."

Jess has been going on and on for the past hour about Jarrett, her ex-teacher-turned-not-boyfriend. She was dancing with the girls earlier, but eventually made her way over to the bar where I set up camp, and it was like she was coming to the confessional. She unleashed all of her anxiety in about two full breaths.

"I'm upset because I *like* him," she draws out her words, as if I should already know this is a huge issue.

"And? Isn't that the point?"

She shakes her head, chocolate eyes on the stirrer in her drink as the bass from the live band thumps through the bar. "I just have a feeling I'm setting myself up to get hurt. Remember how I got my nickname?"

I make a face, thinking back to our freshmen year when Jess told every single guy she hooked up with that she loved him. She used to fall hard and fast and with abandon. She wasn't afraid of being hurt, she wasn't afraid of them not loving her back, she wasn't afraid of anything. I guess the same could be said about her now — about not being afraid — but the truth is, I think her tough, I-don't-give-a-shit attitude is a mask over the fear she developed the moment she became known as J-Love.

"I think Jarrett is different. I mean, I haven't really had the chance to get to know him, but I do know you. And it's been years since you've had feelings for a guy. Maybe it's okay to let them happen. Maybe there's a reason."

"Maybe," she says softly, hiccupping.

I laugh. "Give me this." Pulling her half-empty glass from her hands, I nod toward where Skyler and Cassie are dancing in front of the large stage in the middle of the bar. "Go dance and have fun. Relax. It's Spring Break. You can figure everything out with Jarrett when we get back."

Jess smiles, her eyes glossy, hair wild. "Mmkay." With that, she slides off her barstool and stumbles over to the dance floor, throwing her hands up and shouting something I can't quite make out as soon as she reaches our group.

I watch them all dancing and laughing, stirring the remains of Jess' drink on the bar. Skyler starts moonwalking when the band plays the first notes of *Smooth Criminal* and Ashlei pops off her snapback, tipping it over and holding it out to the crowd like she's taking tips for the performance. I can't help but smile.

In a little while, I'll get up and go dance with them. I enjoy dancing, whether drunk or not. Right now, though, I'd rather sit and watch Clinton and Shawna grinding on each other, because torturing myself is apparently a favorite pastime of mine.

I don't know why seeing them together upsets me. Is it because I have feelings for Clinton? I chew on that thought, assessing my heart rate and stomach knots.

No, I don't think that's it.

I mean, I care for him, but I never wanted to date him. I never expected us to be more than a friendly date that night at semi-formal. Still, seeing his hands tangled in Shawna's purple locks and her lips on his neck makes me feel... something.

Jealous?

Angry?

Sad?

All of the above?

As I'm ticking through the possibilities in my mind, Clinton's eyes lift to mine and I'm caught staring. I snap my attention back to Jess' drink and lift it to my lips, sucking down the smallest sip, just enough to look like I wasn't being a creep without making me want to drink the rest.

But Clinton stops dancing, kissing Shawna's temple and leaving her with Skyler before crossing the room to me.

Shit.

"Thought you weren't drinking," his voice booms as he reaches the bar, his eyes on the bartender instead of me. He nods his head once to the short, dark-haired pixie with tattoos and she gets to work on two drinks that I assume he's been ordering all night — one for him, one for Shawna.

"I'm not." He glances at the drink in my hand from the corner of his eye, brow cocked. "It's Jess'. I'm just holding it."

"Ah."

I stir the drink faster, nervous, before dropping my hands into my lap and clasping them tight. "Having fun?"

"Yep. You would be, too, if you'd loosen up a little bit."

I wince. "I'm having fun."

"Clearly," he scoffs. Sliding a twenty toward the bartender, he takes the drinks from her hands and shakes his head when she asks if he wants change. "Come on. Take this drink and come dance with us. It's Spring Break, Ex."

"Isn't that Shawna's drink?"

"She still has one," he says, holding one of the mixed drinks toward me. It's clear, something with Sprite, I imagine. "Here."

I bite my lip, wondering if maybe he's right. I can have a few drinks and be okay, right? But when my eyes flick to his and a flash of smaller, younger eyes assaults me, I squeeze my own tight.

Would our baby have had his eyes?

His nose?

His skin?

And I realize that maybe that's why I feel something when I see him with Shawna – because he is supposed to be a father. *My* child's father.

The child I killed.

I shake my head, hands clasping tighter. "Thanks, Bear, but I'm okay."

For a moment he watches me, jaw set. He turns just a fraction like he's going to let it go, but then he whips back around. "This is fucking ridiculous, Erin. We hooked up, okay? We had sex. It's not the end of the world and I'm not going to tell anyone. And, whether you stay sober as a judge or get shitfaced tonight, I'm never going to sleep with you again, okay? So stop looking at me like you have to worry about ending up in my bed tonight." His words slam into me like a Mack truck and my mouth pops open as he scowls, rolling his eyes. "Get over yourself."

My nose burns, but I stand before the sensation can reach my eyes. Pulling my purse over my shoulder, I straighten, chest to his. "Fuck you, Bear."

With that, I turn on my heel and push through the crowd of drunk college students to the street. I don't slow down, I don't apologize, and I don't look back at him or anyone else who might have seen the exchange.

I'm done.

***

Less than an hour later, I'm tossing my bag into the back of a Cadillac Escalade sent by my father. I told him I was terribly sick and I needed to get back to campus and he called out a driver from the airport without another question. After shooting a text to Skyler with the same bogus excuse, I let the driver help me into the backseat and sigh as he shuts the door behind me.

Sinking into the cool leather seats, I cross my arms tight over my chest, not even bothering to brush away the few strands of hair falling into my eyes. My chest feels like it's being squeezed by a boa constrictor and no matter how I focus on my breathing, I can't steady it out. Clinton's words slap me over and over again, the anger behind them washing over me in treacherous waves.

I should have told him.

He doesn't understand because I never did. I never will.

Clinton thinks I'm upset that we hooked up, that I'm ashamed or scared or embarrassed by it to the point that I refuse to drink again. He doesn't know that I'm terrified of letting another drop of alcohol hit my system because it could mean losing a part of myself again. It could mean having an amazing night with a great guy without being smart enough to use protection. It could mean one night of fun in exchange for one day of anguish, my back sticky on a paper-covered bed, my feet propped up on cold, unforgiving stirrups.

My heart races, the emotion I've been fighting so hard to keep down threatening to break the surface. Hands fumbling, I rip my phone from my Michael Kors purse and dial his number before I can stop myself. My knee bounces as the phone rings over and over, sending me closer to voicemail.

But then, he answers.

"Hello?"

I stop breathing, stop shaking, stop everything. Eyes wide, I clutch the phone tighter at the sound of his voice.

"Hello? Anyone there?"

Now that I have him on the phone, I don't even know what to say. All I know is that Kip Jackson was the only boy to ever make me feel truly loved. Even though it was years ago, he's the only person I want to call when life gets too hard to handle. But I haven't talked to him since that summer, the one when we fell in love and then I chased him away just as quickly.

There's a shift on the other end and then the line goes dead with a soft, quiet click. I let the cool device drop into my lap, bringing one trembling hand to my lips. And then, I stop fighting. Taking one last breath, I let the pressure rumbling through my chest and up into my throat break through. Loud, ugly, and painful, as so often hidden hurt is, I allow it to consume me.

I finally let myself cry.

Bear

I feel a little shitty when I wake up on the last day of Spring Break. Even after taking a long, hot shower, popping a couple of Advils and drinking an entire Gatorade, I still feel the effects of our week weighing on me. For once, I'm actually looking forward to a day without boozing. I know we'll all go hard one last time on Duval Street tonight, but today, I'm spending time with Shawna.

Away from everyone else.

But, the hangover and dehydration aren't the only reasons I'm feeling like a particularly ripe ass today. Skyler called me this morning to tell me Erin left last night, so Shawna could ride home in our van instead of trying to find a flight home. I should have been happy that I would get to be next to her on the way back, but instead all I felt was an insufferable amount of guilt. Erin wasn't sick, she was hurt.

Because I was a giant bag of dicks.

Sighing, I pull another Gatorade from the fridge and take a few swigs before splaying my palms out on the counter. I didn't mean to lash out at her, especially knowing how sensitive she is, but I was tired of feeling like I did something wrong by hooking up with her. I know I remember the night of semi-formal a little better than she does, but she wanted me. *She* was the one who asked me back to the house. *She* peeled my clothes off. I definitely didn't stop her, hell — I enjoyed myself. But she's making me feel like a criminal and it needs to stop.

Still, I could have waited until I wasn't shitfaced to talk to her about it.

Maybe she caught feelings. Maybe she's jealous seeing me with Shawna. I actually laugh out loud at that, knowing there's no way in hell Erin would ever want to actually *be* with me. She's got her eyes set on a doctor or a lawyer, I'm sure, and even that won't be until after she's reigned as president of KKB.

A loud chorus of laughter from the other room shakes my thoughts and I grab my Gatorade, making my way toward the noise. Several of my brothers are gathered around my Little's laptop, pointing and talking over each other. Josh is furiously typing and clicking away, almost like he's playing a game.

"What are you guys doing?"

Half of them go sheet white and they all stop talking. Instantly, I know they're up to no good.

"Nothing. Just watching YouTube videos," Josh lies. I know it's a lie, I can see right through his blushing ginger cheeks, even if he did bake on the fake tanner this week. I narrow my eyes.

"Do I need to remind you guys about the warning Alec hand-delivered to us before Spring Break? If any of you fuckers get us suspended, I'll personally kick all of your asses."

One of the pledges gulps and Alex, a sophomore pledge who seems to be the leader of the new class, salutes me. "Aye aye, captain." He's a cocky son of a bitch, that's for sure, but he's the only reason we're all in this swanky house for Spring Break, so I can't exactly bitch at the moment.

Everyone fights back laughter just as Shawna slides up next to me, pulling my arm around her shoulder. "Hey, you ready?"

My eyes still hard on my brothers, I give them one last pointed look before turning and pulling Shawna with me. I don't have time to deal with their bullshit today. "Yeah, let's do this."

"So where are we going?" she asks when we're outside. I pat down my pockets, checking to make sure I have my phone and wallet.

"Anything but Smathers Beach."

She giggles, pushing her sunglasses up the bridge of her nose and lacing her hand in mine. I'm so used to seeing her in her regular glasses it almost feels weird to see her in shades. I much prefer having full visibility of her green eyes. "Can we start with breakfast? I'm starving."

"Breakfast it is," I oblige, kissing her hair as we walk.

We don't even look up anything on our phones, just stroll into the first brunch place we find, which just so happens to have unlimited mimosas until noon. And that's how the rest of the day goes. We don't plan, we don't rush — we just take our time and enjoy a little of everything Key West has to offer. We rent bikes, riding them through the shaded streets between colorful houses and stopping at the major tourist spots, like Mile Marker 0 and the Southernmost Point. At sunset, we park our bikes by Mallory Square and find a place on the edge of the water right behind where a man dressed like Captain Jack Sparrow is collecting tips for photos.

As the sun sinks over the water, musical performers serenading us as it does, I pull Shawna in closer, wrapping both arms around her middle and resting my chin on her shoulder. For once, I kind of just want to stay in tonight, take her back to the house, take her slow and steady between the sheets all night long. The crazy thing is that I'm not even scared of the way she makes me feel.

"I'm not ready to go back to reality," she says with a sigh, leaning her head back against me. I rub the smooth skin on her arms with my thumbs as the sky breaks out into a red glow. I feel the same way. When we go back, it's tests and homework and social events. Family Weekend is right around the corner, which means I have to get everything figured out for my brother's stay. But here, in Key West, we don't have any responsibilities. We get to be who we want and do what we want, even if just for a week.

"Stay with me in paradise for a little while longer," I whisper into her ear, my nose in her hair. She smells like tequila and pineapples, my little island girl for at least a few more hours.

Shawna twists in my arms, pulling off her sunglasses to look me in the eyes. We don't say anything, but that one look between us tells me we're both completely out of our element here.

"Maybe we can bring paradise back with us." A smile curls at the left side of her mouth and I slide my hand into her hair. She leans in, pressing her lips to mine just as the square breaks out in applause, the last of the sun sinking away.

Jess

"Are you sure you haven't seen it?" Jess calls out again, this time tossing the same pillows she just rummaged through on one side of the room to the other. "It's Vera Bradley, Can–"

"Canyon print, small backpack, with your name embroidered in yellow I know, Lei, and no, for the one-hundredth time, I haven't seen it," I cut her off. "Jesus, just chill. You can get another Vera bag."

She huffs, standing with her hands hooked on her hips, her hair in a crazy bun as she sweeps the corners of the room with her eyes. "It's not the bag I'm worried about."

"Was your wallet in it?"

"No."

"Your phone?"

"No, it was just something important," she says, frustrated, digging through Skyler's bag now. I roll my eyes, still thumbing through social media on my phone.

"God, if I didn't know you better I'd say it was stashed with drug money." I laugh, shaking my head.

"Could you at least fucking pretend to help me find it?" she snaps, her eyes wild. "You're just sitting there being a giant bitch, which usually I don't mind, but for once in your life can you help me without making me feel like shit in the process?"

"Excuse me?" I scoff, uncrossing my feet on the bed and sitting up straighter. "I am always there for you. If anything, you're the one who always holds me at ten-foot-distance. So don't take your period out on me because you can't find a fucking backpack."

"Whatever, Jess."

"Yeah. Whatever," I repeat, snatching my drink off the nightstand and walking my happy ass downstairs. "Let me know when you're ready."

Everyone else is already on Duval Street, but I agreed to stay back with Ashlei so she could look for her bag without everyone being there. Now, I'm wishing I would have let her do it on her own. She's already being dishonest about whatever is happening with Bo, and now I get the feeling she's hiding something else. At this point, I'm tired of trying to step around the fact that she's being secretive. She knows it, I know it, and I'm sure she can feel that I'm getting tired of it.

Just as my foot hits the bottom step, my phone screen lights up with Jarrett's number.

"Come get me," I answer and he chuckles.

"Over it, are you?"

"Beyond. What are you doing?"

"I just got out of the shower, have to work at the bar tonight. But I was... thinking of you."

The way he says the words flips my stomach. "Were you now?"

"Let's just say I'm more than a little worked up at the moment," he replies, his voice husky. "Are you alone?"

Ashlei curses from upstairs and a loud clatter breaks out. Clearly we're going to be here a while, might as well get my kicks.

"Not right now, but I could be."

"Find a room. I'll call you back." Jarrett ends the call before I have the chance to ask why he needed to end it. Confused, I keep my phone in my hand and duck inside the small half-bathroom downstairs, flicking on the light and checking my appearance in the mirror. If I'm going to be sending him pictures, I definitely want to make them drool-worthy. Luckily, there are about a million makeup bags lined up on the counter, so I reapply my red lipstick and darken my lashes. As soon as I pop the lid back on Skyler's mascara, my phone buzzes.

This time, with a video chat request.

Oh.

"Hi," I say as Jarrett's blurry face slowly comes into view. I almost forgot how incredibly sexy he is. The only view I have is of the top of his shoulders, covered with tats, and his heart-stopping, demanding dark eyes. He's still in his bathroom, the mirror fogged up behind him and small beads of water from his shower gathered on his neck.

"Goddamn, I miss you," he breathes, his eyes searching mine. "Take your clothes off."

I almost laugh, but he's not joking, there's no playful tone to his voice — he meant what he said. His eyes hooded, he bites his lip as I set up my phone on the counter, my hands pulling my hair down from the loose hair tie I had it in.

I shimmy out of my jean shorts first, letting them drop to the floor and eying him through my lashes as I hook my thumbs in the band of my panties and pull them down next. My blouse is light, and I peel it off with ease, unhooking my bra and shaking it off each arm quickly. Jarrett's eyes never leave me, his breaths coming harder.

He moves from the bathroom to his bedroom, propping himself up against his headboard. The camera blanks for just a moment before the view switches and I see him sprawled out in his sheets, his hard body still damp from the shower. Slowly, he unwraps his towel and lets it fall to the side, and I moan when I see how hard he is. He grips himself, stroking slowly as he grows even harder, and suddenly I can't breathe.

"I want you so bad," I whisper, palming my breasts and imagining his hands on me, instead. Each time he strokes, he grows harder, longer, thicker, his fist opening around his shaft as his thumb grazes the tip. I drop to my knees in front of the phone and insert two fingers between my lips, eyes on the lens as I suck my own flesh. Jarrett groans, flipping the camera and adjusting his phone so that I have the most glorious view — his hard cock in his hand, his slick abs and chest, his bottom lip pinned between his teeth as he strokes and watches me.

"Take those wet fingers and fuck yourself with them," he demands, his forearm muscles flexing under the tattooed skin. Grabbing my phone, I lean back against the door and spread my legs wide, taking my time dragging the lens down my body until it lands between my legs. Slowly, my eyes still on his dick, I spread my lips and slide one finger inside, my head falling back at the sensation.

"Oh fuck," Jarrett breathes. "You're always so tight."

"You're always too big," I moan, dipping another finger inside as Jarrett quickens his pace.

"I want to bury my face in that pussy," he husks and the filth turns me on. I let my legs fall open wider, moving up to circle my clit before plunging my fingers back inside. "Taste yourself."

I pull my fingers out and slowly trail them up my stomach, pausing to work my nipples between the slick tips before sliding them in my mouth. Jarrett groans and the guttural noise sends a jolt through me. I'm so fucking hot it's uncomfortable. Squirming, I bite my lip and fuck myself with my fingers again, this time steadying my rhythm, reaching for the orgasm I feel mounting.

"Do you even know how sexy you are?" Jarrett asks, his voice raspy as he pumps. When his hand rolls over the tip of his cock it grazes the abs just above his naval. His every inch is on full display, and all I want is him inside me right now. "You make me so weak, Jess. So fucking weak."

I try so hard to stay quiet, but I know Ashlei must hear my screams as I tumble over the edge, pulling my fingers out to circle my clit and lengthen the ride. Jarrett comes with me, flexing his hips into his hand one last time before grunting out his release. I never thought it would be so seductive to watch him shudder and hear him moan my name as he busts on his abs. I keep my eyes glued on the screen, fascinated, feeling powerful and sexy as hell.

Our breaths are both loud, our limbs weak as we clean up. Jarrett brings the screen to his face, biting his lip. "Hurry home tomorrow."

"Cancel all your plans until Monday."

He chuckles, his eyes low and sedated. "Have fun tonight."

I blow him a kiss and end the call, staring at all my clothes on the floor and laughing to myself. *Did I just video sex my boyfriend in a bathroom?*

Oh my God, did I just call him my boyfriend?

Shaking my head, I quickly dress and burst through the bathroom door, ready to storm upstairs and drag Ashlei down to Duval Street. Instead, I find a sticky note on my purse.

Left without you. Didn't want to interrupt. ;) – Lei

"That little bitch," I whisper with a laugh, wondering if she's still mad at me. I hate fighting with her, and now that I've worked off some tension, I realize I was a little harsh upstairs. Locking up behind me, I scamper down to the street and flag down the first cab I see to shuttle me down to the bars. I'll make it up to Ashlei tonight. Our *last* night. Spring Break is almost over.

My phone pings and when I slide the screen, a full photo of Jarrett in just his board shorts pops up. He's holding the phone to show his reflection in the mirror and my eyes stick hard on the area where his lower abs meet his hip flexors, forming that glorious V.

– A little something to get you through the night. –

I drag my teeth over my bottom lip, shaking my head before tucking my phone away. For once, I can't wait to get back to campus.

Adam

My favorite time to be on the beach is after midnight, when the water is calmer, the sand cooler, and the conversation deeper. Leaning back on my palms, the heels of my feet just barely touching the sand at the edge of my blanket, I listen to the waves roll in.

The last night of Spring Break is coming to an end.

I thought it would be weird, coming with Skyler, her sisters, and Omega Chi Beta without a single other brother of my own. Somehow, though, I managed to have the best time of my life. It was never weird, it was a constant high. Funny enough, I'm one of the last ones standing tonight. It has to be at least three in the morning and the only other people on the beach that I recognize are Cassie, Ashlei, and Bo. They're all gathered around the last beer pong table set up on Smathers Beach, playing against three Omega Chis I don't recognize.

We started our night on Duval Street but moved the population from half the bars to the beach around midnight, wanting to take over the Key West sand one last time. Skyler and Jess turned in pretty early, both exhausted from the week, and Clinton dragged Shawna off not too long after. But I'm still buzzed, not ready to give up vacation just yet.

"Hey." Cassie's voice catches me off guard, I didn't realize she'd stopped playing. Lifting my eyes up her long, lean legs, I note the way the beach fire makes the edges of her silhouetted hair glow a fierce orange. She points back at Bo and Ashlei. "I think we're about to head out."

I frown, nodding. "Okay. I have a key."

"You're not coming with us?"

I shrug, rolling my neck a little and turning back toward the water. "I don't know, I'm not really tired."

"Me either," she says.

"Hang out with me?"

Even with the fire light behind her and her face hidden by the dark night sky, I see the faintest smile. "Okay. One sec." She jogs back over to the girls, saying something I can't quite hear before hugging them both and watching them leave. The last straggling Omega Chi brothers follow suit and then it's just me and Cassie. As she makes her way back across the sand, a familiar ache settles in my chest. It's the same one I've been dealing with every night sleeping next to her — like heartburn, but worse.

I slide over, making more room on my blanket for her to sit. She plops down, pulling her knees up to her chest and threading her arms under her thighs. "I can't believe it's over."

"It's not," I correct. "Not yet."

She grins, laying her cheek on her knees, her green eyes curious as she watches me. She's quiet for a while before she bursts out in a fit of laughter. "I still can't believe you danced on stage at the Red Garter."

"Hey, I got a few dollar bills in the waistband of my boxers that night," I tease, throwing her a wink.

"Yeah. Until the security guards threw you out." She laughs harder, her lightly-tanned cheeks flushing.

"I love how I'm getting picked on by the girl who took fifty-seven seconds to do a beer bong."

"It was my first one!" She smacks my arm and I grin, pulling her head under my arm and ruffling her wild red hair. She pokes me hard in my chest until I release her, both of us still chuckling.

"It really was an amazing trip," she breathes, stretching her legs out on the blanket, her eyes on the waves, mine glued on her. I've never seen her look so free before. Even with her pink lips chapped from the sun and fresh freckles on her cheeks, she's absolutely beautiful in the low glow from the half-moon. Crossing her arms over her chest, she shivers slightly.

"Are you cold?"

"A little."

I smile, opening my arm. "Come here." Her green eyes assess me, as if she's afraid of my touch. "I radiate heat like a werewolf. Seriously, come here."

Cassie hesitates, but slides over, letting me wrap my arms around her. She settles into my grasp and sighs. "Wow. You really are warm."

"Told you."

A small curve meets her lips and she rests her head against my chest. The moment she does, I feel the energy change. I can't explain it. It's like the ocean blanketed us in an electric mist the minute her skin met mine. My throat constricts as I battle with what I should do and what I want to. I don't know if it's the moonlight or the sand or the energy from the night, but I give up trying to fight my urge when it comes to her. I don't want to fight it tonight. I want it to consume me.

Attempting to swallow the lump in my throat, I lift my hand from where it was holding tight to her middle and trail it up her arm, rendering chills in my wake. She stiffens when my fingers graze the bottom of her chin and I lift it, just slightly, tilting my own down toward her. My thumb grazes her jaw and her emerald eyes flick to mine, pupils large and dark. She holds my gaze, her breaths as hard as mine when she lets her eyes fall to my lips.

"What are you doing?" she breathes, so quiet against the sound of the waves that I almost don't hear her.

"Kissing you."

I feel her heart stop and start again with a kick beneath my forearm as I lean in closer, my hand sliding into her hair.

"Adam," she starts. "You're drunk."

"Just because I'm drunk doesn't mean I'm stupid, and I'd be stupid not to kiss you right now."

My hands frame her face and I pull her into me, our lips barely touching before her hand finds the center of my chest. "I have a boyfriend."

I rest my forehead against hers, breaths sharp as they escape my open lips just centimeters from hers. "So tell me to stop."

I wait, expecting to hear the word and praying I won't. My hands slide back into her hair, tilting her mouth up to mine, and her eyes plead with me for something I'm not sure I can give before she lets them flutter closed. Permission granted, I close the distance, pressing my lips to hers as the energy band snaps around us.

Our first kiss flashes through my mind and I let my hands fall to her hips, pulling her closer, knowing it will never be close enough. It's then that I realize Cassie took a piece of me with her that night and she never gave it back. I never asked for it back. And something tells me she'll always have it, no matter what happens after this.

Her fingers weave into my hair, tugging, her back arching toward me as my tongue glides between her lips to meet her own. She whimpers, soft and sweet, and I'm thankful we're sitting because that sound alone would have brought me to my knees. I tug at the belt loop on her shorts and she takes the cue, straddling me, every inch of her shaking as everything we've held back for so long breaks through the fog we've tried to cover it with.

I take my time, massaging her tongue with my own, peppering her neck with kisses, her jaw, sucking the skin behind her ear before finding her mouth again. My hands are everywhere, holding her while she trembles beneath each new touch. She flexes her hips against mine and I wince, my fingertips gripping her hard to stop her from doing it again. It's too much. I know we can't take it there, not tonight, not when she's technically someone else's. Tonight, I'll kiss her, for as long as she'll let me, and hope that, eventually, she'll be able to give me all of her. I'll be able to give her all of me.

Tomorrow will come, and neither of us can stop that. But for now, on a blanket in the sand, beneath a sky of stars, we have tonight.

We have tonight.

Ashlei

I'm so fucking sick.

I wish it was from the alcohol, or sun poisoning, or anything else in the world except the true source. I've tried talking myself down, soothing my nerves, sourcing my options but the truth is I have none.

I lost the backpack.

My chest stings as the realization sinks in and I press my forehead to the bus window. I misplaced my ticket to freedom like it was a spare set of car keys. I looked everywhere, I called everyone, I retraced my steps and dug through every bag in our suite. It's gone. The money is gone.

Xavier is going to kill me.

I mean he might *literally* kill me.

Bo's head is heavy on my shoulder, her breaths long and steady as we pull back into campus. The entire ride home was silent, save for the old 80s rock music keeping the driver of our bus awake. When we stop in front of the Kappa Kappa Beta house, I shrug Bo awake and she wipes at the corner of her mouth, scrubbing her hands down her face.

"I'm so tired."

"Come on, we can take a nap."

She smiles sweetly at me before we shuffle off the bus behind the rest of our sisters. Every step feels weighted as my mind races with what my next moves need to be. I was so close, *so* close to being done with Kya and Hayden and Xavier and every fucking nightmare that's been wrecking my life for months. My only saving grace is that I didn't lose all of the money, but I still lost over a third of it, which is enough to get me into an even deeper hole with a very dangerous man. Every new thought drives the knife in deeper and tears sting my eyes. I suck my lips between my teeth, fighting them back, just as several of my sisters' phones ping all at once.

A chorus of varying ringtones surrounds us on the front lawn of our house and glances are exchanged as we pull out our phones. Mine is in my bag, so I lean over Bo's as she slides the notification. It's a group text from a short-code number.

– OMEGA CHI BETA SPRING BREAK CONQUESTS. CLICK TO VIEW. –

Bo eyes me with a bent brow before tapping the link. When she does, her hand flies to her mouth.

It's a website.

With photos and videos of every girl fucked inside Alex's Spring Break mansion.

My stomach sinks deeper and deeper as our sisters turn one by one, their eyes landing hard on us as a sweat breaks at the nape of my neck. I catch the betrayal beneath Jess' hurt expression and feel the knife twist once again.

Because right there on the homepage is a looping video of their top conquest.

Me and Bo.

EPISODE 5

"What are SISTERS FOR?"

Bear

If ever it were true that Bear hugs are the best hugs, right now would be that moment. Wrapping my arms around my baby brother, I clap him hard on the back, holding him longer than usual and fighting back the sting of emotions threatening to form as tears. We're in the middle of the airport and I know I'm probably embarrassing him, but I don't give a shit. It's the start of Family Weekend and my baby brother is here.

My baby brother is *here*.

"Nice to see you too, loser," he mumbles into my chest, voice cracking a bit less than our last long phone call. He weaves his way out of my grasp and I ruffle his hair.

"Don't act like you're too cool to hug your big bro."

"Well, if you didn't hug like Aunt Shonda at Easter," he teases and I sock him hard on the arm, making him yelp and rub the spot with a smile on his face. My little brother is not-so-little anymore. At just thirteen, the top of his head reaches my shoulders and he's started to bulk, though his frame is still pretty lean in comparison to mine. His curly hair is medium length and unruly, his skin as dark as mine, eyes and nose virtually identical. Anyone who looked at us would know we're brothers, and I catch Skyler ogling our similarities from the corner of my eye.

"Clayton, this is Skyler Thorne. She's the one I'm always telling you about."

"Damn," he draws out the word, eyes devouring Skyler in her small, tight white shorts and loose tank top. "Please tell me I'm bunking with you this weekend, sweetheart."

I thump him on the head and he shoots me a glare, but Skyler just laughs.

"You couldn't handle a night in my bed, Baby Bear."

He grimaces. "Ugh, please tell me that's not going to be my nickname."

"What? I think it's cute," Skyler defends. Clayton's shoulders fall and Skyler fights back a smile as I grab his duffle bag and throw it over my shoulder.

"Come on," I say, steering us toward the large automatic doors that lead out to the taxi cabs. "Your big brother is taking you to a college party."

"What?! No way!" Clayton's dark eyes light up and he holds his hand out until Skyler smacks it with a high five. "Time to get wasted. Make sure you call up all the hottest sorority babes because Baby Bear is looking for someone to hibernate with tonight." He howls and it echoes off the concrete walls of the parking garage.

"Going to get a thirteen-year-old drunk?" Skyler asks me quietly, cocking a brow.

"I bought some non-alcoholic beer. What he doesn't know won't hurt him." I wink and she shakes her head, a few strands falling from the messy bun she's paired with her casual appearance. I love her like this—no makeup, hair up, wearing the first thing she found in her closet. Skyler Thorne in her natural element, ladies and gents.

"I smell trouble."

"Nah, he'll be fine. He's a Pennington."

I beam at Skyler before hailing a cab and climbing in the back with her and Clayton. I throw my arm around his shoulders and tease him about girls and video games and everything else simple in his life because it makes me feel like home. *He* makes me feel like home. The good part of home that I miss.

When we get to the Omega Chi house, I give Clayton the tour while Skyler sets us up for a game of beer pong, complete with cups filled to the brim with Clayton's special beer on one side.

"This place is amazing," he says with wonder as we finally drop his bag off in my room. "No wonder you never come home."

I frown, trying not to read too much into that assessment. "Ready for your first game of beer pong?"

He laughs. "I'm ready for *a* game of beer pong."

"Wait, you've played before?"

Clayton shrugs, like it's no big deal. "Maybe."

It honestly doesn't surprise me that he's already played, because that's the way it was where I grew up in Pittsburgh—where he's growing up right now. I was exposed to drinking and drugs well before my pre-teen years—mostly courtesy of our own family—and I know he's no stranger to it, either. I can only hope he's smart about his choices, and judging by the way he looks up to me, I feel confident that he is.

Smirking, I grab a fresh pack of pong balls out of my dresser and break it open, tossing one up in the air. "Fine. I guess I don't need to take it easy on you, then."

He grins back just as cockily and I wonder how much of myself I've rubbed off on him over the years.

We play three back-to-back games before Clayton realizes his beer isn't doing what it should be. Skyler and I are playing on a team and I paired him with a hot little Zeta, but she's probably doing more to distract him than help him. Her name is Jazmine, though everyone around campus calls her Jazzy, and she keeps running her long manicured nails through Clayton's tight curls and touching his arm over the table. If his skin wasn't so dark, I'd swear he was blushing.

I finally concede and let him drink a little Bud Light, but not in beer pong, because after a few games he'd probably be shitfaced. The last thing our fraternity needs is to get caught with a drunk minor at our house. Frowning, I realize I haven't been able to talk to Skyler much about how her sisters are handling everything with the Spring Break debacle, so I leave Clayton where he's set up on a bean bag playing video games with Josh and go search for her.

It's a Thursday night and everyone is still recovering from Spring Break, so the house is surprisingly dead. Well, for our house, anyway. I can hear Clayton's laughs over the video game sound effects as I round the corner into our kitchen and lean against the counter next to Skyler.

"Tequila?" I ask, eyes on the shot glass pinched between her fingers.

She nods, her blue eyes dull and tired. "It's been that kind of week."

"The blogs?"

She throws the liquid down her throat, eyes squinting against the burn as she reaches for a lime slice. "Partly. I mean, I can't say I'm exactly thrilled to be gaining the reputation as a heartbreaker, but it's not the biggest thing on my plate right now."

"The website?"

She nods, quiet as she refills her shot glass. I push off the counter long enough to retrieve one for me and slide it up next to hers to fill, too. "We kicked him out, you know? Alex." I blow out a long breath through my nose, my hands gripping the edge of the counter as I think about the website he made from Spring Break detailing all his conquests and a few of our other brothers'. I knew I didn't like that cocky son of a bitch, but I didn't know he was a fucking idiot. He's lucky Florida doesn't have laws against "revenge porn" yet, though our alumni brothers made sure to warn us that those laws are well on their way to being passed. Even though it was only one brother's idea, several were involved, and it reflected on our entire chapter as a whole. So, naturally, Alec already called a meeting with nationals, and now, we await our fate. "Thank God he hadn't been sworn in as a brother yet. He doesn't deserve our letters."

"That's the fucking truth." She clinks her glass to mine and we toss them back, hissing through our teeth as we slam them back on the counter. "It was fucked up what he did, but I think our sisters are a little more shocked by Bo and Ashlei. No one knew. I mean, Jess suspected but . . ." She shrugs. "We've never had this situation before, you know? At least not openly. They're our sisters, but they're dating each other. Let's just say some are handling it better than others. And Jess has already almost fought the half of our chapter stupid enough to be vocal about their disapproval."

"Shit, I didn't even think about that."

"Erin is going crazy trying to figure out what to do. Everyone on the executive board is."

I feel a pang of guilt chase the tequila at the mention of Erin's name, remembering how I lashed out on her on Spring Break. I haven't talked to her since. "It's not like they can kick them out, right? They didn't do anything wrong. They couldn't have known he had a camera set up in that room."

"No, they didn't do anything wrong, but some of the girls on exec don't think it's okay for them to date. It's a big ordeal." She sighs. "I don't know. I just hope it doesn't tear any of us apart."

"It won't," I assure her, wrapping her in my arms. She inhales a deep, shaky breath as I rest my chin on her head. "I know my KKB girls, and the bond you guys have is too strong to be broken by something like this."

"I hope you're right."

"I am." I kiss her forehead before we make our way back to the living room, joining Clayton and the rest of my brothers around the television. For the rest of the night, my brothers tell Clayton stories about me and give him tips on how to score girls, like they have any credibility in that area. It's all laughter and good vibes, and in so many ways it feels like a piece of me that I've been missing is finally in the same room again.

I never want to let the feeling go.

***

I'm not sure what time it is when I feel her crawl into bed with me.

I left my window open, knowing she would want me tonight since we haven't seen each other all day. Clayton is sleeping on the giant bean bag in the Omega Chi loft, and as soon as he passed out, I shot off a text to Shawna to let her know the offer was open.

As if it ever wasn't anymore.

She doesn't speak when she climbs under the covers, already undressed, already panting with need. She just slips her warm hand beneath the band of my boxer briefs and drags her tongue along the edge of my jaw until I meet her mouth with my own. She inhales stiffly when our lips touch and her grip on me tightens, intoxication flowing through the point of contact straight into my blood stream. Shawna always brings me to the best kind of high, but having her hands on me when I'm balancing on the edge of sleep is fucking incredible.

My hands find her hips and I grip her hard, pulling her to straddle me without my mouth breaking contact with hers. She pulls my briefs down just enough for me to kick them the rest of the way off and then she pushes off my chest. Palming me, she places me at her wet entrance, pausing for just the smallest second. It's long enough for me to peek up at her through heavy eyelids and see her bathed in the dim moonlight streaming through my window, reminding me of our first night together on my birthday. She arches her back as I flex my hips and push inside her, my hands still holding her firmly in place.

We moan together, the same numbing electricity rolling over each of us. I let her work me slow, her thighs tensing beneath my rough fingertips as she does. Her hands are on my chest, balancing, her head is back, hair falling down her back, the purple ends catching the light in a metallic glimmer. I slide my hands up to frame her small waist, trail them over her hard, pierced nipples, and hook them behind her neck before pulling her down to me.

I kiss her softly, her hair falling all around us as I gently take the lead. Rocking my hips deeper, soft whimpers escape her lips and find refuge on mine. My hands on the move again, chills break in their wake as they snake down her lower back to grip her ass firmly, controlling her movements. She willingly lets me take the reins. Her teeth bite the sensitive skin on my neck just below my ear and I hiss, pumping into her harder, driving us both toward the apex.

When I know we're both close, I pull her forehead to mine, eyes searching, breaths coming hard as I keep our rhythm steady. There are words suspended between us in a space they may never escape, and though neither of us dare speak them out loud, our bodies scream them between the sheets as I rock once, twice, three times, reaching new depths. We hold each other tighter, nails in skin, eyes still wide as the final spark ignites and burns us to the core. We ride out the flames, scorching together, caught in the fire.

A blistering inferno rages in my bedroom, and we gladly go down together in the blaze.

Skyler

It's such a contrast to see the same sisters who were barely clothed and completely sloshed just over a week ago completely sober, dressed in our school colors, ribbons in their hair as they greet the constant stream of parents entering our house. I'm on the front line, handing out programs to smiling faces as they file in out of the Florida heat. My parents aren't among them, since last minute work issues kept them from making the trip down for Family Weekend, but Erin has volunteered her mom as tribute to keep me company—almost too eagerly, actually.

I find out very quickly why.

After an introductory speech from my Grand Big, Kelsey, the parents get tours of the house while sipping lemonade and Erin introduces me to a thin, older version of herself.

"Mom, this is Skyler, my Little," Erin says, gesturing to me.

"Elizabeth Xander." I take her dainty hand in my own and attempt a shake, but she stops me short with a tight, brief squeeze. "Pleasure, I'm sure."

"I've heard so much about you," I volunteer, my eyes catching Erin's. She rolls them behind her mom's back and I grin. "Would you like to see our rooms?"

Elizabeth shakes her head, scouring the living room of the house with an upturned nose. Her dark blonde hair looks just like Erin's, especially since it's pulled back into a tight bun, throwing more attention to the strand of pearls draped over her collar bone. She and Erin are both in brightly colored Lily Pulitzer dresses and wedges, and suddenly I wish I'd let Erin dress me this morning. I'm in jean shorts and a white tank top with our letters on it.

"No need, I had the full tour last year."

"We should probably head over to the tailgate, anyway," Erin adds. Her mother nods and they link arms, leading the way.

Family Weekend is packed with random events for students and their parents, including everything from guest lectures to fraternity parties. The biggest event, however, is the baseball game tailgate. The grassy event area right beside the baseball stadium is transformed into the ultimate tailgate experience, food and booze included, and we all pack the stands for the night's game. Well, those of us who make it past the day drinking, anyway.

Elizabeth talks the entire walk over, chatting with us about her latest shopping trips and Botox treatments. Anytime Erin attempts bringing up her position in the sorority or her classes, her mother loses interest immediately, tapping away on her phone or changing the subject back to something superficial. It's clear she doesn't approve of Erin's major or career choice.

"Oh my, am I seeing double?" A smooth voice drawls from behind us just as we reach the edge of the tailgate yard. Bright orange, teal, and white tents pepper the grass and our Student Government President speaks loudly over the microphone system, welcoming the parents to PSU. When we turn, Erin smiles at Landon, her latest fling and the owner of the smooth voice spitting out clichés. Still, her smile seems bleak, the same way it's been for weeks, and I wonder how badly the stress of the Omega Chi website is getting to her.

"Hi," she says sweetly and Landon grasps her gently by the elbow, pulling her just close enough to kiss her cheek before turning to Elizabeth. His blonde hair is almost too perfectly styled and his freshly tanned skin from Spring Break contrasts harshly with the pastels of his polo and frat shorts.

"You didn't tell me you had a sister, Ex," he flirts, reaching for her mom's hand. She's all smiles as he lifts it to his mouth for a kiss. Erin and I exchange glances. *Is this guy serious right now?*

"Aren't you sweet as pie. I'm Elizabeth Xander, Erin's mother. And you are?"

"Landon Turner, ma'am."

"What a strong name," she says, giggling, eyes bright. "Are you Erin's boyfriend?"

"Mother," Erin scolds, cheeks blushing a light shade of pink.

Landon doesn't miss a beat. He pulls Erin in under his arm and smiles a bright, charming, country smile—all toothy and genuine. "Just friends for now, ma'am. But I'm working on her."

Elizabeth's brows shoot up and she grins at Erin. "Well heavens, child, give in already!"

We all laugh, me mostly to ease the awkwardness, and Erin leads us to a shaded picnic table near the alumni tent. It's a little too warm today, the sun shining high in the sky without a cloud to block it. I'm already sweating slightly from the walk over and gladly take the fresh bottle of water offered to us by the volunteers as we sit down.

"So, Landon, what's your major?" Erin's mom asks, sipping from her own bottle. She's leaning over the dark teal picnic table, ready to devour whatever he says. Of course, when he tells her he's pre-med with a focus in plastic surgery, his Ken doll smile locked in place and his hand running through his blonde hair, she practically sits in his lap.

She lets him ramble on and I lean in to whisper to Erin. "You okay?"

"Fine. This is actually tame for her, believe it or not."

"I think she's planning your wedding."

"Like I said, tame."

We both giggle but neither Landon nor Elizabeth notice us. Draining the rest of my water, I tip the empty plastic toward Erin. "I'm going to get a refill and see if I can track down the other girls. Find me later?"

She nods and I don't even bother interrupting the conversation between Landon and Erin's mom to excuse myself. After tossing my empty bottle in one of the recycling bins, I snatch a turkey wrap off the alumni table and walk the tents. It's kind of funny seeing the parents on campus. Some of them are starry-eyed, possibly setting foot on a college campus for the first time while others look comfortable as they chat about the "glory days" of PSU. I smile, realizing my parents belong to that first group. Skott, my older brother, never went to college. He just left straight for the Peace Corps after high school. I'm the first and *only* one in our family to ever attend a university, which makes me feel strangely like a pioneer for the Thornes.

I wouldn't even be here if it weren't for poker, and now that I'm getting noticed by big poker blogs and reporters, the two worlds are crossing more than I ever thought they would. Adam was right to call it off with me before this summer, because there's no way I'll have time for him. Or anyone else, for that matter. I feel like I'm at the precipice of something huge, and now is my time to make a name for myself, so I'm filling my schedule with tournaments all summer long. If I have it my way, I'll have next year's tuition paid off by July so I can start focusing on bigger and better things.

Like the American Poker Club Tournament.

A light breeze rolls across the tailgate yard and blows my hair back as I round the second row of tents, mind still wandering. It's a tempting thought, entering the APC tourney. I'm not prepared enough to enter it this year. Hell, I don't even have a third of the entry fee. But if I play my cards right, I just might be able to enter the one next May, and if I won or even placed in the top three, I'd be set. No more having to work tournaments at night and be a sorority girl during the day. I could get my parents completely out of debt and then some, tuition for the rest of my time at PSU would be paid, and I could focus on my major and figure out what I want to do with my life.

The thought makes me giddy.

"Hey heartbreaker," Adam says, bumping into me from the side and stirring me from my thoughts. His signature goofy grin is firmly in place, his dark hair a little unruly and a light sweat is breaking on his forehead.

"Oh God, not you, too. I really hope that's not my new nickname."

He shrugs, falling in line with my rhythm. "I don't know, I think it fits pretty perfectly."

"Says the one who broke up with me."

"That's not what the tabloids are saying."

I blanch. "What?"

Adam's shit-eating grin grows wider and when I realize he's joking, I shove him hard into the pole of a passing tent. He laughs, dodging it easily and scooping me up into a hug from behind. "You should have seen your face!"

"You're an asshole."

He drops me back to the ground easily and we walk the yard until we find my sisters, talking the entire time about Spring Break and his upcoming chapter elections. It's nice to know we can still be friends with no awkward feelings between us. Adam Brooks is a nice guy to have in your corner, and I'm glad I didn't screw that up by tagging him as my boyfriend for a few months.

I realize it may be quite a while before I let anyone hold that title again, because the truth is, my heart is already taken. Poker is my boyfriend, and we're taking our relationship to the next level this summer. It's getting serious between us, and Poker is one jealous son-of-a-bitch who hates the idea of sharing me. Probably smart, since the last thing I want to be known as if I make it to the tournament next May is a slut or a man-eater. If I'm going to get my name out of the headlines for my dating lifestyle and into the limelight for my skills, I've got some work to do.

I feel some big changes on the horizon.

And I've got my game face on.

Ashlei

They say avoiding your problems won't make them go away, but what happens when you have too many problems to face them all at once?

That's the question I've been battling with since Spring Break. First and foremost, I had to deal with the Omega Chi website—there was no running away from that. Once we hit campus, the website was texted to virtually everyone, and those who didn't get the original text eventually found out from the masses. Gossip like that spreads like a wildfire at PSU, and with a threesome on the front page, there was plenty of juice to fuel the flames.

So, like my mom always taught me, I focused on one thing at a time—starting with Bo and the website. As I ignore yet another text from Xavier and slip my phone back into my pocket, I try to reassure myself that mom's philosophy will pull through. If it's one thing at a time, I'd rather start with Bo than Xavier.

Ralph's is more packed than usual, but with a rather different crowd. The baseball game is over and all the students and parents have migrated north to everyone's favorite bar. As they do every year, the owners of Ralph's have set up karaoke on the same stage where we held the KKB auction just a couple of months ago and my dad is currently belting out *Paradise by the Dashboard Light*. His dark curls sway a bit as he animates the Meatloaf hit and Mom loops her arm through mine, bending over in a fit of laughter at our table. We're the same size, twins by practically every feature, and I can't help but mirror her laugh when my dad dramatically dips the microphone at the end.

"Bravo!" Mom yells as the bar erupts into whistles and catcalls. Dad takes a bow and hops off the stage, strutting back over to our table with a Cheshire grin. He kisses my mom's forehead and flops down on the bench across from her, taking a long swig from his beer mug.

"Well now I see where Ashlei gets her performance skills from," Skyler jokes, throwing my dad a high five. They've been buddied up all night, like two peas in a pod. In fact, my parents have been getting along with everyone—even Bo's parents. Erin and her mom went out to a late dinner with Landon after the baseball game and Cassie took her parents to watch Grayson play at Cup O' Joe's, but Skyler, Bo, her parents, my parents and I all came out to Ralph's to continue the night's festivities. I have yet to see Jess or her family, but that's been normal lately.

It's strange. Jess has been sticking up for me and Bo more than anyone in the chapter, yet she hasn't said one word to me since the day the news about the website broke. I can't say I blame her, because I know she feels betrayed. We're best friends and Bo is her Little. For many reasons, we should have told her, but we didn't get the chance. She'll come around, she just needs time. Jess is the kind of person who has to go through her own process, and she can't be swayed by anyone else.

"You're up next, sweetie," Dad says, nodding at Mom. She snorts.

"You wish. I wouldn't get on that stage if you paid me."

"Oh yeah?" Dad rubs his chin, bright green eyes lifting to the dingy ceiling of the bar. "What if that Michael Kors watch you've been wanting was up for grabs?"

Mom's eyes widen. "Don't play with my emotions."

"Come on, Mom!" I coax her further. "We can do a duet. Spice Girls or something equally as cliché."

She chews her lip, contemplating. Her eyes find Dad again and she points a freshly manicured finger in his direction. "You swear about the watch?"

Dad holds up two fingers. "On my honor."

Mom jumps up and skips to the stage and I follow. She selects *Turn Back Time* by Cher and we sound absolutely horrible together, but it's the first time I've done something with my mom, just the two of us, in longer than I can remember. I'm always hidden behind my sisters, and as shitty as it is, part of me is thankful that neither of them could make it this weekend. For once, the attention is on me, and I don't care how petty and immature it is to want that because I do. I need it right now.

I told my parents that I'm bisexual last night.

I expected Dad to scream and Mom to cry, but instead they gave each other a knowing look as if I didn't even have to say the words out loud. They both hugged me and we talked all night, each word making me feel more and more okay. I even told them about the website, though I begged them not to say anything to Bo's parents until she felt comfortable enough to tell them herself—if that day ever even came.

So maybe it's the fact that I finally opened up to them that makes me feel like I'm part of the family again. Still, I didn't tell them everything—I conveniently left out that I'm indebted to a drug lord and I lost a third of what I owe him a little over a week ago.

Baby steps.

I've been so caught up dealing with the website scandal that I really haven't had time to figure out what I'm going to do about Xavier. If I know him as well as I think I do, his patience is wearing thin, and it's only a matter of time before he shows up at my door demanding his money. After my parents leave, I'll have to face the music and figure it out.

I just have no idea where to even start.

Dad pays up just like he said he would, ordering Mom's watch right on his phone once we're back at the table. Bo's parents have the same look on their face that's been there all night—a cross between amused and terrified. Apart from her skin tone, Bo looks nothing like them. Her eyes are wide, pinched just a bit at the corners, her smile big and bright, hair sleek. Her parents, on the other hand, rarely smile, their narrow eyes always surveying the surroundings like they're looking for escape routes.

"Well shit, looks like I missed the invitation to the party."

We're all mid-laugh when we turn and find Jess, solo, her eyes glossy and low, a half-empty beer bottle in her hand. I don't have to look at her longer than two seconds to know she's shitfaced. And, judging by the sneer on her lips, she's still pissed at me.

"Jess!" My dad jumps up first with Mom right behind him and they each wrap her in a hug, but her eyes don't leave mine. "It's so nice to see you. Are your parents here? I'd love to buy your dad a beer." Jess and I have spent a lot of time at each other's houses on breaks, and our parents are close because of it. I wonder if Jess told her parents about me and Bo. For some reason, the thought of them disapproving upsets me more than anyone else.

Dad looks around Jess' shoulder like he expects them to appear, but Jess just tilts her bottle to her lips and sloshes it back. "Nah, they went back to the hotel. Maybe you'll see them tomorrow."

Bo shifts in her seat, uneasy under Jess' glare. Her parents seem to pick up her vibes, too, because they're assessing Jess like she's a threat rather than a sister.

"They didn't drop you at the house on their way?" Skyler asks, and I know she's picking up the same cues I am. Jess is swaying, even with one hand firmly propped on the edge of our table, and she simply shakes her head no. Skyler smiles, but with caution. "Well I was just about to get a cab, so we can ride back together."

"We should probably get you guys back to the hotel, too," Bo says to her mom and dad as she stands. Her parents do the same but Jess stumbles over to them quickly.

"Oh no, I just got here!" She trips over the leg of a chair just as she reaches them and I eye Skyler, silently making a plan to get her out of here—and fast. "Are these your parents, Little? You have to introduce me!" But instead of waiting for an introduction, Jess throws her arms around Bo's mother first before fist bumping her father. They don't even try to hide their shock, they just let their mouths hang open before pinning Bo under a disapproving glare.

"Māmā, Bàba, this is Jess. She's my Big Sister in the sorority."

Bo's mother bows just slightly but her father narrows his eyes further before spouting off something in Chinese to Bo.

"Please, at least join me for one drink before you leave. We've just met," Jess says, motioning for them to take a seat. Bo looks to me for help but I just shrug, feeling as helpless as she does. Painting on a forced smile as everyone sits back down, Jess turns to my mom. "How was your day? What did you do?"

"Oh we had a wonderful time! We toured the house and sat front row at the game. Oh, and then Ron did karaoke!"

Dad smacks her leg playfully. "So did you! Should I pull up the video on my phone, Cher?"

Mom cackles, reaching out to touch Jess' arm, clearly oblivious to the tension at the table. Jess just listens patiently, sipping from her beer intermittently.

"Ashlei sang with me. She was actually kind of amazing. Who knew our little princess was keeping her singing talents a secret?"

Jess laughs with Mom, waving her empty beer bottle at a passing waitress. "Oh, she's quite good at keeping secrets."

"Jess," Skyler warns, silently signaling to the same waitress not to bring her another damn drop.

"What?" Jess scoffs, balancing the bottle between her forefinger and the table. "The girl should get an award. Do they have one for that sort of thing? We could always make one." Her lazy eyes find mine again. "*Most Likely to be a Lying Bitch*—Ashlei Daniels."

"We're leaving," Bo snaps, pushing her chair back again as her parents lift themselves from the bench.

"I think I know what this is about, Jess, and I understand why you're upset," my dad says, his hands up just a bit. When I filled my parents in on the website last night, I told them my suspicions that Jess was far from okay with the whole situation. He's talking to her like she's about to jump off the ledge of a building. Right about now, I wish she would. "But maybe we should talk about this later."

"Huh," Jess surmises, chewing on Dad's words. "I don't know. Now seems like the perfect fucking time to talk about it, actually. Especially since we've got the whole fam damily here." She gestures to Bo and her parents and suddenly my entire body is alert. I feel it—something bad is about to happen.

"What is she talking about, Bo?" her mom asks, brows bent inward in confusion.

"Nothing, Māmā. Let's go."

"What, you don't know?" Jess interjects before barking out a loud laugh. "Oh, please, let me be the one to fill you in."

"Jess!" Skyler hisses just as I warn, "That's enough, J-Love." My parents and I stand together, ready to escort Jess out to a cab.

"You see, your lovely daughter here, my precious, *sweet* Little, has been keeping a secret from me. From all of us, actually."

"You don't know what you're saying," my mom tries, but Jess just keeps talking louder.

"Don't worry, she's not alone, because Ashlei was part of all of this, too."

"Big, please," Bo pleads.

"But now, their secret's been leaked—because they're all over a website. And wasn't *that* just the peachiest way to find out that two of my best friends are lesbians." She pauses and my stomach sinks through the floor. "Together."

Everyone is silent for a stretched moment and as Jess' face crumples, I know she regretted the words she said before they even left her mouth. But now it's too late. And after just three quiet seconds, chaos erupts.

Bo's hand flies to her mouth as her parents start screaming at her in Chinese while my parents scream at Jess in English. Skyler pinches the bridge of her nose and I flop back down into my seat, feeling the weight heavy on my chest. I can't breathe, I can't speak, I can't think.

"What the fuck is wrong with you?!" Bo yells so loud her voice cracks and tears break on her cheeks. Her parents are still screaming, fingers waving, faces red with anger. Bo snatches her purse off the table and I shake myself out of my trance, jumping up to pull her into me.

"I'm so sorry."

When I touch her, her parents go absolutely ballistic and she rips away from my grasp.

"Not now." Bo snaps as her parents shove her toward the door.

"Just call me later, it'll be okay," I lie, calling out after her. She turns just enough for the light to catch the fresh tears on her cheeks and I suck my bottom lip between my teeth, knowing in my gut that nothing is okay, least of all this.

Whipping around, I pin Jess with my glare, chest heaving as what she did finally settles in. "Are you fucking happy, Jess? Is this what you wanted? You aired our dirty laundry so now you can feel better about yours?"

Jess' face is sheet white and her palms grip the edge of the table hard.

"We all know you're still fucking your teacher, but guess what? We're your sisters. And we know you'll tell us when *you're* ready, just like Bo and I would have told you. It's not our fault that website happened, but thanks for making an already shitty situation ten times shittier."

"I think I'm going to be sick." Jess gags into the back of her wrist and takes off for the bathroom, parting the sea of drunk parents on wobbly ankles.

Skyler's shoulders sag and she lets out a long sigh. "I'm so sorry, guys."

"It's not your fault," my dad assures her, running a hand through his thick hair, the curls bouncing right back into place. "She was hurt and upset and she acted irrationally. It happens."

"She's a bitch," I correct him and he scolds me with his eyes, but I just cross my arms over my chest.

"You better go check on her, sweetie." My mom motions toward the bathroom and Skyler nods, giving my arm a squeeze on her way.

Dad lets out a breath through his nose before crossing to me and pulling me into his arms. He wraps me in a tight hug, the one he used to save for the bad days, and I fold into him, squeezing my eyes tight against the pain.

"It'll be okay, baby girl," he whispers into my hair, rocking me gently. "Her parents will understand. That's their daughter, and they'll support her. No matter what."

I sniff, shaking my head against his chest. "Nice speech. Now tell me what you really think they'll do."

Dad just pulls me closer and Mom rubs my back, her sad eyes connecting with mine. He doesn't have to say a word.

The answer is in the silence.

Bear

The best thing about going to school in Florida is the spring weather. While the rest of the country is still battling with cold fronts and snow, we're sitting pretty at eighty-five degrees under a partly-cloudy sky. There's a light breeze rolling through the palm trees and Clayton inhales a deep breath, letting it go with a grin on his face. It's the last day of Family Weekend, and as my little brother and I walk across campus to the College Showcase, I can't help but smile along with him. It's been amazing having him here.

"We should do this more often," I say, tossing my arm over his shoulder. "Maybe you could fly down for Shark Week this summer."

"That would be so awesome!" He shakes his head, eyes hidden behind Omega Chi branded sunglasses. "I can't wait to go to college . . . to get out of Pittsburgh."

I squeeze his shoulder firmly before dropping my arm and tucking my hands in my pockets. "You'll be out of there soon enough, little brother. Just try to stay focused on your grades and sports while you're there. Set up your future."

He nods, squinting slightly as the sun peeks around a cloud. "I will." When he turns to me, his expression is hard. "Once I leave, I'm never going back, Clinton."

I swallow, knowing exactly where he is right now. I remember the feeling. I thought the longer I was at Palm South, the more it would fade away, but I can still remember every minute of hating life when I was waiting for high school to end. "I know, baby brother. I don't blame you. I only go back because you're there."

Clayton's brows furrow as we round the fountain and make our way toward the Student Union. "Our family sucks."

I offer a short laugh. "Yeah, unfortunately you can't choose your blood family, but you'll always have me." Smiling, I nudge him. "And when you rush, you get to pick a whole new band of brothers—ones who also don't suck. Then, one day, you'll find a girl, and she'll make all the other girls feel so obsolete. You'll marry her, you'll have kids, and then before you know it, you have your own family." I adjust the backpack of beer on my back, pulling the straps down so it adjusts higher on my shoulders. "And it'll be up to you, then, to make sure that family doesn't suck like ours did."

Clayton smiles up at me, just a slight tug at the corner of his lips, but enough to let me know he needed to hear that. I pull him in for a noogie just as we reach the first row of tents outside the union. The fraternities and sororities always make up the entire first row, and when I spot Adam at the Alpha Sigma tent, I whistle through my teeth.

"Glad to see you're still alive after Spring Break, Brooks." I clap him on the back and he flips me the bird, but with a smile. "This is my little brother, Clayton."

Adam shakes Clayton's hand, lifting his sunglasses up into his hair. "Oh shit, there's another generation of you? President Whittington is going to have a heart attack when your name comes across the admissions desk."

I chuckle. "Just wait until he realizes Clayton is rushing, too."

"God help us all."

We all laugh for a second before Adam breaks the conversation long enough to talk to the mom of a pledge. He hands her a few pamphlets about their founders and heritage and runs over their philanthropic events before she nods and smiles, letting her son lead her to the food set up behind the tent. When Adam turns back to us, his smile fades, his eyes adjusting on something behind us rather than on our faces. He flicks his sunglasses back down and I spin to see what he's looking at. When I find Cassie, her parents, and Grayson laughing as they make their way down the line of tents, I turn to Adam again, narrowing my eyes.

"Hey guys!" Cassie says cheerily when they reach us. I watch as her face transforms from ecstatic when she sees me to curious when she notices Clayton to absolutely terrified when she realizes Adam is behind us. Or maybe that's nervous I'm seeing. Maybe both.

Something is weird between those two.

"Hey," I greet, pulling her in for a hug. "Cassie, this is my little brother, Clayton."

Clayton reaches out for her hand, sliding his sunglasses down his nose just enough to peek at her over the top of the shades. "Well hello, Beautiful. You can call me Baby Bear. How do you feel about younger men, sweetheart?"

Cassie's mom blushes and covers her smile as her dad lets out a loud belly laugh. Her dad is odd-looking, sporting the same fiery red hair that Cassie has except with bronze skin and not a freckle in sight. Her mom, on the other hand, has light blonde hair and green eyes with pale skin, the apples of her cheeks peppered with freckles. It's like Cassie is literally the perfect mix of the two.

"Damn, I need to step up my game," Grayson says, reaching out his hand to shake Clayton's next. "Sorry, Baby Bear, but this little lady is taken at the moment."

Clayton shrugs. "We'll see what the story is in four-and-a-half years when I turn eighteen." Cassie's parents laugh again, but Adam's mouth is still in a thin line, his eyes hard on where Cassie's hand is grasped firmly in Grayson's.

I introduce myself to Cassie's parents next and then they turn to Adam, expectant. He shifts, gripping the fliers in his hand a little too tightly as Cassie finally clears her throat. "Mom, Dad, this is Adam Brooks. He's going to be the president of Alpha Sigma next year."

Adam forces a smile, one that's all teeth and charming as fuck. The kid is good, but I can still see that he's hiding something. I knew the night of the Fratalina Wine Mixer. He's lucky he was smart enough to call it off with Skyler. "Well, we'll see. Elections haven't happened yet."

"We all know it'll be you," Cassie says again with a sweet smile, but her eyes look stressed, too, as they connect with Adam's.

We chat for a while in what feels like a pleasant manner, though Adam, Cassie and I feel the awkward tension that lies beneath it. After Grayson tells Cassie's dad how he works to pay for his tuition and everyone leans in for more, Adam excuses himself to go talk to a group of Alpha Sigma parents, but not until he and Cassie share another glance that says nothing but screams something fucked up all at once.

I catch Cassie's eyes with my own after Adam's gone and she flushes, tucking a strand of hair behind her ear and looping her arm through Grayson's, her attention snapping back to him. It's then that I notice a familiar face at a tent two rows over behind Cassie.

A familiar face, but that's all that's familiar about her.

Shawna's once-purple hair is now all black, falling straight down to her shoulders where it curls in soft waves. Her glasses are replaced with contacts, her normally casual and grungy style opted out in exchange for a knee-length white skirt and light yellow, button-up blouse. She's even wearing wedges, which I didn't realize she owned at all. Still, even with the changes, she's fucking gorgeous, and a shit-eating grin spreads on my face at the sight of her.

"Be right back," I murmur to Clayton before sprinting across the union to the tent she and who I assume are her parents are gathered around. I'm light on my feet, careful to watch the angle at which I approach. When I know I'm safe and she hasn't seen me, I close the distance and scoop her into my arms from behind, spinning her around. She squeals, but not in the way I wanted, before wriggling out of my arms. I drop her gently to the ground and kiss her cheek, but she backs away quickly, her cheeks hot, a nervous smile on her face.

"Hi, Clinton," she says, her bright green eyes darting to her parents before reconnecting with mine. "It's nice to see you."

"It's nice to see *you*," I respond with a chuckle. She must be joking, I don't think I've ever seen her be so formal. Realizing maybe it's her parents, I throw her a wink and slip on my professional face. "Sir, ma'am, my name is Clinton Pennington."

I extend my right hand to her father first, but his eyes don't leave his daughter and my hand remains empty. Her mother reaches her dainty hand across her husband to give mine a light squeeze. "Pleasure, dear. And how do you two know each other?" She phrases the question to her daughter, not to me. Neither of them will look at me.

"Oh we're just project partners in art class, Momma. Clinton is actually really great. He's got a lot of talent."

Her parents' brows shoot up in synchrony, their lips tight, but satisfied at their daughter's response. It's as if their eyebrows have a direct connection to my stomach—they rise, my stomach falls.

What the fuck is happening.

"I have a lot of talent, do I?" I don't even bother hiding my sarcasm as I snap the question at Shawna. All the little pieces are clicking into place as my heart rate accelerates, my nose flaring along with the beat.

"Momma, Daddy, I'll be right back. Clinton and I need to discuss an assignment that's due this week. Why don't I meet you at the alumni tent?"

They both nod, their eyes raking me disapprovingly once more before Shawna pulls me in the opposite direction. I barely let them get out of earshot before I rip away from her grasp.

"What the fuck was that, Shawna?" I seethe. "Your *project partner*? Are you fucking kidding me?"

"Bear, please."

"Oh, *now* I'm Bear to you. What, that didn't sound as impressive to say to Mommy and Daddy? I guess I can thank my deadbeat dad for his last name, at least."

"Stop!" she screams, her eyes glossing over. She's never seen this side of me before. "You don't understand."

"Clearly. Although, I'd love to hear your explanation. Please," I scoff, motioning my hand toward her before crossing my arms over my chest. Her bottom lip quivers as I close myself off to her, and it's almost enough to make me apologize.

"My parents are old-fashioned . . ." She trails off, eyes on her fingers as she wrings them together. "We're from Mississippi, and where I grew up, there weren't many . . . there wasn't much . . . diversity."

She peeks up at me through her lashes, brows furrowed, eyes guilty and ashamed. It takes me a moment to understand as I squint at her, the sun beaming behind her black hair, framing her in a silhouette. When the anchor drops, pulling my chest along with it, I have to force a breath.

"It's because I'm black."

Shawna cringes, one arm crossing her chest as the other lifts her hand to cover her mouth. I watch as her eyes fill to the brim with tears, but I feel no urge to soothe her.

"They hate me already because of the color of my skin, don't they?"

Shawna just shakes her head, refusing to answer my question and answering it all the same.

I lick my bottom lip against a manic smile, clenching my fists where they're still crossed over my chest. "And you?"

"What about me?" she asks softly, her brows pinched in confusion.

"Do you have an opinion about me based on my race?"

"What? No!" Two tears stream out of her left eye, one after the other, the stream falling vertically before breaking right at her jaw line. "I thought that was obvious."

"Then tell them." I point two fingers straight over at where her parents are standing at the alumni tent, not even bothering to see if they're looking at us. "Walk over to them right now and tell them what you told me last week. Tell them you're falling in love with me. Tell them I'm not your project partner, I'm your boyfriend."

She chokes on a sob, biting her lips together. "I can't." She hiccups the words, just above a whisper. "Please, just let me explain."

"I think I've heard plenty." I don't look at her again before walking straight past her back to the Alpha Sigma tent. I *can't* look at her. Still, I hear her calling my name as I stride, her tears breaking on the one harsh syllable.

"Who was that," Clayton asks as I hook my hand around his elbow, pulling him away from the A Sig tent. I'm on a mission to find my own brothers now. It's been a long time since I've drowned myself in a bottle of liquor to find the numb I used to crave so often, but I feel that same want creeping into my bloodstream now.

"No one."

"No one," Clayton deadpans, struggling to keep up with me. "So, you ran up and wrapped your arms around her, but you don't know her?"

His words dig into my chest like a rusty butter knife and I suck in a breath, desperate for air, for relief.

"Not anymore."

Skyler

I've always thought of Erin as the mom of our group. She's the one who has her head on straight, the one with the conscience, the one who knows what to wear and what to say and what not to drink. But she's been absent since Spring Break, tied up in executive board shit half the time and tied up in Landon the other half. I've barely seen her, other than the awkward twenty minutes with her and her real mom, and I'm not even sure she knows what happened last night between Jess and Ashlei. Which means it's my turn to step up to the plate and put on my mom pants.

Jess hasn't moved out of her bed all day, so I'm not surprised when I push through our bedroom door and see her still buried under the covers. It's just after five in the evening, the campus slowly draining itself of parents. Jess' didn't even bother sticking around for today's events, they just left me some cash for Jess and told me to send their love. They assume she's hungover, but I know the truth—she's feeling guilty.

As she should.

I leave the big light out, but click on the small lamp on my bedside table before climbing into bed next to Jess. She doesn't fight me, just lets me slide under the sheets until we're nose-to-nose. I'm silent for a moment, noting the smeared mascara around her tired brown eyes.

"I brought wine," I finally say, reaching into the bag I pulled under the covers with us. The brown paper crinkles as I reveal a sweet moscato.

Jess cringes. "Get that away from me."

"Oh, so you don't want to drink anymore?" I nod, twisting off the top. Buying a bottle that needed a cork popped would have alerted Mom Cindy. I lift the bottle to my lips, shrugging. "I was so sure you were hell-bent on drinking yourself into stupidity."

"I think I already hit that town last night."

"I think you stayed in a hotel overnight and they named the city after you."

She sighs, sniffling as her eyes connect with mine. "I get it, okay?"

"I don't think you do, Jess."

She throws the covers off of us in a huff, the cool air rushing in. "If you came here to lecture me, you can get the fuck out."

"It's my room, too."

"Don't be a bitch."

"*Me?*"

She groans, snatching a pillow up and covering her face with it. "You're not going away, are you?" she mumbles. I just wait, taking another pull from the wine bottle until she tosses the pillow back down. She exhales like a horse, her lips flapping dramatically. "I fucked up."

"Mm hmm."

"So now what?"

"I was going to ask you the same thing."

Jess flips over to rest on her left elbow, her greasy blonde hair falling over her eyes. She brushes it back behind her ear slowly. "I was pissed, Skyler. They both hid that shit for who knows how long and then they get busted, on camera, and act like nothing happened. I've had to stick up for them against all of our sisters who are calling for them to be kicked out of KKB meanwhile I'm pissed at them, myself. And meanwhile, they've been like two fucking mice, not saying a word, not apologizing. It's bullshit."

"What exactly are they supposed to be apologizing for?"

"For lying! For, for . . ." she trails off, her hands waving wildly as she grasps for something else to be pissed about. "All of it!"

Pressing my lips together, I lean up against the headboard of her bed and take another sip of the wine. When I offer it to Jess again, she grimaces and pushes it back toward me.

"Listen, they don't have anything to be sorry for. So what if they're in a relationship? It's no different than you being in a relationship with your teacher and not telling any of us about it."

"We're not in a relationship. And that's different."

"You so are, and no, it's not. And what, they're supposed to be apologizing for getting caught on camera having sex with one lucky son-of-a-bitch on Spring Break? I hooked up last week, too. I could have been taped just as easily. They're not at fault here, Jess."

"Oh, so I'm just some crazy mean bitch, then?"

"Don't be dramatic."

She eyes the bottle in my hand like she's almost tempted to take a drink, but thinks better of it. Squeezing her eyes shut, she covers them with the heels of her hands and blows out a long, slow breath. "I was wasted."

"That's still not an apology."

She huffs. "Fine, I was wrong."

I nod, satisfied, tipping the bottle back once more. "I'm glad you see it now, but I'm not the one you need to be saying that to."

She whimpers, falling forward until her head is in my lap. I run my fingers through her hair as she speaks into the covers, her voice muffled. "She hates me. They both do. Where do I even start?"

"Just be honest with them, J-Love. And apologize, don't make excuses. That's all you can do. They'll either forgive you or tell you to go to hell. Either way, you have to say you're sorry—and mean it."

She swallows, but nods, leaning up to face me again. "I should go find Ashlei."

Wrinkling my nose, I eye the shirt she was wearing last night paired with underwear that could have that same reputation for all I know. "You should shower first."

Jess laughs, smacking me with a pillow, but then her mouth pulls to the side. She leans into me, wrapping her lean arms around me and leaning her head on my shoulder. I hold her for a minute, trying to be the strength she needs. "Thank you, Skyler."

Petting her hair, I offer a reassuring smile. "What are sisters for?"

***

An hour later, Clinton is unloading Clayton's bag from the cab as we stand on the curb outside of the departing flights terminal. They've both been joking around the entire cab ride, but Clinton filled me in on what happened with Shawna just before we piled into the car, so I'm itching to talk to him more about it. Though judging by his forced playfulness with his brother, I can tell he isn't. I wonder if it's one of those situations where I'll need to let him come to me again, the same way I had to wait with his family drama last semester.

It's not that I think racism is dead—I'd be naïve to honestly believe that. Still, I've never been so up close and personal to it before. Shawna seemed so into Clinton, she seemed like a down to earth chick. The fact that she let her prejudiced parents break them apart throttles me.

I can only imagine how Clinton feels.

"I think that Zeta wants me," Clayton says with a sly grin as the cab pulls away and we make our way inside. "She gave me her phone number."

"Oh yeah? Let me see." I hold out my hand and Clayton places his cell phone into my palm, a number pulled up on the screen under the name *Ass-tastic Jazzy*. I chuckle at the name, but full on laugh when I see the number. "Oh, Baby Bear."

"What?!" He looks alarmed, snatching the phone away like I've deleted the number.

"That's the Loser Line."

His brows tug inward over his chocolate irises. "What's that?"

"It's a phone number the local radio station gives out to girls so they can blow off losers. If you call that number and leave a voicemail, they'll probably play it on the air," Clinton explains.

Clayton narrows his eyes and snaps his fingers together. "What a minx. She's playing hard to get."

Clinton nudges him with a grin as I roll my eyes.

The Penningtons are something else.

We check Clayton's bag and make our way toward security, the mood shifting. There's something about seeing boys express emotion that really gets to me. I've never seen my father cry, nor have I stuck around long enough to see any of my exes cry, either. But I feel the weight of Clayton's departure, and Clinton keeps pressing his lips together and chewing the skin next to his thumb nail, fighting back what I'm positive would be tears if he'd let them fall.

"Well, I guess this is it, little bro," he finally says as we reach the security line. Clayton adjusts the small backpack he's using as a carry-on over his shoulder, his eyes on his shoes. "Did you call to make sure Mom would be there to pick you up?"

"Nah, Mac's mom is coming to get me."

Clinton frowns. "Are you staying there again tonight?"

When Clayton twists his mouth and lifts his eyes to mine, my heart stops before he even says a word.

Uh oh.

"I'm sort of staying there every night . . ."

It takes two-and-a-half seconds for Clinton to catch on, and when he does, I watch his nose flare as his fists tighten at his sides. "What are you talking about?"

"Don't be mad," Clayton pleads, holding his hands up. "Mac's family is cool with it. They think of me like a son, and I'm doing chores and stuff to help out around the house."

"Mac's mom I understand, but I have a really fucking hard time believing *our* mom is okay with this." I remember Clinton telling me over Winter Break that his mom never let him leave when he wanted to, even the time his aunt offered her spare bedroom up. His mom needs to feel in control of her kids' lives, no matter how dangerous that may be.

"Well, I wouldn't know."

Clinton and I exchange questioning glances. "What do you mean, Baby Bear?" I ask.

He sighs, his dark fingers fidgeting with the straps of his backpack. "She never came home in December. Neither did Carleton."

Shit.

Clinton's anger disappears as all emotions drain from his face. It's the palest I've ever seen him. "Are you telling me you've been living with Mac since December and you haven't told me?" Clayton doesn't dare answer and I don't dare move. I'm almost afraid to breathe.

For a moment, Clinton just nods, short little nods as his eyes scan the airport, looking everywhere but at Clayton. He chews the insides of his lips and I see the wheels spinning.

"I'm coming home with you. Right now."

"No!" Clayton yells at the same time as I grab Clinton's arm.

"Bear, just relax a second."

"Skyler," he warns and I pull my hand away. He turns his attention back to his brother. "I'm coming. End of story."

"Please, don't." Clayton's eyes brim with tears, his age showing more than it has all weekend. I keep forgetting he's only thirteen. That realization only makes my heart ache more. "You're the only one in our family who has their shit together. I can't wait to get out of Pittsburgh and be with you. If you come home and throw this semester away, you'll fall back and have to take extra classes to catch up or stay another year, and that's *if* you even ever come back. I don't want that for you, for me, for either of us."

"I'm not going to let you live by yourself. Without a mom, without any fucking family."

"I have a family," he pleads. "Mac and his sister and their parents. They make dinner every night, did you know that? I didn't think anyone did that anymore." He smiles, his eyes still glossy, his movements animated as he tries to make his big brother see his side. "And we play video games and go do fun things on the weekend. There's no smoke in the house, no drugs, no fighting."

Clinton crosses his arms, still staring somewhere behind his little brother. Suddenly, his eyes grow wide. "Where are the boys?"

I snap my attention back to Clayton, the realization that Carleton has two sons hitting me as hard and fast as it hit Clinton.

"They're with Tara. They're okay, she's taking care of them. I see them on the weekends."

Clinton exhales a breath, letting me know it's okay I do the same. I think Tara is the mom, but I'm not sure. My eyes find Clinton again. Noting his steadier breathing, I take the opportunity to give my input.

"Bear, he's right. You can't just leave Palm South. I know this isn't easy to hear, but look at Clayton." I point in his direction. "He's fine. He's better than fine."

"I should be there for him."

"You *are*," Clayton emphasizes. "By being here and being the man I hope to be, you're there for me. That's what I need from you right now."

I nod, still not believing how wise Clayton is for such a young kid. "Listen, let's plan a trip home to see him this summer. You can see where he's staying and if you decide then that it's not good enough, then you can stay. I won't even ask you twice to come back." The words sting as they leave my lips, but I know they're necessary. Clinton needs to hear that he has options, especially when it comes to the last family member he really cares about.

"I'll have Mac's mom call you as soon as I get home so you can talk. She's been wanting me to tell you."

"But you didn't," Clinton throws back.

"And this is why."

Clinton shakes his head, his arms still tight over his chest. When his eyes turn to mine, they ask me for permission I'm not sure I can really give. But I smile, giving a short nod to let him know I think it's okay—and truly, I do.

Blowing out a long breath, he pulls his little brother into him and crushes his arms around the smaller version of himself. They hold each other tight and I lean in long enough to ruffle Clayton's curls.

"I'll give you two a minute. Catch you later, Baby Bear. Don't grow up too much before I see you again."

"Afraid you'll want to date me, Sky?"

Clinton finally laughs and I just shoot Clayton a wink before excusing myself. I wait on a small bench as they say their goodbyes, pretending to look through my phone, though I'm too aware of the moment being shared between them to really do anything else. After a while, Clinton makes his way back toward me and I stand to meet him, his eyes still not meeting mine.

Clayton waves at us once more as he hands his ID to the TSA agent and Bear sighs. Sliding my hand into his, I lean my head on his shoulder and he tightens his grip around my fingers.

"Everything is falling to shit, Skyler."

I kiss his arm, squeezing his hand just once. "We'll get through it together. We always do."

He peeks down at me, the smallest smile curving over his lips as he tucks me under his arm. When Clayton finally disappears from view on the other side of security, Clinton pulls me all the way into him, his large frame folding into me. He doesn't sob, but he clutches me tight, using me to steady himself.

"I don't know what I'd do without you," he finally whispers, sniffling as he straightens once more. The left side of my mouth quirks up and I tug him toward the exit.

"Ditto, Bear. Ditto."

Ashlei

My eyes are closed, the sand cold on the back of my thighs as I face the ocean and listen to the waves crashing on the beach. They're not gently rolling in tonight, they're slapping the wet sand, rolling over one another in a race to meet their demise. I don't see or hear her take her place in the sand next to me. I just feel her. Our souls are at war right now, and it's as if my entire body is set on alert just from her nearness.

"How'd you find me?" I finally ask with a sigh. It's not like the beach is a normal place for me to go when I need to get away, that's more Skyler's thing than mine. I'm usually at the gym or, when I danced, at the studio. Even now as I try to find solace in the quietness of the beach at night, I'm mostly annoyed by the sand sticking to my ass and the salt water spritzing my hair.

"Bo told me," Jess answers, her voice quiet. She's sober.

"I'm surprised she's even talking to you."

She offers a short laugh and I open my eyes, letting them land on where her fingers are tracing the sand. "I'm not sure that 'fuck off' counts as talking."

"So she didn't tell you?"

"She didn't have to. I saw the sand on her feet and guessed. Or hoped, rather."

I'm torn between the urge to cry and the overwhelming want to slap her hard across the face. Before Bo, Jess was my best friend in the sorority. I thought she still was. Yes, things have been tired and tense between us since my situation all started last semester, but I never questioned that she would ever hurt me. Now I don't just feel blindsided, but I feel betrayed, too.

"Are you two okay?" Jess asks, and I can tell the question feels strange on her lips.

I shrug, picking up a small shell and using it to carve through the soft sand. My heart aches as I ask myself to answer her question honestly. Bo was just here, maybe two hours ago, and as much as I want us to be okay, we're not. Not even close.

"She's hurt. She's scared. The website hit her hard and this . . . *you* nearly killed her."

Jess swallows, pulling her knees up and tucking her hands under her thighs. "I am so, *so* sorry, Lei. I know that's not enough. It wasn't enough when I told Bo tonight, either, and I'm not really asking for forgiveness. I'm just letting you both know that I regret what I said and how I said it and if I could take it all back, I would. But I can't. So, I'm sorry. And I hope that in time, I can earn back your trust. Both of you."

I don't look at her yet, I can't. I just nod along with her words, tears blurring the line where the light sand meets the dark water. I'm waiting for it—the *but*—the part where she says it's my fault she exploded the way she did. In a way, I sort of agree with her. In another way, I think she's completely full of shit.

After a few moments of silence, I get impatient. Pulling my knees in to mirror her, I finally turn my head, resting my cheek on my knees and connecting my eyes with hers. I find more remorse there than I thought I would. "But?"

Jess breathes out slowly. "No buts. I was wrong."

"Yes you fucking were," I spit out, my voice shaky as the tears break down my cheeks. Her lip quivers, too, and I squeeze my eyes shut against the pain, pulling my arms up to my knees and burying my head between them. Sobs rack my body as the waves rack the shore and I cry with them, both of us losing a part of ourselves, both of us struggling to begin once again.

Hesitantly, Jess' hand touches my back. She waits, ready for me to jerk away, but when I don't, she pulls me flush against her and I cry harder.

"Shhh," she whispers, her fingers running through my hair. She's crying, too. "I'm sorry. I'm so sorry. You're right, I have been hiding Jarrett from you—from all of you. I saw you and Bo kiss at formal and instead of being an adult and asking you to talk to me about it, I figured two could play that game. So we've been shutting each other out for months now, seeing who could be the most secretive. But I don't want to play anymore, Lei. I love you. I miss my best friend."

"I miss you, too," I cry, my hands fisting in her loose t-shirt. My ribs ache with the force of my sobs but I let them hurt me. I let it all sink in.

"Ashlei, let me in. I know there's more you're battling with. I've known it since last semester. First, I pushed you, but you kept it all locked away. So then I gave up asking, and then I saw the Bo thing and I just got so angry. I'm sorry I did that, I wasn't a good sister. But I'm here, right now, and I can help you—with whatever is happening. But you have to let me in, first."

I think I understand why Skyler goes to the ocean when she's struggling, now. It feels like a place where you can be reborn—where you can change. The only person I've let in is Bo, and I haven't even let her all the way in. I've been so set on handling it on my own, afraid of what everyone would think of me, afraid of being a failure. But now, the website has already done that for me. Some of my sisters are judging me, the entire campus has seen me at my most vulnerable, and no matter what happens to the asshole who videotaped us, I'll never have that peace of mind back again. Our secret was no longer ours to keep after that night. And no matter how I try to avoid Xavier, I have to face him eventually—soon. I may not have been ready to come out as a bisexual yet, but that wasn't even my biggest demon. Xavier is.

Wouldn't it be easier to face him if I weren't alone?

Straightening, I wipe my nose against my bare wrist and pull my eyes to Jess'. I inhale a shaky breath that doesn't quite reach my ribs and then, with her hand squeezing mine, I tell her everything. I tell her about pole dancing, how much I loved it, how much I miss it now because of a stupid decision I made with a stupid boy. I tell her about getting shoved out of the car and waking up that night, realizing I was making a mistake, but I was too late. Jess still holds tight to my hand, not an ounce of judgement in her eyes.

I tell her about the first payment, how I lied to my parents, how I let Bo help me and we thought we figured it out together, but then Kya showed up and blew up my entire world. Every word leaves me feeling more broken and somehow fixable at the same time.

I can't look at her when I tell her I did dance for money—once—just enough for me to realize I couldn't do it. I still can't lift my eyes to hers as I tell her about the deals I made with the devil—the payments, the stolen money from our auction, how I asked him to hit me, how I sold drugs on Spring Break. By the time I'm completely caught up, telling her how I lost over a third of the money I owe him and I know any day now he's going to give up trying to call me and send someone to bring me to him, I can't place how I feel. Relieved? Terrified? I'm not sure.

I don't know how long I've been talking. My voice is scratchy, my throat sore, my eyes puffy. Jess' hand is still firmly holding mine.

"I don't know what to do anymore," I whisper, shaking my head as my eyes stay fixed on our hands. "I've tried for so long to figure this out on my own. I was afraid of the judgement, afraid of the consequences. I was so ruled by fear that I kept digging deeper and deeper into a hole I fell into accidentally but stayed in by choice." Realization hits me like a freight train. "This is my fault, Jess. This is all my fault."

"Hey," she says as I start to cry again, her free hand finding my chin. She lifts my head, but I keep my eyes shut. "Look at me, Lei."

Shaking my head, I force a breath and finally crack my eyes open, her blurred face coming into view slowly.

"It's okay. Do you hear me?" She leans in closer, her chocolate eyes connecting hard with mine. "It is *okay*."

It's like those words are all I've been wanting for months now, I just didn't know I needed them. I didn't know what to even ask for. Now that she's said it, my heart finally realizes.

I just want to be okay.

"I wish you would have come to me sooner, Lei. I can't believe you've been going through this on your own." She hugs me close to her chest again and I wrap my arms around her shoulders.

Sniffling, I stare out into the dark ocean, feeling better but not saved yet. "Jess, what am I going to do? He's going to come looking for me. He's killed people before." I choke on the words, gripping her shirt between my fingers. "He could kill *me*."

Everything is heavy—the air, my arms, those words. Jess peels me off of her and frames my arms with her hands, holding me tight, forcing my eyes to hers. Though the mascara stains under her eyes and her body shakes with mine, she no longer looks remorseful or sad. She looks determined—fierce—the Jess I know slowly rising to the surface again. Her eyes narrow, her lips pursed, and slowly, she nods.

"I have a plan."

EPISODE 6

"Time to Kiss Spring Semester GOODBYE IN STYLE."

Jess

Hysterical laughter.

That's what's coming from my mouth right now as Jarrett stares at me from his side of the bed, brows furrowed, lips pressed together in a thin line. He's not amused, and nothing he said was funny, but I can't stop laughing.

It's a nervous habit I've always had. I'm not good with handling serious situations. Anytime I'm uncomfortable or freaked out, I crack a joke or laugh uncontrollably. In both situations, I piss someone off.

And Jarrett is the last person I want to make mad.

Throwing the covers off, he shakes his head and leaves the bed. I instantly miss him, especially as his tight ass stalks toward his closet. Reaching out, I try to fight the giggles. "Wait, Jarrett." Still giggling. "I'm sorry."

"This isn't fucking funny, Jess. Not anymore," he snaps, hastily stepping into a pair of boxer briefs and yanking them up to his hips. My eyes are glued to the deep V of his lower abdomen still left exposed, the one I was dragging my tongue across just moments ago. Before Jarrett asked me—in all seriousness, my hands grasped in his as he kissed my knuckles—to be his girlfriend.

His legit girlfriend—not a fuck buddy, not a friend with benefits, not something we don't title. He wants it all.

And I don't think I can give it to him.

"I know," I say, clearing my throat. The early morning light is trying to break through the navy blue curtains of his bedroom, bathing us in the cool glow of dawn. Another fit of laughter threatens to break loose but I twist my face to fight it down. "It's a nervous habit. I can't really control it."

He sighs, pulling a pair of jeans off a hanger and throwing them on just as quickly as his boxer briefs, the metal hanger still flailing against the others. "I don't understand why you even hesitated when I asked. Are you not essentially my girlfriend already?"

"You know it's not the same."

"Oh? It's not?" He fastens his belt and then slowly crosses the room to me, sitting on the edge of his bed and framing me with his fists pressed into the comforter. "Do you want anyone else? Do you want *me* to be with anyone else? Do you think about me every minute you're not with me? Do you see me in your future? Do you want me here with you in your present?" His dark eyes drink me in, begging for me to argue with him. I can't. "Can you honestly answer 'no' to any of those questions? Even one?"

I'm not laughing anymore.

My breath leaves my chest in a slow exhale along with one word. "No."

"Then fucking *be* with me," he pleads earnestly, the veins in his arms protruding. "I'm tired of this game. You're mine. I'm yours. I want every fucking person in our lives to know that. And I don't want to have to watch you leave my house every morning wondering if you'll come back again."

My breathing accelerates and I pin my bottom lip between my teeth. He makes it sound so easy. *Just be with me.* But it's never that easy. What if the whole reason he loves being with me is because he doesn't have me—not really, not all the way? Or what if, just like how I gained my nickname, I tell him yes, then tell him I love him, and eventually he's gone—just like all the others. Jarrett is possessive over me now, I can't imagine how that would transfer into him being my actual boyfriend. Would he let me go to fraternity parties without him? Would he want to meet my parents?

"You'll lose your job," I try, knowing it's the bottom line from my list of excuses.

Jarrett scoffs. "The semester is all but over, Jess. I'll have a new job within the next few weeks."

"Still, this could damage your reputation."

"It won't. We started dating after I was your teacher, not during that semester. And I wasn't even technically your teacher. I'm a student. A grad student."

"But I'm still here. I have years to go. Don't you want to find a successful woman with her shit together?" Even suggesting he be with someone else makes my stomach lurch.

Jarrett pushes back from where he was angled over me and runs his hands over his bald head, his eyes on the bathroom door. I watch as the tattoos on his arms flex with the movement. They seem angry at me, too.

"Fucking Christ, Jess. How many times do I have to tell you?" He drops his hands to the bed, exhausted. His chest is heaving as he connects his eyes with mine. Suddenly, I'm too aware of my messy, freshly-fucked hair and what I'm sure is smeared makeup. I tuck my knees up to my chest. "I want *you.* I haven't looked at a single other fucking woman since the moment you strolled into the bar looking for me. You didn't know it that night, you didn't know it was me you wanted, but I did. I knew it when I saw the look in your eyes and the determination in your walk. I wanted you then, I want you now, and if you just fucking *let me in—*" His voice cuts off, his fists tightening.

An unfamiliar sting hits my nose and eyes but I sniff it away. *Am I about to cry?* Oh hell no. I'm Jess Vonnegut and I do *not* do emotions—not like this. I have too much shit going on with Ashlei right now as it is. I should be focusing on how I'm going to help her out of the disaster she's found herself in, not on this. Why do we have to figure all of this out right now?

"I thought we were fine the way we were. The way we *are*. Why isn't this enough for you?"

He pauses, a long, slow breath expelling from his lips as he stands. "I don't know. I thought I could do this, not put a title on it, just be whatever we are. But I can't anymore." He crosses back to his closet and tugs a long-sleeved button-up down, shrugging it over his shoulders. On the third button, he stops, peering up at me with a pained expression. "I love you, Jess."

I swallow.

"I do," he continues, his fingers working the buttons again. "And it's okay if you don't feel the same. But I need this from you. I need you to be mine—completely." He's still getting dressed, as if the words slipping from his lips in the process aren't life-changing. He snaps on his watch and grabs his nice shoes, the ones he often wears to class. It's Friday, so he's a little more casual than usual, but just barely.

"And if I can't?" I sit up on my knees, pulling the sheets over my still-naked chest. "Would you rather not have me at all if you can't have me as your girlfriend? Does the title really make that much of a difference to you?"

He halts at his bedroom door, his back to me, shoulders taught.

"It's not just a title. If it were, you wouldn't be fighting it as much as you are."

He's right. I know he's right. Somewhere, deep inside my gut, I feel my own soul screaming at me to tell him yes. But I can't.

"You didn't answer my question."

He sighs, snatching his keys off the small table just outside his bedroom door. "I don't have to, you already know the answer." With that, he crosses the apartment and swings open the front door. His hand gripping the knob, he lifts his eyes to mine again, the space between us deafening. "So?"

My heart races so fast I have to balance my palms on the bed to keep myself upright. I'm not ready to be his girlfriend. I can't be his girlfriend. It's too much, it's too fast, it's too uncertain. I want what we have now, but he's saying that's not an option any longer. Why? What changed? My head is spinning, the room following suit. When my wild eyes find his again, I know I don't have to answer his question, either.

He bites his bottom lip, eyes falling to the floor as one, short laugh echoes through the apartment. Jarrett shakes his head swiftly and turns, calling out behind him. "Lock up before you leave."

He doesn't slam the door. He doesn't need to. It's there, sitting naked in the sheets still warm from sex, that I realize I've been fooling myself all along. Jarrett and I have always wanted different things. How stupid could I have been to think we could just avoid our questions simply because we already knew the answers?

I almost call out for him but stop myself, thinking better of it. Instead, I whisper to myself.

"He loves me?"

A smile touches my lips before reality chases it away. Jarrett loves me, but he's asking me to love him back. He's asking me to give more than we agreed on. We made a deal last semester, and that was working for me. I thought it was working for him. And now, because I won't be his girlfriend, I can't have him at all.

My stomach lurches and I sit up, planting my bare feet on the floor, letting the sheet fall to the side. I need a clear mind today and I know I'm not going to get it. I'm meeting with Ashlei in an hour to finalize our plan for Xavier, and yet now, there's only one thought in my head.

Can I really let Jarrett Locke walk out of my life?

Adam

"And that's why I'm proud to announce that the newest president of Alpha Sigma by an overwhelming vote is Adam Brooks."

The chapter room erupts in cheers, Jeremy going especially wild and hooting loudly over everyone as I stand and make my way to the front of the room. It feels like I'm walking in slow motion, trying to take it all in and feeling like it's impossible to do.

Ever since I rushed Alpha Sigma, I've been busting my ass to make us a top fraternity on campus again. We once were, especially in the 90s, but we fell off along the way. It hasn't been easy and the job is far from done, but now, I'll have more resources to make the difference I want to make. I finally let myself smile, wishing my grandfather could be here to see me. I'm doing it. I'm making something of my organization, of myself.

Clay forces a smile as he shakes my hand. I know he hates this, passing the crown to me, but in a way I think he saw it coming. He had to. He's graduating in just a few short weeks, so it really shouldn't bother him, but it does. I grin smugly, pulling him in to clap him on the back as the cheers continue. I hold him there a moment, squeezing his hand tighter than necessary.

"If you ever so much as fucking look at Cassie McBee again, you'll need reconstructive surgery to get back that fake ass smile of yours. Understand?"

Clay is normally cocky, but I catch the swallow he forces down as he pulls away. He doesn't meet my eyes, just motions toward me with both hands and a smile facing our brothers, making the room go crazy once more. Something tells me I won't have to warn him twice.

After a short speech and photo of me along with the new executive board, my brothers disperse, slipping back into finals mode as we all prepare for the end of the semester. I should feel elated, I should want to go get celebratory drinks, I should be making calls—but there's only one person I want to talk to right now. One person I *need* to talk to.

Pulling my phone from my pocket, I type out a quick text to Cassie, praying she'll actually respond. We've barely talked since Spring Break. I came back on such a high, which makes no sense because all I had done was complicate whatever relationship we have further. We kissed, it was amazing, but what does that really mean? Apparently, to her—nothing. She was back in Grayson's arms as soon as we returned. I wondered why she wasn't returning my calls, but Family Weekend answered that question for me. I may not deserve to know what that night meant to her, but I have to ask anyway.

My phone pings with a text from her saying she's at the KKB house and to come to the back kitchen door. Steeling myself, I tuck my phone back in my pocket and start the walk down Greek Row, words I want to say scrolling through my mind like movie credits the entire time. But when I knock softly on the back door and she lets me in, her soft red curls pulled in a low ponytail over her shoulder and her legs exposed in a tiny pair of plaid sleep shorts, everything I planned to say leaves me instantly—like a candle flame snuffed out by a lid.

"Congrats," she says first with a genuine grin before pulling me in for a hug, like she hasn't been ignoring me for weeks. I'm almost too shocked to hug her back, but slowly, my arms wrap around her and I hold her tight against me, inhaling the tropical scent from her hair. She always smells like paradise.

"News travels fast."

She giggles, pulling back and crossing her arms over her chest, framing the small bit of cleavage exposed by her tank top. "Come on, how long have you been at PSU? You know better than I do."

"True story."

"Well, I wish we could have a shot to celebrate, but, you know, house rules and all." She points a thumb over her shoulder. "Want a root beer?"

I laugh. "Do you *have* a root beer?"

Cassie rolls her eyes as if it's obvious. "Of course. It's my favorite drink."

"Interesting. Well in that case, make it a double." I like that it's easy between us right now, especially after the tension during Family Weekend. Still, I'm not just going to slip back into the friend zone. I have to talk to her about what happened.

She chuckles, arms still crossed until she reaches the refrigerator. Pulling out two tall glasses and filling them to the top with the foamy dark liquid, she slides one down the counter to me as she lifts the other to her own lips. The bubbles stick at the corners of her mouth for just a moment before she licks them away.

"I forgot how much I love root beer," I say, taking a sip myself.

Her eyebrows shoot up and she points at me over her glass. "See? You're welcome."

As our smiles settle, I grip the glass a little tighter. "I didn't come here to celebrate."

"I figured," she responds, eyes on her own hands. "Listen, I get it. It was Spring Break, we were both drinking. It's all good."

I cock a brow, setting my glass down on the kitchen island. It's Sunday night and the house is mostly quiet, save for the faint sound of giggling coming from the rooms upstairs.

"It wasn't a mistake, Cassie. It wasn't an accident or a drunken decision. Ever since I kissed you at the concert last semester, I've wanted to do it again."

She wants me to apologize for the kiss. She thinks I regret it. I don't.

"How can you say that?" she asks, green eyes wide. "You were with Skyler."

"I know, I know." I pinch the bridge of my nose, not really knowing how to explain what I need to. "It's not that I didn't care for her—that I don't *still* care for her. But I also care about you. And that night on the beach, it was like the biggest moment of clarity for me."

Cassie drops her glass to the counter and brings her fingernails to her teeth, nibbling, eyes on the tile floor.

"You can't do this, Adam. I mean, what are you even asking me?" Her voice is shaky when she finally speaks.

"I don't know." I sigh, knowing none of this is coming out right. But what do I really expect? I was dating her Big Sister just a few short weeks ago and now, what? I'm going to ask her to be with me? "I guess I'm just saying that I get what you said at the Fratalina Wine Mixer now." I shrug, lifting my eyes to hers. "You confuse me, too."

"I'm with Grayson."

She says those three words like they won't puncture my lungs, stealing my breath. "Let me take you to formal. Please. Give me . . . I don't know, give me one night."

"One night for what?" She stands straighter, tucking a loose strand of hair behind her ear. "Didn't you hear me? I'm with Grayson. *He's* taking me to formal."

I wince, inching toward her. She's basically telling me to eat shit and die but I can't let it go. Grabbing the crook of her elbow, I force her to look at me, hoping my eyes will be able to say what my words can't. "Shit, Cassie. Did it mean nothing to you? Was this all one-sided?"

She chews the inside of her cheek and I can see her debating whether she should tell me the truth or not. I already know it meant something to her, too, but I need to hear it. I don't want the lies between us anymore, the secrets, the hidden thoughts. I want it all on the table. I want her exposed.

"It doesn't matter. You just broke up with Skyler because you knew you were going to get president. You weren't going to have time for her, so what makes you think you'll have time for me?"

I open my mouth to respond, but snap it shut again. I don't have an answer for that. And as I'm trying my damndest to find one, someone rounds the corner into the kitchen.

"Where's my beautiful redhead?"

I drop Cassie's arm and grab my glass, quickly lifting it to my lips and keeping my eyes on her as she gazes behind me at Grayson. For a moment she just stares at him, but then slowly, she forces a smile. "Hi. I didn't know you were coming over."

"Clearly," he snaps and I grit my teeth. This isn't good. "Brooks." He says my name as a greeting and a threat all at the same time.

Turning in place, I tilt my glass toward him and take another drink. I don't feel like pretending to give a shit that he's here.

He runs a hand over his beard and looks to Cassie once more. "Can we talk?"

She nods, eyes flicking to me quickly before following him out of the kitchen. I think this is where I'm supposed to leave. Or apologize. Or do anything but what I'm actually doing, which is leaning up against the kitchen counter, straining my ears to hear their conversation in the next room.

It's all muffled voices, but every now and then Grayson's voice will boom out loud enough for me to hear. Mostly, when he's saying my name.

This isn't good.

Sighing, I dump the remains of my glass down the drain and flatten my palms on the counter, eyes closed. She wants him. She doesn't want me. Do I even have a right to be upset about that? I've been with Skyler all this time, not realizing that I wanted Cassie, too. Or did I realize it and just ignore it? I'm not sure. It's not fair for me to ask her for anything now, not when she's right about my time. And even if I did have the time, do I deserve hers?

"Can you even deny it?! Look me in the eyes right now and tell me you feel nothing for him." Grayson's voice echoes into the kitchen and I'm sure I'm not the only one in the house who hears him. I strain my ears for her answer, but hear nothing until the front door slams.

Shit.

After a moment, Cassie shuffles back into the kitchen, the skin under her eyes red and puffy. Seeing her like that breaks me.

"Cassie," I breathe her name, crossing the room in two full strides to pull her into me. But the moment my hands find her waist, she shrugs away like I'm a flame set to burn her. She crosses her arms tight over her middle, shielding herself from me—the threat, the danger, the problem.

"You need to go."

My chest deflates. "Just—"

"Adam." She cuts me off, her voice loud but laced with uncertainty. "You need to *go*."

Everything in me screams for me not to leave, to force her to talk to me, but I've pushed her enough this semester. I didn't realize the pain I was putting her through, and now that it's all come to the surface, it's all I can do to not kick my own ass. I may want to hold her right now, but it's not what she wants. It's time to let me be the one who hurts if it means she gets what she needs.

"I'm sorry," I whisper, as if it's enough, as if I really know what I'm apologizing for. Am I sorry I kissed her? Hell no. Am I sorry she's hurt right now? That I'm part of the reason? An ache in my chest answers that question for me.

I pause when my hand is on the back doorknob, words still left unsaid, but I push them back down and force myself forward through the door.

It's not the first time I've left her without saying everything I wanted to, but it's the first time I've worried I may never get the chance again.

Bear

Rain pounds hard on the pavement as I run, chest tight, legs burning across campus. I've been going for hours now. I stopped tracking after the first three miles. Every inch of my body is screaming for me to stop but I need the pain right now, I need it to consume me until it numbs me from my thoughts. I didn't even bring my headphones. I don't want the distraction, I just want the pain.

Though the rain is cold, the evening air is still warm from another spring day in Florida. My sneakers rub new blisters on my heels with every push, adding to the collection I've been building in the last week and a half since I last saw Shawna.

I'm not stupid enough to think racism doesn't exist. I know it does. I've been the subject of it more times in my life than I care to recall. Still, Shawna was different—or so I thought. She opened me up in a way no one ever had before. She was everything I'd been looking for in a girl, everything I thought I'd never find. To find out all of that was an illusion, a dream shattered by reality in the form of her parents, killed me. Skyler tried to convince me I should give her a chance, let her explain. But what is there to explain, really? This is exactly why I don't let myself get caught up in the girls I fuck. If I hadn't learned my lesson before, I damn sure won't forget now.

My hoodie is soaked, so I rip the zipper down and toss it in the yard of the Omega Chi house as I run past. Through the downpour, a faint voice calls out my name.

"Bear! Wait!"

I stop, squinting through the rain until Shawna's frame comes into focus. She's sprinting toward me, the rain assaulting her along the way. Her long hair sticks to her neck and chest as she reaches me, chest heaving. The ends of her jet black hair are purple once again and rain drops gather at the top of her glasses before sliding down the lenses.

For a long minute, she just stares at me, her breaths coming hard as she peers up at me through the rain. She's so goddamn beautiful it takes every ounce of control left in me not to crash my mouth to hers and claim her as mine, even though she clearly isn't.

"I prefer to work out alone," I finally say, speaking loud enough to drown out the weather. A soft rumble of thunder sounds in the distance and I shift from one foot to the other, feeling the aches settle in every inch of my body the longer I stand there.

"I'm sorry!" She screams over the rain. "I was a complete asshole at Family Weekend. You were right to leave. You're right to hate me right now. But you don't understand my parents, you don't understand my family. It's complicated, Bear."

"It doesn't have to be. You're your own person, Shawna. Man the fuck up and tell them what matters to you. *Who* matters to you."

She rakes her fingers back through her soaked hair, squinting up to the sky. "Can we go somewhere to talk?"

"Depends. Are you going to call your parents and tell them we're together?"

"It's not that easy."

"Actually, it is. It really fucking is," I correct her.

"I don't want to lose you over this. Please," she pleads, her icy hands reaching out to grasp my forearms. "I just need some time."

"Do you know how fucking hard it is to hear the first girl I've ever come close to loving tell me she needs *time* to not be ashamed of me?" I ask, ripping my arms away from her. "It's simple, Shawna. You either care about me enough to stand up to your parents and stop giving two shits what they think about the color of my skin or you don't. There is no in-between."

"I can't just tell them like that! They'll cut me off, they'll disown me. Didn't you see the way they looked at me when you were there? How do I look them in the eyes and tell them their only baby girl is dating a black man?"

My neck snaps back as if her words slapped me hard across the face. "Wow. I didn't realize that was something so devastating."

Her lip quivers and as much as I probably should feel sorry for her, I don't. I've been cut off from my parents since before I was old enough to make money on my own. In the downpour, it becomes clear to me just how different Shawna and I truly are.

"I didn't mean it like that," she tries, wringing her hair over her shoulder. "I just . . . I need time. I can't tell them yet, but I will."

"And I'm just supposed to wait around until you find the courage?" I ask incredulously. "Well, that's something *I* can't do. We're done, Shawna. It's over."

Her face twists, but I can't tell if tears fall or if it's just the rain. I may have a weak spot for women, I may want to take care of everyone around me, but there comes a point where I have to shut others out to take care of myself. With my little brother living on his own, my mom and older brother nowhere to be found, and my fraternity under strict watch from nationals, I don't have any room left to deal with racist assholes—especially if the girl I would consider putting up with them for doesn't have the nerve to stand up to them with me.

"Take care of yourself." They're the last words I say to her before my feet are pushing off the pavement once more, my body finding its rhythm. I don't know if it's something I should be proud of, but I have the innate capability to shut people out of my life at the flip of a switch. With every drop of rain that hits my skin, I feel Shawna wash away, leaving nothing but memories behind.

***

Less than an hour later, I push through the doors at Ralph's, still soaking wet from the rain. I'm sore, I smell like complete ass, but I have zero fucks to give as I slide up to the bar and order my first drink. A few girls at a high-top table in front of me are giggling, their eyes glued to where my tank top is stuck on my chest. Crazy how I have *go fuck yourself* written all over my face but all they notice are my swollen muscles. I'd be terrified of me right now if I were them.

The male bartender slides me my beer and my check, not even asking if I want to open a tab. He eyes me under his backward hat with disgust before turning to the other end of the bar where a small crowd is gathered. I throw back half the beer when I realize who's drawing all the attention.

Alex.

"If you thought the video was hot, you should have seen it in person," he says loudly, a bit of his drink flopping out of his mug and onto the floor. The crowd of guys around him is eating up every word. I scan them,, making sure none of them are brothers, and breathe easier when I don't find a single one. It's a good thing, because then I would have had to kick their asses, too.

I stand, my bar stool scraping the floor as I push my way around it toward him.

"I mean, she was just straight up finger-banging the Asian chick while I pounded her from behind. Fucking Spring Break man." He high fives some douchebag behind him right before his eyes connect with mine.

He gulps. I smirk.

"Hey, whoa, Bear. I'm just kidding. We're just having a little fun, right guys?" He looks around for help, eyes wide, but everyone just clears out. I don't even have to say a word. He knows. They all do.

"You've got a lot of fucking nerve showing your face here," I snarl, snatching him by the collar of his Omega Chi shirt. "And these letters? You don't *ever* get to fucking wear them. Ever."

"I'm sorry. I'll leave." He's shaking. It only fuels me more. My entire body comes to life as adrenaline soars through my veins. I need a release, and Alex's face seems like the perfect way to get it.

"It's a little too late for that." I hear the bartender from before holler something out to his manager just as I throw the first punch, my fist connecting with Alex's jaw with a sickening crack. I throw another into his stomach before shoving him to the ground and pinning his arms down. Each punch is for someone new—Ashlei, Bo, Skyler, Erin, Omega Chi. My knuckles sting as they split open from the force, but I welcome the pain.

"Jesus Christ, Bear, that's enough!" I'm finally tugged back, but my hand around Alex's shirt collar rips it with me. I expect to find my brothers behind me, but it's Adam and Jeremy, instead. I use the shirt to wipe the blood from my hands, chest, and face before tossing it over my shoulder.

"If you show your face again," I start to threaten, but Alex is unconscious. I don't even know when I knocked him out. Bouncers grab my arms but I shake them loose and walk myself out, Adam and Jeremy on my heels. No one in the bar says a word, the crowd parting like the red sea with every step I take.

When I'm outside, the rain still dripping from the trees as the clouds clear, Adam approaches me hesitantly. "Hey, you okay?"

Shawna may have been the reason I walked into this bar, but with every punch I threw, I felt her leave my system. It's the end of the semester, the promise of summer so close I can taste it. Alex deserved to have his ass kicked, and the fact that he served as the perfect release for me was only a bonus. I may get knocked down, I may walk through hell, but no one can ever say I don't handle my own. I'm Clinton Fucking Pennington, and though Shawna is the one with the phoenix inked into her skin, it's me rising from her ashes this time.

The left side of my mouth quirks up just marginally. "Never better."

Ashlei

"Listen, let's just go cut the balls off this motherfucker and then we'll go dress shopping, okay?" Jess says, squeezing my hand once before climbing out of the cab in front of Xavier's club. I follow, but stay frozen in place as the yellow car pulls away, letting the gray, rainy day surround me.

"I can't believe you did this for me," I whisper. I've been trying to talk her out of her plan the entire ride over, but unsuccessfully. I know my freedom is just minutes away, but I can't shake the overwhelming feeling of guilt for letting Jess help me reach it.

"Lei," she says my name with a smile, not an ounce of nervousness apparent as she frames my shoulders with her hands. Her blonde hair is pulled into a tight, high ponytail, accenting her cheekbones. "Dude. I'm your sister. I'm your fucking *best friend*. You shouldn't be struggling to believe I'd do this for you. If anything, *I* can't believe you waited this long to ask me to help. You put yourself through hell trying to handle this on your own when I was literally right down the hall."

"It's dangerous, Jess. I didn't want to get anyone else involved. And I was ashamed," I respond softly. "I still am."

"You wanted to do it alone. I get it," she says. "But that's the best thing about being in a sorority. It's like having an entire army of lipstick-wearing badasses behind you." I laugh a little, though my eyes blur with tears. "You're a Kappa Kappa Beta, Ashlei. You never have to face anything alone again."

She pulls me in for a hug and I squeeze her so tight she coughs, tapping my shoulder like a wrestler tapping out of a match.

"Come on, the mall closes in four hours. Let's get this over with."

Jess checks her lipstick on her phone camera as we cross the parking lot to the same bouncer who's always guarding the backdoor. He doesn't even ask who I am this time, just shakes his head as if he knows I won't be coming out alive. Xavier has been looking for me—he knows that just as well as I do.

Jess takes in our surroundings as I lead her back to Xavier's office, my hands still trembling even with her by my side.

"You danced here?" she asks softly, her eyes wide as she meets mine. I just nod in response. Jess reaches out for my hand and squeezes it tight as we reach Xavier's office door. He's bent over his computer, a cigar in his mouth as he hammers away at the keys.

"What?" He hollers out, eyes glancing up at us quickly before going back to the screen. Once realization hits, he pauses, a slow smirk growing above the stubble on his chin. He sits back, lacing his fingers together and propping his elbows on the armrests of his chair as his pulls his eyes to us again. "Well, well. Look who finally decided to show up."

Jess rolls her eyes, clearly not affected by a man who has killed before. Who could easily kill again. "Here's your money, asshole. All of it." She slaps the thick envelope down on his desk, unimpressed. "Now call your watch dogs off Ashlei and take a good look at her tight ass because the last time you'll see it is when we turn around and walk out of this shithole of a club."

Xavier's brows shoot up to his forehead and he barks out a laugh. "I see you brought your bull dog."

"I'm more of a pit bull, actually." She smiles with her eyes, hooking me by the elbow and steering me toward the exit. "Do you want to count that before we go or no?"

"I don't have to count it to know it's not enough. It's a late payment, which means I need interest."

"All the money she owed you before you made your disgusting little deal is in there, plus an additional ten-thousand." Jess spouts off the numbers like they don't affect her, like she didn't sell her prized possession to get that money. Her BMW now belongs to some Botoxed-out bimbo in South Beach, but Jess didn't even flinch when she handed over the keys.

I've never felt so loved in my life.

"And what makes you think that's enough, princess?"

Jess grits her teeth together, dropping my arm and crossing the room to plant her hands on his desk. She leans over and Xavier sneaks a look at her cleavage before his eyes lift up to hers, a sneer still firmly in place.

"It's plenty. And in case you don't know who I am, my name is Jess Vonnegut. That last name ring a bell?" She waits as Xavier files through the names in his head. "My family has won in court before and we can do it again. You forced a young college girl to dance in your club and pay you every penny she earned for drugs she wasn't even responsible for losing. Your death threats might have scared her for this long, but let me assure you—I don't feel one ounce of fear when I look into your beady little eyes." Standing, she presses her finger into the envelope. "The money is here, and unless you want to find out what a crazy son of a bitch my father can be when his little *princess* is fucked with, I suggest you take it and let us go."

Xavier sniffs, clearly more familiar with Jess' family lawsuit than I am. In fact, I don't think anyone really knows how Jess came into money. Whatever it was, Xavier doesn't taunt her further.

"Get the fuck out of my club."

"Gladly," she sings sweetly. "Come on, Lei."

She holds my hand the entire way out, and once we make it to the parking lot, the heavy metal door slamming shut behind us, I take a breath. It fills my lungs to capacity, overwhelming me with oxygen I feel like I've been deprived of for months. Sensing my emotions, Jess calls a cab quickly before pulling me into her.

"Shhh," she whispers into my hair. "It's okay. It's over. It's all over now."

I feel like I should cry, but instead, I laugh. Hard. Uncontrollably. Jess laughs with me, and before I know it, tears do leave my eyes—but not from sadness. I'm elated.

I'm free.

"I don't even know what to do right now," I squeak out between giggles. "This feels so unreal."

"It's real, babe. And now, we hit the mall and buy some sexy dresses and killer heels to match." She smiles, but it's tight. Now that my situation is resolved, I think she's finally letting herself think about her own. She hasn't spoken to Jarrett in almost a week.

"Jess," I start, but she shakes her head.

"Not today. Let's just shop, okay?"

Sighing, I nod. "Okay. Deal."

The same yellow taxi cab pulls in and we climb inside, the leather seats sticking to the back of my thighs just a bit. Folding my hands in my lap, I shake my head, still unable to stop smiling. The last eight months of my life have been ruled by monsters, and now, finally, I'm free of their claws. Finally, I can be me again—Ashlei Daniels—sister, friend, girlfriend.

My smile falters at that last thought. *Hopefully* girlfriend. Now that Xavier is behind me, I can focus on Bo and what comes next for us. As much as I've been through this semester, I've dragged Bo through the gutter with me. I convinced her to have that threesome when it was clear she was only doing it for me, and now, the consequences of my selfishness have stolen her smile that I loved so much.

Jess helped me rid myself of one demon, but now it's up to me to chase away the other one still lurking around. I'm going to make it right. I have to.

"Ready?" Jess asks me when the cab comes to a stop in front of the food court. She reaches a few twenties over the seat into the cabbie's hand before turning to me with a reassuring smile.

Taking a deep breath, I nod. "Ready."

Skyler

"I swear, I'm going to gouge my eyes out before this semester ends," Cassie says, flopping her head down on my desk. "Studying is hard."

I laugh. "Formal is tonight, Little. Just put your notes away and work on it tomorrow."

"Says the communications major."

"Hey! I have tests, too," I defend, but she peeks up at me through her red locks with a smirk. We both know her classes are harder than mine, even if she is a year younger. I toss a highlighter at her. "Whatever. I'm changing my major anyway." The truth is I have no idea what I want to do with my life. Right now, I'm trying to focus on poker and paying my tuition. The American Poker Club tournament pops into my head again and I let myself daydream about what it would be like to not have to worry about money again.

Could I really win it? Could I really take home the grand prize of the largest poker tournament in the nation?

Part of me thinks I could, but the larger part wonders if I'll ever be good enough. I've stacked my summer with tournaments, some bigger than I've ever done before, so I guess the time to show up or shut up has arrived.

At this point, I feel like I'm on the edge of something . . . something I can't quite grasp yet. I can either keep pushing through the fog to find out what it is or I can stay in my comfort zone and go along like I have been.

I've never been one for comfort zones.

Cassie smiles and closes her textbook with a snap, tucking it inside her messenger bag along with the fifty neon-colored notecards she's been reciting all afternoon. Jess swings through the door at the same time and bounds toward me.

"I just realized you and I are going stag to formal tonight." She bounces on the bed excitedly. "Girl fucking power, bitch. I packed us each a flask. Let's get wild!"

"Except I'm not going stag." I point out.

Jess' face falls. "What? I thought you and Adam broke up!"

"We did. Which means . . ." I wait for her to fill in the blank.

"Ugh," she groans. "You're bringing Bear. Of course you're fucking bringing Bear." Waving her hands, she dismisses me quickly. "Fine. More alcohol for me."

"So because I have a date, I don't get booze?"

"Your date can buy your booze, hussy."

Cassie laughs, shaking her head as she pulls her messenger bag over her shoulder. "If it helps, J-Love, I'm going alone, too. I just want to spend time with my sisters. Maybe I can finally take my sister's advice and stay away from boys."

"I hear you on that one," I chime in. The only boy I plan on having anything to do with for quite a while is Bear. He needs me right now after the whole Shawna Shit Show, not to mention his family. For now, my best friend is the only guy I need. No more *Skyler the Heartbreaker* headlines. If I have anything to do with it, those tabloids are going to start to notice me for my talent, not my dating life.

"Wait, what happened to Grayson?" Jess asks.

Her pale fingers fidget with the strap on her bag as her eyes dart toward the door. "It's complicated. I'm going to go grab my makeup bag. Be right back."

She's out the door before I can ask anything else and Jess and I share a glance. "Wonder what that's about."

Jess shrugs. "No clue. That tatted up man-bun piece of sex candy is definitely not one I'd let get away easily."

I cross my arms over my chest and cock a brow. "Funny. I seem to recall you giving up a pretty hot tatted up piece of sex candy yourself."

"Don't, Skyler," she warns, pointing a finger in my direction as she crosses to her closet. She pulls out the clear plastic bag housing her formal dress and lays it across the bed with her back still to me.

"Jess, just call him."

"And say what? He wants me to be his girlfriend or nothing at all."

"So be his girlfriend, you idiot."

She sighs. "He's my teacher."

"*Was*. And technically, he was the Graduate Assistant, which isn't even the same thing."

"I don't do boyfriends."

"And? That's a personal choice, which means you can change it."

Jess rolls her eyes, yanking her dress out of the plastic bag forcefully. "He's about to graduate and have a job. I'm still in college. It'd be weird."

"Says who?"

"Says me. It's not like I could bring him to socials or frat parties."

"Actually, you could. Sisters bring their boyfriends from other schools and stuff all the time. No one would care that he's a couple years older. You act like he's fifty." I grab a pillow and hug it close to my chest, resting my chin on the edge.

"I'd probably hurt him. Or he'd hurt me."

"Again, that's a choice. And you could literally hurt anyone around you at any point in time. Need I remind you of Family Weekend?"

"Which is exactly why I need to keep him in the little box I have him in now. He knows what to expect and so do I."

"Except that he's not trying to live in that box anymore," I argue.

"Ugh you're so exhausting!"

"Well, are you done yet?"

"I'm scared, okay?!" she screams, her hands flying into the air. She holds them there for a moment, her chest heaving, wild eyes searching mine. Finally, she lets them fall, raking her nails back through her messy bun. It falls with the force and she ties it up again before crossing her arms. "I haven't had a boyfriend since the day I found out why everyone calls me J-Love. I've embraced the name, turned it from an embarrassing one to a badass one. Everyone thinks I fall in love too fast and chase guys away? Fine, I'll make *them* fall in love and chase *me*, instead. I flipped a switch, Skyler, and I don't want to go back to where I was before. I was pathetic. I was weak. I was—"

"Normal, Jess," I breathe, hopping off my bed. "You were a normal girl. We all fall in love, sometimes too fast, sometimes not fast enough. We get reputations, we go for the wrong guys and we survive on heartbreak diets when it all goes wrong. We lean on our sisters and we pick ourselves back up just to do it all over again because if we don't, what's the point? It's okay that you love Jarrett."

"I—"

"Yes, you do. And you should. What's more, he should know how you feel because he feels the same way and you guys are just being stupid trying to be together without actually *being* together."

Her face crumples and she buries it in her hands, standing in the middle of our room, exposed. "I do love him."

I pull her in for a hug, squishing my cheek to her head. "I know."

"I'm just so fucking scared."

"That's okay, too."

She sighs, shaking her head against my chest before standing tall again. "He put his feelings out there so easily when I know it wasn't that easy for him to do. We both thought we knew what we were getting into and somewhere along the way we just . . . I don't know. We fell deeper."

"Listen, you've spent this last semester hiding him from us while trying to figure it all out on your own. Before that, you were both hiding because he was your teacher. You've spent all this time feeling like being together was something to be ashamed of when really it should be celebrated."

She sniffs, wiping her nose with the back of her wrist. "You're right. You're so right. God, he probably feels so fucking rejected right now when really he's everything I want. He's *all* I want." Her eyes lift to mine. "I'm going to go tell him. Right now."

"Right now?" I ask as she sprints for her Keds, yanking them on one foot and then the other.

"Yep. Right now."

"What about formal?"

She laughs as she swings our bedroom door open. "Fuck formal."

But before she can exit, Erin and Cassie usher in a red-faced, snotty-nosed Ashlei. She's sobbing, using both my Little and my Big to hold her steady.

"Oh my God, what happened?" Jess asks, dropping the purse she'd just picked up and rushing to help them.

"No idea. I just found her in our room like this," Erin answers. They help Ashlei into Jess' bed and she curls up into a ball, pulling the comforter up to her chin, eyes still squeezed shut. Erin sits on the edge of the bed and pets her hair, murmuring soothing words for a while as the rest of us stand around watching, waiting.

Slowly, Ashlei's cries soften, until she's not crying at all. None of us push, we just let her take the time she needs. Every now and then when we think she's going to speak, she closes her eyes tight again and fights back another wave of tears.

"Bo left," she finally whispers, her voice dry and croaky.

"What do you mean she left?" Jess asks from behind Erin. Cassie and I share concerned looks as Erin rubs Ashlei's back, coaxing her forward.

"She left. She dropped. She's going back home, or to another college, I don't know—she wouldn't really say. But she's gone. She's leaving KKB, she's leaving Palm South. She's done."

We all gasp, questions flying from everyone.

What? Why? When?

Ashlei cringes away from the noise, burrowing herself into the covers more before Erin snaps her fingers and glares at all of us to shut up. Ashlei takes a deep breath, exhaling it shakily. "It was too much. It was all too much for her. The website, Family Weekend, me, us, all of it. And her parents are on her ass. She just can't take it anymore." Ashlei laughs, though nothing is funny right now. "I can't even blame her."

Jess's brows pull inward and she connects eyes with me, guilt evident in her features. Suddenly, Jarrett can wait.

Because when your sister is hurting, you drop everything to be whatever she needs in that moment.

No one says sorry, because Ashlei already knows we are. Jess jumps up into the bed with her and scoots between the wall and Ashlei's back, tugging her close and wrapping her arms tightly around her middle. Erin leans her head down to their shoulders as Cassie and I crowd our way in, too. For a long while we just hold each other, a KKB shield around Ashlei as we let her grieve her loss. Jess cries with her, knowing she was part of the reason for the loss and also mourning herself. Bo was her Little, and she didn't even say goodbye.

"Let's blow formal," Cassie says finally. "We can rent movies and get wine and junk food."

Ashlei shakes her head, sitting up slowly as we all disperse from her like a flower's petals falling back.

"I want to go." She chews her lip, grabbing Jess' hand in hers. "I'm going to miss Bo, but it was her decision to leave and I respect it." Ashlei sniffs, looking around at each of us with a small smile. "Tonight is about more than her. It's about celebrating another semester with my sisters, who I learned recently care about me more than anyone else." Jess squeezes her hand. "We may go through hell when we face life on our own, but together, we can build a bridge over that bitch."

We all laugh and I wipe a tear from the corner of my eye, knowing her words are true. The Kappa Kappa Beta girls may get into trouble. We may try to handle the world on our shoulders and party hard all at the same time, but we're a force to be reckoned with. We're a unit. We're a family.

"On that note," Jess says, popping out of her bed with a bright smile. "I've got the liquor, who's doing our makeup?"

"On it!" Erin chimes, thrusting her finger into the air before speeding out of the room to grab her giant makeup case. And just like that, the room is alive again, everyone talking and laughing, wiping tears, pulling out dresses.

Time to kiss spring semester goodbye in style.

Erin

As the Kappa Kappa Beta house fills up with sisters and their dates, everyone dressed to perfection, I can't help but feel displaced. It's almost as if I'm under water, the sounds muffled, vision slightly blurred. I'm here, but I don't feel *here*.

The past few weeks have been exhausting. I finally let myself break on the way home from Key West, and I guess in a way it's good that I got it out of my system then because I've had no time for myself since. With the Omega Chi website and recruitment preparations, not to mention studying for finals, I haven't had time to breathe let alone think.

Still, Bo leaving so unexpectedly has me shaken. Did she feel the same way I do right now—like an outsider? Was the website combined with her parents just too much for her to handle? I wonder if her shoulders feel lighter now. I wonder what would happen if *I* just packed up my room after this semester and never came back. Would I feel better?

I know the answer before my mind has even finished the question. I can't quit, it's not in me—it's not who I am.

Besides, now is the time for me to shine and prove I'm ready to be president next year. I'm the Recruitment Chair, which means all summer I'll be focusing on planning our fall rush. I'll be responsible for the clothing, the music, the food, the entertaining—everything. And more than that, I'll be responsible for the next pledge class of Kappa Kappa Beta.

That makes me smile.

As shitty as the semester has been, Ashlei was right when she said the KKBs are a special family. Eventually, this fog I've been living in will clear and I'll be back to having fun with my sisters. It may take me a little time, but something tells me spending the summer planning recruitment will put me back in the spirit. We already have an amazing organization, one of the best on campus, and I look forward to being a part of what makes our family grow even stronger.

"Ready, gorgeous?" Landon asks, his hands framing my upper arms from behind as he plants a kiss on my cheek. I jump a little, stirred from my daze, but smile back at him over my bare shoulder.

"Yeah, I just need a minute."

"I'll go grab us a seat on the bus," he says sweetly, leaning in for a longer kiss on my lips. He looks handsome tonight, his blonde hair styled perfectly in a swoop, his jaw freshly shaven. He selected a beige tuxedo with light blue accents to match my dress and I can't help but feel a little like Cinderella with her prince.

When Landon's gone again, I scan the room for the rest of the girls, knowing we'll all want to stick together tonight after what happened with Ashlei. When I find them at the photo booth, my heart stops and kicks back into rhythm quickly at the sight of Clinton standing with them. He's just off to the side, his eyes on me as Skyler, Jess, Ashlei, and Cassie crowd around the green screen with silly props.

I don't know why I can't look away from him.

Maybe it's because he's looking at me, *really* looking at me, for the first time since Spring Break. Maybe it's because he's absolutely mouthwatering in the light gray tuxedo he's wearing. Or maybe it's because the anger I felt behind his eyes last time we spoke is completely gone, replaced instead by something else. Sadness? Curiosity?

Remorse?

He grabs one of the speech bubble props and a marker and scribbles something out before holding it in perfect position, so that it appears the message is coming from his lips.

Sorry for being a giant bag of dicks.

I laugh out loud, covering my mouth with my fingertips as I shake my head from across the chapter room. He quirks a smile from the left side of his mouth and shrugs. I shrug, too. Then, I mouth, "It's okay."

Skyler loops her arm through his, tugging him toward the bus, so he throws me one last wink before following her. Slipping into our downstairs guest bathroom, I check my makeup one last time. My lips are nude but glossy, eyeshadow natural yet complementing. My hair is pulled up off my neck and twisted into a side bun held together with bobby pins, accenting my bare collarbone from my strapless gown. The light blue sequins sparkle in the low light of the bathroom and I turn, checking the back one last time before shutting off the light and making my way out to the buses.

There are three large charter buses ready to take us all to the location for formal. Landon taps on the back window from the third one and I smile up at him, waving to the girls who are already climbing onto the one in front of us.

"See you guys there!" I call out and they all smile and wave back. It's then that I notice Adam is here, too. I didn't realize anyone had invited him.

When I reach the back of the bus, I slide into the seat next to Landon and he greets me with a longer, steamier kiss than before. If we keep on this track, I know exactly where this night will lead.

And I'm not sure I'm ready for that.

"Whoa, easy," I say with a giggle, pulling back from his kiss. "At least let me take a few pictures before you smudge my lip gloss."

Landon grins, his eyes low from pre-gaming. "Fine. On one condition."

"And that is?"

His grin widens. "Turn around."

I do as he says, tucking my knees up slightly as I turn my back to him. When his strong hands find my shoulders and he begins to massage my tense muscles, I moan out loud.

"Oh my *God*," I breathe. "That feels amazing."

"Mmm," Landon groans with me, kissing the soft skin just below my ear. "You've been so stressed lately, Ex. I know you've had a lot going on with the website and with recruitment, but for tonight, even if it's *just* for tonight, you should let loose. Try to enjoy yourself. We're only young once, you know." He plants another kiss and it spreads warmth through my chilled skin.

"I don't know, I'm on the executive board. I don't want to get too crazy . . ."

"You won't. Just relax. Here," he says, squeezing my shoulders once more before removing his hands. I turn in my seat to face him as he pulls a leather-bound flask from the inside of his jacket. "This should help."

Chewing my bottom lip, I eye the flask before lifting my gaze to Landon. He looks so happy, so content, and he's been a complete gentleman to me all semester. I'm not even sure why he's stuck around for as long as he has. Maybe he knew I needed someone to lean on. Maybe he's a sort of gift from the gods for putting me through such hell lately.

"You know what," I concede, taking the flask from his hand. "You're right. I think I should loosen up a bit. The semester is almost over and I feel like I haven't had one ounce of fun this entire time." I cheers to him and he pulls a different flask out, tapping the lip of mine with his.

"Cheers, baby."

We both knock back a few swigs, me cringing as the liquid burns my throat. I shake it off quickly and plaster on a smile, throwing my fist in the air. "Let's party!"

The entire bus erupts with my declaration and Landon's eyes devour me, lighting my insides on fire more than the alcohol. Maybe I have been too uptight lately. I tried the whole staying-sober-to-maintain-control thing during Spring Break and look where that got me. Is it possible I've been going about this all wrong?

It's time to let go of everything that's been plaguing me. What's done is done, and Clinton's apology somehow made me feel like everything will be okay. For the first time this semester, I'm going to enjoy myself.

Landon tips his flask once more and I follow his lead, this time pulling him in for a long kiss once the liquid settles in my stomach. His hands find my waist and grip tight as I snake my fingers into the back of his hair, pulling him closer, needing his escape. With each stroke of his tongue against mine, I feel the water clearing. With each brush of his skin against mine, I feel less and less stressed. It's like my mind and body are screaming together for me to let go, to live life tonight. So, when Landon pulls back, his brows pinched together and his eyes on my mouth, I answer his question without him having to ask it.

"Screw the lip gloss."

Cassie

I can still feel that night.

If I close my eyes, like I am right now, I can go back there so easily, as if I never left. The sand between my toes, the damp ocean air in my hair, the hot night sticking to the skin of my thighs just below the hem of my dress. And if I run my fingertips across the same places he touched me in the sand under the stars, it's like he's still here. My thumb brushes my bottom lip and I feel his teeth biting the same spot. My fingers slide shakily to grip the back of my neck and I feel his handprint, instead.

And when I open my eyes again, just before my vision clears, I swear I can still see his eyes.

"You okay, Little?" Skyler asks just as I pop my eyes open. Warm brown eyes flash in the mirror before being chased away by reality. "You have a headache or something? I think I might have some Advil."

Skyler starts sifting through her clutch and I force a smile, shaking my head. "No, no, I'm fine, Big. Just a little sore from . . . yoga," I lie.

"Well, at least the soreness paid off. You look amazing tonight." She smiles before leaning forward in the bathroom mirror to fix her lipstick. I follow suit, smoothing my hands over the sleek black fabric of my dress. My arms are covered with thin lace that trails up to my shoulders before breaking into a conservative top. Everything is covered, the black framing and slimming me all the way down to the middle of my thigh where it breaks for one, long slit—just enough for my pale leg and strappy gold shoes to peek through. My normally frizzy, crazy red hair is tamed, softly curled, and falling lightly over one shoulder. Erin did my makeup, and whatever eyeshadow she used sets my emerald eyes ablaze against it. I feel beautiful, yet at the same time, inadequate.

Because I'm here alone.

Grayson should be here, waiting for me on the dance floor, tattoos covered by a tuxedo jacket. But he broke up with me, and I can't even blame him for it. How do you stay with someone when they can't deny they have feelings for someone else?

Skyler and I finish our touchups and rejoin our group in the ballroom. I thought the semi-formal venue was beautiful, but this? This is absolutely breathtaking. Our executive board rented out a private plantation, and the fact that this house used to entertain one family and their guests is mind blowing. It's huge and regal, the grand architecture giving off a royal feel with just a hint of southern hospitality. The ballroom is fit for a princess or a wedding, which I imagine it's probably played home to both at some point.

Skyler runs off to Erin as soon as we get back inside, who, surprisingly, is having more fun than any of us. She must have pre-gamed pretty hard on the bus because when she piled off it, her eyes were low, hair mussed, and she was clearly ready to party. She was the first on the dance floor and hasn't left since. She may be a little tipsier than the rest of us but I don't think anyone is even judging because she deserves this. It's nice to see her smiling, dancing, letting go.

"Hi." His voice is low, timid, hesitant. I consider ignoring him, since that tactic has been working in my favor all night so far, but with him so close, it's nearly impossible now.

"Hi, Adam." I keep my eyes on the dance floor, watching as Erin and Skyler captivate everyone around them.

"Need a drink?"

As much as I don't want him to be the one to get me a drink, I really do need one right now, so I concede. "Sure."

We walk in silence over to the bar and Adam slides up first, ordering us two Maker's & Cokes. I almost open my mouth to argue with him, to ask him why he thinks I'd want to drink that, but the truth is whiskey is necessary to get through tonight. Apparently, he gets that. Besides, any words I had on my tongue disappeared when he looked back over his shoulder at me and crooked that signature smile of his. Adam in board shorts or a frat tank is one thing, but seeing him in a perfectly-fitting tux, complete with bowtie, makes my knees weak, no matter how loudly I yell at them to hold it together.

"Having fun?"

I clasp my hands together and stare down at my fingers, noting how the light reflects off the gold polish. "Mm hmm."

He hands me my drink and I take it without looking up, sipping from the skinny black straw and letting the liquid burn, just like it did before Spring Break.

"Cassie . . ." he starts, but I cut him off.

"So who are you here with, anyway?" I ask, snapping my head up to look him in the eyes. His brow drops low as he swallows, shifting.

"No one."

I scoff. "What do you mean, 'no one'? You can't just come to the Kappa Kappa Beta formal without someone inviting . . ." my words trail off as I note his nervous eyes watching those close enough to us to overhear. "Oh my God. Did you sneak into formal?"

He pauses, a guilty grin spreading on his lips. "Maybe."

"Why? To try to get me to talk to you?"

"No," he says quickly, but his eyes drop to his drink. "Yes. Well, kind of." He blows out a long, slow breath before lifting his gaze to me once more. "I just had to apologize. I want you to know I'm sorry, for whatever that's worth."

"For?"

"For . . ." He clearly hasn't thought that far. Maybe he didn't think he'd get the chance to say he was sorry, and now that I let him get it out, he's wondering what exactly he apologized for in the first place. "I don't know, Cassie. I'm not sorry for kissing you," he says the words easily, like they don't rob my next breath. "I probably should be, but I'm not."

"So then what are you apologizing for?" I ask again, softer this time.

"Hurting you. Confusing you. Making you cry." He shrugs. "Should I go on? I'm sure you could help me build the list of things I should be sorry for."

My brows pinch together as I study his face. I find nothing but sincerity. My eyes flick down to the water beading on the outside of my glass and I laugh a little before peeking up at him through my lashes. "I can't believe you snuck into my formal."

He smiles with me, relief exhaling from his chest. "How else could I dance with you?"

Adam holds out his hand just as the slow melody of a familiar song starts to play. I chew my cheek, debating if I should, and just as I reach my hand out to place it in his, I pause, sucking in a breath when my eyes focus behind him. It's not the DJ playing the acoustic tune.

It's Grayson.

"Good evening, Kappa Kappa Betas," his gruff voice speaks into the microphone and my sisters all cheer, half of them visibly swooning as Grayson's eyes scan the crowd. I've only seen him play in the coffee shop, but he always looks comfortable there—confident. Right now, he's plucking away at the strings, missing a few notes here and there, finding his footing, cheeks slightly flushed behind his beard.

He's nervous.

But when his gray-blue eyes finally find me, he smiles, radiant, as if he found exactly what he was looking for. "I'm sorry to interrupt your formal, and I promise to let the DJ get you back to dancing, but first, I have a little story to tell you. Is that okay?"

More cheers. I abandon my glass on the bar and slowly walk toward the stage, eyes never leaving his.

"Some of you already know that a certain redheaded sister of yours played hard to get the first time I saw her in Cup O' Joes." A few giggles break out and all eyes turn to me. "I almost gave up on her, I almost took no for an answer. But something inside me wouldn't let me let *her* walk away." A collective *aww*. "Now I knew that she would be sweet, that she would be fun. But I never could have known that she would bring a light to my life that no one else ever could." He swallows and stops strumming just long enough to run a hand over his beard. "Sorry, nervous habit." More laughs.

He starts again, the chords stronger, more sure. "Cassie, I knew letting you walk away that first time would be a mistake, and yet I made the even bigger mistake of walking away from *you*. And I regret it. Because here's the thing . . ." His strums turn even more familiar and I can't fight the smile on my lips when the tune of Train's *Hey Soul Sister* comes together. "I don't want to miss a single thing you do tonight."

With that, he kicks the beat in and starts crooning out the first set of lyrics, everyone in the room singing with him. All the girls rush around me, their arms enclosing me and making me sway but I can't stop staring at Grayson and he won't stop staring at me. His smile is bright, his eyes hopeful as he puts his heart on the line in front of my entire chapter. Each word he sings, each note that finds my ears sends me even higher. I'm light, almost too light on my feet and I grab ahold of Skyler's arm so I don't float away. When the last note plays, Grayson jumps down from the stage, landing hard on both feet before pulling his guitar overhead and leaving it behind. He stands there in front of the stage, heart open, and I don't waste one second before crossing the space between us and throwing my arms around his neck, pressing my lips against his to the sound of applause.

"I thought," I try, but he stops me.

"I know. I did, too." He kisses me again, hands fisting at the lower back of my dress as mine slide into his beard. "I just decided that he can't have you. Not yet. Not until I do everything in my power to prove to you that I deserve you more than he does."

It's like his words have a direct connection to my heartbeat. It hammers hard against my chest, ringing my ears as I try to focus on his words. *He can't have you.*

But what if he already does?

Grayson wraps me in his arms as the DJ plays the next track, kicking the room back into action. When he pulls back, a crowd of my sisters engulfs us, all wanting to talk to Grayson. He just smiles his charming smile and answers all their questions as I hang on his arm, wondering how he's so perfect. But my stomach sinks a little when I catch sight of Adam's back as he pushes through one of the exits. He just apologized to me and I walked away without so much as an *apology accepted*.

"I'll be right back, going to grab us drinks," I say to Grayson, lifting up on my toes to kiss his cheek swiftly. His brows pull inward for just a moment before he smiles and nods, listening again to one of the sisters in my pledge class as she tells him she's been looking into guitar lessons.

My hands are shaking slightly as I push through the same door Adam just did moments ago, finding myself alone with him in the large, fully-stocked house library. He's facing the far bookshelf, hands in his pocket, eyes focused straight ahead like he's picking out his next read. The door shuts softly behind me, blocking out the noise until only our breathing can be heard.

"Adam . . ."

"Don't," he says, back still to me.

"What?"

He turns, dark eyes determined. "Don't. Don't say my name like that. Like you're about to tell me I'm too late. Like you're about to look me in the goddamn eyes and tell me you're back with him."

My lips quiver as I press them tightly together. "Adam, we talked about this."

"Just wait for me," he pleads, louder this time, his feet moving toward me. "Maybe it won't be crazy as president. Maybe I'll have plenty of time. Maybe all that shit was just me grasping at something to break up with Skyler because I knew deep down that it's *you* I should be with." His breaths are labored, chest heaving.

I close my eyes tight. "It's not the right time, Adam."

"Why? Because of him?" He gestures to the ballroom.

"It's not fair of you to ask me to give him up when I never asked that of you with Skyler!" My voice cracks. "You're *president* now. You can't ask me to wait for you to figure out if that means you'll have time for me or not. It's not fair."

"Of course it's not *fair*, Cassie!" Adam scoffs. "Is anything with us? How the hell do you ever expect me to not be selfish when it comes to you?" His tongue jets out to wet his lips and his hands find his waist. He hangs his head, shaking it just slightly.

"The timing isn't right," I whisper again.

He snaps his eye to mine again. "What if you fall in love with him?" His hands fly up. "Don't answer that." And I don't, because the truth is, I could.

The truth is I might already be on my way.

For a moment, we just stand there, Adam's fingers pinching the bridge of his nose while mine grip the edges of my dress like it'll somehow hold me steady.

"I should probably get back out there," I say softly and he just nods, too much, as if he's trying to convince himself of something. I make to turn, but stop myself. "I still want to be friends, Adam."

He winces, a low groan leaving him as if I just threw a punch straight into his stomach. I guess in a way I did.

There's nothing more to say, so I make a move toward the door.

"Cassie," he calls out, his hand catching the crook of my elbow as I turn. My eyes focus on the point of contact, noting the slight tremble in his hands as they glue me to this spot. "Just because the timing isn't right for us now doesn't mean it never will be."

I squeeze my eyes tight as he leans forward, pressing his lips to my forehead before letting me go. He crosses the room quickly, not looking back once, and when the door closes behind him and I'm left alone, the skin his lips touched burns almost as much as my heart.

Bear

Everything's going to be okay.

It's taken me a while to get to this point, but I know it's the truth. I'm finally feeling lighter, laughing and dancing with Skyler to an old 90s hip hop song as I celebrate the end of another semester. We're on the brink of summer, and in just a couple of weeks I'll be on my way home to spend time with Clayton.

Shawna hurt me, I can't deny that. I won't act like I'm too tough to be affected by a girl. The truth is, I cared about her—a lot. But at the end of the day, I look out for number one—me. So, I let her go that night in the rain, and this summer, I'll focus on my family and come back to PSU regrouped, centered, and ready to take on whatever new challenges may come.

"Shit, Bear," Skyler says, grabbing my arm. "You're bleeding." She holds up my fist where the cuts from Alex have split open.

"Fuck," I murmur, pressing my other hand over the wounds. "Be right back."

I weave through the crowded dance floor and head straight for the bathroom, pushing the door open with my back and flipping the water on with my elbow before submerging my hand under the faucet. When the blood flow is under control, I wrap a paper towel around my knuckles and apply pressure, the stinging a reminder of the trouble I caused by fighting Alex.

Omega Chi has been under watch for a while now. It's one thing to party hard, but to get busted for the website and then put the kid responsible for it in the hospital? That's something nationals won't tolerate, even if the little bastard did deserve every hit.

I was called into a conference call with Alec, several other alumni brothers and the president of our national chapter earlier this week. I've never really taken anything they said seriously before now, but they all made it clear that this is it—we're on our last chance. One more strike, and we're out. They told me to take the summer to cool off and figure out what's important to Omega Chi as an organization. Matt just handed over the presidency to my Little's close friend, Taylor, and as much as I like him as a beer pong partner, I'm worried about him as president. I hope we can team up to get our fraternity back in line, but I'll worry more about that later. Tonight, I'm going to dance with my best friend and take shots and say goodbye to spring semester.

One of the workers with the plantation helps me find gauze and we wrap my knuckles before I make my way back toward the ballroom. A loud burst of laughter from down the hall catches my attention on the way and I slow, watching as Landon and two of his Mu Beta Chi brothers exit a room at the far end. His brothers share a high five as Landon takes a long pull from his flask, checking over his shoulder for something in the room they just exited. When another brother joins them, sweat on his forehead, hands adjusting his dress shirt back into his pants, my stomach drops.

Something isn't right.

Landon sniffs, eyes catching mine just briefly before he nods toward the exit and his brothers follow quickly. Before I know what I'm doing, I let my feet carry me toward the room. Every step feels weighted, slow, like I'm walking through quicksand. My heart is hammering in my ears, adrenaline coursing through my veins and telling me I should walk away. Those primal instincts deep within me are screaming *danger* but I can't stop walking. My hand finds the hard wood of the door and I pause, waiting for permission that never comes. Then, slowly, I push it open with a creak.

What I find knocks the breath from my chest.

That's the only thing that happens quickly, and in the next few moments where I'm not breathing, everything else comes slow in a steady rhythm with my heartbeat.

One beat, Erin, face down on a pool table. Another beat, her mascara stained on her cheeks, brown eyes wide open, staring at me like I'm not real. A third beat, her light blue dress, torn in the back, bunched above her waist. The fourth and final beat, her lacey white panties around her ankles, strained against her silver heels still planted firmly on the floor.

One breath, inhaled slowly and exhaled like fire through my nose as my fists clench, breaking the cuts on my knuckles open once more.

"I'll fucking murder them."

I turn fast, eyes searching for Landon and his brothers as Erin calls out my name.

"Bear!"

"I'll fucking murder them!" I repeat, running in the direction I watched them leave, but Erin's voice stops me.

"Bear, don't leave me!" she cries, and the sound rips through my chest like the sharpest blade. I choke on my next breath, torn between chasing after them and staying with her. A soft whimper is all it takes to make my decision for me.

"Fuck!"

I rush through the door, shutting it quickly behind me before crossing quickly to Erin. She hasn't moved except for to squeeze her eyes shut tightly as fresh tears mark her cheeks. My hands gently find the edge of her dress on the table and I pull it down, covering her shaking legs, closing my eyes along with her and forcing another breath to stop myself from leaving her again.

I'll fucking murder them.

I rip my phone from my pocket.

"I'm calling 911."

"No," she says softly, quickly.

"Yes, Erin."

"Bear, please, stop," she says a little louder, her palms finding the table as she tries to push herself up. The bruises already forming on her arms fuel the fire searing my chest. Erin was having fun tonight, she was smiling, she was dancing, she was wild.

And that's when it hits me.

"They drugged you," I whisper. She pauses, stomach still to the table. Her hesitation is answer enough. "I'm calling, Erin."

"No."

"Yes, goddamn it."

"No!" she screams it this time, standing straight, fresh tears falling with the force. "It's my body, Bear! And I said no!"

A sob breaks through and she doubles over, clutching her stomach as she sinks down to the floor, ankles still bound together by lace. I go down with her, trying to lessen the fall with my arms as I pull her into me. Slowly, I slide her underwear up, but she stops me.

"Take them off. Get them off of me."

I rip the fabric and quickly tuck them inside my jacket, wrapping my arms around her again. I don't know what to do. I don't know what to say. All the skits from PSU freshman orientation and years of sex education come flying at me but none of it feels right. "We have to call 911, Erin."

"And what?" she asks, lifting her tear-stained face to me, blue dress crumpled around her. It's the most heartbreaking thing I've ever seen, like I'm holding a princess broken beyond repair. "This isn't a movie or a fucking seminar, Bear. This is real life. And in real life, rich boys with even richer parents and lawyers don't go away for raping a sorority girl." The word *rape* spits from her lips like poison. "They'll say I wanted it, they'll say I planned it, they'll say I consented, they'll say I was drunk on my own, they'll say whatever they have to because it's four of them against one of me. You weren't here, you can't say without a doubt that you saw them do anything. It's me versus them. And in this world, when the *me* is a girl known for being emotionally unstable and the *them* is a group of privileged white men, they win, Bear." She sniffs, leaning her head against my chest. "They win."

My hand finds her hair and I pull her close, as close as I can, trying to protect her from a monster I was too late to fight. "Erin, you're still . . . you're not thinking right."

"Please," she begs, fists curling in my dress shirt. "Just take me home. Please, Bear. Please. *Please.*" She says the word over and over, each time softer, her frail body rocking in my arms. "Please."

"Okay," I finally say, letting myself feel her pain. I take it in, take it as my own, let it overtake my urge to do what I've been taught is the right thing. "Okay."

***

Erin asks me to take her to my room, knowing her house will soon be flooded with sisters soon, so I do. She asks me to help her undress, so I do. She asks me to burn her dress, so I do. But when she turns on my shower, I quickly turn it back off, keeping my eyes on hers.

"If you're going to shower, if you're really not going to tell anyone, then I need you to promise me something."

Her eyes are so tired, so red, yet tears still pool and spill over. She doesn't ask me what the promise is, she hasn't said much at all.

"Erin, you have to get tested. They could have given you something." I feel weird saying it, but I can't just let her wash away all evidence without a promise that she'll take care of herself. I'm already going against every principle in my being. "A disease . . ."

"A baby?" she finishes for me, laughing a bit. I can't understand why. She shakes her head, leaning over to turn on the shower again. "They used condoms."

"I don't care." I shut it off. She turns it on again but my hand covers hers. "I'm serious, Erin. Promise me."

She swallows, and the way her eyes connect with mine makes me feel like our souls are tied together in a way that can never be undone from this day forward.

"Okay."

I nod, dropping my hand and leaving to let her shower in peace but she reaches out for my arm. "Wait." I pause. "Can you . . . will you . . ."

I turn, brows pinched together as the realization of what she's asking settles in. But I won't leave her, not if what she needs is for me to be here right now. I peel my shirt off in response and Erin watches me for just a moment before stepping behind the curtain.

The water is scalding, almost too hot to bear, but I let it burn us both as she scrubs their hands off her skin. The bruises are really starting to show now and her pale skin turns redder and redder as she scrubs, her tears mixing with the water from the showerhead. Tentatively, I take the rag from her hands and slowly run it over her tender skin. My touches are gentle, and she closes her eyes, lips quivering as I try to help her shed the last few hours.

I'm not sure how long we stay in the shower together. The water runs cold and still we stay, shivering together, crying as one. When her tears stop, I turn the water off and wrap her in a towel, carrying her to my room. I find a t-shirt and boxer shorts and she slips them on, crawling into my sheets and reaching out for me again.

So I hold her, all night, through the tears and the silence and the nightmares and the pain. I hold her close, tight, and I whisper the same words over and over and over again until we have no choice but to believe them, until I have no choice but to never rest until they're true.

"Everything's going to be okay."

Erin

How much weight can one girl hold before she crumples beneath it, spent, too tired to even care if it crushes her?

I've been strong before. I've held myself together through experiences that should have killed me. But now, it's as if that girl is a distant memory, or as if she never really existed at all. I'm just a shell now. A cracked, rusted shell.

I can't shower enough. I can't scrub enough. I can't cry enough. *Nothing* is enough to cleanse me of that night. Nothing ever will be.

I think I broke Clinton, too.

He brought me back to life just enough to let me breathe on my own, though anything else feels impossible, and I asked him to go against everything he stands for. But he did it. For me. And I wonder how much of himself he gave up just to let me hold tight to the last little shred of what was left of me.

I've been holed up in my room since the morning after when I walked in a daze back to the house. I left long enough to take my last final and that's it. The girls think I'm sick, and I let them think whatever they want to. Clinton checks on me from time to time but I ignore him for the most part, only responding enough to let him know I'm alive, though maybe that's a lie, too.

But today, like a child, I called my mother. I showed her my scraped knees and asked her to bandage them. I asked her to fix me. Instead, she cried. And I cried with her. Now, we sit quiet on the phone together, both still sniffling as I curl into myself under my sheets.

"Are you packed?" she finally asks.

"I am."

She sniffs, clearing her throat. "Good. I'm sending a car now. Listen to me." Her voice cracks a bit and a new wave of tears rush in on me. "You are a strong, brave, incredible young lady. You have way too much ahead of you to let four spoiled little punks take your life away." I tuck my knees up closer to my chest and exhale loudly to ward off a sob. "So you're going to come home, and we're going to figure this out together. Do you hear me? You are not broken, Erin Xander. You need to harden your heart, baby girl. Take everything you feel right now and hone it, use it to push you toward what you want most in life. *Take* what you want. Take what you need. Right now, you feel like you've been robbed, right?" I nod, even though she can't see me. "So, take back what's yours."

"I don't know how," I whisper, wanting to believe her but feeling the exact opposite of her words. Is this what bravery looks like? A scared little girl curled up in sheets like they'll be her saving grace?

There's a weighted pause on the other end before Mom's voice comes through again, stronger than before.

"I do. And I'll teach you. Just come home, baby."

So I do.

And going home isn't the hard part. I go willingly, hopefully.

It's coming back to PSU that won't be easy.

And *if* I do make it back, the truth remains that I won't be the same girl everyone knew before. That girl is dead.

Can a new one be reborn?

Jess

I've been practicing.

I've been working every word over and over in my head for the last week since formal. I want this to be perfect, I want this moment to be as big as I feel like it should be. So when Jarrett opens his door dressed in nothing but relaxed, navy blue sweat pants that hang low on his hips, I close my eyes to stop myself from getting distracted.

"Jess?"

"Don't talk," I say quickly, eyes still closed. "I just need to get this all out, okay?" I crack one eye open just long enough to make sure he's still there. And he is, in all his sexy, tattooed glory, brow cocked, an amused look on his face. I close my eyes again, blowing out one long breath.

"I've been stupid. I've been fighting you on this whole relationship thing and giving you every excuse I could think of because the truth is that I'm scared. I'm terrified, actually. That I'll hurt you, that you'll hurt me, that we'll fail miserably or worse—actually make it together." I'm rambling. I'm an idiot. I keep going. "Because if we do make it together, then that means we give each other even more power to break one another. And that's fucking scary, okay? So, I'm sorry I've been a little crybaby bitch. I sucked on a pacifier for a few weeks and pulled up my big girl panties and now I'm ready. I'm still scared," I clarified. "But I'm ready to do this. I want to be your girlfriend." I wait, chest heaving, but no response comes. "Jarrett?"

When I open my eyes to make sure I'm not talking to a closed door, Jarrett comes into view slowly, one arm crossed over his chest and the other holding his hand over his perfect mouth as he fights back laughter.

"This isn't funny, Jarrett!" I scream, my hands flying up. "I'm serious! I love you! I fucking—"

Jarrett's mouth crashes down hard on mine, stealing my next words along with my breath. His hands wrap around my hips with ease and he yanks me inside his apartment, slamming the door closed behind us before throwing me up against it. A picture frame on the same wall falls to the floor, glass cracking as I wrap my legs around his waist and lock ankles. I tug him closer, my nails digging into his bare back, our breaths heavy and desperate.

His mouth is eager as he tastes my lips, my neck, the swell of my breasts. His hips pin mine against the door and he lifts my arms, pulling my tank top up and over my head before flinging it to the side. His expert fingers snap my bra off quickly, letting it fall to the floor as he lifts me once more and carries me to the bedroom. We barely reach the bed before he tosses me onto it, the comforter expelling around me in a *whoosh.*

Jarrett makes quick work of my jean shorts, stripping them off my legs and yanking his own pants to the floor as I lean up to kiss his abs. I take him in my hand, stroking him from the tip all the way down to the base and back, my tongue still tracing figure eights on his chiseled abdomen. Jarrett groans before pushing me back into the bed, his hands gripping my skin as he drags my panties down my thighs, my calves, all the way to my ankles. He lets them drop before wrapping his long fingers around my ankles once more, pulling my legs up one by one to rest on his shoulders. Planting one soft kiss on the inside of my left ankle, he smirks, the tug of his lips tied to the longing building inside me. My thighs tense and tingle as he flexes his hips forward, his hard on pressed against my slit, teasing.

"Jarrett," I breathe his name as my hands find my breasts. He watches as I frame my nipples, tugging each of them gently. Groaning, his hands grip my thighs hard and he pulls me to the edge of the bed, answering my call, filling me with one solid thrust.

"Fuck," he drags the word out, his hands sliding up my ribs, my breasts before holding tight to my shoulders and pulling me toward his second thrust. With my ankles on his shoulders, he hits me deeper than I've ever felt him before. He works me slow and steady, letting me feel every inch as he pulls all the way out before sliding back inside.

His hands slide up higher, cradling my neck and stretching my legs further as he leans in close to my chest. Jarrett's pace intensifies, his eyes dark, wide, and locked on mine as his slides the thumb from his right hand in to hook the corner of my mouth. I suck hard, letting it go with a pop and his eyes roll back as his hips roll forward.

"I want you to come like this," he demands, trailing his hands down my body as he straightens his stance. The same thumb that was just in my mouth finds my clit and I reward him with a sharp cry of pleasure.

"Only if you come with me."

He smiles, biting his lower lip as his thumb applies more pressure. Every circle sends a jolt through me, my need pulsing in time with his movement. "Always so fucking stubborn."

"You love it," I shoot back and he slows, his smile falling.

"I love *you*."

I eye him through heavy lids, my sexy, bald, tattooed boyfriend.

Boyfriend.

Yeah, I could get used to that.

"I love you, too."

He stops, dropping my ankles off his shoulders and pulling me up to meet his lips. His kiss tells me more than his words do, and I let it speak freely, wrapping my arms around his neck and tugging him closer.

"Turn around," he demands, smacking my ass. I giggle, doing as he says, but when one hand grips the bend at my waist and the other positions him behind me, the laughter is gone, replaced by a carnal need only Jarrett makes me feel.

He rocks in slowly, but picks up speed quickly, his hands pulling my hips back to meet his own again and again. When his palm finds the center of my back and he presses me face down into the sheets, I grip them with my fists and hold on tight as I find my climax. I call out his name, chest tight as I ride the wave for as long as I can. Jarrett comes right behind me, and hearing him moan sends an aftershock through my core.

When we're both spent, Jarrett falls into the sheets with me, pulling me to straddle his waist. His hands slide into my hair and he kisses me, softer this time, longer kisses followed by short ones, like the most beautiful cadence.

"Mine," he whispers between kisses, smiling. "Thank *fuck* you're finally mine."

***

"Well, looks like another semester bites the dust, girls," I say, tossing the last of my bags into my rental car. It feels weird to not be loading up the Bimmer for my trip home, but I don't regret giving her up one bit. I would do it all over again, if it meant Ashlei's freedom from Xavier. Even with Bo leaving, she still seems so much happier—lighter—and I look forward to her getting back to the old Ashlei.

Cassie shakes her head, squinting under the bright beams of the Florida sun. The first day of summer may be over a month away, but it's sweltering already. "I can't believe I'll be a sophomore when we all come back."

"THEY GROW UP SO FAST," Skyler fake blubbers, pulling Cassie into a crushing hug.

"I'm not ready to go home," Ashlei says with a sigh as Skyler and Cassie break, still laughing. "It doesn't feel like it's time yet. So much has changed, it feels anti-climactic to just pack up this semester in a duffle bag and head home for three months."

"Tell me about it. I turn twenty-one in two weeks and I won't even have anyone there to celebrate with, unless you count my grams. Which, I mean, the lady can party but . . ."

Ashlei and Cassie laugh but Skyler is just staring at me.

"What?" I ask. "Why are you looking at me like your dad just found your vibrator?"

"What if we just don't go home?" Skyler asks, looking around at each of us. "I mean, not yet. Jess' birthday is in two weeks. What if we . . . I don't know, what if we went somewhere? My place, or anywhere, really. Two of us are newly single while the other two are freshly wifed up. I feel like we should celebrate, kick the summer off in style." At first I shake my head, but the more she talks, the more I think she might have a brilliant idea. "I mean come on. It's J-Love's twenty-first birthday. We can't just *not* be there for it."

"I have a flight in like three hours," Cassie points out.

"So? Cancel it," Skyler challenges.

"Well, I'm in no rush to get home. I say let's do it." Ashlei smiles and Skyler throws her a high-five before turning to me.

"Oh come on, like you even have to ask me," I scoff. "Jarrett already left for his summer internship, so it's not like I have the possibility of getting banged anytime soon. Therefore, I'll need lots of alcohol."

They both grin and then it's just Cassie left. She bites her cheek. "What about Erin? Did she leave already?"

Skyler frowns. "Yeah, she was pretty sick, I guess. I feel like she was just ready to get out of here after all the executive board drama."

Cassie nods, debating. "Well . . . I'm sure my parents can change the flight."

"Yes!" Skyler and I cheer together and we all grab Cassie in another hug. She laughs, throwing her head back as we crowd in around her. She has so much fucking hair that I cough on a strand of the red beast and everyone laughs harder.

"Fuck yes! Pile in, bitches. Let's take this thing back to the rental car place and trade it in for something with more room. Then, we're calling my parents and telling them not to book the beach house in New Smyrna for the next three weeks."

"Shotgun!" Skyler yells, hoisting her bag over her shoulder and running toward the car. Everyone is talking all at once, cramming bags into the trunk and fitting extras on laps. The girls start making phone calls as I pull out of the KKB house, adjusting my rearview mirror when we pull away.

"Someone text Erin. Tell her to meet us there," I say, rolling our windows down to let the warm breeze fill the space between us.

"On it!" Ashlei replies, ending the call with her dad and typing out a text immediately.

As I flick my shades down over my eyes, I take one last glance at campus fading behind us, watching how the bright orange of the setting sun casts it in a fiery glow. My eyes find Cassie's in the rearview and I take the time to look around at my sisters, all of us smiling, all of us leaving Palm South University different than we arrived.

Each and every one of us has climbed a mountain this semester, some with less equipment and rougher paths. But here we are, standing together at the top, and suddenly it feels like there's nothing that can stop us now.

It's going to be one hell of a summer.

A note from the author

I'm writing this note with shaky hands and a heavy heart. This season of *Palm South University* covered a lot of serious topics, including the sexual assault of Erin Xander in this episode. While this was an important part of Erin's journey and story to tell, it's equally important for you, as a reader, to understand that there are options if you ever find yourself in this terrifying situation or one similar to it.

If you become a victim of sexual assault, call 911 or RAINN at 1–800–656-HOPE immediately.

Just like Erin's situation, four out of five rapes are committed by someone known to the victim. Similarly, 68% of rapes are not reported to the police, and 98% of rapists never spend a day in jail or prison. And unfortunately, a college campus isn't always a safe place, as women 18–24 who are enrolled in college are 3 times more likely than women in general to suffer from sexual violence.

If you're like Erin, you may feel that it's useless to tell anyone—no one will believe you, they'll say it was your fault, they'll embarrass you and end up winning in the end, anyway. But no matter what, you must understand that it is **not your fault** and **there is help** available.

I hope you never find yourself in this situation or never have in the past, but if you're reading this and you feel isolated and alone, please, reach out to someone. Reach out to *me*. I am always here, and I care about you—every single one of you.

Take care of your mind, your body, and your soul. You're the only one who can.

For more information and resources, please visit *www.rainn.org*.

Palm South UNIVERSITY

PLEDGE

BOOK 3

EPISODE 1

THANKSGIVING

Jess

Worst.
Friendsgiving.
Ever.

I thought it was my best idea since I'd decided to change my major, to get the gang together to overdose on mashed potatoes and red wine, especially since my original plans for the holiday had fallen as flat as my hair in the Florida humidity. I couldn't be with Jarrett, so I'd be with everyone else I cared about. It seemed genius at the time.

But here I am, sitting in the proof that I was very, very wrong.

We're all gathered around a long, folding table usually used for beer pong, though now it's covered in a deep red table cloth with gold accents and several plates of food. I say *all* lightly, because Ashlei is halfway across the country due to her stupid internship and Erin is MIA.

Her...and the turkey she was supposed to bring.

"Maybe we should just start," Skyler suggests, smiling softly, though her blue eyes are strained. The bags under them tell me she hasn't been sleeping. "I'm sure she'll be here soon. We can at least eat the sides while they're hot."

Clinton scoffs, crossing his hard, dark arms over his chest as he rolls his eyes. "Oh, right, because you always know what's best, don't you, Sky?"

Skyler's face crumples. "Bear, please. I apologized. Can we just... can't we have a nice meal?"

All eyes are on Clinton, mine shooting daggers as we wait for his answer. He's been a prick since he walked in the door, and though I have no idea what happened, I'm almost positive he's being a little bitch about whatever is going on.

Then again, that could just be because right now every man in the entire world is the enemy to me. I hate them. I hate how they make us feel things, how they make promises they can't keep, how they have a gift for building us up with hope only to let us down in the end.

And I'm not even on my period. God help the poor suckers who hit on me the next time I am.

Clinton picks up his fork like he's ready to play nice, at least for a while, but then he grits his teeth and drops it back to the table again. The legs of his chair scrape against the hardwood floor of the chapter room as he pushes back and stands.

"How the fuck are we supposed to have Thanksgiving without a goddamn turkey," he growls, and without another look at any of us, he steamrolls out the back door, letting in the tiniest sliver of the setting sun before the door closes behind him.

Skyler sighs. "He's not mad about the turkey," she explains, standing up for him even when he's being a giant dick to her. "He's just worried about his little brother and..."

"It's fine, Big," Cassie says, offering a soft smile. "I agree, we should just eat."

"Yeah, who says you can't make a meal out of green bean casserole?" Adam chimes in, and for some reason Grayson is giving him a death glare from across the table. I know they had some tension between them after the dodgeball tournament, but was it really so much that he's still not over it? "Challenge accepted."

Skyler nods, but she's chewing her lip between her teeth, eyes on the door Clinton just blew out of. Adam starts, piling mashed potatoes and gravy on his plate first before passing the serving dish to Skyler. She glances at it briefly, then pushes back from the table with another sigh.

"I'm sorry, I just need to check on him. I'll be back."

So, she skips out the door, too, which leaves me alone with the peanut gallery: Cassie, Adam, and Grayson.

Joy.

Adam swallows, offering the dish across the table to Cassie, instead. I'm kneading my temple now, eyes closed until I hear my phone buzz on the table. My hands fly, unlocking the screen quickly and expecting to see Jarrett's name, only to find a sorry ass excuse from Erin.

- Sorry, got caught up with some Panhellenic stuff. I'll be there soon! -

I grumble, but before I can even text back, another chair scrapes against the floor.

"Oh, for Christ's sake, what now?!"

It's Grayson who's standing now, jaw all tense and chest puffed out. I'll admit, he's still a sexy motherfucker with that man bun and those steel eyes, but even he's not immune to my man-hating today.

"I can't do this anymore, Cassie," he says, eyes hard on Adam across the table. "You have to choose. Him," he snarls, thrusting a hand toward Adam. "Or me."

"Andddd, that's my cue." This time it's me who stands, tossing my napkin on my still-empty plate. "You guys can have your pissing match. I'm going to get a cheeseburger."

Tossing my long, freshly highlighted hair over my shoulder, I snag a dinner roll and take a large bite before saluting them and walking out the opposite door the other two had exited. I roll my eyes as soon as the door closes behind me, crossing through the sorority house and taking the stairs two at a time up to my room.

I hit the speed dial for Jarrett, switching my phone to speaker before dropping it to my bed and filtering through the clothing options in my closet. By the second ring, I'm stripped free of the tea-length dress I'd had on. By the fourth, my favorite pair of skin-tight jeans are hugging my hips. And by the time his voicemail picks up, my boobs are pushed up to the heavens and barely covered with a black crop top that criss-crosses over my cleavage.

Huffing, I end the call before the beep, stepping into a high pair of candy red pumps and checking my reflection in the mirror. I run my fingers through my hair, swiping my purse from where it hangs off my closet door and fishing through it for the lipstick that matches the shoes.

Rubbing my lips together with approval, I give myself one last look before adding my last accessory — a smile that screams trouble.

Jarrett is busy. I get it, really, I do. But he could at least call. He could at least *text*, especially considering we were supposed to be together today.

But if he wants to play hard to get with his attention and affection, I'm not afraid to step up to the table and play the game. I have tricks up my sleeve, ones he isn't exactly oblivious to. Still, maybe he's forgotten. Maybe he needs a reminder.

If he's going to sleep on me, then I don't really have much of a choice anymore.

Time to wake that motherfucker up.

THREE MONTHS EARLIER

Cassie

I'm officially a sophomore.

It seems impossible that an entire year has gone by since I first stepped foot on the Palm South University campus, and even more impossible that I'm now on the other side of recruitment. If I thought it was hard rushing as a freshman — choosing a sorority to call my home — I clearly had no idea what it was like to stay up late every night for two full weeks practicing and preparing for rush as a *sister*.

Erin wants the best pledge class Kappa Kappa Beta has ever seen, and she's stopping at nothing to get the most premier girls. Top GPAs, athletes, dancers, pre-med, pre-law, previous class officers, and yearbook editors — she wants them all. We've been studying bios for weeks, and with only two days left before the girls make a decision, Erin is pushing us even harder to lock in the new members.

With all the chaos, it's a miracle I was even able to sneak out. I'm exhausted, I barely have a voice left, and all I want to do is sip a cup of coffee in a quiet coffee shop and kiss my boyfriend whom I haven't seen all summer.

But apparently, quiet is out of the question.

Pushing through the crowded coffee shop, I keep checking the time on my phone, knowing I won't have long before Erin will be blowing it up wondering where I went. I've never seen Cup O' Joe's so packed before. There are girls in every bit of free space, some sitting at tables while others line the walls. None of it makes sense until Grayson comes into view, and when he croons out a smooth note from the Maroon 5 song he's currently playing, I have a feeling this is going to be the new normal.

The longest sigh leaves my lips as I take him in, noting how his eyes look brighter with the tan still bronzing his skin from the summer. His hair is pulled back, bun messy, beard clean and trimmed, guitar strapped over one shoulder like it's an actual limb and not an object he can take off.

"Can I help you?" I hear the barista at the counter ask when it's finally my turn to step up and order, but I can't tear my gaze from Grayson.

I wait for his blue eyes to connect with mine, but they keep wandering the crowd as he sings to every single girl like they're the only ones in the room. I can't deny there's a sting in my chest every time he winks or gives them that same sexy smile he hooked me with last semester, but I try to remind myself it's all now part of the show.

As if he senses my discomfort, Grayson furrows his eyebrows, and he searches the crowd until he finds me.

Then, he smiles.

A radiant, too-hot-for-a-coffee-shop, drop-your-panties-now smile.

"Get that girl a caramel latte," he says, nodding to the barista behind the counter. "And don't let her leave before I kiss her breathless."

He keeps that smile on his face and his eyes on me as he finishes the song, but he's not the only one watching me now. Every girl in the room is staring, eyes flicking from me to Grayson and back again, likely wondering how in the hell I landed him.

I'm still trying to figure it out, too.

When he plays the last note, the whole shop cheers, whistles ringing out, but I barely register them. All I can see is Grayson jumping down from the stage, his stride confident, eyes on my mouth. All I can hear is the beat of my heart in my ears matching each step he takes. All I can smell is his cologne, and I remember sleeping in it, in his sheets, in his arms. And when he finally reaches me, hands framing my face as I taste him for the first time in months, all I can feel is everything.

Longing, excitement, fear, relief, passion — all wrapped into one kiss in a crowded coffee shop where only the two of us exist.

When he pulls back, forehead still pressed against mine and hands on my cheeks, I smile. "Well, mission accomplished. Officially breathless."

He smiles, pecking my nose and pulling me into his chest for a hug. "God, I've missed you."

"I've missed you, too, rock star. Speaking of which," I add, eyeing the girls around us as they throw knives at me with their eyes. "I think you're going to start a riot in here if you don't let me go."

He laughs, shifting to pull me under one arm and leading me through the crowd to a blessedly empty table in the back corner. It's marked with a *reserved* sign, and Grayson slides it aside when we sit down in the two chairs behind it.

"They'll live. It's crazy, though, isn't it? That video, Cassie... it changed everything."

"You had the magic formula," I remind him. "You, shirtless, lights turned down low, acoustic guitar, and an original song better than anything on the radio right now. All it took was that one YouTube fangirl to share it on Facebook and all her groupies attacked."

He chuckles as the barista from behind the counter sets down two matching coffee cups, smiling at both of us before leaving us alone again.

"I guess. But seven-hundred thousand views in less than two months?" He shakes his head, reaching for his coffee to take a sip. "It's crazy. I maxed out on Facebook friends, Cassie. Like... I can't add anymore. It's insanity."

My heart skips as I watch him, eyes all glowy and smile wider than I've ever seen it. He's like a puppy in a blanket — too damn adorable not to kiss.

So, I lean in, taking his coffee from his hands to set it back on the table as I thread my hands behind his neck. His lips are sweet, sticky with caramel, and I lick them clean before letting him slide his tongue between my teeth.

Grayson moans into my mouth, arms wrapping around me and sliding down to palm my ass. His knee is right between mine, and when he pulls me closer, I catch just the slightest bit of friction that makes me whimper.

"Come over tonight," he whispers, slowing our kiss enough to say the words.

I groan. "I can't. Recruitment, remember? I actually snuck out to be here..." I check the time on my phone. One missed text from Erin, soon to be five, I imagine. "I should probably get back."

Grayson pouts, but he doesn't get to throw much of a fit before they're announcing him back up on the stage.

"What about Sunday, then? I'm playing at this swanky new restaurant downtown and I want you there as my date."

I bite my lip, debating my options. Bid Day is Saturday, but there are usually Sunday Funday celebrations at all the houses the day after, too.

"Please?" Grayson adds, pulling me closer. "I need you there."

Smiling, I run my fingers through the hair at the back of his neck with a nod. I'm sure Erin will have something to say about me not being present, but she'll get over it. I've been in her captivity for over two weeks now.

"I wouldn't miss it."

He smiles, leaning in to kiss me once more before pulling me up to stand with him. "Have fun pillow fighting or making necklaces or whatever it is they have you doing over there."

I smack his arm and he sneaks in another peck on my nose, adjusting his hair in the messy tie he has it in as he jogs toward the stage. Allowing myself one last minute of gawking at him as he straps on his guitar, I debate staying a little longer. That is, until a string of three texts come in from Erin all at once.

Sighing, I give Grayson one last longing look before taking my coffee to go for the walk back to the house.

***

"There you are," Erin says as soon as I walk through the door, her voice tight with annoyance.

Sisters are running all over the place, some of them balancing protein bars in one hand and bios in the other. Just because the potential new members are done for the day doesn't mean we're even close, and that fact is cemented when Erin thrusts a thick packet into my chest.

"I need you to run this down to the Alpha Sig house and get it to Adam. Then come right back because we're doing dress check for tomorrow and I'll need you to help me fix the sisters who apparently don't understand what *cerulean blue* means."

She rolls her eyes, tucking a misplaced blonde strand of hair behind her ear before checking two items off the list on her clipboard.

All I can do is stand there and gape at her.

"Why are you still standing here?" she snaps, then she closes her eyes and forces a breath. "God, sorry. I didn't mean that to sound as bitchy as it did. I'm just stressed. You okay?"

I nod, forcing the swallow I couldn't seem to get a grip on before. "Yeah, I just... is there anyone else who could maybe run this down to Alpha Sig? I was actually hoping to take a shower before—"

I don't even get the rest of my pathetic excuse out before Erin cuts me off.

"I need you to do this, G-Little. Please. I've already got Jess, Lei, and your Big off doing other pertinent things and honestly I'm too exhausted to even try to find someone else I trust enough to deliver that packet without somehow getting lost at one of the campus bars." She sighs, pinching the bridge of her nose and closing her eyes again. "Please?"

I clear my throat, holding the packet up with a forced smile. "Of course, it's no problem. Be right back."

"Thank you," she says, squeezing my arm before jetting off toward the kitchen, yelling out demands at every sister she passes along the way.

The walk to the Alpha Sigma house is short, but I feel every step like an agonizing hour at the gym. I haven't seen Adam since the dance last semester, the dance where I walked out on him, where I chose Grayson. Just thinking about that night, about the look on his face right before he walked out that door — it sucker-punches me right square in the gut.

"Just because the timing isn't right for us now doesn't mean it never will be."

I shake the memory from my head as I turn, walking up the drive to the large, wooden door with his letters proudly displayed on the front. Taking one last shaky breath, I walk through the door.

Had this been last year, I likely would have knocked. But I'm not a freshman anymore, and I know well enough now that you don't knock when you go to a fraternity house. I don't even stop to say hi to the guys playing foosball in the living room, just walk straight toward the back hall. Adam will be in the president's suite now, and I'm going to drop this stupid packet on his bed and leave. That's it. The end.

Except as soon as I round the corner leading to the hall, my plan goes up in flames.

Adam is walking toward me, head down as he uses a small towel to dry his hair, wearing only a slightly larger towel tied low around his hips. I freeze, breath catching as I watch the water droplets fall from his shoulders to his chest to his abdomen, all the way down to the hem of the towel. When he's less than ten feet in front of me he looks up, eyes widening at the sight of me.

And then he freezes, too.

"Cassie?" he asks, tossing the small towel over his shoulder. "What are you doing here?"

My eyes are still glued to his chest, to the new muscles stretching over his ribs and abdomen. He's filled out over the summer. His hair is a little longer, his arms a little bulkier, and his skin just as dark as the day we came back from spring break.

I have no clue how long I stare, but it's long enough for him to follow my gaze down to his chest, which immediately makes me flush and squeeze my eyes closed tight. I thrust the packet out toward his chest that I can't stop looking at and turn, practically sprinting for the door.

"Hey, wait," Adam calls out behind me, but I just throw an awkward wave over my shoulder and plow through the front door and out into the humid August air.

I inhale a deep breath, shaking my head and burying my face in my hands.

God, what was that?

I've seen Adam shirtless before — plenty of times, actually. So then why did I just act like a sixteen-year-old virgin seeing her first boy sans clothing? All summer I'd been hoping Adam and I could be friends again this semester, get rid of all the tension between us and go back to how we were before. Zero awkwardness, that's what I was aiming for.

My arrow didn't even hit the target, let alone the bullseye.

Bear

Weightlifting, partying, and fucking.

Three things I do better than anyone else.

I finished the first one early this morning, I'll be doing the second one later tonight, and the last? Well, it's like they always say — there's no time like the present.

"Oh, fuck, Bear. Don't stop. Don't... stop..."

Lacy bites her lip hard as she rides me, hands wrapped up in her hair and thighs tense as she tightens around me. I grip her hips harder, pulling her down as I thrust my hips, hitting her deeper, deep enough to make her scream my name as she comes.

She may not be the brightest color in the crayon box, but one thing I can always depend on with Lacy? She's down to fuck. Down to *just* fuck. She'd had a moment last year where she wanted more, but it was brief, and now I know I can count on her when I need a distraction or a release.

And she can count on me.

"God," she sighs, rolling off me, chest still heaving. "You've ruined me for other guys, you know that, right? Your cock is a fucking treasure."

"Yeah?" I ask, standing and pulling her small wrist until she's standing, too. "Why don't you show me just how valuable it is to you."

She smirks, tongue running the length of her bottom lip before she drops to her knees. She keeps her dark brown eyes locked on mine as she swirls her tongue over the head and I moan, flexing my hips. Lacy takes the cue, swallowing me whole, gagging a little as I groan again.

It's so fucking hot staring down at her, brown skin smooth and shining with a thin sheen of sweat as she works my cock with her hands and mouth. Every time she flicks her eyes up to look at me and takes me in her throat I surge closer to climax, and when one hand cups my balls and squeezes, I curse, pulling out of her mouth.

"Open," I command and she does, closing her eyes and stretching her mouth open wide, tongue out, breasts perky and waiting. I pump myself twice more and then I bust, coming on her mouth, her neck, her nipples. Lacy trails her fingers along the pearly white lines as I finish, tucking one finger in her mouth and sucking it clean before opening her eyes and grinning up at me.

"Fuck." I breathe the word, falling back onto my bed as she giggles and scampers to my bathroom. A few minutes later she returns with a towel, wiping herself clean before handing it to me.

And this is my favorite part.

Because Lacy doesn't ask to cuddle, or talk, or for me to text her later. She just pulls her dress on, tucks her bra into her purse, and slips on her sandals.

"See you around, Bear."

She winks, and then she's gone.

Perfect.

It's been a hell of a summer. Getting my little brother, Clayton, set up at his best friend's house and making sure he had everything he needed for the school year was challenging. I hated that I wasn't there for him, even if Mac's family was. Still, he made it clear last year that the last thing he wanted was for me to give up PSU and move back to Pittsburgh. So, I'm trying to let it go, to give him the respect and trust he's asking for, and do everything I can from Florida for now.

Then there's the fact that I'm a junior now. Classes aren't going to be a breeze anymore, and studying is *not* among my list of things I'm good at. I'm excited for the advanced art classes and harnessing my skills in the Adobe Creative Suite, but I've also heard horror stories about my professors this semester.

Sighing, I try to drop the stress and float on the high from getting my rocks off with one of the hottest chicks on campus as I make my way to the shower. But as soon as the hot water hits my bare back, another girl floods my mind.

Erin.

I wash my body quickly, trying not to think about her too much until I'm out of the space we shared after formal last semester. I won't ever be able to shower without that memory sparking to life, and now that I'm back in the exact shower it happened in, it's even harder to push the thought away.

When I'm dressed, I realize I still have plenty of time before the party starts, so I swipe my wallet off my desk and make my way down to the Kappa Kappa Beta house. It's after nine now, which means the girls rushing are halfway across campus making their final selections before bid day. It's likely a mad house over at KKB, but I don't care.

I need to see her.

***

"You're joking, right?"

Ashlei laughs, arms crossed as she rests her weight on one hip. The house is bustling behind her, all her sisters still dressed in all black cocktail dresses from Pref Night.

"I just need five minutes."

"You *do* realize how impossible that is, right? To see the recruitment chair on Pref Night? Even for five minutes?"

She wasn't being rude, just simply stating facts, and the truth is I knew it before even walking down.

"Humor me. Just ask her."

Ashlei opens her mouth, likely to shut me down again, but then I spot Erin behind her as she zooms by, clipboard in hand.

"Better yet, I'll ask. Excuse me."

I slide past Ashlei before she has the chance to stop me and fall in step with Erin.

"Hey, Dictator Xander."

Erin's face screws up in confusion as she whips around to face me. When she realizes who it is, she pauses, but only for a second. If I would have blinked, I'd have missed it.

"I don't have time to talk, Bear."

"I see that," I muse, walking with her as she continues barking orders at every girl we pass. "How was your summer?"

"I just said I don't have time to talk."

"Come on, just five minutes."

She huffs, propping her clipboard on her hip and coming to a halt. "My summer was fine. Recruitment has been busy, but fantastic. We're going to have the best pledge class this campus has ever seen. I'm all signed up for classes, my immune system is being pushed to its limits but I'm overdosing on vitamin C, and yes, I cut my hair. I think that just about covers it, right?"

Erin starts walking again and I chuckle, jogging to catch up with her. "My summer was great, too. Thanks for asking."

"Can we do this another time?" she asks, distracted by the long list on her clipboard. She turns to head for the chapter room but I reach for her, gently catching her elbow.

But gentle or not, the touch triggers Erin in the absolute worst way.

She jerks back, eyes wide and fists clenching together as she drops her board. It clatters to the floor and I hold my hands up, palms open, and take three steps back.

Erin watches me, swallowing hard, and the fear in her eyes is like a nail gun to my chest.

"Sorry," I say softly, bending to retrieve her clipboard.

She takes it with shaky hands, tucking her hair behind her ear.

"I just wanted to make sure you were okay."

"I'm fine."

I give her a pointed look. We both know she's not fine, but she's clearly not ready to talk about what happened last semester, so I opt for distraction, instead.

"You should come to the O Chi house tonight, let loose a little."

This time it's her who deadpans. "It's the night before Bid Day, Bear. I'm not going to a fucking party."

"Come on, you know half your sisters are going to sneak out and be there, too. You guys need a break. The hard part is over."

"I'm not going," she says, her answer final. "And five minutes is up. I'll see you around."

With that, she slips right back into her role as Recruitment Chair, and further from the girl I was afraid she'd never be again.

"Goddamn it!"

I throw my phone across the room with a roar, watching as it bounces off Skyler's bed and plops down to the floor anticlimactically. Having a shatter-proof phone case is not helping in this moment of rage.

Skyler pokes her head out of the bathroom, curling wand still wrapped around one strand of hair as she eyes the phone and then cocks one eyebrow at me. "Bad horoscope again?"

"No," I huff. "Jarrett got a job."

"And that made you hurl your phone at my pillows?"

"Not a job here. They offered him a job at the nonprofit agency he's been interning at all summer. And that fucker took it!" I punch my pillow, crossing my arms over my chest like a child. I'm whining like a little bitch, but I can't help it.

Skyler drops her curling wand on the counter and pads over to me, hopping up onto the bed as Ashlei leans a hip on the doorframe. She's still brushing her teeth, all of us getting ready to go to the first Omega Chi party of the year.

"This is a good thing, Jess. He's worked hard and it's paying off now."

"Yeah, but this was supposed to be temporary — this whole long-distance thing. Now he's there for, what? A year? Two? Forever?" I flop back against my pillows and pull one to cover my face, muffling my next selfish whine. "I don't want to be in a long-distance relationship."

It's silent a moment before the pillow is pulled from my face and I find myself staring up at Ashlei, her blonde hair straight as a pin and falling all around her face as she points her toothbrush down at me. "You love him, remember? You'll make it work. It's going to be hard," she concedes, glancing at Skyler who nods with a sympathetic smile. "But he's crazy about you, Jess. And you're crazy about him. Don't make him feel guilty for following his dreams."

I sigh. "I know. You're right. But I'm not ready to admit that to him, yet. Right now I just want to be mad and whiney and drunk. I've got the first two down so can we work on that third?"

Skyler grins and Ashlei pops her toothbrush back in her mouth, speaking around the bristles. "Now *that* we can do."

We finish getting ready just before eleven, and without even trying to convince Erin to come with us, we sneak down the stairs and out the back kitchen door, waiting to pull on our high heels until we're safely outside.

Skyler and Ashlei chat as we make the short walk to Omega Chi, Skyler telling us about the national poker tournament she's thinking of entering while Ashlei talks about how nervous she is to start her internship next week. It reminds me that since I changed my major so late, I won't even be able to intern until next summer, at the earliest. My boyfriend is off kicking ass and taking names, already working in the government sector for a top nonprofit, and I can't even apply to be someone's intern bitch yet.

It's not that I'm not happy for him, because I am — I know he deserves this and I know it will make him happy. It's just that *I* want to make him happy, too. And I'm not sure how long I can do that from more than a thousand miles away. Still, I try to remind myself that a plane ride to New York City is short, and it doesn't have to be hard. If we both put in the effort, it won't be. It's fine. It'll all be fine.

I need to seal that mindset with a shot.

"SKYLER FUCKING THORNE!"

We don't even make it up the sidewalk and into the house before Clinton comes barreling out, throwing Skyler over his shoulder and spinning her around as she squeals and kicks. I laugh, and instantly I feel back at home. I can always count on Palm South University for drunken shenanigans and distractions from girly feelings.

"Alright," Clinton says, dropping Skyler's feet back to the sidewalk. "Let's get you three to the kegs. Time for the KKB girls to get this party started."

We throw our fists into the air with a shout and follow him through the house, the three of us lining up on the backside of the kegs, hands braced on the cool metal handles. Clinton grabs Skyler's ankles just as two of his brothers slide up behind me and Ashlei, and the next thing I know, our feet are in the air, taps are in our mouths, and every thought of Jarrett is erased.

At least for now.

***

"I love you two," I slur with a smile.

"Aww, we love you, too, babe," Ashlei says, but when she turns and finds me staring down at my two beautiful boobs, she snorts. "Oh, my God, you are not talking to your rack right now."

"What? I *do* love them. I mean, seriously, have you seen them?" I shimmy my top down a little more and push my chest toward her. "What's not to love?"

"They are always there for you."

"*Always*," I agree, hugging them again. "Through thick and thin. I can't even stay mad at them for the boob sweat terror of the summer."

Skyler giggles, handing us another Jell-O shot just as a loud chant begins to break out in the backyard.

We follow the noise, arms slung around each other and still giggling as we take our shots. When we reach the back, there's a large crowd gathered around the trampoline that surfaced at the Omega Chi house sometime over the summer. Everyone is staring up, and when we follow their gaze, we find a freshman perched on the roof.

Well, I assume he's a freshman, anyway, judging by the fact that he's in nothing but his tighty whities and is wearing a pirate hat.

"Do it, do it, do it!" the crowd chants. I glance at Skyler, whose face is twisted up in concern as she stares up at the naked pirate.

"This isn't a good idea," Ashlei says, her voice soft, but neither of us have time to respond before Clinton pushes through the crowd to join the three of us.

"What's going on?"

I nod up to the freshman. "I think he's going to jump from the roof down to the trampoline."

"What?" Clinton turns, and then his eyes widen as he screams out, "No!"

But it's too late.

The pirate jumps to the roar of at least a hundred people, all of them throwing their red plastic cups full of beer into the air with approval. He hits the trampoline, body flailing as he tries to gain control, but the bounce is too high. He flies forward as the cheers turn to gasps, and then he hits the concrete with a sickening crack.

"Oh, my God." Ashlei covers her mouth with her hands as Clinton curses and pushes through the screaming crowd, rushing to the side of the freshman and hollering for someone to call an ambulance.

Skyler pulls out her phone. "You guys gather up any KKBs you see and get out of here. There's too much underage drinking going on and Erin will flip her shit if any of our sisters get caught here."

"What about you?" I ask.

"I'm going to stay back with Bear. Don't worry," she says when Ashlei and I both start to protest. "I'll be out of here by the time the cops show. I just need to calm Bear down."

We both nod, jogging off in the opposite direction as she runs toward Clinton and the now lifeless pirate. We gather all the sisters we see, ditching drinks and shoving them toward the door until we're all stumbling back up Greek Row. When we get to the house, we all take our shoes off and tiptoe inside, retreating to our rooms or to the chapter room where sisters are camped out in sleeping bags for recruitment week.

"You going to be okay?" Ashlei whispers when we make it upstairs. "I'm going to wake Erin and tell her what happened. She needs to know before the morning and I can tell her we got all our sisters home safe."

"Yeah, I'm going to wait up for Skyler. I'll see you in the morning."

We hug, both of us sobered up from the chaos, and then I retreat to my room, chucking my heels into my closet and falling onto my bed with a sigh.

The silence is deafening, my ears ringing from the music blasting all night as my thoughts race to the sound. I hope the freshman is okay, I hope Skyler gets out of there, I hope the Omega Chi brothers don't get suspended. That last one is a futile hope, because after the shit they pulled during Spring Break last year, the ice they're skating on is thin enough to crack with a finger flick.

My phone lights up with a text from Skyler that she's safe in Clinton's room but that she can't leave yet. I sigh with relief, firing a text back and telling her I'll wait up, then I find Jarrett's number and request a video chat.

"Jess?" he croaks out, voice thick with sleep as his dark screen comes into focus. He flicks on a low lamp beside him and sits up in bed. Shirtless. "Everything okay?"

"Oh, shit, I'm sorry," I whisper. "It's late, I can call you in the morning."

He leans up more, a sleepy smirk on his beautiful face. I trace every feature — the stubble on his jaw, his lazy, sexy brown eyes. I've missed him, and seeing him sends an ache through my chest at the realization that this may be the *only* way I see him for a long time.

"I'm up, beautiful." His face falls a little. "Are you okay? Are... are *we* okay?"

I sigh, propping my head on one palm as I balance my phone in the other. "We're okay. I'm sorry I even made you think otherwise. I was being a selfish, whiney bitch and I'm sorry."

"Don't be sorry," he says, rubbing a hand over his smooth head. "It's a lot to think about. For both of us. I know I should have talked to you about it sooner, but it was a decision I needed to make on my own."

"I know," I assured him. "And you made the right choice. I support you, Jarrett. One-hundred percent."

Jarrett smiles, his eyes soft on mine until he trails them down to where my cleavage is in full view of the camera. "You went out tonight."

"I did."

"You look amazing," he says, shaking his head. "God, I miss you."

"Hold that thought." I pause our video chat long enough to text Skyler, asking for an ETA. When she says she'll be there for at least another hour, I smirk, pulling the video chat back up as I slide one strap of my dress down off my shoulder. I bite my lip, eyes on Jarrett's as I slide the other strap down and shimmy the fabric down to rest just below the hem of my bra. Jarrett swallows, running a hand down his chest and abs before it disappears out of camera view and he moans, flexing his hips.

"Show me just how much you miss me."

Jarrett moves his phone down, the new angle showing me his hard-on through his boxer briefs as he strokes it under the fabric with one hand. I groan, eyes on his tattoos as I flip until I'm on my back and slip one hand under the lacy fabric of my panties.

We tease each other with our words and touches, sending chills through the airwaves with our moans, all the while fucking ourselves and imagining we're fucking each other.

And maybe this is all I have for a while, but I'm okay with it. Because Jarrett is mine, and I'm his, and that's all that really matters.

Cassie

It's a little surreal, standing in the backyard and watching our new Kappa Kappa Beta sisters. Well, they're not quite sisters yet, but they've accepted their bids, and I still remember what that feels like. They've all changed into swim suits and cover ups, and now they're taking pictures, throwing up the KKB hand sign and starting friendships that will last long after we leave Palm South.

I can't believe it's already been a year since I was in their shoes, and thinking back on everything that's happened in the last year, I can't help but smile. It's been a wild ride, and I know there's still so much left to come.

"You sure you don't want to take a Little Sister this semester?" Skyler asks, sidling up next to me and offering me a sip from her Tervis tumbler. We're not supposed to drink at the KKB house, but the rules are always broken on Bid Day, and I take a long pull before handing it back to her.

"Yeah, I'm sure. My classes are going to be really tough this year and I just want to get my footing before I try to be a mentor for anyone else."

"That's fair," she says, smiling.

She looks tired, eyes outlined by dark circles. I didn't go to the Omega Chi party last night, but news about what happened made its way across campus by the time I woke up. Skyler was at the O Chi house all night, trying to make sure Clinton was okay, which I'm sure isn't the case.

"I think it's smart of you to focus on yourself for a while. Better than ending up like me."

"What does that mean?" I ask, nudging her. "You're the most bad-ass person I know."

She chuckles, running a hand roughly through her hair and twisting it over her shoulder. "A bad ass without a major. I have no idea what I'm doing, Little."

I frown, rubbing her arm gently. "You'll figure it out. You've got plenty of time."

She nods, smiling softly, but then a yawn overtakes her. "I can't believe I'm being this lame, but I'm going to sneak upstairs for a nap. If Erin asks, can you just tell her I'm not feeling well?"

"Don't worry about her, she's got plenty to keep her busy," I say, nodding to where Erin is coordinating a group photo of the new recruits. She wanted the best of the best, and she got them. I'm proud of her, and I know I'm not the only one.

Skyler yawns again, offering me a half wave before ducking inside.

And then someone bumps into me from behind, knocking me off balance.

"Whoa!" A deep voice says, and I know the voice, know it too well, which is probably why my entire body reacts at the feel of two strong hands steadying me. "Sorry about that."

I spin, his hands still on my waist as I peer up at him. "You're kidding, right?"

Adam grins, and my stomach twists into a tight sailor's knot. "Couldn't help myself. Had to reenact the first time we met."

"You're so stupid," I say with a laugh, pushing two hands into his chest to put distance between us.

He removes his hands from my hips, tucking them into the pockets of his navy blue and white swim trunks, instead. I trace the muscles of his arms, remembering what they looked like without a t-shirt covering them. How has he changed so much over just one summer? It's like he left Palm South University a boy and came back a man.

I have no idea how to act around him now, not after how last semester ended. We crossed over the feather-light line drawn between friendship and something more, and now I don't know what to do without its boundaries.

"How are your classes this semester? Full schedule?" he finally asks, pushing his sunglasses up onto his head.

"Yeah, I'm sure you'll find me in the library most of the year. I have more lab hours than a white rat."

He chuckles. "Well, before classes take over your life, can I ask you for a favor?"

"Uh-oh."

Adam takes a step toward me, pulling his hands from his pockets to place them together over his chest in a *please* gesture. "Just do this one thing for me and I'll owe you."

"Spit it out already," I tease.

"We're gearing up for the concert, since the one I hosted last year ended up being such a success. But now, it's year two, and whereas last year no one had any idea of what to expect, this year, they're going to want bigger and better. I'm working on the lineups and I've got the bar covered, but one of the biggest complaints last year was the guys-to-girls ratio. If you haven't noticed, a lot of the fraternities aren't exactly a fan of little Alpha Sigma excelling at something."

I sigh. "That's so stupid. We're all a part of the Greek community, why is it always some big competition?"

"I don't know," he answers. "But I need your help. I have a reservation in front of the Student Union three days this week to campaign for the concert. I can get the girls," he says with a cocky smirk. I roll my eyes as he continues. "But I could really use your help with the guys."

"You realize I'm like the literal last person in the world to depend on for good flirting, right?"

Adam throws his head back with a deep laugh before settling his eyes on mine again. "I beg to differ. You know you've got that sweet, innocent, naturally pretty thing down pat. And after that stunt you pulled last year? I know you can rock the hell out of a pair of leather leggings, too."

I blush, completely unable to swallow as one hand reaches up to twirl a piece of my red hair. "I don't know... Why don't you ask Skyler?"

"I don't want to ask Skyler," Adam answers easily. I wait for more, but he just stands there, watching me, waiting.

It feels dangerous, accepting his proposal, but I have no idea why. Everything with Adam somehow feels forbidden, even when it's as innocent as handing out fliers for a concert. Still, the way he's looking at me, I know this isn't about the concert. It's about our friendship — the one we used to have, the one we both thought we'd lost, the one we both can't live without.

"You owe me, Adam."

"Yes!" He fist pumps the air, pulling me in for a hug and spinning me around as I continue yelling at him.

"I mean it! You owe me *big* time. And I'm not wearing leather leggings. Or high heels. And I'm not missing class, either."

"Just be there as your schedule allows, Red." Adam sticks out his tongue, dodging my little fists as I attempt to punish him for using the nickname I hate the most.

"Don't push your luck!"

"Fine, fine," he says, grabbing my wrists gently to stop the punches. He looks down at me, our chests close together, laughs subsiding as he releases my wrists again. "Thank you."

"You're welcome."

He flicks his shades over his eyes after a moment, backing away slowly.

"Oh, and Cassie?" he asks, grin growing wider as he grabs the hem of his t-shirt with both hands.

I follow the motion, eyes stuck for a second before I rip them away. "Don't you dare."

"Welcome *back* to PSU!" He smirks, stripping his shirt over his head and tossing it back at me before sprinting toward the blow-up waterslide, just like he did the first time we met. He rushes down it to a roar of screams from my sisters and I bite back a laugh, watching him all the way to the end. When he shakes the water off his hair at the end and grins back at me, my stomach dips.

I've missed him.

I think I already knew it before, but I finally allow myself to admit it. Maybe it doesn't have to be him or Grayson, maybe we *can* still be friends. He doesn't seem fazed by what happened last semester, so why am I overthinking it?

So, I drop the thought, along with Adam's shirt, and then I peel my own sundress off and take off running. When my stomach hits the slide and I fly down to the end, water spraying and sisters cheering, I decide not to take anything too seriously this semester.

Time to make my second year at PSU even better than the first.

***

"I don't like it," Grayson says the next night after his show. It's a little past midnight and we both have our first classes in the morning, but neither of us could say goodbye after the show ended, so we popped in a movie at his place. A movie we watched all of two minutes before talking over it, instead.

I lean up on one elbow, looking down at Grayson sprawled out next to me in his sheets that smell like him — coffee and cinnamon. His brows are pinched together, forming a deep line between them that I smooth one thumb over before running it across his bottom lip and kissing him there.

"It's just handing out fliers," I assure him.

"Yeah, handing out fliers with a guy who has the hots for you."

"He does not have the hots for me," I say with a laugh, though I'm not sure if that's the absolute truth or not. I know he had feelings last semester, but the way he acted with me yesterday? It felt like old times. "We're friends, Grayson. We have been since my very first day in KKB. And he's asking me for a favor. He wouldn't do that if he didn't need me."

Grayson grumbles, but then rolls me until he's the one on top, sliding his knee between my legs to part them. "Fine," he says, kissing me with the word. "But enough about him. Let's talk about this sexy little dress you wore to my show tonight."

He trails one hand down the side of the sleek fabric where a diamond-shaped cut out lets him feel the skin of my waist. I giggle at the touch, wrapping my arms around his neck as he maneuvers himself until he's settled between my legs.

"You were amazing, by the way. That crowd was huge for a fancy schmancy restaurant."

"You know what else is huge," he says, smirking against my lips as he thrusts his jeans against me. The movement pushes my dress up my thighs, exposing my pink cotton thong.

I swallow hard, heart picking up speed with every kiss Grayson sweeps across my collarbone before sucking my lip between his teeth again. When he grinds into me, the friction catching, I moan into his lips without a single ounce of control.

He groans, rolling into me again and pulling my dress up higher until it rests above my hips. And though I want him so bad it physically hurts, that broken shard Clay shoved deep into my heart last year is still there, and it rubs a sharp pain against my ribs as my breathing grows shallow.

"Wait," I whisper, pressing my hands into his chest to give us a little space.

Grayson drops his forehead to mine, our breaths mixing in a sweet scent between us as he does exactly what I asked. I don't know what to say now, or what to do — only that I'm not ready for what he's ready for. The one and only guy I've ever had sex with betrayed me, and I still don't know how to let that go.

"It's okay," he whispers back after a moment, running his thumb along my jawline before cupping my chin up toward him. "We can take it slow. I just want to make you feel good."

The way he says the words, the way his eyes glow like a rare turquoise in the soft lighting of his bedroom, the way a single strand of his hair hangs down over his forehead — it's too much. Chills race from where his thumb grazes my skin all the way to my toes, and he notices, smirking at the reaction I can't help but have to him.

"I want to make you feel good, too."

"You do," he answers quickly. "Every time we're together I feel good, Cassie. And I can wait. Right now, tonight, I want to show you how much it meant to me that you came to my show tonight."

I smile, leaning up to press my lips to his. Grayson kisses me softly at first, but then one hand trails down my ribs, my hip, down to where my dress is bunched, and when one of his fingers grazes the hem of my panties, I gasp into his mouth.

He kisses me harder, tongue sweeping into my mouth as that same finger slips under the cotton fabric, running the slick line of me.

"Fuck," he groans, dipping the finger between my lips. "I love this, I love how wet I make you."

And with that, he pushes not one, but two fingers, all the way inside.

I arch my back, hands flying from where I was grasping his neck to grip the covers instead. Just his fingers alone stretch me, and thoughts of what it would feel like if it was actually him inside me spark another wave of chills.

Grayson works his fingers as he kisses down my neck, biting at the small swell of my breast before nestling between my legs. He pulls his fingers out long enough to strip my panties off and brace my thighs on his shoulders, and then he looks up at me with a wicked grin, and disappears beneath the fabric of my dress.

His hot breath is all I feel at first, and then the rough pad of his tongue as he runs it from my opening to my clit. He sucks when he reaches it, and I arch up off the bed, moaning loud, reaching for a pillow to mute the noise. I pull one over my mouth but Grayson reaches up and throws it across the room.

"I want to hear you when I make you come."

"Oh, God," is all I manage before his tongue is on me again, this time aided by the help of his fingers. He slides two of them deep inside me again, working them in a rhythm, his tongue drawing circles and teeth biting with just the right tender pressure to make me squirm beneath the touch.

I lean up on my elbows and look down at him, his auburn hair between my pale white thighs, his hungry eyes gazing back up at me as he brings me closer to ecstasy with his mouth. It's too much to watch him, so I fall back again, this time reaching down to pull his hair and guide him to the sweet spot.

The first and last guy to go down on me was Clay, and he was a drunken mess after the Halloween party at Ralph's. I'd faked an orgasm just to get it to end, but I know I won't have to fake it with Grayson. Not with his tongue moving like that, or his hands touching me like that, or his moans vibrating through me to my very core.

When my breathing is scarce, hands twisted in the sheets, Grayson pushes his fingers in even deeper and wiggles them quickly, hitting my G-spot in rapid fire as his tongue flicks my clit in sync. And that's the magic combination.

I feel myself pulse around his fingers as the moans leave my lips, his name riding them like waves as they crash into the four walls around us. I can't see, can't feel —everything is like a numb, icy, burning fire. He wanted to hear me, and I'm pretty sure his roommates are hearing me, too, but I don't care — I want him to know exactly what he's doing to me.

He slows his movements as my breaths even out, kissing my clit softly before climbing up my body to kiss my mouth, instead. I taste myself on him and moan, arching into him.

"Remind me to never miss a show of yours," I pant into his lips. "Ever."

He laughs, and then we kiss and talk until my eyelids are too heavy to hold. And when I fall asleep on his chest, his arms wrapped around me tight, I know I'm the luckiest girl at Palm South University.

Bear

I hate him.

I fucking *hate* him.

The literal last person I want to see, ever, is standing behind the podium at our first Omega Chi Beta chapter of the semester. Alec Carriker is a highly respected alumni of O Chi, but he's still a Class A douchebucket. He only shows up when there's a threat to be made or a wrist-slap to be given.

Unfortunately for us, I think it's past that this time.

"I want you all to know that I don't want to be here tonight," he starts once the room is quiet, his brows bent low as he surveys my brothers. "Least of all to deliver the news I have. But I have tried for a year now to warn you about what would happen if you didn't get your shit together, and not a single one of you listened to me."

Someone makes a snarky comment in the back of the room which garners a few stifled laughs, and Alec fumes, shaking his head before raising his voice.

"The Palm South University chapter of Omega Chi Beta has been suspended."

That shuts up the brothers in the back.

That shuts up everyone.

Even me.

Because though I was pissed the last time Alec told us we were on a probation period, I can't even be mad this time. We fucked up. *Bad.* And I knew this was coming before I even saw Alec stroll in.

"Riley Butler just turned eighteen a month ago. He has been away from home for all of one-hundred hours. And now? Now he's in the hospital with two broken ribs, a fractured wrist, and a severe concussion."

The heaviness of the reality settles over the room like a thick fog, weighing us down into our seats.

"And you can try to say it's not your fault, that you just threw a party, that you're not responsible for what a dumb freshman does after drinking his first beer, but the truth is, you are. You *are* responsible — for anything that happens at that house or to any of your brothers or anyone trying to *become* a brother."

At that, a few of us look around with questioning eyes.

"That's right. Riley was going to pledge in the spring, and a few of you knew that, because he told the police officers at the hospital that two guys told him this was a pre-pledge test."

"Jesus fucking Christ," I mumble, sinking down into my chair as I shake my head in disbelief.

I don't even register the rest of Alec's news. Everything is muted by the fact that the fraternity I love is on suspension. I hear Alec say that it will be a year minimum, and that's all it takes for me to tune out every other sentence that comes after. Because none of it matters, not anymore.

Chapter is called early, without a single ounce of good news, and I'm the first to bolt out of the room and down the hall to my bedroom. I throw on a pair of gym shorts and a PSU t-shirt quickly before tugging on my sneakers and blowing back out the front door.

I need a release. I need to zone out. I need to make every inch of my fucking body burn.

But when I round the Student Union and veer off toward the gym, I get that burn in the worst way possible.

Because Shawna is walking toward me.

"You've got to be fucking kidding me."

Shawna managed to crack through my exterior last semester, and I fell for her. Hard. But when her parents came for family weekend, she showed me her true colors — and they were the ugliest shades.

I see her before she sees me, which gives me just enough time to trace the edges of her new, shorter purple hair before I zero in on her glasses. The glasses that always drove me crazy in the best way. The glasses framing her big brown eyes as they stare back at me.

I stop, and she does, too — watching me as she waits for me to make the first move.

But I can't deal with her, not right now. Maybe not ever. So, I turn the volume on my iPod up higher and jog to the right, taking the longer way to the gym, not even giving her a second look before the decision was made.

***

I feel marginally better after a two-hour session at the gym, and my body is on fire just like I wanted. The last few steps into the O Chi house are brutal, and all I want is a shower and my bed.

When I walk inside and find a dozen brothers lugging in a keg, the fire coursing through my muscles boils my blood, instead.

"What the fuck is this?" I ask, pointing to the metal as two sophomores carry it past me and toward the back door. I shove one of them until he loses his balance and drops his half, forcing the other to do the same.

"Calm down, Bear," Patrick says from behind me. He's in my pledge class and we're both given credit for the best of the O Chi parties, but right now I just want to murder him. "It's just one keg and we told a few sorority chicks to come over tonight. Nothing big."

"Are you guys really that stupid? Are my *brothers* really *this fucking dumb?!"*

"Bear, it's fine. It's—"

"IT'S NOT FINE!" I snap, ripping my earphones out of my ears and heaving my iPod across the room. It hits the wall and shatters, making my brothers jump as I try but fail to calm down. "Don't you get it? We're suspended. There is only one punishment past this and it's losing our letters forever. Losing. Our. *Letters*, you fucking dickwads."

More of my brothers have filtered in from the back hallways and chapter room, and since I have their attention, I decide to say everything I need to.

"You can be mad at Alec and the other alums and nationals all you want, but the truth is we did this to ourselves. And now we need to suck it up and deal with the consequences for a year so we can get this chapter back to being the greatest one on campus like it once was."

"That's easy for you to say," I hear from the back. When a few brothers step aside, our new president, Richard, steps forward. "Some of us are seniors. Some of us don't get another year."

His words sober me. I was supposed to be a senior this year, too, but due to fucking up in classes when I was too busy partying, I'll be a fifth year senior. Still, I stand even straighter before firing back.

"Then I suggest you step up as the fucking president, *Dick*, and figure out a way to make the most of this fraternity and what time you have left here before you're gone. But don't drag an entire chapter with more than a hundred years of history down just because you can't snuff your ego and go party somewhere else. This isn't about you, or about me," I say, sweeping a hand over the entire room. "Or about any of us. It's about those letters." I point to the ΩXB letters that hang on our door. "And this chapter. And this university. It's about all the brothers who came before us, the ones who stand with us, and the ones who will only come after us if we can turn this sinking ship around and put life back into its sails.

"Now to some of you, none of that may mean a single damn thing. But to me?" I shake my head, letting my hands fall at my side. "It means everything. So, as long as I'm in this house, as long as I have anything to say about it, I'm not going to let any of you throw a brotherhood away out of pure stupidity."

The room is silent, most of my brothers staring at the laces on their shoes as I push past them toward my room.

"Get that fucking keg out of this house or I'll knock all of you out with it."

Flying down the hall, I slam my bedroom door closed behind me and rip my shirt up and over my head, kicking my shorts off next and taking the hottest, fastest shower I can manage. When I'm dressed again, I collapse into bed, staring up at the dark ceiling with a million thoughts racing through my head.

I don't try to digest any of them — not the ones of Erin, or Shawna, or Omega Chi or Riley, the kid I never got to meet who probably hates our fraternity now. I just let them all fly at me, taking turns for my attention, none of them getting it for long before another shoves it out of the way.

I'm not sure how long I lie there before there's a hard knock at my door and it creaks open, a stream of light leaking in.

"What."

"Hey, it's Richard."

I sigh, letting my head drop to the right so I can see him as I repeat myself. "What."

"I'm sorry," he says, voice low. "We all are. You're right. We were being stupid, and we care about these letters just as much as you do. The keg is gone, and we're going to come up with some kick-ass philanthropy ideas for this semester and next to make the most of our situation. And we'll party at the other houses or at Ralph's or off campus, and even then, we'll behave." He pauses. "Thanks for helping us see straight."

I nod, looking back up at the ceiling. "Let me know how I can help with the philanthropy."

"We will. Oh, and," he says with a chuckle. "Lacy is here. Should I send her back?"

"Not tonight."

He chuckles again. "Alright. Night, Bear." And then the small stream of light is gone.

I roll over toward the wall, shifting until I'm under the sheets. I'm just about to doze off when my door opens again and a shadow slips through, closing it behind them.

"Lacy, I'm really not in the mood. Not even for a blow job as good as yours."

"How about a best friend cuddle buddy, instead?"

Skyler hops over me, sliding between me and the wall and wiggles her way under the covers. She watches me for a moment, only the light from the streetlights outside my window helping me see her face at all. After a moment I sigh, holding my arms out for her to come closer.

She nuzzles into my side and I wrap her in my famous Bear Hug, setting my chin on the top of her head as she hugs me back.

"You okay?" she asks.

"Not even a little bit."

She hugs me tighter. "You will be."

I sigh, feeling the smallest bit of relief wash over me. Because Skyler Thorne is the only one I actually believe when she says that.

It's not going to be easy, and I have no idea where to even start, but I'm going to help my brothers turn this chapter around. Palm South University only knows us as the party boys, but they're about to see us in a brand new light.

And with that final thought, I tug Skyler closer, and finally fall asleep.

EPISODE 2

Ashlei

This semester is going to be different.

That's all I can repeat in my head as I heave the large glass door open to enter one of the tallest buildings downtown, the building where my new internship is, the building where my new life begins.

My dainty, nude heels clack against the marble floor as I pass by the reception desk, smiling at the young man sitting behind it. His name is Christopher and he was the one who gave me my parking garage pass when I'd accepted the internship. He eyes my first-day outfit, throwing me a subtle thumbs-up with a wink as I strut past him with a wide smile toward the elevators.

On the outside, I look completely put together — pairing my favorite strappy Steve Maddens with the brand-new, navy blue Imporio Armani trench coat dress I begged Mom and Dad to buy me for this internship specifically. The sleeves of it are cuffed up to right under my elbow, and I love the way I feel with one hand in the pocket of it as my heels click across the floor.

I cinched the waist of it this morning with a thick, gold-plated belt, the deep V neckline of the dress dipping down to end only a few inches above it. My jewelry is simple, long blonde hair softly curled, and makeup natural. I don't look nervous, not even a little bit. I look like I belong here, striding right beside the other young professionals, coffee in hand, ready to take on the world.

But inside, I'm completely freaking out.

I toss my half-empty iced coffee into a trashcan on my way to the elevators, casually hooking my damp palm around the base of my small purse as I unclasp it and dig for a mint. I'm not sure why I'm so nervous. I *never* got nervous when I pole danced, not even at regionals, so why does the first day of an internship have my knees unsteady?

Maybe it's because I feel like I have something to prove this semester. There is no Hayden, no drugs, no Xavier, and — though this one actually hurts more than I admit — no Bo. It'd taken me most of the summer to realize that Bo leaving PSU wasn't the end of the world, though it felt like it. In fact, in a way, I'm kind of grateful. Because for the first time in my college career, I have no distractions. I'm single, I don't owe anyone a single thing, and I've landed an internship at one of the most reputable event agencies in South Florida.

The nervous energy flowing through me is almost palpable as I step into one of the six elevators, so I let out a long exhale as the doors start to close.

But then a dark hand reaches in to stop them.

The doors slowly slide back open, and when they reveal the man attached to the hand, I'm glad I got in one last calming breath because there's absolutely no way I'm breathing now.

There's only one word to accurately describe him: Pristine.

Everything about him is sharp — the edge of his short fade, the line of his nose, the angle of his cleanly shaven jaw. My eyes skate over every inch of him, focus shifting from his broad shoulders to the button of his charcoal suit jacket as he uses one hand to fasten it before stepping inside the elevator with me. He reminds me of Clinton, the same smooth skin and full lips, but Mr. Pristine is a little taller and leaner. I chance another glance at him as the doors begin to close, and he tugs his shades off, tucking them into the front pocket of his jacket before acknowledging me with a smirk and dark, intense eyes.

I swallow, eyes shifting to focus on the white light illuminating floor thirty-two as we start to ascend. I'm absolutely not looking at his reflection in the doors of the elevator. Totally not noticing that his eyes are still on me, roaming my skin the way mine just did his. And when his tongue sweeps his bottom lip subtly, almost so imperceptibly I'm not even sure I really saw it, my thighs *definitely* don't clench together under my dress.

I'm one-hundred percent cool.

Until he speaks, that is.

"So, you're on an elevator with a complete stranger for approximately twenty-five seconds," he says, the deep baritone of his voice filling the small space between us. I'm still staring at the way his suit tapers at his waist in the elevator door reflection. "Do you A, ride up in awkward silence, or B, tell this stranger why your hands are shaking."

My eyes snap to his, and he smiles a little wider, knowing he got my attention. I watch him for a moment, his demeanor so cool and calm, and then I clear my throat, facing forward again. I have no idea what to say to that. And if I ignore him much longer, he'll assume I picked option A. Which is probably the option I *should* choose, but after a few long seconds, I figure *what the hell?* Might as well get it out to someone, and why not a stranger?

And so, my nervous energy flows out like word vomit.

"Today is the first day of my internship for what I consider to be the best corporate event agency in Florida and I'm just... I'm nervous, which is weird for me because I'm *never* nervous, like when I used to pole dance I never once got nervous before I went on stage." I pause, eyes widening at what I'd said just as one of Mr. Pristine's eyebrows shoots up to his hairline. "It was competitive pole dancing," I clarify. "Like fitness."

He's still smirking.

Floor seventeen.

"Anyway, I've just had a shit year and this semester I'm determined to turn things around. I want to walk into this internship and impress every single person I talk to — boss, colleague, client, and everyone in-between. So, I guess I'm okay with the fact that my hands are trembling now, so long as they're steady as stone when I start shaking *other* peoples' hands."

He nods, tongue pressing against the inside of his cheek as he eyes me with what feels like respect as the elevator comes to a halt with a soft ding. The doors swing open, and I offer him one last shrug and a smile.

"Wow, that actually helped. Thanks for being the smokin' hot stranger in the elevator," I say, stepping off as he holds the doors open.

His eyes spark with even more intensity when I pass him, my arm grazing his jacket. "My pleasure. Thanks for choosing option B."

I chuckle, giving him an awkward, small wave goodbye.

But then he steps off the elevator, too.

"Oh, and welcome to the best agency in South Florida," he says, still smirking as he uses his badge to enter through the sleek metal doors under the *Okay, Cool Event Agency* sign. I catch the door before it can close, mouth gaping wide, eyes glued to his back as he walks down the row of cubes.

"Hi!" a chipper voice says, snapping me back to reality. The voice belongs to a short, curvy girl around my age with dark blonde hair and freckles lining her cheeks. "You must be one of the interns. I'm Mykayla, the receptionist for *Okay, Cool.* I see you already met our CEO, so we can skip his office on the tour."

"CEO?" I ask, voice a little squeaky as my eyes jet to Mr. Pristine's back again. He turns his head just as his hand finds the handle to an office all the way at the other end, and damn it if he doesn't smirk again as he pushes the door open and disappears inside.

"Yeah, that's Brandon Church — Mr. Church to us," she adds with a wink. "Come on, let's grab some coffee and I'll take you around and introduce you to everyone. Your manager won't be in for another hour or so."

"Fantastic," I murmur. Then I follow her to the break room, all the while wondering why the universe hates me.

Adam

I flop down on my bed with a sigh, closing my eyes and reveling in the silence.

Being president of Alpha Sigma is amazing, but damn is it busy. We've only been back at PSU for a little over a week and we're already in full swing, working on preparing for our second annual concert, signing up for philanthropy event after philanthropy event, and now with the suspension of Omega Chi, planning a full calendar of socials and parties. I told the guys when they elected me that we were going to make a name for Alpha Sigma this year, and already I can feel that promise coming to life.

It's rewarding, but it's also exhausting, so I cherish the feel of my cool comforter against my back and close my eyes, letting out a long breath.

As much as I enjoy the quiet, it doesn't take long for the flurry of thoughts in my head to dissipate, leaving only one left. The one I can never escape, not even in my sleep.

Cassie.

It was a long summer without her, with only the last conversation between us to keep me company while I wondered what she was doing. I didn't know what to expect this semester, and after she basically sprinted out of here the first time we saw each other, I figured there was no way in hell we'd have a chance at friendship again.

But she'd showed up when I asked her to, helping me spread the word about the concert by handing out fliers in front of the Student Union. It's been fun hanging out with her, and every day we spend together I feel more and more of the awkwardness disappear.

Still, it doesn't change the fact that she's still Grayson's, and I have no idea how to handle that.

I inhale another deep breath, wondering if I have enough time to catch a nap, but of course, the silence doesn't last long enough for me to find out.

Two loud knocks hit my door before it swings open and Jeremy flies in. "We have a problem."

"Shhh," I tell him as he kicks the door closed behind him and flops down in my desk chair, ripping his laptop from his backpack in the process.

"Wha—"

"Sixty seconds," I say, cutting him off. "Just... let me have sixty seconds of silence and then you can tell me about the problem."

Jeremy huffs, sitting back in my chair and crossing his arms over his chest. I give him a slight nod and close my eyes again, but he's too fidgety for me to enjoy the rest. He can't stop huffing, and his knee is bouncing, foot tapping against the hardwood floor. I get it, he's under a lot of stress, too, being my right-hand man and second-in-command. It's pretty awesome running the fraternity with one of my best friends, but at the same time, I'm learning a lot about our leadership styles.

For instance, Jeremy has about as much grip on handling stress as bald tires have on a rainy road.

I laugh, sitting up and moving to the edge of my bed to face him well before the full minute has passed. "Okay, Jeremy. What's the problem?"

He blows out a breath and grabs his laptop, flipping the top open. "Futile Destiny pulled out of the show."

"What?! They're our headliner!"

"*Were,*" Jeremy says, shaking his head and typing away on his laptop. "They were our headliner. And now we don't have one."

I sigh, scrubbing a hand over my face. "The concert is in three days. What the hell are we going to do."

Jeremy watches me for a minute, and he doesn't even have to open his mouth for me to know what's coming next.

"Ugh, don't even say it."

"I don't think we have a choice now, Adam." Jeremy sets his laptop aside and leans forward, elbows resting on his knees. "Look, I know he's not your favorite person, but... if we don't book another headliner, we're going to have to cancel the concert. Tickets won't sell without one, and those who already bought them will want a refund if we don't find a replacement."

I want to argue with him, convince him we have other options, but I know I can't — not without putting the concert in jeopardy and failing at my first big challenge as president.

"I know," I admit dejectedly.

"Do you want me to ask him?"

"No," I answer, standing and swiping my wallet off my desk. *So much for a break.* "I'll go. Cassie said he's playing at the coffee shop today. Maybe if she's there, she can help me convince him."

"Probably not a bad idea to have her giving him a nudge, all things considered."

I grunt in answer, clapping him on the shoulder as I pass. "Don't worry, I'll handle it."

***

Cup O' Joe's is packed when I walk in, and I squeeze between groups of people — mostly girls — standing around with their eyes on the stage. Grayson is belting out *Butterfly* by Jason Mraz and I can practically see the panties dropping to the floor with every note he sings.

I roll my eyes, the taste of disdain for having to be here at all growing more sour than a rotten lemon in my mouth. One thing I've learned about being president is that you have to make sacrifices, and you have to do shit you don't want to. Still, even though I know I'm out of choices and this is my only chance to save the concert, I don't want to be here. I don't want to ask Grayson for anything, least of all to headline my show, but here I am.

Swallowing down the last bit of pride I have, I keep pushing through the crowd until I spot Cassie.

Her unruly red hair is braided to the side, the ends of it frayed out in all directions. She aimlessly plays with the ends of it with one hand while the other holds her coffee cup on the table, thumb tapping along to the beat of Grayson's guitar. She's seated at a table in the back right corner, eyes on the stage, though they seem distant, as if she's somewhere else entirely.

My stomach drops at the sight of her, just like it always has. Every step takes me closer to her and further from any semblance of calm I had managed to have when I walked in the door.

"You're pretty good at that," I say when I reach her, shaking her from her thoughts as I nod toward her tapping thumb. "Ever ask Grayson if he needs a drummer?"

Cassie's eyes brighten, as if seeing me is a relief, and my pulse kicks up a notch as I take the empty seat next to her.

"Yeah, right. A girl on stage with him would ruin all of this," she says, sweeping a hand over the crowd.

I nod, brows pinching together as I look around. Girls are huddled together in packs of three or more in every space of the shop, eyes locked on Grayson, camera phones at the ready as they giggle and will him to look at them with their longing gazes.

"Yeah, this is a little intense. Is it hard for you at all?"

She shrugs. "Nah, it's all just for show. I know he's still mine at the end of the night."

The words leave her lips easily enough, slicing my skin with the precision of them, but something in her eyes tells me she doesn't believe them as much as I do.

I clear my throat. "Hey, thanks for all your help with the concert. I really appreciate it. I know you have plenty of other things you'd rather be doing than hanging out with me and sweating your ass off handing out fliers."

Cassie smiles, wrinkling her nose at me. "Ah, it wasn't that bad. Mild torture, at most."

Our eyes connect and I hold her stare, silently thanking her again, wondering if she sees the other words laying just beneath the surface. Words I've never said, words she's never heard. Silence always seems to be the way Cassie and I say what we need to say most.

The song ends to a roar from the coffee shop crowd, and Cassie's attention snaps back to the stage as she claps along with them. When I turn, Grayson is staring directly at us, eyes narrowed as he hangs his guitar on the stand. He forces a smile and waves at the crowd, which makes them go even crazier, and then he jumps down into the masses, making a beeline for our table.

Hands reach for him as he passes, and he politely dismisses each one, focus undeterred until he's swooping Cassie up from her chair and into his arms.

He kisses her hard, which earns him a few groans from the girls standing nearby and a hard eye roll from me. I stand to join them and wait for his power play of possession to end.

Cassie is flushed bright red when he finally pulls back, tucking her under his arm before finally turning to me with a wry grin. "Oh, hey, Adam. Surprised to see you here. Let me guess, more *fliers* to hand out?"

It's clear he's not happy about the fact that I asked Cassie for help with the show, which kills my optimism that he'll be willing to help me out himself. Still, I'm not leaving the shop until I do everything I can to save the concert.

"Came to see you, actually."

His brows shoot up right along with Cassie's.

"You came to see me play," he deadpans. "Really."

I crack my neck, standing a little straighter and biting back the smart ass comments I want to send flying back at him. "Really. We've had a lot of requests for you for the concert, and after hearing you myself, I can see why," I lie, forcing what I'm sure is the fakest smile I've ever had on my face. "How do you feel about headlining the show?"

Cassie's eyes light up. "Oh, my God, that's amazing!" She turns to look up at Grayson, but his eyes are still narrowed, jaw set. "Did you hear that?"

"I thought Futile Destiny was your headliner," he says, ignoring Cassie's enthusiasm.

"They were," I confirm. "Past tense."

"They're okay with stepping down to opener so I can headline?"

I clear my throat again, shoving my hands into my pockets. "They had some other opportunities, so they were cool with it."

At that, Grayson barks out a laugh, his arm still dangling over Cassie's shoulder. "So, what you mean to say is they pulled out and now you're fucked."

I grit my teeth, ready to say *fuck it* and find someone else when Cassie steps out from under his arm and turns to face him.

"Grayson, this is a great opportunity. They've already sold three thousand tickets. That's twice what they sold last year, and that's more people you can potentially turn into fans."

Grayson is still smirking, eyes narrowed at me like he has me all figured out. And right now, as much as I hate it, he holds the power.

Cassie tugs his sleeve and he looks down at her with a sigh. "You want me to do it?"

She nods. "I do. I always feel like my Greek life stuff is so separate from you, but this is a great way for you to be a part of it. And you'd be the headliner!"

He eyes me again before smiling down at her and pulling her in for a kiss. "Okay, I'll do it for you, then."

She lights up, this time pulling *him* down for a kiss, and I nearly double over from the pain of watching it. I've seen them dance together, seen them kiss, but this is the first time I've seen what I've been trying to ignore all along.

She's falling for him, and there's nothing I can do about it.

"Cool," I finally say, clearing my throat. "I'll have Jeremy call you tonight with details."

"Wait," Grayson says as I turn to leave. "I want five bucks a head minimum. And I want a booth set up for merchandise sales."

"It's for charity," Cassie says to him softly, her hand squeezing where it holds his hip.

"Oh, well... fine. No charge per head. But I need a merch table. My agent won't agree to it without one."

I scoff, trying my best to hide it. One viral video and the guy's douche level skyrockets to ten. "Whatever you need. Just let Jeremy know and he'll make it happen. Thanks for agreeing, Grayson. Glad to have you."

I offer him a hand, determined not to let him see how much it pains me to work with him. And the truth is, I really am thankful he agreed to help. The show would have tanked without him, so if I have to bite down my pride and play nice for the next week, I'll do it.

Besides, he clearly makes Cassie happy, and as much as that kills me, it's all I want. Her happiness. Even if I can't be the one responsible for it.

Grayson shakes my hand firmly. "Happy to help."

He wraps Cassie up for one last, ridiculously long kiss before making his way back to the stage. And then I'm alone with her again, alone as we can be in a crowded coffee shop, and suddenly it's too hard to breathe.

"Thanks for the help with that," I say. "See you around."

"Hey, wait!"

I pause, forcing a swallow and facing her again. One deep red strand has fallen loose from her braid, hanging diagonally across her forehead, begging for me to sweep it aside. I shove my hands back in my pockets to avoid it.

"Do you... can I help at all? Want me to print up more fliers or take tickets at the door?"

And though we could use the help with taking tickets, I know without a doubt I can't take it from her. Not after seeing her with Grayson, not after knowing how deep she's in it with him. I thought I could handle it, wait on the sidelines, but it turns out I have absolutely zero chill when it comes to Cassie.

"We're good, but thanks. Enjoy your coffee."

I bolt for the door before she can respond, weaving through the crowd until I'm finally able to breathe in the hot summer air outside. The first breath I take is sticky and painful, and I wipe the sweat from my brow, storming back to the house with a new determination.

Cassie isn't mine.

That fact hasn't been more clear than it is right now, and though it's like filleting my heart slice by painful slice, I know I have to let her go. I have to let the idea of *us* go.

So, with every step, I do just that – dropping every memory, every fantasy, every shred of hope I have. I take the long way back to the house. I replay her kissing him until I'm almost too nauseous to keep walking. And even after all of it, when I reach the house and jet straight back to my bedroom, flopping down into the cool sheets, I know I've failed.

I still can't shake the very last piece.

And I know I never will.

You know that shin, pink skin that makes up a scar? The kind that is a little bit thinner, yet somehow a little more resilient? The kind that marks you forever with a warning sign, with a memory, with a reminder? Well, I am covered in that skin, from head to toe, and I've never felt more beautiful.

The summer made me stronger.

I left Palm South University last semester broken. Shattered. Completely and utterly destroyed. I didn't know if I'd come back – hell, I didn't know if I'd *survive*. But here I am, stronger than ever, and it's all thanks to my mom.

She helped me take the pain and the fear and transform them into drive and determination. It took months of tough love and reality checks that hurt almost worse than what had happened with Landon, but I was finally standing on my own.

And this semester, I was standing even taller.

I realize this is the best part about my new scarred skin as I apply the last bit of my foundation, working it into my skin with a makeup sponge and a soft smile on my face. The best part about my scars is that no one else can see them but me.

And *that* is power.

"I just don't understand why she won't take a Little," I say to Skyler again as I dig through my makeup bag for my eyebrow pencil. "I mean, I get that she's got a tough schedule this semester, but so does everyone else. This is prime time to add to the family. And if she ends up taking a Little next year, that's one less year they'll have together and she'll be so young when she takes president like the rest of our family. It'll make everything more difficult for her. It just doesn't make sense. You *always* take a Little after your first year. You just do."

"Ex," Skyler sighs my nickname, sitting up on the edge of my bed. "Please, can we just let it go? Cassie wants to wait and we need to support her. It's fine, our line will be fine, the presidency legacy will be fine, it'll all be *fine*. Just chill."

I would roll my eyes if I wasn't currently lining them. "Fine. I'll let it go. But I think it's a mistake, especially since this is the best pledge class we've ever had."

"All thanks to you," Skyler reminds me with a wink.

It's a transparent attempt to change the subject and drive me back to Happy Town, but I let it happen. Mostly because the first goal I wanted to accomplish with my newfound determination was to land us the most amazing girls KKB had ever seen, and I'd succeeded.

"I still can't believe it," I say, grabbing my mascara next. Skyler is still in her pajamas, but I have the first Panhellenic all-chapter meeting in thirty minutes, and I plan to make a statement when I walk in. "Highest average GPA, highest percentage of athletes, highest percentage of on-campus involvement. We're going to be unstoppable this semester."

"You killed it. I've never seen a recruitment run so smoothly, Big." Skyler beams as I brush the last of my lashes. "You definitely don't have to worry about getting president now. It's a definite."

I smile. "You think?"

"I *know.*"

Suddenly my bedroom door flies open and Jess tumbles into the room, jumping onto Ashlei's bed across from where Skyler is sitting.

"HE'S COMING!"

She bounces on the bed, the floppy mess of hair piled in a bun on her head jumping right along with her as she claps her hands.

"Jesus?" Skyler asks.

"Close. Jarrett!"

This time we all squeal with her, and she falls back on the bed, legs kicking in the air.

"He's coming to visit and he'll be here a whole week! Andddd, I'm going to introduce him to everyone! No more secrets. I want every single person to know I'm his and he's mine."

"You could always get t-shirts made," I offer.

Jess tosses a pillow in my direction, but it thumps against my closet door and slides down pathetically. "Whatever, Ex. Not even the best of sarcasm can get me down today. My *boyfriend* is coming to town!"

Skyler and I both laugh and then I turn to rummage through my closet while Jess goes on and on about what they'll do while he's here. I know it's a big step for them, since most of their relationship has been kept a secret due to his job on campus. Now that he's working up north, there's nothing to hide, and I'm happy for Jess.

A small part of me wonders if I'll ever know that happiness. The thought of letting another guy in, letting him close, seems so impossible it's like imagining winning the lottery. Fun to think about, but depressing all the same.

My phone buzzes on my desk just as I pull on my favorite Lilly Pulitzer dress and I check my reflection before swiping it off the desk. Clinton's name is framed by a small box, and I swallow, heart kicking against my chest as I slide my thumb across the screen.

- Hey, you, what are you doing for your birthday next week? Big 2-1 deserves a bad-ass party. -

I stare at his text, a mixture of emotions swirling inside me. Clinton was the one who saved me the night of formal, the one who held me together when the last thread snapped. I'm forever thankful for him holding me, for him taking care of me, and most of all, for him not telling anyone else what happened. I knew when I asked him for that, it would be hard for him to do, but he did it because he cared about me.

Still, I don't need any man — not even him — and what's more, I know the minute we're alone, he'll want me to talk. He'll want me to tell him I'm okay, to tell him what I've done to work through what happened.

But I can't reopen that wound.

I won't.

So I ignore the text, dropping my phone into my purse and slinging it over my shoulder before turning back to the girls. "Okay, first Panhellenic meeting. Wish me luck!"

"Good luck!" they both say in unison, and I slip back into business mode without a second thought.

Ashlei

I am exhausted.

It's only Tuesday but I feel like I've worked an entire week. Between classes, the sorority, and my internship, I have exactly twenty minutes of downtime each day, and I usually use it peeing.

And it's only been a week since my internship started.

I guess most people would be complaining, wishing they had more time to sleep or party, but honestly? I'm thriving. It reminds me of when I had pole dancing taking up my time, giving me purpose — a goal to work toward. I'm working alongside three other interns this semester, and I'm determined to be the best. Blame it on always being in competition with my sisters growing up or maybe just on the fact that I have something to prove this semester, but I'm all in.

Which is part of the reason I'm the last to leave the office.

We had a meeting first thing this morning to discuss the event all the interns would be working on, a product launch for a local, high-end skincare line. The only information we'd really been given was the date of the event and a packet with information on the new line they're launching, so I spent the rest of the day researching the company, founders, mission statement, and current marketing struggles. It might have been a little excessive since we'd only be involved in the launch event, but in my opinion, they booked *Okay, Cool* because they want the best, and I'm determined to give it to them.

To meet their needs, I need to understand them.

And then, I can find a way to exceed them.

Balancing my binder now stuffed full with the research I've done all day, I dig through my purse for my phone to call Cassie. We're supposed to meet at Ralph's to talk about Erin's surprise party at seven and I'm already ten minutes late. But when I finally fish it out, I lose the grip on my binder, and it tumbles to the floor, hitting the toe of my high heel in the process before spewing paper all around me.

"Oh, for fuck's sake," I yell, eyes rolling up to the ceiling before I let out an exasperated sigh and kneel down to start retrieving the pages. I hadn't taken the time to hole punch them and actually put them *inside* the three-pronged binder, and now I'm paying the price for it.

My phone lights up with a text from Cassie and I angrily thumb out a response before tossing my phone back in my purse, gathering the paper and trying to keep at least some of the organization I'd worked all day on. I'm so grumbly I don't even register the cherry-brown Ermenegildo Zegna shoes until I'm trying to swipe up a page trapped underneath them.

I pause, fingers still on the paper as my eyes trail up the beige suit pants, skipping the open jacket altogether to land on Mr. Church's face. His hands are resting easily in his pockets, Carolina blue dress shirt exposed and navy tie loosened around his neck as he smirks down at me.

Me.

The intern.

Who is currently on her hands and knees in a pencil skirt.

"I didn't realize we were keeping the interns so late," he booms, bending to my level as he helps gather the last of the pages.

I just gape at him for a moment before clearing my throat and shoving the papers in my binder, not taking the time to keep them in order anymore. My fingers brush his when he hands me the stack he's gathered and I keep my eyes on the binder, cheeks flush with heat.

"*Bare•ly?"* he asks, nodding to my binder as he stands. "Didn't you just get assigned to their event this morning?"

I nod, attempting to stand without flashing him my underwear or breaking my neck. He reaches down for me, one hand grabbing the binder from my grasp as the other stabilizes my elbow.

"Yeah, I just wanted to get a head start on the event. I don't know much about them yet."

"Looks like you will soon," he says, handing the binder back to me when I'm fully standing. "You know, most interns just wait to be told what to do when we assign them their event clients." He checks his watch before lifting a brow back at me. "And most of them leave well before five."

"Guess I'm not like most interns," I offer with a shy smile and a shrug.

"I'm starting to realize that."

He takes a moment to really look at me then, and the heat I feel from his gaze is unlike anything I've ever experienced. It's not a look just reserved for me, either. I've seen him give it to plenty of other people just in my first week. It's not him coming onto me or checking me out, it's just how he is naturally — intense, ablaze, striking.

"Mr. Church, I'm really sorry about that first day in the elevator. I... well, clearly I was nervous, and I didn't know who you were, and—"

"That was the best part," he says, hand finding the small of my back as he leads us to the elevators. "You didn't know who I was, so I got to see you unfiltered. It's rare for me to see anyone that way. I liked it."

"You liked watching me make a fool of myself?"

He chuckles as the doors slide open and we both step inside.

"You didn't make a fool of yourself. You made an impression. There's a difference."

I nod, biting my lips between my teeth for the rest of the ride down. When the doors open again, we both walk in silence until we're out of the lobby and standing in the warm evening air.

"Thanks for your help," I say, sheepishly holding my binder up. "I'll see you in the morning."

"Have a good night, Miss Daniels."

And where I need to turn left for the garage, he turns right, unlocking a pearl white Acura NSX parked in the reserved section with a soft beep before sliding inside. I can't even move another inch toward the garage until I hear him rev it to life, the engine roaring and purring under his touch. It idles for a minute, my eyes on the blacked-out windows, wondering if the ones inside it are focused on me, too.

When I finally turn, the engine hums again as he throws it in reverse, and it takes every ounce of self-control I have to not watch him drive away.

***

"Okay, now that Erin's party details are hammered out, I have a favor to ask you," Cassie says, ordering us another round of margaritas. Ralph's ended up being packed so we moved to the Mexican restaurant just off campus, and after two margaritas I was thankful for the switch. Nothing makes a long day better quite like tequila.

"Ah, so that's why you've been buttering me up with chips and queso."

"*And* Patrón," she adds with a wave of her finger.

"Fine, I'm as buttered as toast. What's the favor?"

"Okay, so ever since Grayson agreed to headline the Alpha Sigma concert, I've been trying to think of ways to make it even better than last year. Not that Adam doesn't already have that covered, but I just..." She pauses, tucking her wild hair behind her ear. "I know it was hard for him to ask Grayson to help, since they don't exactly get along, and I want to try to take some of the stress off him."

"That's really sweet, Cass. Why don't they get along, anyway?"

She shrugs, but something in her eyes gives me the impression there's something she's not saying. "Who knows. Boys are dumb."

"Indeed. So what's the favor?"

"Okay, so I pitched this idea to him and he's in, but he doesn't have time to do anything else. I told him I'd handle it, but... well, I need your help."

"Just spit it out already."

"I need you to auction a date." She throws her hands up when I start to object. "Just hear me out. It's almost exactly like the KKB auction we have every spring except instead of auctioning just the girl, we auction the whole package. So, basically they bet on the 'date' but the catch is that the girl auctioning it off has to go on the date with them. So, it takes the pressure off them for deciding what to do and it's a little bonus, like paying for the activity itself instead of just the girl."

"It sounds great, but I seriously can't, Cassie. I barely have time to breathe, as it is, this semester."

"*Please,*" she begs, sliding my new margarita to me when the waitress drops it off. "All I'm asking for is two nights — this Friday for the concert, and then whatever night the guy picks for the date. I already have the date items to auction so you don't even have to worry about that."

"What is the date?"

"It's a four-car experience at *Palm South Exotic Auto Racing*. You'll basically just have to sit shot gun while the guy gets wet over driving fast sports cars."

I blow out a sigh, taking another, longer drink from my glass. "Fine. I stayed late tonight so I should be able to head out on time Friday as long as my manager is okay with it."

Cassie squeals. "Thank you, thank you, *thank you*. I owe you."

"Yeah, you do, and as you can see, I happily take queso as payment," I say, popping another chip in my mouth with a grin. "How are you and Grayson, anyway? I know you're excited about the show, but it can't be easy having all those girls drooling over him all the time."

Cassie's face falls. "It's not really the girls who bother me. I just don't see him much anymore, and anytime we are together, it's always me watching him from the crowd at the coffee shop or a local show. We haven't had a single date all semester."

I frown. "That's kind of shitty."

"Yeah," she agrees, but shakes it off. "But I get it, and I'm sure we'll spend more time together once the semester settles down a little."

"Have you guys had sex yet?"

Cassie blushes, and I can't help but laugh. She gets so nervous talking about anything sexual.

"Not yet..."

"But?" I probe, sensing more to her statement.

"Well, he did go down on me."

I clink my oversized glass to hers. "Atta girl! How was it?"

She flushes even harder. "Magical. His tongue is just... wow."

"Ugh," I groan. "I haven't had attention down there in way too long."

"Not since Bo?" Cassie asks, and we both fall silent at the mention of her name.

I stir the ice in my margarita, the same part of my heart aching at the loss of her. "Not since Bo."

"Any new girls or guys catching your eye this semester?"

For some reason, Mr. Church's smoldering smirk flashes into my mind at her question, but I shake it off. "Nope. Just focusing on my internship and getting myself stable for once."

"I like that," Cassie says with a smile, lifting her glass this time. "To getting our shit together."

I laugh, tilting my glass toward her.

"I'll drink to that."

Adam

Where the crowd is, everything is perfect.

We more than doubled our ticket sales once Grayson was announced as the headliner, which called for a last-minute relocation to the park near the Student Union. The stage is set up right in front of the large fountain, lights bright enough and speakers loud enough to make it feel like a summertime festival. And in front of the stage are more than seven-thousand students, alumni, and local residents with their hands in the air, screaming as Titanium Rush starts their set.

But backstage, everything is a mess.

"Where the fuck is Grayson?!" I scream into my headset, flipping through the documents on my tablet until I find the one that confirms we asked him to be here before the openers went on. His contact information isn't listed, only a number for his "agent."

Tool.

"No one's seen him," Jeremy's voice crackles through the headphone piece as two brothers zip past me with the banner backdrop for Grayson. "We tried calling the number for his agent but it's going straight to voicemail."

"How many songs does Titanium Rush have in their set list?"

"Six."

I curse, jogging down the stairs backstage and veering toward the auction booth. "I'll work on getting ahold of him, you guys come up with a plan to stall. We still have a few auctions to go up for bidding but after that we're screwed."

"We're on it."

My feet are quick as I make my way to where Cassie is working the auction table, taking the money from the bidders and explaining how to claim the prizes. It was her idea, and though I didn't want her help or to be around her more than what was absolutely necessary, I couldn't turn down an opportunity to rack up a larger donation for our philanthropy.

The sky is clear, still casting a soft blue and purple haze as dusk settles in, but it's hotter than hell. I use the small towel around my shoulder to wipe my face just as I reach Cassie's table.

"We're up to four-thousand dollars with that last set of bidding!" she says excitedly, the red mess of curls on top of her head bouncing a little. Her cheeks are bright red, too, freckles more pronounced in the heat as she blots at her own face with a spare event t-shirt. "I think we'll crack at least five-thousand with the last set."

"Awesome. Now if only we knew where your diva of a boyfriend was, we'd be cruising on Easy Street," I spit back.

Cassie's face falls, her big green eyes softening under bent brows.

I sigh, pinching the bridge of my nose and holding out a hand toward her. "I'm sorry. I think the auction is amazing, Cassie. I do. I'm just a little worried because Grayson still isn't here and Titanium Rush has five songs left after this first one. Is there any way you can try to get ahold of him?"

"It's okay," she says, voice timid. She places a hand on my wrist and squeezes it, not knowing that squeeze is still tied to my heart, too. "I know you're stressed out. Let me try calling him, okay? Can you watch the table for a second?"

I nod and she offers a soft smile before pulling out her phone and walking away from the table.

Leave it to Cassie McBee to still be sweet as sugar when I'm being a complete dick. I don't think that girl has a mean bone in her body, and if she does, I hope I never get to see it. It's one of the things I love most about her, that wide-eyed innocence and kindness.

She's gone longer than I expect, and Titanium Rush finishes their set to a roar from the crowd before half of it disperses to get more booze and the final auction girls take the stage. Skyler is emceeing, which is a perfect job for her since she's quite possibly the most charismatic girl on campus, not to mention one of the hottest. She's wearing tiny, ripped-up jean shorts and one of Grayson's t-shirts tied just under her ribs. I hate seeing her in his shirt, but damn if she doesn't look incredible in it.

"Give it up one more time for Titanium Rush!" she screams into the mic and the crowd goes crazy, cheering and waving their drinks in the air. She continues talking, explaining how the last set of auction items will work, as Jeremy freaks out in my ear.

"WHERE THE FUCK IS HE?!"

"Calm down," I answer, trying to appear unfazed. Someone has to appear calm and collected, even if I feel like throwing up. "Cassie is trying to get ahold of him now. Just gather up how much we've raised so far and be prepared to go on stage with some facts about our philanthropy and the donation they're all helping make tonight if he's not here by the time the auction is over, okay?"

"And if he doesn't show at all?"

My stomach turns. "He'll show."

***

The last three auctions take a while, since they're the most expensive prizes, but when we finally have winners for all three and Jeremy takes the stage with clipboard in shaking hands, I panic.

This motherfucker really isn't going to show.

I know we don't exactly get along — AKA, he's the lucky bastard who managed to land the girl neither one of us deserves — but even for him, this is low. To wreck an entire concert and put the reputation of Alpha Sigma at stake like this? It's a completely different level of disrespect, one I won't let him forget.

Blowing out a long, hot breath, I push the button on my headset. "Just keep talking. I'm on my way up there to break the bad news."

Jeremy pauses mid-sentence on stage, his eyes jetting to mine through the crowd, and I shrug. Nothing to do now but apologize and hope there isn't a riot.

He swallows, forcing a smile as he continues talking about where the money from tonight will go and what it will fund.

"He's here," Cassie says, sniffling a little as she tosses her phone on the table. "He and Cal, his agent, just pulled up. They're parking back behind the stage now, I told him not to worry about a parking ticket, that we'd handle it."

"Oh, thank fucking Christ." I turn back toward the stage and push the button for my headset. "He's here. Stall a little longer, Jeremy, then you can announce him. Carter, you copy?"

"Here," Carter's staticky voice answers.

"Grayson is parking backstage. Get him set up as fast as you can and have the other brothers take care of his car."

"On it."

I let out a long breath of relief, scrubbing a hand over my face and turning back to Cassie. "God, thank you so much." But when I see her, *really* see her, my heart stops. "Wait, are you crying?"

"I'm fine," she whispers, holding her head high as she gently wipes a tear from her cheek. Her smile is as weak as her lie. "He's here, all is good. The show goes on and all that, right?"

Her face crumples, and I reach for her on instinct, pulling her into me and wrapping my arms around her. Her shoulders shake just slightly, her cries nearly silent as I hold her.

"Shhh," I whisper, kissing her forehead before pulling her in tighter and resting my chin on her head. "It's okay. Want me to kick his ass? Put auto-tune on his mic?"

She laughs into my chest. "He was just kind of snappy with me and said some things he didn't mean. He's got a lot going on. I get it, I do. He's just a little... different. That's all. But when we're alone, he's the same Grayson I know and lo—"

She doesn't finish the sentence, stiffening in my arms at the realization of the word that almost slipped out. I just hold her tighter and pretend like I didn't notice, like it wasn't a shotgun shell to the gut.

"Who the hell was that who bid on me?!"

Ashlei rushes the table in a flurry, eyes searching the crowd as Cassie sniffs and pulls away from me, crossing her arms over her chest. "Oh, the guy who bid ten-thousand out the gate? Yeah, we're all dying to know who he was, too."

"That's just insane," Ashlei says, hands flying. She pauses when she looks at Cassie again, no doubt noticing the red blotchy skin under her eyes, but she doesn't push for answers — not in front of me. Instead, she shakes her head and crosses her arms to mimic Cassie. "I mean, honestly, what college kid has that kind of money to throw around? And for an auto racing date that's worth *maybe* fifteen-hundred, if even."

"Maybe it was you who made it worth more to them?" I offer, trying to stick up for the poor sap.

She scoffs. "That's even more ridiculous."

A young girl with the biggest tits I've ever seen stuffed into a small tank top skips over to the table, handing us a check with a wide grin. "This is for the auto racing date with Ashlei Daniels," she says with a high-pitched voice.

"Mykayla?!"

She blinks, turning to Ashlei. "Oh! Hey, you. Good job up there. This event is really cool! I never really did any of this when I was in school. I lived at home and really only came to campus for class. Are you sticking around for Grayson Anderson? He is *so* swoon-worthy."

Cassie chews the inside of her cheek and I reach for her, grabbing her hand behind the table where no one can see. I smooth my thumb over her wrist and she closes her eyes with a sigh before squeezing my hand in return.

"Yeah, he's a hunk," Ashlei deadpans. "Mykayla, why did you bid on me?! And ten-thousand dollars?! Are you insane?!"

"Oh!" Mykayla shakes her head, dark blonde hair framing her rack as she giggles. "No, silly, it wasn't me. I'm here on behalf of Mr. Church."

Ashlei's face goes sheet white as Cassie and I exchange a look and a shrug.

"Mr. Church bid on me?"

"Uh-huh," Mykayla says, dragging out the words and bouncing on her heels. "He heard me talking about the concert and the auction. I just thought it was *so nice* of you to donate your time like that. And to risk going on a date with some random guy you don't know? That takes guts. He agreed, and he wanted to help the cause, so he sent me with a check. Isn't he the best boss ever?"

This time, Ashlei's face flushes red, and she slowly closes her mouth that has been hanging open since Mykayla started talking. "He's something."

Cassie gives Ashlei a look that says they'll be talking later just as Jeremy calls me backstage through my headpiece.

"I have to run," I say, nodding to Ashlei and Mykayla before turning to Cassie. The lights on the stage go black and the crowd roars, more than seven-thousand people on their feet for the asshole who made my favorite girl cry. I keep my eyes on her, ignoring the first note from Grayson's guitar. "You going to be okay?"

Cassie nods. "I'll be fine." She watches me, questions dancing in her eyes as the stage lights up again and the crowd goes even crazier. "Thank you, Adam."

"I'm always here," I remind her. Then, I lean forward, kissing her cheek with the same promise before jogging toward the stage.

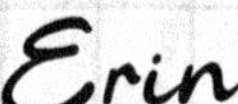

Erin

A few days after the Alpha Sigma concert, I turn twenty-one almost silently and without fuss — exactly how I want it. My sorority sisters bake me an adorable pink cake with white, polka-dot frosting, and my parents call me to let me know they've wired some birthday money into my account, but other than that, it's a normal Monday.

It's perfect.

Around nine, I'm just about to take off my makeup and pull out my planner to see what Tuesday has in store when my phone lights up with a text from Skyler.

- SOS. I know it's your birthday but I need you. Can you throw on something cute and come to Ralph's? -

I groan, thumbing out a polite "no" as fast as I can, but before I can send it, another one from her comes through.

- Please. It's important. You know I wouldn't ask you to come if it wasn't. -

This time I groan louder, but I know I can't leave my Little hanging. She's pretty self-sufficient, even when she has boy or family drama going on, so the fact that she's asking for me tells me she really does need someone.

I send a text back telling her to give me twenty minutes, rummaging through my clothes hamper to pull out the same dress I'd worn all day. It's a little too pink for Ralph's, but I don't feel like putting together another outfit, so it'll do.

When my makeup is touched up and my hair is re-straightened, I grab my phone and purse and head downstairs. The house is surprisingly quiet, only a few sisters studying silently in our small house library, and I wave at them on my way out the door.

There are usually cabs waiting all along Greek Row on the weekends to shuttle students to Ralph's and other off-campus bars, but since it's a Monday, I have to call one, and I wait patiently at the pickup point at the end of the road, going through social media on my phone as I wait.

I glance up when a cab from a different company than the one I ordered pulls up, dropping three tipsy students off before it pulls away again. Two of them stagger toward Greek Row, but the other stands completely frozen, eyes on me.

"Erin?"

I squint through the darkness, and when he takes two steps toward me and the light from the street light catches his face, my entire body goes into fight or flight mode. The hair on my arms sticks straight up, a chill racing from my heart to my toes as my pulse races to catch it. I want to run. I want to knee him in the balls. But more than anything, I don't want to do either of those things.

Because the last thing I want to give him is the satisfaction of knowing he's had any kind of effect on me at all.

"Oh, hi, Landon," I say casually, dropping my gaze back to my phone and pretending like I'm typing out a status update.

"Well, I'll be damned. Can't believe we're running into each other," he offers with a laugh that makes me want to grind my teeth and punch him in the mouth all at once. "How was your summer?"

"Fine."

Every inch of me squirms the closer he moves toward me, and a small part of me dares him to try something. I took self-defense classes all summer long and I'm dying to use them on him if he even so much as puts a pinky finger on me.

"Hey, look, I'm actually glad I ran into you. I wanted to thank you," he says, and I pause, fingers still hovering over my phone. "For being cool about what happened that night of formal. We were all so drunk," he adds with a laugh. A fucking *laugh*. "And it just got a little crazy. I appreciate you not being dramatic about it and causing more trouble than there needed to be."

Nausea rolls through me like a bad shot of alcohol, burning its way down my throat and back up again as I fight against it. My blood is cold, hands shaking as I grip my phone harder.

How fucking *dare* he.

The urge to send my knee flying into his groin and break his nose is almost too strong to contain now, but I use everything my mother taught me and do just that, settling for a sinister laugh of my own before tucking my phone away inside my purse just as my cab pulls up.

I step toward him, looking straight into his eyes, which makes him take a full step back.

"No worries. Your dick is so small, I barely felt anything, anyway."

His smile drops, and I blow him a kiss and wave my fingers in his face before dipping inside the back of the cab.

"Ralph's," I say to the driver, and then I nearly pass out, black and white spots invading my vision as I press one clammy hand hard against my forehead. I focus on my breathing, inhaling for eight seconds before holding the breath and letting it go even slower. I knew I would eventually run into Landon, but the way he just acted — so casual, like what happened didn't matter — it hurt worse than if he were cruel about it.

The farther we drive away, the harder it gets to breathe. I just want to go home, to my bed, but then I hear my mom's voice telling me to be strong, to not let that fucker get even one ounce of power from my emotions.

He hurt me, and now I want revenge.

In the back of this cab, I vow that I'll get it this semester. I don't know how, or when, but I will. And until then, I'll remind him every chance I get that what he did to me doesn't change who I am.

But even lies with intentions to heal are still lies.

My heart's still racing when the cab drops me off, and I walk as best I can with my ankles still shaking as I make my way to the entrance. Before I can tug the door open, Clinton flies out it, ushering me to the side of the building while casting a look over his shoulder to make sure he wasn't seen.

"Uh, hi to you, too, Bear. Care to tell me why you're blocking my entrance to Ralph's and sneaking around like a 007 agent?"

"Skyler doesn't need you," he says. "There's a surprise party inside. For your birthday."

My racing heart stops altogether at his words, deflating like a balloon as I cover my face with one hand and groan. "No. No, no, no, I don't *want* a party."

"I know. I know, that's why I stopped you before you went in. I didn't want you to get overwhelmed."

He's dressed in a bright orange polo and dark jeans, his sneakers matching his shirt, and a flat-billed hat finishing off the look. His cologne is strong and sweet, making me want to curl into him, my body reacting to the way his large arms nearly burst out of his sleeves before I can remind myself why that's a stupid reaction to have.

"Look," he says, bending down a little to catch my eyes with his. His hands find my arms and he steadies me, squeezing them gently. "Just pop in, act surprised, stay for a drink and then you can fake sick and I'll take you home, okay?"

"No," I say automatically. Ten minutes ago, I could have done what he was asking, but after running into Landon, just standing on my own is taking everything I have. "I can't."

"Come on," he urges. "Your sisters planned this for you. It's your twenty-first birthday, Erin. Just have a drink and—"

"I DON'T WANT A DRINK!" I scream, breaking loose from his hold on me. "That last time I drank I was fucking *raped*, Bear," I remind him, my voice cracking on the word as tears threaten to break. I hold them back, not wanting to let the pain out. "And the time before that, I..."

My voice trails off, realizing what I was about to say, but Clinton doesn't let it go.

"You what? Slept with me?"

I shake my head, biting back the tears and wishing I could tell him it's so much more than that. If he only knew what happened after, he would understand.

But it would also kill him.

And he doesn't deserve that.

He scoffs, crossing his arms over his chest with his eyes on the parking lot behind me. "Fine. Just leave. I'll tell them you got food poisoning and you were throwing up the minute the cab dropped you off so I sent you back."

I nod, glancing at him with the only thank you I have in my eyes. I can't say another word, and he doesn't ask for one, just sighs and shakes his head as he starts toward the entrance again. I take out my phone to call the cab back, but before I can dial the number, his voice stops me.

"I know what happened that night, Erin. I was there. I saw it," he reminds me, his voice the shaky one now. "That's why I'm here. That's why I'm pushing. You may have toughened your skin over the summer and shoved all your feelings on it down into some box with a bolted lid, but one day that lid is going to pop off from the pressure, and I just want you to know you have someone to go to when it does."

His words are like numbing cream, drying up my tears as I hold the phone to my ear to order another cab and he disappears inside again without another look from me. He may believe he's right, but I can't — because going through the pain of opening that box again would be more than I could handle. It would kill me, and I'm not ready to die.

So, as I climb into the back of the new cab, I seal the box shut a little tighter, add a few more bolts, and swallow back the tears I never want to let fall again.

Maybe someone can see my scars, after all.

EPISODE 3

Skyler

I have no idea what I'm doing.

Not just in the current moment as I pack my books for a day full of classes, but in life, in general. Up until right now, the only thing I've ever known to be certain is that I love to play poker. Period. The end. But that's about all I have.

Sure, I like to flirt with boys and party with my sisters, but unfortunately, there's neither a career path for those kinds of hobbies nor is there anything such as a Professional Paddleboarder or Dynamite Donut Eater that I'm aware of. So, over the summer, I asked myself if poker was really what I wanted to do for the rest of my life, because it was the only sure thing I had that could potentially be a career.

It wasn't an easy question to answer.

I love poker, that much is easy for anyone to see. But can I imagine a life of always traveling, always hustling, always wondering if I'd make the next tournament or be able to perform in it? Can I see myself getting married or raising a family and somehow battling poker tabloids at the same time?

I don't have those answers, and I didn't find them over the summer. So, I filled my schedule with classes in all fields of study, hoping to find something that will stick. My first two years at Palm South University were a breeze, mostly filled with general education courses that were similar to high school in content, just more intense. But this semester, I'll be diving into five different subject areas to see if anything sticks.

God, help me.

"You're a mess," Ashlei says with a laugh as she watches me pack my books for the day.

I have my Nonprofit Organizations class today, inspired by Jarrett's most recent job acquisition, followed by Judicial Process and Politics, just in case I want to go pre-law, and finally, Stagecraft I. My mother was into theatre when she was in high school, so I figured maybe it's in my blood. And this is just for my Monday and Wednesday classes. On Tuesdays and Thursdays, I have Principles of Advertising and Introduction to Elementary Education.

Something is bound to stick.

"It's like being at a delicious buffet," I say defensively, zipping up my blue and green Vera Bradley bag when all my books are in place. "I have to load up my plate and try a little of everything before I can decide what I actually want to eat a substantial amount of. In the end, I'll be stuffed and happy."

"Or you'll vomit."

I glare at her as she hops down from Jess's bed, linking arms with me with a laugh.

"I'm just giving you a hard time. I'm glad you're exploring options, Sky. It'll be fun."

"Not as fun as your bad-ass internship," I counter as we make our way downstairs.

It's a bustling Monday morning in the sorority house, girls flying every which way, hair half-done and protein bars in hand. Some are heading out to the gym, some coming back, the rest of us somewhere between classes, internships, jobs, or on-campus activities. Erin was out the door by six AM, which surprises absolutely no one.

"It really has been such a blast, but the real work is starting now. I thought I was busy before," Ashlei says with a sigh. "I had no idea. I want to knock the socks off of this client when we meet with them in a few weeks to pitch the event launch concepts."

"You'll do amazing," I assure her, squeezing her arm before breaking our link as she heads toward the door and I toward the kitchen. "Still on for a girly movie night?"

"Definitely. I'll smuggle in some wine."

"My girl."

Ashlei throws me a wink and then she's out the door, and I make my way to the kitchen, snagging a banana and to-go cup of coffee for my walk to the Business building.

Even in the sticky September morning air, it feels good to be back on the PSU campus. The classes are challenging, the boys are hotter than Hades, and the parties are just as wild as ever. It's home, but there is one thing missing.

Clinton's smile.

I haven't seen it, the *real* Clinton smile, ever since Omega Chi was put on a one-year suspension. I can't blame him for feeling down, and even though he's been trying his best to put on a happy face at the Alpha Sigma parties and social events, I know inside he's miserable. Between his little brother living with a friend in Pittsburgh and everything going on with his fraternity, it's a wonder he can even force a fake smile.

But that's what he's wearing nowadays, and today is no different as I round the corner of the Student Union and meet him in our usual place. We walk to the Business building together every Monday and Wednesday, me for my first class of the day and him for his second, hence meeting outside of the Union instead of on Greek Row.

Clinton is leaned up against the dark brick at the side of the building, his gaze distant as I make my way toward him. He still looks as fresh as ever, red and black Air Jordans matching the Nike design on his casual t-shirt and Omega Chi hat turned a little to the side. He's grown a little scruff on his chin since the beginning of the semester, and I run a knuckle over it when I reach him.

"So manly with your little beard," I tease.

He shakes his head, ridding himself of whatever thoughts he was focused on before I got there and smiles down at me, though it's still not the real smile I know and love. "The ladies like a little friction, if you know what I mean."

"Gross," I say with a laugh, nudging him. "But also true."

This time he laughs, throwing his arm over my shoulders as we make our way across campus.

There are few people in the world I love as much as Clinton, which is why it breaks my heart that no matter what we talk about, and no matter what he *says* about how he's feeling, I can read the truth in his eyes. He's sad, he's broken, and when I get that way, I know the only thing that makes me feel better is going home for a while.

So, when he drops me off at my classroom, I pull out my phone before class starts and book two flights to Pittsburgh for next weekend, screenshotting the confirmation and texting it to Clinton.

- Pack your bags. It's time for a bestie trip.

Cassie

"You know," Erin says, a little out of breath as she wipes the sweat from her forehead. "Guys complain about sweaty balls, but they have no idea the torture of sweaty underboob."

I chuckle, glancing up at her from where I'm seated on the turf that stretches in front of the fountain. Less than two weeks ago it was the setting for the Alpha Sigma concert, and in less than a week it will be home to the Kappa Kappa Beta Dodgeball Tournament.

"At least we have a little cloud cover," I offer optimistically.

"Ugh, it's just so muggy," she counters, squinting up at the sky before watching me hammer in another peg for the fence we're putting up to outline the dodgeball court boundaries. "When you're finished here, can you come help me with the referee stands?"

"Absolutely! Be right over."

"Thanks," she says, still eyeing me. She watches me work for another moment before throwing up her hands in exasperation. "How are you this cheery when we're all sweating like pigs and working like men in this God-awful Florida heat? It's gross. And it's creeping me out. Stop it."

I laugh, shrugging as I stand and dust the grass off the back of my shorts. "I can't help it. Grayson is finally taking me on a date tonight. Nothing can bring me down today, Ex. Not even underboob sweat."

"Ugh, fine. Can you at least fake a frown for me?"

I give her my best scowl, but we both end up breaking into giggles as we maneuver through the field of girls toward the referee stands.

"So, where's Mr. Perfect taking you?"

"There's a really fancy steakhouse on the water that he wants to take me to for dinner, and then we're going to walk the beach and you know... I'm sure we'll end up back at his place."

I blush, biting my lip at the thought of Grayson's hands on me. After the rough few weeks we've had, I'm looking forward to having one-on-one time with him, to having time with *my* Grayson — not the one who lives on stage.

"Okay, now I understand why you're all smiley," Erin says, flipping through a few pages of her clipboard. "Think you guys will finally have sex?"

My cheeks heat even more. "I don't know... maybe. I guess we'll see how the night goes. But if I were a betting woman like Skyler... well, I'd put my money on yes."

Erin eyes me for a second, her brows bent like she's worried about my decision. But that doesn't make any sense, since she's more pro-Grayson than anyone.

Her eyes are soft as she grabs my elbow and squeezes it gently. "Well, just be careful, okay, Grandlittle? Protection and all that."

"Oh, my God. Stop mothering me and go boss someone around. That'll make you feel better."

She laughs, but it's small and soft. "Can't argue with that logic. Let me know before you head out for your big date, okay?"

"Will do."

Erin watches me for a moment more with a slight smile, then she snaps back into business mode, flipping through the pages on her clipboard once more and barking out orders at every girl she passes as she crosses the field.

My stomach catches flight with butterflies as I get to work on the referee stand, helping two of our newer sisters build it from the ground up. It's actually a nice distraction to work with my hands for a while, especially considering my mind is completely in the clouds. I can't stop imagining what the night will be like, what he'll wear, how the food will taste, what conversation we'll have, how amazing it will feel to have my hand in his as we walk the beach at night.

Grayson has been so busy, and after our little fight at the Alpha Sigma concert, we really need the alone time. He was stressed that night, running from his solo performance at a coffee shop in an upscale neighborhood back to campus for the concert. He didn't answer my calls the first few times I tried to reach him, and when he finally called me back, he went off on me for blowing up his phone when I knew he was at another performance. The truth was I hadn't remembered it was supposed to go that late, and I was just trying to help Adam.

I can still hear the bite in his voice, the snap of it, a sound so unfamiliar to me. He'd blamed me for putting the pressure on him by making him agree to do the Alpha Sigma concert, and said some things about Greek life that I always knew he felt, but never thought he would say. It hurt, and made me feel about two inches tall.

Grayson apologized, of course, and he held me that night after the concert, kissing away any last tears I had to shed over our fight. Then he promised me more dates and more time spent together, and I promised to be more understanding of his new lifestyle.

I'm beginning to realize that relationships take work. Sure, the passion and butterflies are amazing, but to really survive as a couple, you have to compromise. You have to work together. And I'm happy to do that with Grayson, because I believe in us. And the more I learn about him, the more I fall for him.

I think I might be falling in love.

The admission makes me giddy again, and I bite back the stupid smile spreading on my face as I try to keep up with the conversation my sisters are having about what outfits they want to wear for our next social. But when the last stand is finished and I'm free to go back to the house and get ready for my date, I let the butterflies take me over, wings tickling my ribs as I practically skip home.

I scan through my outfit options the entire way back, wondering what he will wear, wondering how he will look when he sees me all dressed up. I imagine his fingers sliding the straps of my favorite emerald green dress down over my shoulders, my eyes fluttering shut at the thought of his hands moving to the long zipper on the side. It's impossible to know how everything will happen, but one thing I know for sure.

Tonight will be amazing.

***

Tonight is the worst night of my life.

Okay, that might be a little dramatic, but it's definitely in the top five. Here I am, dressed in my favorite green dress just like I imagined, except there won't be any hands sliding it off me tonight. My hair is pulled into an elegant up-do, a few tendrils hanging to frame my face, which is absolutely flawless after an hour of makeup application, and I borrowed Erin's beautiful nude heels that wrap at the ankle with a ribbon. But none of it matters.

Because Grayson bailed.

He was sweet about it, of course, and regretful. His agent booked him a last-minute show and he couldn't turn it down. He promised he'd make it up to me and told me there'd be a ticket at the door with my name on it if I wanted to show up, but I politely declined. I tried to hide my disappointment, but I know he saw right through me.

And the bigger part of me hoped he did.

But now I'm all dressed up with nothing to do, salivating for a delicious steak I won't get to eat, and yearning to be held on the beach by my boyfriend who is across town on a stage singing to a group of swooning girls, instead.

Sighing, I pull my phone from my clutch, thumbing through the contacts to find Skyler's name. I know she'll know exactly what to say to make me feel better, but for some reason I can't get my thumb to drop the last inch to dial her number. I don't even want to talk to anyone, I just want to be miserable.

Pity party, table for one.

So, I let my feet carry me, the adorable heels feeling more and more like medieval torture devices with every step as I meander aimlessly around campus with my mind on Grayson. I wonder if this is really our new normal, if this is how it's going to be now — cancelled plans and IOUs.

My stomach growls as I pass the food court, so I head for my favorite pizza place, the bell above the door announcing my arrival with a sad ding. Pie Heaven sells pizza slices the size of your face, and that's exactly the kind of cure I need right now.

"Two Hawaiians," I say when I reach the counter, knowing full well there's absolutely zero chance of me finishing two slices but ready to give it the college try, anyway. "And a garlic knot. And a large Coke."

The girl behind the counter lifts one eyebrow at me, looking behind me like I brought a friend.

"Nope, no one else, honey. It's just me and a testy appetite, so stop judging and tell me what I owe you."

A laugh breaks loose at a booth to my right and I snap my head to the source of it, heart stopping when I find Adam staring back at me.

"Easy, killer," he says, lifting himself from the booth and pulling his wallet from his pocket. He slides the cashier his card, eyeing me with amusement as she runs it through the machine. "You and that testy appetite of yours want some company?"

I try to glare at him, but a smile breaks loose and I flop into the booth dramatically. He chuckles, bringing the tray with my pizza and drink over to the table before sliding in on the other side.

"Wanna talk about it?" he asks, pushing the parmesan cheese and red pepper flakes toward me.

I shake fresh parmesan on my first slice and shrug, keeping my eyes on the pizza. "Grayson and I were supposed to go on a date tonight but he bailed last minute. It's fine," I say quickly, feeling a little bad talking about Grayson to Adam. Even if I am upset, I already know how Adam feels about Grayson. "He apologized and he's going to make it up to me, but I'm just a little bummed."

"That's understandable," he says, the weight of his eyes still on me as I take my first bite. "But sometimes things come up. I'm sure he's just as sad as you are that he had to cancel."

I pause mid-bite, glancing up at Adam. *There has to be a hint of sarcasm there somewhere,* I think, but find no traces when I search his eyes. He seems genuine, and for some reason that brings the dead butterflies in the pit of my stomach back to life.

"You look beautiful, by the way," he says, his voice softer.

I swallow, cheeks flushing as I reach for my drink.

"Thank you, Adam."

He smiles, finishing off his own pizza before changing the subject. He asks me how my classes are going and tells me all about the concert aftermath and his time as president so far. I fill him in on the dodgeball tournament prep and he tells me about the summer spent with his aunt, the one whom he lived with after his grandpa passed away. After an hour passes, the sadness I felt from Grayson cancelling is like a dull ache in the back of my mind. After two, it's gone completely, and I'm laughing and eating too much instead of feeling sorry for myself.

"I was thinking about going back to the A Sig house and putting on a movie," Adam says when the same cashier who rang us up starts wiping down tables and putting the chairs on top. It's almost eleven. "You're more than welcome to join, if you want to."

His eyes are hopeful as he waits for my response, and a wave rushes through me at the thought of spending more time with him. We always have so much fun, but a bigger part of me knows it's the feeling I have when I'm with him that I want to hold onto. I should feel guilty for wanting it at all, but I don't.

Still, I have a head on my shoulders, and I know when to walk away from trouble.

"I think I should probably get back to the house," I say, gathering our empty plates onto one tray. "I have class pretty early."

Adam smiles, shrugging it off. "No biggie. Maybe another time."

We clean up our table and Adam waves to a guy back in the kitchen before holding the door open for me, the bell sounding a little less sad this time as I step into the warm summer night.

Adam walks me to the Kappa Kappa Beta house, carrying the conversation easily until we reach the front steps. I turn to face him, folding my arms over my chest as he slides his hands easily into his pockets with his eyes on mine. It's quiet on campus now, only a few other students still out, the soft rush of water from the fountain filling most of the silence.

"Thank you for tonight," I say softly.

He watches me for a moment longer, and instead of responding, he untucks his hands from his pockets and reaches for me, pulling me into his chest.

I hate this feeling.

It's the feeling reserved for Adam, the one only he can elicit from me. He owns it. No one else has ever made my body react the way it does when we're in situations like this, his arms around me, my head on his chest, boundaries between us that feel invisible and like barbed wire all at once. He looks at me, my stomach tightens. He holds me, my chest aches. He lets me go, whispering a goodnight before turning to walk away, and everything I've ever known about how to breathe disappears.

I hate this feeling.

I hope it never goes away.

Jess

The airport is surprisingly busy for a Wednesday evening, men in business suits and families dressed in Mickey Mouse gear speeding by me in both directions as I wait at the bottom of the escalator.

Jarrett's plane landed ten minutes ago, which means he should be coming down the escalator toward baggage claim any second now. I can't stop bouncing, my hands a little shaky as I wring them together and watch the top of the moving stairs, waiting to see that glorious bald head.

Boys never make me nervous — ever. But I haven't seen Jarrett since he left for his internship at the very beginning of the summer, and that was right after I admitted out loud that I loved him. Sure, video chatting has been a nice distraction, but it's no substitute for the real thing. Just imagining his hands on me, his lips on mine, his body — so hard, covered with tattoos... it's enough to make me come in a crowded airport before even setting eyes on him.

I pull out my phone, checking the time once more before shoving it in my back pocket again. A few more minutes pass and I debate calling him, but just as I go to grab my phone again, he appears at the top of the escalator.

And time stops.

Seconds stretch and tick as I take him in — his tan, smooth head, the scruff lining his jaw, the way his simple, navy t-shirt hugs the muscles on his arms and chest, tapering off at his narrow waist. And when my eyes find his, when the corner of his mouth quirks up in a small smirk, I can't take it anymore.

I run to him.

"Excuse me, sorry, excuse me." I push through the other travelers on the stairs, working against gravity as they move down and I try to move up...up to him.

Jarrett cracks a wider smile watching me struggle, nearly laughing by the time I reach him and throw my arms around his neck, pressing my lips to his with a sigh of relief. His strong arm holds me close and lifts me from the ground, my feet dangling just a few inches above the escalator stairs as he kisses me with everyone watching. His other hand dips into my hair as one arm holds me steady against him, and I tug him closer by his shirt, wanting more, needing him closer.

"I've missed you so much," I whisper against his lips, kissing him before he can answer.

He wraps both arms around me when we reach the bottom of the escalator, making sure we're on solid ground before he drops my feet down. I'm still holding his shirt, feeling the fabric between my fingers, rolling it around to make sure it's real.

He's here.

"I've missed you, too," he says, pulling back to look into my eyes. His are still the same deep mocha, gold spiraling out from each pupil as he scans my body the way I did his. "Let's grab my bag and get out of here."

We can't keep our hands off each other, not the entire time we wait in baggage claim or on the walk to the taxi lane as I run over everything I have planned for the long weekend. We only have five days together, and I plan to make the most of it.

"I can't believe you're going to introduce me to your sisters," he says when we slide into the backseat of a black sedan. I tell the driver the address of Jarrett's hotel and she smiles politely with a nod.

"It's about damn time."

"Well, we couldn't exactly broadcast our relationship before."

"No," I agree. "But now, I'm going to show you off like a pack of gel pens at show and tell. Everyone on campus is going to know you're mine by the time you leave."

Jarrett chuckles, eyeing the driver's rearview mirror before leaning in to nuzzle my neck. "You wanna show me off, huh?" His voice is low and gravelly, one hand sliding up the inside of my thigh and up to the hem of my jean shorts.

My eyes flutter closed at the contact of his skin on mine, chills racing up to my core. "Mm-hmm," I manage in answer.

"What if I don't want to leave the hotel room?"

He slips two fingers up under the denim fabric of my shorts, brushing the tips against my panties. I bite my lip hard, squirming under his touch, eyes opening just enough to make sure the driver isn't looking at us in her mirror.

I can't even respond, especially when his lips find my neck again. He kisses me softly, fingers running along the edge of my panties before he dips them inside. My lips are pinned between my teeth to hold back my moans, but when Jarrett circles my clit twice and then slides both fingers inside me at once, I nearly combust, letting out a loud pant as my eyes snap open.

The driver glances back at us and Jarrett rests his head on my shoulder. I offer her a smile and she narrows her eyes, but focuses them back on the road again, and as soon as she does, Jarrett withdraws his fingers and slides them in again, wiggling his fingertips to curl against my G-spot.

He continues his slow, quiet assault the entire drive, and by the time we reach the hotel, I'm two feather-light touches away from orgasming in the back of a fucking taxi cab.

Jarrett pays the driver as I sprint inside to the front desk, checking in with weak knees and an unbearable ache between my thighs. I swipe the keys from the counter as soon as the girl tells me our room number and barrel back outside, grabbing Jarrett's hand and leading him inside through the lobby to the elevators.

"Room 813," I pant as the elevator doors close, pushing him against the wall. I cover his mouth with mine as he fumbles to push the button for the eighth floor. He runs his hands down my ribs and to my ass, cupping it firmly and pulling me flush against him as we ride up. The seam of my jean shorts rubs me in the spot I'm aching most and I gasp into his mouth, my orgasm already within reach. One more touch and I'll fall apart.

Jarrett's lips don't leave mine as we stumble down the hall to our room, him pulling his suitcase behind him as my hands get to work on his belt. He taps the plastic card to the scanner on our door and shoves us through, dropping his suitcase right behind the door before picking me up and carrying me to one of the beds.

"Two beds?" he asks, breaking our kiss long enough to appraise the room.

"I asked for a king, probably a mistake. Want me to run downstairs and have them fix it?"

"Are you kidding?" he asks, looking back down at me with a wicked grin. "I'm going to fuck you on both of them." He drops down on top of me, sucking the skin on my neck between his teeth and letting it go with a pop as I cry out at the sensation. "And then the floor. And the shower." He kisses me again. "And that chair over there." Another kiss. "And that desk. *Definitely* that fucking desk."

I giggle against his mouth as he unzips my shorts and tugs them down my thighs. I've missed him, mind and soul, but it's his body that calls to mine first, begging to be touched, to be fucked. My eyes can't devour him long enough, can't get their fill of him before he touches me in a way that has them fluttering closed again.

I wiggle my legs back and forth to help him with my shorts, making quick work of my tank top and bra in the process. When he hooks his thumbs under the lace of my panties and slides them down my legs, slowly pulling them one by one from each ankle at the end, he runs his tongue across his bottom lip and pulls me up until I'm on my knees in front of him.

"I want that perfect fucking pussy on my face," he growls, tugging my hair back with both hands and running his tongue along my jaw. "Now."

And this is why I want everyone to know this man is mine.

Jarrett moves quickly until he's on his back on the bed and I rip his shirt up and over his head, tossing it to the side before crawling up his body. I take my time, reveling in the feel of him underneath me. The man I was never supposed to have, now the only one I ever want.

What has he done to me?

I kiss every tattoo on the way up, tracing the ones I know with my tongue, eyeing the new ones with appreciation until both of my knees are braced on either side of his face.

And then, his mouth is on me.

I gasp at the feel of him, my orgasm already so close I can feel the first tingles climbing. His tongue circles my clit before he sucks it gently between his teeth, hands smacking my ass and pulling me closer to him. I arch my back, crying out with loud moans as I ride his face. Each swirl of his tongue sends me closer to the edge, and when he slides two fingers deep inside me, working them like I'm riding his dick, I go flying.

His name is on my lips as I cry out, nails digging into the headboard, orgasm rocking me from the inside out. A numbing fire consumes every inch of me until I shake and shudder around him, and I barely have time to recover before he flips us.

Jarrett kisses me hard, the taste of me fresh on his tongue, his hands hard on my thighs as he drags me to the edge of the bed. He breaks contact long enough to strip out of his jeans and boxer briefs and then my ankles are on his shoulders and he slides inside me mercilessly, filling me with a moan, his head dropping back.

"Oh, my God," I moan with him, fists twisting in the sheets as he wraps his hands around my thighs and pounds into me again. Every thrust hits deeper, and Jarrett lets my ankles fall to the side, leaning down to suck one nipple between his teeth as he curls his back, pushing in again and again, each time with more purpose than the last.

And it's this I'll never get enough of. The touching, the kissing, the fucking. It's this that reminds me that no matter the distance or the time, what we have is real. It sparks to life as soon as we're together again, like no time has passed, like nothing can ever come between us.

Unstoppable. That's what we are.

Pressing a hand hard into Jarrett's chest, I push him back until he slips out of me, the backs of his legs hitting the edge of the opposite bed. I follow, dropping to my knees in front of him, running my hands along the hard length of him in appreciation.

"I've missed this fucking dick so much," I say, glancing up at Jarrett. He smirks, but as soon as I wrap my mouth around the tip of him, any trace of a smile fades and his eyes roll back as he groans.

I work him into my mouth slowly, sliding down farther each time until he's coated and wet. When I slide my lips all the way down to the base of him, fighting against the gag, he curses, flexing his hips forward. I pull back, circling my tongue over his crown before dipping down again, this time holding my breath so he can fuck my throat.

When I palm his tight balls, I know he's close, but he grabs me by the arms and yanks me up, kissing me hard once before spinning me around until my hands are braced on the other bed we've yet to fuck on.

I climb up, braced on my hands and knees, and Jarrett slides his wet cock down the line of my ass before slipping inside my pussy again. He feels bigger in this position, every inch of him stretching me open as I arch my back and flip my hair back for him to grab.

"I want you to come again," he pants, hips rolling and pushing him in deeper.

"Fuck, I don't know if I can."

"Do you trust me?" he asks, tugging my hair and leaning down to suck the skin of my neck.

I gasp, his cock so deep inside me now I'm seeing stars. "Yes," I breathe, and Jarrett runs his thumb along my bottom lip before dipping it inside my mouth. I suck it gently, rolling my tongue all the way down to the knuckle and back.

Jarrett groans, pulling his thumb from my mouth and sliding his hand down my back, over my ass. Then, before I have time to register it, I feel a pinch, and that same thumb slides inside my ass.

"Oh, fuck," I cry out, the new sensation rocking through me. He pounds in deeper, thumb working in the same rhythm, and it only takes seconds for me to fall apart again. I come hard, fire scorching me from the inside, and my moans are all it takes for Jarrett to come with me.

We ride out our orgasms until the very last tingle, Jarrett slowly removing his thumb, both of us panting for air when he drops to the bed beside me and pulls me into his chest.

I'm completely sated, thighs and hip flexors already sore as I trace my fingers over his abdomen and up to his chest, outlining the fresh ink there. It's a brightly colored hourglass piece, sharp reds and purples lining the wings that frame the glass, the sand trickling down slowly, top half more full than the bottom.

"I love this," I whisper softly, still running my fingertips over the swollen skin.

Jarrett pulls me closer, pressing his lips to my forehead. "And I love you."

I smile, rolling until I'm on top of him, my hair falling down to frame us under the curtains. "Well, two beds down. But we didn't make it to the floor... or the shower... or the chair... or the desk."

"Oh," Jarrett says with a smirk, hand sliding along my jaw before tucking into my hair and pulling my lips to his. "That was just round one. We're not leaving this room until morning, I hope you know that."

And so I smile, order us a pizza, and buckle in for round two.

***

"I'm really glad I got to do dinner with you before Bear and I leave for Pittsburgh, Jarrett," Skyler says just as another round of margaritas is dropped off at our table. "Seeing your eyes light up when you talk about your job... I need to find something like that."

Jarrett is completely surrounded by girls as we gobble up the last of our burritos and tacos at the best Mexican place off campus. Skyler and Erin sit across the table while Cassie flanks his left side, Ashlei and I rounding out the right side. And for the last two hours, he's been drilled with questions, and he's handled it like an absolute champ.

"You get like that with poker," Erin points out, tipping her glass toward Skyler.

"Yeah, but can that really be a career? Like, a forever thing?"

"If it's what you really love, why not?" Jarrett asks.

He makes a good point, and Skyler chews her cheek.

"It seems like that's how you feel about your job, Jarrett. Like you really love it and there's nothing else you want or need to be happy," Cassie adds.

Jarrett smirks, casting a glance at me before tucking me under his arm. He presses a kiss into my hair, holding me close. "There is one thing."

The girls sigh in sync, and I can't help but swoon a little myself. After spending all night with him in the hotel last night, I didn't think the trip could get any better. But we spent the day at the beach together, and now he's getting along with all of the people who are important to me.

I thought I couldn't get in any deeper with him, but here I am, sinking without a single care to save myself.

Jarrett tips my chin up and kisses me sweetly before turning the conversation back to Cassie and her plans to go pre-med. All I can do is watch him, eyes memorizing the sharp edges of his nose, the line of his jaw, the curve of his small smile as he listens to my best friends tell him about themselves. An ache rolls through me at the thought of him leaving again, not knowing when I'll see him, not knowing how long we'll be long distance.

Jarrett is so good at being alone. He was a loner when I met him, perfectly content in his one-bedroom apartment taking care of himself. He's had to his entire life, ever since his mother passed away when he was thirteen. I didn't even know he'd gone through that, not until he was taking care of me when I was sick last semester.

He's self-sufficient. Independent. Completely fine on his own.

But I need him.

Before Jarrett, I didn't need anyone, either. I *wanted* guys, sure — but just to get me off. I was perfectly content doing it myself if the right guy wasn't around, and when they were around, that was all I needed them for.

But Jarrett snuck inside my heart. He opened me up when I was sure the doors were locked forever. I was like a succulent, needing little attention to survive, and now he's transformed me into a weak little rose in the palm of his hand, desperate for his care.

I've never felt so vulnerable, and it scares the ever-loving shit out of me.

"I've got this," Jarrett says when the waitress brings our bill, and all of the girls light up, their eyes catching mine. They know it, too — how deep I'm in — and I wonder if they're happy for me or worried how they'll save me when it all goes up in flames.

Jarrett holds me close to him as we walk the short distance to Ralph's, one hand tucked into the back pocket of my jeans. We fall a little behind the group, and I feel him watching me.

"Stop overthinking," he says. "You've got self-sabotage written all over that beautiful face of yours."

I chuckle, leaning into him. "I'm just going to miss you, that's all."

"I just got here."

"But you'll still leave in three days."

Jarrett frowns, pulling me to a stop when we reach the parking lot of Ralph's. I wave the other girls to go in without us, keeping my eyes on my feet when it's just Jarrett and me.

"Do you remember what you asked me that day I took care of you when you had that nasty sinus infection?" Jarrett asks, knuckle finding my chin and forcing me to look at him. "You asked me how long it would take you to chase me away. And what was my answer?"

"You can't chase someone who's not running."

Jarrett nods, his dark eyes searching mine. "I'm still not running, Jess. Distance hasn't changed the way I feel about you, and it won't change our relationship if we don't let it. I know this is hard." He pauses, Adam's apple bobbing in his throat. "I know I'm asking you to love a man you can't always touch, and I know that's not fair."

"And I know how important this opportunity is to you," I counter, leaning into his touch.

He frames my face with his hand, thumb rubbing the line of my jaw. "You're important to me, too."

"I know."

For a long moment he just holds me, and I watch him, knowing I'm not making it easier for him to stick to his decision when I make him doubt us in any way.

"We're going to make it through this," I whisper. "I won't lie and say I'm not scared, but we'll be okay. I know we will."

Jarrett sighs, relief washing over him as he tugs me into his chest and wraps his arms all the way around me. I inhale the smell of him, wishing I could bottle it up, wishing I could keep us in this moment forever.

"Want to throw me in the back closet for old time's sake?" I ask with a grin, pulling back from his hold and grabbing his hand to lead him inside.

He smacks my ass with a smile of his own. "You've got to find some cowgirl boots first. You know, to keep the memory authentic."

I laugh as we dip inside the glass doors, joining the girls along with Clinton, Adam, and a whole slew of their brothers. And the rest of the night is easy, Jarrett getting along with everyone he talks to, and me letting go of my fears, if even just for the night. We dance and laugh, drink and play, and when last call comes and goes and I'm back in the sheets with Jarrett, I know only one thing really matters.

I'm in love with a man who loves me, too.

Whether it's forever or just for right now, I vow to make the most of every minute I can say that.

Skyler

It's a beautiful, sunny day in Franklin Park, a borough right outside of Pittsburgh where Mac's family lives. We're all seated at a large picnic table in their backyard, plates of ribs and potato salad and everything in-between piled high around us.

Clinton warned me that the weather was pretty unpredictable in Pittsburgh in September, so I packed everything from shorts to a thick rain jacket, but we were welcomed by a temperature in the mid-seventies and blue skies with puffy white clouds slowly flowing by. After melting in South Florida for the past few months, it's a nice change.

What's even nicer is the change I've seen in Clinton.

It's been a short trip, but even just a few days spent with his baby brother has brightened him back into the Clinton I know and love. We went to a Pirates game, let Mac and Clayton show us around their new school, and even took the cable car up the Duquesne Incline for touristy pictures since this is my first time to the city. But the truth is it wouldn't have mattered what we did while we were here. Just being with Clayton has made Clinton smile again, and that's all I ever wanted.

"Needless to say, she's begging for me to take her to homecoming," Clayton says, finishing his story about a girl in his math class. He scoops a big heap of macaroni and cheese onto his plate before passing the bowl to his big brother. "But I mean, I don't want to rush into anything. I've got decisions to make. So many choices, you know?"

Mac rolls his eyes. "Yeah, so many. Her, your right hand, however will you choose?"

Everyone laughs, except Clayton, who grabs a toothpick from the small holder and pegs Mac in the nose with it.

"Clayton likes to pretend like he's such a little thug," Mac's mom says, her voice sweet and slow like molasses. She's a little shorter than me, with a tiny button nose and dark freckles on the apples of her caramel cheeks. "But he's a good kid. Finished eighth grade with straight A's last year and seems to be on the same path in high school. And he does it all while juggling football, too."

"It's true," Mac's sister, Kia, agrees. "Already making a name for himself and he's only been in high school for a couple of months."

"Yeah, makes me look bad. Thanks a lot, Clayton," Mac chimes in.

It's hard to tell if Clayton is blushing, but he wears a shy smile, forking up a few macaroni noodles before popping them in his mouth.

Clinton is beaming, his chest puffed out with pride like a dad. "That's my baby brother. What position are you playing now that you're in high school?"

"Wide receiver."

"And what are your stats so far this season?"

He shrugs. "Well, we've only had a few games, but so far I've got a little over three-hundred receiving yards and four touchdowns."

"That's really good, Baby Bear," I say, winking with the use of his favorite nickname. "Especially for a freshman."

Clinton's smile takes up his entire face, and he puts his fork down, turning to his little brother in earnest. "I'm really proud of you, Clayton. Keep up this hard work and you'll get to go to any college you want to."

"I want to go to PSU," he says easily, mirroring Clinton's smile. "Just like you."

It's a private moment between big brother and little brother, and Mac's dad feels it, too, turning the conversation to me to give them a moment as Clinton claps Clayton on the shoulder with pride in his eyes.

"So, Skyler," Mr. Harrison says between bites of his ribs, his fingers covered in barbecue sauce. "Bear tells us you're entering a pretty big poker tournament this upcoming summer."

"I haven't officially decided yet, but I'm seriously considering it."

"What's holding you back?" he asks, pushing his glasses up the bridge of his long nose. Such a simple question with such a complicated answer.

"It's just a lot more intense than the tournaments I've been in so far. Don't get me wrong, I think I'm ready, but at the same time it's a lot of money to potentially lose."

"Or potentially win," Clinton counters.

I blush, squeezing a little lemon in my iced tea before taking a drink. "I just want to think about it for a while longer, but I'm leaning toward entering. I'm confident in my skills, so really, what do I have to lose?"

"Ah, worst thing that could happen is you get humbled a little," Mrs. Harrison says. "And from what Bear has told us about you, you're already humble and kind anyway. So, my bet is that you'll end up winning or at least give it hell trying, which is a great experience either way."

"Very true, Mrs. Harrison." I smile, my wheels turning the rest of dinner as the conversation easily floats from person to person.

Could I really win it?

It's been heavy on my mind all summer, especially after I won a pretty large tournament in Reno at the end of July. But the American Poker Club tournament is a completely different level. All the big players will be there — ones I've defeated and ones I've been defeated by.

The poker blogs are calling me the next big thing in poker, the next big champ. Can I prove them right?

After the ribs are scarfed down and an entire cherry cheesecake is devoured, Clayton and I work on washing the dishes inside while everyone else cleans up the picnic table and grill. I take the job of washing and rinsing while he dries, but after a few minutes of easy conversation, Clayton grows quiet.

"Has it been nice seeing Bear this weekend?" I ask, handing him one of the large casserole dishes.

He smiles, and it's then that I notice how big he is. I just saw him six months ago, but he's already growing more and more into a young man every single day.

"It's always amazing to have him around. I miss him, but I'm glad he trusts me to live with Mac and his family. I was so worried he was going to drop PSU." He turns to me then. "I guess I kind of have you to thank for helping me convince him to stay."

I shrug. "Ah, Bear just wants you to be okay. He still has a level head. Just have to knock some sense into it sometimes," I add with a laugh.

Clayton smiles, but it fades quickly, his eyes on the dish he's drying.

"Are you, Clayton?" I ask after a moment. "Okay, I mean."

He nods. "Yeah. Clinton is doing everything he can to help me while also taking care of his own expenses, but it's rough, you know? Football is expensive. Mac's mom lets me do some chores around the house for a little extra money, but it's not much, and I'm not old enough to get a job anywhere. At least, not at the places I've applied."

"I get that," I say. "Have you talked to Clinton about it?"

He shakes his head quickly, taking the heap of forks I just rinsed from my hand. "No, he's done so much, Skyler. I'll be fine. If I have to sit out a dance or hang back while my friends go to the movies, it won't be the end of the world." He shrugs. "Just four more years and I'll be out of Pittsburgh, anyway."

My heart breaks at his admission, not just because I don't want him to miss out on his high school experience but because he seems in such a rush to grow up.

"Come with me for a sec," I say, drying my hands on the soft gray dish towel before passing it to him.

He does the same, following me back through the house to the front foyer where my purse is hanging on the coat rack. I flip through it for my checkbook, scribbling one out for three-thousand dollars before handing it to him.

His eyes go wide, his head shaking before I can even speak. "I can't, Skyler, I can't take—"

"Yes, you can," I say, pushing it toward him again. "Look, I was a nerd in high school. Like, I had absolutely zero friends, and I couldn't wait to get out of there, just like how you feel right now. But looking back, I wish I would have taken more chances. I wish I would have gone to the dances and the games and been a part of the class instead of just walking across the stage with them as a stranger at the end of it all."

Clayton's eyes soften, and he finally takes the check, folding it once and tucking it in his back pocket.

"I want you to have fun, Clayton. I want you to enjoy high school, and Clinton would want the same thing. We can keep this between us, okay? That way he doesn't stress himself out thinking he's not doing enough and you don't have to worry about missing a dance. Everyone wins."

"What about you?"

"Meh," I say with a wave of my hand. "I'll just enter a local tournament and clean those suckers out one weekend. No big."

Clayton smiles, because he and I both know it *is* a big deal, but I don't care. I'd give anything to Clinton and his family, because they're my family, too.

"Thank you," he whispers.

"Anytime, Baby Bear," I answer, leaning in to give him a hug. He squeezes me tight, a softer version of the Bear Hug I love so much, and I smile into his chest, heart warm and full and happy to help. "Anytime."

***

Later that night, Clinton and I sneak onto the roof of the hotel we're staying at downtown, one I booked us with hotel credits I got as a prize in a tournament last semester. The bright, full moon is shrouded by low-hanging, gray, wispy clouds, setting an eerie yet beautiful setting as we polish off a twelve-pack.

"Okay," I say, cracking the top off my fifth beer just since we've been on the roof. Add this twelve pack to the drinks we had at Mac's house before we left, and I'm already three beers past drunk and going strong. "Never have I ever had a threesome."

Clinton grins, happily taking a drink from his own beer.

"Are you freaking kidding me?! Who, when?!"

"Freshman year," he answers with a shrug, as if having a threesome is commonplace. "I don't even know the girls' names. They were best friends, seniors, and it was on their bucket list before they graduated. I was happy to help them tick that one off."

I snort. "Oh, I'm sure you were. Your turn."

"Never have I ever done anal."

"*Really?*" I answer in surprise. "I mean, I haven't either, but I'm just shocked to hear those words come out of your mouth."

Clinton smirks again, reaching for his seventh and our last beer in the pack. "Well, girls aren't exactly jumping up and down to have nine inches shoved in their ass."

I choke on a laugh, spitting Bud Light out like a fountain in the process. "Oh, my God."

"You asked!"

We both laugh, and Clinton flicks the aluminum top with a pop and a fizz. "Okay, new game. Truth or Dare?"

I blow out a long breath, resting my back against the brick wall behind me, the only separator from us and a twenty-seven floor dive down to the earth. "Truth."

"Pussy."

"And a mighty pretty one, if I do say so myself."

Clinton laughs. "Okay, fine. Who are your conquests this semester?"

"Honestly?" I ask, taking another long pull from my can. "I don't have any. I mean, if I meet someone out one night and we're having fun, I'm not saying I wouldn't go home with him, but right now I'm just focusing on figuring my own shit out. You're the only guy in my life, Bear." I wink, nudging his knee with mine.

He chuckles, leaning forward to cross his arms over his legs. "Same here. Lacy shows up every now and then, but after Shawna..."

"I know."

I don't even make him finish his sentence, because I know more than maybe anyone how much that girl hurt him. He still loves her, still wants her, but after Family Weekend last semester, there's no going back.

"Why can't we just be sexually attracted to each other?" Clinton jokes. "We'd be set."

"I mean, I'm not *not* sexually attracted to you," I counter, words slurring a bit.

Clinton jerks his head up to look at me, eyes wide before they narrow again. "Are you fucking with me?"

My head is fuzzy, thoughts stumbling over one another as I mull it over. Clinton is hot and always has been. The first time I met him, I remember thinking I would absolutely be taking him home at the end of the night. But from the very beginning, we just fell so easily into our friendship, and became a sort of family.

Still, with his insanely stacked body and sexy-as-hell smile, it's impossible to not feel some sort of attraction to him. Even for me.

I swallow, finishing the last of my beer before crushing the can down and tossing it back into the empty case. "Truth or dare, Bear?"

He watches me, my pulse ticking up a bit as I wait for his answer. Clinton and I have never crossed the line between our friendship, and maybe it's just the beer, or maybe it's the way his dri-fit, black t-shirt hugs his massive arms, or the way he drags his teeth across his bottom lip, his eyes on mine, but the line feels blurry tonight.

"Dare," he finally answers.

My stomach drops, brain screaming at me that I'm completely insane, but I say it anyway.

"I dare you to kiss me."

The words barely leave my mouth before Clinton's hand is around my wrist, tugging me forward, my knees hitting the concrete on either side of his thighs as I straddle him. My breaths are erratic, tipsy mind trying to catch up, but it doesn't have time before his hands are in my hair, and then his mouth is on mine.

His lips are so soft, so big, so warm. They're lips I never thought I'd taste, lips that feel foreign as they trail down my jaw to my neck before he sucks the lobe of my ear between his teeth.

I roll my hips against him with a moan, gasping when his hands slide up my ribs under my shirt. His hands are so big they nearly encompass my entire rib cage, his thumbs touching as they graze their way up my stomach, the rest of his fingers wrapped around me. He could completely crush me if he wanted to, and in a way, I want him to.

With all nine inches.

I can't think straight, thoughts trying to fight their way through as I cross my arms and grab the ends of my shirt, flinging it to the side when it's over my head before kissing Clinton again.

I can't believe this is happening. I can't believe this is happening. Holy shit, this is happening.

Clinton flips us, ripping his own shirt off before falling down on top of me again. He traces the edge of my bra with his tongue, biting and sucking the skin of each swell before working his way back up to kiss me. Our breaths are fast and heavy, hands touching, bodies rolling, and when I feel like I'm at the edge of hysteria, he bites my neck hard.

And it's like that bite is tied to reality.

I burst out laughing, Clinton's mouth still on my neck. It's not a cute laugh, either. It's loud and obnoxious, more like a cackle than anything else, but I can't help it. When I realize I'm actually laughing, I flush with embarrassment, which only makes me laugh harder.

Clinton presses up to balance on his palms, eyeing me like I'm crazy before giving in to a fit of laughter, too.

"We are so drunk," I say through the giggles, eyes tearing up.

He laughs even harder, the sound deep and comfortable as he rolls to the side to lie down next to me, his hands grabbing for his stomach. He can't catch air, both of us hysterical.

"That felt so weird, didn't it?" he asks.

"SO weird," I agree, and we both break into another spell of laughter, ribs burning and eyes blurred with tears.

When we finally settle down, I lean into him and he tucks me under his arm, fingers playing with my hair as we watch the clouds float over the moon.

"I love you, Skyler," he says, tone serious.

"I know," I say, giving his middle a slight squeeze. "I love you, too."

"Thank you for this weekend. I finally feel a little like myself again."

"So, my best friend's back?"

He chuckles, kissing my forehead. "Back and better than ever, baby."

I smile with a sigh, closing my eyes and finally letting the booze take me under.

Mission accomplished.

Cassie

"Catch up, slow poke!" I call out behind me, zipping around a couple holding hands on the sidewalk leading to the Student Union. Grayson is trying to longboard for the first time, and I've finally discovered something he's not effortlessly amazing at.

It's oddly satisfying.

"I think my wheels are messed up," he hollers back, running off the sidewalk for the eighth time. He stumbles off the board, picking it up with a huff before jumping on again and pushing toward me.

"You sound like my big sister when I'd beat her at Mario Kart. 'It's the controller! The buttons are broken!'"

Grayson laughs, the loose strands from where his hair is tied back blowing in the breeze as he catches up to me. "You love this, don't you?"

"Just a little."

I stick my tongue out at him, and he launches toward me when we reach the mall where the dodgeball tournament is, tackling me into the grass. We roll a few times before he lands on top of me, brushing my hair from my face, his steel eyes looking right through me.

For a while he just stays here, eyes bouncing from my lips to my hair to my eyes before making another round. It's as if all the answers to every question he's ever asked are written behind the freckles on my cheeks, or weaved into my red hair, or hidden under my smile.

The butterflies that had been sleeping in my stomach slowly flutter to life as I look up at him, the sun rays framing his silhouette above me. Grayson laughs, tracing my jaw with his thumb before leaning down to take my lips with his. I let him kiss me slowly, not even a little concerned about being late to the dodgeball tournament.

"You're lucky you're so cute."

"I think that makes *you* the lucky one," I point out, pecking him on the lips again after he's pulled away.

Grayson grins, helping me stand, and then we both tuck our boards under our arms and make our way toward where the tournament is already beginning.

It's been a tough week for us, especially after Grayson had to bail on our date, which is a big reason why he's here in the first place. He knew he needed to make it up to me, so he entered the dodgeball tournament with a few of his buddies in the music program. It's the first effort he's truly made to be a part of my world, other than the Alpha Sigma concert, which was almost a disaster.

I've changed my schedule around to be at as many of his shows as I can be, whether he's just playing at Cup O' Joe's or at one of the swanky restaurants downtown. But when it comes to Greek events, Grayson usually rolls his eyes or makes jokes. I get it, it's silly to him, and I guess in the long run a dodgeball tournament benefitting our philanthropy probably doesn't seem as important as a show played in front of hundreds of people or a video shoot that goes viral on YouTube.

But it's important to me.

I know he's busy, and I know he has his own priorities, but it means a lot to me that he's moving me up the list. Even if he doesn't fully get it, he's here — and that's a step forward.

"I'm glad you're here," I say as he tucks me under the arm not carrying his board.

He presses a kiss into my hair. "Me, too. Hey," he says, pulling me to a stop at the edge of the first makeshift court. "I'm sorry I haven't been around as much as I should be. This summer just completely changed everything and I'm trying to figure out what it all means."

"I know." I nod, eyes on my feet, but he tilts my chin up.

"I'm going to be around more. I promise. This, us," he says, motioning between us before tapping my nose. "*You* are important to me."

I smile, leaning up on my tiptoes to kiss him before grabbing his hand. "Come on, let's go find your team."

It's a simple promise, one easy to make but hard to keep. In my heart I believe him, but my head screams for me not to touch the hot water that burned last time. But for now, for today, we're together. So, I focus on that as we walk hand-in-hand across the field.

Erin grabs me as soon as we reach the referee tent and latches on to my arm, shooting off a list of things she needs me to do with her eyes scanning her clipboard. Grayson kisses my cheek with a whispered *good luck* before jogging off to his first game, and then the tournament begins.

The rest of the day is a blur.

Erin has me running all over, bouncing back and forth between courts recording scores, filling water jugs, collecting entry money, and whatever else needs to be done. About the only breaks I get are to pee, reapply sunscreen, and chug down a cup of water of my own each time I refill the jugs.

Before I know it, the sun is setting, and we're in the last game of the tournament. But when I walk up to the board where the bracket is displayed and see the last two teams standing, I know the night is far from over.

Because one team is Grayson's. And the other is Adam's.

"You see me killing it out there, baby?" Grayson asks, picking me up in his arms slick with sweat and spinning me around.

I laugh when he drops my feet back to the ground, my eyes still on the scoreboard with a sickening feeling stirring low in my stomach.

But I fake it.

"You're in the final game!"

"Hell yeah, we are!" his friend, Malik, says. He high fives Grayson, running a hand over his short buzz cut. "Those Greek boys don't stand a chance against musicians. We're too good with our hands."

He adds that last line with a wink and a lewd gesture as a group of my sisters walk by, all of them giggling and helping his inflated ego. Suddenly, a bright red dodgeball is thrown directly at Malik and he catches it last second in his stomach with a grunt.

"That's a lot of talk for a future runner-up," Adam says, crossing his arms over his chest with a grin.

Sweat sticks his light-blue team t-shirt to his chest, outlining the ridges of every muscle. With the sleeves ripped off and the sides stretched to hang down low, my eyes can't move from the ebb and flow of his ribs as he catches his breath from the last game. When they finally trace their way back up to his eyes and they're staring back at me, I clear my throat, turning to Grayson.

"So much testosterone. You guys do know the trophy is just plastic, right?" I joke.

The left side of Grayson's mouth quirks up but falls quickly, his glare still pointed at Adam. "I don't care if it's made of paper. It'll be on my bookshelf tonight."

Adam scoffs, still grinning, not looking the least bit intimidated.

Just as Malik puffs his chest out, ready to fire back, Erin strolls up, pointing her glittery pen in all their faces. "Five minutes, boys. Save the shit talking for the game and go get water."

Grayson and Adam are still leering at each other, but Grayson shakes it off, leaning in to kiss my cheek. "Dinner with the winner after this?"

I laugh. "Sounds perfect."

He winks, glaring at Adam once more before jogging off behind Malik.

The tension is still thick once he's gone, and I tuck my hair behind my ears, but luckily Erin isn't the least bit fazed and is already rattling off the last of my duties for the evening. But I can't help but watch Adam as his jaw flexes and without another look in my direction, he heads in the opposite direction of Grayson, and my eyes follow him the entire way.

The last matchup is best three out of five, with the entire crowd of my sisters and other Greek students crowding around court one for the final showdown. The bleachers are full, Kappa Kappa Beta girls lining the boundary edge and cheering for the team they want to win. I just stand in the middle, pretending to help the line judge, not sure which outcome would make me happier. Or if either one will really make me happy at all.

I can feel it. The night isn't going to end well. I just don't know what will spark the bomb.

Each game makes my stomach hurt worse. Grayson's team wins the first and second one, and Adam's team wins the third. Every single guy on both teams is dripping with sweat by the start of the fourth game, and I'm biting my nails down to the beds, watching and overanalyzing the way I feel when things happen.

Grayson gets hit, I cringe. Adam gets hit, I feel like I'm watching a dog get kicked. Grayson's team wins, I smile and clap, all the while watching Adam with a pit in my stomach. Adam's team wins and I sigh with relief, all the while wondering what that means and why I feel it.

My sister once watched a football game between her two favorite teams — the school where she went to undergrad, and the school where she did her Masters. She said she felt sick watching and had no idea whom to cheer for. She thought she would be happy either way, but when her undergrad team won, she was more sad than happy. That's when she realized she felt more connected to her graduate school.

I didn't get it then, but now I do.

"We couldn't have asked for a better finale," Erin says as Adam's team clinches the fourth game. They're jumping up and down celebrating while Grayson huffs and huddles his team up to strategize. "These two teams are brutal. *And* we made it to game five. Here," she says, thrusting the brightly decorated donations bucket toward me. "Go make another round while the crowd is all amped up."

"On it."

I take the bucket from her hand and try to keep my mind busy as I walk up and down the bleachers collecting donations. The fifth and final game starts with my back turned to the court, and I try to keep it that way, wondering with every cheer and boo which team is winning.

But it doesn't take long before I'm standing back beside Erin, bucket full to the brim with donations, and all that's left to do is watch to see who wins.

I play with my hair as the game continues, twirling it around my fingers and chewing the inside of my cheek. Adam's team is down to only him and Jeremy, with Grayson still holding on to his entire team so far. But Jeremy catches two balls thrown at him at once, one in each hand, and with a roar from the crowd, Grayson's team is down to three.

Adam strikes Malik in the leg, and he curses the entire walk to the sideline, leaving only Grayson and Steven, a drummer from one of his friend's bands.

For a while the four circle each other, throwing balls and dodging them just the same, and it feels like there will never be a winner. But then Steven gets antsy, chucking his ball square at Jeremy who catches it easily. He laughs, holding up the ball in one hand with an oversized pouty lip aimed at Steven walking off the court, which earns him a hard ball to the ribs from Grayson.

And then there are two.

This can't get any worse.

"I feel nauseous," I whisper to Erin, but she just laughs, thinking I'm joking, thinking I'm so excited to see who wins. But I'm not. I'm dreading it. Because either way, I'm screwed.

Grayson and Adam tiptoe around each other for a long while — advancing on the line and then backing off, throwing balls at each other's feet and retreating back with eyes ready for the backfire shot. They're both too coordinated, too powerful, and now I'm convinced there really won't be a winner.

Would that be worse or better?

"They've got two minutes before time is called and we declare a tie," Erin says, eyes on the game clock. "That would be super anti-climactic."

Now we're both stressed, and when the clock ticks down to one minute remaining, Erin jumps into action, calling out to the crowd in the bleachers.

"Cheer for your favorite team! We need a winner! Let's count them down! Fifty-seven, fifty-six..."

She continues the chant, the rest of the crowd joining in, half of them screaming for Adam to throw his ball while the other half cheers Grayson's name. The two of them just watch each other, murderous, waiting for the other to make a move while they plan their own.

When the crowd reaches twenty, everyone is on their feet, counting down the clock and screaming even louder for someone to make a move. Then, almost as if in slow motion, Grayson takes three long, fast strides toward Adam, winding up his arm and launching his last ball straight at Adam's knees.

Adam jumps high into the air with a spiral kick, sending him up and over the ball, and when he lands on one foot his arm follows through like a sling shot, ball flying back toward Grayson before his other foot even hits the ground. It all happens so fast, I'm barely able to register the fact that he jumped over the ball, let alone that he sent his own back straight toward Grayson. Grayson's eyes widen at the rebound, too, and though he tries to dodge it, the ball grazes his hip as he bends away from it.

And with nine seconds left, Adam's team wins.

"FUCK!" Grayson roars, picking up the ball that hit him and launching it over the bleachers. No one notices but me, because everyone else is crowding the field to congratulate Adam's team. Erin announces them the winner over the loudspeaker as music plays, the tournament officially over, and I slowly make my way toward Grayson.

He just stands there with his hands on his head, breaths heavy and lips in a flat line as he watches Adam's team celebrate on the other side of the foul line. Malik, Steven, and the rest of the team clap him on the shoulder, dispersing after one of my sisters hands them their silver medals.

"Hey," I say softly when I reach him. I leave my arms crossed over my middle, afraid to touch him yet. "You okay?"

"It's bullshit," Grayson spits, thrusting his hands toward the other team. "Adam was out like twice and the refs didn't call it."

I smile, stepping into him and threading my arms around his slick neck. "The controller buttons are broken," I tease, but he pulls my arms off of him, still scowling.

"It's not fair. It's all rigged for the Greek system. No way would they let a bunch of GDIs win."

GDI is code for *God Damned Independents,* or non-Greeks. I didn't know what it meant until Skyler explained it to me at Ralph's once, and I'm surprised Grayson knows the term at all.

"I'm sorry, babe. Let's just get out of here, okay?"

But before the words are even out of my mouth, Adam jogs over, hand outstretched toward Grayson.

"Hey, man," he says, wide grin on his face. "Good game. Seriously. Your team was smart and it could have gone either way there at the end."

Grayson eyes Adam's hand, but doesn't reach out to shake it.

Adam waits a moment before shrugging, letting his hand drop and turning to face me. My knees nearly buckle at his bright smile, the widest I've seen it all semester, pointed directly at me like a blinding pair of headlights. "So, where do you want to eat? Dinner with the winner, right?"

I roll my eyes at the tease, but when Grayson shoves Adam hard, stepping between the two of us, my hands fly to my mouth with a gasp.

"Back the fuck off, Brooks, before you get more than just a dodgeball to the face."

Adam shoves him back. "Calm down, it was a fucking joke."

"Yeah, well, I'm not laughing. No one is going to dinner with my girl but me."

"That right?" Adam says, stepping forward until he's chest to chest with Grayson. "Because if I recall correctly it was me who had dinner with her when you were too busy playing guitar for your little groupies to take her on a date."

Grayson growls and shoves Adam again and I step between them, pushing my hands hard into each of their chests.

"STOP IT!"

They both pause, chests heaving against my hands, eyes hard on each other and noses flaring.

"It was just a joke," I say to Grayson, who's eyes widen as Adam snickers from the other end. I turn on him next. "And you already won, so how about you go gloat somewhere else and stop being an asshole."

"I tried to shake his hand!" Adam defends.

"Yeah, and then made a joke about taking my girlfriend to dinner."

"Wasn't joking the other night, but then again you weren't around, were you?"

Tossing my hands up with a sigh, I grab my backpack and longboard from behind the referee stand, strapping on the bag and fighting against the urge to punch them both.

"I give up. If you two want to compare dick sizes all night, be my guest. But I'm going to dinner." They both take a step forward and I hold up a hand. "*Alone.*"

And with that, I drop my board to the sidewalk and kick off, leaving them both standing there as equal losers in my eyes.

***

I take my time at dinner, calling Skyler and asking her if she can meet me. She had to miss the dodgeball tournament for a local poker tournament downtown, but she's finished when I call her, so we meet at Tizzy's Tacos.

Two tacos, one bag of chips, and an hour of venting later, and I feel marginally better.

I don't really tell her about Adam, mostly because no one on campus knows about what happened between us last semester, but I do tell her about Grayson. She listens, eating her burrito and offering advice around mouthfuls when appropriate. Even still, nothing is solved when we finish.

So, I take the long route home, zigging and zagging my board across campus, pausing to sit and reflect at the pond by the Student Union. When it's nearly midnight I finally give up on trying to feel better and make my way toward the house. With Bo dropping out unexpectedly last semester, I don't even have a roommate to go home to.

Ashlei is sitting on the front porch steps when I roll up to the house, and she lights up when she sees me.

"Hey, you've got a visitor."

I cock one eyebrow. "A visitor? At midnight?"

She nods, biting her lip with a mischievous smile. "Mmm-hmm. I helped them sneak in. Just... be quiet. And have fun."

With that little nugget of vagueness and a giggle, she hops off the steps and skips inside, leaving me standing in the open door behind her.

Tiptoeing up the stairs with my heart thundering under my ribs, my mind races with what—or rather, *whom*—I'll find in my bedroom. If Ashlei had to sneak them in, it's definitely a guy, but the only question is... which one?

The fact that I even have to ask myself that sends a surge of guilt through me.

As pissed as I am at Adam for making an already tense situation worse earlier at the game, part of me wants to thank him. He finally said what I had yet to fully express to Grayson — he wasn't there for me when I needed him. All week I had looked forward to that date, and when it had all went up in flames, Adam had been the one there putting out the fire.

But Adam isn't mine, either.

Even if I had chosen him over Grayson last semester, if I had given him the chance he'd begged for at formal, I would have ended up with the same disappointment. He's drowning in his new responsibilities as president, just like he thought he would be. I knew he wouldn't have time for me, for us, and Grayson had given me every part of himself last semester.

So, was it fair of me to be upset with him now? He's chasing a dream he's had his entire life. Shouldn't I support that? I know he cares about me, and I care about him. So what if it's not always easy?

With my hand on the doorknob to my bedroom, I realize I don't want to see either one of them on the other side. I'm still mad at the way they acted. And I still have absolutely zero grip on how I'm feeling.

But it doesn't matter, because one of them is waiting. So, with a deep breath, I twist the knob and push through.

And then my breath catches.

My entire room is covered in small candles, bathing my bed in a soft golden light. And as the door closes behind me and I gently drop my longboard and backpack to the ground, my eyes find Grayson's.

He's sitting on my desk chair beside my bed, in only his boxer briefs, hair damp like he's freshly showered and guitar strapped across his chest. He plucks a few chords as he watches me, brows bent inward, tail between his legs.

"Cassie," he starts, the chords finding more of a melody as he speaks. "I am so, so sorry. Not just for being a sore loser earlier and causing a scene at your event, but for making you feel like our time together doesn't matter to me. I should have been there for our date."

I shake my head, opening my mouth to tell him I understand and that he couldn't have missed that show, but he cuts me off.

"No. No excuses, no bullshit about a show or my agent or whatever. I should have been there. And this is my promise to you that from here on out, I will be."

He motions for me to sit on the bed and I do, hands folded together and squeezed between my knees as he keeps his eyes on me and strums out a beautiful song.

It's an original, one that feels like he just wrote it — just for me — and I hang on to every word as he sings to me. It's a song about being scared, about falling in love, about finding who he is in a time when he's not even sure which way is up. And, finally, I get it.

It's not about his music, or about me — it's about him. Grayson is growing into himself, and with that comes figuring out how to balance it all. He's finally getting everything he's worked for and now he's not sure how to handle it. But he tells me with his music how much he cares, and how he's sorry, and he promises to do better, though I realize in that moment it doesn't get much better than him.

When he thumbs out the last note of the song, I reach for him, sliding his guitar strap up and over his head and placing it gently beside the chair before straddling him. I thread my hands behind his neck, fingers playing with the soft tendrils of hair there as my eyes search his.

"That was beautiful."

He swallows, framing my face with one large hand, his thumb running the length of my jaw. "Not as beautiful as you."

Grayson's eyes flick to my lips, and slowly, as if he doesn't think he deserves to, he pulls me into him until his lips are pressed against my own. He kisses me patiently at first, soft and hesitantly, but when I roll my hips against him and tug on his hair, he groans, kissing me harder, with more need, more passion.

And for the rest of the night, that's how he apologizes — with a kiss, a lick, a suck, a touch. And I accept with a sigh, a moan, an arch, a *yes*. He promises me more with his hands on my waist, and I remind him he's always enough with my mouth on his skin.

I still want to wait to go all the way, and Grayson respects it, bringing me to ecstasy without taking me past my comfort zone. He shows me how much he wants me with every single movement and I show him, too, touching him in new ways, tasting him for the first time.

When we're both spent, holding each other as our breaths even out and the dawn begins to break, a light feather of realization floats down slowly in my heart.

I'm falling in love with Grayson Anderson.

I only hope he's there to catch me when I do.

Jess

"Being a girl is the absolute fucking worst!"

I flail around on my bed, kicking up the covers and swinging my arms like a toddler as Ashlei chuckles from her front row seat to my pity show. She's perched on the edge of Skyler's bed, sitting on her hands, shaking her head as I detail every thought I've had in my pea brain the past two weeks since Jarrett left.

"He's probably just busy with his job, Jess. He treated you like an absolute queen when he was here," she points out. "It's not like he went home and said, 'Fuck that bitch.'"

"I don't know," I counter, sitting up on the bed and tucking my knees up to my chin. "He did go out to Ralph's with all of us, and we are certifiably insane."

"I thought it was a pretty low-key night."

"Skyler kept hiding under tables, grabbing people's legs and shouting, 'SHARK ATTACK!'" I deadpan.

Ashlei snorts.

"And Bear jumped up on stage and started dry-humping the DJ while begging him to play *Party in the U.S.A.*"

"Okay, so maybe we scared him off and he took a hammer to his phone so you couldn't trace him."

I bury my face in my hands, something between a groan and a whine squeaking through my lips.

"I'm kidding," Ashlei says, hopping down from Skyler's bed to come sit next to me. She places a hand on my back and rubs gently. "Seriously, he's crazy about you. Just chill."

"He hasn't called me since he left two weeks ago, Lei." I sniff, leaning my cheek on my knee to look up at her. "His texts have been short, if he even texts back at all. How the hell am I supposed to do this long-distance thing with communication like that?"

She frowns, rubbing my back in response.

"What if he's cheating on me," I whisper, stomach turning and threatening to forfeit the pizza I shoved inside it earlier. "Oh, God, I couldn't handle that. I couldn't."

"He's not cheating on you."

"How do you know?"

"I only had to spend one night with the two of you to see there's not another girl in this world who has his attention, babe. Just try to relax. He'll call, and you'll talk it out, and it'll be fine. Okay?"

I nod, cheek rubbing against my knee pathetically. "Tell me about your internship. I've sucked up enough of the air in the room."

Ashlei smiles. "It's been amazing so far. I feel like I'm really standing out..." Her voice fades off a little, a slight blush hitting her cheeks. "The CEO knows my name, so I guess that's saying something, right?"

"Uh, yeah. That's amazing. I'm so proud of you! What's it like, being an intern?"

"Thank you," she says, and then blows out a short breath. "And it's exhausting. The other interns are pretty slack-ish when it comes to the account we've been assigned, but I don't want to be just another intern, so I'm busting my ass to stand out."

"You always stand out," I say, nudging her. "Why do you think you're my best friend? I don't just let any basic bitch have that title."

Ashlei scrunches her nose with a grin right as my phone vibrates, and I panic, tossing the covers off the bed until I find it hiding underneath.

"Oh, my God, it's him."

"Answer it. I'm going down the hall to Ex's room, just come get me when you're done."

I nod, not even taking my eyes off the screen with his name and a picture of us on the beach filling it. When the door closes behind Ashlei, I take a deep breath and answer.

"Hello?"

"Hey, babe," Jarrett says on a breath. "God, it's good to hear your voice."

I flop back into the sheets, head hitting my pillow with a *poof.* "Jarrett, where have you been? You haven't called in two weeks... and you've barely been texting me."

"I know," he answers with a sigh. I imagine him running a hand over his smooth head, his elbows propped on his knees. "I know. I'm so sorry. Jenny and I got assigned to a project as soon as the wheels on my plane home touched down and we've been drowning in work ever since. I've barely had time to sleep."

I try to swallow but come up dry, my stomach twisting.

"Jess?"

"Yeah," I croak, fighting the tears pooling in my eyes. My emotions are more unstable than an alcoholic at an open bar.

"Talk to me."

"What am I supposed to say right now?" I ask, sitting up in bed. "Two weeks ago you were telling me I'm everything you want, and then you go back to New York and you're so *busy* with *Jenny* that you can't call me or answer a text with more than one word?" I try masking the pain in my voice, but I know it's ringing out loud and clear. "I mean, what is there to even say?"

"Please, try to understand," he begs, exhausted. "This job is important to me, to my career, and yes, I made a choice to throw myself into this project and do it right. Just because I was busy for a couple of weeks doesn't mean I love you any less."

"You've been spending every hour of every day for the past two weeks with another woman," I point out. "How would you feel if the shoe was on the opposite foot? What if I said I'd been too busy *studying* with Bear to call you."

"I'd say, 'Bear studies?'"

"Not funny."

Jarrett sighs. "Jenny is just my co-worker, Jess. I'm going to have to work with females sometimes, and your jealousy doesn't make this distance thing any easier."

"Wow," I say with a click of my tongue.

"What happened to what we talked about when I was there? Where's the trust? Where's the belief that we can make it?"

"Belief is like a flower, Jarrett, and mine hasn't been watered for two weeks."

Jarrett's voice is muffled, as if he's running a hand over his mouth before responding. "I can't do this. I don't have time for it. I'm stressed out, I've barely slept, I don't even have time to *eat* right now, unless you count coffee as a food item."

I pinch the bridge of my nose, shaking my head as we both sit silent on the phone. *He can't do this. It's over. We're done.*

"So... you're breaking up with me?"

"*What?*" Jarrett laughs. "No, God, no. Are you breaking up with me?"

"No!" I cry quickly, letting the tears run.

Jarrett sighs into the other end. "I wish I could hold you right now. I'm sorry, Jess. Look, what about this..." His voice trails off and I hear the clicking of keys in the background. "Come see me for Thanksgiving. We can do the holiday in the city, and you can meet Jenny and everyone else I work with. I want you to be a part of this journey, too. I want you to understand, and to feel comfortable." He pauses. "And more than anything, I want you to see that even when I'm gone, even when you're not with me, I never stop loving you."

I choke on a sob, smiling through it. "I love you, too. I'm sorry."

"Don't be. I promise to call you more. I owe you that. I know this is hard."

"I don't want to be the needy girlfriend," I say with a sniff. "I don't want to stress you out more than you already are. Just... I don't know, send me a text while you're pooping."

He chuckles. "I can do that."

"And book that plane ticket."

"Already done. I'll forward you the itinerary."

I wipe my nose with the back of my wrist, heartbeat settling back to a steady rate as I pull the covers over my legs. "Sorry I'm such a hot mess."

There's a soft laugh on the other end, and I'm comforted by the sound, by the clarity the phone call has brought me.

"As long as you're my hot mess, you'll never hear me complain."

EPISODE 4

Bear

"I just heard two girls reprimanding their drunk friend in the bathroom because she admitted to spitting instead of swallowing," my Little, Josh, says as he stumbles back up to the bar at Ralph's.

"What a time to be alive."

"I poked my head inside and tried to get her number."

"Which one?" I ask, sliding him his beer and shot glass to continue power hour. One shot of beer every sixty seconds, cued by the DJ changing the song playing.

"Honestly? Whichever one answered."

I laugh, cheers-ing my shot glass full of beer toward him as the song changes before throwing it back.

It feels good to be at Ralph's, surrounded by my brothers who are all trying their best to make our probation situation not suck. They seem to have really listened to me when I went off about keeping our letters alive. Ever since then, we've all been focused on doing what we can for our philanthropy, showing support at other Greek functions even if we can't participate, and of course, partying anywhere and everywhere we're allowed to. Ralph's is basically the Omega Chi house now, and on power hour night, anything can happen.

Josh whistles, his eyes on someone over my shoulder. "Damn, Skyler. How are you going to show up looking that fine and not let me take you out?"

I turn, smiling at my best friend as she rolls her eyes and slides onto the barstool next to me. Her long chestnut hair is down and straight, eyes framed by dark shadow and thick mascara, and legs on full display in the tiny ripped-up jean shorts she's wearing. She paired it with a Guns N' Roses t-shirt cropped at her midriff, and I don't blame Josh for wishing she'd give him a chance.

Skyler is a catch. Any man with eyes can see it. Even me, which is probably why I drunkenly made out with her on a roof in Pittsburgh a month ago before we both burst into hysterical laughter. We're just too close to fuck, and I didn't even know that was a thing until her. I've never been genuine friends with a girl, but with Skyler, it's effortless. I love her, I care about her, and I want to be around her all the time. But for the first time, we crossed that line into something more, and we both found out quickly that it just isn't us.

We're best friends — *just* friends — and I love that about us.

I don't have to pretend with Skyler, and she doesn't have to pretend with me. I don't know what I'd do without her.

"You're seventeen minutes behind," I say, sliding a shot glass toward her and pouring a fresh beer from the pitcher. "Time to catch up."

"Is that a challenge?"

I just raise my eyebrows in response, throwing my hands up like the decision is all hers. And of course, because she's Skyler Fucking Thorne, she chugs the full cup before refilling it again, just in time to throw back a shot when the song changes again.

For the first time since the semester started, everything finally feels okay. Sure, it would be better if we weren't on probation, but for what the situation is, everything is pretty great. And when

Lacy walks through the door at the end of power hour, I can't help but feel like my lucky stars are all aligned.

Josh is nearly passed out on the bar, talking to a pineapple cup that some freshman girl on her first social left behind, and Skyler is dancing with her sisters near the DJ. Lacy eyes me when she walks in, smirking in my direction, but of course she doesn't come to me first. No, I'll be her stop at the end of the night, which is exactly how I want it.

That is, until another girl catches my eye.

Suddenly, the room is spinning, and it takes every ounce of willpower I have left not to throw up. I wish it was the beer making my stomach turn, but it's the pair of bright green eyes framed by dark glasses staring at me from across the bar.

Shawna's violet hair is twisted into a messy knot on top of her head, the way she used to style it after we'd fucked for hours under the sheets. She's dressed simple in a tight, short black dress — one that hugs her curves, highlighting the barbells of her nipple piercings through the thin fabric. My balls ache at just the slight view I have of them across the dark room, and the fact that she still has an effect on me makes my jaw clench.

With a shake of my head, I down the rest of my beer, slamming the plastic cup on the bar before making a beeline across the dance floor for Lacy. Her friend points over her shoulder at me, and she turns just in time for me to catch her mouth with mine.

She's surprised at first, hands frozen at her side, but when I slide my tongue inside her mouth and pull her body flush against mine, she relaxes, wrapping her arms around my neck. Alcohol swims in my system, mixing with the adrenaline and anger, stirring up a dangerous concoction as Lacy bites my lower lip between her teeth.

I slide my hands down her small back, cupping her ass and pulling until she grinds against my leg. She shudders at the friction, a breathy *fuck* escaping her lips before I silence her again. And when I kiss down her neck, my eyes find Shawna again, satisfaction flooding through when I see she's still watching.

She grabs her purse, saying something to the group of girls she's with before eyeing me like a homeless puppy again. I push Lacy back, standing tall, not taking my eyes off Shawna as she pushes her way through the crowd toward the door.

Lacy watches me confused, but when her gaze follows mine, she shakes her head before facing me again. "Un-fucking-believable."

She slaps me hard across the face, which zaps my attention back to her, but luckily Shawna is already gone and doesn't see the aftermath. I stretch out my jaw, rubbing it with one hand, heavy eyes finding Lacy again. I wish I cared. I wish I was sorry.

"Look, I've been cool with our arrangement. You want to fuck at two in the morning and not have to wake up to me the next day? Fine. But *that*," she says, motioning to where Shawna just disappeared out the door and back to me. "That's not okay. You may like to fuck me like I don't have feelings, Bear, but I'm still a goddamn human."

She eyes me like a rodent, shaking her head before turning on her heel and stomping away, and I'm left watching the door and knowing only two things are true in this moment.

One, I am an asshole.

And two, I'm not over Shawna Ballentine. No matter how much I want to be.

Erin

October in South Florida is a funny thing.

Most days it still feels like summer, the sun hot, the air like a wet blanket slapping you in the face when you step out of the blessed air conditioning and onto the sidewalk to walk to class. Coffee shops are selling pumpkin-flavored lattes and football season is in full swing, yet it's still impossible for it to feel like fall in Florida because the weather hasn't changed.

But some days, some years, a miracle happens, and a "cool front" blows in after an afternoon shower, giving Florida residents a few days of weather *just* cool enough to wear jeans and a light scarf or sleeves past the elbow.

Today is one of those days, and Jess and I are taking full advantage, sitting outside at one of our favorite brunch restaurants just off campus, both of us wearing designer boots that hit our knees and drinking warm coffee — without sweating.

"I wish this weather would last," Jess says with a sigh, crossing one leg over the other as our waitress tops off our coffee. "It finally feels a little like fall."

I chuckle. "We don't *get* a fall. We get two to three months between summers where it's slightly less miserable. And usually that's January into March."

"Oh, don't get me wrong," Jess clarifies, dumping two spoonfuls of sugar into her fresh coffee. "I love Florida weather, especially in the spring, but it's nice to break out the cute winter clothes from time to time."

"Well, you get a whole fourteen days combined of that in a year, I'd say. So enjoy."

"At least we don't have to worry about it not being warm enough for the Alpha Sigma Halloween party," Jess says. "I can't believe they stepped up. I guess when Omega Chi is suspended, someone has to."

I nod. "Yeah, and Adam has had something to prove since he rushed as a freshman. Between the concert that's now one of the biggest fall events and all the parties he's been throwing to supplement the O Chi's being out of commission? He's definitely making a name for the fraternity."

"What are we dressing up as? We need to get creative, since it's a boat party."

"Mermaids?" I suggest, taking a sip of my black coffee.

"Nah, everyone will do that. Too obvious."

"Skyler and Bear are doing *Baywatch.*"

Jess rolls her eyes. "Of course they are. And those hot fuckers will actually be able to pull it off, too."

"We could do beach Barbies."

She scrunches her nose, holding her cup of coffee to her lips again. I watch the steam rise while she contemplates.

"Oh!" She snaps. "What if we did like the Chiquita banana girl? You know, we could all wear different color swim suits, like I wear orange, you yellow, Ashlei pink, Cassie green, and then we make cute head wraps with fake fruit the same color. We could pick all that up at the craft store."

"I'm pretty sure Cassie is doing a couples' costume with Grayson, but I'm in! And I'm sure Lei would be, too."

"Ugh," Jess groans. "Cassie and Grayson are disgustingly cute."

"Don't you hate them?"

"So much."

I laugh. "But you and Jarrett are pretty gross, too."

At that she smiles, stirring her coffee with her eyes on the spoon. "Yeah, I just wish we could be gross more often."

"How's that going? The long distance?"

Jess sighs. "It's fine. We had a rough patch after he left. He got caught up in a work project and it was like pulling teeth to get him to text back or call me for a couple of weeks. But we talked it out and he promised to be better at communicating, which he has been. And he's flying me up to see him for Thanksgiving."

"Oh, my God! Thanksgiving in the city!"

"I know!" Jess squeals. "I'm so excited. And he's going to introduce me to his whole team, too. I can't wait."

"It'll be here before you know it," I say, my stomach twisting with a strange but familiar longing. It never fails to surprise me when Kip Jackson pops into my head, especially because it's usually at the most peculiar of times. Like now, hearing about Jess and Jarrett, wondering if Kip and I could have made it long distance if I wouldn't have gone completely batshit crazy.

I loved him. I know that now, and I think I knew it then, but it was my first time being in love. I was fresh out of high school, on my way to college, and I was so insecure that thoughts of him cheating on me or leaving me overtook every other rational thought I had. I would go through his phone, scream at him when he didn't come over when he said he would...

We were just kids, and the first two months of our summer affair had been absolute bliss. He was working for my grandparents on harvest in Kansas and I was there visiting. It was almost too perfect, right out of a country song or a rom-com movie.

But then I'd ruined it.

And now, I'll never know if what we had was real, if it could have survived had I nurtured it instead of torched it with a flame thrower.

The loud purr of an engine shakes me from my thoughts and Jess and I both turn in the direction of it, our smiles falling when we see who's responsible for the noise.

Landon pulls into a parking spot at the pizza place next door in a brand new Corvette Stingray, his brothers crowding him with whistles and cheers. I swallow, eyes narrowing as Jess scoffs.

"Looks like *someone's* overcompensating."

"Clearly."

Jess stirs her coffee again, taking a sip before settling her eyes on me. "What ever happened between you two, anyway?"

My stomach lurches again, this time for a completely different reason, but I don't miss a beat. "Meh, he was fun for formal, but I've got too much to focus on this semester. Elections are coming up soon."

"Mmm," Jess says with a nod. "You ready to take your Big's place as president? Continue the family tradition?"

I wink. "Born ready."

"I figured. I swear it's actually in your blood. If you do half of what you did as recruitment chair as president, our sorority is going to be unstoppable."

"That's the plan."

Jess watches me for a minute, smiling. "I'm really proud of you, Ex. Seriously."

My heart warms, and I reach for her hand, squeezing it gently in response.

For a while we just sit and drink our coffee, but my eyes keep wandering to Landon and his brothers, all still crowded around the new car. But I'm not glaring or huffing — no, I'm smiling. Because where I was stumped on how to exact my revenge before, the answer now is crystal clear, thanks to what I would bet money on is a gift from Mommy and Daddy.

Suddenly, I have a plan, one I know will hit him where it hurts.

Now, the only question is — when?

Adam

"Ouch!" I yelp, hopping on one foot as the other throbs from me slamming it against the corner of my dresser. "Fuck. Shit. Fuck."

I hop over to my bed, stripping my clothes off and leaving them on the floor before crawling under the sheets. The slight cold front that blew in last week is definitely gone, evidenced by the sweat glossing my lower back, so I kick the sheets off and lie staring up at my ceiling, watching the tiles turn like the hands of a clock.

I'm drunk.

It's been a while since I could say that, and now that the multiple shots of Fireball are swimming in my stomach as the room spins, I forget why I wanted this in the first place.

I've been stressed since the semester started. Between my new role as president, the concert, and Omega Chi being suspended, I've had my hands full with everything from philanthropy work and nationals relations to keg parties and now, hosting the biggest Halloween bash PSU has ever seen. We've rented out twenty boats with captains to take us out to the sand bar, all drinks included, and every Greek student on campus is stoked.

Except me.

It's not that I'm not excited everyone is buzzing about Alpha Sigma, or that we're going to throw a killer party, but balancing all of it has been more of a struggle than I thought.

So, Jeremy made me take a night off, dragged me to Ralph's, and got me completely shit-faced. *You need a break*, he'd said. But what he couldn't have known is that every time I drink, I *do* forget about the presidency for a while, but I never forget about her.

Being busy helps me keep my mind off Cassie. It's one of the reasons I try not to take a break or slow down, even when the stress is high. It's easier to pretend what I told her last semester about being busy with the presidency is true than to admit to myself that it's not.

I never would have been too busy for her, but now it doesn't matter. I lost my chance.

Sober me knows that.

Drunk me begs to differ.

There isn't even one small part of me that tries to argue or reason with my drunk logic as I blindly reach for my phone on the bedside table. It's just past one in the morning, but that doesn't stop me either. I thumb through my contacts and find hers easily, a picture of us from Spring Break last year filling the screen as I switch to speaker phone.

The rings fill my room, and I close my eyes, trying to stop the room from spinning for just one second. This is stupid. I know that. But all I can do is hope she answers.

When the ringing stops, my eyes flutter open again.

"Hello?" she whispers.

I smile at the sound of her voice, placing the phone on my chest and resting my hands under my head. "What was your favorite game to play as a kid?"

There's a pause on the other end, then the slight sound of papers shuffling.

"Adam, it's one o' clock in the morning."

"And you're awake."

She laughs. "Well, yes. I'm studying. But why are you calling me to ask me about my childhood at one in the morning?"

"I've just been thinking about it. When I was a kid, I used to love to ride my bike. I'd get on it the second I got off the school bus and ride it until the street lights came on. I also used to play this game with my grandpa, before he passed, where he would name a country and I'd have to figure out the capitol, the native language, and the political makeup. Then he'd teach me common phrases in that language. I know how to say *hello, goodbye, thank you, please,* and *do you speak English?* in fourteen different languages."

"You're drunk," Cassie answers simply.

"Maybe. Humor me, anyway."

She sighs, more shuffling noises coming from her end. "Hold on. Let me go outside."

I listen as she packs up her bag, imagining her bright red hair piled on top of her head, her flashcards spread out on the table at the Greek library. After a moment, I hear the soft sound of a door closing, and then the familiar quiet rush from the fountain in the background.

"Operation," she says finally.

"Like the board game with the guy and the big red nose and all the open body parts?"

She laughs. "That's the one. Even back then, I knew I wanted to be a doctor. My mom said I used to write letters to Hasbro telling them their game was broken, because I absolutely did *not* touch the metal sides but I was buzzed. And I went on to tell them how frustrating that is for a steady surgeon hand and that the surgery room should be free of such awful noises. I suggested they use something softer, like a cat meowing or a bird chirp to indicate the sides had been touched."

A laugh barrels out of me. "Why am I not surprised?"

"So, how do you say *hello* in Portuguese?"

"Olá," I answer. "Or oi, or alô."

"At least you got some useful information out of your favorite game. I only learned how to curse at a young age. Stupid Hasbro."

I chuckle, but then silence falls over both of us. I got her to answer, but now that I have her on the phone, the sharp ache in my stomach is rolling strong. Because I don't really have her, but I want her so bad it hurts.

"Here's another one in Portuguese. Desculpe."

"And what does that mean?" she asks.

I swallow, inching up to lean against my headboard and balancing my phone in one hand. "I'm sorry."

She doesn't respond, so I continue.

"I really was just making a joke at the dodgeball tournament, but I also knew what I was doing. I wanted to get under Grayson's skin, and I was gloating off the win. I was an asshole, and you didn't deserve to be stuck in the middle of that."

"Thank you," she whispers, then she sighs. "I'm sorry, too. I shouldn't have had dinner with you the night he bailed on me. We're a couple, we're going to have fights, and I shouldn't have found comfort in you when he let me down. That's not fair to him." She pauses. "Or to you."

The knife in my side twists in a little deeper, and I shift at the pain.

"But I want to be there for you... I always have been. We're friends."

"I know," she answers quickly.

"But he doesn't want us to be, does he?" I finish for her.

"Can you blame him?"

I can't, but I hate it all the same, so I don't answer her question.

"Have you slept with him?"

She scoffs. "Wow. That is none of your business, Adam."

"I'm sorry. Shit, I'm sorry, don't hang up." I pinch the bridge of my nose, trying to shake my way through the drunken fog clouding my head. "I just... I can't stop thinking about you. Not since that night on Spring Break. And I know you're with Grayson, and I know you care about him, but it doesn't change the fact that I want you."

She inhales a stiff breath. "Adam..."

"I want to know everything about you, Cassie. Everything. Your fears, your secrets, your hopes, and your dreams. I want to know how many kids you want or if you even want any at all. Do you want to travel the world or stay in the same small town forever? And who are you when no one is around, when it's just you and your favorite playlist? What's playing, who's singing to you when you're sad, and who do you dance to when you're happy?"

There's a sniff on the other end, but I can't stop.

"I want to know all of that and more. Does he? Does he know the real you? Does he want to?"

I hear her sniff again and my heart clenches. Sitting up straighter in bed, I close my eyes, trying to reach for her across the airwaves. Does she feel me? Is she reaching for me, too?

My answer comes in the form of a soft click, and then the sniffling is gone, and the fountain is muted, and it's just me alone in my bed again. In the morning, I'll be hungover.

In more ways than one.

Ashlei

My sisters and I used to play a game with our pencils when we were younger. We'd grab them by the eraser and wiggle them slightly in the air, pencil held horizontally, and it'd give the illusion that the pencil was made of rubber. We'd watch that pencil for hours, giggling and pretending like we were magicians.

I'm playing that game right now, though not by choice, because Mr. Church just asked me to stay back after an all-staff meeting. As the room clears, everyone casting eyes back in my direction, the pencil in my hand is just as rubbery as my knees taking shaky steps toward where he's seated at the head of the long board table. I tuck it inside my notebook as I take the seat next to him.

It's been six weeks since the Alpha Sigma concert. Six weeks since the CEO of the event agency I intern for "bought" me for a date at a Greek function at a school he's ten years too old to go to. Six weeks with no explanation as to why, with no mention of it at all — with not a single word said to me *period.*

But that six-week silence was just broken.

In front of the entire agency.

I force a steady breath as the last person exits, the door shutting behind them with a soft click as Mr. Church turns to face me. It's hard to keep my eyes trained on his, to not notice the hard edges of his jaw or the perfect slope of his nose as he smiles easily, as if the two of us being alone in the same room doesn't faze him in the least bit.

"I know you probably have some work to wrap up before you get out of here for the weekend, so I'll try to make this quick," he starts, his posture relaxed as he kicks back a little in his chair, unfastening the two buttons on his cobalt blue suit jacket. It falls open, exposing his crisp white dress shirt beneath it as he steeples his fingers, eyes still locked on me. "You did a great job at the event pitch meeting with *Bare•ly* last week."

I swallow, ankles crossed and hands holding tight to the portfolio notebook balanced in my lap. "Thank you, Mr. Church. That means a lot to me."

His eyes spark a little when I say his name. "I wasn't the only one impressed. Mrs. Delure spoke with your manager earlier this week to get more of the details hammered out for the event, including the lead event planner, and she asked specifically for you."

My mouth falls slack. "She... are you serious?"

"I am."

For a second I just stare at him, but then I laugh, covering my wide smile with my hand as I shake my head. "I can't believe that."

Mr. Church chuckles, too. "Neither could your manager, which is why she came to me to ask if it was even possible. We've never had an intern in such an influential role before. She's worried you might not be prepared to do the job effectively."

My smile falters. "Oh..."

"I, however, am not."

My eyes find his then, and they're like lasers piercing straight through me. It's as if every secret

I've ever hidden, every dark thought I've ever had is easily accessible to him. But he doesn't look away. He leans in closer.

"You made an impression on me in that elevator, Miss Daniels, and every day since. You can do this. And that's why I told your manager to make you the lead event planner. You'll have a team of three — two associates and one other intern. We've never done this before, and you're going to be met with resistance. I know you can handle it, but before I announce it to the staff, I need to know *you* know it, too."

I tighten my grip around my notebook, knuckles white from the force as my heart thumps like a kick drum under my ribs. I think of the other associates on the project, of how they've already turned their noses up at me when I've excelled. My manager said they're just threatened, but with this news, I know I'd have a new, larger target on my back.

But I didn't come here to make friends. I came here to learn, to prove myself, and to stand out.

I want to be the best, and I won't get there without taking risks.

"I'm ready. I can do this, Mr. Church."

He smiles, kicking back in his chair again. "That's what I hoped you'd say. I'll send the email on Monday. I'm going to have to explain why we're letting an intern take the lead event planner role, but with Mrs. Delure asking for you by name, it should be easy to do. And if anyone gives you a problem over it, just come to me."

I blush, tucking my hair behind one ear. "No offense, Mr. Church, but running to tattle to the CEO probably won't earn me any respect points. I'll be okay. I'm no stranger to gossip or bullying," I add with a laugh. "I've got pretty thick skin."

He watches me, tapping his steepled index fingers together. "I don't doubt that."

I've never been so pinned by a gaze before. I physically *can't* move, can't speak, can't do anything other than stare back at him, wishing I could read his mind.

"Do you have plans tomorrow?"

At that I laugh. "Honestly? Don't judge me, but I plan on staying in bed all day. We finally have a Saturday without a sorority event and I have two months' worth of sleep to catch up on."

Mr. Church smiles. "Would you consider getting out of bed around two if I promised to have you home in time to get a full eight-hour rest?"

Wait.

Did he just say have me home? As in, he would be taking me somewhere?

I just stare at him, finally blinking after what I'm sure is a full minute.

He cocks an eyebrow. "The auto racing date? I do believe I was the highest bidder."

I'm still staring. What am I even supposed to say? I want to ask him why he did it, why he hasn't mentioned it until now, and more than anything, I want to know how it's even remotely appropriate for him to spend a Saturday with an intern.

Because I know it's not.

And maybe I should say no. Maybe I should politely decline, thank him for his donation and hand him his tickets to the auto racing place, insisting he ask someone else to accompany him.

But I don't do any of that.

"Okay."

His other eyebrow shoots up to join the first before a grin breaks on his stunning face. "Okay, then. May I pick you up?"

I just nod, the room suddenly too hot, and I stand to end our meeting. But when I do, the pencil I'd tucked into my notebook spills onto the floor. We both bend down at the same time to retrieve it, our noses just inches apart as our fingers brush.

We both pause, his hand on the pencil and mine still over his. When he looks up at me, I meet his gaze, holding it there with unanswered questions until his eyes flick to my lips and back again.

Clearing his throat, he hands me the pencil and stands, helping me up. "Tomorrow at noon. Kappa Kappa Beta house, correct?"

Something between an *uh-huh* and a squeak leaves my lips and I dash out the door, trying to calm my walk as I make my way through the office with multiple pairs of eyes watching the entire way. I can't catch my breath, my heart threatening to sprint right out of my chest and across the office. I just agreed to a date with my CEO. Tomorrow.

In what world is that ever a good idea?

***

Just as promised, Mr. Church pulls up at twelve on the dot in his Acura NSX. I'm thankful for the mid-seventies, not-a-cloud-in-the-sky weather, because all of my sisters are at the beach getting their tans ready for Halloween. If they were home, they'd all be lined up at the windows as soon as they heard that engine purr.

I'm still questioning my decision the entire walk down the sidewalk to his car, one thumb hooked into the strap of my purse to keep me from playing with my hair. I spent the entire morning figuring out what to wear, curling my hair to perfection, and applying my makeup to look natural but flawless. I tried on more outfits than I care to admit before I landed on my favorite black body suit, slim cut with thin spaghetti straps and a deep v-neck. Paired with a bleach-washed pair of ripped-up shorts and my white Keds, I feel sexy without being obvious. I topped it off with a thin, gold headband and reflective aviator glasses, which I'm thankful for when Mr. Church steps out of the car.

He rounds the car, opening my door and waiting with one hand still on the handle as I take in his casual attire. I'm so used to seeing him in a full-on suit ensemble that I almost don't believe it's him in the fitted light jeans and simple white t-shirt, covered only by an unbuttoned red and blue flannel shirt cuffed at his forearms.

I stop when I reach him, swallowing past the sticky knot in my throat. "Hi."

"Glad to see you were able to get out of your pajamas," he teases, holding his hand for mine to help me inside the car. When I'm safely in, he shuts the door behind me, jogging around to his side.

I marvel at the white and black leather interior, the stitching wide and bold, the entire world muted inside his car that costs more than my entire tuition. I let my eyes wander the dashboard and middle console controls, anything to keep from noticing how ridiculously sexy he looks kicked back in the driver seat with one hand on the wheel and the other resting easy on his thigh as he turns to me.

"Ready?"

I laugh out a shaky breath. "Ready as I'll ever be, Mr. Church."

He shakes his head with a grin. "You can call me Brandon, if you'd like," he adds quickly.

"Brandon," I say, trying it out with a nod. But then I crack out a laugh. "Feels kind of weird."

A shadow passes over his dark eyes. "I'm sure the more you say it, the more comfortable it will feel."

And there it is again. The look. The piercing gaze that strips me of any reply other than an open mouth as he throws the car in drive.

I keep my hand tucked under my thighs the entire drive to the auto racing venue, mostly looking out the window as we breeze through town. Wale's *Ambition* album beats through the speakers, Mr. Church — er, *Brandon* — rapping along, thumbing to the beat of the bass on his steering wheel.

Every now and then, he casts a glance in my direction, but neither of us makes conversation. When we pull into the parking lot, he doesn't find a spot, but drives through the back alley and up to a locked gate instead.

I frown, scanning the empty race track inside. "Are they open today?"

"Sort of," Brandon answers, nodding to a young man inside the gate as he removes the locks and motions for Brandon to drive forward.

We pull in slowly, right onto the massive track, and Brandon puts the car in park just before the white and black checkered painted block on the track. He steps out first, smiling at my dumbfounded expression as he rounds the car to open my door.

"I don't understand," I say as I take his hand and step out. "Why is no one else here?"

"Ah, Mr. Church!" a voice calls from our right. I turn to find an older man with dark hair, peppered with gray, jogging toward us. He's dressed in khaki pants and a navy blue polo, his skin a deep shade of olive and smile bright under his mustache. "So thrilled to have you back. Always a pleasure."

Brandon meets his extended hand with a firm shake. "Pleasure's all mine, Rodalfo. This is Ashlei Daniels," he adds, motioning to me. Rodalfo takes my hand and lifts it to his lips for a kiss. "She'll be riding shotgun today."

"Welcome, Ashlei," he says, squeezing my hand once more before releasing it. "I would say you are a lucky lady to ride beside Mr. Church in such a beautiful car, but perhaps it is Mr. Church who is the lucky one."

Rodalfo winks as a blush sweeps my cheeks, and I'm not sure if it's that blush or Rodalfo's comments responsible for the smile on Brandon's face.

"Well, the track is cleared for the entire day, so she's all yours for as long as you want her. I'll have the boys run out helmets, if you'd like?"

"Please," Brandon answers, and Rodalfo jogs off again, leaving us alone.

"I didn't realize those tickets were so powerful," I say, crossing my arms and waiting for an explanation.

Brandon just shrugs. "Let's just say they know me here."

"So, why pay ten thousand dollars for the tickets, then?" I press.

He smiles, bullet gray Ray Bans lifting on his cheeks with the expression. "I wasn't bidding on the tickets."

I falter, surprised by his boldness. It's the first time he's admitted that he wanted this date with me. After six weeks of silence, I don't know how to even begin to respond.

But with his next comment, I don't have to.

"It was for charity, remember?" He grins even wider, taking two helmets from the same young man who opened the gate for us and handing me the smaller one. "Hope you're ready for a ride, Miss Daniels."

I can't help but smile back, shaking my head before pulling the helmet on. "Show me what you got, *Brandon*."

He bellows out a laugh, leading me back to the car.

As we both strap in, I adjust my helmet tighter, nerves hitting me at the realization that we're about to be speeding around the track. "Is it safe to drive your car? Don't they have like... extra seatbelts and padding in the ones they race here?"

Brandon ignites the engine, raising a brow in my direction. "Don't you trust me?"

"Should I?"

The words shoot out before I can stop them, and Brandon watches me, debating the answer. "I think that's something you have to decide for yourself."

And with that, he faces forward, revving the engine as the lights change colors in front of us. My breath hitches when they turn green and I don't have time to exhale before I'm flattened against the seat.

For the first five seconds, I completely freak out.

Internally, that is, because I can't manage a breath, let alone a scream as we race from zero to over one-hundred miles per hour in less time than it takes to spell my name. It's almost painful as the laws of physics work against us, crushing my bones into the seat, my body seemingly left on the starting line instead of inside the car.

When we round the first corner of the track, we decelerate just long enough for me to catch my breath.

And then, I laugh.

Not a cute giggle or a soft chuckle, but a full-on, head-thrown-back, tears-in-my-eyes laugh. Adrenaline rushes through me at the speed of light, crashing with my nerves to ignite an uncontrollable sense of euphoria.

Brandon glances at me quickly before smiling, too, and punches the gas again. I wrap my hands around the chest strap of my seatbelt, trying to focus on the track as we fly down it. The bleachers on the sidelines blur together as we pass, almost like we're traveling through time and space. It's the most exhilarating experience I've ever had.

And I've done cocaine, so that's saying something.

I can't stop laughing, and I don't — not until I lose track of how many laps we've done and Brandon slows us to a stop at the starting line again.

"That was incredible!" I scream, even though I don't have to anymore. My ears are ringing, everything still muted. I tear my helmet off and shake my hair out, smiling wide at Brandon as he removes his, too.

"Have fun?"

"Are you *kidding*?! Let's go again!"

He laughs, removing his sunglasses to wipe them clean with his shirt. Then he lifts his chocolate eyes to mine. "Wanna drive?"

***

It was hard to get me off the track after that.

We spent the entire afternoon and well into the evening taking turns driving, competing on who could get to one-hundred the fastest or who had the fastest zero-to-sixty or lap time. I couldn't believe he trusted me enough to let me drive his car, especially at such high speeds, but he didn't seem to be even the slightest bit worried.

When my stomach was growling loud enough for him to hear it, I begrudgingly said goodbye to Rodalfo and his crew, and we grabbed a quick bite at a café nearby before heading back to campus.

We shared casual conversation over dinner, mostly about my pole dancing since he'd been curious since I'd mentioned it. I left out all the drama, of course, but it was nice to talk to someone about one of my passions. It made me realize how much I missed it, and now I find myself wanting to look up local classes again, even if just for weekend workouts.

But the drive back to campus was quiet, leaving my brain room to run over the long list of thoughts I've been avoiding all day — like why the CEO of a successful event agency wanted to take his intern on a date, or what this means, or what we do next. Was it even really a date? Did he really just donate to charity as a nice gesture? And if it was something more... does he expect something now? It doesn't make sense, why a powerful, sexy-as-hell man like him would risk his reputation and more to get me in bed.

And that's all it could possibly be, right?

I'm a full ten years younger than he is. Other than my body, I'm not sure what else I could offer him that another, older, more mature woman couldn't.

I shake the thoughts from my head as Brandon pulls around to the back of the sorority house, finding a parking spot under a large tree covered in Spanish moss before cutting the engine. When the silence envelopes us, the nerves that had disappeared on the race track are back again, and I sit on my hands to keep from wringing them together.

"Thank you for joining me today," he says, voice low and steady as he eyes me from the driver seat.

"Thanks for letting me drive," I reply with a laugh. "It was fun."

I swallow as his eyes rake over me, all the way down to where my hands are tucked under my thighs before they find mine again. "I make you nervous."

Blowing out a breath, I shake my head. "You confuse me."

"How so?"

My stomach turns, hands forming fists between the seat and my skin. "The auction, not talking to me for over a month, the lead event planner position... and now today? I just..." My voice fades as I glance at him through my lashes. "What are we doing, Mr. Church?"

He inhales a stiff breath at his last name rolling off my lips, lips that his eyes are on now. "I don't know what I was thinking sending Mykayla to the auction. I came to my senses that weekend and decided ignoring you was best for both of us."

"What changed?"

His Adam's apple bobs hard in his throat as he leans in closer, hand reaching forward until his fingertips brush my jaw. I freeze at the touch, his skin like a shock to my entire system, zipping a hot line of wire straight down between my clenched thighs.

"I discovered you're impossible to ignore."

His lips find mine in a frenzy, hot and wet and demanding as I struggle to catch my breath. But my hands are already fisting in his hair, pulling him closer. I moan into his kiss, crawling over the middle console to straddle him as his hands wrap around my ribs. When I roll my hips, friction sparking between us, we both groan and Brandon sucks my lip between his teeth, biting hard enough to draw blood.

Kissing him is intoxicating, like the strongest shot of tequila injected straight into a blood vein. My head spins with every touch of his skin on mine, blurring right and wrong together, no and yes as one. But when his hands yank at my body suit, unclasping the buttons that fasten it below my shorts and pulling the fabric free, I clasp my own over his wrists to stop him.

I break our kiss, our foreheads still pressed together, heavy breaths escaping our parted lips and fogging up the windows as his hands grip the freshly exposed skin of my hips.

"I'm sorry," I murmur, reaching blindly over the console for my purse and flinging his door open before crawling out of his lap. My body aches at the loss of his touch as soon as I'm free of him, but I focus on placing one foot in front of the other, blocking out everything else. He doesn't chase me and I don't look back, my heart pounding mercilessly in my ears as I race inside the house.

I push through the back kitchen door, shutting it quickly and pressing my back against it before sliding down to the ground. Pinching my eyes shut, I shake my head, still caught up in the feel of him while my brain battles to remind me why what I just did was a very, very bad move.

But he kissed me first.

I sigh, burying my face in my hands.

What the fuck am I doing?

Bear

"Sounds like my little brother," I say to Mac's mom with a laugh, adjusting the phone between my opposite shoulder and ear as I lay out the rest of my costume on my bed. She just finished telling me how he had two girls fighting over who he'd take to homecoming, so he told them whoever could kiss better would be the lucky lady on his arm.

Little bastard got two, steaming hot kisses from girls trying to prove something, and then invited them both to go, anyway.

And they agreed.

"He's something," she agrees with a chuckle of her own.

"Thank you again, Mrs. Harrison, for taking Clayton in and treating him like your own. I don't..." I pause, trying to find the words. "I'm not sure I'll ever be able to tell you what it means to me. To us."

"He's a good kid," she says easily. "Easy to love, and easy to care for. We wouldn't want him anywhere else but with us."

I smile, chest tightening, and distantly I wonder if my mom ever thinks about him — about any of us. I wonder where she is. The only reason I even know she's alive at all is because her and Carleton check in on his kids from time to time, long enough to send money or ask for it — depending on which side of the gambling ring they're on that day.

"What about you?" Mac's mom asks. "How is school?"

I rummage through my bathroom drawer for my suite mate's tanning oil, tossing it on the bed. "It's school. Classes are tough this semester, but luckily our fraternity is on probation, so I have more time to study."

She clucks her tongue. "I'm sure you're still finding ways to get in trouble."

"Dressing up as David Hasselhoff circa 1989 as we speak."

"Oh, God." She snorts. "Do I even want to know?"

"Skyler and I are dressing up as the *Baywatch* cast for a Halloween boat party today."

"That sounds like so much fun!" She sighs. "I'm really happy you have Skyler. And what she did for Clayton... I know he'll never forget it. She's a great friend, Clinton."

I frown, tossing my black Omega Chi sunglasses on the bed with the rest of my costume. "What do you mean?"

"Oh, my...she didn't tell you?" She sighs again, murmuring softly. "Humble on top of everything else."

"Tell me what?"

There's a pause, and for some reason my blood pressure ticks up a notch, like I'm about to hear something I don't want to, my body preparing me for bad news before my brain even thinks it's necessary.

"Clayton was in a rough place before your visit. My husband and I... well, we help him all that we can, and of course, you send him money every chance you get. And you worked the whole summer. But football is expensive, and he was going to have to make some tough decisions."

"He didn't tell me any of this," I shoot back. "Does he need money? I can... I'll get a job. I'll sell some stuff."

"You don't have to," she says quickly. "Skyler cut him a check, Clinton. She told him to chase his dreams and enjoy his high school years because she didn't get the chance to."

She keeps talking, telling me how much it was for, how they're holding the money and only giving him what he needs when he needs it. She tells me how Clayton is also looking for a job after football season ends, but I can't hear any of it over the ringing in my ears.

Skyler gave my little brother money, without telling me, without *asking* me if it was okay.

"Like I said," Mrs. Harrison says, snapping my attention back to her. "She's a great friend."

"Yeah," I clip. "I have to go. Please, tell Clayton to call me tomorrow."

"I will..." she says hesitantly, and before she can ask any questions, I end the call, gripping the phone hard in my fist.

I debate throwing it, but focus my rage on the person responsible instead of an inanimate object.

Everything is a blur as I walk to the Kappa Kappa Beta house, nostrils flaring the entire way. A small, quiet part of me tells me I'm probably overreacting, but the larger, screaming part reminds me that what Skyler did isn't okay. Maybe she had good intentions and just wanted to help, but Clayton is *my* brother, and my responsibility. I can take care of him without her help, and she knew I'd be upset by her helping, which is exactly why she didn't tell me.

I pound on the front door when I reach the house, working my clenched fists together as I wait for someone to answer. A girl I don't recognize, likely a new member, opens the door with wide eyes.

"Skyler. Now."

"Oh, I think she's getting ready for the Halloween party. Could you maybe—"

"NOW!" I roar, and she yelps, skittering off with the door open behind her.

A few other sisters pass concerned looks my way as they walk by, but eventually Skyler emerges, half-dressed in her *Baywatch* gear. She has her red one-piece on and half a face of makeup, her hair in a clip like she'd only begun to work on it.

Her brows pinch together when she sees me and she steps onto the porch with me, pulling the door closed behind her. "Bear? What's going on?"

"You gave Clayton three-thousand dollars?"

The words spit from my mouth like venom, and Skyler's face drains of color.

"Bear... listen, I just wanted to—"

"Help? Well, you should have fucking came to me first. He's my fucking brother and I can take care of him."

"I know you can. I never said you couldn't."

"Well, that's what you fucking implied by going behind my back like that."

She winces. "Come on, you know it wasn't like that."

"Wasn't it?" I challenge. "God, Skyler, you're so fucking selfish you can't even see it when you're in the wrong. There's a reason you didn't tell me, and it's because you *knew* I'd be pissed. And now that you're caught, all you can do is defend yourself. An apology wasn't even on your radar, was it?"

Skyler swallows, her eyes brimming with unshed tears.

"You call yourself my best friend, but best friends don't do this to each other." I shake my head, looking at the girl I thought I knew for what feels like the first time. "You should have come to me."

"I'm sorry," she quivers, but I just hold my hands up to stop her.

"It's too late for that now. Have fun at the party."

Without another look in her direction, I storm off the porch, feeling more alone than ever before.

Erin

I am way too sober to be balancing a huge wreath of fake fruit on my head.

The costumes Jess came up with for us turned out to be perfect, each of us able to pick out swim suits that complement our figures along with colors that look best on us. My tan is contrasted next to my bright yellow one-piece with a deep v-neck that goes all the way down to just between my hips, showing a little cleavage and my flat stomach. The arches of the fabric on the legs are high, too, giving my thighs and butt some action.

Although most people have no idea what we were going for and keep calling us "the Fanta girls," we look hot, and that's what matters most at a college Halloween party.

Well, usually.

I don't really care to draw attention to my body anymore, not when the desire to have someone touch it died right along with a part of me the night of formal last semester. I haven't gone a day without remembering that night, without reliving it — not since it happened. I wonder if there will ever be a day that I won't remember.

Shaking the thought from my head, I reach for my Bubba Keg from Spring Break last semester, taking a long pull from the straw as I kick back in my small beach chair. It's just water, but no one has to know that. I've done a pretty good job of evading shots up until this point, claiming I have to keep my head on straight and not party too hard with elections coming up soon. No one has pressed me.

The day is just as perfect as our costumes, the sun peeking in and out between fluffy white clouds as a breeze rolls onto the sandbar from the water. Hundreds of students litter the sand, some soaking up the sun while others play drinking games. All the Alpha Sigma boats are anchored down around the sandbar, swaying over the waves, loud music coming from each and every one of them. Half of the party is on the boats, the other half spilling out into the water and up onto the sandbar. Everyone is dressed up, having found ways to creatively turn classic Halloween costumes into beach wear, and even though it's just past two in the afternoon, most of the attendees are already smashed. The event turned out amazing, and I know Adam must be proud.

I want to be a president like that.

"The *Vamps and Tramps* boat is handing out Jell-O shots!" Jess screams excitedly, catching her breath from where she's jogged over from the other side of the sandbar. She reaches down for her own Bubba Keg in the chair next to me, draining it. "Come on. They're delicious."

She grabs my hand but I laugh, pulling back from her grasp. "Pass. Trying not to get completely tanked, remember?"

Jess pouts. "You don't even seem buzzed."

"Oh, I am," I lie, squinting my eyes before pushing my sunglasses up onto my head. "Drunk eyes. About to take a nap in this chair."

She laughs. "I'll probably do the same soon. Your tan is looking amazing, by the way."

Smiling, I put my sunglasses back on and nod toward where Ashlei and Skyler are playing a game of flip cup in the middle of the sandbar. "You should grab the other Fanta girls, though. Skyler can use all the shots she can stomach after what happened with Bear."

"Ugh, what the fuck was that, anyway? Skyler won't say a word about it."

"No idea," I answer. "But she's sad, so we should try to distract her with booze."

"My specialty," Jess says, wiggling her butt a little as she skips away. "You should at least come hang out on the boat!" she calls back behind her.

"Be there in a sec!"

I watch her run off, grabbing Ashlei and Skyler from their table on the way to the boat she'd pointed out. With a sigh, I reach for my phone, pulling up Kip's name before I know what I'm doing.

- Hey, stranger, long time no talk. -

I stare at the text, finger hovering over the send button. I'm not sure why it's him I want to text, or why he's the person I want to comfort me, or why I even need comforting at all. We haven't talked in almost four years, and I'm *fine*. Classes are going great, I recruited the best KKB class our school has seen, and I have a plan to get revenge on Landon.

But still I feel so... empty.

Numb.

I'm not myself, and I know I'm not the only one who's noticed it. And since I've pushed Clinton away and all the girls have their own drama to deal with, I've successfully isolated myself — especially after ditching out on my birthday.

And maybe this is for the best. Maybe, like my mom taught me, there's power in not leaning on anyone, in not exposing my weak spots.

No one knows what happened last semester other than Clinton, and I think he finally understands that I'm not going to talk about it. And I *do* feel marginally better each day... or at least, it's easier to pretend I do. Maybe this is my skin thickening, my scar healing even more, that shiny pink skin stretching and tightening to form a hard shell.

Every time I've given in before, I've been taught a lesson on why I shouldn't. Drinking and partying leads to bad decisions, which leads to horrific consequences. I don't want to experience them anymore.

And if that means being a loner, then so be it.

I have the presidency to focus on, anyway. In a little over a month my sisters will vote on who will take my Big's place, and if I have anything to do with it, there will be a clear choice.

Me.

So, instead of joining Jess, Ashlei and Skyler on the boat, I lean up to adjust the back of my chair and flip over onto my stomach to even out my tan.

Adam

Of course, she did.

That's the theme of the night, because even though I should be focusing on how kick ass the Alpha Sigma Halloween boat party turned out, I can't focus on anything or any*one* but Cassie.

Of course, she showed up to the boat dock with Grayson, and of course, they took the boat I *wasn't* on to get out to the sandbar. Of course, she wore a tight, incredibly sexy, white, two-piece swim suit, one that crosses over her chest in just the right way to remind me how hot that body of hers is, the one she usually hides under modest dresses and blouses. Of course, she dressed up as Cleopatra, complete with a golden headband that makes her green eyes even more distracting than usual. Of course, she stayed on the opposite end of the sandbar, cozying up with Grayson in a beach chair and tossing her head back like he was the funniest man in the whole goddamn world.

Of course, she did.

I've been trying to ignore her, trying to enjoy myself, but it's been largely unsuccessful. Play a game of beer pong, search out Cassie in the crowd. Judge the costume contest, watch Cassie dance with Grayson on the *Mummies and Mimosas* boat. Do a keg stand, hear Cassie's laugh from across the sandbar as she slides off one of the boat slides into the ocean.

It's maddening, especially since the last time I talked to her I made a complete and total ass of myself.

And the strangest thing is that all day, all I want is for her to come talk to me.

Until the exact moment she does.

"Hey, you," she says, wading out into the water to where I'm standing. The sun is starting to set, so all eyes are on the shoreline in the distance, watching as bright oranges and pinks streak the sky.

I swallow, tucking one hand into the pocket of my board shorts, the other holding my red plastic cup of beer. "Well, if it isn't Queen Cleopatra. Nice headdress." I tap the gold piece hanging over the bridge of her nose with my finger and she giggles.

"Thanks. And you're..." She pauses, eying my open collared, relaxed fit, white shirt tucked into my dark blue board shorts. A simple, red cloth belt separates the two, and a sword is fastened to my hip. "A rookie pirate?"

I laugh. "Prince Eric, but thanks for crushing my spirits."

"Prince Eric," she deadpans, and I shrug, offering her a sheepish smile. "A little late for that, don't you think?"

The weight of those words slam into my chest like a boulder, and I lift my cup to my lips instead of answering her, eyes back on the sunset. She dressed up as the Little Mermaid last year, and instead of dressing up as Prince Eric then, I'd chosen Danny Zuko from *Grease* to match Skyler.

"Having fun?" I ask after a moment.

"*So* much fun," she says, crossing her arms lightly over her middle and facing the sunset, too. "You really are making a name for Alpha Sigma, Adam. You should be proud."

I don't know why it hurts when she says those words, when she says anything, really. It's like hearing any semblance of love from her kills me, like it'd almost be easier if she just hated me.

"I am, of some things, at least. Not so much about that phone call I made." I peek at her in my peripheral.

"We all drunk dial sometimes," she answers easily, eyes still on the shoreline.

Grayson comes splashing through the water and picks Cassie up from behind, spinning her around as she kicks and squeals. "There's my queen!"

"Put me down, you animal," she teases.

When he drops her feet back into the water, she pecks him on the lips, and I tear my eyes away, thankful I have my sunglasses to hide behind.

"Hey, Brooks," Grayson says, as if he just saw me standing there. He's dressed as Mark Anthony, Cleopatra's one true love, and suddenly I feel a little foolish in my own costume. "Great party. Seriously. And, hey, no hard feelings about the dodgeball game. You guys won fair and square." He holds out his hand toward me. "Truce?"

I grit my teeth, wanting more than anything to smack his hand away and tell him to eat a dick, but I grab his hand and shake it firmly instead. "Yeah, man, and thanks."

He turns back to Cassie. "The first boat is about to head back to shore," he says, twisting a strand of her hair between two fingers. "I was thinking maybe we should be on it... take this party back to my place." He runs those same two fingers across her collarbone and over her shoulder, trailing them all the way down her arm before tucking them into the band of her swimsuit bottoms.

Chugging the rest of my beer, I keep my eyes on the sun, now starting to dip beneath the clouds just above the horizon. Every muscle in my entire body is tense, so much so that I'm sure I'll wake up sore in the morning.

"Yeah," she answers breathily, and my cup cracks in my grip. "Just give me a minute. I'll meet you by our beach chairs?"

I feel Grayson's stare drilling into the side of my head, but ignore it, pretending like I'm not listening to their conversation. "Okay. But hurry, they're loading people up now."

"I'll be right there," she promises, kissing him once more before he's wading back up to the sandbar.

I don't know how long we stand there, silent, her eyes on me and mine focused in the distance. In my mind it's both forever and just a split second, so I'm not sure which it really is before I completely lose all common sense and rationality.

"You're going to sleep with him."

It's not a question. I don't want her to answer, but she does, anyway.

"He's my boyfriend, Adam..."

I grit my teeth so hard a sharp pain rips through my jaw and I crush the empty cup in my hand, the broken edges of the plastic digging into my palm.

"Don't," I say, finally turning to face her. "Don't leave with him, Cassie."

Her bottom lip is pinned between her teeth and I use every ounce of willpower I have left to keep from pulling her into me and sucking that lip between mine, instead. She feels like mine, even when she's not. And I don't know how to make that go away. Or, if I even want to.

"How can you ask that of me?"

I push a heavy breath through my nose, pinching the bridge of it with a shake of my head. "I don't know. I guess the real answer is that I can't, not really, but I am anyway."

"I think I love him," she whispers, watching where she's wringing her hands together before looking up at me through dark lashes.

I scrub a hand over my face, feeling so out of control I want to scream. It's like being trapped in a slow-motion car crash with a broken seatbelt.

"I don't know what to say to that."

She scoffs, dropping her hand to her thigh with a slap. "Unbelievable." She shakes her head. "You don't have to say a damn thing to that, Adam, because it doesn't matter what you think about it. It's how I feel. And, yes, I'm leaving with him tonight. That's where your need to know ends."

"He doesn't deserve you," I spit, desperate, latching onto anything I think will make her stay, knowing nothing will.

"And you do?" she asks on a laugh. Stepping closer, she lowers her voice. "This isn't your decision to make, Adam. You don't own me."

I press my lips into a hard line, and when she turns for the shore I involuntarily reach for her, just late enough to not even brush her skin before she's too far gone. I watch her leave, watch her walk all the way up to the shore, to Grayson, who wraps her in his arms with a long kiss. His stare lands on me afterward, making sure I saw, and then he tucks her under his arm and steers her toward the boat loading up to leave.

And just before she steps on, Cassie looks back at me, and what I find in her eyes almost knocks me to my knees. Because it's not love, or apology — but pity, and I feel it all the way to my core.

She knows it as well as I do.

It's *her* who owns me.

***

There are only five yachts left on the sandbar by the time midnight hits, and the captains we hired to drive tell us we have one hour left before they need to take us in. Not that I need another hour to get tanked, because I landed there roughly twenty minutes after Cassie was gone.

A little beer sloshes out of my cup and into the water below as I take a drink, elbows resting on the rail at the back of the *Gin and Jack-O-Lantern* yacht. I watch the shore with heavy eyes, knowing she's there somewhere, in bed with another man. I don't want to torture myself, don't want to be pathetic, but I'm powerless to change the way I feel — at least for the night.

So, I let it happen, let the longing fill me from the inside out, suffocating to the point of barely breathing.

Who needs air anyway, right?

"You're looking very Hamlet for someone who just hosted the best party of the year."

Skyler slides up next to me, stealing my beer from my hand and lifting it to her lips. My hand is still molded to the shape of the cup even though it's gone now, and I hold it out over the rail, the shore lights blurring a bit as I turn to face her.

"Hi, stranger."

She smiles. "Hi, yourself."

Skyler and I broke up on civil terms last semester, even going so far as to fuck one last time before we called it quits. Still, we've barely spoken since, not even sharing more than a few "likes" on social media over the summer and no more than two words since school started back.

I can't explain why, but breath comes a little easier with her beside me.

"You're not a Fanta girl like the rest of your crew," I observe, eyeing the red Spandex one-piece painted on her body.

"Baywatch," she answers on a sigh. "Bear was supposed to be my David Hasselhoff, but he's not talking to me as of twelve hours ago, so..."

"What happened?"

She scrunches her nose. "I don't really want to talk about it, honestly. If that's okay."

I nod, stealing my beer back and taking a pull. For a while we just stand there together, listening to the water lap against the back of the boat. The party seems to have died down a little, but there's a small bonfire in the middle of the sandbar, and everyone who's still conscious is gathered around it. Everyone but me and Skyler, anyway.

"So, how have you been?" she asks, breaking the silence. "I see you're kicking ass at president, just like we all knew you would."

I give her a crooked smile, eyes still on the shore. "It's keeping me busy just like I thought it would, but I'm happy," I lie.

Skyler nods. "I get that. I'm pretty much in an exclusive relationship with poker."

"Is he at least good in bed?"

She snorts. "I wish. How about you, you find any time to date or at least have a little fun between throwing all your awesome parties and philanthropy events?"

"I barely find time to shower, let alone date."

Skyler laughs.

"Besides, I doubt there's a single girl out there who would be okay to show up at odd hours of the night, fuck, and then leave. Not without feeling used or demanding a cuddle session, first."

"No time to cuddle either, Brooks?" she teases.

I smile, taking another drink from my cup before passing it to her. "Savage, I know."

"Why can't that be a thing, though?" she asks on a sigh. "Why is there this big stigma against casual sex. At the end of the day, we're animals. And we have needs. Is it so bad to find a release in someone without taking them to dinner first or making them breakfast after?"

"Right? Like what's wrong with catching a nice orgasm and then catching some Zs?"

Skyler tosses her head back on a laugh, and I chuckle, too, distracted from thoughts of Cassie, at least temporarily.

"I miss you," she says, still smiling as her hair blows behind her in the soft breeze.

I nudge her. "Miss you, too."

Skyler is still watching me, and when I turn to meet her gaze, my eyes drop to where her tongue is wetting her lips.

A rush of memories floods through me all at once — Skyler spread out in my sheets, my hand between her thighs, her nails raking down my back. I flick my gaze back to hers and find hooded eyes, watching me, waiting.

The next thing I know we're stumbling inside the yacht, fumbling our way down the stairs into the bottom cabin, a tangle of arms and mouths and hands. I slam her against the door in the bottom cabin as soon as the door is shut and locked behind us.

"Just tonight, no one needs to know," she says, sliding the straps of her one-piece off her shoulders and peeling it down to the floor. She kisses me hard as soon as she's naked, hiking one leg up over my thigh.

I run my hand down between her spread legs, brushing her wet center just enough to earn a soft moan from her lips. "Just tonight. No breakfast."

She laughs into my mouth, spinning until I'm the one pressed against the door. "I hate eggs, anyway." And with that, she drops to her knees, pulling at the strings on my board shorts as I make quick work of the buttons on my shirt, tossing it somewhere into the dark. I don't even know where we are or what kind of room it is. It's pitch black, no windows, just the two of us feeling and touching and tasting.

Every breath is amplified as I kick out of my shorts once she drops them to my ankles, and before I can even prepare for it, her mouth is wrapped around my cock.

"Oh, fuck," I groan as she rolls her tongue over the crown before sliding her lips down to my base. I've never met a girl who gives better head than Skyler Thorne, and I'm immediately reminded of that fact as one hand grabs my balls and she pulls me all the way to the back of her throat.

I'm thankful for the alcohol coating my system, because otherwise I likely would have come right then.

Fisting my hands in her hair, I let her take the lead, head hitting the door behind me with a *thunk* as my drunken senses are overwhelmed with the way her mouth feels. When she starts using her hand in sync with her mouth, it's too much. I reach for her arms blindly, pulling her up until our lips are sealed together again.

Even though it's been months since I've touched her, she still feels familiar — a little like home, a little like my favorite vacation spot. I reach down for the backs of her thighs and lift, letting her wrap herself around me as I stumble forward into the darkness for something to fuck her on. There's a clamor of dishes when we hit a counter, and it's then I realize we're in a small kitchen.

Perfect.

Skyler giggles and kisses down my neck as I feel my way along the countertop. Finding a flat-top stove completely clear, I slide her up onto it, leaning her back and thrusting two fingers deep inside her wet pussy as soon as my lips take hers.

She cries out, hooking one leg over my shoulder to give me better access as I pull my fingers out and slide them back in. Her nails grab at my neck, my back, pulling me closer, wanting more, and I'm all too eager to deliver. I push my fingers in deeper, sucking her lip between my teeth and wiggling my fingertips deep inside, hitting the spot that used to always send her tumbling.

"Oh, God, yes," she pants, breaking our kiss and whispering her pleas into my ear. "Deeper, yes."

I growl, thrusting deeper, and she clenches around me, biting my shoulder to muffle her moans as she comes on my fingers.

It's such a powerful feeling, making someone else fall apart, and I revel in it, pulling her to stand before spinning her around and bending her over the stovetop. I slap her ass, more than ready to fuck her, and it's only when I line up at her wet entrance that I realize I don't have a condom.

"Fuck," I curse, dropping my head to her back. "I, uh… I wasn't exactly prepared for you tonight."

Skyler laughs, spinning to face me again before kissing me hard. "I could say the same. Nice to know you still remember what buttons to push."

She runs her tongue along my bottom lip before reaching down between us to wrap her hand around my shaft. She pumps long and slow, gripping me firmly in her small hands as I thrust into her.

And then she drops to her knees again.

But in that exact moment, my mind decides to be a dick again, because I can't help but wonder if Cassie is on her knees right now, too.

I try to shake her from my thoughts, try to clear them, but it's useless once she's in that space again.

Skyler keeps working me, dropping her mouth to my tip and swirling her tongue around and around. And I know it's Skyler down there, but I can't help but feel in the darkness like it could be Cassie. Imagining it's her hands on my shaft meeting her perfect little mouth, that it's her moan vibrating over my cock as she takes me deep in her throat — it's all it takes to push me to the edge.

I grunt out my release, fighting the urge to call out Cassie's name as I come in Skyler's mouth. But she's all I see. She's all I feel. She's all I want.

When I'm finished, Skyler uses my arms to climb her way back to standing, swallowing like a champ and giggling as I come down from my high. "I have no idea where any of our clothes are."

I laugh at that, feeling through the darkness for my board shorts. When I find them, I dig in the pockets for the water-proof Ziploc bag my phone is in and click on the flashlight, helping Skyler locate her bathing suit.

We get dressed quickly, both of us still smiling, but before I can open the door to lead us back upstairs Skyler pushes me back against the fridge, shoving her tongue in my mouth. She kisses me like a punctuation mark, like she needs to do it just in case I get any ideas. And when she pulls back, the light from my phone illuminates her just enough for me to catch the wink she throws.

"See you around, Brooks."

She bites her lip, shaking her head as she slips out the door and lets it close behind her.

And I just turn the flashlight off, letting the darkness consume me.

Ashlei

"You killed that!" Mykayla whisper yells at me as the last few of our colleagues leave the boardroom. Two of them, Kimberly and Sam, watch me with narrowed eyes as they mumble to each other, and Mykayla follows my gaze to them. "Don't let them get to you. Jealousy is a virus, babe, and those two are sick as hell."

She laughs at her own joke, adjusting her breasts in the tight dress she's wearing before collecting her papers and binder from the table.

"But seriously, that was awesome. No wonder they made you lead event planner. If you're not careful, you might leave here with a job before you're ready for one," she says.

I rub my temples with my pointer and middle fingers, still feeling hungover even though the Alpha Sigma Halloween party was six days ago. "Thank you, Mykayla. Although if I did get offered a job, something tells me I wouldn't have any friends here."

"You'd have me," she reminds me cheerily.

When the table is clear, we turn out the lights in the boardroom and make our way back to the intern cubes, Mykayla chatting the entire way about the Halloween bar crawl she did over the weekend. I'm listening attentively until we round the corner by the break room and Brandon is walking our direction.

My breath catches at the sight of him, all suited up like I'm used to, but now that I've seen him outside of work, I can't help but long to see his arms in a casual white t-shirt.

Mykayla keeps talking, her voice muted to me now as my eyes stick like sap to Brandon. But he keeps his on the papers in his hands, shuffling through them as he passes right by us without so much as a glance up, and my heart sinks right along with my hope.

He hasn't said a word to me since our... whatever that was, and that was the weekend before Halloween. He still sent the email about me being the lead event planner on the *Bare•ly* project the following Monday when we came in, but not a word was said to me otherwise. Not that I can blame him much after I left him with a massive case of blue balls in the back of my sorority house.

But what was I supposed to do?

I panicked. I needed to think straight, to make sense of it all, and I'd even decided that I would tell him we couldn't do this. It was risky — for both of us.

It looked like I wouldn't have to tell him that, because he'd decided for us. But I wasn't so sure I liked the decision, now.

Being a girl sucks.

"Want to grab a drink after work?" Mykayla asks when we reach her reception desk, just before my cube. "It's Happy Hour down at The Lift."

I shake my head, pointing to the stack of binders in my arms. "I've got a hot date with a catalog of chair and linen choices."

She laughs. "Make sure you wear your sexiest bra for that."

"Already got it on." I wink, heading for my desk as Mykayla waves me away with a grin.

The rest of the afternoon passes quickly, which seems to be a pattern now that I've secured the lead event planner position. It's just past five when I wrap up the last email I needed to send and I power down my Mac with a yawn, packing up my oversized handbag before slinging it over my shoulder.

Mykayla is still at her desk when I pass by, and I call out a goodnight to her before rounding the corner toward the elevators. But before I can push the button, she stops me.

"I'm so glad I didn't miss you on your way out," she says, calling me over to her desk. "You're going to flip your shit when I tell you what just happened."

I force a smile, a little too tired to hear office gossip, but I adjust my bag on my shoulder and ask anyway. "What's that?"

"Okay, so, there's a huge event agency award conference in Atlanta every Thanksgiving. It's mostly for agencies in the southeast region, and I'm sure you can imagine, we clean up in pretty much every category. Mr. Church always attends, they usually have him give a keynote speech, and basically he just spends the holiday rubbing elbows with other big wigs in the event industry and bringing back any trends he thinks we should jump on. Anyway," she says, shaking her head with a wave of her hands. "That doesn't really matter. What *does* matter is that he usually goes alone, but this year he requested a plus one."

She looks at me expectantly, her bottom lip pinned between her teeth as she bounces in her chair. When I just offer a raised eyebrow, she leans forward over her desk.

"He requested *you*."

My heart stops, kicking back to life a few seconds later as I stare blankly back at Mykayla. "He did?"

She nods excitedly. "Mm-hmm. But I need an answer from you on whether or not you want to go. Like... well, pretty much like now. He's going to offer it to someone else if you decline. Which you should totally *not* do, if that was even an option in your mind. This has never happened before. It's a big opportunity."

I'm suddenly too aware of my posture, and I have the distinct feeling someone is watching me. When my eyes trail down the row of cubes to Brandon's office, he's watching me from the door, his dark eyes piercing a laser line straight to me. Mykayla goes over the dates and details, clicking through the information on her computer, but I keep my eyes on his.

"So, what do you think? Do you want to go or should I ask the next in line?"

I tear my eyes from Brandon's, swallowing past the wad of sandpaper in my throat. "Well, I guess I'd be stupid to say no."

She bounces again, a squeak escaping her mouth as she softly claps her little hands together. "I'm so excited for you! I'll tell him you've accepted. I hope you'll take a break from your hot date tonight to have a celebratory drink, because this is huge."

I try to smile, but it falls too quickly as I glance toward his office again. I try to make sense of the request, or of the look he's giving me now, but it's all I can do to hold tight to Mykayla's desk and not let my weak knees crash to the floor. The way he's watching me, I'm not sure if I should be excited or scared. His gaze is dark, hungry, and I feel it through my skin, my veins, all the way down to my bones.

I thank Mykayla, turning for the elevators again. When I look back at Brandon, he holds my gaze with his own before shutting his office door, leaving me to stare at the sleek metal door just as the elevator dings its arrival.

***

A few days later, I shove an abnormally large bite of salad in my mouth just as Jess blows through the kitchen door with a growl.

"Boys are the root of all evil, Lei," she says, tossing her phone onto the kitchen island. It slides across and hits my bowl with a *tink*, which causes her to pause and eye the contents. "Ew. Is that your dinner? Because if so, it personally offends me."

I laugh around my mouthful, swallowing before reaching for my water bottle. "Listen, I eat so horrifically at my internship all week that all I want when I get home is something without carbs and grease."

"You're not human."

"Tell me why boys are stupid today," I say, shoveling another mound of kale into my mouth and effectively changing the subject.

"Ugh," she huffs. "Jarrett had to postpone my trip to see him, so I'm not going up to New York for Thanksgiving anymore." She tries to hold her anger, but it slips, leaving a sadness in its place that makes me pause mid-bite and drop my fork back into my bowl. Jess is a pretty tough girl, especially when it comes to handling guys, so to see her with glossy hazel eyes and a wrinkle between her eyebrows makes my chest ache.

"Oh, Jess, I'm so sorry." I reach for her wrist, squeezing it once. "What happened?"

She shrugs, eyes on her hands as she picks at her deep red nail polish. "Work. What always happens?"

Nodding, I take another bite, trying to find the right words to soothe her. I know how important work can be to someone who has a drive and passion, someone who wants to succeed, but at the same time I can't imagine coming second to that. It takes someone who is really understanding and patient, someone who is secure in who they are and what they have with their significant other.

"Are you okay?" I finally ask.

As if those words snap her back into the kitchen with me, Jess lets out a long, loud breath, shaking her head. "Yeah, I am. I really am. I get it, and I know he didn't want to have to cancel. I'm just making the most of the situation," she adds, popping her hands on the counter before forcing a smile my way. "Which is why I was looking for you. Tell your parents you're not coming home for break. We're having a Friendsgiving."

I choke a little. "A what?"

"Friendsgiving! Oh, come on, like you haven't seen every episode of *Friends.*" She waves me off. "Anyway, I already tracked down the rest of the crew and they're all in. Erin, Skyler, Cassie. I even let her invite Grayson and convinced Bear to put aside his differences with Skyler, whatever the hell is going on there." We both exchange a look then. "Adam might come, too."

I clear my throat, which is suddenly dry. "Jess, I'm so sorry but... I can't come."

"Your parents will understand, dude. Just tell them the situation. They love me!"

"I know they do," I agree, playing with the soggy remains of my salad before pushing it away from me. "But it's not them. It's my internship."

She blinks.

"I got invited to go to a conference over the holiday, and it's a pretty big deal. Usually just our CEO goes, but he invited me along with him. I think..." I swallow. "I think I'm really making an impression on him."

That's one way to put it.

"Well, shit." Jess plops down on the bar stool next to me, dropping her head into her hands. "I can't even be mad at you for that."

I chuckle. "Sorry."

She sighs, sitting up again and turning to me with a smile. "It's okay. Really. That's awesome, Lei, and I'm really proud of you. I knew you were going to knock their socks off."

With that she grabs for her phone, checking the screen before huffing again and flipping it over to face down on the counter.

"Waiting for a text from Jarrett?"

She nods. "I love him so much. It scares the shit out of me because I legitimately feel crazy."

"Want me to play some Beyoncé so you can twerk it out to *Crazy in Love* and get it out of your system?"

"Shut up," she says on a laugh, but then she leans her head on my shoulder and I rest mine against hers, petting her hair. "Just tell me everything is going to be okay."

"Everything's going to be okay," I assure her, and maybe myself a little, too. Because in just a few short weeks, I'll be on a plane to Atlanta with my hot CEO. The same CEO who had his tongue in my mouth and his hands under my shirt two weeks ago.

I stare at my salad, suddenly craving something with a lot more anxiety-calming power.

"How do you feel about walking to Froggy's for a triple scoop cone?"

Jess hops down off her stool, tucking her phone into her back pocket as she points in my direction. "*Now* you're speaking my language."

And with that, we link arms and head out the back door, both of us hoping like hell that ice cream is the answer to all our problems.

EPISODE 5

Ashlei

"Have a good Thanksgiving," Hannah, one of the other interns, says to me as she hooks her messenger bag on her shoulder. "Can't wait to hear about the trip!"

I smile, my stomach doing a backflip at the mention of the trip with Brandon. It's the last Friday in the office before the holiday, though we don't leave for Atlanta until Tuesday. The rest of the office has the entire week off until the Monday after the holiday.

"Thanks, Hannah. Enjoy your holiday, too."

When she's gone, Kimberly pushes her chair in under her desk and turns to me with a tight smile. "Yeah, can't wait to hear about the trip. You must be *so* excited."

She narrows her eyes, but it doesn't take her resting bitch face for me to know how she feels about me. She hasn't been the least bit shy in telling everyone exactly why she thinks I got invited on the trip, along with the lead event planner position. But the gossip she's spreading about me "sleeping my way to the top" doesn't faze me. My dad prepared me for this over the summer — the way others would react to someone who was driven to succeed. And being that I'm a woman, being successful usually means I'll either be painted as a slut or a bitch, depending on my leadership style.

Still, I can't help but feel a little uneasy as Brandon comes up behind me, placing a hand on my shoulder, Kimberly's eyes glued to the spot where he's touching my bare skin. Because the truth is that while I may not be sleeping with him on a mission, I am attracted to him. And we did cross a line.

One that seems completely nonexistent now.

"Can I speak with you before you leave, Miss Daniels?" Brandon asks, voice commanding attention as always.

Kimberly purses her lips, cocking one eyebrow at me like she has me all figured out before snatching her blazer off the back of her chair and swinging it over her arm. "Happy Thanksgiving, Mr. Church," she says as she passes, and I close my eyes tight before turning to face him.

"Yes, Mr. Church?" I ask, looking up at him from my chair.

The corner of his mouth twitches a bit at the sound of his name as he casually puts his hands in the pockets of his slacks. "I just wanted to make sure you have the itinerary and everything else you need for our trip on Tuesday."

I hold up the folder Mykayla left with me earlier. "All set. I have a dress for the award ceremony and business attire for the conference. I also printed out a few copies of your speech, just in case we need it to review or anything." His eyes widen just slightly at that. "I haven't read it," I assure him.

Brandon relaxes a bit, nodding. "Okay, then. Be at the hangar at four sharp on Tuesday afternoon. They'll have light snacks and refreshments on the jet but we'll have dinner once we've landed in Atlanta."

I swallow, still a little freaked out that I'll be riding in his private jet. "Sounds good. I won't be late."

Brandon just watches me then, his eyes flicking down to where my legs are crossed, exposed in the pencil skirt I'm wearing, before he lazily pulls his gaze back up to my own. "Looking forward to it."

My skin burns from where his eyes just roamed and I squirm in my chair, uncrossing my legs just to cross them the other way. He smirks, like he knows exactly what he's doing to me, before finally turning for the elevators.

"Don't stay all night," he throws back behind him. "I've already got you working on a holiday week. At least take the full weekend off."

I relax just a hair, smiling. "I'm out of here in ten. Promise."

He pushes the down arrow for the elevators, tossing me a wink before the doors slide open and he steps on, leaving me and a few girls in Corporate Relations as the last ones in the office.

The tension between us since our date at the auto racing track has been like an electric wire pulled taut, threatening to break and spark a fire at the slightest contact. Every look he's cast in my direction during meetings, his gaze always hard and steady, seems to pull it tighter and tighter, the coils stretched to their limits.

Something tells me when those doors close on that private jet, leaving just the two of us alone again, we won't have a chance in hell of keeping it from snapping.

***

A few hours later, Jess tries unsuccessfully to catch a kernel of popcorn in her mouth after launching it up in the air. It hits her nose and bounces to the floor next to Skyler's freshly painted toenails and Jess eyes it for a moment before shrugging and digging into the bowl again.

"I'm so glad we decided to do this," Skyler says, blowing on her turquoise nails. We're all sprawled out in the floor space between the two beds in her and Jess's room, mountains of pillows and blankets surrounding us along with three bottles of wine we smuggled in and an ungodly amount of junk food. "It feels like it's been forever since we had a girls' night."

"It has been," Erin agrees. "I mean between me preparing for the election, you racking up money to pay the entry fee for that poker tournament, Ashlei spending all her time at her internship and Jess loading up her plate with extra classes since she switched her major, none of us have had a free Friday since the semester started."

"I just wish Cassie was here, too," I say, still clicking through the movies on the small TV in the corner near Skyler's bed.

"I know. Poor thing, midterms have her so stressed out. She's been at the Greek library every night for the past two weeks and her last midterm isn't until *Wednesday*," Skyler says.

"The day before Thanksgiving? What a dick professor!" Jess shakes her head. "Shouldn't even be allowed. I'm already done with mine."

"Is that why you've been in a better mood?" I ask, settling on *Pretty Woman* and pushing the play button on the remote. "Or did you and a certain tattooed hottie make up?"

She sighs, tucking her knees up to her chest and shoving another handful of popcorn in her mouth. "It's not his fault he got put on another project so soon. Well," she clarifies, swallowing. "I guess *technically* it is, because he's so damn good at his job. But I know he wouldn't have cancelled unless he absolutely had to. It's hard right now," she admits. "But I love him and I know he loves me, so I'm just trying to focus on that."

"Good girl," Erin says.

Jess claps her hands together. "Plus, Friendsgiving! It's going to be so much fun. Erin, you're still getting the turkey, right?"

"Picking it up that morning from the place my mom ordered from. She said they're the best in town."

"Maybe Bear will actually talk to me then," Skyler says on a sigh. "You know, being that the holiday spirit will be flowing and all."

Erin and Jess both frown, all of us eyeing each other as Skyler keeps her gaze on her nails.

"Do you want to talk about it?" I try, knowing it's probably useless. She hasn't told any of us the details of why Clinton is suddenly acting like she is dead to him, which likely means it's something personal, something only the two of them need to know.

She shakes her head. "Not tonight. I'd rather talk about happy stuff, like this awesome trip you're taking for your internship. Jess, feed me popcorn, my nails are still wet," she adds and Jess laughs, obliging as everyone's attention turns to me.

"It's not a big deal, really. It's just this award banquet thing and Mr. Church will be giving a keynote speech. There's a conference, too, but nothing special."

"Lies," Jess says, popping another popcorn puff into Skyler's mouth. "Stop selling yourself short. You said this is the first time he's ever invited anyone else to attend with him, and you're an *intern*, Lei."

"Oh, my God," Skyler says around a mouthful. "Is he the smoking hot guy who dropped ten thousand bucks on you at the Alpha Sigma concert auction? I saw him pick you up a few weeks ago."

"You didn't tell me he bid on you." Jess narrows her eyes.

"He was just doing it for the charity, guys. He's a philanthropic man."

Skyler laughs. "Mmm-hmm. Is he a God-fearing man, too? Because Lord, take me to church." She fans herself while Erin cracks up.

"You're shameless, Skyler."

Jess ignores Erin's comment, typing away on her phone. "Oh, my God, I just Googled him. Holy shit, Lei! Why didn't you tell me how fucking hot this guy is?!"

Erin and Skyler gather around her phone while I bury my face in my hands. "Because I'm trying my hardest *not* to notice how bangable my CEO is."

"Yeah," Erin scoffs. "Good luck with that."

They all giggle at my misfortune and I just shake my head, eventually giving in and laughing, too. "I'm screwed, huh?"

"Yup," they all agree in sync, Jess tossing popcorn at me while we all laugh even harder. It's like coming home to a warm fire and hot chocolate after walking through the snow, having a girls' night with my three best friends. I'm reminded that no matter what happens to any of us, we always have each other, and that's a pretty amazing thing.

We go through three movies, three bottles of wine, and at least three-thousand calories in salty snacks and chocolate by the time the night is over. Erin is the first to pass out, followed closely by Jess and Skyler, the three of them sleeping with pillows propped up against legs and shoulders in a sort of cuddle pit on the floor. Empty snack wrappers litter the space around them, only the soft glow from the television illuminating their peaceful faces.

I smile, pulling out my phone and snapping a picture of them before uploading it to social media with the caption, "Love my girls. #GNI." Then, I adjust my pillow against Erin's back and curl up, too.

Cassie

I've never climbed a mountain, or run a marathon, or jumped out of a plane just hoping a parachute would open and help me float down safely to the ground. I've never seen the breathtaking islands of Greece or the first snow on the mountains in Colorado, and I've never backpacked across Europe discovering new sights with every turn.

But I have been touched and loved by Grayson Anderson.

I imagine it's the same feeling — the rush of adrenaline, the high not even the best drug could provide, the sense of impossibility, like there's no way this moment is actually happening, that this is actually real. It's a combination of discovery and familiarity, of passion and vulnerability, and I haven't been able to get enough of it since the night we left the Halloween party.

Now, the Sunday before Thanksgiving, Grayson and I are still in bed even though it's almost noon. It's a cool and rainy day, the dark clouds casting a soft gray light across his entire room, but we've been too wrapped up in the covers and each other to care what the weather is like outside. Grayson has already brought me to ecstasy twice in the last twelve hours — once last night and once this morning—but here he is again, face between my thighs and legs hooked over his shoulders as he tries for number three.

I moan as he slips one finger just barely inside me, sweeping his tongue hot and flat over my clit at the same time. It's so sensitive after all the action it's had lately that just him blowing on it makes my entire body tingle. He works his finger slowly, knowing I'm tender, and takes his time building my pleasure. It's almost like I'm in a dream, a weird state of feeling everything and feeling nothing at all, my eyes low and lazy, heart stuck somewhere between a gallop and a flat line.

"Please," I whisper, tugging on his hair to pull him back up my body. He plants kisses across my skin the entire way — on my hips, my ribs, my breast, my neck, until he eventually settles between my legs, capturing my mouth with his.

"Please what?"

I dig my heels into his backside, aching to have him inside me again.

His grin is devilish as he kisses me harder, the tip of him running the line of me, the tease nearly killing me. "I want you to come again."

Everything goes hazy at those words, like a zap to all my senses, effectively muting them before sparking them all back to life at once. "I don't know if I can."

"You can," he answers quickly, and then slowly, with every centimeter stretching me wider around him, he slips all the way inside me. "You will."

The way he feels inside me without a barrier between us overwhelms me every time. My eyes flutter shut, back arching up off the bed as he withdraws slowly and opens me wider the second time he pushes inside. We'd used a condom the first few times, but since we're both clean and are exclusive to each other, we'd decided we wanted to have the full feeling of just the two of us.

And, God, what a feeling it is.

Grayson groans when he finally stretches me to fit all of him all the way inside, dropping his face into my neck and sucking the skin there. "Fuck, you feel so amazing, Cassie."

He works me slow and steady, so different from the way he took me mercilessly last night. It's as if he's matching the slow tempo of the rain pattering on his windowsill. In and out, a kiss and a touch, a sigh and a moan, a boy and a girl.

When he gently rolls until I'm sitting on top, thighs straddled on each side of him, his hands find my waist as he helps me ride, guiding me to match the rhythm he had before. I lean forward over him, elbows braced on either side of his head as I kiss him, wondering if he feels the way I do in this moment. Pure bliss.

When he starts rocking into me deeper, friction catching me in the perfect spot, I feel my orgasm mounting. But it feels just out of reach, like my body is too exhausted to extend a hand out even one inch farther to capture it.

"I'm so close," I breathe into his mouth, kissing him again as he flexes his hips.

Grayson speeds up, just a little, just enough to turn embers to fire. As it catches, billowing through me like an explosion, I gasp against his kisses, whimpering, pleading — for what, I'm not sure. And when the fire has run its course, I collapse, heavy on Grayson's chest as he kisses me softer, slowing his pace.

I rest for a moment before pushing up off his chest to sit straight up, riding him slow again, ready to bring him with me. He's already close, I can tell by the way his face twists up, his eyes closing as his hands grip my hips tighter. When they work their way up to grab both of my breasts, he curses, bucking into me with more force, and then he comes, my name a breath of a whisper on his lips.

Best. Sunday. Ever.

We both groan as I roll over, breaking our connection and spreading out in the sheets next to him as I try to catch my breath. Grayson just reaches his pinky out to graze mine, our eyes on the ceiling, hearts still racing.

"Be right back," I say, kissing his cheek before hopping up and limping to his bathroom. I'm so sore, so I take my time, relieving myself first before running a warm wash cloth along where I ache the most.

When I make my way back into the bedroom, Grayson still hasn't moved. He beckons me over to the bed and I crawl back under the sheets, letting him pull me under his arm with my head resting on his chest.

"I wish I could stay in bed with you all day," I say wistfully, watching the rain wash down the window through his sheer curtains.

He kisses my hair, running his fingers gently through it. "I do, too. I'm not even a little bit ready to play at this coffee bar tonight. It's probably going to be slow with the rain, anyway."

"At least you don't have to study," I grumble.

He laughs, pulling me in for one more kiss before I stand, searching for my clothes. I find my cotton boy shorts first by the foot of the bed and tug them on.

"Are you going to the Greek library again?" he asks, chin propped on his hand, shamelessly watching me as I pull my lacy bralette over my head and adjust it into place.

"Yeah," I answer with a sigh. "I practically live there now. Adam is meeting me there in a few hours, though, so at least I'll have some company."

I pull my Kappa Kappa Beta tank top over my head, and when my eyes find Grayson's again, his smile is completely gone, his body tense.

"You're hanging out with Adam tonight?"

"*Studying* with Adam," I correct him. "Not exactly my version of hanging out or having any fun whatsoever."

Grayson is quiet a moment as I search for my jeans.

"I don't like it," he says finally.

I sigh, finally spotting my jeans draped over his desk chair. I swipe them off and tug them on one leg at a time. "He's my friend, Grayson. And we're just studying. I thought you guys were cool now?" I'd watched them shake hands the night of the Halloween party, and though I knew they'd never be best friends, I hoped they could at least be cordial.

"I can study with you," he tries.

"You're busy tonight. And literally every night until my final."

"Well, isn't studying more of a solo sport anyway? Maybe you should just hang out in your room."

"Grayson," I deadpan.

"Well!" He huffs, throwing the sheets off him and yanking on his boxer briefs before running a hand through his hair, frustrated. "Try seeing this from my point of view, Cassie. How would you feel if there was a girl I knew before I met you whom I spent time with? *Alone*. Without you. A girl who you *knew* had more than friendly feelings for me."

"Adam doesn't—"

"Cassie." He stops me, face flat as he challenges me to finish my sentence.

Sighing, I sink down onto the bed next to him, pulling my hair into a braid over my right shoulder. "It's just... I care about him, too, Grayson. He's one of my best friends, and I'm sorry if that hurts to hear but it's true. He's been there for me through a lot of tough times and..." I shrug, not sure what else to say. "I don't want to upset you, but I don't want to lose my friendship with him, either."

Grayson's jaw tenses, but he pulls me to face him, taking both my hands in his. "I'm not asking you to not be friends with him, okay? I just... what if, at least for a while, you see him when we're all together? It would make me feel a lot more comfortable. Please," he pleads, eyes earnest. "You're going to see him at Jess' Friendsgiving thing when we're all there. Can you study with one of your sisters? I know it seems silly to you, but it matters to me."

Those last words squeeze my heart. I try to put myself in his shoes, imagine how it would feel if he had an Adam, and I had to know they were alone together in an empty library. I know I'd be uncomfortable, too, even if he assured me they were just friends.

Jealousy is an untamable beast.

"Okay," I concede. "I'll cancel with Adam and tell him I decided to study off campus."

"Thank you," Grayson says, smile back as he brings my hands to his lips and kisses them. "Now go study, future Dr. McBee."

He pops me on the ass as I stand and I swat at his hand with a laugh, grabbing my backpack off his desk. But when I'm outside, balancing an umbrella in one hand as I type out a text to Adam with the other, I can't help the sick feeling that washes over me. It feels a little like abandoning Adam, like making a choice I never intended to make between two important people in my life.

Of course Adam writes back right away, completely understanding, even cracking a joke at my expense. Because that's who Adam is — kind, forgiving, always there, even when I maybe don't deserve him to be.

Grayson said he only wants me to see Adam in group settings for now, just until he's comfortable. But will that day ever really come? And if it doesn't, do I have a right to be upset?

Can I have a strong relationship with my boyfriend without sacrificing my friendship with Adam?

I don't have the answer.

And something tells me I wouldn't like it if I did.

Jess

My eyes are winged, lips painted a deep red, and hair curled to perfection as I jump into bed. Normally I wouldn't go all out for a night in, but Jarrett and I have a video chat date set to start in less than five minutes, and I want to make him want me so bad he's booking a plane ticket.

Okay, so I know that's not possible right now, but if I can at the very least make him say, "*Damn*," I'll be happy.

I'm dressed in nothing but a lacy thong as I dive under the sheets, thankful Skyler has another poker tournament keeping her busy and out of our room for the evening. I pull my top sheet up over my chest, leaving just the sweetest view of cleavage in the camera line before dialing Jarrett's number.

My face fills the screen as it waits for him to connect and I touch up my hair again, running my fingers over the curls. But when the phone rings for almost a full minute before disconnecting completely without an answer, I frown.

He said eight o'clock, right?

I check our text messages and the time on my phone again, just to be sure.

Sighing, I lay my phone on my lap and wait, convincing myself he's probably just getting out of the shower or something. But when ten minutes goes by without a call back, I try again.

No answer.

When it's half past eight and there's not even a text from him, my excitement fades into disappointment and uncertainty.

- Hey, we still on for tonight? -

I send the text, heart flipping in my chest when I immediately see the three bouncing dots that tell me he's texting back.

- One sec. -

I smile, flipping on my camera to check my lipstick and fluff my hair again, but when his name finally fills my screen along with a picture of us from his last visit, it's a regular phone call, not a video one.

"Hey, babe," he says immediately when I answer, though I can barely hear him over the loud music and laughter behind him. "I'm stepping outside, just give me a second." My heart sinks, the background noise clearing when he's outside, replaced by the soft, almost muted sound of traffic. "Sorry about that. How are you?"

"I'm fine. Aren't we video chatting tonight?"

Jarrett sighs into the phone. "I'm so sorry, Jess. I completely forgot. Today was absolute hell at the office. We're in crunch time for this project and they had assigned Matt to help me and Jenny, but he's been sick for a week now, so it's just the two of us again and we're beat. We ended up stopping for a drink after work."

All the warmth drains from my face, slipping slowly down my neck. "Oh."

"It's just a drink, Jess," he assures me. "We're both under a lot of pressure right now and needed to take a break before we both lose our damn minds."

I swallow despite the knot in my throat, nodding even though he can't see me.

He sighs. "You're pissed, aren't you?"

At that I close both of my eyes tight, two twin tears rolling down opposite cheeks. "Just tell me the truth, Jarrett. Are you and Jenny... are you messing around with her?"

"What?!" Jarrett huffs. "No. And I told you this last time you accused me of it. I've had a shit day at work and I needed a beer. So did she. So, now we're taking *one* fucking hour to decompress and I don't understand why I can't do that without you throwing a childish fit over it!"

His words only slice me deeper, more tears pouring hot down my face as I wipe at my nose. "I miss you!" I scream back. "Is that my crime? That I miss you and I'm sad when you blow off our date to have a drink at a bar with another woman? How would you feel if you were me?"

"I'd be understanding," he snaps back. "And I'd tell you I'm sorry to hear you had a bad day, and I'd ask you to call me later when you get home."

"Bullshit," I whisper, sniffing and batting at the tears on my face. "That's bullshit and you know it."

"All I *know* right now is that I'm tired of having the same argument. Nothing I say is going to make you believe me."

"Actions speak a lot louder than words."

He barks out a laugh. "Wow. I can't believe we're having this conversation."

I shake my head, heart breaking with every cold word that leaves his lips. "We're not anymore." And with that, I hang up the phone, dropping my face into my pillow and letting my tears consume me.

Every breath burns my lungs, like the air is left toxic from our fight. I know he's working hard, and I understand that need to relieve the stress, but it doesn't change the fact that he forgot about me — about our date — and that hurts more than anything.

He didn't even apologize, I think, which makes the tears come harder.

I should be on a plane tonight, a plane that would take me to him, into his arms, the place where I feel safe and comforted and okay. But instead, I'm crying alone in my bed, wondering why we're even doing this to each other anymore. Maybe he'd be happier without me breathing down his back, needing his constant reassurance. Maybe I'd be happier without him breaking promises, without feeling like a nuisance more than a girlfriend.

Just the thought of living without him makes me curl into myself tighter, shaking my head as a new wave of tears rush down my face, soaking my pillow. I've never loved anyone the way I love Jarrett, and I know I wouldn't be happier without him. I'd be miserable.

But does he feel the same?

Ashlei

Mr. Church must be hungry.

That's all I can think as I cross my legs even tighter, fighting against the heat building between them. It's hard enough not to squirm sitting in a board meeting with Brandon at the head of the table, but with just a small table separating us in a private jet it's damn near impossible.

I'd shown up at the hangar on time, just as promised, and we'd quickly loaded up into the jet, the personnel taking care of our bags and offering us a glass of champagne as we stepped inside. I'd found it hard not to gasp when I boarded, seeing the beautiful leather interior, complete with three sets of comfortable, reclining chairs with tables between them, and one long couch. The leather was a cross of beige and black, cut with thickly sewn stitching that reminded me of Brandon's car interior. There were dark brown and maroon suede pillows on the couch and one small one in each chair, pulling all the aesthetics together, making it scream business and comfort all at once.

Brandon had taken a seat at the back set of chairs, the one across from the couch, and I'd followed suit, sitting across the small table from him. He'd been quiet as the flight crew explained our route and how long it would take, offering us more refreshments, and he'd remained silent until just after takeoff. Once we were in the air, he'd started small talk — literally talking about the weather in Atlanta and asking how my midterms went — before he fell back into a quiet state.

Except this time, his eyes weren't on the newspaper.

They were on me.

And *that* is when I decided that he must be hungry, and that our first stop when we land will most certainly be a restaurant. Because the way he looked at me, the way he's *still* looking at me, is like he's a starved man and I'm a surf n' turf buffet of the highest quality.

I glance at the small screen behind Brandon's head, one with a map of our route and a little white airplane to show us where we are. It also details how fast we're going and our approximate arrival time, which isn't too long, being that the trip from Miami to Atlanta is a quick one in a jet. I try to keep my focus on that little screen, but I feel him in my peripheral, boring a hole into my skin with his gaze.

"I have a proposal for you, Miss Daniels."

Are we back to last names now?

I snap my attention to him, swallowing hard as he steeples his fingers over his lap, his eyes dark and intense.

"And what's that, Mr. Church?"

He smirks. "For the past month, the two of us have been acting like what happened between us didn't happen. Which is professional, and certainly the right thing to do."

I search his face for signs of sarcasm, but find none. So, I just nod in agreement. "Yes."

"Yes," he echoes me. Pausing, he watches me for a moment before leaning forward over the small table between us, his hands disappearing underneath it. "However, I'm in quite a predicament, Miss Daniels. Because it seems that you have awakened a rather persistent itch, one that I don't see going away until I give in and scratch it."

Warmth crawls up my neck, burning my cheeks as I reach for my champagne glass on the table, draining the last sip of it. Every nerve of my body is at full attention, hanging on his words, waiting for what he'll say next.

"Now, I could live with this itch," he says, catching my eyes with his before trailing them down over my chest. "But, judging by the way you're clenching your thighs together under this table..." He leans forward a little more, and then I feel the warmth of his finger — just one — as it brushes the inside of my knee so slightly I'm almost sure I'm imagining it. "And the way your cheeks flush when I touch you, something tells me you've got an itch to scratch, too."

It takes everything in me, including a tight grip on the armrests of my chair and a tight closing of my eyes, not to moan when the one finger on the inside of my knee turns into a flat, hot palm, sliding just an inch up, just enough to brush the hem of my skirt.

"So, what's your proposal, Mr. Church?" The words leave my lips in something like a whisper and a groan, my eyelids cracking open again as I find his gaze.

"Until this jet touches down in Miami again, you're mine," he nearly growls the words, running his tongue along his bottom lip as he eyes mine. "And I'm yours. No boundaries, no rules, no thought of consequences. Just two people scratching an itch and keeping a little secret." He shrugs. "And when we land back in reality, it's hands off again. Responsible. Professional."

My breaths are silent, almost nonexistent as I watch him, debating. "And you think we'll be able to do that," I challenge, uncrossing my legs to spread them just an inch. His nose flares at the bold act, his hand skating up a centimeter more. "You think you'll be able to fuck me this week and let me go on Sunday night? That you'll be able to see me in the office every day, knowing you'll never touch me again?"

I run my fingers through my hair and trail the tips of them down over my neck, my collarbone, running them along the neckline of my blouse with my lip pinned between my teeth.

Brandon inhales a stiff breath, eyes on fire. "I think I'd rather know that torture than continue living in this one."

My brain is in overdrive, ticking through the possibilities and the consequences if we were caught, but the overwhelming thought pushing everything else down is that the likelihood of us getting caught is slim to none. As long as we keep our hands to ourselves when we're in public, and we go back to normal when we're in the office again, no one would need to know.

And, *God*, how I want to taste him again, to touch him again, to know what he feels like inside me.

Fuck it.

"No one finds out. And when we land again, I'm off limits. No looking at me across the boardroom like you want to fuck me on the table while everyone watches."

"You have my word," he says, smirking. "So, do we have a deal?"

He doesn't move his hand any higher, doesn't lick his lips or raise an eyebrow — he simply waits.

"We have a deal."

The last word doesn't even leave my lips before Brandon clears our glasses and his newspaper off the table in one sweep of his arm, sending them crashing to the floor before flipping the table between us up to hook on the wall. He drops to his knees in front of me, and then his hands are in my hair, and his mouth is on mine, tongue sweeping in to claim me like I was never anyone else's, like I'll never be anyone else's again.

I'm still catching my breath against his kisses when his hands trail their way down, following the curves of my body until both palms are pressed on the inside of my knees. He pushes them apart, earning a gasp from me as he slides his hands up my inner thighs, pushing my skirt up with them.

"This is really stupid of us," I pant as he kisses his way down my neck, hands still climbing. "You know that, right?"

"Completely idiotic," he agrees, then he fists the bunched up fabric of my skirt and yanks until my ass is hanging off the edge of the seat.

With slow precision, he unfastens each button on my blouse, tugging it from where it was tucked into my skirt and leaving it open, exposing my simple nude bra. Brandon pulls the cups down until my breasts spill out of the top, pulling both of my nipples between his fingers and thumbs as I arch into his touch with a moan.

"You are so fucking sexy," he growls, and then his hands drop to my thighs as he reaches up under my skirt for my panties, ripping them down my legs until they fall around my ankles. I can't even step out of them before his face is buried between my thighs.

A string of curse words leave my lips on a breath as he runs his tongue along the length of me, swirling my clit at the top before diving between my lips like I'm his last meal. My heart is racing like his NSX, running laps as my breaths struggle to keep up, my hands grasping for anything to hold onto — the arms of the chair, the sleeves of his dress shirt, the last shred of my morals. But I can't catch my grip, not on any of it, so I let go, let him pull me down, two sinners in the clouds just waiting for the fall into hell.

Brandon is an expert with his tongue, sucking and teasing my clit until my legs are quivering on either side of his face. But when he runs two warm fingertips up my inner thigh, coating them in my wetness before sliding them inside, I learn he's an expert with his hands, too.

"Come here," he husks, wiggling his fingers deep inside me as his free hand pulls me in to kiss him. His mouth is hot on mine, his kisses hard and demanding as he pushes me closer and closer to release. Every part of me is held captive — his hand locked behind my neck, holding my mouth to his, his fingers inside me, his eyes devouring what little of me is left.

And I let him take me, let him tease me and ruin me and claim me until it's too much.

"Enough."

I press my hands hard into his chest, pushing him off me, his fingers taking my breath with them as he slips out and lands with his back against his chair. He eyes me with a wild gaze, licking his lips as I crawl out of my seat and across the floor, propping myself on my knees in front of him as I rip at his belt, desperate to have him as naked as I am.

He helps me, lifting his hips when I finish with the zipper and kicking off his dress shoes, allowing me to pull his pants down and off, flinging them to the side before I spread my legs over his thighs to straddle him. Just the length of him pressed against my center makes my breath catch. I haven't been with a man since Spring Break, since everything with Bo and me went up in flames. The thought of her shocks my system, coming out of nowhere, and I quickly shove her to the back of my mind again, fingers frantically working the buttons of Brandon's dress shirt as he fumbles in the pockets of his discarded pants for a condom.

"Up," he commands when he finds one, ripping the package open with his teeth.

I lift my hips, pressing my lips to his as I pull his dress shirt open, running my hands along the length of his hard chest, his defined abdomen, my nails digging into his flesh.

His hands disappear between us for just a fraction of a second, strapping the condom on before they find my waist, gripping hard, and he lines up the crown of him with the wet opening of me.

And for a moment, everything stops, time suspended between us, our breaths slowing before stopping altogether. My arms wrapped around his neck and his hands framing my face, foreheads pressed together, Brandon searches my eyes with his own, asking permission again.

Slowly, with my mouth finding his again, I slide down, the hard length of him stretching me open centimeter by aching centimeter.

I wince against the pain, laced with overwhelming pleasure, my body in shock at the feel of being reopened after so many months. I dig my nails into his back even more, working as slow as I can to fit him all the way inside.

"Goddamn, Ashlei," he groans, brows bent together and hands gripping my waist like that's the only control he has to stop himself from slamming into me. When I finally sink all the way down, the base of me touching the base of him, we both let out a long, almost pained breath.

The first time I tried cocaine, I remember feeling shock and understanding all at once — the rush of blood, the lightheadedness, the intense awareness, the awakening. Still, I hadn't found it difficult to walk away from. But with Brandon's arms wrapping all the way around me, his hands curling on my shoulders, head buried in my chest as he flexes his hips into me, stealing my breath again, I realize distantly that *this* is a real high. This is the high addicts are born from. Walking away from this, from him, won't be simple. Part of me wonders if it will even be possible at all.

Like a light switch, I turn off my thoughts of the future, surrendering to the now as I ride Brandon steadily, my orgasm mounting with every brush of my clit against him, with every deep thrust of him inside me. When his hands find my ass and squeeze, pulling me harder against him as he sucks the sensitive skin around my nipple, my breath catches and I hold it there, reaching blindly for my climax.

"Say my name when you come," he growls, sucking my nipple hard before moving up to kiss the skin under my ear. "I want to hear it."

"Oh, fuck, Mr.—"

"No." He cuts my words short, stopping his movements altogether. "Wrong name."

I writhe in his lap, the sensation that had been rising fading off as I try desperately to hold onto it. I rock against him, crying out, nails digging into his arms. "Please," I beg. "I'm so close."

He answers my plea, thrusting hard and deep, and sparks fly behind my pinched eyelids, flames licking my skin from the inside out as I come apart. "Oh, God, Brandon. Fuck. Don't stop."

He groans at his name, pumping harder, and as I ride out my climax, he finds his. The groans escaping his lips are enough to ignite my orgasm for another round, both of us gripping onto each other, pushing and pulling and scratching and digging until we're both spent, collapsing into each other in a heap of shallow breaths.

When it's over, the high receding, my body sore and aching in all the right places, Brandon holds me in his lap. He kisses the skin on my shoulder, soothing his fingertips over my back as I rest. When I peek up at the screen behind him, I see we only have a half an hour before the jet will land in Atlanta.

"We should get dressed," I whisper.

Brandon pulls back, searching my eyes with his own. "Is that really what you're thinking right now?"

"Well, we land soon," I point out, feeling a little self-conscious. "Why, what are you thinking?"

He pauses, eyes flicking to the ceiling as he thinks. "I'm hungry."

A laugh rips from my throat and Brandon chuckles, too, pulling me into him for one last kiss.

I knew it.

Cassie

"Maybe we should just start," Skyler suggests, her wary eyes on Jess as she waits for her to blow. We've all been waiting, the tension like a cloud of gnats hovering around us at the Friendsgiving table. "I'm sure she'll be here soon. We can at least eat the sides while they're hot."

Erin was supposed to be here already — with the missing turkey — and with both her and Ashlei missing in action coupled with the fact that Jess is only throwing this because her boyfriend cancelled her trip to see him, it's not exactly a joyous occasion. I'm thankful Grayson is here with me, at least.

Clinton scoffs, crossing his arms with a hard roll of his eyes. "Oh, right, because you always know what's best, don't you, Sky?"

Skyler's face crumples and my heart aches seeing my Big like that. She's always so strong, so sure, but Clinton is her best friend. Their fight is taking a toll on her and we all know it.

"Bear, please. I apologized. Can we just... can't we have a nice meal?"

Everyone watches Clinton carefully, like a bomb with three seconds left on the timer and a red wire about to be cut.

After a moment, he picks up his fork, but before I can even let out a sigh of relief he grits his teeth and drops it back to the table again.

"How the fuck are we supposed to have Thanksgiving without a goddamn turkey," he growls as he stands, and without another look at any of us, he blows out the back door.

My eyes find Skyler's and I reach for her wrist, squeezing it gently.

"He's not mad about the turkey," she explains on a sigh. "He's just worried about his little brother and..."

"It's fine, Big," I say, smiling sympathetically. "I agree, we should just eat."

"Yeah, who says you can't make a meal out of green bean casserole?" Adam chimes in. "Challenge accepted."

My eyes find his then, silently thanking him. He just winks, reaching forward for the mashed potatoes and piling them on his plate to get things started. But when he tries to pass the dish to Skyler, she's still staring at the door Clinton just left through.

With a shake of her head, she drops her napkin onto her empty plate and pushes back from the table. "I'm sorry, I just need to check on him. I'll be back."

Jess watches her leave with murderous eyes, and when the door swings shut again and it's just the four of us — Jess, Adam, Grayson, and myself — the swarm of gnats buzzes even louder than before.

Adam swallows, offering the dish across the table to me, instead, as Jess drops her head into her hands, kneading her temples.

I take the dish from Adam, our fingers brushing just slightly. I can't stop the flush that colors my cheeks. We haven't had a chance to talk face to face since Halloween, not after Grayson asked me to cancel our study date, and I feel Adam's eyes burning into me from across the table. There have always been way more questions in those eyes of his than I've ever had answers for.

Jess's phone buzzes on the table and I say a silent prayer that it's Erin with news on the turkey, trying to keep spirits up until she can get here. But before I can even serve myself a scoop of mashed potatoes, Grayson's chair scrapes against the floor as he stands.

"Oh, for Christ's sake, what now?!" Jess huffs.

I pause with the bowl in my hands, looking up at Grayson as he glares at Adam across the table.

"I can't do this anymore, Cassie," he says, and my heart sinks as I follow his gaze to Adam and back again. "You have to choose. Him," he snarls, thrusting a hand toward Adam. "Or me."

"Andddd, that's my cue." Jess stands, throwing her napkin down and waving her hands. "You guys can have your pissing match. I'm going to get a cheeseburger."

But I can't even ask her to stay, or tell her I'm sorry, or do anything other than stare blankly up at Grayson, wondering what the hell is going on.

"Grayson—"

"No," he clips, jaw set. "No, I'm serious. I can't just fucking sit here while he drools over you from across the table."

"Maybe I should leave," Adam tries, placing his hands on the table to stand.

"Sit the fuck down," Grayson growls at him, turning to me next. "This is getting settled. Tonight. I thought I could deal with you guys being friends, but his lack of respect for our relationship isn't going to make that possible. I don't want you around him, Cassie," he says, the sentence like a punctuation. He's like an alien in this moment, a foreigner I don't recognize.

"Please," I whisper, reaching for his hand, but he jerks it away.

"Don't want her around me?" Adam sneers, chair flying behind him as he stands to match Grayson's stance. "I was her friend before she even knew you *existed*."

Grayson scoffs. "Friend, my ass."

"Guys, please." My voice is so small compared to theirs, like a bird chirp competing with a train horn.

"Sounds like someone's threatened," Adam shoots back. "Don't worry, Grayson. Can't steal a girl who doesn't want to be stolen. You should be fine, since you spend so much time with her and really make her a priority in your life."

"Not helping, Adam!" I shout as Grayson beats his fists on the table.

"Enough!" he growls, turning to me with wild eyes. "Do you love me?"

My voice cracks, throat thick with an unswallowable knot. "Of course."

"I'm about to walk out that door." He thrusts his finger toward the back door, the one Skyler and Clinton both blew out of earlier. "And if you love me like you say you do, you'll come with me."

He glares at Adam once more before doing exactly as he said he would. He doesn't look back, doesn't wait for me to come, just plows through the door, letting in the last sliver of fading sunlight before it shuts again, leaving Adam and me alone.

I don't know how much time passes, how many times my heart beats and breaks before I look up from my hands at him. Seconds stretch into years, years reduced to just seconds as I watch one of my best friends try not to fall apart. The skin is stretched tight over his jaw, his eyes hard on the door, fists clenched at his side.

"Adam," I whisper, throat raw.

"Just go."

My eyes flood with tears, Adam's face blurring as my heart splits in two, one jagged half breaking away from the other. "Please," I beg. "Look at me."

"What?" he snaps, tearing his eyes from the door to find mine. His chest is heaving, nose flaring. "You love him, right? So, go."

I choke on a sob, tears spilling down my cheeks like boiling hot water, and I feel every scar they leave behind. "I don't want it to be this way."

"Well, it is." His voice breaks but he clenches his jaw against it. "Go, Cassie."

I cry harder, shaking my head.

"Go!"

Ripping myself from the chair, I try to ignore the pain in his voice as I turn my back on him, following Grayson out the back door. Something crashes to the floor behind me just before the door shuts, but I don't look back. My arms crossed tight over my middle, I close my eyes, shuddering on a breath that burns with unfair reality more than it heals with oxygen.

I spot Grayson across the street, seated on a bench outside the Communications building. He breathes a sigh of relief when he sees me, standing, knowing then that I loved him enough to do as he asked. But with every step toward him, I hate myself more.

How long did I really expect it to last? How long could I expect Grayson to understand, knowing the way Adam feels... the way I feel?

It's not unfair, what Grayson's asking. It's not unfair of him to feel the way he feels. But I still hate it all the same.

Because Adam was right — I didn't lie. I do love Grayson.

But my heart still splits in two, because the words I didn't say before I let him believe I chose another man over him will forever haunt me.

I do love him, but I love you, too.

Jess

By the time I make it to Ralph's and see how completely dead it is inside, the fire I had in my belly when I stormed out of the KKB house is all but ash. Suddenly it doesn't seem like a brilliant idea to push Jarrett's buttons, and seeing as how there are only three other small groups of people in the bar other than myself, there aren't exactly a lot of options for pawns in my game.

There's a small group of girls, all giggling and playing pool, having their version of a Friendsgiving, I assume. I recognize Landon, the guy Erin had a fling with last year, in the corner with some of his buddies. He's off limits since he was with Erin, but even more so, the guy gives me the creeps. Other than that, I don't see anyone standing out.

Maybe it's because none of the guys, no matter how hot they are, hold a candle to Jarrett.

Sighing, I order a vodka tonic and drop my phone onto the bar top in front of me, dropping my head into my hands with my eyes still on it, willing it to ring.

Jarrett hasn't talked to me since our fight on Monday.

He has a right to be pissed, and I'm fully prepared to apologize, but I also won't deny that I'm a little disappointed *he* hasn't apologized yet, either. And now, a little after seven on Thanksgiving, he's still yet to call me. Or answer my call.

The bartender is a slight little thing that I assume to be my age, probably staying around campus just because someone has to serve the poor suckers like me who stumble in here on a holiday weekend. She pops my drink down in front of me and then kicks back against the register at the other end of the bar, texting away on her phone with a giant grin. She looks like she's texting someone she cares about, someone who cares about her. I know that goofy grin.

I used to wear it.

Twirling the ice in my glass with the plastic stirrer, I keep my eyes on my phone, pushing the home button every now and then just to make sure I didn't somehow miss a text. I'm so focused on my pathetic pity party that I don't even notice the guy who sits down next to me until he speaks.

"You know, I've tried that method," he says, breaking my daze. I glance over at him, eyes widening at the bright, boy-next-door smile I find there.

"Excuse me?"

He nods toward my phone on the bar. "The whole *stare at it until it does something* method. I've tried it. Usually leads to sucking down booze like water and drunk texting someone I know I shouldn't."

For the first time tonight, a tiny smile breaks on my face, and I don't even hide it as I take the time to check this guy out. The first thing I notice is his smile — I have never been so attracted to someone's teeth before. They're bright white and perfectly straight, like a dentist commercial, and one little dimple pops on his left cheek when that smile reaches its full wattage. All his features are dark — the jet-black mop of hair on his head, the deep brown of his eyes, the glorious tan skin stretched out over the amazing muscles on his arms, the perfect-length stubble on his jaw. This guy is the definition of tall, dark, and handsome — and suddenly, my game face is back on.

"Maybe I want to send drunk texts."

He laughs. "No, you don't. No one wakes up the morning after sending five unanswered texts in a row happy about it."

This time it's him who lets his eyes wander, and though it feels nice to be devoured by his eyes, it doesn't change the fact that he isn't Jarrett. Every guy just seems so... *blah*, compared to Jarrett. He's ruined me.

"I'm Jess," I say when his eyes finally reach mine again.

"Greg. You're in Kappa Kappa Beta, right?" He motions for the bartender, holding up his empty beer bottle before turning to face me again.

"I am. Are you Greek?"

"Omega Chi Beta."

"Oh, shit, the probation boys," I tease. "I have a really good friend in your fraternity — Bear. Although, he's kind of pissing me off currently."

Greg rolls his eyes. "He's been pissing pretty much everyone off since the beginning of the semester. I think he's just taking the probation thing hard. He's helped us a lot, though. There were still a lot of brothers being stupid after the meeting with nationals — me included — but he reminded us what's at stake. Still," he adds, tipping his new beer toward the bartender before taking a long pull. "His attitude is a lot to handle."

"I think he and Skyler got into some kind of fight, but neither one of them is saying why."

"Doesn't surprise me. Those two are pretty tight, even if they aren't getting along right now." His lips find his bottle again, eyes still on me. "Anyway, enough about them. Tell me about you. Any particular reason you're in Ralph's on Thanksgiving instead of home with family?"

"Ugh," I stick the plastic stirrer in my drink like a dagger, fishing out an ice cube before popping it in my mouth. "That's a long story. You should probably answer that question first."

"My parents took a cruise for the holiday," he answers easily. "So, I stayed here to party with a few brothers. But if I had to guess by the way you're watching your phone, your reason involves a guy, doesn't it?"

I chew my ice cube. "Maybe."

"Boyfriend?"

I pause mid-crunch, swirling the cold remains of the cube with my tongue as I debate how to answer. I could easily lie, play the game I was set on playing when I walked in the door, but suddenly it all feels stupid. So, I just answer with a nod.

"Ah, figures," he says, a defeated smile on his face as he peels the label off his beer bottle. "Doesn't make sense for a girl who looks like you to be single."

"You're sweet." I watch him for a moment, waiting for him to make some excuse to walk away. "Guess now that you know I have a boyfriend, in your mind I've practically sprouted three heads and a dick now, huh?"

He chokes on a laugh, that damn dimple making an appearance again. "Not at all. I was actually going to ask if you would still be okay with a little company tonight. You can talk to me about him, if you want," he offers with a shrug. "Or, I can talk your ear off with turtle facts."

This time it's me who nearly chokes. "I'm sorry?"

"Biology major," he answers. "I'm doing a marine mammal and sea turtle rescue internship next summer, so I've been studying, upping my turtle game."

I laugh, finally feeling marginally better and oddly thankful that Greg wandered into Ralph's tonight. "Okay, you have my attention. Hit me with a turtle fact."

And, so he does. For the rest of the night, we make easy conversation, first with his hilarious but fascinating knowledge of sea turtles and eventually we end up talking about our families, our majors, our love for pizza, our favorite songs and movies. I lose count of how many drinks we both have as well as how many laughs we share. All I know is that it feels good to sit in a bar with an attractive boy who can't stop staring at me but is respectful enough not to make any moves since I have a boyfriend. It's refreshing, and maybe some attention was all I needed, after all.

A loud commotion breaks the spell Greg has me under somewhere around midnight. We eye each other cautiously before abandoning our drinks at the bar and rushing outside. Landon is cursing and screaming, his buddies all gathered around him trying to calm him down. When Greg and I step around the first row of cars in the parking lot, we see why.

"Oh, my God." I cover my mouth, trying to hide my smile and fight down the laugh I feel coming on.

"WHOEVER DID THIS IS DEAD, DO YOU HEAR ME?!" Landon screams, grabbing his friend's beer bottle and hurling it across the parking lot. It hits the brick wall of Ralph's and shatters, splinters of glass raining down on the sidewalk like a parade in his honor. "DEAD."

"I wish I would have grabbed my phone off the bar," I say to Greg, eyes wandering over Landon's car. "I so need a picture of this."

"Something tells me you'll see one on social media in about two minutes," he says, nodding to the group of girls who were playing pool earlier. They all have their phones out, giggling and snapping pictures before Landon sees them and roars for them to put their phones away. I can't blame him for being mad, but even more than that, I want to know the genius behind the prank.

His entire car is covered in dildos.

And not just any kind of dildo — tiny, micro-penis dildos, all Saran Wrapped to his hood, his doors, the roof, the windows. It's impossible to even get inside the car without breaking through the cellophane first, and thus breaking loose at least a hundred tiny, rubber dicks. The tires are shredded, the windshield busted, and nearly all the paint has been keyed up. And to top it all off? There's a message, loud and clear, written in bright red paint on the hood.

Now the outside matches the inside. Go fuck yourself.

I'm still laughing when the police show up and Greg and I dip back inside Ralph's, finding our place back at the bar and slipping easily back into the conversation we were holding before. The night is turning out to be much better than it started.

"We should take a picture," he says about an hour after the dildo commotion, smacking his palms on the bar. "To commemorate one of the best Thanksgivings I've had in a long time."

I chuckle. "A Turkey Day selfie, huh?"

"Absolutely." He pulls his phone out of his pocket, flipping the camera to face us before reaching down and grabbing the edge of my barstool. He pulls me closer to him, hand finding the small of my back as he holds the phone up. "Say turtle."

I laugh, and he snaps the picture with my hand on his chest, my eyes staring up at him, mid-laugh. His smile is wide and lazy, both of us clearly a little intoxicated, but as we both look the picture over, I can't help but think we look cute together.

"Are you allowed to be here?" he asks.

"What do you mean?"

"I was going to post it," he says, nodding toward the picture. My barstool is still touching his, our bodies brushing. "Can I tag you?"

It's funny, how the exact thing I was going to do — the mission I had been on — ended up happening even after I'd dropped the notion. I had my goal set on coming in here and finding some poor sap to use to make Jarrett jealous, but I'd gotten so caught up just having fun with Greg, I'd dropped the initial thought.

Frowning, I realize I haven't checked my phone in a while, and I turn, grabbing it off the bar and clicking the home screen.

No missed texts.

No missed calls.

My heart sinking, I drop the phone back to the bar with a sigh, turning back to Greg with what I'm sure is a pathetic smile. "You know what? Tag me."

"You sure?" he asks, eyeing my phone before finding my gaze again.

"Positive."

He watches me a moment more, his eyes flicking to my lips, but he swallows and tears his gaze away and back to his phone. I watch him type out a caption, draining the last of my vodka tonic as the loading bar fills on his phone, and then the screen re-loads and he grins.

"Posted."

Ashlei

"Everyone always asks me, 'Why *Okay, Cool*?'" Brandon starts, kicking off his keynote speech in front of a ballroom of at least a thousand people, all eyes fixed on him. "And it's my favorite story to tell."

I'm seated just a few tables from the stage, my heel grazing the dance floor that stretches out in front of the stage, separating me from the tables on the other side of it. Looking up at Brandon in his deep red suit with golden accents, tie and pocket handkerchief popping as bright accents, he looks absolutely regal. But as handsome as he looks on that stage, I know the man *beneath* the suit now.

I know the abs that stretch from his rib cage down to the deep V, cut at an angle that leads me right to eight inches of heaven. I know the striking compass tattoo that hugs his left tricep, the imprint his teeth leave on his lip when he bites it hard enough, and the sounds he makes when he's on the brink of ecstasy.

The last few days with Brandon have been pure bliss — from sneaking long, hot, passionate kisses in dark corners and hidden hallways during the conference to not even leaving our hotel room on Thanksgiving, we've both been making the most of our "no rules" weekend. I'm deliciously sore and satisfied, yet never truly sated, always wanting more of him. Even now, as I try to focus on his speech, I can't wait to get him back to the room for our last night together before reality hits.

"It's no secret that growing up in foster care isn't fun," he continues, and a heavier weight settles over the room at his words. "It's hard growing up not feeling valued, or important, or like you belong anywhere in the world. It's even harder when you're surrounded by opportunities to maybe find a sort of family, but you know those opportunities are bad — and likely to land you in jail."

My heart aches as I watch Brandon strip his soul bare in front of an entire crowd of people. I promised him I wouldn't read his speech before he gave it tonight, and I kept my word. Now, I'm hanging on to everything he's saying, wanting to know him more, even though I know I shouldn't.

"I won't lie, I don't know how much longer I would have been able to stay out of trouble had it not been for a young entrepreneur who found me by the grace of God and kept a steady head on my shoulder. His name was Darnell Cohen, and he owned a small but reputable catering company in the town I grew up in." He clears his throat. "He was twenty-five when he offered me my first job. I was only fourteen.

"Darnell didn't have to take a chance on a kid with dirty shoes and a bad attitude, but he did. He gave me somewhere to be after school, a way to make money, and more than that, a brotherhood. He was my big brother in every sense of the word. And the more years I worked under him, the more I realized that he was exactly the kind of man I wanted to be — intelligent, humble, kind, and giving."

I smile at that, because in my mind, Brandon is all of those things to a T.

"'Okay, cool,' was Darnell's answer to everything," Brandon continues with a smile. "When I had a new idea for the business? 'Okay, cool. Let's do it.' When I was late for an event? 'Okay, cool. Don't let it happen again.' When something went wrong and everyone else stressed out? 'Okay, cool. Let me think for a second, I can fix this.' Even when the most beautiful woman I'd ever seen gave me her number to give to him... 'Okay, cool. I'll call her later.'"

The room laughs a little at that, and I cover my smile with my hand, completely enraptured with Brandon's speech.

But when the laughter dies down, his eyes soften, and he smooths his hands over the podium. "And when I came to him on my eighteenth birthday, not able to stay even one more day in my foster home, and asked him for a place to stay... he didn't even hesitate." Brandon lifts his eyes to the audience again. "'Okay, cool. Let's get you into college.'"

I swallow, my throat thick with emotion, my hands aching to reach out to him.

"And, he did," Brandon continues. "He helped me get into college, and helped me realize that just because I'd come from nothing didn't mean I had nothing to become." He pauses. "Darnell was thirty-two when he was murdered."

The entire room inhales a breath, none of us letting go of it as we watch Brandon on stage.

"He was just in the wrong gas station at the wrong time, trying to save the life of a young cashier. And, he did...by sacrificing his own."

Silence.

"So," he continues after a moment, sniffing. "*Okay, Cool* is just one of the many ways I honor Darnell with my life, trying to hold onto his memory for as long as I can and show the world who he was, and who he helped me become."

Brandon continues on to talk about chasing dreams despite obstacles, and rising above the circumstances life hands you, and eventually finishes with his final words of advice for event industry entrepreneurs like himself. It's a moving speech, one that earns him a standing ovation at the end, and his eyes are on me as he smiles and exits the stage to the sound of the string quartet band starting up again.

I'm still standing when he finally reaches our table again, which isn't until after he's stopped by nearly every person he passes, all wanting to shake his hand and tell him how wonderful his speech was. He blows out a long breath when he makes it to his seat, dropping his notecards onto the table and kissing my cheek before we both sit.

"At the risk of repeating what everyone else just said, your speech was... beautiful, Brandon."

He reaches for his drink — a Manhattan — and takes a quick sip. "Thank you. But I'm glad it's over," he adds with a laugh. "Now I can finally enjoy myself."

"You were nervous?" I ask, surprised.

"Always. Speaking in front of a large crowd is not my idea of a good time."

I laugh, placing the delicate white linen napkin over my lap just as the first course of dinner is served. "Well, I would have never guessed. You looked casual and comfortable up there." I pause. "Did you picture everyone in their underwear?"

"Just you," he fires back with a wink.

Brandon is the center of attention all through dinner, the three other couples seated with us asking him question after question that lead to story after story. By the time dessert is finished and our drinks are refilled, I can tell he's ready for a break, so I take a longer sip from my champagne glass and stand.

"Dance with me?" I ask.

His eyes fire up with a mix of relief and hunger, and he wipes the corners of his mouth with his napkin before laying it gently beside his plate. "It would be my honor. Excuse me," he says to the rest of the table, and they all lift their glasses or offer us polite smiles and nods as I take his arm.

"Thank you," he says when we take our places on the dance floor, one of his large hands finding the bare skin at the small of my back as he takes my hand in the other. "I'm going to need a solid week of introverting when we get back to South Florida."

I smile as we start to dance, not even surprised that he moves so smoothly with me in his arms. The man is astounding. "I'll need a week of recovery, myself," I tease.

Brandon's eyes spark, a devilish grin spreading on his face. "I won't apologize for that." His eyes sweep over me, landing on mine just as he twirls me out and pulls me back into his arms. "You look absolutely stunning tonight, by the way."

"This old thing?" I tease, gesturing to the floor-length gold dress I'd picked out for the evening. The high neckline is conservative, my simple earrings and natural makeup complementing the look, but the back of the dress is virtually non-existent, the fabric sweeping wide and low before meeting in a V just above my tailbone. The dress hugs my curves all the way down to the middle of my thigh before sweeping out just slightly, a low slit revealing my left leg and heel when I walk.

"I've been imagining all the ways I can strip you out of it," Brandon admits.

"Even while on stage?"

"*Especially* while on stage."

I laugh, spinning under his arm again before wrapping my arm back around his shoulders. "Our last night," I remind him, eyes searching his for a sign of... well, anything — sadness, excitement, regret, fear, hope.

He swallows. "We'll have to make it count."

"Back to reality tomorrow."

He nods as the band finishes the song, still holding me in his arms when the last note plays. "Indeed."

The room claps politely, the band smiling in thanks before striking up the next melody, but time is frozen where Brandon holds me in the middle of the dance floor. The way his hand grips the skin on my lower back — just slightly, enough to send a wave of chills over my arms — has me anxious to get back to the room.

If we really only have one more night together, I don't want to waste a single second more of it here.

"I'm suddenly very tired," I breathe, my eyes flashing over his lips.

Brandon grins. "Then let's get you to bed, Miss Daniels."

That night, Brandon touches me slower, longer, with more intent and purpose than before. It's as if he's memorizing the way every inch of my body feels beneath his, the way my breaths enter and exit my lungs, the way my lips move over the moans and whispers of his name.

And I memorize him, too — wondering how I'll ever let him go once our jet lands back in South Florida.

We knew the game we were playing was dangerous before we even dealt the cards, and now here we are, nearing the end, both of us winners and losers in equal measure. It's time to pack up. Time to go home. Time to keep our promises, leaving our brief time together in the past, in a memory, never to be relived.

But with Brandon's lips on my skin, his hands on my waist, his breaths in my ear — I can't help but feel like this game is *far* from over.

EPISODE 6

Ashlei

I knew after Thanksgiving, the rest of the semester would fly by. There were only a few weeks left, after all, and now here I am, packing up the last of my belongings in the little cube I've called home all semester.

The Monday after the holiday had started off with a bang, the entire team full on mashed potatoes and drive to make the *Bare•ly* event successful. We'd all joined forces and thrown our all into it, and two weeks later, we'd rocked that event like I knew we would all along. It was chic, elegant, modern and classy — everything our clients had asked for. And for the first time, I'd been in charge of an event from beginning to end, handling the crises as they came and putting out fires left and right, all while never dropping the illusion that everything was going exactly as planned. It was a perfect launch party, and Mrs. Delure had assured me I had a high recommendation letter coming from her whenever I graduated and set out looking for my first job.

"I knew you'd be the last intern out of here," Mykayla says, propping her hip against the wall of my cube as she watches me pack up. "But then again, I knew you'd be different from the other interns the moment I met you."

I toss my sticky notepads into the box, the contents now threatening to spill over the top, and pause to face her. "Aw, Mykayla. I'm going to miss you."

"Same here, girly. But," she clarifies, stepping into my cube with outstretched arms. "I'm serious about you coming to Happy Hour with us every now and then. Your sorority sisters can share."

I laugh, hugging her tight. "Absolutely. You have my number. I'm there anytime."

She sighs, squeezing me once before letting me go. "I'm going to finish up some emails and then we can walk out together, if you're finished?" she asks, eyes on my now very empty desk.

Picking up the last highlighter and tossing it into a vacant corner of the box, I nod. "Yep. I guess this is it..." I swallow, glancing at the office down the hall with the door still open. "I just need to say my goodbyes to Mr. Church and I'll be ready."

Saying his name out loud makes my stomach lurch, though Mykayla is oblivious, taking my box from the desk. "I'll hold this for you. Poor Mr. Church, hope you don't make him cry. He's already going to be here working all weekend long. Add that to the fact that his favorite intern is leaving?" She smiles, nudging me. "You were everyone's favorite, truthfully."

"Oh, stop." I laugh. "Why is he working all weekend?"

She shrugs. "I dunno, last minute event or something. He mentioned it in passing and I told him to let me know if he needed anything, but you know him. He'll work his weekend alone in quiet, suffering, and leave the rest of us alone."

"Yeah..." My eyes find his office again, his face hidden but hands visible as they type away on his keyboard. "Sounds like him."

"Anyway, let me go send these emails and you go say goodbye. See you in a sec!" And with that, she trots off.

When she's gone, I blow out a long, shaky breath, flattening my palms over the skirt of the same dress I wore on day one. Flashes of Brandon in the elevator, of our first exchange, mingle with the intimate way I came to know him over Thanksgiving break as I walk slowly down the hall toward his office. It's after five on a Friday, leaving only a handful of associates in the office. Usually he's gone by now, but something tells me he was waiting for me to come say goodbye.

True to our word, we haven't crossed any lines since the jet touched down back in Miami that Sunday after the holiday. He's kept his gaze neutral in meetings, just like I asked, and with so much of my focus being on the *Bare•ly* event, I only really had time to pine over him in the privacy of mine and Erin's room at the sorority house.

But I'm not immune to him. My breath still hitches when our hands brush, my heart still skips when he calls my name at an event or in the office, and my body still aches with need for him every night when I lie down in my empty bed.

I wonder if he aches for me, too.

He seems so unfazed by me now, like he truly did itch his scratch and has no want or need for me anymore other than to be a good intern. His gaze never lingers over mine longer than it should, he never winks when no one is looking, he never texts me late at night with wistful thoughts. He has kept his word, and I never thought that would hurt as much as it has.

"Mr. Church?" I rap my knuckles on the doorframe to his office, causing him to pause mid-type and look at me. Just that glance alone nearly has me doubling over. "Sorry to bother you, I'm just... I'm about to head out, and I wanted to say goodbye."

His expression is blank, completely void of emotion. He watches me for a moment before standing, fastening the button at the bottom of his suit jacket and stepping around his desk. "It's been a pleasure having you on the team, Miss Daniels," he says, extending his hand for mine. "If you ever need a reference — or anything at all — don't hesitate to give us a call."

My heart sinks, pulling my smile with it as I let him take my hand. He shakes it firmly, like he would anyone else, and I try not to let it show just how badly that hurts. "The pleasure has been mine. I can't thank you enough for the opportunity."

His jaw ticks, like he's biting back the words he can't say — the words I long to hear. I try to hold onto his hand longer, try to feel connected to him for as long as I can, but he pulls back after our handshake, sliding his hands into the pockets of his slacks with his eyes still on me.

"Bye, then," I say, excusing myself. When I'm just past the door, he calls out my name.

"Miss Daniels?"

I turn, finding just a hint of longing in his dark eyes, like he's fighting with every ounce of power he has to keep his hands in his pockets and off of me. It was the look I asked him not to give me, the one I missed, the one I wasn't sure still existed.

"Keep in touch, okay?"

Smiling, I nod, holding his gaze for as long as he'll let me before finally turning for good. I walk slowly down the hallway, hoping he's watching, and when I reach Mykayla's desk, she's already waiting and holding my box for me.

"Ready?"

On an exhale, I nod, looking around the office with an ache in my chest. "Ready."

As we wait for the elevators, I feel his eyes on me, but I wait until Mykayla steps in and it's my turn to let him know it. My eyes find his down the hall, and without any words exchanged, I finally feel it.

He's going to miss me, too.

He smiles, offering me a slight wave, and I smile in return before stepping onto the elevator, all the while wondering if that's the last time I'll ever see Mr. Church.

Skyler

"Ugh, this sucks," I say to my empty room, scrolling through the list of classes still available for spring semester. After filling my schedule with a whole array of classes this semester, I still haven't found anything I'm passionate about — nothing I would want to make a career of, at least — and so here I am, on a Friday night, throwing darts at a spinning wheel again and hoping something sticks.

This semester has been hard.

Classes have been weird, none of them meshing together which, surprisingly, made studying even more difficult than usual. Poker has been consuming my life, especially since I officially decided to enter the big tournament next May. I haven't paid my entry fee yet, but I did give an exclusive interview to one of my favorite poker blogs. Now the poker world is buzzing about my entry, and it's crunch time.

Clinton *still* isn't talking to me, ignoring all my apology texts and voicemails. And, in the strangest turn of events, I haven't had a boy to occupy my time, other than the now two drunken times I've found myself hooking up with Adam. If it wasn't for him being cool with a no-strings drunk hookup situation, I likely would have gone mad from No D Disease by now.

Sighing, I pull the trigger and sign up for my last class — Writing for Television. And with my course load full, I snap my laptop shut, head collapsing on top of it once it's closed with my hair splayed all around me. My phone buzzes from the corner of my desk and I reach for it blindly, peeking through my hair at the name on the screen.

And then I sit up straight, eyes widening.

Sliding the message open from the home screen, Clinton's contact opens, showing me all the unanswered texts I've sent since Halloween. But now, right under the last one, is a text from him.

- Can you come over? -

I don't even bother running a brush through my hair or changing out of the leggings and tank top I have on before I'm running down the stairs and out the door. I'm about halfway down Greek Row when I realize I *also* didn't stop to put a bra on, but I don't turn back, because all that matters in this moment is that Clinton texted me, and he wants to talk to me, and that's all I care about.

My mind is running wild with all the things I'll say when I get to his room — how sorry I am, how I never meant to upset him, how I'll make Clayton do some kind of work for the money if that will help, or let Clinton pay me back if he wants. But I don't get a chance to say any of it, because when I burst through the Omega Chi Beta doors, the entire house is full of brothers.

And all of them are staring at me.

Josh, Clinton's Little, steps forward first, eyeing my outfit with appreciation and a wink that makes me roll my eyes before the first word leaves his mouth.

"Skyler, Bear called on all of us to help him, because apparently he's been a real fucking idiot and not a very good best friend lately," he starts, and it's then that I realize every brother in the room is holding a notecard in their hands. "He didn't want to just apologize, he wanted you to know how special you are to him. So, he wrote down something for every day that you guys haven't talked."

He holds up the notecard in his hand with a goofy smile and my hands fly to my mouth, eyes glossing. I am *not* a cryer, but damnit if the tears don't gather, anyway.

"You are, by far, the best poker player this country has ever seen, and I can't wait to see you take the title in May," Josh reads, and then another brother steps forward, reading from his card next.

"No one cuddles better than you do." The guys all laugh as he steps back, and then another card is read. And another. And another.

"There's no one I'd rather split a twelve-pack with."

"I would go to war for you if you asked."

"Your laugh is the best sound in the world, and the only thing that makes me feel better on a shitty day."

"There isn't a girl on campus who looks better in cut-off shorts and a sorority jersey."

A slew of whistles rings out at that and I laugh, blushing.

The list goes on and on, some of the cards making me smile, some making me laugh, and others making it really difficult not to cry. And after every brother standing in the living room and on the stairs lining to the upstairs has read their card, Clinton steps out from the back hallway, walking straight up to me.

"No matter how many cards I write, I could never truly tell you what you mean to me, Skyler," he says, apologies in his eyes before he even says them. "You are my family — no, you're *more* than family. You're my best friend, and I'm so sorry I let you think for even one second that you don't mean everything in the world to me, because you do. I am so, so sorry for being a giant dick. Will you please let me make it up to you by taking you to Semi-formal and being the best date you could ever ask for?"

I sniff, nodding with tears blurring my vision before launching at him. He catches me easily, wrapping me in the fiercest Bear Hug yet.

"You owe me *so* many burritos for this."

All the guys laugh again, clapping and cheering, and Clinton high fives them and thanks a few as he tucks me under his arm, leading me back to his bedroom. I can still hear the guys laughing and joking with each other, reading the cards with girly voices as Clinton shuts the door behind us.

"Seriously, Skyler. I am so sorry."

"No, no," I shake my head, wrapping my small arms around him again and resting my head in the dip of his chest. "*I'm* sorry. I should have asked you before I did what I did. At the very least, I should have told you. It was selfish and stupid and—"

"It wasn't selfish," he says, cutting me off. "It was sweet and kind, and something I would have done for your family in the reverse. I just... I was upset, he's my brother and I want to be the one to help him, to protect him. I needed a little bit of time to see past my pride, Skyler. And I'm sorry I took so long."

He squeezes me tight, and when he pulls back, I grab his large hand and drag him to his bed, climbing in first and sighing with relief when he slides in behind me and wraps me in his arms again.

"I've missed you so much, Bear. Everything has been so hard without you." My voice sounds small, weak.

"I know," he says, kissing my hair. "I'm so sorry. Tell me everything. How many hearts have you broken since Halloween?"

I laugh. "Zero. Poker has been my only serious relationship this semester."

"Well, who knows. Maybe next semester, some guy will sweep you off your feet and you'll have a date in Vegas."

Rolling my eyes, I twist in his arms and snuggle into his chest, his chin fitting on top of my head like we're the last two puzzle pieces. And for the rest of the night, he catches me up on his life — including how his brother is doing in Pittsburgh — and I tell him my fears about the tournament, and how hard it will be to earn the last bit of the entry money.

Suddenly, everything is right in the world again.

I have no idea what next semester holds, or the rest of my life, for that matter. Maybe I'll figure out my major, maybe I'll win the poker tournament, or maybe I'll still be a confused girl with a best friend who will support me no matter what happens.

And that's more than okay with me.

Jess

When I get a text from Skyler saying she's staying at Clinton's for the night, I breathe a sigh of relief, typing out a text to her that Jarrett and I are finally going to video chat in less than an hour. She wishes me luck and then I plug my phone into the charger, letting it get juiced as I do my makeup in the bathroom.

The last time we were supposed to video chat, I had been so excited.

Now, all I am is sick.

I ended up texting Jarrett the day after Thanksgiving, apologizing for everything and telling him I would give him his space, and to just call me when he was caught up on the project and a little less stressed out. I told him we could see each other over Christmas break, and that I understood, and that we would be okay. I thought it was the right thing to do — the mature thing to do — but when all he wrote back was a simple *thanks*, I wondered if it was already too late, if he would ever forgive me.

Ever since he went back to New York after coming to visit, everything with us has been so rocky. Between the communication breakdown and the long distance, my heart is raw and aching. He can't hold me to make me feel better, and I can't kiss him with my apologies. We can't just jump in his truck and drive to the beach, splitting a joint and having sex until the sun rises. Everything about our relationship is different, and I'm not sure who we are in this new space.

As shitty as it is, Greg has been a huge help keeping my mind off Jarrett the last couple of weeks. He's listened to me talk about Jarrett, offering advice when he had it and just a shoulder to lean on when he had nothing to say. He's funny, and kind, and I appreciate his company. And maybe a small part of me realizes that I just enjoy the fact that a man cares about me, and is attracted to me, and is giving me attention.

Something else inside me, something deep in the trenches of thoughts I like to leave *un*thought, tells me this phone call is either going to make or break me and Jarrett. And as much as I have a whole string of apologies ready to go, I also have questions, and concerns, and things *I* want to talk about. I understand his side of things, how he needs me to be able to trust him and understand how demanding his job is, but relationships are about compromise — and I need love and support, too.

I feel so unlike myself, so vulnerable and defeated. The girls have started to notice, too — wondering where my spunk has gone, and I know I won't get back to myself until I face whatever is about to happen with Jarrett.

When my makeup is flawless and my hair is straightened, I slip on a pair of sleep shorts and a tank top, propping my laptop up on my desk to wait for his call. And when his picture and name fill the screen at exactly ten o'clock, I take a deep breath and answer.

The screen is fuzzy at first, and when it clears, Jarrett is sitting at his small kitchen table, giving me a view of practically his entire studio apartment. The city lights burn through the window behind him, mixing with the low light of his apartment to cast him in a soft glow. Finally seeing his face, his lips, his eyes — it hurts as much as it heals.

"Hi," I breathe, a weary smile finding my lips.

"Hi."

I watch him for a moment, wishing so badly he was here. I just want to touch him, to hold him, to have him hold me. "I wish I could jump through this screen right now."

His eyes are sad, defeated, and he only nods in response.

It's strange, how someone you love can seem so foreign in moments like these, moments when everything hangs in the balance.

Steeling myself, I sit up a little straighter and start my long list of apologies. "Listen, I am so sorry I went off on you for missing our date. That was an immature reaction and a little dramatic and I wish I could take it back. I know you had a long day and I know you can't help what projects you get put on or whom with. I want to be more supportive, but... I need you to understand my side of things, too. I need—"

"It's over."

I pause, mouth still hanging open, the words I'd planned to say next frozen in my throat. I close my mouth, open it again, nose flaring and eyes watering as I try to convince myself I didn't just hear the man I love tell me he doesn't want to be with me anymore.

"Wh-what?"

"It's over, Jess. We, this," he motions to the screen and back to himself. "I can't... I won't do this anymore."

Shock rips through me, my head shaking of its own accord. I knew this phone call wouldn't be pretty, I knew he was upset, I knew there were things to be said and to be decided but still, even if I pretended to prepare for the worst, I didn't actually think it would happen.

How can Jarrett break up with me? After all we've been through, after all he's said, after all we've promised?

"Jarrett, we can work through this. I said I'm sorry, I... I'll try harder. I'll do better. It's just a silly fight, it isn't—"

"I saw the picture." His eyes bore holes through mine from thousands of miles away, the heart he always keeps sheltered now bloody and marred on his sleeve for me to see. "I don't play these games. I put up with you parading other guys in front of me last year, trying to make me jealous, playing me like I'm just another guy to you but I thought we were past that."

Panic rises in my throat like bile. "He's just a friend, Jarrett. I met him that night, we just talked. I swear, that's all."

"But you went into that bar on a mission, didn't you? A mission to find a poor sap to twirl around your finger and make me jealous. You thought it'd make me call you. You thought it'd make me, what? Worship you?"

I shake my head frantically, tears rushing my eyes and billowing down my cheeks before I can stop them. "I didn't... Yes, I wanted your attention, but I didn't do anything with him. I promise. And he posted the picture, not me."

"But he tagged you," Jarrett points out. "Which I'm sure you asked him to do."

"Please," I beg, reaching out to touch the screen. "Just let me come see you. Let's talk about this in person. You don't mean this, you don't—"

"YOU HAD ME, JESS!" he yells, his face twisting as I choke on a sob. "You had me, and now you don't. It shouldn't be like this, I shouldn't have to choose between you and my career, or worry about how you'll react to me *working* with another female. It's just like the surf lessons last year. Nothing I say to you and nothing I do will ever convince you that I am yours, and I have continually paid the price. Do you know how sick I've been, wondering what you did with that guy to get back at me?"

"I didn't," I try, but my voice breaks.

"I love you. And you said you loved me, too." He shakes his head, jaw tight. "This isn't how you treat someone you love."

"I'm sorry," I choke, letting the tears run. "I'm so sorry."

"Me, too," he says, finally lifting his eyes to mine. He searches them, looking for the girl he knew, the girl he fell in love with. When he shakes his head, I know he's come up empty handed. "I have to go."

"Jarrett, please."

But the screen just goes dark like the rest of my world.

***

I've read about these sensory deprivation tanks, where you lie in a tub of water filled with Epson salt to make you float in a soundproof pod with no light. You just float there, completely weightless, emerging on the other side of the experience almost as if in a trance. Some claim it has healing effects, others claim hallucination.

That's the closest comparison I can make to how I feel right now, lying on my bedroom floor, in the exact same place I fell last night after Jarrett ended our call. I only know it's morning because light started breaking through the curtains at some point, though I have no idea how long ago that was. Everything is numb. Everything is on fire. My eyes sting and burn, my brain replaying every word he said, every word he didn't. But somewhere in the numb of the night, I came to a conclusion.

I don't want to fall apart.

I earned my nickname, J-Love, because when I was younger I said I loved pretty much any guy who gave me his attention. And though what I had with Jarrett was much realer than that, in the end, I can't help but feel like I lost a little part of myself with him, too. I don't want to let the end of our relationship be the end of me.

I know I'll need to break, and cry, and I know in the deepest part of my being that there is no getting over Jarrett. Not really. He will always own a part of my heart, and losing him will forever be one of my biggest regrets. But I want to grieve in silence, alone.

Jess Vonnegut is a bad ass. She is a vixen, a fighter, a man-eater, a tough bitch. She doesn't stop the party for any drama, and she doesn't stop her life for any boy.

Swiping at my face as if it isn't already dry, I crawl to the desk and pull my phone down, sinking against the drawers as I type out a text to Greg.

- Take a break from studying turtle facts tonight and go to Semi-formal with me. -

I drop the phone to the floor beside me, kneading my temples, my head throbbing between my fingers. When my phone buzzes, I unlock it quickly, smiling as much as I physically can in this moment at his response.

- I'll bring the vodka. -

And I'm not sure how much longer I lie there before eventually peeling myself off the floor, along with what's left of my dignity, holding onto it as tight as I can. Soon, the girls are all getting ready, music blasting, makeup and hair product everywhere. I tell them about Jarrett with a straight face, my tears all spilled last night, and they console me. Ashlei asks if I want to skip Semi. Skyler wants me to talk about it. But I decline both offers, telling them I already invited Greg, and I'm fine.

It's a lie, and they know it, but they don't press me on it.

At least for tonight, I'm going to be okay. I'm going to dance and sing, laugh and party, and pretend like everything will be okay. I'll fake it until I make it — make it back home, that is. And then, I'll have three weeks of winter break to get over it.

That's that.

When the limos are pulling up outside, I pull up Jarrett's name and type out one last text before blocking his number and tucking my phone in my clutch, ripping the Band-Aid off, ready to scab and heal.

- I will always love you. -

Bear

"Chug! Chug! Chug!"

I hear my brothers chanting as Skyler and I race to see who finishes our beer first, which is ridiculous, really, because she's a tiny little peanut compared to me. It's kind of comical watching her throw down when she's dressed to the nines, beer dripping down her chin and landing on the large gold necklace she's paired with her burgundy dress. In the end, I finish first, wiping my mouth with the back of my wrist and joining in with my brothers chanting as she finishes.

She's just as smiley as she would have been had she won, holding up her empty glass in victory as her sisters cheer. Then she grabs my hand, pulling me back out onto the dance floor.

Everything is back to normal now that I finally manned up and apologized to Skyler. She deserved it way earlier than it happened, but thankfully she'd still accepted. Once I talked to my baby brother and heard the whole story from him, I knew I was being an ass — hell, I knew it before then — but it helped me clear my mind enough to realize I was in the wrong.

So, I booked a flight home in a little over a week for winter break to stay at Mac's place and help Clayton find a job, or at least some way to earn some extra cash. I also made it clear that next time he was worried about money, I wanted him to come to me — even if he felt like I was busy or he didn't want to bother me. Then, I got my brothers together and made a plan to apologize to Skyler.

The semester hasn't exactly been the best for me, with Omega Chi being on probation and the fight with Skyler, but I finally feel like everything is falling back into place. We still get to recruit new members in the spring, which means we'll all be busy when we get back to campus. Add in the facts that I get to spend a few weeks with my brother and Skyler and I are good again, and I'm finding plenty to be thankful for.

Skyler starts the cabbage patch when the DJ spins a disco track and I follow suit, pointing one finger up into the air before crossing it over my hip to point down and back up again. Jess and Ashlei join us, along with Greg and a few of my other brothers, and we make a dance circle, taking turns doing ridiculous dance moves in the middle to a crowd of cheers.

When a slow song comes on, most of the floor clears, making way for couples. Jess and Greg stay on the floor while Ashlei, Skyler, and I make our way back to our table.

"I'm going to run to the restroom," Skyler says, pointing over her shoulder. "Grab us fresh beers and meet back here?"

"On it."

She skips off with Ashlei's arm linked in hers and I head toward the bar at the far end of the ballroom.

Semi-formal is always a little more casual than Formal held in the spring, but everyone still dresses up, and the setting is always some sort of fancy hotel or venue with a ballroom. This one also has a garden, one that connects to the back end of the ballroom where one of the bars is, and when I glance out the door as I wait in line and spot Erin sitting alone on one of the benches, I frown.

Abandoning my spot in line, I dip through the glass double doors, the heat of the night hitting me as soon as they close behind me. It may be December, but it's still South Florida, and there's a thin sheen of sweat gathering on the back of Erin's slender neck as she stares down at her lap, rolling something over and over in her hands.

It's just the two of us outside — probably because ties and tight dresses already make you sweat enough without adding humidity to them — so I take the open seat next to her on the detailed metal bench.

For a moment I let my eyes roam the garden, taking in the low-hanging trees and wide array of bright flowers. There are a few bird baths, too — the water gently running from each of them serving as the only soundtrack as I try to think of what to say to her. Erin and I haven't spoken since the night of her birthday, and she made it pretty clear that she didn't want my help... or maybe even my friendship. But I can't just walk away from her, not when she's hurting — even if she denies that she is.

"My mom used to have a garden," I say finally, my voice soft and low. "When I was younger. Maybe like five or six or so? Before the drugs became more important to her than anything else."

Erin pauses rolling whatever it is she's holding and clasps her hands over it tight, listening.

"I would help her sometimes. She didn't grow flowers as much as like vegetables and stuff. I remember we had fresh tomatoes in our dinners almost every night — in a salad, on a sandwich, mashed up into chili — whatever." I shake my head. "The garden just turned into a dried-up mess of weeds after she got into drugs, though."

"I'm sorry," Erin whispers.

"It's okay. I really don't think about her much, honestly. But something about this garden struck that memory, I guess."

Erin nods and I finally look down at her, taking in the soft shape of her face, the rosy tint of her cheeks, the long slender slope of her nose. She's always had such a classy and regal look about her, which fits perfectly with the all-black pantsuit she's wearing tonight. It's cut deep in the front, right between her chest, but tastefully so, and the back is open, too. Something tells me she decided to wear pants instead of a dress for a reason, a statement of sorts, even if she's the only one she's making it for.

"You look gorgeous tonight, Erin," I say, still watching her.

"Thank you."

I pause, waiting to see if she'll talk, but when she doesn't, I try for humor. "What? Not going to compliment me on my dope threads?" I pull at the cuffs of the gray, black and white plaid jacket I paired with an all-black dress shirt and forest green dress slacks, popping my collar with a grin.

Erin eyes me, a soft smile cracking at the edges of her lips. "It's a wonder what wearing something other than basketball shorts can do."

"I think there was a compliment in there somewhere."

She smiles a little more but it drops from her face too quickly, reminding me that she's still a sad girl sitting alone on a bench at her Semi-formal.

"What's on your mind?" I ask, nudging her gently.

Erin shakes her head, fists closed tight around the object of her hand. "Did you hear about Landon's car?"

My fists clench just at the mention of his name. "Yeah. Fucker deserved it."

"I did it," she says quickly, lifting her eyes to look at mine for just a split second before focusing on her hands again. "I thought it would make me feel better, to get some sort of revenge." She shrugs. "But it just made me feel worse. Because there's absolutely nothing I could ever do to him that would be as horrible as what he did to me."

It's like a fiery arrow is shot straight into my chest at her words and I reach my hand out, grazing her lower back just enough to let her know I'm here. "You could press charges."

She scoffs. "Don't, Bear."

I know her stance on it already — that she feels like it doesn't matter what she says or does, he'll get away with it. She was drunk, they'll say she was "asking for it." And even if they did give him jail time or anything else, it wouldn't make her feel better, and then she'd just be the poor girl who was raped. These are all things she's told me multiple times since that night, but I hate hearing them, hate that she believes them... hate that in many ways, she's right. Our justice system doesn't seek much justice for rape victims, not the way it should.

Erin laughs a little. "And then, to add insult to injury, I was walking by the Student Union earlier and this perky little sophomore on the Orientation Team stops me, telling me that they're fighting back against sexual assault on campus. And she hands me this," she says, opening her hand and holding up a small, teal and orange whistle — PSU's school colors. "'It's a *rape whistle,'* she said." Erin laughs again. "Like this will save anyone. Like this will make it stop."

Suddenly, Erin pops the whistle in her mouth and starts blowing it, loud shrieks piercing the otherwise quiet night around us. She blows it over and over again, her eyes welling with tears, face red when I finally take her in my arms and hold her tight to my chest.

She keeps blowing it, and to drive her point home further, no one inside the ballroom even looks our way. She might as well be whispering.

Finally, the whistle falls from her mouth and she catches it in her hands, choking on a sob as she leans into my chest.

"It's okay," I whisper, running my hand over her hair as I hold her tighter. "I'm so sorry, Erin."

She lets me hold her for a short minute before she's shoving me off, wiping at her face like she's stupid for crying. "Whatever. I was just making a point. Even if I would have had this," she spits, holding up the whistle again. "This stupid *thing*, I would have maybe been able to blow it twice before it would have been ripped from my mouth. And that's *if* I could even manage to get it out of my clutch. And, even if I did, no one would have heard me."

"I was too late," I say, fists clenching at my side again. "I should have known something was off. I should have found you earlier."

"How would you have known?" she challenges, looking at me again. "The door was shut. The music in the ballroom was loud. There's nothing you could have done." She hiccups, wiping at her face again. "There's nothing anyone could have done, other than Landon and his friends." Her face twists. "I don't even know their names."

I reach for her again but she pulls away, standing.

"You need to talk to someone, Erin."

"I'm fine."

"Clearly," I deadpan. "You're going to break if you don't get this off your chest and start working through it."

She laughs, eyes brimming over again. "I'm already fucking broken."

"You're not broken, but you are losing yourself."

"Yeah?" she asks, patronizing me. "Well, maybe I'll like the new girl I find. Maybe she'll be stronger and not take any shit."

"Or maybe she'll be a cold shell of the amazing girl I used to know. And dead inside," I counter.

Erin's eyes catch mine then, her face as smooth as stone. "Better to be dead inside than live with this pain anymore."

My heart is too broken to say another word before she turns, tucking the whistle into her clutch and walking back inside the ballroom.

Cassie

My strapless dress is a giant pain in my ass.

I tug it up by the sides again, for what feels like the fiftieth time, as I wait for Ashlei to finish touching up her lipstick. It's a beautiful dress — navy blue with gold sequins and studs swirled in a floral design over the sweetheart neckline down to my waist, where the navy tulle flares off and ends right above my knees. But I purchased it before Thanksgiving, and I've lost too much weight since then for it to fit properly.

Not that I'm *trying* to lose weight, but apparently it's a side effect of losing someone you care about.

Ever since Thanksgiving, everything has felt off. Grayson and I *seem* fine by all accounts — we're having great sex, spending more time together, making plans for the future — but it's like I'm only living with half of myself turned on, like the other half is stuck in a dark coma. I can't study to save my life, which is not conducive to the final exams I have coming up. I can't eat, I can barely sleep. Because the truth of the matter is I made a choice that day, on Thanksgiving — one that I didn't want to make. And now I'm facing the cold, hard truth of it all.

I don't want to live without Adam in my life.

But I have to in order to keep Grayson.

Adam hasn't spoken to me since that day — hasn't even tried to. He understood, he knew I didn't want to do it but that I had to. Still, everything has been so empty without him. Even tonight, not seeing him staring holes into the back of my head from across the dance floor bothers me. Is that selfish? Probably, but I want him here.

I'm not allowed to want that, but I do.

"Is it just me, or does Semi kind of suck this year?" Ashlei asks on a sigh, popping her violet lips together before dropping her lipstick back in her clutch.

"It's not just you."

She turns to me, head tilted to the side. "Well, I'm stag, so I know a little of the reason why it sucks for me. Why does it suck for you?"

Where to begin?

I smile, waving her off. "We've just had better venues, that's all. And I'm so tired from all the studying I've been doing lately."

"Ugh," Ashlei agrees, linking her arm through mine to head back out to the ballroom. "You really have been hitting the books. Remind me again why you chose biology for a major?"

"Damn aspirations to be a doctor."

"Oh, yeah." She giggles. "That."

We make it back out to the dance floor just in time to hear the music shift to a slower rhythm, once again causing a mass exodus from the dance floor. Clinton ends up keeping Skyler out there this time, and everyone is laughing at the two of them doing some sort of fake waltz to a slow Usher song.

I search for Grayson, wanting nothing more than to just be held by him as we sway back and forth on the dance floor. I feel so weird lately, and being close to him is one of the only things that helps. It reminds me why I made the choice I did, why I sacrificed someone who means something to me. Grayson is the first boy I've ever truly loved, and who loves me, too. It's powerful and addictive, like the best kind of drug, and all I want tonight is to drown in him.

"Hey, have you seen Grayson?" I ask Jess and her date, Greg. It's still a little weird seeing her with someone other than Jarrett, but she's smiling and seems happy, so I'm thankful he's here.

"Oh! Him and his friend — Malik? — went outside to the garden to sneak a few drinks from their flasks, I think," Jess answers, letting Greg pull her up from her seat at the table and onto the dance floor.

"Thanks!"

I walk as fast as I can in my high heels toward the entrance to the garden at the back of the ballroom, pushing through the double doors to find an empty bench. I frown, letting the doors close behind me as I look for Grayson. The garden is small, but the winding path leads back a ways, so I follow it, guessing he and Malik are probably hiding out somewhere.

When the stiff stench of marijuana hits my nose, I know I've found *someone*, but I'm a little surprised when I spot Grayson through the tall bushes near the back corner taking a joint from Malik's hand and holding it to his lips.

The sight of it stops me still in my tracks, my heart thundering in my ears. It's not that I necessarily have anything against smoking, but I never knew Grayson was into it. He never told me. And in this moment, it feels a lot like something he should have told me.

It feels a lot like something he's hiding.

My feet are still glued to the garden path when Grayson passes the joint back to Malik, his voice strange as he tries to hold in the smoke and talk at the same time. "I mean, don't get me wrong. It's not like I see her being a forever sort of thing." He blows out a cloud of smoke, checking over his shoulder at the opening in the path. "She's just college, and I get that. But at least now he's out of my way."

"I'm surprised you were cool about it for as long as you were," Malik says. "That kid has it bad for her. She's lying if she says she doesn't see it."

Grayson shakes his head, dipping into his jacket for his flask. "I don't know. Cassie is just kind of naïve like that. I'm not sure she really sees it, but I do. Which is why I put my foot down and put an end to it."

My throat closes at the mention of my name, heart still racing. I shouldn't be eavesdropping, but now I can't stop.

"Atta boy," Malik says, handing the joint back to Grayson as a puff of smoke leaves his lips. "Speaking of complications, is that groupie finally leaving you alone?"

"Ugh, I wish. That girl cannot take a hint. If only she was as bright as that neon pink hair of hers."

Malik chuckles. "Hey, at least she gives good head. You going to miss that?"

My stomach lurches as Grayson grins, taking a hit from the joint and passing it back. "Nah. Surprisingly, Cassie is pretty hot in bed."

"Now that she's actually fucking you, that is. Think she'll ever find out about the groupie?"

"No way. She knows I love her. Alexis was just a stress relief until Cassie was ready. Had to get it from somewhere, you know?" he jokes, and Malik grins with approval. "Once Cassie let me hit, I stopped texting Alexis altogether."

"Wow, what a great boyfriend," I spit, rounding the bushes until Malik can see me. His eyes widen and Grayson turns, all the color draining from his face when he sees me, too. "To give up your hook ups with a groupie once you got in my pants. So charming."

My voice is just as shaky as my hands and I hate it, rolling them into fists as I try to stand tall, trying to control the racing of my heart long enough to put Grayson in his place. I ran from the last guy who fucked me over, letting him make a fool of me.

Not this time.

"Cassie, I don't know what you heard but—"

"Don't touch me," I seethe, cutting Grayson off mid-sentence as his hands reach out for me. "You'll never touch me again. I hope she was worth it."

"Come on—"

"No!" I shake my head, eyes bouncing between Grayson's like I've never seen him before in my life, like he's a stranger who somehow has the power to break my heart. "No, I'm not listening to another word. And you asked me to give up my friendship with Adam because — what — *your* conscience wouldn't let you sleep at night?"

Grayson swallows, joint still burning in his hand as he pleads with his eyes for me to see him, to want him, to listen to him — but I do none of the above.

"Is she why you were late to the Alpha Sigma concert?" I shake my head, the need to cry burning at the back of my throat and eyes but I refuse to give in. "Is she why you cancelled our date that night?"

He swallows, lips in a flat line and face ashen, which is all the answer I need.

I choke, almost breaking down before shaking it off. "I knew you were a performer," I say, holding my chin up. "But had I known you were playing me like your fucking guitar, I would have stopped buying tickets to the shows a long time ago."

"Cassie, just please—"

"Go fuck yourself, Grayson."

I turn without another look in his direction, not stopping when he calls my name or sprints after me. I snatch my clutch off the table, fighting back tears as Ashlei and Jess swarm me, asking what's wrong. Skyler is there next, pushing Grayson away as he tries to break through the crowd to get to me.

"I just want to leave," I choke out, trying so hard not to cry I can't breathe from holding the tears in.

"Let's go." Skyler grabs my hand, telling Clinton to call us a cab and meet on the curb outside. She holds me in her arms as we walk, not asking any questions, knowing I can't talk in that moment.

It's not when we make it outside that I let myself cry. It's not in the cab ride home, or in Skyler's arms as she hugs me tight at the house. No, it's not until well after midnight, when I've finished telling her what happened and walked numbly up to my room, stripping out of my dress and removing my makeup before slipping into my sheets that I finally break down.

Because my sheets smell like him.

It's like those sheets are covered in betrayal and lies and every breath is me suffocating in them, fighting for oxygen that doesn't exist. I let the tears fall, choking on the toxic air and hugging my arms tight around my middle, as if they can somehow squeeze out the pain racking through me.

I loved him.

No, that's a lie, because it implies past tense. I *love* him — here and now, writhing in sheets that smell like him and replaying the words he said that broke my heart — I still love him. It's the worst feeling, to love someone who has hurt you. But love isn't a pencil mark. It can't be erased so easily.

I wonder if I'll ever be able to erase it at all.

It's with that aching thought that I cry myself into the worst sleep of my life.

Ashlei

After Cassie, Skyler, and Clinton leave, I'm basically alone with Jess and her date.

Erin is here, too, but she's pre-occupied, running around taking care of girls who are too drunk and getting in those last few good impressions before we vote for president. I know she's going to get it — hell, we all do — but it doesn't stop her from taking on the role of KKB Mom tonight.

And then there's me.

Feeling amazing in a beige fit and flare dress that hugs my neck and dips down low in the back, with just a few strings tying it together, and rolling completely stag.

It wouldn't be so bad if my mind wasn't focused on the absolute last person it should be — the one person I can't have. I survived my internship, I only have two finals left and both of them should be easy as pie, I'm healthy and happier than I've been in a long time. By all accounts, I should be ecstatic tonight, but I can't stop thinking about Brandon.

"I think we're going to head out," Jess says, her hand around Greg's as they come back to the table from where they'd been dancing.

I frown, searching Jess' eyes for a sign of the breakdown I know is coming. She loved Jarrett, and she may be trying to put on the tough bitch act, but I see right through it. "Okay. Are you guys going to be alright?"

Jess smiles, but it's weak. "Yeah, we'll be fine. See you later at the house?"

I nod, eyes softening. Jess just shrugs when Greg turns, heading toward where the first bus is loading up to leave.

I love you, I mouth to her, and she smiles, offering a half-wave before following Greg.

For a moment I just sit at the table by myself, sipping on my fruity cocktail and watching everyone on the dance floor. I could leave on the first bus, too, I suppose, but what would I be leaving for? Erin is still here, which means I'd be going home from my Semi-formal *early* just to sit alone in my room.

And then it hits me.

"Why can't I be with him?"

I actually say the words out loud before I clamp my hand over my mouth, smiling under it at my ridiculousness, but my mind keeps rolling the thought over and over. My internship is over, he's not my boss anymore. Why *couldn't* we have a thing, even if just a casual hookup thing, now that I'm no longer his employee?

Checking the time on my phone, I jump up, motioning to Erin that I'm heading out before bolting for the doors. I bypass the bus and jump into the first taxi cab waiting, giving the address of the office to the driver as I adjust my makeup in my small compact mirror.

Mykayla said he's working late all weekend long, so I take the chance, saying a silent prayer that he's still there while my stomach somersaults with every passing mile.

***

I don't have keys to let me into the building anymore, but luckily the night guard recognizes me and lets me in, walking me to the elevator in casual conversation. When the doors finally shut and I'm on my way up to the thirty-second floor, I feel so nauseous I actually press a hand to my stomach, trying to soothe it along with my nerves.

Please, be here. Please, be here.

When the elevator dings and the doors open, I shoot out of them, turning right immediately and jetting down the hall toward his office. His light is the only one on, and when I drop my clutch on a desk as I pass, he leans back in his chair, peering down the hallway with knitted eyebrows.

Then his eyes go wide.

It's like the hallway is my runway, my heels carrying me down it like a force of nature — a hurricane heading straight for him. And just as fast as the surprise flits across his face, it's gone again, and he's standing, rounding his desk to meet me at the door with a hunger in his eyes so dark I shiver. He's in the doorway just a split second before I am and then I'm in his arms, mine wrapped around his neck, our mouths crashing together like the first bolt of lightning.

It's like the universe around us bubbles out before zapping back into focus, pulling both of us into its gravity with a sizzling snap of energy. I can't calm my breaths, panting louder and louder as Brandon's lips move from mine down my neck, over my exposed shoulder, his hands frantic as he tries to untie my dress in the back.

"I can't figure this thing out," he pants, kissing me again.

"Leave it on."

Dropping to my knees, I rip at his belt and the buttons on his slacks until they're loose, pulling his pants and boxer briefs down his legs in one swift motion. He doesn't even have time to kick out of them before my hands are wrapped around his hard length, pulling him to my lips.

Brandon groans as I swirl my tongue over his crown, flicking at the sensitive skin under it before dragging my tongue all the way down to his base with my eyes locked on his. He drops his head back with another moan, hips flexing into my hands. I'm high off the power he gives me, the power to make him lose control, the power to bring him to ecstasy with just my hands, my mouth, my body. It's addicting, and I don't want to let it go.

Moving my hands from his shaft to his ass, I pull him in deep, guiding his hands into my hair to take control. He's careful not to hurt me, working his hips slowly and pulling at my hair as I open my throat for him. When he hits the back and I gag, he curses, ripping me up from the floor and spinning me around until my palms are flat on his desk.

Chills race up my thighs as I wait, lips already swollen and heart galloping full speed. Just being in his proximity lights my skin on fire, the anticipation of him touching me almost as pleasurable as the actual act of it.

There's a faint rip of a condom wrapper behind me and then his feet hit the inside of my ankles, making me spread my legs wider. One hand comes down on my back, pushing me flat to the desk, and then that same hand drags slowly down my back to the skirt of my dress, flipping it up and over.

Brandon groans with appreciation, running his palm over the apple of my ass before smacking it with a force that has me biting my lip and stifling my own moan. He smacks it again and I gasp, arching off the desk until my back is pressed against his chest. With his lips tracing my neck, he slides one hand under my skirt, moving my lacy thong to the side enough to run a single finger along my wet slit.

"Goddamn, you're ready," he breathes.

"I've been thinking about you all night."

He grins against the skin at my neck, biting it with a growl. "Yeah? What have you been thinking about?"

I blindly reach behind me, feeling along his thigh until I hold his hard cock in my hand again. "This," I pant, stroking him against my ass. "And this," I add, arching back until just the tip of him grazes my entrance.

Brandon yanks back, dropping to his knees long enough to pull my thong to the floor before standing again, rolling the condom over himself. He takes one of my thighs in his hand, propping it up on the desk and pushing me forward until my chest is on the cool metal again. With one heel still planted on the ground and the other spread wide over the desk, he flips my skirt up, and then with one powerful thrust, he's all the way inside me.

I cry out as my hips hit the desk with the force, the sensation of being full combined with being in an open office overwhelming me. I suddenly realize anyone could walk in on us at any minute, but I don't give a single flying fuck. Let the whole world watch, for all I care. All I know in this moment is I want Brandon Church, and right now at least, he's mine.

Brandon smacks my ass before sliding inside again, his hands moving to the bend of my hips, holding on with a tight grip as he pounds me into the desk over and over again. My hands writhe on the edges of the desk, desperate for something to ground me as he lifts me higher and higher. I'm so worked up from not having him that I'm already close to coming, and he must sense it, because he pulls out long enough to flip me over, hiking my thighs up onto his forearms with my back on the desk before slamming into me again.

It feels so dirty and forbidden — him still in his dress shirt and me in my dress, the bottom of it hiked up enough to allow him access to my pussy and nothing more.

"This wasn't supposed to happen again," Brandon says, his voice a deep growl as he leans down over the desk. He captures my mouth with his, hips still rocking inside me, hitting me at a new depth with my hips angled up toward his like this.

I whimper, so overwhelmed by the feel of him that I don't have words. "Neither one of us are the type to follow rules."

He grins, kissing me again before lifting himself to standing again, still hitting me at the point of pressure I need the most. When I close my eyes, my climax just within reach, he runs his hand down over my breasts, my ribs, sliding it under my skirt to press his thumb to my clit.

I gasp at the added pressure, and when he starts circling it faster and faster, still pushing into me, it's the perfect combination to send me flying into the most powerful orgasm of my life.

Arching up off the desk, I reach for his neck, pulling his mouth to mine and panting into his kiss as I ride out my orgasm. Every nerve is on fire, my legs trembling where they're wrapped around him, and his hands fist in my hair as I finish. It's the sweetest release, the one only he can give me, and I savor it every inch of the float down.

"On your knees," he says when my breathing evens out, lifting me from the desk to stand. I do as he demands, dropping to my knees with my eyes locked on his as I take him in my mouth again. My pussy is still throbbing between my thighs and I clench them tight, already ready for another round.

His eyes close, head falling back as he guides my mouth over him. I work my hands in rhythm with my mouth, sucking and licking him closer and closer to climax. When his hips start moving slower, his hands fisted hard in my hair, I reach down and cup his balls, rolling them gently, and he lets out a guttural groan as he comes in my mouth.

"Jesus Christ," he moans, hands still in my hair as I swallow his release. When he's finished, I sit back on my heels, looking up at him and licking my lips clean.

He collapses on the floor next to me, leaning his back against the desk with a heaving chest. For a moment he just focuses on his breathing, his elbows resting on his knees, and I move to sit next to him. He pulls me under one arm, both of us silent for a while, but then he looks down at me, eyes dark and wild.

"Why did you come here?"

I wipe at the corner of his mouth where my lipstick stained it, erasing the violet smear with my thumb. "Because I wanted you. I wanted you so bad I couldn't stand it, and then I realized I'm not your intern anymore." I shrug. "I was in a cab before I could think any further than that."

The left corner of his mouth quirks up in a grin, his eyes roaming over me with appreciation. "You look thoroughly fucked."

I laugh, leaning up to kiss him. "That's because I am."

He keeps his mouth on mine, hand framing my face as he kisses me slowly, his tongue rolling over mine in a soft rhythm. When he pulls back, his brows are bent again, eyes searching mine. "I have to tell you something."

"Uh-oh."

He pulls me into his lap until I'm straddling him, brushing my nest of hair out of my face. "Your manager came to me this past week, before you left, saying she wants to extend your internship another semester."

I blink, a mixture of emotions kicking in. On the one hand, that's amazing — Mykayla said they've never invited an intern back for a second semester. But on the other hand, what does it mean that she suggested it, but I never heard of it until now?

"I told her I would think about it," he says. "And honestly, up until the very moment you walked out, I wasn't sure I could do it. I wasn't sure I could get a single ounce of work done if I had you around here for another five months."

My eyes drop to his chest. "I understand that."

"But you deserve to be here, Ashlei," he continues, knuckles lifting my chin until my eyes are on his again. "So, I'm going to offer you the internship. I don't want to let this... this lust between us get in the way of your career and your dreams."

"We can still be together," I try, but he's already shaking his head. "No one has to know. We can keep it a secret."

"And risk ruining the empire I've built and even more importantly, your reputation as a professional?" He runs his thumb along the edge of my jaw. "Ashlei, if someone found out about us, I would be judged, yes. People would probably call me a whole host of names, but at the end of the day, I would still be their boss, and they'd still respect me. But you?" His eyes soften. "Every opportunity you've had while you've been here, you've earned. But if anyone found out about us, it wouldn't matter how amazing you are at your job. All of that would be erased in everyone's mind and all they would see when they look at you is a girl who slept her way through her career. They would call you a slut and a whore and worse. And there would be nothing I could say or do to change their view of you."

"I don't care what people call me."

"But you do care if people respect you," he counters, and my chest deflates at the truth of it. "You're a hard worker, one of the most impressive interns we've ever had. Don't throw that away."

My eyes trace the stitching on his dress shirt again, fingers playing at the holes between the buttons. "So, what does this mean?"

He sighs, pulling me into him and pressing his lips against mine. "It means I'm going to call you on Monday and offer to extend your internship. And if you take it, then this... *we* can't happen again."

"What do you want me to say when you call?"

He thumbs my cheek, a soft smile on his lips. "I want you to do what you would if I was just the CEO at a company you interned at for a semester, calling to offer you an opportunity not handed out lightly. And nothing more." He motions between us. "This isn't a factor to consider, Ashlei. You can't let it be."

My heart breaks at his words, for selfish reasons I'm not even ashamed to admit. I want the internship, I want to keep moving forward in my career, but I want him, too.

And I hate that I can't have both.

"Now, come here," he whispers, pulling my lips to his again. With a gentle rock of his hips, I feel him harden between my legs. "If this is the last time I get to touch you, I'm far from finished."

Erin

"To our brand new cap-ee-tan and fearless leader, Erin 'Ex' Xanders," Jess says, lifting her margarita high in the air. "May you still remember how to party even in your role of responsibility."

"Here, here!" Skyler cheers, and the rest of the girls lift their glasses with a laugh as I do the same.

"Seriously, congratulations, Grand Big. I'm so proud of you." Cassie smiles, taking a sip of her drink before reaching for a chip.

"Thank you, guys. I couldn't have done this without you."

With elections and finals being over, it only made sense for all of us to get together one last time for margaritas and queso before going our separate ways for winter break. It's tradition, spending the last hours of each semester together, and just like every other time, we're all leaving PSU with a little more growth under our belts.

After having my complete meltdown with Clinton at Semi-formal, I finally feel like I've completely shut down, like I've blocked out that part of my life and looked into the future. Getting revenge didn't help me feel better, but I'm convinced that letting it all go and leaving it behind will. So, now that I'm president, I know I'll have plenty of other things to focus on.

Unlocking my phone as Skyler tells the girls about her poker tournament schedule for the break, I read over the unsent text I typed out to Clinton last night.

- I'm sorry for how I acted, I know you're just trying to help. Please... let me handle this the way I need to. It's not your mess to clean up. -

My thumb hovers over the send button and I finally push it, locking my phone as soon as the text is sent.

"How are you holding up, Jess?" Skyler asks, switching the focus of conversation off of her. "It looked like you had fun with Greg at the dance."

"I did," Jess answers quickly, stirring the ice in her nearly empty glass. "He's really nice. I'll be fine, it's not like I expected me and Jarrett to last forever."

We all exchange glances, landing back on Jess with a deadpan expression.

"What?!" She huffs. "I'm serious. It's fine, guys. Cassie has more of a right to be upset than me right now."

It's a shady attempt to change the subject again but it works, Skyler rubbing Cassie's back. "She's going to stay with me for a few days before heading home for break."

"You guys going up to your parents' place?" I ask Skyler.

She nods. "Yeah, we're leaving tomorrow afternoon."

Cassie looks like absolute hell, like she hasn't slept or eaten in weeks. Her face is pale, dark circles dulling her usually bright green eyes. "It just makes me sick to think about, you know?" she says softly. "He would be with her, touching her, and then lie in bed with me. It just feels so personal..."

All of us wince at her confession, reaching out to squeeze her arm or rub her back.

"He's an asshole, and he doesn't deserve you," Ashlei says. "He's just proof that some guys never stop playing games."

Cassie swallows. "It was never a game to me. I feel so stupid."

"Don't," I chime in. "Don't let a boy make you feel stupid. Ever."

Cassie nods, the table silent now. We take turns sipping from our glasses or eating chips, all of us thinking about our own games we've played over the years, and the battle wounds they've left behind.

A text from Clinton pings on my phone and I glance down, relieved that he responded.

- Okay, Ex. Have a good winter break. Call me anytime. -

- I will, and you, too, Bear. XO. -

"In other news," Ashlei says as I tuck my phone back in my purse. "*Okay, Cool* offered me an extension on my internship. I'll be going back again next semester!"

"What?!" Jess and I say in unison. "That's amazing!"

"Congrats, Lei. That's a big deal," Skyler chimes in.

"Thank you. I'm really excited," she says, tucking her hair behind her ear with a blush. "It's going to be hard, balancing everything again, but I think I can do it."

"I know you can," Jess says, hoisting up her glass again. "Looks like we need another toast!"

We all lift our glasses with a laugh, and Jess clears her throat.

"To this amazing group of bad-ass lady bosses conquering the world and taking absolute zero shit," she says, looking all of us in the eyes. "You bitches inspire me, and I love every single one of you."

"Cheers!"

As I clink my glass with theirs, I feel myself shedding the final layers of my old self, settling into the new Erin Xanders. And maybe that's what that scarred skin was — it was old skin, skin that needed to be shed to find my true self. I'm not scared anymore, and I'm not giving up on me, either. Maybe I just need to toughen up, to stop putting everyone else before me and start focusing on number one.

I will not be defined by what has happened to me, only by what I do to overcome it.

This is it — this is what I've been working for my entire college career. I'm going to be president of Kappa Kappa Beta, and as far as I'm concerned, my new story begins right now.

Adam

I knew she was here before I even heard the knock.

It was a gentle rap of the knuckles on my window, nothing more, no demand or urgency in the sound. It was a soft, regretful notion, an apology, a plead for forgiveness. It struck me to the bone when I heard it, so much so that I'm still lying here in my bed, eyes on the ceiling, heart pounding hard in my chest as I work up the courage to go to my window.

I heard about what happened between her and Grayson the day after Semi-formal, and two things struck me at the same time — one, the need to run to her, to hold her, to make her okay again — and two, the outrageous and uncontrollable urge to break Grayson's jaw.

I'd wanted to give into both, but I'd stayed strong, doing neither. I knew Cassie well enough to know she wouldn't want me to run to her before she was ready to see me, and a small part of me wondered if she ever would again. She'd chosen Grayson over me, and although I wanted to believe she didn't have a choice, that she didn't want to, it still hurt. It still felt permanent.

And as much as I would have loved crushing my fist into Grayson's face, I knew that wouldn't have made Cassie happy, either. It would have only made things worse for her.

So, I've waited, my hope fading like a dying glow stick of light with each passing day. I leave to spend winter break at my aunt's house tomorrow, and I'd almost given up on Cassie.

But here she is.

Kicking my sheets off, I pad over to the window in just my boxer briefs, pulling the string on the blinds until I'm standing face to face with the only girl I've ever loved and hated simultaneously. I love everything about her, but hate the power she holds over me. The sweetest contradiction.

She's standing in a simple, white tank top and plaid sleep shorts, her hair tied up in a mess of curls on top of her head as her swollen eyes take me in. I reach down, heaving the window open, the light breeze of the night sweeping into my room as I stare at Cassie. She watches me, too, lip quivering as she shrugs and lets out a long sigh of a breath.

I just reach out with both hands, helping her climb inside just like I did almost exactly a year ago to the day.

And just like last time, she kicks off her Keds by the foot of my bed, climbing into it first and pulling the sheets up to her shoulders. I slide in behind her, hesitant at first until she reaches back for my arm, pulling it around her middle. With a relieved sigh, I pull her closer, fitting my body to hers and holding her tight.

"You were right."

The same three words she said to me last year, and they hurt just as bad this time around.

"I wish I wasn't."

I squeeze her a little tighter, fitting us a little more together, hoping she feels some sort of comfort from the fact that I'm here.

"I'm so sorry, Adam," she whispers, her voice breaking on my name.

Only the moon lights up my room, but it's enough for me to see the first tear slide down her cheek. I catch it with my thumb, wiping it away before pulling her even closer. "It's okay. I'm here."

"You always are." She squeezes her eyes closed. "I don't deserve it."

"You're always here for me, too," I remind her. "Even when I'm an asshole."

She twists in the sheets to face me, one hand pressed into my chest as she looks up at me. "I just left you there. I let him make me choose. I gave you up, and for what? To keep a relationship with a guy who was cheating on me for months." Two tears escape one right after the other, chasing each other down until they drop to my pillow. "I was miserable without you, Adam."

I swallow, my chest aching as my hand finds her hip, resting there. "I was, too."

"I'm not crying because of him," she says, waiting until my eyes are locked on hers again before continuing. "He hurt me, yes. But not as bad as I hurt myself by making a decision I didn't want to make, one that I didn't believe in. I'm just so sorry. Please, please forgive me, Adam."

"Shh," I whisper, pulling her into me and pressing a kiss into her hair. "It's over, we're okay. I'm here."

Cassie fists her hands in the sheets wrapped around us, digging her head into my chest. For a while I just hold her there, one hand pulling strands of hair from her hair tie as I run my fingers through it, the other rubbing soft, slow circles on her lower back.

"What now?" Cassie whispers into the darkness, her breath on the skin of my chest.

"We don't have to figure that out tonight."

She stiffens in my arms, her breathing nearly stopping altogether as she pushes away from me just enough to lift her head. I look down at her, too — our lips just centimeters apart as she searches my eyes with her own. I swallow, gripping her waist with one hand just as she closes the space between us, her lips finding mine on a sigh.

If time was a train, this is what it would feel like for it to slam on its brakes.

I've waited so long to touch her again, to hold her, to kiss her that it almost feels like a dream. It's as if my body isn't my body, my hands aren't my hands, my lips aren't my lips — like I'm watching it all from above. I wince as her mouth opens for me, my tongue sliding in to meet hers, and that's when the reality hits me.

She's here, she's in my bed — in my arms.

It's almost too much, too much history and pain and unexplainable pleasure rolled into one single moment. She melts in my arms as I deepen the kiss, one hand running the length of my abdomen before tucking into the band of my briefs.

I inhale a breath and hold it there, tongue still working hers as I flip us, sliding up between her thighs, her red hair spilling out of her hair tie and over my pillow. She moans when I kiss down her neck, sucking the skin just behind her ear as her nails dig into my back. Our breaths are so loud and heated, years of wanting pouring out without a filter now, my sheets the stage for the show long overdue. Cassie flexes her hips against me, the hot center of her meeting the bulge in my briefs, and I groan, pulling back.

Her eyes widen as I take a pause, squeezing my eyes shut, trying to think clearly.

"You don't... you don't want to..."

"Oh, I want to," I clarify quickly, cock aching at the thought of being inside her. But I lift my eyes to hers, running my thumb over her swollen bottom lip. "Trust me, I want to. But the first time I take you, I want it to be us — just us. No exes, no drama, no pain. I just... I know I'll never forget our first time, and I want to make it worth remembering."

Cassie swallows, nodding with tears misting her eyes as she pulls me down to kiss her again. She kisses me with all the unanswered questions we've shared, with all the *what ifs* and *what nows*.

"Don't let go tonight, okay?"

"I'm never letting go again," I answer, resting between her thighs again as I kiss her lips like I've never tasted them before, like tonight is all I have.

I slide one hand under the cotton of her tank top, groaning with appreciation when I feel she's not wearing a bra. My hands roam over every inch of her, palming her breasts before moving down to grip her waist again. Cassie arches off the bed, offering her neck to my mouth, nails digging into the flesh of my shoulders like she's holding on for dear life.

And for the rest of the night, we explore each other, kissing and touching with our clothes staying completely intact, even when it's nearly impossible to do. I take my time with her, showing her I'm in no rush, that I'm not going anywhere — and I hope she can say the same.

For the last year and a half, we've danced around each other, never fully giving in, always something or some*one* in the way. But now that I have her, now that there's nothing but scraps of cloth between us, I know there's no way I can ever let her go. I meant what I said about not figuring anything out tonight, but in my heart, I know as well as she does that this is it — this is our time.

Cassie McBee is finally mine, and I have always been hers.

With my heart in her hands, Cassie pulls me closer as the sun rises through my window, sealing that thought with the sweetest, most perfect kiss.

Palm South
UNIVERSITY

LEGACY

BOOK 4

EPISODE 1

Jess

"So, we should start taking bets on which pledge will have the best game?" I ask Skyler as we make our way through the pledge tents. I balance our tray of cookies in one hand as I use the other to pull my strappy hoodie down and show off the girls a little more. It's chilly for Florida — hovering right around fifty-five — but it doesn't stop me from showing a little flesh.

I mean, I *do* have a reputation to uphold.

Flags with Greek letters fly high from all the tents around us as we weave between the different frats, the field lit up by the industrial-size lights that have been set up all week. The entire PSU Greek Life organization is out in full force, all of us donning our letters with pride, gathering like a bunch of hyenas at a damn watering hole. And I'm wearing the biggest smile on my face, passing out winks like candy, because I'm right back in my element.

It's fraternity rush, my favorite thing about coming back to Palm South University for spring semester.

And there are boys *everywhere.*

Rush used to be my mecca. It used to be my playground, jackpot, my pond full of fish, if you will.

There's always fresh meat to be found, and all the *current* brothers are at the top of their top game, too. Rush is a time of bromancing, of convincing other guys how great you are, how cool you are, how much they need you in their organization or, if you're already a brother, how much they need to be in *yours*.

Of course, part of that game is showing off what girls you can land. Back in my prime, I loved to play in the game, to be the arm candy hanging on a brother's arm or, sometimes, even the arm of a freshman. Hey, if I could help them get into the frat they wanted? Well, I saw it as my civic duty.

It was a simple game, one I dominated easily, and one I loved to be a part of.

But that was before Jarrett, and I realized over winter break that my life would forever be separated into those two categories: before Jarrett, and after him. I remembered easily what life was like before I met him, remembered the way I used to be, and I could still close my eyes and feel every ounce of happiness, and pain, that I'd felt while being *in* his arms — while being his.

But life after Jarrett? I don't understand that beast yet.

I'm like a baby gazelle, trying to figure out how to walk and run away from lions at the same time. All I can do is put one foot in front of the other and pray for a miracle.

"Aren't we a little old for freshmen, J-Love?" Skyler asks with a roll of her eyes. She's also wearing a Kappa Kappa Beta hoodie, but hers actually covers the goodies.

"Hey! Some of them are sophomores. I heard there are even a few juniors this year."

"What happened to Greg? I thought things were getting *serious*," she mocks, nudging me.

Hearing his name makes my stomach flip, like butterflies are trying to give it liftoff but fail halfway up so it just tumbles on top of itself.

Greg and I haven't talked since semi-formal, and though I had fun with him, I can't help but feel like he's part of the reason I lost Jarrett — even though I *know* that's not true. It isn't his fault I went into that bar on Thanksgiving on a mission and found him, and it definitely isn't his fault that he played into my hand exactly the way I wanted him to.

My plan had worked, and then it had backfired, and I'd lost the most important human to ever exist in my life.

I scoff, trying to play it off. "Yeah right. He was fun for semi-formal, but I lost interest over Christmas break."

That's a lie.

"I'm ready for a new toy."

Also a lie.

Skyler laughs. "You're relentless. You do realize you're the Recruitment Chair now, right? You should probably be setting the standard for our sorority, which I don't think includes scamming on fresh meat."

"There are more eyes on your Big than on me, Sky," I remind her. "Besides, maybe I'm trying to recruit all the skanks this semester." I shimmy my hips a little just to drive that point home, making Skyler laugh.

"Yeah, like that would ever fly with Ex or Lei."

Erin is president this year — the title she's been fighting for since she arrived at Palm South — and she's already taken her new position so seriously that I wonder if I'll ever get to see the *old* Erin again. Believe it or not, she did party once, and even though she's always had her eye on the prize when it came to getting president, she stiffened up even more than usual last semester.

Our recruiting styles would *definitely* be different.

"Come on," Skyler says as I link my arm in hers. "Let's go drop off these cookies and start making the rounds."

As we head toward the Omega Chi tent, I let my mind wonder over what Skyler just said as my eyes wander over the fresh meat at the fraternity rush buffet. She's right — I do need to keep my shit together. Erin won't settle for me getting into too much trouble, not now that I'm our recruitment chair. That thought also sobers me, because I'm officially in my last year at Palm South University.

Since I changed my major late and took a position with the sorority, I'll be graduating after fall semester instead of this May. Even still, that's less than three-hundred-and-fifty days until I walk across the stage and leave PSU behind, until I start a new chapter, a new life.

I thought I had it figured out.

It sounds ludicrous now, that I had hung up my dreams once I'd fallen in love with Jarrett, but it was true. I was perfectly content to graduate and move wherever the fuck he was — New York, Atlanta, Papua New Guinea — it didn't matter, as long as he was there.

But now, there is no Jarrett.

Now, there's just Jess Vonnegut, and that bitch is a mess.

Clinton starts in on Skyler as soon as we reach the Omega Chi tent, and I take the opportunity to pull out my phone while they banter back and forth. My finger finds Jarrett's text messages easily, and I stare at the last one I ever sent him.

- I will always love you. -

My stomach sinks, unlike the flip it did at the mention of Greg's name. No, this time it just falls like a thousand-pound anvil, crushing those poor butterflies beneath it and breaking all their wings in the process.

What everyone already knows is that I fucked up. I lost Jarrett, he broke up with me over a fucking video chat session, and I took Greg to semi-formal, basically only because I didn't want to sit home and sulk. They know I was devastated by losing him, and they know I've never loved a boy until him.

What they don't know is that over Christmas break, I flew to New York to try to see him. And I did.

But he didn't see me.

I had it all planned — the words I would say to win him back, the case I would plead, the promises I would make. But nothing mattered once I finally found him, because he was at a bar with another woman, the one I presumed to be Jenny, his co-worker he'd told me I was crazy for feeling any kind of jealousy toward.

His tongue being halfway down her throat assured me that feeling existed for a reason.

I'm not sure how long I stood there, staring at him from across the crowded bar, watching as they kissed, and held hands, and laughed. It was like he wasn't heartbroken at all, like he never had been, like I was so far in his past that he couldn't even recall my name.

When I left New York City, I vowed to leave my broken heart behind, too. I vowed to return to Palm South as the *old* Jess Vonnegut, the man eating, take-no-shit, bad-ass bitch.

But like I said before — that was *before* Jarrett, and this is after.

Everything is different now.

My attention snaps back to the Omega Chi tent when I hear Skyler talking about the poker tournament she entered that takes place at the end of this semester. Clinton makes some comment to the new pledges gathered around him about her winning every tournament, and she quickly corrects him.

"Not *every* tournament."

I see doubt creep in over her bright blue eyes, and I pull my shit together, eager to squash it.

"Not yet, you mean. We all know you're going to take it all this year," I say, and Clinton nods in agreement.

Skyler smiles, a little light coming back into her eyes, but I know we're all going to have to be there for her this semester. This is a tournament unlike any other she's entered before — higher entry fee, higher stakes — and we have to have her back.

The three of us make our way to the back of the tent, cookies in hand, and Skyler changes gears back to rush. Clinton is telling her all about the new guys rushing, including a few promising guys for the intramural football team, but it's not until he mentions the hot new transfer that both mine and Skyler's ears perk up.

"Transfer?" she asks. "Who the hell transfers to Palm South?"

Clinton laughs, his bright white teeth blazing against his dark skin as he shakes his head, just as confused as we are. "Right? That's what I said. But, apparently he's got a pretty impressive resume. I heard he's a Creative Writing major, though, so my money is on him going Alpha Sigma."

My eyes skirt to the Alpha Sigma tent as they continue talking, and I see a big crowd gathered around it. I can't help but think of Adam, of the legacy he's already built as president — hell, the one he started building *before* he even got the gig. Between his concerts and last year's Halloween party, they've really made a name for themselves.

One of Clinton's brothers, Willie, pops up beside Skyler, joining in the conversation about the all-mighty transfer. I swear, fraternity rush is the only time you'll ever hear guys getting all gooey over other dudes.

"Okay, where is this guy?" I finally ask, scanning the courtyard. "I need to see what all the fuss is about."

Skyler chuckles. "I'm going back to the house to see if my Little is done studying yet. Behave yourself, Jess," she says pointedly.

"No promises."

I'm still on my tiptoes scanning the crowd when she disappears into it, and Clinton and Willie go back to talking to the freshmen. Shrugging when I don't immediately spot some hypnotizingly hot transfer student, I give up, turning to make my way toward the Mu Beta Chi tent, and that's when I run straight into a brick wall.

Or rather, a man as hard as one.

Greg smiles at me, one corner of his mouth pulling up in a lazy, sexy smirk, which makes that damn dimple pop on his cheek. His dark hair blows a little in the wind, and he tucks his hands into his pockets easily, like he's not the least bit affected by my proximity.

I try to pretend the same.

I was serious about what I said to Skyler earlier, that Greg was just for fun, that he wasn't anything special to get my panties in a knot over. But the truth was that the last time I saw him, I was fresh off my break up, and he was just there to pick up the pieces.

Now, though the hole in my heart still gapes from where Jarrett used to be, I can't deny that those damn butterflies aren't trying their damnedest to sprout back to life under the weight of the anvil.

"Hey, stranger," he says, his eyes flicking down to my cleavage and back up again.

My cheeks heat, and I find my stupid gazelle legs standing a little taller, a little straighter — all at the sight of a beautiful boy with dark eyes.

He was just a distraction last semester, a fill for the void, a patch over the hole.

But maybe, just maybe, his job isn't done yet.

Cassie

I am totally cool.

The girls convinced me to come out of my study hole, even though classes haven't even officially started, and join them for fraternity rush. I was just trying to get ahead of my classes, to get a jump start.

I was totally *not* avoiding Adam.

And now that the party has moved from the courtyard to the Alpha Sigma house, I'm totally cool! My palms aren't sweating at *all,* and though my swinging legs with my hands tucked under them might make me *appear* nervous, I'm actually completely fine. I'm just sitting on the kitchen counter in the Alpha Sigma house in very close proximity to Adam and I'm not even concerned a little bit.

Totally cool.

Skyler, on the other hand, looks very concerned about the fact that there is a parade of sorority girls around the new transfer everyone is talking about.

I eye him from our vantage point in the kitchen, the steam from Skyler's skin making *me* a little hot in my long-sleeve shirt. It's not hard to see why he's causing a commotion — the kid is hot. His blue eyes are almost as bright as my Big's, his muscles lean and tanned, and his blond hair is tussled in that *maybe I just had sex, maybe I just woke up, maybe I used a ton of hair product to get it this way, but you'll never know* kind of way. He's also sporting a pair of black-framed glasses that, for some odd reason, really do it for me — and apparently every other girl here, too.

Kip Jackson is the new, shiny toy at Palm South University, and also the newest pledge to Alpha Sigma.

And currently, he's being circled like a bucket of chum, and the Zeta girls are the sharks.

"You know, I think I could rock those glasses he has on," I say after a moment, trying to get Skyler to talk about the very obvious elephant in the room. She hasn't been able to get into much of a conversation with me ever since Kip walked into the party, and the way she's staring at him, I know he's gotten under her skin.

"I think he looks ridiculous."

Liar, I think, but I just smirk.

"I love nerds. And do you see his arms? Something tells me he's not just a book reading, chess playing kind of nerd."

I know I'm pushing all the right buttons when Skyler bites her lip, leaning against the kitchen counter with her eyes still fixed on him. "I think you might be reading into this a little too much, Little Nug."

"Maybe," I agree. "But at least I'm not denying his hotness when I'm clearly affected."

Skyler fights against a smile, but in the end, it cracks her face in half like an egg. She snatches a ping pong ball off the counter next to her and tosses it at me. "Shut up."

I laugh, dodging her attack, but my feet keep swinging as I watch her digest her feelings. Suddenly, her eyes widen at a bottle of tequila sitting next to me, and she swipes it from the counter before heading toward the fridge.

"You know what?" she says. "You're right. He is delicious — like a cool slice of key lime pie on a hot summer day. And have you ever known me to turn down key lime pie?"

I laugh, shaking my head. "Nope, never."

"Exactly. Which is precisely why I can't start now. After all, I have a very demanding sweet tooth."

"Right," I agree, tossing her the shaker of salt from behind me. "I mean, you have a reputation to uphold. You can't let other girls go scamming on your pie."

"Indeed." Skyler winks at me, her feet already well on their way to the path toward the new kid. "I'm glad we talked this out, Little Nug. Thanks for being my voice of reason."

"What are Littles for?"

With one last grin in my direction, Skyler turns, her eyes locked on Kip. I can't hear what's said between them, but the next thing I know, the crowd is gathering around the two of them at the foosball table. And I may not know exactly what game they're playing yet, but I know without a doubt that there's no way in hell my Big won't be the one who wins in the end.

The crowd grows around where Kip and Skyler are setting up a game at the foosball table, so I hop down from the counter, making my way toward the commotion. But before I can get too close, the hairs on my arms stand at full attention, a familiar rush of emotion flooding me from head to toe.

I feel his eyes on me before I see them.

Swallowing, I lift my gaze to the table, and standing next to Jess in the center of the action is Adam.

His dark hair is flushed over in a soft wave, like he just ran his hands back through it, and those dark eyes I've been lost in more than once swallow me like a black hole from across the room. His skin is still bronze, though not quite as tan as it was before he left for winter break, and as my eyes roam over the lean muscles of his arms, a flash of our last night together before break hits me like a strike of lightning.

I feel his body, hard and warm, wrapped around me under the sheets that smelled like him. I hear his voice whispering my name, telling me it will all be okay, groaning against the urge to have me the way he wanted to. I see his dark, long lashes on the apples of his cheeks as I peeked my eyes open mid-kiss, his lips still on mine, his hands gripping my hips like he had to hold onto them for dear life so he wouldn't move those hands anywhere else.

We'd given in. He was right about Grayson, about the man I'd trusted with my heart, with my body, but he hadn't taken the opportunity to say *I told you so*. Instead, he'd held me, and kissed me, and cherished me like I was so precious, so fragile, that every move had to be planned and plotted and practiced before he could ever actually make it.

I'd always loved him, and I'd finally admitted it.

But after that amazing night, after he swore he was never letting go of me again, he disappeared.

I hadn't heard from him since.

The room snaps back like a warped rubber band and I take in a sharp breath, inhaling a burning gulp of oxygen with my eyes finding Adam's again. There's a pained bend in his eyebrows, an apology behind his eyes — or perhaps an explanation? He holds my gaze as long as he can, saying more in that silent stretch of time than he did all break.

That's the way it has always been with us — we spoke in longing glances, in soft, seemingly innocent touches, in the quietest of moments. Words could never say what we needed to so we let our actions and our eyes be our voices.

I can't be sure how much time passes as we stand there, staring across the room at one another like there's still some barrier between us, but after a few moments, or maybe a few years, Adam's expression softens.

And he smiles.

That smile, that soft, slow spread of his lips over his mesmerizing face, it's all I need to feel every tight muscle in my body unwind at the same time.

I exhale, smiling in return, the weight on my chest lifted like a cement block turned to a helium balloon in the snap of his fingers. He holds my eyes, that smile still in place, and holds up one finger, letting me know we'll talk when the game is over.

I still feel a slight pressure, the same one I always feel in his proximity, as he holds up the little white ball between Kip and Skyler. He drops it in after a moment, and the game begins.

I should be watching Skyler in her element as she whoops the new guy's butt in a game of foosball, should be laughing and cheering with the rest of the crowd, but I can't take my eyes off Adam. I can't stop the parade of questions storming through me, like his smile released the flood gates I hadn't even noticed were holding so much back.

How was his break? What did he do? Where did he go?

Did he think of me?

What are we now?

Are we anything at all?

It's not until the very last score that I even register what's happening, and I blink back into the moment just in time to see Skyler throw her hands up in victory. I rush to her, Jess and I engulfing her in a group hug at the same time as I finally tear my attention away from Adam — at least, for the moment.

Skyler won — and now, it's time for Kip Jackson to take a shot of tequila and accept his defeat.

"Grab me a knife, will you, Little Nug?" Skyler says, the bottle of tequila and a lime in her hands.

I skip off to the kitchen, returning to find my Big sitting on one of the tables that was just being used for beer pong. There are empty, red Solo cups scattered on the floor all around her, and Kip is just staring at her with one brow cocked in question.

Oh boy, this poor kid has no idea what he's gotten himself into.

Skyler takes the knife from me with a smirk still firmly in place. She slices the lime into four equal wedges, and then like no one else is in the room, she takes Kip's hand and licks the skin between his pointer finger and thumb with her eyes locked on his.

I swear, the guy practically falls to his knees right then and there.

"I said you had to take a shot of tequila if you lost," she says, lying back on the table. "I didn't say you'd get to shoot it out of a shot glass."

She pops one of the lime wedges in her mouth as the room erupts into a fit of cheers, and Kip just stands there with his mouth open. Jess and I start our sorority chant, the guys hooping and hollering as Skyler lifts her shirt up and tucks it under her bra, revealing her tight, toned stomach. She pours the tequila over her exposed skin, the liquid pooling in her navel, and once the bottle is back on the table, all eyes are on Kip.

He seems to be stuck in some sort of spell, standing there over Skyler, and I can't say I blame the poor sucker. I've seen my Big in action, both with Adam and plenty of other guys on campus, and I know how impossible it is for anyone — especially of the male persuasion — to say no to her. When one of his brothers smacks him on the arm, it seems to jolt him back to the moment, and he licks his hand to another roar from the crowd.

Then, his mouth is on Skyler's stomach, sucking up every drop of tequila before he sucks the lime in her mouth and kisses her like they're the only two in the room.

I laugh, cheering again as the crowd starts to disperse. Kip and Skyler continue making out, oblivious to the party still happening around them, and Jess nudges me as she heads toward the kitchen.

"Okay, I think *I* need a shot after that. You in?"

"Right behind ya."

She weaves through the crowd toward the kitchen, me on her heels, but before I can slip through the opening and join her, I feel a strong, warm hand graze my hip.

I close my eyes, that hand grounding me to the spot where I stand, paralyzing me.

His lips graze the back of my neck, his chest pressed against my back as he whispers the first words since the night I spent in his bed.

"Hey there, Red."

I fight against the smile cracking my face in two, spinning with his hand never leaving my hip, and then I'm face to face with the one guy I've always belonged to, yet never truly had.

I shove his shoulder, still smiling. "Don't even start with that," I warn, referring to the stupid nickname that every single person uses for the redheads in their life. He teased me with it the first semester we met, and never fails to use it to get under my skin when he gets the chance.

Adam just grins, his eyes a little glossy from drinking, the chocolate around his pupils shining in the dim light of the party. He swallows, tucking his hands in the pockets of his jeans, and then we stand there — staring, smiling, shaking a little like two middle schoolers who were just dared to do seven minutes in heaven.

After a moment, I laugh, tucking a strand of my wild, fiery hair behind one ear. "How was your break?"

Adam leans in, his brows pinched together as he yells over the music and cheers coming from the game of flip cup taking place behind us. "What?"

"I said, how was your break?" I yell in return.

He smiles, looking around at all the chaos surrounding us before he reaches forward and grabs my hand without a second thought. Adam turns, leading me through the crowd toward the back yard, all the while completely oblivious to the wave of electricity he just sent crashing through me with the touch of his hand.

I stare at his fingers laced with mine as he tugs me through the sea of students, smiling so big my cheeks hurt.

When we finally break through the crowd, Adam drops my hand to open the sliding glass door, and we step outside into the blissfully quiet night.

He shuts the door behind us, muffling the music and laughter from inside, and then it's just the two of us alone on the empty patio.

The night air seems to buzz to life, warm and sticky between us even though it's below fifty now and entirely too cold for any Floridian to be outside. The party rages on inside, but out here, it's just me and Adam.

"There," he says, guiding me over to where a small fire pit is going in the corner of the yard. "Maybe now we can actually hear each other."

"Yeah, it's a little crazy in there."

Adam plops down in one of the chairs around the fire, and I stand, unsure where to sit. Do I take the chair across the fire? The one next to him?

But I don't have time to make the decision before Adam makes it for me, reaching for my hand and pulling me easily down into his lap. He wraps his arms around me, blocking the cool wind, his eyes reflecting the low flicker of the fire.

"Hi," he says.

I let out a long breath, smiling like a fool again. "Hi."

"You're nervous."

"I am," I admit on a soft laugh. "I don't know why."

"It's just me."

"I know, but..." I bite my lower lip, eyes searching his as my stomach drops to my feet. The stinging reminder that he never called, never texted, never said anything to me after the night we spent together resurfaces, and my confidence shakes under the weight of it. "What happened? I never heard from you after... you know, after everything."

Adam's eyes widen, his arms tightening around me. "Oh, God, Cassie. I'm so sorry, I thought that's what you needed. I was just giving you some space," he says quickly.

My eyes fall to my lap, but he thumbs my chin quickly, pulling my gaze back to him.

"I meant every word I said that night," he says, sincerity laced through every word. "I'm here, Cassie, and I'm not going anywhere. I'm not letting go. But, I also don't want to rush things," he adds. "You've been through a lot, and I wanted to give you the time to process all of that."

"So, you don't want to be a rebound," I whisper.

Adam chuckles. "I know I'm not a rebound," he says, running one hand down my arm. He laces his fingers through my own, squeezing. "But, I also know that you've been hurt. Grayson hurt you. It's okay to admit that, and it's okay to take some time to sort through your feelings on all of it."

"I don't need time," I say quickly. "I need you."

"No, you don't."

My heart sinks further, in danger of drowning, but Adam squeezes my hand again.

"Cassie, you don't need me. You don't need anyone, because you're an incredible girl on your own. You're smart — *so* fucking smart — and beautiful, and funny, and charming." He offers me a soft smile. "You're unlike any girl I know. And *that's* why I think it's important for us to take this slow," he says. "Because I want you to take the time you need to remember all of those things, to get back to Cassie McBee."

My heart squeezes, and I smile, tears pooling in my eyes.

He's right.

All break long, instead of thinking about me, about my goals, about the things I want for myself this semester, I just sat around thinking about Adam. As soon as Grayson was gone, I filled that void with Adam, not even taking the time to process what happened, to let myself be hurt, or to stand on my own two feet again.

I was perfectly content crawling on bruised knees into Adam's arms, to let him hold me and lean on him instead of standing on my own first.

The fact that *he* won't let me do that shows me more than anything that he cares about me more than Grayson ever did.

"Don't worry about me right now, because you've got me — I'm right here, and I'm yours. I'm not going anywhere."

I sigh, nodding and leaning into his chest.

"I just missed you," I confess. "But you're right. We should take it slow." I shake my head against his chest. "I mean, Grayson stuff aside, you used to date my Big and she has no idea I even had a crush on you."

"You had a crush on me, huh?" Adam asks, smirking.

I pinch his side. "Shut up. I'm just saying, I should probably talk to her about everything before we make things official, too."

He shifts, pulling me close until my eyes are locked on his again. His hands frame my face, the tips of his fingers brushing back into my hair.

"Hey, don't worry about any of that right now, okay? Skyler will be fine, and you have plenty of time to tell her. Right now, I want you to focus on *you*."

I nod, leaning my forehead against his. My chest is still tight, anxiety gripping my ribcage with force, but I know Adam's right. It's only been a few weeks since my break up with Grayson, since I found out the man I said I loved cheated on me just because I wouldn't *give it up* fast enough.

My stomach turns.

Maybe I wanted to crawl to Adam because I knew it'd be easier, knew his arms would be waiting, and he'd know all the right words to say. I fled to his window that night because I knew he'd be there, just like he was the semester before, when Clay took my virginity and then slept with my roommate.

My dating record sucks.

A sigh flushes an anxious breath from my lips, and I nuzzle into Adam more, aching at the thought of taking thing slow with him when all I want is to lose myself in his warmth.

"Can I still kiss you?" I whisper after a moment.

Adam shakes his head, fingers gripping my hair a little tighter.

"You never have to ask. Kiss me anytime you want, Red."

I laugh, shoving my hands into his chest to push him away but he wraps his arms around me, pulling me in tighter, and then without warning, his lips cover mine.

That kiss steals my next breath, holding it hostage as my hands fist in Adam's hoodie. I tug and tug, wanting him closer, needing more of him — and he gives without question.

He always has.

One hand finds the back of my neck, pulling me into him as the other warms the exposed sliver of skin under the back of my sweatshirt. And he doesn't rush, doesn't devour me, his lips taking their time tasting and kissing and exploring. I'm reminded of the night spent in his sheets, and every nerve in my body begs me to pull him back into his room to relive that night, to take it to the next level.

But I can't.

Because Adam is right, and as much as I want his hands on every inch of my body, I want to feel okay again, more.

I want to stand again, to walk, to run free — on my own.

Then, when the time is right, I'll fall into Adam's arms.

And I know without a doubt that he'll be there to catch me when I do.

Skyler

"These shoes are too much," I argue with Ashlei, who just wrangled me into a dress and wedges for the first day of class. She's dressed to the nines, of course, but she also has an internship downtown and a reason to be wearing stilettos.

I, however, do not find it at all necessary to wear shoes with a heel when I expect to walk at least a mile.

"Your legs look *killer* in those shoes paired with that dress," she argues, touching up her lipstick. "Please? Just try it. For me."

Turning in the mirror again, I can't say that I disagree with her. My legs are tan from all the paddle boarding time I got in over winter break, and the yellow dress with a simple sweetheart neckline she's dressed me in looks perfect with the wedges. I'm all legs and collarbone and toned arms, and my hair is down and softly curled.

Still, I feel a little overdressed.

"I'm just going to class."

"Yes, but you never know who you might run into."

A flash of the new guy I made out with at the Alpha Sigma house last night hits me, and I smile. *Maybe I'll run into* him.

"Here," Cassie says, popping up from her seat on Jess's bed to hand me the one and only strand of pearls I own. "Add these. They're the perfect accessory."

I do as she says, but it just makes me scrunch my nose up more. "This feels like a lot."

"They're perfect!" Cassie argues, her red hair bobbing a little as she bounces with excitement.

"It's syllabus week, it won't be that long of a day anyway." Ashlei pokes her bottom lip out as she tucks her lipstick back in her bag. "Pleeeease."

I huff. "Fine. But next time I want a drink at Ralph's at ten o'clock on an internship night, you both have to come."

"Deal," they agree in unison.

"Are you heading to your internship now?" I ask Ashlei, packing up my bag.

She shakes her head. "It's a later report for me today, since I don't have to do the orientation that all the new interns will have to do. I'm going to hang out with Erin for a bit and then I'll head downtown."

"I'll probably come back to the house between classes, so I'll see you in a bit."

"Sounds good! See ya later, Legs," she teases, swatting my ass as she skips out of mine and Jess's room. My Little does the same thing, and I laugh, waving them both off before I make my way downstairs.

I'm running late as I hobble-speedwalk across campus to my first class — Writing for Television. Once again, I have an eclectic mix of classes this semester, my feeble attempt to figure out what the hell I'm doing with my life after college.

If I'm being honest with myself, all I really thought about over break was the American Poker Club Tournament. I officially announced my entrance, and even though I haven't fully paid the fee to enter yet, the poker blogs and magazines are already eating it up. I'll be one of the few females in the tournament, and by far the youngest.

But for once — at least, for *now* — they're all talking about how I'm one to beat, not just a hot girl who plays cards, but an actual contender.

It's a step in the right direction, however small.

So, as much as I *do* want to figure out what my next steps are after college, all I've been able to think about is poker.

Well, at least, until the new transfer showed up.

I met Kip Jackson last night at fraternity rush, and about an hour after making fun of his glasses and his name, he was sucking tequila out of my belly button and licking lime juice from my lips.

I smile, biting my lower lip at the memory of that kiss. I'm no stranger to the buzz of a first kiss, of a first night with a guy, but this was different — it was *more*. The moment our lips met, I swear I felt a million bolts of electricity course through me in a smooth, vibrant wave. I'm not even sure how long we made out before he pulled away, but I know it was long enough for me to decide he is *absolutely* my new target for this semester.

I'll have Kip Jackson wrapped around my finger soon enough.

I ended up texting him late last night, thanks to Adam forking over his new pledge's number, but we haven't really talked since then. The ball is in his court. If he wants a date, he'll ask for it.

He better.

I skip into class right after the professor, who tosses his belongings down on his desk and starts writing on the whiteboard. Scanning the classroom, I try to find a place in the back, but sigh when I see all the seats are taken. I'm used to taking classes with at least one sorority sister, having someone to walk into class with and sit with all semester, not to mention, a study buddy. But with this class, I'm on my own.

At least, that's what I think — until I spot Kip a few rows back.

God, he's even sexier than I remember. I decided after I met him that it's not his hair, which is a soft, rugged blond styled messy and casual like I love. And I don't think it's necessarily his lean, toned arms or easy, confident smile that sets him apart, either.

No — it's his eyes. *Definitely* his eyes. They're an electric blue, ocean-like just like mine, and they're framed by black, plastic frames that make them impossible to ignore. Except, he's not wearing those glasses today. Instead, those eyes stand out all on their own, twinkling under the fluorescent light as he watches me from his desk.

I glance at his full lips, that memory of them being pressed against my own sparking to life again. Smirking, I make my way up the steps and slide into the open seat next to him.

"Where's mine?" I ask, eyeing the coffee cup at the corner of his desk.

He follows my gaze to the cup before giving me a smirk of his own. "Sorry, they didn't have tequila. I checked."

"Damn them," I exasperate. "I need to run for Student Council so I can change that."

I don't have time to flirt as much as I'd like, but Kip is still smiling at me when the professor claps his hands together and starts in on his lecture.

I feel a little uneasy being in a classroom full of writers, almost like a poser in some way. The first question Dr. O'Neal asks is, "Why do we write?" It only takes a couple of people being shot down with their attempts at responding to that question for me to know that I have no *chance* of offering any kind of worthy answer.

Kip watches me as I fidget with my pencil, silently begging the professor to move on from this and back to the syllabus. For some reason, I'm completely petrified that he'll decide to call on someone from the class roster or just spot my discomfort and shine it under a spotlight.

It's an unfounded anxiety, I realize, but I can't quiet it.

Luckily, I don't have to, because when Mr. Sexy Four Eyes opens his mouth to give *his* answer, I'm in a complete trance along with the rest of the class and the professor.

"I guess I can't speak for everyone in here," he starts, like he's unsure, though everything about the way he's sitting and speaking screams confidence. His shoulders are back, head high, easy smile in place as he drapes one ankle over the opposite knee. "But I write for a purpose — a purpose that changes each time. Sometimes it's to evoke laughter, sometimes to make people think, sometimes to bring a feeling to life like romance or pain, and always — no matter what the topic — to entertain."

The professor smiles, pointing his marker at Kip with approval before he drones on about something else. I don't even hear it, because I'm too busy staring at Kip's mouth again.

"You kind of have this all figured out, don't you?" I tease.

"I like to think I know what my passions are, yes," he answers, his aqua eyes skirting to mine.

"Passion can be a dangerous thing."

He smiles, turning his attention back to Dr. O'Neal. "What's life without a little danger?"

And just like that, our little game of cat and mouse is back on.

***

After class, the professor asks Kip to stay back, so I wait for him outside of the Visual Arts Building. I can't help myself — he's just too delicious *not* to play with. When he emerges from the double doors, he grins at the sight of me, tucking his hands into the pockets of his hunter green shorts.

"You really are stalking me."

I shrug, still leaning casually against the brick of the building. "You should be so lucky, Four Eyes. Speaking of which, where are your specks today?"

"Contacts," he says. "I'm heading to the gym after my last class today, and they don't fare well with sweat."

The image of him sweating, the muscles in his arms bulging as he bench presses more than I weigh makes me chew my cheek.

How long until I can get him in bed with me?

"You're weird," I assess after a moment, because he is — he is truly a strange creature, one I've never experienced at Palm South University. Usually, the guys here fit easily into a box: Jock, Nerd, Frat Daddy, Rock Star Wannabe, Loser, etc. But Kip?

He doesn't fit in. He stands out.

And he owns that shit like a boss.

"You like it," he challenges, to which I just roll my eyes, turning on my heel for Greek Row.

"Skyler!" he calls out after me, and I smile, hiding it before I turn back to face him. "How do you take your coffee? For next week."

"Trying to be a gentleman now?"

He shrugs, and even though it's kind of a lame game to play, I can't resist the chance to toy with him more.

"I only like one thing on the Starbucks menu. You seem to have everything else figured out, let's see if you can guess what it is."

I turn just as another smile threatens to break on my face, and he calls out behind me again.

"Will I see you before then?"

I only offer him a glance over my shoulder, batting my long lashes with a soft shrug.

Who knows, Kip Jackson — maybe you'll see me before then, maybe you won't.

I'm still floating on the Kip Cloud when I make it back to the sorority house, thankful I survived the trek in my wedges. But before I have the time to kick the God-forsaken shoes off my feet, Jess grabs my arm, dragging me through the house.

"Ex just texted us and said to meet in her room ASAP. Sounds important."

"Crisis with Spring Break planning?"

Jess tries not to laugh, but fails. "I'm sure it's something equally as serious, knowing your Big."

I smile, grateful that I'm still at the point in my life where Spring Break is my biggest worry. At least, for now. It won't be long before all I'll be able to think about is the poker tournament, and how much is riding on it.

I love PSU, and I'm next in line to be president of Kappa Kappa Beta.

But in order for that to happen, I have to be able to *stay* at Palm South.

And in order for *that* to happen, I have to win this tournament.

No pressure.

Erin

What the hell is this feeling?

That's all I can think while I wait for the girls to get to my room.

My chest is prickly, like the air inside my lungs is electric, sending little waves of static through every breath. I can't stop smiling, and there's almost a little... dance? Skip? In every step I take. I know I've felt this feeling before, yet it's foreign and confusing, like my body forgot how to feel it and thus is having a hard time computing.

Is this... excitement? Hope? *Both*?

I smile, shaking my head against my own giddiness.

Calm down, Erin.

But how can I?

Kip Jackson is at Palm South University.

Kip Jackson — my first love, perhaps the *only* boy I've ever loved. Kip Jackson — the one I've wanted to lean on ever since we broke up, the one who always rushes back to my mind when the emotions get to be too much.

I lost him, and I've never forgiven myself for it. He's the best guy I've ever dated, and yet, I thought he was destined to be the one who got away.

But now, I finally have my second chance.

Because Kip Jackson is at Palm South University.

Ashlei and Cassie fly through my door first, Cassie hopping up on my bed as Ashlei tries as delicately as she can to sit in my bean bag chair.

"What's going on, Ex?" she asks, but I just pull up my desk chair to form a semi-circle.

"Let's wait until the other girls get here."

As if on cue, Jess pounces through my door next, taking the spot on my bed next to Cassie. Skyler is the last to join us, and she shuts my door behind her, kicking off her wedges before plopping down on the floor to complete our circle.

In a dress.

"Ew, put your snatch away, Little," I tease.

Jess throws a pillow at Skyler from where she sits on the bed, and my Little glances down at her exposed thong as a blush shades her cheeks.

"Did you just call my treasure box a snatch?"

"Did you just call it a treasure box?" Cassie counters.

"Would you prefer I say vagasaurus? That's my personal favorite nickname," Skyler says matter-of-factly, tucking the pillow Jess threw into her lap to shield her underwear from view.

The girls all chuckle, though Jess looks appalled.

"Do you really call it that?" she asks Skyler.

"Among many other things, yes."

"Like what?" Jess pokes, her brows still pinched together in a mixture of curiosity and disgust.

"I don't know... hoohah, muffin, pink canoe."

"Juice box, kitty, hot pocket," Cassie adds.

Ashlei sits up a little straighter, running her hands over her tight pencil skirt before chiming in. "Tampon tamer, magic bean, cubby hole. I heard someone call it a finger hut once. My personal favorite is vajayjay."

"Oh! That's another one I use frequently, Lei. Nice."

Skyler practically air-high-fives Ashlei from across the room, and what started off as a fun joke suddenly starts to annoy me. The skin on my neck tingles, and my left leg bounces where it rests over my right one.

Don't they realize we have more important things to discuss?

"I seriously have never used any of these," Jess says. "I say vagina. Or occasionally I get a little *Jersey Shore* and say co-cah."

"Or cho-cha like Missy Elliot?" Skyler asks.

"Yes!" Jess and Cassie say in unison, and then everyone explodes into another fit of laughter — me included.

"Can we stop talking about penis fly traps for like two seconds?" I finally say, but I can't deny that it feels good to laugh.

When was the last time I did?

"This is serious!" I add for good measure, but my straight face cracks into another smile which just makes all the girls laugh harder. Snatching a handful of highlighters off my desk, I peg each one of them with a different color to a chorus of more laughter.

Finally, Jess wipes tears from her eyes, settling the room. "Okay, Ex, what's going on?"

I exhale long and slow, folding my hands in my lap and sitting up straighter. Time to get down to business.

"Did I ever tell you guys about the summer before my senior year of high school?"

My Grand-Little stops digging around for snacks in my bedside table long enough to answer. "Isn't that the summer you spent with your grandparents?"

"Yes. It was the summer I wanted to find myself, that I wanted to sort of break free from everything I thought I was."

I close my eyes briefly, smiling a little at the memory of that summer — the Kansas wheat fields, the hot sun, the constant breeze that ruffled Kip's blond hair. I can still feel the way his calloused hands fit in mine after long days on harvest, can still smell the country air as we passed long nights on a blanket under the stars behind my grandparents' house.

"I had just ended a two-year relationship," I continue. "And I was in a strange place." My voice fades as I realize how tough I thought *that* time in my life had been...

If only I would have known what was still to happen to me in the future.

I shake my head. "Well, I met a boy that summer..."

"Oh!" Ashlei says, snapping her fingers. "I remember the story! He was the Army brat, right?"

"He wasn't a *brat,* you brat," I say, narrowing my eyes at her as I fight back a smile. "But yes, he did live on the base by my grandparents' house. He was amazing — everything I needed that summer. We spent practically every night together and as cliché as it sounds, I fell in love with him." I smile. "Well, as in love as I could be at that age. It was the perfect summer romance."

I'm still kind of lost in my memory when Skyler's voice breaks through the fog.

"Not that this isn't romantic and touching, but is there a reason you're telling us this?"

Standing, I let the warm light within me beam through. "You are not going to believe this," I say. "The boy I met that summer? He's *here...* like here, as in he's a student at Palm South!"

"What?" Ashlei pops up. "Isn't that impossible? We know pretty much everyone on this campus."

"Not the new students," I point out, waiting for them to catch on. When they don't, I sigh. "He's a *transfer!*"

My chest prickles with those damn bolts of electricity again, and I press a hand to the center of it, smiling.

"He just moved here. I heard Adam talking about his new pledges this morning outside of the Greek library and I just kind of casually asked about him — where he was from, what he was like — it's definitely him, girls!"

Ashlei's face lights up, but the room is quiet for me having just dropped such exciting news. Provided, I was *possibly* being a little dramatic about the whole thing, but it's been so long since

I've been excited about — well, *anything* — that I kind of expected a little more gusto in the reaction to my news.

For some reason, Jess and Cassie are watching Skyler, who looks like she's about to throw up.

"What?" Ashlei asks before I can. "Why are you guys acting so weird?"

"Nothing," Skyler says quickly. "We know him. Well, we met him. Last night."

"At rush?!" I ask excitedly. My stomach flips at the thought of seeing him again, of just *casually* running into him with the girls.

"Oh my God, Kip? Is that you? How's it going? Oh, have you met our president, Erin Xanders? Oh, you HAVE?"

Skyler nods. "Yep. He was nice."

"That's one way to put it, Sky," Jess adds, snickering. She nudges Cassie, like there's some sort of inside joke under those words, but Cassie just coughs uncomfortably.

What the hell?

"Okay, what the hell happened, Little?" I ask, turning on Skyler.

She groans, face flopping into the pillow in her lap. Her next words are muffled through it. "Nothing. We played foosball."

"And he lost, so she made him take a shot of tequila..." Jess says.

My anxiety eases a little. So they met, and maybe they flirted a bit. Doesn't surprise me that my Little had the new kid taking a shot of tequila to welcome him to PSU.

But then Jess continues, and my stomach sinks with her words.

"...Off her body."

The first thought through my head is *school your features.* If I learned anything from my mother over last summer, it was that ninety-five percent of a woman's power comes from how well she responds to potentially emotional situations. *Think like a man,* she'd put it — though I like to think it's more thinking like a *woman* — a strong, logical woman not ruled by her emotions.

So, even though the thought of Kip running his tongue over my Little's stomach makes me want to punch her in the nose and then run off crying, I simply take a breath, and start thinking.

"Oh," I say first, as calmly as I can. I need something to do with my hands, so I walk toward my closet, running my fingers over the different Lily Pulitzer dresses inside. "Well, that's okay. I mean, you didn't know. How could you?"

And though those words shake as they leave my lips, they're true. Skyler wouldn't hurt me, and she definitely wouldn't have a guy I'm still obsessed over take a body shot off her.

Still, jealousy is an evil bitch, and she's got her claws in me deep now.

All I can think about is him touching her, and her touching him, and both of them smiling and laughing and... *God,* what if he liked it?

What if he likes *her*?

"I swear I didn't, Big," Skyler says. "You know I wouldn't have done it if I had known."

"No, no, it's okay," I say deftly, because now my wheels are turning over that last thought.

What if he likes her?

What if he likes her?

And just like that, an idea snaps into place like the last piece of a puzzle.

What. If. He. Likes. *Her.*

"Actually," I say, turning to face them all again as hope finds me. "No — this is good. This is perfect."

"Um, how is this even remotely in the same category as good?" Cassie asks.

I dart to the planner on my desk, flipping it open as I try my best to explain. The idea is a little crazy, but crazy just might work.

"Well, Kip and I didn't exactly have the best ending that summer. I may have acted a little immature, at best," I admit, thinking of how I would look through his phone, letting my jealousy get the better of me until I blew up on him.

I was young, emotional, naïve — I didn't know what I had until I lost it.

Finding the date I was looking for, I tap the highlighted event, spinning to face the girls again.

"This is perfect. I don't think he would want to talk to me, let alone get back together right now. I need him to come around more, to see how I've grown and how respected I am here. I want him to see that four years has done me well."

"Absolutely! You're the shit," Jess says, but she still looks concerned. "But, I'm lost on how this has anything to do with your Little having lover boy's tongue in her mouth."

Skyler groans, stuffing her head back into the pillow while I try again not to give into my urge to scratch her eyes out for so much as *looking* at Kip.

What the hell is wrong with me?

"Because," I say, calm again, my features smooth. I carefully take a seat on the floor in front of Skyler, knowing before I say the words how insane my little idea is. "She's going to be the one to get him to come back to me. She's the bait."

Skyler's head snaps up, her wide, blue eyes meeting mine.

"*What?* No way!" She jumps up from the floor, tossing the pillow she's been hiding behind on the bed. "I mistakenly made out with your high school... whatever he was, but I'm not involved in this."

I pop up, ready to plead my case. "You are now! He knows you now," I argue. "He's obviously interested, and you're the best shot I have at getting him to hang around me in a natural way without it looking like I'm insane. Or a creeper. Or both."

It's true. I had pulled the girls together to think of ways for me to get him back, to work out a plan. Though this isn't *exactly* how I pictured things going down, it just might be crazy enough to work.

"Big, you can't be serious," Skyler says. "What am I supposed to do... woo him? Flirt him into following me around like a puppy and then blow him off so you can pick up the pieces?"

I pause, digesting her suggestion. "I hadn't thought it out quite that far, but yes."

"No," Skyler says immediately, tossing her hands up. "I'm leaving this room and we can just pretend like last night and this conversation didn't happen."

She turns to leave, and like an out-of-body-experience, I watch in horror from the corner of the room as the next words leave my mouth.

"You want to be president next year, don't you?"

It's like all the air is sucked out of the room with that question. Skyler is stiff as a rod, and when I come to, back in my own body again, Jess is the first person I hear.

"Ex," she warns. She's telling me to back off, that I've gone too far, but she doesn't understand. *No one* understands.

This is the only speck of joy I've managed to find since I was violated in the worst possible way a woman can be. It's been almost a year since it happened, and I still exist in a dark hole of nothingness, where the thought of being happy again feels so ludicrous I don't even allow myself to consider it.

But then, Kip showed up at Palm South University.

I won't let this chance pass me by.

"No, I'm serious," I say. "You have to make a lot of sacrifices as president, Little. You have to do a lot of stuff you really don't want to do. This position is not for the weak or the scared or the selfish."

The irony of that last sentence isn't lost on me, considering I *was* weak, I *am* scared, and right now, I'm also proving to be very, very selfish.

"You want to be next in line?" I ask her. "It's time to start proving you can take it, that you belong in this room when I leave. You need to step up, Little."

And just like that, I become the villain I never knew I could be.

Skyler's face crumples, but she nods. "Can I at least think about it?"

Thinking back to my original plan, I glance at the date still highlighted in the open planner on my desk. "I tell you what, the date auction is Saturday. Let's see if you made the impression I think you did. If he bids the highest and wins the date with you, then the game starts and you play him right into my hand."

"I have a tournament that night, Big," she complains. "I wasn't even going to go to the auction."

"Well, now you are going — and you're getting auctioned off. If he bids the highest, then you're doing this." My words are absolute — final.

"And if he doesn't?" she asks.

I shrug, confident enough in my assessment that I won't have to worry about that possibility. "Then you're off the hook. I want it to be easy for you to get him to come around, and bidding the highest at a date auction is pretty much the most simple way to get a girl on a date. If he doesn't try and succeed to do just that with you, then there's no point in you making it awkward and throwing yourself at him. But," I counter. "If he dragged his tongue up your stomach, I seriously doubt he'll let you go on a date with anyone else."

It's my attempt at a joke, to lighten the mood, but Skyler doesn't crack so much as a small smile.

Can I blame her? This is possibly *the* worst thing I've done in my life… and that's saying something, considering my actions after I slept with Clinton.

"Fine," Skyler concedes. "But if he doesn't make the highest bid, then I'm off the hook and you're on your own to reel in your fish."

Hope floods me again. *She's actually going to help!*

Well, not that I actually gave her an option, but whatever.

"Absolutely, no questions asked." I hold out my hand to shake Skyler's, and when the deal is sealed, I can't help the excitement that pours through me like liquid gold. I turn back to the other girls, practically squealing. "This is going to be fun!"

But even as I say the words, I know in my heart that this is going to be anything but fun for Skyler.

Her face falls again as she leaves the room, and I silently vow to make it up to her.

I owe you one, Little.

Ashlei

A couple hours after Erin's emergency meeting, I'm swinging through the doors to one of the tallest buildings downtown with the biggest smile on my face. The *click clack* of my stilettos on the marble floor of the lobby comfort me, a calm, soothing sense of home washing over me as I make my way toward the elevator. That elevator will take me all the way up to the thirty-second floor, back to *Okay, Cool*, back to a place where I feel confident and respected, back to opportunity.

And back to Brandon Church.

A shallow breath fills my lungs as I press a hand to my stomach at the thought of him. I run my fingers over the buttons on my rose-pink blouse, biting my lower lip against the smile threatening to break on my face. When the elevator doors open, I step inside confidently, a blush creeping over my cheeks at the memory of my first time inside it.

That was the day I met Brandon Church.

That was the day everything changed.

I sigh, giving into my smile as the doors start to close, but just like last semester, a hand darts in to stop them.

Only this one isn't the strong, dark hand of the CEO who makes my panties drip with want. It's a lighter hand, more feminine and delicate, with long, shiny, black pointy nails.

The silver doors open again, and the last person I expect to see greets me with a wicked smile.

"Hello, Ashlei."

"Kimberly," I manage as a response, straightening as she steps onto the elevator with me. I wait for her to choose a different floor, to explain what the hell she's doing back in this building, but she simply smiles wider at my apparent confusion.

Kimberly Marks was an intern with me last semester, and it was no secret that she absolutely hated me. She started rumors about me and Brandon, and although they weren't completely *un*-true, they also had no proof to back them up. Most of the associates couldn't stand Kimberly — me included.

So then *why* was she on her way back to *Okay, Cool* with me?

Kimberly had cut her hair since I'd last seen her, the long, brown locks of curls chopped high and tight into a masculine fade. It accents her high cheek bones and slender nose even more, and leaves her slender collarbone exposed in her simple, scoop-neck, black dress. Her heels are a matte black, too, making her entire appearance dark and commanding.

She's taller than me by several inches, even though my heels are higher than hers, and she seems to take pride in the way she gets to look down her nose at me to answer the questions I haven't even asked aloud.

"What?" she asks, one thin, dark eyebrow raised in pity. "Did you think you were the only intern they invited back for another semester?" She clucks her tongue, turning back toward the elevator doors. "They asked me to come back, too — and unlike you, *I* wasn't asked to extend because of the quality of my blow jobs."

The corner of her red-stained lips quirks up at her little comment, and though my first instinct is to shove my stiletto heel up her ass, I simply smile back in a *bless your heart* kind of way, just like Mom always taught me.

"Well, congratulations, Kimberly. I look forward to working with you again," I lie through my teeth. And just as the elevator dings, letting us know we hit the thirty-second floor, I step forward, making sure she understands her place *behind* me. "And thank you for the compliment on my skillset. It's *so nice* to have the support of another professional, mature businesswoman."

As the doors slide open, Kimberly steps up right behind me, her next threat hot on the skin of my neck.

"You were the top intern last semester, Daniels, but it should have been me. And now that I've been invited back for a second chance to prove that, you better believe I'll do whatever it takes. I'm on to you," she seethes. "So watch yourself, because I'm not backing down, and I won't be overshadowed by the office slut again this semester."

Her words sting, even though I try not to give them power. Still, I don't offer her so much as another glance, let alone more of my time. I simply *click* and *clack* my way off that elevator and back into the place that feels like home — and I don't bother holding the door open for her on my way in.

"ASHLEI!"

Mykayla throws her arms around me as soon as I make it inside, her ginormous breasts pressing against my stomach as she nuzzles into me.

"I'm so, *so* happy you're back. I've missed you so much! How was your break? How's the sorority? I love that skirt on you, and oh, my God, you're so *tan*."

I chuckle, pulling back from our embrace with a smile that mirrors hers. "I'm happy to see you, too, Mykayla."

Kimberly slinks by behind us, narrowing her eyes at me and Mykayla as she makes her way to our section of cubicles. Mykayla notices the ugly look and scoffs, pointing her thumb over her shoulder at where Kimberly's back just disappeared around the corner.

"What the hell? What is *she* doing back here?"

"Hell if I know," I say on a sigh. "She seems pretty fixated on my demise, though."

Mykayla snorts, rounding the welcome counter back to her chair and plopping down. She hands me my new name tag and office key fob with a gentle roll of her eyes. "Whatever. She's peanut butter and jealous — has been since the moment she met you. Anyway, the other interns are almost finished in their morning orientation and then we'll all break for lunch. Sit with me? Let's catch up before the afternoon briefing!"

"You got it. I think I'll walk around, say hi to everyone before then," I say, pulse ticking up speed as I glance down the hall at Brandon's office. The door is cracked, just enough for me to see his strong hand clicking away at his keyboard inside.

"Perfect. Holly should be back by the internship cubes already, if you want to start with her."

I nod, knowing my manager's desk *should* be the first place I stop, but ever since the last time Brandon's hands splayed the small of my back, since the night I ditched my own formal and opted for him plowing me over the side of his desk, instead — he's all I've been able to think about.

He said it was the last time he'd be able to touch me. He swore we'd have to behave ourselves, that we couldn't see each other again — not like that.

But it was like telling a bird not to fly, or urging the wind not to blow — impossible, ridiculous, and absolutely futile.

I would have Brandon Church again. Of that, I was sure.

"I'll make my way back there in a moment," I finally say, my eyes still on his office door. "Figure I might as well say hi to Mr. Church while I'm out this way."

Mykayla follows my gaze, shrugging. "Sure. He's been locked in there all day, I'm sure he'd be happy for a break and a chance to welcome you back." She smiles up at me, completely oblivious — *thank God*. "See you at lunch!"

Then, she gets right back to work like I'm no longer standing there, her little smile in place as she files through a massive stack of paper on her desk.

My throat is dry and sticky, my ability to swallow temporarily thwarted as I slowly make my way back to Brandon's office. Each step has my heart beating a little faster, and my hands do anything but stay at my sides — they slide over my long, slick pony tail, smooth down the sides of my pencil skirt, fidget with my necklace. By the time I make it to his door, my knuckles softly rapping on the sleek, cool metal, I'm not sure if I want to smile, dance, or throw up.

"Come in," Brandon says without looking up from his monitor.

I wedge my hip between the door and the glass of his office window, leaning against the silver pane and crossing my arms casually over my middle. "Good afternoon, Mr. Church."

His hands stop, his eyes still locked on his screen. I watch his face, searching for a sign of recognition, of delight, of want — of *anything*, but he keeps all of his features completely schooled. His fingers go back to typing, only the slightest tick in his dark, strong jaw letting me know he registered my words at all.

"Miss Daniels," he says calmly. "Nice to have you back. How was your winter break?"

"Uneventful," I say, lowering my voice a little. "I was pretty sore, after all the *dancing* I did the night of my formal. Spent a lot of time recovering from that."

There it is, I think, noting the slight twitch at the corner of Brandon's mouth. He wants to smile, wants to tease me back, but he doesn't. Instead, he clears his throat, keeping his eyes glued to his screen.

"Well, we're glad to have you back at *Okay, Cool*. I have to finish this report, but I'll see you at the briefing later?"

"Are you sure I can't help with your report?" I ask, voice seductive and laced with intention.

In the next second, I feel like a foolish little girl, because Brandon huffs, shaking his head as he pounds on the keys harder.

"No, Miss Daniels, you can't help. This is a report being crafted by the CEO, it's not exactly internship busy work material."

I snap back at the briskness of his tone, standing straight as shame shades my cheeks.

"Right. Of course. I didn't mean to... I apologize, Mr. Church."

He gives a curt nod. "No need to apologize. Have a good afternoon."

My heart deflates like a sad, whining balloon. Brandon still won't look at me, and though I knew he was serious when he said he wouldn't be touching me again, the bigger part of me assumed that was just a cover — a way for him to say he *tried* to stay away from me once he finally gave in.

Judging by the way he won't even look at me now, I realize I was wrong. He didn't say those words last semester as a tease, or a joke, or a challenge.

He meant what he said, and for the first time in my life, I wish a man would have lied to me.

"You, too," I say softly, dejected.

My heart beats too loudly in my ears as I shuffle my way back to the internship cubicles, my heels clicking along the marble once more.

But now, the sound doesn't bring me comfort.

It just breaks my heart.

Bear

"I know it's upsetting, but remember how you got here in the first place," Alec says to a full, groaning chapter room on Friday night. He holds up his hands to try to silent my brothers, but it's a futile attempt. Everyone is already anxious to get out to the bars, being that it's our first weekend since rush, but with Alec's news, that anxiousness turns more to anger.

Alec is the most hated alumni of Omega Chi Beta, mostly because he was the one to deliver us our asses on a silver platter last year in the form of a chapter suspension. And with the news he just delivered, his reputation isn't getting any better.

Because even after minding our Ps and Qs last fall, we're *still* suspended.

And my brothers are pissed.

After a semester of good deeds, we all thought we'd be back in action this year. But it turns out one semester doesn't undo years of getting ourselves into trouble, and honestly, I can't say I'm surprised.

"Look," Alec says louder, calming the room. "You guys did great in the fall. Your philanthropic efforts were spot on, and you stayed out of trouble once the suspension was put into place. I know another semester feels like a lifetime, but if you can hold it together, you'll be back to full status next fall."

The room erupts in groans again, and I'm secretly thankful that our first chapter doesn't include any of the new guys who decided to pledge Omega Chi. They'd be changing their minds real quick if they saw us right now.

"What about the seniors?" one brother asks above the rest.

"Yeah, what about Spring Break?"

That causes another unified growl of disapproval, and Alec looks a little sorry then, scanning the faces of the other alumni advisors behind him. One of them says something to him that none of us can hear over all our brothers bitching and moaning, and Alec comes back to the mic with his hands up again.

"I'll try my best to get you permission for Spring Break, but even if you *can* do something as a chapter, it will most likely have to be with another fraternity, too." Alec kills the protests to that before they can even start. "OR, you can not go at all, the choice will be yours — *if* I can convince nationals that you deserve a Spring Break."

We all pack up our shit in relative silence when chapter ends, a solemn disappointment settling over all of us. The Omega Chi Beta brothers were the top fraternity on campus, until our suspension, and now we're quickly being replaced — or at least rivaled — by Alpha Sigma. My brothers hate it, and so do I, but there's not much we can do.

"This fucking blows," my Little, Josh, says as we push through the chapter doors and out into the cool night air. It's our first chapter, less than a week of classes under our belt in the new semester, and now that rush is over, there's not much for us to look forward to.

"It'll be alright," I assure him, adjusting my book bag on my shoulder. "We'll just have to party off campus or at other frat houses like we did last year."

"Oh yeah, let's just continue to go to Alpha Sigma parties and help them elevate their status above ours. Sounds great."

"Better than not partying at all, am I right?"

Josh frowns, not happy about that point. He runs a hand over his curly, ginger hair, a frustrated sigh leaving his lips.

"Whatever. I just hope we get to go on Spring Break."

"I think Alec is actually in our corner this semester," I say. "Let's just hope nationals will listen to him."

"We'll find out."

Josh looks at me, taking in my haggard appearance. I know I look haggard, because I slept half the day away and woke up just in time to throw on business slacks and a button up for chapter. It was my first chance to catch up on rest since last semester ended, after spending winter break up in Pittsburgh helping my little brother, Clayton, find a part-time job.

"You need to get laid," Josh says when we turn onto Greek Row.

I chuckle. "I don't think I have the energy to fuck anyone right now."

"Well, you better take a nap and find some. And fast. Because you look like shit."

"Thanks, Little."

"I'm serious," he continues, unapologetically. "You spent your entire winter break helping out your fam, which is admirable, man, and I think it's awesome that you're there for your little bro. But seriously dude, you're Clinton Pennington. You're M.O. is weightlifting, partying, and fucking — and I haven't seen you do much of any of that in a while."

I frown, considering his assessment. With Omega Chi being suspended, I have toned down on the partying, and after the little stunt I pulled with Shawna in front of Lacey last semester, I'm not getting any tail from her anymore. The combination of worrying about my brother and feeling sick over treating Skyler like shit had me sitting in my room playing video games more than lifting weights at the end of last semester.

In a way, I guess you could say I'd let myself go.

"I'm just in a funk," I finally say. "I'll be fine."

"Here," Josh says, thumbing out a text on his phone. Mine pings in the next instant. "I just sent you an invite for this dating app everyone is talking about. It's exclusive to PSU, and it's literally like shopping for a fuck buddy. You just swipe right on a girl's picture if you're interested, and swipe left if you're not. If you match, then you can see their phone number and they can see yours. It's up to one of you to make a move then."

"Sounds creepy."

"It's efficient," he argues. "And I've already fucked three girls this week."

I raise my brows, and as sad as it is, he has my attention.

"I'll think about it."

Josh opens the door to our house, letting me in first before he holds up his phone again. "Don't think about it, do it. Seriously, Bear. You spend so much time taking care of everyone else — the fraternity, your family — but what you *need* to spend some time doing is getting your dick wet."

"That almost sounded sincere."

Josh just shrugs. "Hey, I'm nothing if not honest. Download the app. And come out to the Kappa Kappa Beta date auction tonight. You need to get out of your room."

He doesn't give me a chance to respond before he's jogging up the stairs to his room.

I sigh when I'm inside my own room down the hall, dropping my bag at the door and taking in the small space. It's the same room I've had since I joined Omega Chi, same bedspread, same décor. The same gaming system rests underneath the same TV, the same paddle with the same letters hanging above my bed.

So much in that room is exactly the same as it was the day I moved in, and yet the man who sleeps inside it every night couldn't be further from the boy he was that day.

I flop down on my bed, eyes on the ceiling as my Little's words play on repeat in my head.

In a way, he's right.

I can't help but take care of the people around me, it's just who I am. Between my brothers and my family, I haven't had energy for much else. Add in the fact that Erin *still* won't let me in to talk about what happened last year, and you could say the amount of space left in my energy tank for dating is pretty nonexistent.

But as much as I want to blame it on time and energy, the truth of why I've avoided anyone other than Lacy hovers over me like a blinking neon sign.

I'm not over Shawna.

Just bringing her memory to mind makes my chest tighten, and I roll on my side, staring at my phone on the bedside table.

Have I even *tried* to get over her? To forget her?

I know that answer before I even ask the question, but it doesn't make it hurt any less.

I don't do feelings. Before Shawna, the most a girl had ever gotten out of me was more than one night in my bed. But *after* her? Well, no girl had a shot in *hell* of getting anything at all from me. Lacy had been there, sure — but as a distraction, as a mutual understanding. We didn't talk, didn't hang out, didn't go on dates. We banged, and then she left. The end.

But I'd ruined that.

Huffing, I swipe my phone off the table, opening up Josh's text and clicking the link inside it.

I don't know if I'm ready for dating, or even finding a fuck buddy, but I decide to give it a shot, anyway.

My brother is fine — he's got a job now and still has plenty of cash leftover from the generous gift Skyler gave him last semester. My brothers are stuck on suspension, and there's nothing more I can do about that right now. And Erin? Well, she doesn't want my help — no matter how much I want to give it.

It's a new semester, a new year, and maybe it's time I get back to basics — back to Bear.

So, I make a new gym plan, order some protein powder online, and then I download the stupid motherfucking app and start swiping.

Adam

It has never been so difficult to keep my damn hands to myself.

The Kappa Kappa Beta Date Auction will always remind me of Cassie, no matter what, because I can't help but think back to her first year when she was auctioned off. She was so shy and timid, so scared, so completely oblivious to the fact that she is seriously sexy and adorable and way too intelligent for any of the poor suckers here at PSU.

And now, watching her from the crowd while she scurries around Ralph's, helping Erin and the MC, Chelsea, with whatever they need, I practically have to sit on my hands to keep from rushing to her. All I want to do is shove her behind the stage curtains, hike one leg up, and slide my fingers under the tiny skirt she's wearing to find out what kind of panties are underneath it. Are they lace? Cotton? A thong or boy shorts?

Is she even wearing any at all?

I groan out loud at that possibility, which has Jeremy's eyes following mine to where Cassie is looking over a clipboard with her Grand Big.

He whistles, nudging my elbow with his. "Damn. Cassie's looking good tonight." He takes a tentative sip of his beer, watching me out of the corner of his eye. "Don't you think?"

"Shut up, Jeremy."

He chuckles. "Come on, man. You're watching her like you're something between a lovesick puppy and a possessive, ravenous bear that hasn't eaten since it went into hibernation."

I sigh, eyebrows lifting at the surprising accurateness of his assessment.

"Are you guys dating now or what?"

"Or what," I answer, taking a drink from my own bottle.

"What the hell is stopping you now? She's single, *you're* single, you both want to bang each other or eat the other's face off, depending on how you decipher those weird looks you give each other across the room. What's the issue?"

"There's no issue," I defend. "We're not together, but we're not *not* together either."

"Then what the fuck are you?"

"Complicated," I murmur, taking another drink.

Jeremy watches with me as Cassie scans the room, looking for something. She glances past us before doubling back, and when our eyes lock, a slow, dazzling smile spreads on her strawberry-pink lips. She waves, tucking a strand of her curly hair behind one ear, and I tip my bottle toward her in greeting with the same stupid grin on my face.

"She wants to fuck," Jeremy says, and I punch him hard in the chest. He bends with an *oof,* but just laughs it off. "I mean seriously, dude. Did you see her all playing with her hair and eye-fucking you from across the room? What is so complicated about that?"

"Look," I say with a sigh, pointing my bottle in his face. "Every single guy at PSU who has gone after Cassie has had one thing on their mind — getting in her pants. Clay took her virginity, and then embarrassed her in front of the entire Greek system by showing up to the end of the semester party with her *roommate*. Then," I say hurriedly, cutting off Jeremy's attempt to argue with me.

"She falls in love with our closest thing to a campus rock star, and he swoons her out of her panties with his bullshit sensitivity and acoustic guitar, and she finds out he was cheating on her with some groupie the entire time."

Jeremy opens his mouth again, but I shake my head.

"I have wanted Cassie longer than I was even able to admit to myself, and yes, while all the doors are open right now, I also don't want to be just another guy on the long list of ones who have disappointed her. So, while I desperately want to sleep with her, I respect her more than that, and I know she needs some time to figure shit out after what happened last semester."

I swallow, thinking back to how hard Cassie cried in my arms that night she crawled through my window. I'll be damned if I'm ever the reason for tears like that.

"She's the most incredible girl I've ever known, Jeremy. I've fucked up in the past, lost her when I had the chance to have her, hurt her when all I wanted was to heal her. Now that we're both single, I have the chance to do this right. So, I'm moving slow, and I'm giving her space to find herself again before she finds who she is with me."

Jeremy half-smiles, his expression something between pity and understanding. "I get it, dude. And it's admirable. I don't envy you or your blue balls," he adds quickly. "But, I get it."

I nod, taking a longer pull from my beer before Chelsea takes the stage again, ready to auction off the next KKB sister.

She starts by talking about the philanthropy again, and as she reads off statistics of the past few years with how much their fundraising has helped the local chapter, I think over what I just said to Jeremy, memories of my talk with my aunt over the break still loud in my head.

"A good woman is worth waiting for," she'd told me after I'd spilled out my heart. My aunt was like a mother to me, just like my grandfather had been like a dad. Now that he was gone, she was all I had, and she'd listened patiently as I'd told her everything about Cassie.

It made sense, what she said, about Cassie needing to find herself again. I knew what it was like to emerge on the other end of a break up wondering who you even were without the person who'd been the other half of your life for so long. I'd felt it when I broke up with Skyler, and even more so when I'd split from my long-time high school girlfriend before coming to PSU.

It's tricky, navigating the waters post-relationship, and while I want nothing more than for Cassie to dive straight into me, I know she needs some space, some time to remember how to swim again. I don't want her to drown *in* me — I want her to thrive *with* me.

A loud roar from the crowd snaps me back to the present moment, and when my eyes find Skyler in a bright pink dress on stage, I can't help but laugh and cheer with them.

She looks wildly uncomfortable in that dress, but her confident *I'm Skyler Fucking Thorne* face is firmly in place, and more cat calls and whistles ring out as she does a little spin for the crowd. I'm surprised they convinced her to even participate in the auction, but it was a good call on their part — Skyler would easily be their biggest moneymaker.

After she lists off some of Skyler's "selling points," Chelsea starts the bidding at fifty bucks.

The first paddle belongs to Josh, Clinton's Little in Omega Chi Beta, and I roll my eyes. That kid has had a crush on Skyler since the beginning of time. He's also had absolutely zero chance of ever getting her on a date.

When Chelsea calls for one-hundred dollars, I put my own paddle up.

Skyler's eyes widen, but when she realizes it's me, she shakes her head, pointing at me with a smile. I just shrug. Hey, the least I can do is *try* to save her from the literal last person she would want to win her.

When he bids two-hundred, I shove my paddle up one more time to outbid him, someone in the back outbidding me next, and then it's back to Josh at four-hundred.

Too rich for my blood.

I bow out, throwing my hands up in surrender. Though Skyler and I discovered very quickly that we're much better as friends than anything else, I still love her — more like a sister, I suppose. I did my best to save her from having to go on a date with Clinton's beefhead little brother, but she might be screwed.

Suddenly, someone calls out from the back, and I turn to find one of our new pledges — Kip Jackson — holding up his beer as he becomes the new highest bidder at five-hundred dollars.

"Damn it, Kip," I murmur under my breath.

Jeremy turns, laughing when he sees Kip climbing up onto the bar. Josh bid it up to six-hundred dollars, but Kip swiftly defeats him when he thrusts his arm up again and bids one-thousand.

"Why do you look so upset?" Jeremy asks, cheersing Kip from afar as the bar erupts into cheers. "That's a lot of money to charity."

"He's a pledge," I remind Jeremy. "He should be laying low, learning the ropes before he's thrusting himself into the spotlight like that."

"Oh, come on." Jeremy scoffs. "He's a junior, not a freshmen like most pledges. And I like him. He's got guts. Reminds me of you when you first joined."

I grimace at the comparison, though I can't figure out exactly why. I'm the one who recruited Kip, who wanted him to rush Alpha Sigma. But along the way, I learned he's a little pretentious, and while Jeremy might see his attitude as *enthusiasm,* I saw it as him not knowing his place.

Ugh. I sound like Clay.

Thinking back to the douchebag who was president when I was trying to make strides for Alpha Sigma makes my lip curl even more, especially after what he did to Cassie. I don't want to be anything like him, and yet here I am, hating on a pledge who just did a pretty awesome thing not only for KKB and their charity, but for our organization, too.

"Going once? Going twice?" Chelsea bangs the gavel against the podium. "Sold! To the Alpha Sig pledge in the glasses!"

Everyone laughs a little as I sigh, shoving down my pride and clapping along with the rest of the bar. I frown a little at the sigh of Skyler fleeing the stage so quickly. She's smiling, waving at the crowd like she should, but something in her eyes says she's not happy about something.

Probably the fact that her Big made her do the auction at all.

She's never been the kind of girl to get all dolled up and stand on stage to be bid on. She's more of the ripped-up jeans and t-shirt kind of gal.

I'm still watching as Kip chases Skyler out the front doors, and if anything, I can at least be happy for *her* — even if I am annoyed at Kip. She made it clear he was her new target for the semester, and this is a sure way to make sure she gets more time with him. Skyler deserves to be happy, and if a new transfer with glasses is going to do it for her, then I wish her the best.

My eyes find Cassie's in the crowd again, and she's right back to work now that the auction is over, helping Erin collect the winning bids and organize clean-up. Even though she seems a bit overwhelmed, her smile is genuine, and I can feel her happiness from across the room. She's getting back to the old her, finding herself, and as much as I want to drag her back to my bedroom tonight, I don't mind watching that happiness from afar for a while.

When the time is right, we'll be together — but there's no need to rush.

I'm not going anywhere.

Skyler

Kip Jackson is about as subtle as a fog horn in a museum.

I somehow managed to make it to the small poker tournament I originally had planned *before* Erin saddled me into the date auction. The only problem is that Kip wiggled his way into my cab, too. And now, on top of my plan of getting Clinton's Little, Josh, to buy me tonight so that I wouldn't be stuck playing Erin's game anymore falling through, I'm also stuck with Kip distracting me from the bar while I'm trying to focus on winning the next hand.

He doesn't fit in, not in this little shit hole bar. It's closed off to the public, only accessible with a secret password, and the clientele are *far* from anything remotely close to Kip. Everything in here is dark — the lighting, the liquor, the tattoos on the guy sitting at the bar, eyeing me like a snake now that I've taken his money and booted him out of the tournament. It's okay that my bright pink dress stands out — hell, it even plays in my favor, since distracting the other players and playing up my naiveté is part of my poker game.

But Kip? He needs to blend in, to not cause a scene.

And he's failing.

Not too long into the game, I beat out one of the toughest players at the table with a flush, one he thought was a bluff. He, of course, threw a big fit about his loss, which I'm used to. But Kip looked like he was about to jump out of his skin and across the bar to pummel the guy when it all went down. I had to shoot lasers at him with my eyes to get him to sit back down.

Now, an hour later, and it's down to just me and the guy I've been strategically flirting with all night — Luke. He's dressed pretty fratty in his khaki shorts straight from The Gap and his bro tank, complete with dark Oakley sunglasses and a ball cap turned around backward on his fat head.

He's had his eyes on me all night, and though I've been playing into his flirting banter, it's pure strategy — he doesn't have a shot in hell with me.

Still, I'm a little nervous now that I've just called his bet. He's all in, which means if I win this hand, I win it all — one step closer to paying off my entry fee for the APC tournament. But if he wins, I'm down to just twelve-hundred dollars to try to battle back to the top with.

Luke's been making comments about me being Barbie all night — which I can't really blame him for, seeing as how I'm still sporting the bright pink dress the girls dressed me in for the auction. Still, I can't resist the urge to throw that shit back in his face when he lays his hand down, smug as hell.

He has a straight, and that's all fine and dandy.

But I've got a four of a kind.

"Oh, Ken," I tease. "Barbie never bluffs."

Spreading the cards out on the table, I reveal my hand, and my opponent's jaw drops as the tiny bar erupts in a mixture of laughter and applause. I graciously accept the congratulations from those who offer, quickly swiping up the envelope with my cash in it as soon as the dealer places it in front of me.

I need to get out of here — need to get *Kip* out of here — and fast.

"That was a good game," the dealer says as I stand and tuck the envelope of cash in my clutch. "You know, you look familiar. Do you play a lot around here?"

I quickly shake my head. "No, but I have a familiar face. A lot of people think they know me."

I know he doesn't believe me, but thankfully, he doesn't push further. "I guess that's it. Well, at any rate, good job tonight."

I thank him, glancing at Kip briefly to let him know it's time to go before I make my way toward the door.

My one, explicit rule for allowing him to come with me to the tournament was that he stay cool and pretend like he doesn't know me. If these guys found out it was me, Skyler Thorne, one of the hottest women in poker who came to clear out their pockets at a tiny little tournament, we'd have trouble. Somehow, we've managed to skate by without anyone noticing, but I still won't feel at ease until we're back in a cab.

"Wait a second," Luke says, blocking my exit as he grabs my arm. "You're Skyler, aren't you?"

Though my heart skips at his recognition, I rip my arm free, stepping around him with ease. "Nope, I'm Barbie, remember?"

Luke grabs my arm again, but before I can defend myself, Kip is sprinting across the room.

"Don't touch her," he growls out, and I internally groan.

Damn it, Kip.

While I want to admit that it's a little hot how possessive his icy blue eyes are as he pins Luke with them, I'm more than a little aggravated. We need to get out of this bar without causing a scene, and this is *not* how we do it.

"Who the fuck are you?" Luke asks when Kip steps into his space.

"He's leaving," I say quickly. "We both are. Let's go," I say to Kip next, shoving him toward the door.

"Hey, I thought we were going out after this," Luke says, his arm wrapping around my waist from behind. "You just hustled me, the least you can do is put out tonight."

I narrow my eyes, ready to lay into him, but my blond-haired, blue-eyed bull dog attacks before I can.

Kip shoves Luke back, *hard*, sending him flying into the poker table. The chips scatter in his wake, a drink splashing over the side and onto the felt, and then all hell breaks loose.

"Take that shit outside!" the dealer yells.

"Yeah, let's go, playboy." Luke pushes himself off the table, launching at Kip, who rushes toward him, too.

I throw my hands out just in time to catch Kip's advance, shoving him back toward the door as I grit through my teeth. "Go. Now."

"I'm not going to let this asshole put his hands all over you."

Swoon.

Ugh, stop it, Skyler.

I shove Kip harder, making him stumble back toward the door. Once we're safely outside, the little bit of weakness Kip gave me with his possessiveness morphs back into annoyed anger. There's a cab waiting, one Kip was instructed to call at the end of the tournament, and I climb inside it, immediately smacking his chest once the door is closed behind us.

"What the fuck, Kip?! You almost screwed everything up!"

"I wasn't just going to stand there and watch that shit happen, Skyler!" he says, his breath hot on my skin.

Our bodies are too close, and I scoot away, putting distance between us in the backseat.

"I don't care if you did take that douchebag's money, he shouldn't have put his hands on you."

Do not swoon. Do not give in.

"I told you, I can handle myself," I remind him, crossing my arms and looking out the window. I don't know if I'm more frustrated at the fact that he almost blew the tournament for me, or at the fact that I still desperately want him, except now, I'm not allowed to have him.

Now, I have to play him like a game of poker – right into my Big's hands.

"I don't need you to save me, Kip," I say quieter.

For a while, we sit in silence, and I try to let that truth sink in. Kip is not mine, he never *will* be mine. And now, I'm stuck in a game I never intended to play, with a heart who doesn't even realize it's in the game, too.

Great.

"Hey," Kip says after a while, reaching over to place one hand on my thigh. Warmth spreads from that point of contact down to my toes, and I fight the urge to shiver. "Listen, I'm sorry."

I smack his hand away. "Whatever."

"Shit, Skyler," he says, exasperated. "I don't know what you want from me. I'm into you, okay?"

My heart squeezes.

"I'm sorry I didn't sit back and let some Abercrombie model-wannabe molest you. Next time, I'll back off. Just, come on, I don't want to end the night like this. Come home with me."

At that, my eyes widen.

"Are you serious?" I ask, finally facing him again.

"Not like that," he clarifies quickly, his hands up like he comes in peace.

Yeah, right. That motherfucker came in like a hurricane.

"It's almost four in the morning and I know you've got to be hungry. Let me make us breakfast."

As if on cue, my stomach growls, reminding me that I didn't even eat before the auction because my nerves were so shot. Still, I haven't had time to digest the night, to digest the fact that my big plan of having Josh win me in the auction backfired, and now Erin's little game is in place — with me as the pawn.

I turn toward the window again, hoping he'll just drop it, but Kip scoots closer to me, instead. He sets his chin on my shoulder, his big, puppy dog eyes begging me through the reflection in the glass.

"I make killer chocolate chip waffles."

I try not to smile, but he's just so damn adorable, it's practically impossible.

"I'll strip down to my boxers and wear an apron for you," he adds, and I pinch my lips together, still trying to fight.

Kip leans in a little closer, his voice just a whisper in my ear with his next sentence.

"What if I told you I had bacon?"

I can't help it — I laugh. Kip knows he's won, but still, I shove him away, shaking my head. "You're the biggest nerd, you know that?"

"I've been called worse. So," he says, eyes hopeful. "Waffles and bacon? Please? I promise to keep my hands to myself and you can punch me if I start to annoy you."

I sigh, debating my options. I really *am* hungry, and as much as I want time to figure out what the hell to do with my feelings toward Kip, I'd also be lying if I said I didn't want to spend more time with him.

"Fine," I concede. "But only because I love bacon."

EPISODE 2

Erin

"Okay, we have a few visitors tonight before we end chapter," I announce to my sisters Sunday evening. They're all a bit cranky after a particularly long chapter, so I put on my best smile to help them get through the last half hour. It's been a hectic week since our date auction, and with Valentine's Day around the corner, every sister has more pressing things on their mind.

Like who will be bringing them roses.

"Please welcome the lovely ladies of Zeta Pi Alpha." I initiate the applause, which my sisters mirror as the ZPA girls make their way into our house. They're the first in a line of visitors who want our attention tonight. Now that the semester is in full swing, we're getting invited to participate in philanthropic events, dances, socials, and more.

Once the girls leave, the Omega Chi Beta brothers enter, and my stomach knots when I see Clinton for the first time.

He's dressed in his chapter best, donning charcoal gray dress slacks and a relaxed, cream button-down with the top button undone. The sleeves are pushed up his massive forearms, exposing the muscle there, and I can't help but notice he's been bulking up since the last time I saw him.

There's always a kind of magnetism I feel around Clinton, like no matter the time and place, I could always depend on him to be there when I need him. I can close my eyes and still see him in the soft light on the garden balcony at our semi-formal, feel his arms around me as I finally let out every tear I'd been holding back over what had happened.

He told me to go see someone, begged me to talk about it.

But it's not that simple.

His dark eyes are soft as he smiles and sings along with his brothers, but those eyes have seen darkness. They've seen horror, they've seen hardship, and yet he still finds a way to smile bright enough to light up an entire room.

I don't know how he does it, and I can't watch anyone but him as they make their way through the room, handing out roses as they sing.

They sound terrible, but they look nice — and that's all that matters when it comes to fraternity serenades.

I'm at the front of the room, so Clinton makes it to me last, and he pauses in front of me, offering me the very last rose from his bundle. He's still singing, though his eyes are different now — tinged with sadness at the corners instead of the joy I'd watched moments before.

I wonder if he'll ever be able to look at me without feeling sad, without experiencing some sort of pity.

After what I put him through, I can't imagine how he ever could.

I take the rose from his hands, my creamy fingers brushing the rough skin of his dark hand, and he finally offers me a soft smile as their song ends. Then, he turns to face the room with the rest of his brothers.

"Ladies of Kappa Kappa Beta," their president says. "I am pleased to inform you that our national chapter has granted us permission to attend Spring Break with you, thanks to our good behavior last semester."

All the brothers make lewd gestures at that, and everyone laughs.

"We can't wait to party with you like we always do, and until then, feel free to use our new pledges to do your homework or rub you down with tanning oil — whichever item is most pressing on your to-do list."

A few whistles ring out at that, and I shake my head, hurrying them along with a few snaps of my fingers. Once they make their way out of the room, it's Alpha Sigma's turn to come in, and if I thought the pull I felt to Clinton was strong, it's nothing compared to what I feel when Kip Jackson walks into the room.

Kip Jackson.

The only boy I've ever loved, the only boy I've ever wanted to save me.

The only chance at happiness I have left.

His blue eyes barely even skirt to mine before he's turned around, facing the rest of my sisters as his president introduces them, but just that tiny glance has me reeling back to the summer we were together. I can still see those eyes outlined by a black night sky, his smile bright and wide just before he kissed me.

I've seen him around campus a few times since I heard he was here, but we still haven't had the chance to speak. I'm not even sure if he knows I'm here, but being that he's in Greek life, I don't see how he could *not* have heard of me. I'm the president of the top sorority.

Still, whether he's heard of me being here or not, he hasn't searched me out, which confirms my suspicion that he probably doesn't really care to see me. After the way I acted at the end of our relationship, fueled by jealousy, I can't blame him.

All my money is on Skyler.

Just like I suspected, he outbid everyone at the date auction to "win" Skyler. But, to my knowledge, they haven't gone on the date yet. Once they do, the plan will be in motion, and my last-ditch effort to get Kip back in my arms will either do just that or blow up in my face entirely.

Am I crazy?

The thought passes my mind, just like it has several times since I asked Skyler for her help. I even gave her an out at the auction, right before she went on stage. But, she assured me she was fine, and she was all in to help me.

Sometimes I'm sure I don't deserve her.

Staring at the back of Kip's head doesn't make him turn around to look at me again, so I scan the faces of my sisters. When I spot Skyler, I see *her* eyes are fixed on Kip, too.

And I know without a doubt that he's looking right back at her.

"The brothers of Alpha Sigma would like to welcome back the lovely ladies of Kappa Kappa Beta to Palm South for spring semester," Adam says, gleaming at the new additions to his fraternity. They're all dressed in the same khaki pants, light blue button-ups and navy and white striped bow ties. "We proudly present our new pledges."

He reads off all their names before telling us that they've all prepared a little something to introduce themselves. The next ten minutes is pure laughter, with each pledge using poem, song, or stunt form to tell us their hobbies and interests — most of which include meeting girls.

Kip is the last pledge to perform, and when he steps forward, I feel all the oxygen available in the room pull toward him, like he's the only source of life.

"Hit it, boys!" he says, which cues his pledge brothers to break into a chorus of beatboxing. I have to stifle a laugh at their ridiculous movements, each of them acting like a B Boy right out of the 90s as they circle my sisters and add to the rhythm, whether it be with bass, snaps, or some other sound.

And then, with his eyes on Skyler, Kip starts to rap.

Let me tell you a story about this girl I met,
She had the bluest eyes that were hard to forget.
She challenged me to a game of foosball,
Little did I know that I would lose all.

I scoff at that. *Lame.*

Cinderella stole a kiss and then she ran away,
So I gave her some space for a couple of days.
Then I took a thousand bucks and I played my cards right,
I bought a date with the princess last Saturday night.

My stomach drops at the mention of that kiss. I knew he'd taken a shot off her body, and even though no one specifically *said* it, Jess had eluded to Skyler having her tongue down Kip's throat. Still, it stings to hear *him* say it, to hear him rap about it like it was the best kiss of his life.

I want to be the best kiss of his life.

And now here I am to collect my prize,
No more running and no more lies.
It's been over a week and now I'm ready for my date,
So what'ya say, Skyler Thorne, can I pick you up at eight?

His brothers make the beat drop and the entire chapter room goes wild. I'm a little delayed, my eyes glued to the back of his head as everything around me morphs, the cheers muted, claps in slow motion. Shaking my head, I join in on the applause, my eyes finding Skyler along with everyone else.

She seems just as shocked as I am, her bottom lip pinned between her teeth as she watches Kip. I can't tell if she's pissed or swooning.

When Skyler's eyes find mine, I nod toward Kip, urging her to accept his date. As much as it makes my stomach curdle like an Irish Car Bomb not taken fast enough, it's the only way to get the plan in motion.

If I want Kip, this is part of it. Skyler will have him coming around us more, and then once she breaks things off, he'll be looking for someone to lean on, someone to confide in.

Enter: me.

"About time you did this the right way, pledge," Skyler finally says, appearing as confident as ever. "I guess you can take me out. Friday night. And seven, not eight."

She winks at him as everyone cheers, and I watch them staring at each other as Kip makes his way out the door with the rest of his brothers. His gaze never leaves her, and her eyes stay fixed on his, and I feel a little like celebrating and a little like throwing up all at once.

I adjourn chapter as soon as they're gone, rushing up the stairs after Skyler and the rest of the girls. Ashlei's pouring out of her room as soon as I make it upstairs, and we squeal together before bursting through the door to Jess and Skyler's room.

"This is so perfect, Little!" I say immediately as Ashlei pops up into Jess's bed with her. "I knew you would come through. I've been so busy getting everything situated for the semester that I haven't had time to check in and here you are outperforming what I could even imagine!"

My chest tightens, but I smile through the discomfort.

Pulling Skyler in for a hug, I assure myself again that this will work — this *will* be worth it.

"I knew there was a reason I picked you as my Little. You're a bad ass, just like me."

Skyler squeezes me back as the girls laugh, and I hold her a little tighter, thanking her as much as I can in that embrace for what she's doing for me. Even though I truly do believe Skyler *is* a bad ass, I know what I'm asking her to do isn't easy.

"Where do you think he'll take you on the date?" Ashlei asks, her eyes wide as I release Skyler.

"The better question is what are you going to *wear*?" Jess chimes in.

I launch into theories with them, the excitement and giddiness taking over me. When Skyler says she wants to get some sleep, Ashlei and I skip down to my room and rummage through my closet, trying to find the perfect outfit for Skyler to wear.

Sitting there on my bed, watching Ashlei pull out dress after dress, I finally let it hit me.

This is it.

In less than a week, they'll go on their first date, and it'll all start. I'll be one step closer to being with Kip again. My smile falters, brows pinching together as the reality of it sinks in. Kip will be on a date. With Skyler. And then, because of *me*, she'll pull him in, get him close enough to care about her, and then break his heart.

For me.

I should be happy. That giddiness I had before, that smile, it should be all I can register.

It's working, the plan is in place...

So then why do I feel like the scum of the Earth?

Jess

A girl has needs.

The last time I had that one, steadfast thought on repeat in my dirty little pea brain, I met Jarrett. I never could have known what would come from that, but I'm pretty sure I know exactly what will come of tonight.

After chapter, I half-walked, half-skipped down Greek Row to the Omega Chi house. Greg asked me if I wanted to come by to "study" tonight, and I have a pretty good idea what that's code for.

"Study" equals "take our pants off and see what happens."

So, I decided not to wear pants at all, opting to stay in the same little black dress I wore to chapter. It's a little formal for the occasion, since we have to wear business casual for chapter, but it's also easier access.

Priorities.

Greg meets me at the door after I shoot out a text to let him know I'm walking up, and he leans against the frame, smirking as his eyes take in my legs.

"A little overdressed for studying," he muses. "And you didn't bring any textbooks."

"I don't really need them for the subject I'm studying tonight," I banter back, pausing in front of him. My eyes drink him in — the black sweat pants hanging on his hips, the large, heather gray Omega Chi t-shirt with the sleeves ripped off, arm holes gaping so far down I have full view of his glorious washboard abs.

"That so?"

"Mm-hmm," I assure him, tapping my temple. "All up here."

"And what subject is it that you're studying?"

"Anatomy."

He chokes out a laugh, shaking his head and holding the door wide for me as I slip under his arm and into the house. He tosses that same arm over my shoulder, guiding me through the hallway back to his room with my arm pressed against his bare ribcage — also exposed by that artfully shredded t-shirt.

"I really do have to study," he says. "I started my internship, and hatching season is coming up soon."

"That's right," I mused, snapping my fingers. "I forgot how much you nerd out over turtles."

"Don't act like it doesn't turn you on."

"Oh, it definitely does," I agree as he ushers me inside his room. "Which is exactly why I didn't bring anything to study, nor did I wear panties under this dress."

Greg groans, sitting on the edge of his bed with my hands still in his. He pulls me to stand right between his legs, his eyes roaming over my curves appreciatively.

"You just sit there and talk about turtles," I tell him, guiding his hand up my inner thigh. He bites his lip, shaking his head as he follows the movement with his eyes. "And I'll do my own kind of homework."

Standing over him, his hand inching closer and closer to my heated and severely underused treasure box, as Skyler would call it — I realize Greg is actually *insanely* hot. His features are all *so* dark — and delicious. From his caramel skin to his jet black, messy hair, he's like sin wrapped up in an ice cream cone. Add in his eyes, black and wide, like deep, bottomless pools of water, and his smirk, devilish enough to melt even the chastest of panties — and I can't figure out how I ever *didn't* notice his sex appeal.

I should have realized all of this the first night we met at Ralph's, but then again, my heart belonged to Jarrett that night. I couldn't think of any other guy in any kind of sexual way, not in the entire time I was dating Jarrett. I was literally broken when it came to having those thoughts.

And while my heart might still belong to Jarrett, it's different now, knowing he doesn't want it — knowing he's holding on firmly to another woman's heart now, and most likely holding on to a lot more than that at the present moment.

So, when Greg slides his hand up a little more, his fingers brushing my slick heat, I moan with him at the feel of it, closing my eyes and letting go.

Greg may not be Jarrett, but he *is* a sexy, fun, single male with his hand between my legs.

And right now, that's all I need, anyway.

As soon as he feels how wet I am, Greg stands, yanking my wrists over my head as he crashes his mouth to mine. He tastes like beer, like he's been drunk since noon, and I feel his kiss like an intoxicating shot of alcohol warming every single limb. His lips are firm but warm, his breaths coming harder now — which, coincidentally, leads to him growing harder in a completely different way, too. I lean forward, pressing my stomach into his erection, and he groans at the contact.

Running his rough hands down over my arms, he hooks them in the hem of my dress and yanks up, breaking our kiss long enough to strip me out of the black fabric and drop it to the floor. My bra comes off next, an easy snap of his fingers sending it down to the floor next to my dress.

I wait for it to hit, that shock of electricity I always felt when Jarrett touched me, but it never does. My heart is racing, my clit swollen and throbbing, just waiting for Greg to touch me. But it feels a little empty, a little detached — a little like every other guy felt *before* Jarrett.

Again, I'm reminded of how my life was severed by that man.

Shoving him out of my mind, I push my hands into Greg's chest until he's sitting on the bed again. I rip his shirt over his head, nodding to his sweat pants as I toss the shirt over the back of his desk chair. Greg just smirks, lifting his hips enough to take off his pants and briefs in one sweep of motion, and when his hard-on springs free, all I can do is lick my lips.

I drop to my knees, giving Greg a wicked grin as I take him in one hand and tease the tip of him with my tongue. He's not quite as big as Jarrett, and he leans a little to the left, but it's still a beautiful cock — and definitely a tool I can work with.

Greg leans back on his palms, watching me with rapt attention as I take him inside my mouth. My brows pinch together as I figure out how to fit him inside, working with his unique shape, and once I find the magic combo, he lets out a steely, "Fuckkk."

"Don't let me keep you from studying," I tease, releasing him from my lips with a pop. "Come on. Tell me about hatching season."

Something between a laugh and a curse escapes his lips as I take him inside my mouth again.

"I can't," he manages, his breaths labored.

Greg flexes his hips into my slick hand when I take my mouth off again, eyes meeting his.

"Come on. Talk turtle to me."

He spits out another laugh, but it dies quickly when I strengthen my grip, sliding down from his tip to his base. With a growl, he leans forward, hands wrapping around my upper arms as he tosses me onto the bed.

"We're done talking."

"Oh, are we?" I tease, spreading my legs wide open for him to see. He's on his knees above me, one hand stroking his cock as his eyes roam over my breasts, down my stomach, his pupils dilating when he takes in my wet pussy.

Greg bends forward, which gives me hope that he's going to spend some time downtown returning the favor I just paid, but instead, he grips my ass, yanking hard until my wet entrance is lined up with his ready member.

"Tell you what," he says, teasing the slick skin between my lips with his crown. "If you can say a word after this, you can talk about whatever the hell you want."

It's right on the tip of my tongue, the smart-ass remark to his challenge, but everything is wiped from rational thought when he slides all the way inside me — all at once, balls deep, not a single centimeter of space left between us as he groans in ecstasy and I try desperately to catch my next breath.

Before I can so much as moan, he's withdrawing, plummeting inside me again with just as much gusto. He feels even deeper somehow, and when he lifts my ankles up to rest on his shoulders, I finally cry out, the sensation too much — but in the *best* fucking way.

Greg works himself to a release within minutes, and I fake mine, just to give him credit for surprising me. The poor guy likely didn't stand a chance of getting me off, anyway — not tonight, at least. With Jarrett, it was easy to come. Hell, just looking into his eyes while he whispered that he loved me was enough to send me skyrocketing.

Still, when Greg rolls off of me, kissing my neck with a chuckle before retreating to the bathroom to clean up, I smile. And when he comes back with a hot wash cloth, wiping between my legs carefully, I smile a little wider. And when he hands me a pair of his boxers and an oversized sweater, when we crawl into bed — me with my phone, him with his textbook — I rest my head on his chest and revel in the comfortable silence between us.

Greg holds me while he studies, his fingers drawing circles on my shoulder, and I turn the page for him when he asks me to. Sometime after midnight, I pull the book from his sleeping hands, kiss his cheek, and slip out of the Omega Chi house.

He may not be Jarrett, but no one ever will be. And when I'm with Greg, I feel a little less shitty.

I'll take what I can get.

Adam

"What happened to going easy on the pledges?" Jeremy asks me, his voice low as we circle our new members. They're all standing huddled together in a kiddy pool full of ice water in the middle of our chapter room, teeth chattering as they silently pray not to be the next one I call on. "I mean, don't get me wrong," he adds with a chuckle. "This is priceless entertainment, but I thought you said you were going to run the pledge process differently when you were president."

"And I have been," I remind him. "But, some things are tradition — like the camping trip."

"And this particularly torturous brand of hazing."

"Exactly."

Jeremy smirks. "I will say, this might be the best pledge class we've ever had. Between Kade showing athletic promise and Kip already making such a big splash, we're on everyone's radar. Let's just hope they can keep their GPAs up."

Something twists in my stomach at the mention of Kip, a foreign feeling I can't fully digest.

"We shall see." I make my way toward Kip next, that same uncomfortable swell in my gut as I approach him.

"Go easy on him," Jeremy warns as I close in, but I brush him off.

"Pledge Jackson," I say, pausing to stand in front of him. His glasses slip down his nose a bit, and he pushes them back up, his eyes as confident as they can be as he shivers his ass off, waiting for my question. "Name the three founders of Alpha Sigma who helped the sisters of Pi Gamma Zeta sneak out of their dorms when they were founding their sorority."

Kip forces a breath, and for some reason, I find myself silently wishing for him to screw up. Of course, that would earn him some groans and possibly a few punches from his fellow pledges. If they answer wrong, we start back over, and we go until they can answer ten questions in a row without missing one.

It seems cruel to anyone outside of the Greek system, but anyone who has had to earn their letters, to learn about how their organization was founded and discover a new kind of respect for the gentlemen who paved the way — they understand. These potential new members aren't getting hazed for fun. They're being tested, not just on their knowledge, but on their loyalty.

Alpha Sigma was quickly becoming a top fraternity on campus, and I would do whatever I could to ensure this next group of guys would add to that, that they would help us continue to build a legacy.

"Harry Winters, Edward Sanders, and..." Kip's voice fades, his eyes rolling up to the ceiling as he tries to grasp for the last name.

"Ten. Nine." I start a countdown, just to give him a little pressure, a little push. The rest of his pledge brothers groan, some of them cursing while others encourage Kip that he can do it. They're a small group, only eight of them, and they're already forming the bonds of brotherhood.

"Clarence Bell?" he finally says, the answer more of a question.

For a moment I just stand there, making him sweat his answer, but then I nod, moving down the line to the next pledge. Kip lets out a relieved breath, along with the rest of his brothers, but they still have one more question to answer correctly before they're out of the ice pool.

Jeremy suggests Christopher, our youngest pledge. He answers his question correctly, and all at once, the pledges tumble out of the water as our brothers toss them towels and bring them hot water to sip on. We push them to their limits, but we're still careful with them. The last thing we want is to end up like Omega Chi for not being smart with our pledging process.

"Can I ask you something?" Jeremy says, handing me two cups of hot water to deliver.

"You already did."

He smiles a little, rubbing the back of his neck. Jeremy is never nervous when it comes to talking to me. Hell, he's one of my best friends. So, the fact that he can't look me in the eyes when he asks his next question puts me on edge.

"What's your deal with Kip?"

I swallow, my eyes flicking over to where he and Kade are sitting on the couch, chatting and waiting for their water as they warm their feet.

"I don't have a deal with him."

"You're pretty hard on him," Jeremy argues. "Like, more so than the other pledges. Is it because he's got a thing going with Skyler?"

"No?" I say, but it doesn't come out confidently, and Jeremy cocks a brow. I sigh. "I don't know. Maybe. There's just something about him that irks me. I can't figure it out. I mean, I'm the one who wanted him to pledge, but he's just... he's so *showy*. And he's got all this attention on him already. He's not laying low, not working hard like the rest of the pledges. It's like he has this sense of entitlement or something."

"I think he's just confident," Jeremy says. "I mean... I hate to say it again, Adam, but..."

"If you say he reminds you of me again, I'll nut tap you."

Jeremy chuckles, tossing his hands up in surrender. "I'm just saying. He's a great pledge, and he's going to be a great brother, if he makes it through your tests, anyway." He lets his hands drop to his sides, tucking them in his pockets. "If it is about Skyler, just talk to him. Let him know whatever it is that you need to tell him. You're his president, man, and he wants to impress you. Don't make it harder on him than it already is."

I huff, aggravated both at the thought of talking to Kip and that Jeremy is right. I care about Skyler, she's one of my best friends, so maybe part of my annoyance toward Kip has to do with her. Then again, maybe it has to do with the fact that, like Jeremy said, he reminds me a little of myself.

Do I feel threatened?

I shake off the possibility of that. If jealousy has anything to do with my attitude toward him, I sure as hell wouldn't be admitting it to Jeremy — or even myself, for that matter.

With two cups of hot water in hand, I make my way toward where Kip and Kade are sitting, and their conversation comes to a grinding halt once I reach them.

"Kip, can I talk to you for a second?" I ask once they have their hot water.

Kade jumps up like my words were lava spilling on the floor at his feet, rushing to join the other pledges by the pool table. Kip follows him with his eyes like he wished he'd stayed, and I'm reminded of Jeremy's words as I take the seat next to him.

Don't be a dick, Adam. Don't be like Clay.

"Are you taking Skyler out tonight?" I ask, remembering from his little stunt at Kappa Kappa Beta's chapter that their date is supposed to be this evening.

Kip takes a drink of his hot water, simply nodding in lieu of an answer.

I sigh, running my hands back through my hair as I grasp for the right words to say. "Listen, I don't have claims on her or anything, but I still care about her," I say honestly. "And I swear to God, if you fuck her over, I will personally fuck you up."

So much for not being a dick.

The words fly out before I have the chance to run them through my head, to digest them and decipher a way to say them in a more respectful way. Still, I find myself watching Kip confidently, as if those words were exactly what I planned to say.

Kip swallows down his frustration, and I can't help but admire the way he's able to school his features and say his next words calmly and respectfully.

"You won't have to do that."

I search his eyes for a sign of a lie there, but find nothing. Satisfied, and frankly out of words to say, I just nod, standing and leaving him alone as I make my way back to Jeremy.

"Well, that looked like it went well," he says, his eyes on Kip behind me.

"I'm working on it, okay?"

Jeremy chuckles. "Okay. By the way, a cute little redhead just showed up asking for you."

I can't hide the smile that that news spreads on my face, and Jeremy waggles his eyebrows in response to it, as if he knows something no one else does.

"And on that note, I'm officially off duty," I say, walking backward toward the front door. "Can you handle wrapping all this up?"

"I got it, El Presidente. Go have fun."

I roll my eyes, turning away from him, but he calls out again.

"No. Seriously. Please, for the love of God and for all our sakes, have some fun."

I flip him off over my shoulder, tucking that little finger away as soon as I round the corner and see Cassie standing in the foyer.

Her back is to me, her unruly red hair pulled over one shoulder of her emerald green hoodie as she mindlessly twists the strands into a braid. She scans the picture of our founders hanging on the wall, her Keds turned inward a little, legs covered by a pair of dark jeans.

Sliding my hands into my pockets, I slip up behind her, my lips close to her neck as I eye the picture over her head.

"Back then, they were told not to smile when they took pictures," I say, and she jumps a little, but then a small smile spreads on her lips. "What's my excuse going to be when all the pledges from this semester look just as miserable in their photograph?"

Cassie turns, one eyebrow climbing toward her hairline. "I guess the rumors about you being a dictator president to the new guys are true, then, huh?"

"Hey, can't make it easy on them," I say with a shrug.

Her green eyes twinkle as she smiles wider, the gold flecks in those green irises even more pronounced thanks to the deep shade of her hoodie. "Can't make it anything less than brutal, from what I've heard."

"Yeah, yeah," I say, exasperated. I pull her under my arm for a hug, inhaling the scent of her strawberry shampoo. "Jeremy's already on my ass, okay? I'll ease up."

"Do whatever you want," she says when we pull away, my hand finding hers. "You're a great president, Adam. Whatever you think is best, I believe it."

A warm surge of pride tickles my ribcage as I tug her back toward my room.

"Alright, enough of that. I didn't ask you over to talk about Greek stuff."

"What *did* you invite me over for?"

"Mind-blowing sex."

She balks at my attempt at dry humor, coming to a complete stop inside my bedroom. A deep blush shades her cheeks, crawling quickly down her neck as she opens her mouth to respond and closes it again without a single peep coming out.

I chuckle, shutting the door behind us and plopping down on my bed, patting the spot next to me. "Kidding. Come here."

She lets out a breath, but her body is still tense as she sits next to me.

"I got you something. Close your eyes."

Cassie watches me curiously, her nervousness easing as confusion takes its place.

"Close your eyes," I say again, leaning in to peck her lips.

She giggles, finally letting her lids flutter closed as I grab her wrists, turning her palms toward the ceiling. Once I'm sure she's not looking, I reach behind my headboard for the gift, laying it in her lap where her hands are waiting.

Cassie's brows pull together once the board touches her palms. "It's kind of heavy. What is it?"

"Open your eyes and find out."

When she does, the little smile on her face fades instantly, her lips parting as her eyes sweep over the wood in her hand.

"Adam..." she says, my name just a breath on her lips. She pulls her hands from under the gift — a long board — and runs her fingertips over the designs splashed over the bottom of it. "Did you... did you make this?"

"I did. Well," I clarify quickly, one hand finding the back of my neck. "I mean, I didn't make the long board, of course, but I did the design. It's decoupage, or whatever it's called."

She smiles a little as I butcher the word, her eyes still glued to the board as she trails her fingers over each design.

"I did the Palm South University crest, of course," I say, pointing to it. "And then your letters — KKB — and I tried to make the whole thing in your colors. Lots of blues and golds. And I put some doctor stuff on there, see the stethoscope?"

She pauses when her fingers touch the bottom of the board — the Key West section.

"Dolphins," she muses, her eyes flicking up to meet mine. "Like the ones we saw when we did the boat trip."

"Yeah," I admit, heat tingeing my neck. "I put a little of us on there. Not too much, I wanted it to be mostly you, but I added the dolphins. And pizza from Moon Pie." I point to the oversized slice of Hawaiian. "Just a few things."

There are pictures of her with her sisters, the largest being one of her and Skyler last Spring Break, and she eyes each one of them before landing on a small one of us near the middle of the board. It's from one of the intramural football games she came to watch, right after I tackle hugged her in my dirty gear as she tried unsuccessfully to shove me away.

Cassie laughs, though tears flood her eyes. "It's so... perfect. I can't believe you did this." She looks at me then, swallowing. "Thank you, Adam."

"You're welcome. I hope you like it."

"I love it," she says quickly, running her hand over the board again. Then, she slips it carefully down to the floor, the nerves back on her face as she faces me again.

"What?" I ask, searching the unspoken questions in her eyes.

"I was just thinking..." she says, her voice a whisper as she scoots closer to me on the bed. One hand reaches forward, playing with the hem of my polo. "That first thing you said, about why you brought me here... you said you were kidding... but... maybe, it doesn't have to be a joke."

Her eyes flick up to mine then, wide and hopeful, and her cool hand slips under the fabric of my shirt, her fingertips brushing against my abdomen as I suck in a breath.

"Cassie..."

"We don't have to go all the way," she says hurriedly, but she slips her fingertips between the band of my jeans and my boxers, making every thought in my brain turn to fuzz. "I just... Adam, I can't go another second without you touching me. I mean," she clarifies, scooting even closer, one of her ankles crossing over mine. "*Really* touching me."

I growl out my next breath, my hand covering hers. I wrap my fingers around her wrist, pulling her forward, and she climbs into my lap without another word. When her thighs straddle mine, she rolls her hips hard, and I press my forehead to hers.

"Wait."

She pauses, her hands fisting in my hair as her eyes find mine.

"I just, before we go any further, I want you to know that every single chance I get to touch you, every chance I get to put my hands where you don't let any other hands go, it means... everything to me."

She swallows, the corners of her mouth turning up a bit.

"Does that mean you'll touch me where you haven't before?"

The question is just a whisper, but it pains me like it was blown through an air horn. I wince, gripping the thick fabric of her hoodie as I pull her flush against me.

"If you'll let me, yes."

"Please," she whispers immediately, rolling her hips again. Then, her lips land on mine, soft and inviting, and I know there's nothing else I can do but give her what she needs.

It's all I can manage to repeat my conversation with my aunt in my head, to remind myself *why* I'm waiting, why I'm going slow, as Cassie intensifies our kiss. She's all hands and moans, breaths and touches. Her hands rip at my clothes, my hair, my skin, her lips devouring mine. But I keep my pace, forcing her to slow down, asking her to trust me.

We've waited so long, had so many years — so many *people* between us — but I'd wait twice as long, and suffer through twice as much, if it meant I got to have her in the long run.

That's why I take my time, and that's why I promise myself again that I can make her feel good without hurting her, that I can give without taking, that I can go slow and make every moment with her count.

At the end of it all, when Cassie McBee looks back on her life, she will never forget the moments of us. She'll remember every word, every touch, every kiss — and in those moments, she'll find no pain — only the brightest joy.

That's the promise I vow to keep.

Cassie strips my shirt over my head, and I roll us until she's beneath me, her red hair splayed out against the light blue cotton of my pillowcases. I don't realize I'm trembling until I reach for the hem of her hoodie, helping her ease out of it. She lays back again, her chest heaving under the simple white tank top covering her bra.

For a moment, I just stare at her, eyes slowly climbing over every curve of her. When I make it back to her eyes, they're underlined by bright red cheeks and a shy smile.

"No one looks at me the way you do," she whispers.

"I'd kill them if they did."

She laughs, helping me as I work the button and zipper on her jeans. I pull the stiff fabric down over her hips, her thighs, until I can peel the denim off her calves and let it fall to the floor. A soft, mint green pair of cotton panties is the only barrier now between my eyes and the place I ache to touch Cassie most, and the weight of that is like a bag of bricks on my chest.

I force a shaky breath, dragging one finger over the cotton before dipping it just a centimeter underneath, brushing the soft, bare skin of her that rests underneath. Cassie arches into the touch, her eyes fluttering closed as both fists twist in my comforter.

I'm still trembling as I slip my thumbs under each strap of her panties, stripping them down slowly. I don't even know where I drop them, because my eyes are too busy devouring the newly exposed view — one I've never seen before. Cassie blushes deeper as my eyes greedily take her in — every inch, every freckle, every single centimeter of pale, white skin.

She still has her tank top and bra on, and as much as I want to see all of her exposed, I don't move to dispose of those last two articles. They're all that keep me from feasting on all of her, and I know if I had her completely naked in my bed, I wouldn't have the strength to stop until I was so deep inside her that I became a permanent mark.

Instead, I kiss my way slowly down her arms, shoving her tank top up enough to lick a line down her stomach, and then I settle between her legs. Her emerald pools never leave me as I hoist her thighs up, the backs of them resting on my shoulders, and I hold her gaze as my tongue flicks out, just marginally, just enough for the first taste.

We both moan, the sounds mixing together in a symphony of pleasure and pain.

I close my eyes, steeling a breath before I lower my mouth again, this time running my tongue long and flat against her. From her slick opening all the way up to her tender, swollen bud, I taste her, the heat from my next breath making goosebumps explode over her legs.

She whimpers, writhing under my hands pinned at her waist. I just hold her steady, lips closing over her clit as I suck gently. Cassie's legs quiver more, her fists twisting in my comforter more until they fly into my hair with the same pressure.

It would be a bold-face lie if I said I never imagined what Cassie would taste like, what she'd look like if I ever got the chance to throw her down on my bed and ravage her the way I wanted to. But everything I'd ever imagined, every wet dream I'd ever had was so wrong, so far off, I almost laugh.

She's so much sweeter than I imagined, and the vision of her in my bed is enough to make *me* come, even without her touching me. Her cheeks had started as a dusty pink, but they grow a deeper shade by the second, with each and every touch of my tongue adding another drop of crimson under her freckles. Her eyes, closed tight, hypnotize me every time they fly open, finding me there between her legs with my mouth fastened on her. Her hands, weaved into my hair, tug and grip, and I feel every movement like a direct electric spark to my dick.

My hands slide from her hips to grip the tops of her thighs as I pull her closer, swirling my tongue over her clit before I lick her with a flat tongue from bottom to top again. I moan with the motion, causing a new wave of goosebumps as she writhes beneath me.

"Adam," she whispers, my name such a sweet, torturous plea on her lips that I groan again, sucking her clit with more force between my teeth.

I could taste her forever like this — devouring her like she's my last meal, or maybe my first, or maybe both all in one. But she's close. I can tell by the way she moves under my touch, but the heat in her cheeks, by the way her eyes squeeze shut, the muscles in her legs tensing as she reaches for the finish line in sight.

And I want her to detonate under my touch.

Slowly, I run the fingertips of my right hand down over her inner thigh, my tongue still working her clit as my fingers find her slick entrance. My middle finger dances there, soaking up her sweet wetness, with just enough pressure for the tip of it to dip inside her.

Cassie moans louder, her fingers tangling in my hair with her plea. She wants more, she wants me inside her, and even though I know it will practically kill me — I answer her request like it's all I've wanted to do in my entire life.

With as much composure as I can manage, I slip that middle finger inside her.

We both moan when my first knuckle disappears, and when she squeezes around the full finger, coating my second knuckle with her desire, I curse out loud at the tight feel of her.

"Fuck, Cassie," I breathe, withdrawing my finger slowly just to slide it back inside her. I curl the tip of it, brushing her sensitive G-spot as she arches off the bed. "I thought I knew... I thought I was ready to feel you like this, but *God*, it's killing me." I kiss her mound. "You're fucking perfect."

She moans at my words, fingers flying from my hair back to the comforter as she grasps for something to hold onto. But it's too late. With a few more curls of my finger and a gentle suck of her clit between my teeth, she comes for me, flying into oblivion with only my hands to root her back to Earth.

Cassie doesn't scream like a porn star, or fake moan with the sole purpose of putting on a show. Instead, all the blood in her cheeks rushes down to her clit, swelling in my mouth as she whimpers through her almost-silent release. She calls my name under the soft, hushed groans of pleasure, her breaths shallow and heated, and when she's done, her entire body collapses into a satiated heap in my hands.

And I feel like I've just run a marathon in the desert heat.

I smile, kissing her tender clit softly as I withdraw my finger and crawl up to kiss her parted lips. Her breaths even out slowly, her mouth seeking mine between exhales. Every time her tongue swirls in a dance with mine, she smiles a little more, like tasting herself on me is too good to be true.

I nuzzle into her neck as I roll her to one side, her back to me as she faces my wall and I wrap myself around her. We fit together so easily, so perfectly, my knees tucking into the backs of hers in an immaculate seam. I sigh into the back of her neck, kissing it softly before tugging her more into my chest.

Cassie rolls her hips, her bottom brushing against the swollen head of my cock as I inhale a stiff groan.

"Your turn," she whispers, hand reaching back, but I wrap my fingers around her wrist to stop her.

"Not tonight. Tonight, it's about you."

She rolls in my arms, looking up at me with a pout that I *know* got her whatever she wanted growing up.

"But I want to touch you, too. I want to taste you, too."

My eyes nearly cross at the thought of that, of her lips around me, her mouth taking me inside her. I groan, adjusting my throbbing hard-on under my jeans as I kiss her forehead.

"You will. But not tonight, okay?" Pulling back, I brush her hair out of her face, running the pad of my thumb over her blushed cheeks. "I meant what I said about going slow. We have all the time in the world to touch each other, to explore each other. But right now, I just want to hold you. I just want to make you feel safe."

Tears well in her eyes, and she shakes her head, burying her face into my chest.

We don't say another word, but her fingertips circle the skin on my back as I run my own through her unruly curls. I'm not sure how long she's in my arms before her breaths even out, her chest rising and falling in a slow rhythm as she falls asleep. I don't dare move, not even when my left arm screams at me before becoming numb altogether.

I hold that girl all night long like she's my entire world.

And that's when I realize she is.

This motherfucker is crazy.

That's the first thing that pops into my head when I descend the stairs and see Kip waiting for me at the bottom of them — in his pajamas.

Here I am in high heels that already make my arches ache, and a black dress so tight I won't be able to eat more than a piece of cheese without busting out of it, and this motherfucker is in flannel sleep pants.

Flannel sleep pants that hang on his hips in a way that shouldn't even be legal, but that's beside the point.

I should have said no to this date. I didn't really have a choice — not with Erin giving me the death eye when he asked me in front of our entire chapter — but I should have found a way. Because I knew, I *knew* after last weekend that I was in trouble.

After the tournament, I went back to Kip's house and let him make me breakfast. Okay, fine. No big deal. It's just pancakes and bacon, right?

Wrong. *So* wrong.

Blame it on the high from winning the tournament, or maybe on the late-night hour, but something shifted during that breakfast-slash-dinner. Kip watched me in a different way, a mixture of respect and longing, and I tried desperately to keep my feelings at bay.

He's just a boy, I'd tried to tell myself. *There are plenty of others like him.*

But that's where I'd had to laugh at myself, because I knew it wasn't true. I've dated around PSU. Hell, I've even dipped my toes into other university's fishing pool, thanks to Spring Break ventures. And one thing I knew for sure, *especially* after he made me breakfast and walked on the beach with me as the sun rose, was that there were not plenty of others out there like Kip.

I'm pretty sure there aren't any. Period.

I watch his face as I make my way down the stairs, eyes tracing over the slight stubble on his chin, fixating on those damn glasses that make my knees do wobbly things. He looked so different in the morning light as the sun rose over the coast, and even though I was *sure* he wanted to take me home to try to get some, he didn't.

We talked.

About our family, our background, our goals. And, for the first time ever, I found someone other than my parents and Bear who seemed genuinely interested in my poker life.

He offered to help me, to get me prepped for the tournament, and that little offer did fluttery things to my stomach, the same way his stupid glasses do wobbly things to my knees. Not even my sisters had ever offered to help me with poker. Sure, they've supported me from afar, but even that has been slim.

Kip saw what I wanted, what I desired, and he wanted to help me achieve it.

This motherfucker is breaking down my body — more importantly, my mind — and it is *not* okay.

"Um, hi?" I ask, one eyebrow cocking up at his appearance when I hit the last step.

His blond hair is ruffled more than usual, a lazy, sleepy smirk resting on his face. It's that same face he had when he propositioned me for a date in front of my entire sorority. It's also the same stupid face keeping me awake late at night when I should be sleeping and *not* thinking about Kip motherfucking Jackson.

"Did I wake you?"

"I told you to stay in your sweats," he says easily, referring to my half-ass attempt to bail on our date earlier. I tried to avoid it at all costs — especially after the week of torture I'd had since the last time we'd hung out. Class, I could survive. Seeing him around Greek Row? No big deal. But knowing it would be just the two of us tonight? Doing very date-like things?

Nope. SOS. Cannot deal.

My original plan was to just avoid giving him the little date he'd "won" altogether. I thought maybe he'd drop it, maybe he'd forget. I thought maybe Erin would forget, too, with how much she has on her plate this semester.

But then, Kip showed up at our chapter and rapped — yes, *rapped* his plea to take me out. In front of everyone. In front of Erin.

I had no choice but to say yes, and I've been dreading this night ever since I agreed to it. I even completely ditched last night, but he wouldn't let it go.

We rescheduled for tonight, and even still, I tried to bail earlier, to reschedule. I said I was tired. I said I wanted to stay in my sweats, and he told me that was fine. He told me to stay in my PJs.

Of course, I was kidding.

But this. Mother. Fucker.

"Go change," he instructs.

"What? But we're going on a date."

"Your point? Go change, damnit, or we're going to be late."

"For what, a slumber party?"

Kip's eyes narrow, though a playful smirk plays at the corner of his lips. He steps toward me, and before I even register that I should take a step back, his hands find the small of my back.

"You know I like it when you're feisty," he husks. "So unless you want me to do very non-friend-zone things to you, I suggest you go change. And quickly."

All the blood drains from my cheeks. I feel it like cold, icy water slicking down my spine.

This. This is what I knew I couldn't handle, what I knew I needed to avoid. I can't handle him looking at me like this — like he wants to lick every inch of skin I have exposed in the little black dress I'm wearing, and then some.

"You said hands to yourself," I remind him, referring to our texts, to the promise he made me that even though this was a date, he wouldn't try to be more than friends. I tried to set up boundaries between us, to give us some sort of line to stay behind when it came to being around one another. I had to try *something,* anything not to test the little resistance I had when it came to him. "You promised."

"Then don't make me break my word," he muses, releasing me.

Fire.

Hot, burning, dangerous fire — *that's* what Kip Jackson is.

Erin wants me to lure him in, to get him to fall for me so she can pick up the pieces when I break him. I'm trying to save him. I'm trying to warn him, to keep my distance so we can stay just friends, so I can prove to Erin that her plan has no merit.

I can't break someone's heart if they don't give it to me, right?

But standing at the bottom of those stairs, all I see is fire. Fire I'm about to jump into like it's a deep pool of water, instead. He wants me, and I want him, and there is no fucking way any of this will end well.

For a moment, I debate my options. Could I fake a stroke? Run upstairs and lock myself inside my room for the entire semester? Nothing sticks as I grasp for straws, and Kip just waits, that stupid smirk on his face as I have a complete panic attack under a cool façade.

Finally, I huff, frustrated as I climb back up the stairs and change into sweats. I throw my hair up in a messy bun, too, before trotting back downstairs to join Kip.

Then, we're in a cab on our way to whatever place he has planned for our date, and all I can think about is Erin.

"If you want to be president, you have to make sacrifices."

I love her, and I *do* want to be president — but can I really do this? Can I really get close to Kip — close enough to hurt him — without also hurting myself in the process?

I know the answer to that question, and I feel more uncertainty bubbling up like acid in my stomach with each mile we drive away from campus as more questions pop in to take its place.

Erin has a plan, and once she has her heart set on something, there's no deterring her. There's no reasoning with her, either.

But... what if I can't follow through with my end of the deal?

Something tells me I'll find out the answer to *that* question soon enough.

And I probably won't like what I find.

***

As we wait for our check at Bella's, the cute little Italian place off campus, my knee bounces. To Kip, it probably looks like I'm nervous, like I'm still concerned with the fact that we're in our pajamas at a nice restaurant, like I'm scared we might run into someone I know.

But really, I'm wishing he would just stop talking.

Not because I don't love the sound of his voice, the smooth baritone of it, or because what he's saying is stupid or immature or rude. No, quite the opposite, actually.

Every time he opens that beautiful mouth of his, I want to listen. I want to believe the words he's saying, like that he thinks I look exquisite with no makeup on and my hair up in a bird's nest of a bun. Or that he sees me as a girl meant to stand out when all I've ever wanted to do at PSU is blend in.

Bella's is quaint, half indoors and half out, close enough to the beach to smell the salt on the breeze. I trace the hanging white lights twinkling against the night sky as Kip continues staring at me.

"Why are you watching me like that?" I ask him after a moment, noticing his gaze on my skin.

"I can't look at you?"

"Not like that, you can't."

He just grins, finishing off the last of the wine in his glass before standing and smoothing his hands over his wrinkled tank top. My eyes flick to his flannel pants again, to the delicious way they hug his hips, but then my eyes shoot up to his.

"What are you doing?"

This isn't good. This is *not* good. Kip has that look, that same mischievous look he had before he jumped on the bar and won me at the auction. The same look he had before he rapped to my entire sorority.

"Ella Mae," he says, his voice deep with a fake southern drawl.

Or is that midwestern?

Honestly, I have no fucking clue and I can't really think straight enough to figure it out because in the next instant, his hand grabs mine, and all I can do is stare at that point of contact.

"I know we've only been together for 'bout a year now, but I feel like you're my whole world."

I don't know how he's not laughing — especially with what I'm sure is a quite hysterical expression on my face. I'm watching him like he just sprouted a second head, or like he's talking in some fake accent super loudly while everyone around us watches.

Oh, wait, that's actually happening.

"I wanna drive our RV all over 'Merica and see everything with you. I can't imagine sharin' my pork rinds with anyone else. And, well, I guess what I'm sayin' is..."

Kip drops down to one knee, fishing a piece of trash out of his pocket. When he presents it to me like a prized pig, I realize he's twisted a piece of straw wrapper into a sort of ring.

Oh, my God.

I'll kill him.

"Will you marry me?"

The entire restaurant is wrapped around that little finger of his, some of them squealing or gasping or offering a collective chorus of *"awww"* that makes my skin crawl. Me? I'm too busy trying to figure out if I can somehow strangle Kip with my eyes somehow.

"I know it's just a straw wrapper," he continues. "Heck, I never have been able to give you the finer things in life. But I promise to buy you a real nice ring when we can afford it. I'll buy you whatever ring you want! Just please, make me the happiest man this side of the Mississippi River and say yes."

It's hard to say how long I sit there, staring at his stupid, adorable face while everyone around me encourages me to say yes. I think very seriously about throwing something at him, or standing up and just walking right out, leaving him to sit there on his knee like a dumb ass alone in a room of strangers.

But then, I realize something that makes my stomach curl in on itself like a snake.

I want to laugh.

This is fun. It's fun-*ny*. And what's worse? I haven't had fun since Erin told me about her little plan, since my semester got flipped upside down in an instant.

The last time I smiled — *truly* smiled — and felt giddy like this was when I realized Kip and I were in the same class, right before Erin's emergency meeting.

I blink, and a flash of Kip grinning down at me before he licked a line of salt up my abdomen hits me out of nowhere.

All I can do is smile.

I slap a hand over my mouth, forcing fake tears in my eyes as I throw all the warnings out the window. "Oh, gosh, Tommy. I wouldn't spend my life with anyone else. Yes, a thousand times, yes!"

I bolt out of my chair, flinging myself into his lap as I throw my arms around his neck and pull him close. The restaurant erupts into applause and whistles, and Kip smirks, his lips brushing my shoulder as we hold each other.

"Nicely played, Ella Mae," he whispers.

I dig my knuckle into his rib before he yanks me to stand with him, facing the restaurant with a cocky grin.

"Kiss! Kiss!"

The chant starts somewhere in the back, but soon enough, it's all I hear as everyone in the restaurant joins in. I feel the blush on my cheeks before I even turn to Kip, sure that he'll wave everyone off and we'll gracefully exit. But when his aqua eyes find mine, they drink me in like a healing elixir, and his smile is genuine as he reaches for me, dipping me back in a dramatic fashion to more cheers.

His lips seek mine without a moment of hesitation, both of us caught up in the fake proposal. But the moment we connect, the *second* we kiss, every ounce of fakeness, or pretending, fades away in a flash, leaving us submerged in the thick, cool grips of reality.

One of Kip's hands is splayed across my lower back, holding me flush against him as our lips fuse together as one. I breathe him in deep, chills racing from the point where our mouths meet all the way down to my ankles. It's just like before, like our kiss the first night we met, except this time, the electricity is amplified like it's designed to kill.

Perhaps, I think as Kip grips me a little tighter, it is.

I nearly pass out, not another breath passing through me until Kip tilts me up again, the world coming back into focus. Someone snaps a picture, and that flash blinds me as much as the kiss. I just stand there, watching Kip with flushed cheeks as he pays our bill and grabs my hand, pulling me through the crowd and back into the Florida night.

The air is a little chilled when it touches my hot cheeks, and it's like that pinch of cold yanks me back to reality with enough force to knock my next breath out of reach. I don't say a word as we wait for the cab Kip called for us, and once we're inside it, I go off on him, fighting against every urge I have to laugh and feigning annoyance, instead.

I have to be annoyed, because otherwise, I'll be forced to acknowledge the other feelings resting below that pretense.

Like want.

And need.

And the cold realization that I'm in big, *big* trouble.

Erin

For the first time since I was raped, I'm drunk.

I've avoided alcohol like most college students avoid homework, knowing all too well what can happen when I lose control of my body, of my mind. I've had absolutely no desire to even have *a* drink, let alone several.

Until tonight.

I knew I shouldn't have followed Kip and Skyler. I knew I shouldn't have creeped on their date like some kind of psycho. But, then again, I've known since the moment this harebrained scheme formed in my head that I was tiptoeing on the line between *I'm okay* and *I'm completely insane*, but it didn't stop me.

Maybe I really am going crazy, but I can't find the will to care — let alone stop.

And so, I'd broken my dry spell, no longer able to survive the night sober after I watched them fake kiss at Bella's Italian Restaurant.

If I told my mom what I was doing, she'd likely pull me out of school and drag me kicking and screaming back home. But it was her who told me to channel my emotions, to put them to use, to find what makes me happy and cling onto that.

Well, Kip makes me happy. At least, he *did*, when we were younger, and I know he will again.

I just have to get to him.

And Skyler is supposed to be helping me do that.

I shift on the couch in our sorority common room, my stomach rolling as I finish off the last of the tequila I poured in a small tea cup, just in case anyone walked in. My thoughts swim in my intoxicated mind, fuzzy and unclear, and I try to pick them out of the murky water as they pass.

It's after two now, and Skyler should be rolling in any minute.

I know, because I watched them from afar as she and Kip said goodnight. I listened to him ask her to stay, to her saying she couldn't, all the while fighting off the urge to upchuck my dinner on the beach.

Sighing, I run the tip of my index finger along the lip of my tea cup, eyes on the small bit of liquid left in a ring around the bottom. Skyler was trying to keep her distance from Kip — that much I could tell with how she responded to his fake proposal at dinner. It was adorable, absolutely swoon-worthy for any girl trying to resist his charm. But Skyler had played it like a pro, only joining in at the very end to join his charade.

That hadn't been hard to watch.

In fact, not even that first kiss had been. I watched him dip her back in a dramatic fashion, watched his hands grip the small of her back as they kissed for the crowd, and though it stung, I knew it was all part of the show.

But then, I followed them to the beach, to the pier, and everything from that point on became a torturous affair.

I never would have labeled myself as a masochist before tonight, but that's the only word suitable for what I'd inflicted. I'd followed them around, watching from afar as Kip tried unsuccessfully to win Skyler a giant teddy bear before *she* finally became the one to pull it off. I tried to breathe normally as I watched them float up to the sky in a bucket on the Ferris wheel, tried to ignore the jealousy flaring in me as they laughed at the top, and I tried not to pass out altogether when I saw their lips still locked together as they floated toward the bottom again. Skyler had broken their kiss first, jumping off Kip's lap and running her hands through her messy hair, but I knew as much as she did in that moment that she was in trouble.

She was falling for him. He was falling for her.

And my plan was quickly getting sidelined.

A very small, very quiet voice in my head told me I should stop the charade altogether. I should tell Skyler she's off the hook, free to do whatever she wanted with Kip. I should move on, leaving my past in the past.

But that voice was like a quiet whisper compared to the other one, the one screaming like a freight train for me to hold onto this one, small sliver of possible happiness.

It's been such a long year, filled with so much pain, and all I want is to feel whole again.

I hear my mom's voice in my head again as I ask myself how many people I'll have to hurt in the process, and I can't find it in myself to care.

I steel my emotions as the front door creaks open, Skyler sneaking through it as quietly as she can. I deposit the empty tea cup on the table beside the couch, reaffirming my plan to pull her head back in the game. She had a fun night. She's distracted. She's possibly thinking of all the ways she can ask me to call everything off.

This is my chance to get us back on track.

Just before she hits the stairs, I find my voice, the sound of it almost foreign as I call after her.

"Good night?"

I can't disguise the touch of bitterness in my words, but Skyler doesn't seem to catch it as she clutches her heart and lets out a sigh of relief when she sees me on the couch.

"Holy shit, Big. You scared the living hell out of me."

"Sorry," I say with a smile, willing all the calmness I can from my inner pool of strength. "I was waiting up, wanted to know how it went tonight."

Skyler eyes me like she doesn't believe that for a second. My Little is smart, and she's careful with her word choice as she falls down into the cushions next to me, her pink cheeks framed by the long hair now falling out of her messy bun.

Effortlessly beautiful, that's what Skyler is. She doesn't need makeup, or a dress, or a strand of pearls. She's the kind of girl who can roll out of bed and have a man falling to his knees with want.

Kip was proof of that.

"It was nice," she says, her eyes soft on mine. "We went to dinner and to the pier, nothing special."

Liar.

The thought screams through me, but I force a smile, swallowing past the sandpaper knot in my throat.

"Good."

Skyler watches me for a long moment, like she's trying to decipher the thoughts in my head. If only she knew how difficult that was, how long I'd tried to untangle the sticky web of them.

There's a touch of something behind her blue irises... pity, maybe? But I don't let it sink in, don't let my heart soften at the sight of it. And when she moves to stand, saying she wants to turn in for the night, I drop that hard shield over my heart again.

"Wait."

Skyler turns, waiting for my next words.

"Has he asked you to the A Sig Valentine's Day dance yet?"

"No," she answers, her voice hesitant. "And I doubt he will."

"No, he definitely will," I assure her, a hint of bitterness back in my words. I cross my arms tight over my chest, testing my next words before I say them aloud. "When he does, you'll say yes. And that's the night you blow him off. I'll be there with Chance Griffins. It'll be perfect. Chance is a dog and will surely do *something* to piss me off," I think out loud, the plan forming as the words tumble out. "Kip will be heartbroken, and by the end of the night, we'll be consoling each other between the sheets."

Skyler's calm expression cracks a little at that, and I can't help but cringe with her.

Did those words really just come out of my mouth?

I'm distantly aware of how far I've fallen from the girl I used to know as I watch Skyler, looking for any sign of defiance, all the while wondering how the hell I got here.

"Okay, sounds like a plan," she says after a moment.

I nod, something between a smile and a grimace finding my lips as I lean back into the couch again. I wait for Skyler to make her way up the stairs, but she just watches me instead.

Then, slowly, she sits back down beside me and pulls me in for a hug.

I stiffen in her arms, warning bells going off at her proximity. But then her warmth transfers into me, and I break, leaning into her as I rest my head on her chest.

The urge to cry washes over me like a tsunami, but I swallow it down.

"You okay, Big?" Skyler whispers.

I sigh, one word slipping through my lips easily. "No."

After that, I'm not sure what to say.

I was raped.

I thought I was okay, but I'm not.

No one knows except Bear, and he can't help me. No one can. No one but me. But I don't know how *to help me.*

I'm scared.

I feel used. I feel broken. I feel ruined.

I don't know who I am anymore.

I hate myself for what I'm doing to you.

I don't know how to stop.

Each thought flicks in and out of range like low-flying birds, close enough to see but too far away to touch, to catch and hold onto.

So, I lie, instead.

Seems to be the only thing I'm good at doing, anymore.

"I'm stressed the fuck out," I say. "Being president is amazing, but it's a lot of work. I'm falling behind in class already and I feel like my social life is consumed with meetings and philanthropy work."

And stalking you and Kip.

"I'm happy," I whisper, the lie coming from my lips so effortlessly I surprise myself. "But, I don't know..."

"Can you take a break?" Skyler asks, her *Mrs. Fix-It* brain already kicking into high gear. "Let J-Love and Lei handle some of the weight for a while? I know you like to be in control, but maybe just let a few of the smaller things go so you have more time."

"Yeah, I guess I could," I say, my heart aching a little as she holds me tighter.

Here I am using her for my own agenda, and she can't help herself but to try to help *me* feel better.

The world doesn't deserve Skyler Thorne.

"You know how I am, though," I continue "I just feel like if I don't do everything, it'll all get messed up."

"I know, Big," she says with a laugh. "But trust me, the girls know what they're doing. Your G-Little is pretty smart, too. You should ask her for help."

I should probably also jump off a cliff because I'm quite possibly the worst human being to ever walk the Earth.

"Really?" I ask distantly.

"Seriously. She's amazing. I really hope you two can get to know each other more."

"I do, too," I say, this time genuine. Cassie and I used to spend more time together, studying and talking, sharing our mutual love for our majors. But after what happened last semester, I shut everyone out — her included.

Another wave of tequila rushes through me as my eyes find focus on my toes, and I finally let myself ask something real, bridging the gap between me and Skyler in a rare moment of vulnerability.

"Do you hate me for what I'm making you do?" I ask, my voice just a whisper. "Be honest."

Skyler tenses, one hand still rubbing my back as her eyes fall to the floor with mine. "No," she says on a long breath. "I mean, I'd be lying if I said it didn't bother me to play him this way, but I want to be president. I want to keep our Greek line tradition. And I know that you would do the same thing for me."

Her admission warms my heart, and I smile — because it's true. I would do the same for her. There's something special about the bond between sisters, and I know what she means by wanting to keep our Greek traditions alive. I know how much that want can grow deep within a heart, how deep the roots can be.

"It's about sacrifice sometimes," Skyler continues. "And I'm pretty selfish all the time, so it's a good lesson."

I want to argue with her, because in my opinion, Skyler is the least selfish person I know. But my words stick in my throat, and before I can fight back again, the tears I've been holding back pool in my eyes.

I wipe away the first tear before it can fall past the apple of my cheek. "Ugh, sorry. I'm such an emotional wreck right now." I watch her, forcing a smile. "You just make me so proud, Little. You're going to be an awesome president." I swallow, knowing that if nothing else I've said tonight is true, that definitely is. "I love you."

"I love you, too," she says, wrapping me in another hug.

When we pull back, I eye her sweat pants, my curiosity from the entire night getting the best of me. I was horrified when I saw them both dressed in pajamas in public.

"What are you wearing?"

A laugh bursts out of her, and she shakes her head. "It's a long story."

But she tells it, filling me in on the night as carefully as she can. And though it burns to hear her talk about Kip, I feel a touch of comfort at the fact that the plan has been solidified again.

We know the next steps. And with the Valentine's Day dance being just around the corner, I allow hope to bloom in my chest again, small and feeble, but blooming nonetheless.

Kip Jackson will be back in my life soon enough.

And then, hopefully, I'll find happiness again, too.

The next morning, I somehow manage to peel myself out of bed just before sunrise. I'd like to say it's paddle boarding that made it possible to survive on less than four hours of sleep, but it'd be a lie if I didn't also include the blond-haired, blue-eyed boy waiting for me at the edge of the water.

The sun is still painting bright colors across the sky as I make my way toward Kip on the beach, paddle board in tow. It was a sick form of compromise that we agreed to — in exchange for me not staying with him last night, I agreed to show him how to paddle board today.

Stupid.

I knew I was in trouble after our kiss at Bella's, but then the pier had happened. We walked around laughing and playing games like a couple of high schoolers, and then, with no one watching, with no fake proposal as an excuse, Kip had kissed me at the top of the Ferris wheel.

My heart flutters at the thought of it, though I try my best to hold its wings down to keep it from taking flight. It's nearly impossible, especially now, staring at his back as he watches the sun rise over the waves. His hands are tucked easily into the pockets of his board shorts, his white t-shirt blowing in the breeze, bronze skin shining in the morning light, a brand new paddle board in the sand by his feet. The man is too beautiful for his own good, too sexy for me to even try to resist.

And I *had* tried.

But with him opening me up the way he is, asking me questions no one else ever has, breaking through walls no one else even knew existed... I'm helpless.

And at the top of that wheel, with his eyes on me and the lights casting him in a soft glow, it all seemed very simple.

I couldn't *not* kiss him.

That's just all there was to it.

Of course, I'd realized my mistake in the cab back to the sorority house, chastising myself for letting it go too far. And to top it all off, Erin had been waiting for me after our date, and she had the next part of her little plan in place. All I needed was one conversation with her to be brought back to reality, to be sobered up to what I was actually doing.

I have less than two weeks until the Valentine's Day dance, until the night when everything with Kip will end.

Thirteen days.

So, maybe it's a sick kind of self-flagellation, but I choose to ignore that ominous date when I should have it in the forefront of my mind. I choose to shove it down, bury it under the sand, and live in my fantasy a little while longer.

At least for today, I'm just going to enjoy the time I have with Kip. I'm going to pretend like we're just a boy and a girl, enjoying the sunrise on a couple of paddle boards. It'll all be fine.

Sure.

"Sorry I'm late," I say when I'm close enough for Kip to hear.

He turns at the sound of my voice, his blue eyes widening a little at the sight of me as he scans me from head to toe.

"Yeah, you better be sorry," he says with a grin, his gaze sweeping over the sunrise again as I sidle up beside him. "It's half past early as fuck and we agreed to meet at the ass crack of dawn. Way to make me wait."

I smile at his joke, dropping my board into the sand beside his. Without another word, and without a warning I probably should have given him, I strip my light blue tank top over my head and pop the button on my jean shorts, shimmying them down over my hips.

Kip watches my every move.

I know before I meet his eyes. I feel the heat of his gaze on my skin more than I do the rising sun, and when I finally look his way, I can't stop my grin at his dumbfounded expression.

"You just going to stand there and ogle my boobs all day or are we doing this?"

"Can't I do both?" he quips back quickly, and I shake my head with a laugh, making my way toward the water without checking to see if he's following.

It's been so long since I've been able to spend time on my board, I audibly sigh once we're out past the easy waves and gliding on the smooth water as the sun rises over the beach. I start out on my knees, showing Kip how to catch his balance and maneuver the waves before we both stand. Surprisingly, Kip catches on pretty quickly, and doesn't fall even once as we paddle parallel to the shoreline.

We're both quiet for the most part, enjoying the sounds of the beach waking up — the soft crash of the water on the shore, the high chirp of the birds, the distant sounds of the ships coming to life. When I notice a thin sheen of sweat gathering on Kip's defined abdomen, I nod toward a sand bar not too far away and we make our way toward it, both popping off our boards once the water is shallow enough.

We hydrate with the water I brought for us, both of us watching as more and more people make their way onto the sandy beach in the distance. Kip is quiet, but I feel him watching me, that same heat sparking on my skin like it did before when I stripped out of my shorts. Only this time, I hear questions he's not asking, and it makes me more curious about him.

I try to talk myself out of more conversation. *Just enjoy being close to him and keep that distance in place*, I silently warn myself. But the more we stand there, the more I want to know. And when I cast a casual glance his way as I tuck my water bottle away again, I can't help myself.

"So, what's your story, Kip?" I ask as he leans his elbows over his board.

"What do you mean? My story?"

I shrug, wiggling my toes in the sand. The sand bar is a little mushier than the sand that lines the beach, but the water is crystal clear, and I can see all the way down to my pink toe nail polish.

"I mean, why did you move out here? Why did you transfer to Palm South of all places? Where are you from? What do you like to do? You know, besides lick tequila off strange girls."

"Hey," he defends quickly. "That was not my fault. And who's worse off here — me or the strange girl?"

My throat warms, remembering the way it felt to have his wet tongue tracing lines on my stomach. "I think I got the better end of the deal."

"And I tend to disagree."

Kip's eyes fall to my stomach, half of it covered by the water, and my cheeks flush. But I just watch him, waiting for his response to my question.

"Let's see," he finally says, looking up at the white, whispy clouds floating by us. "I transferred to Palm South because I wanted to get out of the Midwest. And because Palm South has a pretty decent screenwriting program, which is what I want to do with my life. It's not the last stop by any means, but it's a good transition."

I smile, thinking about how Kip is in our Writing for Television class. It's only been a few weeks and I already know I won't be changing my major to anything related to writing, but it has been fun to read his pieces, to listen to him talk about his passion with Dr. O'Neal.

"It also helps that I could get away from my dad," he adds, his voice a little softer.

"Uh-oh, Daddy drama?"

Kip snorts. "Well, he's an Army Major General, if that gives you any idea."

"Yeesh," I say, raising both eyebrows at that. "Sounds fun."

"Yeah, real fun. I mean, I love him and everything," he says quickly. "He's my dad, he's a *good* dad in the sense of the word, but he just wants to live his dream through me and I'm over trying to be what he wants. It's nice to be out here away from his constant glare of disapproval."

My stomach twists at that as I try to imagine being in his shoes. My family and I may not have had much, but we had love. My mom and dad have always been supportive of me, and though I help them with their bills, they've tried everything they can to get me *not* to do that. They want me to live my own life, to do what makes me happy. But helping them is part of what makes me happy.

"What dream?" I ask after a moment.

"Huh?"

"His dream?" I ask, cocking a brow. "That he wants to live through you? What is it?"

"Uh..."

Kip's eyes widen, and I watch with curiosity as he scans the water with his breath coming a little harder, like he said something he wasn't supposed to. Playing poker lets me pick up on peoples' quirks easy, read when they're uncomfortable or, worse, when they're lying.

And something tells me there's a thin veil of dishonesty over his next words.

"Being in a fraternity," he says. "College, the whole thing. He went straight into the service after high school and I guess he always wanted to go. So he's had this big dream for me ever since I was little. Perfect school, perfect fraternity, you know."

He shrugs, his eyes still on the water as I watch him, trying to decipher the truth. It makes sense, what he said about his dad wanting that experience. Still... he's hiding something.

I pop back up on my paddle board, stretching until my back is pressed against the warmth of it. I breathe in a deep sigh, letting one leg hang in the water as I reach out toward Kip with the opposite hand.

"Hold me so I won't float away?"

Kip swallows, a smirk finding his lips as his hand wraps around mine. And just like every time the boy touches me, my skin sparks to life under his fingertips, a constant rush of energy flowing through me and cycling back toward him.

"So," I say, letting my eyes fall up to the sky. I stare at the white clouds through the safety of my sunglasses, bringing the conversation back around. "If it were up to you, would you be in a fraternity?"

"Maybe. I guess I don't really know. It's just always been ingrained in me that I would go to college and be in a fraternity. I've never really had the chance to think if I'd actually like it. But, at least being here, I can do what he wants and still do what I want, too. I don't have to live under his scrutiny, his constant judging of whether I'm doing the right thing or not."

I smile, holding his hand a little tighter. "I think you've got life figured out, Kip Jackson. At least, you seem like you do. You know what you want to do in life, you're not afraid to be who you want to be — I think your dad should be proud of you."

The words slip out before I realize the magnitude of them, and I feel the moment they hit Kip. His hand stiffens in mine, just a pause, and then his thumb rubs against my palm.

"You know, I liked the you that came out last night," he says, switching gears. "The care-free, I-don't-give-a-shit Skyler."

I shake my head, thinking of how he had me screaming — yes, literally *screaming* — at the top of the Ferris wheel. I can't remember the last time I let loose like that, that I let go of caring what other people thought of me.

"I still can't believe I let you take me around town in my freaking sweat pants."

"You looked hot in those sweat pants. And I dare you to tell me you didn't have fun."

I let my head fall toward him at that, my cheek resting on the paddle board. "I did have fun."

It's honest, and Kip raises his brows like he knew that all along. Then, he props himself up on his board, mirroring me as he lays the opposite way, his feet toward the end where my head is. We're still linked together, our hands wrapped around one another, eyes focused on the sky above.

We talk for a while longer, Kip telling me more about the kind of shows he'd like to write in the future. When the sun is higher in the sky, making me sweat even with my leg in the water, I suggest we head back to shore.

But before I have the chance to even stand fully on my board, Kip tackles me into the water.

"What the hell, Kip?!" I say on a laugh, splashing him when my head is above water again. "You're such a jerk."

He's chuckling, but the laughter dies in both of our throats when he steps into me, one hand finding the small of my back as he pulls me into him. My chest brushes his, my heart hammering so hard at his proximity that I'm sure he feels every beat.

Kip watches me, his eyes halfway hidden under his sunglasses, but I catch the exact moment when he moves a centimeter closer, his mouth on a track for mine. I close my eyes, screaming at myself internally that I should pull away, I should get back on my board, I should get away from him.

His lips brush mine, so softly I almost convince myself I didn't feel them at all...

And then, that motherfucker snaps my top off with a tug of the string.

I jerk back, hands flying to my chest just before the triangle-shaped fabric slips off. Kip laughs, already retreating toward his board.

"Oh my God! Kip!"

"Race you back!" he yells over his shoulder, and then he's on his board and half-ass paddling away.

I want to scream, but all I can do is laugh as I hastily re-tie my top and jump on my own board, catching up to him not even a full twenty-yards later. I beat him back to shore without breaking a sweat, and I stand on the beach where the water breaks over the sand, shaking my head at him as he walks his board up.

"You work pretty well with your clothes off," he teases. Water drips off his chest and down his abdomen, soaking his board shorts. A few droplets sneak under the band of his briefs beneath them, and I've never been more jealous of water in my entire life.

"You know you'll pay for that, right?"

He shrugs. "We'll see."

My eyes find the edge of his shorts again, noting the deep V that points down to an area of Kip I can only imagine is as impressive as the rest of him. And though I shouldn't, I find myself genuinely hoping I *do* get the chance to pay him back.

There are worse things I could see than Kip Jackson naked.

***

It's after noon when Kip clears the dishes from the turkey sandwiches he made us, and I'm back in the kitchen where he fed me pancakes and bacon at four in the morning thinking the exact same thing I thought last time I was here.

I should go.

Truthfully, the words were in my mind when I agreed to come back to his place after we rinsed off our paddle boards. I should have just gone back to the sorority house. But he'd begged me, saying his place is closer, that he wanted to feed me, that it was Sunday and I had nothing better to do, anyway.

Which was true.

So, I agreed, but now that I'm here, fed and sleepy from the sun and from a lack of rest last night, I hear the voice even louder.

I should go.

"Why don't we take a shower and watch a movie?" Kip suggests.

"I don't have any clothes here besides the ones I have on now," I say, my excuse weak. "And they're all sandy."

"You can borrow a pair of boxers and a shirt of mine."

I chew my lip, trying to listen to that little voice inside me when the other, louder one is telling me that a movie with Kip sounds pretty perfect.

"I don't know, I'm pretty tired," I finally say, adding a yawn for emphasis.

"So am I," he says, standing. He reaches for my hands and tugs me up with him. "So maybe we watch a movie and maybe we take a nap." He shrugs, as if it's simple. His blue eyes twinkle a little, a mischievous tell as they search mine. "Don't leave yet. I barely see you during the week and I know there's not many weekends where you don't have sorority stuff going on."

God, if looks could kill. Not that he's looking at me like he wants to kill me. No, it's more like he wants to hold me, and kiss me, and get to know me more. But *that* look kills me more right now.

It's like a rusty, jagged knife straight to the throat. If he knew what I was doing to him, what Erin had planned, he'd hate us.

Both of us.

"I actually have a sisterhood event tonight," I admit.

"See?" He tugs my wrist, leading me toward his bedroom as alarms go off in my mind like a fucking pinball machine.

His apartment is small — a little studio close to the beach, with nothing but a curtain separating his "bedroom" from his small living area and kitchen. But it's cozy, and with a keyboard in one corner and various albums spread out on the shelf opposite his bed, it's very him. Simple, masculine, artsy.

Kip.

Kip drops my hand long enough to rummage through his dresser, pulling free a clean shirt and pair of boxers that he tosses to me without giving me another chance to argue.

He points to the bathroom behind me. "Towels are above the toilet in the cabinet, shampoo and shit's in there."

But I can't move. I'm still trying to convince myself to leave, to *run*, but I just stand there, instead.

"Come on," he says, moving toward me until he's close enough to touch. His fingers reach out, pushing a few strands of my salty hair out of my eyes. "Just for a few hours. You'll feel better once you shower and I know you're tired. You're not going to get any sleep if you go home to your sorority house."

At that, I let out a long breath and nod. "You're probably right about that."

Kip's smile is that of a winner, and he nudges me toward the bathroom again.

"Fine," I finally concede, the little voice inside me throwing her hands up in surrender. "But just for a little while. And no trying to ambush me in the shower, either," I warn.

"I promise," he says, hands held up high. "You can shower in peace."

I narrow my eyes at him. "Mm-hmm."

He's still smiling when I finally step inside the bathroom and close the door between us, his eyes disappearing on the other side.

I strip out of my clothes quickly, turning the water all the way hot in his shower before standing in front of the mirror over his bathroom cabinet. I stare at my hollow, tired eyes as the steam fills up the room, sighing with a shake of my head.

"This is not smart," I whisper, almost in a mocking voice.

Still, I step inside the shower, convincing myself everything will be fine. I'll rinse off, get dressed in *his* boxers, in a shirt that smells like *him*, and then we'll just lie around. I'll catch a nap, maybe watch a movie. No harm, no foul.

But before I can even realize how stupid I am for thinking any of that is possible, my entire body freezes at the sound of a soft knock on the door.

I haven't even pulled his shower curtain closed yet. I'm just standing there, the water hitting my stomach and running down my bare thighs as I turn my head — slowly, carefully — like I'm scared of what I'll find.

And I should have been scared.

Two bright, turquoise eyes stare at me through a barely-cracked door, and I swallow, not moving to cover myself like I should.

Kip pushes the door open a little farther, but his eyes don't skate down my naked body. He keeps his gaze locked on my own eyes, swallowing, and I watch his Adam's apple bob in his throat as I wait. For what, I'm not sure — an explanation? An invitation? A demand to get the fuck out of here before we both do something we can't take back?

Erin's voice pops into my head briefly, just long enough to make my stomach roll before it disappears along with every other rational thought at his next words.

"I suck at keeping promises," he admits, his voice low, mixing with the sound of the water raining down around me in the shower.

My breath catches, the lump in my throat too hard to swallow past when I admit my own secret to him.

"And I suck at pretending like I don't want you."

Kip's eyelids flutter a little, his jaw ticking under the skin as he moves toward me — slowly, cautiously, like I might bolt if he takes even one step too far.

"You want me?"

I should feel exposed, embarrassed, standing here naked in front of him. But I don't. I feel wanted, desired, and powerful as hell.

Still, I tremble as I let out something between a laugh and a whimper at the truth. "Kip, I've wanted you since the first time I felt your mouth on my skin. Maybe even a little before that." I press my lips together, knowing I should stop, knowing I should grab the towel hanging on the rack beside Kip and get the hell out of his apartment.

But I can't.

Not now.

"I hate pretending like I don't want you," I whisper. "But I don't know how to do this. It's dangerous, you and me. Being together. Like this." I tell him, wishing I could tell him exactly *why* it's dangerous.

But if he knew, if he *really* knew, he'd hate me.

I already do.

Kip is so close now, his hands reaching forward slowly until they cradle my face between them. I want to sigh, to lean into that touch, but I keep my eyes trained on his.

"This is about Erin, isn't it?"

At that, my chest deflates like a popped balloon, my knees nearly giving in under the weight.

Shit. He knows. He fucking knows. Oh, God.

Kip shakes his head, his eyes still hard on mine. "Listen, Erin is in the past for me. I'm sure she's telling you and everyone else to stay away from me, staking her claim — but she doesn't have a claim over me. I am not hers."

Another sickening wave washes over me the more he talks. *I wish* it was that simple, that it was just that she told me to stay away from him. I thought he knew, I thought he somehow figured out her plan, but he has no idea.

He has no idea how important my sorority is to me — my sisters, my line, my Big and my Little, my legacy as future president. He has no idea how much power Erin holds, or how much I love her, how much I would do anything for her — even this. Even as much as it hurts. Because she's one of my best friends.

They've always said, *sisters before misters*. And it's been easy, up until now, to follow that rule.

But staring at Kip, feeling his hands on me, I don't know how *not* to break that rule now.

"You don't understand," I say, my voice shaking. How do I even *begin* to explain it to him?

"I do," he interrupts, lifting my chin. "Are you going to let her dictate who you like? Who you touch? Just because she's your Big, because she's president of your sorority?"

"It's so much more than that," I try, ripping my gaze from his. "It would be easier if you just let me go, if we just stopped this right now. We could save a lot of hurt, a lot of pain."

"Skyler," he says on a huff. He lifts my chin again, forcing me to look at him when I'm trying to do anything but. "I want you. If what you said is true just now, then you want me, too. I don't care about Erin, I don't care about your sorority or my fraternity — not right now. Right now, I care about the fact that you're here, with me, in my shower, and I want you."

The hand not holding my chin in place slips down, down, over my arm to hold my naked waist.

"Now," he breathes. "Tell me you don't want me. Tell me you want me to stop."

His hand drops a little lower, his fingertip brushing over my clit so softly, so lightly, I inhale a warm, steamy breath and don't let it go.

"Tell me to let you go. Tell me to stop, Skyler."

I can't stop shaking, my eyes watching his as I try to find the right words to get me out of the hell I'm currently burning in. Erin will be devastated if she even finds out this much has happened, let alone anything else. I knew her well before Kip, before he came in and flipped my entire world upside down.

I owe it to my Big to stop. Right now.

But the truth slips from my mouth in a whisper, and I know I'll have to suffer the consequences.

"I can't."

Kip shakes his head. "You have to tell me to stop, Skyler, or I won't be able to. Once I feel you, once I taste you, I won't be able to stop then. If you don't want this, you have to tell me now."

But I do want this.

And that's all I hold onto, that simple truth, no matter how fucked up and selfish it is.

"I want this. I want you."

And just like that, with those six, simple, unapologetic words, all bets are off between me and Kip Jackson.

My hands are in his hair before I can register that I told them to go there, pulling and tugging, his lips hard on mine as Kip pushes me against the shower wall. He's inside the shower with me in the next second, still in his board shorts, not taking the time to strip them off before letting the water crash down on him, too. Steam swirls around us, our breaths making it heavier — hands touching, lips kissing, tongues licking. We're a mess of sighs and moans, the kiss without a doubt the most passionate one of my life.

I've never been a believer in love at first sight. It sounds crazy to even consider that I could be in love with Kip. But the way I feel with his lips on mine, the foreign, never-before-felt electricity that buzzes through me *every single time* we touch — it has to be a sign. It's not just because he's forbidden, because he's technically off limits to me — if it was, I wouldn't have felt it that first night he sucked tequila off my stomach. And it's not just because he's quite possibly the sexiest man I've ever known, with his icy blue eyes, his perfectly mussed hair, his strong, stubble-lined jaw. No, it's something more — something unexplainable, something I'm sure I'll never quite figure out.

Kip feels like forever, and I can't even call him mine.

Pinning my wrists above my head, Kip slides two fingers inside me quickly, the movement easy and fluid as he fills me to the hilt. I suck in a breath, the rush of blood heavy in my head before it all rushes straight back to where his fingers are buried deep inside. His cock strains against the wet fabric of his shorts into my stomach as his fingers work, steady and smooth, his mouth sucking and biting up and down my neck.

Thoughts are fleeting, all sense of time and rationality lost the more Kip touches me. I can't even touch him *back,* not with my wrists pinned above my head, so I just wrap my hands into fists and hold on, letting everything I feel escape in breathy moans through my parted lips.

Kip moans his approval as his kisses fall lower, and his eyes find mine just as he sucks one tender, puckered nipple between his teeth. My back arches off the wet wall, into the hot stream of water, and the new angle of Kip's hand has his palm giving my clit just the friction it needs.

"Oh, fuck," I breathe, almost a whimper, maybe a plea. "*Kip*. Yes. More."

The moment the word leaves my mouth, I realize that's exactly what I want. What I need.

More.

Ripping my wrists free, I immediately grab the strings on Kip's board shorts, untying them in an instant before I tug the shorts over his hips. The deep V I admired from above the hem of his shorts shoots down farther, the lean muscle framing where I want to see him most. And when the shorts fall into a wet heap at his feet, his hard-on springs forward, granting my wish with more enthusiasm than I could have imagined.

I've seen enough cocks to know a good one when it's in front of me, and Kip's is so hard, so long and thick, the head of it glistening with just a drop of pre-cum, that I nearly lose my mind with the want to drop to my knees and take him inside my mouth. I want to taste every inch of it, feel that perfectly mushroomed head hitting the back of my throat, lick up the thick vein lining the top.

When I reach forward, wrapping one hand around him with a firm grip, Kip's hand stills inside me, his fingers immobilized.

"Oh, fuck," he groans. His hips flex forward as I roll my hand from his tip to his base, slow at first before picking up rhythm as the water helps lubricate each pump.

Kip's fingers start moving again, this time with more fervor, the heel of his hand pressing more into my clit. He kisses me hard, sucking my bottom lip between his teeth and holding it there. Each time he works harder with his hand, so do I, each of us rushing closer to the edge.

My breaths are shallow, hollow, not a single one of them deep enough to provide enough oxygen. I feel the fire of my orgasm threatening to catch, each new rub of his palm on my clit another spark, another flick of the match. I feel my grip on him loosening, my focus lost, and Kip kisses my neck before growling out his next words against the slick skin.

"This is about you. I want you to come. Come on my fingers so I can taste you."

"Oh, God."

His words are so dirty, so unfiltered, they make my knees quiver under the pressure of them.

I finally let my hand drop from his rigid cock, my fingers pressing into the slick wall behind me, instead, as I try to find something to hold onto before I fly over the edge of my release.

Suddenly, Kip pulls me up into his arms, bending so I'm cradled inside them before he steps out of the shower, carrying me into his bedroom with my body dripping water and marking a trail along the way. He drops me into the ruffled sheets, his mouth finding my skin in the next instant as he kisses down my stomach, biting the inside of my thighs before his tongue circles around my clit.

Oh. My. God.

If I thought the man knew how to work his hand, it's nothing compared to how he is with his tongue. It's like he knows every move to make, every spot to hit, like I drew up a personal map for him and he's writing the instruction manual. My legs tremble, thighs shaking on either side of his face as his blue eyes watch me like they're just *daring* me to come.

I've never been one to back down from a dare.

He plunges two fingers back inside me, and just a few curls of them combined with his tongue on my clit sends me spiraling. My toes spread, numb as all the blood in my body rushes to where Kip touches me. My vision grows black, and I have no idea if I'm screaming his name or if I'm completely silent. I feel myself pulsing around him, and my vision comes back just in time to see his grin turn wicked as he keeps his tongue working, his fingers in perfect rhythm, pushing and pushing until every ounce of my orgasm is spilled onto his fingers.

My tense muscles all let loose at once, my legs falling limp, and Kip carefully removes his fingers, causing another tremble. He softly kisses his way back up my body, and when he's balanced on one elbow above me, his blue eyes hard on mine, he smiles, slipping his still-soaked fingers inside his lips and licking them clean.

Goddamn.

I close my eyes, savoring the feel of that moment, of being desired *that* much. Kip's lips are on mine, pushing and eager, his tongue slipping in so I can taste myself there. And it feels a little like an hour, a little like only a second before his warmth leaves me as he moves to grab the towel I'd laid out in the bathroom.

As soon as he's gone, as soon as his hands are no longer on me, the spell is broken.

My heart ticks up a notch, the thumps hitting harder against my ribcage as the reality of what I've done settles in like a slow, cold flood. I watch the water rise higher, knowing it will suffocate me soon, and yet I still can't move.

I've betrayed Erin. I've betrayed Kip. I've put my *own* heart at risk. Because now that he's touched me, now that I know what it feels like to have a piece of him, I want all of him.

I *need* all of him.

But I can't have him.

In the moment, I convinced myself that I could. I told myself it would be fine, just let go, just exist with him now — here — in this moment. But here I am, sitting in the cold, merciless flood waters of the truth.

I'm royally fucked.

Kip is still smiling when he emerges from the bathroom, helping me dry off in a warm, fuzzy towel before helping me get dressed in his boxers and a t-shirt. He pulls me into the bed with him, tucking me close with his body in a perfect seam with mine. His knees fold into the space behind mine, his chest hot on my back, his arms wrapped around me like a body pillow.

I still my movements, closing my eyes and holding back the hot tears pooling behind my eyes. I've never felt more safe, more at home, than I do in his arms right now.

But he's not my home.

When he thinks I'm asleep, Kip lets himself drift off, too. I wait until I can say his name without him stirring, and then I peel myself out of his grip, slipping into the living area to redress. I leave his clothes folded on the bed next to him, watching his chest rise and fall as he sleeps for a long moment before I sigh, biting my lip against the urge to cry and crawl back into bed with him.

Then, I leave.

Because I'm Skyler Thorne. And like I've told every guy I've been with at PSU, Skyler Thorne doesn't sex and sleep.

Though for the first time, I want to.

And *that's* the worst part.

Cassie

"You look like you're on Cloud Mystery Man."

Erin's voice jars me from where I'm working on separating and stapling the packets for this week's Panhellenic meeting, and I pause, eyes meeting hers. My brows pull inward as I try to decipher what she means.

"What?"

Erin smirks, tucking her dark blonde hair behind one ear. She's typing away on her laptop, working on her agenda for the meeting, but her eyes hold mine for a moment before they return to the screen.

"You've got that look. That one that says there's a boy."

My eyes pop open wider, and Erin doesn't even look at me when she chuckles at the response.

"Don't worry," she says quickly. "I'm not going to press you on telling me who it is. I'm just saying, you had your heart broken by Grayson at semi-formal, and you popped back so quickly." One of her neatly manicured eyebrows lifts. "That doesn't happen unless there's someone else helping speed the healing process."

Heat sparks on my neck, crawling up to my cheeks as I let my eyes fall back to the packet I'm assembling. Flashes of Adam hit me hard, my stomach fluttering at the memory of his hands on me last night. We're in Erin's room now, but I know that just down the hall, the long board Adam made me sits propped beside my bed.

She's right.

I am on a cloud, floating high and free, intoxicated by what it feels like to be with Adam. He touched me last night like no one ever has — patiently, adoringly, like all he'd ever wanted in his life was to have that pleasure, and now that he was experiencing it, he would take his time memorizing every minute, every second.

My eyes flutter close, a soft smile spreading on my lips as I remember how he looked staring up at me, his mouth on the most sensitive part of me. I wanted to return the favor. I wanted to taste him so badly it *hurt,* like the lady version of blue balls. But, Adam's taking his time with me. He's moving slow, and not with the same, false intentions that Grayson had said he wanted to move slow with. *He'd* been getting some on the side.

No, Adam is mine, even if we aren't official yet.

... right?

I swallow at the possibility that he might be fooling around with someone else, though I know in my heart that it couldn't be true. Still, if he *is* only faithful to me... then *why* can't we just be together?

I've asked myself that a hundred times.

I believe him when he says he wants to move slow, when he wants me to focus on me, but then he goes and makes me a personalized long board. He holds my hand, he calls me every single night and texts me all through the day.

He's my boyfriend by all accounts... except the public admission.

"I think I just saw every single possible girly emotion cross over your face in a span of twenty seconds."

I snap my head toward Erin, forgetting she was even in the room until the moment she speaks.

She smirks, shaking her head. "If you want to talk about it, I'm here."

I let out a breath, returning her smile. Erin and I haven't hung out in a long time — not like this. I was surprised when she texted me this morning — or rather, *very* late last night — asking me if I had some time to help her prepare for the meeting this week. She wanted to catch up, she said, and I was excited to get some time alone with my Grand Big.

Still, what can I even say? If I tell her about me and Adam, she'll be the first one. And she's Skyler's Big. Will she understand, will she question when Adam and I started to feel this way? He never cheated on Skyler with me... but then again, he did kiss me less than a week after they broke up.

My stomach turns.

"Have you ever been in love?" I ask Erin instead of divulging my situation.

She pauses, her fingers hovering over her keys for a moment before she starts typing again.

"Once."

"Kip?"

Erin nods, her eyes softer now, tinged with a hint of sorrow.

"He was the first boy I ever loved... the only one. But, I messed it up."

I watch her with a sympathetic gaze, though I can't say I agree with her plan to get him back. Tangling Skyler up in her mess doesn't seem fair to me. But, Skyler is a big girl, and she agreed to it on her own free will. I keep telling her I'm here if she wants to talk about it, encouraging her to call it off if she needs to. That's all I can do — be there. I can't make the decision for her.

And watching Erin now, noting the sadness in her features, I know she must feel like this is the only way. I try to put myself in her shoes. If Adam slipped out of my grasp, would I ever do something as crazy to try to get him back?

I know that answer without even asking the question aloud. I would. In a heartbeat.

I'd do whatever it took.

"Do you think your plan will work?"

She shrugs. "I don't know. I hope, of course. I think it will. But it's hard to say. Until I have him alone, until I see what it feels like to be with him, I can't be sure."

"What do you mean?"

Erin presses her lips together, thinking. "Well, if there's anything I've learned in my dating experience, it's that if a guy wants to be with you — *really* wants to be with you — then he will be. So, if after Skyler pulls this off, Kip doesn't show interest? Well, then I'll know."

Though I hear what Erin says about Kip, I can't help but think about Adam.

He says he wants to be with me, that I mean everything to him... but he also says we should wait. He says I need to focus on myself.

Is that really what he means?

Or is it that he doesn't want to be with me at all?

I swallow, mind racing.

What if he just doesn't want to hurt me?

The thought grows from nothing, but sprouts to life like Jack's magic bean stalk, flying high into the sky and past the clouds with its realness. It's something Adam would do — keep me at a distance, do everything he could to be there for me and help me heal. He cares about me, that much is easy to see... but does he really want to be with me?

If he does, wouldn't he already *be* with me?

"Do you really think it's that simple?" I ask Erin. "I mean, what if you knew Kip cared about you. What if you were hanging out and he was telling you everything you needed to hear, but he wanted to wait a while before making things official. Would you wait?"

Erin scoffs. "Hell no. I mean we'd date, of course. But once the feelings were there for me? I'd ask him if he felt the same. And if he did, we'd be together. It's that simple. I'm not down to play that *what are we* bullshit. Been there, done that, bought the t-shirt." She chuckles, shaking her head. "I'm too grown to play those games."

My tongue is thick and sticky in my mouth, impossible to swallow past.

Erin's eyes flick to me, her brows pinching together when she notes my expression.

"He's toying with you, isn't he? Your Mystery Man."

I don't respond.

Erin sighs, closing the lid on her laptop to face me completely. "Look. Here's the truth. You want it?"

I just look at her, still unable to speak.

She dips until her eyes are at the same level as mine, a mixture of sympathy and hard-hitting realness reflected in her gaze. "The truth is, if you're not sure what you are to him, then you're nothing. A man who wants to be with you will be with you. Period. He won't be able to stomach the thought of anyone else being with you, therefore, he'll make you his. If it doesn't make him sick not to call you his girlfriend, if he doesn't feel some kind of sense of urgency to claim you, to mark you as his own, then he doesn't really want you. He's waiting for someone better to come along. He's getting what he can out of you because you're there, and he knows he can, but in the end?" She shakes her head. "Men are quite simple to figure out. And trust me when I say if he loved you, or even liked you — you'd know. There wouldn't be anything to question." She sits back, shrugging simply, as if it was all common sense. "A real man would never make you question what you mean to him."

Her last sentence hits me like a hot, deadly bullet to the chest. I lose my next breath at the impact of it, simply staring at her without a word to offer in response.

Because she's right.

It makes sense. Adam wants me to take time to "find myself" again, or whatever. But I can do that *with* him. I can be his girlfriend and still take time to heal. In fact, why wouldn't he want to be a bigger part of that?

He has the power to heal me, and yet he's only using part of it.

It's not that I don't see the value in being alone, in taking time to reconnect with myself... but the thing is, I'm *not* alone. We text all the time, call every night, hang out alone, and do very girlfriend-slash-boyfriend things.

Like stick our tongues down each other's throats.

And lick places not seen by the sun.

He's with me, in practically every sense of the word, and I'm not going to let him play this game.

As soon as I realize it, as soon as I make the decision, I'm up off the floor, shaking out my achy legs from sitting crosslegged for so long.

"I need to run an errand real quick," I say to Erin, casting a quick glance in the mirror at my hair. It's messy, my cheeks flushed, but I don't take time to fix it. "You okay for a little bit? I'll be back."

Erin smirks, like she knows, and opens her laptop again. "I'll be here, Grand Little. Just going to stop by Skyler's room here in a bit and see how her morning with Kip went."

"Okay," I say, not even really hearing her over the rushing rapids in my ears. "I'll be back."

Then, I'm flying down the stairs, out the door, and down Greek Row. My eyes are hot on the Alpha Sigma house, the words I'll say forming in my head so quickly that they disappear before I can practice them and get them on my tongue, ready to throw at Adam. But it doesn't matter. No matter how I say it, I will demand answers — and I won't leave until I get them.

I knock hard on the door, annoyed when it doesn't just open at the push of my hand. It's a fraternity house, for God's sake. They *never* lock their door. Beating my fist harder, I keep knocking and knocking, still to no avail.

The sun is setting off in the distance, the air growing cooler with its descent as Greek Row is cast in a low, orange light. Walking around to the backyard gate, I peek through one of the slits in the wooden planks, finding no bodies there, either.

Weird.

When I knock directly on his bedroom window without an answer, I give up, huffing as I rip my phone from my pocket.

- Hey. We need to talk. Where are you? -

But he doesn't answer.

Not that minute, not that night, not even that week.

And with each passing day, with each minute that goes by with him ignoring me, acting like what happened between us Friday night was *nothing*, I get the answer to my unasked question — louder than I wanted, with a harsher reality than I could have imagined.

He got into my pants, and just like Clay, he disappeared.

Without a word.

Without so much as an *I'm sorry, I can't do this.* Without an explanation. Without a care that he would break my heart in the process, just like every boy to touch it before him.

And suddenly, all the bullshit he served me on his shiny, golden platter rolls in my stomach, threatening to come back up.

I thought, when I was ready, I could fall into his arms and trust that he'd be there to catch me. But the truth is much harder to swallow.

The truth is, I fell a long time ago.

And Adam was never really there.

EPISODE 3

Cassie

Two-hundred and sixteen.

That's how many hours have passed since I went to the Alpha Sigma house, seeking Adam, needing answers. That's how many hours have passed since I sent him a text, telling him we needed to talk. That's how many hours have passed, and I haven't heard a single word from him — not a date, not a phone call, not a text, not even a stupid smoke signal.

Nothing.

And now, on the precipice of a holiday centered around love, all I feel in my heart is bitter, icky resentment.

"I hate Valentine's Day," I say to Skyler, for probably the fifth time this week, as another romantic comedy starts on her television.

It's a Monday — a rainy one, at that — and after my two morning classes were done, I slipped into Skyler's room and crawled into bed with her, taking solace in watching other romances play out on the screen.

"I mean seriously, whose bright idea was it to make a day to single out the already miserably single?" I pout.

"Oh, stop," Skyler says quickly. "Last year, Valentine's Day was the best day ever to you."

"Yeah, well," I say, reaching for our half-eaten bowl of popcorn. "That was because I had not one, but *two* guys fighting for my attention."

The words slip out before I have the chance to stop them, and I freeze, eyes wide with the realization of my admission. Skyler knows about Grayson, obviously. She knows he won me in the bid auction right before Valentine's Day last year. But what she *doesn't* know is that her boyfriend at the time had also given me a pep talk backstage before the auction. I was nervous as hell, and Adam made me feel like the most wanted girl on campus.

He always has made me feel like that — wanted, desired — and not just for my looks.

I sigh, something between longing and frustration washing through me in a tumbling wave.

If Skyler catches on to me mentioning two guys, she doesn't say anything. So, I continue talking, hoping to keep her from asking who the other one was.

"How is it that Valentine's Day is in four days and I don't have a single option?"

I don't know why I'm even complaining about not having a Valentine's Day date. Maybe it's because I know the Alpha Sigma boys are having a dance, and maybe I assumed I'd be at that dance with Adam.

Then again, I never would have thought he could touch me the way he did and then disappear on me.

That longing twists harder toward anger, and I toss a kernel of popcorn in my mouth to keep from growling.

I should be focusing on me. That's what Adam said, right?

But maybe *that's* exactly why I want a date for Valentine's Day. Because I don't want to do what Adam thinks is right, not after he made me call his name with his head between my thighs and then hasn't talked to me for a week.

A *week*.

It's petty, I realize, that I want to get his attention, to make him angry, to make him talk to me out of jealousy if nothing more. But I can't help it.

Adam brings out the worst in me, just as he does the best. It's a dangerous, messed up kind of tango.

Skyler starts in on how she's not surprised I don't have a date, considering how crazy my schedule is with my major. But before we can get too deep into the conversation and figure out a solution to my dateless problem, the door swings open, and Jess flies in like the Tasmanian Devil in a tornado of rage.

"OH MY FUCKING GOD I'M GOING TO KILL SOMEONE!"

My instinct is to shield the popcorn from her, like she might come after it next since she's already thrown her hoodie across the room. "What the hell?"

Jess paces, her face pink, hair mussed. "Greg. Fucking *Greg*."

"What did he do?"

"It's what he *didn't* do," Jess says, flopping back onto her bed.

Skyler and I just exchange glances, waiting for her to continue. When she doesn't, Skyler clears her throat.

"Uh, care to divulge, J-Love?"

"I've got a really bad case of the Blue Bean, ladies. A major Violet Vulva."

I just blink, thinking maybe it's just me who doesn't understand. When I chance a glance at Skyler, her brows are pinched together tight, her expression just as confused as mine.

Jess peeks over her boobs at us, sighing and throwing herself up to sit when we don't immediately react.

"Blue balls!" she screams. "I have blue balls. Like, fucking bruised, swollen, black and blue balls."

I suck my lips between my teeth, fighting back the laugh that wants to break free. Usually, it would be no problem to laugh with Jess, but she looks more than a little frustrated right now.

Skyler peeks at me, and then holding back her own laugh, she squeaks out, "Would you like me to rub them for you?"

I break down, laughing so loud I'm a little embarrassed at the sound of it. Skyler cracks up when I do, tears streaking down her face as Jess tosses pillows across the room at us. One of them whacks Skyler in the head, which makes me laugh harder.

"Witches!" she yells as we burst into another fit of laughter.

"Sorry," Skyler says first, clearing her throat. I'm still trying to gain composure. "Sorry, Jess. Tell us what happened."

"No. Fuck you."

"Wait," I say when Jess covers her face with her sheets. "Does it really hurt?"

"Yes, fuckhead, it really hearts. I'm so worked up I'm pretty sure putting on sweat pants is going to make me orgasm."

"Well shit, let me at least put on *Magic Mike* or something," Skyler says, flipping through the channels.

Another pillow flies toward us.

"I hate you," Jess wallows. "What am I going to do? Like seriously, I'm going to kill him. *Murder* him. Hang him from the Omega Chi Beta roof."

When I ask her to explain what happened, Skyler and I both sit and listen attentively — half because we want to be there for her, and half because I personally find it fascinating as hell. Jess is a man killer. The fact that a guy left *her* hanging without an orgasm? It seems impossible.

And yet, he did.

Her frustration grows into a whine as she explains that he was finger banging her when his roommate walked in, and instead of telling him to get out, Greg stopped messing around with Jess and started playing video games with his roommate, talking about getting a pizza and this week's intramural game.

With her still there.

Ouch.

"Ugh!" Jess says, punching her pillow just as Erin and Ashlei walk into the room. "My pussy is so swollen right now I'm pretty sure it's hanging out the side of my thong."

"Ew! What the fuck, J-Love?" Erin asks, grimacing. That causes another roar of laughter from me and Skyler.

"Apparently we missed something," Ashlei muses.

"You don't even want to know, Lei," Skyler says.

Erin and Ashlei make themselves comfortable, Ashlei climbing into bed with Jess to play with her hair, and then the conversation switches with just one question to the most dreaded topic of conversation this semester.

Kip.

"Has Kip asked you to the dance yet?"

Erin stares at Skyler, the question silencing all of our laughter like a splash of water to a match flame.

I watch my Big, my heart twisting at the sight of her white face. I've tried to get her to talk about the whole situation, to tell Erin she needs out, but Skyler has always been good at shutting down when she's hurting.

If she doesn't talk about it, the pain doesn't exist, right?

"Uh, no..." Skyler finally answers, swallowing.

"What about your date last Sunday? He didn't ask then?"

"That wasn't a date. I taught him how to paddle board, that's all. And no, he didn't ask. And I haven't talked to him since." Skyler answers atomically, like a robot set to respond to demands.

"Why not?"

Skyler's eyes skirt to mine, and I smile, trying to give her comfort.

"I don't know. I may or may not have left his place without saying anything. And then he texted me and I didn't answer. And then he didn't show up for class Thursday, so I tried texting him and acting like everything was cool, but he didn't answer me. I think he's pissed. I don't blame him."

"What the hell?!" Erin asks, clearly upset, but Ashlei speaks over her, asking, "When was this?"

Skyler's eyes flick from Erin's to Ashlei's, and she seems to decide Ashlei is the safer one to answer.

"Last Sunday is when I saw him. I texted him Thursday after class."

"Aren't the A Sigs on their retreat thingy?" Ashlei asks. "You know, how they disappear every spring semester with the new pledges?"

"Holy crap, I didn't even think of that," Skyler says, and my stomach drops as the same thought passes through me.

Could it be *that's* why I haven't heard from Adam?

Every year, the Alpha Sigs disappear with their new pledges, finishing their initiation process. They return after about a week or so, throwing the New Member Bonfire to celebrate the new brothers.

It makes sense...

He's the president. If they're on that retreat, he would be leading them. And if they all had to surrender their phones, I imagine he would stay off his, just to set the example.

But could he not have told me before he left?

"I haven't seen Adam since last weekend now that I think about it..." I murmur, and Skyler nods, but then she snaps her head in my direction, one brow quirking up.

Shit.

She's probably wondering why the hell I would care that I hadn't talked to Adam in a week. We're just friends in her eyes, after all, and she doesn't even know the *half* of how deep our "friendship" runs.

"See?" Erin says, taking the attention off me. "I bet he's not mad at you. He probably disappeared not too long after you left that day."

"Maybe. Ex, I don't know about this anymore," Skyler breathes, and I perk up, hopeful that she'll tell Erin what's really been on her heart.

Tell *all* of us, really.

"I feel like he's going to get too caught up... I'm really starting to learn a lot about him and he's asking a lot about me. It's getting serious — and fast."

"Good," Erin says quickly. She stands, and with that motion, it's like all the power shifts in the room again — right back into the palm of her hands. "That's exactly what we want, isn't it? The faster and harder he falls, the more devastated he will be and the more he'll want what we had back. What we had was simple, true, uncomplicated," Erin says, her eyes lighting up, a small smile reaching her lips. It falls quickly as she shakes her head, as if she's afraid to submit to the feeling. "After the mess you leave him in, he'll be begging for that back."

Fuck.

I wince, and for the first time, the respect I've always had for my Grand Big wanes.

It's not fair what she's asking Skyler to do, and I reach under the covers, squeezing my Big's hand to let her know I'm there. I can't get her out of this mess, but I can at least be there for her, let her know she's not alone.

"Okay," Skyler manages, her voice strained.

Erin goes on, talking to Skyler about the importance of the presidency and knowing how hard it is to make sacrifices along the way. I think it's all complete bullshit, especially since *I'm* supposed to fill that role one day and have absolutely no desire — at least, not now.

So, of course, my thoughts drift to Adam.

My stomach flips with the first thought of him, the realization that he maybe *wasn't* being a complete asshole and ignoring me all week. Half of me can't wait to see him, to see if he texts me as soon as they're back, if I see him at the bonfire. The other half of me can't stop replaying what Erin said last week.

"A real man would never make you question what you mean to him."

I wish I could talk to Skyler, take her mind off Kip and Erin and ask for her advice. She has been through so much with guys, and she knows how Adam is in a relationship. If anyone could help me untangle the knots in my stomach, it's her.

But even as the thought passes through me, I know it's selfish — and the timing couldn't be worse.

I can't talk to Skyler about him, about *us* — not now. With the Kip and Erin drama surrounding her like an Army set to attack, the last thing she needs is to hear that I'm in love with her ex-boyfriend.

And that I was even when he was hers.

With that realization, I button my lips, holding my tongue with the resolve to just wait. Wait to see what he says, to see when he comes back, to see why he didn't tell me he was leaving in the first place.

It's all I can do.

Sit and wait.

I hate this game.

Ashlei

Growing up as the middle child, competitiveness has always been a part of who I am. I was always working to stand out, to not be ignored or forgotten. It was easy for my parents to forget about me, with having an incredibly smart oldest daughter and an incredibly athletic youngest one. I was still there, excelling at nearly everything I did, but it was nothing my parents cared about.

So, when my internship was extended, my parents beamed like it was the first solid thing I'd ever accomplished in my life. Dad bragged about me at the country club over winter break, saying I would be the best event planner in south Florida, and Mom took me shopping for more amazing outfits to help me feel as great on the outside as I did on the inside when I walked into *Okay, Cool.*

But if they could see me today, I know they'd be disappointed.

It's Wednesday, which usually means everyone is in great spirits. We're halfway to the weekend, the hardest meetings of the week are done, and for all intents and purposes, it's a good day of the week. But today? Well, today feels a hell of a lot like a Monday.

"Do you have that report on Kiki Kween's athletic apparel line yet?" Kimberly asks, swinging into my cube like an unwanted, buzzing gnat.

I sigh, still tapping away on my keyboard and not even glancing up at her. "Working on it now."

"It was due to me EOD yesterday," she says, using the acronym for *end of day* like it makes her more powerful. She checks her watch. "And it's already three."

"I'll get it to you."

There's no use in telling her that Holly assigned me two other, more pressing tasks since we last divvied up the responsibilities for the Kiki Kween account. Or that I'm on my period, cramping like a sonofabitch and trying not to die. None of it would matter to Kimberly, and the last thing I'd ever do is admit any kind of weakness to her.

Instead, I aim for indifference, like I don't really care that I missed a deadline that *she* made after we were assigned the account.

"When?"

"Soon."

Kimberly rolls her eyes, a frustrated huff leaving her bright pink lips as she stomps away. When she's gone, I let out my own sigh, slumping back in my chair before closing my eyes and rubbing my temples.

It's been a hell of a week.

Between my classes and the internship, I've barely had time to eat. Add in the fact that Erin has been *extra* demanding since she became president, expecting more of me as her right-hand woman, and you could say that I might be in six feet of water with no heels to get me high enough to breathe. But this is who I am, and this is what women like me do — we push, we work hard, and we don't make excuses.

Even when we really, *really* want to.

I let my hands fall from my temples, palms smacking my skirt-covered thighs before I reach into my purse for two more Midol. I pop them in my mouth, chasing them with a swish of water, and then I nearly spit it out when I glance up at the source of the new shadow over my desk.

Brandon.

I somehow manage to swallow the pills, though they feel dry in my throat despite the water. Brandon's brows are pulled low over his fierce eyes, one hand clutching a stack of papers as the other rests calmly in the loose pocket of his robin's egg blue slacks. Those slacks hang *way* too deliciously on his hips, his all-white dress shirt buttoned up to his neck, the top button left undone, sleeves rolled up to his elbows.

I'm checking him out. Blatantly, unapologetically. I can't help it. His dark skin contrasts with the light colors in his outfit choice, and the way he's looking at me is a cross between anger and desire. Anger wins out, the tiny flash of want slipping from behind them as he drops the papers to my desk with a *thwap*.

"Good afternoon, Mr. Church."

"Do you know what these are?" he asks, ignoring my greeting.

Immediately, all the blood drains from my face, another cramp rolling through me. I'm pretty sure it's not the crimson tide's fault this time.

"I..." I stammer, picking up the papers and flipping through them. I recognize some of the reports, ones I'd worked on with Kimberly, including our first assessment of the athletic line. There are also countless emails from her to him, all with my name as the subject. I furrow my brows. "Well, sir, it looks like some of my reports from—"

"From the accounts you've been assigned to this semester? Yes. There are also countless emails from Kimberly to me, with explicit, color-coded mistakes you've made. From typos in a report to missing deadlines and everything in-between." My stomach drops as his eyes grow colder. "I've received at least three every single week."

My jaw pops open, but I clamp it shut again, swallowing down the urge to curse her name and rip her greasy hair from her skull.

"Sir, I apologize if Kimberly has been bothering you with this. Holly has had me working on a lot of different projects, outside of the ones Kimberly and I have been assigned to work together on, and I—"

"I don't want excuses, Miss Daniels. What I want is to not have to open an email with your name as the subject line from her ever again. I don't care what that takes on your end, just make sure it happens. I'm the CEO of a Fortune 500 company. I don't have time to read emails about an intern not doing her job."

Heat climbs up my neck, tingeing my cheeks as I press my lips into a thin line. "Yes, sir."

Brandon's jaw ticks at that, but if it affects him the way I mean for it to, he doesn't show it. Instead, he turns on the heels of his designer, leather shoes, and I watch his muscular back until it disappears around the corner.

My stomach rolls again, this time with a new kind of sickness, and I let out a long, pained sigh. I'm not sure if it's because of my period, or if it's because every possible chance I'd held onto that Brandon *might* come back to me, that he might let his wall down and let me back in, just disappeared into a cloud of smoke, but I'm done.

With Kimberly, with Brandon, with the whole fucking day.

I set up an out-of-office early email and pack up my bag, not even bothering to stop by Kimberly's desk on my way out. The only people I do say anything to is Holly, who takes one look at me and believes me when I say I'm not feeling well, and Mykayla, who offers to kick Kimberly in the twat for me.

I almost take her up on it.

When I regretfully decline, she gives me a hug, and I ride the elevator down to the lobby in silence, fighting back the urge to cry.

I consider myself a strong woman. A fierce storm. A force to be reckoned with.

But today? Right now?

I'm just a girl.

A sad, hormonal girl who needs three things and three things only: a bed, a movie, and a two-pound bag of gummy bears.

And I give myself all three.

***

I call out of work the next day.

I know I shouldn't, that technically speaking, my cramps are gone and I should get my ass to work. But the truth is, my ego hurts worse than my uterus ever did.

Brandon treated me like the gum on the bottom of his shoe, and I'm not ready to face him again. Not yet.

So, I ditch work, and Jess and I spend the morning hanging out, rummaging through her closet and Skyler's to find Sky the perfect outfit for tonight's New Member bonfire.

"I tried talking Erin out of all of this," Jess says, pulling another hoodie option from Skyler's closet. "This whole Kip thing."

"Yeah?"

She nods. "Yeah. I mean, I don't even think she heard a word I said, or if she did, she chose to carefully ignore all my questions and warnings." Jess sighs. "She's really set on this."

"I know. I tried talking to her, too — after Monday's little scene with Sky. I mean, we *all* knew she was uncomfortable, and Erin was unusually cold that night."

"She was. She *has* been, with this whole plan. It's like she's possessed."

"The things we do for boys," I said with a sigh, plucking two pairs of ripped jeans from Jess's closet. "We can't get her to see reason, not until she at least tries this crazy shit. All we can do is be there for Skyler and Erin *both* when this all goes up in flames."

"It will go up in flames, won't it?"

I nod. "I don't see any other possible ending. I sure as shit don't see it ending the way Erin thinks it will."

Jess frowns, pausing where her hands are hovering over a long maxi skirt Skyler wore last Spring Break. "This sucks."

"Indeed."

As if her ears were burning, Skyler walks through the door, and Jess and I exchange a *let's do this* power glance before I straighten my shoulders and toss her a handful of the hoodies we picked out. "Oh good, you're home. Try these on."

Skyler blinks as the hoodies hit her arms, a few of them falling to the floor. For a moment she just stares at them, then her blue eyes roll up to the ceiling.

"Are you seriously dressing me up for the bonfire? It's a bonfire... like, outside, in the dirt."

"And?" Jess says. "You need to look fucking hot, Sky. Try these on so we can see which one flatters you more and then we can pick accessories. And you're lucky it's in the dirt. We'll settle for cute boots, though wedges would look much better."

"You're not freezing my toes off to look cute at a New Member bonfire."

"I *said* we'll settle for boots, grumpy pants," Jess repeats. "Did you forget that Kip is going to be there and you haven't talked to him or seen him in over a week?"

I cringe, opening my mouth to smooth over Jess's hasty words and let Skyler know we're here for *her*, to help, but it's too late.

Skyler blinks, the movement more aggressive than it should be allowed to be before she claps her hands together. "Oh! Kip is going to be there? Well I'll be damned. Must have slipped my mind."

She pulls the first hoodie option over her head, and immediately Jess and I shake our heads, knowing it isn't the one.

"We're just trying to help," I offer as she strips it off again, moving to the next. It's a light blue zip up with hot pink KKB letters over the chest. When she zips it up, it frames her rack perfectly, and I try my best to bring some positivity back in the room. "Oh, I love that one! Brings out the blue in your eyes and you could show some cleavage. Put that one in the maybe pile."

"I know you're trying to help," Skyler admits on a sigh, tossing the blue zip up where I told her to. "I appreciate it, I do. I'm just..."

"Nervous? Scared?" Jess probes.

"Yes."

Jess and I exchange sad looks as Skyler's eyes fall to the floor. She's the most confident out of all of us — at least, it's always seemed that way. Whether it was kissing a boy from another university on Spring Break or answering a dare to jump on stage and do karaoke in nothing but a swim suit, Skyler made it all look easy.

But now, standing in the room with her hair a mess from ripping another hoodie off, I can see her true colors.

Skyler is scared. She's hurting. And she hates it.

"I just really need to push him away tonight while also making him think I'm still completely into him. It's a mess... *I'm* a mess."

Jess swallows, nodding to me to let me know she'll take the lead. "Hey, you got this, Sky. Who has the best poker face in the game? Who can bluff their way out of a speeding ticket? Who can play every single boy for a complete fool and leave them begging for more?"

Skyler is silent, so I move toward her, handing her another hoodie option. "You, that's who. I've never seen a girl who can play the dating game as well as you do. You get to have the fun you want without all the drama because somehow you keep every guy at just the right distance." I smile. "Don't let this kid get under your skin. You're so close to being done with this stupid game and then you can focus on the tournament in May and more importantly, Spring Break."

We all chuckle at that, and I rub Skyler's back encouragingly.

"You girls are right," she says, a little color returning to her cheeks. "I do this all the time, I don't know why I'm letting him get to me."

"Just brush him off. Pick out a pair of ripped, tight-as-fuck jeans and a hot sweater and we'll do your hair and makeup. You'll look and feel sexy and invincible, and before you know it, you'll be breaking his heart and moving on. End of story, next book."

Jess tries to make it sound easy, though all three of us feel the weight of the impending task. Skyler has a lot on her shoulders, and I know we all just want it to be over with.

Skyler still looks a little sick, and for the first time, the thought crosses my mind — does she *really* like Kip?

I mean, I heard about the night they met, about the tequila shot. I heard about their first date, about the paddle boarding. But from a distance, it all just seemed like part of the plan.

Staring at her now, at the slump in her shoulders, the bags under her eyes, I can't help but wonder if there's more to her side than she's telling us.

If I were in her shoes, if I liked a boy whom Erin liked first, one she'd laid claim to... could I walk away so easily?

I knew the answer before I even asked the question in my mind. The thought of her saying she wanted Brandon, even if it was after I'd first met him, it made me want to punch her in the tit and throw up all at once.

And she doesn't even *know* Brandon.

Skyler sighs, bringing me back to the current moment. "Okay, let's do this. Make me pretty."

I shake my head, swallowing back the urge to cry with her out of solidarity.

Stupid period.

"You're already pretty," I tell her. "We're just going to make you *feel* it."

And we do. After a tight hug and a couple hours of primping, Skyler is hot enough to spark that bisexual side of me and make *me* want to kiss her. I know without a doubt that Kip will be putty in her hands tonight, especially after she sets her game face in place.

None of us can help her out of the particularly sticky situation she's in, but we *can* be there to help her survive along the way. So, I hold her hand and Jess rubs her shoulders, giving her our final pep talks before setting her loose.

Skyler Thorne, set to win her next big game.

At least, we hope.

Skyler

My stomach should be in knots.

I should be shaking, the way I was when I left Kip's apartment last Sunday after what transpired between us. I should be staring at him across the flames of this fire right now and remembering what it felt like to have his hand between my thighs.

But my poker face is on.

Jess and Ashlei gave me a little pep talk before the fire, and it was exactly what I needed to hear. I've been in my head all week about Kip, wondering where he'd gone, wondering what he'd been thinking. *I* was the one who walked out on him, who left him guessing, and for a while, I was thankful that he hadn't pursued me. I thought maybe I got my point across, that we could end this little game early.

But then he didn't show up to class on Thursday.

That made me worry. It wasn't until Ashlei reminded us about the Alpha Sigma initiation camping trip that I was able to rest a little easier. Of course, that was also the night that Erin hammered home that she had *not* forgotten about Kip, or the game, and I was still very much a pawn.

Until I walked through my bedroom door and found Ashlei and Jess waiting for me, my day had been shit. I couldn't stop thinking about Kip, about what I was expected to do. I didn't know how to separate my heart from my bond with Erin, the promise I'd made her.

But the girls were right.

They reminded me who I am, how good I am at playing the game when I need to. I may have let myself get a little too caught up with Kip, let myself fall a little too far into the trenches, but now, tonight, I have control again.

Now, I just need to keep it.

Ever since the girls and I showed up to the bonfire — fashionably late, of course — Kip's eyes have been glued to me. He's trying so hard to pretend like he's not fazed by me being here, like he doesn't care that I didn't come up to him immediately, or that I've been talking to Adam and Cassie for the past forty-five minutes instead of him. But I see what he doesn't think I do.

I see him crush his plastic red cup when he sees Adam's hand touch my knee, splashing beer all over his friend. Adam and I are friends, nothing more, but to anyone who doesn't know us, I could easily see why it may be perceived as flirting.

So, being the power holder, I play right into that hand.

I nudge Adam when he teases me and Cassie, reminding us of the "Slip N Slide Sisters" days. I let the wind blow my hair over my face, dramatically blowing at it so Adam will shove it out of my eyes and make fun of me. And everything is working exactly how I want it to.

Just when I think he'll spontaneously combust, Kip's eyes lock on mine across the fire again as Adam gets up, telling me and Cassie he'll be back. He heads for the portable bathrooms on the other end of the fire, and as soon as his ass is up off the bench, Kip drains the last of his beer and storms toward me.

Here we go.

I remain calm, sipping on my beer and turning to face Cassie. "He's walking over here."

"Who?" Cassie asks.

Erin takes Adam's seat, and she leans in to catch the conversation.

"Kip," I answer.

Cassie's eyes widen, and Erin freezes before she's searching the crowd. She finds him quickly — I imagine because he's currently racing toward us like a pissed off bull.

"He's been here this whole time?" Cassie asks.

I almost snort. "Oh yeah."

She glances at him, then her eyes widen more, her voice lowering. "Oh my God, he's like Hulk raging his way over here."

"Shhh." I cut her off just as he reaches us, my eyes slowly making their way up to him, as if I'm surprised to see him, even though we've been trading glances across the party all night.

His lean chest is heaving under his new hoodie, the double-stitched Alpha Sigma letters rising and falling with every heated breath. His icy blue eyes watch mine from behind his glasses, the frames of them just as thick and strangely irresistible as I remember. He pinches his brows together, opening his mouth and closing it again like he's not sure what to say, or like he knows *exactly* what he wants to say but is trying to talk himself out of it.

I see it written all over him, question after question, the most confused expression I've ever seen him wear. It reminds me of my male opponents after I show my cards and they realize they've lost to a girl.

He has no idea who he's tangoing with.

One of Kip's brothers ask him if he's okay, but he doesn't so much as flick his eyes away from mine. He keeps those hypnotizing irises locked in on me, and Erin and Cassie watch him like they expect he'll explode at any minute.

I just smile.

I expect him to ask to talk to me, to perhaps grab my hand and pull me away from the crowd.

What I *don't* expect is for him to make a scene.

"I know I'm probably supposed to say I'm sorry right now, but I'm not going to. I'm not sorry about what happened between us last Sunday, Skyler."

My eyes threaten to bulge out of my head, but I school my expression, calming my racing heart. I feel Erin's heated eyes on mine, imploring me to look her way so she can ask me what the hell Kip's referring to, but I'm locked into the game now.

"I am sorry that I had to leave, that I couldn't talk to you afterward, but you left me first. Remember that. I woke up and you weren't there."

Erin is going to kill me.

"I'm sorry for that," Kip continues, his jaw ticking. "I'm sorry that I didn't chase after you or call you or make sure you were okay, but I'm not sorry about what happened. I don't regret it. I want to do it again. Right now, actually."

My cheeks flame at that, some of the students around us giggling at that, drawing their own conclusions. A few of his brothers hoot out their approvals, too.

I need to stop this soon. I need to take back control.

"I don't care about what people think, Skyler. I know you do, but I don't."

His words sting a little — both with the truth of them and his public delivery. It's one thing I envy about Kip — the way he seems to give absolutely zero fucks about what anyone else thinks.

And already, with just a few sentences, he's got my game face slipping.

"I'm not sorry. I want you. I want—"

Before he can finish his sentence, I shove my cup of beer into Cassie's hands and stand, taking a fistful of his hoodie and pulling him down until his mouth crashes into mine. There's a mixture of cheering and laughing around us, whistles ringing out, and in the back of my mind I know it must kill Erin to see me kissing him.

But this is all part of *her* game. If I'm going to shut him up, if I'm going to keep the control I somehow managed to get tonight, I have to act now.

I thread my arms around Kip's neck, his own hands pulling me tighter against him. When I pull back, both of us a little breathless, I run my hands through his hair with a smile.

"I've missed you," I say, which is more true than I care to admit. "Take me to the dance tomorrow."

I don't ask — I demand. That's where Erin wants this all to end? Fine. I'm more ready than she is at this point.

Kip watches me, his eyes lighting up and smile brightening at my request. But as I try to hold my poker face steady, his brows bend together slightly, his eyes searching mine like he senses that something is off, something is different.

So, I force an even bigger smile.

Play it off, Skyler. Don't let him see how you really feel.

"Like that was even an option," he answers, kissing me again.

I lean into the kiss, letting myself revel in the feel of his hands on my waist, his tongue dancing over mine. Someone yells for us to get a room, and I laugh, Kip tugging on my hand to pull me away from the fire. I glance over my shoulder as he pulls me away, and it's just in time to see Erin storming off in the opposite direction.

Shit.

"Don't worry about that," Kip says, his knuckle finding my chin and tilting it up once we're away from the fire. "She'll be okay."

A sigh leaves my lips as I watch Erin disappear across the crowd, the sound of the party muted now that Kip and I have migrated away from the action. I want to run to her, to explain, to see if she's okay. But in the end, what she *really* wants from me right now is for me to follow through on what I promised.

So, I throw on my best fake smile, turning back to Kip.

"Yeah, she'll be fine," I say, slipping my hands into the front pocket of my hoodie. Away from the fire, the chill of the night creeps in stronger. "So, you're officially a brother huh?"

Kip watches me curiously, his eyes searching mine.

He can tell.

He's reading me like an all-caps word on a giant billboard sign. I don't know what it is about my poker face that's slipping, but something is giving me away. It takes every ounce of willpower I have to try again, to solidify that smile, to force the joy into my eyes. It must work, because though Kip doesn't seem completely convinced everything is okay, he finally mirrors my smile.

"Nah, I stole this sweater from Goodwill. Don't tell."

I lift a finger to my lips in a *shhh* symbol. "Your secret is safe with me."

It's a deliberate move, one I know will take his attention to my lips, to the way they felt on his skin last Sunday — and it works. Kip swallows, his Adam's apple bobbing hard in his throat before he leans forward, taking my face between his hands. He pulls me into him, his soft lips pressing into mine, and when he slides his tongue between them, I moan, leaning into him more.

This is fake. This is not real. You don't really feel that tingling, it doesn't really feel that good, you don't really want him to take you home right now. It's a game. It's a game.

"Come home with me," he murmurs between kisses, and all I can do is kiss him harder.

Yes. Take me.

Pressing my hands to his chest, I pause for air, for clarity. I can't think with his lips on me like that, with his hands pulling, his mouth demanding.

"I can't."

He sighs. "Stop overthinking it and do what you want to do."

"It's not that easy."

My game plan slips, and suddenly I want to tell him everything. I want to tell him that there's more to this than he could ever understand, that he needs to walk away — no, he needs to *run*.

But before I can process the thought, a bright, assaulting flash strikes us both like a bolt of lightning.

Kip grabs me protectively, his arms surrounding me, both of our hearts ticking up a notch.

"You two are so cute together."

The voice is distant, unfamiliar, and with the bright flash still blinding me, I can't make out who it belongs to. Slowly, the fire behind their silhouette brings their frame into view, and I swallow hard.

"New boyfriend again, Skyler? Will he be with you in Vegas?"

"Shit," I murmur, my hand blindly reaching for Kip's. I yank it hard, steering him toward Greek Row. As soon as we catch our bearings, I start running, and Kip follows, still glancing over his shoulder as more flashes ring out.

The photographer follows for a short while, shooting out more questions, but we lose him once I take us through the Omega Chi Beta back yard. I keep running, just in case, not stopping until we're tucked away safely in the family bathroom of Hawthorne Hall.

We stand there, quietly, save for our breathing. Kip asks me what's going on but I cut him off quickly, pressing a hand over his mouth. Once I'm sure we've lost him, we let ourselves back out into the cool night, and I keep my eyes away from Kip's.

Great.

As if the night wasn't already bad enough, *of course* a reporter would show up. Dad told me I should be on the lookout for them, that they'd be seeking me out again now that it was public knowledge that I'm in the tournament this May. Still, I thought after they were banned from campus, I wouldn't have anything to worry about.

Then again, *technically*, the bonfire was right off campus.

I sigh.

"What the fuck was that?" Kip asks, his breathing still evening out as we make our way toward the sorority house.

"Probably a reporter," I answer, voice flat. "Or a freelance photographer low on funds. Or maybe there's another *Hottest Poker Players* issue coming out from some played-out magazine. I always seem to end up on those shitty lists."

The words flow out freely, my poker face temporarily stunned as the real pain in my heart slips through.

I'm entered in one of the biggest tournaments in the world. I've proven that I can handle my own, that I can be competition for even the top players in the industry.

And yet still, all they care about is what I look like and who I'm dating.

"What are you talking about?" Kip asks.

"This happened last year before I played a pretty massive tournament in Atlantic City," I say with a sigh. "My parents told me it would probably happen again and maybe be even worse with this one in Vegas, but I guess I didn't think they would find me here. They're not supposed to be allowed on campus, but technically the bonfire isn't on campus, is it? Fuck."

I repeat the words I'd thought silently aloud, and the more I think about it, the more upset I am.

I just want to be left alone. I don't want to be their pawn, or Erin's, or anyone else's.

How did I end up here?

Thoughts are hitting me faster than I can process them, and suddenly, Kip traps my wrist in his hand, pulling me back until I'm crushed into his chest, both of his arms around me. He holds me tight, rocking me gently, his lips finding my hair as he presses a soft kiss there.

And I let him hold me.

I'm tempted to cry, but I use every last bit of mental strength I have left not to. Instead, I focus on my breathing, letting it even out as Kip holds me, his warmth surrounding me as we stand in the yard of the sorority house. Everyone is at the bonfire, so I'm not worried about anyone seeing.

But I *am* worried about what I'm feeling.

Because I feel safe.

And I've never felt that with a boy before.

"It's all good," he says after a moment, pulling me back to look at me. "They're gone now and we can talk to the Dean tomorrow about this. Or President Whittington. They'll take care of it."

I nod, though my wheels are still spinning. "Okay."

Kip doesn't seem convinced by my verbal agreement. His eyes search mine, the light from the front porch just barely illuminating his eyes.

"Hey, look at me."

I suck in a deep breath, holding it in my chest before I let my gaze find his.

"The only thing you need to worry about right now is picking out a dress for tomorrow night, okay? I'll handle talking to the president." He smiles, so confident in the fact that he can take care of me.

And I so desperately want to let him.

"Pick you up at seven?"

I let myself study him for a moment, my eyes sweeping over his mussed hair, his high cheek bones, his strong jaw. I hover over his lips, still tasting them on my own.

And then, I force a smile, putting my poker face back on.

"Actually, Adam and some of your brothers are coming in a limo to pick a lot of my sisters up. Could we ride with them? It would be so fun!"

I can tell Kip hates the idea of sharing me with anyone, especially a car full of people, but he nods. "Okay, yeah. I'll talk to Adam."

"Okay."

I smile again, lifting up on my toes to peck his lips before turning for the door. I need to get inside. I need to put distance between us, to put my resolve back in place.

Thankfully, Kip doesn't follow me. He doesn't tug my wrist and pull me back, deepen the kiss, ask me again to come home with him. *Thank God,* I think, because I doubt I could decline again.

I don't feel the weight on my chest recede until I'm inside the house, the door closed behind me, serving as a barrier between me and Kip. And even then, the weight only lifts a little, just enough to let me breathe.

I don't even bother taking a shower.

As soon as I'm up the stairs, I strip out of my hoodie, kick off my boots, and face plant on my bed. When my cheek hits the cool cotton of my pillow, I know the truth. It screams at me, taking over every other thought now that I'm alone, and it won't let me rest until I look it in the eye — until I acknowledge it.

I can't do this.

I can't play this game anymore. I can't pretend I don't have feelings for Kip, and I can't lure him in just to hurt him. I have to tell Erin that I need out.

I have to tell her I like him.

Taking a deep breath, I let the weight of *that* settle in on me.

And only then, in a dark room without a single other sister in the house, I finally let myself cry.

Adam

"You did good," Jeremy says, slapping me on the back before giving my shoulder a squeeze.

He scans the bonfire with me, hundreds of Greek students gathered to celebrate our new members. It's my first New Member bonfire as president, and the pride I feel swelling in my chest is almost too much to bear. I can't help the goofy grin on my face, the warm, fuzzy cloud floating through me — though that might be the alcohol.

"Thank you. And it wasn't just me. *We* did good."

"We did, didn't we?" Jeremy smiles wider, shaking his head. "I think this is our best pledge class yet. This is *definitely* the best turnout for the fire, that's for sure."

I nod in agreement, taking another drink from the red Solo cup in my hand. The night is still going strong, the kegs slowly tapping out one by one as the hours stretch into early morning. And as proud as I am of Jeremy and myself, of our leaders, I'm even more proud of our pledges.

It wasn't easy, what we asked of them.

Dropping your cell phone for more than an hour is hard for our generation to do, let alone giving it up for over a week. Add in the fact that we put them through a little hell, a little bonding, and a *lot* of brotherhood testing out at the cabin, and it's no wonder they're all wearing their new letters like a badge of honor tonight.

My eyes skirt to where Cassie is, where I left her moments ago with Skyler. I'd sat and talked with them for almost an hour, loving the way Cassie seemed to be letting herself have a little fun, but I knew from the moment I sat down that she wanted to talk to me — and I couldn't blame her. I had some explaining to do.

I wanted to tell her I was leaving after we hooked up last week. The last thing I wanted her thinking was that I would do that and then stop returning her texts — and I had turned on my phone to one from her saying we needed to talk. My stomach had dropped at that, but I knew she'd understand once I explained.

I was the president, and I had to lead by example. If the pledges couldn't be on their phones, I wouldn't be on mine, either.

Still, I feel her eyes from across the fire, hear the plea behind them. She needs answers, and when Kip and Skyler disappear, Erin heading off in the other direction, it leaves her all alone on the bench we were just sitting at together.

I take another drink, hoping the beer will somehow give me the right words to say.

"I'm going to go see about a girl," I say to Jeremy.

His brows knit together, but when his gaze follows mine to Cassie, he smirks. "Have fun, El Presidente. You deserve it."

I hold up my cup toward him with a little nod, and then one hand slips into my jeans pocket as I make my way to Cassie.

Her eyes widen a little when she notices me moving across the lot, and she looks around for someone to talk to, someone to save her from having to stare at me while I walk her way. I can't help but smile at how easily she wears her nerves, her cheeks flushing the closer I get, fingers brushing her hair behind her ear. She takes a sip from her cup, balancing it on one shaking knee as she looks anywhere but at me until I'm right in front of her.

"Hey, you," I say, plopping down beside her where Skyler sat before. She'd been between us then, a barrier, but with nothing between us now, that same familiar buzz surges to life as soon as her eyes find mine.

"Hey."

I sigh, hating the way she's looking at me, like I can't be trusted, like I'm not the person she thought I was. It's everything I've been trying to avoid. I want to be a man of my word with her, want to be different from the others, and yet I know without asking that I've hurt her.

"I'm sorry," I say immediately.

Her eyes widen, the emerald flecks of them flickering in the fire light. "You are?"

"Yes, I am," I say, smirking. "I know the week must have been hard for you, with me not responding to your text. You had no idea where I went, and I didn't tell you I was leaving. But, I want you to understand that Alpha Sigma and my brothers are important to me. I wanted to tell you, but I had told everyone else in leadership that they were explicitly forbidden from telling *anyone* what the date was for us to leave for the trip. I wanted to lead by example." I shrug, scratching at my neck. "Although, saying that out loud sounds a little silly. I know I could have told you and you wouldn't have told anyone else."

"I wouldn't have."

I search her eyes, wanting so desperately to reach for her. "I really am sorry, Cassie. I wanted to tell you, but I was trying to do right by my fraternity. And I hope you know now that I'm back, that you know where I was, that everything is okay between us. I meant what I said to you last week," I promise, and then I lower my voice, leaning in closer. "And I meant every single touch, too."

Cassie inhales a shallow breath, her bottom lip trembling slightly. Her knees clench together, but then her eyes rip away from mine, hands slipping under the backs of her thighs as she stares down at her Keds.

"Talk to me," I beg her, scooting closer. Our legs brush, the energy transferring between us.

"You said everything is okay between us," she whispers. "But... is it really?"

"Of course, it is."

I shake my head, finally giving into the urge to reach for her. I grab her wrist, pulling one hand from under her leg and into my grip, but she slides it away immediately, tucking her hair behind her ear before sitting on the hand again.

"Cassie... what's wrong?"

She rolls her eyes, letting out an exhausted huff. "How can you even ask me that when you know the answer?" Her eyes land hard on mine, the pain ridden in them. "Why aren't we together, Adam? Why don't you want me to be your girlfriend?"

"I do," I assure her. "When the time is right."

"What does that even mean?" She throws her hands up, letting them smack her thighs when they fall. "You know, Erin said something to me last week that really hit me hard. She said, if a guy wants to be with you, then he will be. And a real man won't make you wonder what you mean to him."

Her words are like a slap to the face, and I flinch back at the sting of them.

"You don't know what you mean to me?"

"Not anymore," she answers quickly, and then her hands are tucked under her thighs again, her little shoulders shrugging as she looks down at the dirt. "Maybe not ever, really."

I drag a hand over my jaw, closing my eyes as I search for the right thing to say, to make her understand. Right now, it feels like everything she just said stole my breath, my will to speak along with it.

How can I make her understand?

To tell her I don't want to just be another Grayson or Clay would insult her. She knows I'm not them, and it's like me telling her that she needs to have better judgment, that she needs to take a step back and evaluate before jumping in. But I don't mean it that way. I only want her to be happy — *truly* happy — with herself, and with me.

I can't tell her I'm doing this for her, because I know as much as she does that she's a strong, resilient girl. She can make her own decisions, and I *honor* those choices.

I just want her to take a moment for herself.

I want her to know that I will wait, that there's no rush.

Sitting next to her now, her bottom lip sucked between her teeth, I have to remind myself again exactly *why* I want to wait.

"I don't know how to explain this in words," I say softly, resting my hand on her knee. I don't reach for her hand again, but I crave the connection, the need to let her feel me when I speak. "And I may not ever be able to fully explain it. But, my grandfather taught me that actions speak louder than words. And you've heard a *lot* of talk, Cassie."

She sniffs, eyes still on the dirt.

"You heard Clay tell you you could trust him, that he wouldn't hurt you — but his actions proved you wrong. You heard Grayson when he said he loved you, that he would take care of you, that you were safe — but then *his* actions proved you wrong again. And now here I am," I say modestly, shaking my head as I swallow past the knot in my throat. "Just another boy completely fascinated with you, who has loved you for *so* long — longer than I should have. And I'm telling you all those same things."

Cassie slowly pulls her gaze to mine, her shiny green eyes shielded under bent brows.

"You can trust me," I say, repeating what I know those other boys said. "I won't hurt you. I love you, I want to take care of you, and you're safe with me." I swallow again, harder this time. "I mean every word, Cassie. But give me the chance to prove it to you. Let me show you I mean it, while you take the time to heal those scars the other guys left. Do I want to help? Absolutely. But I know your strength, and I know the girl who existed *before* those scars were left. She's different now — stronger, smarter, even more beautiful, somehow." I smile at that, and the corner of her own mouth twitches up. "And I want her to remember that. I want *you* to spend some well-deserved time on yourself because I care about you. *That's* the first step for me in my actions speaking louder than my words. Because as much as I want to wrap you up in my arms and tell everyone that you're my girl, what I want *more* is for you to be happy, to be free, to be *you*."

Cassie smiles then, her eyes glossing over so much that one tear leaks free.

"You're not just mine," I tell her, wiping the tear away with the pad of my thumb. "You belong to *you*. Take this time, just heal a little, and know I'm always here. I'm not going anywhere. Those guys lied when they said you were their girl, when they said you were the only one they wanted. When I say it, when we make it official, you'll know in your heart that there's no possible way it could be a lie." I shrug. "You'll know, because even without saying it, without anyone else knowing, it's already true."

It's as if my words break her, because Cassie's face warps, and then she buries it in her palms, her shoulders shaking a little. I pull her into me, not worried about the eyes around us now. Most of her sisters are gone, and anyone who's still partying is too far gone to care what's happening around them, anyway.

Cassie's hands grip at my hoodie, pulling me closer as she rests her face in the crook of my neck.

"I'm sorry," she says with a sniff. "I'm such a mess."

"No, you're not."

"I am," she insists, pulling back to look at me. "I've been going crazy, convincing myself that you didn't really care about me, that it was all a lie. And why? Because that's what I've been conditioned to do. That's what those other guys taught me. So I was so quick to just assume that you would do the same." She shakes her head. "I'm so sorry. I assumed the worst of you, when all you've done is prove to me that you care."

"That's not true."

She sniffs again, watching me.

"Cassie, I've hurt you, too. When I was with Skyler, when you were with Grayson, and so many times between. What we have? It hasn't come easy." I chuckle. "Not even close. And it's okay that you feel the way you do. That's why I want to prove to you with my actions what I mean with my words."

She lets out a long, exasperated sigh, nodding. "I do, too."

"Hey," I say, rubbing my hands on her sweater-covered arms. "Why don't you come to the dance tomorrow night? Take my extra ticket. We don't have to tell anyone that you're my date. You can just come and hang out with your sisters, and maybe save me a few dances."

Cassie smiles. "Really? I was hoping I could go, but wasn't sure if you'd ask."

"Really. And you know what else?"

She shakes her head.

"I'm going to book you a spa day for this weekend. Go get your shoulders rubbed, a little face mask action." She shakes her head, eyes wide like I can't possibly spend my money on her. "Don't even try to argue, I'm doing it. And you're going."

She laughs, still sniffling. "You're impossible."

"I know. But, it's Valentine's Day. As much as I want to take you out on a date and then take you back and do *very* not-safe-for-work things to you, I think this year it should be a little different. This year, maybe you spend the holiday of love loving yourself a little."

Cassie shakes her head, a bright smile breaking through as she slips her hand into mine. "I like that idea."

"Yeah?"

She nods. "Yeah."

"Good. It's settled then. We have a big limo picking up some other sisters from your house tomorrow. I'll save you a seat."

"Okay," she says, smiling. And then, she just watches me, her big green eyes nearly doubling in size as she searches me. It's like she's checking to see if I'm real, or memorizing the moment to hold onto forever.

Maybe both.

And it's the first time I feel like maybe my plan is working. Maybe I really can show her with my actions what she means to me, instead of just telling her. Maybe I really can treat her like the woman she's always deserved to be treated like.

Cassie McBee has never been loved the right way, and I vow to be the one to break that streak.

I vow to be the first one to really love her, to really *be* loved by her.

And, hopefully, the last one, too.

Erin

The sun hasn't completely shed its light over the university, hasn't spilled in through our large kitchen window, but yet still I stand at the counter, eyes on my phone, two names fighting for attention.

I didn't try to sleep last night — not after seeing Skyler pull Kip in for a kiss, or hearing him talk about how he isn't sorry for what they did. Whatever it was, he wanted to do it again, and as much as I know it's all part of the plan *I* set up, I couldn't stomach it.

So, I did what I do best. I fled.

Drinking hadn't helped last time I'd felt that ickiness settling in my stomach after their date at the pier, so I tried running, instead. Stopping by the sorority house long enough to change into long pants and a light long-sleeve shirt, I set out across campus, running along the dimly lit paths until my muscles were screaming at me to stop. Every step took a tiny bit of the pain, every sharp breath through my lungs gave a little bit of strength. When I hit the reflection pond on campus, I stopped, collapsing in a heap on the grassy hill that overlooked it.

I close my eyes, one hand wrapped around my steaming mug of hot chocolate as I go back to that moment, to the stars spread above me, the cool, wet grass on my neck, my breaths shallow but sure.

It was then that I realized it wasn't the kiss that hurt me the most. It was the *way* they kissed — the way Skyler tried to fake it, but gave into Kip with every second that passed, melting into his arms. It's the way Kip spilled his heart out to her before she shut him up with her mouth on his, and the relief that spilled off of him when she was pressed against him.

Sobs racked through me on that hill, every fear and damning emotion surging over me like a tidal wave. I had no choice but to succumb to it, to let it roll me under its powerful waves before it spit me out. And when it did, I sniffed, wiping my eyes dry and staring up at the unblinking stars in the sky as I realized the truth.

I was stupid to think this was ever a game.

He likes her. And she likes him.

And now, I have to figure out what to do about it.

My eyes flutter open again, the first bit of sunlight slipping inside our small sorority kitchen. I stare at my phone again, debating my options.

The first person I want to call is Clinton.

We haven't talked since the semester started, but he always said he'd be there for me if I needed him. And I need him. *Bad.* He'd know what to say, how to help me see sanity, to make the right decision.

But that's the problem.

As much as I need him, as much as I should pick up the phone and call him or storm down Greek Row and right into his bedroom, I don't want to. *Because* he would tell me the right thing to do.

And right now, I don't want to be right.

Right now, I want Kip Jackson to be mine again. I want to find happiness with him, the kind of naïve, untouched happiness we had before. I want to remember what it feels like to be held by a man and not flinch away from his touch, to be kissed because I asked for it, not have my lips taken greedily and without mercy.

I want to be taken to bed, softly and gently, and cherished. I want to feel Kip's hands on me, his lips, his eyes...

Clinton would talk me out of the whole thing, and although that might be what I *should* do, I don't.

Instead, I pick up my phone and dial person number two.

Mom.

"It's early, Erin," she answers gruffly.

"I need you."

There's shuffling on the other end, and I hear my father's voice murmur something before my mom covers the phone to answer. A door clicks, and I imagine her retreating into her master bathroom, perching on the edge of her deep bath tub.

"Okay, I'm here. What happened?"

She still sounds slightly annoyed by me waking her, but the fact that she's still on the line brings me comfort. I sigh, feeling stronger already just by hearing her voice. She was the only one I could lean on after what happened, the only one who knew how to take what I felt and turn it into something I could control, something I could manage.

As sick as it sounds, that horrifying day brought me closer to my mom, and for that, I'm thankful.

"It's nothing big," I say quickly, to ease her mind. "There's something I want, something I feel like might really help me find some happiness again."

"Okay," she says softly. "Well, you know you can do anything you put your mind to. If there's something you want, take it. Make it yours. Make it happen."

"I know, I know, and I have been trying. I have a plan in place, a way to get what I want, but..." My voice fades, my eyes losing focus on the marshmallows floating in my hot chocolate. "I'm hurting someone I care about in the process. And I'm afraid that the more I use her, the more she'll hate me in the end."

"A sister?"

I sigh. "Yes. A very close sister."

"Oh, Erin," Mom says, the annoyance back in her voice. "Listen to me. College is such a small, temporary part of your life. I know these girls feel like they're everything to you right now, but one day, you won't even talk to ninety percent of them. Don't let your emotions and feelings stand in the way of your goals. What does that get you? Where has it ever landed you before?"

Every word she says is like a little prick of a needle, like motherly acupuncture, a mixture of discomfort, pain, and relief.

Maybe I want to hear someone tell me what I'm doing is okay.

Maybe I knew she'd be the one to say it.

"I think it's really hard on her," I say, not sure if I want my mom to hear it or myself. "But we're so close, and what I want is within reach. I'm just not sure if, ethically, the way I've gone about it is okay."

"Well, ethics aren't everything," Mom answers matter-of-factly. "Listen to me. You've had things taken from you, Erin. You've given when you didn't want to. This is karma, the balance of the universe. Now, it's your turn to take a little, to get back what you desire to make yourself happy again. And that doesn't always happen without a few fires along the way — fires that burn people you care about."

"That doesn't sound right to me."

"It's not always about being right. Sometimes, it's about the end game. Let me ask you this. When you close your eyes and think about reaching that goal, about getting what you want, how do you feel?"

I do as she says, an overwhelming wave of warmth and joy washing over me when I picture myself back in Kip's arms, his blue eyes looking into mine, his lips kissing the soft skin of my neck.

"I feel..." I shake my head, eyes opening with a new resolve. "I feel perfect. I feel whole again."

"Then you have your answer."

I swallow. "I think she wants out of the plan. I'm not sure how to get her to see it through."

"Well, you got her to agree somehow, didn't you? Think about what motivates her, what her weaknesses are, and play into them. Remind her why she agreed, why this is important not just for you, but for her, too." Mom pauses. "You're smarter than you think you are, Erin. You're just a little soft. Don't let what happened to you play into that softness. Let it harden you — your heart, your resolve — and take what you want from this world."

In the back of my mind, I realize the twisted, questionable morals that my mother's advice is laced with, but in this moment, I can't find it in me to dissect it. She said exactly what I needed to hear — what I *wanted* to hear.

She gave me permission, encouragement, and any thought of backing out is long gone.

When I end the call with Mom, I make another mug of hot chocolate, leaning one hip against the counter and watching the sun rise through the kitchen window as I formulate a new plan. I know Skyler's weaknesses — her desire to fit in, her need to fulfill our Greek line's legacy of being the next president. Before she came to Palm South University, she was a no one. Here, she's everything.

But a reputation is a futile thing.

And a delicate, self-conscience girl is easy to prey on.

I almost shutter at that thought as it rolls through me, at how easily I think it, but I don't have time to digest it before the universe hands me my first test.

Skyler shuffles into the kitchen, hair a rats nest on top of her head as her eyes widen when they land on me. It's early, the rest of the house sleeping, and she likely imagined she'd find the kitchen empty.

It's now or never.

"Hot chocolate?" I ask her, lifting my mug a little.

Skyler smiles, but it falls quickly as she props herself on the counter beside me. "I think I need something stronger."

It should scare me, how quickly I shove my emotions down into a box, slamming the lid shut and taping the edges for good measure. I can see it all over Skyler's face, her desire to talk to me, to tell me she wants out. It's in the knit of her brows, in the way she chews on her bottom lip. This is it — my last chance to get her to seal the deal.

So, I set a plan into place, not questioning a single step in it as it forms.

First, I have to break her down, tap into *her* emotions. Skyler is perhaps the most caring human being I know, soft at the heart no matter how she tries to hide it. And, unlike me, she doesn't possess the will to box her emotions away. Sure, she may be able to disguise them with a poker face now and then, but in the end? They always overwhelm her.

"It's funny, you know," I say, grabbing another mug from the cupboard and starting a cup of coffee for her on our Keurig. "Parents. Kids. The whole relationship that exists there."

"I'm not sure I'm following, Big."

I sigh, debating my next words before I say them as I detangle my hair with a wave of my hand through it. It's a delicate balance, what I'm about to do. I need to tap into her sympathy for me while also relaying my warning, my threat — or rather, my promise.

She's not getting out of this.

"I mean, we grow up looking up to our parents. We envy them, build our dreams and our goals around who they are and who they aren't. But do we ever really make them happy? Or proud? They say we do, but would they really tell us if we failed them?"

I turn again, pulling the fresh cup of coffee from the Keurig and handing it to Skyler. She holds it in her hands, the steam wafting up as she thinks.

"I don't think we can fail them," she finally says. "I think just by existing, we make them proud. They see themselves in us."

I see my in, my way to tap into her sympathy for me, to get her putting me above her own wants and needs.

And as selfish as it is, as fucked up as I've become, I take it.

Scoffing, I take another sip of my hot chocolate. "All my parents see when they look at me is a blurred, imperfect reflection of what they wish I was. I feel it. They don't say it, but their eyes do. They're ashamed of me."

And that was true, this time last year. My parents were only concerned with me finding a husband in college, nothing more. But after what happened to me, my mom finally understood, finally got behind me and supported me getting a degree I loved and forging my own path.

Still, Skyler is close with her parents. She's helped them in times of need, and she understands family obligation and pride. So, I continue.

"I know, right? It doesn't make sense, does it? Most parents would be proud of me, I guess. But then again, most parents didn't dream of their baby girl growing up and getting a MRS degree and banging a rich lawyer or doctor or whatever. You would think I shot a puppy by telling them I'd rather *be* a lawyer than marry one."

It's silent a moment, and I hear Skyler's wheels turning. Her initial worry that was laden on her features when she walked into the kitchen is gone, and I've successfully pushed those thoughts aside long enough to get her to think of how to help me. She wants to make me feel better.

Time to reel her in.

"Ex, you have nothing to be ashamed of and your parents are crazy if they don't see the amazing things you're doing for this campus, this sorority, and for yourself. They come from old money, they're not used to a world where a woman wants to be educated simply because she can be. You're too smart and too damn talented to get married and sit at home. Not that there's anything wrong with that, but it's not your style. Could you imagine that? You would go bat shit crazy. You can't even sit in your pajamas for a full day!

I giggle at that, heart warming a little at her words. Because as much as I may be putting on a show for her, Skyler is being nothing but real with me. She really thinks those things, and that stubborn voice inside me tries to pipe up again, the box rattling, everything threatening to break loose and remind me why I should let Skyler call everything off.

I shove it all back down.

"You have to say that," I say to Skyler, sniffling a little like I might cry at any moment. "You're my little nugget of sunshine."

Skyler watches me a moment, a strange smile on her face. And in that moment, we're just Big and Little, two sisters brought together by circumstance, staying together by choice.

But would she choose to keep that relationship in the end, after this... after Kip?

I could never be sure. And though I should have, I couldn't find it in me to care.

"I don't *have* to say anything," Skyler argues. "Except the truth. And I mean it when I say you are the bomb dot com and your parents are insane if they don't see that. They'll come around and realize that your dreams are just a little different than what they had in mind but that it actually makes you even better than they could have ever imagined. Just wait until family weekend. When they come up here and see everything you've done for Kappa Kappa Beta and for Palm South as a whole, they're going to lose their shit. And your grades are off the charts. You're going to get first pick of law schools and they're going to brag to all their friends at the country club about their amazing daughter who's not only drop dead gorgeous, but a lawyer, to boot."

And with that, I've got her right where I want her.

Step one: complete.

I smile, eyes watering a little as I cross the kitchen and wrap Skyler in a hug. "I love you, Little. Thank you."

"I'll always be honest with you," she says, pulling back and taking a deep breath. "And I'm sorry about last night."

My façade falters, a coldness sweeping over me at the mention of the bonfire.

"It's okay. I know it's part of it, it's part of the game. It's hard to watch, but I get it. You did good last night."

Positive reinforcement. Make her feel like what she's doing is good, that it will lead to something she wants.

"Thanks," Skyler mumbles. "But, I wanted to talk to you about it."

I swallow, alarms ringing in my head as I grasp for how to steer the conversation away from what I know she wants to say. Even after sucking her in with the sympathy card, she still wants to call it off.

Time for the threat.

"I—"

"You know," I say quickly, cutting her off. "I knew this was a crazy plan when it first slipped out of my mouth that night in my room. In fact, that night I stayed up all night thinking about how crazy I was being," I say, and that part is the truth. "But then I realized that I couldn't have had any better luck. I mean, how ironic that my Little just so happened to meet my first love and develop a connection with him?" I ask, reminding her who had him first, who he is to me. "It was almost too perfect."

Skyler watches me carefully, her face neutral.

"And being that you're the best damn poker player around," I say, feeding into her ego, tapping on that most important part of her life. "There literally is no better person for the job."

She swallows. "Ex, that's just the thing. I'm not sure—"

"And you know what else?" I say, not letting her finish. I drop my mug into the sink, turning to lean against the counter again with my eyes hard on Skyler. "I know it's not just about the presidency for you. I know it's because you care about me, because you know what I'm going through right now and you genuinely want to see me happy."

Skyler fumbles her mug a little, just enough to spill a drop of coffee on her sweater, and I know it's sunk in.

I'm reminding her what's at stake.

Not just the presidency, which she wants not only for herself, but for our family, too, but also our friendship. I asked her to do something for me, for girl code, and she agreed.

And I see it all set in as she schools her features, her resolve to tell me she wants out extinguished like a match under a bucket of water.

Handing her a napkin for the spilt coffee, I smile. "I'm so lucky to have you in my life, Little. You know, for a second last night I thought you were actually into him. It was so convincing!" I sigh, letting out a short laugh as I make my way toward the kitchen exit. "But of course, that would be silly," I say at the door, turning to face her again. "I mean, what kind of relationship could you possibly have with him now? If he ever found out about the game, about the set up... I can't even imagine what he'd think, how he'd *feel*." I smile a little, the intention clear as day. "He'd probably never talk to you again."

I watch as Skyler tries to swallow, though I can feel that same tightness in my throat.

I'm being an absolute bitch, the worst I've ever been to Skyler or anyone else in my entire life... and the worst part is...

I like it.

The power surges through me, the overwhelming rush of knowing what I want and taking it, no mercy, no excuses.

"Anyway," I say, still smiling. "I'm so excited for tonight. It's going to be perfect! Come up to my room around four and we can all get ready together. And, Little?"

Skyler looks back up at me from where her eyes had fallen to her lap, face a little white.

"Thank you, for talking to me. You really are one of the best friends I have."

I smile a little wider, knocking once on the door frame before I leave her in the kitchen alone, making my way upstairs.

And just like that, I'm back in control.

Right where I belong.

Bear

I'm going to fucking kill him.

He's my Little, one of my best friends, my brother and my mentee. But none of that matters. Because he made me sign up for this stupid motherfucking dating app, and I am going to *kill* him.

"*Gosh*, this was just so fun," Kimona says, smiling big enough to show me the piece of pepper she's had lodged between her two front teeth all night again. "We have to get together again soon."

"Definitely," I grind out, holding my breath as she leans in for a goodbye hug. This girl has no concept of personal space, which *normally* wouldn't be a big deal. But when she smells like our fraternity house after an intramural game and a keg party, it's an issue.

"Walk me to my car?" she asks when she pulls back.

For a moment, I just let myself stare at her, convincing myself that it's not my fault she bottled all that crazy up in that hot, tight little package and put it on a dating app for me to swipe right on. Her abdomen is lean, all of it showing under her tiny crop top. The ripped-up jeans she's wearing hug her hips, rounding over her firm ass in the perfect way, and her hair is straight as a pin, flowing down behind her shoulders to touch the top of her belt. She's got style, her kicks matching the floral designs on her crop top, and her makeup flawlessly applied.

But that's the thing about online dating — no matter how hot the girl looks, and how well she sells herself in her bio, and how funny she is in text messages — you never really know what you're getting into until you meet her in person.

And boy, did I get myself into a big, steaming pile of horse shit with this one.

Kimona, though cute as hell, is fucking insane.

I'm talking Mike Tyson taking a chunk out of Holyfield's ear crazy.

If her *starting* off our "casual" Friday night date of bowling by bringing me a stuffed bear wearing a t-shirt with her name on it and box of *her* favorite chocolates — because she "just knew I'd share" — for Valentine's Day wasn't weird enough, the fact that she was so genuinely appalled that I didn't buy *her* a gift that she made me buy enough tokens in the arcade to *win* her a teddy bear pretty much sealed the deal.

And this was in the first fifteen minutes.

Forget about the entire two hours of bowling, listening to her talk about her Instagram followers and her crazy fucking friends, who, by the way, ended up *video chatting us* after the first game. One of them drilled me about my background, and the other made me lift up my shirt to show her my abs, to which the third friend, a slender kid with his makeup done better than Kimona, celebrated with a *"Yes, daddy."*

"Um, I actually think I left my jacket inside, so I'm going to run back in. But I'll call you," I told her, offering a hand in a wave.

She started to pout, opening her mouth to ask something else, and then she paused, brows pinching together like she was trying to remember what jacket I'd worn.

The answer was that I *hadn't* worn a jacket. I needed a drink, which they conveniently had at the bar inside the bowling alley.

Before she could say anything else, I turned, booking it toward the bar. I checked over my shoulder to make sure she left, and when she had, I slid into the first barstool at the edge of the bar, running my hands over my fade with a groan.

I'm going to kill him.

It would be one thing if this had been the *first* horrific, nightmare-inducing date from this stupid app. But no, this was now the fifth one in a row. And, sadly, Kimona, as crazy as she is, was the best of those five. Between the girl who neglected to put in her profile her obsession with vampires and desire to have her blood sucked, to the girl who cried about her ex the entire time we were at the nauseating romantic comedy screening — that *she* chose — well, you could say I'm over it.

There *was* a little promise in the date I had last Saturday with a girl who, oddly, reminded me a lot of Shawna — only her hair was pink instead of purple and she didn't wear those sexy glasses I loved so much. But, after two hours of a pretty decent date, I rode home with her in a taxi only for her to tell me it was going to cost me five-hundred dollars to go past that point.

Sighing, I thumb out an angry text to Josh warning him to guard his loins next time I'm around him. Then, I text Skyler, telling her I hope her night at the Alpha Sigma dance is less of a disaster than my fifth and final blind date. She doesn't answer, which doesn't surprise me — she's been *more* than a little occupied with the new transfer since she sank her teeth into him the night they met at rush. We have plans to meet up for breakfast next week, so I decide to fill her in on my dates then, and toss my phone on the bar face down with another long sigh.

"You know, I want so badly to tease you about all that huffing and sighing, but I had a front row viewing of that train wreck and I can't say I blame you. Here," a commanding, yet melodic voice says. "This one's on me."

A tall glass filled to the top with a light, amber-colored beer appears in front of me, and I follow the hand hooked to it.

To a girl so beautiful that I have to actively think about keeping my jaw clamped shut.

Wow.

It's been a long time since a girl has stunned me with her beauty alone. In fact, I can't think of the last time it happened. Perhaps when I met Skyler? As much as I was into Shawna, it wasn't the same kind of beauty. Shawna was different, unique. She stuck out with her purple hair, her glasses, her pierced nipples.

But this girl? This girl is a classic, timeless kind of pretty.

She looks like she walked straight out of a 1970's issue of *Ebony* magazine, her skin dark and smooth, hair just a couple inches longer than mine, framing her face with natural, easily styled curls. She's dressed in the aqua blue bowling alley tank top that all the other girls working there are wearing, paired with a short pair of white shorts, but she adds her own flair with an aqua and orange bandana tied at the front edge of her hair. Large, gold hoop earrings adorn her ears, her makeup natural and slight, but what catches me most is the combination of her smile and her eyes.

That smile, not a bright, blinding one, but a comfortable smirk, like she knows something the rest of the world doesn't. Her plump bottom lip is nude, giving her a natural pout, and the way those lips complement her bright, golden eyes is enough to make me blink to be sure I'm seeing it all as it really is, and not as a dream.

Because she *must* be a dream.

I'm not sure how long I stare at her before my ability to find words comes back, but she's just waiting, watching, that beautiful smile in place as she hangs one hand on her hip.

"You mean you saw that whole thing and didn't send help? What kind of monster are you?"

She chuckles, tossing her hands up to reveal her smooth, light palms. "Hey, it's not my business to get involved in the affairs of customers — even if they are poor sonofabitches dating quite possibly the worst kind of girl."

"We're not dating," I clarified quickly. Then, I tilted my head with a cock of one eyebrow. "Well, *technically*, this was a date. But it was our first one. And our last."

"Bit off more than you could chew, huh?"

"Let's just say I've quickly discovered that online dating is *not* for me."

I take my first drink as she laughs, savoring the cool, refreshing bubbles as much as the sound of her delicate voice.

"Oh God, don't tell me your friends suckered you into downloading one of those atrocious apps."

I point one finger at her like a gun. "Bingo."

"Poor thing. Tell you what, the second one is on me, too," she says, nodding to my already half-empty glass.

Cocking one brow, I take another small sip. "Buying me two beers within the first five minutes of talking to me, huh? Is this what it feels like to be a chick at a bar?"

"Don't get used to it. You're buying on our next date."

I have to swallow slowly not to choke on my beer at that. "I didn't realize we were having a first."

"Well, now you do." She winks, nodding at a customer down the bar to let him know she's on her way over. Then, before she makes her way toward him, she extends her hand for mine. Her nails are nude, just like her lips, but each delicate finger is covered with gold and silver rings. "It's Becca, by the way."

I take her hand in mine, not fighting the smile she brings to the surface after such a shitty night. "Bear. Er—" I pause. "Clinton."

"Which one is it?"

"Both. Clinton is my real name, but my friends call me Bear."

Becca smirks, that same confident, sexy-as-hell one she had when I first laid eyes on her. "Well, let's start with Clinton then." Then she knocks a knuckle on the bar. "Be right back."

She sashays down to the other end of the bar, and I don't dare tear my eyes away from her plump ass, even though I should. Nope, I shamelessly watch her for the rest of the night, whether she's tending to other customers or hanging out in front of me. We talk as much as her busy bar allows, and at the end of the night, she puts her number in my phone — and a kissy face emoji right next to her name.

The next thing I do is delete that fucking app.

Cassie

In hindsight, perhaps using Kade as a secret way to talk about Adam with the girls wasn't my smartest plan.

It started earlier in the week, when I was feeling particularly bummed out *before* my talk with Adam at the bonfire last night. Skyler asked me what was wrong, and in an effort to get her fabulous boy advice, I told her about my flip-flop emotional feelings toward Adam.

Except, I said it was Kade I was feeling them for.

It seemed smart at the time. If I used a code name, then I could talk about my feelings and get them out of my head. I could get advice from my sisters. And Kade is such a flirt, he's already had three "girlfriends" in his short time since joining Alpha Sigma. It would work, I told myself. No one would question it.

And they haven't.

But now, it's a little harder to hold the façade as I carefully craft my words before I say them to Skyler in the bathroom at the Alpha Sig Valentine's Day dance.

To say that I'm frustrated would be a drastic understatement. I huff again, sliding my lip gloss over my lip for the thirteenth time. My lips are shiny. I should put it away, but it's giving me something to do.

Adam sat next to me in the limo on the way to the dance, but other than our conversation there, he hasn't said a word to me.

And he hasn't asked me to dance.

I *know* it's his duty as president to make sure everything is going smoothly, and I know his brothers are here, and his new members, and he's got his hands full. I know all that. But here he is, less than twenty-four hours after preaching all this *actions are louder than words* shit, and in my eyes, he's failing. His words might have said that he thinks I'm beautiful tonight and he can't wait to spin me around the dance floor, but his actions are saying I'm the last thing on his mind.

I should be calm, I should know he'll ask me to dance soon. I should still be comforted by all the wonderful, perfect, amazing things he said to me as he held me by the bonfire last night.

But my anxiety is a nasty, wild beast, and right now, I can't fight against it with an animal as weak as logic.

"So, do you see what I'm saying?" I ask Skyler, continuing our conversation about Adam — AKA, Kade — not asking me to dance yet. I slip my lip gloss back in my purse, turning to watch her finish touching up her mascara. "He's more difficult to read than my fucking biology books."

At least *that* part was true.

"Take control, Little," Skyler says, as if it's easy. As if every girl in the world has the same bad ass, cocky style that she does. "Kade is young. Hot, but young. If you want him, make a move."

Things I want to say:

I *have* made a move, but he wants to take it slow. What's up with that shit?

I understand his motives for wanting to move slow. It's the most amazing, most respectful way I've ever been treated. But I simultaneously hate it.

I feel completely out of control of my emotions and have no idea what is happening.

Oh and PS, it's actually Adam I'm talking about.

Instead, what I *actually* say is, "Ugh. I'm not you, Big. I can't just make a move."

And again, at least that part is true. At this point in our story, I am not asking Adam to dance. He should be asking me.

"I'm confident," I tell Skyler, believing it only about sixty percent in my heart. "But, I'm also traditional. I want him to ask *me*."

I watch her slick the mascara over her lashes one last time, chewing my lip with a question I've been burning to ask her since last night at the bonfire. I know she and Adam are just friends, that they have a close relationship — definitely not a traditional one for exes to have. Still... the way she looked at him, the way she flirted with him...

Does she still like him?

Because I'm almost entirely sure that if the answer to that is yes, I will literally die. And not a cute, movie kind of death. I'm talking the gruesome kind that they can't show on the news.

Kappa Kappa Beta Sister Dies of Heartbreak, Explodes Into Mess of Guts and Feelings.

"Ask me whatever it is you want to ask me before you chew off your bottom lip," Skyler says, grinning at me in the mirror.

I sigh, leaning a hip against the bathroom counter. I debate my next words carefully. I haven't talked to Skyler about Adam in... well, ever. Our entire friendship, or whatever you call it, has been kept away from Skyler — mostly because I was a little ashamed of having feelings for someone who used to be her boyfriend.

But I can't go any longer without knowing.

"Are you and Adam still a thing?" I ask, trying to sound naïve. I aim for somewhere between idle curiosity and bored concern. "Like, when this thing is over with Kip... are you going to date him again?"

A friend would ask another friend that, right? That's normal, right?

Skyler's face warps into confusion as she tucks her mascara away. "What?" she almost scoffs. "No, not even close. Adam was fun last year and we're still good friends, but he's president and doesn't have time for a girlfriend."

Tell me about it.

"And even if he did," Skyler continues. "It wouldn't be me."

"Why?" I say quickly, almost too quickly.

"I don't know," she says with a shrug. "I'm just not into him like that anymore." Suddenly, Skyler turns on me, one brow popped up in curiosity. "Why do you ask?"

I have to focus not to blanch, not to blush, and I'm sure my cheeks shade pink, anyway. But I keep my voice steady, convincing her as much as I can that this is a normal conversation.

"I don't know," I say, shrugging and facing the mirror again. "I was just curious. Just wondering if you'd have someone to fall back on, I guess."

Yeah, that sounds legit.

Blessedly, Erin, Ashlei, and Jess pour into the bathroom, saving me from having to answer any other questions about my sudden interest in Skyler and Adam. Ashlei gets to us first, and she slides right between us, one arm hanging on each of our shoulders.

"J-Love is D-Runk," she announces.

"I am not!" is the immediate argument from Jess, but the words slur a little as she says them. "I'm just having fun. You should try it."

"No Violet Vulva tonight, J-Love?" Skyler asks.

"Nope." Jess holds one finger up, waving it side to side. "Let's just say there's a little garden that's not so innocent anymore."

We all laugh out a mixture of *ew* and *gross*, and through the spew of laughter, Skyler says, "Kip gave me a gift in that garden, you skank. You ruined my Valentine's Day."

"Oh hush, I didn't fuck on your precious glasses, you prude," Jess retorts, referencing the new pair of Ray-Bans Kip gave Skyler as a gift. They're actually perfect for her, and one of the most thoughtful gifts I've ever seen her receive. I eye her as Jess keeps talking, noting the tinge of sadness in her eyes.

She likes him.

It's as clear as day, and we all know it.

My stomach knots, thinking about how this is all going to end.

"Just on the bench where he *gave* them to you," Jess continues, which earns another round of laughter and a playful shove from Skyler.

Jess escapes into one of the stalls to pee as Ashlei leans up agains the wall, taking pressure off her feet in the sky-high heels she's wearing. "Speaking of Kip, how's it going?"

Erin has been surprisingly quiet, just laughing along with everything until that exact moment. She watches Skyler carefully, as if she's ready to catch her should she try to run away — like a lioness hunting a gazelle.

"It's fine. We're having fun, everything is going according to plan."

The words roll off Skyler's tongue easy enough, but we all know it's a lie.

Even Erin.

Which is why I can't contain my reaction to what she says next.

"The dance is almost over. I think you should do it soon. Use Adam."

The room tilts, the laughter of other girls around us suddenly too loud, the lights too bright. I'm sure my knees will buckle at any moment, and I grab the counter to hold myself up.

"What?!"

That's the word out of my mouth — and it's the same one out of Skyler's. She turns to look at me, as if it's strange for *me* to react in that way, and with her now knowing about me and Adam, I guess it kind of is.

But I can't look at her.

All I can do is gape at Erin, silently begging her with my gaze to reconsider what she's asking, to come up with a new plan.

"Why would I use Adam?" Skyler asks Erin, though she's still watching me.

"It's believable," Erin answers easily. "It's obvious Adam still has a thing for you, so tell Kip you have feelings for him, too. Tell him you were using him to make Adam jealous and it worked."

That tilt turns into a full spin, warping my reality like a washing machine set to high speed. I grip the counter more firmly, my only assurance that I'm not actually tumbling to the floor of the bathroom. Every breath comes shallower, every blink invades my vision with more blackness that doesn't recede when my eyes are open again. I tell myself to calm down, to breathe, but I can't do either.

This cannot be happening.

I think I tell the girls I need air. I think I tell Skyler good luck. I think I tell Erin to go fuck herself. Maybe I say nothing at all. I don't know anything for sure, not until I'm outside, in the garden, away from the noise and the reality of what's about to happen.

It'll be fine. Adam cares about you, he wants to be with you. He's not going to be with Skyler just because she says she wants him back.

I say the words in my head, even risking it and speaking a few of them out loud. But they do nothing to soothe my racing heart, because the truth of the matter is I don't know any of those things for sure.

Do I trust him? Yes. Do I believe that he feels what he says he does for me? Without a doubt.

But things between us have been muddled enough without any interference. What will happen when Adam hears Skyler say she wants him again? Will it stir something inside him, wake him up to a feeling he thought was gone that has always existed?

Will he want her, too?

My mouth waters, almost as if its sweating, and heat rushes away from my face, leaving it clammy and cool. I'm sick. I'm absolutely sick at the thought, at the possibility of losing Adam again — losing him before I've even had him at all. I force a breath, closing my eyes for five long seconds to try to find calmness, to find assurance, to find peace.

But what I actually find is the nearest bush, just in time to pull my hair back and forfeit my dinner.

Adam

I sigh as the first drink I've had all evening is handed to me over the bar, and when I take that first sip, I close my eyes and savor the taste. It's just a Bud Light, but after a long night of running around making sure everything was going according to plan, it tastes like heaven.

I'm not sure why I thought it was a good idea to have our Valentine's Day dance the day after our New Member bonfire, but I feel the ramifications of that choice as I take another, longer pull of my beer. It feels like I haven't caught a breath since I sat on the bench with Cassie last night. Between the catering for dinner being all wrong, the bars only being half stocked and us having to figure out how to get them *fully* stocked, and watching the under-age new members to make sure they weren't doing anything stupid — like trying to give a fake ID to one of these bartenders — and you could say I'm more than a little stressed.

But, Jeremy has stepped in, taking over the last of our night's worries, and I'm on strict orders to enjoy myself — even if it is just for the last couple of hours.

So, beer in hand, I make my way through the room on a hunt for the one girl I've been thinking about all night.

When the limo pulled up in front of the KKB house earlier, there were way too many pretty girls on the lawn waiting for us. I mean, between Skyler in her killer red sequin number and Ashlei in her jet black, slinky thing, it was all I could do to get my brothers to stop drooling and howling like a bunch of animals when we piled out of the limo to let them get in.

Part of me was glad Skyler was dressed to kill, because while most of my brothers' eyes were on her, mine were stuck like lasers on Cassie.

I had to laugh a little when I first saw her, because just like the first dance I'd seen her at, the one where Skyler had been my date, she was wearing white while Skyler wore red. Only this time, her dress wasn't quite so conservative. The front neckline dipped dramatically between her small breasts, showing freckles I didn't yet know existed, ones I wasn't sure I wanted anyone else to know about, either. The white fabric hugged her slim waist, rouching around her hips before it flowed down to her slender ankles strapped into nude heels.

She was an angel, just like she had been at that first dance.

I'd kept my promise to her, giving her space to enjoy the dance with her sisters and not worry about me. Honestly, I had my hands full anyway, so it was a little easier to do than I had thought it would be once I saw her in that dress. But now that I finally have a second to breathe, she's the only thing I can think about.

I don't care if I promised I'd give her the night with her sisters, with herself. I have to get her in my arms.

I have to get her on that dance floor.

A slow song comes on as I search for her, trying to spot her bright red hair in the sea of blondes and brunettes. I seek that white dress, hands aching to hold her, but the entire song plays through and I still don't see her. I look outside in the garden, check the bars, even ask a girl to yell out her name in the bathroom.

Nothing.

I'm just about to double check the garden when I notice a small crowd gathering around the bar across the dance floor. Curious, I make my way toward the commotion, and when I notice Skyler and Kip in the center of it, my throat tightens.

Skyler's face is cold as she says something to Kip, something that makes everyone around them start whispering to each other, trying to appear like they're not eavesdropping. He reaches for her, but she steps back, and my stomach sinks again.

What did this motherfucker do?

My jaw is set, lips pressed together as I get close enough to hear what's going on. But it's a blessing and a curse when I reach my destination. My curiosity is cured, and I finally know what's going on, but at her next words, everything I thought I knew goes up in flames.

"It's done, Kip," Skyler says, her voice shaky, emotion threatening to overtake her. "I don't need you anymore. I just wanted to get back at Adam. I wanted to make him jealous. And it worked. And now I don't need you."

My beer slips in my hands, and I grip it just in time to save it from crashing to the floor.

What the actual fuck did she just say?

My knee-jerk reaction is to laugh, because she clearly has to be joking. Skyler and I haven't had more than a late night, drunken hookup since we broke up last year. We're friends, sure, but I know without a doubt that she doesn't have feelings for me.

"Is this a joke?" Kip asks, his thoughts mirroring mine.

"No, it's not a fucking joke, Kip," Skyler says, her voice louder.

The crowd thickens, and the president side of me says I need to shut this down. *Now*. But I'm rooted to where I stand, only capable of hanging on to her next words, waiting for an explanation as much as Kip is.

"I don't feel anything for you. I never have, okay?" She says, and though her words are convincing to the entire room, I note the way her voice shakes, the way her hands tremble.

What's going on?

She looks on the verge of tears, and I watch for more signs as she continues.

"I've been in love with Adam since last year and that hasn't changed. Now that I have his attention again, I don't need you. It was fun, but it's over."

A slew of heads turn in my direction then, and I swallow, heat rising up my neck like a bug.

First, she says she's made me jealous — which is entirely false. Now, she says she has my attention, that she's been in *love* with me since last year?

Something is up.

In the back of my mind, I wonder if maybe she's telling the truth. Have I been so blind to not see that she still likes me? Sure, we've hooked up, and yes, we still flirt with each other. But that's just who we are. That's just how our relationship is.

Right?

Dread seeps through me at the possibility that I may have been reading it all wrong, that I may have been leading Skyler on without even knowing it. She thrusts a box into Kip's hand, telling him to take whatever it is back, that she doesn't want it anymore. And then, as Kip stares down at that box, Skyler pushes through the crowd and out the front doors.

Fuck.

My wheels turn faster than I can keep up with, turning over words and thoughts that can't find traction before another one knocks them out of the way. I'm still watching those doors when Kip lets out a frustrated growl, and he goes barreling toward them, too. I follow without thinking, without having a plan, the only driving motivator being my need to know what the hell is going on.

By the time I make it outside, Kip and Skyler are standing at the far end of the car loop, Kip's hand cradling Skyler's face. She's crying, yet leaning into his touch, as if he's the source of the pain and yet the only way to heal it all at once.

I swallow, watching them from a distance, but when she pulls back again, when more tears slip from her blue eyes, I can't watch any longer.

"Hey, man," I say, grabbing Kip by the shoulders to guide him toward the venue. "I think you need to go back inside."

I'm just trying to dissolve the tension, but I realize my mistake as soon as its made when Kip shrugs me off forcefully, turning on me like I'm the dog that shit in his yard.

"Don't fucking touch me."

My defenses kick in automatically, chest broadening as I set my jaw. "You don't want to do this, Kip. Don't lose your head right now."

I try that gentle reminder of whom he's talking to, of where he is, but it only adds fuel to the fire.

"Fuck you."

The words barely meet my ears before I'm shoved back hard. Skyler screams out for Kip to stop, and I'm not in control of my body anymore as I spring back toward him, shoving just as hard.

His eyes are menacing as some of our brothers step between us, Kade holding Kip back as Jeremy does the same with me.

"Calm down," he whispers.

I thrust a hand toward Kip. "I'm calm! It's this motherfucker raging out, not me."

Jeremy gives me a warning look, and I concede, throwing my hands up to let them all know I'm fine as they work on cooling Kip off. The only person I care about right now is the girl crying behind me, anyway.

Turning, I find her with her hands over her mouth, tears streaking her black mascara over her cheeks. I have no idea what's going on, why she's so upset, why she's calling things off with Kip when it's clear she still cares about him. And I *definitely* have no idea how I got pulled into this mess.

But what I do know is that Skyler needs to go home, to get away from Kip and this dance, and I make it my mission to do just that.

"Come on," I tell her softly, offering her my arm. "Let's get out of here."

She takes it as Kip surges toward me again, our brothers holding him back, and she casts one last glance over her shoulder before I open the door to one of the waiting cabs, ushering her inside. She slides across the seat, making room for me to dip in with her, and as soon as the door shuts behind us, she breaks.

I grit my teeth against the sound of her tears, pulling her into me immediately and rocking her as one hand smooths over her back. She's practically sweating, her skin hot to the touch, and she fists my dress shirt as her tears stain my shoulder.

"I'm sorry, I'm so sorry. I'm sorry. I'm sorry."

She says it over and over, and I'm almost positive it's not me she's apologizing to.

So, I just hold her, rocking her, letting her know that whatever it is, it's going to be okay. I don't pry, don't question what happened, or why my name was brought up as an excuse to break up with Kip. Who knows, maybe she just didn't want to be with him anymore and didn't have an excuse to break up.

But even as I think it, I know it's a lie. If that were the case, Skyler would be partying still, not crying on my shoulder.

Sighing, I tuck her a little closer, knowing I won't get answers for a while.

But one thing I know for sure is that Skyler is my friend — nothing more — and she needs me right now. So, if she needs me, I'll be here. Just like I told Cassie, I want to be a man of my word, I want my actions to speak louder than any promise I've ever made.

When Skyler is back at the sorority house and safely tucked away in her bed, I pull out my phone to call Cassie. There's no answer, so I leave a voicemail.

"Hey, it's me," I say on a sigh, tucking my free hand in my pocket as I make my way down Greek Row toward the A Sig house. I open my mouth to say something else, but for some reason, no words come.

Where were you tonight?

Are you okay?

Are we *okay?*

I consider telling her that I got Skyler home safely, but for some reason, it almost feels as if that would make things worse.

But I can't figure out why.

After too many seconds pass, I settle on asking her to call me back, and then I hang up.

And I wait.

Ashlei

"Shit," I murmur under my breath the morning after the Alpha Sigma dance, clenching the pole as hard as I can with my thighs. But it's too late. I'm already slipping out of the spin I attempted, and I throw my hand out in time to catch myself before I face plant on the mat.

When my entire body reaches the floor, I flop out on my back, letting hot air through my flat lips like a balloon deflating after a birthday party. Pretty much sums up how I feel about everything right now.

Karen chuckles, bending down to pat my stomach twice before standing tall and hanging her hands on her hips. "You're not going to be able to just jump back up on here and do everything you were doing a year ago," she says, the ring on her left eyebrow lifting.

"I know, but I didn't think I'd be *this* out of shape."

"You're not out of shape. You're in fantastic shape, honestly," she says, eyes scanning my exposed body. In pole, I never wear more than tiny dance shorts and a strappy sports bra. "But you haven't had to lift all of your body weight and then invert and spin and make it look pretty in over a year. It's going to take some time. And some *practice*."

I sigh again, scrubbing my hands down my face before reaching one hand up. Karen takes it, tugging me up to stand again.

"Twenty more minutes and then call it quits for today. You can come back tomorrow, okay?"

I nod, thanking her again for letting me come to her studio for an open pole session on such late notice. I was thankful to find another pole studio near school — one *not* connected to the awful memories of what happened at my last one — and the fact that she could get me in this morning was everything I needed after the Valentine's dance.

Last year, I spent Valentine's Day with Bo.

And last night, she called me.

The same feeling moves through me when I think about the call as did when it came through — like a little bug crawling down my neck and venturing all the way down my spine. I rub down the pole with a rag and alcohol, then I climb up again, this time working on tucks and other strength-building poses as I try to process.

Just seeing her name light up my phone screen was panic-inducing enough, but when I connected the call and the video came in clear, showing a face that seemed almost like a ghost to me after a year, I couldn't breathe. Literally, I stood there with my mouth hanging open and didn't take a single breath for a full minute.

Bo had smiled, reminding me with just that simple notion how much I'd loved her, and then I had to try not to throw up as she told me how happy she was. She told me she's up in New York City now, enrolled in a fashion school, and I marveled at how she looked almost nothing like the Bo I knew before. Her hair was a bright, almost neon pink, cut short and shaved on one side, and she had a piercing in the little dip at the bottom of her lip.

Just about the time I figured out how to breathe normally again, she told me she has a girlfriend.

My hands slip a little as that same feeling rolls through me, but I grip the pole tighter, using my shoulders and lower abs to swing myself up and around the pole until my feet land gracefully on the mat. I walk slowly around it, feeling out my new grip before launching myself back up.

It's not that I'm not happy for Bo, that I don't feel a little better knowing she's alive and happy, but I think I realized when she called me that *I'm* not happy — not the way I should be, anyway. Between Kimberly and the drama at work, trying to put fires out in sorority land, and not having anything to fuel me in my spare time — like pole used to — I feel a little aimless.

And, underneath all those shallow reasons for my unhappiness lies the real truth.

I miss Brandon.

I still want him, which is absolutely ridiculous after the way he's given me the cold shoulder at work. The memory of his biting remarks earlier this week make me grunt as I release my hands from the pole, inverting backward and holding myself with the strength of my legs and core alone. And it's there, hanging upside down doing something I used to love so much, something that feels so challenging an unfamiliar to me now, that I realize I've lost myself.

For the next fifteen minutes, I try to clear my head, focusing only on using my body to practice old spins and climbs. After a quick cool down, I pay Karen for the drop-in session and we set up a training schedule.

"You know, we're looking at going to competition later this year," Karen says, handing me my credit card back. "Think you'd be interested? You're already better rusty than half the girls on our team."

I smile, swallowing down the memories of my last competition. "Thank you, that's very flattering, but this time around I'm just doing pole for me. No competitions."

Karen watches me curiously, her almost gray eyes searching mine. "Okay, I can respect that. But let me know if you ever change your mind."

"I will. And hey, thank you again for today. I really needed it."

She chuckles, eyeing the new bruises already showing on my arms and legs. "Well, now you'll probably need an ice bath and some Arnica."

"No shit," I agree with a laugh of my own as I tug on my loose-fitting travel pants over my tiny shorts. Adjusting the strap of my gym bag over my shoulder, I give her a little wave and make my way through the studio hall and back out into the Florida heat.

It's a beautiful morning, just past nine now, and I plug in my headphones to start the walk back to campus. The studio was only a little over a mile away, so I took the walk this morning to warm up.

This one, I need to clear my head.

I scan the windows of the little shops I pass as I weave through downtown, enjoying the cool breeze mixing with the sunshine hitting my shoulders. I work through my plan for the week, starting with a beach day with the girls tomorrow and then back on the grind early Monday morning. Pulling out my phone, I jot down when I'll go to pole between work and class. My chest feels lighter with every step, and the more my plan falls into place, the easier my breaths come. I know pole isn't the answer to everything, but it's the first step to getting a little of the old me back.

I drop my phone back into my pocket, hooking one thumb on the strap of my gym bag as I go back to scanning the shops. My mind drifts from Bo back to Brandon, and my stomach turns.

I miss him.

My hand itches to grab my phone again, to call him and ask to see him. What's the worst that could happen? He says no and I feel just as annoyed and hurt as I do now? The possibility that he might say yes is enough to shove that fear down, but when I ask myself if I can truly handle another rejection from him right now, I know the answer without saying it out loud.

Taking that roll of my stomach as a sign from the universe, I decide to wait, to talk to him on Monday in the office, instead. At least there, I can't break down crying asking him if he ever thinks of me anymore. Maybe I'll have a small chance of keeping my shit together.

The decision is made, but when my eyes flit through the next shop, I wonder if I was reading the sign from the universe all wrong.

Because there he is.

As if he's a mirage, or as if my soul called to him without asking permission first, I spot Brandon standing inside a suit store, his beautiful, chiseled jaw casting a shadow down his neck as he appraises himself in a mirror.

My feet stop working.

I just stand there and gape from the sidewalk, watching Brandon eyeing himself in the full-length mirror as a shorter, slightly chubby man takes measurements along his inseam and then jots down notes in a little notebook. Brandon's eyes are hard, the irises scrutinizing as he scans the new suit. It's a creamy beige, complementing the caramel tones of his complexion, and even now — before it's been tailored — it fits him in a way that should be illegal.

I lick my lips, remembering how hard the body is underneath all that fabric, and it's as if that little spark I taste on my lips shocks him, too. He pauses, flattening a palm over his abdomen before lifting his eyes to the window beyond the mirror he's staring into, the window where I stand.

His gaze hits me like a wave of fire, burning me from the inside out.

I pluck the neck of my tank top away from my skin, a bead of sweat dripping down the back of my neck. I swallow, wrapping both hands around the front strap of my bag to keep them from nervously fidgeting. Somehow, I manage a smile, but Brandon doesn't smile back. Instead, he says something to the man working on his suit, and then he steps down from the platform, his feet moving him quickly toward the door.

Toward me.

I steal a breath before he opens the glass door, and when we're face to face on the sidewalk, I smile, squinting a little at the sun streaming in behind him.

"Fancy meeting you here."

Brandon tucks his hands easily into the pockets of his slacks, ones that hang on his hips a little now but I know will fit like a glove once he's done. It's the way all his suits fit — tailored to perfection, hugging every asset.

"Fancy, indeed," he says, his voice smooth and steady as his eyes rake over me. I catch a slight tick in his jaw then, especially when he takes in my tiny sports bra. "You're dressed... interestingly."

I glance down at the bra, my abdomen still exposed, but I at least took the time to throw on travel pants over my skimpy shorts.

"Ah, yeah. I just got done with a pole session, actually."

Brandon lifts a brow. "Pole? You went back?"

"I went back," I say, voice soft. Then, I shrug, running a hand over my high pony tail. "It's just been a really stressful couple of weeks, and I needed to blow off some steam. I suck, though," I say quickly. "My body is out of shape. I have a lot of work to do to get back to where I was."

"You are not out of shape."

"You didn't see me try to climb a pole."

"I'd like to."

I clench my teeth together to keep my mouth from gaping open again, and Brandon just watches me, his gaze smoldering.

"What's wrong?" he asks after a moment.

Um, besides the fact that you just said you'd like to see me climb a pole?

"You said you went to clear your head," he clarifies when I don't respond. "What's wrong, what's been going on?"

I sigh, turning so I don't have to look at him when I lie. "Nothing. I'm fine. Just a little stressed from work and stuff."

"Just because you're not looking at me doesn't mean I don't know when you're lying."

His voice is lower, and when he takes a step closer, my façade breaks. Tears prick my eyes, everything I haven't been facing welling up at the absolute worst time possible. I sniff, holding it all in, trying my damnedest to pull myself together even as my vision floods.

"Really, I'm fine," I say, but my voice is weak — pathetic.

Brandon reaches for me, but stops himself short, tucking his hands back in his pockets as he watches me. My eyes stay focused on the sidewalk, and I sniff again.

"What are you doing today?"

I glance at him then, but then my gaze is right back on the ground. "I don't know, I have some homework."

"Can it wait?" he asks, almost hopeful. "I want to show you something."

And when I pull my eyes back to his, watching him through my wet lashes, I know there isn't a chance in hell I could say no. The way those dark pools swallow me is just all kinds of wrong. I feel like a tiny little guppy trying to swim upstream in white water rapids — completely helpless.

"What do you want to show me?"

***

"Oh, my God. You're kidding, right?"

I gape at the monstrous boat in front of us, taking in the crisp white build of it, contrasted by large, dark, tinted windows. The railing spans the top deck, silver and shiny, complementing the wood flooring and accents. It's the kind of boat I've only seen in movies, the kind I've only dreamed about ever being this close to — let alone being *on.*

Brandon hands his bag to one of the crew members who just met us at the bottom of the ramp, ignoring my question. My eyes widen even more when he says something to the woman in Spanish, and she nods with a bright smile, taking the bag and greeting me with a shy smile before she heads back up the ramp.

Brandon smirks when he sees my mouth hanging open. "What?"

"Don't *what* me," I chastise. "Usually when someone says they want to show you something, it's an old family photograph, or a cool, limited edition comic book, or maybe even a secret place where they go to think. They literally never mean, 'Let me show you my *yacht.*'"

He chuckles, rolling up the sleeve of his loose, white, button-up shirt and revealing a dark, toned forearm. That button-up shirt is paired casually with a pair of baby blue shorts that end just above his knee, his boat shoes pulling off the sailor look he has going. It was the outfit he changed back into after leaving the suit for the tailor, and I wonder if he had plans to come out here before he saw me or if he was just dressed and ready.

"Are you just going to stare at me or can we get on board now?"

"I think I'll just stay here and stare."

He smiles at that, showing me his perfect teeth as he gestures one hand toward the ramp.

"Seriously, I don't have a swim suit or anything. I wasn't prepared for a boat day."

"We have everything on board."

I scoff, crossing my arms over my chest. "Oh, so you've just got swim suits waiting in every size so you can entertain whatever lady you have with you, huh?"

"Maybe."

Anger flares deep in my belly, boiling my skin. "That's disgusting."

He laughs, stepping into my space as his eyes descend on mine. "I called ahead and asked Marietta to go down the street and grab you one from one of the tourist shops, okay? Now, stop being such an adorable pain in my ass and get on the boat."

I chew my lip, which makes his gaze fall to my mouth.

And if the sun was hot before, it's absolute fire now.

Brandon keeps his eyes fixed on my lips as he swallows, stepping back and gesturing toward the ramp again. This time, I step onto it, making my way toward the boat with him following close behind.

I can't take everything in, it all happens so quickly. My eyes try to take in every accent, every luxurious corner of the yacht as the captain and crew greet us. They each shake Brandon's hand first, and then mine, and the next thing I know I've got a glass of champagne in my hand, a beach towel laid over one arm, and directions to a room inside that has a swim suit waiting for me.

Well, this day turned around quickly.

"Why don't you go get changed," Brandon says, nodding inside. "I'm going to speak with the captain, and then I'll meet you on the top deck?"

I shake my head, still looking around. "This isn't a boat, this is like a... home. A *mansion.*" My eyes widen when I glance over his shoulder. "Oh my God, is that a pool? A pool, on a boat." I press a hand to my forehead. "What even."

Brandon watches my little meltdown with amusement, standing just as confidently and casually as he had on the sidewalk outside the tailor.

"Trust me, it's a lot more exciting once we get out on the water. Go, change, then meet me up top."

I think I nod, though I can't be sure. I just let my feet guide me inside, following Marietta's instructions until I find a beautiful bedroom. It's like the master bed and bath of a mansion, a grand California king bed sprawled out in the middle of the room with gorgeous views out the large tinted window. A tiny, white bikini is laid out on the deep burgundy comforter, and I hold up the top with one eyebrow quirked.

"Nice," I murmur, realizing how much my tits are going to spill out of the fabric. I may not be a super curvy girl, but I'm blessed enough for my athletic figure.

When I hold up the bottoms — which might as well have been just a thong — I laugh.

But once I'm dressed in the suit, staring at my reflection in the full-length mirror fixed to the wall opposite the foot of the bed, I smirk.

"Damn, girl," I say, turning to see my tan backside before taking in the full-frontal view again. Thank goodness Erin has been obsessed with getting sun lately. The suit reveals a little bit of my tan lines from my other suit, but it fits perfectly, almost as if it was tailored for me.

Thanks, Marietta.

Tossing the towel back over my arm, I take a sip of my champagne and carry it with me as I make my way up to the top deck.

Of course, I can't get to the top deck without first passing the massive dining area, the living area — complete with the biggest flat-screen TV I've seen in my entire life — and that damn pool. There are chairs lining the edge of it, but I find Brandon casually reclining on a couch on the very top deck, his bare feet kicked up on the table in front of him and his arms lining the back cushions as he stares out at the water.

I didn't even realize we were moving, but up here on the top deck, it's easy to see the water spreading for the nose of the yacht. The blue is reflected in the lenses of Brandon's dark sunglasses, and I watch him for longer than I should before finally dropping my towel next to him.

He glances up, and when he does, I swear I see his eyes widen even through his dark shades. But he doesn't let his neck move, doesn't give away whether his gaze is roaming my body or staying fixed on my face. My cheeks warm regardless, and I cross my arms over my middle with a shrug.

"Thank you for the suit, Mr. Church."

He just stares for a solid thirty seconds more, and then he clears his throat, patting the cushion next to him.

"It's no problem. Here, sit." When I do, he holds up his glass of champagne toward mine. "And you can call me Brandon, Miss Daniels."

My heart leaps into my throat, but I hold my glass just a little away from his. "Is that only for today?"

His smile falls a little at that, and in lieu of answering, he just clinks his glass to mine.

"To secret getaways."

I swallow, holding his gaze as we both take a sip of the crisp bubbles.

And for the next hour, not another word is said.

Brandon asks Marietta to put on his playlist, which includes everything from Chance the Rapper and Kendrick Lamar to The Dirty Heads and Sublime. He sings along to every song that comes on, tapping his feet on the table, and I sprawl out on the circular couch next to his. As the sun warms my skin, and the champagne warms my blood, I let out a content sigh and soak in the day.

Sometime after I flip onto my stomach, I doze off, and Brandon wakes me with a gentle sweep of my hair off my slick forehead.

"How do you feel about some lunch?" he asks, the sun serving as a halo around his silhouetted frame.

My stomach grumbles before I have the chance to respond, and we both chuckle.

"There's my answer," he says, holding out a hand to help me up off the couch. When I slide my fingers into his palm, he tugs me up, catching me in his arms once I'm standing. His Adam's apple bobs hard in his throat, and he lets me go slowly, stepping back with a hand gesture to the lower deck. "After you."

I debate wrapping my towel around me, but leave it behind, saying a little prayer to the cellulite gods that my ass looks good as I strut inside. Brandon follows behind me, and when I stop at the sight of our lunch spread with a gasp, he runs right into my backside with an *oof*.

"Sorry," I murmur, but I still can't move. "You said lunch. I thought, like, sandwiches."

My eyes scan the massive spread, complete with what looks like a full raw bar of oysters and crab legs. There is more champagne waiting where our plates are set up, and a bowl of fruit large enough to feed ten easily makes my mouth water. I eye the juicy watermelon, the bright strawberries, the crisp grapes.

"I love how surprised you are by all of this," he says, moving past me to the table. He pulls one chair out, holding out a hand to help me sit. "Sometimes I feel like I take it for granted."

"I don't think I ever could," I say, still amazed as I take my seat, eyeing the rest of the table.

"You think that, but even when you come from humble beginnings, it's easy to get used to this kind of life. If you don't take the time to appreciate it, that is." Brandon sits across from me, unfolding his napkin onto his lap. "I'm glad you came out here with me. Makes me slow down and really take it all in, the way I used to."

"What was it like the first time you set foot on this monster?" I ask.

I go to lay my own napkin out, but it feels strange setting it across my bare thighs. Marietta seems to pick up on my discomfort, and she exits her post at the far corner of the dining area, returning quickly with a plush, beige robe.

"Oh, thank you," I tell her as she helps me put the robe on. Brandon watches every move of my body with a tense jaw, not speaking until I'm seated again.

"The first time I set foot on this, I was twenty-seven," he says. "Single, on top of the world — at least, it felt like it."

"Did you have a big yacht party with all your friends?"

He smirks, plucking a grape from the bowl between us. "Not really my style."

"You're telling me you came out on this thing all by yourself?"

He nods. "I did. We took it to... Bimini, I want to say?"

"The Bahamas," Marietta corrects from her corner. "Bimini was our second trip."

"Ah, that's right."

I shake my head, using the tongs to fish out a collection of fruit onto my own plate. I pop a strawberry between my lips, trying to imagine his life.

"Do you ever have anyone else out here?"

Brandon shifts. "I have. Clients, mostly. But, there have been friends, too."

"Female friends?" I pry.

He doesn't answer, just sips his champagne as if he knows better than I do that I don't want to hear his response to that.

My cheeks flame, and I follow his guide, sipping from my own glass. "Well, thank you for inviting me out today. This is... incredible."

And it is. I truly am thankful to be spending the day with him, especially after the week I've had. But as we talk through lunch and make our way back out to the top deck, I can't help but wonder what changed. Why the sudden friendliness, the sudden olive branch? And does it only exist here, or will he be friendly in the office, too?

More than that, can I handle being *only* friends with Brandon?

This, the laughter and stories on a beautiful yacht, it almost hurts worse than him shrugging me off in the office. At least there, I can put him in a box. The Mr. Church box. My boss, my CEO — *not* my friend, and certainly nothing more.

But now?

My mind is spinning with the confusion of it a few hours after lunch when Brandon asks if I'd like a tour.

"We're heading back toward shore, but it will take a while. We'll probably get to see the sun set over Miami before we dock," he explains as I wrap my robe around me again, following him inside the yacht. "I guess I should have started with this tour, huh?"

"It's okay, I've enjoyed just lounging on the deck."

"Me, too."

He slides his sunglasses up onto his head with those words, his dark eyes finding mine as we cross the threshold inside. I tuck a strand of hair behind my ear, trying to hold his gaze but finding it impossible to do so without leaning up to kiss him.

God, I want to kiss him.

I can feel his lips on mine like they were just there, only seconds ago. I remember the firm, yet soft press of them against mine. I remember the way he smells after sex, the way a thin sheen of sweat always gathers on his chest and abdomen after we finish. I remember the way he feels inside me, when he stretches me open.

Clenching my thighs, I tear my eyes away from his, blinking away the very not-safe-for-work thoughts.

"So, where do we start?"

Brandon takes his time, weaving us in and out of the yacht. He takes me through the entertainment areas — both dining and gaming — and out to each of the two decks I hadn't visited yet. One of them hosts the pool, while the other is a mostly-shaded bar and lounging area similar to the top deck, but with more seating.

Inside, we tour the back kitchen, the captain's post, and the crew quarters. Then, Brandon takes me through the meeting space he had designed for clients, the various bedrooms and bathrooms, and then, at the end of the tour, we're back in the first room I entered when we boarded.

The master bedroom.

Brandon pauses at the door as I wander the room, really taking it in this time around. I note the gold and burgundy accents, the way the setting sun casts a soft, orange glow over the entire room. The master bath is visible from the bed, the two rooms joined, no walls between them. I eye the large tub, wondering what it'd be like to soak in it, wondering if he's ever had another woman in it before me.

I spot a picture frame on a small dresser to the left of the bed, and I carefully pick it up, my fingers brushing over the photo inside it.

"Is this Darnell?" I ask, eyes flicking back and forth between a younger Brandon and a tall, strikingly handsome man with his arm around Brandon's shoulders. I remember Darnell from his speech at the award banquet in Atlanta, the man who took Brandon under his wing as a young kid.

They look like brothers, their smiles wide, both of them dressed in basketball shorts and loose-fitting t-shirts. Brandon holds a basketball under one arm, the street court laid out in the background behind them.

"Yes."

His voice is soft, and suddenly the vibe in the room changes. The air is sucked out with that word, leaving us in a hot, sticky vacuum where breaths are limited.

Gently placing the frame back on the dresser, I turn, pulling my robe tighter around me. There's an entire room between us, yet I feel the warmth of Brandon's breath like he's only inches away.

"Why did you bring me out here today?" I finally ask, my voice barely a whisper.

"Because you were sad. Because you needed to get away."

"Since when is my emotional state any of your concern?" I bite back, though my voice is still subdued. I shrug before adding, "It certainly hasn't been since I came back to *Okay, Cool.*"

Brandon stands taller, his eyes never leaving mine, hands still casually tucked in his pockets. "I want you to be happy, Ashlei."

I shiver at the sound of my name on his tongue, but close my eyes against the feel of it.

"That's not true."

"It is," he implores, taking one step. It's such a small movement, I almost question he took it at all. "I've always wanted that, from the moment I met you."

"No." I shake my head, opening my eyes again to find his boring into me from across the room. "If that were true, you wouldn't ignore me. You wouldn't treat me the way you do." I swallow. "You reprimanded me like... like..."

"Like one of my employees who didn't do her job correctly?"

I clench my jaw to keep it from popping open.

"I—"

"Don't you understand?" he asks, cutting me off as he walks purposefully toward me. "I *have* to do that, treat you like you're just another employee. It's the only thing I can control. That office," he says, pointing one hand back toward shore, "is the only goddamn place where I have any semblance of power over you." He takes a larger step, and then another, until he's only a few feet away. "In every other place," he says, chest heaving. "In every other time — you consume me. You *own* me."

I swallow, back hitting the curved glass of the window. My hands press into it for stability, but the next step Brandon takes puts us chest to chest. Breathing is impossible, and my knees are so weak they tremble under the weight of my body, ready to collapse.

"When I'm in my car, you're in my head. When I'm at the gym, trying to sweat you out of my system, your eyes are all I see. When I'm in my bed, I imagine your hair splayed over my pillows the way it fell over the pillows in Atlanta. And when I give in? When I finally fuck myself, and let out all the tension you cause, it's *you* I think of when I come. Your mouth," he says, reaching out to touch my lips with his fingers. I gasp, opening them just enough to taste his skin. "Your body, your tight, always-wet, always-ready pussy. It's you I think of, Ashlei. Always. Ever since I met you, and ever since I touched you, it's only been worse."

He pulls his fingers away, running his hands down my shoulders until they hook behind my elbows. Pressing off the glass, I lean into him, pushing onto my toes so my whisper reaches his ear.

"Touch me again."

He groans, letting his forehead drop to mine, our breaths heavy and heated between us. "This is dangerous. You know that. We talked about it — what people would say about you, if anyone found out."

"Who said anyone has to know?" I ask, sliding my hands over his chest. I hook my fingertips in the band of his shorts, tugging him forward, our lips nearly touching as he groans again. "That toast earlier, it was to secret getaways, right?"

Brandon blows out a breath. "It can only be here. It can only be when we're not at the office. We can't have a relationship, Ashlei."

He pulls back enough to look me in the eyes when he delivers his next blow.

"You won't be mine," he says. "And I can never be yours."

I swallow those words like knives, letting them shred permanent marks into my throat on the way down. But, despite how they hurt, despite how hard I know it will be, there's only one thought on my mind. Only one thing matters.

So, I lean in again, my lips touching his as I repeat my plea.

"Touch. Me. Again."

Then, I bite his thick lower lip, pulling it between my teeth and sucking before I release it with a pop.

Brandon full on growls, bending just enough to palm the back of my thighs and lift me. My back hits the glass, my throbbing middle presses against his solid bulge, my ankles clasp behind him, and his lips finally claim me — all of me — regardless of what he said.

I'm already his.

The burst of want that surges through me with his lips on mine is palpable, like the hot lick of a flame held only inches from my skin. I feel it crawl over every centimeter of my body, leaving goosebumps in its wake. Everything I remembered — the feel of him, the taste, the smell — it all crashes back over me like the sweetest burn.

Brandon pulls his lips away long enough to rip the tie loose from my robe. I tug it off my shoulders, letting it fall to the floor before my arms are back around his neck, pulling him closer, needing his mouth on mine again. He kisses me for just a second before his lips travel down, down, over my neck, my collarbone, to the gentle swell of my breast. One finger pulls the top away, his tongue flicking in to brush my nipple as I arch into him, and then his arms are around me again.

He lifts me, tossing me to the bed as if I weigh nothing, and with his eyes still on me, he slowly unbuttons his shirt.

"Take that off," he says, glancing at my top.

I sit on the bed, knees clenched together to fight the release already building as I watch him undo his shirt. Each button reveals a new sliver of his hard abdomen, and I keep my eyes there as I reach back for the clasp of my top. Once it's unsnapped, I pull the tie around my neck, and my breasts spring free just as Brandon tugs his shirt down off his shoulders.

He inhales deep, his tongue sneaking out to lick his lower lip as he stares unabashedly at my exposed chest. His hard-on twitches under his shorts, and his hands immediately move there next, flicking the button and pulling the zipper down in one fluid motion.

"That, too," he says, nodding to the bottom half of my bikini.

He lets his shorts fall to his ankles, tugging his briefs off next before kicking them both to the side.

And then, Mr. Church is gloriously naked, and gloriously hard — all for me.

I bite my lip, lying back on the bed and lifting my hips enough to slowly strip my bottoms down my legs. Then, I peel them off one ankle, letting them hang on the other as I lean back on my elbows and spread my legs for him.

Brandon lets out a pained breath, one hand stroking his impossibly hard erection as he stares at the wet pool between my thighs. I watch his hand roll over his shaft, his fist tightening over his mushroom tip before pushing down again.

"This is such a bad idea," he rasps.

"The worst," I moan in return, shifting my weight to one elbow. I use my free hand to spread my lips, letting my head fall back as I slip one finger inside me.

"We should stop."

My head pops up at that. "Damn it, Mr. Church, touch me. *Now.*"

And it's then that I see the power he was talking about, like I hold the handle to a leash tied around his neck. He jolts forward, one hand lifting me from the small of my back until he's between my legs, balancing on his elbows over me, my lips kissing down his shoulders.

There's no warning, no foreplay, no fingers or mouths on either of us. Just one slip of his hand between us, lining him up with my entrance, and then he thrusts inside me — hard and greedy and relentless.

"Fuuuuck," he groans, stopping once he's filled me all the way. My legs tighten around him, my nails scratching down his back to give him some of my pain. "I thought I had just imagined how tight you were."

He withdraws, flexing in again and finding new depth somehow. Each new flex of his hips has our breaths coming harder, his arms trembling around me, my legs mirroring the same pleasure as I squeeze him tight.

Maybe the fact that it's so bad to be with him is what makes it so fucking hot. He's my boss. I'm his intern. I shouldn't be on his yacht. He shouldn't have his mouth around my nipple. I shouldn't have his cock buried deep inside me.

But the things we shouldn't do were everything we wanted to do, and neither of us was used to hearing the word no.

Brandon's tongue is just as expert as I remember — the way he rolls it over each of my nipples, the thick warmth of it dragging up my breasts to claim my mouth again. He kisses me like I'm his only possession, the last thing he has left in this world — like he'll never let me go.

Pressing my hands into his chest, I lean up off the bed, giving him the signal to roll us. And when I'm on top, sitting on my throne, I glare down at him with a wicked grin before lifting off him and lowering back down. It's so slow, the pace I take, the way he stretches me open even more in the new position. Brandon's fingers dig into my hips, sure to leave bruises just like the pole did this morning, but I don't care.

"Always a tease," he whispers, his eyes rolling back.

"You love it."

Brandon spanks my ass, thrusting his hips up to meet my slow torture. The new depth elicits a loud, crying moan from me, but he doesn't stop his assault. Faster and faster his hips move, and when his thumb finds my clit, circling with just the slightest pressure, I come apart from the inside.

And I don't see stars, I don't feel numbness. No, it's like I float above my body in that moment. I see the water, the sun setting over the shore, Brandon splayed beneath me, a satisfied smirk on his lips as I call out his name with every new wave.

I am floating, so high I could never truly come back down to Earth. I'll forever exist in this new purgatory — a sweet kind of heavenly hell with Mr. Church as the only god.

Like a snap of a rubber band, my universe warps, and I'm catching my breath at the end of my orgasm, shaking as my hands reach for stability on Brandon's chest. He smirks wider, biting his lower lip, and then all the control I had is ripped away again.

He flips me, rolling me onto my stomach with one smooth motion, his legs straddling mine. Brandon palms my ass, appreciating the firmness of it with another smack before he spreads my cheeks apart. My own legs are sealed together under him, making it even tighter when he presses into me from behind, filling me to the hilt. I'm so wet from my own release that he slides right in, but I'm swollen, sated, and every inch of him feels like a mile.

"Oh, God. Please. Come for me," I plead, a mixture of pain and ecstasy ringing through me as he thrusts inside again.

He groans, balancing on his fists as his hips work. "Fuck, you feel so incredible like this. So tight. So fucking wet."

"Please," I repeat, just as he hits a new depth. "Oh, *God*."

He picks up his pace, hips working as his breaths shallow out. A few grunts, his forearms tightening, and then one last, long thrust inside me as he finds his release. He spills into me, pressing so deep I'd surely have twins if I weren't on the pill. And when he's done, his arms cave, just a little, and he lowers himself down onto me as he softens inside.

The weight of his slick, hot body presses me into the comforter, and I sigh, a smile splitting my face as pleasure rolls through us.

"Whoops," I say.

Brandon chuckles, rolling off me and onto one elbow. He watches me as I stare back under a curtain of sex hair, still grinning.

"You're impossible."

I crawl toward him, pressing my lips to his in a long, slow kiss. "And you're insatiable."

"Also true."

When I pull back, Brandon runs his fingertips over my bare shoulder and down the curve of my back, tracing a circle on my hip before dragging them back up. He watches me, eyes searching mine before he asks the question we've been avoiding.

"So, now what?"

Now what, indeed.

Erin

I've never had an ulcer, but at just twenty-one years old, I might be experiencing my first.

There's a gnawing, intense pinch in my stomach as I eye Skyler in my right peripheral, watching the waves crash in the reflection of her aviator sunglasses. She's been staring out at the water, not saying a word to any of us since we got to the beach. We're all lined up in a row — me, Ashlei, Jess, Cassie, and at the far end, as far as she can be away from me — Skyler.

We haven't spoken since Friday, since the night my plan went up in the most catastrophic of fires. Not only did Skyler have to make a public scene, including making an early exit with Adam, but Kip *also* left — which was not part of the plan. I expected him to run to me, or at the very least, to stay at the dance. I could have found him later, comforted him as he got wasted, been there for him as he tried to make sense of what happened with Skyler. I expected it to be a slow transition, but a transition, nonetheless.

But, he'd just left. He'd left without so much as a glance in my direction. And I haven't heard from him since.

And Skyler isn't talking to me either.

Cool.

It's a beautiful Sunday, one of those days in Florida where I'm more than thankful I don't live anywhere else in the country. There's a blizzard up north, meanwhile it's sunny and in the seventies here in South Florida.

In February.

I sigh, tearing my eyes away from Skyler to take another drink as Jess continues her story.

"I don't know, he's fun, and the sex is good, but..." She pauses, chewing her lip. "It's just..."

"He's not Jarrett," Ashlei finishes for her.

Jess lets out a long exhale, sucking the vodka and pink lemonade mix up through the straw in her tumbler. "He's just not Jarrett."

I smile, reaching over Ashlei to swat Jess's knee playfully. "Hey, don't overthink it so much. Do you like this guy? Greg?"

"Yes," she says, circling the lid of her tumbler with her index finger.

"The sex is good, you like hanging out, he makes you laugh... right?"

She nods.

"Well," I continue with a shrug. "Then, maybe instead of trying to distract yourself from Jarrett with him, you actually try to let yourself *date* him — like, for real. I mean, have you guys talked about that at all?"

"We haven't. And it's weird because I thought we were just kind of hook-up buddies or whatever, but we talk every day. He calls me all the time, and we hang out almost every night. He talks to me about his internship, about his family. He's really been letting me in."

"And have you done the same?"

At that, Jess frowns. "No. To tell you the truth, I'm a little scared."

Cassie glances over at us, like that statement resonates with her, but she doesn't say a word. She's been just as quiet as Skyler since the dance on Friday, and we had to drag them both out today. She watches us for a moment before watching the water again, sitting in content silence with Skyler.

"It's okay to be scared," Ashlei says, the wind blowing her hair over her shades before it whips it back again. "Dating is scary. I mean, seriously, is there anything more terrifying than showing someone your heart and just hoping they'll stick around after they see the crazy shit inside it?"

We're all quiet at that.

Jess sighs after a moment. "He did ask me to go see a movie this week, one of the new superhero ones."

"Sounds date-ish," I assess. "You should go."

She nods, chewing her cheek as if she's giving herself a pep talk in her head. "Okay. I'll go. Why shouldn't I try to move on?" She pauses. "I mean, it clearly didn't take Jarrett long to."

Ashlei squeezes Jess's knee, and I just take a sip of my drink. Sometimes, there are no words to cool the sting of betrayal, especially from someone you loved as much as Jess loved Jarrett.

I reapply my tanning oil as Ashlei changes the subject, filling us in on the terror of a coworker she's interning with this semester. I'm forming my advice for her in my head, ready to relay some of what my mom taught me over the years, but everything washes away when a shadow crosses over us and we all turn to find the source.

Kip.

In nothing but a pair of red, white, and blue board shorts and his reflective aviators, I have a hard time not letting my jaw drop the way the rest of the girls did. His hair is mussed, being continually tussled by the wind, and he tucks his hands in his pockets easily as a cocky grin spreads over his face.

"Afternoon, ladies."

I swallow, the act strained against the lump forming in my throat. I trace the sexy stubble on his jaw, let my eyes crawl over the tan skin stretched over his abdomen muscles, and when my eyes find his again, I smile.

"Well, hello there, handsome," I say, hope blooming in my chest as I hold up one hand to shield the sun streaming in from behind him. I shouldn't have hope so easily, shouldn't assume anything. He could be here for Skyler. He could ask her if they can talk.

But I can't help it, because though those things might be a possibility, his eyes are locked on me right now.

Me.

Not Skyler.

And my fractured heart can't help but hold onto that.

"You girls need a drink?" he asks, thumbing over his shoulder to where his brothers are set up down the beach. "We've got a cooler up by the volleyball net."

"We're all set, thanks," Jess says quickly, but I don't take my eyes off Kip.

And he can't seem to take his eyes off me.

He smiles. "Well, if you run out, you know where to find us." He glances at Jess when he says that, but then his focus is right back on me. "Erin, are you free tonight?"

My heart leaps up into my throat, thumping an unsteady rhythm somewhere right under my tongue as I try not to squeal out loud.

"I was thinking maybe we could catch up. I haven't really had a chance to talk to you since I got here, and before that it had been at least two years since we had a conversation. What do you think? Wanna grab a bottle of Jack and reminisce on the good ol' days of harvest?"

That hope that had popped its head up before jumps out completely now, filling my chest with a new, lighter breath. I wonder if I have literal hearts in my eyes, and I'm thankful for the sunglasses covering them — just in case.

Holy shit. It worked. The plan actually worked.

"You bring the bottle and I'll make my grandma's famous sandwiches," I say, focusing on keeping my breaths steady. "They'll be the perfect ingredients to travel back in time."

Kip nods, a smirk curving up the right side of his beautiful lips. "I can hardly wait. Pick you up at seven?"

Seven!

I need to shower. I need to do my hair. I need to pick up new lipstick. Oh my *God,* what will I wear?

"It's a date," I say, my mind racing with everything I need to get done. It's still circling and circling as Kip holds up his hand in a slight wave, turning his back on us without another word to rejoin his brothers.

Oh. My. *God.*

I turn toward the girls, finally letting my mouth pop open. "Did that just happen?!"

Ashlei and Jess smile, Jess nodding as she removes her sunglasses and gazes down the beach where Kip just walked. "Uh, yeah. Holy shit."

"I can't believe it! It *worked*, girls. It actually worked!"

Cassie is still watching the waves, but she forces a smile, glancing over at me quickly before returning her gaze. "Congrats, G-Big. Mission accomplished."

I shake my head, mouth still open as I try to process it. "I can't believe it actually worked. And I couldn't have done any of this without you, Little," I say, tears springing in my eyes as I turn to face her. I take my sunglasses off, letting my emotion show. "I mean that. I know this was so hard, and that you had to do something that made you really uncomfortable. But I..." Words fail me, and I laugh, still shaking my head. "I can't ever tell you how much this means to me, how much I needed this. Thank you, Skyler. Thank you."

Ashlei squeezes my forearm as Jess smiles in my direction, and even Cassie gives me a little quirk of her lips, though she still seems lost in her own world.

Skyler just watches me for a moment, and I wonder if her eyes are on me or on where Kip just walked behind me.

"Of course," she says after a moment, her voice soft. She clears her throat, smiling for the first time since Friday. "It was hard, but it's over now. And you got what you wanted all along. I'm so happy for you."

I search for a hint of sarcasm, but find nothing. Skyler seems genuine, her smile true, her eyes kind as she takes off her own shades.

"Thank you."

She smiles a little wider, holding up her empty cup with a rattle of the ice. "I'm going to go refill. Be right back."

"I'll come, too," Jess says, popping up with her.

When they're gone, Ashlei and I talk excitedly about what I should wear, and my mind runs wild with possibilities of what the night might hold. Will we talk all night, reminiscing about old times? Will he tell me all about his life since I left, about how he missed me after that summer, about how he's thought about me so much since then? Will I tell him about the times I called, when I never said a word, or will I keep that to myself? Will he hold me and tell me everything's okay, that he's here now, that he's back in my life for good?

Oh God, will he *kiss* me?

I cover my mouth with one hand at that, touching my lips with my fingertips and not even fighting against my smile.

I'm going on a date with Kip Jackson.

I never thought I'd ever get to say those words again, let alone say them and they be true.

But I am.

And finally, after a year of suffering, a year of nothing but regret and painful reminders of all the scars PSU has given me, I see a soft light at the end of the long, dark tunnel.

Happiness.

And it's finally within reach.

EPISODE 4

Erin

The last time I went on an actual date, I was raped.

It's a blunt and sad truth, but a truth, nonetheless.

The last time I got dressed up for a boy, with the intention of having a good time and possibly growing in a relationship with him, he betrayed me in the absolute worst way — and changed my life forever.

When I put on my lipstick tonight, I could still feel how it had smeared across my jaw that night, when Landon's hand covered my mouth, forcing me to hold in screams that wouldn't come, anyway. When I slipped into my heels, I remembered how much the balls of my feet had hurt as they bent me over the table, thighs digging into the corners, their hands pinning me in place.

Those were memories I would never shake, nightmares I would never escape.

But tonight, almost a year later, I'm finally trying again. I'm finally putting on the lipstick, and the heels, and the smile — believing for the first time since that night that my heart may be able to bloom again, that those walls might be able to open.

I'm on a date — a *real* date — with a boy I know I can trust.

It's such a foreign feeling, walking with my arm looped in Kip's as we make our way toward the small paint store. It's our third time hanging out this week, though this is technically our first *date*. On Sunday night, after the day at the beach, we just hung out at his apartment, catching up, eating my grandmother's famous sandwiches while Kip sipped on whiskey. I listened to him recount the years we'd lost between us, and he seemed to hang on my every word as I caught him up on my life. It was nothing special — no fancy restaurants or expensive entertainment — just a boy and a girl laughing and existing together.

I walked home on cloud nine that night, head floaty and stomach flipping as I replayed every look, every word, every single moment. And when he texted me, asking to see me again, I clutched my phone to my chest like a love-sick teenager. Since then, we've texted all day and all night, every day since Sunday.

In some ways, reconnecting with Kip over the last few days has felt like no time has passed at all, like we're still those same kids spending the summer together and falling in love. But, in other ways, it feels like we're strangers now — like we've only scratched the surface of everything we need to know about one another.

I love that part the most.

The thought of re-discovering Kip excites me — and I can't remember the last time something truly made me giddy with hope and joy the way being with him does. It's a little naïve, I realize, as I tighten my grip on his arm. But isn't that where love is born — somewhere between hope, happiness, and blind trust?

I decide not to overthink it — for once in my life — and focus, instead, on how his hard bicep feels under my arms as we reach the door of the art boutique. There are canvases displayed along the windows, showing local talent as well as group party projects — the paintings of everything from hot air balloons and palm tree beach scenes to abstract shapes and realistic self-portraits. I smile a little, eyes roaming the mini masterpieces as Kip covers my small hand with his when we reach the door.

"Are you sure you're okay with getting a little messy?" he asks, eyeing my outfit again.

I knew pairing high, sexy heels with my bright pink, business casual shorts was a risk. I had no idea what we were doing, but the girls all assured me I looked hot, and I figured it was dressy, yet casual enough, to pass for whatever we did.

"I'm sure," I say, leaning into him a bit with the word. "I've never done this before. Have you?"

"Nope. It'll be a first for both of us." He grins, holding the door open to usher me inside first. "After you."

For a moment, I just stand there, staring at the boy holding the door for me. Maybe it's *him* that's the real masterpiece, here. Dressed simply in a dark pair of jeans, a black, v-neck t-shirt, and a backward white-on-white ball cap, he looks confident, sexy, and cool. Add in his classic, black-framed glasses and the little grin he's giving me as he waits for me to step over the threshold, and it's all I can do to not float away.

He's the same boy I fell for, and yet so much more — like a sketch that painted itself in my absence, showing me the colors I never would have thought to paint it with.

I wonder if he can paint me to life, too.

There are a few other couples already seated in the studio when we walk in, and a bright, cheery woman greets us before the door even shuts behind Kip.

"Hi! Welcome to *The Fuzzy Canvas!* I'm Regina," she says, waving at us with one paint-covered hand. Her hair is a bright auburn, her cheeks speckled with freckles and her eyes wide, endless pools of green. She reminds me a little of Ms. Frizzle off *The Magic School Bus*, her hair wild and smile a little too big. "Take a seat wherever you'd like, and go ahead and put on an apron. We have a few others joining us and then we'll get started."

Kip and I thank her before taking the back corner seats, and as I tie a paint-splattered apron around my waist, watching Kip do the same, I smile.

"I'm really excited," I say. "Thank you for asking me out tonight."

"Of course," he answers easily. "It's been nice reconnecting this week."

"It really has been," I agree, taking my seat first. Regina brings us each a full glass of red wine, but I slide mine behind my canvas and out of sight. "You know, I wasn't sure how you would feel about me... after the way everything went down."

"What do you mean?"

I shrug. "I just, I know I didn't handle our break-up in the most graceful way. I was young, Kip — jealous, insecure. And you were the first boy I loved. It was just... I was a mess."

"Hey," he says quickly, taking the seat next to me and pulling my hands into his. He levels his aqua eyes with mine, crooked smirk falling on his lips. "We were *both* young, and I'm sure there are things we both wish we had said, or done, or maybe *not* have said or done," he adds and we both laugh a little. "But, the past is the past. Tonight, we're older, we're a little wiser, and," he says, holding his glass up. "We can drink. Legally. So, let's cheers to that."

I smile, reaching for my glass behind the canvas. I tap it to his, but instead of taking a drink when he does, I place it back in its original place."

"Not a red wine fan?" Kip asks, one brow quirked as he sets his own glass down.

"I don't really drink."

"At all?" He presses his lips together, digesting that. "Huh. Don't take this the wrong way, but that's kind of impressive — especially considering you're in a sorority."

I chuckle. "Yeah, well, I *used* to drink, but I learned the hard way how alcohol can impair judgment and get you caught up in situations you don't want to be in."

Kip watches me curiously when those words slip out, and suddenly his eyes are too much for me to handle. I drop my gaze to the floor, shaking my head and turning toward my canvas.

"Anyway, speaking of Greek life, how do you like being an official brother of Alpha Sigma?"

Kip lets me change the subject, and the conversation flows like that all night — back and forth, the two of us swapping stories in-between taking painting instructions from Regina. We're working on painting a beautiful sunset scene, contrasted by the silhouette of a tree in the foreground. When we're finished and push the canvases together, our two tree shapes will make a heart, and the birds we painted on the limbs will join each other, too.

"This is fun," I say when we're almost finished, painting a little bow on my bird's head. "I needed it."

Kip sighs, his chest deflating long and slow as he drags his fat brush over his sunset, deepening the reds in his sky. "Tell me about it."

"Rough week for you, too, huh?"

He shrugs, eyes still on the canvas. "Rough semester, honestly."

Swallowing, I dip my paint brush into our jar of water, rinsing it off as my heart ticks up speed. "That have anything to do with Skyler?"

Kip's hand stills over the canvas, his jaw clenching, but he doesn't answer. Instead, he makes a broader swoop with his brush, pressing a little too hard and creasing the canvas as he works.

"It's okay," I assure him, wiping my hands on my apron. "We can talk about it, about her, if you want. I know that must have been hard."

My stomach rolls at the reminder of what I put him through — of what I put *Skyler* through. Now that it's all over, I should feel better about it all. I should feel like I've won. I mean, here I am, on a date with Kip, reliving old memories and making new ones, too. Still, I can't help but feel like there's a curtain between us, like he's putting on some kind of performance, not letting me in completely.

I know how hard that can be to do after you've been hurt.

"Nothing to talk about," Kip says, his words curt. "We weren't official or anything. She's into Adam, I guess. It's whatever."

His words sound blasé, but the way his brush strokes grow more aggressive give him away.

"Besides, her being out of the way leaves more time for me and you, doesn't it?"

He glances sideways at me then, his smirk sexy, eyes low, and my cheeks flame at his insinuation. For a split second, my heart feels whole again — my soul reconnected to my body — and before I even realize I'm thinking it, two words slip out in an almost-silent whisper.

"Fix me."

I balk when the words hang between us — both mortified that I spoke them out loud and confused as to why I thought them at all.

Kip frowns. "What?"

Clearing my throat, I pick a small brush back up, fixing the little leaves on my tree. "Nothing, just realized I didn't do these very well."

Kip looks at my tree. "I think it's perfect. And, look," he says, sliding his canvas over to mine. Our little trees align, making the heart complete, and our birds join each other at the bottom point. "We make a pretty good team."

"We do, don't we?" I ask.

Our noses are so close, his lips near enough to mine that I feel every hot breath he takes. I lean in, just a little, hoping he'll kiss me — hoping he'll seal in this happiness with his lips and never let that hole in my heart be empty again. His eyes flick to my lips, the irises dancing back and forth before they find my gaze again.

"Oh, this is *beautiful!*" Regina says, popping up between us.

Kip straightens, clearing his throat as he drops his paint brush in the water jar and smiles up at her. "Thank you. We had a great teacher."

"Oh, aren't you sweet!" she giggles the word, swatting at his shoulder with a wide, blushing smile before moving on to the next couple.

I glare at her as she passes, the moment gone, Kip's mouth too far away from mine now.

Kip holds my hand on the cab ride home, and just like a gentleman, he walks me to the door at the sorority house as a gaggle of my sisters stare at us out the various windows. But, he doesn't move to kiss me before he leaves, pulling me in for a long hug, instead.

"Thank you," I whisper into his chest. "For tonight. It was perfect."

"I'm glad you had fun," he says, pulling back with a grin. "I'll text you when I get home?"

I nod, biting my lip. "Please do."

He goes to pull away, but I hold his hand, tugging him back. When his eyes meet mine, I push past my nerves and lean in, pressing my lips to his before I have the chance to psyche myself out.

Kip stiffens, the kiss not really returned at first. But then, his lips soften, and his hands move up my arms, one sliding behind my neck as the other cradles my cheek. The kiss is soft, sweet, nothing too passionate or earth-shattering. But it's nice.

And it's a kiss I asked for, one I wanted.

When he pulls away, Kip smirks, nudging my chin with his knuckle gently. "Goodnight, Ex."

"'Night," I whisper back, my voice light and airy as I watch him trot down the steps of our front porch.

I'm not sure how long I stand there, or what I say to all the girls waiting inside when I finally make my way in. I'm not sure of anything, really, except how good it feels to kick my heels off and flop down into the plush comforter of my bed. When my back hits it, my eyes on the ceiling, a smile splits my face in two, my stomach light and giddy.

And it's then that I realize why I asked him to fix me.

It's because I know he can.

Jess

This son-of-a-bitch.

This crooked-dick, turtle-loving, lying son-of-a-bitch.

Swiping another handful of nuts out of the bar bowl, I crunch them a little too aggressively, staring across Ralph's at Greg. Every time he laughs, flashing that ridiculously beautiful smile of his, I imagine what he'd look like if I slammed his face into the bar and he lost a few of those pretty teeth.

It may be borderline psycho bitch how long I've been here, at the other end of the bar, angrily eating bar nuts and drinking my beer and wondering when this son-of-a-bitch is going to look up and realize that the girl he bailed on is at the same place he is. This guy owes me a drink and a mind-blowing orgasm after leaving me with a serious case of the lady blue balls last week, and that was all supposed to be rectified tonight.

Except, he was "sick," and had to bail last minute.

I check for signs of illness as he pounds back another shot with a group of his fraternity brothers. He doesn't look sweaty, or clammy, and by the way he's drinking, I'd say there's no chance in hell that he has a stomachache. Nope, this son-of-a-bitch looks healthy as can be, and he also looks like he's not the least bit bothered that he lied to me less than an hour ago, or that he's left my vulva a throbbing violet for over a week now.

Bastard.

For the past five minutes, I've been trying to convince myself that it isn't worth saying anything. So what, he blew me off? Point taken. He's not interested. No big deal, moving forward, on to the next poor guy.

But for some reason, I can't let it go.

Maybe it's because I haven't been bailed on since I sprouted boobs sophomore year of high school, or maybe it's because I'm particularly sensitive after being dumped by Jarett, or hell — maybe it's just because I'm three days away from being visited by the crimson tide. Regardless, I can't seem to find the common sense or couth to keep my ass planted or get up only long enough to get the hell out of this bar.

Nope, instead, I swallow down a few more nuts, slam back the rest of my beer, and storm toward the group of Omega Chis.

They're all crowded together around a high-top table, playing various drinking games, and I have to shove a few of the smaller ones aside to reach Greg. When I do, I thrust my finger into his shoulder with a hard poke, hanging my hands on my hips as he turns around to face me.

His eyebrows are bent together at first, as if he doesn't realize who I am, and then he smiles, dimple and all. "Oh, hey, Jess."

Oh, hey, Jess?

This son-of-a-bitch.

"Didn't realize they had doctors at Ralph's now," I deadpan. "Looks like they work fast, too, because you don't seem sick at all. It's a miracle!"

I throw my hands up at that last part, not even bothering to hide my flair for the dramatic. Greg's brothers all watch me before giving each other wide-eyed looks. They go back to drinking their beers, albeit a bit uncomfortably, as Greg crosses his arms over his chest.

"What's your deal?"

"What's my *deal?*" I repeat incredulously. "We were supposed to go out tonight. We had a date. You literally told me less than an hour ago that you were sick, and then I find you here drinking like a frat boy."

"I am a frat boy."

I narrow my eyes.

"I don't get what the big deal is. I had a change of plans."

"You *lied* to me, asshole."

"And?" he asks, like I don't have a point. "Like you've never lied to get out of a date with a dude before? Come on, J-Love. I know about your reputation."

At that, a few of his brothers let out low *oooohs* and my jaw pops open. I clamp it shut quickly, face heating with rage.

Two can play this game, buddy.

"Oh, you've heard about my *reputation*, huh? Well, I wish I would have heard about yours. If I'd have known you have a dick that leans west and doesn't get the job done, I could have saved myself the trouble."

Greg's eyes widen, his hand reaching out to wrap around my wrist and drag me away from the table as his brothers burst into a fit of laughter. They're still cracking jokes when Greg pulls me into the corner near the DJ booth, his expression cold as stone.

"Not cool."

"Yeah? Well, neither is you bailing on me. What the fuck, Greg? You should have just told me you had other plans."

"Why are you acting like you're my girlfriend?"

His question stops me short, and I open my mouth to pop back at him but nothing leaves my lips.

"We met when you had a boyfriend, Jess," he says, twisting the knife more. "And we've never had that talk. Yeah, we hooked up a few times, we've had some fun, but honestly, I thought we were just friends." He shrugs. "Look, I'm sorry I lied to you about tonight or whatever, but I don't owe you anything, and I don't expect anything from you, either."

"We text every day," I finally say, though I know the argument is weak before I even give it. "And we talk about shit. And bang. How are we not in a relationship status where you at least owe me the truth if you bail on me?"

"That's not what I'm looking for," Greg says easily. "I thought it was a kind of *see ya when I see ya* thing. I have fun with you, don't get me wrong, but I don't want a relationship." He cocks one brow, lips pulling to the side. "And from the sounds of it, you *shouldn't* be in one — at least, not right now."

"What the hell is that supposed to mean?"

"Let's just cut the shit. I was a distraction for you, which I was fine with, since I'm not looking for anything, anyway. But somewhere along the way, you started lying to yourself, saying I was what you wanted when you know that's not true. We have fun, but we're not relationship material."

I swallow, crossing my arms.

"And you're not over Jarrett."

He says the words so easily, like they won't hit me like rusty scissors straight to the heart.

"Which is fine," he continues. "I'm not saying you all of a sudden should be. But, take the time to figure that shit out. If you did, I think you'd realize how crazy you're acting right now."

My nostrils flare, fists clenching as I open my mouth to show this son-of-a-bitch just how crazy I can be, but he holds up his hands quickly to calm me.

"I didn't mean that disrespectfully, okay? You're a cool girl, and that's the only reason I used that verbiage, because I know that if the *real* you — the you I met here last Thanksgiving — was here, she'd tell you the same thing. You're not yourself right now."

"Are you telling me to eat a fucking Snickers bar?"

He laughs, reaching out to pull me into a hug. I'm still stiff in his arms, my own crossed over my chest, but as he chuckles again, I soften.

"Just take a breath, okay?"

I sigh, groaning as I lean into him a little more. For a moment, he just holds me, and when he lets me go, my desire to punch him in the groin has decreased by at least forty percent.

"You're still a dick," I say, pointing at him with my index finger. "But, you're not entirely wrong. We never had any kind of talk about what we expected out of each other, and I shouldn't have assumed."

"You shouldn't have, but I also shouldn't have lied. So, for that, I'm sorry."

I nod, still grumpy as I wave him off. "Go take shots and be a frat boy."

Greg gives me another hug and ruffles my hair like a stupid older brother before he rejoins his brothers, and I pay my tab quietly, mood sinking by the second. When I'm finally in a cab heading back toward the sorority house, I sigh, staring out the window and digesting Greg's words.

That son-of-a-bitch was right.

And I hate it.

Thumbing through the pictures my phone, I hover over one of me and Jarrett, taken in bed at the hotel he booked when he came to visit last semester. I trace the lines of his smile, the stubble on his jaw, the ink splayed across his bicep where he cradles his head on the pillow. And then there's me — my smile genuine and wide, my eyes tired but sated. I miss that girl.

I miss that boy even more.

I click the side button on my phone when we pull up to the house, making the screen go dark as I pay the driver and climb out of the car. My mind is still racing as I climb the stairs, crawling into my bed as quietly as I can so as not to wake Skyler.

I thought using Greg as a distraction would help, that it would be part of my healing, but the truth is I wasn't using him to distract me — I was trying to use him to replace Jarrett.

And that's impossible to do.

I need to move on — *really* move on — and that starts with focusing on me.

So, starting tomorrow, that's exactly what I plan to do.

Bear

I can't help but chuckle as Skyler barrels toward me, her entire face covered by a scarf wrapped at least eight times from her neck to her ears. Her arms are crossed tight, brows furrowed as I swing the door to the cafeteria open when she reaches me.

"Gah!" she huffs, still bouncing and rubbing her hands together once she's inside. "How is it that it was seventy-six degrees yesterday, and then this morning, it's forty-eight?! I can't handle this."

I take my spot in line behind her, savoring the smell of bacon as we shuffle along behind the other students. It's been a while since we've met for breakfast in the old university cafeteria, but I haven't spent one-on-one time with Skyler since the semester started, and this was the only time we could both make work this week.

"Psh, Floridian. You wouldn't last ten minutes in a Pennsylvania winter," I tease.

She sticks her tongue out at m e, swiping a plate from the stack before handing one back to me. "You're damn right I wouldn't. Who wants to live in Pennsylvania, anyway?"

At that, I laugh. "Hell if I know. I got out of there as soon as I turned eighteen," I point out. And while it wasn't necessarily because of the weather, it is true that I couldn't wait to leave that state. Still, thinking about my little brother living back there makes me miss it. I wish I could be there for him while he grows up. But, he has Mac and his family. I'm grateful for that.

"My point, exactly." Skyler smiles, popping a blueberry muffin onto her tray before we split up, making our way down the buffet line.

Once our plates are piled high with more breakfast than either of us can actually eat, we settle into a small table by the window facing the library. I watch Skyler take her first bite — mostly because I can tell she hasn't been eating. Or sleeping, from the looks of it. Something has been off about her all semester, and after the shit show I heard happened at the Alpha Sigma dance, I knew she needed some Bear time.

Maybe a hug or two, too.

"So, how are you?" I ask once she's devoured half of her muffin. I keep my eyes on my plate, building a sandwich out of my eggs, bacon, and toast. "I'm still kind of pissed that we haven't hung out since Rush week."

Skyler cringes. "I know, I suck and I'm sorry. But I'm good. Counting down the days to Spring Break." She picks at the wrapper of her muffin, her long, dark hair falling in a curtain around her face. She's trying to force a smile — one she should know won't fool me. "You?"

"Cut the shit, Sky."

Her eyes grow wide, brows bending together like she doesn't know what I'm talking about.

"I know what happened Friday night... everyone on Greek Row is talking about it. So, are you going to tell me how you are — for real — or am I going to have to tickle it out of you?"

She smiles, making a joke about the last time I tickled her, which ended with her pissing herself. It was hilarious. And though the smile she wears now is smaller than her fake one — at least it's real.

Skyler chews her lip, and I just take a bite of my sandwich, giving her time to think through what she wants to say.

"Bear, honestly, I'm okay," she says on a sigh, picking at her muffin wrapper again. "I'm not good and I'm not bad, I'm just okay. That's all I can really say right now. I love you, and I know you're here for me, but I just really don't want to talk about it."

I've heard those words before.

A flash of Erin comes to mind, but I push her away, focusing on Skyler.

"I got involved in something I never should have agreed to, and now I'm paying for it," she continues, a slight shrug finding her shoulders. "It's my fault, so it would be stupid to ask for sympathy from anyone. Even you."

My chest squeezes, my next breath a sort of sigh as I lean back in my seat and force a smile. Skyler is my best friend, and hearing that she's hurting and feels like nothing can be done about it kills me — especially since she does everything she can to help her friends when they're in the same position.

Me included.

"I'm sorry, Sky," I say after a beat. "I don't know what you got yourself into, but I know you don't look like someone who just blew off a guy after using him to get back at an ex," I say, repeating what I heard happened at the dance with Adam and Kip. "You look like someone who was on the *other* end of the break-up, actually."

She shrugs, her eyes empty. "Well, there's a lot behind the situation that nobody knows."

The way her shoulders slump, the gloss of her eyes, the pain creasing her every feature — it's enough to make me want to convince her to skip school and just let me hold her all day.

Because she's lying, and we both know it.

"You like him, don't you?"

She closes her eyes, forcing a swallow.

"All that shit about Adam was bull crap. I know you, and you were over Adam the week after you broke things off."

Skyler crosses her arms over her chest, sinking down in her seat. "Yeah," she whispers. "I do like him."

I sigh. The transfer didn't seem like a big deal to me — hell, I didn't want him in Omega Chi at all. But, after getting to know him at some of the Greek events, I can see why Skyler is into him. He's cool, a good balance of both nerd and jock that we don't see around PSU very much. And, from what I could tell, he was treating Skyler like she should be treated. He liked her — a lot.

So, if she liked him, too, then what the hell is going on?

"But it doesn't matter," Skyler continues, answering my question. "Because Ex is into him and they have a past. And now they're talking, which was what she wanted from the start. So, whatever, my part is done, I guess."

I cock a brow, everything clicking into place as she talks.

"So, you were playing him for your Big?" I ask. "Shit, I should have known."

Erin is desperate for something — *anything* — to make her feel happy again. It doesn't surprise me that she would go for a guy from her past, one who made her feel good. And using Skyler? That's a no-brainer. The girl plays poker for a living. If anyone is going to be a part of an Erin scheme and pull it off, it's her.

"No one has a better poker face than you," I muse aloud.

Skyler chuckles, though there's no humor in the situation. "Yeah, well, my poker face pretty much goes to shit when I'm around him." She shakes her head. "I'm pretty sure he knows I fed him a lie, but he doesn't know the truth so he won't call me out completely. But, then again, he moved on to her pretty quickly," she points out, her expression turning sour. "So, maybe that was his plan all along, too."

Bullshit.

I know dudes, and I know the games they play when they want a chick to want them back. The biggest, easiest target to hit with any girl is her jealousy button.

"I don't think it's like that," I say, washing down another bite of food with a swig of OJ. "I mean, I don't know the kid, but I saw him at the auction and the bonfire. He put himself out there for you and, to me, it seemed like he didn't give two fucks about what anyone else thought. Including

Erin." I shrug. "I think he's just trying to get to you by talking to her now. Does he know about their past?"

Skyler nods, frowning as she considers my point.

"Well, then this is probably his way of calling you on your bluff. You said you wanted Adam all along, and maybe he knows that's bullshit, so he's pulling the oldest trick in the book to see if you get jealous."

She's still nodding, and I can hear the wheels turning in her head from across the table. "You might be onto something, Bear."

"I mean, I *am* a genius," I tease. "You should know that by now."

Skyler doesn't eat much more the rest of breakfast, and I keep the conversation light by talking about my brothers — mostly about how we can't wait for Spring Break, since we've been starved from fun on probation. I leave out the details of my horrific dating app encounters, knowing I can save those for another time, and though Skyler still seems lost in her own little world when we begin to make our way outside, it doesn't bother me.

She's been there for me when I needed her most, and I'm just glad I can return the favor.

"Thanks for asking me to meet this morning, Bear," she says when we drop our trays by the door. She wraps her scarf around her again, smiling up at me. "I've missed you."

"You know I had to check on my baby sister," I say. "Just stay away from pledges and maybe we can hang out more. I couldn't have you cramping my style before."

She punches me in the shoulder as we push through the doors outside, and even I shiver a little against the cold whip of wind. Florida winters — gotta love the inconsistency.

"Trust me," she says. "I'm staying away from boys for a while."

"Yeah, good luck with that," I say, laughing. "I have a feeling you and Nerd Boy aren't done causing drama in Greek world just yet."

"What's college without a little drama?"

I smirk, tugging on her wrist until she's wrapped in my arms. "Just be careful with that heart of yours, okay?"

"I'll try."

I squeeze her hard, and she sighs.

"Your hugs are the best."

"You're biased."

"Doesn't mean I'm not right."

I chuckle, releasing my grip. "Get to class, and text me later. Let me know how everything works out."

"I will. Love you," she says, and then she's pulling her phone out, typing out a text as she bolts across campus.

Tucking my hands in the pockets of my coat, I veer off in the opposite direction, making my way toward my Digital Imaging Fundamentals class. I only make it a few steps before I stop dead in my tracks, just a few feet away from a smirking Becca.

One hand hangs on her hip as she cocks a brow up at me, her eyes playful and wide. I can't help but return her smile, and my eyes flick to her lips as her first words ride out on a cloud of breath.

"So," she says. "Did you lose your phone, break it, or just forget how to use it? Because I *know* you haven't texted me yet because you haven't wanted to."

She's still smiling, though her neck weaves a little with each word, adding sass to her appraisal of me.

I laugh, holding up my hands in mock surrender. "It's only been a few days, I didn't want to seem eager."

"Mm-hmm," she muses, brow climbing higher on her forehead. "That was Friday, it's been five days — almost a week."

Touché.

She's right, I have wanted to text her — since the very moment she put her number in my phone next to a little kissy emoji, actually. Still, something warned me to wait, to give it time, to remember what happened last time I rushed into something without thinking it through. Sure, Becca is gorgeous — stunning, even — but Shawna was just as hot.

And that girl nearly killed me.

"You're right," I say. "I'm—"

"What was that?" she asks, stepping closer with the most adorable little grin. "Could you say it again, a little louder for the people in the back, please?"

For a moment I just stare down at her, a stupid smile locked on my face, and then I laugh, rolling my eyes and repeating my sentiment. "You're right."

"Ahh," she says, inhaling deep like my words are a delicious meal she's about to devour. "I could get used to that."

"I'm sure you could," I muse, smiling. "I'm sorry I didn't call yet, I just wasn't sure what to say."

"How about, 'Gee, Becca. I sure had a good time the other night. How about you let me take you out on a proper date this weekend?'"

"Since when am I a cowboy from an old western?"

"Just let me live out my fantasy here."

I laugh, and Becca nudges me, crossing her arms over her chest.

"I'm serious. Take me on a date. A real one, not one where you use my bar to lick your wounds from a date gone wrong and I foot the tab."

"Hey, you didn't even let me try to pay for those."

"And I told you you could pay me back," she reminds me. "On a *date*."

I nod, hands sliding into my pockets as I smile down at her. I'm pretty sure my face is going to break any second now, my cheeks hurt so much, but I can't help it. Becca is different — bold and witty, sexy yet classy. On the surface, she's everything I want in a girl.

So why am I being such a pussy about getting to know her better?

"Okay," I say after a moment. "Gee, Becca. I sure had a good time the other night."

She cracks out a laugh at my imitation of her.

"How about you let me take you out on a proper date this weekend?"

"That's better."

"How's my accent?"

"Terrible, but luckily your biceps make up for what you lack in acting skills."

I laugh again, shaking my head.

"Pick me up at eight on Saturday. There's this coffee shop by my place that has open mic night."

"Wow," I say. "A girl who not only tells me what time to pick her up, but where to take her, too. You make it too easy on me."

"Apparently, I have to, otherwise I'll be old and gray by the time you figure out how to use a phone again." She rolls her eyes, but winks at me playfully. "Now, text me, so I can text back with my address."

"I will," I say. "Looking forward to Saturday."

But she doesn't move.

"No, I mean, text me *right now*," she says, motioning to my pocket. "Because I don't trust that you actually will."

I smirk, biting my lower lip as I take out my phone and hold it up for her to see. Then, I slide it open with one thumb, text her a bear emoji, and drop my phone back in my pocket as hers pings with a notification.

Satisfied at the text, she smiles, nodding and adjusting her bag on her shoulder. "Alright, then. See you on Saturday, cowboy."

I watch her walk away, her hips swinging in a natural rhythm. Once she's around the corner of the library, I finally shake my head, making my way across campus again. I'm going to be late, but I don't give a fuck — because I have a date. A *real* date, with a girl who isn't a psycho off a dating app.

My phone lights up with two back-to-back texts from her a few moments later — one with her address, and the other with one last subtle hint for our date.

- I hate flowers, but I love donuts. Don't fuck up. -

A girl after my own heart.

Ashlei

"So, are you *actually* going to come to happy hour tonight, or are you just saying that so I'll leave you alone?" Mykayla cocks a brow, tossing her lipstick in her purse before slugging it over her shoulder. "Because this is like the eighteenth time I've asked you, and you've always said no, and I feel like you're lying now that you've said yes because it's just too good to be true."

I roll my eyes. "Stop being dramatic. I'll be there, okay? Promise." I move a hand over the stack of files on my desk. "I'm just reviewing a few things for the meeting Monday morning with our new client and then I'll be right down."

"Just come now. It's almost seven, everyone else is gone. It's *Friday*, for Christ's sake."

"I'll just be twenty minutes or so. I promise."

"Mm-hmm," she muses. "If you're not down there in an hour, I'm coming up to drag you down myself."

I laugh. "Permission granted to do so, but you won't have to."

Mykayla smiles, waving a hand over her shoulder as she rounds the cubicles and swings through the front office door. When she's gone, I sigh, kicking my heels off and stretching my sore arches out as I filter through the files.

It's been a long week, and with Kimberly still on my heels and doing everything she can to outshine me, my competitiveness is in high gear. Last week, I was slipping, falling behind on projects and just not feeling like myself. But after my run in with Brandon on Sunday and a few more pole sessions, I'm feeling back to the old me — powerful, ready to take on anything.

Including a snobby, bitchy intern.

I feel her watching my every move, especially when I'm around Brandon. After Sunday, I was hoping to steal a few glances in our meetings, or maybe pass sexy notes between the folders of our reports we passed back and forth. But with Kimberly around, it's impossible. Any time I talk to Brandon in a meeting or pass him in the hallway, I'm guaranteed to find her eyes staring back at me in the next instant. She's like a hawk, trained on me as her prey, and she's just waiting for one false step to attack.

A normal mouse might be a little weaker, a little quicker to relent. But not me.

I take notes on our new clients, making speaking points I want to be sure to remember for when we speak on Monday. It's more than I need to do right now, but if I give myself the weekend to think, I'll be ready to shine on Monday, to grab their attention in a fresh, new way. It's my hope that they'll want me as their event coordinator, the same way *Bare•ly* did last semester. If there's a full-time job opening up in the near future at *Okay, Cool,* it has my name on it.

I'll make sure of it.

"Sore?"

My heart leaps into my throat, hair standing on end as I jump in my seat at the sound of Brandon's voice. I don't register that it's him until after I've spun around in my chair, one hand pressed to my chest and eyes wide as I try to catch my breath.

He just smirks, amused.

Pushing out my breath in one long exhale, I drop my head on a laugh. "Jesus Christ. How about a little warning next time?"

"All I did was speak."

"Yeah, but," I argue, hand motioning to the otherwise empty office. "I'm supposed to be the only one here."

"Actually, *no one* is supposed to be here — you included," he points out, leaning against the side of my cubicle. His burnt orange dress shirt is unbuttoned at the top, his sleeves rolled to his elbows like usual, bottom him tucked into a pair of cream dress slacks.

So much for casual Friday.

"Well, looks like I'm not the only one breaking the rule."

Brandon drags his gaze down my neck, following the line of my necklace to where it dips between my breasts in the loose blouse I'm sporting with tight, ripped-up jeans. "We do have a knack for doing that, don't we?"

I bite my lip, ready to spout off a sassy retort when he drops to his knees, wrapping his strong fingers around one of my delicate ankles and tugging until my chair rolls toward him.

And then, he touches my foot.

I rip it back, but his grip is firm, and he eyes me from where he's bent on the floor. It shouldn't feel so right, seeing a man of that power kneeling beneath me, but *damn* does it turn me on.

"What are you doing? I've been sweating in these heels all day. Don't touch." I swat at his hand for good measure.

"Exactly. You've been in heels all day. Let me help."

Brandon presses his thumb into the bottom arch, and I moan, eyes rolling up before I try to pull away again. "Seriously, don't. They're dirty. They probably smell."

He chuckles. "They're fine. Now, sit still and let me make you feel good."

Our eyes catch, and he holds my gaze as his hands move to my foot again, this time digging deep into the arch before smoothing down over the aching ball. I moan, sliding lower into my chair and relenting.

"Good girl."

"Shut up," I murmur, but another roll of his thumbs has me groaning again, each new pressure massaging away the aches. "This might be better than sex."

"Liar."

I cock one brow. "Okay, I said *might*, don't get so huffy. Besides, if you were on the other end of this foot massage, you'd understand."

Brandon is quiet, though he smiles at that, his eyes focused on where his hands are working. I watch him, remembering what those hands felt like on Sunday, the way they lit me on fire with every touch. Just like he promised, he was all business again when we walked through the office doors Monday morning. Still, the energy between us has shifted.

Before, I wasn't sure if he was still into me, if he still wanted me. Now, there was no denying. I knew when we sat in the same room together that it was torture for him not to look at me. And I knew when I wore a skirt that was a little shorter than business appropriate on Wednesday that he was going mad not being able to touch me. And more than anything, I knew the next time we were alone — *truly* alone — he wouldn't be able to resist me.

Power is a dangerous addiction.

"So..." I say when he carefully drops my left foot to the floor, cradling my right in his lap next. The first touch on that foot makes me groan again, the ecstasy renewed. "You taking the boat out this weekend?"

Brandon glances at me from under his brows, smiling as he turns his attention back to my heel. "I've thought about it. Why, you interested?"

"Oh, me?" I ask. "I could never go on my CEO's yacht with him. I mean, that would just be inappropriate, to wear only a bikini around you, and get all *wet*."

He pauses, his hands just cradling my foot as I continue.

"I mean, even if it has been a *long, hard* week... I couldn't possibly *ride* my CEO..." I pause long enough to make him look up at me, his eyes darker, before I continue. "... 's yacht."

"I'll give you something to ride," he murmurs, but I don't even have the chance to laugh before he grabs both ankles in his hands, tugging me to the floor with him and catching me when I tumble down. His lips are on mine in the next second, one hand in my hair, the other palming my ass in my impossibly tight jeans.

"Oh, my," I gasp the words between kisses as Brandon tugs my blouse over one shoulder, licking the skin stretched over the bone. "Mr. Church, we shouldn't. We *can't*. I'm the intern, this is wrong."

"I know you're making a joke right now," he says, nipping my jaw before claiming my mouth again. "But if you haven't noticed, there are consequences for every word you're rasping out between those pretty, strawberry lips of yours."

He thrusts his hips up, letting me feel his firm cock against the seam of my jeans, and I grin, crashing my mouth back on his.

"So, you're saying these consequences are my punishment?"

Brandon growls, smacking my ass and lifting me off of him before he stands and pulls me up to join him. "I'm going to bend you over this desk and show you punishment."

"Wait!"

"Oh, no, you asked for it now," he says, smile wicked as he presses me against the edge of the desk. The pain of it shoots through me, mixing with want and desire in the best concoction.

"No, really," I pant, pressing my hands into his chest. "Not my desk. There's too much shit on it and we're going to have to pick it all up after."

Brandon pauses just long enough to let that sink in before he nods, grabbing my hand and pulling me through the office. We swing into the first empty conference room, not even bothering to shut the door behind us before he does exactly what he promised.

One of his hands grips my hair, the other hooking at the crease of my waist, and then I'm bent over, cheek to the cool, black metal of the long conference table. His hard on presses against my ass, his chest hot on my back as he sucks my ear lobe between his teeth.

"You're going to pay for that little skirt you wore Wednesday," he says. "Among other things."

"Promises, promises," I tease, but all laughter fades from my voice when one hand reaches around, flicks open the button of my jeans, and in the next instant, he pulls them down by the back loop, just enough to expose my ass. He smacks it hard, and I bite my lip against the sting of pleasure, arching my back up into him. "*Yes*," I breathe. "More."

Brandon rears back, smacking the skin again before tugging my jeans down farther. One hand crawls between my thighs, the other pinning my wrists to the table as he slips just the tip of one finger between my wet, throbbing lips.

I gasp at the feel, my knees trapped by my jeans. I can't open wider for him, can't give him better access, and he just teases me more — not fully entering, not filling the depth I ache for him to fill. Instead, that fingertip just tickles my skin, building my desire, the feather-light touch not enough.

"It's maddening, isn't it?" he rasps, leaning down to bite my neck. His finger presses just a centimeter deeper, and I moan, arching my back more as if that will force him all the way inside. "Being so close to something you want, something you desire, and yet not being able to have it?"

Oh, he's good.

That power I thought I held over him is instantly reverted back to the original owner, and Brandon claims it proudly, as if it never left his hands in the first place.

Maybe it never did.

He's the cat, I'm the mouse.

I like when he reminds me.

"Please," I whisper, squirming. "You made your point. Let me touch you. Get inside me."

"Which one first?"

"Both."

He smirks, the curve of his smile on the skin of my neck as he pulls back from the table. In an instant, I'm standing, ripping my jeans and panties down my legs in one fell swoop. I don't bother with my top, reaching for Brandon, instead. He backs me up to the table, lifting me and spreading my legs wide.

"I'll touch you," he promises, his fingertips teasing my throbbing middle again. He pulls them away too quickly, running them up my arm until one hooks between my lips. "But I'm not done punishing you yet. Lie down."

I do as he says, my ass still at the edge of the table as my head hits the other. He walks around the edge of it slowly, unzipping his dress pants and pulling them down to his knees. He stands wide once he's above me at the other end, his erection posed above me, and then he leans forward, gently grabbing my hips and pulling until my head is hanging off the table.

My instinct is to clasp my legs together but he stops me, pressing one hand onto each knee to keep me spread eagle. Then, he stands again, smile wicked as he gazes down at my mouth.

"Open."

Oh.

I swallow, heat pooling between my legs as I do as he demands, opening my mouth slowly with my eyes locked on his. But when he steps forward, the tip of him touching my tongue, all I can see is his glorious shaft, his smooth balls, his slacks stretched around his knees, his designer shoes. I take a breath and hold it as he slides all the way in, slowly, coating himself with my saliva before he hits the back of my throat.

"God*damn*," he groans, withdrawing before flexing his hips into me again. He fills my mouth, pressing into my gag reflex as I gag, my back arching off the table. "Stick your tongue out, hold your breath."

I do as he says, sticking my tongue out as far as I can and holding it there as he drives in again. He's slower this time, careful, and with the new lubrication and angle, he slides even deeper — deeper than I even knew I could fit him.

"Yes," he whispers, his voice heated. "Good girl."

Why does it turn me on so much when he says that?

I've never been dominated like this, and yet I feel no desire to pull the power back into my own hands. I want him to own me, to use me, to find his pleasure in *only* me.

"Do it again," he says, withdrawing to give me a breath. "And hold on, because this might be rough."

I nod, inhaling and pressing my fingertips into the cool metal of the table for grip as I stick my tongue out again. He cradles my neck, sliding in slow and easy, somehow deeper than before, and then he lets out a long, animalistic groan of approval.

"Fuck yes, Ashlei. God, that's incredible."

He holds me there, one of his hands tracing my throat as if he can feel himself inside it. And then, slowly, carefully, he pumps.

In and out, just marginally, his shaft stretching my throat as I hold my breath and ride out his thrusts. It's uncomfortable, yet the powerful feeling of being so desired by him, and so sexually satisfying, has me fighting against the urge to push him away. It's only when my body reacts, when a gag heaves through me that I press one hand into his thigh and he backs off, stroking my hair.

"Are you okay?"

I nod, wiping my mouth. "Yes. More."

He smiles, tracing my lips with his thumb. "That's my girl. Open."

This time when I open, his hard cock slides inside my mouth at the same time as he leans forward and slides two fingers inside my soaked pussy. I moan around him at the feel, the ache inside me growing stronger. He leans forward even more, his cock deeper in my throat, but then his mouth is on my clit.

Another moan surges through me, muffled around the fill of him as he carefully thrusts. I find a breathing pattern, slowly and deliberately pulling oxygen through my nose so as not to gag again. It's hard to do when all I want is to focus on what he's doing between my thighs. His fingers work in and out effortlessly, his tongue circling in perfect rhythm, and when I reach forward to cup his balls in my hand, his guttural groan sends a wave of want through me.

"Oh, fuck, yes, I'm coming," he grunts, and then he thrusts in one last, hard time, and I can't fight the gag as he spills inside me.

His release is warm in my throat, but I swallow it down, and the god that he is — he never stops working me. He sucks my clit between his teeth, sucking and letting me go with a pop as his fingers dive in deeper. He's still coming, his ass flexing, balls throbbing in my hand as he empties. And it's that reaction to what I do to him that makes me come, too.

I can't scream, can't say his name the way I want to as I fall apart under his touch, his cock still in my throat. I just swallow as I can, eyes closed before they burst open with the incredible ecstasy surging through me. My knees shake on the table, my glutes on fire as I squeeze, chasing my release until the very last vibration.

And when we're both sated, when the final wave subsides, Brandon carefully removes his fingers first and stares down at me one last time with his softening cock in my mouth. When he pulls it out, I gag a little, but not a drop of his release is left.

"Damn, girl," he says, holding out one hand. He helps me sit up and spin on the table before my feet find the ground, and he pulls me into him, hugging me tight before his lips press against my forehead. "You are phenomenal."

I smile, inhaling the scent of his cologne on his collar as I blush. "And you are a sadist. That wasn't just punishment, that was downright torture."

"You loved it."

I can't even argue that.

When both of our pants are back on and the conference table wiped down, Brandon walks me back to my desk, watching me pack up my purse.

"Come stay with me this weekend."

I smile. "On your yacht?"

"If you want. Or my apartment, or a hotel, or a fucking hotel in Paris. Where do you want to go?" he asks. "Just say it, and I'll take you there."

My eyes find his, flicking between the golden hue of them, trying my damnedest not to fall in love. Because that's what I feel, I recognize, every time I'm with him. I feel desired, and wanted, and safe, and cared for. And if I'm not careful, I'll make more of this than I should.

"Anywhere?"

"Anywhere."

I smile, shaking my head as I toss my purse strap over my shoulder. "Happy Hour."

He balks.

"You said anywhere," I remind him, one finger extended. "And Mykayla is literally going to burst through that door in five minutes to drag me down if I don't show up."

"I can't go with you."

"Sure you can," I say. "Stay up here another half hour and then casually show up. They'll love it, getting to spend time with you outside of the office."

"Sounds like more work. It's the weekend."

"It'll be *fun*," I promise him, leaning up on my tiptoes to plant a kiss on his lips. "And I'll be there."

He groans, conceding though he makes it seem like I'm twisting his arm. "Fine. And after? Will you come home with me then?"

At that, I press another kiss to his lips, sauntering off with him still standing at my cube.

"If you behave."

I throw him a wink over my shoulder, blowing a kiss before I push through the glass door.

Bear

Just as promised, I show up at Becca's dorm at eight on the dot Saturday night — box of donuts in hand. She smiles when she opens the door to greet me, tapping the lid of the box with one nude fingernail.

"You remembered."

"I already screwed up once, figured I wasn't ready for strike two yet," I say, and she smiles wider, taking the box from my hands and depositing it on a small table near the door behind her.

As she says goodbye to her roommate, I shamelessly check her out, starting with the ample curve of her ass highlighted in a pair of high-waisted, bell-bottom pants. They're a thin fabric, flowy at the bottom and too tight for church at her hips. When she swings around, joining me in the hallway, I step back enough to let her out, but don't stop my visual assault.

I'm blatantly staring at the way her simple white crop top hugs her rack when she crosses her arms, pushing them up a little more.

"Either you haven't been laid in a long time, or you're not used to a girl with curves like me," she muses.

My eyes flash to hers, meeting her cocky smirk with my own.

"Both. Definitely both."

She laughs, threading her arm through mine as we make our way down the hall and out into the fresh, cool night. Her earrings jingle a little as we walk, and she watches me from her peripheral as I take in her natural hair, styled in a beautiful afro and framed by a unique headband.

"The coffee shop is just a few blocks down and around the corner," she says, smiling and keeping her eyes forward. "Unless you'd rather just stare at me all night instead of watching the open mic."

"Sorry," I say, but it's an insincere apology. I'm not sorry at all. "It's just, you're unlike any other girl I've seen. That sounds lame and cliché, but I don't really know how else to say it. You're just... strikingly beautiful, Becca."

"Oh, stop it," she says, swatting at my arm playfully. Then, she leans in and whispers, "Tell me more."

We both laugh.

"So, no working at the bowling alley tonight, huh?"

"My one Saturday off in the past three months," she says. "Hence why I was so adamant about you taking me on a date."

I chuckle. "Yeah, definitely can't say that you're subtle."

"Never promised to be." She winks, tightening her grip on my bicep a little. "So, Bear-er-Clinton, why the hell were you on a dating app?"

I smile at her reference to me telling her what my name was the night we met.

"Honestly, I have no fucking idea. My fraternity brother suckered me into it, said I've been grumpy lately due to my lack of..." I almost say pussy, catching myself at the last second. "*Dating*."

"He said you needed to get laid."

"He did," I admit on a laugh.

"And why haven't you had a lady friend in your bed in a while?"

I scratch the back of my neck, a little uncomfortable at how fast the conversation has gone toward my lack of sex in the past year. "Let's just say I was getting it on a regular basis, but then circumstances changed."

"You were dumped."

"Technically, I did the dumping, but yeah... same shit."

I feel Becca watching me as we round the corner, and I shift to the other side of her so I'm walking on the edge closest to the street. That earns me a smile.

"Ah, I see," she says after a moment. "So, you had a girl break your heart, decided *fuck that shit*, and swore off every other girl."

I clear my throat. "Kind of. I was hooking up with this one girl, not exclusively or anything, but it didn't last long."

"Probably because you were still hung up on the other girl, huh?"

I stop, turning to face her as we reach the coffee shop. "It's like you've read the book on my love life."

Becca snorts, both eyebrows raising. "Well, let's just say I could have wrote it."

"Someone break your heart, too?"

Her face falls then, and she shrugs. "We've all had our hearts broken, and probably done some breaking, ourselves. But, I'm not focusing on what the past has held for me anymore," she says, decidedly, her chin lifting and her eyes finding mine. "I like how the future looks better."

I smile, eyes washing over the beautiful angles of her face highlighted under the neon buzz of the coffee shop logo.

"Me, too."

I gently guide Becca inside the shop with a hand at the small of her back, keeping it there until we find an empty table near the front corner of the stage. There's a young guy with long, blond, almost dreaded hair playing a set of bongos as we find our seat, his raspy voice fitting in the cool vibe of the shop. Our waitress stops by to take our order with a smile, and once coffee is on the way, I take the time to look around.

It's like a psychic and a hippie got married and made this place their love baby.

The menu is filled with tea and coffee of all different flavors, each with its unique, "star-given" name. The wall is covered with photography from around the world, mostly in shaded hues of sepia, and behind those photos hang large, yoga-inspired tapestry sheets. The ceiling is dotted with tiny, luminescent lights that give the appearance of us being under the stars, and with the lights dimmed low other than the spotlight on stage, Becca's face glows in a mixture of warmth and shadows.

"You come here a lot?" I ask, still taking in the décor. There's a faint scent of burning wood and essential oil, likely from the incense lining the bar.

"At least a couple times a week," she answers, waving to one of the bartenders. "It has a great vibe, doesn't it?"

I shift in my chair. "It's... interesting."

Becca chuckles. "I take it you're not really connected with spirit and the universe, huh?"

"Not particularly."

"Well, don't be scared. I won't force you to get a tarot card reading or anything."

I smile, leaning back a little in my cushioned chair as our waitress drops off our orders. I opted for coffee, but Becca chose tea, and she pours the steaming hot water from the little tea pot they brought her as I consider my next words.

"I'm surprised you haven't asked me my sign yet."

"Oh, I don't have to. I already know."

I balk at that, watching as she dunks the little bag of herbs into the hot water. "Bullshit. How?"

She smiles, eyes on her tea. "It's in the way you carry yourself. You're practical, very grounded. You seem to think before you speak or act, and you're aware of how your actions affect those around you. You're not necessarily an *overly* caring person, because you watch your own back, but you also don't intend to run people over in your path. It's not that you don't have emotions — because you do — but you're not ruled by them, you don't let them deter you from your main focus."

I shift.

So far, she isn't wrong.

"You're a bit shy, a little reserved, but at the same time, open to the possibilities around you." She continues, chuckling. "Like going on horrendous dating app dates, or meeting a weird girl in a hippie coffee shop."

I smile. "Hmm," I muse, thinking over her assessment. "So you think you have me all figured out, then?"

"No, not even close," she says quickly, slipping her fingers around the handle of her mug. "But, I know enough to hope I get to discover more."

Well, that was adorable.

"You never did say what you think my sign is."

"Capricorn."

I blanch, lifting my coffee for the first sip. "That's pretty impressive. And what's yours?"

"Pisces."

"I'll have to research the sign to figure you out."

She lifts her tea, taking the first light sip. "Or, you could just get to know me yourself. It's way more fun than reading astrology books, I promise."

"Oh, that I don't doubt."

We both pause our conversation to clap as our friend on the bongos finishes up, and a soft music fills the shop as they prep the mic for the next performer.

"Tarot card reading, huh?" I ask, taking another drink of coffee. It's warm and nutty, with just a touch of cinnamon. "You must do that all the time."

"I do. Tarot cards are fun, they help you when you're navigating through trying times, when you have a question or are unsure about a path to take. But, my favorite, personally, is palm reading."

"That so?"

She nods, sipping her tea. "I had mine read at a young age, and I've had follow-up readings. I loved it so much I actually studied it so I can do it on my own."

"Wait," I say, holding out my hand in a pausing motion. "You're telling me you read palms?"

"I do."

I raise my brows, setting my coffee down and propping one elbow on the table before handing her my right palm. "Do me."

She cocks a brow back. "Right here? Now? I think we might get kicked out, but I mean, I'm not opposed."

I smirk, shaking my head at her joke, though I can't deny that my dick hardens at the thought of her mounting me right here and now. "My palm. Read my palm."

"I don't know if you're ready for that," she says.

"Humor me."

She narrows her eyes, taking one more sip of her tea before sliding it to the side and grabbing my hand in hers. "Okay, but don't say I didn't warn you."

I watch Becca as she studies my palm, taking any excuse I can get to study *her*. As much as I wouldn't mind having her ankles hanging over my shoulders as I plow into her, I oddly find myself wanting to just stay up all night *talking* to her, instead. What makes her mind tick? What was she like as a kid, what does she want to be as an adult, who broke her heart, and where does he live so I can break his fucking face?

Or thank him, because now, she's sitting here with me.

I don't believe in love at first sight.

To me, that's ludicrous. I barely believe in *love,* period, let alone in falling into it without knowing someone.

But, something inside me shifted the night I met Becca, and I feel that same stirring now as I watch her brow crease in concentration, her eyes flying over the different lines on my palm. It's like a cold pool of water in the depths of my chest, coming to life as hot water mixes in, warming me from the inside out. It's like finding something I never knew I lost, something I forgot about, or maybe never even realized existed.

It's like a strange recognition, an unfamiliar thing I knew all along.

"So," she says after a moment, scooting forward in her seat. "The first thing I notice is that you have an earth shape to your hand, which makes sense, considering how you're an earth sign. With palm reading, it signifies to me that you've been shaped a lot by what has happened to you — more so than anything you've learned from, say, reading, or school. You've learned by living."

I nod, the truth of that sinking in deeper than she could ever know.

She goes on to assess three different lines on my hand — the "head" line, the "life" line, and the "heart" line. And while I walk into the reading skeptical, I find myself leaning more and more into her as she traces the lines on my hand, telling me what they speak to her. She points out how the shortness in my head line tells me that I prefer more physically demanding tasks, and that I throw myself into physical work when I have difficult decisions to make or when I'm hurting. That wakes me up, the truth of it so real it sends a tingle down my back.

On and on she goes, pointing out how my life line tells her that I keep distance and caution in my relationships, and also that my heart line indicates that I have difficulty expressing my feelings, even when I'm aware of them. Each new word from her lips has me reeling, my wheels spinning as I conjure up example after example of how her assessment is true. Am I reaching for this stuff, or is she actually onto something? I can't be sure, but all I know by the time she grins up at me, watching the different shades of confusion on my face, is that she's an incredible girl.

Weird, but incredible.

"So, what do you think?" she asks as they announce the next performer — a young girl who will read slam poetry.

"I think that's some crazy shit."

She laughs. "It is. There are more lines, too, but I'll go easy on you for this first one." She furrows her brows, pulling my hand back to her. "Wait. There is one other thing here... it's kind of troubling."

"What is it?" I ask, leaning forward.

"Well, see the way this line curves?" she asks.

I nod, focusing on that line as she continues.

"It's troubling, because that tells me that there's someone in your life you've wanted to kiss, but haven't. Someone you want to touch, to feel, but you've refrained. It's a terrible, pent-up energy, and it should be rectified immediately."

I let out a soft laugh, shaking my head at my embarrassing eagerness, which only makes her teasing funnier. When my eyes find hers, she smirks, the light glossing off her irises.

"Real smooth."

She shrugs, waiting, and I lean across the table, lifting my palm from her hands. My thumb finds her chin, tipping it up just a bit, and then I close the distance between us, pressing my lips to hers.

There's a curve in her mouth during our first kiss, a sweet smile that permeates into my own lips like honey. She giggles when I break away, just marginally, enough to lick my lips and dive back in for more. It's a kiss I never could have had with Shawna, or Lacy, or any other girl. It's a kiss reserved for books and movies, for sappy, romantic guys who don't refer to girls as bitches and fantasize about banging them the first time they meet.

What's happening to me?

I vaguely recognize that I should care, I should give a damn that my chest is light, my heart kicking as her hands wrap around my neck. She pulls me in closer, nipping at my bottom lip, and suddenly that ravaging beast inside me is awake again. He kicks the sappy bastard who preceded him out in a flash, and I slide my tongue along the crease of Becca's lips until she lets me inside. Our tongues swirl, a soft moan leaving her mouth for mine, and as the performer begins her first poem, we back away, our breaths heavy between us.

"What does my palm say now?" I ask, offering her the same hand.

She blushes, tracing one finger down the middle of it before tapping it twice. "It says you need another coffee, because it's going to be a *long* night."

Now *that's* a future I can get on board with.

Skyler

My mother told me about Murphy's Law when I was seventeen.

I still remember that day — how I'd woken up late, missed the bus to my field trip and had to stay back while the rest of my classmates went to a local museum, then I'd broken my sandal, having to use duct tape to temporarily fix it for the day. When I got home, thinking that the bad day was over, I discovered that I had lost my wallet somewhere between school and home — and it had all my babysitting money in it. The final straw was when Mom brought me my laundry later, showing me one of my favorite shirts with a rip in the side from the washing machine.

That's when I'd lost it.

Mom held me as I cried, soothing me as she told me about Murphy's Law, about when you just have a day where nothing can go right. But, she said the best thing about it was that I would go to bed, and the day would end, and I'd wake up to a fresh new start tomorrow.

I'd thought that was the worst day ever, thought I knew how bad Murphy's Law could get.

But today proved me wrong.

Kip is on my heels as I storm toward a waiting cab outside the downtown casino, and I slide in without a word or a glance in his direction. My eyes focus somewhere beyond the glass, on nothing in particular, as I try and fail repeatedly to calm my racing heart.

I blew it.

I blew a tournament that I should have easily won, not only missing out on the opportunity to stack up my savings for the entry fee in Vegas, but also giving the tabloids plenty to write about. I can already see the headlines.

Skyler Thorne on Tilt at Local Tournament — Pressure Too Much?

I sigh, leaning my head against the back of the seat. It bounces a little as Kip climbs in next to me, and I'm reminded that now I have to share a ride home with him, with the guy I want to blame for everything tonight, even though I know it's my fault.

I can't look at him when he shuts the door behind him. I can't do anything but sit there and wonder how the hell this all happened.

Last week after my breakfast with Clinton, I'd gone straight to class to find Kip waiting for me in our usual spot — with a coffee for me in hand. It had become a running joke between us, him trying to guess what kind of coffee I drink — which is ironic, considering I only drink hot chocolate. But after the dance, I figured that would stop. Hell, I figured he wouldn't even *look* at me, let alone invite me to sit next to him.

But he'd been there, and he'd acted like nothing was wrong. In fact, *he'd* apologized, told me he understood my feelings for Adam and respected them, and asked if we could be friends.

Friends.

I laugh a little, my breath hitting the cool glass at the fog. How naïve I was to believe I could go back to being Kip Jackson's *friend* after having his tongue down my throat.

But for some idiotic reason, I'd agreed — and not just to being friends. He'd also asked me to do the tournament tonight, telling me it would be good practice, and a great way to make some cash for the entry fee. He wasn't wrong, but honestly, this tournament wasn't even on my radar until he suggested it.

I'd said yes as if I had nothing to lose.

Maybe it was because I didn't want to lose *him*.

Selfishly, I wanted to hold onto him — however I could, even if it wasn't the way I wanted to. I told myself this was better than nothing, that being with him in any capacity was better than not having him at all.

Wrong.

So, so wrong.

If I hadn't figured it out when my stomach rolled every time he came to the house for Erin over the past week, or how I felt like throwing up when I saw her name pop up as a text message on his phone, then I definitely got my reality slap to the face earlier today at the gym.

There I was, just minding my business on my way to spin class when I saw Kip in the weight room. He was already dripping sweat, his arms and chest bulging as he did reps, and for a while, I just stared. That's when I first realized it. I felt a rolling wave of something unfamiliar, yet something I placed immediately.

Mine.

The thought had crossed my mind unashamedly, and I didn't even take the time to process it before I jogged over to him, ripping his headphones out of his ears and making light conversation. That's what we'd been doing since we had our truce. The conversation stayed surface level, nothing deep, nothing too emotional.

But he'd flirted with me.

His eyes couldn't stay off my cleavage in my workout tank, and I'd felt that heat of his gaze all the way to my core. Trying my best to shift the conversation into safe territory, I'd asked him if he wanted to take spin with me to get in some cardio. He'd smiled, that same sexy smirk I'd come to love, but his words were delivered like a bullet to the chest.

"I got in plenty of cardio earlier, trust me."

It was a casual enough response, but the implication behind it was murderous. He'd been with Erin this morning. I knew because she'd come in from seeing him high as a kite and giddy as a lottery winner. If he'd gotten in cardio, I was pretty sure I knew exactly how he'd done so.

And that was it.

That stupid, ridiculous scene was what threw me for the rest of the day. I bailed on spin class early, dodged across campus, and let myself stew. Then, when it was time for the tournament, I'd dressed in my classic jeans and black hoodie and I'd settled into my pre-tournament rituals like I had a shot in hell of getting out of my head and into the game.

Fat chance in hell of that.

Kip didn't even glance at me in the cab as he told the driver the address, and I couldn't blame him. I'd been nothing short of sassy to him all night long. From him trying to coach me before the tournament to him slipping up and saying my name in the bar, getting me roped into an interview with a reporter who overheard him, I made it clear that Kip wasn't welcome in my head that night.

Or in my heart.

It's only when I close my eyes and take a deep breath, trying to reconcile with the fact that the tournament is over and there's nothing I can do about it, that I realize *which* address Kip gave the driver.

My eyes pop open.

"Wait," I say, turning to Kip. "She needs to take me home first. It's on the way."

"You're coming home with me tonight."

My cheeks betray me in a blush, but I use the heat to fuel my anger. "What? Um, no," I correct him. "Not happening."

I lean forward, ready to spout off my address to the driver when Kip's hand reaches for my elbow.

"Damnit, Skyler, you're coming home with me or I'm going to call that reporter and tell her I was the guy from the bonfire."

My eyes widen, stomach sinking at the headlines that would run with that. Lacy, the reporter from earlier, had asked if Kip was the guy I'd been caught kissing at the bonfire. We'd played it off, me making a joke about it being cute that she thought I was only kissing one guy. I told her I didn't even remember his name, and Kip played along.

If only that were actually true, maybe I wouldn't be in this mess.

"And I can tell her way more fun stories about you than what she got earlier," Kip finishes, his threat clear.

My mouth pops open, something between disbelief and intense hurt passing through me. He wouldn't do that to me, would he? I mean, I knew I hurt him at the dance, but he wouldn't put my career on the line...

Right?

"You wouldn't do that," I challenge.

Without so much as a second of hesitation, Kip pulls Lacy's business card from his pocket, holding it like a weapon between his fingertips.

I just stare at that little card, wishing I could set it on fire with my gaze, and then I throw myself against the seat like a child throwing a tantrum.

"You're a Class A douche right now."

"You can insult me all you want, but you're still coming home with me."

"Why do you want me to come home with you, anyway?" I argue, crossing my arms over my chest. And before I can stop myself from the pettiness, the next words slip out. "Wouldn't you rather call *Erin?*"

Kip isn't phased in the slightest.

"I'm not asking you to come home with me for sex, Skyler," he chastises, like I truly am a child throwing a fit. "I'm your friend, and whether you want to let me or not, I'm helping you get ready for May and we need to talk about tonight."

I barely register the last of his explanation, because I'm too busy focusing on the first blip that came out of his mouth. I gave him a chance to prove me wrong, to ask me what the hell I was talking about when I referenced how Erin should be the one he's calling for a late-night booty call. Instead, he'd only proven my suspicions right.

He's had sex with Erin.

That bullet from before is lodged somewhere in my throat, making it impossible to swallow. Bile rises anyway, my stomach churning. But as much as I want to break down and sob, my poker face is in full effect.

We pull up to Kip's apartment, and I whip around to face him fully as the driver brings us to a stop.

"You aren't *asking* me anything," I remind him. "You're blackmailing me."

I throw open my door, the weight of it bouncing off the hinges before I stand and slam it shut again. Leaning down to glare at him through the window, I steady my voice as much as I can to deliver my final blow.

"And it's so nice to know that if it were Erin here, it would be for sex. Sorry I'm cock-blocking your *cardio* plans."

Then, I storm off toward his apartment, realizing I've just cornered myself and admitted I'm affected by who he has sex with.

Fuck.

So much for my poker face.

***

Kip is hot on my heels when I reach his apartment door. I try but fail to open it, huffing like my flagrant annoyance and anger will save me from the fact that I just put my foot in my big, stupid mouth.

Before that moment, Kip had no idea why I wasn't on my game tonight. It could have been anything — a sorority event, my family, school. But no, I just lit up a bright neon sign that said *he* is the one on my mind, the reason I'm so off, the reason I couldn't keep my shit together and win the tournament.

I'm supposed to be into Adam — *that* was the role I agreed to play. That's what Kip is supposed to think. And if that was the case, then there is absolutely no reason I should be upset about him being with Erin.

I'm not supposed to care about him.

I *told* him I didn't care.

And now, I've fucked everything up.

"Skyler," Kip says my name again, out of breath as he jogs up the last of the steps after me.

I cross my arms over my chest defiantly. "Just open the damn door."

He huffs, shoving the key in the lock and swinging the door open. "What the fuck, Skyler?" he yells when we're inside, tossing his keys on the table by the door. His hands run through his hair next, pulling a little like I'm driving him mad. "Why are you mad at me?"

My eyes skirt to the bedroom, to the bed where Kip put his hands on me.

The same one he fucked Erin in.

Ugh.

"You wanted this, didn't you?" he presses when I don't answer. "We're friends. You have Adam, and I've moved on. I haven't made this weird. I didn't hold what happened against you and I didn't make shit awkward. I moved on and you got what you wanted, because clearly Adam wants you."

His voice cracks a little at that.

"I see him texting you every fucking day, and he's always talking about you. This is it." He tosses his hands up, letting them slap against his thighs when they land again. "You asked for this. So, why does it matter who I'm fucking?"

And there it is.

I assumed before, and after his admission in the car, I may have been reaching. But with those words, I know with absolute certainty.

I'm not allowed to care that he's fucked Erin. That was the plan, that was what I signed up for.

I'm not allowed to care.

But that doesn't change the fact that I do.

"Let's just drop it, okay, Kip?" I beg, crossing my arms over my middle to try to suffocate my urge to vomit.

One quick glance at Kip has me wishing I could sink into the floor and disappear. He's just standing there across the room, arms outstretched, chest heaving as he watches me under bent brows. He's sporting a light green t-shirt, one that sets his icy eyes ablaze in the low light of his apartment.

He's absolutely beautiful.

And absolutely off-limits.

"Let's just talk about the tournament," I try. "And then we can both go to sleep and clear our heads."

"No." The word is more of a growl, his jaw tense when it leaves his lips. "Fuck that."

He takes a few steps toward me and I instinctively back up, finding the wall with my back and then my palms.

"I don't know what fucking game you're playing," he spits. "But I'm calling it tonight. Why do you care about me and Erin?"

"Kip, please..."

"You broke me that night, Skyler."

My chest tightens at the rasp in his voice, the earnest honesty. He moves closer, and I pin my bottom lip between my teeth, willing it not to quiver. I roll my eyes up toward the ceiling, fighting against the urge to cry, to break and tell him everything.

Kip taps his fist on his chest. "Everything I felt between us," he says, voice thick with emotion. "Everything I *know* is here, you told me it didn't exist. And you know what? I knew it was bullshit. I *knew* it. The words were coming from your lips, and it was your eyes I was looking into as each one slammed into me, but it wasn't *you* I was hearing. So," he says. One step closer. "Now's your chance to tell me — why do you care?"

I shake my head as tears blur my vision. Kip takes another step, the warmth from his chest warming my own.

"Was it Erin?"

All I can do is focus on each breath. In and out, inhale and exhale.

Do not cry.

Do. Not. Break.

But one tear breaks loose, scarring my cheek with its wet betrayal. It might be an invisible scar, but I'll feel this tear forever. And that's the thing about scars. They're like skid marks on the highway. No one slows down enough to see the painful proof that something happened. But the road? The road will always remember. The road can't forget, no matter how many times it's repaved.

"Was it?" Kip repeats. "Or was it that you were starting to feel something, too?"

I swallow, my eyes on his, trying and failing to meet his challenging stare with my own.

"I know you, Skyler," he whispers. "I know who you pretend to be in front of all these people." He sweeps his hand behind him, toward campus. "And I know who you *really* are."

His eyes soften a little then, and he leans forward, the electricity sparking between us. I focus on his eyes, willing myself not to notice the thick bulge of his neck, the tightness in his biceps, the heaving of his chest.

"I know the you who doesn't fit in because you were never meant to. You were *born* to stand out. You want to pretend like you're untouchable and nothing can phase you with those people? Play around with a few frat boys, dress up in frilly dresses and keep your reputation? Fine," he says. "But don't sit here and feed *me* that bullshit. I see you, Skyler. I. See. You."

His hands find my arms, tenderly, but I jump anyway. His cool palms slide up, slowly, covering me with goosebumps as he runs them over my shoulders, my neck, until my face is cradled between them. More tears fall, landing between us as I keep my chin high and my eyes on his.

"Why do you care?" he asks again, his voice low.

"I don't."

"Liar."

My entire body trembles as I lick my lip and pull my eyes to the ceiling again. My next confession slips out in a whisper, a solemn admission I wish I didn't have to make.

"I don't want to."

"But you do."

I can't answer. I just swallow, closing my eyes and setting two new tears free.

"This is a no-limit game, Skyler," Kip says. "Neither of us went into it thinking we would be here, but now we've got everything on the table because we're both too stubborn to give in. I raise, you call. You raise, I call." He shakes his head. "Back and forth, always in this fucking game. You want to win? Fine. Take it. Take everything I have, but I'm not the one who's going to walk away the real loser."

I can't breathe. My chest squeezes, my breaths like fire instead of oxygen in my lungs.

"If you don't wake up and realize what you're feeling — what *we're* feeling — is real, then it's you I feel sorry for," he says, taking a tentative step back. His eyes never leave mine. "It's *you* who loses."

His words are an ice bucket of water, poured over an already trembling me, the truth of them permeating my skin like they'll forever be a part of me now.

Kip turns, throwing his hands up and letting them rest on his head as he faces the door. For a moment, I just watch his back, the ebbs and flows of the muscles as he breathes. I feel sick as I squeeze my eyes shut, holding back the sob stuck tight in my throat. My next move isn't clear — not even close. It's like staring into murky, black water and trying to find the one and only shiny penny on the bottom.

He's right.

We are in a game, and if he knew everything I've done to play this hand, if he knew about Erin, about the deal, he would hate me.

Which is why I can't tell him.

And though my stomach sinks at that, at a truth I have to bury away and never let him see, my hands stop trembling. My breaths come more even as I open my eyes, lifting my gaze, and the endless flow of tears halt.

Because I'm done playing the game.

I can't imagine it, moving on without him, walking away like I don't give a damn. I can't imagine a world where his hands don't touch me, where his eyes don't light up at the sight of me, where I'm not the one responsible for that sexy smirk.

Kip is mine. He has been since the moment we met.

And I can't just walk away.

Not even for Erin.

"I care," I say quietly, weakly, like a prized fighter tapping out in a choke hold. "I've cared about you for *so* long."

Kip doesn't face me, but his shoulders pull back, his stance straightening.

"I care that I hurt you, I care that even though I did, you still stuck around, and yes," I admit, pushing away from the wall until I'm standing straight, too. "I care that Erin was here, that she was in your bed, because I don't want anyone else in your bed but me."

The dam doesn't just crack — it crumbles, the once solid walls tumbling down and letting everything out that I'd fought to hold back.

"I don't want anyone else in your *arms* but me," I continue. "I want to be the only girl in your head when you wake up and I… I was petrified, okay?" My stomach twists. "I thought if I told you I wanted Adam, you would leave me alone. I thought you'd be pissed off and you'd be out of my life completely and I wouldn't have to worry about feeling this. And on the beach?" I shake my head. "I actually *wanted* you to be with Erin. It made sense. I figured it was your plan all along."

Kip scoffs at that, still not facing me.

"No, I'm serious. It makes sense." My insecurities float to the surface, and for once, I don't cover them with a cocky façade. "Compared to her, I'm nothing. And I was happy for you. At least, that's what I told myself. But I don't know what to do, Kip, because I *do* care about you." I swallow. "But I can't."

"Why?" He finally faces me, and his aqua eyes are still wild, their intensity locked in on me.

"It's complicated."

What more can I say without telling him the truth?

Kip watches me for a beat, and then a long, frustrated sigh breaks through his flat lips. He takes one step toward me, then another, shaking his head as he descends. "I didn't have sex with Erin, Skyler."

My heart skips.

"I don't *want* Erin," he says, his strides more purposeful. He's so close, and he isn't stopping this time. "It's *you* I want."

My back hits the wall, his chest meeting mine, hips pinning me where he wants me. Every breath that leaves my lungs threatens to never return.

"And less than three weeks ago, you stood in that shower and told me you wanted me, too. So stop being scared, stop caring what other people think, and for once in your life, take what you want."

My eyes flick to his lips, their demand still hot on my ears as I press forward, closing the distance between us and slamming my mouth on his. We both inhale a breath, long and sharp, our hands reaching, pushing, pulling, all the want and need pouring out of us in one passionate flood.

And I don't just fall into him — I leap.

I jump, head first, more sure than I've ever been that this is right, no matter how wrong it feels. I can't think of Erin, or of what I'll do tomorrow when I wake up and realize all that I've said that I can't think back.

All I can think, all I can see, all I can *feel* is him.

That electricity that sparked between us when we shared our first kiss roars back to life, its energy so powerfully overwhelming my knees buckle from the shock of it. Kip is there in an instant, leaning into me, his hands rounding over my hips until they cup my ass and lift. The force of him pinning me to the wall steals my breath, but I wrap my legs around him, pulling him closer, needing more.

My fingers claw at his shirt, the breaths heavy in my chest as the hunger builds to an impossible level. He pulls it over his head effortlessly and lets it fall to the ground before his eyes meet mine.

And we both stop.

I see the questions, the uncertainty, the wonder if he's going to wake up to an empty bed again. And right now, I can't promise him anything, so I don't speak. And he doesn't push.

We both know what this is and what it isn't, and that's enough.

I grab the bottom of my hoodie and pull it over my head, taking my small tank top with it. Kip's eyes fall to my chest and I feel his hard bulge between my hips. Moaning at his reaction to me, I grab his neck and pull his mouth to mine again. The first time Kip touched me, I was caught off guard. I was timid and afraid and overwhelmed with guilt. Now, I still know it's wrong, but I don't care. I don't feel ashamed. I don't feel guilty.

I just feel… alive.

Kip thrusts his hips into me, kissing his way down my neck. When he bites down, I hiss with the mixture of pleasure and pain.

"Fuck, Skyler," Kip growls, his scruff against my skin making me shiver. "If you keep making noises like that, this is going to be over before it even starts."

Our breaths are hard, our skin slick with sweat. Warning bells sound in my head — or are those church bells? I can't decipher if they're joyous or haunted with warnings of danger.

"Hang on, let me grab something," Kip says, starting to drop me to the floor.

I shake my head, wrapping my arms around his neck tighter. "I'm on the pill."

"Thank fuck," he groans, pulling me in his arms and moving us quickly to the couch. He throws me down, towering over me, lust rolling off him like steam.

I lean up and make quick work of the button on his jeans before tugging them down and over his hips. They fall to the floor, exposing Kip's more than ample bulge straining against his cotton boxers, and I groan with appreciation. Slowly, I run my hands up his thighs and palm him through the fabric, his head falling back as a deep groan escapes his throat.

Last time, it was him who pleasured me, who brought me to ecstasy with his hands alone.

Time to repay the favor.

Moving my fingertips to the band just below his waistline, I tug them down and his erection springs free, sending a warm pulse of need between my thighs. My eyes find his again as I move my lips to his head, slowly swirling my tongue around the tip before running it along his length.

"Fuck," he whispers, dragging out the word. I take it as my cue and suck harder.

Blow jobs have always been my gift, and it might as well be Kip's birthday tonight.

He curses again as I pull him all the way into my mouth, feeling myself grow wetter at the taste of him. I want to devour him completely, to banish every other woman from his memory with my mouth.

Grabbing his ass in both hands, I pull him into me forcefully, his dick hitting the back of my throat. He curses louder this time and pulls out quickly before lifting me to my feet, his eyes wide and wild like he was close to coming, like if he hadn't yanked me to my feet, this would have all been over already.

I smile up at him wickedly, licking my lips and wiping the corners with my fingers.

He runs the pad of his thumb along my bottom lip, shaking his head. "You know exactly what you can do with this mouth of yours, don't you?"

Slowly, he runs his hand down the front of my body before tucking his fingertips in the band of my jeans.

"Take these off."

I do as he says, kicking them to join the rest of our clothes piling up around us. Before I have the chance to look at him again, his mouth finds mine and his hand slips beneath the lacy fabric of my panties. He dips two fingers inside me quickly and I moan against his lips, my legs weakening at the touch.

"I've got some talents of my own, you know." He grins, working his fingers as his palm rubs against my clit. My breath is already labored, my body dangerously close to the edge of release.

Kip uses his free hand to unclasp my bra and sends it flying across the room, an expert move I didn't expect, and it only fuels my desire more. When one hot hand palms my breast as he continues his assault between my thighs, I moan.

"Goddamn, you are so fucking wet, Sky."

Desperate, my hands find his cock again and I move in time with his fingers inside me. Our breaths mingle together, both of us wide-eyed as the heat builds. So long I've wondered what this would feel like, what it would do to me if I just threw caution to the wind and gave in to my need for him.

Now that I know, I know there's no going back.

Kip removes his fingers without warning, spinning me around and using his palm to push my upper back down and bend me over the couch. His hands run down my hips and over my ass, hooking my panties with his fingers and pulling them down to just above my knees before letting them fall.

I look back at him, completely exposed in this position as he kisses the backs of my thighs, his eyes locked on mine with reverence. When he stands, he grips himself in one hand, using the other to slide a finger inside me again. I bite my lip and let my head fall back and he quickly withdraws and grabs my hair instead, tugging it with force.

When he positions himself at my entrance, my breath catches, every inch trembling with the need to feel all of him. I'm so far past what's right and wrong I can't even see the line anymore. I just breathe him in, the need to be under him, to be claimed. Arching my back, I push my ass against him, the tip of his dick just barely slipping inside me.

Kip groans at the feel of it, and I hiss as he tugs my hair again, gripping it in his fist.

"I'm going to take you, Skyler," he husks. "But I need you to know that once I do, I'm going to own you. You're going to be mine. This game between us? The rules are going to change."

"Take me," I whisper, the words leaving my lips before I have the chance to decide if I mean them or not.

"Is that what you want?" He tugs my hair a little more, his lips by my ear now. I feel his breath hot on my skin and chills race down my body.

"Take me, Kip. Now."

He growls, biting down on my neck before pushing inside me — not slowly, but all at once, like a man on a mission to take back what's his. I cry out as he fills me, again and again, my fists gripping the sofa as the pleasure pulses through me. Kip releases my hair, his hands trailing down my back before gripping my hips. He slams into me harder, pushing deeper as my orgasm builds.

"God, you're so beautiful, Skyler," he breathes, his breath strained. "So fucking sexy."

I don't even attempt to hide my moans now and they ring out in his apartment, the sounds echoing off the walls as we move. He leans down and palms my breasts in his hands, pulling me up and against him. Moving slower now, he kisses my neck as his hand falls to my clit. He applies just a little pressure but it shoots straight through me, my entire body igniting at the touch.

I moan louder, my breaths uneven until he finally pushes me over the edge I've been dancing on with him since the first moment we met. His mouth finds mine and I moan into his lips as I come, my legs shaking against him, all of my weight supported in his arms. Waves of heat roll through me and every sense is dulled, my orgasm owning me completely.

Just like him.

"That was so fucking hot," Kip says, kissing down my neck before flipping me over. He grabs my hips and lifts them to meet his before pushing into me again, before my orgasm has even fully resided. The intensity throttles me, every nerve jumping to life at the sensation of him stretching me open again. He's even deeper now, my hips elevated as he pounds into me.

His eyes cascade over every inch of my body as if he can't get enough of me, as if he's never seen anything he's wanted more. He's the musician, and I his muse — the one he's been chasing his entire life.

He palms my breasts, pushing into me once more before he finds his release with a groan and my name on his lips. His eyes roll back and I drag my nails down the muscles flexed in his arms as he comes inside me, our bodies trembling together.

And for one, blissful moment, we're sated and complete.

Then, my anxiety rears its ugly head like it never truly left at all, but just watched from the corner, waiting to pounce as soon as the pheromones were gone.

I reach up and pull Kip down on top of me, kissing him hard as we come down from the high, like those punishing kisses can band all other thoughts. But as our breaths begin to even out, the weight of the night folds in on us.

Kip wraps me tighter in his arms, pulling me into his chest as if he feels it, too. As if he's trying to protect us from the inevitable reality we have to return to.

My fingertips slowly run the length of his abs and chest, leaving a trail of goosebumps in their wake. He runs his fingers through my hair and we both submit to our thoughts, nervous to say anything out loud.

"Kip," I start, but he pulls me in tighter, shaking his head.

"Not tonight, Skyler. Just... let's not ruin tonight."

I nod, nuzzling into him more.

We know that when the sun rises, it'll shed light on everything the darkness consumed tonight. Silently, we consider what that means.

We both know what this is and what it isn't.

But the question remains – can we live with that, or is it time to change the rules?

***

"Wake up," a voice says.

I stir a bit, the soft sound of rain pattering against the window as I stretch. Soft lips touch my shoulder and my eyes flutter open. I smile as Kip kisses up my neck to just behind my ear, my entire body coming alive at the touch.

"Mornin'," he says, pulling back and resting on an elbow. The shadows from the rain on the window dance over his skin and I stare in awe, mesmerized by his effortless beauty.

Suddenly, it hits me.

Everything that corresponded between us last night flashes through my head and I blanch, eyes wide in horror as I bolt upright.

Kip frowns, sitting up with me, one hand reaching out to touch me. I pull the sheets higher, covering myself, my eyes darting around the room for my clothes.

"Don't do that," he says softly, shaking his head. "Don't look at me like you just made a mistake."

I try to make my face change, to relax my breathing, to find the calm that I had last night but I can't. Kip's expression looks pained as he rolls to the other side of the bed, his feet hitting the floor. He runs his hands through his hair.

"Fuck, Skyler."

"No, wait, just..." I lean up, relieved when I realize I'm wearing his shirt and I'm not naked like I thought. Slowly, I crawl over to Kip, tucking my hands under his arms to place them on his chest as I plant small kisses on his back. He stiffens at first, but each kiss unties the knots of tension just a little more. "I'm sorry. I don't regret last night. I don't."

It's true, I don't regret it, but I still know that I should. Erin is one-hundred percent into Kip and falling faster than the first time and I had sex with him. Worse than that, it wasn't a one-time thing. I knew it last night, Kip knew it, too – and we both know it right now.

Something changed last night.

The presidency aside, my relationship with all my sisters is at risk now. I broke girl code.

And I just wish I was sorry about it.

I pull away, sighing as I move to sit next to him. "I don't know what to do," I admit, glancing over at him.

He turns to me, worry still laden on his face as if he's battling with his own guilt. Maybe he does care about Erin? Or maybe there's something else behind those furrowed brows.

"If I told you I was an asshole, that I'm going to end up hurting you and this is all going to end just as fucked up as it started, would you hate me? Would you leave?"

I bite my lip, the bluntness of his words slamming into me like a club. *If only he knows.*

"Am I stupid if I tell you I don't think it's possible for me to hate you?"

He sighs, as if he knew I'd answer that way and it makes him hate himself even more.

I shrug, leaning down to look into his eyes again. "I already tried."

His hand finds mine and for a few moments we just sit there, staring ahead and letting the rain pour down outside. Finally, Kip speaks again. "I'm going to call things off with Erin."

I nod, feeling a mixture of guilt and relief. I don't want him to be with Erin. "We still need to keep this a secret for a while," I say, gently rubbing his fingers between mine. "I think after a while, Erin and my sisters and just everyone in general will be okay with us being together. But right now, it's going to be too obvious. Erin would know we hooked up when you were together. She would hate me. Everyone would hate *us*."

"I'm not with her, not the way you're putting it, anyway. I'm going to make that clear to her, too," Kip says quickly, turning to face me. "And why does it matter what everyone else thinks?" He's saying the words like he wants us to be together now, but there's still something in his eyes that tells me he's not sure that's what he wants, either.

"It's not that easy, Kip. They're my sisters and I'm in line to be the president next year. I can't lead a sorority of girls who don't trust me." My eyes fall to the floor. "Plus, Erin is my Big. We've had some issues this year but I love her, I don't want to hurt her."

Her face flashes in my mind, the girl who convinced me to rush Kappa Kappa Beta, who held my hand and helped me change everything I wanted to change about myself. I went from nobody to one of the most popular girls on our campus. She was instrumental in that transformation.

And I've betrayed her.

Kip nods, sighing as he reaches out and pulls me into him. "I know, I'm sorry. You're right. Laying low for a while is a good idea. I'm sure Adam would be pissed, too. You need to figure out what to say to him."

I roll my eyes. "Ugh, I don't know how he hasn't gotten the clue yet. I've barely spoken to him. He texts me every minute of the day, it feels like."

That's been the most surprising part of this, how eager Adam has been to talk to me, to get inside my head. He's been trying to get me to talk to him about what's really going on since the dance. Not that I can blame him, after what I said, but he and I *both* know that we could never be more than friends again. We tried, and it just doesn't work. Hooking up a few times? Sure. But past that, nothing exists.

I should have just told him I was drunk, that I didn't mean what I said about still being into him. But with Erin breathing down my neck and watching every little piece of her puzzle closely, there was no way.

I had a part to play, and up until last night, I'd played it perfectly.

Best poker face in the game.

A smile curls on Kip's face. "Is it bad that I kind of look forward to seeing his face when he realizes you're with me?"

I nudge him playfully and he pulls me in tighter, laughing.

"Just saying, he thinks you played me to get him back. It's going to be sweet revenge to prove that assumption incorrect."

I roll my eyes again and Kip pulls me back onto the bed quickly, wrapping his arms around me. I laugh and push at his shoulders but give in too easily, not really wanting to get away from him in the first place. His smile fades slowly and his eyes search mine as he moves a strand of fallen hair from my face.

There's a storm brewing in those blue eyes of his, but I can't figure out if I should be afraid or excited for the rain to pour.

"Stay with me today," he says, leaning up on one elbow.

I nod in response and he leans down again, pressing his lips to mine.

The rain sounds softer now, replaced by the internal buzz I feel when Kip kisses me. I've decided he's one of those kissers who really takes his time. He runs his hands through my hair and moves his lips slowly against mine, his tongue sweeping in at the perfect time to cause my breath to catch. He touches my face, my neck, my lower back. When it's natural, he catches my bottom lip between his teeth, tugging just enough to make my stomach flip.

Kip kisses me like I'm a goddess, like he's lucky to even be near me, let alone with his lips on mine.

And with Kip, I *feel* like a goddess.

Beautiful.

Invincible.

Immortal.

But the truth is, I'm not a goddess. I can break. I know that, and yet I'm still here, wrapped in the arms of the one who could shatter me into pieces.

I guess I should start praying now.

Erin

"Are you okay?"

I blink, those words oozing over me like sick, poisonous slime.

How many times have I been asked that, if I'm okay, like that's the only way to be? To live? Do I not deserve to be happy, or elated, or glowing with indestructible joy?

The answer to that question, it appears, is no. I am forever destined to exist somewhere between okay and not okay, never surpassing, never able to exist in a state of being that surpasses that purgatory.

Okay, or not okay.

And right now, I am *not* okay.

Kip watches me, his brows furrowed, hands folded over mine between us. He just broke up with me — if you can even call it that, seeing as how according to *him*, we weren't even truly dating.

Since when is making out, going to dinners, seeing movies, hanging out and talking for *hours* not dating? Since when is holding my hand and walking me home not dating? Since when is texting me all day, every day, not dating?

My nose flares as a new wave of anger washes over me, but I hear my mother's cool, calm voice in my head.

Hold your power, baby girl.

I smile, though it's weak on the inside. "I'm okay," I lie. "And, I understand."

"You do?"

I nod, clearing my throat and pulling my hands from his. "It was all a little fast. Maybe we can start over, go slower. Start as friends."

Kip nods, but his face folds, like he already knows there's no way he'll ever be with me. My stomach turns.

"Yeah, friends. I like that plan."

I smile again, but it falls too quickly. "Well, I have to run. Panhellenic meeting soon. I'll see you around? Spring Break is just a few days away."

"Yeah, it'll be fun," Kip says, standing with me, but his brows are still pinched together in concern. "Thanks for being so cool about this, Erin. Are you sure you're okay?"

That fucking word.

"Mm-hmm." I pull my purse strap over one shoulder. "Bye, Kip."

I don't linger on his eyes, or his strong, square jaw as I turn and strut away from him, my kitten heels click-clacking across the tile floor of the coffee shop. He couldn't even "not-break-up" with me in private. No, he had to do it at Cup O' Joes, where everyone could see, where everyone could watch me do everything I can to hold it together when all I want is to fall apart.

If I broke, if I just gave in and slumped down into a pile of nothing on the floor, would anyone help me stand again? Would anyone pick up the pieces?

Clinton would.

The thought passes like a flash of lightning, strong and shocking and gone in an instant, leaving only the roll of thunder in its place. I swallow, shaking him from my thoughts as I make my way across campus, back to the sorority house.

"Okay, Erin," I whisper to myself, holding my chin high. "New plan. That's all you need, a new plan."

I think over everything Kip said, how he told me things didn't feel right, that he wasn't interested, and he thought we should just be friends. I scour our text messages, our dates, looking for some sign I missed — but I come up empty. He'd seemed interested, touching me when we were in public, kissing me when we were alone, rubbing my shoulders and losing afternoons with me as we watched movies and caught up. He even listened to me talk about sorority drama, which I knew was torture for any guy.

So, then, *what happened*?

I chew my cheek, the methodical click and clack of my heels soothing my thoughts.

Maybe he's just scared, freaked out by how much he's feeling. I've heard of guys backing out for that reason more times than I can count. Maybe he likes me so much, he doesn't know how to deal.

But when I round the corner onto Greek Row and see Skyler on the front lawn, I pause.

Of course.

I watch her throw back her head in a strong laugh, she and Jess soaking up sun rays on our front lawn. They clink their plastic tumblers together, sipping a light pink liquid, and I laugh out loud at my stupidity.

It's her.

It *has* to be her.

All of a sudden, out of nowhere, Kip breaks up with me. And all of a sudden, out of nowhere, Skyler is back to her happy-go-lucky self after weeks of sulking.

Something happened.

I can't believe I didn't see it, can't believe *they* were stupid enough to think I never would.

Skyler's laugh reaches my ear, and I clench my fists, forcing a smile as I straighten my back and find my pace again. Kip mentioned something about him helping Skyler with a tournament on Friday night, and my bet is *that* is where something happened — where something changed.

I smirk.

They think this is over? They think I'm going to just lie down, roll over and forget any of this happened? That I'm just going to move on, and maybe *one day* they can date, and I'll be just fine?

As if.

I'm Erin Xander, and I decided almost a year ago that for the rest of my life, I would take what I wanted — just as others had taken from me.

And I want Kip Jackson.

I'll get him back. There's no question, no doubt in my mind. They may think I've played all my cards, but I'm smarter than they give me credit for.

Kip loves me. He did when we were kids, and he still does now. Once Skyler is out of the way, he'll realize that.

Now, I just have to sit and wait for the perfect time to play my ace.

Game on.

EPISODE 5

Ashlei

Spring Break.

It's the Holy Grail of college, the one week every student looks forward to. For seven, blissful days, there are no exams, no homework, no fraternity or sorority events, and, though I haven't decided if it's a good thing or not yet — no internships.

So, it's no surprise to me that at the end of my last day in the office before break, I get called into Mr. Church's office.

I made sure I was the last one to leave again today, knowing it would be my last chance to see Brandon before I left. I also made sure to wear a skirt that's just a little too short, and a little too tight, and my hair up in a clip that I know he's dying to unfasten so he can see my hair spill over my shoulders.

After our last weekend together, I've got him under my spell.

And he's got me under his.

I tried to tell myself before that it was just our dynamite sex keeping us entwined, but after spending two days in his luxury downtown sky-rise condo, I couldn't lie to myself anymore. Brandon didn't just fuck me and then kick me out the door. No, he made me breakfast, and took me out on his boat, and rubbed my feet after a long night of dancing in the VIP section of one of his favorite clubs. He drove me to pole practice Sunday evening, kissing me in the car where the tinted windows hid us before watching me leave, knowing we wouldn't touch again for a while.

But this is what we signed up for, this cat and mouse game, this hiding in the shadows romance. For now, at least while I'm his intern, it's the safest bet. Not that he would lose his career, but his reputation might suffer for a while if he were discovered. And me?

Well, I'd be fucked. As in, all up in the booty hole, no lube, kind of fucked.

That should be the loudest thought in my head as I walk quickly and purposefully across the office toward his door.

I should be thinking of someone catching us, of what would happen if we had to pull footage off these cameras for some reason, what I would do if everything I've worked for at *Okay, Cool* came crashing to the ground — all because of my sex life.

But I can't.

All I can think about is his white dress shirt, top three buttons unfastened, sleeves rolled like they always are at the end of the day. All I can see is his dark, wicked eyes watching me as I ride him in his office chair. Slowly, step by step, the closer I get to his office, the more he overtakes every sense.

He's poison dressed as a delicious apple, and I'm powerless to resist temptation.

I have to have a bite.

I smooth my skirt and brush my hair out of my face as I near his door, rapping my knuckles just twice on the frame when I reach it.

"Mr. Church?" I ask innocently, batting my lashes. "You wanted to see me?"

Brandon smirks, kicking back in his chair and letting his eyes roam me shamelessly.

"I did. Come in," he commands, and that's the way his voice always is — demanding, deep and powerful and impossible to disobey. "Have a seat."

I do as he says, making a show of crossing my legs, one stiletto hanging between us as I fold my hands in my lap. Brandon eyes that heel, tracing the arch of it before his eyes flow all the way up my legs to my skirt.

They snap to my eyes next.

"I know you've been focused on Spring Break," he says, "But it's come to my attention that you're past due on a very important task you were given." Brandon pauses, his eyes growing dark. "You know I'm not a fan of missed deadlines."

Immediately, I scan through everything I'd had on my to-do list for the week, knowing there was absolutely no way I left anything off. But as Brandon's grin grows wider the more I pinch my brows together, I realize his accusation is part of the game.

He does love to play boss.

"Oh, my," I breathe, feigning disappointment in myself. "I'm so sorry, Mr. Church. It's just been such a busy week, I couldn't get everything done. But I'll make sure to handle it first thing on my return."

Brandon rests his elbow on one arm rest, twirling a pen between his fingers as he watches me. "I'm afraid that won't be enough, Ms. Daniels."

Why does that work for me? Why does him using my last name, talking to me like I'm just the intern, and looking at me like a hot apple pie mix into the perfect concoction to get me wet? When we're alone, in his apartment or on the boat, the way he makes love to me is reverent. It's slow and romantic, calculated and pure, like a slow Sunday morning bang every single time.

But here? In his office? Or on his jet? He's Mr. Church, and I'm Ms. Daniels — and we both know which one holds the power.

"I'm sorry," I breathe again, biting my lower lip and leaning forward enough to show a hint of cleavage. I hold my eyes open wide, my head tilted down a little as I look up at him through my lashes. "Are you going to punish me, Mr. Church?"

When the word *punish* leaves my lips, Brandon's eyelids flutter a bit, his nose flaring. And when I use his favorite name, the one that holds that power, he shakes his head, a lustrous gaze fixed hard on my mouth.

"I'm afraid I have no other choice."

His hands shoot out, grabbing the armrests of my chair and tugging until my legs are between his. As soon as those hands move from the chair to my thighs, sliding up the sensitive skin to spread me open, I reach for the collar of his shirt and pull his mouth to mine.

We both exhale the moment our lips touch, Brandon's hands still steadfast on their mission to reach my center. His pinky finger brushes the lace of my thong and I moan, bucking my hips, ready for more.

Always ready for *so* much more of him.

And he delivers, slipping one finger under the lace when I lift my hips again, a ragged *please* escaping my lips. But before that finger can dip all the way inside me, before that void is filled, Brandon's eyes widen at something behind me. He yanks his hand back like he's touched fire, his face ashen, and when I glance over my shoulder, I regretfully understand why.

"Well, well, well," Kimberly says, tongue pressing into her cheek as she glares at us with a satisfied grin. I thought I hated seeing that spiky hair and messy lipstick every morning, but it's nothing compared to the sinking stone I feel in my gut looking at her now.

Shit.

She crosses her arms over her chest, casually leaning a hip against the door frame. "I would say I'm surprised, but I called this from day one."

"Ms. Marks, it's after hours. You shouldn't—"

"I shouldn't *what,* Mr. Church?" she asks defiantly, chin raised high. "Please, I'm *dying* to hear you tell me what *I* shouldn't be doing right now."

At first, I swear I see Brandon shrink in size, his shoulders deflating a little like he's ready to accept defeat. But I know this man, and I know he doesn't react to someone trying to exert power over him well.

Unless it's me. And I'm naked.

"You shouldn't assume things," he finishes, standing.

As soon as he does, the power shifts, like the wind switching directions mid-storm. He stands so tall, so straight, his eyes on Kimberly like she just interrupted a meeting instead of walked in on him with his hand up my skirt.

"It's late, it's been a long week, and it's Spring Break. You should go," he says calmly, and I pull energy from him, straightening my shoulders and smiling at Kimberly like she has nothing on us, even though we both know we're in deep shit. "And consider the consequences of your actions, or your words, should you choose to utilize either."

Kimberly swallows, her confident stance weakened for a split second before she shakes her head, that wry grin back in place. "Oh, I will. Trust me when I say I will." She snaps her menacing gaze to me next. "Your days are numbered, slut."

She turns on the heel of her suede pumps, and damn it if she doesn't keep the cocky swing in her walk all the way to the front office doors. When they close behind her, the relief I thought we'd find once she was gone isn't there. In fact, the air is thicker, coated with a hot, wet heat like the Florida humidity — sticky and heavy and uncomfortable.

I just close my eyes, finally letting out a long, weighted breath.

"I'll fire her."

Brandon speaks first, his words punctuated and sure.

"I'll fire her immediately, have her manager call her tomorrow and tell her not to come back after Spring Break."

"You can't fire her," I say with a sigh, kneading my temples.

"I can, and I will."

"No." My voice is louder, eyes hard when I tilt my chin up to find his gaze. "That's a law suit waiting to happen, Brandon. There are cameras, and logs of our key access into the building. She'd have too much against us, and then you'd really put your career — your business — in jeopardy."

He shakes his head, frown firm. "I don't care. She can't take me down."

"She could, if you fire her," I quickly correct. "But if you just wait and let me handle this—"

"I can't *wait,*" he says incredulously, dropping back into his chair with a huff. He reaches for my hands, pulling them into his own with his eyes locked on mine, brows bent. "Don't you understand what this means, Ashlei? This could... this *will* ruin you. If she talks, if she tells *anyone*, you're in danger. Me?" He shakes his head. "I'll be fine. Even if you left, even if I had to submit to a slew of rumors or whatever, this is my business. *I* make the rules. Sleeping with the intern wouldn't hurt me. Hell, the guys would high five me, and the women would probably ask where the line is to be next."

The truth in his assessment stings like a slap to the face, and I swallow, nodding in agreement.

"That's all true. You would be fine, but my name, my reputation would be damaged. I wouldn't be able to stay here," I say quickly. "And, if I left, I'd have to go somewhere far enough away that they don't know about *Okay, Cool...* or what happened... *is happening* between us."

"So, out of the southeastern United States," he says gruffly, a curt shake of his head. "No. Absolutely not. We have to do something. I can't let this... I can't let *her...*" his voice fades, and he swallows hard. For the first time since his speech in Atlanta, emotion strangles him — all because he can't bear the thought of me being hurt.

Am I allowed to swoon right now? Because... SWOON.

"I know," I say, squeezing his hands. "I know. But, I think I have a plan."

"You do?"

I nod, the thought still forming in my head, like a caterpillar wrapping itself in a cocoon.

"But, you have to trust me," I say, forcing him to meet my eyes again. "And you have to wait."

"*Wait,*" he says, already shaking his head again. "We can't wait. She could run out and tell someone tonight. She could be telling someone right *now.*"

"She could, but she won't. Kimberly is smart," I say, believing it more when I say it. "And she's calculated. She's been waiting for this, to get something on me, to prove what she's always suspected — and she's not going to waste it as soon as she has it by just telling anyone who will listen. No, she's going to sit on it, and she's going to come up with the perfect time to take me down."

"And when would that be?"

I swallow, almost smiling at the obviousness of my enemy. "The staff meeting on Monday. That's when they're announcing who the event coordinator is for the project we've been splitting. If it goes to me, which we both know it will, she'll do it then."

"Fuck!" Brandon runs his hands over his head, kicking back in his chair. "I hate this. I fucking hate this. I'm so, *so* sorry, Ashlei. I shouldn't have—"

"Don't," I cut him off.

Brandon swallows, his eyes searching mine.

"Don't tell me you shouldn't have touched me, or kissed me, or made me feel the way you have. I've been happier in the past few months with you than I have the past few years before I knew you existed," I admit, voice rough. "And I'm not letting some *girl* set on taking down a fellow female co-worker because of her own insecurities ruin that."

For a moment he just watches me, his eyes softening as the left side of his mouth quirks up in a soft smile. He rolls closer to me, framing my cheeks in his hands and planting a long, sweet kiss on my lips.

"You're amazing, you know that?"

He rests his forehead against mine as I smile, the heaviness gone if even for just a moment.

"Okay, I won't fire her," he concedes, as if that was still an option on the table. "What's your plan?"

I don't have the full answer to that question yet, but as it forms slowly in my mind, I see it playing out the way I want it to more and more clearly. It will take patience, and courage, and the timing has to be perfect. With one wrong move, or one mistake on my assumption of my opponent, everything I've worked for could go up in a dumpster fire.

"Simple," I say, trying to convince myself of the same. "We beat her to the punch line."

Bear

"How do you look like this," I ask Becca, one hand sweeping over her ridiculous physique, "when you eat donuts like *that*."

She bites off another hunk of the maple bacon donut she's devouring, grinning at me as much as she can with her mouth still full. Her eyes are shielded by round sunglasses, straight out of the seventies just like everything else about her, as we people watch on a bench in front of the fountain. I leave for the Spring Break cruise tomorrow, and it's my last chance to see her before I go.

On a shrug, she licks the frosting off her fingers and swallows. "Donuts don't count as calories."

"Tell that to the gut you're going to give me if I continue eating them with you." I pat my stomach — still hard as stone under my t-shirt.

She laughs. "Whatever. Pretty sure you could eat twice as many donuts as I do and not workout for three weeks and you'd *still* have that six-pack."

"What makes you think I have a six-pack under here?" I lift a brow. "Not like you've seen."

"Not like I haven't *tried* to see," Becca counters with a sassy head swivel. She opens up wide for the last bite, wiping her hands together and sending dry glaze all over the cement beneath us.

I don't have anything to retort to that. The fact that I've been dating Becca for almost two weeks now and we haven't hooked up is a miracle. The fact that she's *wanted* to and I've insisted we wait is a goddamn oxymoron. I'm Clinton Pennington — fucking is one of my favorite hobbies. But, everything feels different with Becca, and after Shawna, I know how fast *different* can turn into *gut-wrenchingly painful*.

"You'll see it soon enough."

"Mm-hmm," she grumbles, clearly not convinced.

"You will," I promise. "Trust me, I want to do..." I shake my head, eyes roaming down her body and back up again. She's wearing a bright orange dress, modest at the top but so short I know just a few more inches would reveal everything I want to see. "*So* many inappropriate things to you. But, I've never done slow before," I confess. "And, honestly, you're the first girl I've wanted to try with."

At that, Becca smiles, nudging me with her shoulder. She doesn't lean away again, but stays close, her skin as warm against mine as the sunshine. "Don't think saying cute shit like that is going to get you out of banging me for very long."

A laugh bursts out of me.

"I mean it," she continues, poking me in the chest. "I want the goods."

"Oh, you'll get them."

She crinkles her nose, pressing up on the bench until her lips meet mine. That first touch is always overwhelming to every sense, and for a moment I'm paralyzed, just breathing and kissing the most beautiful girl in the world. Then, my hands find her hair, and I pull her closer, realizing again how much I don't want to let her go — not even for a short cruise.

When she pulls back, Becca's eyes catch on something behind me, and she cringes. "Damn, poor girl."

I turn, searching the courtyard until I spot a girl with a mess of shit at her feet — books, pens, highlighters, planners, a Diet Coke can — the contents of that sprayed all over everything else on the ground. She huffs, letting her head fall back before dropping to her hands and knees. And when she does, she pulls her hair over one shoulder, and my heart squeezes painfully in my chest.

Erin.

"I know her," I murmur, carefully maneuvering until my arm is out from behind Becca's shoulders. I hop up, jogging over to where Erin is still retrieving everything that fell from her bag.

"I'm fine, I've got it," she says before even looking up, but I bend down anyway, working on the pens and highlighters as she stacks the papers.

Erin huffs, grimacing a little as she falls from her knees to her hip, grimacing a little as her skin scrapes against the sidewalk.

"I said, I'm—"

She stops when she sees it's me, a glimmer of something passing over her as she takes me in. Her eyes graze my shoulders, my chest, before they land on my own eyes.

"Fine?" I finish for her. "I know. Erin Xanders is the queen of *fine*."

She narrows her eyes at first, but then she smirks, covering her face with her hands as I continue picking up her stuff. "Ugh," she groans. "Is it Spring Break yet?"

I laugh. "Almost. Here," I say, handing her everything I've gathered. She shoves it into her bag, picking up the last book and forcing it inside, too. When I'm standing again, I hold out a hand, helping her upright.

"Thank you."

I nod, tucking my hands in my pockets. And then we're just standing there — me staring at her, her staring at me, and all I want to do is ask every question she still hasn't answered. I want to know if she's gotten help, if she's okay, if she's even remotely close to the girl I once knew who looked like her and wore her name.

Something is wrong.

I know what Erin looks like when she's hiding something, when she's hurting — but this is different. This is something deeper, another scar, another permanent mark on her that she's trying to learn to wear with the same grace as she does her others. The longer I watch her — the bags under her eyes, her nails chewed down to the nub, skin pale and slick — the more questions I have.

And she feels them.

Her cheeks flush, eyes skirting to the ground as she tucks a strand of hair behind her ear. "I'm fine, Bear. Really. You can stop looking at me like a charity case."

"I'm looking at you like a friend," I correct her. "Don't expect me to ever stop doing that."

She peeks up at me through her lashes, her brows bent, but then her gaze draws to my left.

"Hey," Becca says, sliding up beside me. Her arm wraps under mine, hand folding over my bicep as she eyes Erin curiously. "Everything okay?"

"Actually, you might want to take a picture and mark the date and time," I say. "Not very often you catch Erin Xanders anywhere outside the lines of perfect, poised, on time, and put together."

Erin laughs, shaking her head before reaching her hand out for Becca. "Hi, I'm Erin."

"Becca," she answers, eyes finding me before resting back on Erin. "Did you guys used to date or something?"

"Oh, God, no," Erin says quickly, and my jaw tenses, though I can't place the discomfort.

We *didn't* date, but she doesn't have to say it so sure, like it's impossible to fathom.

"Erin is the president of Kappa Kappa Sigma," I explain. "We're friends."

"That's the sorority you're going on Spring Break with, right?"

"It is," I confirm, noting that Erin can't stop staring at Becca. Her eyes sweep over every inch, and she shifts, tucking the strap of her messenger bag back in place.

"Yep," she echoes. "And I'm late for my last final, so I better be going. I'll see you tomorrow, Bear." She won't meet my gaze, barely glancing at me before she's smiling back at Becca. "It was nice to meet you."

And then she turns, strutting off in the same hurried fashion she always has.

I watch her go, a frustrated sigh leaving my lips before I turn back to Becca. She has her weight balanced on one hip, arms crossed, and one brow cocked as she peers up at me.

"Just friends, huh?"

"It's complicated," I try. "I promise, we never dated. But, we did hook up. Once."

"Hmm."

But instead of diving more into whatever the hell Erin and I were — *are?* — I take the chance to tease Becca.

"Wait..." I stroke my chin with my fingers and thumb, grinning. "Are you *jealous*?"

She shoves me in lieu of an answer, already storming back to our bench, but I grab her from behind and lift, crushing her into me with a classic Bear hug from behind.

"Put me down!" She laughs, pounding her little fists on my forearms. "Ugh, you're so infuriating."

"But how turned on are you right now?" I whisper against the skin of her neck.

That just earns me another punch.

When we're back on the bench, Becca tells me about her plans for the week, and I kiss her goodbye just a short hour later, wishing she was going to be on the boat taking me to the islands tomorrow. But on my walk back to the house, it's another girl on my mind.

One who maybe never left it in the first place.

I'll have a whole week with Erin on this cruise, and one thing I know for sure is I'm done playing this *I'm fine, I promise* game. This week, I'll get her to talk. She's gone long enough shoving everyone away, and I won't stand back and watch her deteriorate any longer.

This time, she'll let me in.

I won't take no for an answer.

Cassie

I hate him.

I absolutely, without a doubt, whole-heartedly hate him.

Just standing within fifty feet of him now makes my jaw ache, my teeth are clenched so tight. Adam is laughing and smiling and goofing off with his brothers like he doesn't have a care in the world. And maybe he doesn't. Maybe, to him, everything is fine. Because to his knowledge, I've been "working on me," and everything between us is just fine.

I laugh.

Sure, he's assured me that there's nothing between him and Skyler, that they're just friends and he has no idea why she would ever say she had feelings for him. He's assured me that he's just trying to be there for her — *as a friend* — and there's nothing to worry about.

Of course, *I* know the background behind why Skyler said what she did about still being in love with Adam. I know the real plan behind her actions, the real motive, fueled by Erin — but Adam doesn't. And the fact that he still cares about her enough to run out of his own dance for *her* without even spending one full minute with *me*? Well, call me petty, but that hurts.

And no matter what he says, it's not okay.

I've done all the "me" stuff I can stomach. I've done yoga, and spa days, and long evenings on my longboard cruising the campus. I've studied, aced my midterms, picked up meditation and even pinned more than thirty-five possibilities for cutting my hair this summer. I'm over it, the me time, and whether *he* thinks I'm ready or not — I want *us* time now.

If Adam wants me, if he cares about me the way he says he does, then time is up.

All the games end this week.

But first, I have to play my own.

My stomach churns a little as I watch him, playing over my sister's words in my head. I called her yesterday, needing to talk to someone about Adam and actually use his name. The other girls still don't know about me and Adam, but my sister? She's a safe place.

"For the record, before I tell you anything else, I think you're being stupid," my sister, Claire, had said.

"*Me*? It's *him* who's being stupid! He's texting my Big, who he *used to date*, Claire."

"I get that, but have you seen his texts to her? Is he sending dick pics and asking her to make out?" She didn't let me respond. "No, he's not. He's being a *friend* to her, just like he told you he was." Claire had clucked her tongue then. "Adam is being mature beyond his years, if you ask me. I can't think of one single guy who tried to date me in college and told me I should take some time to focus on myself, or held me in their arms and said anything even close to as sweet as everything he's told you. If anything, they wanted me to lose myself in them, to do whatever they wanted to do. I'm telling you, if you're still single when you're my age, you'll kill for a guy like Adam."

I'd huffed, staring at my pile of clothes on my bed, still trying to figure out what to pack for Spring Break.

"Just help me," I had begged, my voice soft. "Please."

And with that, Claire had cracked, giving me advice that I should have already known myself.

"It's the oldest trick in the book, but there's a reason that sucker is still in there. Men are simple creatures, and boys are even more so. It's simple, really — you just need to make him jealous. If you think he's sleeping on you, if you think he's too comfortable or not moving fast enough, show him that other people are noticing you and you've got options."

"But I don't," I'd quickly pointed out.

"Doesn't matter. It can be a friend or one of *his* friends — anyone. Doesn't matter what they look like or what kind of connection you have. If there's another guy even *talking* to you, trust me, Adam will notice."

And so, I'd stewed on that advice overnight, packing and repacking and staying up way too late to feel functional on my first day of Spring Break. I still hadn't had any idea of what I'd do, of when I'd make my move.

But now, staring across the deck at Adam, Kade, and their other brothers, I know the time is now.

The cruise ship is buzzing with the energy of Spring Break, so similar to my first one last year and yet heightened somehow. This isn't just a road trip to Key West — it's an all-inclusive *cruise.* For the next five days, our only obligation is to drink, party, and soak up the sun.

It's college bliss.

And I'm damn sure not spending it alone.

As soon as the safety drill ends, we all disperse, making our way to various parts of the ship. The girls and I are on a mission to snag prime real estate at the pool, and as soon as we make it to the top deck, I spy my first opportunity.

I grab Skyler's arm, tugging her toward Adam and his brothers before I can talk myself out of my next move. Without warning, I launch myself at Kade's back, wrapping my arms around his neck and my legs around his waist in a forced piggyback ride.

"It's Spring Break, bitches!" I yell, loud enough to cause several people to turn around and look — Adam included.

He smiles at first when he realizes it's me, but his eyes darken at the sight of my legs wrapped around Kade, of his hands holding my thighs in place as he adjusts me on his back. Kade laughs, smacking my butt playfully, and Adam's jaw clenching is the last thing I see before I pull my attention back to the task at hand.

"Where's our shots?" I ask.

I don't even realize it's Kip standing next to Kade, not until I glance over and see that's who Skyler jumped on, mirroring me. For a second, I see it — how good they would have been together, had it not been for Erin. And even though I know he's called things off with Erin, we all know there's no chance for Skyler now. It'd be against girl code, and I know my Big well enough to know she'd never break that.

"I've been on this boat for seven-and-a-half minutes now and I still don't have a frozen, fruity drink in my hand," Skyler chimes in.

Kip stares up at her over his shoulder, a wry grin on his face. "Well, that sounds like a problem I can solve."

The next thing I know, I'm hanging on for dear life as Kade and Kip take off sprinting toward the bar. I squeal extra loud as we pass Adam and his brothers, but I don't take my eyes off the bar, acting like I don't even realize we passed him.

"Okay, transportation complete," Kade says, dropping me to my feet once we make it to the pool bar. "Now the only question is — which shot?"

"Hmmm... something fruity."

The bartender overhears, holding up an "okay" sign with his fingers to let us know he's got just the thing. Kade and I chat while she makes our drinks, and anytime I can, I touch his arm, laugh at his jokes, stare into his eyes. I'm pleasantly aware of the other set of eyes locked on me at the present moment, and that only fuels my fire.

"To Spring Break," Kade says, holding up his shot glass to mine.

"May we survive it."

He laughs. "Hear, hear!"

We down the shot, Kade howling when his is down, and then he winks at me before trotting over to join his group of brothers. Skyler is preoccupied with Kip at the bar, so I sip my piña colada, waiting for her to finish up so we can make our way to the pool.

And just like always — I feel him before I see him.

I wonder if that will ever go away, the way my body reacts to Adam before I should even know he's nearby. Will he ever be able to surprise me, to catch me off guard, or will my hair always stand on end, my stomach always tighten, my heart always skip before picking up a notch?

"Happy Spring Break," he says, tapping his knuckles on the bar.

"Yep."

The word leaves my mouth with a pop, and I take another drink, not so much as glancing his way.

"You okay?"

"I'm great!" I force a smile, finally meeting his eyes. "How about you?"

Two lines form between his brows, like he can't figure out if he should believe me or not. And he shouldn't. He definitely shouldn't.

"I'm good... I saw you with Kade," he says, broaching the subject like Mr. Subtle himself. "I didn't realize you two knew each other."

On the outside, I'm calm and cool, merely shrugging and taking another sip of my drink. But inside, I'm wearing the most satisfied grin.

"Oh, yeah, we met at rush," I say coolly. "I didn't really talk to him much until the Valentine's Day dance. We hung out a lot that night."

I practically shoot lasers at him with that last line, making my message clear. It's been almost a month since that dance, and I'm still not over the fact that he ran out with Skyler that night. Yes, he explained later. And yes, we've hung out since. But still, I know he's texting Skyler, and I know I'm tired of the *let's take this slow* bullshit.

"Oh," Adam answers.

He pauses a moment, sliding closer to me, his pinky finger brushing mine. And as much as I want to hold his hand, as much as I want to hear what he has to say next, I cut him off with his mouth still open.

"Well, have fun today."

I turn, linking my arm in Skyler's and guiding her toward the pool where Erin, Ashlei, and Jess are already set up. We dip our feet in the cool water, clinking our glasses together and celebrating the start of the best week of spring semester.

I don't have to glance over my shoulder to know Adam is still watching, and I hope like hell he's feeling even a margin of the kind of hurt he made me feel the night of the dance. I've never done anything like this before, never been about playing games, but if that's the way to get his attention, I'm damn sure not above it.

I served the ball, now it's his move.

He better choose it wisely.

Skyler

Spring Break.

Every year, we count down the days until this magnificent week. Every year, we push our diets, tan as much as we can, and buy way too many clothes because we have "nothing to wear" — regardless of our closets being stuffed full of clothes.

But this year? I'd almost forgotten.

I've been so focused on Kip, on trying *not* to focus on him, that I forgot how much fun Spring Break is. I forgot that I'd have the week with my sisters, that I'd have the chance to earn my entry fee for the tournament by doing the small tournaments on board, that I'd have days in the sun and nights dancing the hours away with my favorite people in life.

But I could never forget that *he* would be here, too.

It's been a week since Kip and I hooked up, since the night of the tournament downtown, and ever since then, we've played our cards as carefully as we could. A few stolen glances here and there, a hot kiss in the Greek library, a few text messages — all disguised by putting different names on our phone numbers just in case. I feel like I'm cheating on someone, even though I'm single, but I don't want to hurt Erin.

I *can't* hurt her.

Until she gives me the sign that she's fully over Kip, this will have to do. I tell myself I can handle it, I can keep everything on the down low, can control myself around big groups of people and sneak around to touch him the way I want to. But when he slides up behind me as I place another bet at the roulette table, I know I'm walking a very thin, very dangerous line.

"Why black number four?" he asks over my shoulder.

His breath warms my neck, and I smile, keeping my composure as best I can and focusing on my chips laying on the table.

"It's a long story," I answer, taking a marginal step back — enough to touch him, just a little bit, our bodies sparking to life at the contact.

"I'm in no rush. I'm actually on vacation, believe it or not."

I roll my eyes, taking a sip of my drink as other players place their bets.

"My dad has this formula," I say, smiling at the mention of him. It's been a while since I've talked to either of my parents, and I miss them. They were my best friends before I had any at all. "He uses it to find out people's lucky numbers. He used to do it all the time, sort of like his party trick, I guess."

Kip is so warm behind me, so close, I nearly forget what I was saying. But I shake my head, brushing it off.

"Anyway, obviously he figured mine out the day I was born, and it's been drilled into my head ever since then that my lucky number is four." I shrug. "When I played little league sports, four was always my number. If anyone asks me to choose a number between one and ten, that's my go-to — always. I have a tattoo with it, I purposefully buy scratch-offs that are the fourth ones on the roll, I mean, literally anything involving numbers leads me straight to number four."

I smile, knowing how superstitious and, frankly, ridiculous I sound, but continuing regardless.

"And, honestly," I say. "It really is lucky for me. I've won a lot of money by betting horses racing with the number four and on the scratch-offs, too."

I pause, turning to face him to deliver the last of my story. His strikingly blue eyes meet mine with a glittering interest, and my knees shake, my hands reaching for his forearms to steady myself.

"Except, something weird happens in poker," I say, doing my best not to drop my focus from the story to how delicious he looks in his crisp white button-up and navy blue dress pants. "For whatever reason, anytime I'm dealt a black number four in poker, whether it's a spade or a club, I lose the hand. No shit," I say, holding up my hands. "Even if I have a pair of aces in the hole, if a four comes up — I know I'm going to lose." I chuckle. "Kind of ironic, isn't it? My lucky number screws me in the game I need it most."

Turning back toward the table, I gesture toward my bet. "So, because I'm superstitious and a little crazy, I play black number four on roulette. Every time. I guess I'm convinced that if a black four can hit for me here, it'll reverse my luck with the cards."

"Has it ever hit for you before?" Kip asks.

I scrunch my nose, half because I can't believe he's actually interested in this stupid, crazy story and half because I realize my theory about number four always being lucky except for poker is a little flawed.

"No, it hasn't," I finally concede. "So, I guess my lucky number is kind of cursed in this game, too."

Kip doesn't answer, but instead reaches into his pocket for his wallet. Before I can even register it, he flicks a crisp one-hundred-dollar bill on the table. The dealer exchanges it for one black chip, and Kip's eyes find mine as he plucks it from the green.

"Maybe you're just not betting enough," he muses, voice low. "Maybe your lucky number feels cheated."

And then, he slaps that one-hundred-dollar chip right on top of my measley one dollar one.

I'm already shaking my head when I turn to face him, my eyes wide with worry. "Kip! Don't do that, that's so much money." My heart races, knowing he's about to lose a hundred dollars all because of some stupid superstition of mine. "It won't hit, it never does, I don't want to be the reason you lose that!"

"No more bets," the dealer says behind us, and all eyes move to the ball spinning on the number wheel — except for mine.

"Too late now." Kip grins, and I just groan, covering my face with my hands.

"Oh, my God. I can't breathe."

Kip laughs, but I can't hear anything past the *click-click-clicking* of the ball on the wheel as it rolls over the wooden wheel. It'll drop any moment now.

"You have a tattoo?" Kip asks. "I don't know how I missed that."

I laugh at his stupid attempt to distract me, still covering my face with my hands. "If you're still talking to me after this, maybe I'll show you later."

Kip leans in closer, his voice a growling whisper. "Looking forward to it."

Heat creeps up my neck as I nudge him, but I still can't take my hands down. I know the ball is going to land anywhere but on the number we bet on, and it makes me sick to think about how Kip will look at me once he realizes I cost him a hundred bucks. The ball hits one of the silver knobs, the sound as distinct as my own mother's voice, and the bouncing begins.

My heart kicks up another notch, beating painfully hard in my chest.

"I seriously can't breathe," I whisper, and Kip's hand slides down to my hip. He squeezes it gently, but doesn't say a word.

And then, a gasp from the other players at the table as the dealer announces the winning bet.

"Black four."

Chaos. Complete and utter chaos.

Everyone at the table cheers, regardless of their own bets as I throw my hands up into the air and stare at the ball resting in the little black crevice of number four on the wheel. I still don't believe it, not when I wrap my arm around Kip, not when we jump up and down screaming like a couple of lunatics, and not when the dealer puts the little glass marker on top of our bets, sealing the deal.

"OH MY GOD! That did not just happen!" I stare at the marker, blinking over and over, the reality not sinking in. "Kip, that's like three thousand dollars," I whisper, turning back to him with my hands fisting his dress shirt. "Holy shit!"

The rest of the table laughs, my whisper anything but discreet. Even the dealer cracks a smile as she calls the pit boss over to check the pile of chips she's piled up for Kip.

"Well, I guess we better find a really awesome way to spend it tomorrow on the island, huh?" Kip says, spinning me around to face him again. "See?" His eyes zero in on me, that same flood of weakness consuming my knees. "You just needed to have a little more faith in your number. That's all."

I smile, throat tightening with emotion. There are so many things I want to say to him, so many places I want to take him, so many things I wish I could take back, and so much time lost I wish I could have again. How is it that my entire life was turned upside down by a transfer, a silly boy with blue eyes, blond hair, and glasses? He walked onto our campus and into my life and nothing was ever the same.

I know it never will be again.

"I think I just needed you," I argue. "Maybe you're my lucky charm."

His face falls a little, a shadow of something similar to guilt crossing over him before he grins. It happens so fast, I know I must have imagined it, but I wonder what was going through his mind.

"I'll take that title," he says. "Am I the kind of lucky charm you never take off? You know, the kind you shower with?"

Kip waggles his brows and I just roll my eyes, turning to collect chips from the dealer. There are a few more congratulations from the players at the table and then new bets are placed, our win forgotten.

When I face him again, my eyes trail his entire body, knowing that what lies underneath those clothes far outweighs the threads.

"Well, I did say I'd show you my tattoo," I tease.

Kip bites his lip, and just like that, we're racing to find our next hiding spot.

I can't wait to have his lips on me, to have his hands on me, to have his body on mine. And more than anything, I can't wait until Erin gives me even one small sign that she's over him.

Because I can't wait until he's mine — *truly* mine — for everyone to see.

Cassie

On the second night of Spring Break, I press a cool hand to my cheek, sipping on my frozen daiquiri as I attempt to soothe my sunburn. It's not bad, just a light blush of pink over my face, arms, and legs, but it's enough for me to feel it. My cool hand only soothes it for a moment, a temporary fix before the burn singes through and leaves my hand just as hot.

Yesterday, I got so drunk I ended up turning in early after dinner. Then, today, we partied on the island, Kip blowing the money he won last night on a couple of cabanas for his brothers and our sisters. Again, I found myself drinking to forget about Adam, to try to avoid him *and* my feelings.

Now, sitting at the bar with my sisters as we try to turn our day drinking into a successful night, I feel silly.

No, I feel stupid.

Before I came to Palm South, I rarely ever drank. I'd had a few wine coolers, stolen from my mom's stash, but other than that, I'd never indulged. And while I love having a great time with my sisters, I've never used alcohol before as a way to avoid, as an attempt to feel better.

I found out quickly it doesn't work.

If anything, the more I drink, the worse I feel. The game I'm playing with Kade to make Adam jealous only adds to how shitty I feel, and I just want it all over with.

I just want to talk to Adam.

Sighing, I push past the sickening drop of my stomach as I finish off my drink and stand, searching the piano bar for the one guy I've been avoiding.

"You okay?" Ashlei asks, eying my empty glass. "Need another drink?"

My stomach rolls at the thought of it. "I think I just need some fresh air. I'll be back."

She frowns, but nods. "Okay, babe. Let me know if you need anything."

I somehow manage a smile, and then I'm shoving through the crowd of fraternity brothers and sorority sisters, making my way toward the deck. Adam comes into view once I cross the room, and at the sight of me, his face falls, brows bending together. He pushes off where he was leaning on the wall, meeting me in the middle of the room with his hands in his pockets.

The red polo he's wearing blazes against his tan biceps, and I watch the muscles flex and move as he makes his way toward me. His hair is mussed, as if he didn't even shower after spending a day on the island. He looks like he just threw on new clothes and embraced the salty waves, and somehow, he looks even sexier than if he were all dressed up, hair gelled back and bow tie in place. And I can't stop staring at his arms, wishing I was in them, wishing they were my place to call home.

"Hey," he says over the sound of a new song starting when he reaches me. The entire room erupts into cheers before I can answer, a drunken choir pouring out the first verse of "Tiny Dancer."

"Hi."

I cross one arm over my middle, holding onto my opposite elbow and staring down at my open-toed heels. I paired them with a pair of white, high-waisted shorts and an Easter yellow crop top. I wanted to stand out, to make him notice me.

Now I just want to hide.

I should say something, I realize as we stand there — starting with an apology. But all I can do is stand there, staring at my feet, and even that is a task. If I wasn't using every ounce of strength I have left, I'd be on my knees, or curled into the fetal position, begging him to leave me alone.

Begging him to never leave.

Adam doesn't say a word, just gently grabs my hand and guides me through the crowd, the same direction I was heading before I saw him. In a matter of moments, we're out of the bar and on the outside deck, the rambunctious sound of music and singing replaced with the soft crash of the waves against the ship.

My hands wrap around the railing, the cool metal soothing as much as it is shocking. And I can't look at him, can't bear to have him look at me — not after how I've acted.

"You okay?" he asks after a moment, sliding up to rest his elbows on the railing next to me.

I pinch my eyes shut, willing myself not to cry. "I think we both know the answer to that."

"Cassie..."

His hand moves for mine, but I rip it away as soon as our fingers brush.

"No," I say, voice firm. I lift my eyes to his, swallowing down my nerves. "No, I get to talk this time."

Adam doesn't argue, his face ridden with a mixture of apology and shame before I even start talking.

"I can't do this anymore, Adam. I can't."

My voice breaks, tears filling my eyes, though I don't blink to let them fall. Instead, I hold my shoulders back, standing straighter.

"I know you want me to focus on me, but I have. I've had months to myself, and I appreciate that you pushed me to do that, that you encouraged me to find myself again, to be happy *alone* — without a boyfriend." I sniff. "But I love you," I whisper, and that breaks me, two tears spilling down my hot cheeks as Adam's shoulders crumple. "And I don't want to be without you anymore."

Adam steps forward, his arms reaching out for me and pulling me into his chest. He wraps me in the tightest hug, one that tells me more than words that he doesn't want to be without me, either. And even though I'm still hurting, comfort sneaks in, warming me from the inside out.

"I don't want to play the games," I say through my tears. "I don't want to wonder what you're texting Skyler, or why you can touch me but not *be* with me. I don't want to do anymore yoga or meditation or post anymore stupid Facebook statuses about having my 'me time'."

Adam chuckles, and I can't help the smile that cracks through my tears.

"I don't want to flirt with other guys to make you mad."

He sighs, stroking my hair with one hand before planting a kiss to my forehead. "That worked very well, by the way."

"I'm sorry," I whisper, pulling back just enough to look up into his eyes. "I did that to hurt you, even when I know you would never do anything to hurt me. I wanted a reaction. I wanted you to care."

"I've always cared."

I watch him for a moment before softly shrugging. "I couldn't tell."

Adam sighs again, framing my face with his hands as his thumbs wipe away the tears from my cheeks.

"I'm so, so sorry, Cassie. For everything. I thought I knew what was best for you, thought I was doing the right thing by having you take some time for yourself. But all I did was hurt us both."

I swallow, leaning into his touch.

"I meant everything I said about you spending time on *you*, and I'm glad you have. But, I was wrong for chasing Skyler out of the dance, for putting her above you even though that was not my intention. I care about her, Cassie," he says, and the words are like ice picks through my heart. "I do. But as a *friend* only. I won't lie, her profession of love for me threw me. For a moment, I wondered if I'd read our entire relationship wrong. But, there's something going on between her and Kip, and I know I was just part of her game." He smirks. "Your Big is really good at playing those, too."

I scoff. "Don't I know it."

"But, I focused on making sure *she* was okay," he confesses. "When I should have been focusing on you. And I can't take that back, but I can apologize. I am truly sorry, and I don't ever want you to feel like you're anything but the most important girl in my life." His thumb swipes away a fresh tear, one corner of his mouth quirking into a soft smile. "Because you are, Cassie. You are everything to me."

"Then let me in," I whisper. "Please, Adam. Let me in. Be with me."

"Would you stop?" he says, laughing and wiping away more tears. "I'm trying to do the apologize and grovel thing and you're just being so damn adorable I can't focus."

I smile, but can't help crying even more as he pulls me into him. He hugs me tight, kissing my hair.

"I'm yours, Cassie McBee," he whispers. "I always have been. I always will be."

He lifts my chin with his knuckle, and when his lips touch mine, every game, every fight, every ounce of hurt that's ever existed between us melts into a puddle at our feet. I press onto my toes, strengthening our kiss, my arms wrapping around his shoulders and pulling him closer.

"I love you," he says softly, the words hot on my mouth. "I know I haven't shown you that, not in the right way, but I promise that from this moment on, I will do everything I can to prove it to you."

"You better."

We both laugh at that, and then he kisses me again, and for the first time since the semester started, I finally feel whole again.

I finally feel okay.

Erin

For the first time, I hate that my plan is falling into place.

Ever since Kip broke up with me, I have been scheming to get him back. I knew I would, it was just a matter of time.

And the first step in my plan? Prove myself right about Skyler.

I had to know she had betrayed me, that she was the reason he broke up with me. I knew it in my gut the moment he said we were done, but I had to play my cards right. I opened up to Skyler, told her I understood and I was sorry I ever put her through my stupid plan. And tonight, getting ready for our second night out on Spring Break, I mentioned being ready to move on — to bring a guy home. I put up the front that I was over Kip, and just like I knew she would, Skyler took the bait.

She's been staring at him all night.

At least for the past week, they've been *trying* to hide their relationship. Tonight, there might as well be a blinking neon heart hanging over them with arrows pointed at each of their heads.

And even though I know it's working, even though I know she'll reveal everything soon, it hurts. I thought it wouldn't, thought I could be strong enough to brush it off. But when I watch him watch her, I know they've touched. When I see her smile at him, I know they've laughed.

And in my heart, I know my own Little betrayed me.

It wasn't fair, what I asked of her, but I never imagined she'd go behind my back and be with Kip, anyway. What hurts the most is that she did it while I was still *with* him — before I even had the chance to see if we could make it work. Kip is *mine,* he's supposed to be with me, but she just couldn't stand it.

I know I hurt her, and I know I'm not perfect — but what she did to me is worse.

I've been drinking too much. I realized that earlier on the island, but lost the ability to care. Instead, I kept drinking, and now, at almost midnight, everything is blurry. I can't even hide my glares toward Skyler, or my longing stares toward Kip. I can't hide the fact that I'm two seconds away from losing my shit. But I have to.

I have to hold it together.

The piano bar is packed to the brim, and after the third round of "Benny and the Jets", I'm about ready to throw in the towel for the night and head up to my room. But just when the thought crosses my mind, I see Kip being shoved toward the piano by his brothers, all of them chanting his name.

I blink through the fog in my head, leaning against the bar as I focus on Kip. He slides behind the piano with a wry grin as the cruise ship pianist stands, microphone in hand.

"Ladies and gentlemen, I'm told we have a pretty good piano player here on board from Palm South University," he says. The entire bar erupts into cheers — even the brothers of Omega Chi. Somehow, a sort of bond has been formed between the opposing fraternities, though I'm skeptical it will last past this week.

Kip seems almost shy at the piano, his cheeks reddening as everyone starts chanting his name. I open my mouth to join in, but can't be sure if I actually do.

I'm really, *really* drunk.

After a moment, his hands move over the keys, a soft melody filling the bar. "Go easy on me, guys," he says into the microphone, and every girl — including me — melts into a puddle on the floor.

How could we not?

Kip's wearing a hot pink button-up, the sleeves shoved up to his elbows, hair mussed, and of course, he's wearing his damn glasses — which apparently make every girl weak. But all I can stare at is the eyes *behind* those frames as he starts playing a familiar song, and as soon as he leans into the mic and sings the first line, the entire bar goes silent.

And his eyes lock onto Skyler.

My stomach rolls, every shot of alcohol threatening to make a reappearance as he belts out the ballad. He doesn't take his eyes of Skyler, and every smooth croon of his voice enhances my urge to vomit. I know I'll never hear this Michael Bublé song the same again, and I know I'll never want to.

I hate it. I hate him.

I hate *her*.

As it always does when I'm drinking, time passes in a morphed loop, the song seeming to replay over and over even when Kip finishes and stands from behind the piano. The bar is alive with cheers, everyone clapping and chanting his name again, but that's nothing compared to how loud they are when Skyler jumps behind the piano with him.

Then, time slows down.

Every cheer morphs, the sounds muted, and I watch in slow motion as Skyler grabs Kip by his collar and pulls his lips to hers. Somehow, I know the crowd is louder, but I only hear a ringing in my ears. I blink, trying to decipher what I feel, but everything is numb. Just like it was when I aborted my child. Just like it was when four men pushed inside of me without me saying they could.

It's defense mode, a method of survival.

I'm no longer a human with feelings and fears. I'm a machine — an unbreakable force.

Or maybe I'm nothing at all.

"Ex..." Jess starts, her hand reaching for my wrist. "You okay?"

I sniff, forcing a smile and blinking away the fog. "I'm good! I'm going to go find someone to fuck."

Ashlei's eyes widen at that. "Maybe you should just chill tonight, you've been drinking a lot."

"I'm fine."

"I don't know, Grand Big," Cassie chimes in. "Maybe we should just go back to the room."

"I said, I'm *fine,*" I say louder. "If you girls want to call it a night, be my guest. I'm going to the club."

I don't wait for them to answer before I'm pushing through the crowd, avoiding Kip and Skyler at all costs. A hand wraps around my wrist from behind, and I whip around, ready to unleash my anger on Jess and tell her to fuck off and leave me alone.

But it isn't Jess.

It's Clinton.

His grip on me softens, but he doesn't let me go, his brows bent into a hard line over his dark eyes.

"Let me go," I demand, but I don't rip away from him. I don't have the strength.

"Only if you talk to me."

I scoff. "What is there to talk about?"

"I don't know, maybe you should tell me. Because clearly you're not okay right now." He shakes his head. "What's going on? What's happening with you and Sky, with you and this new kid?"

I finally rip my wrist from his hands, tucking my arms over my chest. "Doesn't matter."

"It does to me."

My heart squeezes, façade dropping at his words. I trail my eyes up his broad chest to lock on his, and the sympathy I find there, the genuine care — it nearly kills me. I want to fall into him, to break in his arms, to let him fix me.

But he can't.

No one can.

"Please, Erin," he tries again, his hand reaching for mine.

I let him take it, let him thread his fingers with my own. Black and white, large and small, hard and soft. We don't make sense, and yet Clinton is the only one who can make me feel anything at all anymore.

"Talk to me. Let me help you. I..." He pauses, wetting his lips. "You're not alone, okay? Even when you feel like you are. I'm here."

My eyelids flutter, the threat of tears stinging my throat so strongly I nearly let them fall. But instead, I pull my hand from his, my mother's voice loud in my foggy mind as I steel myself.

"I am alone," I whisper. "And I prefer it that way."

His chest deflates. "Erin."

"Goodnight, Bear."

I turn and leave him behind, along with the rest of my morals. It's like I lost the very last piece of myself in that bar, in that moment, and now I'm just the black, charred shell of a woman who once was. I only want justice. I only want what's rightfully mine.

I only want revenge.

And I don't care who I hurt, or who I lose — I will get it.

Jess

"Anddd she's back, ladies and gents!" Ashlei announces, smacking my hand in a high five as I wipe leftover beer from my mouth.

I let out a loud belch, slamming down my empty cup on the pool bar. "Back and better than ever."

"Gross."

"You love me."

"Also true."

Ashlei taps the bar, and the bartender refills our cups before we make our way back to our lounge chairs at the edge of the pool. Ashlei slides into hers gracefully as I plop down on mine, crossing my ankles with a satisfied sigh.

"Spring Break fixes everything. It's science."

Ashlei chuckles. "It is a pretty great medicine. I'm glad you're feeling better, babe. I've missed you."

"I've been right here," I argue, poking out my bottom lip.

"I know, but you've been distracted. Heartbreak diet and all." Ashlei shrugs. "And then you were trying to use Greg as a distraction, which took up all your time. I'm just saying, I'm glad I have my feisty best friend back."

"Me, too."

We both smile, and I cheers her cup with mine before taking a swig.

"How's the internship going?" I ask as we both kick back.

Ashlei sprays her legs with tanning oil, rubbing it in as her lips pull to one side. "It's... good. A little challenging this semester, but nothing I can't handle."

"Damn straight. You're Ashlei Davison — Certified Bad Ass. But what's been going on?"

She sighs, tossing the tanning oil back in her beach bag and leaning back. "Just some drama with another intern. She was with me last semester, too. She has it out for me for some reason, just determined to take me down."

"Want me to cut her?"

Ashlei chokes on a laugh. "No, but thanks. With Kimberly, I've learned I have to fight dirty just like she does. Dirty, but gracefully, if that makes any sense."

"Of course. Brain fighting instead of fist fighting."

"You could say that."

"Well, I'm here if you need to talk out any plans. How's that hot ass CEO of yours? You let him bend you over a desk yet?"

Ashlei coughs on her beer, wiping foam from her lips as she faces me. "What? No, of course not."

I cock a brow. "I was kidding..." Then, I gasp. "WAIT! Have you *actually* let him bend you over a desk? Oh, my God, Ashlei, you better spill the juice. NOW."

"Shhhh," she spits, looking around us like anyone is at all interested in our conversation.

"Oh, stop. Everyone's drunk. And *you're* hiding something. Spill. Now."

She groans, setting her beer on the table between us before covering her face with her hands. "Fine. I'm banging him."

"YOU LITTLE OFFICE WHORE!" I scream, and she smacks me as I laugh. "Oh, my God. I'm so happy. And so proud. Tell me more! Tell me *everything*."

And though I have to pull every little detail out of her, Ashlei gives me the dirt, making me gasp over and over again the more she reveals. By the end of her story, when I'm all caught up, I'm pretty sure I could catch flies with how big my mouth is hanging open.

"So, let me get this straight. You've been banging your fine ass CEO since last semester — on his private jets and his fucking *yacht*, AND in the office — and you never told me?"

Ashlei rolls her eyes. "That's what you're taking from all this?"

"Well, that's clearly what's most important, here."

"Oh, my bad. I thought what was most important was that Kimberly *saw us* and my entire career is in jeopardy. How silly of me."

I wave her off. "No way. Like you said, you've got a plan. Put that bitch on blast when you get back. If you own what you and Mr. Church have before she has the chance to throw you under the bus, *she's* the one who will look like an idiot."

"I hope so."

"I know so. Now," I say, draining my beer. "Go get us another round, and then I want details on the yacht sex because seriously what the fuck."

Ashlei laughs, shaking her head and taking my empty cup before prancing off toward the bar.

Stretching in my chair, I let my head drop back and tap my bare toes to the beat of the steel drum the band is playing on the pool deck. The sun warms my skin, blending with the heat from the alcohol, and I smile. Greg was a wake-up call, and ever since he handed me my ass at Ralph's, I've been on a mission to get back to the old me. It hasn't been easy, since most of my nights end with me thinking about Jarrett, no matter how hard I try not to. But, the more time passes, the easier it gets. And the more drinks I have, the more I remember what it felt like to be single — the *before Jarrett* era.

Spring Break? Well, it's exactly what I needed. Sunshine, booze, and quality time with my sisters. This is what college is about. This is what Jess Vonnegut does best.

This is my element.

At least, until I'm suddenly covered in shade.

I scowl, lifting my head and pulling my sunglasses down to peer at the shadow-inducing figure. "Oh, God. Not you again."

Kade smirks, holding his arms open wide. "You know you missed me."

"Like I miss a yeast infection."

His arms drop, his face screwing up in confusion as he considers what I've said. Then, he points a finger at me. "That's gross. But you're still hot."

He plops down in Ashlei's seat, giving me my sun back in exchange for an annoying new neighbor.

An annoyingly *hot* neighbor, too — but annoying, nonetheless.

"What's shakin', sexy?"

"Ugh."

I reach for my drink, and then remember I don't have one, which leaves me groaning again. Kade just smiles, handing me his beer, and I take a large swig before handing it back to him.

I met Kade on the island yesterday, hanging out with Kip and his brothers in their cabanas. I'd seen him around, knew he was a new Alpha Sigma brother, but yesterday he was like a fly I couldn't get rid of. He hovered around me, playing drinking games and following me every time I went to the water. He even pulled me out to dance at the club last night, which apparently I was too intoxicated to say no to.

He's so young. And so annoying.

And yet for some reason, I'm intrigued by him.

Maybe it's his goofy, somehow sexy grin that is permanently plastered on his face. Maybe it's his ridiculously cheesy pick-up lines, or his blatant ogling of my tits when he thinks I'm not looking. He's like a little kid, one I want to take under my wing.

And simultaneously give a wedgie.

"I thought I got rid of you after yesterday."

"Nah," Kade answers, resting his hands behind his head. "After watching you do three beer bongs in a row in that skimpy little bikini you wore yesterday, you're stuck with me. Sorry, not sorry, princess."

I scan his built frame, which — in my opinion — doesn't match his personality. He looks like a beef head, tattoos sprawling down his left side and bicep, his dark hair cut short and gelled like a *Jersey Shore* cast member. But his goofy ass grin combats all of that hard muscle, the only evidence I need that he's still just a kid.

"Don't call me that."

"What should I call you, then? Please, tell me the dirty nicknames you love." He rolls over, resting his chin on one hand as he leans in. "I bet you want to call me Daddy, huh? I'm down for that, just so you know."

I try to roll my eyes again, but a laugh bursts out of me before I get the chance. "Who *are* you? Does that ever work for you? Like, ever?"

Kade shrugs. "Wouldn't you like to know."

"How old are you?"

"Twenty-one in September, gorgeous."

"You're a baby."

"Does that make you a cougar?"

I shake my head, ready to pop off a retort when Kade chuckles and holds his hands up, rolling over on his back again.

"I'm just kidding. But seriously, how are you today? Working on that tan, I see."

I'm so annoyed, and yet I smile.

Why do I smile?

"I'm fine," I answer, clipped. "Don't you have somewhere to be? Some brothers to annoy or something?"

"I do, but I'd rather sit here and stare at you."

I shake my head again, but can't help the blush that spreads on my cheeks. *God,* he's so young, and so fucking childish. Why is that somehow adorable and infuriating all at once?

Kade reaches out, his thumb brushing my cheek. "Was that a blush I saw?"

"Don't flatter yourself." I smack his hand away.

"God, I love when you get angry. That little scowl, those pursed lips." He groans. "I just want you to sit on my face."

My mouth pops open, body jolting off the back of my chair as I sit up straight and stare at him in shock. "Do you *hear* yourself? You're like an over-eager puppy dog."

"Mmm, want to put a leash on me and train me to be a good boy?"

"Jesus Christ." I cover my face with my hands, but can't help but laugh. I may or may not be covering another blush, too, because the thought of Kade on his hands and knees for me with a leash around his neck does tingly things to my nether regions.

What the fuck is wrong with me?

"That'll be ten dollars," Ashlei says, delivering me my new drink and a breath of relief.

"How about I pay you in ass smacks?"

"My favorite."

She hands me my beer, staring at Kade in her chair with a raised brow.

"Oh!" He jumps up, gesturing to the now-empty chair like it's a throne. "M'lady. I was just leaving. Your friend here wants to tie me up, and I'm just not ready for that."

"GO AWAY."

He laughs, and Ashlei watches me with a curious smile as Kade bows to me.

Brat.

"As you wish, my queen. See you in the dungeon of pain."

"I hate you."

"More like you wish you did."

And with that, he slides his aviators down his nose and winks before jogging back over to his brothers.

"What the hell was that?" Ashlei asks, taking her seat again.

"Nothing. That was nothing," I say quickly, cheersing her cup with mine. "Drink up, betch."

I chug before she can say anything else, and ignore the damn puppy dog eyes locked on me from across the pool.

Adam

"This is the literal worst time to have to pee," Cassie says, bouncing a little as she watches Skyler shove all her chips in. It's the final table of the tournament onboard, and it's down to Skyler and one older guy from Germany.

I chuckle. "You better go now. He's going to take a moment to call, and then the cards will come quickly if he does. They'll both flip their hands over."

"I can hold it," she says, but as she does, her face goes ash white and she squeezes her knees together.

"Go pee, crazy girl." I shove her toward the bathrooms.

"Yeah, girl. Trust me when I say you do *not* want to deal with a UTI," Jess chimes in.

At that, Cassie's eyes widen and she bites her lip. Then, a soft curse under her breath.

"I'll be *right* back. Don't let them end this without me!"

She half runs, half wobbles off toward the bathroom as Jess and I chuckle before turning back toward the table. It's a fairly small crowd gathered for the final table, and the only ones from PSU are me, Kip, Clinton, Jess, Ashlei, Cassie, and Erin. We're the Skyler Thorne fan club, and we've been the most obnoxious of the night. Now that it's down to just two, I know we're about to go wild.

Because Skyler *will* win this thing. There's no doubt in my mind.

"God, she's got to be sweating so bad," Ashlei whispers, her hands over her lips. "I can't imagine the pressure. That's so much money on the line."

Clinton crosses his arms over his chest. "Nah, she's cool as a cucumber. That's part of what makes her game so incredible to watch — she never shows her tells."

"Oh, shit, he called." Jess points to the table as the guy from Germany shoves his chips in, and then both him and Skyler flip their cards over. When they do, everyone in the little crowd except for us laughs.

He has a queen, king suited.

Skyler has a pair of fours.

"Shit," I murmur, but Kip smiles, nodding like it's the best hand she's had.

"This is perfect," he says.

"How so? There's a queen and king on the table. That's *two pair* — and she has one," Jess argues.

Kip just smiles wider. "I have faith."

A hush falls over all of us as the dealer burns one card before turning the next. Nine of hearts. No help for either of them. One more card is burned, and Skyler can't even look. She watches Kip instead, and I can't help but grin. I'm glad they've finally figured their shit out, and now that they've made it public that they're a thing, they both seem happier.

I wonder if the same will happen for me and Cassie.

I check over my shoulder for her, but there's no movement from the bathroom.

"Come on, babe. Get back out here," I whisper under my breath.

But, it's too late. The dealer burns and turns, and then, the entire room gasps.

Four of spades.

Three of a kind for Skyler.

Everyone claps in a polite manner, but I can't help letting out a whistle. Clinton follows up with a classic "Bear howl" until one of the ushers quiets us down.

She did it. I knew she would.

Skyler stands and shakes hands with her opponent, and I turn to Kip, wanting to tell him he better take that girl to celebrate. But when I do, he's already talking to someone else.

Erin.

"You think you know her, but you don't," she says, her voice low, but just loud enough for me to overhear.

I furrow my brows, moving closer as my eyes flick to Skyler and back. She's still shaking hands with other people at the table, oblivious to her Big standing so close to her boyfriend.

"You think she really likes you, but she only hooked up with you because I told her to. For me. I wanted you back, Kip, and I used her as bait to get you around more. I told her to date you. And I told her to kiss you. And I told her to invite you to the dance and to break up with you there, too. It was all a game."

My stomach sinks, and when I look back at Skyler, there's no denying she's feeling the same thing. Her eyes are wide, locked on Erin, her face pale white.

"No," Kip tries, shaking his head. "What we have is real. Skyler wouldn't..."

"She wouldn't?" Erin interrupts. Then, she gestures to Skyler. "Go ahead. Ask her."

And when Skyler and Kip's eyes lock, the guilt written all over her face, Kip shuts down. His eyes harden, his mouth flattening to a thin line, and without another word, he turns, pushing through the crowd.

"Kip! Wait!"

Skyler tries to run after him, but he's already gone by the time she reaches us, and tears flood her eyes as she grabs Erin.

"What did you do?! What did you tell him?!"

Erin is stoic, her jaw set. "I told him about our deal, about everything. He needed to know, Little. It wasn't fair for him to think what you have is real."

"Damn, Ex," Jess murmurs, stepping back. "That's fucked up."

I doubt Erin hears her. I doubt Skyler does, either. They just stare at each other, while the rest of us stare at them. I always knew Erin was tough, that she was uptight, and some would even say she's a bit bitchy. But I never, *never* thought she would do anything to hurt Skyler.

"What the hell is wrong with you?!" Skyler yells, tears streaming down her cheeks. "Why would you do this to me?! What we have *is* real, Erin. I've never felt anything more real in my life. It was real before I knew you dated him that summer and it was real the whole time I was trying to play your stupid game."

Erin just stands straighter, unaffected. "He needed to know," she repeats, but this time, her voice is softer — just a whisper.

Skyler backs away, her eyes like lasers. "I *hate* you," she spits. "How dare you call yourself my Big. A Big is someone who loves their Little, sets an example for them, cares for them, guides them." She shakes her head. "All you did was use me."

Ashlei covers her mouth, tears in her own eyes as Jess grabs her other hand.

"Don't ever talk to me again," Skyler finishes, sniffing and wiping her cheek with the back of her wrist. Then, she turns, racing toward the elevators.

My eyes shoot to Clinton, sure he'd be the first to take off after her, but to my surprise, he's pulling Erin away, consoling her under one arm as Ashlei holds Jess back.

"Just let her go. She needs to be alone."

And that may be true, but I can't let her. I can't let her think she's alone in this.

With one last glance toward the bathroom, Cassie still not emerging, I curse under my breath and take off sprinting.

Skyler is pushing the elevator button wildly when I reach her, and I wrap my arms around her from behind, shushing her as I try to soothe her cries.

"Shh, it's okay. It's okay, Sky. I'm here."

When she hears my voice, she relaxes, and I hold her until the elevator door opens before ushering her inside.

She's like a wild animal, her eyes rimmed in mascara as she tucks into the corner of the elevator. I just watch her, wondering what to say, wondering what the hell happened between her, Kip, and Erin. It's apparent that what Erin said isn't wrong, but it can't be right. There has to be more to it, a side yet to be seen.

When we reach the floor for Skyler's room, she bolts off and I follow, slipping inside her room behind her. She immediately flops onto the bed, tucking her legs up and burying her face in her arms as more tears rack through her.

It's hard to see Skyler Thorne broken. She's the toughest girl I know, and nothing can get to her — least of all a guy. If I told anyone who wasn't there tonight that a boy made her cry, made her lose her shit, no one would believe me. She's untouchable, unstoppable, and unbreakable.

At least, she was.

Until tonight.

Until Kip Jackson.

I sigh, carefully sitting on the bed next to her and gently resting my hand on her back. "Are you okay?"

As soon as the words are out of my mouth, I curse, shaking my head as she cries harder.

Of course, she's not okay, genius.

"I know, stupid question. I'm here, Skyler. I'm right here. I'm not going anywhere."

Skyler sniffs, turning until her wet cheek is resting on her knees. Our eyes meet for just a split second before there's a soft click at the door. It swings open, and I expect to see Kip, or possibly Erin, but it's neither.

It's Cassie.

Her eyes are on Skyler first, her brows bent in worry, but when those emerald eyes float to me, they harden, all worry fading into anger.

"What are you doing here?"

Shit.

I swallow, taking my hand from Skyler's back and holding them both up. "I just came to check on her."

It's the truth, and I shouldn't feel guilty for that, but the way Cassie's glaring at me tells me it's a statement I'll regret.

"Of course, you did."

Her words are menacing, and my shoulders slump. I plead with her with my eyes, begging her to understand, to see that Skyler needed someone. I didn't do anything inappropriate, nothing that a friend wouldn't do.

I open my mouth to explain when Cassie cuts me off.

"Can you leave us alone, please?"

My throat tightens, but I nod, standing and offering Skyler one last look to let her know it'll all be okay. That earns me an eye roll from Cassie and a stiff shove toward the door.

"Stay here," she whispers to me when I'm outside the door, low enough that Skyler can't hear. Her eyes are still shooting venom at me. "I have words for my Big, but you're next."

"Can—" I try, but the door slams shut, cutting my plea short.

Shit.

I sigh, running my hands back through my hair as my back hits the wall next to their door. I slide down, elbows meeting my knees, eyes on my shoes.

I fucked up.

Again.

No, I shouldn't be sorry for making sure Skyler is okay, but the problem with that scenario is that, once again, I didn't think of how my actions would affect Cassie before I made my move. I ran after Skyler, wanting to make sure she was okay, when I could have easily waited a few more minutes for Cassie. I could have ran to the bathroom, beat on the door or had someone go in after her. We could have gone after Skyler *together*.

But none of that occurred to me in that moment.

I think it was my grandfather who always said hindsight is twenty-twenty, and it's always easier to see our mistakes after they've already been made.

I've never wished for a time machine more.

I begged Cassie to trust me, to let me show her I loved her with my actions instead of my words. And just last night, I promised her I'd prove to her how much she meant to me.

I didn't even make it twenty-four hours before fucking it all up.

I groan, knocking my head back against the wall. "Idiot."

What are only minutes feel like hours as I wait for Cassie. I can't hear what's happening inside, but when the door does open, it swings back against their wall inside and Skyler takes off sprinting down the hall, not so much as a glance in my direction before she's gone.

Cassie emerges next, her eyes on where Skyler just disappeared before they fall to me. I jump up, brushing my jeans off and moving toward her instinctively.

"Cassie, I—"

She just holds up her hand, eyes squeezed shut as she looks away from me. "No."

"Please, just let me—"

"Explain?" She finishes, her eyes snapping back to me. "Why should I? Once again, you picked her over me, Adam. You left *me* behind to make sure she was okay."

God. When she says it like that, it makes my stomach curdle like sour milk.

"I know," I confess, swallowing. "I know, and I'm so sorry. I wasn't thinking, I just saw how hurt she was and no one went after her and—"

"And so you did."

My jaw clenches, and I shove my hands in my pockets, eyes dropping to the floor like the sad, guilty dog that I am.

"You told me to let actions speak louder than words," she whispers. "Well, your actions have been screaming for months. I just haven't listened."

My chest splits open with her words, the truth of them cutting me like a knife. I shake my head, eyes watering as I find hers again. "Cassie, please. I'm sorry. Just give me—"

"I'm not *giving* you anything," she spits, her own eyes flooding. "Not anymore. From this moment on, you have to earn it. You have to earn *me.*" Then, she turns, waving one hand behind her without another look in my direction. "Don't follow me."

And she doesn't run. She doesn't jog. She just walks, slowly and purposefully with her head held high — away. Away from me. Away from us.

All I can do is watch, falling more in love with every step she takes, my heart aching and reaching for her, begging my feet to move, my mouth to work. But I do as she asked. I don't follow her. I just stand there, knowing in my heart the one and only gut-wrenching truth.

I blew it.

Skyler

Life is a funny thing.

The way it shifts, changes, flowing easily from complete bliss to complete and utter chaos. One day there are kisses, and laughter, and long nights spent between the sheets, and little love notes left on napkins. The very next, there are tears, and promises broken, and two chests aching with the pain of lies.

It happens so fast, and yet in slow motion, it seems.

But I can't change what's happened. I can't go back to yesterday, to Kip's arms around me, to his lips on mine. And I can't take back what I've done, the lies I've told, the deal I agreed to just to appease Erin. All I can do is take my Little's advice.

"Stop running from this secret, from this stupid game. Make him understand. Show him how you really feel. Don't give up on him. Have faith."

Those words cycle through my head on repeat, over and over, each time growing louder as my feet carry me across the ship. Clinton calls out for me as I run past, but I keep going, my heart pounding hard and fast in my ears.

I can't lose him.

I *won't* lose him.

When I round the corner toward the stairs, I slam right into Kade, knocking us both off balance before he catches me at the elbows. His eyes watch me under bent brows, taking in my erratic breathing, and he doesn't even ask. He just points.

"He went up to the top deck," he says, but then his face breaks. "He's a mess, Skyler. He wouldn't listen to anything I said."

I swallow, nodding before taking off again. My legs are weak, the tears still drying on my face as I sprint through the ship and up the stairs four decks to the top.

When I reach the top floor, I run even harder, my ribs aching, chest heaving as my legs pump faster and faster. The wind whips my hair around wildly, the moonlight casting an eerie glow over the water as I scan the deck for Kip. I have no idea what I'm going to say when I reach him, words won't form in my head as I run. All I know is that I have to find him. I have to explain.

I can't lose him.

I *won't* lose him.

This game ends tonight.

My chest is burning when I finally spot him, his back hunched, arms resting on the railing as he stares at the light cast over the waves by the moon. I push harder, sprinting through the pain, but it's even harder to breathe when he turns to face me.

Kip's eyes are wide, searching, and when recognition hits him — when he realizes it's me — the hardness that falls over his features is enough to knock what little breath I had right out of my chest. He shakes his head, turning to face the water again as my run slows to a walk, and then to nothing.

I stand there and watch him.

He stands there and watches the water.

And now I need to speak, and I have no idea where to start.

Kip won't turn to face me, like even *looking* at me makes him sick — and I can't blame him. I'm still trying to catch my breath, bending at the waist for a moment before standing as tall as I can.

"Kip, please," I start, breath still ragged. "Let me explain."

Even as the words leave my mouth, I know how pathetic they are. And as he should, Kip just laughs.

"Don't bother, Skyler," he says, voice low but firm. "You played your game, and you played it really fucking well."

I cringe.

"Are you sure you're sold on the poker world?" he continues. "Because with the performance you gave, I think you might want to move to Hollywood."

Ouch.

His words are harsh, and even though I deserve them, it doesn't lessen the sting. I want to retreat into myself, to throw my hands up in surrender and crawl back to my room with my tail between my legs to cry the night away.

But that's not me.

That's not what Skyler Fucking Thorne does.

So, instead, I reach for his arm and whip him around to face me.

"Okay, you're mad," I say. "And you deserve to be. But don't you dare treat me like that. You're going to let me explain myself and you're not going to say a word until I finish, and *then* you can make up your mind about me."

"I don't have to—"

"Damn it, Kip!" I cut him off, desperation slipping through my voice as it cracks. "Let me fight for you!"

My heart squeezes, tears stinging my nose, but I don't let them show.

"If you don't want me after you hear me out, I'll let you go," I concede, swallowing the awful possibility of that like a jagged, dry pill. "But I'm not going to do that until I know I've fought to keep you."

Kip's jaw ticks, his eyes flickering over mine. I wait, wondering if he'll shrug me off, if he'll turn back around, but when he just stands there, I take a deep breath and a step closer.

To which he takes a step back.

I roll my lips together, closing my eyes as I confess. "It's true," I say, and instantly anger shades his face. "But it's not what you think," I add quickly. "The night I met you, Kip, I wanted you. For *me*. You completely captured me. And then when I saw you in class, I knew it would only be a matter of time before you would be mine."

"Cocky, are we?" he clips.

I narrow my eyes. "Right after that, I went back to the sorority house and Erin called us into her room. She told us the story about you guys that summer and then she dropped the bomb that you were here. And when she said your name, everything changed. She came up with this..." I wave one hand in the air. "Sick game, and like a fool, I agreed. But Kip," I plead, stepping closer again. "I *tried* to get out of it. I gave Bear's Little money to buy me at the auction. I tried to stay away from you. I tried to make you not want to be around me, but the more I tried to avoid you, the more I fell for you. And that?" I smile, just barely, a reaction of the heart. "*That* was not a game. That wasn't fake, it wasn't a lie, it wasn't pretend."

My hands shake as I confess everything, washing my slate clean yet revealing all the inky smudges forever left behind. My eyes flood with tears, and I have to take a calming breath to hold them there.

"Kip," I whisper his name as I take another step. He doesn't move, doesn't back away this time. "That night at the dance, it broke me, too. And seeing you with Erin? It..." I shake my head, and it releases the tears I was trying so desperately to keep at bay. "I can't even explain what it did to me. I've never cared about anyone the way I care about you. I would have just let any other guy go without so much as a second glance." The truth of that rings like a bell in my ears, and I realize another truth as the words slip from my lips. "But you have changed me."

He's changed me.

The weight of that sits on my chest, but not like an uncomfortable pressure. No, more like a blanket, like a warmth, a comfort, a piece of me that had been missing and now is found.

"You've opened up the side of me that I have tried so desperately to hide and I'm not even sure why," I confess, thinking about my time at PSU, how I've tried so hard to just fit in and blend. "You like me when I'm being *me,* no matter what I'm wearing or who I'm with or what I'm doing. You care about my love for poker and no one has ever taken the time to appreciate what I love the way you have."

His face morphs at that, a shade of something coloring his anger. Is it remorse? Sympathy? Whatever it is, I take it as my cue to slip through the crack in his walls.

"You made it impossible to play Erin's game because you came at me so fiercely and without apologies and you..." I choke. "You made me love you, Kip."

Oh my God, I said it. I said I loved him.

I don't have time to panic, because it's true, and the truth is all I can offer Kip right now.

"And I'm sorry. I'm so, so sorry for what I've done," I continue, tears streaming, heart squeezing. "But I'm not sorry for loving you."

Kip's hands snap out for me and in the next instant, I'm in his arms, his body engulfing mine as I melt into him and completely break. I fist my hands in his shirt, my tears soaking his shoulder as relief pours through me like sweet champagne.

"I'm so sorry," I repeat, words muffled by his shirt.

Kip kisses my hair, his lips lingering there as he forces a long exhale. "Stop, it's okay. It's okay."

"It's not okay," I argue, pulling back. "None of it was okay and I knew it then just as much as I know it now. But it's over, and I promise I will never lie to you again. I don't want to keep anything from you. Ever. You've always given me nothing but honesty, and that's what I want to give to you. I'm sorry. Please, please forgive me."

Kip's nose flares, his own eyes glossing over as he pulls me back into him. It's indescribable, what I feel when his arms are wrapped around me, when my ear is pressed against his chest, his heartbeats connecting to mine.

"I do," he says softly, stroking my hair back as he kisses my forehead. "I forgive you."

I didn't know I had more weight to give him until those words slipped free, and I melt into him even more, my knees weak, hands gripping onto him for dear life. Kip takes my weight easily, his stance never wavering. Slowly, he pulls back, his eyes searching mine.

"I love you, too," he whispers.

My lip quivers, more tears slipping free, but this time from a different well. I smile, shaking my head as Kip wipes them away with his thumb.

"I don't deserve you," he adds. "I'll never be good enough for you, but I love you, nonetheless."

He presses his lips to mine before I can argue, and I kiss him hard in return, sealing our vows of love in the only way we really can. Kip's hands slip to frame my face, his own kisses coming harder as heat builds between us. We're all hands and grips, breaths and groans, and when he presses my back against the railing, his grip tight on my hips as he trails kisses from my lips to my jaw and down my neck, I whisper the only thing I want in the world right now.

"Take me back to your room."

***

"Get out," Kip says firmly when we burst through the door of his room.

Kade smirks, his eyes bouncing between us before he hops off the bed. That smirk grows to a shit-eating grin as he swipes a flask off the dresser and tips it at us with a wink on his way out.

I smile back, a blush shading my cheeks. Kip just rolls his eyes and shuts the door as soon as Kade is gone.

When we're finally alone, that same electricity that always exists between us buzzes back to life, charging the room with a familiar, magnetic heat. Kip slows his movements, making his way to a phone plugged in by the bed with a long exhale.

"Do you like Ed Sheeran at all?"

I shrug, taking a seat on the edge of his bed and tucking my hands under my thighs. "I don't know, I've never really listened to him, honestly."

Why am I so nervous?

The answer to that hits me almost as soon as I think to question it. I'm not ashamed to say I've had plenty of sex in my short twenty-one years of life, but I've never made love.

I've never had sex with someone I loved.

Truly loved.

I swallow when a soft melody fills the room, and Kip turns the volume up a few pegs, his eyes hot on mine when he turns around again. He reaches for me, pulling me to stand easily before slipping his hands to frame my face again. He searches my eyes, lips finding mine with a tender, delicate pressure that makes my knees shake.

When I open my mouth, his tongue slides inside, stealing both of our next breaths. When we let them go, it's on a sigh that mixes between us, my hands finding their way up into his messy, wind-blown hair. Kip reaches for the hem of my hoodie, fingering it softly at first before breaking our kiss long enough to strip it over my head.

He smiles when he sees I'm in nothing but my bra once it's gone. "Were you planning on taking this off at all tonight?"

"I was hoping you'd be the one to do it."

Kip smirks, his eyes hungry as he slowly unbuttons my jeans. He takes my mouth with his before tugging them over my hips, my ass, my thighs. They fall to my ankles and, keeping my eyes on his, I slip my thumbs in the band of my panties, peeling them down my legs next.

His eyes follow the movement, Adam's apple bobbing hard in his throat as I step out of them, snapping off my bra in a fluid motion next, and then I'm standing in front of him completely bare.

Completely ready for him.

Time slows, dancing with us to the soft croon of Ed Sheeran's voice as I cross the space between us. I slip my hands under his shirt, moaning in appreciation at the hot, hard muscles underneath. I remember all too well how they feel, how they look... how they taste.

Kip's eyes roll back when my fingertips trace the line of his boxers, his hands reaching for the back neck of his shirt quickly. He discards it as I untie his board shorts, my heart beating in my throat with every move. I've touched Kip before, felt him inside me, witnessed his head buried between my legs. But every touch is amplified this time — slower, more purposeful, with a weight only three little words can add.

He loves me.

He *loves* me.

I smile, that thought on repeat as Kip pulls his shorts and boxers down swiftly, shoving them to the side once they're on the floor. And then, it's just us, body to body, skin on skin.

We stare.

His eyes devour me, racing over every curve before locking back on my eyes. I see the same blue of mine reflected in his, like two oceans meeting, joining as one. There's no rush, no frantic urgency. Tonight, we take our time, letting the music pace our touches, our breaths, our love.

I reach forward, fingertips brushing his jaw before I drop them to his chest, tracing that valley between the muscles of his abdomen. I let them rest just above the line of his hips, waiting.

"You're so fucking gorgeous," Kip whispers, our foreheads brushing.

I just smile, holding onto him as I lower myself back down to the edge of the bed. Then, slowly, I crawl my way up the bed to the pillows, watching him over my shoulder as I move. His eyes on me are like the strongest shot of espresso, the caffeine buzzing through me as I spread myself across the bed. I touch one edge of the bed with my left toes, and then the other with my right, legs wide open as I beckon Kip with one finger.

He shakes his head, like he can't believe I'm real — that *this* is real — that we are real. Time stretches as he kisses his way up my body, starting at my ankle and touching every inch he can with his lips until he reaches my mouth. He sucks my bottom lip between his teeth, grinding his stiff and ready member against my clit with just enough pressure to make me moan into his kiss.

Kip slows, circling his hips, the friction a perfect tease for both of us. When I reach down, gripping him between us and pressing him to my wet entrance, we both pause, inhaling a breath and locking eyes as just the tip of him slides between my folds.

A beat in time.

A second.

A breath.

And then, slowly, with his eyes still on mine, Kip pushes forward, filling me in one, slick flex.

Just like that, everything fades away.

The music is gone, the lights extinguished like match flames, the ship and the bed and anything that isn't our bodies, our hearts, our souls — gone. We're floating, suspended in a moment, in a body-consuming, earth-shattering, life-altering speck of time where everything changes. Kip is a part of me now, and I, a part of him, and neither one of us will ever live without that part being with us ever again.

I moan, dragging my nails down his back as he presses all the way in. Our bodies are sealed together in a seam, sweat slicking our movements as Kip withdraws and flexes, over and over, again and again. He plants kisses as I breathe and moan, his lips brushing my neck, my collarbone, the swell of my breasts. It's all I can do to hold onto his biceps, feeling each rock of his hips like an earthquake of pleasure and powerful emotion.

And for the rest of the night, we make love. Like two virgins, discovering each other in a brand-new light, a brand new way. It's my first time making love like this, and I know without a doubt that it's his. I see it in the way his eyes search mine, in the gentle touches of his hands, in the soft melody of our breaths mixing together.

I laid my cards on the table, and I lost my heart in the bet.

It belongs to Kip Jackson now.

It belongs to him forever.

Cassie

Last time I was in Key West, Adam kissed me.

I close my eyes, feeling the salty ocean air breeze across my face as that night comes back in blinding color. I remember the way he looked at me before his lips met mine, that crease in his brows, like he knew he shouldn't but he couldn't help himself. I remember the way we both exhaled, the way my stomach flipped, how my hands shook as I climbed to straddle him on that dark, secluded beach.

All we did was kiss.

But it wasn't *just* kissing.

It was an exchange of souls, a trading of hearts. I gave him mine, and he handed me his, and even though things were complicated then — I was with Grayson, he'd just broken up with Skyler — we made a silent promise not to hurt each other.

And we both lied.

My eyes flutter open, and I sigh, leaning over the railing and letting my eyes drift lazily along the different vendors set up at Mallory Square below us. It's the last day of our cruise, and we all spent the day frolicking on Duval Street before retreating to the boat just in time to push off from shore. I watch as the last few people board the ship, the door shutting, and the captain announces we'll pull away in just ten short minutes.

There's a party on the pool deck, and all of my sisters are down there making the most of their last night. They're day drunk and happy, celebrating an incredible trip, and I should be with them.

But I can't be.

I can't fake a smile anymore, or shove another shot down my throat when everything I taste makes me want to vomit. The truth is, I can't stop thinking about Adam, about last night, about what we said and what we *didn't* say. Everything's a mess.

First and foremost, me.

So, I snuck up to the very top deck, and while the party rages on just below me, I watch the coastline below, thinking of the last time I was in Key West and how I'd been just as much of a mess then.

Yet, somehow, I'd been happier.

Being with Adam, no matter how wrong it was, always made me happier.

I sigh, trailing one finger over the cool railing. Suddenly, there's a loud clanking noise behind me, followed by a curse muttered under someone's breath. I turn, one brow cocked as I take in Adam shuffling toward me, a giant, black duffle bag hanging from his shoulder. It hits his thigh, bouncing off awkwardly, and he curses again before dropping it to the deck when he's standing a few feet away from me.

My instinct is to laugh, to smile and ask him what the hell he's doing, but as soon as the thought passes my mind, my smile dies before it's even born. His messy hair, his dark, intoxicating eyes — shadowed and dark, as if he hasn't slept — they make me want to forget what happened. They make me want to throw my arms around him, kiss him, hold him, spend the night in his arms.

But I refuse to do any of that.

Instead, I cross my arms over my chest, leaning one hip against the railing as I face him.

"I've been looking everywhere for you," he pants, running a flustered hand back through his hair as he eyes the duffle bag at his feet. He points to it like a curse. "Dragging this sonofabitch with me."

I shift, glancing at the bag before I take in his haggard appearance again. Though I know it's impossible, it almost feels like he's lost muscle mass since yesterday, like he's shrunk three inches, his entire body shriveling away before my very eyes. He hasn't slept, that much I know.

He can join the club.

"I just needed some time to think," I answer softly.

Adam swallows, nodding just once. "Good. I'm glad you're up here, away from everyone." He pauses, wringing his hands together. "Cassie, I am so sorry for hurting you. Again."

I close my eyes on his words, pressing my fingers to my temple. "Adam..."

"No, please. *Please,*" he begs. "Just, I know you said I have to earn it. Earn *you.* And you're right. Can you please just give me the next five minutes to try to do just that?" Adam's shoulders fall. "Or at least, to try to *start*, anyway."

I don't nod, don't give him a verbal agreement, but I also don't turn away. I just fold my arms over my chest again, eyes falling to the bag at his feet before they settle on his tired eyes once more.

Adam sighs, his shoulders tugging back like he's preparing to deliver a speech he's practiced for years. His eyes level with mine, tender and soft, just like they always are when he looks at me. They're like home, that familiar, comfortable peace that exists in no other place, in no other person.

Just him.

Always.

"Ever since we met, we've played games with each other's hearts," he starts, reaching into the bag at his feet. He pulls out the board game, Clue, and holds it between his hands. "At first, I didn't have a clue how to handle what I felt for you."

A smile threatens to break on my lips, but I cover it with my fingertips, trying with all my might not to let the fact that Adam is insanely adorable affect me.

"If I'm being honest," he continues. "I think I did know, I think I always have. But, I was scared."

He reaches into the bag again, this time pulling out the board game, Snakes and Ladders.

"Our entire relationship has been full of ups and downs. It seems like when I climb a ladder to reach you, you slide down into a pit of snakes." He coughs. "Clay, Grayson." He coughs again.

I smirk.

"And just when I slide down to you, just when our hands touch, it's like you climb a ladder, and you're out of reach again." He pauses, shaking his head. "It's like we're always just out of reach."

He drops the box, reaching in to pull out Chess, next.

"So, I try and try to set up a strategy, to put all the pieces in place. I convinced myself if I waited, if I let Grayson fuck up on his own, you'd be with me in the end. But I couldn't stop myself from interfering. And even though, in time, he did end up proving that he was a douchebag," he says, holding up one finger. "I shouldn't have tried to rush that. I shouldn't have been wishing for him to hurt you, Cassie, just because I wanted the chance to have you."

My heart twists with the thought of Grayson, that wound still tender, still healing.

"As if that wasn't bad enough," he says, reaching in the bag for a little foam football. "When I finally had you, instead of being your teammate, I tried to be your coach, instead. I tried to tell you how to run your plays, how to live your life, how to find yourself — when, honestly, it was just because I was scared."

I frown, tilting my head to one side.

"I was," he repeats, nodding. "*God*, Cassie, I was petrified to be with you. To love you. Because I knew that somehow, some way, I'd fuck it all up and I'd lose you. Up until this point, I've never had the chance to make you mine — not truly. And the fact of the matter is that even though it's all I've wanted since the very moment I met you, it's also my biggest fear. To have you, *really* have you, and then lose you. For good."

I roll my lips, fighting against the tears blurring my vision as Adam pours his heart out to me. It makes sense, that fear, because I know I've had it, too. But the more he talks, the more he explains, the more my heart retreats.

"And I know," he says, dropping the football and pulling a small, wooden bat out next. "That I haven't just had three strikes. No, I've had three strike*outs.* I haven't lost just one at bat, I've lost an entire game."

He rears back, holding the bat high above his head before slamming it down on the deck.

I jump, he screams, the bat staying fully in tact as he drops it to the deck and rubs his right wrist.

"Oh, my God, Adam, are you okay?"

I move toward him, but he holds up one hand to stop me, gritting through the pain.

"Stop," he grunts. "I'm trying to grand gesture here, okay?"

I chuckle, shaking my head and leaning back against the rail to let him finish.

Adam shakes his head, cursing as he shoves the still-whole bat back into the bag. "What I'm trying to say is, I'm done playing games, Cassie. With your head, with your heart, with our relationship. I want to be with you. *Really* be with you — no matter what the risk, no matter what the odds, no matter what the future might hold."

He's shaking now as he bends to retrieve one last box, and he holds it up with a sad, hopeful smile.

"I don't know everything. I don't know if we'll make it, or if you'll change your mind, or if I'll be a perfect boyfriend or fuck up time and time again." He shrugs. "I can't predict what will happen. All I *do* know is that I love you, Cassie McBee."

I choke on a sob, the tears flooding my eyes and spilling over without a chance to hold them at bay.

"I *love* you," he repeats, stepping forward, the game still between his hands. "And if we are stuck in the game of Life," he says, tapping the box. "There's no one else I want to play it with."

Smiling, I cover my mouth with one hand, glancing at the box as he drops it at his feet and steps toward me. His hands reach for mine, both of us shaking, and when his thumbs smooth over the skin of my wrists, I sigh.

"I can't take back anything that I've done, but I can tell you that I am sorry. And I can promise you that I will do everything I can to not be so fucking stupid anymore," he says, and we both chuckle. "If you will give me the chance, I will love you like you deserve to be loved."

More tears slip from my eyes as my head falls forward, and he meets me in the middle, our foreheads touching, eyes closing. Adam rubs my hands with his, pulling me closer, his arms slipping around me and pulling me into him.

And I want to stay.

I want to stay right here, in his arms, in the comfort of his words forever. I want to plant a flag, plant some roots, and settle down for life. Because in my heart I know that he's it — he's all I've ever wanted, and he's everything that's wrong and right and all that I desire. Adam Brooks is my soul mate.

But he's my Kryptonite, too.

I reach around my back, unlacing his fingers and dropping them at his side before I step back. My heart aches in protest the moment we break contact, but I stamp that little sucker down, letting my head lead this time.

"I'm sorry, Adam," I whisper.

I glance at him with the words, and immediately wish I hadn't. The way his face breaks, the slump in his shoulders, the tremor of his hands as he reaches for me again, shake me to my very core. But I step back, away, swiping the new tears from my cheeks.

"I don't believe you."

Silence.

Not just between us, but in the entire world. It's like with those four words, I stole time and space, created a vacuum that took everything away. There are no breaths, no sun setting off in the distance, no music playing below, nowhere to exist after this moment.

It's all gone.

Adam's eyes well, and I can't even beg him not to cry, knowing it will break me, before one tear slides down his cheek, running the length of his jaw and falling to the deck below.

"You don't mean that," he croaks, shaking his head. "You don't... you can't..."

"I do," I say, swallowing down a fresh wave of tears. "I'm sorry, Adam. I'm sorry. I just can't do this anymore."

The vacuum breaks, the noise crashes back in all at once, the sun sets in the distance, and I turn away from the boy I've always turned to.

Then, I run.

EPISODE 6

Adam

"Come on, man," Jeremy says, kicking my foot where it hangs off the side of my bed. "You've got to stop moping."

"Fuck off."

He chuckles, sitting at the foot of my bed with a sigh. "Look, you pulled out all the stops and it didn't work. So, you didn't get the girl," he says, shrugging. "I hate to tell you, but you're not the only one in history for that to happen to. You're not the first, and you definitely won't be the last."

"Is this supposed to make me feel better?" I ask, eyes glued to the ceiling. I'm still in the same flannel pants and white t-shirt that I changed into when we got home from the cruise. It's a little more dingy yellow than white, now.

"It's supposed to let you know that this won't kill you."

"I beg to differ."

Jeremy sighs again, and I just let out another painful breath. That's how every single breath has been since I watched Cassie run away from me on the top deck of that cruise ship.

I don't believe you.

My chest shrinks again, as if the bones of my rib cage want nothing more than to puncture each one of my lungs and put me out of my misery.

"Have you tried talking to her?"

I shake my head.

"You should."

"She ran away from me, Jeremy," I say, not taking my gaze from the ceiling. "*Ran.* Like the thought of being around me for even a split second more would make her crawl out of her skin."

"She's scared."

At that, I laugh, though the whole situation is anything but funny. "She should be. I'm an asshole. I've done nothing but hurt her when all I want is to make her happy."

"You're being such a chick."

I don't acknowledge that. There's nothing more to say.

Jeremy punches my leg in a brotherly way, standing and shoving his hands in his pockets. "Alright, man. I'll leave you alone. Just... try to take a shower before Chapter tomorrow night, okay?"

The door to my bedroom opens and closes, and then I'm alone — the way I'll likely stay forever.

God, I really am pathetic.

But I can't help it. I was barely putty in Cassie's hands the day I went to her, putting my heart on the line — putting *everything* on the line. I was held together by bubble gum and hope, and she popped both.

I've gone through every emotion since that day.

At first, I was devastated. I cried. *Cried.* I'm a man, one raised by a grandfather who warned me that men don't cry. And yet, I did. Then, once the sadness had faded, I got angry. How could she walk away from me, from us, when I apologized for *everything*? How could she just throw it all away?

Guilt came next, because I knew *exactly* why she could throw it all away. I told her to listen to my actions, and then I let them speak loud and clear. In my mind, I was showing her my love, but in reality, I was only showing her time and time again that she was never the number-one priority in my life. Even though she *was,* I didn't show it.

I wished I could go back, go back to the dance and not chase after Skyler. I wished I could take Cassie in my arms instead, twirl her around the dance floor, remind her I would always be there. I wished I could go back to the poker tournament, let Skyler go on her own, wait for Cassie and go to her and Skyler's room *together.*

So many mistakes. So many moments I wish I could re-do. So many things I wish I could take back.

And after that guilt subsided, I landed in some sticky kind of acceptance. Except it wasn't the healing kind. No, the kind of acceptance I found myself in was the kind that swallows you whole, that pulls you into a deep, tar-like darkness, its hands around your throat, suffocating you with your new reality.

I've laid here inside it ever since.

Right now, it's still cold. It's still dark and unfamiliar, like a reality that couldn't possibly be mine. But over time, I imagine it'll come to feel like home.

Over time, I imagine I'll have to learn how to let her go.

My bedroom door opens again, and I sigh, closing my eyes on that painful exhale. "Jeremy, just drop it. Please. Let me wallow in peace."

"Whatcha wallowing about?"

My eyes snap open at the sound of her voice, almost as if it's a dream, as if I just realized I'm sleeping but now I'm half awake, wondering if I want to stay in the dream or shake myself to consciousness.

Slowly, I raise up onto my elbows, and when my eyes land on Cassie, my chest tightens, heart jumping to life at the sight of her.

Her ginger hair is piled into a curly, messy bun, a few tendrils framing her face in a haphazard manner as she folds her arms over her middle. Her eyes skate the floor before those emerald gems lock onto mine, and her brows bend, pink lips pulling to one side.

"Can I sit?" she asks, nodding toward the bed.

I scramble up to the headboard, scooting over and making room for her. "Of course. Here, sit. Please."

She smiles, sitting at the edge of the bed, one leg propped on the sheets while the other remains grounded. Her eyes search mine, taking in what I'm sure are dark, sleepless circles by now. Cassie's face breaks, tears glossing her pupils before she blinks them away.

"Adam, I'm so sorry. I shouldn't have run from you, I shouldn't have left you like that."

"Stop," I say quickly, holding up one hand on a breath. "Trust me, I deserved that. And more. I don't..." I swallow. "I don't blame you for leaving, for not believing me. You don't have a reason to, not after all I've done."

She smiles, but it falls quickly, eyes still glossed as she whispers, "That's just the problem, though. Even though I shouldn't, I can't help it." Cassie shrugs. "I do."

I frown. "You do what?"

"Believe you," she says it on a whispered laugh, a shake of her head like she can't believe it's the truth. Then, she lowers her voice even more. "Want you. Need you." She pauses. "Love you."

I gape at her.

Full on, eyes wide, mouth open gape.

"What are you saying right now?"

She smiles, shaking her head with something between a shrug and a shiver touching her shoulders. "I'm saying that it doesn't matter what you've done to me, what I've done to you. It doesn't matter if we've both hurt each other, if we've both messed up. It doesn't matter that we can't go back in time and make this story — *our* story — perfect." She sniffs, her eyes flooding again as she watches me. "What we have is the messiest, stupidest, most fucked-up thing I've ever heard of and yet, I can't let it go."

I let out a breath, reaching for her hands, my fingers wrapping around hers as two tears slip from her eyes.

"I can't let *you* go, Adam. Not even if I wanted to."

I steal her next words with a kiss, tasting the salty wetness of her tears on her lips as they meet mine. She chokes — whether on a laugh or a sob, I can't be sure — but her hands reach around my neck, fingertips slipping into my hair as she pulls me closer.

"Don't let me go," I whisper, kissing that plea as soon as it leaves my mouth and touches hers. "Please, Cassie. Don't let me go."

She laughs, climbing into my lap and kissing me harder. My hands slip into the back pockets of her jean shorts, and she gasps, pushing her hands into my chest.

"But, if we're doing this, we're *doing* it." She says, one brow raising. "I mean like I'm your girlfriend, you're my boyfriend, there is no other girl above me and no other guy above you."

I cock an eyebrow back at her. "You act like any of that is a deal breaker."

"And, I want to take it slow," she says, resting her hands on my shoulders. "We've rushed through so much, made decisions without thinking... that stops now. From here on, I want to be a team."

"Me, too."

"Okay," she says, as if she's stood her ground. Her brows are set, eyes determined.

"Okay," I agree, and I can't help but smirk. "Can I kiss you now, boss?"

Her eyes soften, a smile touching her lips, too, before she lowers them to mine.

"It's like you said earlier this semester," she whispers against my lips. "You never have to ask."

And just like an 80's movie, I thrust my fist into the air, earning me a chuckle before I steal her next laugh with an even deeper kiss.

I got the girl.

Thank *fuck*, I got the girl.

Erin

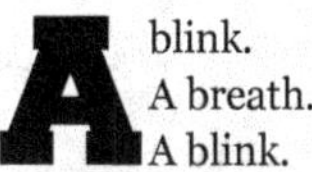

A blink.

A breath.

A blink.

Repeat.

I stare at my planner, willing it to clear itself, or to check off the items highlighted in a dozen different colors without me having to participate. All I want to do, all I can manage, is to blink, breathe, blink, repeat.

Classes start back up tomorrow.

I should have stood tall as a leader tonight, running our post-Spring Break Chapter, but I cancelled it.

Because I couldn't stand up there in front of all my sisters and pretend like I deserved to be there.

Not after what I did.

As soon as the words slipped from my mouth, I regretted them. I almost stopped mid-sentence, almost turned and left Kip standing there wondering what the hell I was going to say. But it was like word vomit, unable to stop once I started upchucking the truth.

My parents never told me it was right to tell the truth, but somewhere along the way, I learned that. Church, maybe? A teacher? A friend? Wherever that lesson came from, I'm sure there was a little asterisk somewhere that said, "Always tell the truth — *if* that truth is yours to tell."

And what I told Kip? That was not my truth to tell.

Sure, I was a part of it — the "plan." Hell, I was the source of it. But, I knew just as well as everyone else after seeing Kip and Skyler that night at the piano bar that they were in love. I was out of the picture. There *was* no chance for me and Kip anymore.

But I couldn't stop.

I wanted him so badly, wanted *happiness* so badly, that I couldn't see reason.

And now, I have to own up to that. To *my* truth.

A blink.

A breath.

A blink.

Repeat.

Somehow, I peel myself out of my office chair and let my feet carry me on autopilot down the hall to Skyler and Jess's room. The girls all freeze inside when I swing the door open, my eyes gracing each one of them.

Ashlei, Jess, Cassie, Skyler — all snuggled up, spending a lazy Sunday watching movies.

Without me.

"Little," I finally say, my voice a croak. "Can I talk to you?"

The realization of how bad I must look sinks in as the girls' brows bend in pity, their eyes skating over my worn and tired features. I cross one arm over my stomach, holding the elbow of the opposite, feeling like an injured bird on display at a zoo.

"About what?"

Skyler's voice is a clip, her jaw set.

I just watch her, silently begging her to give me the chance to explain.

She sighs, throwing the covers off her and Cassie in a dramatic fashion before hopping off the bed. I don't even look at the other girls before I turn, and Skyler follows me back to my room.

Skyler pauses at the entrance, her arms crossed, body language as closed off as I imagine her heart is to me right now.

"Come sit down," I try, gesturing to the bed.

"I'll stand."

I sigh. "Leave it to you to make this even harder than it already is."

As soon as the words leave my mouth, I internally curse. They aren't *my* words — they're my mother's. I hear her more in every move I make nowadays. But, for once, I understand her.

Easier to point a finger at the other person than admit my own part in the game.

Only, Skyler isn't me. She won't just sit back and let me speak to her the way my mother speaks to me. She won't let me — won't let *anyone* — talk to her like that.

She crosses the room in less than a second, and yet I feel the palm of her hand against my cheek in slow motion, the sting of it somehow lost by the time I register what happened. My hand flies up, covering the cheek she struck, and while my immediate reaction is to strike back, I simply nod.

Skyler stands there, chest heaving, face beet red as she dares me to get mad, to lash out. But she and I both know I won't.

"Fair enough," I say, rubbing my cheek. "I deserved that. But I'm not the only one at fault here, Little."

Skyler laughs, throwing her hands up and turning to leave without another word.

"Wait!" I plead, stopping her just before she hits my door. "Please, let's just talk about this. I'm not saying it was your fault, I know it's mostly mine, but just let me speak. We have to work this out." My chest squeezes. "You can't be mad at me forever."

"The hell I can't."

Her face morphs in that moment, a darkness I've never seen in my Little emerging like a dragon.

"You're a *bitch*, Ex."

Her words are like another slap to the face, and I stagger back at the force of them.

"I'm your Little. Your *Little*. You're supposed to take care of me, to help me through college, to be my mentor in all things. Instead, you wrapped me up in this twisted game that you *knew* I was uncomfortable playing."

The more she speaks, the more my brain scrambles, quickly building my defense. I should be listening to her, should be heeding her words, but I can't help but hold up my mirror to reflect back at her.

"And when it was all finally over," she continues, "and we could move on, you gave me one last jab with your knife like the last thing you wanted to see was for me to come out of this whole mess alive. I don't owe you anything, Erin. Nothing."

"I know that, okay?!"

The words burst from my lips in a high-pitched, desperate scream. I step toward her, hands out in a plea for understanding.

A blink.

A breath.

A blink.

Repeat.

Except this time, with the blinks, my cheeks are wet. With the breath, a sob.

"You think I don't see that what I've done is pathetic and disgusting?" I choke out. "I can't even talk to anyone I know about how I feel because I'm ashamed to admit what I asked you to do. And on the cruise? Yeah, I made one of the worst choices of my entire life, Little. I fucked up."

My next breath is stolen, chest stinging painfully as I gasp for air on another sob.

"And I am so, so sorry," I croak. "I'm sorry for what I asked you to do, for the way I've treated you, for what I did earlier this week. I'm sorry for all of it. I love you, Little."

Skyler swallows hard as I succumb to another wave of tears, my skin hot and itchy with emotion. Sniffing, I inhale a deep, cleansing breath, wiping the tears from my cheeks with the back of my sleeve.

"But you hurt me too, Little," I say, finally looking her in the eye again. "You could have stopped this. You could have told me from the beginning that you couldn't do it, that you didn't want to. At the auction, I told you before it even started that we didn't have to do this," I remind her. "You could have stopped it."

That seems to sober Skyler, and she blinks, holding her chin almost defiantly high.

"And when I was getting caught up in Kip and thinking everything was working," I say, voice thick with emotion again at the realization that everything I thought I felt from him was all a lie. "You could have warned me that it wasn't. You could have told me the truth. But instead, you snuck behind my back and pulled him back to you. You played our own little game so that you could come out of this whole thing unscathed."

"You threatened me with the presidency!"

"And you knew that with or without me, you could get elected!" I throw back.

Skyler's jaw clenches, the air thickening with a hot, electric charge.

"Stop trying to make it sound like you were defenseless in all this, Sky. You didn't stop it, and you damn sure didn't do anything to make it right in the end. You would have never told Kip. Yeah, it wasn't my place to tell him," I admit. "But he deserved to know. If you two are going to be together, he should be able to choose to be with you knowing the truth."

"God, do you hear yourself?" Skyler throws her hands up, exhausted. "You manipulated me, Erin. You know what, I will give you one thing — I should have stopped it," she confesses. "But I couldn't. I didn't have the strength — not until after Kip made me realize to stop caring so much about what you and all the people on this campus think of me."

She shakes her head as I digest her words, wondering what intention lies beneath them. Does she think I judge her, that I don't love her for who she is? Because that couldn't be further from the truth. If anything, I look up to her. I wish I could be more like her, not the other way around.

"I don't know if I want to be president next year," she adds, voice softer. "But *if* I run, it will be because *I* want to. Not because our family has been in this room for as long as anyone can remember, not because everyone would talk if I didn't run, and damn sure not because you want me to."

Skyler points at me with one straight, damning finger. When she lets it drop again, she just stares at me like I'm a monster.

And I can't even argue that I'm not.

I nod, sniffling. "Look, I don't want to fight anymore," I say pathetically. "I'm sorry, okay? I'm sorry for everything. I know it's not going to be like a light switch for you to forgive me, but please just tell me you'll try," I plead, eyes searching hers for the same girl I sat with on pledge night, the same girl I helped become the young woman she is now. "I'm human, I made a mistake. But I love you, Sky. And whether you think I do or not, I love you regardless of what you wear, or who you're with, or what position you hold."

Skyler's bottom lip quivers at that, but she just holds her chin higher.

"We all do," I add, gesturing to the girls down the hall. "We're your sisters, Skyler. You may think we judge you based on those things, but we don't."

She swallows, nodding a bit as her eyes gloss. "I love you, too, Big. And I forgive you." She pauses. "I'm not ready to move back to where we were before, but I'm willing to try if you are."

A smile splits my face, and I nod.

"But don't ever put me in this kind of position again, Ex," she warns.

"Never."

Skyler nods. "Okay."

"Okay," I agree, still smiling. But as soon as she turns and leaves my bedroom, that smile dissipates, like cotton candy in a bowl of cold water.

What the hell is wrong with me?

She's only just left the room, and yet I can't help but replay my so-called apology — one that she gracefully accepted even when I didn't deserve it. I can't even *apologize* right. I can't even accept fault for the mistakes I've made without pointing two fingers right back at the person I'm apologizing to.

My mom has hardened me into the same kind of woman she is.

Cold.

Heartless.

Selfish.

In my attempt to heal, to survive what happened to me, I took advice from the one woman I never wanted to be. And just as I suspected, it's lonely in her shoes.

It's lonely in mine.

I don't even realize what I'm doing until I'm halfway down Greek Row, tears still stained on my cheeks, hair pulled up in a messy pony tail and shoes not matching my sundress. A few girls gape at me as I pass, no doubt wondering if it's even me. Surely, that can't be Erin Xanders, the most put-together girl on campus.

Surely, those can't be her tears on her cheeks.

Surely, that can't be her hair, thrown up haphazardly over a face completely void of makeup.

I shove through the door of the Omega Chi house, and on my way down to Clinton's room, I run into him in the hallway. His cologne invades my senses before his full body comes into view, and I can't help but scan him — hat to matching sneakers. He looks incredible, like he's going on a date, like he's ready to make panties melt off with one little second of eye contact and a smirk.

I should leave.

I should leave him alone.

I should let him be happy.

But one glance at me has his brows furrowing, his hands reaching for me before I can stop the tears from pooling in my eyes. They slip over easily as he pulls me into him, dampening his button-up shirt.

He just kisses my hair.

"I'm here," he whispers, holding me tight. "I'm right here."

A blink.

A breath.

A blink.

Repeat.

And then, I break.

Skyler

When Wednesay rolls around, the first week of classes post-Spring Break back in full swing, Kip and I finally get together for the first time since he kissed me goodbye after the cruise ended. We've texted, but he's blown me off every time we had plans to hang out. He kept saying he was dealing with something, and though I told him I was there to help, he just asked for space.

So, I gave it to him.

But now that I'm finally with him, I can't help but feel uneasy as one thought repeats like a record in my mind.

Kip is different.

I don't know how else to describe it. He's *physically* here — he cooked me dinner, held me close while we watched a movie, kissed me just as slow and sensual as ever before loving me between his sheets — but mentally, he's gone.

And for the life of me, I can't figure out how to pull him back to Earth.

"Are you sure we're okay?" I ask for what has to be at least the tenth time. I'm sure it's annoying, but it can't be half as frustrating as him avoiding whatever it is that's bothering him.

We're still lying in bed, our bodies tangled up together. He pulls me in a little closer and kisses my forehead. "We're fine, babe."

"Just fine?" I lean up to look at him, taking in his messy blond hair — the hair I had my hands in not too long ago. He sighs, gently moving me off of him as he stands and pulls on his boxers. I watch as the muscles in his back ebb and flow with the movement, like a hypnotizing song lulling me into a trance.

"Sky, please, I'm asking you to just not push right now."

My stomach aches at his words. I hate this. We're not fighting, but something is off and he won't tell me what. And perhaps the feeling souring in my stomach the most is that this is uncharted territory for us.

We've never been here before.

We've been pissed at each other, sure, but all *those* times we were apart. Now, we're together and something is wrong, but what?

"Are you still mad at me? For the Erin thing?"

He laughs a little, running his fingers through his tousled hair. "No, Skyler. I told you I forgave you for that and I meant it. I'm not even thinking about it anymore. It's done."

I swallow, hating the possibility of his answer to my next question. "Are you done with me?"

His eyes grow wide and he crosses the room to sit on the bed with me again. "What? No, baby. Are you kidding me? You're the only thing keeping me grounded right now, the only thing getting me out of bed in the morning." His diamond eyes are pained, his jaw tense as he lets out a long breath. "I don't deserve you, Skyler."

"I don't understand, why do you keep saying that?"

He opens his mouth to say something, but then stops himself, shaking his head. "I can't get into it tonight, okay? I love you, Skyler." My stomach still flutters at those words. "I do, *so* fucking much. But I'm going through a lot right now. And I want to tell you, I *will* tell you, but I can't tell you tonight."

My stomach drops.

"I know that's not fair, but I'm asking you to be okay with it. For me."

Kip lifts my hand in his to his lips and kisses my fingers, waiting for me to reply.

I nod softly. "Okay."

He smiles and pulls me in for a long, slow kiss, and that's all it takes for every thought to blur.

"I'm going to jump in the shower real quick. Want to join?" He winks, and for just a second the playful Kip is back, but even still, he's hidden behind sad, hooded eyes.

"I have to turn in that paper before midnight. Let me finish and submit it real quick and then I'll be there."

"Don't keep me waiting too long." He leans up and kisses me again before turning toward the bathroom, shutting the door behind him.

I sigh, leaning over the bed for my bag and retrieving my laptop. I don't like that he won't tell me what's going on, but whatever it is, it's something he's not ready to deal with just yet. I can respect that. I've been there before.

And when he *is* ready, I'll be here.

With my mind made up to just let it go and let him come to me when he wants to, I shift my focus to the paper I should have turned in *before* I let Kip distract me in his bed all day. It's written, and ready to go for the most part, but I have to add a few finishing thoughts and get it submitted before the clock strikes midnight.

Cinderella essay, ladies and gents.

When I open my laptop and click the power button, nothing happens. I try a few more times and curse under my breath when I realize it's dead. I didn't bring my charger with me, and my stomach sinks when I check the clock.

Twenty minutes until midnight.

Shit.

I scan the room for Kip's laptop and find it set up on the small desk pushed against the far wall. Quickly, I grab my computer and take it to the desk, pulling the cord from his laptop and trying it in mine.

Nothing.

Double shit.

I knew it was a long shot that it would work for mine, too, but it was worth a try. I have the paper in my email, I just need to format it and add a few sentences in the conclusion. Why didn't I just do this before I left the house? Idiot.

Can brunettes have blonde moments?

"Kip?" I call out over my shoulder, opening his laptop. "What's the password on your laptop? Mine's dead and I forgot my charger."

He doesn't answer, the shower muting my question. I go to open the door to ask him again when his home screen pops up without asking for a password.

"Perfect," I murmur, double clicking the Internet Explorer icon. I log into my email and pull up the paper before quickly formatting it and typing out my final thoughts. By the time I send the email to my professor, there's less than two minutes left until midnight.

Talk about a close call.

"Sky?" Kip calls over the shower.

"I'm coming!"

I exit the browser window and start to close the laptop screen again when a folder in the right-hand corner of the desktop catches my eye.

It's labeled with my name.

I glance back over my shoulder at the bathroom, but the door is still closed, the shower running as an unsettling feeling finds home in my chest.

I know it's wrong, snooping through his stuff, but my curiosity overwhelms my conscience and I double click the folder until a list of documents pops up.

I squint at the screen, taking in the contents like I'm looking through text messages that prove my boyfriend is cheating. But there are no emails from other girls, no nude pictures — though there *are* photos.

Of me.

Playing poker.

I scan through them, noting how serious I look with my hoodie pulled over my hair. I recognize the video that he took that night I blew the tournament downtown, right before we came back here and he blew my mind.

I breathe a sigh of relief.

It's just the research he's been doing to help me prep for May.

Wow, he made an entire folder for me. He wasn't kidding about wanting to help.

I click on the Word document labeled FILE and when it fills the screen, one large photo pops up. It's the headshot I took for a blog site last year. Written above my head in bold letters is my name in all caps.

Okay, this is weird...

I scroll through the file, reading the text under each category.

CLASS SCHEDULE.
PAST RELATIONSHIPS.
HOME LIFE.
HOBBIES.
TOURNAMENT STANDINGS.
BLOG ARTICLES.
SOCIAL MEDIA.
VIDEO RESEARCH.
LIVE FEEDBACK.

The more I scroll, the faster my heart races. Under the regular text in each category, there are short notes written out in red.

Wears sunglasses to hide eyes – possible tell?

Lip quivers slightly when she has a pocket pair.

Easily distracted by emotions – work her up before tournament?

Bothered by blogs referring to her looks. Pay blogger for racy interview/find pictures?

Main reason is for family – parents not well off. Cares a lot about what other people think.

My throat constricts, my attempt at a swallow thwarted by the sick feeling that everything I think I know about Kip Jackson is a lie.

I scroll and read and scroll and read until I feel I might throw up. When I reach the end of the document, there's a small line of text written in bold.

Remember, Son – head in the game. Get her close, but don't get caught up. Break her down, find her weaknesses, and beat her in May or give it hell trying. You help me with my dream, I help you with yours. UCLA is waiting. – Dad

I stand so fast I knock the top of my thighs on the bottom of the desk, but the pain is masked by the panic racing through me. I cover my mouth, shaking my head as tears rush to my eyes.

No.

Oh my God, please, *please* no.

"Sorry, Sky, but I was turning into a raisin in there," Kip says, opening the bathroom door as steam floats up around him. He's relaxed and smiling, a navy blue towel wrapped around his waist.

But the only color I see is red.

Kip stops short when he sees my face. "What happened?" He moves toward me but I back away, shaking my head violently. "What's going on?"

My eyes find his computer and he follows my stare, swallowing hard when he sees the file pulled up on the screen. For a moment, he says nothing, and it feels like the entire world has stopped — like everything and everyone is waiting for what will happen next. My heart drums loud in my ears, my hands shaking, eyes blurred from tears.

"Skyler," he finally says, moving toward me with his arms outstretched, palms facing up like I'm a wild animal and he knows the slightest move could scare me away. "I can explain."

"Don't." I shake my head more, the room spinning as my stomach lurches. My voice is low, too low. Scratchy. Weak.

He takes another step toward me and it's like he crossed over the force field that was holding me back.

I back up to the wall, doubling over as I scream at the top of my lungs. "Don't fucking touch me!"

My breaths are ragged, strained under the pressure of my world collapsing. When I look back up at Kip, his jaw is clenched and his eyes laden with pain. "I wasn't going to go through with it, I was going to tell you and call the whole thing off," he says quickly. "Yes, that's why I came to Palm South, but when I met you, I knew I could never do what my dad was asking me to."

"Then why didn't you tell me?"

He swallows. "It's complicated."

"Are you serious?" I ask, incredulous. Not even a full week ago, we agreed — no more lies, no more games. It was supposed to be us. It was supposed to be *real.*

I've never felt more foolish in my entire life.

Shaking my head, I lift myself from the wall and stand straighter. "Whatever, I don't even care. Just tell me you aren't registered for the tournament. Tell me this was something stupid you were involved in when I was being stupid with Erin. Tell me we can put all this stupidity behind us and move on."

Kip doesn't respond, his nose flaring as he presses his lips together in a hard line. I watch as the muscles over his abdomen flex with every breath. "I can't."

My heart slows, the beats coming at a reduced pace but with more force than I've ever felt. Every thump knocks me forward a little, jerking my body with it.

"What?"

He swallows. "I am registered for the tournament."

"But you're not going, right?" I press. "Not anymore. Not after you promised me you wouldn't hurt me. Not after you told me you loved me. Not after we became *us.* Right?" I ask the questions without breathing. Breath doesn't exist in my body at this point. "*Right?*"

Kip doesn't move. He doesn't swallow or blink or flinch, but one single tear rolls down the left side of his face and under his cheek.

And I know that one tear is saying more than any words can.

"I'm sorry, Skyler."

He doesn't look away from me or hang his head. He just kills me with his baby blues, keeping me locked in their glare as he waits for my next move.

And I don't know what to do.

I want to throw something at him, I want to kill him, I want to cry and scream and rip his apartment to shreds.

But more than that, I want to run to him.

I want him to hold me and make the pain tearing my chest apart disappear. I want him to fix it. To fix me.

But he won't.

Because he can't.

Because he never loved me enough to care in the first place.

The reality of everything crashes down on me in one large, soul-crushing wave. I start breathing faster, inhaling the water instead of oxygen, panic washing through me as the wave takes me under the current, pulling me down, down, down.

I look at him one last time, memorizing the words I read in the file and relating them to his face. His beautiful smile ties into his lies, his lips into his broken promises, his eyes into the pain I feel right now in this moment.

Without another word, I turn and run out of his apartment, flying across the parking lot and across campus. He doesn't come after me and I don't wait to see if he will. I just run. I know I'll have to send someone back to get my stuff tomorrow, but I couldn't stay in that room one second longer.

For minutes, or maybe hours, it's just my feet against the pavement. It's just the air assaulting my lungs, every breath burning more than the last. It's just image after image of Kip — of his eyes, his stupid glasses, his panty-melting smile. A torturous cycle of images and touches on replay, but now, with flashes of the truth between them.

The file.

My face.

His father's words.

The tear on his cheek that told me all I needed to know.

Kip betrayed me, he lied to me — I was just a means to an end.

When I reach the house, my legs are burning and my feet are raw from running on the concrete. I put my hand on the doorknob but don't turn it. Everything hits me and I fall to my knees, leaning my forehead against the door as I give in to the flood of tears escaping my eyes. I squeeze them tight, trying to will the tears to stay away, but they seep through the cracks and pull me down further into the dark hole Kip shoved me in.

Everything was a lie.

Helping me with poker, asking about my past, about my dreams. Kissing me, touching me, making me want him and making me think he wanted me, too. The words, the promises, every single feeling.

This is the game changer.

This is the part where everything I thought I knew about the game gets shattered into tiny pieces and I'm left reeling, trying to pick them up and glue them back together, to force them to make sense to me again. I thought I had it in the bag, I thought I was sitting on Lucky Street with nothing but good days and smooth sailing ahead.

But I'm in stormy water.

Deep, treacherous, Kip-infested water.

And I don't think anyone is strong enough to survive this storm.

Ashlei

Brandon is looking at me like a dog he's about to put down.

His eyes are laden with concern, brows pinched together, jaw tense and lips thinned into a flat line to keep him from saying the multitude of things I know he wants to. He rests his hands on my shoulders, gently rubbing — up, and then down — like he wishes he could somehow change my mind with that touch.

"Stop looking at me like that."

"I'm just not sure about this," he confesses, swallowing hard, his dark eyes searching mine. "We have no control over how that room will respond. It could be a disaster."

"Or, it could be the end of all our worries," I counter.

He rolls his lips together, skepticism rolling off him in waves.

"Look," I whisper, stepping closer to him. "Whether they react the way I want them to is irrelevant at this point, because the truth of the matter is that Kimberly knows. Okay? She knows about us, and she's going to out us."

"She hasn't yet."

"Because she's been waiting for the perfect time, for the opportunity that would hurt us most."

Brandon frowns. He knows it's true.

"And I'm not going down like that," I finish, sneaking a kiss on his cheek before pulling back and straightening my blazer. "If anyone's going to tell my story, it's me. Period."

"You could ruin your career," he says softly, solemnly.

My rib cage squeezes, but I just smooth my hands over my skirt next, holding my shoulders back, my chin high.

"Trust me, I've been through much worse than this." I blink, Xavier's face flashing behind hot lids. "I've been through real ruin. And if I can survive that, if I can rebuild from ashes, I can damn sure rebuild from sexist, judgmental assholes."

I sniff, grabbing my folder and clipboard from Brandon's desk.

"Ready?"

But he's just watching me.

A smile spreads on his face as he makes his way around his desk, framing my face with his hands. "This," he whispers, eyes flicking back and forth between mine. "*This* is why I can't leave you alone."

I let out my next breath on a sigh, smiling a little as I lean into his hand. I kiss his palm, stealing another breath before holding out my arm not wrapped around my binder.

"Well," I say. "How do I look?"

"Like a woman on a mission."

"Perfect." I nod, swallowing down any doubt or fear that's left. "Let's do this."

My knees don't shake as I strut my ass out of Brandon's office, ignoring the curious stares that I'm sure sprouted from us being in there alone — with the door closed. But I don't care, because I'm about to set the record straight.

Kimberly falls into step right beside me, a wicked smirk on her face as she lowers her voice.

"You're going down, Daniels. Hope you've enjoyed this semester, because it's the last one you'll ever have at *Okay, Cool.*" She laughs. "Or anywhere, if I have it my way."

I fake fear, coming to a complete halt as she stalks past me. She spins, raising her eyebrows at me as she walks backwards.

"Nice knowing ya."

Then, she rolls her eyes and laughs, continuing on into the conference room.

Once she's gone, I smile.

Good luck with that, sweetheart.

I hold back for as long as I can, filling my tumbler with water and stopping at a few desks on my way to the meeting. It's two minutes past ten when I swing into the giant conference room, already packed wall to wall with virtually everyone in the company. I offer a few smiles and hellos, but mostly keep my head down, not even acknowledging Mykayla when she waves me over to sit by her.

And it's her unassuming smile that gives me my first jolt of guilt.

She's my friend — one of my closest — and I've kept this from her for almost a year now. Even if I *do* keep my job, will I have any friends left here?

I don't have time to answer that question, to get sad, to talk myself out of my decision before Brandon stands at the head of the table.

"Welcome, everyone," he says, his signature smile in place — though I know him well enough to see he's forcing it. "We're nearing the end of the semester for our interns, and, thanks to them, we just secured the *Palm South Luxury Suites* account. Please, help me thank and congratulate them."

Everyone politely claps, Mykayla letting out a few rowdy hoots that earn her some laughs and elbow nudges. She catches my eyes from across the table, holding both of her thumbs up, her mouth open in an ecstatic smile.

I smile back as best I can.

"As they prepare themselves for summer break and the next step in their event planning career, I invite them each to speak a little about their time here, what they've learned, and what they hope to accomplish in the future," Brandon says, unfastening the button on his blazer before taking a seat.

Kimberly smirks at me, hands braced on her chair to stand when Brandon speaks up again.

"Ashlei," he says, eyes on his folder and not on me, one leg crossed over the other like it's just a casual day in the office and I'm not about to completely expose us. "Why don't you start?"

Kimberly pauses, already half out of her chair. "Sir, I thought I could—"

"Thank you, Mr. Church," I say louder, cutting her off as I stand.

She sits back down with a murderous glare locked on me as I clear my throat, shuffling through the papers I wrote notes on. But once she's sitting again, she smirks, as if she knows there's nothing I can say to get myself out of the hole I dug.

And honestly, she very well could be right.

But I hold onto the small, feather-light streak of hope I built my plan on, and I tuck my notes away in my binder.

"I had some notes," I say, gesturing to the pile of paper I just tucked away. "I had all these things I wanted to say, but the truth is there really aren't any words for all this company — and you all — have done for me."

I'm met with smiles, Mykayla even giving a soft *awww* as she clutches her heart.

"The truth is, I was in a dark place before I started my internship last semester. And throwing myself into event planning, into a company and a task that makes me happy, it saved me in more ways than I can ever explain. I turned everything around — my attitude, my life — and I found purpose again."

I glance at Brandon, just long enough to catch his understanding eyes, and I hold onto the burst of energy they give me as I clear my throat again.

"You know, what I love most about this company is that we're not really like an office," I say. "We're a family."

I scan the faces of all the people around me, some I know well and others who I've only just met. Regardless of how *well* know them, my statement is true — the *Okay, Cool* crew is a family, and the moment you start for them, you're part of it.

"We work hard together. We celebrate together when one of us succeeds, and we buck up and pitch in to help when one of us is down. We don't turn our backs on each other, and we don't try to climb over one another." I direct my gaze at Kimberly with that point. "No matter what, we always see that the team is bigger than the individual, and I truly believe that's why we continue to win account after account, and award after award."

"Hear, hear!" my manager says, and everyone chuckles.

My hands tremble a little, and I fold them together in front of me, willing the bad ass, confident bitch who just stood in Brandon's office to stay with me a little longer.

"As a woman in this industry," I say. "Well, in any industry, really — I have been faced with a lot of choices." I laugh a little, lifting my brows on a joke. "My mother's voice is loud in my head every time I step off those elevators. 'Don't be too firm, they'll call you a bitch. Don't be too emotional, they'll say you can't handle the pressure. Don't wear clothes that are too masculine or baggy, you want to command attention. Don't wear clothes that are too tight, or too low cut, they'll say you're sleeping your way to the top.'"

The room grows quiet as soon as the word *bitch* slips from my mouth, and I feel the solemn weight overtake us all. A few women nod as I speak, a few others smile knowingly.

Kimberly just glares at me.

"And we're not alone, you know? Guys," I say, gesturing to the men in the room. "I know you face your own kind of hell, your own kind of judgment, especially when it comes to *being a man*, as my father likes to say." I shrug. "There's no room for anxiety or feelings when you're supposed to be dominating everything with masculinity and power every day."

"Preach, honey," Mario, one of our other interns, says. He snaps with the words, which lightens the mood a bit, earning a chorus of laughter from the room.

I smile, but my stomach rolls as I take one last breath and say what I need to say.

"That judgment," I start. "That expectation is what makes it hard for me to tell you what I'm about to."

Mykayla eyes me curiously, leaning forward in her chair as the rest of the room falls silent again.

"Mr. Church and I are in a relationship."

I hold my head high as those words tumble out, my shoulders back, spine straight. And I don't blink or close my eyes or let any tinge of color shade my cheeks.

But the whole room goes nuts.

"*What?!*"

"Oh, my God."

"No way," I hear Mykayla's voice mutter, almost a whisper. I glance at her with an apology in my eyes as Kimberly stands up.

"I knew it! I knew it all along!" She smiles, pointing her finger up at the ceiling. "I was going to tell you all. I saw them together. In his office!"

That earns another gasp, all eyes turning to Brandon, who just sits calmly at the head of the table. His eyes find mine, the worry there thicker than before as he holds up both of his hands to silent the room again.

"It's true," I say, voice loud, commanding the attention back to me. "Kimberly did see us, and she did threaten to out us. She's been using it as blackmail, as she is so proud to claim."

That shifts the judgmental eyes to her, and she sits back down slowly, a cowardly shade of red on her neck.

"Because, come on," I say with a scoff. "*What* a stereotype, am I right? The CEO hooking up with the intern. Classic." I press my hand to my chest. "I clearly *must* be a whore, one who doesn't offer anything to this company other than how far my legs can spread. And, obviously," I add, pointing to Brandon next. "Mr. Church *must* be a mysoginistic, horny predator taking advantage of the women who work underneath him."

That shuts the room completely up, and I watch as one by one, eyes start to turn from judgmental to ashamed, from angry to sad.

"Right?" I press. "There's no way we could have actually have found a genuine connection, or that what we've built together has been completely outside of the realm of where we work, and what position we hold. I mean, that would make us human." I scoff again. "How ridiculous, right?"

Mykayla frowns, her eyes falling to where her hands lay in her lap.

It seems no one else can look at me anymore, either.

"Joanne," I say, calling on one of the women in accounting. "Has Mr. Church ever made a pass at you?"

Her eyes bulge. "What? Of course not." She shakes her head. "Mr. Church has always been nothing but professional and caring toward me."

"How about you, Valerie?" I ask next, pointing to a younger associate from marketing. "Surely, he's cornered you, offered you a raise for a blow job, right?"

Brandon raises a brow in warning of my language, but he doesn't understand that this is how the punches hit hardest.

Valerie shakes her head. "No. Never." She sinks a little lower in her chair. "In fact, he helped me once, when I was behind on rent. He gave me an advance and let me pay it back over time." She smiles at him then. "He didn't ask for a single thing in return."

I nod, tracing the other female faces in the room.

"Can any woman, or man, in here stand and say that Mr. Church has made them ever feel uncomfortable? That he's ever approached them with sexual intention or tried to use his power in a way to get what he wants?"

Silence.

Kimberly's eyes sweep the room, too, only hers are shaded with horror, like she's watching her entire plan burn down like a flimsy house.

"And what about me?" I ask, my eyes glossing over a bit. I inhale a stiff breath and hold those fucking tears back like a boss bitch. "Have I done nothing valuable for this company, for any of you?"

More silence, heads hanging, eyes averted.

"I know this is shocking, and Mr. Church and I both realized when we first got involved that it was a dangerous idea. We tried to stop, several times, but the fact of the matter is that you can't tell love to live within the boundaries you draw for it." My heart skips at the fact that I mentioned the L word, but I don't let anyone dwell on it — least of all Brandon. "We care about each other, and because we work in an office of *family*, we didn't let the fact that he is my boss stop that.

"Now, you can say what you want about me, about us, and you can call me all the names in the book if that will make you feel better. You can cast your stones at me, and I promise, I will not cast them back." I swallow, sniffing back the threat of emotion. "But I am not ashamed of the work I've done here, nor am I ashamed of the way I feel for a man who, just like this job, saved me in more ways than he'll ever know."

My heart surges with that, like the power of that simple truth is enough, no matter what happens next.

"I want to apologize to all of you," I continue. "But not for how I feel for Mr. Church, or how he feels for me. I apologize for hiding it, for not respecting you all enough to tell you *before* we were caught and threatened. I should have come to you sooner, and for that, I am sorry."

I try to capture Mykayla's eyes again, but she refuses to look up, and I'm left staring at the only person in the room who can stand to look at me.

Brandon.

"I am a good woman," I say. "And he is a good man. And we are human. I hope that our family will understand that, but if you don't, there's no need for any drama. I will quietly pack my things and I will leave, without even one word of argument, if *any* of you are not okay with what I've told you."

"And I will step down as CEO, and revert to being only a silent owner," Brandon chimes in.

I balk, his statement not part of our plan. "Brandon, you can't—"

"I played just as big a role in this as you did, Ashlei," he says, eyes hard on me as he stands. His chest is broad, stance powerful as he refastens his blazer and straightens his shoulders. "And if you have to lose something you love, then I should, too. Just because you're a woman, you do not own the fault. Just because you're a woman, you do not go down in this alone."

I've never wanted to fuck him more in my life.

God*damn,* feminism is sexy.

I smile, eyes watering more than I want to allow as I watch him stand up for me — literally.

With nothing more for either of us to say, we stand defenseless in front of our peers, waiting. The room is quiet, nothing breaking the silence other than the occasional shuffling of papers or cough. After what feels like a weighted hour, Mykayla finally stands — though she's just barely taller than the woman sitting next to her even when she's on her feet.

"I just want to say something," she says, eyes on the table before she lifts them to me.

I hold my breath, preparing myself for the verbal lashing. She's my friend, and I left her in the dark. She's my friend, and in a way, I betrayed her. Not only did I not tell her, but I mishandled her trust, and I know a simple apology would never fix that.

Mykayla shakes her head, her brows furrowed. But then, she sort of smiles.

"That was the bravest, most amazing act of womanhood and humanity that I have ever witnessed in person."

My chest tightens, and I cover my mouth with one hand, stifling my need to cry.

"Ashlei, you are *such* an amazing woman. You're powerful, and courageous, and you get shit done and you balance a million different things on your plate better than I can balance three." A few soft chuckles as Mykayla sweeps the room with her hand. "There isn't a single person here who could say that you are nothing but a *whore* or whatever, because it'd be a bold-faced lie. You have done more as an intern than most of us have done with years of being fully employed."

I smile, dropping my hand back to clasp with the other one in front of me. "Thank you, Mykayla."

"And, Mr. Church," she says, turning to him next. "Excuse my language, but to be frank — whatever gets your dick wet is none of our business."

My jaw pops open as Brandon fights to hide a smile, and the mood in the room lifts again, notch by notch. More people lift their eyes, a few of them smiling, a few laughing.

"You are the best boss any of us could ask for. You're here every day, usually longer hours than we are, and you do whatever it takes to make sure your work family is okay. No, *more* than okay. You're our friend first and our boss second, and you run one hell of a company, if I do say so myself."

There's a chorus of head nods and soft claps to that.

"So, no. I'm not going to pass judgment on you. I appreciate you telling us, even though there honestly is no reason you should ever feel like you have to." She turns to Kimberly then. "And any woman wanting to out you for the disgusting reasons you just listed is the only person, in my opinion, who should have to answer for their actions. We should be building each other up and moving forward," she adds, eyes hard. "Not tearing each other down and setting us all back fifty years."

The women in the room cheer at that, a few of them clapping Mykayla on the back as she sits down again, a shit-eating grin on her face.

Kimberly just shrinks down farther into her chair.

"So, are we done here?" Mykayla adds. "We still have five other interns to hear from and this girl right here is ready for lunch."

A few more laughs ring out, and Brandon and I smile at each other before glancing around the room. No one else speaks, just smiles and nods, letting us know we're still in the family.

Not a single stone is cast.

Kimberly swipes her binder from the table, hurrying out of the room as Brandon and I take our seat again. She doesn't look up from the floor until she's out the door, and though I should feel like I've won, I can't help but feel bad for her, too.

Meh, she'll be fine.

Glancing at his folder, Brandon folds his hands together on the table, sliding me one last smile before he addresses the room.

"Alright, then," he says. "Who's next?"

***

"I'll just be a second," I say, hopping out of Brandon's convertible and jogging toward the apartment building. I pop up the steps with a smile on my face, rapping my knuckles on the door.

As I wait, I run over my plan in my head. There are only a couple weeks of classes left, and now that I have my drama handled, I can finally start being a better friend to my sisters.

Starting with Skyler.

The poor girl has been moping around the sorority house like a lost kitten for weeks now, and I can't sit back and let her be sad anymore without trying to fix it. Something happened with her and Kip — though she won't tell us *what* — and I'm determined to make them get out of their own way.

God knows they fought hard enough to be together in the first place, it doesn't make sense for them to throw it away now.

The door swings open, and Kip doesn't show a single ounce of emotion or any kind of reaction when he sees it's me. He's sweating profusely, likely from another run — he's been running all over campus since the break up — and his hair is a damp, blond, ratted nest. I trace his features, noting how hollow his cheeks are, how his eyes sag, the skin beneath them shiny and purple like he's been in a fist fight. He's got a full chin of stubble, and as soon as the door opened, I could smell him.

And not in a good way.

"You look like shit," I say, letting myself inside his apartment. He's still standing at the door as I survey the space — dishes piling up in the sink, clothes strewn everywhere, trash overflowing. "So does your apartment."

"What do you want, Ashlei?" he asks when the front door is closed again. "You already go all of Skyler's things out of here."

I nod, eyes softening a little as I take him in again. Poor sap. Skyler sent me back the day after she'd left his apartment in a hurry. She wouldn't tell me why she couldn't go back, and I tried my best not to pry. Still, he looked shitty that morning, his questions aimed at me like bullets as I gathered up her things. But now? He just looks... void. Void of light. Void of happiness.

Void of life.

"I came to check on you," I say with a sigh. "I figured if you were half as bad as Skyler, you'd probably need me to force you into the shower. Which is kind of what it's looking like right now," I add, eyeing his dingy clothes.

Kip glances down, but doesn't respond.

"Kade says he never sees you anymore," I continue. "And you won't talk to anyone. You can't hold yourself up in here, Kip."

Kip blinks, but other than that simple, automatic body reaction, there's nothing.

"I can do whatever I need to do to get through this, Ashlei," he finally says, voice hoarse as he gestures to his messy apartment. "And this is part of the process."

I shake my head. "I don't understand, what exactly happened between you two? Skyler won't talk about it, and you're both acting like you still *want* to be together... so why not just *be* together?"

Kip swallows, his eyes sad. "It's complicated."

"Sounds familiar," I murmur with a roll of my eyes. "Listen, the KKB formal is on Saturday. Come with me."

That gets a reaction.

Kip cocks a brow, his eyes wide. "Are you serious?"

"Not like that," I clarify. "I know Skyler wants you there, but she's not going to ask. Maybe if you come with me, you can talk to her and figure this shit out. You're both making yourselves sick, and it's not healthy."

He crosses his arms, seemingly considering the offer. "Is she going with anyone?"

"Bear," I answer. "As *friends*."

I know I'm overstepping, putting my nose deep in Skyler's business when she asked me to just drop it. But, I know my girl, and she's in love with this kid. She's trying not to be, trying to just let him go and be the tough bad ass she always has been, but she can't help it. She's head over heels, and from what I can tell, he feels the same about her.

If I've learned anything, it's that life is too short to let stupid games get in the way of love.

Kip is quiet, thinking. After a moment, he shifts his weight, eyes finding mine. "It's Saturday?"

I nod.

He watches me for a moment, like he's checking to see if I'm setting him up with some kind of trap. Finally, he sighs, running fingers back through his hair. How he manages to get them through without getting caught in a tangle is beyond me.

"Okay."

I smile, feeling more victorious than I should, considering I have no idea what will happen once he's actually at the dance. "Wear something nice, it's formal attire. And for Pete's sake, take a shower. You smell like complete ass."

Kip chuckles.

"We don't need to ride together or anything," I add. "Just meet me at the venue. I'll text you the address."

Kip nods, moving toward the door as I make my way that direction. But once it's open, I pause, holding one hand on the knob as I face him.

"Skyler loves you, you know?" I say, watching how those words wash over him. His face breaks, his fist clenching at his side like it kills him to know it. "Whatever is happening between you two, I can see that hasn't changed."

I watch him for a moment longer, but when he doesn't respond, I decide my job is done for the day. I got him to agree to come to the dance, and that will set up his chance to make things right. So, I smile once more, close the door behind me, and jog back down the steps.

"All good?" Brandon asks when I slide back into the passenger seat.

I take a moment just to stare at him before I reach for my seatbelt, taking in his smooth skin, his soft, crooked smile, his relaxed posture as he grips the wheel with one hand, the other already reaching for my thigh.

Swoon.

"Yep, all good. At least, for now."

"Do I even want to know what you're getting yourself into now?" he asks once my belt is clicked.

"Probably not."

Brandon just smirks, throwing the car in drive and cruising down toward the dock. With the semester coming to a close, we planned one last day on the yacht to relax before my finals kick into high gear. I've been looking forward to this day all week, but now that it's here, I can't help but feel a sinking in my stomach.

It says with me all the way to the dock, and well into our day on the yacht. I feel it niggling at me as we lounge by the pool, let it keep me from eating much when we sit down for dinner, and barely manage to fight past it to get an orgasm when Brandon takes me from behind on the top deck, my chest hanging over the railing, hair swinging.

But when we're back in bed, curled up together and softly running our fingers over one another, I can't ignore it anymore.

Now that the cat's out of the bag and we're no longer keeping our relationship a secret, I can't help but wonder what we are. It seems like the most juvenile thing to ask, even before the words make it from my brain to my mouth, but I have to ask.

I have to know.

"Brandon," I whisper, fingertips dancing on his bare chest.

His eyes are closed, a sleepy smile on his face as he plays with my hair. "Mmm?"

"Can I ask you something?"

"No, I'm not ready for round two yet."

I smack his chest playfully before lightly running my fingertips over the skin again. "I'm serious."

"So am I," he says, still smirking.

I roll my eyes, finger stilling as I swallow down the nerves. "I was just... I was thinking, about us. About how we don't have to hide anymore. And, well... I just, I don't know how it works at your age, but at mine, everyone plays all these games. It's like, you can be dating someone but not actually *dating* them, like not *just* them. It's all this open-ended *are we, or are we not* nonsense and..." I pause, forcing a breath. "I'm rambling."

Brandon finally opens his eyes, cocking one brow. "What's your question, Ashlei?"

I frown, biting my lower lip. "Are we... are we exclusive?"

He watches me a moment, his brows tugging inward. And then, he laughs.

Laughs.

And not just a little laugh, but a full on, head thrown back against the pillow, one hand over his stomach laugh.

"I'm serious!" I say, rolling away from him defensively. But he snags my wrist with one hand, tugging me back into him and wrapping both his arms around me.

"I'm sorry," he says, still laughing as he kisses my hair. "It's just, it's so ridiculous that you think I have even done so much as *think* about another woman since the day I met you."

The stiffness I held against his hold melts in an instant, my entire body molding to fit his as I let out a sigh of relief. My cheeks flush, and Brandon pulls back, returning my smile.

"Are you saying you want to be my girlfriend?"

I shrug, keeping my eyes on the fingertip I run over his chest again. "Do you want me to be your girlfriend?"

"Honestly," he says, thumb brushing my cheek until I look at him again. "I kind of thought you already were."

That earns him a wide smile, and the corner of his mouth pulls to the side before he leans down, pressing that smirk to meet my smile in a perfect kiss.

And just like that, I have a boyfriend.

One who actually cares about me, who wouldn't hurt me, who wouldn't use me. And, most importantly...

One I don't have to hide.

Jess

"What a shit show."

I shake my head, taking another sip of my old fashioned, rolling the amber liquid around in the glass as I watch Kip on the dance floor.

To say I was shocked when he showed up at our formal tonight would be an understatement. For reasons I *still* don't understand, even after Ashlei explained her plan to me, she invited Kip to be her date. Of course, in her mind, it was a way for Kip to be able to talk to Skyler, for them to work out whatever has been going on between them.

But I know better.

I know my girl Sky, and she's on a mission tonight. Mission Forget Kip Ever Existed. These types of missions are dangerous, and usually consist of large volumes of alcohol, kissing random guys who *aren't* Kip, and blacking out by the end of the night.

So, I can't help but sigh in pity as Kip watches Skyler walk away from him. She had just been dancing with him, but from where I'm standing, it looked more like she was chewing his ass and reminding him that his chances to be with her are long gone.

Poor sap.

As if it isn't already bad enough, Erin slides up, asking Kip to dance next. I can't even watch that disaster.

Waving a hand like I can't be bothered, I turn toward our table, ready to make my way to a chair so I can kick off my high heels for a bit. But instead, I'm met with a goofy smile and two full shot glasses.

"Well, if it isn't Venus herself."

I flatten my lips, blinking twice at Kade before I answer. "What does that even mean."

"It means you're the goddess of sex, of course," he says. "And love and fertility and some other shit, too, but that's not the point."

I shove past him, rolling my eyes and draining the last of my old fashioned. I drop it on the first table I pass as he jogs to catch up to me, spilling a little of the two shots he's balancing.

"Come on, look at you. That gold dress, the vine headband. You *do* look like Venus."

"Stop talking."

"Fine," he grinds, stepping in front of me so I can't keep walking away. "How about we drink, instead."

Kade holds a shot toward me, and I eye it suspiciously before taking notice of how good he looks in his tuxedo tonight. All his tattoos are covered, which I actually hate, but how tall, dark, and handsome he looks somewhat makes up for it. His usually unruly hair is gelled and styled, curling a bit at the top. He's sporting an all-black suit, his beige dress shirt and gold pocket square matching me a little too much.

He looks down at the shots again, waggling his brows in an annoyingly adorable manner. "Eh? Come on."

"Ugh, fine," I say, but when I go to snag a shot glass from his hand, he pulls both away.

"First, a toast." His brows furrow. "Or, rather, a proposition."

I groan, slapping one hand against my forehead and dragging it down dramatically.

"Just, hear me out," he says. "You're here this summer, right?"

"I am... creeper, how did you know that?"

He ignores my question. "I've been thinking about what you said on the cruise... about my game. And as much as it pains me to say this... you're right."

At that, I stand a little straighter, folding my arms over my chest. "Okay, you said the magic words. I'm listening."

"I *am* eager, and I spit a bunch of cheesy lines because, frankly, it's all I know. I was raised by two older, bonehead brothers who treat girls like absolute garbage. I learned how to flirt from them, how to land a date, how to hold a relationship. And, as you can see, that's working out just peachy for me."

"Please tell me they didn't also give you advice on how to fuck."

He cringes.

"Jesus Christ."

"I know," he says quickly. "I know. It's bad. Which is why, I was thinking..." He steps closer, a stupid smirk on his face. "What if you helped me? What if you were my teacher of sorts."

I balk, jaw flopping open as my eyes double in size. "You're kidding," I say, but Kade just stares, biting his lip and bouncing on his toes a little. "Wow, you're actually not."

"Look, I know it sounds..."

"Stupid? Crazy? Like there's absolutely nothing in it for me and it's never going to happen?"

"Out of the ordinary," he finishes. "But, you're wrong about there not being anything in it for you. First of all, you get the satisfaction of taking an over-eager puppy under your wing and turning him into a panty-melting beast of a dog."

I roll my eyes.

"And, you get free, no-strings-attached sex whenever you want it."

At that, I laugh. "Because that's so hard to find."

"I'm clean, there's no danger in banging me. And we're friends."

"News to me."

Kade narrows his eyes. "Fine. What do you want in exchange. What will it take for you to say yes?"

I'm tempted to just tell him to get lost, but something about his little proposal piques my interest. Here's this massively built, incredibly sexy, young kid asking for me to help him get better at flirting. And dating. And fucking. He may be annoying as hell, but I saw the bulge in his swim trunks on Spring Break, and I know that equipment is *more* than enough to help a girl get by.

And there's something about his eyes, about his tattoos, about his bulging biceps that remind me of Jarrett, and I wonder if he could fuck me like him, too. With a little training, of course.

My thighs clench at the thought. I need to get laid, *bad*, but that's not reason enough to say yes to these kinds of shenanigans.

... Is it?

"Do you have a car?" I finally ask.

"I do."

"What kind?"

He quirks a brow. "A Camaro."

"Convertible?"

"Uh-huh."

"Good, it's mine now," I say. "You can drop the keys off tomorrow. I had to sell mine to help a friend out, and I need wheels going into the summer and my last semester."

I wait for him to argue, sure my request is too steep. But, to my surprise, he grits his teeth and nods with a somewhat genuine smile.

"Fine. Car's yours. Anything else?"

"You have to actually listen," I say, holding up one manicured finger. "And at least *try* not to completely annoy me every time we're together."

"I'll do my best. So, we have a deal?"

I narrow my eyes, but finally sigh, snatching the shot glass out of his left hand. "We have a deal. Here's to your helpless game, and my sanity in trying to fix it."

Kade chuckles, clinking his glass to mine before we both throw them back and seal the deal.

Lord help me.

Skyler

I'm good at this game.

The *"ignore him, get wasted, dance with every other guy and make him want to crawl out of his skin with jealousy"* game.

It's the most natural, comfortable thing, slipping into that role tonight. I didn't expect to see Kip at *my* formal, the one place where I was supposed to be able to let loose with my sisters and Clinton and just forget about Kip for a while.

But of course, he showed up.

At first, I tried ignoring him. Then, I got so annoyed by his presence that I pulled him into a dance and demanded to know why he was there.

"I wanted to see you, to talk to you. I feel like I owe you an explanation."

Oh, you fucking think?

Just remembering his stupid, sad eyes when he tried to explain himself makes me throw back another shot angrily. Then, I'm grabbing another guy and dragging him to the dance floor. I have no idea who he is. It doesn't matter. All that *does* matter is that he's got his hands on my hips, his crotch pressed against my ass, and Kip has to watch it and know there's nothing he can do about it.

Take that, asshole.

It's petty, and childish, but I can't help it. All semester long, Kip preached to me to stop caring what other people think of me, to stand up for myself and be who *I* want to be — regardless of what anyone else has to say about it. So, to find out he's letting his father play him like a puppet because *he's* afraid of disappointing him?

He's a hypocrite, and now I'm determined to drink and dance until I forget he ever existed.

My head rushes, vision fuzzy and legs heavy as I try to keep up with the swaying rhythm set by the guy behind me. His hands crawl up my ribs, grabbing the silk of my dress as I lean more of my weight on him. I kind of feel like throwing up, kind of feel like taking someone home — and in the back of my mind, I hear my dignity begging me to come to my senses.

"'Scuse me," I slur to the guy, shoving off him and stumbling toward the stage. The DJ claps his hands and changes up the beat when I make my way up to stand next to him, and there's a crowd of guys below me, hooting and hollering, my own little fan show.

In my mind, I try to convince myself that they want me because I'm such a catch, because I'm such a great dancer and my dress looks amazing. But I know the truth. Somewhere deep down, I know they just see a drunk girl who they can easily get in their bed.

But no one is getting in my bed. Not for a long time. Maybe not ever.

Not after Kip Jackson.

I let him in, let him obliterate my walls like they were made of paper instead of stone. I trusted him, confessed all my lies, thought we were starting over with a clean slate. But all this time, he was playing me.

All this time, I was just a game.

The sting of that drives me as I dance, the cheers from below fueling my pettiness. And when I look up past the crowd and see Kip's back, see him walking away, I know I've won. He can't take anymore. He's leaving.

Why do I suddenly want him to stay?

I shove that thought down, throwing my hands up and closing my eyes as I dance. I sway my hips, spinning slowly to the beat. But my foot slips, and then there's no floor beneath it, and the next thing I know, I'm falling.

For a moment, it's almost as I I'm suspended in time, as if my body is floating down to the hard ground below the stage like a feather. I watch the faces twist around me, the eyes growing wide, the mouths closing into tight *o's* as they watch in horror.

But I feel nothing.

Not when my body hits the floor.

Not when my vision goes dark.

And not when I come to again, however many minutes later, and see Kip's ocean blue eyes staring down at me.

"Fuck, Skyler," he says, pulling me to his chest. I'm still on the floor, but he's holding me in his arms, my head on his shoulder as he wipes my hair from my face. "You scared the shit out of me."

My heart skips a beat, warmth crashing over me as my traitorous body clings to Kip like he's my only lifeline.

"Ouch," I manage, and there's a little ring of laughter around me. I can't even focus my vision enough to see who's there. Someone presses a cool washcloth to the back of my neck and I sigh, head spinning, body aching.

"Let's get you home," Kip whispers in my ear, and all I can do is nod, holding onto him tighter as he lifts me.

I hear my sisters telling him to let them know we made it home safely, but I just curl into him more. I feel hands touching my back, but I just curl into him more. Clinton tells me to call him in the morning and I nod, but then, I curl into Kip more. And when we're in a cab, the engine humming me to sleep as we make our way across town, I hold onto him, wishing I never had to let go.

Wishing he was still the boy who loved me, instead of the one who caused me pain.

I don't know how far we are from the venue when I lift my head, my eyes struggling to focus on his as he stares back at me. And I don't know what I'm thinking when I lean into him again, this time pressing my lips to his, my entire body buzzing to life with the electric charge that's always existed between us. Kip inhales a breath, and I do, too, holding it in my burning chest as I try to deepen the kiss.

But he breaks it.

"Skyler," he says when he pulls back, and just the way he says my name is the worst rejection I've ever felt.

I swallow, waiting for him to take it back, to kiss me, too. But his brows pull together, his eyes searching mine.

"You're drunk," he finally says, shaking his head. "You don't want to kiss me."

And I wish he was right. I wish that were true.

But no matter how he's hurt me, no matter what I *should* feel, I can't help it.

I still want him.

"Yes, I do," I whisper, eyes blurring from tears instead of alcohol as I push off his lap and slide across the back seat to the opposite window. I stare at the car lights passing on the other side of the road, rolling my lips together to keep from crying.

How did I get here?

I can't wrap my head around it, how I started the semester with only one thing on my mind — the tournament — and yet ended it with a boy somehow ruling more of me than poker ever has. I just want him to take it all back, to tell me he's not entering the tournament, that he loves me more than he loves playing me for his father's entertainment. I don't even understand it all, what his dad wants from him, why it means so much.

I want answers, and yet I don't want anything else from Kip at all.

Other than maybe for him to go back in time and never come into my life at all.

"You know," I say after a moment, sniffing. "This just might be the worst downswing I've ever experienced."

I turn to him again, waiting until his eyes are on mine before I continue.

"I never could have expected I'd lose so much of my self betting on you."

I know the words cut him deep. His eyes sag, brows pinching together. One of his hands twitches, like he wants to reach for me, but I just turn away again, staring out the window and waiting for the ride to end.

But Kip is just like me.

He can't let go.

"I love you."

His words fly into space without warning, and I choke on a sob I didn't expect, shaking my head and trying with all my might to fight off the wave of tears. But I can't fight anymore, and as the first tears wet my cheeks, my heart twists in defeat.

"Well, I fucking hate you."

"No, you don't."

I face him again, my chest tight, tears hot on my face. "I want to."

God, do I want to. I don't think I've ever wished for anything more than to disconnect from my feelings in this moment, to take his face and associate it with pain and betrayal instead of love and comfort.

Kip just swallows, his mouth opening like he wants to say something before he snaps it shut again. And when we pull up to the KKB house, he jumps out, quickly making his way around to my door. In an instant, his arm is around my waist, mine over his shoulder as he peels me out of the cab and helps me up to the porch.

"Are you okay?" he asks when we make it. "Are you going to be sick?"

And I just laugh, because the irony of the boy causing me the most pain asking if alcohol is going to be the reason I have a shit night is just too much.

"I'm fine," I bite, pulling out of his grasp to stand on my own. "I've been drunk a few times before, you know."

"I just want you to be okay."

"I find that hard to believe."

Kip swallows, stepping back with a slight nod as he shoves his hands in his pockets and stares at his shoes. There are so many words hanging between us, suspended in a void we can't quite reach. There's so much still left to say, and yet, there's nothing more to say at all.

A fresh tear streaks down my cheek without warning, and I swipe it away, wishing I could do the same to the love I feel for Kip. Glancing at my phone, I see it's just past midnight — on a date I know I'll never forget, not since the cruise when Kip had me figure out what his lucky number was.

"See you in Vegas," I say, reaching for the door handle when I turn. But I pause, heart squeezing as I look back over my shoulder. "Oh, and happy birthday."

I close the door behind me, climb the stairs, and crawl into bed still in my dress, hoping sleep will kill the pain.

Thankfully, I don't dream of Kip.

That's the only mercy I'm shown.

***

When I check into my room at the Aria the night before the tournament, I can't help but feel like a bird in the pouring down rain — so desperate to fly, yet with no means to get off the ground.

I'm broken, and I just wish the only thing that could fix me wasn't the one thing I need to stay away from.

The past month has been absolute hell.

I somehow managed to make it through the rest of the semester and finish out my classes, but just barely. Practicing for the tournament has been nothing but me playing like complete shit. I'm off my game, and it's not a secret, anymore.

I drop my luggage and sit down on the bed, looking around at the beautiful room. I have an incredible view of the Strip from my window and the bed is luxurious. Whites and purples cover the room and every amenity is top of the line and brand new. The Aria is one of the newer hotels on the Strip and this is the first year they've hosted the American Poker Club Tournament. I just wish I had someone here to celebrate this amazing room with me.

I thought it would be Kip here with me.

I planned on asking him to join me before everything happened. My Little was going to come, but I knew she wanted to get a head start on her summer classes, so I told her it was okay. I'm sure the other girls would have come, too, but to be honest, I was tired of them asking if I was okay.

Why is it that I can hold everything together until someone asks me that one question? I'm fine... until you ask me if I'm fine.

Then I'm not fine, at all.

It's the exact same feeling when I think about Kip calling me. He checked on me the day after formal, and I basically told him to fuck off. And though part of me wished he would fight me on it, he didn't.

He's left me alone just like I asked him to.

Isn't it funny how sometimes we tell someone to fuck off, but then wish more than anything that they would just call?

I sigh, still looking around the room as I try to prepare myself for the night. They're hosting a tournament pre-party tonight downstairs, and even though I don't want to go, I know I need to make an appearance.

For one, everyone in the blogosphere has been talking about how I've been off my game, so I need to try to fake that I'm fine so they see I'm still here to compete.

And two, I want to scope out my competition. A lot of people register last minute, just like I did, and I want to see who I'm going to be facing the next two days.

I pull out the black cocktail dress I packed for the party and slip it on, curling my hair and touching up my makeup before heading downstairs. The party is already packed and I run into a few friends from past tournaments almost immediately. When I say *friends*, I mean either competition or other female players. For some reason, we all gravitate to one another. I guess because we all understand what it's like to be on the "hot or not" list.

Stupid sexist magazines.

I grab a plate of hors d'oeuvres, even though I haven't really eaten anything in the past three weeks, and snag a glass of honey whiskey from the bartender before finding a table near the back of the room. The lights are off, but there's multicolored uplighting and lights that move with the music from the DJ. On any other day, I would be stoked to be here. I would be taking in everything and how amazing it is here in Vegas, one of my favorite places in the world, but right now I just can't. I need to get myself pulled together before tomorrow.

I just really don't know how.

"This seat taken?" he asks, and I know it's Kip without even looking up from my plate. I shake my head and he sits down. For some reason, I still can't look up.

"Hi," he says softly, and I find the strength to pull my eyes to his. He's dressed in a long-sleeve, white button-up and black vest, and of course he's wearing his glasses.

Perfect.

The sleeves of his shirt are rolled up to his elbows, his hair styled perfectly, and his skin is a beautiful bronze. Maybe he's been lounging by the pool living the good life. I don't know, but whatever he's been doing, he looks amazing.

And I know I look like shit.

"Hi."

He takes a pull of his drink, surveying me. "You look beautiful tonight."

I really want to make some smart-ass comment back to him, but I just don't think it's worth it. And I need my head on straight tomorrow. I can't let him faze me tonight.

"Thank you. So do you."

He cocks a brow. "You think I'm beautiful, huh?"

I roll my eyes, but a smile threatens at the corners of my mouth and it's the first time I've had that urge in a while. "Like a shark before he eats his prey."

"So, what you're saying is that I'm like Sparky?"

I laugh a little at his reference to the little stuffed shark I won him on our first date, forgoing playing with my food on my plate and taking a drink instead. "Sparky is fluffier than you. I think I like him more."

"Hey, I've put on a few pounds. I might be fighting Sparky for that fluffy title here pretty soon."

He doesn't look like he's put on even a single ounce. In fact, he looks like he's lost weight —

especially in his face. It's then that I take a closer look at him — the bags under his eyes, the tired expression behind his smile. Maybe this hasn't been as easy for him as I thought.

"Skyler, I need to talk to you."

I close my eyes, setting my drink on the table. "Please don't do this, Kip. Not before tomorrow."

"It's not about us," he clarifies, but then he bites the inside of his lip a little. "Well, not entirely. I just need you to know something before tomorrow, before we start this tournament. I want you to understand."

Pulling the glass to my lips, I drain the rest of my whiskey and cross my arms on the table, bracing for impact. I have no idea what he could possibly say to make me understand why he's here, why he's doing this to me. But, I remember running to him on our cruise, desperate to make him understand the whole Erin situation when I knew I didn't even deserve him listening to a word I said.

I owe him the same courtesy.

"Skyler," he starts, and the way he says my name is almost too much. It's almost enough for me to get up and walk out. "I did come to Palm South to seek you out. My dad has been watching you play for years and when he found out you were entering this tournament, or well, rumored to be, anyway — he made me a deal. If I came to this school and got close enough to you to learn how to take you down at this tournament, he would pay for me to go to my dream school — UCLA."

He pauses, probably reading the confusion on my face. *Why the hell would his dad target* me *of all players?*

"Please don't take it personally," he says quickly. "My dad doesn't have a vendetta against you or anything, it's just that he thinks you're the best in the game right now. And you're also one of the youngest. I don't know," he says, scratching the back of his neck. "I guess he felt like if everything he's taught me about the game could help me beat you or at least keep up and compete, he would be 'beating the best', in a way."

I'm oddly flattered, but still can't understand how Kip could go through with that deal — not after he actually met me, after we fell in love.

Or was it only *me* who did the falling?

"He even made that crazy fucking file that you found." Kip says, running his fingers through his hair. "It's like he's living through me. And I didn't understand that before, not for a long time. But I get it now."

He shakes his head, almost as if he's jumping to something too quickly — something he's not ready to say yet.

"Anyway, I've been going to community college the past couple of years because I couldn't afford anything else without my dad's help. And I know there are loans and I could work, but to be honest, I just didn't think it through. I was lazy, I was selfish, and I wanted my father's help. So, when he offered it, I jumped on the chance."

I inhale a deep breath and lift my glass, trying to suck the remaining whiskey from the ice cubes. Kip pauses for a moment, his attention falling to my mouth as I swirl the cube around inside. A surge runs straight through me when I realize why he's distracted. And no matter how much I try not to like it, I love the power I still have over him.

So, I grab another cube.

But he tears his eyes away, continuing. "When I met you that night at rush, I didn't know who you were. You have to know that," he pleads earnestly. "I found out that night when I went back to my apartment. That first night between us was all us — you didn't know about Erin, I didn't know about you — it was just us and the way we felt together."

My chest squeezes, stomach tightening, too, at the thought of seeing him for the first time that night. I can close my eyes and still feel his tongue on my stomach, licking up the tequila before he kissed me.

I shiver, but don't say a word.

"When I did find out it was you my dad had sent me to Palm South for, I almost called it off then," Kip says, licking his lips. "I fell for you that first night, Skyler. The first time my eyes found yours. When you called me a nerd and said I looked like a Matthew." He laughs a little and I do, too. "You had me. Right then."

We both sit silent for just a second, just a split second after that laugh before he takes a breath and continues.

"But it's my dad, and this was his deal. For a while, I let that drive me. Then, when I was close to calling everything off because I was starting to fall for you, you ended it at the dance. And then I was more determined than ever to take you down. But then things changed again, and fuck." He runs his hands through his hair again and lets out a puff of air. "Everything was just such a mess, Skyler. My head was fucked up. But I tried calling my dad to tell him the deal was off before the cruise."

I sit up a little straighter at his words. "You did?"

He nods. "Yes. But, he didn't answer, and I should have known then that something was wrong." Kip swallows hard and his eyes grow darker. "But I called him as soon as we got off the boat, Skyler. And my mom answered. And once again, when I thought I was done with his game, shit got more complicated."

I inhale, waiting for him to continue. Something tells me what he's about to say is difficult for him, and even though I still feel that little pang of anger deep in my stomach, I try to give him the time he needs to gather the words.

"My dad is sick, Skyler." He chokes on the words a little, his façade breaking. "He has lung cancer. And he's not going to live much longer."

And just like that, there's no oxygen left in the room.

My chest tightens again, this time from a completely different kind of pain. I think of my own dad, of what I would do if the same were true for him, and it's too much to bear. Tears immediately sting the backs of my eyes, but I hold them back, because this isn't my time to cry. This is my time to listen and be there for Kip, even if I'm not sure I can be.

His dad is sick.

And now, suddenly, everything between us seems so small.

"Oh my God, Kip." I shake my head, reaching out to grab his hand in mine. He flinches at first, but then he takes mine in his and squeezes like it's the last thing in life he has to hold on to. "I'm so sorry. I'm such a bitch. *God*, I'm sorry."

He shakes his head. "No, you're not. I didn't tell you. I was going to that night at formal, but you weren't exactly in the best state."

He eyes me for a second and I blush, looking down at the table. I made an ass of myself that night and I know it.

"I know this doesn't change anything between us. I know I still betrayed you, lied to you, earned your trust when I didn't deserve it. I know that," he says, his voice fading. "But, I wanted you to understand. I needed you to be able to look at me from across the table tomorrow and know that I'm here for my dad, not because I don't love you. Because I do. I love you, Skyler."

He pulls me across the table and our lips meet in the middle, his hands moving to either side of my face. I let him kiss me and I kiss him back, but my heart is still torn. I still don't know what to believe. I don't know what was real between us and what was an act.

I'm still broken.

I wish this kiss alone could put me back together, but it can't.

When he pulls back, he runs the pad of his thumb over my cheek once before dropping his hands. We both stand there for a moment, and I know this very well could be the last time I stand this close to him. We'll be at the tournament together, but there's no telling if either of us will even make it far enough to sit at the same table together. And after this, he'll be gone from Palm South.

From me.

"Is your dad here?"

He hangs his head. "He can't travel right now. He's watching from home."

A pain shoots through my heart and I bite my lips together. "I'm sure he's proud of you."

Kip nods, trying to smile but failing. Finally, he looks up at me once more, his diamond blue eyes glimmering in the soft light. "For the record, I hope you win tomorrow."

I cock my brow and he leans in, kissing my forehead.

"I want to win for my dad, yes," he says, eyes still on me. "But, more than anything, I want to see you happy. And if that means you kick my ass tomorrow, then so be it."

My skin stings from where his lips touched my head, and my fingers move to the spot as he reaches into his pocket, pulling out a long, slender case. He hands it to me and I know what it is without even opening it.

"Good luck, number four."

He winks before turning and walking away. I watch as he walks across the room until he disappears behind the doors and I lose sight of him. Then, I grab what was left of his drink and down it, open the case, and try not to show any emotion.

Inside are the same glasses he got me before, though I know he smashed that pair, so this is a new one. On the top left of the left lens, there are four gold dots, just like my freckle tattoo. I swallow hard, closing the case again before sitting back in my chair.

For some reason, I find myself wondering if Kip has a tell.

What is the sign that he's bluffing? I can always spot it, a person's giveaway. Always. I can read every single human being I meet.

But not him.

Why? When he tells me he loves me, why do I believe it's true? Yet, there's still something warning me that maybe, just *maybe*, he's bluffing.

But what could his tell be?

Is it the way he kisses me? The way he runs his hands through my hair? The way his eyes shift from dark blue to sky blue? The way he smiles when I touch him?

What is it that will give me the true answer?

I need another drink.

I head back to my room not too long after that, exhausted from our conversation. My heart and soul ache for him and what he's going through. I can't imagine losing either one of my parents, and knowing what a big part his dad played in his life, I know this isn't easy for him.

As if I'm a glutton for punishment, I pull his oversized black t-shirt from my bag and slip it over my head, taking everything else off. I don't know why I packed this, why I kept it after all this time, but there's something about it that brings me comfort.

Wrapping up in the covers of the bed, I pull the shirt to my nose and inhale his scent, closing my eyes as tears start to gather again. I hate crying, and I hate crying over him more than anything else. But, lately, it seems it's all I can do.

I don't know what to think. I don't know what to feel. He told me he loved me tonight and I believe him, I just don't know what that means. I understand why he's in the tournament still, but how do I know what was real between us and what wasn't? Does he really love me, or did he just get caught up in his game?

As I drift off to sleep, I think about love. Love is like the wind, someone once told me, because it's felt and not seen. But I think you actually can see it. You see love just the same way that you see the wind — by the way it moves other things. Love has moved me, it's changed me, and I can see it more clearly than the sun in the sky. Clearly, love has moved Kip, too.

The question is, will love move us together, or sweep us apart?

Cassie

"Remind me again why I agreed to let you torture me."

Adam chuckles, smacking my ass as I pass him on my way up the stairs. He's on his way down.

Bastard.

"You agreed to let me *train* you," he corrects, turning all the way around to face me, but he keeps jogging down the stairs, anyway. Backwards.

Bastard.

"And, for what it's worth, your ass looks great in those shorts."

I smack that ass he's referencing before flipping him off, and he just laughs harder, turning the corner down the next set of stairs.

It's summer, which is usually my time to go back to Arizona and be lazy by the pool. But with my biology major picking up speed and medical schools getting tougher to get into by the day, I don't have time to mess around anymore. I signed up for a full set of summer classes, and since Adam was elected to be president for a second term — an achievement never before seen in Alpha Sigma's history on campus — he decided to stay with me to gear up for the next year.

He also agreed to train me, when I chopped half my hair off and said I wanted to add a fitness routine to my study schedule so I wasn't inside sitting so much.

Mistakes were made.

So, here we are, at nine o'clock at night on a Thursday running up and down the stairs of the tallest parking garage on campus, stopping on every floor to do different body weight reps.

And, here *I* am, dying.

After the last round of dumbbell squats on the top floor, I flop down on the warm concrete, chest heaving. There are a few clouds in the sky tonight, the moon casting a magical glow through them, and I watch them float by as my breathing steadies.

"You okay, there, Red?" Adam asks, taking a seat next to me.

"If I had the energy," I pant. "I'd punch you so hard right now."

"What? It's your favorite nickname."

I just glare at him.

He chuckles, leaning back until he's lying next to me. His hand reaches for mine, but I yank it away.

"I'm sweaty and gross."

"More like sweaty and adorable," he argues. "Come here."

He reaches for me, trying to pull me into his chest, but I wiggle free.

"Seriously, I'm soaked. And sweaty."

Adam gives me a pointed look, one brow cocked as he taps his chest. "Your sweaty, smelly head. Here. Now."

I groan, but give in, letting him pull me into his warm body. He somehow still smells like soap, even after an hour of working out, and as much as I want to hate it, I can't help but inhale his scent and snuggle into him.

"That's better."

For a while, Adam just holds me while we watch the clouds, his fingers playing in my new, short hair. I chopped it all the way above my shoulders, the curly edges of it framing my chin, and it's too short now to even bother trying to put it in a pony tail.

"I can't believe we're here," Adam muses, his voice soft.

"On top of a parking garage?"

He smirks. "I mean *here,* together. Really together. No other guys, no other girls, no one and nothing between us. We're just... us."

At that, I sigh, snuggling into his chest more. "It is pretty crazy."

"Did you ever think we'd actually get here?"

I snort. "Honestly? No."

"Really?"

"I was wrapped up in Grayson," I say, trying to defend my thoughts. "And you had the presidency, and before that, you had Skyler. I don't know, I just kind of felt like it was never in the cards for us. Half the time I wasn't even sure how you felt about me."

"Well, then you weren't paying attention."

"More like you're harder to read than my biology books."

Adam leans up on one elbow, his brows bending together slightly as his eyes search mine. "I always knew we'd be together. Eventually. When the time was right."

"You did?"

He nods, a little smirk climbing on his lips. "I did."

"How could you be so sure?" I ask, pushing up to sit with him.

Adam stares off in the distance, his lips pressed together in thought. Then, slowly, he smiles, and a shrug finds his shoulders. "I don't know. I guess the best way to explain it is that when we weren't together, you were always on my mind — even when I was busy, or dating someone else, or mad at you for choosing Grayson."

I blush at that, but Adam keeps going.

"You were always what I was thinking about. And when I was with you, when I could see you, it felt like this piece of me that was missing when you were gone just snapped back into place. Now, don't get me wrong," he says, cocking a brow as his eyes find mine again. "That little piece of me shook with anger when I had to watch Grayson with you."

I bite my lip, cheeks flooding with more heat.

"But," he continues, thumbing my blushing skin before pulling my chin up. "I only felt like me when that piece was alive, when I was with you — even when it hurt." He lowers his mouth to mine, and after stealing one small kiss and my breath along with it, he smiles. "*That's* how I knew."

Adam kisses me again, this time pressing into my lips until I opened them to let his tongue inside. He smooths his over mine, one hand cradling my neck as he deepens the kiss. My body reacts automatically — leaning in, heart picking up speed, stomach fluttering. By the time he pulls back, my desire to take things slow that I've managed to hold onto since we made up after Spring Break is depleted to dust.

"Well, now that you know," I whisper. "And *I* know, where do we go from here?"

Adam's dark eyes sparkle in the low light of the moon, and he pops up onto his feet without warning, hands wrapping around his mouth to make a megaphone.

"I LOVE CASSIE MCBEE!"

His scream echoes off the walls of the parking garage, so loud I jump and my heart picks up for a completely different reason. But he just keeps going.

"CASSIE MCBEE IS MY GIRLFRIEND, AND I'M HER BOYFRIEND, AND EVERYONE ELSE CAN JUST FUCK THE HELL OFF!"

I laugh, scrambling to my feet and ripping his arms down to break the megaphone. "Oh, my God. Shhhh, stop."

My entire neck lights with heat as he screams again, megaphone or not.

"CASSIE MCBEE IS MINE, MOTHERFUCKERS! *MINE.* YOU HEAR ME, BOYS OF PSU?"

Thrusting up onto my tiptoes, I press my lips to his, shutting him up the only way I know how before I blush so hard I get a sunburn. Adam laughs against my lips, wrapping his arms around me and swinging me in a circle before he lets my sneakers touch the ground again.

"There," he says, kissing my nose. "Now, you know, I know, and so does everyone else." He brushes my short hair behind one ear, shaking his head as his eyes trace the features of my face, like he can't believe the words he's about to say. "You're mine," he whispers, bending until our foreheads meet. "And I'm never giving you up. Ever."

I giggle, kissing him again as I wrap my arms around his neck. "Take me home, stupid."

"Yes, ma'am."

Adam takes my hand, stopping to pack up the small equipment we brought with us and shove it into his duffle bag on our way downstairs. We're laughing and talking as we make our way across campus, but when we turn onto Greek Row, something shifts.

The energy around us picks up a static charge, one familiar and yet different tonight. It's that same electricity that lets me know when Adam is around me before he's even said a word, but tonight, it feels powered by an unstoppable magnetic field. I lean into Adam, and his arm wraps around my waist, and as we walk down the silent street, most of the Greek students already gone for the summer, we fall silent, too.

And I know.

I know tonight is the night I give myself to Adam, and he gives me another piece of him, too. Tonight, we'll make another promise.

And this time, I know we'll keep it.

The Alpha Sigma house is quiet when we step inside. There are only a few other brothers staying in the house over summer, and all of them are upstairs in the second-floor rooms. Adam drops his duffle bag by the front door and holds my hand tight as we walk down the dark hallway to his room.

Once we're inside, I slip out of my sneakers and socks, and Adam strips his shirt over his head. I trace the lean muscles of his abdomen, a flash of last semester hitting me hard. I remember running into him rush week when I had to bring him a file from Erin, and how even then, when I was with Grayson, I couldn't help the way Adam affected me.

His eyes meet mine when I trail my way back up, and he smirks, crossing the room until his hands rest on my hips.

"Shower?" he asks, voice low. The only light in his room is from a small, bedside lamp, and it casts his skin in a warm, orange glow.

I nod, and Adam fingers the hem of my tank top before peeling it from my slick skin. I lift my arms, keeping my eyes on his as he strips the fabric over my head and lets it fall to the floor. He swallows, eyes flashing to my breasts, and I keep my hands in the air until he peels my bra off, too.

When the cool air hits my nipples, they peak, rushing a wave of goose bumps down my arms, my ribs, my legs, all the way to my ankles. Adam watches them, chest heaving as he steps closer, his fingertips reaching for my shorts next.

I close my eyes, trying to savor every touch, featherlight or bruising, like I can store this moment and relive it anytime I want. So long, I've wondered what it would be like. So long, I've hoped it would happen — one day, just me and Adam.

And when someday becomes tonight, it's almost too much to bear.

Adam drops to his knees, his eyes on mine as he slips his fingertips beneath the band of my shorts and pulls them slowly over my hips, my ass, letting them fall down to the floor once they're free from my thighs. I step out of them, and when Adam stands again, I'm completely naked in front of him.

For the first time.

He lets out a shaky breath, hands reaching for me before he stops himself, rolling his hands into fists at his side, instead. His eyes roam over my exposed flesh, his erection straining more and more beneath his shorts as he does. And as much as part of me wants to hide, wants to skip the shower and jump under the covers of his bed, instead — it's the way he looks at me, the way he's *always* looked at me, that makes me stand tall and confident, welcoming his appreciative stare.

"Now I remember why I never let you get naked in front of me before," he whispers.

"Why's that?"

"Because I knew if you took off all your clothes, I wouldn't be able to let you leave without taking all of *you*."

I swallow, stepping closer to him, my trembling hands reaching forward for his shorts. I slip one hand beneath the band, the other sliding over his bulge as his eyes flutter shut at the contact.

"Take all of me," I whisper, meeting his gaze when his eyes open again. "Here. Tonight."

He opens his mouth, but I shake my head, kissing him to stop his words.

"Don't ask me if I'm sure," I breathe against his lips. "I want you. Now. And I wouldn't say it if I wasn't sure."

With that, I push his shorts over his hips, taking his briefs with him, and in seconds, he's naked with me.

I don't look down, don't let myself see what I've always wanted to until Adam leads us into his small shower. He runs the water hot before stepping inside, and then he reaches back for my hand, pulling me in with him. I step under the stream, and then — only then — do I let myself look down.

My walls clench at the sight of his stiff member, the size of it even more than I expected. I've felt it under sheets and clothing, felt the warmth of it pressed against me when we made out. But to see it, to see *him* fully exposed from head to toe, every muscle in his body hard and wanting, with me as the desired target... it sends a rush through me so powerful, my knees buckle at the force.

Adam's arms wrap around me just in time, his chest pressing against mine as he sweeps my wet hair from my face. His eyes search mine, that heavy, magnetic charge descending on us even under the water.

"Do you remember what I said to you earlier this semester?" he asks, voice low in my ear as he spins me to face the faucet. His erection presses into my lower back, and my breath catches, eyes shutting on a sigh. "When you let me touch you, do you remember?"

My head is foggy, thoughts nonexistent as every molecule of my brain focuses on how his hands feel sliding with the water over my hips, up my ribs, his warm palms cupping my breasts. "Um... you said... you said..." I try, but my breath is too ragged, my heart beating too fast for a single thought to catch.

"I said before we went any further, I wanted you to know that every single chance I get to touch you, every chance I get to put my hands where you don't let any other hands go, it means everything to me."

"Yes, that." I pant.

Adam chuckles, his hands still massaging my breasts under the warm stream. When he rolls my nipples between his thumbs and pointer fingers, I hiss, arching my back off his chest and leaning into the touch.

"I just wanted to remind you," he says, sucking my earlobe between his teeth. One hand keeps rolling over my left breast, but the other slides down with the water over my navel, down below my hips, his hot fingertips slipping between my thighs easily. "I want to make you feel good, Cassie," he whispers. His fingers slide farther between my legs, the tip of one of them slipping inside me, and I moan, the sensation of it rocking me from head to toe. "I want to make you *come*," he says a little softer, and my knees shake, legs parting wider to let his fingers press inside me more. "But first, I had to make sure you remembered."

"I remember," I pant, one hand flying back into his hair behind me while the other braces on the wall. "Now *please*, Adam. Touch me."

My voice is light and raspy, more seductive than I even knew I could manage, and it drives a growl out of Adam so deep I feel it rumble through his chest as his two fingers finally slide inside me. The way he enters me, my back pressed against his chest, his arms wrapped around me — one between my legs, one flicking my sensitive nipple — it's so much more than anything I've felt before. It's like he's completely consumed me, like we're one together. When my hand slips behind me, gripping his hard on and pumping in time with his hand, I can't decide if I'm touching him, or still touching *me* — because I feel everything I'm doing to him, too.

"Fuck," he draws out, biting my neck with another groan. His fingers dive deeper inside me, and I squeeze my hand over him tighter, relishing in the feel of the water over his soft skin as I pulse. I remember how I felt the first time Adam touched me, the first time his fingers were inside me, his mouth on my clit — but it's nothing compared to my first time touching *him*.

And now that I've had a taste, I want more.

Adam's fingers slip from inside me when I push away from him, spinning and holding onto his arms as I lower to my knees. His eyes widen, hands gripping my arms like he wants to pull me back up. And when I'm level with his hard, wet cock, I realize I have no idea what I'm doing.

"Cassie..." he warns.

"I want to taste you," I whisper, looking up at him through my lashes from where I sit on my knees. "The way you've tasted me."

His nose flares, hands pulling my wet hair back as I grip him firmly in one hand. The water streams down Adam's back, his chest, dripping down his abdomen to where my hand grips his shaft. I pulse once, wrapping around him at the base, and then slowly, I lower my lips to his tip.

He tastes salty on my tongue, and as I swirl it around his tip and lick down to where my hand rests, I wonder what I tasted like to him. The memory of his head between my thighs, his magical tongue licking and sucking my clit, makes my thighs clench. And when I look up at Adam again, my tongue running along his base, and watch his eyes flutter shut as his head tilts back, a new wave of want pulses through me.

"Is this okay?" I ask, flicking under his crown with the tip of my tongue. "Am I doing it right?"

Adam pauses, his head lifting slowly as his eyes find mine. "Is this... is this your first time?"

I nod. "Doing this, yes. I've never... can you help me? Tell me what you like."

Adam shakes with a guttural moan as I wrap my mouth around him again, this time taking him in my throat as far as I can. It's not far, and I gag a little, eyes watering as I withdraw and suck his tip.

"Is that okay?"

"God, Cassie, you're going to make me come in this shower before I've even been inside you if you keep looking up at me like that."

He groans, gripping my forearms tight and pulling me to stand again. Then, his mouth is devouring mine hungrily, like his last breath exists somewhere inside me and he's on a mission to steal it back.

"We can revisit that another time," he breathes. "Right now, I need you."

He reaches behind him to kill the water, thrusting the shower curtain back and hastily wrapping a towel around him. He pulls one out for me, but when he turns to face me again, it's as if time completely stops.

Adam pauses, holding my towel in his hand, and our eyes stay connected without either of us taking another step. Water drips from his hair down his jaw, to his chest, and I know he's watching the same waterfall over my own body. He swallows, as if he's just realized what we're about to do, and then slowly, carefully, he wraps me in the towel and helps me out of the shower.

I'm still dripping as Adam lowers me into his bed, my wet hair splaying out over his pillow, hands clutching the towel over my chest. I was just naked and on my knees for him, but suddenly, I'm more exposed. Suddenly, it's not just his fingers inside me, or me going down on him. It's not just a shower. It's not just sex.

It's me, and Adam, for the first time.

It's years of wanting, of never knowing, of always hoping. It's an immeasurable time of hurt, of pain, of broken promises — and an equal amount of time making that right. It's late nights eating pizza, him being there for me when Grayson wasn't. It's our first kiss on a dark beach in Key West, his hands on me when they shouldn't have been. It's him knowing better than I did what I needed this semester, and holding back on what *he* wanted just to make sure I was okay.

It's love.

And that's more intimate than the touches, the kisses, the feel of his body against mine. It's what makes this time different than any other.

It's what makes tonight *more.*

Adam swallows from where he towers above me, balancing on his forearms. He shifts his weight to one of them, kissing my hands where they clutch my towel before slowly peeling them back. I fist them in the sheets, instead, as he drops the edges of my towel to each side, and then his eyes are on me, his mouth descending.

He kisses my neck, my collarbone, the swell of my breast. His hands grip my ribs, my waist, my hips and my thighs. It's like he can't kiss everywhere he wants, can't grab me tight enough, and when his hips settle between mine, the slick, hard tip of him pressing against the wet, swollen entrance of me — we both stop.

Kissing. Breathing. Feeling.

For that one moment, we're suspended in time, and nothing or no one else exists.

Adam's hand shakes as he reaches past my left shoulder and into his bedside table drawer for a condom. I just hold onto his shoulders, watching the mix of nerves and desire play across his face as he slips it on. When his weight is back on his forearms, his hips pressed against mine again, and his eyes float to mine, we both inhale a deep breath together.

"I love you," he whispers, and his entire body trembles with the words.

"I love you, too."

The laughter is gone. The playfulness? Left behind in the shower. It's all heat and love and wonder as Adam presses his lips to mine, and slowly, with intent and care and purpose — he pushes inside me for the first time.

He fills me with our mouths fused together, stretching me inch by blissful inch with each withdrawal and flex of his hips. My nails dig into his shoulders, his back, my toes curling under the sheets. When it's too much, I gasp for air from our kiss, eyes closing as he plants gentle kisses down my neck.

It's nothing like I expected, feeling the weight of him between my legs. It's more — *so* much more. It's the love behind his eyes as he watches me, the tenderness of his shaking hands as they cradle my face, the careful way he enters me each and every time, pressing deep, but not too hard, letting us each feel every single centimeter. It's everything I've always wanted sex to be, and everything I thought it never *could* be.

"Are you okay?" Adam asks, eyes finding mine.

I nod, kissing him again, my heels digging into his behind to press him deeper inside me. When he fills me again, I gasp, a rush of heat warming my entire body. "Yes," I breathe. "More."

And he delivers.

More and more, flex after flex, moan after moan, until I'm so ready to come I almost don't want to. This feeling — this rush of pleasure right before it all ends — *this* is what I love the most.

Adam shifts his weight to one arm, wrapping the other around my thigh and lifting it until one leg is on his shoulder. In the new position, I'm even tighter than before, and both of us groan at the sensation.

"Adam..." I breathe, nails dragging down his back. He thrusts a little harder, the friction catching my clit in the perfect way, and I pull him closer, down into me, like I can't come until we're seamed together. "Yes. Oh, God, *yes*."

Moans I've never heard before somehow spill from me, my cries loud and unabashed as I come harder than ever before. My vision goes black, a rush of blood flowing from every vein in my body straight to the pulsing need between my legs. I shudder, gripping Adam tight as I spiral out into space, and my moans drive him over his edge, taking him down with me.

He buries his head between my neck and my shoulder, his breath hot on my skin as we find our releases together. My name leaves his lips in a sigh, his falls from mine in a prayer, and when we emerge on the other side, in a new time, a new place, a new existence.

It's the after, the now, the impossible that somehow slipped within our reach.

And we take our first breaths together.

***

The next night, I'm ridiculously happy and deliciously sore, crowded into Erin's bed with her, Jess, and Ashlei as we FaceTime Skyler in Vegas. She just wrapped up the first day of the tournament, but we're all more focused on what she just told us about Kip.

None of us knew what happened with Skyler and Kip after the cruise. We all thought everything was smooth sailing once the Erin drama was out in the open. But, they had a big blow out, and now that she's revealed *why*, none of us can wrap our heads around it.

Kip's dad sent him to PSU specifically to meet Skyler, to get to know her — to get to know her *game*. He wanted Kip to beat her at the tournament in Vegas, and Skyler found a file on his computer detailing the whole thing. It makes complete sense to us now that she blew him off and wanted nothing to do with him, but as soon as she dropped that bomb on us, she dropped another.

And this one has more kick.

Kip's father has cancer.

So, what started as a deal between them, as a way for Kip to get the tuition money he needed for his dream school, turned into his father's dying wish. And suddenly, nothing is black and white.

I'm beginning to learn that nothing in life is.

"Not to sound like your mother," I say after a while, the subject changed. "But you look too thin. Are you eating out there in Vegas?"

Skyler laughs a little, bringing color to her ashen face. Her eyes are tired, hair in a messy bun, and I can tell she hasn't been sleeping as much as she needs to to win a tournament.

"Trust me," she says. "It's just the camera. I've eaten at like five buffets already."

"Sounds like heaven to me," Jess pipes in. She takes a swig of the bottle of wine we snuck in and passes it to Erin. Skyler salutes us with a drink from her own bottle on the other end.

"I just wish we could be there," Ashlei says, her face falling. "You should have someone there to cheer you on."

"I know you girls will cheer me on at the watch party tomorrow, and honestly that will probably be more fun than the viewing section here. Send me pictures! I want to see everyone."

"You know we will," Ashlei says.

My phone lights up with a text from Adam and I blush, smiling as I tuck it under the covers.

"Bear has been planning this thing for months. I'm pretty sure he bought enough kegs for the entire city instead of just the school. Which, by the way, literally the entire school will be there." Ashlei smiles, shaking her head. "We are all so fucking proud of you."

"Thanks." Skyler says with a small smile, but it falls a bit when her eyes land on Erin. "What are you thinking so hard about, Big?"

Every time Skyler addresses Erin, or the other way around, we can't help but all get a little stiff. Things are still tense between them after everything that happened. I'm glad they apologized to each other and agreed to make amends, but something tells me it won't be anything they can resolve overnight. Or even over a summer.

Erin sighs. "I just can't get over what you told us about Kip's dad."

Jess and Ashlei exchange glances, their eyes wide. *Why is she bringing up Kip again? We just moved past this.*

"What do you mean?"

Erin shakes her head. "They were just so close when I knew him back in high school. His dad was everything to him. He was so afraid to be who he was because he wanted to be everything his *dad* wanted him to be. I was in the process of finding myself that summer, but Kip couldn't join me in that because he was trying to find how he fit in his father's picture." Erin pauses, her brows pinching together, eyes on her hands. "I know he's come a long way from that, but I also know this can't be easy for him. I just can't believe he's even there."

"Well, isn't that precisely *why* he's there?" I point out. "I don't think he would be if this wouldn't have happened."

"Can we not talk about this?" Skyler pinches the bridge of her nose, her eyes closing on the other end of the video call.

Jess gives Erin a pointed look before jumping up from the bed, pulling the wine bottle with her.

"Whatever," she says. "Forget all that. To you, Skyler Fucking Thorne." She lifts the bottle to the screen. "Kick ass tomorrow and then get back here so we can throw a huge rager with all that money."

We all laugh and Jess takes a pull of her bottle as Skyler lifts hers, too. "I love you girls. Thank you."

Ashlei shrugs. "That's what we're here for."

"Do you guys mind if I talk to Little alone?"

Skyler's eyes find mine in the screen, a silence falling over us as the other girls nod in understanding. They all blow kisses at the screen and offer various forms of advice before leaving the room. Then, it's just me and Skyler.

She inhales a shaky breath, her eyes watering, and I immediately shake my head.

"Do not cry on me, Big."

She blows out the breath. "I'm trying not to. Little, I don't know what the hell I'm doing. This tournament means everything to me, or it *did*, anyway. But now, I'm not sure what matters most to me anymore." She buries her face in her hands, as if admitting that out loud scares her more than anything ever has in her life.

"I think you do know."

I offer Skyler a soft smile as she looks back up, wishing more than anything that I could say what I'm about to say to her in person.

"Skyler, you were going to pretty much be done with tournaments after this, right?" I ask, remembering what she'd told us last semester. She just wanted to get enough to finish paying off her tuition for her remaining time at PSU, and to set her family up a little more. After that, she wanted to focus on *her* future — on what that looked like.

Skyler nods, blinking against the tears pooling in her eyes.

"You want this more than anything not for the title, but for your family. You want to pay off school at Palm South and help your parents out. I get that, I totally do," I say. "But, Sky, it's not up to you to set your parents up for life. And you and I both know that it wouldn't take first place for you to be able to pay off your tuition. Don't let the pressure of winning get to you. Just play like I know you know how to and let the cards fall where they're meant to fall."

Skyler bites her lower lip, considering my advice. Maybe she hasn't thought of that before, how winning at almost *any* point now would give her a great pot of cash to come home with. Or, maybe she's known all along, but she doesn't know how to handle her new feelings. Poker has been everything to her for so long. She's never put a boy above it.

Sometimes, love makes us forget who we are. But others? It shows us who we've wanted to be all along. I've felt that with Adam, and just by looking at my Big, I know she feels it, too.

Poor girl. Here's hoping she doesn't have to go through what we did.

"What are you going to do about Kip?" I ask her after a moment.

She shrugs. "What is there to do? It's over."

"I call bullshit."

Huffing, Skyler takes a long drink from the bottle of wine. "It is! How could I ever forgive him for what he did? How do I know what's been real and what was just a game?"

I roll my eyes, because I remember those exact same excuses coming from my own mouth. "Oh, please. Every single moment between the two of you has been one-hundred percent real and you know it." I lean in toward the screen. "Look at me, Big. I have known you for two years now and I've never seen you like this with a guy. *Ever*. You may not be sure about what's happening between you and Kip, but I am. When he says he loves you, he means it — and I think you know that, too."

"I don't though, that's what's so hard!" Skyler practically yells, slamming the wine bottle down on her bedside table in frustration. "I would never have guessed he was playing this game, Little. Never. Everything with him felt so real, so genuine, so unlike anything I've ever had before. If it was so easy for him to pull off this whole scheme without me knowing the difference, wouldn't it be just as easy for him to make me believe he loved me when he didn't?"

I shake my head. "But then why would he still be trying to convince you? If it was all just a game, why would he bother?"

Skyler scoffs. "He's probably trying to get under my skin for tomorrow."

"You and I both know that's complete crap," I say firmly. Leaning in more, I make sure her eyes are on mine when I say my next sentence. "You're scared, Skyler. I know you are and it's okay to be scared. But remember, some of life's best experiences are masked as terrifying leaps of faith."

Her face softens at that.

"Just please, *please* — think about what you want before tomorrow," I beg her. "Think about what matters to you. What *really* matters."

Skyler nods, and I can only imagine how she must feel with all the thoughts in her head warring against each other. Poker used to be simple for her, it used to be the *only* sure thing. Now, everything she thought she knew about what she wanted, about *who* mattered in her life, has been flipped upside down.

But she can do this, she can make her way out. She just has to decide what result she wants in the end.

"I love you, Big," I tell her. "We'll all be watching tomorrow. Just know you have a team rooting for you, no matter what happens."

And with that, we end the call, and all eyes at Palm South University are watching Vegas.

Bear

"Come on, Sky. Come on."

I press my fingertips into the bridge of my nose, my hands steepled around my mouth as I pray. It's the final table in Vegas, and at almost eleven our time — about eight o'clock theirs — Skyler just went all in.

There are three players left — her, Kip, and some douchebag named Brandon who just stood up to challenge her. Honestly, Brandon probably *isn't* a douchebag. For all I know, he could be a sweet country boy from Missouri trying to win money for his high school sweetheart to go to college or to get his sick grandma the care she needs.

But right now, he's up against my best friend.

Therefore: douchebag.

"Is this how you get during football season?" Becca teases from beside me, popping a Dorito in her mouth. "If so, I might be busy for like all of fall."

I smirk, blowing out a breath and leaning back on the couch. I throw my arm around her, pulling her into me.

"It's just Skyler. She's like a little sister to me, and I know how bad she wants this."

"Well, from what you told me, the guy she's been dating all semester wants it just as bad. Wonder what she'll do about that."

I frown, eyes flicking to Kip as his face fills the screen. Then, the camera is back on the cards, and I don't have time to think about how I'm torn between ripping Kip a new asshole and giving him a Bear Hug. My parents are shit humans, but I've seen what good family can look like. It looks like Mac and his family, like Skyler and hers. And I can't imagine being in Kip's shoes after what Erin told me about his dad.

Luckily, it's none of my business, and I'm completely content in staying the hell out of it.

The dealer reveals a Jack of spades, and everyone in the room groans. At least, everyone who's paying attention. The rager ended up being bigger than even *I* expected, and half of the crowd is gathered around the various TVs in the house while the other half plays drinking games, dances, and parties outside.

"Fuck," I murmur, running my free hand back over my head.

"So, what does that mean?" Becca asks. "Is she done?"

"Not yet, but he has three Jacks now. She needs a heart on this last card or she's fucked."

Becca turns back toward the screen just in time for the dealer to turn the river, and when I see it's a nine of hearts, I jump up from the couch at the same time Skyler thrusts her fist in the air. The entire house cheers, even people not paying attention knowing something good must have happened. It's a deafening roar, one I hope Skyler can hear from Vegas.

"Atta fucking girl, Sky!" I holler, and Becca holds up both hands for a high ten.

"That's so crazy!" she says, running her hands through her hair, eyes wide. "So now it's just her and that guy? Like, one of them is walking away the winner of this whole thing?"

"Yep," I say, still buzzing off the win. Skyler shakes hands with Brandon, but then her eyes focus on Kip, and I can see her jaw tighten on the screen. My stomach falls. "It all comes down to this."

There's a mad dash to the kitchen for beer refills and snacks before the last round starts. And in my rush to get back to my spot on the couch with a fresh beer for me and Becca, I nearly run over Erin.

"Ooof!" she exclaims as I hold the beers out above her head, doing my best not to spill them all over her.

"Shit, Erin, I'm sorry."

"No, no, I'm sorry. I wasn't looking where I was going," she says, and then she starts giggling. Erin Xanders, who I haven't seen laugh in over a year, is *giggling*.

"Uh..." I bend down to look into her glazed eyes. "Are you okay?"

"Oh, I'm *fantastic!*" she says, clapping her hands down on my shoulders. She kisses each one of my cheeks and pulls back with a grin plastered on her face as she runs her hands back through her hair. "I've had a few beers. I can't remember the last time I had *beer*," she says. "And Skyler is doing so good. And Kip is there, so that's super fun. And I had the best brownie of my *life* and now I'm going back to get more."

"Brownie?" I follow her gaze to the plate of baked goods behind me in the kitchen, and my eyes double in size when I look at her again. "Oh, shit, Erin. Those are pot brownies."

I expect her to freak out, to go into paranoid mode about being within even twenty feet of drugs. But she just smiles, and shrugs. "Ah. Well, that explains why I feel so great then, doesn't it?"

"Um, yeah..." Glancing behind her, I see Becca watching us, but she pulls her gaze away as soon as mine finds hers. "Are you sure you're okay? Maybe you should come sit down in the living room for a bit."

"I will. I'm just going to get some water," Erin says, smacking her tongue to the roof of her mouth. "I'm thirsty."

She grins again and I can't help but chuckle. "Alright. See you in there."

Erin makes her way into the kitchen as I take my seat next to Becca again, handing her the beer I managed to save. She takes her first sip as a new hand is dealt to Kip and Skyler.

"You missed it," she says, licking her lips as she sets her cup down on the table. "They had these hot bitches bringing out piles of money and shit."

"Damn it!" I say, making a big deal of it even though I could care less. I prop my arm around her shoulders on the couch. "Maybe you can get half-naked later and give me a replay."

"Only if you get *all the way* naked," she says, brow arched.

I just laugh, bending to kiss her full, nude lips before turning my attention back to the screen. Erin plops down in one of the chairs down the couch from us, spilling a little water as she giggles and tries to focus on the television. I watch her for a moment, caught somewhere between happy for her that she's smiling and worried for her because I know drugs can become an addiction when it feels like there's nothing else happy in life. And for Erin, right now, I know that's how she feels.

She finally came to me.

After all this time running, after all this time saying she was fine, she finally came to me after she and Skyler made up. And I held her, and she talked, and cried, and even though we haven't figured everything out yet, it's a step.

I feel like she can get better, like she can be okay again.

I feel like I can help her get there.

"She okay?" Becca asks, noticing my gaze.

I clear my throat and take another sip of my beer. "She's good. Just ate a pot brownie by mistake."

Becca laughs. "Oh, God. Been there." She leans into me, her eyes on mine while I keep my gaze on the screen. "Hey... I don't have to worry about her, right?"

"What?" I snap my eyes to hers, immediately shaking my head as I drop my beer to the table again. "Of course not."

"Okay," Becca says, fingers playing with the hem of my t-shirt. "I just wanted to check. I know we're not official or anything, but... I like you, Bear. And I've been second place before." She swallows, her eyes on where her hand twists in my shirt. "Too many times, actually. And I'm not doing it again."

I tilt her chin up with my knuckle, making sure her eyes are on mine when I say my next words. "Hey, you're not second place with me. You're first. Hell, you're the *only* place, there aren't even any other competitors."

She smiles, leaning into my touch.

"I know we're taking it slower than either of us is used to," I say, searching her golden eyes. I let myself trace the smooth features of her face, the curls of her hair. "But, it's not because I have feelings for anyone else. It's because I have a *lot* of feelings for you, and I want to take my time exploring them. Just like you've been second place before, I've rushed in and felt safe sooner than I should have," I admit, a flash of Shawna hitting me out of nowhere. "I just want to do it right this time."

"Me, too," Becca says. She leans up, pressing her lips to mine. "Just keep it real with me, okay?"

"Always."

She snuggles into my side, and then the entire house is sucked into what's happening in Vegas.

***

A little past midnight, the stacks are almost completely even in Vegas. It's easy to see both players are tired, even with the jokes they've been throwing back and forth at each other, and we all know it's going to be over soon.

"I better piss now or forever hold my peace," I murmur, slipping my arm from around Becca.

"Gross. Did not need to know."

"Hey, you said to keep it one-hundred."

"For future reference, that doesn't include your digestion status."

I shrug, throwing her a wink as I make my way toward the hall. "Your loss."

I jog down the hallway first, but the bathroom in my room is in use — and not in the way I need to use it. I smirk when I hear the moans and thumps, tapping the door with an, "Atta boy," before heading for the bathroom upstairs. It's usually the cleanest, and after the kind of party we've had tonight, I know the co-ed ones downstairs have to be a mess.

I don't bother locking the door behind me, knowing I won't be long. I realize that was a mistake not even a full minute later when I'm still zipping up my fly and the door bursts open.

Erin flies through, shoving me to the side just in time to drop to her knees and vomit in the toilet I just pissed in.

"Jesus Christ, Ex," I say, rinsing my hands quickly before drying them and bending to hold her hair back. I reach her just in time for her to heave again, and I cringe at the sight, looking away but still holding her hair and rubbing her back. "It's okay, get it all out."

"I don't understand," she groans, leaning her cheek on the toilet seat.

"Don't do that."

I try to get her to sit up again, but she swats me away, groaning again.

"I felt fine, I felt great."

I chuckle, dropping to the floor next to her. "Yeah, well, you drank and *then* ate a pot brownie. The spins were inevitable."

She opens her eyes, blinking a few times. "So, you feel the room spinning, too?"

I don't have time to answer before she's head in the toilet again, dry heaving. I just smile and rub her back. *Poor girl.*

"It's okay, just get it all out and you'll feel better after a night of sleep."

Erin doesn't get anything up that time, so she rests her cheek on the toilet seat again. Her eyes are glazed and out of focus as she looks up at me, and a smile splits her face. Then, she giggles before full on laughing.

"Still high, huh?" I ask with a smile.

"No, no, it's just..." She shakes her head, waving her hand at me before it lands on my arm. She squeezes it tight, her warm hand smoothing over my bicep as her eyes search mine. "It's just, the last time I was throwing up in this bathroom, it was because I was pregnant with your baby."

There's a loud commotion downstairs, a mixture of cheers and groans, but all I hear is ringing. All I see is Erin's smiling face, staring back at me without a single ounce of embarrassment or regret over what she just said. She doesn't realize it. She probably doesn't even remember it, and it just happened.

But I'll never forget it.

"What did you just say?"

Suddenly, her eyes go wide, like her words finally registered. Her breathing accelerates as I drop my hand from her back.

"Erin. What the fuck did you just say to me." I shake my head, grabbing her wrist and pulling her up to look at me. "Was that a joke?"

"Oh, God."

Her eyes bulge again just as the door swings open, and my Little grimaces at the sight of Erin's puke in the toilet before his eyes find mine.

"Shit, man."

"Get out, Josh." I point to the door he just came through, my voice firm.

"I'm going, man, trust me. I just thought you should know. Skyler lost," he says.

My stomach drops even lower, head falling back a bit as a sigh leaves my chest. *Shit.* She lost, and I wasn't even there to watch it.

Josh shrugs, his eyes sympathetic. "Sorry, man. It's all over."

He shuts the door, and as soon as we're alone again, Erin finds a little more to throw up.

Skyler

- Meet me at the Bellagio. 11:30. -

I stare at Kip's text when I'm fully dressed, debating if I should actually meet him or just crawl back into the hot bathtub. His message is the only one I've looked at, choosing to ignore the multitude of other texts and calls until the morning when I can face them. They'll all want answers, they'll want to know what happened, they'll want to congratulate me on second place even when they're secretly wondering why the hell I didn't take first.

Only Kip and I know that.

I'm already late, if I do want to meet him, but I still don't rush. Instead, I sit on the bed, replaying the night. I close my eyes, see Kip sitting across from me, see his eyes widen when I go all in with a pair of black fours on the table. It's my cursed hand in poker. He and I both knew it was over right then, but what *he* doesn't know is that was the exact moment I realized it didn't matter.

The title didn't matter.

The only thing that did was *him.*

The second-place check is plenty to pay off my tuition, set my family up, and then some. It was what I came for. The title would have just been a bonus for me, a decorative medal for my ego. But to Kip? It was everything.

So, I went from being his opponent to being his teammate, and we won the tournament *together* — for his dad.

I sigh, opening my eyes again to stare at the black television screen hanging above the desk. Not even an hour ago, I watched Kip's face fill that screen, his eyes tired but his smile wide as he talked to the reporter.

"I'm not really sure how I feel just yet," he'd said, laughing.

It was a charming laugh that I was sure was melting panties across the country.

"I just..." He'd paused, biting down on his bottom lip and looking up for a second to compose himself. *"I just want to dedicate this to my father, Oliver Jackson Sr. Thank you for sacrificing your dream so that I could have mine. I didn't win this tournament today. You did. I love you."*

The announcers went on and on about Kip's dad and his condition and I wondered how they found out. Did Kip reveal it in one of his pre-tournament interviews? Had they been talking about it while we were at the final table? Regardless, I know one thing is certain — this will make for one of the best headlines in the tournament's history.

FISH TAKES HOME GRAND PRIZE, HONORS FATHER WITH WIN.

I smile, finally standing and inhaling a long, slow breath. "Okay. Let's get this over with."

I take my time making my way downstairs, and don't rush as I walk the Strip to the Bellagio. It's not too far from the Aria, and my stomach flips with every step as I let myself overthink what he wants to talk about. Does he want to know if I threw the tournament? Does he want to know if I'm okay after the loss?

Does he want to tell me he still loves me, that he wants to be with me?

I shake the possibility from my head, trying to remind myself that everything between us was just a game for him. It was a means to an end, and even if *I* still love him — and perhaps, always will — it doesn't mean he feels the same.

And that's okay.

For once, I'm not asking what's in this for me. For once, I care about someone else's happiness more than mine.

To me, that's what love really is.

The strip is alive as I walk toward the fountain, the lights bright and energy buzzing. Groups pass me in a blur, smiles and laughter blending together with the distant dings from the slot machines to create the Vegas symphony. I just smile, tucking my hands in my pockets and scanning the crowd for Kip. A warm breeze tickles my neck when I find him, and suddenly my feet are lead. All I can do is stand and stare.

He's facing the fountain, his shoulders slumped like he's convinced himself I'm not going to show. His hair is mussed, and even from the back, I spy the black frames of his glasses — those stupid glasses that proved to be such a weakness for me.

Kip turns, looking over the shoulder farthest from me, his face searching the crowd. When he turns over the other one, his eyes catch on mine just as another breeze whips through my hair.

A minute stretches between us, dancing like a year, with his diamond blue eyes locked on mine.

My breaths are shallow but steady, and I finally force my feet to move, carrying me toward him without our gaze ever breaking. He stands straighter as I make my way toward him, wiping his palms on his dark jeans. He's nervous, and suddenly, I am, too.

When I'm just a few feet in front of him, Kip's face washes over like a ghost, like he can't find a single word to say now that I'm here. So, I let out a breath, and I say the first word.

"Hi."

My voice is barely above a whisper, but it visibly stabilizes Kip. He finally breathes again, though his eyes are still heavy, never leaving mine.

"Hi."

I tuck the blowing strands of my hair behind my ear, chewing the inside of my lip. "Congratulations," I finally offer, smiling a little.

"Thanks."

He returns the smile, but it doesn't stick, doesn't warm me from the inside out like his smiles used to do. Instead, it settles us into a long moment of silence, the two of us standing and staring, not knowing what to do.

Kip shoves his hands into his pockets, shaking his head just slightly as his eyes continue to search mine, like he's sure he'll find all the answers there. "Skyler..." He says my name like a curse. "Why did you do it?"

My heart skips a beat before kicking back into gear, but I don't let an ounce of emotion show on my face.

"Do what?"

"Don't make me say it. You know what."

I shrug. "Maybe I was trying to have more faith in our lucky number."

"You knew before he even dealt those fours in the flop that I had a pocket pair. Don't act like you didn't," Kip says, his eyes level. Then, his brows bend together, his eyes still on mine. "Why did you let me win?"

I sigh, crossing my arms over my middle. "Because, Kip," I say, wishing I didn't have to explain. It was easy to make the decision, but to defend it? Not so much. "I knew you wanted this for your dad, and, frankly you deserved it."

"And you didn't?"

"I didn't say that." I huff, anger surging up inside me.

Can't he see it? Can't he see the real reason I made the decision I did?

"My reasons for wanting to win were no better than yours," he says, stepping a little closer. "Skyler, this was important to you and your family."

"Well, maybe it wasn't as important to me as you!" I yell, and as soon as the words leave my mouth, I know there's no going back now.

A few bystanders glance our way before skittering apart, and I shift my weight, pulling a strand of hair between my fingers. I don't want to look at Kip, don't want to see his face after what I just said, but I can't look anywhere else.

"Are you saying you're not important to me?"

"No," I answer. "I'm saying you didn't have a choice. I did. The runner-up prize is plenty for me to pay off school and set my family up, Kip." I shake my head, still playing with my hair. "And even if it wasn't, it wouldn't matter. You did this for your dad, for his dying wish. If it were me in your shoes, I know you would have done the same."

Silence.

I can't take my eyes off his, no matter how badly I want to find comfort in staring anywhere else but at him. His blue pools are wide with wonder, like he can't believe I would do that for him.

Like he can't believe I'm real.

"So, what does this mean?" he finally asks.

I shrug. "I don't know. It means you won and I lost, I guess."

"I don't know if I agree with that."

His answer is so quick, so sure, that I can't do anything other than tilt my head as I try to digest it.

"I may have won the tournament," he breathes, taking another small step toward me. "But did I lose you?"

For the first time tonight, I let myself look at the ground and away from him. My heart thumps hard in my chest, the beats echoing in my ears.

"I don't know where we go from here, Kip," I whisper, tears stinging behind my eyes. "I don't know if we can come back from this. We lied. Both of us. We played games and even though all the cards are on the table now, I don't know if this is a game we can finish playing and still survive."

I look up just in time to see Kip's bottom lip quiver as he looks up to the sky, willing himself not to give into his emotions. Slowly, he levels his gaze with me again, his chest deflating on a long breath.

"I'm sorry, Skyler. For everything," he says, voice raspy and desperate. "And I know those two words won't do anything to heal the fucking hole I've punched in you, but I mean them. And if you let me, I will spend the rest of my life making sure you know that nothing in this world is more important to me than you are. Nothing."

He pauses, debating his next words as I try to swallow the ones he just said.

Did he just say the rest of his life? As in, forever? As in...

"You've changed everything about my life," he says, pulling me out of my head and back to the moment. "Every dream I thought I had means nothing to me now if you're not a part of them, too. I've never opened myself up to love, I've never let anything get in the way of my career. But you came in and turned all that into nothing. You obliterated everything I thought was important. All that matters to me, Skyler, is you."

My heart flutters to life, like a hot air balloon being fired up into the sky. But my biggest insecurities are still standing on top of it, digging their heels in, and I let them win as my eyes fall to the ground again.

"How do I know what was real and what wasn't? How do I know when you were getting to know me because you wanted to, as opposed to when you were just playing a game?"

Kips moves closer but I step away, keeping the space between us. I know he wants to pull me into him, to wrap those perfect arms around me and make me melt into him. But I can't. The moment he touches me, it's all over.

And before I let him touch me again, I have to be sure.

"Everything was real, Skyler," he breathes. "It was real when we kissed the night we met and the electricity shocked us both. It was real when I asked you about your past. It was real when I helped you figure out who you really are and told you not to be ashamed of her. It was real when you ripped my fucking heart out at the Valentine's Day dance," he chokes, as if just the memory of that night is enough to make him want to throw himself in front of a train. "When I touched you for the first time, when we fought because we cared too much about each other, when we made sacrifices and decisions we weren't proud of — all of that was real. This," he says, stepping toward me. I don't back away this time. "*We*, are real."

Listen to him, my heart screams. *You love him, you idiot.*

But my walls are still up, the wire on top buzzing with an electric charge as if to remind me how bad it hurt the last time I let them down, let him inside them.

My heart and my brain are at war, and I don't know who I want to win.

"Let's let Fate decide," Kip says after a moment, and then his hand is in front of me, a shiny, black die balanced on his palm. "Roll the die. If it's a four, we give this game another round. If it's anything else, we walk away."

I eye him, doing the easy math in my head as he stands there with his heart on his sleeve. "You know those odds are really terrible, right?"

But Kip just shrugs, his eyes calm. "I'm confident in our number."

I study him for a long moment, eyes sweeping over the stubble on his jaw, the messy ends of his blond hair blowing in the wind before finding his eyes again. Then, slowly, I take the die from his hand.

This is crazy, I think, shaking my head as I roll the die around in my hand. But I let it go anyway, the black plastic sliding across the concrete at our feet.

Time warps again, as it always does with Kip, and we both watch that plastic bounce around from side to side until it knocks against a man's shoe. When it finally falls, I close my eyes on a sigh, my heart squeezing hard in my chest.

Six.

When I open my eyes again, I will Kip to look at me, but he can't look away from the die on the ground. He just stares at it, as if he can change what number is showing with his glare alone. The crowd continues to grow around us, laughter and conversation floating in as we exist in our own little bubble of silence.

And just like tonight in the tournament, I have a moment of clarity.

The devastation on his face, the bravery it took to ask me to meet him tonight, to say the words he has... it's all the proof I need. What happened between us *was* real, and no matter how badly my walls want to protect me, the truth is that he's worth the risk.

I'd feel the pain all over again, if it meant I got to be with him in the end.

So, I bend, retrieving the die from where it rests between us. I offer it to Kip at first, but he doesn't move for it, and just when I see his hand twitch forward, I rear back, throwing it with all my might and sending it sailing over his head.

Whipping around, Kip watches the die splash into the fountain while I watch him, knowing this is the moment when it all changes. He turns to face me again, eyes wide, brows bent together in question.

"I'm done leaving my life to chance," I say, smiling and shaking my head as the tears that threatened before blur my vision. "Black number four can suck it."

I close the space between us in the next breath, Kip's arms wrapping around me as I crash my mouth to his. His hands slide into my hair, pulling me closer, deepening the kiss as I fist my hands in his shirt. We're completely lost in the moment, in each other, when suddenly music spills out from the fountain speakers and the show begins.

Neither of us look up to see it.

We lose ourselves in each other, touching and feeling and kissing as the water shoots up into the night sky until someone near us clears their throat, pulling us back to reality.

"I love you," Kip breathes, the pad of his thumb skating over my bottom lip as his eyes flick between mine. "I'm so fucking sorry, Skyler."

"Stop." I shake my head. "We both played a stupid game."

"I promise to never gamble with your heart again, Ella Mae."

At that, I smile, remembering that night of our first date. We were both hiding so much, fighting our own demons, and yet we couldn't help it even then.

We were destined to be together, to love each other.

It was always in the cards for us.

"Deal," I say as Kip grabs my hand. He pulls me away from the fountain and toward the Strip, walking me back to our hotel without even asking. We both want to be alone, away from the crowds, away from anyone who isn't us.

"I can't believe you let me watch that die roll like that, when you knew it didn't even matter."

I laugh. "It was fun to watch you sweat."

Kip squeezes my hand.

"That was super cheesy, by the way," I add, glancing back at the fountains still going off.

"What? You're not impressed with that impeccable timing?"

"How did you know I wouldn't be dumping your ass when the fountains went off like that?"

Kip frowns, pulling me into him and knuckling my head. I laugh and push him off, smile fading a bit when his blue eyes lock on mine again.

"I knew you couldn't resist this."

I roll my eyes. "Please."

But when he presses his lips to mine again, his fingertips skating down my arms to grip my waist and pull me into him, I know he's right. He sucks my bottom lip between his teeth, biting it gently and eliciting a moan from deep within me.

"You couldn't resist me if you tried."

I smile, pulling back just enough to take in those stupid black frames surrounding his eyes. Looking back on the semester, on all the games, I can't wrap my head around how far we've come. He was just supposed to be a blond-haired, blue-eyed boy to play with, a new toy to keep me occupied on the weekends. And somehow, he got under my skin. Somehow, he became so much more.

He became my everything.

And I can't resist the urge to bring everything full circle.

So, I lean in, eyes mischievous and hands around his waist as I whisper against his lips.

"Wanna bet?"

Jess

"I'm so obsessed with your new haircut, Little," Skyler says, pulling on one of Cassie's curls and letting it bounce back into place.

"Same. Makes me want to chop mine," I chime in. "But, you know, that means less to pull on when I'm getting banged from the back. So... priorities."

The girls all laugh at that, Ashlei tossing a handful of popcorn at me.

"I'm going to miss this," Cassie says, leaning her head on Skyler's shoulder. We're all piled together on the sorority couch, enjoying one last movie day before we split up. Cassie and I are both sticking around for the rest of the summer, but the other girls are leaving, and it'll be two months before we see them again.

"I love summer," I say. "But, I wish I could spend more of it with you girls."

"Me, too. It's been an... *interesting* semester." Erin's cheeks flush. "Thank you for not completely disowning me after the major bitch I've been."

Skyler shifts uncomfortably, not saying anything, so I lean over and pull Erin under one arm. "Ah, we've all had our period before. Rest assured, we'll pay you back sometime in the future."

She smiles, leaning her head on my shoulder.

"So, Cassie, you're sticking around here for summer classes... and Adam is here, too?" I waggle my brows. "Bow chicka wow wow."

She flushes a deep red, pulling her blanket up to her chin. "You just can't go a day without trying to get me to divulge the details of my sex life, can you?"

"My lady blue balls need rubbing, Cass." I flex my hips toward her and the girls all laugh while she swats me away.

"Thought Kade was rubbing those balls for you," Ashlei points out.

"Oh, please," I scoff. "More like I'm trying my best to teach him how to even get a girl to talk to him for more than three minutes. We're so far away from bang town, it's not even funny."

"I still can't believe you agreed to train him," she says.

"Yeah, well, I can't believe you're officially dating the hottest, richest CEO this side of the Florida-Georgia line."

"Seriously!" Erin chimes in, smacking Ashlei. "How the hell did you keep that a secret from us for almost a year?"

Ashlei just smiles, popping a kernel into her mouth. "Some things are too good to share, my friends."

"Selfish whore," I murmur, and the girls all burst into laughter again.

"Skyler, are you going up north with Kip?" Erin asks, and the weight of his father's illness settles over us like a cloud.

"I am," she says, eyes on her hands as she picks at a stray string on her blanket. "I'm a little nervous, a little scared, but mostly, I just want to be there for Kip. It's going to be weird, meeting the man who sent him here to take me down, but at the same time, I understand him. And at the end of the day, being a support system for Kip is what matters most to me."

"He's lucky to have you, Little," Erin says, sincerity in her eyes. And when she reaches over to grab Skyler's hand, Ashlei and I exchange a worried glance.

For a moment, Skyler just stares at it, like she's debating flicking Erin's hand away and immediately flipping her off. But instead, she sighs, squeezing her Big's hand with a soft, resigned smile. "Thank you."

I let out a breath of relief.

"And what about you, G Big?" Cassie asks. "What are your plans for the summer?"

Erin swallows, her gaze finding the television screen. "Therapy."

"*What*?" We all gasp in unison, eyes locked on Erin as we wait for her to explain.

"There's a lot I've been through in the past year that I haven't talked to anyone about..." she says, her voice soft. "Not even you girls. And, it's time. I need to work through it if I'm ever going to move forward."

"What happened?" I ask, leaning into her. "You can tell us."

"I know, I know I can," she says, finally returning our gazes with a slight smile. "But, it's not the right time. When it is, when I'm ready, I'll come to you. I promise."

Ashlei leans over my lap, squeezing Erin's knee as I try to search her eyes for some sort of answer.

"Well, when that time comes, we'll be here."

"Thank you."

For a while, we're just silent, staring at the television screen without even registering what's on it. Finally, Skyler jumps up, clapping her hands together.

"Alright, enough of that shit." She skips away and up the stairs, returning moments later with a half-empty bottle of whiskey. "We're ending this semester on a high note. Time to belly up, bitches."

"Oh, God. I can't even *think* about alcohol right now," Erin says with a wince.

"You don't have to think about it," Skyler says. "You just have to drink it."

"I'll grab glasses!" Cassie sprints off to the kitchen, and when she's back, she lines up five shot glasses as Skyler tops them off with the amber liquid. We each grab one when they're full, holding them together over the coffee table with a mixture of sadness and joy in our eyes.

"We only have one more semester together before you three bitches graduate," Skyler says, eyes flashing over me, Ashlei, and Erin. "So, here's to making the most of it — the Kappa Kappa Beta way."

Ashlei thrusts her glass higher. "To parties."

"To movie days," Cassie chimes in.

Skyler pushes her glass in next. "To love — in all its forms."

"And to sex, because... well, it's us."

They all laugh at my addition, and then our eyes are on Erin, hers on her glass, like her thoughts are far off in space. Finally, she blinks, swallowing a little as she joins our glasses with hers.

"To friends," she says, her voice light. "Who are always there for us, no matter how bad we fuck up."

Skyler's eyes soften, and she clinks her shot glass to her Big's. "Hear, hear."

We toss the liquid back, me throwing my hands up in the air with a *woo* and Skyler joining in with a high five while the rest of the girls grimace. We all laugh, stacking the glasses and piling back on the couch just in time for a new chick flick to start.

And as another semester comes to an end, I glance around at my sisters, heart squeezing at the thought of living a life without them. I only have one more semester with them, and in less than a year, I'll be graduated — thrust into the real world whether I like it or not.

But the truth is, I know I don't have to worry, because I'll never have to live without them.

My Kappa Kappa Beta sisters are my sisters for life — through college and beyond.

So, for now, I vow to make the most of the time we have left. I'll have a kick-ass summer with Cassie, recruit some more bad-ass bitches in the fall, and when my time as officer is over and it's time to walk across that stage, I'll do so holding hands with the girls who matter most.

In the meantime, there are parties that need raging, kegs that need draining, and boys who need banging. Those are my duties as Jess "J-Love" Vonnegut, and I can't wait to honor my university.

Buckle up, Palm South University.

You ain't seen nothing yet.

Palm South
UNIVERSITY

RITUAL

BOOK 5

EPISODE 1

Jess

"Fuck off, Kade."

A laugh bubbles out of him, and I flick my right foot up to my ass long enough to snatch the heel off it and hold it up over my head in a threat to squash him like a bug.

Kade holds up his hands, eyes bulging out of his head. "Jess, come on," he says, but that motherfucker is still smirking. "Look, I've apologized. I've all but groveled at your feet, for Christ's sake. I *know* I was an asshole."

"It's not about you being an asshole," I seethe, still holding my weapon of choice ready to strike. "It's that you wasted my time."

"I'm an idiot."

"You act like that's news to me."

He softens, that stupid smirk still on his face as he takes a step closer to me. I cock an eyebrow in warning, holding the shoe up a little higher, but he reaches for it, gently lowering it until it's between us and no longer a threat.

"Look, I really am sorry," he says, more sincerely. "I asked for your help and then I blew you off. I can't help it, I'm a stupid boy."

I scoff.

"But I'm serious now. And I want another chance."

Inside me, there's a bear growling and tearing trees to shreds. On the outside, I'm cool as a cucumber. Kade is a junior who I met last semester when he rushed Alpha Sigma. He's close friends with Kip, Skyler's boyfriend, which made him part of our group pretty fast.

When I first met him, I was annoyed with everything he was.

The more he talked to me and flashed his corny pickup lines, the more that annoyance turned to something between curiosity and the urge to bang him.

And when he made a proposition that I should hang out with him this summer, teach him how to have better game and how to be better in bed, in exchange for getting to drive his car and have guaranteed sex anytime I wanted it? Well, I thought it was the most ridiculous idea I'd ever heard of.

And yet, I'd agreed — for no other reason than I was bored and needed a distraction from Jarrett and the heartbreak that was forever lingering in his absence.

It had seemed like a good idea.

Until this twat rag blew me off and made *me* look like the idiot.

"Well, good for you," I snap, tugging my heel back on and crossing my arms. "But I don't give second chances. Now, if you'll excuse me, I have a recruitment to run."

Before I can shut the door in his face, Kade blocks it with his hands.

And then, the motherfucker falls to his knees.

"Oh, *please*, Jess," he says, so loudly that his voice echoes off the walls in the Kappa Kappa Beta house foyer. "Please, give me another chance. There's nothing I want more than to rub your body down and learn your kinky ways."

My eyes bulge, and I kick my heel right into the middle of his chest until he tumbles backward onto the house porch. I slam the door shut behind us, fuming.

"There are *potential new members* in there, you asshat."

He's still flat on his back, holding up his hands in surrender.

And I hate myself a little, because in that moment, he looks a little like he did the first night I threw him down on his bed and rode him until he moaned my name.

"Get up," I said, pretending to be disgusted. "You look like a fool."

"Only a fool for you."

I roll my eyes, sighing with as much dramatic flare as I can manage when he's standing again. "Why should I give you another chance? This whole..." I wave my hand at him. "*Training* thing was your idea in the first place, and then you bail. What are you even looking for? What's the motive here?"

"I already told you," he says, stepping into me. "I know I flaked this summer. There was..." He swallows, looking down Greek Row as if it were a hall of ghosts. "I had some family stuff to handle, and I wasn't in my right state of mind. Okay?"

He looks like a puppy that's just been kicked, and I hate that I care.

"But I mean it this time. I have zero game, and I need your help. Plus," he says, smirking as he steps more into me. His hand creeps up my arm, tucking a strand of my hair behind one ear. "After our first round, you can't tell me you don't want more, too."

Heat snakes up my neck from where his fingers brush the sensitive skin, and my eyes flutter before I shove him back with two hands.

"I can get hot sex from anyone I want," I remind him.

"I know that."

"Then you also know that you're wasting your time."

"Jess," he says, seemingly exhausted now. "Come on. I'm sorry. I have now *literally* groveled at your feet." He swallows. "I need this."

I narrow my eyes, annoyance mixing with the ridiculous attraction I have for this kid and making me want to slap myself. When I first agreed to this *insane* proposition at our formal last semester, it was because I was in a dire state. I was still heartbroken over Jarrett, and — if I were being completely honest — I was fascinated by the thought of being in power over this young buck. I would be his teacher, his Dom, his sexual sensei.

Above all, he would be a distraction from Jarrett.

And after our first romp in the sack to gauge just what kind of lessons would be needed, I discovered that bulge I'd seen in his swim trunks at Spring Break was just the tip — and not of the iceberg.

But now, I was busy with recruitment. And when it was over, I'd be busy with my last semester of college. Plus, this little fucker had *played* me. It was all his idea, for me to help him with his game, teach him how to flirt and date and fuck like a pro — and then he'd bailed. After one round, he flaked.

Still, I can't deny the way my body is heated at the sight of his tattoos peeking out from under his tight t-shirt — tattoos that I know spread across his chest and abdomen and down the length of his muscular back. It should be illegal for a kid this young to be this ripped, but even if it was, I have a feeling Kade would break the law.

I appraise him, and before the words are out of my mouth, I wonder if I'm conceding because I want to, because I feel bad for him, or because I'm annoyed and need him off my porch so I can get back to recruiting the best damn rush class our sorority has ever seen.

"*Fine,*" I grit, but before Kade can thrust his fist all the way into the air, I wrap my hand around it and hold it firmly. "But you *will* follow through with your part of the deal this time."

He raises an eyebrow.

"The car," I remind him. "I want your keys. Now."

"I don't have them on me."

"Then I guess we're done here." I turn to head back inside, but Kade rounds me quickly, holding up his hands.

"Wait, wait, wait," he says, fishing his keys from his pocket. He holds them out to me with a cringe. "Please, don't wreck it."

I smile wickedly, snatching the keys from his grasp before I press up on my toes. "Oh, sweetheart. The only thing I plan on wrecking is you."

I thread my hands into his hair, tugging with enough force to make him suck in a breath through his teeth before my mouth covers his. I kiss him like I hate him, and I know I'll fuck him the same way later.

"Don't touch your dick until the next time I see you," I whisper against his mouth before I bite his bottom lip. "Don't masturbate, don't edge, don't even hold it any longer than you have to to piss. Understand me?"

Kade swallows, and I don't miss the twitch of his already-growing erection in his basketball shorts. "There she is," he whispers on a grin.

I grin back, leaning in like I'm going to kiss him again, but then I shove him away and maneuver around him, pushing through the front door of the Kappa Kappa Beta house and shutting it again before he can say a word.

You want to play, Kade Brewer?

Fine.

Let's play.

Bear

Family.

That one word can mean so many things.

It can mean a house on a hill with two parents who adore you, and an older sibling who cares for you, and grandparents and aunts and uncles who gather near for holidays. It can mean someone to lean on — always — no matter what you're going through. It can mean safety, and comfort, and support.

Family can also mean a mother addicted to drugs and gambling, and an older brother who follows in her footsteps. It can mean the parents of your best friend taking you in as their own, like my little brother and Mac. Like me and Skyler.

It can mean never really feeling like you had a family at all, and so you build one at the college you go to, surrounding yourself with fraternity brothers and sorority girls and making your own dysfunctional unit.

Or it can mean a baby, one of your own.

One never born.

One you never knew existed — not before it was too late to have a say in whether it stayed that way or not.

It's the Saturday before fall semester, and I should be happy. It's my senior year, my fraternity is *finally* off suspension, I'm in the best shape I've ever been in, and I've got the hottest, smartest, kindest girl I've ever known wrapped around me in my bed. Skyler is here, too, sitting in the bean bag on my floor with her feet propped up on my desk as she relays her summer to us. She and Becca have become friends — my two favorite girls — and yet, still, there's a hollowness inside me.

Because down Greek Row, there's a girl who carried my child inside her.

A girl who never let that child be born.

"I will say this," Skyler says, letting her legs drop to the floor as she sinks even lower into the bean bag. "I am *so* glad rush is over. I usually love Bid Day, but I was exhausted today."

"Maybe you're getting old," Becca offers

"I am. I most certainly am."

"And you're still considering running for president?" Becca asks

Skyler frowns, a strand of her long, brown hair falling into her face. "As crazy as it sounds, I am. I know Erin and I went through a lot of shit last year, and I wasn't sure if I'd ever want to have anything to do with the presidency after that. But... I love KKB. That's my family. And to lead them for a year? That would be an honor."

I listen to them talk in a sort of numb daze, broken up time to time only by them saying Erin's name. Every time I hear the two syllables, a zing of something hot and uncomfortable assaults my chest.

"You okay, babe?" Becca asks me quietly when Skyler pulls out her phone. I bet money she's texting Kip. With him being at school in California, they're committed to the long-distance relationship thing — and I am not envious of the work that goes with that.

"I'm good," I assure her, rubbing her back before I press a kiss to the sunshine yellow bandana tied around her hair and covering her forehead. "Just going to run to the bathroom real quick."

"Okay," she says, smiling at me, but I see the worry etched in her eyes.

When I slip out from under the covers, Skyler whistles.

"Hot *damn*, Bear," she says, eyeing me from head to toe. "I didn't think it was possible for you to get more beastly than you already were. What the hell have you been eating?"

"He eats like The Rock now," Becca answers for me. "I swear, I counted one morning, and the man had *eight* whole wheat pancakes. And a half a pound of turkey bacon."

Skyler whines. "Not fair. If I ate like that, I'd have an ass the size of Texas."

"Ain't nothing wrong with that," Becca says, smacking her own ass.

When I don't so much as chuckle, Skyler eyes me warily, but I avoid her eyes.

"He's also been working out like a mad man," Becca continues, but I snuff out her next sentence with the gentle *snick* of the bathroom door closing, reveling in the time alone.

After I piss, I wash my hands and dry them before splaying them on the bathroom counter. My eyes find those of my reflection, and I hold my own gaze, searching for the man I used to be in the mirror. But he's not there, he's not *anywhere* — not anymore.

They say there are moments in your life that change everything. I could look back and name a few in mine — when Mom first asked me for money, and when she and my older brother bailed on life, leaving behind my nephews and my little brother, Clayton. I could even peg my breakup with Shawna as one that changed me, and the night I saw Erin raped definitely fell into that category, too.

But finding out I had fathered a child with her, one that she never told me about, one that she aborted — it didn't just change me.

It fucked me all the way up.

I search my dead eyes for a sign of humanity, of someone still capable of feeling, but come up short. Becca is the only person I've been able to be even close to myself with over the summer, but even she can't break through entirely.

I can't discern what I feel. It's like a never-ending tornado, one that has lifted everything in my life up into the air — me included — and is just tossing me around, dropping me and picking me back up again, not sure where it wants to leave everything when it finally dissipates.

In the past few months, I've cycled through everything from anger and guilt, to crushing depression and horrifically sad understanding. I want to hate Erin, but I also want to run to her. I want to shake her and demand answers, but I also want to hug her and tell her there's no need, that I already understand.

And in the process of these cycles, of this tornado, I've lost myself completely.

I sigh, scrubbing my hands over my face before I shove through the door and back into my bedroom. Skyler is gone, and Becca sits on my bed in one of my t-shirts, her legs tucked under her.

For a long while, she just stares at me, her eyes speaking to mine without a single word being said.

Then, she leans back, pulls her knees up to her chest, and slowly, seductively, she lets them fall open, revealing that she doesn't have a pair of panties on under that shirt.

"I know we've been taking it slow," she whispers, and I see her throat constrict as she swallows. "But I feel how lost you are right now, Clinton. And I want you to find yourself in me."

My eyes trail her slight curves visible even in the loose fabric of my t-shirt, and when my gaze settles on the wet heat between her legs, I will myself to feel something — anything. Because that's my M.O. If I have something to run from, I find solace in fucking, and working out, and drinking myself into oblivion.

But the desire I yearn to feel for Becca is subdued, suffocated by the vision of another girl I'd been inside of — one I'd "lost myself" in when I was running from something.

Erin Xander.

Still, I can't walk out on Becca — not with her vulnerability on full display like this. So, I shove my own fears and anxieties out, ignoring the anger and the desire for answers I'll never get to questions I should never, ever ask.

In the end, it was Erin's body, and it was her choice.

I find as much resolve from that fact as I can, and in two strides, I'm standing over Becca, sliding my hands up her shins, over her knees, along the warm, smooth skin of her inner thighs. And for the first time since we started dating, I slide my palm over her clit, my fingers dipping between her wet lips.

She shivers, hands fisting in my shirt and holding onto me for dear life as her eyes flutter shut. She lets her head fall back when I press my fingers inside her, slowly, tentatively, and I will myself to be present. I will my dick to stand at attention, will my brain to focus on the beautiful woman giving herself to me.

But everything feels dead.

Lifeless.

Empty.

"I want tonight to be about you," I say with a groan, escaping her hands just before they dip below the band of my sweatpants. She pouts for only a moment before I'm on my knees, tugging her ass to the edge of the bed. "Let me discover you."

At that, her eyes heat with desire again, and she smirks, letting me have my way with her.

And I do.

I take my time, testing out what makes her writhe. Is it when I flick my tongue over her clit, or when I roll it hot and flat along her seam? Is it when my fingers just barely enter her, or when they curl deep inside? Does she like it when I bite her and grip her hard and give her bruises, or does she want me slow and soft and romantic, does she want care and concern?

I find the answers to every single one of my questions, but I do so with a sort of distant, numb version of myself — as if I have a clone, and I'm in a room miles away controlling him.

I asked Becca to take it slow because I'd been hurt before. Because I felt so much for her. Because I knew she was special, and I didn't want to fuck it all up by moving fast.

I'd waited so long to touch her this way.

And yet, I feel nothing.

Becca's nails dig into my flesh. Her body writhes in my sheets. Her cries are heard through the entire Omega Chi house before she grabs one of my pillows and bites down hard to subdue them.

She comes with her hands in my hair and my name on her lips.

And still, I am numb.

Cassie

The excitement that courses through my veins on the first day of a new semester is a neon flashing sign for how big of a nerd I am.

Fortunately, I've gotten pretty good at hiding my geeked-out joy, though if anyone looked close enough, I'm sure they'd see it.

I'm sure they'd see my hands shaking a little as I unpack my new notebook and fresh pack of Le Pens, ordering them in color on my desk, ready to mark up the syllabus once the professor hands it out. They'd see my smile — not overly obnoxious or visibly excited, but permanent in its place. They'd see that my new, short hair is perfectly styled and that I had this outfit laid out a week in advance. They'd see the foot hanging where my legs are crossed under my desk, swinging slightly, and the cool, calm collectiveness I'm faking as I open my laptop — just in case I need to take notes there, too.

It's junior year, and I'm not messing around.

I'm finally out of all of the general education classes, and *firmly* in the core curriculum that will get me my bio med degree. This isn't even the prerequisites we're talking about. I'm *done* with biology I and II, with organic chemistry, with my first labs. I'm officially in the classes that *really* matter, the ones where I don't just like getting As, but where I will *need* them if I have any prayer of getting into the medical schools on my dream list.

This is it. The big leagues.

And I'm ready.

I uncap the deep blue Le Pen first, writing *Genetics* in perfectly neat handwriting at the top of my notebook, and feeling a zip of excitement run through my veins just as a familiar voice speaks my name.

"Cassie?"

All the joy fades instantly when I look up and find Grayson standing in front of my desk, something between a smile and a cringe on his face.

"Hi," he says when I don't respond.

"What the hell are you doing here?"

I can't help the bitterness in my voice when I finally speak, and a few students around us cast us weary glances as Grayson cocks a brow.

"Same as you, I'd expect." He holds up his notebook with a black pen hooked in the spiral ring.

I narrow my eyes. "You're a music major. Why are you in *Genetics*?"

What was left of his smile slides off his face like a runny egg. His eyes harden — eyes the color of a deep sapphire.

Eyes I used to long for, to lose hours in.

To lose *myself* in.

"Yeah, well, let's just say I *was* a music major, but my father decided that wasn't an option anymore."

My heart squeezes with something close to sympathy before my head snuffs it out with a firm boot heel. "Okay. That still doesn't explain how you've met the pre-reqs for this class."

"I took a lot last semester and over the summer. You would know that if you were still speaking to me."

My jaw clenches. "Why in God's name would I *ever* talk to you again?" I shake my head, throwing my hands up. "I don't know why I'm talking to you now!"

More people turn to look at us, and I blush, ignoring him as I turn my attention back to my pen and notebook.

"Cassie, I'm sorry—"

"Just leave me alone, Grayson."

He stands there for a long while, and I ignore him dutifully until he finally concedes and takes a seat somewhere behind me.

And from that moment on, my focus is shot.

It's impossible not to think about the fact that I'm in the same room, the same class, the same fucking *lab* with my ex-boyfriend who cheated on me and made a fool of me, and almost cost me my relationship with the one man who truly loves me. No matter how I try, every part of my mind and body is unpleasantly aware of my proximity to that danger.

I sit there with my jaw clenched, my brain a whir of angry nonsense as I try to listen to the professor warn us that we're in for a challenging semester. I take notes, mark up my syllabus, and add important dates to my calendar on my laptop, all while trying to pretend I don't care that Grayson is a few seats behind me.

When the professor dismisses us, I bolt out of that room like it's on fire, not giving Grayson the chance to even attempt to talk to me again. It's not until I'm a hundred yards away from the science building and nearly to the student union that I take a calming breath, releasing the tension in my chest.

As soon as I do, I'm lifted from behind and spun around in a frenzied circle.

I scream, swatting at the arms around me until I'm dropped back to the Earth. When I turn and find a sexy, lazily smiling Adam, I shove him hard in the chest.

"Asshole! You scared the living hell out of me!"

He chuckles, wrapping me in a warm hug and kissing my nose as I pout. "I'm sorry, babe. I just couldn't resist. I haven't seen you since this morning. I missed you."

"You saw me three hours ago," I say, but already I'm smiling and leaning into his chest with a sigh. I wrap my arms around his waist and rest my head under his.

"Three hours is too long." He pulls back, grabbing my hand as we continue making our way toward the student union. "How was class?"

Anxiety rips through me — and this time, not from having Grayson in the same room with me, but with the decision of whether or not I should tell *Adam* that he was in the same room with me. I glance at him from the corner of my eyes, swallowing.

"It was fine."

"*Fine*?" he asks with a smirk. "You were practically bouncing like a little kid about to ride a carousel when I dropped you off in front of the science building. How come you're not smiling like a loon now?"

I blow out a breath. "It's an advanced Genetics class, Adam, not a carnival. Excuse me if I'm not excited about the massive amount of lab work I'll have this semester."

I inwardly cringe at the way I snapped at him, but he just stops walking, pulling me to a halt, too, and framing my face with his hands.

"Hey, I'm sorry," he says — even though it's *me* who should be apologizing. His brown eyes search mine. "Are you okay? Did something happen?"

I sigh, shaking my head and leaning my forehead against his. "I'm just a little stressed with the new workload, I think."

It's a lie. A blatant lie. And I can't figure out why I'm making it. I should just tell him what happened, tell him Grayson is in my class and it freaked me out to see him after everything.

But Adam and I are *finally* happy. We're finally together — *really* together. We've spent the whole summer falling in love and getting even closer than we ever were before. And for the first time since we met, there's no one and nothing between us.

And I don't want to ruin it.

Adam kisses my forehead, pulling me in for a long hug with his chin balanced on the crown of my head. "That's understandable, Red."

I pinch his side and he makes an *oaf!* sound before chucking and hugging me tighter.

"How about we grab lunch, I'll walk you to your next class, and then when you're done we can go get Moon Pie pizza and hide away in my bed for the rest of the night?"

I pull back and peer up at him. "I thought we were going to work out after class?"

He shrugs, a smirk on his too-hot-for-his-own-good face. "We can work extra hard tomorrow. Tonight, I want to hold my beautiful, amazing, smart, incredible girlfriend and make all her stress go away." He leans in, grabbing my ass as he whispers in my ear. "And I know *many* ways to do it."

I shove him away with a roll of my eyes, pretending to be annoyed, but as soon as he's away from me I'm grabbing his hand and holding it tight. I lean up to kiss his cheek. "You're perfect."

"That's you, baby girl. Now," he says, opening the door to the boisterous student union. "What's for lunch?"

Jess

"Alright, ladies," Erin says, highlighting something on her clipboard before smiling at the group of our sorority sisters gathered in her bedroom. "I think that's it for today. Thank you for meeting with me. I think it's important that we're all on the same page heading into our first Sunday Chapter of the semester tomorrow — *especially* since we'll have the most fantastic group of new members this sorority has ever seen, thanks to J-Love."

I smile and pretend like I'm blushing, waving off the little round of applause from the other executive board members.

"Oh, stop. You're too kind."

"Don't play modest," Ashlei teases. "We all know you're not."

I toss one of Erin's pillows at her, and then everyone is dismissed.

Ashlei kisses both me and Erin on the cheek before being one of the first to bolt out of the room. It's Saturday, which is about the only day she and her sexy, suit-wearing CEO can get in some hump time nowadays, and she doesn't play coy when she lets us know that's *exactly* where she's heading. But I hang around until everyone else is gone and it's just me and Erin.

"Great first meeting, Prez," I say, reaching into her secret stash of snacks in her bedside table drawer. I crack open a bag of white cheddar popcorn and shove a handful in my mouth. "On a scale of one to ten, how ready are you for this semester to be over?"

She smiles, still jotting something down in her planner. "You know I love being president, and I'm in no rush to graduate, either. But, I'll admit," she says with a sigh, finally looking at me. "It's been a rough few months, and I'm not excited to be back in the full swing of things."

I frown, wiping my hands together to dust off the cheese powder before I hop off her bed. I lean against the foot of it right in front of where she's seated in her desk chair. "How are you, Ex?" I ask. "I mean, really."

Erin sighs, capping her highlighter and shutting her planner. "I'm okay. I actually have group therapy in about an hour, so I need to get ready for that."

"Group therapy?" I ask. "I know you were seeing a therapist over the summer, but I didn't realize it was a group thing."

"This is part of my overall recovery plan," she explains. "Something my therapist recommended. It's been good," she adds quickly, and I don't miss something curious in her eyes as she smiles. "Strange... but good."

I smile in return, but my heart aches for my best friend. She hasn't been herself in what feels like at least a year, and I hardly noticed because I'd been caught up in my own shit. I was caught up in Jarrett, in Greg, in Kade. I had no idea what Erin had been through, or why she hadn't told any of us, but I was glad she was getting help.

"You know you can talk to me," I say, barely above a whisper. "I love you, and I would never judge."

"I know," she says, and she stands, wrapping me in a hug that surprises me. I wrap my arms around her hesitantly while she squeezes me tight. "And I will. One day."

When she releases me, she hangs her hands on her hips, eyes on her closet. "Welp. Time to figure out what the hell to wear."

"To therapy?" I smirk, pushing myself off the bed to stand. "I'm sure what you have on is fine, Ex."

"Well, I might go to dinner after, so I just want to be prepared for both."

I cock a brow. "Dinner? With who?"

Her eyes widen as she finds me, but she shrugs quickly. "Just some kids from therapy."

She doesn't elaborate, and I take it as a cue that she doesn't want me prying, so I drop it, but not before giving her a look that I know lets *her* know that I know.

Something.

I just don't know *what* I know.

"Alright," I say, still eyeing her. "Well, I'll see you at Chapter tomorrow. Love you."

She makes a kissy face, dipping into her closet as I let myself out.

Skyler is nowhere to be found when I make it to our room down the hall, so I put on some music while I get ready. I take my time, brushing my teeth and applying my makeup with care before slicking my long hair back into a fierce, high ponytail. I dig out one of my favorite little black dresses, slipping it on over my head — but only after layering up my new, hot pink lingerie set — complete with a garter belt and stockings.

When I'm dressed, I slip into my high heels and make my way downstairs, a wicked grin on my face as I fire Kade's car to life. It's a short walk down Greek Row to the Alpha Sigma house, but I want to remind him that I'm the one with the power in our little arrangement.

Plus, high heels and long walks are not friends.

I haven't talked to Kade since he showed up on the Kappa Kappa Beta front porch during rush week. Now that recruitment is over and the first week of classes is under my belt, I'm ready to deal with him.

And he may think he's ready, but he's nowhere *near*.

I park my car in the Alpha Sigma parking lot, ignoring the blatant stares and gaping mouths as I strut my ass through the yard, shoving the front door open without knocking.

I know the code, obviously, because I'm fucking J-Love.

Adam is in the living room with a group of his brothers, and they all stop talking when they see me. But I don't acknowledge a single one, keeping my eyes locked on the hallway as I make my way toward it.

Every open door I pass is quickly filled with heads leaning out to watch me walk by, and I smirk at the power I feel rushing through my veins. When I make it to Kade's room, I stand in the doorway, popping my weight onto one hip.

He's on his bed, with two other brothers in the room with him. One is in the bean bag on his floor, and the other is sitting backward in Kade's desk chair, all of their eyes locked on the television screen.

On some stupid video game, to be more exact.

At first, none of them look up, but the one in the bean bag glances toward the door. He looks back to the television, then does a double-take, and his jaw drops as he hits the leg of the kid sitting on the chair.

"What the fuck, you're both going to die," Kade says, still hammering away at the remote control in his hands. He scowls. "What are you losers gaping at?"

Then, he turns and sees me, and all the blood drains from his face.

Carnage ensues on the television screen with the three of them watching me, and I smirk like the devil I am.

"Out," I say simply to the two brothers with their jaws on the floor.

They jump up without question, averting their eyes from me the best they can as they make their way past me and into the hall. As soon as they're gone, I shut the door behind me and turn to face Kade.

He swallows.

"So," I say, walking toward him with my hips swaying slowly and purposefully. His eyes drink in every inch of me, and when I'm right in front of where he's sitting on the edge of his bed, I stop, just out of his reach. "Have you been a good boy?"

His eyes grow hungrier and hungrier, his erection already so hard and strong that his basketball shorts look like a fucking tent.

I reach out and forcefully grab his chin, tugging it up until his eyes are on mine. "Answer me."

"Define good," he rasps out, already panting.

"Did you listen to my instructions when you left the Kappa Kappa Beta house?"

He gives me a look of confusion, and I'm so annoyed I roll my eyes and debate dropping the whole thing.

But, truth be told, I'm turned on, too.

And I'm just getting started.

I release his chin, trailing the long fingernail of my pointer finger down his chest, his abs, running it along his hard shaft as he inhales a stiff breath. "I told you not to touch your dick until I saw you," I remind him, then I grasp his cock hard and squeeze, and he groans, head falling back. "Did you listen?"

"Um..."

I squeeze again, this time in a way that I know probably hurts as much as it makes him feel good.

He winces, but his hips buck against the touch, anyway. "I... I..."

"Don't lie to me."

I stroke him softer, rolling my hand from the tip down to the base, all with the fabric still separating us.

He looks at me again. "I didn't listen."

I cluck my tongue. "Bad boy. I'll have to punish you for that."

To be clear, I have *no* idea where this dominatrix side of me has come from. All I know is that I woke up with the urge to hurt Kade after him blowing me off this summer and then making a show of himself at the KKB house during rush.

But I also woke up with the urge to turn him on, too.

And I guess when you combine the two, you get this.

"On your knees," I say.

He cocks a brow, smirking. "You're joking."

"Now," I say, this time grabbing a fistful of his hair and shoving him down to the ground.

He drops the remote control he still had in his hands, doing as I said, and when he's on his knees looking up at me, the power that rushes through me is so addicting I want to bottle it up and get drunk on it forever.

With one hand on the foot of his bed steadying me, I lift my left leg, pressing my high heel into his chest until his back is against the bed. His eyes greedily take in the view my dress is offering him, and I smirk.

"I hope you're hungry," I state, and then I yank my dress up to my hips, place my high heel on the bed behind his head, and lunge forward until my pussy is hovering over his sweet mouth.

He groans, hands reaching out for my thighs and running the length of them as he appreciates my pink lingerie. The one-piece is crotchless, my pussy framed by the garter belt, and when his finger grazes my clit, my eyes flutter at the contact.

I reach out, fisting my hand in his hair again until his mouth is on the very clit he just brushed.

The rush of heat is instant, the same way it had been our first night in bed together. Kade brings out a power-hungry side of me, one that's controlling and bossy and hellbent on getting an orgasm the way *she* wants it. It's a new and exciting side of myself, one I want to explore more.

And even though he needs help in the flirting and dating and game side of things, I have to give it to him: Kade is a fucking *magician* when it comes to pussy worship.

His tongue is fast and focused, flicking my clit with just the right force to have my orgasm building. When he slides his fingers inside me to help push me to the edge, I lean into the touch, basically riding his damn hand as he continues pleasuring me.

It doesn't take me long to come, and as soon as the orgasm rocks through me and my legs give out from the weight of my body, I pull Kade to stand and shove him back onto his bed.

"Get naked. Now."

I've never seen a man strip faster than he does in that moment, and I stay standing on the edge of the bed, leaning over him when he's fully naked and grabbing his erection in my hands. It's slick with pre-cum, and I run my thumb over the slick tip, coating him with his arousal.

"Fuck," he moans out, writhing in his sheets.

"How badly do you want me to suck your dick right now, Kade?"

"Oh, God," he cries out, eyes shooting open as he finds me. "So fucking bad."

"Yeah?" I ask, and I bend at the waist, taking just the tip of him inside my mouth. I swirl my tongue around his tip, slide it along the length of his base, and cup his balls just as I take him all the way inside my mouth.

He's already close to coming — I can tell from the way his balls hang, tight and high, and the way his legs flex as he tries to catch the orgasm.

So, I suck faster, using my hand in rhythm with my mouth, and Kade flexes and pushes farther inside me, nearly making me gag when he shoves in deep.

"Oh fuck," he moans. "I'm going to come."

And as soon as he says the magic words, I pull off.

Kade's eyes shoot open again, this time in confusion and shock, his body trembling as he reaches for me when I'm already standing and two feet away.

"Wait, no, no, I was so close."

"Were you?" I asked, wiping the corners of my lips innocently. "Aw, that's too bad."

Kade's mouth drops, but before he can say another word, I rush him, straddling him and sitting right down on his cock when my mouth covers his.

His entire body trembles, and I ride him fast and hard, mimicking the pace I'd had with my mouth just moments before. I bite his neck, suck on his ear, nearly draw blood from his bottom lip. It's rough and nasty and hot as *fuck*.

And when his hands tighten around my hips, a guttural groan ripping from his throat, I push myself off of him, breaking every spot of contact all at once.

Kade shakes violently from head to toe, and when I'm standing at the edge of the bed again, I have a glorious view of him ejaculating all over his abs without so much as touching his dick.

"Jesus Christ," he cries out, leaning up on his elbows and assessing the mess he's made on himself. He looks up at me with wild, confused eyes. "What... the fuck... was that?"

I smirk, walking over and pressing my mouth tenderly to his in a long, sweet kiss.

"*That* was payback," I whisper. "The real lessons haven't even started."

He whimpers, reaching out for me but I pull away before he can get a grip.

Then, I tug down my dress until it's covering my hips again, and I don't give him so much as another look when I swing his bedroom door open.

"Don't touch your dick until I see you again."

And with that, I strut my ass out of that house like the goddamn Queen I am.

Bear

Intramural football is just about the only thing keeping me alive.

Once school started, I found that the hole I'd slid into over the summer was deeper than I realized. I couldn't focus in class — which I really need to do, considering I'm in my cornerstone courses now that I'm a senior — and even with most of my nights spent exploring Becca, the hole continued to grow, and I fell in deeper.

It wasn't until the first IM football game with my Omega Chi brothers that a small spark of my old self came back to life.

Now, it's the only thing I look forward to.

The Alpha Sigma quarterback hikes the ball, and I slam into the offensive lineman across from me, overpowering him in seconds and sliding past him. I growl, thighs burning as I run as fast as I can, and I launch for the quarterback, taking him down before he has the chance to throw the ball.

It's my seventh sack of the game.

Cheers break out from the crowd of Greek students watching the game from the sidelines, and I'm almost positive I hear Skyler screaming above all the noise. I don't celebrate, though — in fact, I remain stoic all game as if I'm not even playing at all.

Because the biggest part of me is still numb, no matter how I try to bring it back to life with the things I used to love.

By the time the game is over, we've outscored the A Sigs by seventeen and clenched our second win of the season. I shake hands with the other players and immediately strip out of my helmet and jersey, desperate to get my pads off.

Every muscle is aching. I know I'll need an ice bath and I'll still be paying for it tomorrow, but that pain reminds me that I'm still here.

I'm still breathing.

I'm still alive.

I've barely peeled my pads off when Skyler is on my back, her legs wrapped around me and fist in the air.

"My best friend is a fucking BEAST!" she screams, chanting my name until a small crowd joins in.

I muster the best smile I have, tickling her sides until she falls off me and lands on the ground, hanging her hands on her hips.

She nudges me playfully with a wide smile. "You murdered them today."

"Just doing my job," I said on a shrug.

"Well, you're doing it well. I don't think anyone can overpower you now that you've beefed up to twice your original size — which was already ghastly, by the way." She squeezes my biceps, but when I don't smile, her eyes grow sad. "Hey, I know you already know this, but... you can talk to me. If something is going on."

"It's not."

She frowns. "It's just... you don't seem like yourself since we came back to school. I know I was busy with Kip and his dad over the summer, so I'm sorry if I wasn't—"

"You don't need to apologize, I'm fine," I clip, shoving my shit into my gym bag with more force than necessary. I don't know why I'm pissed that she's asking if I'm okay when, *clearly*, I am not, but for some reason, it fires me up. "I gotta run."

"Bear..."

"I'll see you around."

I don't look at her again, don't let her get another word in before I sling my bag over my shoulder and start the walk across campus to the Omega Chi house. Most of the guys drove, and a few of them offer me rides, but I decline, looking forward to the alone time.

When I pull my phone out of my bag, there's a few missed texts from Becca wishing me luck on the game. She's at work, and her last text asks if I want her to come over after. I don't answer, switching instead to the missed text from my little brother.

Clayton: Call me when you get this.

My stomach drops. Clayton is still living with Mac and his family in Pittsburgh, and though I'm happy he can be with his friends, and I know from my time spent with them that there's no better place for him to be than at Mac's, it still hurts to be so far from him and know he has no one in *our* family.

I dial his number from my favorites list and plug my headphones into the phone jack, popping the buds in my ears just as he answers.

"Hey," he answers, and I can tell by the sound in his voice that my stomach lurching wasn't for nothing.

Something is wrong.

"Hey, Little Bro. Sorry I didn't call sooner, was at an IM game."

"You clobber them?"

"Naturally," I answer. "What's going on?"

I get straight to the point, and Clayton sighs on the other end before I hear what sounds like a door closing and then the faint sounds of him being outside.

"Mom messaged me."

My heart stops, along with my feet, and I stand frozen for what feels like an hour in the middle of the sidewalk trail that leads around our circular-shaped campus before I find the will to speak.

"What the fuck do you mean, she *messaged* you?"

My mother had disappeared the fall semester of my sophomore year — immediately after I'd given her two-thousand dollars, thanks to Skyler's help — and she'd taken my older brother, Carleton, with her. Other than them occasionally checking in with Carleton's wife and two sons, none of us had heard from them. *I* had seen his kids more than he had, and I'd given up on ever seeing Mom again. Hell, I'd lost every ounce of care I had left for her when I realized what she'd done to Clayton.

How could she just leave him there? He was alone, staying on Mac's couch until his parents really took my brother in and made a new home for him.

What kind of mother could leave her teenage son like that, without so much as a phone call every now and then to check in?

"I mean, she messaged me. She's on Facebook now, I guess... she made a new profile."

"What the fuck did she say?" I ask, and already I'd pulled over to one of the benches near the reflection pond, plopping down and pulling up Facebook on my phone. I search her name, gulping when her profile comes up and I realize she sent me a friend request, too.

"She just said, 'Hey, son. It's Mom. How are you?'" Clayton answers, and then he pauses a moment. "I just got the message late last night, around three in the morning or so. I didn't know what to say, so I didn't respond. I wanted to talk to you first."

"Jesus Christ," I mutter, swiping through the few photos she'd uploaded. One is of her on a beach, the other is in front of some old, run-down house. She's somehow even thinner than the last time I saw her, and she's cut all her hair off.

My heart breaks at the sight of her frail form, of her sad, drugged-out eyes.

But then it hardens right back up, remembering what she'd done.

"Don't message her back," I say finally, grabbing my bag as I close Facebook and resume my walk again. "Not until I figure out where she is and what her intentions are."

"Okay," he says, not arguing, but I can hear the disappointment in his voice.

"I know you miss her," I say on a sigh, eyes rolling up to the sky and fists clenching at my sides. I want so badly to hurt my own mother, and I know what a twisted, fucked-up thing that is, but I want her to know this pain we've felt as her kids. "Just let me figure out a few things first, and then you can talk to her if you want. Okay?"

"Yeah," he says. A pause. "I do miss her, but I think I miss who I thought she was. You know? Not who she really is."

I inhale a stiff breath, blowing it out as calmly as I can as I scrub a hand down my face. Clayton is around the same age I was when I realized who my mother truly is, and I remember how badly it killed me.

I hate that it's doing the same to him.

"Hey, we have each other, right?" I remind him. "What else do we need?"

"Not a damn thing."

"That's right."

I change the subject to football, asking how his season is going so far. He's a sophomore and already on the varsity team, a wide receiver with stats more impressive than I ever had when I played in school.

After a while, we end the call, and I walk the rest of the way to the house in a fuming silence. As soon as I get back to the Omega Chi house, I lock myself in my room, text Becca that I'll see her later in the week, and then run a shower so hot my skin is a bright red when I finally emerge.

I might as well have steam wafting off my skin with the anger still sourcing through me, and I can't get my thoughts straight to figure out what I want to do next.

Before I realize what I'm doing, I have my phone in my hand, Erin's name on my screen, and a text message written in the box below it.

Me: Are you free? Really need someone right now.

I stare at the words, eyes welling with tears that burn as I try to figure out why the hell *she* was the one I thought of, why *she* was the name I typed, why *she* was the one I wanted to talk to.

None of it matters, not anymore.

Not since I realized everything I thought we had between us was a lie.

The truth is I can never lean on her.

She's the last person I can trust.

I delete the text, swiping at the one tear that managed to slip free from my eye before it has the chance to roll down my cheek.

Then, without a plan or a single fucking clue as to what I want to say, I open my laptop, pull up Facebook, and message the woman who gave me life.

Cassie

"And… I just feel…" Adam grunts, straining himself up and planting a kiss on my lips before he lowers back down to the ground, his hands behind his head. "A lot… of pressure… you know?"

Another lift. Another kiss.

Sit-ups are my favorite.

"That makes sense," I tell him, holding his feet firmly down to give him support as he lifts again. The sun has just set over campus, and on top of the parking garage where we like to be masochists with our workouts, there's a spectacular view of the pink and purple sky, and the lights flickering on all across town.

I also don't mind the view of his glistening abs, still tan from our days in the sun this summer, flexing and releasing each time he does another sit-up and gives me a kiss.

"You're the first person to ever be president for a second term in Alpha Sig," I remind him. "Anyone would feel pressure."

"I just… think I need… to do something… *different*," he continues, and I chuckle at him trying to speak through the effort.

"Like what?"

He lifts once more, grabbing my face this time and holding me to his mouth for a long, hot kiss that sends a jolt through me before he lets me go. He smiles, tracing my bottom lip before his eyes find mine. "One hundred. Your turn."

"I'm *not* doing a hundred."

"You're doing fifty. Now, come on, switch."

He grabs my breasts and squeezes them through my sports bra before I swat him away and lie back, not ready for my torture.

"Wipe that look off your face, you know you love it," he says.

"I do *not* love it," I argue, doing my first sit-up and kissing him before I lower back down. The first few are easy, but when I get to the tenth, my abdomen fires up in protest. "I'm doing it because I'm a biology major and a future doctor and I need to learn how to put nutrition and fitness in the forefront of my priority list. That doesn't mean I have to *like* it, though."

Adam smiles, kissing my nose on the next sit-up. "You're cute when you're complaining about a workout."

I flip him off, but continue the reps as he starts in on his ideas for his second year as A Sig president. Now that we're a couple of weeks into the school year, I'm in my routine, feeling solid for the first time since I got to Palm South University. Maybe it's because I'm finally in my cornerstone classes, or maybe it's because Adam and I are together, *finally*, without anyone or anything in-between us.

It's crazy what feeling settled in your love life can do for the rest of your life.

"And I was thinking," Adam continues when I'm on my fortieth rep. "Instead of doing the concert like I've done the last two years, what if I changed it up a bit?"

I frown. "That concert... got you... on the map again," I remind him. "It took Alpha Sigma from..." I groan, wrenching myself up and kissing him reluctantly before I lower again. "Nothing... to the talk of Greek Row."

"I know, and I think that's just it. It's served its purpose, you know? But I want to keep things fresh and exciting." He grins, kissing me before I go down for my last three reps. "What do you think about karaoke?"

"Karaoke?" I echo, finishing my last reps and enjoying the long, sweet kiss that follows the end of my torture before I lean back on my hands, sweating, panting. "As in, poor quality instrumental music from a speaker with an amateur singing the words on a monitor in front of them?"

"Exactly. Except, better."

I chuckle. "Okay. I'm listening."

"Picture this," he says, excitement rolling off him. "We set up a huge stage, just like we normally do for the concert, and there's a band set up — drums, guitars, bass, backup singers, all that. Then, each fraternity and sorority gets to compete for the trophy by pulling out their best karaoke skills. We'll encourage them to not only bring out their best singers, but to also go for the entertainment factor — humor, dancing, all of it. Can you imagine how fun that would be?"

I tilt my head, cocking one eyebrow. "Honestly, my sisters *do* love karaoke."

"Who doesn't?"

"You said there'd be a band? So, instead of instrumental, it's a real band?"

"Exactly. I already talked to a local band who does weddings and stuff. They said they can give me a giant list of songs they know for the fraternities and sororities to choose from. And we'll do the lights up just like we do for the concert, and the fog and confetti and all that. It'll *feel* like a real show."

"That's really cool," I muse, smiling.

"And, we'll make more for our charity this way, too. We can charge an entry fee for the fraternities and sororities to enter, and charge a low-ticket price, get prizes donated for the winners — first, second, and third place." He's so excited that he's breathing as hard as he was when we got to the top of the parking garage after running up the stairs. "And if it goes off the way I have it planned, I feel like it would become a new tradition, kind of like the Greek Week games where we all compete."

I lean forward, grabbing his face in mine and kissing him hard. "How did I get such a smart, sexy boyfriend?"

"Well, it wasn't exactly easy."

I snort, but before I can sass back, he's pulling me in closer, wrapping me up in his arms, his love, kissing me like it's the first and the last time at once.

"What about you?" he asks, popping up to stand before he reaches his hand down to help me up, too. "How has the new school year been for you so far? Anything new and exciting in the land of KKB?"

He grabs my shoulder as I grab his, and we both pull up the opposite foot to our butts, stretching our quads.

"We got a great group of new members," I say, frowning. "And the pressure is on from my G-Big to take a Little."

"Ex?"

I nod. "I didn't take one last year, mostly because I just didn't feel ready to, you know? And I guess I do feel ready this year, but... I don't know." I struggle to find the explanation. "It's my junior year, you know? I have a ton of schoolwork, and I don't know if I..." My stomach drops as the root of my concern hits me. "I don't know if I'd be a good Big."

We switch legs, and Adam squeezes my shoulder where he holds me. "Cassie, you're an amazing friend, an amazing sister, a *phenomenal* kisser — er, I mean, girlfriend."

I smirk.

"And I *know* you'd be an amazing Big — but only if you want to be one. Don't feel like you have to just because it's the norm. Take a Little if you want to continue your family line and pass down some traditions, if you want to mentor one of the new girls and help her find her footing in the sorority the way Sky helped you."

I smile. "I really do think I'd like that. I don't know what I would have done without Skyler, maybe dropped out of KKB altogether."

"Well, then, maybe that's your answer. But sleep on it, okay? You have time to think."

I nod, and we finish stretching in a comfortable silence.

"What about school? Your classes as hard as you thought they'd be?" Adam asks as we cross the top of the garage to start making our way back down.

My throat tightens, a jolt of nerves flittering through me at the thought of the past two weeks. Classes have been fine, for the most part. I prepared over the summer, and I've always been one of those students who excelled pretty easily. I'm not intimidated by my cornerstone classes.

But I *am* freaked out about having class with Grayson.

He hasn't tried to talk to me again since that first day, but I feel his energy every time I'm in that classroom with him. It makes my skin crawl.

And as ashamed as I am to admit it to myself, it also makes me sad.

I can't place why, and I never give myself time to think on it before I push him out of my mind and focus on the professor.

But I still have yet to tell Adam about it, and I don't know if I even need to.

Why would it matter? It's just a class together, and I don't even talk to Grayson or anything. It's not like I'm doing anything *wrong*.

Adam glances behind him on our way down the stairs when I don't answer for a while, and I shake my head, smiling.

"Sorry, just tired. Yeah, school is fine. I feel like me staying here over the summer to get ahead was smart."

"You're the smartest girl I know," he says, and when we reach the bottom of the stairs, he grabs my wrist and tugs me into him.

His mouth is on mine in the next instant, his hands in my hair, running through it softly before he tugs it at the end.

"You got homework tonight?" he husks.

"Nothing that can't wait."

"Good," he says, smiling at my shortness of breath as he slips his tongue inside my mouth, swirling and teasing. "Because I think we have some anatomy to study."

"Mmm," I muse, running my hands down his back to hook into the back band of his shorts. "I *do* still need some help in a certain area, come to think of it."

Adam frowns. "And that is?"

I lick my lips, leaning up on my tiptoes to whisper in his ear. "Blow jobs."

A shiver runs through him, and he groans, looking up to the sky as if he needs a god to save him from me. "Jesus Christ, woman. I've got an instant boner and we have to walk all the way across campus."

"Guess you better walk behind me, then," I say, turning and leaning my ass into his hard on.

He groans again, smacking my ass and tucking his erection into the band of his shorts before we start our walk — both of us a little quicker than necessary now that we know what waits for us when we get back to the A Sig house.

Yeah, I think. *No sense in bringing up Grayson.*

We're happy — *finally* — and there's nothing to tell, really. It's just a class together, nothing to concern him over.

For now, I'll keep it to myself.

What's the harm in that?

EPISODE 2

Ashlei

The wood floor of the studio is cool under my bare feet, and I wiggle my toes, reveling in the feel of it as I close my eyes and listen to the music. It's a slow, exotic song, filled with heat and energy, and slowly, my hips begin to sway to the beat.

On my next breath, I lift my arms over my head, rolling them in time with my hips before I trail them down, gliding my fingertips over my body, the song sinking in deeper and deeper.

When my eyes open, I see the center pole four feet in front of me, and I lick my lips, still moving in time with the music as I strut toward it. My right hand reaches out, wrapping around the chrome, and I swing, lifting my feet off the ground and letting the momentum send me spinning.

Everything is lost in moments like these, when I'm in the studio, the music loud, just me and my body dancing and making art. My feet barely hit the floor before I grip the pole in my armpit and lean back, legs tucked before extending into chopper, and then I'm hooking my outside leg and letting the rest of my body hang.

The skin on my inside thigh burns to life, but it's a comforting pain, one that I know from experience will go away the longer I practice. I use my legs and arms to make shapes as the pole spins, and then I swing my inside leg around, hooking it over the pole before my right leg extends.

Leg hang after leg hang, shape after shape, I feel my way through the song. I alternate between tricks in the air to low flow and floor work, and by the time the last beats of the sexy song fade away, I'm dripping in sweat, chest heaving, abdomen contracting and releasing where I lie on my back on the floor.

From the corner of the room, Karen, the studio owner and my own personal torturer — er, trainer — applauds.

"Fantastic work, Ashlei," she says, leaning over and extending a hand to help me up. When I'm on my feet again, she smiles wider. "Truly. I'm amazed at the progress you've made since you first came to our studio."

"All thanks to you," I pant.

She shakes her head. "No way. This is all *you*. You worked hard over the summer. Hard to believe you're the same girl who stumbled her way through basic spins and sits the first time you walked through those doors on Valentine's Day."

I smile, thanking her before she winks and makes her way over to the desk to welcome the girls showing up for her next class.

Karen is nothing like my previous pole studio owner.

She's kind, and caring, and driven and smart. At five-foot-eight, she's almost all beautiful legs and strong, toned arms. I watch her with appreciation as she checks girls in, her wide smile bright against her dark brown skin. Her long, black hair is in a hundred tiny braids and piled into a gorgeous bun on top of her head, all of it contained by a bright headband.

It's as if the yellows and oranges in that headband are her aura, her energy, that bright, sunshine vibe she always gives off.

My muscles are deliciously sore as I throw her a wave over my shoulder on my way out, smiling and thinking about everything she said about my progress. It feels good, the reward slowly showing from all the hard work I've been putting in.

And that smile doubles when I push through the doors that lead onto the sunny downtown street, and I see Brandon's pearl white Acura NSX parked on the curb.

The driver side door opens as soon as I'm on the sidewalk, and he steps out, looking dapper as ever in a custom beige suit, tailored to fit every muscle. His eyes are shielded behind dark square sunglasses, but he takes them off as he rounds the car, opening the passenger side for me with a grin.

"Your chariot, Miss."

I shake my head, handing him my gym bag when he reaches for it before I plant a long, warm kiss on his lips. He wraps his arms around me, inhaling at the contact as if it were his first breath all day.

"Hi, baby," I whisper.

"Hi," he says back, kissing my nose before he releases me. "I missed you."

"Clearly. I don't remember asking you to pick me up," I point out. "*Or* making plans at all today."

"Yeah... about that... get in, let's talk."

I cock a brow, sliding into the passenger seat before he gently shuts the door behind me. He walks around the back, tossing my bag in the small trunk before he's in the driver seat next to me, roaring the engine to life.

"Do you have pole tomorrow?" he asks, checking his side mirror before he pulls onto the road.

"No, I need a rest day."

"And it's Sunday, so you wouldn't have class, right?"

My suspicion rises. "No... but I *do* have Chapter at six."

"Chapter..." he muses, side-eyeing me with a grin. "Damn sorority."

I smack his arm playfully.

"Do you think you could skip it, just this once?"

"Probably not without a death threat from Ex," I say seriously. "But... what are you proposing?"

We pull up to a red light, and Brandon bites his lip before turning to me. "The Bahamas."

"The Bahamas?!"

"The Exumas, technically."

"The *Exumas*," I repeat, sounding like a freaking parrot at this point. "You're proposing we go to the Exumas tonight," I clarify. "As in... the place where you swim with pigs."

"I was thinking more like the place where I fuck you on my yacht and drink fruity cocktails out of coconuts with you on the beach," he says on a smirk, and the light turns green, making him turn back to the road with a shrug. "But if you'd rather swim with pigs..."

I laugh, shaking my head at the ridiculousness of it. I'm tempted to say *We can't just go to the fucking Bahamas, Brandon,* but I know that's a lie.

He has a yacht.

And more money than he knows how to spend.

Technically, we *can* go to the Bahamas.

I'm quiet for a long while, and Brandon glances at me from the corner of his eye before pulling into a random restaurant parking lot. It's a Mexican diner, not even open yet, since it's only ten in the morning. When he's parked, he turns to me, grabbing my hands and pulling them into his lap.

"Look, we've both been busy this summer — you with your exec position in the sorority, and pole... me with this national client we're in the bidding war for... *both* of us working hard at *Okay, Cool* after everything that went down in the spring with Kim... and now, school is back in session, it's the last semester before you graduate, we're both hard at work, and I just..."

He smooths his dark thumbs over my wrists, his eyes that are usually so intense, soft and vulnerable now.

"This might be our last chance to spend some real, quality time together before life gets even crazier than it already is."

My heart melts into a puddle right there on the floorboard of his expensive ass car, and I lean over the console, kissing him long and hard.

"Let's go to the Bahamas," I whisper between kisses. "You're right. Everything else can wait."

He sighs, wrapping his arms around me until he's pulling me into his lap. I squeal and laugh, but then my next breath is stolen by the erection growing in his slacks.

"This would be a lot easier on the yacht," I say, rubbing the seam of my leggings against his hard-on.

"Maybe," he says, sucking on my bottom lip and releasing it with a pop. His lips trail down my neck as my head rolls back. "But these windows are tinted, and you're sexy when you say I'm right."

I bark out a laugh that's stolen with another kiss, knowing tinted windows or not, if anyone walks by, they'll know what's going on in here. I have yet to be fucked by Mr. Church without screaming out his name a time or two.

"How long has it been since you fucked me?" I ask, slipping my hand between us and gripping his cock hard.

He groans, flexing into my fist through the fabric of his slacks. "Too long."

It's only been a week, but I agree with the sentiment, and both of us lose our ability to go slow and take our time with foreplay. Instead, I lift up on my knees just enough to unfasten the button on his slacks and slide the zipper down, then I'm yanking down on his pants and briefs together. He lifts his hips to help me, and as soon as his shaft is free, I turn into a trapeze artist.

"What the hell are you doing?" Brandon asks with a smirk when I start flipping upside down. I pause long enough to peel off my leggings, and then I'm ass up, face down, with my pussy in his face and my arms straddling his thighs.

I don't have to answer his question with words. Instead, I take the tip of him in my mouth, slowly at first, just enough to swirl my tongue and get him wet. He groans, palming my ass cheeks with both hands before smacking them hard.

I yelp, taking him all the way in my throat, and then I'm rewarded with a lash of his tongue on my clit.

It's not easy, balancing on my forearms in what is practically a yoga inversion with my legs straddled around his face, but Brandon holds onto my thighs and ass, taking his share of the weight and making it easier for me to focus on getting him off.

It's been a year now since I met this man, since he stole my breath away in the elevator at *Okay, Cool* and then I spent months trying to avoid him, trying not to give in to his devilish stare and sexy confidence.

But I was a goner from the first time I laid eyes on him, since the first time he laid eyes on *me*.

And I was a fool to ever think otherwise.

"God*damn*, Ashlei," he groans, flexing his hips until his cock bulges in my throat. I do everything to keep from gagging, letting him hold himself there for a long time before he withdraws. Then, he's assaulting my pussy with his tongue, his fingers, burying his face between my thighs.

My legs shiver and quake around him, and when he circles my clit time and time again with his tongue, working it in rhythm with his fingers inside me, I have to take a break from sucking his dick. I have to just hold myself up and let everything else go as an explosion of fire and stars invade my vision, all the blood rushing to where his tongue drives me to climax.

I rock my hips against his mouth, and his free hand grabs my ass and pulls me into him, letting me know he can take it. Each new wave of my orgasm hits harder than the last, and I ride his face until I'm spent, until I'm nothing but a mess of shallow breath and trembling muscles.

When I'm done, Brandon hits a button that sends his seat back a little farther. Then, he leans it back and flips me over in a complicated tangle of limbs until he's on top of me and I'm half bent over the console, half bent over his seat.

Without a chance to catch my breath, he slides inside me from behind, stealing my next breath with the raw sensation of being filled after just climaxing so fucking hard.

I cry out his name, holding onto the leather seats for dear life as he pounds into me hard, harder, over and over, punishing and claiming.

And when he's ready to come, he pulls out of me and flips me back over, climbing up the seat to empty inside my mouth.

I swallow every drop.

Skyler

"NO, NO, *NO*," KIP groans, shaking his head on the screen of my laptop. "You're supposed to take the clothes *off* — not put them *on*."

I chuckle, zipping up my black dress pants and fastening the button at the top before I shove one arm through the long-sleeve, white, button-up top. I lean forward once both arms are in, pushing my cleavage together.

"Take one last look, baby," I tease, biting my lip. "Because in about two minutes, I'll look like a cocktail waiter and your sex drive will die right along with my pride."

Kip chuckles, but his eyes are on my chest with a longing sigh on his lips. "Please don't button up that top."

"But I have to go to work."

"You should come here, instead."

I smile. "To California? Sure, I'll hop the next flight."

"Great. See you soon!"

Kip jokes like he's going to hang up our video chat, but of course he doesn't, and then we're both smiling and staring at each other through the screen, wishing we could touch from across the country.

As horrible as the summer was with his father passing away, I hadn't realized until the new semester started how spoiled we had been. Even after his father had passed, we'd spent time with his mom, in his hometown, falling more in love every single day — while also dealing with the fall-out from the tournament. It didn't take long for the reporters to put the pieces together and realize Kip was the same guy from the bonfire photo that had been leaked of me, and needless to say, we were the juiciest story the poker world had seen in a while — especially once I disappeared off the scene.

In those short months of summer, Kip had become my person. We'd spend nearly every day together, every night in each other's arms, and now we had thousands of miles between us.

And there was just no way around it.

It hurt.

Kip was finally at his dream school — UCLA — chasing his dream of becoming a script writer. And as much as I knew he was where he needed to be, and I was where *I* needed to be at PSU, I hated that those two schools were not in the same zip code.

Or even the same state.

There was only so much a text or a phone call or even a video chat could do.

I stand, shrugging the dress shirt on and start buttoning it from the bottom up. "What are you going to do tonight?"

"Dream about you stripping out of that outfit."

I roll my eyes.

"Alpha Sigma is having a little party to kick off Greek Week," he says after he gets his rise out of me. "Rick and I are going to head that way after our Character Creation class."

"I still can't believe you managed to find not only a fraternity brother with the same major, but then he ends up as your roommate, too."

Kip chuckles. "It's not so weird here, babe. Everyone wants to work in movies or TV or music." He shrugs, a dreamy smile on those perfect lips I love to taste. "That's why I wanted to be here. It feels like home."

My heart rips somehow with a gentle pang of longing, as if his words hurt just as much as they made me proud of him. I still remember our first date, when he opened up to me about his dreams of writing scripts, and now, he's on his way to doing just that.

"What's wrong, Ella Mae," he asks, leaning forward. The movement allows me to see the *Singing in the Rain* movie poster hanging above his bed behind him. "You seem distant tonight."

I sigh, flopping down in the office chair at my desk as I struggle with the red bow tie around my neck. "I don't know. I guess I've just been feeling a little... lost. Now that I'm not playing poker professionally, I feel like one of my limbs has been cut off."

"You still *could* play, you know," he reminds me.

I nod, but fall quiet, because we both know *not* continuing to play was the best move for me. Kip and I made quite the scene in Vegas last year, and really — I've accomplished what I wanted to. Mom and Dad are set up financially, my tuition and *then* some is paid, and I have a solid savings stashed up for when I graduate. Plus — I got the guy.

What more do I need?

Poker has served its purpose for me, and now I want to dive deeper and find out what I want to do with the rest of my life.

But I'm already a senior, and I'm just now thinking about my career after college.

To say I'm behind is an understatement.

"Do you want to talk about it?" Kip asks. "I know you started taking some entrepreneurship and business classes this semester, but we haven't talked about how they're going. Do you like them? Do you feel like they fit you?"

Anxiety flares in my chest, as it often does when I try to find out where I fit in. It's been like that my entire life. The only place I've really been able to find my footing is in Kappa Kappa Beta and the Greek community at Palm South.

Once I graduate, all that will be gone, too.

I shake my head, forcing a smile. "Not right now. I don't really have much to say yet since it's only been a few weeks. Besides," I say, waggling my eyebrows as I pull on the slick, black vest and button it up, standing back with my arms wide. "This sexy thing has a shift to work on the casino boat."

Kip smiles, too, but his blue eyes shine with worry. "I wish I was there to hold you in my arms right now."

My smile falls at that. "Me, too."

A long moment stretches between us, and finally Kip sighs, his smile genuine again. "They're all going to love you. I can't wait to hear how much you make in tips."

"It's going to be keeping my mouth shut when they do something stupid that will be hard."

He barks out a laugh at that. "Nah, don't hold back. School 'em. Maybe they'll tip you more if you give them advice and they win."

I point at him in a *touché* gesture, and then lean forward, blowing him one more kiss. He catches it, holds it, and then throws it up to the sky — something we've done every time we can since his dad passed away. It's a little reminder to keep him in our hearts, and also to live each day to the fullest.

"I'll text you after my shift," I say, knowing that even though it'll be late here, the night will just be getting started in California. "Have fun at the party, but tell Rick to fight the girls off you for me."

"You're the only girl for me and everyone here knows it."

I smile at that, giving him one last longing look before I close the screen on my laptop. Then, I look in the floor-length mirror in the room I share with Jess, adjusting the ridiculous bow tie and sighing at the way the work uniform hides all of my best features. I look like I'm wearing a large potato bag painted black, white, and red.

But as much as I don't have the desire to play poker *professionally*, I can't deny the rush flowing through me at the thought of being around *other* players. I'll be dealing blackjack most of the night, and if I have my charm turned up to a hundred, I'll also be walking out with a pocket full of cash in tips.

It isn't the Friday night I'm used to. I *should* be getting ready to go to a party with Jess and Lei, preparing myself to take shots instead of to take chips. But something tells me this casino boat is where I need to be, that even though I'm not playing poker for money, I'm not quite done with it yet, either.

With a strange, unfamiliar feeling floating in my stomach, I push all my anxious thoughts down and cover my lips in matte red lipstick for good measure. Then, I head to work.

I think of Kip the entire drive.

Adam

"And for Halloween, the sandbar party was a success last year," I say, tapping through the lists of things in my notebook that I wanted to discuss with Jeremy. He sits on my bed, looking bored, tossing my baseball up into the air over and over again while I ramble away. "I think we should do it again. But maybe bigger this time." I pause. "Do you think we could get a DJ out there?"

Jeremy tosses the ball up. "Everyone plays music on their boats," he pointed out. "I think it'd be too much noise."

"But if the DJ was in the *middle*," I pointed out. "It'd be an attraction, something to draw people onto the island more so than just into the boats."

"True." He snatches the ball from the air and sits up. "But first, I think you need to remain focused on this karaoke thing."

"It's pretty much handled," I say, waving him off. That fresh energy I get from making a list, a plan, a new goal rushes through me, and I smile, jotting down more ideas.

"I'm serious, man," he says. "The event is a couple weeks away and there's still so much we haven't nailed down. We need an emcee. We need monitors. We still haven't received the entry fee from half of the fraternities and sororities who've entered. Plus, we haven't talked at all about day-of fundraising tactics."

Jeremy continues on, but my phone buzzes on my desk with a reminder that Cassie's class ends in fifteen minutes, and already, I'm closing up my notebook and packing my bag to go meet her.

"... the food and the..." He stops. "Are you listening to me?"

"Yeah," I answer easily. "I gotta go, but don't worry, okay?" I slap him on the shoulder as I swing my backpack onto mine. "I've got this under control."

Jeremy stops me before I can turn, his hand landing hard on my forearm. "I'm serious, Adam. This is your second year as president — something no one in this fraternity has done before. And I'm just saying, I'm not the only one who notices that you're a little distracted."

I frown. "Distracted?"

"With Cassie."

At that, my expression hardens. "What does she have to do with anything?"

"I'm just saying," he says with his palms out. "You two have always been dancing around each other. This is your first time being *together*, and, well... let's just say it's very apparent that she's the first priority for you right now."

My defenses spike, and I point a finger at my closest fraternity brother, narrowing my gaze. "I've been present for everything. I've been running Chapter, coming up with new ideas for the semester, already planning for Rush that isn't even until the spring, and I literally brainstormed and made this entire karaoke fundraising event come together in just weeks." I shake my head. "I can be happy with Cassie and still get shit done. If anything, she's motivated me to do even *more*."

Jeremy folds his arms over his chest. "You've been here, yes, but you haven't been present. You're always on your phone — texting her, calling her, whatever. You spend more time with her than you do with your brothers. It doesn't matter that you're here making *plans*," he says. "What matters is that you're *here* — really and truly here. When was the last time you played video games in the main room? Stayed for a party instead of hiding out in your room with Cassie? Attended an IM game to just be with your brothers instead of watching it with her and then leaving immediately after to go on a date?"

The more he shoots at me, the more my shoulders slump, guilt sinking in. I haven't even noticed I've been doing any of those things, but as he lists them off, my defenses crumble.

Because he's right.

"I love Cassie," he says when I don't respond. "You know that. I've wanted you two together for years. But... just remember that we're your brothers, and as our president, we need your time, too. *Especially* right now, changing up a concert that's been working to try something new. This was your idea, brother," he says, standing. "So, lean into it and help us pull it off successfully."

I sigh, chest tight with shame. I can always depend on Jeremy to give it to me straight, but I hate what I'm hearing from him in this moment.

"I hear you," I say, gripping his shoulder in one hand as I level my gaze with his. "Thank you for helping me see what I couldn't. I promise, I'm here, and I'll *be* here more. Don't worry about the karaoke event this weekend," I assure him. "I've got this."

Jeremy's lips press together, and he nods once. We exchange a unique handshake we've had since freshman year, and he claps me on the back as we head out of my bedroom.

When we make it to the main room, a bunch of our brothers are gathered on the couches and beanbags, watching two seniors battle it out in a game of Madden on the big screen. They welcome Jeremy easily, scooting over on the couch to make more room for him and handing him a beer out of the ice chest at the edge of the coffee table.

Then there are eyes on me.

"Heading out, Pres?" Kade asks, drinking a beer with his eyes still on the screen. He rushed last spring, in Kip's class, and already he's been showing leadership potential.

Before I can answer, one of my brothers says, "Of course he is. Time to go pick up Cassie from class, right?"

There's a snicker from my other brothers, one I wouldn't have even noticed had Jeremy not just had the conversation with me that he had. Before, I would have laughed it off, said something to the effect of *you bet your ass*. But now, I watch them exchange knowing looks, feeling like an outsider in the family I spent the last year building.

"I'll be back after lunch," I say.

"Yeah. See ya," Kade replies.

And then the attention is back on the game, and I'm invisible.

My mind is spinning the entire walk across campus to the Science Building, and I chase each thought, holding onto it by the tail before it wriggles free and another comes into view.

I love Cassie. I love spending time with her. But have I really been so wrapped up in her this semester that I've been neglecting my brothers?

I know the answer solely from the interaction I just had with them in the house. If Jeremy hadn't pulled my head out of my ass, I'm not sure I would have seen it *even then*.

The truth is I *like* being lost in Cassie. I like that she's my entire world.

But if I'm going to be president, and if Alpha Sigma is as important to me as it always has been, I need to find the balance.

The more I think on it, the more I can't wait to talk to Cassie about it all. She's my best friend, and I know she'll have exactly the right words to say.

When I see her red hair bounce out of the front doors from where I'm sitting on one of the benches fifty yards or so from the building, I smile, my heart already fluttering with relief just from seeing her.

But then my eyes land on the person walking out of the building with her.

The person I hate more than anyone in the world.

Grayson fucking Anderson is walking next to Cassie — so close their arms brush a little as the crowd moves around them.

My heart stops in my throat as I watch them come to a stop in the sea of students leaving the building. Cassie stands with her arms crossed over her books tucked into her chest, and Grayson is talking animatedly, his hands moving, sincerity on his face as he says whatever it is he's saying.

Cassie listens, chewing her lip, and when he's done, she says something in response. I have no idea what it is, but I know he smiles after she's said it, and that alone sends a rip current of anger rushing through me.

I stand, snatching my backpack off the bench and throwing it on my shoulders, determined to march my ass over there and shove Grayson away from her. I want to remind him that he's not welcome to talk to her — *ever* — but before I can move, he salutes her, and she offers him a small wave, and then he turns and walks in the opposite direction.

I pause, watching Cassie as she watches him leave, an unreadable expression in her eyes. After a moment, a big breath leaves her chest, and she turns, searching for something.

For me.

I know that's what her eyes are scanning for, that *she* knows I'm out here somewhere, walking toward her or waiting for her to make her way toward me. I know she's wondering where we'll go for lunch before I walk her to her next class.

But for the first time, I don't want her to find me.

Something indescribable sears through my spine like a hot wire, and I know if I talk to her right now, I'll blow. I don't have the details. I have no idea why Grayson was with her, or what they were talking about, but I know if she walks over to me and I ask her how class was and all she says is *fine* and then pretends like nothing happened and we go to lunch — I won't be able to let it go.

So I don't give her the chance.

With my backpack on my shoulder, I fall into the sea of students and make my way back toward Greek Row, pulling out my phone to send her a text.

Me: Got caught up with A Sig stuff. Text you later.

I shove my phone back in my pocket, ignoring the response buzz that comes through less than sixty seconds later, and keep my head down the rest of my walk.

Why the fuck was she with Grayson? He's a Music major — there's literally no reason for him to be in that building. And why was Cassie talking to him, *listening* to him? I don't care if he was apologizing for what he did to her, or talking about the fucking weather. She *hates* him.

Doesn't she?

Shouldn't she?

It doesn't make sense to me why she would give him even two minutes of her time.

And the worst part is that whatever she said brought a relieved smile to his face, and they'd waved goodbye to each other like they were friends.

Friends.

Just the thought of it sends another chill of rage through me, and I shake my head, letting out an audible, frustrated growl that earns me a few weary glances from the students walking around me.

I need to get back to the house, and I need to get my mind on literally *anything* else.

I'll talk to Cassie about this later, when I've cooled down, when I can be rational.

As I storm through campus, I know I'm lying to myself.

Because rationality doesn't exist in me.

Not when it comes to that motherfucker and my girl.

Cassie

I pack my books and laptop up with more aggression than necessary at the end of Genetics, grumbling to myself as I shove everything in my bag. I've been doing great in this class so far, and effectively avoiding Grayson.

Until today.

Because the professor just assigned us as lab partners.

I inhale a stiff, hot breath and blow it out like a dragon before slugging my bag onto my shoulder. I don't make it two steps from my desk when Grayson jogs down the steps in the classroom to catch up with me.

"So, lab partners," he says on a grin, waggling his brows at me. "Talk about some fucked-up fate, huh?"

"I'm putting in a request for someone else," I growl out, locking eyes on his. "Right now."

"Wait!" He rounds to stand in front of me, reaching out for my arms to grab me and pull me to the side. I rip away from his touch, but let him guide me out of the path of the other students. "Don't do that."

"We can't be lab partners, Grayson."

"Why not?"

"Oh, do I need to remind you? Well, let's see..." I tap my chin, ready to pop off *every* thing he's ever done wrong, but he holds up his hands in surrender before I do.

"You don't have to remind me that I hurt you," he says, sighing. "I just... What about forgiveness?"

I laugh, shaking my head and trying to push past him, but he steps in my way again.

"I'm serious. Look, I hurt you. I fucked you over and you *deserve* to hate me — now and forever."

"Gee, thanks for the permission," I reply flatly.

"I didn't mean to hurt you. I didn't *want* to hurt you." Grayson shoves a hand back over his hair, trailing the length of it before hooking his hand on the back of his neck. His eyes flick back and forth somewhere in the distance. "I was lost. I was fucked up and I acted out and hurt the one person who was there for me. I just... I didn't know what to do. My parents were on me to pick another major, and threatening to pull any and all financial support if I didn't. I was in denial, playing shows, focusing on my music career, all the while knowing it was about to end for good."

Do not feel sorry for him. Do not.

"I don't have enough excuses to make you truly forgive me. And you never have to. But I'm asking you to give me a shot at being your friend."

"My friend," I echo.

"Yes." He sighs, stepping a little closer and lowering his voice. "I know how badly it hurts you to lose people in your life. I remember what you told me about Paris. I remember how badly it hurt you to pick me over Adam when I was being a selfish little boy with you."

That last confession surprises me, because I never thought I'd hear the day when Grayson admitted he was wrong about asking me to choose between him and Adam.

"I don't want to hurt you even more than I already have by disappearing from your life. We had a great friendship, Cassie. And I miss it. Don't you?"

My throat is tight and sticky with the question, and softly, quietly, somewhere deep within me, I hear a distant *yes.*

I shake my head, shoving past him and over to the professor.

"Professor Drumm, sir," I start. "I'm sorry to bother you. But about the lab partner assignment..."

"No changes," he says without looking up at me from his laptop. "It takes a long time for us to pair students, and we do so with careful intent." He glances at me briefly, then over the top of his glasses. "If you've got a problem, figure it out. You'll have to work with a lot of people you don't like when you're a doctor, Ms. McBee."

My next breath is subdued by a smile I force so hard my cheek hurts, and I nod, thanking him before grinding my teeth and bolting out of the classroom.

Grayson is right on my heels.

"Just give me a chance," he pleads. "If I pull anything that makes you uncomfortable, you have permission to deck me in the face."

He holds the doors open for us to exit the science building, and then falls in step next to me.

"We have to be lab partners," he says, pulling me to a stop. "You heard Drumm. There's no getting out of this. So, we can either make an attempt to be friends, or we can both be miserable for the rest of the semester. I know which option sounds better to me," he says with a shrug. "What about you?"

I chew my lip, watching his sincere blue eyes like they're a snake that's been beside me in the grass all this time. I'm equal parts terrified, and sure I'll die from a venomous bite as I am surprised he hasn't struck me down yet. Something close to trust niggles at me from the inside, but it's against a strong warning from every cell in my being.

He's right. I *do* hate losing people. I hate it more than anything.

And as much as what he did hurt me, it killed me more to have someone I loved, someone I gave myself to completely, just disappear from my life overnight.

What if we *could* be friends?

Am I crazy for thinking it's possible?

"We can attempt to be friend*ly*," I decide on, which makes Grayson instantly smile and do a small fist bump by his side. "But I'm not making any promises that I'll be okay with it. I'll try. That's all I can give."

"That's enough," he says. Then, he stands straight and salutes me. "See you Thursday, partner."

I offer a small wave, chest tight even after he's gone. Then, I scan the yard for Adam. Now that Grayson and I are lab partners, it's time to tell Adam what's going on.

I don't find him after a long moment of searching, and I frown as a text comes through my phone saying he got caught up with Alpha Sigma stuff.

He's been stressed out, and I know he has a lot going on with the Alpha Sigma karaoke event coming up *and* the Halloween bash not too far after.

Maybe I should wait until things settle down a little bit.

Maybe by then, I'll know if Grayson is true to his word or not.

With a deep and uncertain sigh, I reply to Adam's text to let him know I'll see him later, and then I make my way to the Student Union to have lunch alone.

Erin

I never eat the donuts or drink the coffee at group therapy.

I don't know why I choose this exact moment to notice that, but as the usual group files in, I stare at the donuts, the various colors of sugar and sugar substitutes, the tiny, individual cups of creamer, the simple red stirrers, and the steaming, black liquid as it flows from the pot and into a Styrofoam cup that's then carried away and I wonder — why do I never get any?

Part of it is vanity, I suppose, because I gave up coffee for fear of stunting my growth and yellowing my teeth, and donuts, well, that one is pretty obvious. I work hard enough to keep my thighs cellulite-free and my hips fitting into a size six, that even thinking about how many miles I'd need to run to work off a donut stresses me out.

But deep down, I think I know it's because that seemingly innocent table spread of caffeine and sugar is a watering hole.

And in my eyes — a trap.

When I come to group, I walk straight to the same chair I've sat in every week, sit down quietly, place my large purse in my lap, and cross my legs.

Then, I wait.

I watch as other members talk to each other while making their perfect cocktail of coffee and sugar and cream, and I smile politely if someone catches me looking — but I never join them.

And yet, I always take my time to get dressed up for session. I change into a different outfit so I'm fresh, redo my makeup and hair if need be, and I always look like I'm ready to go out to dinner after.

Maybe it's because sometimes, I hope I will be.

My vision is blurred and out of focus with my mind buzzing, until a dark shadow crosses between me and the coffee table. It's just a blur of black and gray that whooshes by, but I blink, waking from my daze, and my gaze follows the shadow.

Of course, when my vision focuses once more, I realize the shadow is a human. A boy — around my age, I guess — with olive skin. He's dressed in dark, skinny jeans and a black, long-sleeve shirt that makes *me* sweat thinking about the fact that it's September in South Florida. Those sleeves are crossed over a broad chest, and he stretches out his long legs next, crossing them at the ankles and sinking down into his chair. His face is hidden by the bill of a gray ball cap, pulled down over his eyes, just the hint of stubble on his chin visible to the room.

I've been coming to group therapy all summer, and I haven't seen him before. Everyone *else* in the room I know very well — at least, well *enough*.

There's Cyndi — with an *i*, which she'll remind you nearly every session — a white, middle-aged redhead who has an obsession with the color green and has been plagued with guilt since she backed out of her driveway and accidentally ran over her thirteen-year-old cat. There's Jonathan, the father who put his gambling addiction before his children, and they now want nothing to do with him. There's Kendall, the kleptomaniac — which I smiled at the first time I heard it, because it somehow sounded cute, the combination of her name and her affliction.

There's Sam, the man cheated on by his wife before she divorced him, and Clarence, the quiet old man who always smiles when someone's talking and barely ever says a word about himself. Harper is my favorite, mostly because she always sits next to me and leans in to offer her commentary on everyone's *problems*.

I could go on and on, but the point is that I know everyone in this group.

Except for the new shadow.

I wait for myself to feel something about him, about his newness, but all I can think is that he's very tall, very lean, and very sad.

The last fact is as obvious as the color of his shirt.

I'm still watching him when our group leader, Jackie, clicks the top of her pen and holds the notebook in her lap by the serial binding, her usual cue that we're about to begin. With one last, curious look at our new addition, I turn my attention fully to her, and straighten my back, meeting her smile with my own.

"Hello, everyone," she sings in her calm, soothing voice. "Welcome to group."

There's a murmur of *hellos* from the group — from everyone except our new shadow.

"So, before we get started, I want everyone to get comfortable in your chair, and then I want you to close your eyes."

I want to *roll* my eyes, but I close them as she instructs, reminding myself to remain open to the energy she's trying to give off. That's what my *personal* therapist always says. She knows how I've felt in the past about group therapy, about therapy *in general*, and she always reminds me that I'm on the road to healing, and if I snub my nose at everything I pass on this road, I'll just end up right back where I started.

Once our eyes are closed, Jackie leads us through a breathing exercise, reading off some calming mantras as we tune into our breaths. The more we breathe, the more she speaks in her soothing tone, the more I relax and drift into the open space she wants us to be in.

But suddenly, I feel like someone's watching me.

I creak one eye open, and then the next, glancing around the group at all the other members who have their eyes closed. Jackie is still speaking, and I frown, not knowing what made me feel uneasy and snapped me out of the moment.

Until I lock eyes with the shadow.

He's still in the same pose — long legs outstretched, arms folded across his chest — and his eyes aren't closed like Jackie instructed.

They're wide open, and completely zeroed in on me.

I blink at the boldness of them, of *him* — his gaze and his demeanor. His eyes are a bright, Caribbean water blue — almost see through, almost green, almost gray. They're light and playful as they take me in, and just as Jackie signals for everyone to open their eyes, he smiles at me.

Just a tiny curl of his lips, but it does something to my stomach that I *do not* like.

"Alright," Jackie says, and I tear my eyes from the shadow and back to her. "Who would like to start?"

The group takes turns sharing, then — tentative hands raising before something good or bad from the week is divulged. Jonathan had a phone call with his daughter, though it was short and he could tell she didn't want to talk to him. He felt like it was a step in the right direction, but was seeking advice on how to bridge that conversation gap between them. Kendall had a breakthrough when she was shopping with her sister and resisted the urge to steal a pair of earrings.

It goes like this for nearly an hour, and I listen to everyone speak, nodding in empathy and offering words of encouragement when it feels right. I really do like being in the group, for as much of a fit I threw about going in the first place. I might not be the most talkative, but I do like helping others when I can, and I like feeling like I'm not alone in my struggle to move past all my own shit.

"Erin, what about you?" Jackie asks toward the end of session. "Anything going on with you this week?"

I take a deep breath, adjusting my legs to cross the opposite way as I balance my notebook in my lap. "Well, school is back in session," I remind her and the group. "And sorority life, too. So... it's been interesting, adjusting to having classes and responsibilities again. But it feels good. I'm redoing a wing of our sorority house and helping some of the other sororities plan their philanthropy events. Being president keeps me busy, and I've found when I'm busy, I don't have time to dwell on everything that makes me sad."

"But it's okay to be sad sometimes," Jackie gently reminds me.

I nod. "I know. Trust me, I still go there. But... I don't take out my sadness on the people I love anymore. At least, I'm trying not to. There are still some bridges I'm trying to mend but..." I scratch the back of my neck, thinking of Skyler.

Of Clinton.

"Well, all things in time, I suppose," I finish.

Jackie smiles. "That's exactly right. And what are you working on this week?"

My heart squeezes. "Writing letters. I'm trying to write letters to the people I know I hurt... not necessarily to send, but just to figure out my feelings."

"What happened to you?"

The question is loud and abrupt, and all heads swing to the shadow, who's looking at me with his fierce eyes again.

I swallow. "Sorry?"

"What'd you do? Who'd you hurt? What happened to you to make you come here?"

Jackie smiles apologetically at me, and then she addresses the shadow in a soft tone. "We actually don't encourage questions like that here," she says. "We prefer to let our guests speak about whatever it is that they're comfortable with."

He keeps his eyes on me when he speaks. "That doesn't really make sense, does it? Isn't the whole point of therapy to talk about your shit and work through it?"

"I *have* talked about my shit," I say to him, folding my hands over my notebook. "You weren't here. Sorry you missed the show."

"So, tell me now."

"I don't feel like talking about it today."

"Why not?"

My heart picks up its pace, but this stranger isn't backing down. He just cocks his head, like he's trying to figure me out, like I'm a puzzle to be solved.

"Why don't you tell us about you, instead?" Jackie offers, noting the flush of my cheeks at all the attention.

The shadow smiles then, shrugging before he turns to Jackie. "Okay. I'm Gavin Lindberg. I'm a graduate student at Palm South. And I'm here because I got drunk and slammed my car into a tree with my little sister in the passenger seat. I killed her."

He says the words with conviction, with punctuation, as if each word is a fist he's throwing into our jaws. I feel each punch, and when he's done, he looks at me again.

"I had an abortion that I didn't tell anyone about, and when I finally healed from that, I was gang-raped by a guy I was seeing and three of his fraternity brothers," I say, not backing down from his gaze. "Then, I became the villain, and I hurt everyone I love most."

The room goes completely silent, and my heart beats so loud in my ears I wonder if they can all hear it, too.

Gavin smiles, and so softly under his breath that I almost don't hear him, he says, "There she is."

Jackie wraps up our session a few minutes later with another breathing exercise, and as soon as we're dismissed, various members join in little groups to chat and finish up the last of the donuts. I'm just throwing my purse over my shoulder when I feel body heat behind me.

When I turn, I'm met with those piercing blue eyes up close and personal.

I wait for him to speak, but for the longest time, he just looks at me, his eyes trailing over me from head to toe. It's not in a way that creeps me out, oddly — not like he's checking me out or assessing my size.

Just like he's *seeing* me, like he's taking the time to look at the girl I hide from everyone else.

When his eyes finally trail up to mine again, he slides his hands into the pockets of his dark jeans, and that same crooked grin finds his lips.

"Thanks for sharing," he says.

And then he brushes past me and walks out the door without another word to anyone else.

Ashlei

Walking back into *Okay, Cool* feels a lot like coming home.

I greet everyone on my way in, taking a little more time to chat with MyKayla at the front desk. She catches me up on her online dating ventures, while I fill her in on how Kappa Kappa Beta recruitment was and how classes have been so far. Then, I make my way to my new, *permanent* cube, and I sit down in the chair with my chest swelling as I adjust my little keyboard.

This is *mine.*

I feel it deep in my soul, that earned possession. Now that everyone knows about me and Mr. Church, I'm free from having to hide anything about myself. And with my internship being over, I've fully transitioned into a full-time paid position.

Ashlei Daniels, Account Manager at *Okay, Cool.*

My heart flutters a little with the feel of it. After my internship ended, I offered to extend over the summer, and of course, Brandon okayed it. And in the middle of July, my manager offered me the full-time position.

It wasn't that I was shocked at the offer, but more so that it had come not from Brandon, but from my manager and her team. *They* wanted me here, and not because I gave great blow jobs.

Because I'd *earned* my spot.

Another smile finds my lips as I log into my computer, going through the flurry of emails that came in while I was gone. I took four weeks off between my internship and my first day in my new position, mostly to be there for Jess during recruitment, and to get through syllabus week before work got crazy.

And then, there was the weekend in the Bahamas with Brandon.

I bite my lip as last weekend flashes through my mind — days spent on the boat and exploring the island, nights spent wrapped in the sheets. My skin is still bronzed from the island sun, the tan line left from my swimsuit top visible around my neck, and I run my finger over it with my cheeks flushing.

It had been absolutely perfect, wasting away a few days with him before we both got back to reality. I could still close my eyes and see his eyes dancing in the candlelight over our private dinners served on the yacht, could hear his laughter as I swam with the pigs and one nipped at the strings of my bikini, untying the bottoms, could still feel his warm hands framing my face as he swept his lips over mine on the beach, the moon high and full above us, waves crashing gently at our feet.

I sigh, feeling warmth spread through my chest like that island sunshine.

I've known Brandon for a full year now, and somehow, he still manages to surprise me.

He's still on my mind after I have lunch with MyKayla, so before my first team meeting, I slip into his office, hellbent on sneaking a kiss or two.

That plan is throttled, however, when I walk in and find two, long, tan and toned legs with red-bottom stilettos strapped to the feet hanging from the edge of his desk.

I stop in the doorway, following the line of those legs up to the body attached to them. The girl sitting on the corner of his desk — the desk he'd bent me over too many times to count — is younger than me, by the looks of it, with long, bleach-blonde hair and lips painted the same bright red as the bottom of her Louboutins. She's wearing a chic, black pencil skirt with a crisp, white button-up top that cuffs at her elbows. She has her arms wrapped around a binder, and her eyes on my boyfriend as she laughs.

As he laughs with her.

I'm not sure how long I stand there — it must only be a fraction of a second, though it feels like hours. And when the laughter subsides, Brandon finds me in the doorway, and his smile somehow stretches even wider.

"Well, if it isn't our brand-new account manager," he says, standing and fastening the button of his blazer. He turns his attention back to the girl. "Sophie, this is Ashlei Daniels. She started as an intern, too, and today is her first day as a full-time employee."

Sophie turns her wide, sparkling, honey eyes to me, then.

We're practically twins.

"Wow, so *you're* the famous Ashlei Daniels," she says, genuinely.

She stands then, and I take a breath that doesn't burn quite as badly now that her legs aren't dangling off Brandon's desk anymore.

"Sophie Miller," she says, extending her hand for mine. I shake it with the best smile I can muster. "I've heard a lot about you already."

"Have you, now?" I ask, quirking a brow at Brandon.

"You have a great reputation here," she explains. "I've only been here two weeks and already I've heard your name referenced a million times. It's nice to finally put a face to the name."

The longer she talks, the more I realize I can't figure her out. At first, she seemed bubbly and sweet, but something about the firmness of her handshake, the way her eyes linger on mine, the confidence in the way she holds her shoulders back, in her smile...

It puts me on edge.

It's like she already owns this place and everyone who works here, too.

"That's sweet," I say when our hands release. "It's nice to meet you."

"Sophie is already making a name for *herself*, too," Brandon says, circling his desk to join us on the other side of it. "Two weeks in and she's already brought in a new client."

Brandon smiles at Sophie, and she beams under his gaze like a prized peacock.

I narrow my eyes.

I don't know why jealousy is flaring hot and bird-like in my chest, but it is, and I hate that I feel threatened by this girl just as much as I hate that I had no idea who she was before this very moment.

Why hadn't Brandon mentioned her to me?

Then again, why *would* he?

I've been off work for three weeks. I've repeatedly told him *not* to talk about work around me because it was my break, my time off, my vacation.

Now, I'm back.

And apparently, there's a new girl in town.

Sophie waves him off, blushing — and I swear to God, my fists curl at my sides at the sight of those stupid red cheeks.

"You're too kind, Mr. Church," she says, tucking a strand of hair behind her ear as she peeks up at him through her lashes.

Yes, *peeks up at him*, like a shy little girl.

"I'll get these reports on your desk by the end of the day," she says, patting the binder in her hands. Then, she turns to me, and there's a glint of something in her eyes when she smiles. "It was *so* nice to meet you, Ashlei. I look forward to working together."

I smile, too. "Yes, you too, Sophie."

With one last little wave of her fingers, she's gone, and Brandon pulls me into his arms for a kiss that distracts me long enough to forget why my chest was tight in the first place.

Why did I just feel threatened by a freaking *intern*?

I shake my head at myself, wrapping my arms around Brandon's neck with a sigh. "Hi," I say.

"Hey, you. How's the first day back going?"

"It's busy," I admit. "Took all morning just to catch up on emails and get my calendar in order. I'm about to walk into my first meeting, but I wanted to see you first."

"I'm glad you stopped by," he says, releasing me and putting a work-appropriate distance between us. "We still on for dinner tonight?"

"You bet your sweet ass, we are."

He chuckles. "Good luck at your first meeting, babe."

My heart flutters at the pet name, and he leans in to kiss my cheek before rounding his desk to get back to work. I'm almost to the door of his office when I turn again, watching him, something pulling at a string tied around my chest.

He stops typing, looking at me with a frown. "Everything okay?"

There's a question looming inside that aching chest of mine, but I can't quite figure out what it is. All I *do* know is that it was born from jealousy.

And that that jealousy is unfounded.

So, I force a breath and smile, shaking my head. "Just taking one last look at my hot boyfriend."

Brandon rolls his eyes, balling up a piece of notebook paper on his desk and throwing it at me. I catch it and toss it up in the air before pretending to slam-dunk it in the waste bin by his door.

"See you tonight, cheese ball."

"Tonight," I echo.

And I ignore what's left of that burning question as I make my way down the hall to my meeting.

My best friend is out of orbit.

I've been suspicious of it since the summer, when he all but ignored me. And once we got back to school for fall semester, I knew it was true. He's too quiet, too broody, too shut off. He's not cracking jokes or cracking beers, and both are tell-tale signs that he's not okay.

Which is exactly why I'm flopped on the bean bag in Clinton's room while his legs hang off his bed above me, both of our eyes fixed on his television screen. We're both silent, save for the clicking of buttons as we play some stupid video game that I only marginally understand.

But that silence is about to be broken, because I'm tired of pretending like everything is fine.

"So," I say as our characters traipse through the mystical woods of another world in search of our next mission. "How are classes going so far?"

Clinton grunts in lieu of an answer.

"That good, huh?"

No answer.

"You been spending a lot of time with Becca?"

Again, he doesn't answer, and when I glance at him, he just shrugs.

"How's Baby Bear?" I ask, referring to his little brother.

"Seems good."

I sigh, pausing the game before I pop up off the bean bag and sit on the bed next to him. He scowls at the screen, trying to restart the game on his own controller, but since I'm the one who paused it, the play remains frozen.

"Bear, can we stop? Please?"

"Stop playing?"

I narrow my eyes. "Yes. The video game *and* whatever game it is you've been playing since last semester." I relax my glare on a sigh, reaching over to squeeze his forearm — which is so buff from all his working out that I can barely squeeze it at all. "Something is going on. Talk to me."

Bear drops his shoulder and the controller at that, a long exhale leaving his giant chest as he scrubs his hands over his face. When his hands fall, he stares at the paused television screen, opening his mouth before he closes it again.

"My mom is back."

I blanch, because that was the absolute *last* thing I was expecting him to say. "Back? As in..."

"As in, she messaged Clayton on Facebook a couple weeks ago, and I told him not to answer until I talked to her."

"And did you?"

He nods, just once, barely visible.

I swallow. "What did she say?"

"I asked her what the hell she was doing messaging Clayton, and told her if she was looking for more money to piss the fuck off."

"Fair," I say, but I reach for his hand, squeezing it in my own because I know this kind of callousness doesn't come from my best friend unless he was really, really hurt.

"She said she just wanted to talk, to catch up. She's back in Pittsburgh."

"Shit..."

"I told her to stay away from Clayton. At least, until I can see her and make sure she's clean."

"What'd she say to that?"

Bear finally looks at me then. "She booked me a plane ticket home."

At that, my jaw hinges open. "She... like, she *paid* for it?"

He nods. "I'm going the weekend before Halloween."

A long silence passes between us, and I watch him, searching his eyes for some sort of clue as to what he feels about all of it.

"Want me to go with you?"

He shakes his head immediately. "I need to do this on my own."

"Okay," I whisper. "So... this just happened a couple weeks ago?"

He nods.

"Then... what's been going on before this? You haven't been yourself all summer, all fall semester."

Clinton's jaw ticks, but before he can answer me, his eyes shift to something behind me, and he stands.

I turn, finding my Big standing in the frame of his bedroom door.

Erin is completely put together, as she always is, with a Lily Pulitzer dress and matching bow in her hair. But aside from her perfect makeup and outfit, there's something off about her, too. There has been ever since she betrayed me at Spring Break last year.

But whereas I've felt a calling to find out what's wrong with Bear, I haven't felt anything toward Erin.

Other than the urge to stay away from her.

Her big, brown eyes are locked on Bear, and when I look up at him, he's staring right back at her. Erin's hands are folded in front of her, and she picks at her nails, but Bear just stands stoic, unflinching, his jaw still hard set from our conversation.

I finally clear my throat, addressing Erin. "Uh... what's up?"

Erin blinks, as if I've woken her from a daze, and then her eyes find mine. "I was hoping I could talk to you."

She says the words to me, but her eyes move to Bear's again, and I can't help but feel whatever weird tension is going on between them. I know they were friends before last semester, but I also know that Bear lit her ass up after what she did to me and Kip. I had no idea if they'd ever worked through it.

Judging by the way they're acting now, I'd say it's a big fat *nope*.

"Um, sure," I answer, standing. I turn, giving Bear a big hug and assuring him I'll text later before I make my way to where Erin is.

She and Bear don't exchange a single word.

When we're out of the Omega Chi house and on Greek Row, Erin takes a deep breath, like she'd been stuck on an exhale the entire time we were inside.

"Thank you for talking to me," she starts.

I nod, and for a few steps we're both quiet, other than the clicking of her kitten heels and my sandals on the sidewalk.

"I know things aren't going to get better overnight," she says after a while. "Between us. I know I royally screwed up. I betrayed you, asked you to do something... *horrid*," she whispers, shaking her head. "And then I went full-on crazy and you were in the line of fire."

My nose flares, but I tell myself to listen, to be open to what she has to say.

"But," she continues. "I've been going to therapy for months now, and something I'm really trying to do is make amends with the people I've hurt."

Her expression morphs then, her brows folding together as she casts a glance back at the Omega Chi house. Then, she lets out a long sigh.

"Last semester, when I apologized, it wasn't sincere. I know that now, looking back. I tried to blame you, too — to make it somehow partly your fault that I did what I did to you."

She stops walking, waiting for me to face her, and it's such an interesting sight to behold — this perfectly put-together girl falling apart on Greek Row on a sunny, South Florida day.

"I am so sorry, Sky. Truly," she whispers, her bottom lip quivering. "I'm sorry I asked you to lure Kip in for me, that I manipulated you with the presidency, that I turned on you in front of everyone we know." She chokes on a sob, shaking her head and covering her mouth. "I am truly ashamed. I was in a very, very dark place, but that does not excuse what I did to you. And I hope we can start over, from this moment on. And I don't expect you to forgive me, but I hope one day we can have a friendship again."

My heart breaks at the sight of two tears streaming simultaneously down each of her cheeks, and I sigh, reaching out for her. In the next instant, she's in my arms, holding me so tightly I chuckle.

"I already forgave you," I tell her. "But I appreciate the genuine apology." I pull back then, looking her in the eyes. "And I'm sorry I've been avoiding you. I just... I guess part of me wondered if that version of you I saw last semester was still hanging around. I was a little scared."

"That's fair," she says, sniffing. She pulls a tissue from her purse and wipes daintily at her nose. "That version of me was an absolute monster."

"And who are you now?"

She laughs at that, shaking her head as she folds the tissue. "Figuring that out."

I smile, squeezing her arm. "You said you were in a dark place... what happened?"

"Oh, boy," she says, blowing out a breath and looking around Greek Row. Then, she loops her arm through mine, steering me toward the house once more. "There's a lot more to the story of everything that happened last semester, and before that. But... I can't tell you. Not yet, okay? I'm just... I'm not there yet." She looks at me with a glossy smile. "But I will be. One day. Hopefully soon."

I cover her hand that's looped through my arm, smiling back. "Whenever you're ready."

"Right now, I was kind of thinking... margaritas?"

I nudge her. "Oh, now you're just trying to butter me up."

"Is it working?"

"Add in some chips and guac, and I'll be as buttered as a biscuit."

We both laugh, and just like that, the past is the past.

At least, for now.

Adam

The last two weeks have been hell.

After seeing Cassie with Grayson, I completely lost it. I found myself in one of my old habits — numbing. And I knew it was wrong. I knew it wasn't healthy. But there was literally nothing I could do to stop it.

I *still* can't.

For the last couple of weeks, I've thrown myself into everything Alpha Sigma. I've spent more time with my brothers, worked on our plans for the semester and next, and more than anything, dedicated time and effort to getting everything in order for tonight's event.

The Alpha Sigma Karaoke Showdown.

Jeremy had me worried, after our conversation a couple weeks ago, that I'd made a terrible decision in changing up the event. After all, he was right — the concert *had* been successful for two years. It was part of what got our fraternity on the map again. And as soon as it had a reputation, I get the big idea to go and change it up.

But now, halfway through the event and having already raised more than double what we did with the concert funds last year, I know I've made the right choice.

And still, I feel numb.

It doesn't matter that the event has gone over without a hitch, that every fraternity and sorority showed up to participate and compete, that the crowd is *packed* with students from all over campus, here for the entertainment and the opportunity to help determine the winners.

It's exactly as I imagined it.

Except that in my mind, I always saw Cassie right by my side through it all.

And since that day, I've been avoiding her.

It's not that I don't want to be with her. It's the exact opposite, really. But, the first few times we hung out after I saw her with Grayson, I tried several different ways to get her to bring up that she'd talked to him. I asked about her classes, asked if anything strange had happened, asked if there was anything going on that she needed to talk about. I literally asked her in every single way I could without coming right out with it.

And she hadn't said a word.

She still hasn't told me that she spoke to him. For all she knows, I'm still oblivious to the fact that she's talked to him at all since she found out he cheated on her at her semi-formal last year.

I've tried to understand, tried to give her space, tried to put my anger at bay by throwing myself into other things.

But one thing remains ominously true.

She's hiding something from me, and now, I no longer trust her.

Every day, when that thought crosses my mind, a sharp pain like a knife to the gut passes through me. It happens again as I make my way across the large lawn where we're hosting the concert during intermission. She's standing with some of her sisters and my brothers, smiling and blushing and watching me walk toward her.

And I feel nothing but betrayal.

"There he is!" Kade says from where he's standing in the crowd. He rushes over to me, launching himself high into the air and forcing me to catch him whether I want to or not. When he's cradled in my arms — the beast of a guy — he rubs his knuckles against my skull. "El Presidente, putting on the best damn show this school has seen."

I chuckle, dropping him to the ground to the tune of light applause and other brothers joining in on his sentiments.

It's a moment that should fill me with pride, but instead, I only feel dread. Because the moment Kade is out of my arms, Cassie's in them.

"You're doing amazing!" she squeals, hugging me hard before she presses up on her toes to give me a kiss. Her soft green eyes are bright and wide under the hanging lights spanning the massive length of the yard — a last-minute touch I'd added to make it feel like a backyard barbecue — and her hair is smooth and straight, angling at her chin in a way that makes me stare at her lips.

"Thanks, babe," I say, but I immediately release her.

I don't miss the way she frowns up at me, but luckily I don't have to answer for my actions. Jess is next in line to congratulate me.

"Not bad for an Alpha Sigma shindig," she says, cocking one brow.

"Is there a compliment hidden somewhere in there?"

Kade shakes his head, clapping me on the shoulder. "Trust me, coming from this one?" He points a thumb at Jess. "That *is* a compliment. A high one."

She narrows her gaze at him, but then smiles, poking him hard in the ribs until he releases his hand on my shoulder and throws his arm around hers, instead. She crosses her arms like she's annoyed, but I don't miss the way she leans into him.

I have no idea what the fuck those two are.

They've been doing something close to seeing each other, and something equally as close to being mortal enemies, ever since the end of spring semester. But I've given up on trying to figure them out — especially since I have my own fish to fry.

After a few more notes of congrats, conversation moves away from me, everyone falling back into what they were discussing before I showed up. One of the students we hired to walk around with red plastic cups of beer on fancy serving platters walks past us, and I snag a beer from them, draining half of it in one swallow.

"Need some booze for those nerves, huh?" Cassie teases, threading her arms around me and looking up at me with her gorgeous eyes again. I usually love them, the way they always seem to find me, to light me on fire, to fill me up from the inside.

Now, I just wonder what else they're hiding.

"Something like that," I murmur.

"Everything is perfect," she says, looking around at the packed yard. It's the same place we had the concert in prior years, but we've completely transformed it this time around. The lights strung high above us, criss-crossing the space between the fake plants on either side, make it feel like a private, exclusive event. We found clever ways to weave the casual in with the fancy, the backyard family feels with the black-tie event vibes. Music plays from the stage, where the next groups of karaoke singers are getting set up, and without a doubt, I know that everyone is having a blast. "It's everything you wanted it to be and more."

She's right.

And yet, I'm counting down the minutes until it's over, until I can be alone again.

I sigh, chugging the last of my beer before trading it in for another. Cassie takes it away before I can drink too much.

"Hey," she says on a giggle, raising one eyebrow. "Maybe save the celebrating for *after* the event? You still have to get up there and emcee."

"I'm fine," I say, snatching the beer back from her. I don't mean to, but in the attempt, half of it splashes onto her shirt.

She gasps, stepping back from me, shocked at first, but then laughing. "Jerk," she says, shoving me playfully as she flicks the liquid off her hands. She even pegs me with a few droplets. "You're lucky you're cute. And that I happen to loooove you."

Cassie drags out the word *love*, long and sweet and adorable, coming in to cuddle me again regardless of the wetness of her shirt.

My jaw clenches, heart stopping altogether when I look down at her. "Do you?"

Her smile falls, brows tugging together. "Of course I do." Then, her eyes search mine, her arms tightening where they hold me. "Adam, what's going on? Are you okay?"

I can't help the smile that unleashes itself on my face, and it's an evil one — one accented by a chesty, one-syllable laugh before I drain my beer again. I toss the red cup in the nearby trashcan, shaking my head as I peel Cassie off me.

"I better get back up there."

She grabs my hand and pulls me back. "Adam," she pleads. She doesn't say anything else, but her eyes say everything her mouth isn't.

Talk to me.

Don't push me away.

I love you.

What's wrong?

I swallow, ripping my hand free from her grasp and shaking off the bad mood as I make my way back to the stage. Then, I finish the show, announce a final donation to our philanthropy that blows everyone out of the water, and high-five my brothers after an event well-done.

And I text Cassie, telling her I need to stay back to clean up and to head out without me.

I feel like shit, like an absolute fucking asshole.

But I also feel validated.

I don't want to hurt her. It's the *last* thing I want. But the truth is, she's hurting me. She's had her chance to tell me about Grayson — multiple times — and she hasn't. And maybe I should just ask her about it, but if I'm being honest with myself, I don't think I should have to.

If we're together, if she's my person and I'm hers... shouldn't we be honest with each other, always? No matter what?

That's what's on repeat in my mind as I help my brothers wrap up the event, as we celebrate well into the next morning, as I lie in bed hungover the next afternoon, with my eyes on the ceiling and the girl who's driven me crazy for years the only thing on my mind.

And the truth of what I'm feeling kills me.

Cassie can *say* she loves me all she wants to.

But until her actions line up with those words, I'm not sure I can believe them anymore.

Erin

Bear,

I've started this letter and torn it up a thousand times, it seems. I don't think there are words to say what I need to say to you. I've tried and tried to find the right ones, but I always come up empty-handed.

I guess I should just start by saying that I am sorry.

But, God, that sounds so trite.

I want to roll my eyes at those words. They aren't enough. They don't do justice to how I really feel, to how much I care for you, to how badly it kills me to know that I hurt you.

They do nothing to explain what the choice I made did to me — long before you knew.

So, I'm going to try to explain. I know most of this won't make sense. Most of this won't

The alarm goes off on my phone, a bright, cheerful jingle that signals it's time for me to leave to head to group therapy. I silence it, and then stare at yet another unfinished letter to Clinton. There's a pile of them in the waste bin next to my desk, and I crumple this one up into a ball and toss it in with the others.

The letter is still in my mind as I drive to therapy. The little church it's held in is off campus, just a short, ten-minute drive, but it's long enough to let me mull over the fact that I'm never going to be able to write out what I want to say to Clinton.

"You don't need to send the letters," my therapist had told me at our last session. *"Just write them to the people you've hurt, and say what you're too scared to say to them in person."*

I'd thought the exercise was annoying and cliché at first, but then... it had worked.

At least, sort of.

I'd written a letter to Skyler, and while I didn't give the letter to her, writing it helped me find the courage to talk to her. And now, we had finally taken a real, genuine step to putting everything that happened last semester behind us. I know we have a long way to go yet, but just having the conversation healed me in a way I couldn't fully understand.

Since then, I've written letters to my parents, to my unborn child, to my rapists, and to all of my closest friends — Jess, Lei, Cassie.

But I can't seem to write one for Bear.

If I could have anything in the world, it would be to have my friendship with Bear again. The way we used to be. Before he knew.

I'm still in a fog of thoughts when I make my way into therapy, and just like always, I bypass the donuts and the coffee and take my usual seat, pulling out a notebook and setting my purse in my lap.

And when I look up, Gavin Lindberg is staring at me.

The jolt of those electric blue eyes is enough to stop my next breath, and I stare back at him, unflinchingly, until Jackie asks everyone to find their seats and that we're about to begin. It's only at the sound of her voice that I finally blink, and with that blink, the rest of the room seems to come back to me in a whoosh.

I clear my throat, looking from him to Jackie, instead, and I keep my focus on her or whoever is speaking for the rest of group session. I'm not in the mood to talk today, so I just sit quietly and listen, and smile, and nod, and think.

And *not* look at Gavin Lindberg.

"Alright, that wraps us up for today," Jackie says after our breathing exercise. "Before you go, I want to leave you all with one last thought... this week, while you're going about your normal routine, I want you to ask yourself what you miss about what you perceive as *the old you*. If anything comes to mind, write it down. You don't have to do anything, not yet, I just want you to jot down anything that you used to do, or used to have, that you feel is lacking now."

I chew the inside of my cheek, already mentally noting a dozen things that I miss about the girl I used to be. I decide to write them down later, though — mostly because I'm already late to the Panhellenic meeting and I still need to set the house up for our KKB movie night.

As I'm packing my notebook into my purse, a shadow steps between me and the overhead fluorescent light, and I pause, letting my eyes slowly crawl up to Gavin's waiting face.

I hadn't noticed last week how tall he was, but as I stand, my eyes only coming to the base of his neck, I realize it. He's very tall. And very lean. And very... *dark*. It isn't just his hair or his clothes, but the way he stands, the hidden storm in his eyes, the lines in his face that somehow seem to hold more history than that of an old and tired man.

His skin is a golden brown, almost olive, like he's from the Mediterranean, and since he's not wearing a hat this week, I can see that his hair is a deep, rustic brown. It's short, but a little untidy, with ends sticking up here and there. And just like last week, he's dressed in dark, distressed jeans and a black t-shirt that says *Thy Art is Murder* on it.

"Hi," he says when I shrug my purse over my shoulder.

I swallow. "Hi."

"I wanted to apologize."

"Oh," I say, sweeping my hair behind one ear and over my shoulder.

"Yeah. So... this is me. Apologizing."

"You're doing great."

"I'm really very good. At practically everything. It's a curse."

I smile, and a quiet moment passes between us, with him staring at me and me checking the time on my watch.

"Seriously," he says when I meet his gaze again, shoving his hands in his pockets like they'll betray him if he leaves them dangling free. "Last week... I was a bit prickly. I didn't want to be here, and I... I don't really know why I attacked you like I did, but I'm sorry."

"It's okay," I assure him. "Really. I didn't think it was an attack at all. And, I get it. I didn't want to be here the first few times I came, either."

"And now?"

At that, I sigh, shrugging a little as I look around the room at the fellow misfit toys. "Now, I worry less about what I want, and more about what I need."

When our eyes meet again, there's an understanding there — one unlike any I've ever felt before. It's the kind of universal tug at my heart, at my soul, that makes me feel like I'm tethered to a stranger. Like somehow, there's a piece of me in them, and a piece of them in me.

After a minute, Gavin nods, and then without another word, he brushes past me and toward the door.

I stand for a second, face screwing up in a bit of confusion at the abrupt exit. But when I shake my head and turn to head for the door myself, I nearly run into Gavin where he's stopped and turned around.

I manage to put the brakes on before I run straight into his chest, but we're still a little too close for two people who just met when he looks down the crooked bridge of his nose at me and asks, "Would you like to have dinner with me?"

My eyes shoot open wide.

"Next week," he says when I don't answer. "After group. We can go wherever you want, unless it's Italian or Indian food because I hate both."

I bite my lip against the laugh that comes from me then, because it's both unexpected and absolutely lovely. I forgot what it feels like, to laugh like that, to feel joy fizzing in your chest like champagne bubbles.

At the sight of my smile, the side of Gavin's lips tug up, too, until he's wearing a shy smirk that somehow fits him perfectly.

"Sure," I say.

I debate offering him my number, but I don't have the chance. As soon as I agree, his smile ticks up a bit more, and then he nods at me, turns, and rushes out the door.

And I stand there in his dust, still a little sad from earlier, a little confused from our interaction, and a little something else, too.

Though I can't quite put my finger on what.

EPISODE 3

Cassie

If you would have told me ten months ago that I would be sitting next to Grayson Anderson, listening to him play a new song, *without* wanting to strangle him and spit in his eye — I would have told you you were crazy.

Almost a year later, and I can still close my eyes and see him outside of semi-formal last year, talking to Malik, admitting that he had been screwing some girl named Alexis while we'd been dating.

While I'd been falling in love with him.

While I'd been trusting him.

While I'd been thinking about giving myself to him fully.

And once I had, he'd apparently told that girl to kick rocks — but that didn't change the fact that all the time I was dedicating to him, he was giving to someone else.

He'd cheated on me. He'd broken my heart. And I'd sworn I'd never forgive him.

But here I am, sitting next to him on the bench outside the science building, listening to him strum on his guitar and watching strands of his long hair fall out of the bun at the nape of his neck, into his face.

For the first couple weeks of class, I dutifully ignored him. Unfortunately for *me*, we were assigned lab partners during week three — which made it impossible to ignore him any further, unless I wanted to fail Genetics.

And I don't fail *anything*.

Still, I wasn't keen on the idea, and only conceded after Professor Drumm said I didn't have a prayer in changing partners, anyway.

Grayson asked me for forgiveness. He asked me for friendship.

And damn it if that doesn't hit some super soft bruise inside me that I didn't even realize existed.

Something I learned from my older sister is that holding onto a grudge, or something that hurt you, is useless. Giving anyone or anything that power only strips you of it and holds you back.

So, when Grayson poured his heart out, trying to get me to understand that he was in a bad place, I listened. When he told me his parents were already on his ass to change his major back then, at the same time his music career was taking off, I could see the internal struggle he must have been facing. And when he promised me he never meant to hurt me, and that if he could take it all back, he would — I believed him.

I don't have to forgive him, and I told him that much. But he asked for a chance for a friendship, and because I don't know how to stay mad at people who hurt me, I'm giving him one.

Or at least, I'm trying.

"That was really good," I say when he finishes the last note of the song. "Are you going to record it?"

Grayson sweeps his hair back off his face, something of a grin on his lips. "No more recording for me. I just do it for fun."

It's the middle of October, which should mean boots and scarves and pumpkin-spiced lattes — but in South Florida, it just feels like Summer Part Two. It's fifteen minutes until noon and I'm already sweating, my thighs sticking to the bench we're sitting on.

"Why? Just because you changed your major doesn't mean you can't still focus on your music."

"It does when I'm already behind in credits, and science might as well be another language to me," he argues. Then, he nudges me where I sit beside him on the bench. "Unlike you, brainiac."

"So *that's* what happened here — you bribed the professor to be my lab partner so you could pass, huh?"

"Damn it, you caught me."

Something in my stomach twisted at that, because the last time I *caught him*, it'd nearly killed me.

Grayson must have noticed the shift in me, because he set his guitar to the side, crossing his ankle over the opposite knee. "I didn't notice when we were dating just how smart you are," he says. "But I was so far up my own ass, I guess, that I didn't really see much at all."

I nod, because though it didn't feel like it back then, I look back on the time we dated now and see just how wrapped up I was in him. It was always me going to his shows, his place, hanging with his friends. Sure, he came to sorority events after I begged him to, but for the most part, I was happy to lose myself in who he was and not talk about me at all.

With Adam, it's the complete opposite.

He always builds me up, asks me about my classes, about my *dreams*. It's not just the here and now that he's fascinated with, but who I want to be next year, or in five years, or for the rest of my life.

It's like he knows he's going to be there with me, and he's so sure in that fact that he's determined to find out where he fits in my picture so he can step into the role fully.

My heart pinches the more I think about him, because as confident as I was at the beginning of the semester about us, something has changed in the last few weeks.

And I have no idea what's going on with him.

"Yeah, up your ass and probably a few other girls', too," I shoot back at Grayson, arching a brow.

He throws his hands up over his heart like he's been struck. "Ouch. Okay, I deserved that."

"You deserve a whole hell of a lot more than a jab for what you did." I shake my head, crossing my legs as my eyes scan the sidewalks for Adam. "You're just lucky I'm too nice to hand out punishment."

"I lost you."

I blink, turning back to him and finding sincerity laced in his gray eyes.

"Trust me," he whispers. "That was the worst punishment of all."

I swallow, something low and familiar hitting me deep in my belly at the sight of his pain. For so long, that boy had been everything to me. I'd loved him. I'd touched him and let him touch me, too.

God, is it awful that I've sort of missed him?

It's not that I want to be with him — not at *all*. Adam is everything I've wanted since I first stepped foot on this campus, even if we did have to take the long way around to finally be together.

But I miss talking to Grayson, miss listening to him play, miss the connection we've always had so effortlessly.

And I *hate* losing people.

It's the worst feeling in the world, in my opinion. I'd felt it the hardest when I'd lost my childhood best friend, Paris, after she'd betrayed me my freshman year. And it'd reverberated through me when I'd walked away from Grayson in that courtyard, knowing I'd never forgive him, that what we'd had was lost.

But now here we are, *trying* to be friends when it all seemed so impossible even a short month ago.

Something about that fills me with hope.

My gut drops again at the more pressing matter on my conscience — which is that I know when I tell Adam that Grayson and I are rekindling a friendship, he will be less than thrilled. And if there's one scar I don't want to reopen, it's the one that's still fresh from watching Grayson and Adam at each other's throats for an entire semester.

Last time the roles had been reversed.

But I have a feeling it won't matter to Adam that he's the one who has me now.

He still won't want to share.

I wanted to tell him after the first day of class, when I realized Grayson was in the same one. But at the time, there was really nothing to tell. We went to a small campus. It wasn't *that* weird that I ended up in the same class with my ex.

But once we started talking, once he apologized and asked me if we could try to be friends, I knew I needed to tell Adam — and I planned to.

Except he's been so distant.

First, it was the concert, and I didn't want to upset him when he already had so much to focus on. He had been stressed out that night, and it seemed like he'd been that way ever since. We haven't hung out much, and when we have, he's always on his phone, talking to Jeremy about fraternity stuff or working on his outline for Alpha Sigma Chapter or planning his next big thing — the Halloween bash.

But distractions or not, I have to tell him, and soon — which is why I'm not hiding the fact that I'm sitting with Grayson now as I wait for Adam to come by and meet me for lunch, like he used to do every day after this class.

When my phone buzzes in my pocket, I don't have to check it to know it's him saying he won't make it.

He's had some sort of excuse like that for the past couple of weeks, ever since his concert.

I sigh, pulling my phone from my pocket long enough to tell him it's okay and we'll catch up later, but my chest is tight as I do so. Jeremy had let it slip to me that night of the concert that some of the brothers had been giving Adam a hard time about spending so much time with me and not dedicating enough time to the fraternity, and ever since then, he's pulled back, focusing more on them and less on me.

Which is *fine*, I remind myself, because we're together all the time.

I can spare him and let him do his thing as president.

But I can't help but feel like there's something else going on, something he won't tell me...

"You okay?" Grayson asks, nodding toward my death grip on my phone with the open text message still glaring back at me.

I shake my head, finishing my text and shooting it back to Adam before I tuck my phone away again. "I'm fine."

"Mm. *Fine.* That's lady talk for *nothing is okay and I'm two seconds away from burning this whole motherfucking campus down.*"

I roll my eyes, but a soft smile finds my lips. "I really am fine."

"Didn't you say you're waiting on Adam?" he asks casually, picking up his guitar again. "What time is he coming by?"

"He's not," I say, checking my bitter tone as soon as I realize the way I said it. "Uh... he has a fraternity thing I forgot about. Got my days mixed up."

Grayson holds his guitar in his lap, balancing his arms on the top of it and watching me carefully. "Everything okay with you two?"

At that, I chuckle, pulling the strap of my backpack onto one shoulder and standing. "Not happening, Grayson."

"What?" he asks, feigning innocence.

"I know we're trying to be friends again, but you'll never be the one I lean on when there's something going on between me and Adam."

"So there *is* something."

I swallow, heart ticking up a notch at the realization that I let that slip.

"I'll see you Thursday at lab," I say instead of acknowledging his assessment, and I can tell in his eyes that he doesn't want me to go, that he wants to know more about everything I'm not saying, but I turn my back on him and start the walk toward the sorority house without another word.

When I get back to my room, Ashlei, Jess, and Skyler are piled in a fluff of blankets in the middle of the floor, their laptops in front of them. They all smile when I walk in, and Skyler scoots over, patting the space next to her.

"Grab your laptop and take a seat, Little," she says with waggling eyebrows. "It's time to plan our Halloween costumes."

Then, Jess hands me a flyer — one confirming what my own boyfriend hadn't even told me yet.

Alpha Sigma is hosting another Halloween party on the sandbar, and with a live DJ, fireworks show, and open bar sponsored by one of the local clubs, the neon orange flyer promises it will be even bigger and better than last year.

I somehow manage a smile despite the rollercoaster dip of my stomach, and I pull my laptop from my bag, plopping down next to my Big to surf costume ideas as she hands me the open bag of Doritos, taking one before she passes it.

But before I pull up Pinterest, I text Adam.

We need to talk.

Jess

There is no better feeling than having Kade's face buried between my thighs.

My hands are tangled in his hair, grabbing and pulling as I arch off his bed and grind my pelvis against his mouth. He already had a solid foundation in going down, but thanks to my expert teaching, he now knows just how to suck my clit, just how to curl his fingers inside me and make me writhe with aching need.

I finally understand that old saying now.

Hard work pays off.

When he releases the pressure, withdrawing his finger and rubbing the seam of my lips while he kisses inside my knee, I peer up at him through heavy lids, my lips parted, chest heaving.

"No," I whine, trying to drag his head back down. "Don't stop."

Kade smirks, balancing on his elbow with his face still fully between my thighs. Only now, he's stroking me between my wet and swollen lips, his fingertips skating over my clit before they dive back down again.

And all the while, he's sitting there with his stupid smirk, watching the show.

"Someone's close," he muses.

Something between a curse and a moan rips through me when he flattens his palm, rubbing it over the length of me with just enough pressure to have my whole body tensing and releasing at once, making me shiver and shake at the touch. I'm so wet from his mouth and my own desire that his hot skin slicks over me easily, and the more he rubs me, the more I feel that pressure mounting in my core.

Until he stops.

My eyes shoot open at the loss of heat, of connection, the cool air from his ceiling fan wafting over me uncomfortably.

"Damn it, Kade," I say, but before I can even lift my head to properly curse at him, his mouth is on mine, still covered with my salty taste as he backs me into the bed even more somehow.

His hand rests tentatively over me again, cupping me in warmth, and I gasp into his mouth at the sensation.

"If you want to get off," he whispers, sucking my lip between his teeth and holding it there before releasing it with a pop. "You'll have to get there yourself."

I narrow my eyes. "Fuck you," I spit, but then his hand cups me harder, and he moves it just an inch — up and back down — his deep brown eyes firing to life as he watches my eyelids flutter with the touch.

"Fuck my hand, Jess," he whispers, kissing my neck seductively, sucking my earlobe between his teeth. His next whisper is right into the shell of my ear, and it evokes a tsunami of chills over me. "I want you to fuck my hand until you come all over it, and then I can lick my fingers clean."

My mouth parts with a gasp, and in the next second his own covers mine, and he's kissing me hard and demanding, his hand just sitting there between my legs, warm and waiting.

I reach down with my own hands, holding his to me harder, and flex my hips.

Just that one motion has me sucking in a hot, stiff breath, and Kade devours it hungrily, kissing me harder as I buck my hips again.

His hand is so warm, so wet, and I hold it firm between my legs, rocking my hips back and forth, humping his palm as my clit fires to life. I know before a full minute has passed that I could get off just like that, without him even being inside me, but when I'm humping him hard and fast and he surprises me, slipping his middle finger deep and quick inside me before pulling out again, I groan at the feeling of being full.

"More," I pant, writhing under his touch. "I want you to fuck me, Kade."

"Not until you come."

I whimper, but it's silenced as soon as he dives back inside me again — this time with two fingers slipping easily into my soaked hole.

"Jesus Christ," I curse, and then without warning, I flip him over with his hand still cupping me, until the back of his palm is laying on his thick, muscular thigh and I'm straddling his fingers — all the while staring longingly at his thick, perfect, untouched erection.

Just the sight of it standing at attention pulses a new wave of need through me, and Kade's eyes intensify, urging me on. I sit back down on his fingers, feeling them deeper now, and he curls them inside me as I ride his hand the way I want to ride his cock.

The heat from his thighs press into every angle of my inner thighs, his palm hot on my clit, and I lean forward, getting more pressure where I need it and still fucking his fingers. And then everything clinches and releases, hot and fast, a lightning bolt of an orgasm striking me as I cry out.

Kade's hand slaps hard over my mouth, so much that it stings, but I cry into his left palm as I ride his right one, knowing he's just trying to save me from alerting the entire fraternity that he's getting me off.

Not that I care right now.

When my body slows, muscles already sore and aching, he removes his palm from my mouth with a knowing grin on his.

But before I can slump and let my climax lull me under, he sits up, kissing me hard and grabbing my ass firmly in both hands before he smacks it hard and flips me over.

I don't get another breath before he's wrapped in a condom and thrusting inside me — deep and urgent, every thick and pulsing inch filling me in quick, swift thrusts.

Damn, he's a good student.

This motherfucker was helpless just a few months ago, and now he's a sex god — one perfectly tailored to meet my kinky needs.

Maybe this deal wasn't a bad idea, after all.

Kade wraps both fists in my long hair and yanks hard, exposing my throat and cutting off my oxygen enough that I can't even cry out in approval. I'm so fucking turned on I could come again, but I don't have the chance before he pounds his climax into me, pulsing into the condom with subdued groans and his hands still in my hair.

He slows to a complete stop when he's done, releasing my hair, but then his hands pet down my back — slowly, softly, making goosebumps explode over my sensitive skin. He's still inside me, thrusting slowly and purposefully, and already I feel him softening, but he won't stop. Instead, he bends over me, pulling my back flush to his chest as he thrusts as deep inside me as he can with his erection quickly losing steam.

His mouth finds my ear, sucking the lobe, and then he grabs my chin and tilts it until he can claim my mouth.

I hate this kiss.

It's too intimate, too soon after making me come, too close to real feelings that I break it quickly and roll over on to my back, chuckling with a satisfied sigh and closing my eyes.

Kade drops down beside me, still panting, one hand resting on his chest and the other reaching over to rest on my knee.

"Jess?"

"Mm?" I ask, brushing my hair back from my face.

When I creak my eyelids open, he's there balanced above me, something unreadable in his dark eyes.

"I think you're hotter than I've ever fucking seen you right now."

His eyes sweep over me, and a blush shades my cheeks as I cover my face with my hands. It's seven o'clock in the morning and I haven't even brushed my hair, let alone put on a stitch of make-up. I was just horny when I woke up and couldn't wait.

Usually, I dress up in lingerie for this prick — mostly because I like to boss him around in the bed and make him feel like I'm his Dom.

But this morning, *he* took control.

And now, he's got my stomach riding on the wings of butterflies with his stupid, *too-nice-for-a-fuck-buddy* comment.

I shove him away playfully with a roll of my eyes. "Whatever."

Kade laughs, tucking his hands under his head with his gaze on the ceiling. "You should have seen your face, getting all goopy-eyed over that romantic comment."

"You wish."

"Deny it all you want, J-Love," he teases, glancing at me with an arched brow. "But you know damn well that was an A+ move."

I don't deny it, but I *definitely* don't confirm it, either. Kade waits for a moment before giving up with a chuckle, rolling over and grabbing his phone off his nightstand.

"I feel like a Skywalker, conquering the Force."

I snort, but Kade just sits there with that doofus smile, flipping through his texts.

"Might have to pull out all the tricks I've learned on some unsuspecting hottie at the Halloween party next week."

My stomach takes a deep dive off the bed, and my eyes shoot open, throat constricting. I attempt a swallow but come up empty, and then I'm pissed at my body for betraying me, for being affected by what he said when *clearly* we shouldn't be.

I can almost see it — my brain putting her hands on her hips, glaring at my body like *Bitch, what the hell is wrong with you?*

But even as I sit there and convince myself I shouldn't feel the way I do after Kade's little comment, the feeling only sinks in deeper, and I press a hand to my chest, forcing a swallow.

Wait — am I annoyed?

Am I... jealous?

I frown at the thought, because why the *hell* would I be jealous that Kade wants to hook up with some chick at the Halloween party next weekend? It's not like we're dating. It's not like we're even *close* to that. We had a deal — I teach him how to have some fucking game, and he gets me off and lets me drive his car.

Plain and simple.

Except when I turn and see his goofy smile on his face, and another girl's name on his phone screen, my chest tightens, body betraying me once more.

Maybe it's not so simple, after all.

Bear

Sitting in Mr. and Mrs. Harrison's backyard in Franklin Park, it's all I can do to keep my mouth shut and drink my beer while everyone else around me talks and laughs like everything is just peachy keen.

It's a perfect fall day, the bright blue sky virtually cloudless and letting the sun warm us where we sit around the small bonfire Mac's dad built. It's just cool enough to need the fire, and a light sweater, but not so cold that we need to bundle up or that we can't be outside enjoying the evening. I can't help but compare it to the hot and humid October day I left behind in South Florida when I got on the plane that took me back home just a couple days go, and perhaps what guts me is I don't know which one feels like home.

Honestly, neither really does anymore.

I've spent the weekend with my little brother, watching him dominate at his home football game Friday night, and then eating our way around Pittsburgh all day yesterday. It was the closest I've felt to myself since the day Erin told me about our unborn child, but I woke this morning with the same numbness, the same dread swimming in my stomach.

Because we were going to see our mother for the first time in two years.

I'd reached out to her after Clayton told me she was online again, and she asked to see us both. She wanted to explain, wanted to spend time with us, show us how much she'd changed. And while everything inside me wanted to scream at her to go fuck herself all the way off, I knew what my little brother wanted more than anything in the world was a relationship with at least one of his parents.

And since our dad was a piece of shit who took off shortly after Clayton was born, this was the only option.

It's a full house, with Mac and his sister, Kia, their parents, my little brother, me, and — the guest of the day — my mother.

Christine Pennington looks better than I've ever seen her look. Her normally ashen skin is golden brown and healthy, her big brown eyes wide and full of life, her smile no longer the dead one that I'd become accustomed to growing up, but rather one that glows and fills her entire face. She looks nothing like the profile picture on her new Facebook account — the one she'd contacted both me and Clayton on. That woman was skinny and drugged out and sad. The one sitting across the fire from me with a glass of water is healthy and sober and happy.

Still, I don't trust her.

And I don't like the way Clayton so easily does.

"I can't believe you've been in Mexico this whole time," Clayton says after our mother finishes off a story about her and my older brother, Carleton, in Tijuana drinking margaritas the size of their face. He had asked to come today, too, but I'd refused.

One fucked-up family member at a time.

"It was quite a ride," Mom muses, thumbing the condensation off the side of her glass with a smile. "The beaches there, they're just incredible." Her eyes find mine then. "Of course, I'm sure it's nothing compared to the beaches in Florida, right, baby?"

My nostrils flare at the pet name, because she hasn't ever called me her *baby*. Even before she bailed on her family, we had a strained relationship at best. Because unlike my younger brother who saw her as an angel, and my older brother who followed in her footsteps, I saw her for exactly who she was.

A monster.

And I wanted nothing but to get as far away from her as I could.

I take a sip of my beer in lieu of answering, and an awkward silence passes over everyone before Kia steers the conversation toward how Clayton and Mac are both doing so well in football. My shoulders ease a little once it's no longer my mother talking, until she somehow finds a way to bring it all back to her.

"I wish I could have seen you play your freshman year last year," she says to Clayton, reaching over to thumb his cheek. I don't miss the way his eyes light up at the affection. "I bet you were a stud."

"He really was. Made me look bad," Mac comments, nudging his best friend. "But now, we're dominating. Going to take this team all the way to state."

"Well, I can't wait to watch it."

I scoff, crushing the can of beer I just drained and tossing it in the bag for recycling before reaching into the cooler for another.

Everyone is quiet, and Mom looks hurt where she watches me across the fire.

"What?" I ask, cracking the top on my next can. "Disappointed that I'm not playing into your bullshit the way everyone else is?"

"Clinton," Mrs. Harrison warns me, but her husband touches her arm gently, shaking his head to indicate it's not her place. And while I respect the shit out of her for stepping up and caring for my brother like he was her own, right now, it really *isn't* her place.

"I'm not... I wasn't trying to..." Mom stammers.

"You're not what?" I ask, tilting my head. "Spewing off a bunch of lies like you always do? Showing up after ditching your family for two years for some vacation in Mexico and expecting it to all be okay?"

She swallows.

"I was just saying that I'm happy I'll be able to see him play," she whispers.

"Bullshit," I whisper, sucking down half my beer.

"Come on, bro," Clayton begs from across the fire just as Kia excuses herself to the restroom.

"No," I yell, and I surprise myself at how much my voice booms. Everyone else seems shaken, too, their eyes locked on me as I point across the fire at my brother. "Don't let her fool you. Don't let her get in your head with her lies. I've lived through enough of them to tell you that they only get better with age."

"I'm not lying," Mom says defensively, holding her chin high. "And I surely don't appreciate the way you're talking to me or about me right now, Clinton. I'm your mother."

At that, I bark out a loud, barrel-chested laugh. "Oh, are you? Because I thought mothers were supposed to take care of their children, not ask them for money time and time again, and then disappear and not talk to them for two years."

"Alright, Bear, I think that's—" Mr. Harrison starts, but he doesn't get to finish before I stand, towering over the fire and my mother on the other side of it.

"You're a liar, and an addict, and a piece of shit excuse for a mother, and I won't let you tear Clayton up the way you did me." I look at him then. "She won't be at your football games. She won't be here for your prom or senior night or graduation, either. Trust me when I tell you that she came back because she needs something." I turn on my mother again. "And as soon as she gets it, she'll be gone again."

Mom's bottom lip quivers, and I wish I felt a shred of remorse for what I said, but I feel nothing.

She stands, mumbling something about needing to get something out of her car before she excuses herself through the backyard gate. Mac's mom looks at her husband with worried eyes before chasing after her, and then I'm being shoved back by two surprisingly strong hands.

"What the fuck, Bear?!"

"Language, Clayton," Mr. Harrison warns, but he's already ushering Mac inside. "We'll leave you two alone, but just for the record, I don't appreciate any of that kind of disrespectful talk going down in my house. You understand me?" He looks briefly at my little brother, but his glare nearly burns a hole in my skull. "So, you two talk this out and cool down. Now."

I don't respond, but I do nod to let him know I've heard him, and a sliver of guilt seeps into my spoiled gut.

"Seriously, what the hell is wrong with you?" Clayton asks when we're alone. He's almost as tall as me now, with the lean and built body of a wide receiver, instead of the lanky one he'd had as a kid. I see the same shape of my eyes in his own, feel the same blood coursing through our veins, and though I know he's not a child anymore, I can't help but want to protect him like one. "We finally have her back in our lives, and you're doing everything you can to push her away."

"She left us," I remind him. "Our brother left *his* children, too. Now, they're back after two years of barely any word at all, and we're just supposed to listen to their stories, celebrate them, welcome them home with open arms?"

"People make mistakes, Bear," Clayton says. "Haven't you?"

I grit my teeth, looking away from him and at the half-open gate across the yard from us. Through the slit, I can see Mrs. Harrison holding my mother while she cries.

And it pisses me off even more.

"Yes, people *do* make mistakes. But unlike our mother, most people regret them. Most people do whatever they can to make amends and become a better person. But our mother, Clayton?" I point at the gate. "She is a fucking train wreck. She cares about no one but herself, and I know you want to believe her when she says she'll stay, that she'll be a better mother, but believe me when *I* say that she's lying."

"You don't know that."

"But I *do*," I urge, stepping into him and grabbing both his shoulders in my hands. "Who has been there for you your entire life? Who used to feed you when that woman wouldn't, change your diapers, play with you, care for you when you were sick? Who made sure you got up in time for school and got on the bus? Who made sure you took showers and brushed your teeth? Who made sure you were okay when she bailed out of here?" I shake my head, begging him to see it. "I may not be perfect, Clayton, but *I'm* your family. I'm the one you should trust in — not her."

Clayton's eyes grow so tired in the span of my words, that I wonder if I've aged him, if it would be one of those moments like so many I had lived through myself that he'd look back on as a turning point.

"I do trust you," he finally whispers. "And I love you, bro. I do. And maybe you're right. Maybe she'll leave again or make promises she can't keep, but... I don't know. I think she's changed. I think something happened. She seems different, and I know she doesn't deserve it, but I want to give her a second chance. Okay? And that's my choice. Not yours. So if you want to write her off forever, if you want to be an asshole to her and never give her the opportunity to make things right, then that's your decision. I won't force you to do anything you don't want to do. But I'm asking the same courtesy from you."

His eyes are hard on mine, and he shrugs out of my grasp without letting me respond, jogging across the yard and through the gate to join our mother and Mrs. Harrison.

The next breath through my nose is icy cold, and I seethe with the overwhelming urge to run to him and hold him away from our mother and take him away from this place, even if he hates me for doing it.

But he's right.

I can't make choices for him, and he's grown enough now to know the possible consequences of the decisions he's making. And hadn't I done the same, given our mother chance after chance until she'd burned me enough times that I learned not to get close to the fire ever again?

I scrub my hands over my face, trying to soothe my uneven breathing enough to get through the rest of the night. My phone buzzes in my pocket, and I yank it out, expecting to see Becca's warm smile on my screen.

Instead, it's a black screen with the name ERIN XANDER in white letters at the top.

My stomach drops, and I stare at the vibrating device for what feels like an eternity with my heart in my throat. When I don't answer, she goes to voicemail, a *missed call* notification taking the place of her name on the screen. But before I can put the phone back in my pocket, it rings again.

Erin.

I answer quickly this time, snapping back to reality like waking from a dream. "Erin? Are you okay? What's going on?"

"Hey," she answers softly, tentatively. "Oh gosh, yes, I'm fine, I'm sorry if I worried you. I just wasn't sure if my first call came through but... oh, you're probably busy. I'm sorry. I'll just—"

"Don't hang up."

A silent moment passes between us as my racing heart slows to its normal rate, and I run a hand through my short hair, turning away from where I can still see my mom and brother through the backyard gate.

"Did I catch you at a bad time?" Erin finally asks.

I want to laugh, because *every* time is a bad time for me — ever since the last night Erin and I talked.

"Why did you call me, Ex?"

I hear a shaky inhale on the other end, a shuffling of papers. "I'd like to talk to you."

"So, talk."

"Not on the phone," she explains. "I was wondering if we could have dinner."

My heart stops, skipping a few beats before it hammers back to life. "Dinner."

"If that would be okay."

I glance over my shoulder and see Mrs. Harrison and Clayton leading Mom back inside the house, and I nod to my little brother, signaling that I'll be right in.

"I'm out of town."

"Oh..." Erin pauses. "Okay. I'm sorry, I—"

"I'll be back next week."

I swallow, my stomach so fucked up from the emotions of the day, I'm not sure I'll be able to hold down the beer churning inside it.

"Okay," Erin whispers. "How about the Sunday after Halloween? Eros?"

Eros is a small Greek restaurant off campus, and one of my favorites.

"What time?"

"Seven okay?"

I nod, more to myself than to her, as if I need that assurance from myself that I can do this, that I can have dinner with Erin and somehow live through it. "See you then."

I don't wait for a response before I end the call, and I don't allow myself to simmer on the sound of her voice, or the fact that I'll be meeting up with her when I get back to Florida. Instead, I shove the phone in my pocket and put out the bonfire on my way back inside to suffer through whatever time I have left with my mother.

One monster at a time.

"Alright, let's make this happen," I say, blowing a whistle through my teeth when I flip over the bottom card in my dealer stack. The top one was a Jack of spades, and the bottom is a three of hearts.

"Come on, come on," Chelsea says from the edge of the table. I learned earlier tonight that she's in banking, and the hot stud next to her who can't be any older than me is James, her "friend" from out of town.

They've been making out all night between hands, and judging by the ring on her finger, I'd say Chelsea is up to no good.

But it's not for me to judge. My job tonight is to lose as many hands as the cards will let me.

Because the more the Blackjack dealer loses, the more she gets tipped.

Casino Boat 101.

I flip the next card, and it's a two of hearts, giving me a fifteen.

"Bust! Bust! Come on!" Roberto says. He's short and spunky and has been smoking like a chimney all night, but he's also been the only one tipping me between hands.

I like Roberto.

I cringe, eyeing the next card before I flip it with a satisfied grin.

King of clubs.

The table roars, everyone thrusting their hands up into the air and high-fiving each other as I pay out the winnings and clear the cards.

I've been working on the boat for a couple months now, and one thing I've figured out for sure — I love it. I love being on a boat with people letting loose for the night. I love the freedom we all feel in international waters, like nothing is off limits, like the night is forever young. I love the clouds of smoke and the dinging bells of the slot machines and the distant roars of each table when they beat the dealer or get a good roll in Craps.

I may be out of the professional poker scene, but this will always be a part of who I am.

It's my energy. It's my soul. It's the very blood in my veins.

And that's why I'm going to open my *own* casino company when I graduate.

It won't be a real casino, but rather one that can be hired out for parties and weddings and corporate events. I've already got the start of a business plan together, detailing how companies or hosts can purchase fake money that, in turn, the guests can use to gamble. The more money they have at the end of the night, the more entries they get into raffles, or the more they have to use to bid on auction items. It will all be legal, not gambling, per se, but gambling-ish.

And it will all be mine.

Until then, working on the casino cruise will give me more experience dealing different games, which I'll need when it's time to train my *own* dealers.

Plus, it's a good distraction from the fact that Kip is across the country.

He must know that I'm extra in my sad panda feels tonight, because as soon as I wrap up my shift on the boat, stepping back onto the dock and immediately unfastening the tie around my neck, my phone rings.

"Hello, handsome," I sing.

"Hiiiii."

At the long, drawn-out greeting, I grin. "Someone's been drinking."

"And someone *else* has not been sending nudes."

I bark out a laugh, pulling my keys from my purse as I cross the employee parking lot. "That's because someone else has been working."

"Boooooo. Ditch work. Come to California, instead."

"I will, baby. In less than a month now."

"That's so far away."

My heart squeezes. "I know. I miss you, too."

There's a long pause of silence, and then a hiccup that makes me smile again.

"Where are you?"

"At the A Sig house. We had a party tonight."

"Clearly."

"The whole week is a party around Halloween."

"Tell me about it. The A Sig Halloween bash is tomorrow on the sandbar. Everyone has been talking about it all week."

"What are you going to wear?"

"The girls and I are going as pin-up dolls."

There's a groan on the other end, and then what sounds like Kip slapping himself in the face and dragging his hand over it. "You're going to look so hot," he almost whines.

I chuckle. "I'll bring the outfit when I come next month."

"You better."

I sigh, and silence passes between us as I get in my car and fire it to life. There's a roar somewhere in the background where Kip is, and I smile, picturing the madness.

"You sound like you're having fun," I say. "I wish I was there with you."

"Soon," he promises.

"Soon," I echo.

I check the date on my watch, letting my head fall back against the head rest and closing my eyes.

Just twenty-four more days.

Cassie

"God, when they said the Halloween party would be even bigger and better than last year, I doubted it," Skyler confesses, lowering her sunglasses down to the tip of her nose as she looks around the sandbar. "But *damn*, did Alpha Sig deliver."

I glance around with her, and while I can tell she's in awe, I feel mostly overwhelmed by the amount of students crammed onto one speck of sand off the east coast of Florida. The sandbar is usually vacant, save for the occasional boat that might stop there on the weekends, but today, it's crawling with people dressed in swimsuit Halloween costumes. Boats line every bit of the shore, anchored in place, with people standing or floating in the water between each one, and in the center of the sandbar is a DJ, hooked up to a generator and thumping music like a heartbeat out to every inch of the little island.

We couldn't have asked for a more perfect day. It's seventy-five and sunny, the breeze enough to cool us if we get too drunk and hot, but the water still warm enough for us to not freeze our asses off. Ashlei and Jess have already set up camp with their beach chairs and umbrellas and gone in search of booze, and Skyler and I set our stuff next to theirs, saving room for Erin, just in case she shows.

Fluffy white clouds pepper the bright blue sky, giving a slight reprieve from the sun as we splay out our beach towels, but I still pull out my sunscreen to protect my fair skin.

"Adam is really kicking ass as second-term president, isn't he?" Skyler asks, putting her hand out for the sunscreen once I have a dollop in my hand.

I pass it to her, still looking around and trying to ignore the pit in my stomach at the fact that I knew nothing about what to expect today since Adam and I have barely talked, let alone seen each other. "He is, indeed."

"I'm sure the pressure is insane," Skyler says, rubbing lotion on her chest. "No one has ever been president two years in a row."

My stomach twists again, but I force a smile. "Speaking of pressure, how is Kip doing in the film program at UCLA?"

"Oh, kicking ass and taking names, of course. He's working on a script for an online series right now that will go up in competition against the other students in his program. He seems pretty geeked up about it, but won't tell me much."

"When do you get to see him next?"

Skyler frowns a little at that, squeezing more lotion into her hands before passing the bottle to me. "Thanksgiving. I can't believe it's already been two months."

I reach over to squeeze her arm. "But hey, Thanksgiving is just a month away."

"Twenty-three days," Skyler corrects with a smile. "I hope he knows we're not leaving his dorm room."

I snicker. "And *I* hope his roommates have noise-cancelling headphones."

It's only a little past noon, and already the Halloween party is in full swing. Just looking around the island at the multitude of students doing beer bongs and keg stands and hammering back shots tells me most of them won't make it to sunset. Still, I love seeing how creative everyone got with their costumes, finding ways to dress up but in swimsuits. I spot an Indiana Jones, a group of Minions from the *Despicable Me* movie, animals of every kind, superheroes and Disney princesses, Barbies and musicians, even a few puns — like Bear's Little, Josh, who has a lampshade on his head and a box over his shoulders with a table cloth and some random items on top. The front of it says "*one night stand.*"

The girls and I decided to go for something sexy but classy, landing on pin-up dolls. For one, it was easy to transform that into a swimsuit costume, and for two, we could each dress in colors that complemented our different skin and hair colors.

I'm in an emerald two piece, the bottoms high waisted with a frilly trim, the top a shiny sweetheart cut with straps over my shoulders. I curled my short red hair and wrapped a matching green bandana around it to tie at my forehead, and painted my lips a cherry red.

Skyler, on the other hand, is sexy as hell in a yellow one piece that looks more like a man's shirt than a swimsuit. It's loose at the top, with a deep V that accentuates her tan cleavage and toned stomach, but it cinches at her waist and hugs her ass perfectly at the bottom. It looks like a cuffed sleeve where the straps hook around her neck, and the left breast has a pocket, like a work shirt. She's paired it with jean shorts that I'm sure will come off at some point, and her hair is braided into pigtails, each wrapped with yellow bows.

"Speak of the devil, if it isn't the big man on campus," Skyler says with a grin, skipping past me. I turn just in time to see her give Adam a big high-five before hanging her hands on her hips. "This is *bad ass*, my friend. Well done."

"Thank you, thank you," Adam replies, pretending to bow.

"How the hell did you get a DJ on a sandbar?"

"With a very expensive generator and a lot of possible disaster planning."

Skyler chuckles. "Well, it sets the tone, and the open bars, the kegs, the slip and slide..." She whistles her approval. "You've outdone yourself."

"Just wait until the fireworks show." Adam smiles, pride radiating off him. It turns me on to see him like this, exuding power and confidence, and I slide up to him, wrapping my arms around his bare torso.

"I agree," I say, kissing his warm neck. "You knocked it out of the park, babe."

He swallows, putting his arm around my shoulders, but I feel the hesitant way he does it, and it makes my stomach ache. "Thanks, Cass."

"I'm going to get a drink," Skyler says, pointing a thumb over her shoulder. "Want anything, Little?"

"Just a beer for me. And a shot of something fruity, if you're up for it?"

Skyler scoffs. "Like that's even a question. Be right back!"

She skips off, and then it's just me and Adam, and I turn to thread my hands behind his neck and press my lips to his. The kiss is a little too cold and short for my taste, but he keeps his arm around my waist when we break off.

"So... I thought you were going to wear green trunks to match me?" I tease, eyeing his red swim trunks. He has a whistle around his neck and a patch of white sunscreen on his nose, which tells me he went for a lifeguard. "We never do seem to get our Halloween costumes right, do we?"

It's a joke, referencing the fact that he dressed to match Skyler my freshman year, and then last year, dressed up like Prince Eric as if to make up for it, since I had been Ariel from *The Little Mermaid*. But of course, I hadn't worn the same thing twice, and was Cleopatra, with a matching Grayson as my Mark Anthony.

It seems we're always mixing signals, but here in his arms, I don't care. I'm just thankful we've finally gotten out of our own way to be together.

"Yeah, I didn't really have time to shop," he says coldly, shrugging out of my grasp. "I actually need to go check on something at the DJ booth, but I wanted to say hi. I hope you have fun today."

I swallow, shivering at the cool breeze once he's no longer holding me. "You say that like I won't be spending it with you."

Adam runs a hand through his hair, looking off toward the DJ booth before he looks at me again. Of course, I can't see his expression under his dark Ray-Bans, but I don't have to see his eyes to notice the avoidance in them.

"Of course, you will," he says unconvincingly. "But I'll be running around a lot, too. I have to make sure everything runs smoothly."

I nod. "Right."

Adam takes a step toward the DJ booth, but I reach out for his arm, spinning him in place.

"Adam, what's going on?"

He sighs, but before he can say anything, I hold up my hand.

"And don't tell me it's nothing. You've been a class-A prick to me since the night of your concert. I know you got ragged on for spending time with me, and that your fraternity brothers need you around as president. I get that, and I've been supporting it. But it's not fair to be a jerk to me, or to just ignore me completely. Just because you need to be more present at Alpha Sig doesn't mean I get placed on the back burner." I frown, stepping into him and wrapping my hands around his forearm. "I'm still your girlfriend."

Adam chuckles. "Oh, are you?"

"What the hell is that supposed to mean?"

"Oh, nothing — except I wasn't aware that girlfriends lied to their boyfriends about hanging out with their exes."

The blood drains from my face, but I still hold onto him. "I'm not trying to hide anything from you, Adam. I've been trying to talk to you for weeks about it."

"About what? The fact that you're hanging out with Grayson behind my back?"

I inhale a hot breath. "Not behind your back. Like I said, I've been trying to tell you."

Adam scoffs, ripping away from my grasp. "Do you hear yourself, Cassie? You're hanging out with your fucking *ex-boyfriend* who cheated on you and oh, by the way, also came between us."

"I'm not *hanging out with him*, okay? We have a class together, and we've been assigned lab partners, and *yes*, he apologized to me about what happened and I listened, okay? He wants to try to be friends, and I've lost so many people in my life..." I swallow. "I just don't want to write someone off because of past transgressions."

"He's in your Genetics class?"

"Yes."

"And why didn't you tell me? I picked you up for lunch every fucking *day* after that class."

"I've been *trying* to tell you," I fume. "But you've been all caught up in Alpha Sigma stuff and hellbent on ignoring me."

"Oh, so now it's my fault."

"I don't even understand why this is a fight," I say, throwing my hands up.

"You do, Cassie, or you wouldn't have hidden it."

"I *didn't* hide it."

"Well, you certainly didn't tell me outright, did you?"

I know he has a right to be upset — I do, deep down in my gut. But for some reason, I'm defensive, and annoyed, and pissed off that he's accusing me, and that all this time that I thought he was focusing on his fraternity, he was really just ignoring me for sport. To make a point. To drive that point home.

That is *not* how a healthy relationship functions.

"Jesus, Adam," I say, holding my hands out, palms up. "You already won me. Okay? I'm yours. And that's not changing. But I don't want to have to hurt someone, either. I know it's hard to understand but... Grayson is my friend."

"No."

"Adam."

"No," he says again, shaking his head forcefully. "I'm not okay with that."

"He's not a bad guy, okay? I know he fucked up, he hurt me, he was an asshole to you, but he had a lot of shit going on that neither one of us knew about, okay? I mean, would you want someone to judge you in *your* darkest hour?"

Adam grinds his jaw but doesn't reply.

"He's changed," I continue, voice softer. "And he's not asking me on a date or hitting on me. He's asking to be my *friend*."

Adam laughs, crossing his arms as he tongues his cheek. "You actually believe the words you're saying to me right now, don't you?"

I frown. "You know he even asked about us? He asked how we were doing, Adam. He knows we're together, and he's happy for us."

"Bullshit," Adam says, his voice high-pitched and desperate as he thrusts his hands toward me. "It's all bullshit. Are you so blind, Cassie? Of course he asked how we were, because he's just *dying* for one little fuck up on my end so he can slip back into your heart, and then into your pants. He doesn't want to be *friends*. He wants you back."

"But I don't want *him*," I yell in return. "I love *you*, Adam. It's as simple as that. He is not a threat and you know it."

Adam's jaw clenches, and he looks away from me without a response.

My skin prickles with the memory of being in this position before, of having to choose between Adam and Grayson, and my stomach flips violently at the thought of it. I've already lost my best friend, and there was still a gaping hole I was convinced would never be filled again.

If I have the chance to fill the hole Grayson left in me, I want to take it — and I don't understand what I've ever done to make Adam second-guess that he can trust me, that I can be friends with another guy without it being a danger to us.

"There was a time he made me choose between you two," I whisper, crossing my arms over my chest. "Do you remember that?"

I don't miss the way Adam's jaw ticks. "How could I forget."

"Well, then you know why I'm so adamant about this. Making that choice... being in that position..." I swallow, thankful for the sunglasses hiding the tears glossing my eyes. "It *killed* me. It tore me in half. I swore to myself that I would never do that again. I *can't* do that again."

Adam nods, stepping into my space, and he removes his sunglasses for the first time, showing me the pain in his eyes as he stares down his nose at me. "So, you'll do it for him, but not for me?"

My next breath is shaky and burns me from the inside, stinging my nose and making my bottom lip quiver. How can he not understand? How can he not see that I can be friends with Grayson and still be in love with him, still be *his* — completely?

How could he ever ask me to choose, knowing the hell it put me through last time?

I'm not sure how long we stand there, nose to nose, chest to chest, each of us waiting for the other to break. But it doesn't matter, because neither of us does, and it's Adam who shakes his head and pulls back.

He slips his sunglasses back on, pausing when he's a few feet away like he wants to say something, but decides against it. Instead, he takes off toward the DJ booth, speaking into the walkie-talkie that was strapped to his hip, effectively dismissing me and slipping back into president mode.

And I just stand there, watching the muscles of his back as he goes, wondering how we always find ourselves back here, no matter what we do.

Jess

My best friend and I are the most annoyed I've ever known us to be.

We are also at petty level one thousand.

But I don't care.

I don't care that we're both grumbling and being catty little bitches as we watch our respective targets from across the sandbar, each of us leaning back in our beach chairs and soaking up the sun as if it could do anything to warm our cold, black hearts in this moment. I don't care that we're shit talking about someone we don't know to make ourselves feel better. I don't care that we're making up stories in our head to fill in the blank spots for everything we're dying to know.

Sometimes you know you're being a little bitch, and you just can't stop yourself.

And that's where we're at today.

Ashlei's target? The new intern at *Okay, Cool*, who looks absolutely stunning in a flapper swimsuit costume, complete with pearls draped around her neck and a feather in her headband. She honestly looks so much like Lei that they could be doppelgängers, which is likely why my bestie wants to strangle her with the pearls around her neck. She looks like her, has her old gig at the agency, and seems to be making quite the impression on their boss — AKA, Ashlei's boyfriend.

And my target?

The *too-hot-to-be-in-college* Puerto Rican goddess currently hanging on Kade's arm.

I don't even know her name, and I don't need to. All I know is that Kade is making her laugh, and she's rubbing all over him, and he's holding her close, and I can hear his words reverberating like bells in an echo chamber in my mind.

"Might have to pull out all the tricks I've learned on some unsuspecting hottie at the Halloween party..."

I grind my teeth together, and then continue my petty party.

"I mean, honestly, who has tits that big in college? They're like a triple D, and she has a waist the size of a coffee cup."

"Did you know she has already been put on an event account?" Ashlei responds. "I mean, I had to *claw* my way to my own account."

"Sure, she's gorgeous," I continue. "But I bet she's vanilla in bed. He could do better."

"She's got this sweet little angel thing going for her at the office," Ashlei says, shaking her head before she sips on the bright pink straw sticking out of her tumbler. "But I know better. She's got an agenda, I just don't know what it is."

"And besides, *I* taught him everything he knows. So really, if she's falling for his lines, she's falling for me, *technically*."

"She's not even that good at her job." Another lie from Ashlei.

"Whatever, I don't care, he's just a fuck buddy and a free ride, anyway." Another lie from me.

We both fall silent, sipping our drinks angrily and swimming in our petty pool. After another stretch of me trying to ignore Kade and his "unsuspecting hottie" but always finding myself staring at them again, I stand, ditching my cover up on my chair.

"You know, maybe I'll go over there just to make him squirm a little."

"Good idea," Ashlei says, standing. "I think I'll go hang out with our perfect little intern, get better acquainted."

"Not that we care about either of them," I remind us both.

"No, of course not," Ashlei agrees, and then we storm off in the sand in opposite directions.

I don't realize it's a terrible idea, inserting myself into a situation that clearly makes me itchy, until I'm standing right in front of Kade with a fake smile on my lips. He doesn't even notice me at first, which pisses me off, but luckily, I'm patient, and I stand there next to one of his fraternity brothers, blending in until he sees me.

When he does, one eyebrow arches high up into his hairline, and a stupid smirk spreads on his dumb face. "Hey there, J-Love."

Hey there? I'm going to murder him.

"Hey, yourself," I say, still wearing the fake smile. "Nice costume."

Kade is dressed in bright red, flashy shorts that cut off down past his knees and hug him right under where that deep V cuts from his abdomen to the promise land. Around that waist, he's got a giant, heavyweight champion belt, and the way it pairs with the tattoos sprawled out over his entire body, he looks like a younger, hotter version of John Cena — if there even is such a thing.

"Thanks," he says, flexing his biceps, which makes me roll my eyes and wonder why I care that he's hanging all over someone else.

"I absolutely *love* yours," the unfortunately beautiful girl on his arm says, leaning forward to touch one of the curls in my hair without asking. "Pin-up, right? My dad *loves* pin-ups... he has calendars and posters and old tin containers and all kinds of stuff with pin-ups on them."

Ashlei, Skyler, Cassie, and I decided the pin-up idea together. My costume is a one-piece, black-and-white striped, with a cut out where my stomach and back are, the top and bottom connected only by scrappy fabric over my ribs and hips. The top has a zipper down the front of the cleavage, too, which is conveniently zipped low right now, boosting up my tits.

"Thanks, sweetie," I say, smiling at her even though it's killing me to watch her thread her arm through Kade's and draw a fingernail up and down his toned forearm. At first, I thought she was clueless, but the way she's holding onto him and smiling back at me with possession in her eyes tells me she sees me as a threat.

And she should.

I somehow manage to check myself before I can be a bitch, thanks to my feminist side reminding me that I should lift women up, not tear them down — even if I'm jealous of them. But I'm done playing games.

She has something I want, and I'm not leaving without it.

"Kade," I say, turning my attention back to him with my smile still in place. "Can I steal you for a second?"

He shrugs, oblivious, whispering something in his unsuspecting victim's ear before she giggles and runs her hand over his chest, slick with tanning oil. "Hurry back," she says, and then she grabs his junk over his shorts, right there in front of everyone, outlining the thick shaft that I had inside me just days ago.

I turn before rage can seethe through me, not checking to see if Kade is following, because I know he knows better than *not* to. I just stalk toward one of the tents set up for shade reprieve, and when I step inside it, I thank Adam and his fraternity brothers for being smart enough to put fans with water spritzers inside each one of them.

It feels like heaven.

I sigh, turning just as Kade joins me in the tent. It's a large one, with space for at least a couple dozen people, but most everyone is out in the sun or on a boat. There's a couple making out on one of the couches in the corner, but I snap at them and point to the tent flap, and without a word, they exit.

Then, it's just me and Kade.

I cross my arms, mouth twisting to the side as I wait for him to say something.

"Uh..." He looks around, cocking a confused brow. "Am I in trouble or something?"

"What are you doing?"

"Currently? Standing in a tent with you wondering why you look like you want to murder me right now."

"I mean, with Miss Tits for Brains out there." I cringe. "Sorry, I didn't mean that, I'm sure she's lovely and very intelligent and driven and resilient."

Kade chuckles. "I wouldn't know, I just met her."

"Well, you seem to be *very* acquainted, judging by how she just wrapped her hand around your cock in front of your brothers and me and God and everyone else."

A moment of silence passes, and Kade's smirk climbs higher as he crosses his arms over his chest, his stance even cockier with that damn belt hanging around his hips. "Jess... are you *jealous*?"

"No."

"No?" he asks, taking a step toward me. "Because it *kind of* seems like you might be jealous."

"I'm not."

"Then why'd you pull me in here?"

He's still walking toward me, and I take a few steps back, until I run into one of the several cocktail tables set up inside the tent. Just as I do, three Omega Chi brothers stumble into the tent. Kade turns around and points at the door they just came through, and they laugh, all drunk, throwing their hands up before exiting again.

"I haven't done anything wrong, have I?" Kade pushes again when we're alone. "We had a deal, did we not?"

"We did."

"You've been a great instructor; I was just testing out my skills."

I scoff.

His brow arches higher, and he moves into my space, trapping me between his hot, toned body and the table behind me. My hands press into his chest, and he places his palms flat on the table, staring down his nose at me.

"If you want to re-negotiate our terms," he husks. "I'm all ears."

I want to growl. I want to scream and slap him and shove him away and spit on him for good measure.

But I also want him to take those big bear hands of his and put them on every inch of me.

Jesus Christ, what is happening?

And it's then that I realize it.

I like him.

I fucking like him, and I *hate* myself for it, but it's true. Somewhere between all the teasing and fucking and fooling around, I started liking the time we spend together.

And he's right.

I am jealous.

Fuck.

"Fine. I still want to teach you," I say, dragging my nails slowly down his chest to his abdomen. Each inch lower makes his cock twitch, growing where it's pressed against me, and I instantly react to the power I feel from having that effect on him. "Because God knows, you still have a lot to learn."

"I'm sure I do," he says, his voice low and husky.

"But if I'm going to teach you, then I want to reap the benefits."

"And?"

"And..." I say, dragging my fingertips down lower. I slip them under the band of his shorts and revel in the stiff inhale it elicits from him. "I want to be the *only* one who gets to reap the benefits."

I try to shove my hand down his pants, but he stops me, wrapping his hand around my wrist with force. "Meaning?"

"Fuck you, Kade," I say, writhing in his grasp with my swimsuit so wet you would have thought I'd already been in the water. "Don't make me say it."

"If you want me inside you right now," he whispers, using his free hand to skate up the inside of my thighs. His thick knee presses between them, spreading me wider, my back aching where I'm pressed against the table. "You *have* to say it."

"Fuck," I moan, ripping my hands free of his grasp to hold onto his shoulder. His thigh rubs against my swimsuit, the friction heating my clit, and my eyelids flutter at the sensation.

"Come on, Jess," he teases, releasing the belt around his waist with one snap. In the next breath, he reaches into his shorts and pulls his cock out, holding it, throbbing and hard in his hand, right between my thighs. "What. Do. You. Want."

I'm practically salivating, and in that moment, I'd say anything to have his dick inside me.

I convince myself *that's* why I reach up on my tiptoes and bite his lower lip, sucking it between my teeth before I whisper, "Be mine." My hand wraps around his cock, replacing his, and I grab his ass, making him thrust into my grip. "And make me yours, too."

Kade answers with a growl, whipping me around to face the table so fast I have no choice but to brace myself on it. My fingers have barely wrapped around the edges before one of his hands is crooking me at the hips, and the other is yanking my swimsuit to the side, and in the next inhale, I'm filled to the brim — all at once, brutally and punishing, a claiming thrust that kills me as much as it makes me feel alive.

"Oh *God,* you feel so fucking good," he groans, nipping at my ear as his hands find my hips and slam me onto him again. "All that talking made you wet, didn't it, babe?"

"Yes," I whimper, and I want to slap myself because I *don't* whimper for a man. But here I am, putty in his hand, legs shaking and orgasm already building from just a few thrusts.

I reach down and shove my swimsuit farther to the side, rubbing my clit as he pounds into me. It's fast and animalistic, and it takes everything in me to be fucking quiet so not everyone on the beach knows I'm getting railed inside this tent. Not that I particularly care, but I'm at least *trying* to be discreet.

Kade reaches down, hiking one of my legs up to where I'm balanced on just one foot, but he's holding all of my weight, allowing me to spread my legs open wider and rub my clit until I come in a burst of gasps and fire. I quiver and shake in his grasp, and his mouth claims mine, my neck bent so forcefully it hurts, but the kiss is too good to break. And Kade keeps going, pounding into me, forcing me to open wider and wider for him as I ride the waves.

When my climax recedes, I'm even more weak, and I know that if it wasn't for him holding me, I'd collapse to the ground. But we're still kissing, tongues and teeth clashing, biting and licking, until he grunts something that sounds like *coming* and rips himself out of me, whipping me around and forcing me into the sand on my knees.

I don't even think twice, just open my mouth and guide him into it just in time to catch his hot release down my throat. He shoves a little too far down and I gag, but he holds me there, and I squeeze my eyes shut in an attempt to focus and not gag again.

I'm so fucking turned on I want a round two already.

When he's spent, he pulls out of me slowly, trembling, and I swallow, looking up at him with a wicked smile and wiping the corners of my mouth.

"So, you're mine?" I ask, and he just laughs, a lazy smile on his face as he yanks up his shorts and collapses into the sand next to me.

Kade pulls me under his arm, kissing my temple, chest still heaving. "All yours, you devil woman," he says.

Then, he palms my tit with a grin.

"And *these* are all mine."

Bear

The Sunday after Halloween, an entire plate of hummus and tzatziki sits untouched between me and Erin, along with fresh, hot pita bread and a smorgasbord of vegetables. It's been there for at least five minutes now, but neither of us moves for it, and I've nearly drained my first beer as Erin has attempted small talk. The way her eyebrows are drawn together as she watches me from across the table, I have a feeling she's about done with that.

Thank God.

Now we can get this over with.

"Thank you for agreeing to meet me," she says, tentatively tucking a strand of hair behind one ear. Her hair is longer now than it was at the end of last semester, when her head was in the toilet and she told me unknowingly about our baby. She was an absolute wreck that night, but this evening, she looks... calm. At peace. She looks like she's getting sleep and eating.

Still, she watches me with worry etched in every feature, and I find that as fucked up as it is, I like that aspect the most.

Erin clears her throat when I don't answer, folding her hands in her lap with her eyes falling to the hummus plate. "I don't know how to start, so I'm just going to talk. And I know a lot of this might not make sense to you, but... I guess, I just wanted to talk to you. I wanted to explain what happened." She lifted her eyes to me then. "Why I made the choices I made."

I inhale a stiff breath, draining the last of my beer and signaling to the waitress for another. She delivers it promptly, seeing as how there are only a dozen tables inside the small restaurant.

Erin offers a gentle smile as I take my first sip, something like pity in her eyes now.

"When we slept together, neither of us really knew each other. I mean, I asked you to semi-formal on the heels of your fraternity being on probation, and then we accidentally got too drunk and..."

She pauses when I take three dramatically large gulps from my beer, belching before I set the glass back down on the table. Her eyes stick there for a moment before she swallows and continues.

"I mean, neither of us even really remembered it the next morning. Do you recall that? We laughed it off, promised not to tell anyone... it wasn't serious."

"Is there a point here?"

Erin blows out a slow breath. "Bear, we weren't in a relationship. We *still* aren't ready for a child, let alone back then. We're just kids ourselves. And when I found out I was pregnant... I did come to you."

"Bullshit."

"Let me finish," she says, holding up one hand. "I came to you, before I even took the test, actually. I wanted to do it together. I knew we could figure it out. But when I went to you... you were with Shawna."

I frown, tracing back through my memory for what she could possibly be talking about. "I don't understand."

Erin takes all her hair and wraps it over one shoulder, taking a deep breath. "I went back to your room, and I was knocking but you didn't answer, and when I walked in… I didn't know her at the time, but you and Shawna were…" She swallows. "Indisposed."

My gaze hardens.

"And, I don't know, Bear. I just, I felt so fucking silly. Like, we had a one-night stand, and I expected you to hold my hand while I peed on a stick? I mean, these were my *exact* thoughts." She shakes her head. "I felt like a fool. How could I expect that of you, of anyone in college?"

I take another pull of my beer in lieu of answering.

"Anyway, so I took the test alone, and… well… obviously, I was pregnant. But I lied to Jess, who was the only one who even knew I was suspicious about being pregnant. I told her it was a stomach flu. And then…"

She doesn't finish, and I squeeze the glass so hard in my hand, I wonder if I can break it like the Hulk.

Erin's expression softens, and she reaches forward, wrapping her hand around my wrist before I can flinch away. As soon as I feel her warmth, something inside me cracks, and emotion stings my nose, but I fight it back.

"I am so sorry, Bear," she says, her eyes glossing with tears. "I was a coward. I should have come to you. I know that now, but I also know it doesn't change what I did. At the time, I thought it was the right thing to do. And I'm sorry I didn't include you in the decision, but… it was my body. And ultimately, it was my choice."

I shake my head, tearing back from her grasp. "I know it was your choice. And I would have supported it, Ex — even more so if you would have just fucking told me."

She breaks at my words, swiping at the tears streaming down her cheeks furiously. "I know that now. I didn't know that then, but I do now. I know that you were the one who saw I wasn't okay before anyone else. I know that you were the one who saved me when Landon…" Her voice breaks, and another zip of pain splits my chest open. "When he raped me, when his brothers stole every ounce of innocence I had, you were there. You saved me. You kept my secret even when I knew it killed you." She rolls her lips together, more tears tumbling over her cheeks. "You are the most amazing man I know, and you are my best friend. And I am so sorry I hurt you."

Every muscle in my jaw is tight and burning as I fight off the emotion strangling my throat. I just shake my head, over and over, gaze lost in the distance before I finally pull my eyes back to hers.

"Listen. I know you're going to therapy, and I'm really fucking glad you are. Okay? I want you to be okay. I do," I say, and I mean it. "I also know that you're sorry," I continue, forcing a breath. "But that doesn't mean I have to forgive you. So, don't expect me to."

"Bear," her voice cracks, and she reaches for me again, but I'm already up out of my chair, abandoning my napkin on the table, as well as what's left of my beer.

"Excuse me," I murmur, and then I'm gone, out of the restaurant and in the first campus cab I see.

My heart is thundering in my chest as the car carries me to the other side of campus, and then I'm on Becca's doorstep, and as soon as she opens the door and sees me, she invites me in, wrapping me in a warm hug that I completely collapse into.

I'm not sure how long she holds me, how long I have to use every ounce of willpower I have to fight off the tears my body is desperate to let free, but eventually, she grabs me by the hand and pulls me back to her room. Her dorm mate doesn't seem to be around, which I'm thankful for as she closes the door behind us.

She sits us on her bed, wrapping her arms around me and leaning her head on my chest. For the longest time, we just hold each other, and she takes long, exaggerated breaths, cueing me to do the same.

After a while, she whispers, "Is this about the trip?"

I sigh, running my fingers over her hip where I hold her against me. Just feeling her warmth already makes me feel better. "Partly."

"How did it go?"

I swallow. "Well, Clayton is convinced I'm a monster because I don't believe our lying, sack-of-shit mother when she says she's back for good."

"Was she drugged out?"

"No," I admit. "She seems clean, actually. But I don't trust it."

"What's the other part?"

I sigh, debating how much I should tell her. "I just met up with Erin, and we... we had a fight."

Becca stiffens in my grasp, sitting up even when I try to hold her there in my arms. She shakes her head, looking out her window before her eyes land on me. "You saw Erin before you saw me?"

Shit.

I let out a long sigh. "She asked if I'd have dinner with her," I explain. "She wanted to apologize."

"For what?"

Fuck.

Another hot breath leaves my nose, and I roll my lips together, looking anywhere but back at Becca.

"I asked you last semester if there was anything between you and Erin, and you said there wasn't."

"There's not."

"Then why are you holding this..." She waves her hand in the air. "*Grudge* against her? You haven't talked to her or *about* her since the night of Skyler's poker tournament, and now you're meeting her for dinner for her to apologize for... what?"

I swallow.

"What *happened*, Bear?"

Still, I don't answer. And it kills me, because I know Becca is pissed, and hurt, and as much as *I* am angry with Erin, it's still not my place to tell anyone what happened.

Becca shakes her head, sliding off the bed before I can stop her. She stands, crossing her arms and watching me. "Maybe you should look at that."

I frown. "At what?"

"You told me about what happened with you and Shawna, how you never forgave her, even when she came to you *begging* for you to understand. And when you held a grudge against Skyler for half a semester. And how you wrote off your mom completely, and now that she's back and legitimately trying, you won't have any part of it."

Defensiveness prickles in my chest, and I stand up, too, ready to combat her. But she holds up a hand to silence me.

"And, on top of all that, whatever is happening with Erin that she needs to apologize, which — judging by the way you were acting when you first got here — I'm assuming you didn't accept either."

I clamp my mouth shut at that.

Becca shakes her head, her golden eyes thick with confusion and pity as she watches me. "You don't give second chances, even when someone maybe deserves one. Why is that, Bear?"

I blink at the accusation, skin hot and uncomfortable for the way it sinks into my gut like an anchor.

Becca holds her hands out toward me, palms up, desperation in her voice. "Have you never made a mistake? Have you never hurt someone?"

My little brother's words echoed on my girlfriend's lips.

She waits for me to answer and gives me plenty of time to do so. But when I don't, she just shakes her head, tears blurring her vision as she opens her door.

"I think you should go," she whispers, her eyes finding mine. "And maybe think about that. Because we're all human, Bear. We *all* fuck up. I know I have. And if I was never forgiven for my transgressions in the past, I don't know where I'd be today. Besides... holding onto all that anger, all the resentment?" She swallows. "It's tearing you up."

"I'm sorry," I say, moving toward her, but she flinches away, opening the door wider. "Please, don't make me go right now. I need you."

"No," she argues, looking at me pointedly. "What you need is time alone with yourself. You're just too scared to take it."

We stand there, watching each other for what feels like an eternity, and her words melt over me like lava, burning my skin, scarring my heart. Eventually, I nod, and as soon as I'm out her dorm door, she closes and locks it behind me.

For the first time since last semester, I don't feel numb.

For the first time, I feel all the pain, all the betrayal, all the resentment and anger I've been trying to work out of my system with weights and cardio and drinking.

Becca's right.

I do need to be alone.

But I'm fucking terrified of what will happen now that I am.

EPISODE 4

Ashlei

Here's what I know about our precious little shining star of an intern, Sophie Miller.

She's a junior at Palm South University, majoring in Public Relations with a particular interest in working as a publicist for high-profile executives. She's not in a sorority, but seems to be very *in* with the Greek crowd, thanks to dating the president of Zeta Rho Kappa her sophomore year and becoming affectionately known as "one of the guys" in that circle. She's a self-proclaimed country girl from Central Florida, and her favorite party trick is shotgunning a tall boy faster than any guy who tries to compete against her.

Of course, this was all learned at the Halloween party last weekend, when I casually found my way over to her group and infiltrated enemy territory. I shamelessly admit that I was looking for dirt, because Sophie Miller has been too damn perfect at work, and I wanted something to have even a small leg up on her.

Instead, I came to the conclusion that not only is she a stand-out intern, but she's also pretty fun to party with.

Currently, she's at the biggest *Okay, Cool* event of the year — our relatively small and intimate after-party for the Southeastern Advertising Conference held in Miami. It's invite only, costs a thousand dollars a head, with all proceeds benefitting a local charity, and it's reserved for the agencies my beloved boyfriend sees as leaders in the industry. Getting an invite as an agency is like finding Willy Wonka's golden ticket, and being asked to attend as an *Okay, Cool* employee is arguably better than a ten-thousand-dollar bonus.

I know why I'm here.

I landed one of our biggest clients to this date while I was an intern. *I* completely dismantled and rebuilt our current project management team from the ground up, revamping old and outdated systems and ushering us back into our top spot in the industry. *I* am already building a reputation as one of the most competent and creative account managers and creative directors in Florida, and I haven't even graduated yet.

I've earned my spot in this bougie mansion, standing in my brand new, rose gold and crystal-covered Jimmy Choo heels next to a giant pool that no one at this party will enter.

What I can't figure out is why Sophie *Goddamn* Miller is here.

The party is in full swing, even though the conference just ended an hour ago. And though Florida may be immune to the rest of our country's quickly declining temperatures during the holiday season, we're still a victim to the days being shorter, so the sun has already set, and the party's up-lighting and pool-lighting and candles littering every table make for an elegant, sophisticated feel. A jazz trio plays music from the corner of the pool balcony, a pleasant background to the soft buzz of chatter and laughter coming from each little pod of people.

It's the networking event of the year, and that's what I should be doing — networking. I should be rubbing elbows with other creative directors, making proposals for how we could work together to bag large, out-of-our-league clients, or steal the most coveted ones from other agencies who are lacking what we have.

I should *not* be staring death lasers with my eyeballs into the intern, but it's all I can manage to do.

Presently, we're both in a small gathering of executives — including the CEO of Atlanta's hottest agency, *Ball & Pen,* the director of the conference, who also hands out the most sought-after agency awards each year, our CFO, and of course, Brandon.

He's who stands between me and Sophie, one hand tucked into his pocket, and the other wrapped confidently around a glass tumbler of scotch. He and the others are laughing at something, which I miss, because I'm too busy wondering how the hell Sophie weaseled her way into this event and, even more so, how she's standing here in this particular circle.

To make matters even more peachy, Brandon is bragging on her to the group. It's not over the top, just noting a few of her accolades as an intern, but it's enough to make me have to actively keep myself from tapping my heel in annoyance.

I'm debating ways I could make it look like an accident and shove her into the pool, when Brandon puts his hand at the small of my back and smiles down at me, flashing his dazzling smile that somehow looks even more charming in the low lighting and pulling me back to the moment.

"And this one," he says, shaking his head. "Not *only* did she secure the *Bare•ly* account as an intern, but she is also the lead on our top-performing campaign." He pauses, arching a brow at Mrs. Lambert, the CEO of the Atlanta agency. "And she hasn't even graduated yet."

Mrs. Lambert whistles through her teeth as the rest of the group smiles and nods their approval. "That's pretty impressive, Ms. Daniels. You ever get tired of working for this chump, you make sure you find me in Atlanta, okay?"

"Does Atlanta have a beach?"

The group chuckles at that, but Mrs. Lambert tips her glass toward me. "No beach, but if you ever thought about coming to work for me, I'd build one for you right in the middle of the city, if that's what you wanted."

"I'm flattered, Mrs. Lambert," I say, laying a palm over my chest. "But my home is *Okay, Cool.*" I look up at Brandon then. "As long as this one will keep me around, anyway."

Brandon pulls me into his side possessively. "Like I'd ever be stupid enough to let you slip out of my hands."

My heart blooms in my chest as he stares down at me, and then — in front of our little group and for everyone else to see, too — he plants a gentle, adoring kiss on my lips.

Fucking swoon.

He jumps right back into the conversation, steering them toward the conference and how they could improve upon it, but I'm still floating on a cloud with that kiss reverberating through my body. Ever since the end of last semester when the truth about us came out, we haven't had to hide our relationship — and being able to stand next to this man and proudly claim him, to have *him* claim me?

It's the most powerful drug in the world.

I'm still trying to contain the butterflies in my ribcage when my gaze shifts to Sophie, and I'm a little surprised to find her staring back at me, a small smile curved on her ballerina-pink lips. She tilts her glass toward me in a nod of acknowledgement, and I do my best not to frown, offering her my *this-isn't-a-fake-smile-I-swear* smile before I turn my attention to the current speaker in the group.

But Sophie keeps watching me, and when Brandon's assistant comes up to usher him away from our group and to another anxiously waiting to speak with him, the rest of the executives disband, and Sophie stands closer to me, sipping from her champagne glass as we both survey the crowd.

"This event is *wild,* isn't it?" she says after a moment, shaking her head as her bright eyes scan the crowd.

I hate those eyes, because they remind me so much of my own that I want to gouge them out of her head and claim copyright infringement. It pisses me off that her hair is the same platinum blonde as mine, that she has the same taste in high heels, and the same love for high fashion. Hell, we even look like we *planned* our similarities tonight, both of us dressed in sleek, form-fitting and short white dresses with heels that steal the show — mine being the dazzly Jimmy Choos, and hers the same Louboutins she was wearing the first day I saw her in Brandon's office.

She looks incredible, sexy but professional.

And I *loathe* her for it.

"I can't believe Brandon invited me to come," she continues, a longing sigh leaving her chest. "I feel like the luckiest girl in the world."

I growl low in my throat, though I'm praying it's not loud enough that Sophie heard me. "Yes. *Mr. Church* is lovely in that respect," I correct her subtly, reminding her that *no one* at work calls him Brandon — except for me. "He has *such* a big heart for charity."

It's a thinly veiled dig, but if Sophie notices it, she doesn't let me know it.

Instead, she leans in closer, lowering her voice. "I know I won't have much time alone with you tonight, since I'm sure you have so many people to see and talk to, but while I have you, I just have to say..."

And then, that conniving, sneaky little bitch wraps her silky palm around the inside of my elbow.

"The work you've done on the *Bare•ly* account?" She shakes her head in earnest, leveling her gaze with mine. "It is the most inspiring work I've seen done in any agency in the years I've been studying. I was wondering... I have this project I have to do for my cornerstone class on big moves in the industry, and I'd really love to spotlight you and that account in particular. It wouldn't require much, just an interview and maybe some behind-the-scenes brainstorm notes, if you'd be willing to give me access. Just enough for me to put together a ten-minute presentation."

Sophie pauses then, her hand slides down my arm, slowly, each fingernail making contact with my skin. Her eyes follow the gesture, her plump, smooth lips parted slightly, and when she glances back at me, there's something hidden in her lash-covered gaze.

Chills and confusion wash over me in equal measure, and I'm suddenly shocked still, throat tightening with how intimate the touch is. We're in a crowd full of people, but the way she's looking at me, it feels like we're miles and miles away.

"You're just such an inspiration to me," she explains, wrapping her hand around mine until our palms touch. She's not holding my hand, but rather sliding her skin over mine, and she holds my fingertips with her own for just the briefest moment before withdrawing entirely. "It'd truly be an honor to work under you, to get an inside look of what makes you tick."

If anyone were to ask me, I would never admit to my suspicion — but I *swear* her eyes flick to my lips, that there's heat in her gaze when it finds me again, that the curl of her lips is alluding to more than just her desire to use me for a school project.

I clear my throat, inhaling a breath that burns too much for my liking and taking a marginal step back from Sophie. Her grin intensifies, as if she's won some competition I hadn't realized we'd entered into, but I hold my chin high to let her know she hasn't won *shit* in my eyes.

"Thank you," I say first. "And I would be happy to help you with your project. Why don't you swing by my desk on Monday and we can discuss further?"

Sophie's manicured eyebrow inches up, that smile still cemented on her lips. "I'll do that." Her eyes wash over me suggestively, tongue sliding along the inside of her cheek as she does, and now I *know* I'm not imagining things.

This bitch is checking me out.

Is she... *is she hitting on me?*

"Have a good evening, Ms. Daniels," she says, tipping her almost-empty glass with a wink. Then, she plucks the toothpick with an olive at the end of it and pops it into her mouth, sucking on it in a way that makes her lips big and pouty before she turns and leaves me standing at the edge of the pool so shaken up that I'm in danger of falling into it.

And I *keep* standing there, completely alone, with a shocked face I can't even pretend to hide.

What in the ever loving fuck was that?

Erin

Gavin Lindberg has been MIA from every session since the one when he so casually asked me to dinner.

Not that it matters, of course, because I've had my own priorities to focus on. I've spent the last month making amends, apologizing to everyone I've hurt and accepting that as much as I want them to, not everyone will forgive me.

Skyler was first, and she was the easiest — perhaps because she was the one in our group who always seemed to put her friends before herself. I don't think it's in her blood to hold a grudge, and I'm thankful for that, since we're now slowly working toward having a friendship again.

My mother was the next battle, and it was more like a war, because as much as I was apologizing to her for all the hell I'd put her through in the past year, I was also confessing to her that she was responsible for a lot of the deep-seated issues I'd been fighting all my life.

She did *not* like hearing that.

I'm thankful to my mom for how she helped me after Landon and his brothers gang-raped me. It's because of her that I clawed my way out of the deep, bottomless hole that night had put me in and took the reins of my life firmly in my hands once more.

But she also advocated ignoring what had happened and disguised that as strength. We never talked about it, and there was never any room for me to explore what that night did to me, how it permanently changed me, how I would never be the woman I was before. Hell, I wasn't even allowed to say the *word* rape — like I should have been ashamed of it.

To my mom, strength is standing tall and holding your chin high and never letting anyone see that you were a human being with feelings and flaws and hopes and dreams.

You must be steel — cold and hard and resilient.

So, opening up to her was not only difficult for me, but to her it was practically being forced to lie in a bed of needles. She wasn't just annoyed by my emotions, she was uncomfortable when they were aimed at her, which is why I wasn't surprised when she was less then receptive to them.

Still, she forgave me, and she seemed to at least somewhat listen to me, and I hope that, like Skyler, we'll move forward into a new, stronger relationship together.

I'd sat down and talked with everyone close to me — Lei, Jess, and Cassie included. I wasn't ready to tell them everything that had happened to me just yet, but I at least wanted them to know that I was trying.

And then, there was Bear.

I'm not surprised that he reacted the way he did when I asked him to dinner and tried, pathetically, to explain why I murdered our child.

I know it's not as callous as that, that I'm berating myself and not "being kind to myself," as my therapist would urge me to do.

But truthfully? In my heart? That's how I see it.

I took life from my own child, and I'll never forgive myself.

So why does it upset me so much that Bear won't forgive me, either?

He had every right to reject my apology that night we went to dinner, and still, I was shocked by it. Maybe it's because through all the shit I've faced in the past year, he has always been there for me. He's always been the one holding me and assuring me that it's okay, and that I'm not a terrible person, and that I will make it out of the hell I've been imprisoned in.

But he didn't hold me this time.

Hell, he could barely *look* at me.

And it killed me.

So, yeah, I've had plenty of my own shit to occupy my time and energy without worrying about going on a date with Gavin Lindberg.

But I'd be lying if I said I didn't notice he hadn't been around.

I'd be lying if I said I didn't take extra time getting ready for group the week we were supposed to go to dinner, curling my hair and putting on my makeup with precision and picking out one of my favorite fall outfits — dark, skinny jeans, a conservative silky blouse, and my favorite black high heels. And I'd be lying if I said my heart didn't deflate a little when he never showed that night, or the week after, or the week after that.

Maybe that's why I find myself slightly annoyed when he waltzes through the door two minutes before group therapy starts, casting me a smile and a wink as if we're buddies before taking a seat across the circle from me, outstretching his legs and shoving his hands in the pockets of his hoodie. His intense blue eyes watch me curiously, and I just glare back at him, letting my annoyance show until Jackie says we're getting started.

Then, I turn my attention to her, and I leave it there for the rest of the session.

I don't look at Gavin again, not even when he makes his sarcastic and ill-placed comments when someone else is speaking. Jackie warns him a couple times, and he finally shuts up — presumably because he's failing to get my attention like he so desperately seems to want to do.

When the session is over, I promptly grab my belongings and make my way toward the door, not bothering to stop by the table of coffee and donuts that I never touch, or stay back to talk to anyone else in the group.

I make it all the way to the parking lot before the distant sound of my name being called out stops me, and I take a deep breath, turning and finding Gavin slowing from his jog to a walk and eventually to stand just a few feet away from me.

It's dark in the parking lot, save for the streetlights casting warm circles over a few of the spots. Gavin is standing under one of them, and it leaves his face half-shadowed, but I can still see a tinge of remorse in his ocean eyes.

"Geez, you really bolted out of there tonight," he says. "Did I miss the fire?"

I cross my arms, shifting my weight to one hip.

Gavin sighs, grabbing the back of his neck and looking around at the otherwise-empty lot before his embarrassed gaze finds mine again. "Alright, I deserve the silent treatment. I'm sorry I bailed on our dinner. I have the tendency of being an asshole from time to time."

"How unfortunate," I deadpan, turning on my heel and making my way toward my car. I click the button to unlock it, sending a flash of taillights over the lot before Gavin jogs around to stand in front of me, holding his hands out, palms up.

"Erin, wait."

"Honestly, Gavin, I've been busy handling my own shit, okay? If you didn't want to go to dinner with me, you could have just said it. You didn't have to avoid group for almost a month."

"I *do* want to go to dinner with you."

"Clearly." I roll my eyes, pushing past him and opening my car door, but before I can slide inside, Gavin wraps his hand around the top of the window, serving as a barricade.

"I mean it," he says, brows furrowed together as his eyes search mine. "I'm sorry. Truly. I... I've had some personal things going on." He swallows, and I let my guard down marginally at the display of vulnerability. "And I *do* want to go to dinner with you."

I inhale, but otherwise don't respond, waiting.

"Let's go now."

At that, I laugh. "Now?"

"Right now," he says again. "If we go now, I can't bail out."

"Oh, how charming."

"I'm serious," he says when I try to push him out of the way to get in my car. His hand gently holds my forearm — not with enough force to stop me from brushing him off if I really want to, but with enough care to let me know he means what he says. "Let me take you to dinner. Right now. Anywhere you want."

The way he watches me is like he already knows who I am, and I hate that I love it so much. I hate that feeling like I'm being seen makes me want to say yes to any and everything this shadow of a man proposes.

"I don't really know of any good places to eat around here," I finally say. "I spend most of my time on the other side of town, near campus."

"What are you in the mood for?"

I shrug. "Sushi?"

Gavin grins, stepping out of the way and holding the car door open for me. "I know just the place."

***

"Why do I feel like I should be scared for my life or, at the very least, that I will be hugging my toilet later tonight?" I ask, eyeballing the dingy, roughed-up exterior of the brick building Gavin has guided us to. It's small and tucked between a bicycle shop and a barber shop in the part of downtown my parents specifically told me to stay away from when I first started school at PSU. The flickering neon sign above the blacked-out door says something in Japanese, and under it, a simple white banner reads SUSHI in black, all-caps English.

"Trust me, this will be the *best* sushi you'll ever have in your life," Gavin says, holding the door open for me. As soon as he opens it, we're hit with the thumping base of electronic music that would be better suited for a club than for any kind of restaurant, and a large group of people smushed inside, waiting to be seated. It's dim throughout the restaurant, with black lights and disco balls sending flares of light across the room.

I arch a brow, but don't move otherwise.

Gavin chuckles, reaching out for my hand. "Come on. Have a little faith."

Something about his smile makes my chest warm and fuzzy, and I smile in return, letting him take my hand in his and guide me inside. We mutter *excuse me* to several groups, squirming our way to the hostess stand.

Then, Gavin surprises me by speaking Japanese to the hostess, who smiles at him like she knows him — or like she wants to sleep with him, I can't be sure which — before leading us to a corner booth all the way in the back, where the music is a little softer and we have a view of the entire room.

Another surprise to me is that the place is *packed*. Every single table is taken, even though it's after eight now, and the table we're seated at was roped off like it was being held for a VIP. Judging by the long wait at the front, Gavin isn't the only one who's a fan of the sushi here.

I shrug off my jacket once we're seated, folding it once and laying it next to me in the booth. It's very rarely cold in South Florida, but we've been blessed with a cool front that leaves the evenings just chilly enough to wear the jackets and scarves we wear approximately three times a year and leave buried in our closet to stare at longingly for the rest of it.

A waiter swings by and asks what we'd like to drink, to which Gavin responds for me, ordering us both a water and a bottle of saki to share.

"So, you speak Japanese?" I ask when the waiter leaves.

"Surprised?"

"Very," I admit. "I take it you frequent this place a lot, judging by the fact that they gave us a roped-off booth."

"I roomed with the owner's son for a couple of months when I lived in Tokyo."

"You *lived* in Tokyo?"

"Briefly," Gavin says, shrugging as if it's no big deal. "I was thinking about teaching English there, so I stayed with a friend who was doing just that. Wasn't really my thing," he confessed. "But I loved the food, and the culture."

The way he said that, with a shit-eating grin and a wink, made me roll my eyes.

"Let me guess — culture is code for *girls*?"

"You said it, not me," Gavin deflects, holding up the menu with the writing facing me. It's just a simple, half-sheet of paper with a couple dozen items, and the menu is hand-written and photocopied. "Now, what you need to know about this place is that you can't go wrong with anything you order," he says. "But, if you really want to wet your panties, order the mackerel nigiri, the otoro sashimi, and the moon phase roll."

I laugh, folding my hands over my own menu rather than looking at it. "Okay. I trust you."

"Do you?" he challenges, and I love the way his eyes light up, the way his lazy smile spreads on his face.

"To order sushi for me, yes. To be respectful in group therapy or actually show up to take me on the date you asked me on?" I shrug. "Jury's still out."

"Hey, we're here, aren't we?" Gavin argues, gesturing to the restaurant around us.

"Just a few weeks late."

"That's fair," he says, and then the waiter drops off our water and saki, and Gavin pours two small ceramic cups with the hot liquid before passing one to me. "To overdue dates and the beautiful women who concede to them."

I roll my eyes, taking a sip before hugging the small cup between my hands. The smell and taste is delightful, and the warmth of the cup in my cool palms makes me feel oddly cozy inside this dim restaurant that could be a club.

"You were thinking about teaching English," I muse after the drink. "And you mentioned in therapy that you're a grad student. Is that what you're studying now?"

He shakes his head. "Psychology."

I chuckle.

"Fitting, isn't it?" he says with his own smile. Then, a shrug. "I want to be a different kind of grief counselor. I want to work with people who don't believe in the hippie ya-ya bullshit. People like me. People who need their therapy served a little hard up, like a shot of whiskey instead of a tall glass of sweet tea."

I tilt my head. "I like that analogy."

"We'll see how far it gets me."

The waiter stops by again, and Gavin places our order in Japanese before making small talk. By the time the waiter leaves, they seem like best buds.

"So, Erin Xander," he says once we're alone again. "Besides the fact that you're fucked up enough to need group *and* solo therapy, what else should I know about you?"

I nearly choke on my next sip of saki, but laugh despite it. "Wow, you really don't shy away from the dark, do you?"

"Why should I?" He shrugs. "We're all fucked up. It's the brave ones who actually admit it."

"And the ones like us who go to therapy for it, what do you call us?"

"Bored. Self-seeking." He pauses, his blue eyes locking on mine. "Lonely."

My eyes drop to the cup in my hand. "Well, if the fact that you know a little Japanese didn't make me think you were smart, that observation just did." I sigh, ignoring the pinch in my gut when I look at Gavin again. "As far as what you should know about me, I'm the president of Kappa Kappa Beta."

"I don't care."

The comment shocks me quiet, and I stare at smiling, confident Gavin for a moment before hesitantly continuing. "Um... I graduate at the end of this semester, and I'll be attending Grove Law School next summer."

"Don't care about that, either."

I frown. "I love country music, and going to the beach with my friends."

"Bor-ing," he sings, sitting back in his booth and sipping his saki.

"You are such an asshole," I spit, shaking my head. "Seriously, why ask me something and then react like that?"

"I asked what I should know about you."

"And I'm telling you."

He leans forward, elbows on the table and eyes boring into mine. "You're telling me things you think define you — positions you hold, schools you attend, your major, the music you like." Gavin's eyes search mine. "Tell me something real."

My chest is tight when I force my next breath. "I don't know what you want from me."

"Tell me. Something. Real."

Part of me wants to reach over and slap the stupid, knowing look off his face. The other part of me wants to shrink away from his gaze. And somewhere in the deepest, darkest hole of my heart, I see myself reflected in him.

It both terrifies and excites me.

I lean over the table, too — mirroring his stance and leveling my gaze with his. "I've been playing a part for so long, I don't know who I am past the labels I've been given and the credentials I can attach to the back of my name."

Those words linger between us for a moment, and Gavin's eyes soften, his next inhale long and deep.

"That real enough for you?"

Gavin swallows, and then he pushes out of his side of the booth enough to balance on his elbows and meet my lips in the middle of the table.

The kiss is so unexpected that I'm stiff at first, my eyes shooting open wide as he takes my face in his hands, holding me to his mouth, his lips soft and warm. In the next breath, before I can even catalog what I'm feeling or what we're doing, I'm melting into him, sighing into his mouth as I open mine and let his tongue sweep inside.

The lights dim somehow, and the music around us fades until it's no more than a thumping heartbeat pulsing through me. Gavin's hands are possessive and sure, holding me steady as his expert lips move in time with mine. It feels like the entire world has stopped spinning, like everyone in the restaurant has frozen in place in the name of this sacred moment.

When Gavin pulls back, he presses his forehead to mine, and we both exhale shaky breaths that meet between us.

Then, his hands gently release me, thumbs brushing my jaw softly before he sits back in his booth. I lean back in mine, too, and we watch each other for a beat before the world kicks into motion again, and the waiter delivers our order, and Gavin picks up his chopsticks like nothing even happened.

"Alright," he says, smirking with his eyes on me while I fight to catch my breath. He picks up the mackerel nigiri, dipping it ever so slightly in soy sauce before offering it to me. "Are you ready to have your mind blown?"

I think I already have, Gavin Lindberg.

I think I already have.

Jess

The best part about fall in South Florida is that while the rest of the country is already getting snow and temperatures well under fifty degrees, Florida is cooling down just enough to land us in that perfect beach weather zone. Almost every day is sunny, hovering between seventy-five and eight-five, with a cool breeze coming in off the coast.

I smile and soak it all in as the girls and I work on our tan in the back yard of the sorority house. We've all been so busy with classes and work and relationship shit that it's the first time the five of us have really been able to spend quality time together, and while the weather might be cooling down a smidge, it's apparent to me that the drama in our lives never will.

This crew couldn't escape trouble even if we tried.

So far, Cassie has filled us in on her and Adam's fight regarding Grayson, and to be fair, we've all told her that while we understood that she wanted to be friends with Grayson, we understood why Adam flew off the handle. Was he a little overdramatic? Maybe. But when I think back on how I reacted to Jarrett spending time with his female co-workers, I can't blame him.

Hell, Jarrett didn't even fuck those girls, and I was jealous and pissed off. I can't imagine how I would have reacted if I knew they had a past.

Still, Cassie is adamant that she's had to cut friends out of her life before and it's nearly killed her. She almost cried when she told us she couldn't do it again.

And I also understood that.

So, while we tried to help her through that whole ordeal, we also caught up with Ashlei and the weird intern drama going on at *Okay, Cool* and — though she's been mostly coy about it — Erin briefly told us about a new "friend" she's made at group therapy.

I have a feeling that *friend* is going to come with some benefits.

But we can all tell Erin's not ready to talk about it, because she brushes off the topic as soon as it's brought up and shifts the attention to Skyler.

"When do you see Kip next?" Erin asks, reaching for the sunscreen to reapply on her face. Erin has always been the one to take the best care of her skin — not just in the sun, but with her entire regimen that she's had since she was eighteen. If I had to make a bet on which one of us would age the most gracefully, all my money would be on her.

"I'm flying in to see him for Thanksgiving, actually," Skyler says on a longing sigh, fanning herself with her magazine. "And honestly, I'm a little nervous."

"Why?" Cassie asks.

Skyler shrugs. "It's hard to explain. I miss him so much, but I haven't seen him since he started school out there. I don't know... I guess I'm just worried that maybe I won't fit into this new part of his life."

Ashlei scoffs. "Are you kidding? I bet he can't *wait* for you to be there so he can show you around and show you *off* to all his film buddies."

"And *I'm* sure he can't wait to bang your brains out," I chime in. Then, I snap my fingers, leaning up in my chair so I can see her better. "Oh! Maybe you could make a movie of your own."

I waggle my brows, and Skyler rips out a page of her magazine, balls it up, and pegs me in the forehead with it. "Perv."

I stick my tongue out before reaching for my tumbler, which I told our sorority house mom had iced coffee in it but is actually filled with vodka and tonic and a splash of lime juice. "You love me."

"We all bear that curse," Erin agrees, and I reach over to smack her ass where she's tanning it to the tune of giggles.

"Speaking of the spell you've put on us," Cassie says. "Looks like Kade has fallen under the same one, huh?"

I try to bite back a smile, but fail miserably, and then *I blush* and I want to punch myself in the face.

"He's definitely hooked," I say, shaking off the butterflies in my stomach.

"And are you?" Skyler asks.

I sigh, flopping back in my chair dramatically. "God, I don't even know anymore." I shake my head, trying to find the right words. "He annoys the absolute *fuck* out of me. But... he also fascinates me, too. And *God*, the sex..." I pull down my sunglasses so the girls can see how serious I am. "The sex is out of this *world*."

"Better than with Jarrett?" Ashlei asks, and I know she means it as nothing more than a simple comparison, but my heart pounds once, twice, three times hard in my chest.

I swallow. "It was different with Jarrett."

"Different good or different bad?" Skyler asks.

"Just... different. We weren't just fucking. We had a relationship."

"Is that what you want with Kade?" Erin asks.

And the question hits me like a semi-truck.

I freeze, shock still, holding my drink in my hand with the sun warming my skin.

"Jess?" Erin asks.

But I can't respond. I'm too busy turning her question over and over in my head, like the winning numbers of the lottery just waiting to be plucked out.

Holy fucking shit.

Do I want a relationship with Kade?

I mean, obviously, I want more — that much was established when I dragged his ass into the tent during the Halloween party and told him I wanted to be his and for him to be mine. But, at the time, I'd been so focused on the fact that I didn't want him with any other girl, that I hadn't paused to ask myself what *exactly* I wanted from him — other than to fuck me exclusively.

And now that I'd asked myself the question, my reaction told me all I needed to know.

Skyler snaps her fingers in front of my face. "Earth to J-Love."

I groan, sinking back in my chair and abandoning my drink on the table so I can scrub my hands over my face. "Oh, God."

"What?" Cassie asks, worried.

I sigh. "I do."

The girls fall silent, exchanging glances.

"I *do* want a relationship."

At that, Ashlei laughs, reaching over to squeeze my forearm. "You say that like you just realized you're an alcoholic or something. Wanting a relationship isn't bad, babe."

My next swallow is impossible, like I've just eaten forty-five saltines without a glass of water to help out. "It is when I'm pretty fucking certain that is *not* what he wants," I argue. Then, I lock eyes with her. "And that the last time I was in a relationship, I had my heart shattered."

Again, the girls exchange glances, and then Skyler gets up from her chair and sits down at the foot of mine, leaning in to look me in the eyes. "Hey, love is fucking scary, okay? I think if anyone gets that, it's this group of girls."

Everyone nods, and my chest tightens with discomfort. I want to crawl inside a hole and hide forever.

"What if you just asked him?" Skyler suggests.

"Ask him what?"

"Ask him on a date," she says with a shrug. "Or, better yet, *tell him* you're going on a date. See what he says."

My instant reaction is to shake my head and scream out *absolutely not*, but her words slide over me like silk, and I lean into them, wrapping them around myself like a blanket.

Could it be that simple?

Could I just tell Kade what I want, and him reciprocate it?

Everything in my body screams a resounding *hell no*, but already, I'm up out of my chair, throwing on my cover up and sliding into my sandals.

"Where are you going?" Erin asks.

"To the Alpha Sigma house."

"To...?"

I look at all of them. "To tell that motherfucker that he's taking me on a date."

That earns me a burst of laughter, and they each smack my ass and holler out encouragements as I dash out of the backyard and down Greek Row.

I burst into the A Sig house just like I did that first time I came to tease Kade, only this time, the house is mostly empty — likely due to it being such a beautiful day outside. I head straight back to Kade's room, but find it empty, and I frown, hanging my hands on my hips.

Where are you? I text him.

The house. What's up?

Where at in the house?

Outside playing beer pong with the guys.

I weave my way through the house and outside, and there are at least a dozen brothers in their swim trunks, jamming to country music and playing beer pong and having an arm-wrestling competition at a nearby table.

At the sight of me, all the commotion stops.

Kade's right in the middle of a game, and before he can shoot the ping pong ball across the table and into his opponent's cup, I slide in front of him, taking it from his hand.

"What the—"

"I want more."

Kade's smile slips off his face at my words, and he shoves his sunglasses up onto the top of his head, cocking a brow at me. "Um... hi?"

"Hi," I say. "I want more."

"More what?"

"More than mind-blowing, toe-curling, name-screaming sex."

That earns a few whistles and *atta boys* from his brothers, and I flick them all off before crossing my arms over my chest and focusing back on Kade. The noise around us picks up again, as if everyone has gone back to their business while Kade smirks down at me.

"Okay, then," he says, leaning a hip against the table. "What do you want?"

"I want to go on a date."

Kade's eyes trail over me, locking on my cleavage still visible even in my cover up. When his eyes find mine again, his grin widens. "Friday?"

I clear my throat, aiming for nonchalance. "Fine."

With my mission accomplished, I turn, tossing the ping pong ball across the table. It bounces once and sinks into the right back cup, and the boys roar in approval.

I wink at Kade, who's laughing his ass off, and then I waltz *my* ass right on out of there with a victory smile on my face.

Adam

I am the worst pathetic piece of shit.

I run another hand through my greasy hair, feeling that sentence sink into my veins like venom. I haven't slept more than a few hours since the Halloween party, when Cassie told me she wouldn't choose between me and Grayson, and to me, that meant she'd already made a choice.

And once again, it wasn't me.

Eating has been impossible. I've taken to drinking protein shakes with a shit ton of vegetables just to keep my nutrition up because solid food just isn't an option. And currently, though it's gorgeous outside, I'm in my dark bedroom all alone with Thirty Seconds to Mars blasting in my headphones.

I'm perfectly content to waste my day away. It's what I've been doing for the past week and a half, and every day I go without Cassie showing up at my door, I realize I'd be content to do this for the rest of my life. Who needs a presidency? Who needs a college degree? Who needs sunlight or friends or something to live for?

I've hit some lows in my life, but this might be the lowest.

Because for the first time, I've lost Cassie not because of something stupid, but because of something real that we couldn't see eye to eye on.

That we maybe never will.

And I have to decide if this is what will end it all.

I roll over to face my wall, but before I can curl into a fetal position, my headphones are ripped from my ears.

I don't even yell at the offender — especially when I see Jeremy's annoyed expression staring back at me in the dim light of my bedroom. I just sigh and face the wall again, resigned.

"You're wasting your time," I mutter.

"Yeah. And you're wasting your senior year." Jeremy reaches over me, ripping the navy-blue curtains on my window open before I can prepare for it. I shrink away from the sunlight, shielding my eyes and shoving him off my bed.

"Asshole."

"Get up."

He yanks the covers off me, and I try to rip them back, but he chucks them across the room before I can.

"Look. It's been almost two weeks. I'm tired of this shit, and so is everyone else. So, if you need to talk about what happened at the Halloween party, let's talk."

"I don't."

"You don't?" Jeremy deadpans.

When I say nothing, he shakes his head and pulls up my desk chair to sit in front of my bed. He straddles it backward, leaning his arms on the back of it with a heavy sigh.

"Fine. I'll talk." But before he says another word, he reaches over and thunks me on the forehead. "Why are you such a fucking idiot when it comes to Cassie McBee?"

I sit up, a bit stunned and a lot pissed, ready to slug him off his chair, but he easily dodges my fist and shoves me back onto the bed — hard.

"No, you had your chance to talk and didn't say shit. So you sit there and listen."

I'm panting, gritting my teeth, but I know Jeremy well enough to know he's not here out of disrespect.

If anything, he's here because he cares about me.

And that's a helluva lot more than I can say for anyone else.

"Look. I get it. If I had a girlfriend and she was hanging out with her ex-boyfriend, I'd be fucking livid, too. In fact, I probably would have run over to them the first time I saw them together and laid him out. But here's the thing — you sat on it *for weeks*, and grew all this resentment, so much so that by the time you two hashed it out, you were so heated and so far up your own ass that you couldn't even listen to her."

"What the fuck was I supposed to listen to?" I argued. "She told me that no matter what I said or did, she wasn't going to choose between us."

"Because she doesn't think she should have to! And honestly, Adam — do you?"

I blew out a breath like a dragon. "I don't think I even should have had to *ask* her."

Jeremy holds up his hands. "Just think about it for a second. Okay? Do you remember all that fucking shit that went down with her and our stupid asshat for a president?"

I swallow, because I'll never forget the night Cassie climbed into my window and into my bed and I held her against my chest while she cried. She told me I was right about Clay, who had been fucking around with her *and* her high school best friend at the same time. She found out in the crudest way possible at a party after her first semester at PSU, and I'd been there for her.

I'll never forget how crushed she was.

"I remember," I manage on a croak.

"Then you know that this is more than just a simple *him or you* scenario," Jeremy says. "This isn't about her wanting to fuck Grayson or ever be with him again. This is about the fact that she's lost people in her life and it *kills* her. I mean, you know better than anyone that Cassie is the sweetest fucking girl on the planet. She hates being hurt. She hates hurting others. So, when this guy she spent so much time with comes back around and apologizes and she has an opportunity to be friends with him? Of course, she wants to. And I hate to say it, brother," he says, shaking his head. "But it has nothing to do with you."

My chest tightens. "It does, though. It's not fair of her to expect me to be okay with that."

"Really? Just like it's not fair of you to expect her to be okay with you and Skyler still being friends?"

His words slam into me, hard and fast and unexpected, and I sit up slowly in my bed before leaning my back against my headboard. "Fuck."

"Yeah," Jeremy says. "Look, man. I know it's hard. You two have been through some shit, and you don't want to lose her. She doesn't want to lose *you*, either. And I know this is a big thing she's asking of you, to put aside your pride and your jealousy and trust her."

I bite my tongue against the urge to argue that I'm not jealous of that fucking prick, and Jeremy must notice, because he leans down until I look at him again.

"But whether you see it or not, she *already* chose you." He smiles, shaking his head. "Bro, you got her. You got the girl. She's all yours and has been since she came to this campus — regardless of the past."

A deflated breath leaves my chest.

"Do you trust her?" he asks.

"More than anyone."

"Then, what's the problem?"

I swallow, because as much as I want to argue that it's that fucking douchebag musician I don't trust, I know that negates what I just said. Because no matter what *he* tries, Cassie would never lean into it — into *him* — ever again.

Jeremy's right — that girl *is* mine.

And I can't fucking lose her again.

I scrub my hands over my face. "Goddamnit. How the fuck do I make this right?"

Jeremy claps his hand on my shoulder. "Step one, take a shower. You smell like shit, bro. And then, go *talk* to her. And listen this time, too."

I nod, looking at my best friend who should be so tired of my shit, he never speaks to me again, but instead, is always there for me. “I owe you a beer.”

Jeremy scoffs, standing. “More like a keg.”

“Thank you, bro. Seriously.”

“I got you. Now, get your shit together and then come outside and hang with your brothers.”

I nod, and when he’s gone, I pull out my phone and immediately dial Cassie’s number. My heart races in my chest as it rings, and after the seventh one, I’m sent to her voicemail.

“Cassie...” I say after the beep, but then I freeze.

I’m sorry?

I love you?

I take it all back?

Nothing seems right, and I sigh, leaning my forehead against the cool wall. After a few calming breaths, I decide if there’s any way to make this right, it’s not going to be with a simple phone call or text or trip down Greek Row.

I need to show her that I’m serious, that I’m sorry, and that I trust her.

“If you still love me,” I say, my voice low and hoarse. “Then meet me at the marina this Saturday. One hour before sunset.”

I stay on the line for a moment longer, as if somehow she’ll feel me through the phone. When I finally hang up, I take a deep breath and drag myself into the shower.

And while I put together my plan, I pray that Cassie will give me the chance to make things right.

Ashlei

The inside of my thighs are tender and slightly bruised by the time I finish my pole session on Friday.

Getting back into dancing? Easy enough, just a little cardio training and getting my body to remember how it feels to move that way. Revisiting climbing the pole and head up tricks? Not too shabby, a little painful, but for the most part, I got this.

But once I got into training my leg hangs and thigh grips again, my body wanted to divorce me.

I've spent all afternoon upside down, working on my Extended Butterfly, my Scorpio, my leg switches and hip holds, and *God help me,* even my Superman. As much as it hurts to train like this, it also feels good, like I'm making progress and finding my passion again.

Besides, I need a break from my brain.

I haven't stopped turning over what happened between me and Sophie since the *Okay, Cool* after-party. It seems no matter how much I try to focus on work or school or sorority events or pole, that night keeps creeping up on me, and I find myself trying to dissect every word she said, every move she made, wondering if I made it up, or if she really was hitting on me.

And if she was... *what the hell?*

Was she bisexual? Was she just being a bitch, trying to fuck with my head since it's clear that I'm onto her and the way she looks at Brandon?

Did I make it all up, and it's *me* who's the psycho?

I sigh, peeling my high heels and knee pads off and shoving them into my gym bag with more force than necessary, like it's Sophie I'm shoving out of my life.

"Hey now," Karen says, arching an eyebrow as she lowers down to the floor next to me. "It wasn't *that* bad of a training session, was it?"

I offer her a smile. "I'm sorry. Just have a lot on my mind."

"That explains why you asked for two hours of torture instead of just one today." Karen pauses, watching me. "Ashlei, I know we talked about this a few months ago... but I really think you should consider competing again."

I swallow, trying to remain calm when I meet Karen's eyes. "I... I don't think..."

Karen folds her soft fingers over my arm, gentle and calm. "I know what happened with Kitty Heels."

I nearly pass out at the mention of the studio I left behind me, that I've tried to bury for years. In a flash, I see Leslie, Kya, Hayden, the drugs, the threats, the money, the club I tried to work at to save my ass, Jess coming to my rescue.

Another soft squeeze from Karen saves me from blacking out. "Leslie has made a name for herself in this industry — and it's not a good one. Everyone knows the sketchy shit she pulls, and trust me when I say you were the best thing to happen for her and that studio. I know she fucked you over... but don't let her steal this passion from you."

My eyes gloss, and I don't have a single word to say in response.

"You don't have to make a decision now, okay?" Karen says, standing and offering a hand down to help me up, too. "Just think about it. If not competing, maybe you could at least perform. Trust me — if you got on a pole stage?" She shakes her head once I'm standing with her. "You'd captivate the entire audience — me included."

I somehow manage a nod and a smile, and I thank her, grabbing my bag and leaving the studio with my mind whirling with even more thoughts than when I walked in. When I see Brandon's car on the curb, relief sinks into me like sweet honey, and I smile.

"I like this tradition of you picking me up after class," I say when I slide inside the passenger seat. I toss my bag in the back. "But I'm starting to think you might have a fetish for sweaty girls or something."

"I only have a fetish for *one* sweaty girl," he corrects, leaning over the console to give me a deep, passionate kiss. I'm breathless when he pulls back, and his golden eyes settle over me in appreciation. "I was thinking we could do dinner tonight."

"I like that idea."

"In Chicago."

I balk. "*Chicago?*"

He nods on a grin. "There was a last-minute cancellation at one of the most famous restaurants in town, and the owner called me and asked if I wanted the table. It's twenty-four courses of the finest cuisine you'll ever have." He shrugs. "And then, I was thinking I could fuck you on the balcony of my favorite suite in the city."

I lick my lips, crawling over the console enough to thread my fingers around the back of his neck and pull him into me for a kiss. "Are we flying commercial?"

"Come on now," he chastises, nipping my bottom lip. "You know me better than that, Miss Daniels."

I smirk. "Then *you* should know better than to think we'll wait until after dinner to fuck if you're taking me on your private jet again." I pause, letting my hand drop to his belt buckle and drawing a soft line over the seam of his dress pants before whispering. "Mr. Church."

A guttural groan rips from his throat, and then he breaks our kiss suddenly and swiftly, throwing the car in drive and speeding us across town to the airport.

***

I feel night and day better after an evening with Brandon.

Just like I suspected, we'd barely made it through takeoff before Brandon had me pinned against one of the leather couches on the private jet, and once we'd landed in Chicago, we'd spent all dinner staring at each other from across our intimately lit table, my heel tracing up and down his leg under the tablecloth, his eyes devouring me more than the meal.

By the time we get back to the suite downtown, I'm starving for his touch again. It seems I never can get enough.

I've never been to Chicago before, and I decide after just one day in the city that I love it. The architecture is unlike anything I've ever seen, buildings stretching up high into the sky and lining the river, the lake, filling the city with lights. But there are also dozens of parks and recreational areas, so while it's a city, it's somehow greener and fresher than Manhattan — at least, in my opinion.

I'm appreciating the view from our balcony and the crisp, cool air when Brandon joins me, wrapping his arms around me from behind. I rest my head back on his chest as he lets out a deep, content sigh.

"Beautiful, isn't it?" he whispers in my ear.

I nod, letting my eyes trace over the city lights glittering like stars, the river reflecting their glare and making for the most picturesque backdrop.

"You know, it's been almost a year since the first time you took me on that private jet," I remark.

Brandon chuckles, kissing my cheek. "It has, hasn't it? God, I wanted you so bad. I'm surprised I made it that long before touching you."

"You were trying to do the right, moral thing and not fuck your intern."

"Looks like I sold my soul to the devil, then."

I turn in his arms, threading mine around his neck. The way the lights reflect in his eyes warm my chest, and I trace his dark features, falling even more for him every second that we're together. "I'm so happy we found each other."

He nods, knuckles brushing my jaw. "Me, too. I can't believe you thought we weren't exclusive all that time, until you asked me in the spring after we told everyone at the agency about us."

"It's hard," I argue. "When you're my age, everyone plays games."

His eyes are darker when they meet mine again. "Do you know now that I don't?"

I swallow, nodding, leaning into where his hand frames my face.

"And do you know that I love you?"

I close my eyes, fighting back the tears those words drew from me the moment he said them. It's nearly impossible, though, for the joy that strangles me, the relief, the terror and otherworldly ecstasy that consume me at once.

"I do now," I say, opening my eyes and looking into his. "And I love you, too."

Brandon's lips are on mine as soon as I finish speaking, and I breathe in the kiss, the man holding me, the night around us, the moment I'll never forget. I'm so lost in the way his hands feel on my waist, and the way his lips move in time with mine, that I barely register him lifting me into his arms and carrying me inside.

The windows that surround the suite are floor to ceiling, still showcasing the breathtaking city view as Brandon deftly turns out every light and guides me to the California king bed. My knees hit the back of it once he sets me back down on the floor, and I press my hands into his chest, smiling against his kiss.

"I thought you said you wanted to fuck me on the balcony?"

I'm ready for him to give some smart ass comment in response, or to haul my ass back outside, but instead, he swallows, pressing his forehead to mine. "Not now," he husks. "Now, I'm going to make love to you in this bed."

My heart swells in my chest, my throat tight as I run my fingers back to hold his neck and draw him back to my lips. The kiss is gentle and sweet and unlike any other that I've had from this man, and I melt into it, resisting the urge to pinch myself to make sure this is all real.

He takes his time undressing me, peeling my little black dress over my head before reaching into my hair and slowly pulling out each bobby pin that holds it in place. Next, he unclasps my bra, and helps me step out of my heels before slipping my panties down over my ass, my thighs, my ankles, leaving them on the floor.

Between kisses and touches and sighs and licks, he undresses himself, too — and then his arms wrap around me, guiding me down on top of the plush comforter of the bed, the down pillows giving way to the weight of my head.

I don't realize I'm shaking until Brandon holds himself over me and my trembling fingers wrap around his thick, bulging biceps. I hold onto them as an unsteady breath slips through my lips, and Brandon kisses me gently, spreading my legs wider with his. Our bodies are hot where they touch — chest to chest, his arms surrounding me, and mine holding onto him, his thighs between mine, his shaft warm and hard where it slicks between my wet lips.

"Do you remember when I told you on my yacht that the only place I held any power over you was in the office?"

I nod, still holding onto him for dear life with my heart racing in my chest.

"Well, I've decided that's now a lie." He shakes his head, eyes flicking back and forth between mine. "In every possible way, in every place that exists, you are my everything. You hold the power, Ashlei, and I am yours — to bear or to break."

Tears flood my eyes, and this time I don't try to stop them. I have never felt anything in my life like I feel for this man, and I succumb to the feeling of him surrounding me — all of me — now and forever.

"I will never break you," I whisper, reaching up to press my lips to his. He answers me with a passionate kiss in return, and then with a flex of his hips, he's inside me.

I feel him all at once, all-encompassing, the bare length of him filling me up. I gasp into his mouth, and his hands wrap around my shoulders, giving him a better grip to thrust inside me again. Each time he withdraws and pummels in, his pelvis rubs my clit, and I spread my legs even wider, chasing the building fire ready to catch.

Brandon's mouth roams all over me — my neck, my jaw, my chin and lips and ears and breasts. I feel him everywhere, and I run my nails down his back, kiss his skin in return, praying that he feels me just as much.

How can it be that this strong, powerful, successful man wants anything to do with me? How can it be that out of all the women falling at his feet, he chose me to stand by his side, to be his queen, to say the three words every woman wants to hear?

This time last year, I was fighting every urge that begged me to give into my lust for him, and now, he's making love to me in a city halfway across the country, and everyone knows about us, and nobody dares to tell us we can't have each other.

I could never break him, I realize, because we're unbreakable.

As long as we're together, we can't be stopped.

Trembling and holding onto each other with slick, hot hands, Brandon makes love to me for hours in that bed.

And before we leave the next morning, he makes good on his promise to fuck me on the balcony, too.

Jess

The last time I went on a date, it was with Jarrett.

I don't want to compare. Fuck, the whole *point* of dicking around with Kade was to distract myself from the fact that Jarrett had pulverized my heart. And the surprising fact is that it's been working... until now.

Because now, I'm staring in the mirror moments before Kade is picking me up for our first official date, and for some reason, it all feels wrong.

It feels wrong to be thinking about the way my stomach fluttered the first time Jarrett took me on a date, or how he made me come home with him when I was sick just so he could take care of me, or how he flew in from New York and hung out with me and my sorority sisters, which made them fall just as in love with him as I was.

It feels wrong because it's a past, not a future — and tonight, I start something new with *someone* new.

I sigh, rubbing the edge of my lip with my pinky to fix a bit of lipstick smudge. It's slightly cool tonight — for South Florida, at least — so I landed on my favorite pair of Spanx leggings, a burnt orange crop top, and my favorite black booty heels. I layered a cream, high-low cardigan over the top, and did my makeup mostly natural, except for the smoky eye. My blonde hair is down and curled, falling over my shoulders, and I stare back at the golden eyes in the mirror with a pit in my stomach.

Because as much as I'm thinking of Jarrett, perhaps what fucks me up most is that I don't think I miss him anymore.

I don't think my heart breaks as much when I think about him. I don't think I care what he's doing or who he's with anymore.

And more than anything, I don't think I'm sad that it's not him picking me up tonight.

The truth is, I'm *excited* for my date with Kade.

And for some reason, that fucks me up.

That's what feels wrong.

Skyler pops her head into the bathroom, dancing a little with her eyebrows waggling like a cartoon character. "He's here," she whispers. "And he's *smokin'!*"

"Are you hitting on my boyfriend, Sky?"

At that, her mouth pops open. "Oh, I didn't realize he was your *boyfriend*."

My cheeks flame, and I grab the makeup remover wipe I'd used to correct my eyeliner and chuck it at her. She dodges it easy, laughing and teasing me all the way down the stairs. When I hit the bottom one, we both stop, Skyler watching me knowingly as I do everything in my power to keep my jaw from dropping.

Holy fucking shit.

The Kade I'm most familiar with is naked Kade. I'm used to seeing his tattoos sprawling out over every inch of his muscular body, his short hair messy and mussed, his grin goofy and playful. But tonight? Tonight, Kade is in dark, form-fitting jeans, an olive green polo that sets off the color of his hungry eyes, and a brown leather jacket, shoved up just below his elbows, showing off his toned and tattooed forearms. His hair is styled, and that grin that's usually so goofy and carefree is sultry and sexy as hell.

He looks like a *GQ* model, a celebrity, a rock star who could fuck me all the way up.

And I want *all* of him.

"Jess," he says, his eyes roaming over me appreciatively as he shakes his head. I shiver at my name on his tongue, and when his gaze finds mine, that tongue snakes out just enough to wet his bottom lip. "You look gorgeous." He pauses, lowering his voice to just above a whisper. "You always do."

I don't realize we're not alone until that exact moment, because a chorus of *awww's* and *oh my God's* ring out from the sorority sisters clamored in the living room.

That seems to knock me out of my daze, and I roll my eyes, taking the last step off the stairs and crossing my arms in front of him. "That's some line."

"Not a line," he assures me, that sexy smirk back in place. Then, he holds out his arm for me to thread mine through. "Ready?"

Oh, how I want to call him on his obvious show. But then again, I love the way he's holding out an arm for me, the way he came to the house to pick me up, the way he planned an entire night for us.

I meant it when I said I wanted a date.

And he's delivering.

I try to fight a smile, but fail miserably, weaving my hand through the hole in his arm and wrapping my fingers around his bicep. I glance back at Skyler and the other girls when we're at the door, and they're all holding up their thumbs and clapping quietly with glee.

"So, Mr. GQ," I say when I'm buckled into the passenger seat of his hot little Camaro — the one *I've* been driving all semester, thanks to our deal. "What's on the menu tonight?"

It's a purposeful line, one that sets him up to easily say *you* in return. But instead, Kade smiles, firing the engine to life. "I'm going to wine and dine you, beautiful. Just like you deserve."

His eyes find mine then, and then one hand reaches over to hold mine across the console, and he doesn't remove it the entire drive.

***

When Kade told me he was going to wine and dine me, I honestly thought he meant he was going to take me to the equivalent of a fancy Olive Garden downtown. I definitely *did not* expect him to take me to one of the most expensive restaurants on the water, one that sits at the top of a high rise and rotates.

No joke — the restaurant *spins*, giving you a three-sixty view of the city and the coastline as you eat.

On top of that, they're known for incredible tapas, of which Kade orders us a dozen, a rare collection of wine, of which Kade orders us not one, but *two* bottles, and a live jazz trio, to which Kade takes my hand after dinner and leads me out on the dance floor to enjoy.

It's the most magical night.

And it is absolutely not what I expected from him.

I can't help but stare at him when we're back at the table after a few songs, each of us sipping our wine and enjoying the music as we look over the dessert menu. Or rather, as *Kade* looks over the dessert menu and I study him, instead. He looks even more handsome in the candlelight, with the city glowing behind him, and I have to admit, watching him sip red wine turns me on *way* more than seeing him chug a beer at a frat party.

"I feel like I don't even know who you are."

The words blurt out before I can stop them, and Kade lifts a brow, casting me a glance before he's looking at the menu again. "What do you mean?"

"I mean, who the fuck are you?" I ask, gesturing to where he sits. "The Kade I know lives in basketball shorts and flat-bill hats. I didn't even know you had clothes like this in your wardrobe."

Kade chuckles, setting his menu down and lifting his glass to his lips for another sip. "Are you upset about it?"

"No," I answer quickly, shifting. "Just surprised, is all."

"I love surprising you."

"Seriously, Kade," I say on a sigh. "This is... a lot. I'm just... where is the kid who annoyed me at Spring Break last year? Where is the kid who thought telling me he wanted me to sit on his face was a good pick-up line?"

"I was a puppy then, remember?" he says, using the exact words I had. "I've been trained."

"I didn't train you to do all *this*," I argue, gesturing to the table.

Kade leans forward, resting his elbows on the table and folding his hands together. "You said you wanted to be taken on a date," he reminds me. "You also said you wanted to be mine, and wanted me to be yours. Am I missing anything yet?"

I shake my head.

"Well, for me, I don't take any of that lightly. If you're my girl, then I'm not just fucking you in my dorm room and eating burritos wrapped in foil — though that *is* a good time," he adds with a grin. Then, he shrugs. "If you're my girl, then I'm giving you the best that I can."

"Color me impressed."

"Oh, this is just the first date," he says with a grin. "The best is yet to come. And for the record, you may not have liked the proposal when I first gave it, but you *know* damn well that you love sitting on my face."

I roll my eyes, taking a sip of my wine just as the waiter asks us for our order. Kade takes over, ordering three different desserts for us to sample from, and once our menus have been taken and it's just us and our wine, his eyes land on me.

"So, you're graduating soon," he says. "What are you going to do next?"

I chuckle. "Why do you care?"

"Jess, if you want more, you've gotta give me more, too."

His eyes are sincere, and somehow that scares me more than anything.

I swallow another sip of wine, staring at the red liquid in my cup. "Hell if I know. I changed my major last year because one thing I figured out for sure, I do *not* want to go into politics."

Kade snorts. "I can't imagine that ever even being an option for you."

"I thought it was at one point," I admit. "I was a poli sci major, bright-eyed and bushy-tailed and thinking — like everyone else in that major — that I could someday change the world."

"What happened?"

"I'm not sure, honestly. I mean, the classes were hard," I admit, and a vision of Jarrett at the front of the classroom assaults me out of nowhere. I shake it off as soon as it hits. "But I think more than anything, I realized that — like Ashlei — I love to plan and organize events. I think I have more passion for that than anything else."

"So, do you want to go into corporate events and advertising like Ashlei?"

I scoff. "Not a chance. I think... maybe... more like weddings."

Kade's wearing his shocked expression again.

"What?"

"Nothing," he says quickly. "I was just thinking how great you'd be at that."

"Really?"

"Are you kidding? Kappa Kappa Beta just had the best recruitment they've ever seen, thanks to you. And every time you host a KKB event, it's the best one. You have a great knack for attention to detail. Besides," he says, taking a sip of his wine. "If anyone can wrangle a Bridezilla, it's you."

"I'll take that as a compliment."

"You should."

I smile, still watching him with a mixture of confusion and appreciation. It's just so crazy to see this side of him when I'm so used to the other.

"When you blew me off this summer," I say. "You said there was some family stuff going on."

Kade's smile instantly falls, and his gaze drops to his hands. "Yeah."

"What was it?"

He lets out a long sigh, looking around the restaurant. "Remember how I told you last year that I was practically raised by two rowdy older brothers?"

"I do."

"Well... they're half-brothers. Technically. And their dad..." He pauses, jaw ticking.

"We don't have to talk about this if you don't want to."

"No, it's okay," he assures me, and his eyes meet mine. "I want to tell you. I want you to know more about me."

I smile at that, reaching across the table for his hand. And though I've touched every other part of him, this — holding hands across a candle-lit table in a room full of strangers — it somehow feels like the most intimate touch we've shared.

"Our mom got sick when I was really little," he says after a moment. "When she passed away, my brothers went to live with their dad, and I stayed with mine. And let's just say it put a rift in the family, because their dad was an addict and, frankly, a piece of shit. And my dad, while he took care of *me*, didn't really want to take care of my brothers — especially when he found out that my mom had been seeing their dad behind his back once she found out she was sick."

"Whoa."

Kade grimaces. "I know. Family drama is super fun, right?"

I squeeze his hand.

"Anyway, my brothers' dad just got into some trouble this summer, and they called me and asked me to help." He shakes his head, eyes lost somewhere in a memory. "It was the first time I'd seen them in years."

"That must have been hard."

He shrugs. "It was. But our mom was the glue that held us together. Once she passed... we all kind of fell apart."

The waiter brings our desserts then — a key lime pie, a cheesecake, and apple pie a la mode — but when I try to slip my hand out of Kade's to make room for the dishes, he holds fast to me, his eyes begging me not to let go.

So I don't.

We hold hands through dessert, turning the subject to lighter topics and feeding each other sweets and finishing off the last of our wine.

Kade is a little too buzzed to drive at the end of the night, so we take a cab, and when we make it back to the sorority house, he walks me to the door with his hands in his pockets.

"I had a great time tonight, Jess," he says softly when I slide my hands around his neck. His wrap around my waist in the next breath, and he lowers his lips slowly and carefully, the kiss sweet and a little too PG-13 for my liking.

"Well, the night's not over, is it?" I husk, running my hands down his chest and over his abdomen.

Before I can trace the outline of the thick cock I *know* his pants are hiding, he grabs my wrists, stopping me short.

I pout, which earns me a chuckle before Kade kisses me again, a little more passionately this time, which only fuels my desire to get him naked — and fast.

His lips move from my mouth to my jaw, to my neck, and I let my head fall back to allow him better access. When he kisses his way up to the shell of my ear, his breath eliciting chills over every inch of me, I practically pant in anticipation.

That is, until he whispers, "I don't fuck on the first date."

He pulls back with a sexy, knowing smirk, kissing my knuckles on each hand before releasing me.

"Gotta get to at least number three for that," he adds on a wink. "I'll call you tomorrow."

I'm still standing there in shock, mouth open, violet vulva throbbing in my pants. "You're fucking joking, right?"

Kade chuckles, rolling his lips together before he walks off the sorority front porch backward. "Goodnight, gorgeous."

I flick him off, which makes him laugh harder, and then he turns and leaves me there with a wine buzz and no orgasm.

That motherfucker.

But then, I smile.

I really have taught him well.

Adam

She came.

My heart that's been racing since I called Cassie earlier this week — with no reply — heaves a sigh of relief at the sight of her walking down the dock. Her short red hair is curled around her face, and she's bundled in a pair of leggings, an oversized KKB sweatshirt, and simple black boots. We rarely get weather cold enough to wear a sweater in South Florida, but tonight, the breeze is blowing in from the north, and we're on the water, which puts us perfectly in the sixty to sixty-five-degree range.

Perfect cuddle weather, I think.

If she'll let me get close to her, that is.

I jump off the boat and onto the dock, shoving my hands in my pockets as she walks the rest of the way. She stops a few feet in front of me, crossing her arms and looking over the boat before her green eyes find mine.

"Thank you for meeting me."

She nods, looking down at her shoes.

I want to pull her into me. I want to drop to my knees and beg for her forgiveness right here and now. But I rented the boat for a reason, and I've got way more in store for this girl than just a boy begging for forgiveness on a boat dock.

I reach out my hand for hers, and when she hesitantly takes it, I help her onto the boat before climbing on myself. It's nothing fancy, a little twenty-five-foot deck boat that would be perfect for a trip to the sandbar with a group of friends. But tonight, it'll take us to Boca Chita Key.

Cassie takes a seat at the back of the boat, and the fact that she's letting me take her off the mainland tells me more than any words do that I still have a fighting chance here. If I were past the point of no-return, she would have fought me on the shore — or not shown up at all.

So, I put on a little music, deciding on one of her favorite artists — Jack Johnson — and we cruise out into Biscayne Bay, quiet but for the boat, the water, and the melody of "Monsoon."

It only takes about forty-five minutes to get out to the key, and we're greeted first by the lighthouse — one that I hope to take Cassie up in tomorrow, if she doesn't demand I take her back to shore tonight. Chancing a glance back at her from where I'm driving, she's not giving anything away. There's no smile on her face, but she doesn't seem in a hurry to run away, either.

She's waiting for me to make my move.

I just hope it's enough.

After I dock the boat, I grab her hand and walk her quietly onto the tiny island.

"What is this place?" she asks, looking around in wonder at the mangroves, the small, sandy shore, the crystal blue water, made darker by the sun setting over the coast.

"Boca Chita Key."

"I've never heard of it."

I chuckle. "Well, we're in college. I think we focus a little more on classes and partying than on cool places to camp."

"Are we camping here?"

I swallow, pulling her to a stop along the shore. "I hope so." Then, I look behind her.

She follows my gaze, and when she does, a soft gasp slips from her lips. She covers her mouth, and I hold my breath, hoping that reaction means everything I've set up is paying off.

Camping on the island is first-come, first-serve — so I came here early this morning, setting up a tent and working throughout the day to make it the most amazing campsite anyone could ask for. It took a little planning and a *lot* of figuring out how to do everything I wanted with just the power on the generator I bought for the Halloween party, but I pulled it off.

The two-person tent is cast in an orange glow, both from the setting sun and from the white string lights I hung above it. Two chairs wait by the fire, along with everything we need to make hot dogs and s'mores in a cooler and a couple reusable bags. There's a bottle of wine in a bucket of ice that I set up just before going back to the mainland to pick her up, and two plastic wine glasses beside it.

Grabbing Cassie's hand, I guide her toward the site, refilling the ice in the bucket as she looks around more. One peek inside the tent, and I know she's seen that it's filled with blankets and pillows and rose petals for a romantic touch. She closes the flap once more, standing, eyes tracing each and every detail of the scene before she looks at me.

"You did all this?"

My hands find my pockets, and I nod.

Her mouth parts, and she looks around in wonder, shaking her head. "It's beautiful," she whispers. "Are we the only ones out here?"

I look around at the vacant campsites. "It's first-come, first-serve, and there are a few other spots to camp on the key. But it's not really camping season. We very well might be."

She nods, still taking it all in.

Everything about her is stunning in that moment — the glow of the sun on her fiery hair, the freckles dotting her cheeks, her wide, emerald eyes sweeping over the campsite. Everything inside me longs to hold her, and I decide I can't wait another minute.

I swallow, reaching for her and breathing another sigh of relief when she lets me take her hands in my own. "Cassie, I'm sorry. I am so fucking sorry for the way I treated you at the Halloween party — for the way I've treated you most of this semester. We're finally together, finally official, and I take the first opportunity to blow something out of proportion and fuck it all up."

Her eyes well with tears, and she looks between us, rolling her lips together. "No, you had a right to be upset. I should have come to you that first day that I realized Grayson was in my class. I should have just told you from the start, and then maybe we wouldn't be in this mess."

I tilt her chin with my knuckle. "Hey, it's okay. I mean, with the way I reacted... well, it's pretty clear why you were hesitant to tell me."

Cassie sniffs, nodding slightly. "I'm sorry I hurt you, Adam. But I promise — *nothing* is going on between me and Grayson. Nothing ever will again. I'm yours, and I know it doesn't make sense to you, but Grayson wanting to make amends and be friends... it's important to me. It gives me the chance to not lose yet another person in my life. And—"

"I get it."

Her green eyes widen. "You do?"

"I do," I say, smoothing my thumbs over her knuckles. "I didn't, not at first, but luckily I have some pretty great brothers who help me see clearer. I mean, I'm friends with Skyler, and you've *never* been opposed to that — other than when I put her before us, which was fair. But since we cleared that all out, it's been me and you, and Skyler being my friend has never been an issue."

"Of course not," Cassie says, like she's shocked I would think that at all.

God, I love this girl.

"Well, that's just one good example of why I shouldn't have blown up the way I did," I say on a sigh. "You trust me. And though my actions at the Halloween party say otherwise, I trust you, too, Cassie. I know you wouldn't do anything with Grayson, that your heart is mine. I guess I just... I was scared. I thought I was losing you again. And to be honest, I still don't trust that guy."

She chuckles at that. "That's fair."

"But again, I trust *you*," I say. "And that's what matters."

I pull her into me, and she lets me take her into my arms, burying her face in my chest as I breathe in the scent of her.

"So, we're okay? You're not mad at me?"

"We're okay," I tell her, kissing her hair. "I'm sorry."

"I'm sorry, too," she whispers, and then she hugs me tighter and I do the same, and we stay there for a long time, just holding each other while the waves lap at the shore and the mockingbirds sing us a song.

After a while, we peel apart enough for Cassie to ask more about the camping set-up, and I walk her through everything, pouring us each a glass of wine. We make hot dogs and eat s'mores by the fire, listen to music on the portable speaker I brought with me, and catch up on everything we've missed over the semester.

And finally, I feel whole again.

It's late when we climb into the tent, the moon high above us and casting its silvery glow over the water. We leave the flaps of the tent open so we can enjoy the view, taking advantage of the fact that we're alone, and Cassie lays her head on my chest where we lie in the fortress of pillows and blankets.

"I've been so miserable without you," she whispers.

I inhale deep, running my fingers through her hair. "You and me both."

"I hate how well I know that feeling," she says, leaning up on her elbow to look at me. "The feeling of losing you, of wondering if I've lost you forever."

"You could never lose me forever."

"Promise?"

I laugh, kissing her cheek. "I mean, as long as you can put up with my stubborn ass, I'll be around."

"Good," she says on a grin, but as soon as it comes, it falls, and her eyes search mine. She watches me for a long moment, and then in one motion, her hands grab my shoulders and she swings one leg over me until she's sitting in my lap.

Her mouth finds mine, passionate and sure, and as soon as we breathe into that kiss, all the blood rushes to where her center meets mine.

"*God,* I've missed you kissing me," she whispers, grinding her hips. "*Touching* me."

"I hate myself that I wasted all this time."

"Well," she says, rolling again. "You can make up for it now."

Leaning back, she pulls her sweatshirt over her head, leaving my face lined up with her perfect breasts barely covered in a lilac lace bra. I groan in appreciation, running my fingers along the edge of the fabric before I dip underneath and palm her completely.

Her head falls back, mouth open, and she grinds against my erection with just the right friction to have me ready to come in my pants.

Ever since the first time Cassie let me touch her, we've gone slow. We've gone easy. We've taken our time and explored each other, and I made sure — above all else — that she felt good and comfortable and safe.

But the way she's grinding against me, the way she's kissing me and biting my neck and running her nails down my back, I know she doesn't want easy tonight.

And I can deliver whatever she needs.

We're all arms and lips and heavy breathing as we take turns rolling on top of the other, stripping off articles of clothing and letting them get lost in the blankets. When we're bare, I back up into the pillows and pull Cassie onto my lap again, running my hand down between her legs and slipping my fingers between her wet lips.

She moans, arching her back and digging her nails into my shoulders as I press one finger inside without warning.

"Jesus Christ, Cassie," I curse, sucking her neck between my teeth. "You're so fucking wet."

"I want you inside me."

"I am inside you," I say, pressing another finger in to join the first.

I curl them to the tune of another moan, but then she presses her hands into my chest. "No, I want *you,*" she says, running her hand down my abdomen until she's palming me in her grip. Just the feel of her sweet fucking hand around my shaft has me flexing into her grip, pre-cum letting her palm slide up and down me with ease.

"Fuck," I draw out, letting my head fall back. I revel in the feel of her for a split moment before I smack her ass and yank her off of me, rolling her down into the blankets and pressing a hard kiss to her lips. "Hold that thought."

It takes me seconds to find my pants and pull a condom from my wallet, and then the package is torn open and I roll it over my length, loving the way Cassie's eyes heat as she watches me. She licks her lips like she loves what she sees, so I stroke myself in the condom for her, until she's reaching for me.

"Adam..."

"Roll over," I command, and I see the surprise in her eyes before she does as I say. We've only ever fucked face to face, with me on top or her on top, lost in each other's gazes.

But tonight, I can feel her craving for more.

She wants something dirty and carnal. She wants me to claim her and remind her that she's mine.

When she's on her stomach, I straddle her calves and wrap my hands around her hips, yanking until her ass is up in the air. At the same time, I press one hand down on her upper back, keeping her chest and face pressed into the pile of pillows and blankets.

I run my hand over her spine, reveling in the chills that break in my wake, and then I lower to press my chest into her back, sucking on her earlobe as she rolls her ass against my hard-on.

"Are you ready to feel me deep, baby?"

"*Oh, God.*"

I smirk, that answer enough for me, and then I kiss the back of her neck and position myself at her entrance with just a breath of warning before I slam it home.

Cassie cries out, fisting the blankets and squeezing her eyes shut. "Yes," she breathes, and I withdraw, pummeling in again with just as much force.

Her cheeks are already flushed, and the sight of her bent over in the mess of blankets under the glow of the string lights is like something out of a painting. Every curve is outlined, and I run my hands along all of them as I position myself on my knees and take her hips in my hands, pulling her wet pussy over my cock again and again.

"Play with your clit, baby," I say, flexing my hips to fill her again. "Reach down there and play with your pussy while I fuck you."

I've never talked to her like this, and I'm rewarded with a moan and a whimper before one of her hands that was gripping the blankets disappears under her. She strokes that hand over where I'm entering her first, eliciting a sharp inhale from me before I feel her circling her clit.

"God*damn*, you're so hot," I husk, watching her squirm as I fill her.

Cassie's cries echo throughout the entire park as she rubs her clit and rolls her hips, meeting my thrust each time. I'm half-thankful we're alone, half-wishing there was someone else to witness the way my girl can be so sexy when she's completely uninhibited.

"Adam," she says, just above a whisper and just shy of a cry, and then her hips drop, thighs spreading wider as she chases her orgasm. I answer the call by falling onto my hands on either side of her and grinding in even deeper, sucking on her earlobe and kissing over her neck as she screams out.

Her pussy tightens around me, her hand moving fast and furious between her legs. And just the sound of her coming undone has me ready to do the same.

She falls limp when she's spent, her hand pinned under her as I slow just a little, kissing the back of her neck and her shoulders tenderly.

"You good, baby?"

Cassie chuckles. "I'm fucking *great*."

I smile against her skin, still pumping gently in and out of her tight, swollen, soaked pussy. "You ready for me?"

"Please," she cries.

"I don't want to come in this condom."

She stiffens at that, glancing at me over her shoulder as I still. "Where do you want to come?"

"Roll over," I say as I withdraw, peeling the condom off and tossing it to the side as she rolls onto her back. I bite my lip at the sight of the lights casting a glow over her breasts, her lean navel, her thighs, spread and waiting.

"Move down a little," I say, grabbing her hips and helping her slide down until her head is on the blankets instead of the pillows. Then, I crawl up her, straddling her breasts and feeling them against my balls as I grip my shaft tight.

Her eyes are wide, flicking back and forth between my cock and my face as she waits for my next move.

"If this is too much, tell me to stop, okay?"

She nods, and I run my hands through her hair, tugging until her neck is exposed.

"Open your mouth, baby."

When she does, I nearly come on the spot. It's so fucking hot looking down on her plump lips and wet tongue, her eyes watching me, waiting. I position my tip on her tongue first, sliding it around to get it nice and wet before I gently thrust inside.

I groan at the feel of her lips surrounding me, of her tongue sliding along my base, and my hands fall to the pillows above her head to keep me balanced. Slowly, carefully, I withdraw and press inside her again, fucking her mouth with as much restraint as I can manage.

She gags a few times, and I slow, making sure she knows she's in control. But she doesn't ask me to stop. Instead, she grabs my ass, her nails digging into the skin as she guides me inside her again.

"Oh, *fuck*," I groan, my breathing picking up, heart racing. "I need to go a little faster. It won't take long."

She answers by grabbing my ass and pulling me inside her throat deeper, and my eyes flutter shut at the all-encompassing feel of her letting me take her this way. It's so vulnerable and hot, and at the very base of it, it's her saying she trusts me.

Just like I trust her.

With my eyes still shut, I pick up the pace, careful not to go too deep but finding my release building with each wrap of her lips and slip of her tongue. "Oh, fuck," I grunt. "Coming."

And with one last thrust deep into her throat, I spill.

My body shakes, fire consuming me as I black out to everything that isn't Cassie's mouth around my cock. Faintly, I register her gagging, but she holds me inside her as I ride out every last pulse. I withdraw and push back in, again and again, until I'm empty and spent and trembling as I carefully roll off of her and onto my back next to where she lay.

I'm still seeing stars, panting and trying to catch my breath when I look over and see Cassie swallow, wiping the corners of her mouth and smiling at me shyly.

"Fuck *me*," I say, rolling over to pull her into me and kiss all over her. She giggles and wraps herself around me, too, until we're a tangle of slick arms and legs.

"Did you like that?"

"Do you really have to fucking ask?" I laugh.

"I liked it, too," she says, kissing my jaw. "And I liked you taking me from behind."

"That so?" I ask on a smirk. "My little innocent Cassie McBee, a fan of doggy-style."

Her nose wrinkles. "Don't call it that."

"I'll call it whatever you want, babe," I say, pulling her into my chest. "As long as we get to do it again."

She laughs in my arms, and as the world slowly comes back to us, our breaths evening out and the music and sounds of the night finding us inside the tent, I run my fingers through her hair and count my lucky stars that she came tonight, that she forgave me, that I didn't lose her for good.

"I love you," she whispers.

I inhale deep, holding her tighter and vowing to never fuck this up again. "I love you, too."

Erin

"Alright, ladies," I say once the room is quiet, glancing over my notes for tonight's Chapter meeting. "I think that wraps up everything on the agenda. But we do have some visitors tonight. So, phones away, everyone give your full attention, okay? First up, the ladies of Zeta Pi Alpha."

My sisters sit and clap politely as Jess lets five girls from the sorority stand at the front of the room and tell us about their upcoming philanthropy event. I'm half-listening, half-watching my sisters with a proud smile. It's a bigger Chapter night with our visitors, so I booked us one of the large rooms in the Sciences Building. And now that our new members have been officially initiated, the room feels whole, and I love knowing that I'm a part of what made this organization what it is now.

After last semester, Kappa Kappa Beta was awarded the best GPA out of all the sororities on campus. With Jess taking over during recruitment, we had a brand new, all-star pledge class, and with each member of exec mentoring another sister, I have faith that when we hand off the torch at the end of the semester, it'll be with this sorority in the best shape it's ever been in.

I glance at Skyler, knowing that while things are still a bit rocky between us, she's leaning more and more into following in my footsteps — just like I followed in my Big's, and her in her Big's before that. Our family line had a long running as president, and I know it won't end with me.

But it just might end with Cassie.

She decided again not to take a Little this semester, and as much as that pissed me off when she didn't as a sophomore, I accept it now. So what if our line ends with her? If it did, I'd say we've had a pretty badass family line, and every single one of us has left a mark on this sorority.

Besides, I'm done trying to tell others what they should do or judge them based on their decisions.

God knows I wouldn't want anyone judging me based on mine.

After the Zetas leave, I announce that the brothers of Omega Chi are next, and I take a seat off to the right of the podium still in a slight daze.

Until Bear walks in first, leading a group of ten of his brothers to the front of the room.

I stiffen immediately at the sight of him, sitting up straighter in my chair. He winks at Skyler and smiles at various sisters around the room, but then his eyes find mine, and he keeps them on me until the moment he reaches the front of the room and turns to address the chapter.

"Ladies," he says, his booming voice commanding attention as always. "Thank you for having us."

And as he stands there, demanding that power, I can't help but appreciate the way he looks when he's cleaned up for Sunday Chapter. I love Bear in his basketball shorts and muscle tanks, but there's just something about seeing him in dress slacks and a button-up that makes it hard to swallow.

"We know you're busy, and that all of you probably want to get home to enjoy what's left of your Sunday before classes tomorrow, so we won't stay long. We just wanted to wish you good luck on mid-terms, and bring you a little something..."

At that, he looks to the back of the room where one of his brothers is still standing, and he nods, opening the doors. As soon as he does, more and more Omega Chi brothers pile in, each of them holding a dozen roses in one hand and a reusable bag in the other.

The girls all gasp and smile in delight as each Omega Chi brother finds a sister and gives her the roses and bag. A few of the guys are carrying two of each, and they bring the extras to the front of the room to the brothers who were already standing there. When Bear has his in hand, he turns to me, and the smile slips off my face.

The room is abuzz with girls laughing and squealing and kissing cheeks and pulling all the goodies out of their bags — chocolate, salty snacks, a couple of shot-sized alcohol bottles — but I'm so focused on Bear walking toward me that I barely register any of it.

I stand when he's a few feet away, and he pauses, extending the bundle of roses and goody bag. He doesn't say a word as I take them from his hands, but our fingers brush, and I inhale a deep breath at the contact.

"Thank you," I manage.

He nods, and there's something there in his eyes — something I can't quite put my finger on. He looks so sad, so tired, and... maybe a little sorry.

Our dinner flashes in my mind, and my cheeks heat as I tear my gaze from his.

It's all I can do to hold it together through the rest of Chapter once he and his brothers are gone, and as soon as I call it, I gather my belongings and force a smile through small talk with sisters until the room is clear.

I lock up behind me with one thought on my mind — *I need wine.* But when I turn and spot a familiar shadow leaning against the brick building, a completely different thought comes to mind.

"Gavin?" I ask, shaking my head. "What are you doing here?"

He kicks off the wall with a grin. "Picking you up."

"Picking me up?" I cross my arms and arch a brow. "It's a Sunday night. I've got class early in the morning."

"I won't keep you out too late." His eyes flick to the flowers in my hand, but he doesn't address them.

"I take it that means you're not taking no for an answer."

The crook of his lips is all I get as a response, and he holds out his arm, waiting for me to slip mine through it.

***

"I'm sorry," the girl on stage at The Black Lily says, looking around the dimly lit room at all of the patrons. Gavin and I are in the back corner, at a table for two, each of us sipping on warm Earl Grey tea.

I can't take my eyes off the poet on stage, and it seems Gavin can't take his eyes off *me.*

"I'm sorry for distracting you, my shoulders too bare, my thighs too exposed in these shorts. I'm sorry for speaking too loud, my words ugly with truth, your ears sensitive from ignorance."

Each word she says hits like a beat of a drum, the cadence powerful and seductive, and I lean into every line.

"I'm sorry for chasing my dream, how selfish of me, to not ask for permission first."

A few girls snap at that, firing up the energy in the room.

"I'm sorry for leaving you, how careless to stand on my own when you begged me to bend."

"Preach, girl!" someone calls out in the dark.

"I'm sorry for proving you wrong," the poet says, grabbing the mic and raising her voice as her haunting brown eyes sweep the room. "How embarrassing my smile is for you, I'm sure. I'm sorry the flower you tried so long to drown bloomed anyway — that stem, once so fragile and weak, now roots dug deep."

A few more snaps ring out, and I snap, too, completely lost in the moment.

"I'm sorry," she says, louder now, her eyes boring into the crowd. "That I was *never* sorry."

"Yes!"

"Go on, then!"

The poet pauses, lowering the mic back into the stand before she whispers, "And that I never will be."

Applause rings out as she takes a little bow and exits the stage, leaving the mic open once again for the next performer, and I shake my head in awe, leaning back in my chair with my muscles relaxing all at once like I was just holding onto a speeding train for my life rather than listening to spoken word.

"She's amazing," I whisper, glancing at Gavin. "All of these performers are."

"Open mic is pretty cool, huh?"

"Very," I say, reaching for my tea to take a sip. "You come here a lot?"

"Almost every Sunday. It's a cool place on a regular night, too, but... for me? Open mic is where you get the real. The raw. The brave." He nods toward the stage. "It takes a lot of guts to get up there."

"Do you ever?"

He shakes his head easily. "I'm more of the lurk in the corner kind of guy than the one who wants a mic in his hand."

"Fair," I say with a smile. "Thank you for bringing me here."

"Of course."

I study him for a moment while the next performer gets set up — a young man, no older than eighteen if I had to guess, with an acoustic guitar and a wide, unabashed grin.

"Have you thought about our little therapy assignment?"

Gavin frowns. "What assignment?"

I chuckle. "Don't you *ever* listen? Jackie asked us to think about what we miss about the old us."

"Oh," Gavin says with a frown. "Yeah, well, I instantly wrote that off as stupid and never considered it again."

"Why do you think it's stupid?"

"Why do you think it's *not*?"

A little laugh bubbles in my throat. "I don't know. I guess I'm open to any and everything therapy has to offer. I've tried handling this all on my own," I confess. "It didn't work out well."

Gavin watches me curiously. "Okay. Tell me yours. What do you miss about the *you before you were all fucked up*?"

He waves his hands in the air like a fortune teller with those words, making me giggle.

"I miss a lot of things, actually," I say, playing with the handle on my teacup. "I miss when my biggest worry was what to wear to a sorority event. I miss when all my friends trusted me and looked up to me." I swallow. "I miss wanting to have sex."

I can't look at Gavin when I say those words, and they hang between us for a long time before he responds.

"I just miss my sister."

My heart cracks in my chest, and I close my eyes, inhaling a breath before I open them to meet his gaze. For a long while, he watches me unashamed, but slowly, he lowers his eyes to the table, jaw ticking, nose flaring.

He looks so old and tired and broken in that moment that I can't help but reach over and shelter his hand with mine.

Gavin swallows at the contact, covering my knuckles with his thumb, smoothing skin over skin, his eyes flicking up to meet mine. I offer a small smile, squeezing his hand in return.

"Thank you for sharing."

I get a genuine smile for that, and Gavin shakes his head, bringing my knuckles to his lips briefly before he pulls his grasp from mine to reach into his back pocket.

"Alright," he says, slapping a twenty down to pay for our tea and leave a generous tip. He stands then, holding out his hand for mine again. "I promised to get you back early."

"I just need to use the restroom."

"Come on, I'll take you."

Gavin leads me through a dark hallway in the back of the venue, waiting outside the bathroom for me. Then, we slip out the back door, and it's just the two of us alone in the alley.

The breeze is crisp and cool, but my skin is so hot from the adrenaline and the tea that I revel in the feel of it, closing my eyes and inhaling deep.

Gavin slips his hand into mine, pulling me to a stop in the middle of the alley.

"What?" I ask, eyes fluttering open.

His eyes watch me carefully, flicking back and forth, a small crease just above them. He steps into me, slowly, backing me up until I hit the brick wall behind me.

My heart picks up speed with the way his demanding gaze devours me, and when my mouth parts, his fills the space, the kiss soft but sure.

Now my heart is thundering so loudly, it's all I can hear in my ears, and I grip Gavin's shoulders, so afraid I'll pass out at any moment that I can't do anything but hold on. His hands thread with mine, and he pulls them up to either side of my head, leaning into me and licking my bottom lip gently before his mouth captures mine again.

A spark of something hot and electric shoots down between my legs, and it surprises me so much that I stiffen and shy away from it, panic filling my chest.

Gavin seems to notice, and he slows his kiss, pressing his forehead to mine. "Is it okay that I'm kissing you?" he asks on a whisper, pausing with his lips over mine until I answer.

"Yes."

"You're shaking."

I swallow, nodding.

Gavin releases my hands, framing my face and searching my eyes with his. This close, everything about him surrounds me — his dark and soul-piercing eyes, the heat from his chest and his hands on my skin, his scent — vanilla and oak and tobacco, something like a leather shop and a bar.

"No one has touched you since that night."

He says the words softly, kind of like a question and kind of like something he just realized he should have known all along.

I swallow, not sure how to respond, but knowing that my silence is answer enough.

Gavin closes his eyes, blowing out a breath between us before his thumbs trace a line on my jaw. He holds me there for a long time, silent, our chests heaving, and bodies still pressed together in heat and want and — for me, a mix of fear, too.

"I may be a little fucked up, Erin," he says in the dark. "But I won't hurt you."

I close my eyes at his words, fighting back emotion, because against every ounce of logic I've managed to hold onto in my life, I want to believe him.

"Can I..." He swallows, waiting until I open my eyes to look at him again. "I want to touch you. I want to make you feel good." His hands slip down to circle my waist, and my next breath is shaky at the heat they funnel into me. "Can I try, if I promise to stop anytime you want me to?"

Panic zips through me, but it's overpowered by a want so fierce I can't believe I haven't felt it in almost a year now.

"I'll stop if you want me to," he promises again. "Just say the word."

Everything inside me wants to run and hide with as much urgency as I want to wrap myself up in him and lose myself in the way it feels to be wanted and touched and desired. I have no idea which one will win, which one holds the most power.

But there's only one way to find out.

Slowly, I nod, threading my hands back through his hair and pulling his mouth back to mine. He answers with a passionate, bruising kiss, and I surrender.

I'm still wearing my dress from Chapter, and as he slowly kisses me, Gavin slips one warm, rough hand underneath it. I grip his shoulders, holding on as he lifts one of my legs and balances it on his thigh.

His eyes connect with mine between kisses, and I know I'm breathing so loud they can probably hear me inside the club, but I can't control it. I can't do anything but hold on and try not to pass out as Gavin runs his hand up my inner thigh, cupping me over the lace of my panties.

The moment his warmth covers me, I gasp, eyes fluttering and head falling back.

"Are you okay?"

I nod, deftly, and Gavin kisses my neck softly and sweetly before moving the lace of my panties aside and running one finger between my folds.

I inhale stiffly at the feel of his skin on mine, of him touching me where I haven't been touched since the night four boys took what wasn't theirs. I've spent the last year trying to block out that night, to forget their touch, to unhear their laughs and grunts and crude words as they took their turns on me. Most nights I failed. Most nights I laid awake with the nightmare burning in my mind so fiercely that it felt like it was happening all over again.

But tonight is different.

Tonight, as soon as the thought of them comes, it's whisked away by another kiss from Gavin. He holds all of my focus, so much that I can't think of anything else but the way he feels — his lips on mine, his finger pressing against the sensitive bundle of nerves between my legs, his other hand holding me steady, digging into my hip.

Gavin breaks our kiss, eyes on mine as he skates his finger up and down my slick lips, and then — carefully and slowly — he enters me.

I must have blacked out. I must have collapsed in his arms and lost myself in another universe with him. I must have found a piece of me I thought was gone forever. Something out of this world happened, because when I finally come to, Gavin is kissing me to keep me quiet as I ride out an orgasm on his fingers, bucking my hips and digging my nails into his shoulders and crying out against his lips.

The climax is so powerful and electric that I feel it in every muscle, in every bone, in every fiber of my being and corner of my soul. I forgot what it was to feel this way, to be touched and not be scared, to have a man inside me and not be crying and praying for it to end.

Instead, I prayed for it to *never* end.

But it does, and when the climax fades, and the cool breeze of the night sweeps across my hot, slick skin, I whimper, folding into Gavin's arms.

He catches me easily, his fingers withdrawing from inside me slowly and carefully. He puts my panties back in place, drops my leg back to the ground, and wraps me in his arms, surrounding me with his warmth and embrace.

And just when I thought I was okay, I fucking lose it.

Sobs rip through my chest, and I cling to him more, like if he even thinks of letting me go, I'll die. But he doesn't move away. He doesn't flinch or ask me what's wrong or demand that I stop crying. He just pulls me deeper into his chest, wrapping me in his arms as fully as he can and kissing my hair, repeating the same words over and over again until I can finally breathe.

"It's okay. I got you. You're beautiful. You're safe."

"It's okay. I got you. You're beautiful. You're safe."

It's okay.

I got you.

You're beautiful.

You're safe.

EPISODE 5

Bear

I am the equivalent to a dog with its tail tucked firmly between its legs when I knock on Becca's door a week before Thanksgiving.

My heart races in my chest as I wait for her to answer, knowing she's home since I asked permission before coming over. I haven't seen her since the night she booted me out and essentially told me to get my shit together.

And she was right — I did need time alone.

I was also right.

It sucked.

I spent most of the first week wallowing, turning to the classic things that always got me by: drinking, working out, and — since fucking was out of the question with Becca being so pissed off — masturbating.

I had zero shame, and I wasted away seven days without a single urge to do anything about my predicament.

But something happened on that seventh day, like God himself was yanking me up out of my bed and throwing me in the shower and telling me we had work to do. I drove out to the beach that morning and sat there for hours, watching the sun rise, listening to the waves, and — for the first time since last semester — not running from the thoughts inside my head.

I thought about Erin, about our unborn child, about how it hurt me that I hadn't been a part of the conversation and how I also understood how it wouldn't have been my decision anyway. I thought about how I'd been so focused on my own betrayal and hurt that I hadn't thought about the fact that Erin went through that just months before she was raped, and then she slipped into the darkest hole I'd ever seen her in.

She's been fighting her way out of that hole all summer and all fall semester long, going to therapy and trying to make amends with the people she hurt.

And I shut her out.

She's on my list of people to try to make things right with, and next on that list is my little brother.

My mother, too.

That long morning at the beach helped me see that a lot of my anger toward my mother rests in the fact that I'm jealous.

I'm jealous that she never got clean when I was a kid. I'm jealous that I can't be there to get to know her — sober — and have a relationship with her. I'm jealous that my little brother doesn't need me now, that he might very well move out of Mac's place soon and back in with Mom, and then where will that leave me?

And I'm scared.

God, I'm scared. I'm scared of her leaving unexpectedly again and fucking Clayton up. I'm scared of her starting to use again and him getting caught up in it, the way Carleton had. I'm scared of Clayton and Mom becoming close and leaving me somewhere on the outside looking in.

But something I decided that day on the beach was that I wouldn't let fear drive my life.

Over the past few weeks, I've been working on *me*. I've been studying, focusing on school, working out more but drinking less. I've been spending time with my fraternity brothers, video chatting with my family and trying to put my fear aside to form a bond with them in understanding rather than suspicion.

And I've been thinking about how to make things right with Becca.

A deep inhale is my only preparation, and then the door swings open, and I lay eyes on Becca for the first time in weeks.

Her hair is wrapped in an orange and blue bohemian turban, tied in a swirl knot at the front with just a few tendrils of curly hair peeking out around her ears. Her face is void of makeup and she's wearing leggings that I know have holes in the thighs from her wearing them so much, along with one of my hoodies, which nearly knocks the breath out of me because it tells me I have a chance before I've even spoken a single word.

She looks effortlessly beautiful, just like always.

And what makes her even better is that she's even more gorgeous where no one can see her.

Her heart.

Her mind.

Her soul.

"Hi," I whisper after a moment.

"Hey," she says, opening the door a little more for me to walk through.

I go straight back to her bedroom, and when she shuts the door behind us and crosses her arms, waiting, I take my shot.

"Becca, I am so sorry for the way I've been acting this semester. You were right to kick me out that weekend after Halloween. And you were right about me needing time alone."

"I didn't want to, you know," she whispers. "Kick you out. Not see you for weeks."

"I know," I say, and not overthinking it enough to talk myself out of it, I cross the room and pull her into my arms.

She's stiff at first, her arms still crossed between us, but slowly, she unwinds them and wraps them around my back, resting her head on my chest with a sigh.

"I've missed you," she whispers.

"Not as much as I've missed you. I promise you that."

Grabbing my hand, she leads me to the bed, sitting with her legs crossed by her pillows while I take a seat in front of her. "How have you been?"

I blow out a breath, looking around her room at the dream catchers, the moon phase tapestry, the old record player and an open dream journal on her desk. Incense burns on a small slate of wood in the corner, and I smile, loving that that scent will forever remind me of her.

"Shitty," I confess, capturing her golden eyes with mine. "But I've been taking a lot of time to work on myself, and to think about everything that's been fucking me up. I'm not one-hundred-percent better, but... I'm working on it. And that's a step."

"A big step," she agrees. A frown slips over her. "Anything you want to talk about?"

"Yes, but not tonight. If that's okay." I reach for her, pulling her into me as we lie down in her sheets. "Tonight, I just want to hold you, and kiss you, and touch you, and make you feel how important you are to me."

She smiles against my lips as I kiss her. "I like the sound of that."

"And I promise I'll talk to you about everything I've been working through. Oh, and I had an idea."

"Do tell."

"I did a lot of thinking about what you said." I swallow. "About Erin. And it made me realize that I don't know a lot about you and *your* friends, either. And I want to."

I don't miss the way Becca shifts in my arms at the mention of Erin, but I hold onto hope that this idea is a good one.

"What if we host a Friendsgiving?"

"A what?"

"Friendsgiving. It's Thanksgiving but with your friends instead of your family. Jess hosted one last year..." I frown. "Actually, it was kind of a disaster, *but* ours won't be. I was thinking I could invite Erin, and my Little, Josh. I would invite Skyler, but she'll be out of town. But you could bring your friends, too — your roommate, your best friend from high school. You said she'll be in town, right?"

Becca nods. "Yeah... she will be. Are you sure this is a good idea? Did you and Erin work through whatever weirdness is going on between you two?"

"Not yet," I admit. "But... I'm hoping this can kind of be the start of that. And I want you to be a part of it."

She peeks up at me from where I hold her then, a soft smile on her lips. "I think it sounds fun."

"Yeah?"

She nods. "Yeah. I'll let the girls know." Then, she presses her soft, warm lips to mine, leaving them there long enough to send blood rushing to my groin. "Now, you ready to make true on your promise to hold me and kiss me and touch me tonight?"

I groan, rolling her over until I'm pressed between her thighs, hiking one up high so I can nestle into her heat. "I've been ready since the second I walked through that door."

Becca answers me with her hands on my face, pulling me into her kiss, her heel digging into my ass and pulling me in closer. I roll my hips against her heat, and she shudders, gasping into my mouth which is enough to have my erection straining against my basketball shorts.

We took it slow for so long, that even a kiss has me hard and ready to go, and the memory of the first time I tasted her at the beginning of the semester makes me even harder. She was so slick and tight, and the thought of tasting her again is too much to resist.

I kiss my way down her jaw, her neck, helping her sit up enough for me to slide my hoodie over her head, and groaning in appreciation when I see she's not wearing anything under it. Immediately, I drop down on my hands on either side of her, bending to suck and kiss the soft skin of her swelled breasts. Her dark nipples pebble under the touch, and I gently bite each one, sucking the peaks between my teeth.

I'm on my way down her navel, ready to spend the rest of the night, and maybe the rest of my life, with my mouth between her legs when she grabs my shoulders to stop me.

"Bear..."

Her eyes hold mine, her mouth parted, chest heaving. And I know without her saying a word what she wants.

"Tonight?"

She nods, and I don't miss the hard swallow, the way her heart picks up its pace under my lips when I kiss her breast again.

Slowly, I peel her leggings off, dropping them on the floor and taking a moment to kiss up and down her thighs, her calves, even the bones of her ankles. She's completely naked and writhing under my touch, and I allow myself the pleasure of torturing her until she's shoving me to stand up and ripping my clothes off, too.

When we're both bare, she opens her bed table drawer and pulls out a golden foil package, ripping it open without haste and sliding the condom over my length.

It's the first time she's touched me, and her hand rolling that latex over me is nearly enough to make me come already.

I groan, holding her wrist to keep her there even once the condom is in place. Her eyes widen, and she looks up at me through heavy lashes, squeezing a little more, wrapping her small fist around my shaft as best she can.

"Does that feel good?" she whispers, and *that* from her mouth has me groaning and flexing into her hand, my climax building before I've even pressed my tip inside her.

"Yes, baby. Grip it tighter."

She answers my demand, and her lips find my neck on the next thrust into her hand, leaving me biting my lip and imagining how good it's going to feel to finally fuck her after months of taking it slow.

"Do you want me to suck it?" Becca asks in my ear, and I swear to God I have to yank back and throw her on the bed because I feel my orgasm edging for release. She smiles wickedly at me, balanced on her elbows, her legs falling open, perfect brown pussy waiting.

"I don't fuck the way I eat," I say, grabbing her by the hips and yanking her down until her ass is hanging off the bed. I grab my cock in my hand, stroking it once before I line it up at her entrance, both of us moaning at the feel of her slick heat covering the tip. "This won't be gentle."

"Shut up and fuck me already."

I answer with a slam of my hips, filling her to the brim, and she cries out in what I know is both a mixture of ecstasy and pain. And it's not that I want to hurt her. It's just that I don't know how else to take her but hard, fast, and rough — my favorite fucking way.

I groan at the feel of her tight pussy wrapping around me, withdrawing and sinking back into her even deeper. Becca's back arches off the bed, fingers wrapping in the sheets and twisting, neck exposed.

I wrap my hands around that beautiful neck, gripping just enough to hold onto her as I pound without cutting off her air supply. Her fingers wrap around my wrist where I hold her, but the way her eyes heat when they look at me, I know she doesn't want me to take my hand away.

She loves it.

She wants more.

I squeeze just a little tighter, capturing her lips in a bruising kiss and reveling in the way the breath coming from her mouth into mine is strained.

"You like when I choke you, don't you, baby?" I hiss, slowing my pace just a little, just enough to feel every inch of her as I pepper kisses on her jaw. "I know you can't answer me, but the way your pussy is tightening is all I need to know."

Something of a whimper escapes her lips, and her eyelids flutter shut, her thighs somehow opening even more. That tells me she's chasing her orgasm, and I answer that plea by sliding my free hand down between us.

I skate my hand over my cock when I pull out of her, slicking it in her wetness, and then I cup her, rubbing my fingers up and down her clit in time with my thrusts.

"Oh, God," she manages, her voice still strained where I hold her neck. I grin, fucking her harder and rubbing her clit mercilessly the same way I sucked it the night I went down on her.

I don't need verbal affirmation that she's coming. I feel it in the pulses of her walls around my shaft, in the way her nails dig into where she holds my wrist, in the way her eyes roll up, like a spirit is taking over her body.

And if I had any doubt, it's erased when she squirts all over me.

Her eyes fly open at the sensation, and I know without her saying anything that she's never done it before. That makes it even fucking better, and I keep my pace on her clit, loving the way she covers me and the bed and the floor with her desire.

When she's sated and shaking and tapping on my wrist to release, I let her go gently, slowing my pace a little and bending to kiss her neck where I'd held her. I was careful enough to know I wouldn't leave any marks, but I still know it was rough, and I want my tender kisses to assure her she's safe.

"Oh my *God,*" she finally breathes. "I fucking squirted."

"Hell yeah, you did," I growl, biting her earlobe before I stand again. Then, I wrap my hands around her thighs and pull her down the bed again, picking up my pace. "It was the hottest fucking thing I've ever seen."

"I've never done that before. I've never... *oooh, shiiiitttt.*"

Whatever she was going to say is stolen when I start pounding into her deeper and harder, ready for my own release. Her tits bounce wildly, her hands gripping the sheets, and the sight of her writhing and moaning does the trick.

"*Fuuuuck.*"

I burst into the condom so hard I worry I'll break it, the release I've been holding for weeks finding itself inside Becca. It's all I can do to stay standing as I empty, stilling and letting my climax pulse out inside her as I hold onto her thighs for dear life. Stars and numbness take me over, take me under, and by the time I'm finished, there's nothing I can do but collapse on top of her, and she wraps her arms around me, holding me, taking me, kissing my slick skin over and over and over.

I'm not sure how long we lie there, half on the bed, half off, both of us panting and sweating and sated. It's not until she giggles that I manage to pick my head up enough to look at her.

"Well, seems all that waiting had a pretty explosive outcome."

I smirk, using all the effort I have to discard of the condom before rolling us into the bed and wrapping myself full around her. I kiss her forehead, a deep and content sigh leaving both our chests at the same time.

"You're my favorite," I whisper.

Becca nods, holding me tighter, and I know she feels the same.

Cassie

Everything is perfect.

It's a bright contrast against the dark place I was in just a few weeks ago, when Adam and I weren't speaking and I was convinced it was over for us. Completely and utterly over. It seemed we were at an impasse, with him firm in his righteousness and me firm in mine.

But then, just like he always does, Adam surprised me.

His apology and camping night on Boca Chita Key was everything I've come to expect from him, and yet somehow, it still takes my breath away. Because even when I don't deserve his love, he gives it to me — as if he has no other choice.

I knew what I was asking of him was hard when I asked it. Accepting that I wanted to be friends with my ex-boyfriend? That's a sticky demand for *anyone* to make, let alone with the history the three of us had.

But whether it was talking to Jeremy or realizing that he was still friends with Skyler without me having an issue with it, he came around. And more than anything, he showed me that he trusts me, that even if he doesn't love the idea of me being friends with Grayson, he understands why I want to be, and why it's important to me, and most importantly, that he can trust me to keep that friend zone firm.

It means more to me than anything else in our relationship, that earnest trust and support.

And it's a giant step for us as a couple.

My heart has been afloat on the wings of butterflies ever since that night in the tent on the key, and a permanent smile is my favorite accessory. I'm wearing said smile the Sunday before Thanksgiving as the girls and I shop for semi-formal dresses, each of us filtering through the racks at our favorite dress boutique and piling hangers on our arms.

"Well, I'm glad you two worked it out," Skyler says, eyeballing a red, glittery dress before putting it back on the rack. "I was worried there for a second."

"Me, too," Erin confesses. "But then again, I don't think Adam could ever let you go — not now that he finally got you."

I blush, passing up an emerald floor-length dress that caught my eye and running my fingers over a white one, instead. "Well, I want to hold onto him, too. So I guess that's a good thing."

"Indeed, it is," Erin says, squeezing my arm as she passes.

"Gah, why does every dress make my ass look so large?" Jess huffs, dramatically exiting the little dressing room with the curtains flying up behind her. She hangs her hands on her hips, turning around to show us said ass in a tight-fitting and rouched gold dress. "I mean, *look* at this."

She grabs both her cheeks and jiggles them to the tune of our laughter, and Ashlei smacks her ass for good measure. "I'd hit that."

"I'm sure Kade won't mind your ass being highlighted," Skyler remarks, arching a brow before making her way into the dressing room next to Jess.

"He might if it busts through the fabric and everyone else gets to see it, too." Jess mumbles to herself, shaking her head and flinging the curtains back on the dressing room, slipping inside it again.

"How's that going, anyway?" I ask, taking a seat on the bench outside the row of dressing rooms once I have an arm full of dresses. "How was your first real date?"

Jess pokes her head out, giving me a thoughtful look. "Honestly? It was... surprising."

"How so?" Ashlei asks, joining us from where she'd been picking out a couple of short numbers from the return rack.

"He was such a gentleman... all dressed up and fancy. Took me to this super nice restaurant. We talked, laughed, shared feelings and things." She wrinkles her nose. "And, he wouldn't fuck me at the end of the night."

Ashlei balks. "What? Why?"

"He said he won't until the third date."

Erin barks out a laugh from the dressing room. "I like him."

"Anyway," Jess says, disappearing behind the curtain again. "I had a great time. I just also am ready to get these next two dates over with so we can bang again."

I snort a laugh just as Skyler walks out in a rose gold baby doll dress. Ashlei and I both shake our heads in unison.

"Too innocent," Ashlei says. "You look like you're twelve."

"Aw, I thought the color was pretty," Skyler says on a pout, twirling and watching herself in the mirror. When she stops, she nods. "But, you're right. Next!"

"Are you excited for your trip to California on Tuesday, Little?" Erin asks beside her.

"Ugh. I'm *dying*. I feel like I've been staring at the clock since I booked my flight last month." She sighs. "I just can't wait to be in Kip's arms."

"I bet *he* can't wait to be in your pants," Jess murmurs.

I chuckle. "Honestly, I don't know how y'all do it. Just being apart from Adam for a couple weeks drove me insane. And we were still on the same campus. Like, if I *wanted* to see him, I could." I shake my head. "It's got to be maddening to have so much distance between you guys."

"It sucks. A lot," Sky confesses, emerging again at the same time Erin does. They look at each other and burst out into laughter when they see they're in the same dress, and then they're gone again, a wave of curtains floating behind them. "But," she adds. "This is the way it needs to be for now. I've got another year here, and he's just getting started at his dream school. We can make it work."

"Do you think you'll move out to California with him once you graduate?" Lei asks.

Skyler pops her head out of the curtains, frowning. "I hadn't thought of it... but honestly? Maybe. I could get down with the other coast."

"Maybe you could go from paddle boarding to surfing," I suggest.

"What's going on with that intern, Lei?" Jess asks, coming out in a breathtaking high-low sunshine yellow dress. It highlights her bronze skin and showcases her cleavage with the sweetheart, shell bust, and the flowy layers of the skirt seem to swish and sway with every tiny move she makes.

"Oh, Jess," I whisper, still gawking. "*That* is the one."

"Agreed," Ashlei says. "You might as well stop looking now. You won't find better than that. *God*, you look stunning!"

"Is that a *blush* I see?" Skyler teases, poking her head out to see what all the fuss is about.

"Shut up." Jess waves her off, but she can't hide her glow as she looks herself over in the three-split mirror. "It really is pretty."

"You're getting it," Erin says definitively, and then she steps out in a poofy purple dress that we all go silent at before bursting out into a chorus of laughter.

"Yeah. That *ain't* it, sis," Jess says.

Erin's shoulders deflate. "I look like a bridesmaid from 1982."

That earns her another roar of laughter, and when she's in the dressing room again, Jess and I turn to Lei.

She sighs. "The intern is... fine. I guess. She was great at the *Okay, Cool* party, and she said she wants to interview me for some project. She really is good at her job, but... there's something off about her. She's like a fox. I don't trust her." She pauses. "And... I think she might be into me."

"What do you mean *into you*?" Jess probes.

"I mean, I think she might have hit on me at the party."

We all widen our eyes at that.

"I know, I know, it sounds crazy, and maybe it is," she confesses with her hands up. "I don't know. I'll keep y'all posted when I know more, because right now, I'm just confused and jealous."

"Nothing to be jealous of," I assure her. "Especially since Brandon told you he *loves you*."

I sing the last words, and all the girls chime in with *ooh's* and *aww's* that have Ashlei flicking us all off.

"I think I'm seeing someone, too."

We all turn in unison to look at Erin, who's looking back at us in the mirror as she assesses the long violet dress she's wearing. She does a little turn, stopping when she's facing us.

I don't think a single one of us blinks.

"His name is Gavin. He's in my therapy group."

She adds that last part with a little clearing of her throat at the end, and we're all completely silent for a moment longer before Jess squeals and wraps her in a hug.

"Ex! You sly dog, you. Why haven't you told us?"

Erin blushes. "I don't know. I *kind* of told you when we were sunbathing behind the house."

"Ah, the *friend*," Jess teases.

Erin shoots her a glare. "Well, I wasn't sure what it was at first but... we've gone on a few dates and... I don't know. I think I like him."

"You haven't dated anyone seriously since Landon," Skyler observes. "Well, other than my boyfriend, but that was a hot mess."

We all shift a little uncomfortably at that.

"Too soon?" Skyler asks with her arms out.

Erin chuckles. "Yeah, I know... it's been..." She goes silent for a long time, a shadow passing over her eyes, and the girls and I exchange worried glances.

"You know you can talk to us," I whisper, standing to touch my Grand Big's arm. "Whatever it is you've been through, we'd understand."

"I know," she whispers, tears flooding her eyes. "And I will. Someday. Soon."

We all nod, and then Lei wraps her in a hug. "Well, I for one am glad this Gavin guy has caught your attention. I can't wait to meet him."

"And I can't wait for him to fuck your brains out so you'll loosen up a bit in Chapter," Jess adds.

Erin launches at her, tickling her sides before Jess breaks free and takes off. Erin chases her around the dress shop while we all watch and laugh.

Skyler and I exchange a beaming look, and I know we're thinking the same thing.

Our sisters are fucking crazy.

But *damn,* do we love them.

***

Later that night, after Sunday Chapter, Adam and I walk the beach licking on our respective ice cream cones. Mine is mint chocolate chip, his is moose tracks. Our hands that aren't holding our dessert are clasped between us, swinging lightly as we walk.

The stars are non-existent, the clouds wispy, glowing from the moon behind them and adding a moody tone to the beach. It's quiet but for the waves, and our occasional laughter.

When we finish our cones, Adam pulls me into his arms and kisses me breathless, his warm lips a contrast between the cool sand under my bare feet.

And when we sneak away under the pier to make love, that same fluttering of wings sets my chest afloat.

Everything is perfect.

Ashlei

"So, you took the lead, pitched the launch event to Mrs. Delure from *Bare•ly*, and then *she* asked for you to be the lead event planner on the account?" Sophie asks, leaning on one elbow with stars in her eyes.

We're in one of the smaller conference rooms at *Okay, Cool*, finishing up what has been almost an hour of her asking me questions. We've covered everything from how I first became interested in event planning to my studies at Palm South University, from my first day of the internship to my duties today. I've never been watched with such reverence before, never been asked so much about myself as if I had something to offer that wasn't just a pretty face and an occasional creative event idea.

Sophie is making me feel special, like my role here actually matters.

And as the hour ticks by, I wonder if I've made a mistake about her.

I chuckle. "Yeah, that's pretty much exactly how it went."

"Wow," Sophie remarks, sitting back in her chair with a shake of her head. She clicks the top of her pen back and forth, jotting down something in her notebook. "That's pretty impressive. I mean, I feel like I've made strides as an intern, but I can't *imagine* being offered the event planner position on an account. I mean, there's a lot that goes into that."

"Oh, more than you can even think of or try to list out. I had more than a few times where I was sure I was going to land flat on my ass, but somehow managed to pull the event off by the hair of my teeth." I smile. "That was the first time I realized that working in event planning is a lot like trying to put out a house fire with nothing but a bucket of water and a handful of prayers."

"I'm sure you're selling yourself short," Sophie says, tapping her pen on my knee. "From what I hear, you've been rocking that account since the day they placed the first binder of information in your hands."

Appreciation settles in her fierce eyes, and those eyes trail the length of me, her tongue wetting her lips a little as they flow over my legs. I'm dressed in a rose gold, silky blouse and my favorite white pencil skirt, complete with hose underneath, and nude stilettos. Sophie nearly matches me in a skirt and blouse of her own, except her skirt is short, her blouse revealing, and where I'm all light and airy this afternoon, she's all mauve and black, dark and severe, all the way from her black heels to the dark blood shade of her lips.

And the way she just licked them, it looks like she wants to have me for lunch.

The trust she's built over the last hour fizzles out of me like the bubbles of a champagne bottle, and suspicion cools its place, making my skin prickle.

I clear my throat, gathering up the notes and files I'd brought for her to browse through for the interview. "Alright, does that about do it, then?"

"I think so," she says, but I don't miss the disappointment in her voice. "Thank you for taking time out of your day to speak with me. Truly. I appreciate it."

"No problem. You'll have to let me see the final product."

"Absolutely." She clicks her pen, still watching me as I pack up. "Can I ask you one more question? Off the record."

"Sure."

"Are you bisexual?"

I drop the files I'd been about to shove into my bag, sending papers flying around our heels on the floor as I watch her wide-eyed.

"Excuse me?"

"I'm sorry, I know that's forward," she says hurriedly with a blush. "I just... Well, you see, *I'm* bisexual. And I guess I just thought I had a knack for sniffing out another bi. My friends and I always joke that I have a radar of sorts."

She chuckles, and on the surface, she looks pleasant and friendly and like she genuinely is just curious.

But my insides shrivel up in warning.

I swallow, standing and holding my skirt tucked against the back of my thighs as I slowly lower down onto my knees and begin picking up the papers that fell from the file.

Sophie doesn't move an inch to help me.

She just sits in her chair above me, her crossed knees level with my face.

"I don't know that that's work-appropriate conversation," I murmur, focusing on getting the pages back in place.

"I didn't mean any offense. Honestly, I don't think being bisexual is offensive. Do you?"

"No, of course not," I answer quickly.

"Then, what's the big deal?"

What is *the big deal?*

I try to find the answer to that myself but come up empty. What is it about her that sets me off? What is it about her that makes me want to strangle her and be best friends with her all at the same time?

I grind my teeth. "I am."

"You are what?"

I huff, sitting back on my heels and looking up at her with half of the spilled papers in my hands. "Bi."

Her lips curl up slowly. "I knew it."

"But, I'm with Brandon now," I quickly add.

Sophie chuckles. "And I don't blame you for shouting it from the rooftops any time you get a chance. Mr. Church is..." She shakes her head, whistling. "Let's just say I'd let him put it where no man has put it before."

"Watch it," I warn, jaw tight.

"Oh, don't get me wrong," Sophie quickly adds, and then right in front of my face, she uncrosses her legs, spreading them just wide enough to show me a flash of her black panties before she leans forward and balances her elbows on her knees. Her eyes skate over the features of my face before they meet my gaze. "I'd let you fuck my ass, too. If you wanted."

A zip of something hot and electric shoots straight down between my legs.

Sophie's lips part, just barely, enough for her tongue to dart out and wet her lips again as she watches me. From this angle, I can see the mountains of her breasts, the black lace of her bra from where her silk blouse gapes at her neck.

And I'm rendered completely speechless.

Get up.

Get the fuck up and get the fuck out of this room.

But I'm under her spell.

Sophie spreads her legs again, this time lowering one knee to the ground, and then the other, placing one knee between mine. Her leg is warm and smooth as she presses my knees apart, just a little, and she picks up a few stranded sheets of paper as if that's why she was on the floor.

But her eyes don't leave mine.

And when she hands them to me, I hold onto them without moving an inch to put them in the folder, and her eyes flick to my lips.

She leans in.

I lean back.

At least, I want to. I *should.* But maybe I don't at all. Maybe I sit there completely still, shocked, knowing I should move but not knowing how.

Maybe… I lean in, too.

And in what feels like a stolen breath of time, Sophie kisses me.

I know I feel the kiss.

I know I feel her lips on mine, slightly dry from her lipstick but warm and soft all the same. I know I feel her hands shakily resting on my thighs for balance, and her hot breath on mine, and the silk of her blouse as I hold onto her, too. I know I hear her whimper of a moan, and taste that moan on my tongue.

I know I'm present for every searing moment of it.

But I awake on the other side as if I'd blacked out, as if someone had drugged me, as if I'd been betrayed and violated in the worst possible way.

"No!"

I shove her backward, sending her flying to her elbows with a shocked curse. I stand as soon as she's off me, swiping what's left of the papers off the floor and hastily shoving them into the folders before I shove them into my bag.

"Fuck, Sophie. *Fuck*. What the hell was that?"

I'm still packing up my shit, and I wait for her to say something. To apologize. To leap up and beg me not to overreact, not to tell, not to freak out or hold it against her. I expect her to blame it on a moment of passion, or a late night, or a connection she felt through the interview.

But when I finally tug my bag onto my shoulder and look down at her, she's not making any excuse at all.

She's just lying there on her elbows staring up at me.

With the most wicked smile I've ever seen.

I shake my head, frowning at her with a mixture of horror and astonishment whirling inside me. It's like she's the devil or a witch or both wrapped into one, and I can't reconcile the fact that I just fell victim to her spell.

"Stay away from me," I warn.

And then I run out of the conference room to wash her lipstick off my mouth.

Skyler

I was an anxious bundle of nerves the entire flight from Miami to LA.

It had been all I could do just to sit still, to drink the mimosas I'd ordered to help me cope with the fact that I was more nervous than I'd been in recent memory. And now that I'm on the ground in California, tugging my little carry-on luggage behind me in the airport and looking for Kip, I feel equal parts sick and elated.

I haven't seen Kip since we parted ways after the summer, him coming here to UCLA while I went back to Palm South, and as silly as it seems, I'm nervous.

What if he's changed?

What if he's forgotten about me since he's been here?

What if I'm a burden, if he doesn't want me here, if he wishes I would have just stayed in Florida?

What if it's weird between us?

What if we're not meant to be?

I don't know when I became this person, the kind who cares and loves someone so much that these are the kind of thoughts that plague me. Gone is the girl I used to be who could bang a stranger on Spring Break and not think twice about them. Gone is the Skyler Thorne who couldn't be tied down, no matter who tried. And absolutely gone is the version of me who couldn't be hurt by a breakup.

If I lost Kip, I'd lose my mind.

And my heart.

And my soul.

And my grip on life.

That much I know for sure.

I try to school my breathing as I roll through the airport, following the signs for passenger pickup. My stomach is still in a fierce tangle of knots, though.

Until the very moment I see him.

My blond hair, blue-eyed boy is leaning up against his shiny new BMW Z4 — the one he'd bought for himself after winning it all in Vegas — with his hands in his pockets and a sexy smirk on his face. Dark Ray-Bans cover his eyes, and when he sees me, he kicks off from where he's been leaning against the car, strutting toward me confidently in his dark blue jeans and casual, pistachio green long-sleeve, relaxed fit tee.

To anyone else in this airport, he's just another guy. He's just muscles and tan skin and a smile that might make them look twice.

But to me?

He's everything.

I walk slowly at first, returning his smile until the butterflies in my stomach are too loud to ignore any longer. With a laugh, I take off in a jog, abandoning my bag behind me when I'm just a few feet away from him and launching myself into his arms.

He catches me with an easy spin and an easy smile, our lips connecting like magnets, my arms threading around his neck while his hold fast to my waist.

And the moment we touch, the moment I'm in his arms, every nerve and anxiety settles into absolute peace.

In his arms, I'm home.

"Hey there, Ella Mae," he whispers against my lips before capturing them again. A deep and longing sigh leaves his chest when he finally puts me back on the ground, but he doesn't let me go. "Was it just me, or did that flight seem to last years?"

I scoff. "*You* weren't the one who had to sit through the torture of being on it."

"Trust me, it was just as sucky here on the ground waiting for you to land." He kisses my lips too briefly for my taste, squeezing my hand before grabbing the handle of my suitcase and wheeling it to his car. "You ready to see California?"

"I'm ready to see your bedroom," I murmur.

Kip chuckles, opening the passenger side door for me and stealing one last kiss from me as I slide inside. Then, he joins me in the driver seat, laying one hand on the inside of my thigh and the other on the steering wheel and driving us across town to UCLA.

***

Kip's room in the small house he shares with nine of his brothers is almost exactly like his apartment he had when he was at PSU, except it's much smaller, much darker, and has the faint scent of an old library.

The area they refer to as A Sig Quad is a little collection of five houses and a cottage on the same block, each one housing Alpha Sigma brothers close enough to campus to be convenient and yet far enough away to host parties that don't have to follow campus rules. Kip gave me a little tour of the courtyard and common living areas on our way upstairs, and now it's just me and him in the room he shares with Rick.

I smile, fingers gliding over the old wood paneling of the built-in shelves as I look around. "You know, as a millionaire, I'm a little surprised you didn't want to live in some fancy condo on the bay."

"And miss out on this glory?" he asks, propping my suitcase in the corner before waving his hands over the room. "It wouldn't be the same experience to live that far from campus. I mean, look at you. You could easily get your own place on the beach, but you stay at the sorority house."

"Fair. I guess we're both weirdos."

"At least we can be weird together." Kip points a thumb over his shoulder at the door. "You hungry? Want me to make us a couple sandwiches?"

"Oh, I'm hungry, alright," I say with a devious grin, stepping into him and winding my fingers into his hair. I kiss him deeply, inhaling his scent and reveling in the familiar feel of his lips against mine.

He grins. "That's not exactly what I meant."

"When does Rick get home?"

I'm already unfastening his belt, my fingers curling under the hem of his sweater so I can peel it up over his head.

"He's staying with his girlfriend tonight," Kip answers, letting me tug his sweater off before his lips find mine again.

"So it's just us?"

"In this room, yes," Kip says, slowly unwrapping the scarf around my neck. He pauses when it's unwrapped but still over my shoulders, tugging on it until my neck bends and my lips tip up toward his. "But as you saw, there are brothers all over this house."

"I'll be quiet," I promise.

But Kip smirks, shaking his head before he whispers in my ear, "Liar."

I just grin, done talking and joking now that I've got my nails raking down the ridges and valleys of his insane abdomen. I remember watching Kip workout when he was at PSU, and he's somehow bulked up even more here in California, which makes me jealous of all the girls who have been in the gym with him.

That jealousy stings in my chest, fueling me to kiss him harder, drag my nails deeper as they trail over his shoulders and down his back. He hisses in through his teeth, grabbing me by the waist and backing me into the corner of his desk.

A grunt leaves my chest when we hit it, but the next breath is stolen by Kip's lips, and we're a flurry of hands and mouths, undressing and kissing and sucking and biting. Any time I moan or whimper, Kip's hand covers my mouth, and he clamps that hand hard over my panting.

Even still, nothing could muzzle the pleasure coursing through me at feeling him touch me for the first time in months.

When all that's left is his boxer briefs and my panties, Kip flips me around, walking me over to his full-length mirror on the back of the bedroom door. I brace my hands on either side of it just in time to stop my face from hitting it, and Kip grins from behind me, our eyes connected in the mirror.

It's a sight that sends waves of chills over every inch of me, seeing Kip towering behind me, his bare, bulging muscles encompassing me. One arm wraps around my waist and up to palm my breast, and he groans in approval with the full weight of it in his grasp, squeezing and kneading as his lips find my neck and suck hard. His other hand is behind me, and I feel it slowly trail down and over my ass, his fingers slipping between my legs and roughly sliding my lace panties aside.

"God*damn*, you're wet, Sky," he pants, his fingers easily sliding between my lips. He skates them deeper, centimeters at a time, but never enters me — not even a fingertip.

I writhe against the touch, pushing my ass back and up so I can get those fingers inside me. But every time I try, Kip pulls them back just enough to keep me empty and begging.

His hand retracts altogether on a shudder and a sigh from me, but before I can beg for more, I feel Kip shed his briefs and press his length against my ass. His long, thick, pulsing cock lines up in my crease, spreading me open as the hand that was on my breast slides up to grab my neck.

"Open your eyes," he commands, and when I do, the smile on his face is wicked and sexy as hell. "I want to see you when I fill you for the first time in months."

And that's all the warning I get before he slides in, hard and punishing and all at once, filling me to the brim as I shake in his grasp.

The moan that escapes me is impossible to quiet, and Kip squeezes my throat a little tighter in warning, withdrawing his hips just to slam back into me again.

"Shhh, baby," he says in my ear, sucking the lobe between his teeth.

I bite my lip to keep from crying out again, focusing on keeping myself braced over the mirror, my eyes fluttering open and closed again and again, little glimpses of Kip's hand around my throat, his other hand holding my hips as he plows into me from behind.

The way his cock curves, the way he squats just enough to fill me up completely on each thrust, has me seeing stars within seconds. Every new thrust hits that magical spot deep inside me, and the slight pressure of his hand around my neck sends all the blood rushing between my legs.

Fuck, I've missed this.

But I want more before I come.

Peeling his fingers from around my neck, I twist away from him and press my hands into his chest, shoving him backward.

He's panting, chest heaving, cock hard and erect and glistening with my pleasure as I guide him back to the bed. I shove him again until he's on his back, and then I climb up, taking time to slide my pussy over his cock before I continue my trek up, up.

And then, I sit on my boyfriend's god-like, too-handsome-for-his-own-good face.

"Make me come, baby," I whisper, and Kip answers with his hands gripping my ass and pulling my clit to his mouth.

His tongue lashes me like a whip, making me shudder with the way it flicks over that sensitive bundle of nerves. I grab his headboard and hold on for dear life, and when he sucks me, gently, over and over between his teeth, I rock my hips against the pressure, needing more.

"Fuck, I'm close," I groan.

Kip slips his finger inside me long enough to wet it, and then with his mouth still punishing my clit, he slips that same finger right into my ass.

I barely have time to gasp, to let my mouth fall open and my eyes shoot wide and my fingers curl into the headboard before I'm flying off into an orgasm like none I've ever had before. It's not the same as just having my clit rubbed or my g-spot hit. It's shocking and forbidden and a little painful as it rocks through me.

But I fucking love it.

I sit back a little, taking his finger deeper in my ass as I ride out my climax. And I don't give two flying fucks about the other brothers in the house. My screams are loud and wild and desperate, and I give in to every single one.

I've been living on masturbation alone since August.

I'm not being quiet during my first male-generated orgasm in months.

I'm still seeing stars, shaking and pulsing around Kip's finger when he gently removes it, kissing the inside of my thighs.

But I don't have time to rest.

He flips me over, kissing me with lips and a tongue that taste like my pussy before he hikes both of my legs up. My ankles on his shoulders, he slides back inside me, both of us growling at the sensation of him filling me again.

"Oh *fuck,* Sky," he says, pulling out and pressing in all the way. I twist my fists in the sheets and arch into him, begging for more.

He delivers with a harder thrust, a faster rhythm, and his hands reach out to palm both of my bouncing breasts as he fucks me like a man who's been in prison for years.

I see it the moment he crests, the moment that spark catches fire and his orgasm releases. His face screws up, a grunt escaping his lips, and he drops his grip on my tits, pulling his cock out just in time to spill hot cum all over my stomach, my chest, some even shooting up and hitting my chin.

My lips curl into a smile as I watch him come undone, and when he shudders his last breath, holding his wet, still pulsing cock in his hands, his eyes flutter open to find mine.

And I hold his gaze as I swipe a finger through the cum on my chin, sucking that finger into my mouth to taste him.

"*Fuck,*" he groans, shaking his head, and then he's on top of me — sated and limp — while I giggle and kiss all over his shoulders.

We lie there for a long while, both of us coming down from our highs, our muscles already sore and aching for more.

Then Kip leans up on one elbow, his eternal blue eyes searching mine, and he sweeps my hair out of my face, gaze full of adoration.

"I love you," he whispers.

"I love you, too."

It's the sweetest, most tender moment, sealed with a perfect, gentle kiss.

And then a roar of applause breaks out downstairs, hoots and hollers and *atta boys!* so loud it sounds like we're at a football game.

Kip and I lock wide eyes, and then I blush furiously, burying my face in his chest as he laughs and kisses my hair.

"I told you to be quiet."

Indeed, he did.

Whoops.

Bear

"Aw, look at us," Becca teases, kissing my cheek while I carve the turkey. "We're so domesticated."

"Totally. Cooking a half-ass Thanksgiving meal in a frat house kitchen. *So* adult."

She pats my ass, then gets back to whipping the mashed potatoes.

"Yeah, as much as this is awesome for a college Thanksgiving dinner, I have to admit — it ain't my mama's cooking," Amber says, eyeing the green bean casserole suspiciously.

Amber is Becca's best friend, a short little thing with curves for days, wild and beautiful curly black hair, warm brown skin, and a birth mark above her lip that makes her look like a glamorous Hollywood star from the twenties. She and Becca have been friends since they were toddlers, and the way they act together, the way they even mirror each other's gestures makes them seem more like sisters than friends.

Amber goes to school in Boston, but is visiting for the holiday, and watching her with Becca makes my chest warm and fuzzy in a new and unfamiliar way. It's one thing to see her undressed, or to have her all to myself in bed, both of us in sweatpants and lazy smiles. But it's another thing completely to see her with the ones she cares about, the ones she loves, joking and laughing and reminiscing on old stories.

"My mom always makes this *amazing* sweet potato pie," Becca says, still working on the mashed potatoes. "She's given me the recipe, but I swear it never turns out the way hers does."

"That's how my grandma is with her recipes," Amber chimes in. "I think they leave out important ingredients or steps so that we keep coming home for holidays. My grandma's homemade stuffing?" She clicks her tongue, shaking her head. "That shit is *magical*. But she'll never give away her secret."

Becca smiles, giving me a wink when she catches me staring at her. But I just can't help it. Seeing her in the kitchen like that — apron around her waist, natural curls bouncing with every laugh and turn of her head, smile wide and bright and full of love... it hits me hard in the chest, like a fist more than a feeling.

Because I can see it.

I can imagine us together, not just now but in the future, too. I can see her in our house, in our kitchen, with our family and friends gathered around us.

"What?" Becca asks, hanging a hand on her hip the longer I stare.

"You're beautiful."

I steal a kiss from her just as Amber makes a gagging noise. "Alright, that's enough mush for me. I'm going to go watch Josh try to hit on Pamela."

Becca and I chuckle at that. Pamela is Becca's roommate, a sweet, shy, petite little white girl with dark freckles and long, brunette hair she always lets hang a little in front of her face, like she's trying to hide from any and everyone.

Josh has been shooting his shot since the moment she showed up, and it's been the entertainment of the day.

I told everyone that we'd have dinner around four, but that they were welcome to come to the house ahead of time to watch football and hang out. Most of our brothers clear off campus for the break, visiting their families, so we have the entire place to ourselves today.

Becca, Pamela, and Amber got here early, helping prep the food and cook and bake and set up the table. Josh stumbled out of bed around noon and plopped his ass down on the couch to watch football — and try his best to make Pamela uncomfortable, which was undoubtedly working.

But Erin hasn't showed yet, and I can't help but wonder if she will at all.

She'd been surprised to say the least when I called and invited her to Friendsgiving. But after asking if I was sure and if she could bring a friend, she'd agreed, and I'd be lying if I said my stomach hasn't been in knots all day thinking about being around her tonight.

When Becca finishes mashing the potatoes, she washes her hands and dries them on a towel, looking around at the feast we've prepared. "I'd say we make a pretty good team, Chef Pennington."

"You're the chef," I correct her, taking her in my arms and planting a kiss on her nose. "I'm just the big-fisted dummy you boss around to help you."

She chuckles, threading her hands together behind my neck. "This was a good idea, Bear. The girls are having fun — even Pam, despite Josh being up her ass."

I laugh. "Are *you* having fun?"

"I am." She pauses, swallowing. "Is Erin still coming?"

I take a deep breath. "Your guess is as good as mine."

As if on cue, there's commotion from the living room, and Becca and I round the corner to find Erin giving Josh a hug before immediately introducing herself to Pam and Amber.

Herself, and then the tall, brooding guy she brought with her.

"This is Gavin," she explains, and he shakes everyone's hands with an easy grin before tucking his hands back in his pockets. He listens as Josh and Erin chat, his eyes wandering the room.

Until they land on me.

Then, they don't budge.

He and Erin couldn't be more opposite. Where Erin is sunshine embodied, from her shining blonde hair to the mustard yellow dress slimming her waist and cutting off below her knees, he's like the dark side of the moon, dressed in black distressed jeans and a black long-sleeve shirt with the name of some metal band I don't recognize sprawled across his chest.

He nods his chin at me after a moment, and it's as if that notion knocks me out of my spell.

"You must be Bear," he says, stepping around the couch to where Becca and I are. He extends his hand on a comfortable smile. "I'm Gavin, Erin's boyfriend."

I hope I'm hiding it. I hope my jaw isn't as tight as it feels, that my eyes didn't just shoot open as wide as I think they did when I snapped my gaze to Erin's.

She's still standing by the girls and Josh, holding a casserole dish in her hands, her wide brown eyes watching me.

I hope an uncomfortable amount of time hasn't passed as I force a smile and reach out for Gavin's hand, both of us engaging in a crushing grip that tells me he's threatened by me and whispers that I might feel the same about him, too.

"I didn't realize Erin *had* a boyfriend," I comment, and I want to kick myself for how petty it sounds.

"Yeah. From what she tells me, you two don't talk much anymore," Gavin comments. Before I can reply, he pulls his hand from mine and extends it for Becca. "Thanks for having us over."

"It's our pleasure," she says, shaking his hand. "I'm Becca." Then, her eyes land hard on me. "*Bear's* girlfriend."

I know that look. It's the one that says *why the hell didn't you say this before I had to?*

I clear my throat, rounding the couch to where Erin is standing with the casserole dish. I reach out for it. "I told you you didn't have to bring anything."

It comes out harsher than I mean for it to, and I internally curse myself. *Snap out of it, big guy.*

"It's just a sweet corn casserole," she says softly, tucking her hair behind her ear when her hands are free. "It's my mom's specialty."

My stomach tightens.

It seems like everyone has a memory of their mother on this holiday, fond thoughts of cooking in the kitchen and famous recipes.

The only things my mom ever brought around on Thanksgiving were drugs and strangers.

At least, that was always the case when I was younger. But earlier this afternoon when Becca and I were cooking, I got a video call from my little brother, showing me that they were all gathered at Mac's house — including our mother and my older brother and *his* family — laughing and playing games and getting ready to eat their own feast.

Without me.

"Well, thank you," I say after a long pause, shaking off my own shit to focus on the whole reason I had this get-together in the first place. I owe Erin an apology, but not now. Not in front of everyone.

Erin and I watch each other, her shifting her weight before the gaze becomes too much for her, and she looks behind me.

At Gavin.

Who promptly returns to where she's standing, putting his arm around her waist. What pisses me off most is it's not possessive or territorial or aimed toward me at all.

It's comforting and calming, meant for Erin only, and she leans into that touch with a sigh of relief that makes my chest tighten for a completely new reason.

"Alright, let's get this into the kitchen and I think we should be ready to eat," Becca says, taking the casserole from my hands with a warning glare. "Everyone grab your plates."

It's all laughter and catching up and getting to know each other as we fill our plates and gather at the table — a folding table usually used for flip cup and beer pong that has been disguised with a tablecloth, some flowers, and a few candles. The frat house always smells faintly of beer, but the candles help cover it a bit, and though it's far from something Martha Stewart would approve, it's not bad for a college Thanksgiving set-up.

I'm mostly a quiet bystander as everyone talks while we eat — Josh bragging about his IM football stats, Amber and Becca telling us stories from their raucous high school days, Erin and Pamela bonding over their shared love of well-organized planners.

And then there's Gavin.

He's almost as quiet as I am, chiming in time to time only to lay out a well-placed joke or to ask a question about something someone's talking about. Like he cares.

And maybe he does.

Maybe he's a perfectly cool dude with perfectly good intentions with Erin.

But after what she's been through, I can't help but watch him like the big brother she never asked me to be — arms crossed, gaze hard, jaw ticking as I fight back the questions I really want to ask.

Like:

Do you have a criminal record?

How many girls have you cheated on or broken up with?

When was your last serious relationship?

What plans do you have for your life?

What makes you think you deserve the most amazing girl in the world?

I shift uncomfortably as that last thought flitters through me, chugging half my beer in one swallow with Becca's eyes watching.

"So," I say when I set my glass back down, staring at Gavin. "Gavin. How did you and Erin meet?"

Erin smiles at him when he turns to her, and even without being able to see it, I know he grabs her hand under the table and gives it a squeeze.

"She was walking on the beach at sunrise, her hair and skirt blowing back behind her in the breeze as she watched the horizon. And I watched her. I mean, how could I not, with the morning glow on her face like that? I was just out surfing, but I didn't care about the waves once I saw her. I had to know her name. So, I paddled in and hopped off my board and walked straight up to her and said..." He pauses, looking at Erin with a bent brow and making his voice deeper. "*Hello, my queen. It is I, your King, and I have searched this world high and low for you.*"

Erin shoves his chest with a roll of her eyes, still smiling when she looks at me. "We met at therapy."

The girls all laugh, and Amber holds up her glass to Gavin. "You had me going. I was leaning in like *oh my God, what did she say to that?!*"

"I was just about to start taking notes, see if I could pull the same stunt on Perfect Pam here," Josh added, which made the group chuckle again. Well, except for Pam, who blushed and hid behind her hair.

And except for me, too, because I couldn't find it in me to so much as smile.

"What are you in therapy for?"

The room goes silent at my question, and Becca pinches me under the table. "*Bear*," she warns.

"Do you have to be in therapy for one specific reason?" Gavin asks, taking a sip of his wine, completely calm and cool and collected.

"Isn't that kind of the point?"

"The goals of therapy differ greatly, depending on the person. It can be focused on healing, growing, resolving issues, surviving trauma."

"So what's yours?"

"*Bear,*" Erin says this time, her eyes wide.

"A little of everything, I suppose. Do you go to therapy, Bear?" Gavin asks.

"Of course not."

"Oh, so you're perfect? Nothing wrong with you at all, huh? No shit to work through, nothing holding you back from being your best self?"

I don't have an answer to that, which makes me grip my glass harder as I lift it to my lips and drain the last of my beer.

"I think it's great," Becca says, somehow managing a smile when she finally peels her murderous glare away from me.

"Me, too," Amber agrees. "And I think it's awesome that you two met at your most vulnerable. Not a lot of people can say that, you know? We all play games when we first start dating. We hide who we really are in the name of being who we *think* the other person wants us to be."

Becca sips her champagne silently, glancing at me with a sullen look in her eyes as Erin and Gavin smile at each other.

"It is pretty awesome," Gavin agrees. "There's a side of this girl that she doesn't show to anyone but me. And I'll admit, I'm a greedy bastard when it comes to that pile of gold."

The girls visibly swoon, but I just grind my teeth, not able to hold back my sarcastic grunt.

Gavin turns to look at me, arching one brow. "Something else to say, Bear?"

"Not to you."

"Whoa, bro," Josh says, smiling at everyone to try to make the moment lighter. "What's with the hostility? Gavin, did you steal the last of the cranberry sauce or something?"

"Actually, I think I stole the girl he never thought to make his. And now he's regretting his inaction and thinks he can piss on her to scare me off."

My chair grinds against the wooden floor when I stand, towering over Gavin as everyone jumps. I point my finger straight into his chest. "Listen here, you disrespectful little fuck."

"Oh, I'm listening. Go on. Tell me I'm wrong," Gavin challenges with a smirk, not even so much as puffing his chest back at me. He's not threatened, and that somehow pisses me off more.

"I think we should go," Erin says, standing and folding her napkin primly before laying it carefully next to her plate. "Becca, I hope you don't mind if we don't help with clean up."

"Not at all," Becca says, standing too. Only she doesn't fold her napkin — she bunches it in her fist and throws it down on the table with her eyes on me. "In fact, I think Bear can clean up this mess on his own."

She storms out of the room without another look at me, her friends on her tail, Pam looking at me with pity, while Amber's glare matches the one Becca had been giving me all night.

Gavin stands slowly, helping Erin put her camisole sweater on before grabbing her hand and leading her toward the door. "Thanks for dinner," he says to me, winking. "It's been a real treat."

My muscles work before my brain does, and the only thing that stops me from launching at that motherfucker and beating his face in is Josh's hands wrapping around my arms and quickly holding them behind my back in a stiff lock. I shrug against it to no avail, which makes Gavin shake his head with a look like he pities me.

Then they're gone, and it's just me and Josh.

"Damn, bro," he says when they're gone, releasing me. "What the hell was all that?"

And I just breathe like a bull, chest heaving, wishing I knew the goddamn answer myself.

Cassie

I haven't been to Cup O' Joes since Grayson and I broke up, and sitting here for the first time in almost a year, I remember why.

Everything about this place reminds me of when we dated.

I remember the first time I met him, when he bought my coffee and asked for my number and made me blush with his unapologetic gaze.

I remember watching him play a set, looking around the room at the way the girls visibly swooned with every note he played and every word he sang.

I remember sitting in this very seat, at this very table in the back corner of the room, so I could watch but not *be* watched.

Of course, Grayson never let me slide under the radar for long. He loved to call attention to me when he was on stage, or as soon as he got *off* stage, striding back to me and wrapping me in a hug or planting a big kiss on my lips to let everyone in that room know he was taken.

At least, that's what I'd thought.

My stomach sours when I remember something else — that the entire time I'd trusted him, he'd been lying to me.

Shaking that thought off, I take a sip of my coffee, reveling in the sweet taste of their famous caramel mocha that I haven't had since Grayson and I broke up. I've missed it, and the atmosphere of the shop, with students studying and chatting and listening to Grayson play.

He's on stage, crooning out a Maroon 5 song and winking at every girl who casts her wide-eyed gaze up at him. I can't help but chuckle, noting that while he's changed, some things never will.

It's Monday evening, the first day back on campus for most students who went away for the Thanksgiving holiday. With the sun setting earlier now, it's completely dark in the shop, save for the dim industrial lighting and the candles at each table. With Grayson singing and strumming his guitar and the Christmas lights already being hung across campus, there's a feel of the holiday season in the air, and I breathe into it with a smile.

Grayson asked me to come watch him play while we were walking out of lab earlier. He wanted me to be there when he played his newest song, the one he'd been writing and giving me previews of for the past few weeks. I agreed, of course, and invited Adam to join me — which I knew he appreciated as much as he hated.

He doesn't love Grayson and me being friends, but he understands it. He respects it. And that means more to me than he could ever know.

I'm excited for him to see that Grayson and I really *are* just friends, that anything there was between us is firmly in the past. I hope it will set his mind at ease.

And hey, he can kiss me right here in front of Grayson and everyone else.

I don't mind him claiming his territory.

Heat flushes my cheeks at the thought of his kiss, the kind that always burns me and leaves a mark, and I check my watch anxiously. He should have been here by now.

Grayson announces he's going to take a little break, and when he comes back, he'll play a brand-new song. That earns applause and hoots and hollers from just about every girl in the place, and when I look around, I wonder how many of them are here for Grayson, alone.

His hair is tied at the back of his neck, and he's dressed in a leather jacket, forest green relaxed-fit t-shirt and dark jeans. His combat boots set off the rock-star look, and he strides toward me with an easy smile, like he doesn't realize every girl's neck is breaking to watch him as he passes.

"Great set," I say when he sits at the table. "Want me to get you a coffee?"

He opens his mouth to answer, but before he can, the barista drops off a hot Earl Grey tea and a tall glass of ice water. "The usual, Grayson," she says, casting me a cautious glance before she smiles at him again. "You were great up there. Can't wait to hear the new song."

"I'll play it just for you, Wendy."

She bites her lip on a flush, excusing herself without another word.

When Grayson looks at me, he shrugs. "What?"

"Just watching Casanova in action," I say, chuckling.

"Hey, I'm just being nice."

"Mm-hmm." I sip my coffee. "So, your parents know you still play here?"

His eyes darken with the question, and he dunks the bag of tea a few times, watching it steep. "Yeah. Dad says he doesn't care, as long as I've let go of my *fantasy* and am getting good grades."

"I'm sorry, Grayson."

He shrugs. "It's whatever. As long as I keep working on the plan *they* think is best for me, I can play my music. And that's all that matters to me."

"Do you think you'll go back to music once you graduate?"

Another shrug. "I don't know. I want to, of course, but... I mean, maybe it really is a fantasy. Look how many musicians never make a name for themself."

"Do you have to make a name for yourself?" I ask, sitting up straighter when he looks at me confused. "I mean, what if it was always just like this. You and your guitar, small coffee shops, playing music and making people feel good."

Grayson nods. "That'd be alright, I think."

"Then maybe you can have both — the life they want for you, and the life you want, too."

"I guess I never considered that the two could marry."

I shrug. "Just a thought."

"You always were smarter than me."

I scoff at that, biting my tongue to resist the urge to point out that I wasn't smart enough to know he was cheating on me all along.

My next sip of coffee is bitter. *Why the hell do I still care? Why does that thought still bubble to the surface every time I'm with Grayson, making me feel prickly as a cactus?*

I frown.

Will my new friendship with Grayson always be shadowed by that cloud of betrayal?

"What's on your mind?"

I blink, clearing my throat when I realize Grayson has been watching me. "Nothing."

"You've also always been a terrible liar."

"I guess I was just thinking. This place brings back a lot of memories."

Grayson's face slacks. "Yeah. It does for me, too."

The way he watches me now is with a longing so fierce, I feel it like a vibration in the air. I swallow, looking away from him and out at the quad where students are dressing the giant Christmas tree they put up there every year.

"I can't believe it's almost Christmas. This semester has flown by."

"Cassie, don't change the subject."

I frown, looking back at him. "I didn't realize we were on a subject."

"The shop. The memories." He pauses. "You and me."

"Uh..."

Grayson scoots his chair closer to mine, his eyes earnest as they watch me intently, and warning bells ring loud and shrill in my ears.

Oh no...

"I invited you tonight because I wanted to see if you felt it, too — the rush of what we used to be. Because every time I walk through those doors, every time I play here... it takes me under like a tidal wave."

"Grayson," I whisper, shaking my head. "I just came here to support you. As a *friend*."

"You and I have never been friends," he says, covering my knee with his hand. "And you know it."

I swat his hand away quickly, scooting back. "Grayson. Stop. Now. I mean it."

"Don't pretend like you don't miss me," he hisses, frowning and shaking his head like I'm in denial. "I see it. I feel it. And whatever is going on between you and Adam, it's not what we had."

"You're right," I say. "It's so much more than what you and I could ever have even *hoped* to have." I scoff, my chest on fire. "God, I can't believe I fell for this. I can't believe I thought you actually, *genuinely* wanted to be my friend."

"I do want to be your friend," he argues, scooting his chair closer again. Mine is pinned now, and I curse myself for picking that same back corner table I'd always sat at before. "But I want to be more, too. I want you back. I want to prove to you that *I'm* the one you should be with — not that asshat."

"I love him," I whisper-yell. "How *dare* you say these things to me. I stood up for you, you know that? When you didn't deserve it. When Adam questioned me. When he told me I was an idiot for thinking you could ever be just my friend." My mouth falls open, and I shake my head in disbelief at my own stupidity. "He was right. How did I not see it?"

"He sees what I see. What I know you see, too." Grayson puts his hand on my knee again, and this time when I try to swat it away, it doesn't budge. "We're meant for each other, Cassie. And I'm not letting up until you realize you never stopped loving me, and I never stopped loving you, and this — you and me — we're real. We're inevitable."

He takes his hand off my knee, but then it moves for my face, sliding back into my hair with his lips on track for mine.

I rip away, panic searing my chest. "Grayson, no!"

Crack.

I don't register what's happened, not until I blink several times, taking in the people gasping and screaming around us.

And then I see Grayson on the floor.

And Adam on top of him, fist in the air, ready to plow it back into Grayson's already bleeding nose.

"Adam, don't!" I scream, flying out of my chair and down to him. I wrap my arms around his waist and pull, knowing I wouldn't be able to budge him unless he actually wanted to be budged.

Luckily, he lets me pull him up to stand, but his chest is heaving, glare murderous, his eyes nearly popping out of his head as he stares down at Grayson. "YOU MOTHERFUCKER," he screams, grabbing him by the shirt. "HOW DARE YOU TOUCH MY GIRL."

Grayson spits a mouthful of blood to the side before grinning up at Adam. "My girl, first."

A growl rips through Adam, and he lays another crack to Grayson's jaw before I can stop him. I'm screaming and crying and tearing at him to let Grayson go. When he finally does, it's to the tune of the manager yelling for us to take it outside or she'd call campus police. And so, Adam drops his grip, letting Grayson fall back onto the floor.

Then, he storms out without even looking back at me.

I scramble to get my purse where it's hanging off the back of my chair, plucking a twenty out and leaving it on the table before I fly out after Adam. He's already halfway across the quad, and I scream his name over and over, jogging to catch up.

It's not until we're by the reflection pond that Adam stops and turns, and when the weight of his gaze hits me, I stumble back, eyes blurring as I cover my mouth.

"Adam, it's not what you think."

"Oh, it's not?" he challenges, stepping into my chest as I shrink away. He points a finger back at the shop. "So that *wasn't* your so-called *friend* hitting on you, touching you, trying to kiss you?"

I cringe. "I swear, I didn't do anything."

"No, *you* didn't. But that motherfucker sure as hell did."

"I told him not to touch me. I told him to stop."

Adam roars out a growl that makes the students walking by us glance our direction with wide eyes before they scurry off. He throws his hands up in the air, lacing them over his head as he paces.

"What did I tell you? Huh?" Adam throws his arms out toward me, and I wince at his already swollen and bruised knuckles from where he hit Grayson. "I *told* you he didn't want to just be your friend. I *told* you he wanted more, that he had something up his sleeve. But you didn't believe me. You picked him over me."

"That's not fair," I defend. "I didn't *pick* anyone."

"Yes," he argues, stepping into my space again. "Yes, you fucking did. You may not have said the words *I choose Grayson over you*, but that's exactly what you made clear when you told me you *wouldn't* choose me. When you dug your heels in and proved that being friends with that asshole *who cheated on you* was more important than making me feel safe and comfortable."

"You're friends with Skyler!" I scream out, desperation flowing through me. I know the argument is weak before I even finish making it. "How is this not the same?"

"SKYLER DOESN'T TRY TO MAKE OUT WITH ME!"

My nose flares, and I look around at the attention we're calling, reaching out for Adam to calm him.

But he backs away before I can connect.

His chest heaves with the next breath, and he beats on it like an ape. "*I* don't hang out with Skyler after every single fucking class. Hell, I don't even hang out with her *period* — not anymore, not unless we're in a group setting in the same place. And if you asked me right now, right here, to not be friends with her because it made you uncomfortable?" He shakes his head, as if it's obvious. "I would never see her again. No questions asked."

"Adam," I beg, eyes blurring. "I'm sorry. Okay? I was wrong. I thought..." My voice is strangled, and I shake my head. "I... I really thought..."

"That he wanted to be your fucking *friend*? That you two would braid each other's hair and drink coffee and study together and he wouldn't be using every minute to plan how to get your panties on his bedroom floor?"

My chin quivers. "Okay. You've made your point."

"Have I?" He steps into me, staring down his nose. "What's my point, Cassie?"

"I didn't kiss him!" I say loudly, pressing my hands into his chest. "Okay? I didn't come onto him or ask for any of that back there. I didn't do anything wrong. I can't control what *he* did, but why are you so fucking mad at *me*?"

Adam watches me for a long time, breathing slowly, eyes dancing between mine. After a while, he shakes his head, looking at me like I disgust him, like I'm an idiot he feels sorry for, like he can't believe he ever trusted me.

"I'm not mad, Cassie," he says, his voice soft, resigned. "I'm tired."

"Of what?" I ask, throwing my hands out, exasperated.

"Of choosing you when you refuse to choose me back."

I frown, my next breath stuttering out of my chest like the exhaust of a busted old car. His words slice me into ribbons, each piece of me cut so thin and weak that I'm afraid I might blow away in the next breeze.

I hurt him.

I hurt the boy I love.

And all for what?

"Adam, I'm so—" I try, reaching for him, but he just shakes his head, giving me one last hurt look before he turns and walks away.

I cover my mouth, squeezing my eyes shut and freeing the tears before I open them again and watch him walk away from me, his hands in his pockets, head hanging between his shoulders.

And I just let him go.

Because I know in that moment that I don't deserve to ask him to stay.

Skyler

"I've missed this," I say on a wistful sigh, drawing circles on Kip's chest while he plays with my hair. I'm balanced on one elbow, looking down at the masterpiece that is his body. It's early in the morning, and the sun is casting the hills and valleys of his abdomen in shadows and bursts of light.

Perfect.

"What, staying up all night having sex?"

"Well, yes, that," I admit. "But I mean *this* — lying next to you, cuddling, talking." I tap his nose. "Getting to see you in these specs."

Kip smirks, adjusting his black-framed glasses higher on his nose. "I can't see your beautiful face without them."

"You wore contacts a lot this weekend."

I pout with the realization, and Kip laughs, leaning up to kiss my lips briefly. "I didn't realize you loved my glasses so much."

"My four-eyed blond thief."

"Thief?"

"Yeah. You stole my heart."

Kip smiles, shaking his head before he pins me in the sheets and slides between my legs, kissing all over my neck. "That was so fucking cheesy."

"But you loved it."

"I did," he agrees. And then he props himself up on his elbows, his sea blue eyes watching mine. "And I love you."

I answer with another long, telling kiss, inhaling him in and wishing we could stay just like that forever. But my plane leaves in four hours, and by the end of the day, I'll be across the country again.

My chest splits with the anxiety of being away from Kip, especially after having the most perfect week together. He showed me around the UCLA campus, let me get a sneak peek of his current film project, introduced me to all his brothers — who he complained liked me more than they did him. We played beer pong and flip cup and had a very college Thanksgiving, complete with pizzas and whiskey instead of turkey and wine. We spent time at the beach, taking a surf lesson that made me realize I much prefer the warm water of the Atlantic to the freezing water of the Pacific. Not that we don't get glimpses of cool water during the winter months, but for the most part? It's perfect.

Here, you need a wet suit. And that's not nearly as much fun as a bikini.

As much as we saw over the past week and as much as we did, my favorite moments were the ones just like this — me and Kip in his bed, holding each other close, saying more with silence than we ever could with words.

I met Rick the second day I was here, and once we became quick friends, I told him I'd book him a room downtown *and* give him five-hundred dollars if he'd get lost for the week and not tell Kip what I did.

Let's just say I'm a little selfish when it comes to this boy, and I wanted all the alone time we could get.

Kip groans when we break our kiss, holding me tighter. "I don't want you to go."

Another zing of my heart.

"I don't want to go, either."

We both sigh, then fall silent, knowing there's no other choice.

"What if you came to semi-formal in a couple weeks?"

Kip brushes my hair from my face, frowning. "I wish I could, babe. It's finals time, and I've got to submit this project. It's going to take up every hour of my day once you leave."

"Did I distract you this week?"

"Yes," he says quickly, kissing my nose. "But it was worth it."

I sigh, tracing the muscles of his shoulders and traps with my finger. "I'll ask Bear. He's always down for a good time. Although, he's been sort of distant this semester."

"Family stuff?"

"I think that's part of it. But I also think there's more." I pause. "I know it sounds crazy, but... I think something might have happened between him and Erin."

"Erin?" Kip asks, arching a brow. "As in Ex?"

"The very one."

"Why do you think that?"

"I don't know. They just... *look* at each other weird. I know that sounds stupid, but they formed this random friendship, which was odd enough, and now they barely talk and when they're in the same room, it's awkward. I can't explain it."

"Well, let me know what you find out on that."

I sigh. "I will. Erin and I have been talking more, hanging out more... we have a lot of stuff still to work through, but it's getting better."

"Have you made up your mind about the presidency?"

I smile then, my stomach flipping for a completely different reason. "Yeah. I'm going for it."

"Yeah?"

I nod. "I really want to be president, to continue our family tradition. Not even for that reason, honestly. But because I think I could make a difference. And I love KKB. I want to leave a mark before I go."

Kip kisses my neck, tickling my ribs as I giggle and kick him away. "You'll leave one hell of a mark."

From all my writhing, my legs are tangled around his waist, and even though we've been insatiable all week long, I feel him growing hard between my thighs.

I hum my approval, sucking the skin of his neck as I climb my way up to his mouth. But just as we lock into a needy kiss, my phone rings.

"It can wait," I murmur against his lips.

But before we can even get some heavy petting going, my phone rings again.

"Okay, maybe it can't," I groan, rolling over until I can swipe my phone off the nightstand. I frown. "It's Ashlei."

"Answer it."

I nod, hitting the green phone button and putting Ashlei on speaker. "Hey, babe. Kind of indisposed at the moment. Everything okay?"

"No."

As soon as I hear her choked voice, her sobs, I shoot upright. "What happened?"

She cries for so long that I debate texting Jess and telling her to get her ass to wherever Ashlei is — and fast. I'm texting it out when she finally speaks.

"I fucked up. *Bad*, Sky. I don't know what to do."

"Whatever it is, we can figure it out. Take a deep breath."

She does, but then she's crying again. "Sophie... the intern..."

I freeze, Kip and I exchanging glances. I'd filled him in on that whole situation when I first got here. "What did she do?"

"She... she kissed me."

"She *what*?"

"I shoved her off me as soon as I realized what was happening, but I can't even believe it happened *at all*. And when I pushed her back, she had this shit-eating grin, like she'd won something. I have been trying to make sense of it all week, trying to figure out how to tell Brandon. And this morning..." She pauses, a sob breaking through. "This morning, I realized..."

"What, Lei?"

She sniffs. "She was interviewing me for her project. And I just forgot..."

"Forgot *what*?"

Another pause. "She was recording it. She had her phone set up on a tripod to record so she could pay attention to what I was saying."

My heart tripled its pace in my chest, Kip and I sharing another look. I know what she's going to say before she can even get the words out, and the way Kip is looking at me, he knows as well as I do that this is bad fucking news.

"She has our kiss on video, Sky."

Ashlei lets out a long, painful sigh as I scrub a hand back through my hair, trying to think.

"What do I do?"

"It'll be okay. I have a plan," I lie, kicking the covers off and hopping out of Kip's bed. "Just... call Jess. You don't need to be alone right now. And don't talk to Brandon yet. I'll be home by seven tonight, and we'll figure this out."

"I can't lose him," she whispers, her voice breaking again. And I look at Kip, knowing that if I were in her shoes, I'd be ripping at the seams, too.

"You won't."

And I pray that that's not a lie, too.

EPISODE 6

Cassie

"Alright, my favorite little redhead," Skyler says, grabbing my toes from where they stick out from under my comforter. "What do you say we go for a walk?"

"That sounds awful."

She chuckles. "Yeah, well, I'm sure showering does, too, but that's next. Come on."

Skyler rips my comforter off of me before I have the chance to grab it, and I groan, thrashing in my sheets and making a big show of my unhappiness at being forced out of bed.

"Please, just let me sulk in peace. I don't do this often."

"It's been long enough, babe. I let you do nothing but go to class and then come back here and mope for over a week now. But it's time to face the music."

I roll over, face half buried in my pillow. "What if the music really sucks? Like a third-grade orchestra concert kind of suck?"

Skyler smiles, sitting on the edge of my bed and sweeping my messy hair off my cheek. "You just need to talk to him, Little."

"I've tried."

"Tried what, exactly?"

"I texted him after he left that night. I tried calling."

"And then?"

I frown. "I mean, he made it pretty clear he didn't want to talk."

"*Didn't*," she echoes. "Past tense. It's been over a week now. He's had time to cool off and think. And so have you. What's stopping you from going down Greek Row and staying in his room until y'all work this out?"

I sigh, forcing myself into an upright position with more effort than should be necessary. Once I'm leaned back against the headboard, I meet Skyler's gaze. "Honestly?"

She nods.

"I feel like maybe this is a sign from the universe."

"What do you mean?"

"I mean that Adam and I have been a train wreck since forever. When we weren't together, when we were with other people and trying to be friends, when we finally became more than friends... we just keep hurting each other, over and over. We always have some kind of drama, some kind of misunderstanding, some kind of fight." I swallow, eyes flooding with tears when I remember how he turned his back on me by the pond. "That can't be healthy, can it? I mean... are we ever just going to be *okay*?"

Skyler offers a soft smile, scooting over until she's right next to me before pulling me into her arms. I lie there limp for a long while, quivering lip and blurry eyes, and then I finally wrap my arms around her, too.

"You're too smart to think love will ever be easy, Little."

I sigh, resting my head on her shoulder. "But should it always be this hard?"

Skyler frames my arms, pulling back so she can look at me. "You and Adam spent *years* denying what you had between you. Okay? And you were both so damn good at it that I didn't even see it — and I dated the guy." She chuckles. "To go from that, to being together... it's not an easy transition. You have years of history, of hurt, and now you're in this fragile time of building trust."

"And I blew that trust to hell..."

Skyler frowns. "Well, not the words I was going to use, but... kind of."

I sigh, scrubbing my hands over my face. "I don't deserve him."

"Yes, you do," she argues. "And he deserves you. If any two people in the world were meant for each other, it's you guys. But, here's the thing... he's right. You have to choose him over everyone, and he has to do the same. That's the only way you're going to shake your feet free of this muck that's got you guys stuck in the past."

"I didn't choose Grayson over him."

Skyler crosses her arms, releasing mine. "Don't get defensive with me. I'm calling you on your shit, so accept it."

I huff. "I hate you sometimes."

"Why was it so important for you to keep a friendship with Grayson, anyway? The guy cheated on you, Cassie. He was a pretentious asshole, too."

I lean my head back against the headboard. "Do you remember when Clay fucked me over my freshman year, and I lost Paris because of that whole ordeal?"

She nods.

"I never got over that. And it wasn't even Clay I was upset about. Not really. I mean, did he deserve my virginity? No. But what girl loses her innocence in some perfect, magical way? That's not what I was hurt over. What hurt me the most was losing my best friend." My eyes fill with tears again. "I don't like losing people. I just want everyone to love me and stay forever."

Skyler smiles, reaching out to rub my elbow. "That's understandable. We all want to be loved for who we are. But the truth is... you're going to lose people as you grow. A lot of them. Friends, family, people who you thought would be a part of your story forever. The older we get, the less we give a shit about what other people think, and the more we start coming to terms with who we are, what we want, what we stand for." Skyler shrugs. "It's natural to lose people in that process."

I nod, sniffing. "I guess I just believed Grayson. When he said he was sorry, that he wanted to be friends... it felt like getting a second chance. Like I could have Adam and Grayson both."

"Sounds like a lot of work to me," Skyler says. "To be devoted to your boyfriend and also friends with your ex."

I blink. "God, it sounds so stupid when you say it like that."

"It's not stupid," Skyler says gently. "But it was maybe a lapse in judgment. It was acting on the desire to hold onto something in the past, rather than to embrace a new and brighter future."

"A future I blew to smithereens," I say on a sigh.

"Talk to him." Skyler stands, squeezing my shoulder. "Go for a walk, take a shower, and make a plan. Figure out a way to reach him even when he doesn't want to be reached. Because I promise you, he's just as miserable as you are right now. If there's anything I know about Adam, it's that he loves you more than he loves himself. More than he loves Alpha Sigma. More than he loves anything in this world." She smiles. "He doesn't want to lose you, either, Cassie. You guys just have to get out of your own way and stop the bullshit."

"Such wise and kind words of advice," I remark with a grin.

"Feel free to leave a tip in the jar." Skyler winks, patting my arm once more before she leaves me alone with my thoughts — the very ones that have plagued me since the night Adam walked away from me.

God, I'm so thankful for Skyler.

The universe knew what it was doing when it placed us together as Big and Little. I smile, thinking back to the first night we met, that night by the reflection pond when I was torn between which sorority to choose as my home. And now, we were about to be the only two left out of our little group of five. Erin, Lei, and Jess would all be graduating in just a few short weeks.

Everything is about to change.

And it only makes me want to hold onto her and Adam even tighter.

My chest squeezes, because I know Skyler is right — about everything. I know this is a mess that I made. And I know it's on me to figure out how to clean it up.

When it comes to Adam, there's only one way I can think of that I might be able to reach him.

I just hope he'll let me in.

Bear

Becca sounds a little like the teacher in the Charlie Brown cartoons I used to watch with Carleton as a kid.

I know she's saying shit I need to hear. I know I should be latching on to every word, nodding, letting her know I hear her and I understand what she's saying.

But I can't.

Everything feels distant, foggy, like I'm on a cloud of having an out-of-body experience as I sit next to her on the bench by the reflection pond. It's hot and muggy and so far from what December was as a kid growing up in Pennsylvania. It doesn't feel like Christmas is around the corner. It doesn't feel like winter.

And it definitely doesn't feel like Becca is breaking up with me.

But she is.

And I can't even find the words to try to convince her not to.

"Are you even listening to me at *all* right now?" she asks, waving her hand in front of my face before she lets it fall to her thigh with a slap. She sighs, sitting back on the bench, shaking her head with her eyes on the pond. "I don't know why I'm surprised."

"I'm listening."

"Mm-hmm."

I turn to her then, pinning her with my gaze. "What more do I really need to hear past the part of this conversation where you said you don't want to be with me anymore?"

Becca swallows, eyes softening, her eyebrows tugging together to meet in the middle of her forehead. "You do realize I don't *want* to break up with you, right?"

"Not what it seems like right now."

"What choice have you given me?" She throws up her hands, exhausted. "Bear, that Friendsgiving shit... that was the most embarrassing moment of my life. My roommate and my best fucking friend hang out with you for the first time — this guy I've been telling them I'm so head over heels for — and you show your ass being possessive over *some other girl*." She holds her hand out like she's serving me my own ass on a silver platter. "Do you see how this is a problem?"

"I wasn't being possessive."

To that, she only scoffs and crosses her arms, tonguing her cheek when she tears her eyes from me and focuses on the pond again. "Unbelievable."

Shame and guilt sizzle in my chest, like I've just thrown my heart on a grill. I know it's a lie just as much as she does. But I refuse to admit it, because if I admit it to her, I'd have to admit it to myself.

That I care about Erin.

That I care about her as more than just a friend.

That I can't stand to see her with someone else, even if *I'm* with someone else.

That until I work through my feelings with her, I can't be with anyone.

I keep my mouth shut, zipping my lips tight in an effort to keep all those thoughts hidden forever. I'd rather die with them buried inside me than live with them out in the open.

"Look… maybe you should go home for the holidays. Work things out with your family. With *yourself*," she adds, turning and waiting for me to look at her before she continues. "And then, *maybe*, we can talk about being together when you get back. But I don't want to be with you if your heart belongs to someone else, Bear. That's not fair to me *or* to her. So… if you want her, maybe you should tell her that."

My stomach sinks so violently that I nearly retch, because I care for Becca so much that it makes me physically ill to think she can see right through me, that I can hurt her so badly without even meaning to.

"I want *you*, Becca," I say, voice cracking.

"I know. But you *love* her," she says matter of factly, with a shrug in her shoulder. "And as long as that is true, you can't have me."

I suck in a stiff breath, shaking my head as emotion strangles me from the inside. My chest is tight, my jaw thick with tension, my knee bouncing uncontrollably.

I have to stop her.

But I can't.

She's right.

But I can't admit it.

Slowly, Becca leans over, wrapping her arms around my neck. She presses her lips to my cheek, and I close my eyes at the contact, savoring what I know will be our last touch.

"You're a good man, Bear," she whispers. "But you can't keep running and hiding from your truths."

When she pulls back, it's with a sniff and a swipe of her hand over her cheek to wipe away her tears. I wish it was *my* hand wiping them away, but it's not me who gets to comfort her anymore.

I'm not sure I ever really did.

She doesn't say another word. The *goodbye* doesn't ever come. She just stands and bolts, her feet carrying her quickly away from me as I watch her go.

I let out a gasp, one that I can't replace with my next inhale. I'm trying to get oxygen into my lungs and failing every time. Scrubbing my hands back through my hair, I let out a loud, lung-collapsing scream that echoes across campus.

And once again, I am alone.

***

I somehow make it back to my room at the Omega Chi house.

I somehow manage to peel my damp clothes off, the ones I sweated through, and drag myself into the shower.

And when I finally collapse into my bed, I somehow pull out my phone.

And I call Erin.

My heart is in my throat as the line rings, over and over, again and again, with no answer. I hang up when her voicemail clicks on, immediately redialing her number.

"Please," I beg, rolling my lips between my teeth. "Please pick up, Erin."

When her voicemail clicks on again, I sigh, sitting up and moving to the edge of my bed. My legs dangle over, and I stare at my bare feet, waiting for the tone.

"Erin," I say when it clicks, and just saying her fucking name has that same tight emotion gripping my throat. I let out a shaky breath, and with it, anything else I could have said.

Please, I need you.

Come over.

Help.

Instead, I hang up, and dial Skyler.

It takes less than five minutes for her to show up at my door, and she doesn't knock. She just pushes through it, kicks off her sandals and climbs into bed with me.

Usually, it's me curling around her, or holding her to my chest, but this time when she climbs over me, she drags my back to her chest and wraps her tiny arms around me as best she can.

Never in my life have I ever been the little spoon, and I almost laugh out loud at the stupidity of it.

But that laugh comes out as a sob.

And with it, I break.

Skyler doesn't try to shush me as I fall apart. She doesn't try to control my shaking body in her arms or my piercing wails as they rip through the quiet night around us. And if any of my brothers hear me — which I'm almost certain they do — they're wise enough to stay away, to not ask, to pretend like they didn't hear a thing.

For the first time since I was a kid, I cry myself to sleep.

Skyler is still there holding me in the morning.

Ashlei

"You can do this," Skyler assures me on the phone as I press the button that will take me up to Brandon's penthouse.

"You sure about that?"

"He loves you, Lei. Remember? He's not going to walk away from you."

I sigh, leaning my head back against the elevator wall and praying the call doesn't drop on the way up. I need Skyler's voice to keep me calm. "I'm such a fucking handful. Why would he stay? After what happened in the spring... and now this..."

"*This* was not your fault. And dating your boss is not a crime, however taboo it may be."

I shake my head. "I'm trying to put myself in his shoes, if he came to me with this. And I gotta say... I wouldn't be happy."

"Look, he might be mad, okay? He might be hurt. *But*, again, *he loves you*. He's not going anywhere. You two are a team, and you'll figure this out together. Right?"

Silence.

"Lei, I need you to say it."

I sigh. "Right."

The elevator dings, and I force a slow exhale. "I'll call you after."

"You've got this," she says again, and then I end the call just as the elevator doors open.

Brandon's penthouse is unlike any place I've ever been in my life. The first time he brought me here, I had stood in this very elevator and gaped at the expansive space for what felt like an hour while he watched me and chuckled to himself.

The skyrise is right on the bay, with floor-to-ceiling windows that overlook Miami's beaches and beautiful teal water. His floors are a polished white marble, and the exposed air ducts and concrete give it an industrial feel like a New York apartment, but with the elegance and heat of Florida. He'd hired an interior designer to bring his vision to life, which was to make the entire place feel like an art museum. And it's not just the breathtaking art that decorates the walls. Each piece of furniture, each vase, each light fixture — every single aspect of the apartment is art.

And as soon as you walk in, you're part of the show, too.

Tonight, with the soft glow of candles and the fireplace in the center wall where the sitting room is, you can't even see the beaches or the water at all. Instead, it's dark outside the windows, save for the few boats in the distance.

And Brandon is sitting on the couch in front of the fire, scotch in hand, his eyes watching the flames and one ankle crossed over his knee.

It's Friday evening, so it doesn't surprise me that he's still in the same chocolate dress slacks and ice-blue button up that he wore at the office today. Even on casual Friday, the man always dressed to impress.

He was the boss, after all.

"Hey," I say tentatively, setting my purse on the kitchen counter before I make my way over to him.

I seem to shake him out of a spell, and he looks up at me with glazed eyes, accepting the kiss I bend to press on his lips.

"Thanks for letting me come over," I say, folding my hands in my lap once I'm seated next to him.

He nods, but otherwise doesn't say a word, his eyes back on the flames of the fire. I can't blame him for drinking and avoiding eye contact. After all, who responds well to the dreaded words...

We need to talk.

I sigh. "Brandon, something happened that I need you to know about. And it's going to sound crazy, but you have to believe—"

"I already know."

My mouth is still open, ready to recite the speech I'd practiced with Skyler all week — the one where I explain how Sophie had been quietly hitting on me, how she'd plotted out a way to get me alone, how she'd kissed me and made sure to get it on film. I was fully ready to get him prepared and on my side, ready to fight her attempt to take me down.

But those words are all stuck in my throat now, and confusion sweeps over me instead.

"What?"

"You and Sophie made out," he said, taking a sip of his scotch and hissing through his teeth.

"Um..." I think I'm in shock. I think my heart might actually give out. "Well, that's not *exactly* what happened, but—"

"It's not?" Brandon challenges, his eyes finding mine. "Because I saw the video, and I'm *pretty sure* that's exactly what happened."

Confusion turns to defensiveness in my chest as his scowl deepens, and I frown right back. "Why do I feel under attack right now?"

"Oh, I don't know. Maybe because you kissed our intern? Maybe because you cheated on me? Maybe because you waited over a week and *until I already knew* to tell me about it?"

My jaw drops. "Okay, first of all, *she* kissed me. I did not kiss her. And I certainly didn't *cheat* on you."

"No? What is it called when you kiss someone who isn't your boyfriend?"

I grind my teeth together, heart racing in my chest. "I didn't kiss—"

"Goddamnit, Ashlei," he yells, standing and slamming his glass onto the coffee table. What's left of the amber liquid inside sloshes out onto the wood, and Brandon threads his hands over his head, pacing until he's staring out the massive windows over the dark beach.

I just watch him, breath shallow, mind racing trying to catch up.

"I saw the video," he says quietly, turning to face me as his hands slowly come down. "She might have made the move. She might have been the one to lean in. But let me tell you, I've been in that position — when a woman makes a move on me that's unwanted. And what I do in those situations and what *you* did are vastly different. *I* pull away. *I* quickly tell them they are out of line. *I* remind them I'm happily taken, and that they need to respect my boundaries."

"I did the same thing. I told her to stay away from me, I asked her what the hell she was doing."

"*After* you kissed her and grabbed her blouse and moaned like your panties were fucking soaked."

I blink, over and over, my mouth hanging open.

Brandon just shakes his head, turning back toward the window. "We don't have anything to discuss. I took care of it."

"Took... took *care* of it?"

"Sophie came into my office earlier this week and showed me the video," he says, turning to look me in the eyes when he nails me with those words. "She knew what she was doing. She wanted to blackmail you, to blackmail *me*. She said it was sexual harassment and that I had until the end of the week to fire you and hire her, or she'd blast it to every news station in the city."

I stand, picking up the nearest pillow and chucking it across the room. "That little *bitch!*"

Brandon just holds up his hands, closing his eyes and forcing a breath like I'm a petulant little child he's highly annoyed with. "Like I said, it's handled."

"How?"

"Well, lucky for *you*, we record every call our interns make. I had MyKayla scrub all her calls to see if she could find something, and though Sophie might be cunning, she's also conceited. And she told her entire plan to one of her friends on her work cell."

I smirk. "Stupid cunt."

Brandon watches me for a long moment, like he can't believe me, like he doesn't know who it is standing in his living room at all.

"So, she has nothing," I say.

"She has nothing," he echoes. "I played the call for her and told her if she left quietly, I'd write her a letter of recommendation."

"What?" I shake my head, crossing the room to where he is. "Why would you do that?"

"To save your ass!"

My head snaps back at his words, but he's already turned away from me, scrubbing his hand over his face with his eyes focused somewhere on the water.

I sigh, closing my eyes. I knew this was going to suck, and I was right. Still, relief washes through me that Brandon handled it.

I don't know why I'm surprised, why I ever thought he wouldn't.

We're a team, just like Skyler said.

Wrapping my arms around his waist, I rest my cheek on his back, holding him to me. "I'm so sorry this happened. Thank you for handling it."

It's quiet after that but for the crackling of the fire, and I take what feels like my first breath in ages.

"Well, now that that's over with," I say, rounding until I'm standing between him and the window. I thread my arms around his neck, kissing his chin. "Are you ready for your first sorority event tomorrow?" I chuckle. "The girls are going to lose their shit when you show up to semi-formal."

Brandon's jaw ticks, but otherwise there's no response, and my stomach drops with the silence.

"What's wrong?"

"I think we should take a break."

My heart stops. "A... a *break*?"

Brandon closes his eyes, grabbing my hands where they rest behind his neck and peeling them off of him. "Ashlei," he says when his eyes open again. "Consider this your two-week notice to *Okay, Cool*."

Again, I find myself blinking repeatedly, as if I can erase what he just said with my lashes. "You're *firing* me?"

"No. You're resigning. Because you have opportunities elsewhere," he says, looking away from me. He crosses back to the coffee table and picks up what's left of his scotch. "That's the story we're telling. And if you go with it, I'll give you a letter of recommendation to take with you, too."

"A letter of rec—" I nearly vomit, my desperation propelling me forward until I'm in front of Brandon again, my hands around his bicep, urging him to look at me. "Brandon. I don't want a fucking letter of recommendation. I want *you*." Panic sears through me. "I want *us*."

He closes his eyes, and I see the emotion strangling him just as it is me.

"I love you," I whisper.

Brandon grits his teeth at my words, looking up at the ceiling, but I grab his chin and force him to look me in the eyes.

"She kissed *me*."

"Yes. She did," he agrees. "But you're lying to both of us if you say you didn't kiss her back."

I shake my head, tears flooding my eyes in an instant and spilling out over my cheeks before I can even think to stop them. The panic I felt before is a full-on storm now, swirling in my chest, crackling like lightning in my heart, the thunder so loud in my ears I can't hear his words through it.

"It was a mistake," I cry, holding onto him tighter. "I *love you*."

Tears gloss his eyes, but he rips away from me before they fall, leaving me standing in the middle of his living room as he storms across the marble back to his bedroom. "You should leave."

"*Brandon*," I plead.

And then, in one swift moment, he launches his glass across the room.

It hits the corner of the kitchen island and shatters, making me scream and jump back, covering my mouth with eyes as big as saucers.

"GET. OUT." His chest is heaving when his gaze finds me. "NOW!"

I press my other hand over my mouth, crying so hard my chest burns.

"You said you'd never break me," he chokes out, turning away from me before his emotion can show. "And you fucking lied."

"I didn't mean to—"

"Get out," he says, and then he starts beating his fist on the window. "Get out, get out, get out, GET OUT!"

I bite my lip as more tears trickle over my cheeks, but there's no use in trying to make him understand now. All I can do is leave him alone, like he's asking me to.

I rush to the kitchen counter and grab my purse, not even trying to be careful to avoid the glass. At this point, if I get cut, I deserve it.

I deserve every ounce of pain I'm feeling right now.

It doesn't take long for the elevator to ascend, and then I'm in it, and my back is to the wall, eyes on where Brandon stands across the penthouse. He has one hand on the giant window and the other scrubbing back over his head, his shoulders tense and rigid.

He turns just as the elevator doors begin to shut, and he forces a breath, covering his mouth with his hand as the first tear falls down his perfect face.

My eyes close before the doors do.

I can't bear to see the pain I've caused.

I can't bear to watch the only man I've ever loved cry because of me.

And on the way down, I realize it doesn't matter if I watch or not. It's still real. It's still happening. It's still true.

I've lost him.

And I know before the doors open again that I'll never get him back.

Adam

They don't make noise-canceling headphones strong enough to drown out how loud the Alpha Sigma house can get on a Saturday night.

It's especially difficult on this particular Saturday night, when half the sororities on campus are having their semi-formals, and half our brothers are pre-gaming, trying to get drunk enough to not care that they have to wear a tie all night.

Another roar of laughter, followed by the chanting of *Chug! Chug! Chug!* makes me grit my teeth and rip my headphones off, tossing them on my desk as I kick away from it. I don't know who I'm trying to kid. Like I could sit here and study knowing that Cassie is down Greek Row getting ready to go to the Kappa Kappa Beta semi-formal.

Without me.

My chest squeezes hard, but I don't lose my breath this time. In fact, I've become used to it, that aching hollowness inside me that likes to remind me from time to time that I'm alive and suffering.

Cassie and I haven't spoken since the night I walked in on Grayson trying to kiss her at the campus coffee shop.

It's not that she didn't try — at least, at first. She texted me when I left her there at the reflection pond. She tried calling. Once.

But then?

Nothing.

And I know I have no right to be pissed off. If I wanted to talk to her, I should have answered.

I guess I just expected more effort.

I expected her to try harder.

And more than anything, I expected her to choose me the same way I'd chosen her.

Another sickening wave rolls through me, the same one that's made it damn near impossible to eat or sleep since that night. I'm fighting down the urge to dry heave when there's a soft knock at my door.

"Hey, Prez," Kade says, leaning against the door frame. He tucks his hands into the pockets of his slacks, watching me with a sympathetic smile. "You doing okay?"

No one knows the specifics of what happened between me and Cassie, but with Grayson having a broken nose, and Cassie staying away from the house, they could do some simple math and figure it out.

"I'm good," I lie. Then, I whistle, waggling my brows. "Look at you, all cleaned up."

Kade stands tall and adjusts his tie. "I look dapper as fuck, don't I?"

"I'm surprised you can fit those massive biceps of yours into a suit jacket, to be honest."

He shakes his head, staring at said muscles. "I'm going to split a seam by the end of the night."

I chuckle.

Kade relaxes again, leaning against the door frame and nodding to me with his chin. "What about you? Where's your suit?"

I swallow, pretending to go back to the very important papers on my desk. "In my closet."

"You're not going tonight?"

"You already know the answer to that."

Kade sighs, walking in to sit on the edge of my bed. "I know you and I aren't exactly best buddies, Adam. Fuck, if I'm being honest? I hated your ass as a pledge last year."

"Gee, thanks."

"But," he continues. "You've earned my respect since then. And one thing I like most about you is how openly and honestly you love Cassie."

His words surprise me, and I turn in my chair to face him.

"I mean it," he says, smirking as he runs his hand back through his hair. "It's not easy to do that. I am much more of a play games, crack corny pick-up lines, and hide all emotions kind of guy. Or, at least, I *was*."

"Until Jess."

Kade sighs, shaking his head. "That woman will be the death of me."

I smile. "Something about those KKB girls."

"Right? Anyway, I don't know exactly what happened between you and Cassie. But I hope you guys work it out. You make a good pair. And from what I hear, you two went through a lot to get here. I mean, hell, she used me as a pawn last year to cover up the fact that it was actually *you* she was falling for."

I held up my hands. "Don't get me started on what a train wreck last semester was."

Kade laughs, standing. "I won't. Just wanted to let you know I'm here if you need to talk or anything. And, for what it's worth, I think you should crash semi-formal. Show up in a suit and sweep that girl off her feet. She can't say no to you in a tie."

I smile. "Thanks, man. I appreciate it. Have fun with Jess tonight." I tilt my head, assessing him. "You're really into her, aren't you?"

Kade grabs the back of his neck, nodding sheepishly. "On a scale of one to fucking idiot, where do I land if I say I'm already head over heels for the girl?"

"I don't think you're stupid at all."

"Something tells me it won't last," he says, but he shrugs before the moment can get too serious. "But I guess that means I should just make the most of now."

I stand, clapping him on the shoulder. "I think that's the best way to look at it. Besides," I add. "For whatever it's worth, I've never seen her show another fraternity guy the kind of attention she shows you. I think she's just as into you as you are into her."

He smiles, squeezing my shoulder, too, and then he's out the door and I'm alone again.

I sigh, collapsing back into my chair and sinking down until my ass is hanging off it. I stare up at my ceiling as the house grows quiet, all the brothers leaving to hop into their various limos that will take them out tonight.

I debate Kade's suggestion the entire time.

I *could* crash the semi-formal, show up and demand that Cassie talk to me. But... what would I say that I haven't already?

Nothing has changed.

I still want her to choose me.

And the fact that her friendship with Grayson was more important than her relationship with me isn't something I can just forget about — especially if she doesn't even see it the way I do.

You're being stubborn, my brain sings to me for the fiftieth time this week. I don't have time to tell it to shut up before there's a soft rap of knuckles on my window.

My head snaps toward the noise, and I frown, wondering if I imagined it.

When it comes again, I rush out of my chair and leap onto my bed, yanking the cord on my blinds.

And when they open, I'm face to face with Cassie McBee.

She's an absolute vision in the last glow of the setting sun, casting her red hair aflame and igniting the flecks of gold in her emerald eyes. I blink away my shock at the sight of her, opening my window and holding out a hand to help her inside.

She's not wearing a dress, or makeup, or a head of curls like I imagined she would be tonight. Instead, she's in worn-out navy-blue sweatpants and one of my long sleeve Alpha Sigma shirts that she stole from me over the summer when she was cold one night.

And on her feet are the same Keds she wore the first night she crawled into my window two years ago.

That was when she was a freshman, and I was a sophomore, and my room was down the hall and on the other side of the house. That was when my bed was against the wall opposite my window. That was when I was with Skyler, and she'd just had her heart broken by my asshole president.

That was before we were us.

And yet, we'd *always* been us — no matter how we tried to fight it.

Her hand is cold in mine as I help her inside the window, which is a little tougher since my bed is right up against it. But she shimmies in, and once she's inside, she kicks out of her shoes just like she did that first time. I leave the window open, the breeze blowing through the strands coming loose from her messy top knot, and for the longest time, I just watch her and wait.

"Hi," she whispers after a while, pulling her legs to sit criss-cross on my bed.

"Hi."

I want so badly to reach for her, to pull her into me, to kiss her and tell her she doesn't have to say a word. And I decide after approximately two seconds that that's exactly what I'm going to do.

I reach for her at the same time her little bottom lip quivers, and she launches into my arms, letting me wrap her up and cradle her. I inhale her scent, breathe in her heat and her love, and the first relieved sigh leaves my chest since the night we parted.

"I'm so fucking sorry, Cassie."

"*You're* sorry?" She shakes her head, which is still buried in my chest. "It's *me* who was the idiot."

I chuckle. "You're not an idiot."

She pulls back, her eyes meeting mine. "You were right. You were right about Grayson just like you were right about Clay my first semester here. How is it that your asshole radar is so strong and mine is completely broken?"

"Hey, I'm kind of glad it's broken," I tease. "If it wasn't, you might never have started dating me."

She smiles, burying her head in my chest again. "God, I've been so miserable without you."

"Why didn't you come talk to me?"

"I wanted to, but..." She huffs, looking up at me again. "Honestly? I don't like being wrong. And when it comes to me and you, I'm not used to being in this position."

I scoff, tickling her sides as she writhes in my grip. "Wow. You saying you're always right and I'm always wrong?"

She's still laughing, shoving my hands away from her ribs, but then she curls up in my arms even more. "See? I even suck at apologizing."

I kiss her hair, my smile impenetrable. It doesn't matter now that she's in my arms. Nothing else matters.

"You don't need to apologize, Cassie. You *are* right — it was him who made a move on you. You didn't do anything wrong."

"Except trust him. And decide that having a friendship with him was more important than making sure you were okay."

She throws my words from that night back at me, and I sigh, holding her tighter. "I know you didn't mean it that way, though."

"I didn't. But it doesn't change the fact that I hurt you."

I nod, falling quiet for a moment.

"You know, I love that your heart is so big. I love that you forgave him, even after what he did to you, that you wanted to have a friendship with him. I've *always* loved those things about you. If they weren't a part of you, you definitely wouldn't put up with my sorry ass."

She giggles, and the sound makes me want to throw my hands up and rejoice that she's still mine.

"I'm sorry I lost my shit and hit him. I just..." I shake my head, and then shake her gently. "I go *mad* when it comes to you. I can't lose you. I can't live without you."

Cassie peers up at me, her eyes big and soft. "You know, for once, it was me who messed up. You're supposed to let *me* apologize, but you're stealing all my thunder."

I laugh. "Okay. I'm listening."

She sits up and shimmies out of my embrace, facing me completely. "I'm so sorry I dug my heels in about being friends with him. I was holding onto something I shouldn't have. The truth is, I loved Grayson."

Bile hits my throat, but I swallow it down.

"*Did* being the keyword there. I guess there was a part of me that hoped I could have it all... a relationship with you *and* a friendship with him. But I was wrong. I should have known his intentions. And even if those intentions were pure, the fact that it hurt you for me to be with him should have mattered more than anything." She grabs my hands in hers, lifting my knuckles to her lips. "*You* matter more than anything to me. And I'm sorry I didn't prove that with my actions. But I will now. I will for as long as you'll have me."

At that, I bark out a laugh, shaking my head and pulling her into me. "You're crazy if you think I'd ever let you go."

She melts into my arms as I press my lips to hers, and the kiss is a seal of that promise, one I'll continue making over and over again, no matter what shit we go through.

Because if there's anything I know, it's that Cassie McBee is it for me. She always has been. She always will be.

And I'll weather any storm I have to to fight for our love.

"Has he..." I swallow. "Has Grayson talked to you since..."

Cassie scoffs. "Hell no. I mean, he tried reaching out, but I blocked his number and went to Professor Drumm to explain the situation. He told me I can finish out the semester on my own in lab. And Grayson can do the same."

"I'm sorry," I say with a sigh. "Are you going to be okay on your own?"

She arches a brow. "Please. Do you even know me? I'm a friggin' genius."

I laugh, kissing her nose. "Yes. Yes, you are." Tugging on the fabric of her sweatpants, I let the topic of Grayson fizzle out, focusing on the more pressing point, instead. "So, I take it we're not going to semi-formal?"

"Let's be honest — we don't have the best record at these things, anyway."

"Well, maybe we change that. Let's make a pact, right here and now."

Cassie sits up straight. "Okay. Hit me."

"No more fights. No more third parties. No more stupid drama or miscommunication or whatever other bullshit tends to wiggle its way between us." I hold out my pinky. "From now on, it's just me and you."

Cassie loops her pinky through mine. "Me and you."

"Forever."

"Are you proposing, Adam Brooks?"

"Not yet. But you can bet your ass I will someday."

She flushes, shaking her head as she watches me. "And you can bet *your* ass that I'll say yes."

My heart does a leap in my chest at the thought, and I pull her into me, pressing another kiss to her perfect lips.

"So," I say, still holding onto her. "We could lie here, order some greasy food and watch some movies. *Or*, we could crash semi-formal like a couple of bums."

Her eyes widen. "Dressed like *this*?"

"Mm-hmm. Just like this. What do you say?"

Cassie hums, eyes tracing the ceiling before she looks at me with a devilish grin.

And I know her answer before she can even speak.

Erin

It's my last semi-formal.

I don't know why it took so long to hit me, why all semester long I haven't taken the time to stop and really consider the fact that this is it.

This is my last semester of college.

This is my last month at Palm South University.

These are my last few weeks as president of Kappa Kappa Beta.

And after this, a completely new life starts.

"What planet are you on?"

I blink at the question, turning to find a grinning Gavin watching me, amused. His hair is styled for the first time since I've known him, and to my surprise, he showed up at the Kappa Kappa Beta house in a beige suit, one that brings out the blue in his eyes and highlights the dark olive of his skin.

"Hmm?"

"You were lost in space. Just wondering which planet you were on."

I smile, eyes trailing over the room. We rented out a gorgeous and historic hotel downtown for semi this year, and it almost feels like we've stepped back in time in the grand ballroom, the extravagant chandeliers casting a low-lit glow over my sisters and their dates as they dance. Gavin and I are alone at a cocktail table in the corner, and yet I feel so warm and full I could combust.

"The planet where I'm no longer in a sorority," I finally answer. "Where I'm no longer defined by the letters on my shirt or the title I hold."

"Sounds like an awesome planet to me."

I chuckle. "I'm sure it will be great in its own ways, but... I'm really going to miss this."

My heart squeezes the more I look around, and I can't help but smile when I see Cassie and Adam letting loose on the dance floor — both of them in sweat pants and standing out like two sore thumbs in the sea of suits and dresses. But they're laughing and spinning each other and having the time of their lives, and for the first time, I don't give a shit that they broke the rules. I don't care that they're out of dress code and mocking an event with history and purpose.

My smile climbs farther when I spot Jess and Kade making out behind the stage. The way the curtain is hung, no one else can see them, but our table just happens to have a perfect view. And again, I don't find a care in my soul about Jess being scandalous at a sorority event.

Because seriously, who the hell cares?

We're young. And limitless. And gloriously unbound.

It's magical.

And yet, with so much joy and love comes heartbreak in equal measure. Ashlei didn't even come tonight, to her last semi-formal, because she's heartbroken over her breakup with Brandon. And though Skyler is here, it's without Kip, and I know it kills her.

Little does she know that he's going to surprise her in a big way next week.

He called me right after she left California after Thanksgiving and asked me to help set it all up. He wants to surprise her the night she finds out she's president — because we *all* know she will get elected. So, he's flying in, and not just to see her.

But to lavalier her.

Getting a lavalier from your boyfriend is like one step away from an engagement ring, and about the most serious step you can take in college. It's a special ceremony for a silly little necklace that means everything to the two people exchanging it.

And I can't wait to be a part of it.

But tonight, she's solo — well, kind of. Kip might not be here, but just like always, she's got Bear by her side.

My stomach twists when I spot them at a cocktail table across the dance floor, and I tear my eyes away from them before Bear has the chance to lock his on me. We haven't spoken since he showed his ass at the Thanksgiving event he'd planned.

He'd tried calling me, but the truth was that I didn't want to talk to him. Not now. Not after the way he acted toward Gavin.

If anyone in my life knows what I've been through, it's Bear. And if anyone should know what a huge deal it is for me to open up to a guy, to let him in, to *date him* — it should be Bear.

He invited me there after denying my apology, after denying *me* all semester, and then he made me *and* my date feel like complete and total outcasts. It was like we were unwelcome, like we'd shown up despite him trying his best to avoid us.

I don't know what's going on with Bear, but I know one thing — I'm tired of putting in effort that he doesn't reciprocate.

I've tried apologizing.

I've tried explaining.

I've tried mending our friendship.

And he won't have any of it.

You can't force someone to care about you, and you can't always fix what's broken.

"So," Gavin says, wrapping me in his arms and pulling my attention away from the crowd. "What's next for Erin Xander?"

"Hmm... well," I say, lacing my hands behind his neck and looking up at the high ceiling. "Take the next few weeks off after graduation, try to relax I guess, and then sink or swim in law school." I pause. "I'm sure my *parents* are hoping for the former, while I'm praying for the latter."

"You're going to be the most kick ass lawyer to ever exist," he says matter of factly. "But I'm less interested in the school part, and more interested in what you're going to do with these few weeks of freedom you have in-between."

I shrug. "I told you. I'll go home for the holidays, maybe relax by the pool or something."

"Is that what you want to do?"

I tilt my head. "I mean... I want to do a lot of things."

"Like what?"

"I don't know what you mean."

"I mean, what if you didn't just go home and relax. What if you did something you really want to do, or something spontaneous and crazy before you commit yourself to law school?"

"Okay, I'm listening," I say warily. "What do you have in mind."

"What if we got out of here?"

"Like, took a trip?"

Gavin nods.

"You and me?"

Another nod, his smile climbing.

"Where would we go?"

"Anywhere," he answers easily. "In fact... what if we didn't make the decision."

I cock a brow, confused.

"What if we let strangers make it *for* us."

"Okay. You've lost me," I confess.

Gavin kisses my nose, and the notion makes my heart flutter. How is it that this strange, shadow of a man has somehow wiggled his way into my heart?

"Let's make a game of it. Pack a couple bags and just fucking *go*." He snaps his fingers. "I know. We'll go to the airport and pick two strangers. One of them gives us a terminal letter, the other gives us a number, and that's the gate we go to. That's the plane ticket we buy."

I laugh. "You're kidding, right?"

"I'm serious as a heart attack."

I shake my head, still laughing. "What if the flight is to another country?"

"Then we end up in another country," he says easily, on a shrug, nonetheless, as if it's no big deal. "You have a passport, right?"

"Well, yes, but..." I scramble for words, my mind reeling. "We wouldn't know what to pack."

"Pack the essentials. If it's somewhere freezing, we buy a heavier jacket. If it's somewhere warm, we buy a swimsuit."

"You make it sound so easy."

"It can be," he says, tipping my chin with his knuckles, his eyes searching mine. "If you trust me."

My heart surges in my chest, but this time, not from anxiety — but from pure, unadulterated excitement. I can feel the blood pumping through my veins, the unknown possibilities fluttering in my chest.

"This is insane."

"Aren't the best things in life?"

I chuckle, shaking my head again. "I'm scared," I admit.

"I've got you."

It's a promise he seals with a peppering of kisses on my neck, my chin, my jaw as I laugh and wriggle in his grasp. And when he captures my lips with his, I sigh into the kiss, leaning into everything that he is, everything he's brought into my life, everything still yet to come.

On the cusp of a new chapter in an already crazy life, I feel like I'm standing on the edge of a cliff, ready to jump, but terrified of the possible outcome all the same.

And maybe in this scenario, Gavin is the parachute.

All that's left to do now is take the leap and trust him not to let me fall.

Jess

"You okay, Lei?" I ask at our last KKB Chapter of the year — of our *lives*.

Ashlei sniffs, dabbing at the corner of her eyes so she doesn't mess up her makeup. "I'm trying to be."

"Is this about giving up your exec position and getting ready to graduate, or about Brandon?"

She visibly shrinks in size, as if just his name took the breath out of her lungs. And when she peeks a glance at me, it's the most pitiful I've ever seen. "Both," she whispers.

I squeeze her knee. "Hey, you two are going to work it out. Alright? Trust me."

She nods, but I know from our conversations over the past couple of weeks that she doesn't believe me. Brandon hasn't talked to her since the night she came clean about the intern. He's even been avoiding her at the office in her last two weeks there. And as of this weekend, she's a free woman.

Free from work.

Free from school.

Free from a relationship.

And though that could be seen as a fresh, new, and exciting step in life, I know right now all she can feel is heartbroken for everything she's losing.

Honestly, I can't blame her — especially when Kade and I are getting serious, and Erin is dating Gavin. I've been in that position before, when you try everything you can not to look around at everyone else's happiness and compare your lack thereof.

All I can do now is be there for her, and I nudge her to remind her of that just as Erin invites Skyler and the other presidential candidates back into the room.

We all sit and clap, Cassie yelling out *You got this, Big!* from her seat across the aisle. I give a hoot of approval, along with half the chapter, because we all know before Erin even announces it who will be the next Kappa Kappa Beta president.

It couldn't be anyone *but* Skyler Thorne.

It's not even because Erin is president now, and her big was before her, and her grand big before that, etc., etc. It's because no one cares about our sisters and this sorority more than Skyler does. No one else drops whatever they have going on in an instant to be there for their friends the way she does. And no one else could fill Erin's shoes — and maybe even do the job *better*.

"I've already given my sappy thank you speech," Erin says when the room has quieted, and I don't miss her tearing up just like Lei. "But I just have to say one more time that I am truly honored for the privilege you all bestowed upon me this time last year. I hope I made you proud, and I want you to know that I will never forget you — any of you — or this amazing sorority."

I start my favorite Kappa Kappa Beta chant, and sisters slowly chime in, until the whole room is full of laughter and yelling and crying and far too much emotion for me, personally, but damn it if I don't love it all the same.

Even I, Jess Vonnegut, am not immune to the sads that come with graduating college and leaving this part of my life behind.

"Okay okay, enough about me," Erin says, facing Skyler and the two other sisters who were brave enough to run against her for president. "This decision was incredibly tough for all of us. We had to ask ourselves who would be our best leader, who would fight for us, and most of all — who would represent everything we stand for?

"I have nothing but absolute faith that the person who you all chose to place your faith in will far exceed your expectations. This young woman is exciting, fresh, full of ideas and even more — spunk. She's everyone's best friend, confidant, and mentor. She's been through a lot in life, more than most of us will ever face, and she isn't afraid to own every part of her life that's made her who she is."

Erin smiles, and I nearly combust trying to hold in the cheer I know is coming.

"I am proud to announce that the new president of Kappa Kappa Beta is... should I let someone else say it?"

Erin pauses, and I huff, rolling my eyes. But before I can spout off a smart-ass remark, the back doors open, and all my sisters start cheering. I frown at first, standing and cheering along with them as the brothers of Alpha Sigma pour into the room. Half of them are wearing acoustic guitars around their chests, and when Kade slides by the front row and steals a kiss from me, I laugh and bat him away, still confused.

Until I see a familiar face that I haven't seen since last semester.

Well, I'll be damned.

Kip Jackson struts in like he owns the place, and I only look at him for a split second before I find Skyler, who covers her mouth with both hands and tears up immediately. The damn sight of it gets *me* choked up and Lei pokes my ribs, making fun of me as I swat her away like I did Kade.

Damn emotions.

Kip takes Skyler's hand in his, kissing it before thrusting it up into the air. "Ladies of Kappa Kappa Beta, your new president!"

We all clap and cheer and lose our shit, and then the brothers all start swaying — some of them playing guitar, some of them singing the lyrics to "My Girl." Before long, all my sisters join in, too, and when the song finishes, Kip calls our attention back to him long enough to present Skyler with the Alpha Sigma letters on a delicate gold chain.

A lavalier.

"Skyler Thorne, you mean everything to me. You are my world. When we met earlier this year, we were both playing a game that neither of us was prepared to lose. Tricks were played, hearts were broken, but in the end — we somehow made it out alive. Together. I promised to never gamble with your heart again, and this is me showing that promise to the world. Please, make me the happiest man in the world, Ella Mae. Wear my lavalier?"

God, it's just too fucking sweet!

I'm so annoyed that I'm all teary-eyed and gooey as the room cheers again and Kip puts the necklace around Skyler's neck. Kade's eyes find mine, and he winks, giving me a shit-eating grin that tells me he sees just how emotional I am over the whole night.

Damn it all.

"Alright, bitches!" I yell, standing up before I can cry. "Let's go party! Everyone to Ralph's!"

Ashlei laughs as the rest of the sorority cheers in agreement, and then Kade sneaks up behind me, squeezing my hips. I turn, and as much as the old Jess would have thumped him on the nose or shoved him away, it's the last thing I want to do. Instead, I throw my arms around his neck and kiss him for everyone to see, both loving and hating the butterflies in my chest.

This kid was just supposed to be a distraction, a free ride, a little fun in my last semester.

And then the asshole went and stole my heart.

"Someone is all in their feels tonight," he says, kissing my neck.

"Shut up."

"It's okay to be mushy sometimes, Jess. No one will judge you for having a pulse and emotions."

"*I* am judging me," I argue.

Kade chuckles, threading his hand through mine. "Come on, let's go get you drunk. That'll take your mind off your feels. Plus," he adds, sucking my earlobe between his teeth. "Then, I can take advantage of you."

"*Finally* on date 3," I muse.

"Finally."

"We could just skip Ralph's altogether."

"But it was your idea. You just told everyone to go there."

I huff dramatically. "*Fine*. But you're driving."

That earns me a kiss on the cheek, and I lean into Kade, wrapping my arm through his as we make our way to the back of the house and out to the parking lot before making our way down Greek Row to the Alpha Sig house.

"So, classes are over, graduation in just a few days... how are you feeling?"

I sigh. "Weird."

"Going to miss all this?"

"Of course. But, as much as I'm sad, I'm excited, too. I'll have a big girl job soon, and my own apartment, and who knows what else. College has been amazing, but... I'm ready for what's next."

"And what about me?"

I tap his nose. "What about you?"

"You going to miss me, too?"

All the joking is gone, and I see the vulnerability in Kade's eyes like I've never seen it before. I pull him to a stop on the sidewalk, frowning. "I don't have to miss you. I'll still be local. I thought... I mean, I thought we'd stay together."

He lets out a long breath. "You did?"

"Of course, I did, you dummy." I shove him playfully. "What, you think I'd spend all that time and effort morphing you into my perfect little sex god just to let some other girl reap the benefits? No way."

"Hey, I was a sex god *before* you got to me. You just made me better."

"Mm-hmm, whatever you say." I lean up on my tiptoes and press a kiss to his lips. "But seriously, I want to do this. I want to keep dating and see where this goes... that is, if *you* want to. I mean, you're a junior, you still have some time here, and I don't want to hold you back from enjoying it."

"You don't hold me back from anything," he says quickly, sincerely. "You make it *better*."

"That was borderline cheesy."

"You love my cheese."

I roll my eyes, but don't deny that he's right, and after another hot, longing kiss that has me wishing we were already done partying for the night and back in his bed, we continue our walk down Greek Row.

"I just have to run inside and grab my keys. Meet you at the car?" he says when we get to the A Sig house.

I nod, pulling out my phone to text the girls. My feet carry me on autopilot to Kade's parking spot, and it's not until I'm a few feet away from it that I look up.

When I do, I drop my phone.

I can't bend to retrieve it when the glass shatters on the ground. I can't even grasp that it fell at all. I can't do *anything* but stand there as if my feet are cemented to the parking lot, staring, unblinking, unbelieving at the sight in front of me.

My heart races in my ears, pulsing in my throat, consuming me with its erratic, suffocating rhythm. It's all I can focus on, and it's the only thing keeping me upright and alive, because every other organ slowly gives out.

"Jarrett?"

His name is a gasp of a whisper on my lips, and I blink over and over, trying to unsee him, to clear the vision of him leaned up against Kade's car. It *must* be a mirage. It *must* be a hallucination.

Jarrett's eyes are hard on me, brown and endless as ever, his smooth head and sprawling tattoos covering every inch of his arms a sight for sore eyes. I still don't believe he's real, even when he pushes off the car and tucks his hands into his pockets, crossing the small space between us and stopping with just a foot left to go.

His eyes search mine, and my stomach bottoms out.

He bites his lip, and my heart squeezes to a stop before kicking back to life painfully in my chest.

He lets out a breath that reaches my lips, and I inhale it shakily, swallowing it down, my entire body shaking with the familiar scent of it.

Kade's hand on my hip jolts me back to life, and I jump at the contact, breathing heavy and nearly fainting. The only thing that stops me from going down is Kade's arms around me, and he frowns, looking back and forth between me and Jarrett while I try not to pass out again.

"Are you okay?" he asks me, and I think I nod. I think I grip onto his arms to hold myself upright. I think I keep breathing.

What happens next, I only *wish* I could convince myself wasn't real.

Because Kade looks at Jarrett, and Jarrett appraises Kade, and then he says the last thing I ever could have expected.

"Hello, brother."

After that, everything goes dark.

Skyler

"Smile, ladies!"

Cassie holds out her Polaroid camera as far as she can with all of us piled into Erin's queen-size bed, taking a picture with a grunt. When she pulls the photo out and starts waving it around, she frowns.

"You cut off all our faces?" I tease.

"Surprisingly, no — but I look like I'm taking a poop."

"You do not," Erin argues, stealing the picture with a smile. "We all look perfect."

It's the night before graduation for Erin, Ashlei, and Jess, and with all their families coming into town and graduation parties and campus-wide celebrations, this will be our last chance to be all together, just the five of us.

Maybe for a very long time.

My heart twists, and I hug Cassie tight. "Welp, it's just going to be me and you now, Little."

"Hey! We're not dead," Ashlei argues.

"We're not even leaving the zip code," Erin adds.

"Still, it won't be the same without you *here* here," Cassie says with a pouty lip.

We all fall quiet at that, and I roll over to squeeze Jess. "You okay over here?"

"Yeah, I'm sorry," she says on a sigh, scrubbing her hands over her tired face. "I'm trying to be present, but I'd be lying if I said I wasn't all the way fucked up right now."

"I cannot *believe* Jarrett is here," Cassie says.

"*I* can't believe Jarrett and Kade are brothers," Ashlei chimes in.

Jess just groans, rolling until her face is buried in the covers. "Just kill me now."

"What are you going to do?" Erin asks.

"Move to Mexico?" Jess answers hopefully, popping her head up long enough to say the words before she face plants in the pillows again.

I chuckle, sweeping her hair back. "It'll be okay. You're with Kade now. Jarrett lost his chance, right?"

There's a long pause, and the girls and I exchange worried glances.

"Can we just talk about something else for now?" Jess begs.

"Sure. I can join in your misery and remind you again how I fucked up the best thing to ever happen to me," Ashlei offers.

"Lei," Erin says sadly.

"I was just trying to make a joke," Ashlei says, holding her hands up. "But, honestly? I'm doing okay. I think I'm starting to accept it... at least, a little bit. I wish he would talk to me, but I can't force him to." She shrugs. "There's nothing left to do, really, but to pick myself up and move on. Starting with a new job."

"Have you been putting in applications?" I ask, letting her avoid the fact that I *know* she's not okay. Ashlei is a lot like me in that regard — when she's hurting, she doesn't want to make a big show of it. She just wants to pretend like everything is fine and that she's moving on to bigger and better things.

But we'll be here when she needs to fall.

"I haven't had to. As soon as word got out that I was leaving *Okay, Cool,* my phone started ringing off the hook. I've got offers all over Miami *and* in other states, too."

Jess leans up and glares at Ashlei. "You're *not* allowed to leave. Not right now."

Ashlei chuckles. "I'm not going anywhere, Bossy Pants."

Jess face plants into the pillows with another grunt.

"You're going to be amazing, no matter where you end up," Cassie says to Lei. "And, I agree with Jess. I just want you *all* to stay here. Forever."

"Says the one who will leave for med school," I point out.

"Well, when that happens, you all have my permission to leave, also."

We laugh at that, and Erin catches my eyes from across the bed. "So, a little birdie told me that Kip is transferring here for the spring semester?"

I bite my lip, nodding. "That little birdie would be correct. *And*, he'll be here for the summer, too."

"How?" Cassie asks with a frown.

"He's going to be working on his show... about *us*."

"As in, how you two met?" she asks.

"As in everything — how we met, our crazy dating story, the tournament, all of it. His professors loved the concept and want him to bring it to life. He has through the end of the summer to shoot the pilot season, and then he'll submit it to compete for the chance to turn it into an online series hosted through the university."

"Holy shit!" Ashlei says on a grin. "That's a big deal."

"It is," I agree. "I'm so proud of him."

"So, do you get to help with casting?" Erin asks.

I laugh. "Oh, whether he knows it or not, I will be casting *director* — especially when it comes to who plays me."

"They'll never find anyone who comes close to the real thing," Ashlei says.

"What about you, Little? What are you doing for the holidays?" I ask Cassie.

"Adam and I are going to see our families... it'll be the first time for him meeting my parents and me meeting his aunt."

"Wow, big step," Erin says.

"It is... but we're ready. We've both decided this is it — no more games, no more letting other people get between us or standing in our own way. We just want to be together. Zero drama."

"Good luck with that," Jess says, her voice muffled by the comforter.

I pat her ass sympathetically.

"But there's something I wanted to tell you guys..." Cassie continues, biting her lip. "I'm going to graduate early."

Erin cocks a brow. "Really?"

"Yeah. I'm ahead in my classes. My GPA is killer, surely enough to apply to my med schools of choice. Adam graduates next semester, and Big," she says to me, smiling. "I think I want to graduate with you. Next fall."

I beam. "One last year together."

"One last year to raise some serious hell," she agrees.

"I'm proud of you." I wrap her in a hug, and then Erin takes her turn.

"Oh, and I was thinking... I know I'm a little late now, but... what if I *did* take a Little next fall? I'd only have one semester with her, but then she could start her own family, carry on our line."

At that, Erin sits upright, her eyes welling. "Wait. Are you serious? You really want to take a Little?"

Cassie nods. "I really, really do."

Something of a squeal comes from my Big, and then there's more hugging, and Jess makes a comment under her breath about us being entirely too mushy for her current depressed state.

She gets the next round of smushes.

For a long time, we just lie there in bed, cuddling and reminiscing on the past few years. Sometimes we laugh, other times we cry, and through it all, we hold onto each other and the memories we've made.

Everything is about to change.

It feels that way at the end of every semester, but this one is unlike any I've felt before. I'm officially the *president* of Kappa Kappa Beta — a responsibility I won't take lightly — and with Jess, Lei, and Erin graduating, it'll just be me and Cassie left.

The changing of the tides is cold and unfamiliar, and it leaves me wishing I could wrap myself up in what has always been and never let it go.

But this is the way life is. It's constantly ebbing and flowing, throwing us into new waters, testing our ability to float.

One thing I know for sure is that no matter where these girls end up in the world, we'll always have each other.

And as long as that's true, there's nothing we can't survive.

"Welp," Erin says when it's almost midnight, rolling out of bed. "As much as I'd love to just pass out right now, my bag isn't going to pack itself."

I frown. "Don't you mean your entire *room*?"

Erin shakes her head. "Nope. Mom and Dad are going to take care of packing up my room, actually. They're going to store everything at their house until I get back."

Jess sits up, blowing her hair out of her face. "Back? Back from where?"

"I don't know, actually," Erin says with a blush.

The girls and I exchange looks. "Okay..." I say after a minute. "You mind telling us what the hell you're talking about?"

Erin giggles — *giggles,* like a freaking kindergartner. "Gavin and I are going on a trip."

"What?!"

We all say it at once, and then it's a chaos of questions — *Where? For how long? Is this safe?* —before Erin holds out her hands to shush us all.

"We don't know where we're going," she says with a smile. "That's kind of the point."

Jess blinks. "I'm confused."

"We're going to let two strangers in the airport choose our gate, and then we're just going to buy a ticket and... go."

"Go," Ashlei repeats. "You're just going to get on a plane and fly wherever that plane is going with whatever you can fit in that bag." She points at the suitcase Erin has unfolded on the floor.

"Yep."

"Who are you and what have you done with our best friend?" Jess asks.

Erin laughs, jumping back into the bed with us. "I haven't been this excited in a long, long time, you guys. I trust Gavin. And I know it's out of character for me but... hell, I'm about to be in *law school.* There won't be any time for fun." She shrugs. "This is all I have for a while, and he wants to make the most of it."

"I like him," I say, definitively.

"Me, too," she whispers, her eyes meeting mine. "As much as it terrifies me, me too."

Cassie sighs, throwing her arms around all our necks. "I can't believe this is it. This is our last cuddle session in this bed."

"Hey, this bed is about to be *mine,*" I remind her. "Consider it open for cuddle seshes."

Cassie holds out her pinky. "Let's make a promise. Anytime anyone needs us, all they have to do is say the word, and we're right here in this bed. No matter what."

We somehow manage to all loop our pinkies in one giant knot, and then we lean forward to kiss our knuckles, laughing when we bump heads.

And again, I'm reminded that no matter how things change, no matter what bumps lie ahead, I'm surrounded by the strongest, smartest, most badass girls to ever live.

The bonds of sisterhood don't just go away with graduation... and thank God for that.

Because something tells me we're going to need each other more than ever.

Palm South

UNIVERSITY

HAZED

BOOK 6

EPISODE 1

Jess

I am at a whole new level of Hot Mess Express.

Of course, I'm no *stranger* to this state of being. I've been the caboose of that train, the engine, the dozen or so carts in-between. But this? This is another train altogether. No, this is a *jet plane* of hot mess. Or perhaps even a spaceship.

And still, I'd rather sit in this steaming pile of mess than face everything plaguing me head on.

I wonder if this is part of becoming an *"adult."* You graduate from college, move off campus, and instead of actually having your shit together with a badass job and a hot ass fiancé and whatever else you thought would happen, you just end up an even more frazzled version of who you were a month ago when you were still a college student.

From the outside looking in, the unknowing bystander would likely take one look at me and think, "Wow, she's really got it together." After all, my dad hooked me, Lei, and Erin up with a bougie condo in downtown Miami overlooking the beach, with floor-to-ceiling windows that make me feel like an absolute boss, even if it *is* being paid for with Daddy's money. His deal was simple — I'll float you the first year while you figure out what comes next.

Seems simple enough. A fair and generous trade.

Except I don't exactly *know* what I'm going to do now that I've graduated.

I have the degree. I have the internship under my belt and the coursework fresh in my head and all the desire and passion it takes to be a wedding planner.

And still, not a single company has called me in for an interview.

It will just take time, Lei assures me daily. That's easy for her to say. The bitch not only got hired on at *Okay, Cool* after one semester of interning, but promptly got a dozen job offers the second she was let go.

Well, at least I have it going on in the boyfriend department, right? Kade Brewer is everything every girl dreams of — hilarious, smart, driven, incredibly hot, and, thanks in large part to my training, an absolute *god* in the bedroom.

The problem?

I've barely talked to, let alone *seen*, him since we both left campus in December.

It's been four weeks, and bless the sweet man, he's given me my space. He understood when I said I just wanted to spend time with my family after graduation. He understood when I said I just needed some time to get the new place set up with the girls. He understood when I said I just needed time to focus on job applications.

I make an excuse, he says *no problem*.

The asshole.

If only he were demanding I face him, maybe I could be mad at him. Maybe I could blame all my icky feelings and this state I've found myself in on him.

Maybe I could admit the fact that the real reason I've been hiding away is because his big brother is the first man I ever loved, and he just swung back into my life like a wrecking ball.

God, just the thought of that horrid event has me groaning and covering my head with my covers again.

Yes, it's ten past noon and I'm still in bed. Don't come for me.

When the darkness covers me, it's easy to go back to that day. It was my last Kappa Kappa Beta chapter. Erin passed the torch down to Skyler and we were all ready to go party at Ralph's. *I* was ready to ditch it altogether in favor of doing extremely dirty things to Kade.

Until we got to where he'd parked his car at the Alpha Sigma house and I'd found Jarrett leaning up against it.

Jarret fucking Locke.

That bald, tattooed, beautiful bastard was the absolute last person I expected to see, and when he called Kade "brother," I passed out.

Literally, blacked out and hit the concrete.

I guess it was my body's defense mechanism. *Hurry, knock the bitch out so she doesn't have to deal with this!*

And here we are, a month later, and I'm still living that motto.

In all fairness, I really *did* take the holiday break to spend time with my family, and I really *have* been setting up in the new place and job searching.

Did I really need to blow my boyfriend off in the process? No.

But this is my M.O. When something hurts or is confusing, I run from it.

Clearly, I haven't stepped into adulthood quite yet.

My phone buzzes incessantly, keeping me from slipping into my second nap for the day. When I glance at the screen, I see *Front Desk* on the caller ID.

"Good afternoon, Miss Vonnegut," Herb says. He's one of the associates who mans the front desk area in the lobby, signing for packages and letting us know when we have guests.

"Afternoon, Herb," I reply with a fake British accent. I don't really know how it started, but when I met him, I pretended to be British after he greeted me so formally. I'm ninety percent sure he doesn't think I'm *actually* British, but it's still fun to keep up the façade.

"A Mr. Kade Brewer is here for you. Shall I send him up?"

My eyes bulge out of the sockets as I throw the covers off and jump out of bed. "Uh," I say, taking one look at myself in the mirror before promptly cringing. "Can you give me five minutes?"

I don't use the accent.

Damn it, my image is ruined.

"How about ten?"

"You're my favorite, Herb."

He chuckles before ending the call, and I promptly grab a brush and comb through my tangled mess of hair. Once it's secured in a high ponytail, I strip off my sweats and throw on leggings and a sports bra, as if I was doing something active or have plans to. A bit of mascara and tinted moisturizer later, and I'm satisfied.

When I'm looking slightly less hellish, I survey my room, picking up the loose articles of clothing and tossing them in my closet before I haphazardly make my bed. It's not perfect, but not half-bad when two loud knocks sound at the front door.

My feet feel like lead as I drag them down the hall. My room is the last one at the very end, with Erin and Ashlei's framing up either side. My dad was an absolute gem to understand that we'd not only need our own bedrooms, but our own bathrooms, too. And the living area is one giant room where the kitchen, dining room, and sitting area sit as one.

My favorite part of the entire condo is the gas fireplace that serves as a sort of centerpiece under the television and in front of the giant white couch the girls and I picked out together. It's actually cold today — well, cold *for Florida*, anyway, at a brisk fifty-seven degrees — and so the fireplace crackles softly as I pass it on my way to the front door.

Steeling a breath, I force a smile and open it, launching myself into Kade's arms as soon as I see him.

"Hey, you!" I say, wrapping my arms around his neck and inhaling his scent. "What a surprise!"

It's a show at first, my lame attempt to assure him I'm fine, but the moment I'm in his arms and that familiar scent of eucalyptus that always seems to cling to him finds me, I nearly break. I forgot what it was like to have his beastly biceps holding me close, to feel his hard chest softening just for me, to hear the relieved exhale that always came when he held me.

I swallow down the urge to cry right then and there.

"Hi," Kade says — cautiously, like I'm a rabid animal head butting him for pets after just trying to bite his arm off the day before. "Uh, yeah, I just... I haven't heard from you so..." He frowns a little but tries to smile through it. "Thought I'd just pop by."

God, if the smell of him wasn't enough to undo me, the sight of him is doing the trick. I'm not sure how it's possible, but he seems even more ripped than the last time I saw him, his biceps bulging against the sleeves of his olive-green, long-sleeve shirt. That buzzcut he's always had has grown out a bit, giving him a boyish look; his brown hair now mussed like he's been dragging his hands through it.

I instantly want to do the same.

"Well, I'm glad you did. Come in," I say, holding the door open.

Kade walks in with his hands in his pockets, his warm brown eyes scanning the length of the windows. He lets out a whistle. "Well, I'd say this is a step up from the KKB house."

"All thanks to Daddy. Though, if all goes according to plan, I'm hoping the girls and I will be able to afford this place on our own this time next year."

"How's the job hunting going?" Kade asks, looking at the couch like he's going to sit, but then he doesn't.

"Good," I lie, folding my arms over myself across the room from him.

"That's good."

We stand there for a long pause, Kade watching me and me watching the floor. Finally, I let out a sigh, lifting my gaze to his. "Kade, I'm sorry I've been avoiding you."

"Ah, there's the truth."

I shake my head. "I just... seeing Jarrett... finding out he was your *brother*," I add with wide eyes. "It was a lot for me. On top of graduating and moving out and..."

"Hey, I get it," Kade says, moving a little closer to me. "I figured you needed the space, and I've been giving it to you, haven't I?"

I nod.

"But it's been a month, Jess. And the last time we talked, you said..." He swallows, and then laughs, shaking his head at himself. "God, I sound like such a pussy."

"You don't," I insist, and I cross the last bit of space between us, sliding my arms around him and clasping my hands behind his back. "I said I wanted to keep dating, that I wanted to see where this was going."

Kade frowns. "And do you still mean it?"

Something between a laugh and a gasp comes from my lips, and I pull him in closer. "Of course, I do."

Kade sighs with relief, and it's like that finally gives him the green light to hold me in return. His arms fold around me, and he drops his forehead to mine. "Thank God. I thought for sure I was walking into a breakup."

"I'm sorry I made you feel that way." I shake my head. "I'm still... processing. Okay? And I won't lie, I'm kind of a hot mess right now. But, as long as you're willing to be patient with me," I say, lifting my gaze to his. "I still want to be with you."

"I'll be the most patient motherfucker who ever lived."

His lips are on mine in the next breath, hard and demanding, his arms tightening around my waist. Every other thought, every other thing that needs to be discussed is gone in an instant, and I pull him in even more, moaning at the feeling of his kiss after so long.

"God, Jess, I'm already rock hard," he breathes against my mouth, pulling my hips against his pelvis so I can feel him. "I need to be inside you."

I gasp as he bites hard on my bottom lip, and then I'm in his arms, being carried blindly across the living room. It's a good thing Erin and Ashlei aren't home, because I have full faith we aren't making it back to my room.

Kade slams my back against one of the windows, dropping my legs to the floor only long enough to forcefully rip my leggings down to my knees. They hold tight there, though, the traitorous bastards, and Kade is so frustrated with waiting that he growls and slips his hand between my thighs instead of trying to work them down more.

The second his fingers slip between my already-wet lips, I arch off the glass and into the touch.

"*Fuck,*" I groan, and Kade bites and kisses down my neck, sliding his fingers in more until the tips of them tease my entrance.

"There are so many things I want to do to you right now," he whispers between kisses. "I want you sitting on my face. I want to ram my cock down your throat until you gag."

A shock zips through me, and I shiver when he grazes my clit.

"I want to take my time tasting every inch of you. But all that will have to wait," he says, and then he grabs my hips and spins me until my hands flatten against the cool glass. "Because right now," he whispers against the shell of my ear. "I'm going to fuck you hard and come fast, so you better do the same."

He grabs my ponytail then, yanking hard until I have no choice but to arch and stay still. I want to moan. I want to say *yes*. But the way he's holding me, I can barely breathe, let alone speak.

All I can do is wait.

I wait as he fumbles with his belt. I wait as he works the button and zipper of his jeans with one hand. I wait as he runs his fingers along my ass crack and slips one inside my pussy, just to make sure I'm wet and ready.

As if that was an actual question.

And once he confirms his suspicion, he releases my hair just enough to let me breathe, to let me moan, to let me prepare.

Then, he fills me like a flash flood, wiping everything else away.

The first thrust is to the hilt, and his cock stretches my pussy that's been empty for the past month in a mixture of pleasure and pain. I gasp at the feel of it, and when he withdraws and slams into me again, I can already feel my orgasm ready to explode.

"God*damn*," he breathes, slowing his pace. He pulls all the way out, and I know without even turning to look that he's looking down at where my wetness coats him, at where every inch of him glides in and out of me with ease. "You feel so fucking good."

"I thought you said you were going to fuck me hard and come fast?"

A growl rips from Kade's throat, and then he drops his hold on my hair so that both his hands can grip my hips.

And it's all I can do to hold onto that glass and keep my knees from giving out.

True to his word, Kade's thrusts are punishing, his thighs slapping against my ass as he pummels me against the window. And in less than sixty seconds, he pulls out, ripping me around just in time for me to drop to my knees and take his release in my mouth.

It feels like a part of me slipping back into place, watching Kade unleash himself at my mercy. His hands are planted on the window as he grunts his release, his face twisting, and then he's pulsing and convulsing and doing *his* best to stay standing, just like I was.

It's everything I've been missing, that connection with Kade.

And now that it's back, I feel like I am, too.

I'm still wiping the corners of my mouth when Kade picks me up, carrying me through the condo and down the hall with his jeans around his ankles and a promise on his lips to make me come at least three times before dinner.

And he delivers.

We order takeout and stay in the room all night, catching up and watching half a movie before Kade passes out and I get close to doing the same. It'll be nice, I think to myself, to finally get a good night's rest.

But when I turn off the TV and curl up next to Kade, sighing at the way it feels to be wrapped up with him, I'm jolted awake just when I'm about to doze off. It's my phone, buzzing hard and filling my room with light from where it's plugged in on the nightstand.

I know I shouldn't check it. Whatever it is, it can wait. But I roll over to put it on *do not disturb* and freeze at the name on the screen.

Jarrett.

And when I slide my thumb across the screen, it's a four-word text that delivers me yet another sleepless night.

Can I see you?

Cassie

"And obviously, Harvard — *ohhh, yes right there* — would be amazing. Especially if I wanted to go into — *oh, God* — research. But really, I feel like my heart is calling me to Johns Hopkins. *Ughhh, this is amazing.*"

I finally give up, letting my hands drop to my sides from where they were hovering over the keys of my laptop. I close my eyes and sink into the pillows, letting out another moan when Adam presses his thumbs deep into the arch of my left foot.

He chuckles. "That good, huh?"

"You have no idea. I mean, I know I need to get used to this, being on my feet all the time. But after just one week at the hospital..." I groan again as Adam rolls my ankle and massages my heel. "Well, let's just say I've got a whole new appreciation for nurses."

Adam smiles, rubbing my foot with admiration in his eyes. I don't know why it even interests him, sitting on my bed in the Kappa Kappa Beta house while I filter through all the medical school pamphlets I collected over break and compare them with my online research. You would think I was doing a boudoir shoot rather than talking about where I wanted to go for med school.

"No matter where you go, you're going to be amazing," Adam says, switching to my right foot. "But let's just say someone walked in right now and said your life depended on you naming your top three schools. Don't think too hard, just say what your gut tells you."

I grimace. "I don't want to—"

"Cassie, just say it, dammit, or I'll suck on your big toe."

"Ew!"

Adam opens his mouth big as a trout and pretends like he's going to shove my whole foot in his mouth, to which I respond with jerking back so hard I nearly pull him into my lap. He laughs, grabbing my foot and rubbing again with a *go on* look on his face.

I sigh. "Harvard. Johns Hopkins. Duke."

"And if that same person said you can only choose one, your top choice, and it's yours. You'd say..."

I chew my lip for a long while until Adam starts tickling my foot while I writhe and try to break free.

"Johns Hopkins!" I scream, partially begging for mercy. "Johns Hopkins, okay?"

Adam smirks in victory, going back to the massage. "Well, there you have it. You can toss the rest of these pamphlets."

I laugh. "I wish," I say, picking up one for a smaller, lesser-known school in Florida. "But the truth is, the chances of me getting into those places are... well..."

"You'll get in."

"I need to apply to at least ten schools, just to be safe."

"Fine, do what you want," Adam says, and then he starts reeling me in like a fish, using my leg as the pole. "But you're going to get in. You and I both know they'd be crazy not to let you in. With your GPA and the research projects you've already done, plus the fact that you're graduating a whole year early?" He shakes his head. "You're going to be the best damn doctor anyone has ever known."

I welcome the kiss he presses to my lips with the sentiment, and then my cheeks heat as I finally admit out loud what I've been considering for months now. "Or… surgeon."

Adam's eyebrows shoot up into his hairline. "Surgeon, huh?"

I nod. "Am I crazy to think I can do that?"

"Are you kidding?" Adam pulls me into his lap then, covering me in kisses. "I'd let you perform surgery on me *right now,* no training or anything. That's how great I think you'll be."

"You're crazy," I say with a laugh, squirming under his kisses.

"Crazy in love with you."

As corny as the line is, it makes me swoon all the same, and Adam pulls me back into the mountain of pillows on my bed as we stare at each other all googly-eyed.

For once, it feels like Adam and I are on stable ground.

After the hellish semester we endured in the fall — well, really, the hellish semesters, plural, that we've endured ever since we've known each other — it feels amazing to finally just *be together.*

We spent the holiday break with each other's families, going to stay with his aunt first, and then with my parents and sister. I knew I loved Adam before, but there was a whole new level of love uncovered when I walked into the house he grew up in, when I met his aunt who took over after his grandfather passed away, when I saw pictures of Adam growing up, when I made cookies with his aunt and got to know the woman who raised the boy I was so in love with.

And if that wasn't heartwarming enough, watching him play video games with my sister and listening to him talk golf with my dad and watching him load the dishwasher for Mom while she nearly cried at the sight?

Well, that was the icing on the cake.

And now, we're back at PSU, Adam in his last semester before graduation and me going into my last full year, now that I've decided to graduate early.

It feels like a new era.

It feels like everything I could ever want.

"Are you sure you don't need to be at the A Sig house?" I ask, but I'm already wrapping myself up more in him, knowing full well I don't want him to leave. "Fraternity Rush is still under way, and I know you have a lot to do."

"Oh, I have plenty to do," he agrees, but wraps himself up in me just as tight. "Fortunately, I did a lot of it when we first got back, and I've become rather good at delegating. Jeremy is handling everything tonight, and the other brothers are stepping up, too."

"Are you sure?" I ask again.

"Yes, I'm sure, my little parrot," he says, kissing my nose. "Hey, I've got to step back a little this semester and let the other guys get their chance to shine. I've already been the first to ever be president two years in a row." He shrugs. "I'm graduating in just five months. These guys gotta figure out what comes next, and I have to step out of the way in order for that to happen."

I arch a brow. "You're surprisingly… *calm* about all this. You're not going to miss it?"

"Of course, I will. I mean, I feel like I'm largely responsible for turning our entire chapter around, for giving us a new reputation, for getting A Sig back in the game." Adam pauses, his eyes focused somewhere in the distance. "But I think I'm ready for the next chapter in *my* life, and I have faith in my brothers. They're going to be just fine without me."

"And what's next for you?"

Adam watches me for a long time, his eyes flicking back and forth between my own, like there are a million things running through his head and he can't tell me a single one of them.

"I'm not sure," he finally says. "I mean, I majored in Business. Pretty versatile. But… you know… I've been thinking… and I really loved turning our chapter around here, and I know there are a lot of other Alpha Sigma chapters struggling across the nation."

"Oh my God," I say, jolting upright so I can face him. "Are you thinking about being a Field Executive?!"

Adam laughs. "You stole my thunder."

"Babe!" I smack his chest, my smile so big I think it might split my face. "You would be *amazing* at that."

Field Executives are college graduates who go on to work for their fraternity at the national level. They're usually assigned to a chapter for a semester or a year, and their tasks range from everything from recruitment and expansion to best practices for the chapter and spreading historical fraternity knowledge.

Adam wouldn't just be amazing at the job — he was practically *made* for it.

"Don't get so excited," he says, holding up his hands. "They don't hire many guys, and I'm sure I'll be one in a sea of hundreds applying."

"Doesn't matter. One look at what you did here at Palm South, and they'll hire you on the spot. *With* a signing bonus."

Adam laughs as I cuddle up against him again. "A signing bonus, huh? Like a baseball player?"

"Yep. Millions of dollars, just like that." I snap to illustrate.

He laughs again. "You know, my aunt is obsessed with you."

"Is she now?"

"Yep. Which makes two of us." He pins me into the sheets then, kissing all over my neck while I laugh and wriggle beneath him. Just that simple movement fires me up, and Adam pauses where he hovers over me with a wicked smile.

"This semester feels different, doesn't it?"

"It does," he agrees, sweeping my hair from my face.

"You and me, we've been through so much..."

Adam nods, resting on his elbows so that we're chest to chest, stomach to stomach, lined up in every possible way.

"I kind of feel like nothing can stop us now."

At that, Adam smirks, pressing a long kiss against my mouth before he whispers, "It's only up from here, baby."

And then, he peels my shirt up and kisses his way down to show me just how unstoppable we are.

Bear

There's no better view than a redhead sucking your cock.

I don't care what the travel buffs say about mountains and valleys, beaches and lakes, bustling cities or tiny map dot towns. They can say whatever they want about that kind of scenery — I much prefer this one.

My dark hands, twisted in bright copper hair.

Plump lips around my thick length.

Manicured nails digging into my thighs.

A cotton-candy pink tongue, dragged from balls to tip.

I groan and let my head roll back only long enough to keep myself from coming too quickly before my eyes are on Kailey again. I met her earlier this week when Fraternity Rush started and she showed up with a tray full of freshly baked brownies. I loved her hair, her sweet and innocent smile, her long eyelashes.

I especially loved when she blew all that shit away, leaning in to whisper in my ear that she couldn't wait to see what my bedroom looked like.

And now, here we are, and with a hot, wet mouth driving me to the edge of my release, I finally feel like myself again.

"Fuck, I'm going to—"

I don't even get the words out before Kailey takes me all the way down her throat — or at least, as deep as she can go — and I don't miss the gag when I find my release. But, like a champion, she holds me there, and it's the sexiest thing I've seen in a long fucking time.

"Damn, girl," I say when she looks up at me with a wicked smile, swallowing and wiping the corners of her mouth. "That was hot as fuck."

"Glad you enjoyed yourself," she says. Then, she stands and pulls her sweater dress down from where I'd hiked it up over her hips. She checks her makeup in my mirror, running her fingers through the hair I mussed.

"Your turn?" I ask, sliding up behind her. My cock is already soft, but I know plenty of ways to get her off.

"You can get me next time," she says, turning to tap my nose with her pointer finger.

She's already out of my arms and heading for the door when I say, "Oh, so it's like that, huh? You're going to just suck me off and then waltz right out of here?"

Kailey laughs, pointing a thumb over her shoulder. "Can't you hear? There's a party going on out there. Don't worry," she says with a wink as she opens my door. "I'll come to collect soon enough."

I laugh when she blows me a kiss before shutting the door behind her, and when I'm alone, I can't help but appreciate that kind of confidence and ownership of a woman's sexuality.

I think I'm even more turned on now.

With a sigh, I yank on my sweatpants and flop back on my bed, resting my hands behind my head as I look up at the ceiling.

The holiday break was... tough, to say the least. After Becca broke up with me, and Erin refused to talk to me and let me apologize for the whole Friendsgiving mishap, all I could do was go home to Pittsburgh and lick my wounds.

Fortunately, it turned out to be just what I needed.

Being with my brothers and my mom brought me back to myself, and for the first time since I can remember, we're a unit.

Carleton is getting clean, has a full-time job, and even his wife is working at the grocery store down the street from them. My nephews are in school and happy. Clayton is ecstatic after a killer football season and growing more and more into a lady killer every day.

And mom is... *around.* For once.

It's as uncomfortable as it is exciting, having my mom present, getting to know her again after all that has transpired between us. I have Becca to thank for getting me to pull my head out of my ass and realize that giving my mom a chance to right her wrongs was the least I could do.

And to her credit, she really is trying.

So much so that Clayton moved out of Mac's house and in with Mom in her new two-bedroom apartment.

It scared me at first, when they told me the news, but it helped that at least I was there to help them both move in and get settled. I even took Mom to the Goodwill to get furniture and things they needed. Clayton seemed excited to have his own place again. Even though Mac's family had been amazing, I knew it gave him a sense of independence to not have to depend on them anymore.

Still, Mr. and Mrs. Harrison assured me they would still be there, checking in, making sure all was well. And it makes me feel better to know I've got eyes in town even when I'm not there.

And the timing of it all couldn't be better.

It's my last semester at PSU, my last semester as a brother, my last semester of college, period.

This is it.

Just a handful of months filled with classes and partying in equal measure stand between me and graduation.

I have no idea what comes next for me. I feel confident in my skills as a graphic designer at this point, but the question isn't *what* I'll do.

It's *where* I'll do it.

There's a huge part of me that yearns to go back to Pittsburgh, even though I used to swear to myself that I never would. Now that my family is there, mending our past, my thought have shifted and I realize that I want to be there with them.

Pittsburgh is a cool city.

There are plenty of jobs available.

I know Pennsylvania. I miss the cold. I miss seasons, having a fall and winter and spring instead of one perpetual summer with a dash of chill now and then.

And still, there's something holding me here, something that says my time in South Florida isn't over, something that makes my gut churn with a silent whisper of *you can't leave, not yet.*

I feel tethered to this place.

I just haven't quite figured out *why*.

A loud ruckus down the hall breaks me out of my daydream, and I sigh, scrubbing a hand over my head before I hop up and check my reflection in the mirror. I look like a man who just got properly sucked off, and if anything, I kind of like the look more than when I first got ready for tonight.

I don't even bother to change into jeans again, just give myself a swig of mouthwash and then I'm out the door. All the *what comes next* shit running through my head can wait.

Kailey's right. There *is* a party going on.

Time to do it up Clinton Fucking Pennington style.

For one last semester.

Jess

Just remind me one more time that I have nothing to worry about.

I smile a little at the text from Kade, but can't ignore the way my stomach somersaults, too.

You have nothing to worry about. I'll be in your bed in just a few hours.

The little dots bounce on the screen as I check my reflection one last time in the bar bathroom.

I'll keep it warm until then.

With another smile, I tuck my phone away, stilling a breath before I make my way out of the bathroom.

This little beach bar hasn't changed much since the first time I graced its presence. I still remember that night like it was yesterday, strolling in here looking for a little escape from recruitment. I thought I'd find a good fruity cocktail and a guy to fawn over me all night before I had to go back to a house full of screaming sisters.

Instead, I found Jarrett.

A shiver races up my spine at the memory of him behind the bar, the wicked smile he gave me, the confidence, the unforgettable first time of him touching me in his truck in the parking lot.

That memory seems to grow three heads and a dozen eyeballs when I round the corner out of the bathroom hallway and spot Jarrett coming in from outside.

It's chilly tonight, a rare and blessed event in South Florida, so the beach bar that's normally all open and airy has plastic awnings pulled down to keep out the cold as best they can. Jarrett is bundled up in a brown leather jacket and dark distressed jeans. All his tattoos are covered, along with his bald head, thanks to a Patagonia beanie. I can tell the time he's spent in Manhattan has given him more fashion sense just by the outfit and designer boots he's paired with it.

He's my Jarrett, the same one who stole my heart with just one look.

And yet, he's a complete stranger, someone I don't know at all.

His smile is weak when his eyes meet mine, and he makes his way toward me with his hands in the pocket of his jacket.

"Hi," he says, and I have a flashback to our last conversation — the video chat where he broke up with me.

I clear my throat and force a smile. "Hi, yourself."

"Thank you for meeting me."

I nod.

"Shall we?" Jarrett gestures toward the bar, and when we reach it, he pulls out my stool first before taking the one next to me.

It's been about a year and a half since Jarrett left his job at this bar and took the internship in New York, but still, he's like a celebrity when he sits down. The manager comes out and tells the bartender to put our tab on the house, an older woman who worked with Jarrett when he was here comes over to give him a big hug, and even a few patrons pay their respects. When it's finally just the two of us again, he sighs, smiling sheepishly at me.

"So," he says. "My brother has threatened to castrate me if I so much as touch you, but for the record, I really wanted to give you a hug."

I chuckle. "Better not, just to keep the balls safe."

"My thoughts exactly." Jarrett pauses, lifting his beer to his lips for a sip. It makes me happy that even after so long in the city and obviously graduating to better clothing, he still likes an ice-cold Pabst Blue Ribbon. "I will say, I'm glad you didn't pass out when you saw me this time."

My cheeks heat, but I don't really know what to say. *Oh, yeah, that. Sorry. Just wasn't prepared to see my ex-boyfriend whom I had barely gotten over standing next to my current boyfriend's car. Oh, and double whammy, you two end up being brothers!*

I sip my margarita, instead.

Jarrett watches me for a long time, and I feel his eyes crawling over me like they're a laser beam sparking every cell inside me to life. Those warm brown eyes still know just how to make me feel naked as the day I was born.

I sigh, shaking my head and pushing my drink away before I turn to face him head on. "Jarrett, what are we doing here?"

"Having a drink," he says, holding up his beer. "Talking. Catching up."

"Catching up," I deadpan.

Jarrett lets out a sigh of his own, taking a big gulp of his beer before he says, "I don't know, Jess. I wanted to see you. I *needed* to see you."

My heart squeezes in my chest.

"The way things ended between us... I hated it. I *still* hate it. I've thought about it so much since then. I even tried to reach out to you a few times, but... well... I guess you blocked my number. And I don't blame you, I just..."

He doesn't continue for a long while, just stares at where his hand is wrapped around the PBR can.

"I had to block you," I say, my voice barely above a whisper. "Jarrett, I loved you. Fiercely. And I was *broken* after... after..." I swallow, unable to finish my sentence. "I just wanted to move on, and I knew you enough to know there was no changing your mind — not once you'd made it up the way you had."

He nods in understanding, scratching the scruff on his jaw. "We're opening a branch here in Miami," he says. "For the nonprofit. And since I used to live here, they picked me to head the expansion."

I smile genuinely. "That's amazing. Congratulations."

He gives me another weak smile. "Thanks." A swallow. "It's weird. When they told me, I wasn't really excited about leaving New York. I wasn't really able to get excited about *anything* after dealing with my father this summer," he adds with a shake of his head. "But that's a story for another time. What I'm trying to say is that I have sort of been... *numb*. But when they said they were sending me here, there was one little glimpse of light." His eyes find mine then, the depths of them endless. "I knew you'd be here."

I frown, tearing my eyes from his to look at my margarita. I hate the way my stomach tightens at his words, the way my skin heats under his gaze.

"Can I ask you something?"

I nod, still not looking at him.

"What's going on with you and my brother?"

A little laugh escapes me at that. "It's a long story." I pause. "Kind of a humorous one, actually. But... long story short?" I turn to meet his gaze. "We're dating. And I really, really like him."

I can see the flash of pain that hits Jarrett at my words, but he swallows it down, smiling. "I'm glad you're happy. You *deserve* to be happy."

"Thank you."

"For the record," he says, sipping his beer. "He really, really likes you, too."

I chuckle, and my hair falls in front of my face a little before I tuck it behind one ear. When I look back at Jarrett, I can see there are a million things he wants to say.

I think there are a million things I want to say, too.

"Look," he says after a moment. "All the bullshit aside, I know it's too late to apologize for the past. I know it's too late to go back to what we had. And I really don't want anything more than for you to be okay, to be happy, and it's clear that you are." He shrugs. "But if you're okay with it, I'd like to be friends."

"Friends," I repeat with an arched brow. "I think we tried that once before."

He laughs. "Well, things are a bit different now, wouldn't you say?"

I smile and nod, considering his offer. To say that him being back in town knocked the breath out of me would be an understatement. To say that discovering he was Kade's *brother* fucked me up would be the understatement of the *century*.

But to say that I don't want him in my life would be a big, fat lie.

"Do you remember the first time we met here," I ask, looking around with a grin. "And you called me *princess*?"

He wrinkles his nose. "God, I did, didn't I?" A shake of his head. "What weak game."

"Hey, it worked."

He smiles at me, that smile that melted my heart and my panties the first time he flashed it at me. "It did, didn't it?"

"I mean, I called you out for it and did my best to emasculate you but, yes, it did."

"You were such a spitfire," Jarrett says with a remembering smile. "I'd never met anyone like you."

"And have you since?"

"I think you know the answer to that," he says with a laugh.

We just watch each other for a moment after that, and I feel it — the buzzing energy crackling like electricity underneath all the things we don't say.

"I like the idea of being friends," I whisper.

"Yeah?"

I nod. "I've missed you, Jarrett. If I have the chance to have you in my life again, I want to take it."

Another flash of something in his eyes, but it's gone quickly, and then his hand extends for mine. "Friends, then."

I eye his hand. "I thought Kade said he'd castrate you if you touched me."

"True," he says, but leaves his hand extended. "I won't tell if you don't."

It's just a handshake, a simple pump of my hand in his to solidify our agreement, but the moment our skin touches, I hear the distant hum of a thousand warning bells alarming in sync.

As if he hears them, too, Jarrett swallows and pulls his hand from mine, reaching for his beer, instead. "Now," he says, taking a sip. "Tell me what the hell you've been up to this past year."

The conversation is easy from there, and I find that it feels natural, sitting there with Jarrett, him telling me about his life in New York while I fill him in on my last year as a college student. By the end of the night, he's helping me look for jobs and telling me I'm always welcome at the agency if I need somewhere to get started. We're swapping stories and laughing and drinking and everything feels okay.

Maybe Jarrett being back won't be so bad, after all.

Maybe being friends will be easy, now that we've had so much time apart.

Maybe we can all three hang out — me, him, and Kade — one big happy family.

Or maybe I'm still the same walking train wreck I was the night I first walked into this bar, and this whole thing will blow up in my face.

I guess only time will tell.

Cassise

Ralph's is on Spring Break level.

Fraternity rush is officially over, which means new brothers and old ones alike flock to the university bars to celebrate their letters. Music blasts from the speakers, the DJ yelling into the mic about the happy hour pricing, and every inch of the dance floor is packed.

Skyler, Kip, Adam, and I managed to snag a high-top table tucked back in the corner near the billiards tables, and though we still have to scream over the music, it's like we've carved out our own little slice of the bar.

"So, what comes next?" Adam asks Kip after he gives us the rundown of his television series idea. He wants to capture the story of how he and Skyler met and fell in love — including all the lies, games, and poker drama. It's the whole reason he's here and not in California at UCLA, and by the way Skyler is leaning into him all doe-eyed listening to him talk about the project, I know she couldn't care less what he's filming — so long as he's here.

"Casting," he says, nudging Skyler. "And this gal made sure I knew that she'd be Head Bitch in Charge when it came down to this part."

"Damn straight," she says, lifting her beer toward us before she takes a sip. "I've got to make sure the girl who plays me is bad ass enough to fill the role."

"And what about me?" Kip teases with an arched brow. "Think you can cast the right guy to fill my shoes?"

"Never," she answers easily, wrapping her arms around him and kissing his chin as she looks up at him with a tipsy smile. "I'll find a suitable actor, don't you worry. But only I get the real thing."

Adam and I exchange smiles when they practically start making out, but suddenly, a rowdy group of freshmen bump into our table and send our beers sloshing out of the plastic cups containing them.

"Jesus!" Adam yells, steadying the table as the rest of us reach out to hold the beers. Once everything is calm again, we all laugh, shaking our heads.

"I remember my first time in this bar," Kip says, throwing his arm around Skyler with a smile. "It's when I bet on you and won your heart."

"Uh," Skyler says, holding up a finger. "I'm pretty sure all you did was piss me off, and then stalk me when I told you to leave me alone afterward."

"You were going to a sketchy part of town to play in a poker tournament. I had to protect you."

"Oh, really? And how did that work out?"

I laugh, remembering from Skyler's stories that Kip almost got into a fight with a guy Skyler had beaten at the tournament.

"All I know is that *night* didn't end until morning," Kip says, waggling his brows. "With me and you on the beach at sunrise. And for that reason, I'd do it all again, given the chance."

Skyler blushes, shoving Kip playfully before she leans into him. And I know that look on her face when she casts her gaze up at him, her head on his shoulder.

Hopeless.

The girl is just absolutely hopeless.

"I remember my first time at this bar, too," I say, smiling at Skyler. "It was the night I became your Little."

"Oh my *gosh!*" Skyler squeals. "That's right! Awww, I got you a fake ID and everything."

"You did. And *you,*" I say, poking Adam in the ribs. "You danced with Skyler while I pined for you from afar."

"Okay, that's not fair," he says, poking me back. "I didn't know you were *pining* for anything. You played it cool for a girl who was supposedly so smitten."

"Well, I had to! My Big called dibs!"

"Gah, I still can't believe I was so blind to that," Skyler says, shaking her head.

"Can we change the subject?" Kip asks, frowning. "I don't like to think about you two banging." He points between Adam and Skyler, and my nose wrinkles with the notion.

"Yeah, I think that's a time I'd like to forget, too."

"What, you don't like being Eskimo sisters, Little?" Skyler teases, which makes Adam laugh out loud until I elbow him in the side.

Kip pulls Skyler out onto the dance floor, then, leaving me and Adam alone. I take a long pull of the fruity mystery cocktail the bartender poured me for happy hour, and when I set the drink down again, Adam is watching me with a curious smile.

"What?" I ask. "Something on my face?"

I'm already patting my cheeks and the corners of my lips when Adam chuckles, scooting his barstool closer. He slips his knee between my legs, his hands resting on my hips.

"No, you're beautiful."

"Then why are you looking at me like that?"

He shrugs. "Just thinking. Reminiscing." He pauses. "It's just... this is all so *real* now."

I tilt my head.

"That story we were just talking about, it just reminded me how far we've come. I mean, I can still remember the first time I saw you by the slip and slide at the Kappa Kappa Beta house. I can remember thinking you were so cute, but not realizing I actually had feelings for you for *so long*. We played so many games..." He shakes his head. "God, I remember the first time I saw you dancing with Clay. In this bar, Halloween. Do you remember?"

I scoff. "I try to forget everything about him."

"Well, I remember *distinctly* how badly I wanted to rip his head off."

"But you were with Skyler."

"I know. That's the point."

"What is?"

Adam smirks, grabbing my barstool and pulling me closer to him. "That through all the years, no matter who else was in the picture, no matter how many games we've played... it's always been you and me."

He steals my smile with a kiss, long and sensual, one that makes me wish we weren't in a crowded bar full of strangers.

"You're applying to med school," he says, his lips still hovering over mine. "I'm starting to look for a job. We're *both* graduating soon." Adam shakes his head, tucking my hair behind one hear as his warm brown eyes stare into mine. "We're about to start our lives together, Cassie."

I chuckle. "Are you sure you want to, after everything I've put you through?"

"Are you kidding?" Adam shakes his head again, and then his hands are framing my face. "For better or worse, drama free or up to our necks in frustration — I'm yours."

"It's probably going to be the latter, knowing us."

"Probably," Adam agrees. "But as long as I've got you at the end of the day, I'll take every challenge that comes our way."

"That kind of rhymed."

"Poet and didn't even know it."

I laugh, kissing his cheek before I pop out of my chair. "Dance with me, Adam Brooks."

And for the rest of the night, he does.

Bear

"Little, if you don't get your shit together right now, I'm going to put you in a cab and send you back to Greek Row."

My goofy-ass Little, Josh, who is *usually* mouthing off and getting himself into trouble with girls, is currently a sobbing mess in one of the hottest bars downtown.

His red hair is disheveled, and thanks to his fresh spray tan, he's starting to leave streak marks on his face. If it wasn't so pathetic, I'd be laughing.

"I just don't know what I'm going to do without you here," he says, and he grimaces with another wave of emotion.

Until I punch him in the stomach.

He doubles over, coughing, but when he's upright again, he nods. "You're right. I needed that."

"You're going to be fine," I assure him, resting a hand on his shoulder as I inch a shot of whiskey toward him. "You're going to party and hook up with girls and do all the things you've done every year since you joined Omega Chi."

"But you're my partner in crime," he says, shaking his head. "I mean, you're the reason half these guys put up with me."

At that, I laugh. "Hey, that's not true. We all love you — even when you annoy the shit out of us."

He looks down at the shot, not convinced.

"Listen to me," I say, leveling my gaze with his. "You need to stop playing this role you think you have to play, being the jokester all the time. You spit the corny lines to the ladies because you think that's what they expect from you. You're the clown, right?"

Josh nods.

"But I know you, the *real* you," I say, poking his chest. "And you're *actually* funny. Not in the stupid way either. You're also smart. And you've got ideas for this fraternity that you would rather shuffle through me than stand up and say on your own. But this is it, little brother. This is the passing of the torch. You can either let it fall to the ground and extinguish itself, or you can grab it and hold it high and run on. The choice is yours."

The more I talk, the more Josh nods, his brows furrowing together. "Yeah. Yeah, you're right, man."

"Obviously."

He smirks at that, and then he claps a hand on my shoulder. "I really am going to miss you, bro."

"Well, I'm not gone yet," I say, lifting my own shot glass. "So, let's get fucked up while I'm still young and broke and without adult responsibilities."

"Hear, hear!"

We slam back the whiskey, wincing as it burns our esophagi. Then, Josh nods toward a few girls at the other end of the bar.

"Shall we?"

Every single one of the girls looks older than us by at least five years — the perks of being at a bar downtown as opposed to one close to campus. We loaded up two vans with brothers to take on the downtown area, and I have to admit, the women coming out after a long day working at the office in their designer heels and pencil skirts is a fresh and welcome change of scenery.

Still, even with the tallest of the girls batting her lashes at me, her long legs crossed, skirt inched up over her knees — I can't help but feel like something's... *off.*

"You go ahead without me," I say. "I need some air, I think."

Josh frowns, and I can already see him opening his mouth to argue.

"You've got this," I say, giving him a pointed look as I stand.

At that, he zips his lips closed again with a determined nod, and then he brushes past me, puffing his chest out and holding his shoulders back as he approaches the girls.

I should have told him to wipe his fucking face first, but lucky for him, it looks like the blonde of the group is into sensitive guys. She wipes the wetness from his cheeks and even though I can't hear her, I see her lips mouth *what happened, are you okay?*

Josh gives me a wink over his shoulder, and I shake my head on a laugh, knowing he'll be just fine.

One glance around the dark bar and it's easy to see all my brothers are enjoying themselves. They're dancing under the lights on the giant dance floor, hitting on girls older and wiser than them at the bar, competing in beer pong back in the corner. They're all smiles and laughter, living it up.

And for some reason, it makes my chest hurt.

Scrubbing a hand over my fade, I make my way through the crowd and let myself outside. It's not as cold as it has been — the rare cold front that moved through has definitely passed — but it's far from the summertime heat, and I give a sigh of relief when the cool breeze washes over me.

Downtown is bustling with people going to and fro, girls linking arms and giggling as they pass, guys shouting and jumping on each other's backs as they try to get the girls' attention. Music and laughter spill out onto the street from every building, and I smile, leaning my back against the cool brick and taking it all in.

I'm not sure why I felt so claustrophobic inside. Maybe it's because I'm going to miss it all, that I'm sad to be leaving it behind. I'm graduating soon, moving on, leaving the place I've called home for almost four years now. My life will consist of more work and less play, a natural progression.

Even so, I shake my head at myself, because it's not like my life is ending when I leave college. If anything, it's just beginning. I'll have more freedom, no classes or homework, no fraternity events. I'll be able to go wherever I want, do whatever I want. And, if I get the right job, I'll actually have money to do shit with.

I'm still trying to figure out the source of my anxiety when a familiar head of short, blonde hair catches my eye down the street.

It's just a glimmer of the fairy lights hanging over head at first, their glow reflecting in her golden locks. But then she turns, and laughs, her wide, brown eyes shining in the low light of the street.

Erin Xander.

My heart stops in my chest at the sight of her. I haven't seen her since we got back from break. Truthfully, I wondered if I'd ever see her again after Friendsgiving last year. She graduated, and since she wouldn't return any of my calls or texts, I had no idea if she stayed in the area or moved away.

But here she is, shining like the brightest star downtown.

With her arm linked in Gavin's.

I hate that my fingers curl into fists at my sides at the sight of him, that my jaw tenses and my next breath is hotter than the one before it. All I want is to be happy for her, to see that smile on her face and be thankful that someone put it back after so many years of it being absent.

But something in my stomach sours every time I see them together, and I don't know if that will ever change.

Gavin says something to Erin when they're about two bars down from me, and she nods with a smile, blushing at the kiss he lays on her cheek before he disappears inside.

My feet are moving before I even make the conscious decision to go to her.

As soon as I take the first step, my heart is in my throat, and it stays there every inch of the way as I make my way toward her. The closer I get, the more I can see how freshly tanned her skin is, how her long lashes are painted black, her lips a crimson red. The dress she's wearing is somehow both conservative and sexy, the hem of it flowing below her knees, but the V-neck cutting down deep enough to show her cleavage. Those legs of hers are emphasized by the high heels she's wearing, and her hair is slightly curled, just enough of a wave to make it look like she might have just taken a toss in the sheets before coming out.

Maybe she had.

The thought makes me ill.

She's blissfully unaware of me until I'm about ten feet away, and then her brown eyes catch on mine, and the smile on her face slips off like a runny egg.

I stop when there's a foot left between us, and suddenly, I have no idea what the hell I'm doing. I open my mouth, close it again, shove my hands in my pockets and look down the street, clearing my throat. It takes me a long moment to look at her again, and when I do, she's watching me like a nightmare that's come to haunt her again.

I want to be the first one to speak, but I can't.

"Bear," she finally says, and my name is broken on her lips. So much so that she clears her throat, tucking her hair behind her ears before she crosses her arms over her chest. "What are you doing down here?"

"Some of the brothers carpooled out," I answer stupidly. "Wanted a change of scenery."

"Oh," she says, and she tries to smile, but it falls flat.

Her eyes jet over to the door Gavin walked in, and I assume he either went to the bathroom or to get them a drink, since there's an open container pass as long as you stay within the block.

Either way, my time alone with her is limited.

"You look good," I say.

Again, stupidly.

"Oh, thank you," she says with a blush, looking down at her dress.

"Get lots of time at the beach over break?"

She frowns, confused.

"You're tan," I comment. "More so than usual."

So stupid.

"Ah," she says. "Yes, actually, but not here. Um... Gavin and I, we... we took a trip."

"Oh."

"We went to the airport and just let two strangers pick our gate letter and number."

At that, I balk genuinely. "Wow. That's... that's ballsy."

She laughs, and the sound is so sweet, so familiar and yet such a distant memory I almost question if it's real. "It's okay. You can say what you really think — it was crazy. And very unlike me." She pauses then, filling up with a fresh inhale. "And amazing in every possible way."

My stomach twists with jealousy, but I shove the emotion down. "Where did you end up?"

"Ecuador, if you can believe it."

"Wow," I say with another bulging of eyes.

"I know! I know," Erin says, shaking her head. "It was some city we'd never even heard of. Guayaquil? But some quick research while we waited to board and we found this gorgeous beach town. The water was so blue and beautiful, and there were giant turtles and exotic birds, and the music was... oh, and the *food*!"

She can barely contain her smile as she talks about the place, the name of which I miss because I'm too busy telling myself to smile like I mean it, and it takes *all* my effort to do so.

After a while, she falls silent again, and I know my time is running out. It's now or never to say what I have to say.

"Erin, I'm really sorry about what happened at Friendsgiving."

She winces like I've struck her. "It's ok—"

"No." I stop her, holding up a hand. "It's not okay. I know it and so do you."

She rolls her lips together, crossing her arms even tighter over her chest as she waits for me to continue.

"I was an asshole. I acted out of line and I'm sorry for it. I don't blame you for ignoring my calls and my texts. I'd be pissed if I were you, too. But..."

Don't you fucking get emotional, Bear.

But it's useless. My throat nearly closes on itself as I try to fight back the tears stinging the corner of my eyes, and I still a breath before I continue.

"Look, I don't have an excuse, other than I had my own shit going on. But it doesn't matter. All that does is that I'm genuinely sorry that I hurt you." I find her gaze then, and when I see her eyebrows pinched together as she watches me struggle with my emotion, I nearly fall apart. "And I'm glad to see you happy, Erin. I truly am. It's all I've ever wanted."

She sucks in a stiff breath, and I don't miss the glossing of her own eyes. "Bear…"

Behind her, I see Gavin in the bar, making his way through the crowd and back out to the street.

"I just wanted you to know," I say with a sniff, and then I turn and bolt without another word, steering myself back toward the bar where my brothers are. I don't look over my shoulder to see if Erin is watching me leave, or if Gavin is giving her a kiss now that he's reunited with her, or if they're walking hand in hand in the opposite direction.

I can't do anything but forge on.

And as I reach the bar again, ducking inside and welcoming the greeting of smoke and music, I have the most disturbing moment of clarity.

I finally understand why I feel tethered to this place, why it feels impossible to leave.

It's not PSU that's keeping me here. It's not my brothers or the parties or the nostalgia of being a college kid. It's not the bars or the three-story gym on campus or the mostly responsibility-free lifestyle.

It's her.

And now that I see it, I know one thing for sure.

I can't leave here.

Not yet.

And not without her.

EPISODE 2

Erin

"What is it?"

"Open it and find out."

I stare at the giant box Gavin just took out of his car and sat between us in the parking lot, questioning its safety with an arched brow. Other people from therapy are still filing out to their own cars around us, and Gavin tips an imaginary hat at them when they stare at the box with just as much confusion as I am.

"I don't like surprises."

"It's not a surprise," he says on a laugh. "It's a gift. Open it."

I should be used to this kind of behavior from Gavin. I mean, if him suggesting that we take a spontaneous trip where we let strangers pick our destination hadn't proved that already, I'm not sure what would. Still, my stomach is a mess of butterflies as I stare at the gift.

I roll my lips together, slowly inching closer to the box. It's obnoxiously big, so much so that it barely fit in the back seat of Gavin's car, and it's fire-engine red with a bright pink bow on top.

I slip my fingers under the bow first, untying it and letting it fall open to expose the top lid of the box. And when I remove it, I scream.

A cannon of confetti and glitter bursts when I remove the top, making a loud *pop* sound as a flurry of red, pink, purple, and white rains down around me. Gavin is laughing uncontrollably as I try desperately not to have a heart attack, and I throw the box lid directly at him, disappointed when he catches it easily.

"Jerk!"

"I'm sorry," he says, still fighting off laughter. "I didn't know it would be so explosive."

That sends him into another riot of laughter, and though I'm starting to laugh, too, I beat my tiny fists on his chest until he drops the box lid and wraps his arm around me.

"Did you look inside?"

"I didn't have to. The insides jumped out at me!"

He chuckles, nodding toward the box as he shifts me in his arms so I can see.

Inside, there's a fluffy teddy bear with soft beige fur and a red heart clasped between its paws. There are also at least three boxes of chocolate, a bottle of champagne, and a giant cartoon-drawn card that says *will you be my Valentine?*

"Valentine's Day?" I ask, giving Gavin a pointed look when I turn in his arms once more. I thread my hands behind his neck. "You're joking, right? You don't strike me as a man who buys into a consumer-driven, romantic holiday."

"Oh, I absolutely *loathe* the holiday," he agrees with a grin. "But I happen to really like *you*."

I smile. "Is that so?"

"It is. So you see, I'm in a conundrum, because where I would usually spend the holiday playing video games or making fun of couples posting on social media, this year..." He pulls me in closer, his endless blue-green eyes sparkling in the low light from the parking lot streetlamps. "I'd rather be disgustingly cute and couple-y with you."

"What if I *also* hate Valentine's Day?"

"We can have an anti-Valentine's Day."

"And that would entail..."

"Watching *John Tucker Must Die* and pigging out on our favorite snacks in our sweatpants. No candles, no roses, no romance. Just trashy movies, trashy food, and trashy conversation."

I laugh, playing with his hair where it meets the nape of his neck. "You've got this all planned out."

"So, are you in?"

His eyes fall to my lips, and when he bites his, desire rolls through me in a drastic heat wave.

Our trip only lasted ten days, but it was magical in every way. Sure, there was the anxiety of not knowing what to pack, of flying to a country I barely knew anything about, let alone had ever visited before, but overall, it was the most exhilarating trip of my life.

We flew into Ecuador without a single thing planned, using our time in the airports to book a last-minute hotel and car. We decided to drive out to a little beach town called Montañita, and the next ten days were filled with perfectly warm days and cool, pleasant nights. We lounged on the beach, danced in the sand to hypnotic local music, ate some of the best food of my life with spices and flavors I'd never experienced, and talked about everything — our past, our present, what we wanted in our future.

And through it all, Gavin never pushed me past where I was comfortable.

I'd be lying if I said we didn't spend plenty of nights wrapped up in each other, touching and exploring. But we never went all the way. I wasn't quite ready.

But now, I think I am.

And what better time to give myself to Gavin fully than Valentine's Day, even an anti-one?

"I'm in," I answer, and then I press up on my toes to kiss him and seal the deal.

***

Later that night, back at the condo Jess, Ashlei, and I moved into together after I got back from my trip, I take a long, hot shower and join the girls on the couch for popcorn and reality TV. I don't even make it through one episode before I'm yawning and debating how early is *too* early to go to bed. I've got class bright and early in the morning, and if I've learned anything after just the first two weeks of law school, it's that there isn't enough sleep in the world to get me through it.

I somehow manage to make it to nine before I peel myself off the couch and tell the girls goodnight. I brush my teeth and wash my face and sigh with relief when I climb into bed.

Until my phone starts vibrating so hard it nearly falls off the bedside table.

I roll over and snatch it before it does, and then I freeze.

It's Bear.

I swallow, debating if I should answer. I ran into him downtown over the weekend, and seeing him for the first time in nearly a month knocked the breath clean out of me. He finally apologized for Friendsgiving — mostly because I couldn't ignore him when he practically ambushed me in the middle of the street — and while I wanted to still be angry with him, one look at the remorse on his face, at the pain I knew he was in, and the last thing I could be was mad.

Shaking my head, I press the green phone button on my screen and put the phone on speaker, lying back and resting it on my chest.

"Hello?"

There's a shuffling of noise, and then a breathless Bear. "You answered."

And I can't help it.

I smile.

"Indeed, I did." I pause, swallowing down the nerves threading like a yarn ball in my throat. "Everything okay?"

"Oh, yeah." A breath. "Well, no, not exactly."

I frown. "What's going on?"

"I just... I've been thinking a lot since I saw you downtown."

I wait for him to continue, but he doesn't. "Okay..."

"God, now that I have you on the phone, I don't know how to say this."

"Jesus, Bear, you're going to give me a heart attack if you don't just spit it out."

I think I hear a soft laugh, but then the line goes silent.

"Okay, well... here's the truth of it." Another pause. A swallow. "I don't want to lose you, Erin."

I can't explain what those words do to me, how they hit me hard in the chest and steal my next breath, make me pop up straight in bed, make me grip my phone like a lifeline.

"I know we have both... we've put each other through..." He inhales a long breath, lets it go, and I know that he's wishing for the right words to come to him.

I also know from the past that it's impossible, because I've tried to find the right words to say to him more times than I can count.

"Can we please start over? I know that's asking a lot, to try to erase and forget everything... but... I don't want to just go on with my life and pretend like I don't want you in it."

I sigh, sinking back into my pillows as I scrub a hand back through my still-damp hair. "I don't want to forget," I finally croak out.

Bear is silent for a long moment before he says simply, "Oh..."

Silence.

"Well, I'm sorry I called so late," he finally says. "I'll let you get some—"

"I don't want to forget because everything we've been through has made us who we are," I finish. "I know it hasn't all been easy. I've hurt you, you've hurt me, but..." I swallow, and then say it again. "I don't want to forget. I don't think I *could* forget," I add. "Could you?"

"No," he answers, honestly and quickly. "No, I don't think I ever could."

"Then I don't think starting over is an option," I say, playing with the lace hem of my sheets. "But... I don't think that means we can't be friends."

A relieved exhale comes from the other end of the line. "That's all I want, Erin. Just give me the chance to right my wrongs, and we can move forward together."

I smile. "I like the sound of that."

"So, friends?"

"Friends."

"Perfect," he says. And even though I can't see him, I can picture his bright, wide smile when he adds, "I'll have bracelets made."

I bark out a laugh. "I think you'd need more of a necklace to fit around your beastly wrist."

"And more of a ring to fit around your tiny one."

We both chuckle at that, and then the line falls quiet, and I'm suddenly aware of how hard my heart is thumping in my chest.

"Goodnight, Bear."

"Goodnight, Erin."

Ashlei

The clicking of high heels on a marble floor is one of my favorite sounds of all time.

There's just something about that *click, clack, click, clack* that makes me feel powerful as fuck when I strut my ass through the office at *Ball & Pen*.

The new *Ball & Pen*.

In downtown Miami.

Where I'm the HBIC — Head Bitch in Charge.

Okay, so that's not *technically* my title, but it might as well be. Celeste Lambert, whom I met at the *Okay, Cool* Southeast Advertising Conference afterparty last year, was quick to snatch me up when she heard I'd left *Okay, Cool.*

Fortunately, she didn't know the exact reason *why* I had left — no one did — which was about all the mercy I was receiving from Brandon since our breakup.

The thought of him still makes my stomach drop, even in my new bougie office with a view of Bayshore. I was honored to be hired by Mrs. Lambert to essentially head the expansion of *Ball & Pen* with the new Miami office, and I'm already securing high-end clients for us left and right. When it comes to events, especially in the corporate and technology spaces, I'm confident there's no one better than me.

But all that confidence can't heal a broken heart.

Brandon has ignored every single attempt I've made to reach out to him since he kicked me out of his condo after he found out about the stupid kiss-*not*-kiss I shared with the intern last semester. No text or phone call has been answered, and when February first rolled around and I realized it had been nearly two months since our breakup, I realized one gut-wrenching truth.

It's over.

Truly over.

And there's nothing I can do but pick myself up and keep walking.

The timing of what happened between us couldn't have been worse. Spending the holidays with my parents was not what I had in mind. Brandon and I were supposed to go skiing in Colorado. We were supposed to exchange gifts and hang Christmas lights and cozy up together all through the holiday season. We were supposed to ring in the new year in Times Square, sharing a kiss under a rain shower of confetti.

I was supposed to have a Valentine locked in for life.

Instead, I'm alone, and it's all my own fault.

So, while a badass new job doesn't fix heartbreak, it offers a pretty stellar distraction from it, which is better than nothing.

A knock on my door frame jolts me from my thoughts, and I smile when I look up and find my assistant, Jeannie.

Yes, I have an assistant.

HBIC status.

"Ms. Daniels? Is now a good time to go over this week's agenda?"

I usher her in, giving her a pointed look at the formality. "Call me, Lei, Jeannie. I've told you that at least five times now."

"Sorry, Ms.— er, Lei. I've never worked for someone who didn't… um…"

"Need their ego stroked every hour of the day?" I challenge with an arched brow.

That makes her flush furiously, but at least earns me a smile as she takes a seat in the chair opposite me.

Jeannie is sweet. My senior by ten years, she's no stranger to agency life. We've only been working together a month now and I can already tell we'll get along. She understands where I need her to step up and take over and where I need her to give me full reign. She organizes my calendar in a way that makes sense for me, keeps up to date with the latest agency drama so I can deal with it without accidentally involving myself, and doesn't have a problem rolling up her sleeves and diving into the trenches with me when I need a hand.

With jet-black hair, a full-figure frame, and a dazzling smile, she's far from hard on the eyes. But perhaps what I love most about her is — beauty aside — I have absolutely zero desire to fuck her.

And if I've learned anything from my past mistakes with Brandon and that little bitch, Sophie, it's that *that* is a good thing.

"Alright, hit me," I say, typing my password in to wake my computer up again. I go to my calendar to review with Jeannie, making notes of the particular team meetings, client presentations, and events coming up.

We're just about to wrap up when she clears her throat uncomfortably, shifting in her seat. "There's also the matter of the agency arrival event Mrs. Lambert wants you to coordinate."

I wrinkle my nose. "The what?"

Jeannie's flush is almost comical. "She just, she did this in Atlanta, too, when she first opened *Ball & Pen*. And again in Chicago when that branch opened. Basically, it's a hoity-toity affair where we invite all the other event and marketing agencies in the area to come get to know us, talk about possible collaborations, and—"

"Let them know there's a new shiny toy in town and we're here to play?"

Jeannie hangs her head. "Pretty much."

I laugh, leaning back in my chair and crossing my legs. "That woman has some balls," I comment, and then I point my pen at Jeannie. "As do I, which is likely why she hired me." Sitting up straight again, I start typing into my notes app. "Get me a list of five possible venues. I'm thinking rooftop, on the water." I gasp, eyes wide when I find Jeannie. "Or maybe *in* the water. Let's look into chartering a yacht."

I continue typing and rattling off tasks for Jeannie, asking her to look into everything from catering to entertainment and giving her some jumping off points to get started. Once she's armed with a to-do list at least a mile long, she leaves me with forty-five minutes before my first meeting of the week.

The premise of the event has my chest light with excitement, my heart fluttering much the way it does when I'm about to do a pole performance or kiss someone I know I'm going to fuck. This is my favorite part — the brainstorming — other than when it all comes together in the end, of course.

With a little time to kill before I'm needed anywhere else, I decide to take the matter of the guest list into my own hands, and I can't fight off the satisfied smile that spreads on my face with the thought.

After all, I've been working in this industry, in this city, for almost two years now.

And I know *just* who to invite.

Skyler

There's something incredibly hot about watching your man work on what he's passionate about.

I've known about Kip's passion for the film industry ever since before we even officially started dating. I know he's obsessed with television, specifically that he has dreams of creating a series viewers can't help but be obsessed with. I've seen the posters on his walls, the podcasts filling his phone, the documentary DVDs spilling out of his dresser back at UCLA.

But it's something altogether different to see him in his element.

I smile, sipping my coffee as I relax in the casting director's chair Kip made just for me. It was a joke, of course, but I appreciate the fancy place to sit with my fake title on the back anyway. While I've been chiming in now and then with my thoughts, I'm mostly here for support.

And to watch his fine ass in director mode.

I love the way his glasses keep falling down the bridge of his nose as he examines audition notes on his clipboard, his brows furrowed in concentration. I love the messy way his blond hair is styled, the waves mussed from him scrubbing his hands through them. I love the smiles he flashes when he encourages someone auditioning to try again, giving them notes for a better application. I love how even dressed in a white button down and navy dress pants, I can imagine his lean muscles ebbing and flowing beneath the fabric.

More than anything, I just love that he's *here*.

At Palm South.

With me.

I was unsure when he first told me he was going to make a show about our story, about all the games we played, the lies we told, the rough and rocky road we had to take to get to where we are today. But I know this is about more than just us. It's about exploring the grief he feels over losing his father, and the complicated relationship they had while he was alive. It's also a commentary on young love, on college, on finding yourself while also finding a relationship.

Whatever he does with our story, I know it will be amazing. Because it's him creating it.

I smile a little more, inhaling the sweet scent of my latte. I'm in a state of peaceful calm and just taking in all the scenery.

That is, until my doppelgänger walks through the door.

Kip rented the smaller of the three auditoriums on campus for auditions, so everyone is waiting in the hallway until they're called in for their turn. So far, we've seen auditions for Kip, his dad, my parents, Kade, all the girls, and some extras. Kip must have been saving the auditions for me for last.

That makes me smile, too.

Still, the sight of the girl who just walked in makes me dizzy. Her long, brown hair is the same shade as mine, pinpoint straight and parted just how I part my own. Her lashes are a little longer than mine, her skin a bit fairer, and I'd give just about anything to have her amazing lips. But her eyes are the same shade of blue that I see reflected in the mirror every morning, and her tight little athletic body reminds me of how I looked when I was at my prime.

It's unsettling and exciting, all in the same breath.

She looks a little nervous, waiting by the door. Kip is engrossed in a conversation with one of the students he brought on to help with casting, reviewing notes from the last audition. So, when the girl's eyes flick to me, I smile and usher her over, patting the empty chair next to me.

She blushes, looking around for a second before she smiles and makes her way toward me. The closer she gets, the dizzier I feel, but I fight past the feeling with a grin of my own.

"Hey there," I say when she's standing in front of me. "I bet I can guess which part you're going for."

She chuckles, tucking her hair behind one ear. "Skyler Thorne?"

"In the flesh," I answer, waving a hand over myself dramatically. "What's your name?"

"Natalia Colburn."

My brows shoot up. "Wow. You already have a movie-star name."

"Right? That's what I told my parents when I was twelve. I said, *'You already gave me the name. Now I just have to win the lead in the school play.'*"

"And did you?"

At that, Natalia cocked a brow, looking down at herself before she gave me a pointed look. "What do you think?"

I laugh. "I like your spunk, Natalia. Here," I say, patting the chair next to me again. "Have a seat. They're finishing up something anyway."

"Why, thank you," she says, and when she's seated next to me, she shakes her head as she looks around. "This is so cool."

"Yeah?" I ask, looking around with her. "I mean, I think so, but I figured you'd be used to it by now. I'm sure you have been to many auditions."

"Not in *college*, though."

"Ah," I say with a smile. "Freshman."

"And eager as hell to make my mark."

That earned her a laugh. "I know that feeling well. Where are you from?"

"South Dakota," she answers with a grimace. "And yes, it's as bland as it seems. Drama class was all that got me through to graduation."

"Your parents still there?"

At that, her smile slips. "Yeah. Neither one of them has a college education. I'm the first in the family to even attempt a degree." She shrugs, looking down at her fingers folded in her lap. "I want this part so bad. Not just for me, but for them. If I could be a part of a show like this, and it takes off? It opens so many doors. It could launch my career." Her eyes flick to Kip then, and she smiles. "And if there's anything I know about Kip Jackson, it's that he's talented enough to make it happen."

I smile, surprised. "You know of his work already?"

"Oh, yeah. I always do a lot of research into the roles I'm auditioning for, and getting to know the director and producer is step number one. He's done a lot of great things in just one short year out in California. And the fact that his professors sent him here to film his pilot?" She shakes her head. "They know something special when they see it. And I want to be a part of that magic."

Natalia and I share a smile then, just as she's called up to the stage. She gives me a nervous wave goodbye and I tell her to break a leg. Then, I sit back and settle in for her audition.

And I'm blown away.

I don't know if Kip gave her clips of me or an in-depth character description in the casting call or if she has straight up been stalking me, but Natalia nails her impression of me so much so that I can barely keep my jaw off the floor.

Her mannerisms, her voice, her well-delivered jokes and deeply moving monologues when she talks about her family — er, *my* family — about poker, about PSU... it's incredible. Kip has her run a few lines as if she's hanging out with the girls in the sorority house, has her run a part of the scene he wrote for the night he came to watch me at the poker tournament downtown, has her speak a monologue like she's sitting on her paddle board out in the water in the early morning light.

I'm so moved, so touched, so enraptured that I almost feel like I'm having an out-of-body experience.

When she finishes, Kip and the casting director share a knowing smile before excusing her and letting her know they'll be in touch. The minute she's out the door, before they can call in whoever's next, I'm out of my chair and running to Kip.

"Cast her."

His smile is dazzling as ever as he arches a brow at me. "You like her, huh?"

I shake my head. "I don't just like her. I *love* her. She gets it. She gets *me*. And she comes from means that I know she can really understand what it's like to be me."

"I saw you two chatting over there." Kip smiles, looking down at his clipboard. "We have seven other girls outside waiting to audition, though. I think—"

"You said you'd let me have a say in who played me," I remind him.

"I know," he replies with a chuckle. "But you've only seen one girl."

"I don't need to see anyone else to know she's the right choice."

Kip frowns a little, and I huff, throwing my hands toward Dina, his casting director.

"Come on, you had to see it, too," I say to her. "The girl was magic."

Dina bites her lip, looking at her notes before her eyes find Kip's. "She really did have something, Kip. The look is spot on, and the monologue she gave about Skyler's parents..."

"I know," Kip says on a sigh, looking at his own notes. "I almost got teary-eyed."

"See?" I grab his arm and plead, giving him my best puppy dog eyes. "Trust me on this. She's the one."

Kip smirks, then, shaking his head as he tucks me under his arm and presses a kiss to my forehead. "Alright, then. She's the one."

"Yay!"

He laughs when I throw my arms around his neck and kiss him all over.

"Even as great as she is, she's got the toughest part in the show," he says, resting his arms around my hips.

"Because I'm a pain in the ass to understand?'

"No," he says, kissing my nose. "Because there's no one in the world like you."

"Thank goodness for that."

He laughs, and then his lips find mine, and I revel once again in how happy I am that he's here.

Adam

There's something rather unsettling about being in your last semester of college.

It reminds me of high school a little bit, how excited you are at the end of your junior year. You think to yourself *I'm finally a senior! It's my year to rule!* And everything is full of possibility and promise.

But then, you transition into that last semester of your senior year, and something changes.

Something shifts.

Suddenly, you realize that it's the end of an era, a door closing that you can never open again. This time in your life — whether you've loved or hated it — is about to end. Which, of course, means a new chapter is beginning.

It's both exciting and terrifying.

Those emotions on their own are strong, but when you mix them together, it's like having a permanent stomachache. You slow down a little more, look around a little more, appreciate things that maybe you never took the time to throughout the last four years of your life.

I've been to hundreds of Alpha Sigma events by now — dozens of which I've coordinated myself. And sure, I've enjoyed myself. I've thrown myself into event planning, stayed up all night long with my brothers celebrating, lost weeks on end where there was so much going on it was like a blur.

But tonight, at our first annual Valentine's Day Soirée, I'm soaking it all in.

The event was actually Kade's idea, which threw me for a loop because I'd always taken Kade as more of a party brother than one interested in leadership. But something's happened since he's been with Jess. It seems that *he's* transformed, that he's been moved by the urge to do more, to *be* more.

He came to me with the idea a month ago: a Valentine's Day, all-inclusive event that every girl on campus would be dying to go to. There'd be an elegant catered dinner at the house, a quartet band playing old jazz favorites, and an excuse to dress up — which, if I'm being honest, is probably the main allure.

College girls *love* an excuse to dress up.

Now, sitting at my rose-petal-covered table with Cassie as we drink champagne and listen to the band, I can't help but look around at what Kade created in awe. The Alpha Sigma house has been completely transformed, inside and out, with intimate, candle-lit tables lining our hallways, filling our common rooms, and spilling out onto the covered dance floor in the back yard. The tent is strung with fairy lights, too, and there's just something about the jazz band that elevates the whole experience.

It doesn't feel like a college party, like a typical frat event.

It feels sophisticated and grown.

It feels magical.

"You've really outdone yourself tonight, Adam," Cassie says, her green eyes sparkling in the candlelight from our table. I chose one that was outside for us, under the tent, and not too far from the band, and it just so happens to be the most pleasant evening we've had all month — cool, but not cold, with a gentle breeze wafting over the yard.

Cassie always looks radiant, but seeing her in a blush silk gown tapered in all the right places with pearls on her neck and in her ears, her red hair pulled back in an elegant twist of braids and curls, her lips painted a soft pink that makes me want to kiss her senseless... it's enough to make me dizzy just looking at her.

"I wish I could take the credit," I admit honestly, taking a sip of my champagne. "But this is all Kade."

"*Kade?*" She shakes her head, finding him and Jess on the dance floor. He's got one hand holding hers upright, and the other snaked around the small of her back as they sway softly to the music. "I had no idea he had this in him."

"Neither did I."

"Does Jess know?"

I shrug. "He's been pretty humble about it all. Even with the planning, he wasn't trying to really boss anyone around. He took everything on himself that he could, delegated when he needed to, and named it a team effort from the start." My stomach pinches a little. "He's a better man than I am. I would want *all* the credit for an event like this."

Cassie smiles, placing her hand over mine. "I seem to remember you sharing credit for the amazing Alpha Sigma concert you threw that very first year I knew you. And it's become an annual hit."

"With a karaoke twist now."

"Lord, help us all."

I chuckle, smoothing my thumb over her wrist. Cassie locks her gaze on mine for a long while before she's watching the band again, sipping her champagne, and I can see it without her saying a word.

She wants to dance.

Folding my napkin and setting it beside our half-eaten, red velvet cake, I extend my hand for hers, taking her out to the floor to sway alongside Jess and Kade. It's like we start a trend, because before we know it, the entire dance floor is full.

And a bunch of college kids are dancing to a Billie Holiday song.

Who would have thought?

As I hold Cassie in my arms, I can't help but feel that same sentimental bug crawling under my skin. I'll miss being here with her, miss going to frat parties and formals and spring breaks with her. I have no doubt the next chapter in my life holds Cassie in it, but I'd also be stupid to think it wouldn't be different.

Even with all we've been through, college is nothing compared to what waits for us in the real world.

And that fact is thrown in my face every time I go to apply for the Alpha Sigma Field Executive position.

Being a part of the national organization as a college graduate makes my heart race any time I think about it. Some nights, I can't sleep because I get so excited thinking about what campuses I'd be sent to, the young men I'd get to meet and shape, the organizations I could turn around.

But in the same breath, I lose sleep when I remember the sobering facts.

Not only would I be away from Cassie in her last semester as a college student, but none of the schools she wants to apply to for med school have an Alpha Sigma chapter. In fact, most of them don't even have a chapter within a hundred miles.

Which means if I do land my dream job, I'd be far away from my dream girl.

And while I know our love is strong and we have already made it through so many trials, I feel sick at the thought of losing her in exchange for having a career.

"I think I smell smoke."

I arch a brow, snapping back to the present moment when Cassie taps my temple.

She chuckles. "What are you thinking so hard about over there?"

I smile, letting out a long release of a breath. "Lots of things. But most of all, how gorgeous you look tonight."

She blushes, that familiar shade of crimson coloring her cheeks just like it did the first day I met her. "You just want to get me out of this dress."

"Oh, I definitely do. And I intend to as soon as possible. But first," I say when the song ends, doing a dramatic bow as I kiss her hand. "I have some business to attend to."

She giggles, turning to the side to let me kiss her cheek when I'm upright again. Then, I make my way over to Kade, tearing him away from Jess — which is no easy feat — and taking him off to the side of the dance floor. Jess makes her way over to Cassie, taking my seat at our table, and once they're settled, I focus on Kade.

"You did a phenomenal job putting this all together," I say.

He shrugs. "Ah, it was a team effort. I couldn't have done it alone."

"No," I agree. "But it wouldn't be happening at *all* if not for you. This isn't just some frat party, or just another cheesy costume event that anyone could slap together. It has finesse. And I'm being honest when I say no one has impressed me this much since I impressed my own damn self coming up with the A Sig concert idea."

Kade laughs.

"I'm serious, man," I say, shoving my hands in my pockets. I look around at the event, taking it all in. "Have you thought about going for president?"

When I look back at Kade, his jaw is practically on the floor, his eyes wide as he blinks at me repeatedly. "Is that a joke?"

"No," I say with a chuckle of my own. "Come on, man. I mean, you threw this together in less than a month. You have raw leadership skills and the ability to get the guys fired up and excited about something. That *alone* is enough to make a good president, but on top of that, you're smart and motivated and creative. You've got the chops."

Kade frowns, then laughs, shaking his head as he looks around at our brothers and their dates. "I... I don't know, man."

"Well, I do." I clap him on the shoulder. "You don't have to make a decision tonight, okay? Just think about it."

His frown is still in place, but he nods, offering me what smile he can manage. "Thanks, Adam."

I return his nod with a grin, and then make my way back over to Cassie.

If it's our last Valentine's Day together on campus, I'm going to make the most of it.

Erin

"You're so sexy when you've got Dorito dust all over your sweatpants," Gavin says — or rather, *growls*, like he's some sex-craved animal.

I laugh as he climbs on top of me, pressing me into his sheets and kissing all over my neck.

"Sexier than the swimsuit in Ecuador, huh?"

"Oh, a thousand times over."

I chuckle again as he settles in above me, balancing on his elbows with a sleepy, hot-as-hell grin on that perfect face of his. In the low light of his bedroom, those Tahiti-blue eyes of his still seem to glow against his freshly tanned olive skin.

True to his word, we've had the most anti-Valentine's Day evening together. There have been no candles or rose petals, no boxes of chocolate or expensive fancy dinners. Instead, it's been just me and him in his little apartment off campus, more junk food than I've had even on a girls' night in, and — since we really wanted to commit to the anti-holiday thing — we landed on a horror movie instead of a romance one.

It's been weirdly perfect.

"What was your favorite part of the trip?" I ask.

He rolls his eyes. "Come on, you know I hate conversations like this. *What's your favorite color?*" he mocks.

"Humor me, asshole." I pinch his side for good measure.

"Fine," he concedes, then he pulls my hand between his and uses my pointer finger to tap his chin like he's a cartoon character thinking. "I think my favorite part was the plane ride home."

I frown. "What? That's the literal *worst* part. Of any trip!"

"I disagree."

"What could you have possibly enjoyed about it?"

"Well, see, there was a solid hour or so where you were zonked out so hard next to me, your mouth was hanging open and there was a little line of drool from the corner of your lips down to your chin."

My jaw drops, and I try to cover my face with my hands, but Gavin holds onto the one so that I can't. "Oh, my *God*. That's so embarrassing!"

"It was adorable," he disagrees with a chuckle. "And you leaned your head on my shoulder when your neck started to hurt from leaning the other way. And for that little bit of time, we were just two people on a plane, exhausted from vacation, and I had this post-vacation high still humming through my body. It was an unremarkable moment, but the best kind."

I smile softly, leaning up from the pillows long enough to capture his mouth with mine. "Careful," I warned. "That was almost romantic, and we're doing all the opposite today, remember?"

"I bet I can guess your favorite part."

"Hit me."

"It was parasailing."

"Ohhh, that *was* fun. Scary as hell, but fun."

"It wasn't that scary," he argues. "Did I guess right?"

"No, actually."

His eyebrows shoot up. "Do tell, then."

"I thought you hated conversations like this."

"Tell me, or I'll tickle it out of you," he threatens, and he gets me good under the armpits, making me wriggle beneath him as I laugh hysterically. I can't even breathe, let alone speak, until he stops.

"Brat."

"Tell me," he says again, holding his fingers above me and wiggling them in warning.

I chuckle, but then wrap my arms around his biceps where he's holding them above me, and my eyes flick back and forth between his. "The third night of the trip, after we went to that little beach restaurant — you remember the one, where we had a table *on* the actual beach, and our toes in the sand as we ate that fancy lobster tail?"

"I remember," he says, and the corner of his mouth ticks up with the thought.

"Well, we walked back, and had our shoes in our hands. And the moon was full, and we could hear the waves crashing on the shore. And when we got back to our room..." I swallow, not able to look at him directly as I continue, so I stare at his chest, instead. "You undressed me. And you kissed what felt like every possible inch of my body. And then you laid me down and... and... well, you know the rest."

Gavin is smirking when I look up at him again. "I think I forgot, maybe you should remind me."

I smack his chest.

"Oh!" he says, nodding. "You mean when I went down on you for about a half an hour until you climaxed? I guess I remember now."

"Jerk," I say with my cheeks on fire.

"I'm surprised that's your favorite part."

"Well, it was the first time in... a long time," I say, knowing I don't have to be explicit with Gavin for him to know what I mean. That's the benefit of sharing trauma, I suppose.

He nods, and then slowly, he lowers his mouth to mine, kissing me softly at first before the pressure intensifies. My legs part of their own accord, inviting him to fit more snuggly between my hips, and the more we kiss, the harder I feel him grow.

"Gavin," I whisper.

"Mmm?"

"Will you... will you make love to me?"

Gavin pulls back, breaking from the little kisses he was planting all over my neck. The second I see all the color wash from his face, I regret my question.

"Oh, God, I'm sorry," I say, shaking my head. "That sounded so... cheesy and... I mean, will you fuck me?"

But those words sound even worse, and I cringe as I say them, and Gavin shakes his head and immediately rolls off of me so that we can switch positions. He pulls me into his chest, holding me, wrapping me up tight.

"Okay, I know what's going through your head. So first, let me just say do not be ashamed of what you just asked. It was hot as fuck and there's absolutely nothing wrong with you feeling desire and wanting to have sex."

Even though I know his words are meant to soothe me, they just spark my anxiety more, and I find it harder and harder to breathe pressed against him.

"And please know, this is not me rejecting you. This is not me saying that I don't want to lie you down in these sheets and be inside you and make you climax all fucking night, okay?" He stops when I don't answer, maneuvering until he can pull my chin up and look me in the eyes. "Okay?"

I can't fight the tears that well in my eyes, and I sniff and try to nod.

"I'm serious, Erin. I mean it. I wouldn't lie to you and you know that. It's just..." He takes a deep breath. "I know what happened to you and I know, maybe better than most, how much it can fuck you up. I'm so honored you feel comfortable with me enough to ask me to be the first man to touch you since that night. But I want to be sure, too. Okay? And right now, I really think we should stay where we are, and move slow."

All the words he's saying are right. They're honest and true and kind. They're perhaps the nicest thing anyone has ever said to me, and the most respectful.

But I'd be lying if I said they didn't hurt.

"Can I just hold you tonight? And kiss you? And eat more trashy food and stay up way past bedtime even though we both have school tomorrow?"

I chuckle, and I'm thankful the tears don't build enough to actually fall. "Okay."

With a sigh, he pulls me back to his chest, kissing my hair and grabbing the remote. "You're an amazing girl, Erin Xanders."

But as he flips through the movie options, I can't help but feel like the scum of the earth.

Ashlei

B*reathe.*

Don't forget to breathe.

Smile.

Don't forget to smile.

Squeeze.

For the love of God, don't forget to squeeze.

Reminder after reminder pelts me like rubber bullets as I run through my competition routine one last time. *Melt* by Shaed blasts from the studio speakers, reverberating off the walls and filling my soul like the sweetest drug.

I'm already dripping in sweat from running the routine full out five times before — in addition to stretching and training tricks beforehand — but I'm still far from nailing everything perfectly the way I want to.

Competition is one month away, and I don't just want to compete.

I want to medal.

I want to *win*.

The beat builds as I climb the pole, spinning higher and higher.

Point your toes.

Shoulders back and down.

Core engaged.

I take a deep breath as I extend my legs out in a straddle, holding the position strong before I bring my ankles together to sit with my thighs wrapped around the pole. One more breath and then I'm letting go of the pole with my hands, relying on my engaged thighs as I lean back and hang upside down.

Laybacks used to be one of the scariest pole tricks to me. But once I learned them, they quickly became my favorite. Not only are they gorgeous and flowy, but there's so many combinations you can make out of them.

Of course, I maybe could have selected a slightly simpler one for competition.

But where's the fun in that?

Reaching behind me, I grab for the pole, and as soon as I have it in my hands, I loosen my thigh grip until I'm holding on by my ankles, instead.

Iguana pose.

Smile, bitch, smile. Fight the pain.

On a steady breath, I remove my right hand from the pole, swinging it down below where my head hangs. Then, in what most would consider a miraculous feat, I free my shoulder from the pole and twist my body until I'm turned all the way around and facing it.

My hips come back away from the pole, legs extended in straddle.

And *bam* — just like that, I'm in my last trick of the routine, a beautifully extended and strong twist-grip Ayesha.

Nailed it.

Distantly, I hear the applause and cheers from the other girls in the studio. It's open practice time, so everyone is doing their own thing. I asked the instructor to put on my song for the last bit of class, just to get one routine run without my earphones in.

And now, I'm putting on a show.

I come down via a shoulder dismount, crawling on the floor with as much sex appeal as I can manage as tired as I am now. Then, I lie back, arching my back off the ground and staggering my legs for my final pose as the music cuts out.

And the room goes absolutely wild with cheers.

"Holy shit, Lei!"

"That was incredible!"

"So strong!"

"You're totally going to win!"

I'm still on the floor, propped up against the pole now and laughing as girl after girl comes up to congratulate me. I blush and wave them off, but as I try to catch my breath, I can feel it, the adrenaline zinging through my bones.

I did it.

"Well done, babe," Karen, the owner of the studio, says to me as she extends a hand down to help me up from the floor. She's so tall and strong that I feel like a little pixie next to her — even in my eight-inch competition heels.

"Thank you," I pant. "I'm dead."

"I don't doubt it," she says on a chuckle. "But let me tell you this. If you can do what you just did in here on that stage next month?" She clicks her tongue. "You won't just win first place, you'll scare off any girl in the South Florida area from competing in the same level and category as you ever again."

"Well, that wouldn't be very fun. Then what would I do?"

"Teach."

She says the word so easily, so quickly, that I almost think I imagined it. But when I laugh it off, she just arches a brow.

"You're serious?"

"As a heart attack. I know I would hire you in a heartbeat. Every day I get dozens of emails from new clients. Pole fitness is blowing up, thanks to social media. More and more people want to learn. And honestly, we don't have enough instructors to teach them all."

She hands me a towel when we make it over to the cubbies where all our gym bags are, and I swig my water, considering the offer.

"I never thought about teaching before."

"Well, you're incredibly talented, and strong. You know the sport. You've competed multiple times. And you've been through hardship." She frowns a little at that. Karen is familiar with everything that happened with my last studio.

The memory makes my stomach knot.

"I'm just saying, our clients would be lucky to learn from you. So, if you ever get tired of the competition life, you let me know. And hey," she adds with a shrug. "You'll always be a performer. There are shows and clubs around here just dying to book someone as talented as you are."

I smile. "I think I'd be more apt to teach than to perform."

"Well, I think you could do either. Or both, even, if you wanted to."

"I would take a class from you in a heartbeat," one of the girls chimes in from her pole, and then a chorus of agreement rings out across the studio.

I laugh, waving them off. "Thank you, ladies, but... for now, I just want to get through the competition next month."

They smile and nod, and then get back to the last of their practice. But Karen leans in, grabbing my shoulder before she whispers, "You're going to win."

After a cool down, I've got my bag slung over my shoulder and I'm walking out of the studio. I pull my phone out to see a dozen or so missed texts — mostly from the girls checking in on me.

I know they're worried. After all, I was completely alone on Valentine's Day earlier this week, and I haven't even tried to date since everything happened between me and Brandon. The truth is that I'm not ready. And maybe I will be soon, but right now, I just want to focus on myself.

Besides, the new job is keeping me plenty busy — especially with our launch event in the works.

Tucking my phone away, I dig for my keys and unlock my car in the parking lot. And just as I do, I notice a familiar car driving by.

I stop dead in my tracks at the sight of it — the sleek, pearl white Acura NSX. I'd know that car anywhere, and I'd also know just as well as anyone else that there wasn't another one out there like it.

It's one of a kind.

Which means there's no trying to talk myself out of the fact that Brandon is driving by me.

I can't move, my feet rooted to the cement as I try to see through the dark windows. I know it's useless, though. They're tinted so dark no one can see through them — and on purpose.

He's speeding by, probably not even looking around him at all, just focused on getting home after a long day.

Except suddenly, he slams on his brakes.

The car comes to a squealing, smoky stop right in the middle of the road and a good thirty feet before the stoplight ahead — which is green anyway.

My breath hitches in my throat, heart racing loud in my ears.

Does he see me?

Is he going to turn around?

I'm not sure how long we stay like that — him stopped dead in the middle of the road, me rooted in place.

Both of us watching.

Both of us waiting.

But then a car pulls up behind him, and on this downtown street, it's a one-way.

He doesn't move at first, not until the car beeps its horn. Brandon's car jolts forward, and then he's speeding off again.

There's a chance to U-turn at the next light...

But he doesn't.

When I realize he has no intention of turning around, my stomach rolls, and I shake my head at myself for even thinking there was a chance.

For *wanting* him to turn around.

I finally will my feet to move, and then I climb in my car and slam the door shut, peeling out of the parking lot with as much fury as I can.

Maybe I don't need to wait until I'm ready. Maybe the best way to get over Brandon is, as they say, to get under someone else. Maybe a little romp with a stranger would set me right.

With that theory in mind, I head for the bar.

Skyler

"Well, I think that about wraps it up for this week," I say to the rest of the Kappa Kappa Beta Executive Board while glancing at my watch. "Mandy, send me the proposal for Greek Week before you start the applications for event chairs. And Kimberly, make sure you remind Omega Chi that we're excited to do Spring Break together as usual, but they need to get on board with planning ASAP, otherwise they'll get no say in where we go."

The ladies nod, and then it's a shuffling of papers and a flurry of voices as everyone gathers their things to head out of the KKB house library. I check my watch again, knowing Kip and his crew have already been rehearsing for an hour. If I hurry, I can catch the last half before we go to dinner together.

It's been amazing having Kip back at Palm South.

It feels a little like that first semester we met, except without all the drama. When I'm not tied up in Kappa Kappa Beta events and he's not working on the show, we're tangled up in his sheets, or exploring the city together, or spending early mornings out on the water. We're together practically every minute we can be, and I don't miss my "alone time" even a little bit.

I had enough of that over the last semester of us being apart to last me a lifetime.

To say I'm thrilled that I don't have to jump on a five-hour flight just to spend a few stolen days with him is an understatement. And since we're only promised this semester and the summer together, I'm going to make the most of it.

I toss my backpack in my room before jogging down the KKB house stairs two at a time, careful to be extra quiet when I go by our house mom's room so she doesn't come out and ask me a million questions like she loves to do. As soon as I'm on Greek Row and headed toward the auditorium, my cell phone rings.

"Hey, Lei," I answer.

"I'm broken."

I chuckle, waving at a few Omega Chis as I pass them on the sidewalk. "I highly doubt that. I know you well enough to know nothing can break Ashlei Daniels."

"Well, I would have agreed with you before what happened Friday."

"Oh, do tell."

She sighs dramatically. "So, I was coming out of the studio that evening, and I see Brandon's car. It completely fucked me up, Sky. I just stood there awkwardly watching him drive by."

"Oh, babe. I'm sure he didn't see you."

"He slammed on his brakes and froze in the middle of the street for a good sixty seconds."

I grimace. "Okay, so maybe he *did* see you. Did he get out?"

"No! That's what was even weirder. He stopped, and I know he saw me, and I know he saw that I saw *him*. But he just stopped in the middle of the road and then when cars started coming, he sped off. No call, no text, nothing."

"Ouch."

"So I went out."

"Oh?"

"And that's when I realized I'm broken. Because I went to one of my favorite bars, Sky, and I looked good, I felt good, but I..." She sighs again. "I wasn't attracted to a single person in there. Guy, girl, it didn't matter — everyone sucks in comparison to Brandon." She pauses. "I don't think I can have one-night stands anymore."

"Oh, Lei..."

"Don't," she says, and I can almost see her holding her hand up, that beautiful face of hers scrunched up in discontent. "Don't pity me. Just fix me."

I chuckle on a sigh. "Well, first of all — you're not broken. You're *healing*, my love. And those are two very different things."

"Healing is awful."

"It is," I agreed, remembering the pain easily. I was lucky to be happy and on the other side of everything that Kip and I went through, but I'd never forget what it felt like to be in the middle of it all. "Unfortunately, about the only thing that is going to help you is time. And staying busy, which I already know you are. Don't worry about trying to date someone else, or even just have sex with them. Right now, the best thing you can do is focus on yourself and just let each new day slowly erase that pain until you're *truly* ready to let someone else in."

Ashlei is quiet for a long while before she whispers. "And if that day never comes?"

"It will," I promise her.

"I don't want to hurt anymore," she says, and I can hear the emotion strangling her as she holds it all in. "I don't want to think about him."

I sigh, tugging on the door to the auditorium. There are students lining the halls, gathered in groups hunched over laptops or rehearsing. "You may always think about him, Lei, but soon, it won't be all the time. It will be every once in a while, and it'll be memories that bring a smile to your face, because you'll be thankful for the time you shared together — even if it didn't last. But for now, just trust me when I say that every new day you get up and go to work and go to the gym and make it through, you're one step closer to not having him occupy every waking minute of your thoughts."

"I can't wait for that day."

"It'll come," I promise again. "Until then, I think a girls' night is in order. Why don't I come over after you finish up at work tomorrow?"

"Please. I need tequila and hair pets."

"Lucky for you, those are two of my specialties." I smile as I round the corner at the end of the hallway that will lead me to where Kip and his crew are meeting today. "I'll text you with a time."

"Thanks for talking me off the ledge."

"Love you, Lei."

When the line cuts out, I use the camera on my phone to make sure my hair and makeup aren't a complete disaster after the long Monday I've had. Then, I push through the doors and smile when I find Kip leaning against a table with a half-eaten box of pizza on it. His glasses have slipped down to the edge of his nose as he studies what I imagine is the script in his hands, his brows are furrowed together, and his blond hair looks windblown even though I know he's likely been inside most of the day.

My little director.

Everyone in the room looks familiar — producers, writers, directors, the like. But as I make my way toward Kip, I frown.

Because Natalia makes it to him first.

I didn't even realize she was in the room, and when I do, I find myself frowning even more. From what Kip explained to me last night, today would be mostly working on finalizing the shots list and getting applications in for filming permits. They aren't supposed to start shooting until next week.

So why is Natalia here?

And *why* are her glittery fingernails touching my man's arm?

She smiles, making some comment as she leans against the table beside him. I don't like that she touches him at all, but the fact that she lets her hand linger over his forearm for at least thirty seconds makes me want to gouge her eyes out. And the little smile, the batting of her lashes as she laughs at something he said?

It's enough to make me see red.

Before I take another step, I force myself to take three deep breaths. I shake my head at myself, at the jealousy coursing so strongly through my veins. It's hard not to get this way after everything Kip and I have put each other through, but I'm older now — more mature.

More *secure* in our relationship and the fact that I know Kip only has eyes for me.

So what, Natalia is here. She's probably helping with something on their pre-production checklist. And so what, she touched his arm. Maybe she's flirty. Maybe she's trying to butter him up so she can get a good recommendation letter for when she goes out to Los Angeles, herself.

Do they even do recommendation letters in film? I have no freaking clue.

Regardless, she's not a threat.

And treating her like one would be a mistake.

Smile firmly in place again, I make the last of the trek across the room. Kip looks up from his script when I'm roughly ten feet from him, and that brilliant smile of his that I love so much spreads like butter across his perfect face.

"Well, aren't you a sight for sore eyes," he says, setting his clipboard down on the table behind him. Then, he's pushing off from where he was leaned against it, and in the next breath, I'm in his arms.

"Hey, you," I whisper, and I focus on squeezing him tight, on returning his kiss with as much gusto as he gives it.

And on *not* sending eyeball death lasers at the girl he hired to play me in his show.

"Am I running late again?" he asks, checking his watch.

"No, no, I just wanted to come by and see how it was going." I smile. "An extra hand, if you need it."

"Trust me, I've been offering all day," Natalia says, beaming at me.

I bet you have...

"Natalia," I greet with a smile I hope doesn't look as fake as it feels. "Nice to see you again."

"You, too!" She nods at Kip. "Your man here is a workaholic. A bit of a control freak, too."

He gives her a playful glare. "It's my first baby, okay? So I'm a little possessive. Sue me."

"No way! Then I wouldn't get paid." She winks at him, and then her beautiful blue eyes find me. "I'll leave you two be. Kip, let me know if you want me to swing by the library to follow up on the permit."

Kip makes a face. "You wouldn't mind?"

"Are you kidding?" she asks, hopping down from where she was sitting on the edge of the table. Then, her stupid hand is reaching out to touch his arm again. "I told you, I'm happy to help."

He breathes a relieved sigh. "Thank you. It would be one thing off my list today."

"I'm on it." She squeezes his arm, and then her smile is aimed at me again. "See you around, Sky."

"See you."

I keep my smile in place as she walks away, all the while telling myself it's not worth it to tell her she is *not* allowed to call me Sky.

That's reserved for friends.

And I can already tell she is *not* one of those.

Listen, I *know* I sound crazy. But being a girl myself, I know girls. I know the manipulative, sneaky games we play. And I know the way Natalia is looking at Kip and what she'd do if he gave her so much as a yellow light instead of a red one.

"I didn't realize Natalia was joining you today," I said when she was gone, turning my smile to Kip.

He shrugs. "She just showed up and started helping. She seems really eager to be on the project, which is refreshing, if I'm honest." He chuckles then. "Then again, I'm sure she's just trying to get a foot in the door with a future UCLA grad."

"*And* future hot film director in LA," I add, wrapping my arms around his neck. But then I frown. "You know I can help, too. I've offered."

"I know, baby," he says, pressing his lips to mine. I want that kiss to last forever, but he breaks it with a smile as he slips his arms around my hips. "But you're president of the top sorority on campus now. Remember? You've got plenty on your plate. Besides, I've got this all under control."

I return his smile. “Okay. But don’t be afraid to call on me, if you need me. Alright?”

“You got it. Now,” he says, shifting so I’m under his arm and we’re walking toward the door. “I think it’s time for the director to take a break.”

“Oh, yeah?” I arch a brow. “Need a quick stress relief, Mr. Jackson?”

He smirks, leaning in to whisper in my ear, “I really, *really* do. Think you can help?”

My eyes flick to Natalia, and just like I knew I would, I find her staring at me and Kip as he drags me out of the auditorium.

“Trust me, I’m the only girl for the job,” I whisper back, sucking his earlobe between my teeth.

He shivers, biting his lip and murmuring something to one of his writers about taking a fifteen before we push through the door. And I know Natalia is still watching, that she’s wondering just how much competition she’s got.

So before the door shuts behind us, I grab his ass for good measure.

Adam

"What's wrong, Prez?" Bear chides, giving me a cocky grin as he dribbles the basketball. "Tired already?"

I'm bent over, hands on my knees, preparing to guard him again while sweat is pouring off my forehead and dripping from my hair down to the cement.

"Not too tired to block this next shot."

Bear grins even wider, and then he's dribbling the ball back and forth, between his legs, around his back before he breaks away and drives toward the basket. I stay on him the entire time, and when he goes up for the shot — a little jumper not too far from the hoop — I jump with all my might and sling my hand up into the air to block it.

Except I don't.

And when the ball swishes in the net, Bear hoots and hollers in a victory loop as I stand there staring at the hoop with my hands hanging on my hips.

"Tough luck, kid," Bear says, ruffling my hair as he passes me.

I shove him off with a laugh. "You have to admit, for someone who's never played on a team, I didn't do too bad keeping up."

"You did alright," Bear concedes. He jogs to the side of the court, grabbing a water out of the small cooler we brought with us and tossing one to me, too. "Your shooting isn't half bad. It's your ball handling and defense skills that need work."

"Probably too late for me to go pro," I tease, uncapping the water and taking a healthy swig.

We're not even out of February yet and Florida is fucking hot again. With only a few whispy clouds in the sky, the sun has been beating down on us for the last hour while we played. I already know I'll have a gnarly tan line where my basketball shorts hide my hips down to my knees.

And the sock tan. Oof.

Still, with it only being in the low eighties, it's one of those days you can't help but take advantage of. Sooner than we think, it'll be hot enough to fry an egg on this court, and the last thing we'll want to do is be outside for more than thirty minutes unless it's at the pool or the beach.

Bear plops down at the edge of the court, balancing his elbows on his knees as he looks around at the other students playing at various hoops. Water in hand, I lower down next to him, taking another swig.

"I feel like I can tell which ones are freshmen just by looking at them," Bear says, nodding toward one of the smaller groups of guys playing.

"How so?"

"They still have hope in their eyes."

I chuckle, setting my water aside and leaning back on my palms. "Hard to believe this is our last semester, isn't it?"

"Impossible."

"I still remember my orientation." I chuckle. "My aunt was so worried about me staying on campus for the weekend. She was worried I'd party too much."

"At least you had someone who gave a shit. My mom was so blazed out of her mind, I don't even think she realized I was gone until my sophomore year."

I frown. "How's that going, her being back in Pitt?"

He shrugs. "Honestly, I haven't thought much about it since I came back from break. She was good when I was there, and she and my little brother moved into a little apartment. I think if there was anything wrong, he'd let me know. Besides," he adds, taking a drink of water. "I've had other things occupying my mind."

"Job hunting?"

He laughs at that. "I wish it was something that simple."

I nod. "Ah. Must be a girl, then. I was wondering if you were working off some pent-up aggression on me out there."

Bear doesn't say anything, just takes another drink of water.

"You going to tell me who she is?"

"No."

"Okay," I laugh. "Want to talk about why she's driving you mad, then?"

He sighs, shaking his head. "It's my own damn fault I'm in the situation I'm in. I was too stupid to realize how I felt about her until it was too late."

"Hmm," I muse. "I'm very familiar with that predicament."

Bear tries to smirk, but it falls short. "Did you ever think it would be best to give up?" he asks, looking at me. "Did you ever think to leave Cassie alone, to let her be with Grayson and just trust that you weren't the one for her?"

I inhale a long breath. "There were times I wondered, times I thought maybe I was causing her more pain than anything else. And sometimes, that was true." I pause. "But there was always this... *attraction* between us. Not just physical, but magnetic, chemical, all-encompassing. I knew when she was in the same room before I even saw her. And whether I was with someone else or she was, it didn't matter. If she was there, my eyes were on her."

"Creep."

"Tell me about it."

Bear smiles, his eyes drifting across the court again. "I think she's happy with this guy she's dating now, but I can't fight the feeling that he's wrong for her. I just feel like... like he's going to hurt her." He swallows. "And she's been through a whole lifetime of hurt already."

"You want to protect her."

He nods.

"Well, I'll tell you what I learned the hard way — you can't. She's going to make some choices, some mistakes, that will drive you insane to watch. But she has to have the space to make her own decisions, and you have to decide if you want to be there at the end of whatever path she chooses."

"What if she chooses him?"

"Then you're her friend."

"And if I can't be her friend?"

"Then you should walk away from her now."

He lets out a long, slow breath. "I don't like either of those options."

"So, fight for her."

"It's not that easy."

"It is. Trust me, it really is. You can make every excuse in the book for why you shouldn't go after her, why you should let her be. But if she's this ingrained in your thoughts?" I shrug. "You'll never be able to sleep again until you know you gave your all fighting for her."

"I think it has to be smoother than that."

"Oh, I didn't say you don't have to play a few games," I add with a smirk. "If she's with this guy now, let her be with him. Chances are it's something she needs. But... be there for her, too. And if you haven't told her how you feel yet..." I shrug. "Might be time."

"Ugh."

I smile.

"I take it from the way you asked if I was worried about job hunting first that you are?"

"Nice subject change," I tease, but then I sigh, reaching for my water again. "It's just weird. I knew this day would come, but it always seemed so far off. And now that it's here..."

"You don't feel ready."

"I feel ready for work. But I don't feel ready to leave Cassie and be in a long-distance relationship after all it took for us to finally be happy together."

Bear frowns, confused.

"I'm thinking of applying to be a Field Executive for Alpha Sig."

"Whoa," Bear says, and then he gives me a genuine smile. "Man, you'd be great at that."

"That's what Cassie said, too, but she doesn't realize that if I get the job, I'll be sent to whatever university they choose. And out of all the med schools she's applying to, the closest I'd be to her in the most ideal situation would be two-hundred-and-thirty-five miles."

Bear whistles.

"Yeah," I say, grabbing my t-shirt and mopping up the sweat on the back of my neck with it. I let it hang over my shoulders when I'm done. "It just feels stupid, to make a career decision that will take me away from her like that."

"Hey, listen to me. You and Cassie have been through a lot of shit — much, much worse than this. So what, if you get sent to a university in another state while she's in med school? She'll be in *med school*, man." Bear looks at me with wide eyes and arched brows. "Do you know how busy she's going to be?"

I sigh.

"She's not going to have time to do much else than study, *especially* once she gets to clinicals." Bear shrugs, then. "If anything, this is the perfect timing for you to do this job. You know as well as I do that most Field Executives only hold the position for a few years before they move on. So, go for it. You and Cassie can both focus on yourselves while still being together. And hey, it'll make it that much more exciting when you get to see her."

I chew my cheek on a nod. "You do have a point."

"Just apply," he says, clapping me on my shoulder. "And if you get in, then you talk with Cassie and you make a decision *together*." He shakes his head as he stands and offers his hand down to me. "Why do you always make things more complicated than they need to be?"

"Oh, and I'm alone in that?" I ask as he helps me stand.

He narrows his eyes. "Shut up."

I laugh just as he passes me the ball, catching it at my stomach with an *oomf.*

"Let's go. First to twenty-one," Bear calls, and then he's jogging back to the hoop.

***

Later that night, Cassie is giggling while we watch her favorite show between study sessions. She's leaning against the wall with neon-colored cards scattered all over my bed, three different textbooks open, and her hair tied up in a messy bun while I sit against the headboard with my laptop on my thighs.

As I watch her, my stomach twists in warning, heart already aching at the thought of not being this close to her — close enough to walk down the street to her house, close enough to have her in my room every night, close enough to hold her, to touch her, to kiss her, to be there on the bad days and make sure she's celebrating all the great ones, too.

"You okay, babe?" she asks when she catches me staring at her.

"I love you, Cassie McBee."

She smiles, leaning over the pile of study papers long enough to press a kiss on my lips. "Love you more, Adam Brooks."

Then she's laughing again, and I'm staring at the completed Field Executive application on my laptop, mouse hovering over the *send* button.

EPISODE 3

Jess

"Wait, really?!"

There's a chuckle on the other end of the line, and even though I can't see him, I can imagine Kade's sexy-as-hell grin and it makes me want to jump through the phone and right into his pants.

"Really, really."

"Kade Brewer. President of Alpha Sigma." I smirk. "I like the sound of that."

"Well, don't become too fond of it just yet. I have to run for the position first. And then I have to win."

"Which you will."

"You sound like Adam."

"You know, I used to think that kid was pretty dumb, but turns out, he's a genius. They couldn't pick anyone better to step into his shoes once he graduates."

"Wow. J-Love being sweet. This is new."

"Come over and I'll show you just how *sweet* I can be."

I bite my lip, because there are *many,* many ways I could show him, and just thinking of a few makes me squeeze my thighs together against the pussy tingles. I haven't seen Kade since Valentine's Day, which might be a new record for us. But he's had his hands full with classes and fraternity events, and I know all too well how hard that can be to balance on its own.

Let alone adding in a girlfriend who lives thirty minutes away from campus.

"I wish I could," he says with a longing sigh that lets me know he means it. "Adam actually wants me to help with tonight's pledge event. Since we're swearing these guys in soon, that's twenty-nine more votes I'll need to win over."

"Already hot on the campaign trail," I muse, hopping up from where I'd been reclined on the couch. I head to the kitchen, pulling down a wine glass and a bottle of pinot grigio. The sun is already beginning to set, casting the bay in a watercolor swirl of pinks and yellows.

"Well, that's why I wanted to talk to you... before I decided." He pauses. "If I do this, I'm going to be busy. Busier than I already am. And you know that means less time for... us."

"Hey, stop it right now. I'm the last thing that should be worrying you. I mean, I'm a college graduate. I'm busier now than I ever have been."

As I say it, I wrinkle my nose at the job application abandoned on my laptop across the room. So what, I didn't have a job offer yet? So what, I'm still living off my dad's money and pretending like I could afford this insane condo on my own?

Kade doesn't need to know that.

"I just don't want you to feel like I'm not prioritizing you."

"Tell you what," I say, pouring the wine into my glass. As I do, Erin bursts through the front door, and by the crazy bird's nest of hair tied on top of her head and the bags under her eyes, I can tell I'm not the only one who needs wine.

I pull down another glass, nodding to her to sit on the couch.

"Next time I see you, you can show me just how much of a priority I am to you."

"Mmm, I like the sound of that." Somewhere in the background, I hear a deep voice call his name. "I need to run. I'm sorry I can't talk longer."

"Stop apologizing and go win a presidency. I can't wait to be your First Lady."

He chuckles. "You going to wear a pearl necklace?"

"Only if you give it to me... while I'm on my knees."

Kade groans at the same time Erin gives me an *eww* grimace from the living room.

I laugh.

"Don't give me a boner before a fraternity event," Kade says.

"Too late, huh?"

"Devil woman."

"Byeee, sweetie." I make some kissy noises and then end the call, leaving my cell phone on the counter as I grab both freshly filled wine glasses and carry them into the living room.

Erin takes the one with the heaviest pour, and in three gulps, half of it is gone.

My eyes widen as I take the seat next to her. "Bad day?"

Her brown eyes look almost black when they find me in a deadpan expression.

"What happened?" I ask with a chuckle.

She shakes her head, settling into the plush couch with her feet tucked under her and balancing her wine glass on her knee. "Just a long day at school."

"Mm-hmm," I say, taking a sip from my own glass. "What else?"

"That obvious, huh?"

"I'm sure law school is a total drag, but the greasy heap of hair on your head tells me this is guy related."

Erin had let her head fall back against the cushion, but at my assessment, her neck snaps up, her eyes wild when she looks at me. "How the hell could you possibly know that?"

I shrug. "It's my gift. Now," I say, spreading my hand over the couch. "Tell me what happened."

With a sigh and another big swig of wine, Erin tells me about her Valentine's Day with Gavin. It seemed to have gone off perfectly... until the end of the night, when he stopped short of having sex with her. She goes on to tell me that since that night, which was almost two weeks ago now, he's been acting weird, and they haven't hung out other than catching lunch between classes the other day.

Ouch.

"Okay, first of all," I say, holding up my pointer finger. "What kind of asshole doesn't trip over himself at the chance to have sex with you? I mean, *look* at you." I gesture a hand over her body, but then wrinkle my nose. "Okay, well, maybe you're not a sex kitten today, but on a normal occasion?" I scoff. "I've seen grown ass men ready to leave their wives and sell everything they own for a shot with you."

Erin snorts. "I highly doubt that. But regardless... he just said he wants to move slow."

"You've been together for, what... four months now?"

"About," she says. "Depends on what you consider the point we got together."

"Doesn't matter." I shake my head. "You went on a freaking international trip, for God's sake. The fact that you didn't fuck *then* is a miracle. But now?" I take a sip of wine. "And, furthermore, that he's making it *weird* now? Being absent? I don't know, Erin. I don't like it."

Her mouth pulls to one side, and she picks at the cuticles of the fingers holding her wine glass. "There's more to it."

"What more could there possibly be?"

Her eyes flick to mine then, but she pulls them away quickly. "It's complicated. But I guess what I'm saying is I understand why he chose not to that night, but just... I don't know why he's been so distant lately. I'm worried I fucked it up."

"If you fucked it up by wanting to sit on his cock, then I hate to break it to you, but the man is gay."

Erin laughs. "Trust me. He is very much *not* gay."

"Then, he's stupid."

"Jess."

I throw my hands up. "Look, I'll leave it alone if you want me to. It would probably help if you told me the whole story," I add with a pointed look. "But as it stands? If he rejected you, then started acting differently and texting you less, calling you less, *seeing* you less." I take a deep breath. "Those are red flags, Ex. That's fuck-boy behavior."

She frowns, sinking back into the cushions. "But we didn't even fuck. That's what's weird about it."

"You guys need to talk."

"We do," she concedes with a sigh. "But tonight, I just want to finish that bottle of wine, heat up a frozen pizza, and watch a thriller."

I laugh at the last part.

Then, her big brown eyes are on me, lashes batting. "Will you join me?"

My eyes flick to the application on my laptop, and though I know it's not very adult of me, I reach over and close the lid with a *click*.

My bestie needs me.

Reality can wait until morning.

"I'm all yours."

Ashlei

Things couldn't be more perfect.

On this warm February evening in South Florida, a gentle breeze rolling in from the water and brushing my long, curled locks off my neck, it's impossible not to feel proud as I look around at the *Ball & Pen* launch event.

That I planned.

That I coordinated.

That I was one-hundred percent completely in charge of.

And that's going off without a hitch.

At first, I was bummed when we couldn't secure a yacht like I'd envisioned, but everything happens for a reason. In lieu of being on the water, we have a sweeping view of it — plus a dramatic outline of the downtown skyline as the last of the sun sinks over the horizon.

Not only did I book one of the most romantic, intimate rooftops in the city for the event, but my team and I completely transformed it. Dramatic red uplights and canopy-draped silk took what once was just a rooftop with a pool, a bar, and plenty of space to a high-end carnival.

Games of all kinds line the left edge of the pool, except instead of winning a giant stuffed teddy bear, guests could win a cocktail, or a dress rental from the hottest boutique downtown, or a designer watch, or — my personal favorite — a speedy ride in a luxury car across town.

Performers pepper the event space tastefully, everything from drag queens in all their carnival glory to hoopers, Lyra and silks aerialists, and even some of the women I train with at the pole studio.

Deep bass and high-energy lo-fi beats thumps rhythmically through the party, loud enough to dance to, but low enough not to overshadow the conversation. This is the kind of lighting, music, and event space that ignites deep thoughts, gives space for creative work, and illuminates endless possibilities.

I can feel it as I walk around from group to group, introducing myself and my team, checking in on guests and ensuring everyone is having a great time.

And I know the guests can feel it, too.

Jeannie is by my side as I flitter around, clipboard in hand and earpiece tucked inconspicuously in the shell of her ear. Every now and then, she'll tap my shoulder to let me know of a minor issue, ask a question, or let me know of someone's arrival. Otherwise, she's a friendly smile and perfectly timed polite exit at my side.

It's just after eight when I finally get the chance to talk to Mrs. Lambert, who has been tied up with every executive at the event up until this point. She joins me at the east side of the balcony, resting an elbow on the glass railing as she lifts her champagne to her burgundy lips with a smile.

"Ms. Daniels, you completely outdid yourself."

"Too much?" I ask with a smile that tells her I already know her answer.

"I've played host to many events, but none quite as eclectic as this one. If you would have let me in on the planning and told me you were conjuring up a carnival theme, I would have promptly wrinkled my nose and demanded you pivot in another direction. I mean, honestly... *carnivals*?" And just like she said, she wrinkles her perfect nose. "They're dirty and smelly and cheap. But this?" She sighs, looking around the space. "This is magical."

"Mission accomplished."

"To you, my dear," Mrs. Lambert says, lifting her glass to mine. "And the undoubtedly bright future you have with *Ball & Pen.*"

I clink my glass to hers with a smile.

"I'm so glad Brandon Church was stupid enough to let you go," she adds once we've cheersed, chuckling to herself and taking a sip of her champagne. She's completely oblivious to how those words have shocked me still, especially since she's apparently spotted someone across the pool whom she needs to speak with. "Alright, back to the rounds. Let's rendezvous at the office Monday morning before I fly back to Atlanta. I've already had offers to collaborate and there are unhappy clients looking to move their accounts to our firm."

And with a waggle of her brows and a dazzling smile, she's off.

It only takes me a moment to shake off her words once she's gone. If this was me even a year ago, they might have crippled me to the point of not being able to hold it together for the rest of the event. But I've learned a lot in my short life, and one thing I knew for certain was that the show must go on.

And giving power to someone in your past does nothing to grow your future.

Still, even as Jeannie gently touches my elbow and guides me to the next group of guests, I can't help but ruminate on her words.

That rumination grows substantially when I realize Brandon is in the group I'm approaching.

I'm surprised my legs manage to keep working once I spot him. I'm surprised my heart doesn't stop beating at the sight of his warm eyes, crinkled at the edges as he laughs at something the woman next to him said. I'm surprised his brilliant, megawatt smile doesn't steal my breath, that the delicious way his tailored navy suit hugs his shoulders and biceps doesn't make me audibly moan.

He is, in every way, the absolute picture of elegance and power. Strong and confident, enigmatic and sure. It's the kind of aura a king might possess, or a billionaire greeting guests on his private island, or the captain of a championship team.

But I'm holding it together, holding everything steady and confident, myself, even in his midst.

Until the very moment his eyes find mine.

They flick to me easily, accidentally, a casual glance up at the crowd around his little pocket of people as he takes a sip of the amber liquid in his glass. I just so happen to be in his line of vision when he does, and at the sight of me, his hands pause, glass hovering just away from his lips.

I could look away. I could turn to Jeannie and pretend I have something to ask her. I could smile as I pass one group on my way over to his. I could look *anywhere else* than right back at him.

But I don't want to.

I love the way his gaze burns, like a candle flame I can't help but hold my hand over. It's enough to sear my flesh and leave a mark, but it's a price I'll pay to keep this warmth as long as I can.

"Are you going to be okay, talking to your ex-boss?" Jeannie whispers as our heels click along the tile. "I can steer you the other way and avoid them, if you prefer."

I blink, and it's as if that notion snaps Brandon back to reality. He finally sips his drink, and then his eyes are back on the man across from him, and he's smiling like he's been following along the entire time.

"No," I answer confidently. "I've got this."

The small group parts like the sea for Moses when Jeannie and I approach, and everyone is a bustle of greetings and smiles. They congratulate me on a fantastic event, compliment me on the décor and entertainment, and almost immediately, I'm roped into the conversation that was occurring before we came by — how the Super Bowl will be held in Miami next year, and what that will mean for our event industry.

Jeannie and I slide right in, joining the circle and the conversation with ease, and while I chat business with the various executives, I can feel Brandon's eyes on me.

Part of me doesn't want to give him the satisfaction of looking back.

But dammit if I can't help it.

There's a lull in the conversation when I finally peel my eyes up to meet his, and when I do, the muscle in his jaw tenses, his grip tightening around the glass in his hand.

"Mr. Church," I greet with a smile. "It's so lovely that you could join us this evening. I know how busy it must be at *Okay, Cool* with the launch of the work share space downtown."

His Adam's apple bobs hard in his throat, but he manages a smile. "We wouldn't miss it."

I don't miss the *we* instead of *I*, and at that very moment, the woman standing next to him casts a shy smile his way.

Though my heart is sticky and sluggish at the sight, I smile wider. "I don't believe we've met," I say to the woman, extending my hand for hers. She's older than me, but still young enough for me to be impressed that she's at this event, and while she wouldn't capture my attention if I walked past her on a crowded street, she has a girl-next-door kind of charm about her. Her dark blonde hair is pulled back in a tight bun, warm brown eyes friendly and kind, freckles dotting the pale skin of her cheeks. "I'm Ashlei Daniels."

"Oh gosh, I know who you are," she says with flaming red cheeks, but she shakes my hand confidently. "Your reputation proceeds you."

I smile. "Well, hopefully it's a good one."

"Very much so," she says on a breath. "My name is Colleen Sparks. I'm the new lead account manager at *Okay, Cool*. Just moved here from New York."

"Ah," I say with what I hope is a pleasant smile. "My replacement."

The color drains from her face. "Oh, well… I… I, uh…" She looks to Brandon with a grimace like she's said something she shouldn't have, but his gaze is apathetic. He takes a sip of his drink with those eyes burning a hole into the side of my skull.

"We'll have to collaborate sometime," I say to ease the discomfort I've brought to the group. I can almost feel the collective breath of relief when I do. "I love the *Okay, Cool* team, and I know you have talent over there. Together? There's no telling what we could create."

"We'd be honored to work with you," Colleen rushes out.

"If there's time," Brandon says just as quickly, and I can see straight through his forced smile. "It's a busy quarter for us."

Code for: *Don't you dare come back into my life.*

Part of me shrivels up at the rejection, but it's a small part. Sure, I still feel guilty for what I did. And sure, I still love that grumpy man and miss him something terrible.

But I've got the power buzzing under my skin, the kind that can only come from putting on a perfect event and knowing I'm the head bitch in charge, too.

I know I hurt him, but he hurt me, too.

And where I would have stayed to fight for us, he fled.

So no, I don't feel even a little bit sorry when I stand even taller, offer him a pleasant smile and say, "Of course. I understand. Collaboration with the new kid on the block can be scary." I shrug as the group exchanges knowing looks and grins. "But my offer stands, should your schedule clear up at all."

With a smile and a tip of my glass, I excuse myself from the group, then, and it's not until we're on the other side of the pool that I drain every drop of gin from my glass.

Jeannie smirks a little, taking the empty glass from my hand. "I'll refill this." She pauses, arching a brow. "Nice work over there. Mrs. Lambert would be proud."

I just wink at her, and once she's gone, I press a hand to my stomach to catch my breath.

I can feel it still, Brandon's laser-sharp gaze, and when I casually turn to survey the party, I find him staring at me through the gaps in the crowd. Every now and then, someone will walk in front of him or in front of me, somewhere in the way, but all the while, his gaze stays fixed on me.

And it stays that way all night.

No matter where I move, no matter who I'm with, if I look in that general direction, I find those hazel hues locked on me.

So, toward the end of the night, I decide to give him something to stare at.

I know it's juvenile. I *know* I'm playing a game similar to one I would have in college. I'm also completely aware that Brandon is an adult, and it will likely not have the desired effect on him that I'd like.

But I don't care.

I still waltz my ass up to the hottest guy I can find and drag my fingertip down the sleeve of his suit jacket. I still laugh at his stupid jokes and lean in closer when he talks business and draw attention to my lips with every sip of my drink. I still push my cleavage together a little as I find the shell of his ear and whisper *we should go somewhere more private*, and I still let my gaze flick to Brandon's when that man takes my arm in his and steers us toward the exit.

You're doing just fine without me? That's great.

Because *I'm* doing just fine, too.

I don't care if it's partially a lie. In that moment, with the adrenaline and power running through my veins and an incredibly fine specimen pressing his warm palm to the small of my back, it feels true.

And I hope the smirk on my lips as I leave Brandon behind is convincing enough that he believes every bit of it.

Bear

"You just can't go wrong with Key West," Skyler says matter-of-factly.

"I know, but come on — we've *done* Key West. Many times. I think we should switch it up."

Skyler nods. "Fair. The cruise was a hit."

"Again, we've done it. I think we need something... more. Something unexpected."

Skyler's legs are in my lap, both of us sprawled out on a blanket in the back yard of the Kappa Kappa Beta house. It's a beautiful day, sunny and warm, and Skyler has her bikini top paired with her shorts to make the most of it. We've both been busy since school started back — Skyler with presidential duties, me with partying it up my last semester.

And, if I'm being honest, trying not to drive myself insane with thoughts of Erin.

Priorities.

But now, we're down to the wire to hammer out Spring Break details.

"You thinking like international?" Skyler asks, swiping through Spring Break designations on her phone. "We could do Bahamas... or go all out and hit Hawaii."

"Hawaii *would* be cool," I agree, looking through the options pulled up on my own phone screen. "But... expensive, considering we're in Florida. It's basically halfway around the world."

Skyler sighs. "I keep coming back to Key West."

"It's senior year. This is it, Sky. Our last Spring Break."

At that, Skyler looks up at me with a pouty lip and big doe eyes. "I know that, but when you say it... it makes it more real."

"We've got to do it up big."

"Well, if we're there, it's guaranteed to be a shit show."

I laugh. "True. We could always go to Pittsburgh."

"Wanna make out on the roof again, Bear? Because I think my boyfriend might take issue with that."

I bark out a laugh just as my phone screen fills with my little brother's face, all goofy and smiling and sweaty. He sent me the picture last season after they won their conference championship.

"I must have conjured you," I say when I answer the video call. "We were just talking about Spring Break and I mentioned Pittsburgh."

Clayton wrinkles his nose. "Ew. Why on earth would you ever want to come *here* for Spring Break?"

"It was a joke, trust me," I say just as the phone is stolen from my hands.

Skyler pops up to sit on her knees next to me. "Hey, Little Bear!"

"Skyler Thorne," Clayton muses, running his fingers over his chin in appreciation of the view filling his phone screen. "Look at you, hot as ever. That boyfriend of yours still treating you right?"

"Always."

"Well, if that ever changes, you let me know. I'll kick his ass and then sweep you off your feet."

She laughs, sliding her sunglasses down her nose enough to arch a brow at me. "You've really taught him all you know, haven't you?"

I throw my hands up. "Hey, this is all him. Kid's got more game as a high school sophomore than I've had my whole life."

"Still juggling two girlfriends?" Skyler asks.

"Nah, I'm single. Why be tied down when there's so much fun to be had?"

"No arguments here," I chime in. Then, my chest tightens, because Mom walks into the frame behind him.

"Hey, sweetie! Oh, you two look like you're having fun." She smiles, drying her hands on a towel before tossing it over her shoulder and hanging her hands on her hips. She's smiling bigger than she has in years, and she still looks healthy.

Clean.

Which is a good sign.

Even though we made up over break and really worked on us as a family, I can't help that suspicious part of me that sparks to life any time I see her or hear from her. Part of me wants to believe that she's sobered up, that she's here to stay.

The other part of me is waiting for the day Clayton wakes up to an empty apartment and nowhere to go.

"How are you, Mom?"

"Good! Work is going well. And I'm getting to spend lots of quality time with this guy," she adds, smiling down at Clayton as she squeezes his shoulders. "When he's not out causing trouble with the girls, that is."

"Just wait until I turn sixteen and get a car," Clayton says, putting his hands together in prayer. "These girls ain't ready for Clayton Pennington on wheels."

"You better get *yourself* a job if you want a car, little bro."

"Details," he says, waving me off. "Hey, guess what?"

"What?"

"Mom and I are coming to see you for Family Weekend!"

The light on my little brother's face could have illuminated a dark gymnasium, but I can't help the way my stomach sinks at his news.

Skyler gently elbows me out of camera view to snap me back to the moment.

"That's... wow. Really?"

"If it's okay with you," Mom says sheepishly. "I know we didn't really talk about it first. But I booked us flights and a hotel, made sure they were refundable, too." Her smile is sad. "Just in case."

"No, no," I say quickly. "Don't cancel them. I'm happy you're coming."

"Really?" she asks.

I smile and nod, and Clayton throws his fist into the air.

"Yes! I can't *wait* to scope those college hunnies."

"Um, you're still a minor, Little Bear," Skyler reminds me. "Look, but don't touch. Especially if it's one of my sisters. I don't need anyone getting arrested."

"Yeah, yeah," he says. "I'm still waiting on Kip to mess up, anyway."

We all laugh at that.

After a few more minutes of chatting and going over trip details, we end the call, and then Skyler and I are back to planning.

"It'll be fun," Skyler says when I'm silent for a long while. "And if your mom pulls any shit, I'll be here."

"I know," I say, taking a deep breath. "It will be fine. She seems... better. I'm just..."

"Still wary?"

I nod guiltily.

"I think that's normal. She's put you through a lot, Clinton. You don't erase pain and betrayal like that overnight. But hey, at least this way, she'll get to see more of the place that's been your home the last four years. And meet your *other* family."

"Yeah," I agree. With a shake of my head, I start scrolling through Spring Break destinations again. "How's Kip's show going?"

"Ugh," Skyler says, reclining again. She tosses her phone aside, seemingly done with scrolling for inspiration, at least for the moment. "It's going great. He's amazing, as usual, and the whole crew seems inspired by him. They finally started filming after getting all their ducks in a row."

"Why do you sound so angry about it?"

She forces a breath. "Well, I'm ninety percent sure the girl he casted to play me has the hots for him."

I chuckle. "Come on, Sky. You're not actually threatened by some wannabe you, are you? Kip couldn't look at another girl as anything more than a friend if he tried. He's obsessed with you and has been since the first night he laid eyes on you. Or, should I say, the first night he laid a line of tequila, salt, a lime, and his tongue on you."

She flicks me off, but it's with a grin. "I know I'm being ridiculous, but you haven't seen her around him. I liked her the first time we met. Hell, I'm practically the reason she *got* the part. And as soon as she did..." She makes a little notion with her hand that looks like a snake, and the noise came next. "She came right up and bit me in the ass."

"Has she made a move on him?"

"Oh, no — girls aren't that conspicuous." She shakes her head as if I should have known. "But I know the games we play, and I know another player when I see one. I'm not too threatened, but I'm on guard."

"I'm sure she just wants to impress him and make a good show, Sky."

"And *I'm* sure that if she so much as touches my man, I'll rip her hair out." She smiles widely. Then, she wipes away a streak of sweat from her neck. "Ugh. It's freaking *February* and already it's too hot to be outside without a pool nearby."

Her assessment pops an idea into my mind, and I grin, rolling over onto my stomach next to her. "I got it."

"What?"

"Breckenridge."

Skyler frowns. "As in, the ski town?"

"The very one."

Skyler wrinkles her nose. "But it'll be cold. And snowy."

"That's kind of the point," I say with a laugh. "Think about it — we could get cabins with hot tubs, have big firepit parties at night, ski during the day. It'd be different than the usual beach shit — which we do *all the time* anyway, since we live in paradise."

At that, Skyler pops up to rest on her palms behind her. "I actually kind of like the sound of this."

"And I didn't even mention the best part yet."

She arches a brow. "Cute ski bunny outfits?"

"What? No." I shake my head, leaning in to whisper, "*Legal marijuana.*"

Skyler pulls her sunglasses off completely, then, her eyes wide, mouth gaping. "Oh my God, Bear, you're an actual genius."

"Think our brothers and sisters will go for it?"

Skyler grins. "Once we give them our sales pitch? Without a doubt."

"Spring Break Breckenridge, here we come."

With an excited squeal and clap from Skyler, the deal is signed. "Alright, let's talk transportation and lodging. I think we could charter a plane. There would be enough of us. And Jess's dad has some hookups that..."

Skyler goes on, already jotting down a million notes on her phone as her planning nature takes over. But I'm momentarily distracted.

Because on *my* phone is a text from Erin.

Hey, friend. Are you free this weekend?

I type out a yes without even checking my schedule.

Skyler

I was nervous when I was elected president of Kappa Kappa Beta.

I'm sure every girl before me felt the same way, but my anxiety was an acute kind, one born of an unfamiliar sense of dread warning me that maybe I wasn't good enough. I never felt that when I played poker professionally, and I haven't felt it in my job on the casino boat or in my entrepreneurial classes on campus. I hate to say that I'm cocky but, well, if I'm being honest… I kind of am. And honestly? Being that way has paid off for me. I know what I'm worth, what I'm capable of, and I don't shy away from that.

Except when it comes to running the top sorority on campus.

Stepping into Erin's shoes was hard enough on its own, but knowing we had the top GPA, highest attendance and money raised at our philanthropy events, and most active new member class on top of it?

The bar was so high, there wasn't a prayer of jumping over it without a trampoline to help.

That's why I decided to push our annual Kappa Kappa Beta date auction back a couple of months from when we usually hold it. Being that it's our biggest philanthropy event of the semester, I wanted to make sure we did it up big.

And boy, did we.

I held up the tradition of hosting it at Ralph's, of course, but past that, *nothing* is the same. We've got a full band instead of a DJ, uplighting and fairy lights and fresh flowers and a photobooth in the back. On top of my sisters being auctioned off for dates on stage, we also have a live silent auction lining every wall of Ralph's with prizes that range from local restaurant gift cards, to a five-day cruise out of Miami.

We're only halfway through the event and we've already beat last year's total for funds raised for our charity.

Add this to the fact that I just announced a Breckenridge Spring Break, and you could say the ladies of KKB are loving their new president.

When Cassie takes the stage to the roar of applause, I fold my arms over my chest and look around, appreciating the hard work coming together for tonight's event.

I may not have known what I was getting myself into when I took on this position, but by God, I'm figuring it out.

"Alright, next up we have this fiery redhead," Ellie says, gesturing to Cassie. Ellie is one of our newest members from the fall semester rush, and I already know she's well on her way to being on the executive board. She jumped right into the sorority with guns blazing, eager to take on leadership roles.

Cassie stands next to her with a shy smile, holding a giant textbook clutched to her chest with her fake glasses falling down her nose a little bit. She's also wearing a plaid skirt and white button-up shirt like she's at a prep school.

With a little creative directing, I had all the girls dress to play a part this year. We've had the vixen, the party girl, the goody two shoes, and now, the smarty pants.

"Don't let her glasses and biology book fool you, fellas – she's a spitfire and ready for a hot night out on the town!" Ellie says to another roar of applause. "Feast your eyes on the one, the only, Cassie McBee!"

The crowd goes wild, and I throw in a loud hoot and holler of my own, cupping my hands around my mouth like a megaphone. Just as I lower my hands, I'm picked up from behind and spun around as I squeal.

I land back on my feet in front of a smirking Kip, and I narrow my eyes, poking him in the stomach before I leap up into his arms again and press a kiss to his mouth.

"I thought you couldn't make it!"

"Surprise," he says against my smile. Then, with another kiss, he turns me in his arms to face the stage as the bidding starts on Cassie. "Actually, we wrapped up filming today's scenes, and with the auction being one of the next we're working on, Natalia wanted to come get a feel for what it's like."

My body goes rigid at the mention of her name, and I turn over my shoulder to find Natalia wearing a bright smile just behind Kip. She waves excitedly at me, and then her eyes are on the stage, and she's jotting down notes in a notebook as she watches the bidding.

I force a smile. "Great idea."

Natalia grabs Kip's arm from behind, pulling him back and saying something in his ear over the shouting from the crowd. Whatever it is makes Kip laugh, and then he says something back to her, and she laughs, and then shakes her head at me as if to say, *"Gah, this guy, so funny, am I right?"*

I tear my focus from them and turn back toward the stage just as Adam shouts an outrageous two-thousand-dollar bid from the crowd. Cassie's jaw falls open, but no one else is surprised.

That boy is crazy about her.

No one can compete with that bid, so in a snap, Cassie is off the stage and Ellie is bringing out our next sister.

And I'm trying to watch and be happy like I was just moments ago, and *not* focus on the fact that my doppelgänger is standing right behind my boyfriend.

Touching his shoulder.

Whispering in his ear.

Laughing at his jokes.

Making *him* laugh, too.

I crack my neck, annoyed with how jealous I am. I have no reason to be, and yet, I can't seem to shake this gut feeling that tells me Natalia is trouble.

I somehow manage to subdue the feeling as the auction goes on, and when it's intermission, Kip, Natalia, and I take a break in the Ralph's parking lot to get some fresh air.

"Wow!" Natalia says when we're free of most of the crowd. Her eyes are wide as she looks at her notes and then back at the bar. "This really is something. I'm glad we came tonight, because I had no idea how to picture it when I read the script. I mean, guys dropping *thousands* of dollars for a date with a girl?" She shakes her head. "Insane!"

I smile, looping my arm through Kip's. "It's for charity. And besides, most of these guys are using Daddy's money, if you know what I mean."

Natalia chuckles. "Yeah, I definitely don't. I'm here on scholarship and working my ass off just to be here. These kind of kids aren't exactly the type I hang out with."

My neck flares with heat, but I force a breath to subdue it. "Some of them are rich, sure, or come from well-off families. But not all of them. I'm like you, I've had to work to pay my tuition."

"For the record," Kip interjects, holding up one finger. "I outbid that douchebag with my own money just to get you to go on a date with me."

"And *I* paid that douchebag to bid on me because I wanted to make sure you wouldn't win."

"Your plan backfired," Kip says, turning until I'm in his arms.

"In the best way," I agree.

We kiss as Natalia makes a little *aww* sound, and then Kip pulls back with his cheeks flushed. "Excuse me, ladies, I'm going to catch up with some of my brothers. Be right back."

He nods toward a group of Alpha Sigmas on the other side of the parking lot, and then he's off, and Natalia and I are left alone.

"So, did you always want to be in a sorority?" Natalia asks. The way she's poised with her pen and notebook in hand, I feel like I'm having flashbacks to the asshole reporters who used to write about me when I played poker.

Top Ten Hottest Poker Players!

"I don't know about *always*," I say, leaning my back against the brick building. "But, I didn't really have any friends in high school, or feel like I belonged anywhere. So when I came to PSU, it was a chance to start over. I knew I wanted to find a family here. And Kappa Kappa Beta was that for me."

Natalia sighs, shaking her head as she looks around. "It just all feels so foreign to me. Back home in South Dakota, I was always like one of the guys, you know? I hung out with my cousin and his friends, and the few friends of my own I made were all dudes." She frowns. "I've never had any girlfriends."

I fight the urge to scoff, because I have a feeling there are more than a few reasons why she hasn't had many girlfriends.

"You think you might rush?" I ask instead.

"Oh, no," she says quickly, shaking her head. "I'm not one to pay for my friends."

She laughs with the joke, writing something in her notes, but when she looks back up at me and sees the pissed expression, her face goes ashen.

"Oh... shit, Skyler, I didn't mean it like that. I just meant—"

"That you think I pay for my friends?"

She cringes. "Sorry. I shouldn't assume. I just... I don't really *get* all this," she says, waving her hand around. "It all feels fake to me."

I push off the wall, stepping into her space. "I know the feeling, of when something feels *fake*," I say, arching a brow as I eye her up and down. "Or some*one*."

There's a twitch of something in Natalia's eyes then, recognition, like she knows what I'm not saying. She smirks, and then her eyes flick behind me. "Your boyfriend is amazing, you know?" she asks, pulling her gaze back to mine. "He's really going to be something out in Los Angeles." She tilts her head then, fake sympathy washing over her face. "I'm sure you'll really miss him when he goes back and you're still here."

"I'm sure I won't be the only one," I pop off before I can think better of it.

At that, Natalia smiles. "Maybe you can come out to California after graduation and I can show you around."

Confusion furrows my brows.

"Oh, Kip hasn't told you?" Natalia asks, stepping in a bit closer. "I've been accepted to UCLA for the fall semester."

It takes everything in me to show absolutely no emotion at her news, but I know even with a stone-cold expression, there's victory for Natalia in the fact that I have nothing to respond with.

Before I get the chance to figure out what to say, Kip is back, his arm around my shoulder and his lips pressing a warm kiss to my cheek. "Ready to get back in there?"

"Oh, I'll get us a couple beers. I can't wait to hear how much you all raised at the end of the auction!" Natalia says, her smile bright and cheery. She winks at us. "See you two inside."

And then she skips off, and Kip beams like she's his favorite child.

"She's really taking this seriously," he says, shaking his head. "It's not often you find people like her, who are focused at such a young age."

"She's focused, alright," I murmur under my breath.

"Come on," Kip says, squeezing me at his side. "The show can't start without the president."

Natalia is a perfect angel for the rest of the night. She buys me drinks and keeps her distance from Kip, as if now that she knows I'm not too shy to call her on her shit, she wants to make me think I'm crazy by playing completely innocent.

The fact is, she hasn't *really* done anything wrong, or said anything wrong, or put her threat on the table in any substantial way.

But I'm not a fool.

And I'm also not one to fuck with.

They say to keep your friends close and your enemies closer.

Looks like I'm about to have a new best friend.

Jess

This *would* happen to me.

I *would* finally land an interview at one of the top wedding planning firms in the city and then wake up on the morning of the interview sick as a dog.

I *would* go to the interview anyway, hoping they couldn't tell, only to be looked at with wide, bulgy, *don't come too close to me* eyes.

I *would* have what otherwise would have been considered the best interview of my life... and then promptly sneeze and send snot flying into my hand without a tissue anywhere in the room.

Just the memory of my interview this afternoon has me groaning again, and I roll over in bed, sniffling and peeking out from the burial ground I've made with my sheets and comforter. I'm completely burritoed up, save for my eyes, and the hand holding my phone as I scroll through social media.

There's nothing worse than when you've already had a bad day and you scroll through your newsfeed only to discover that everyone else is just out living their best life.

I'm engaged!

I got a new job!

I spent my day on a boat!

Well, good for fucking you.

With a resentful sigh, I pull up the *add a post* tab and snap a picture of me under the covers with my red, puffy eyes and raw nose. I flip the camera off for good measure, and then post it with the caption *being sick sucks*.

So original, Jess.

I don't feel any better once it's posted, even with the flurry of hearts that come in and the waterfall of *feel better* comments. Probably because I know every single one of those people commenting couldn't care less about me in actuality. I'm just another stop on their social media tour, a quick like and obligatory comment, and then they're moving on and I'm forgotten.

Wow, I really am in a sour mood tonight.

A huff of a breath leaves my chest as I scroll a few more times. "Just put the phone down, Jess, and go to bed," I say to myself, and I'm on track to do just that when the little notification lights up in my messages.

When I click them, my heart freezes at the sight of Jarrett's name.

I swallow, opening the message like it's a highly flammable tank of gasoline and I've got a match in my hand.

He sent me a link to my post, and then underneath it, there's just one simple word.

Soup?

My heart picks up its pace from a trot to a gallop, and with a groan, I sit up in bed, staring at his message with two opposing thoughts warring in my head.

No, I should not hang out with my ex-boyfriend.

Well, I'm sick, it's not like I'm going to do anything sexy right now, no matter who's around.

Kade wouldn't like it.

Kade said he's fine with us being friends.

Kade would be here with you if he could be.

But he's not.

It's Jarrett.

It's just *Jarrett, and besides, soup does sound really good...*

That last thought wins out, and I type out a response before throwing my phone across the room like it's a bomb about to go off.

Part of me thinks he won't even really come. I hear my phone buzz across the room and imagine that he said something along the lines of *ha ha, wish I could, feel better*. He's probably out with his friends. He doesn't have time to bring soup to a friend.

But the other, louder part of me reminds me that Jarrett is nothing if not a man of his word.

It's only a half hour later that my phone rings, and the front desk tells me I have a visitor.

"Shit!" I mutter after telling them to send him up and hanging up the phone. I jump up out of bed with my body aching, and then I'm in front of my mirror, staring at the absolute wreck of my reflections. "Double shit."

My half-ass attempt to tame my hair and make myself not look disgusting is subpar at best, but it's all I've got time for before there's a knock at the front door.

I make my way down the hall, and when I answer the door, Jarrett stands on the other side of it looking like trouble with a capital T.

A cool front whipped through South Florida tonight — probably the last we'll have, now that we've tiptoed into the first day of March. And thanks to that, Jarrett's bald head is covered with a black and gray beanie, his tattooed arms shielded by a well-fitted leather jacket, and the dark jeans he's paired it with hug him in all the right places.

Which means I'm thinking *all* the wrong things.

To top it all off, he's got bags full of groceries hanging from his arms and a too-sexy-for-his-own-good smile spreading over his perfect lips.

Jesus Christ, I'm screwed.

Jarrett's eyebrow arches as he takes in the sight of me, and then with that sexy grin still intact, he says, "You look like shit."

I breathe out a laugh as I hold the door open wider, signaling for him to come in. "I feel even worse."

"Symptoms?"

"Congested. Sore throat. Body aches." I sniff on cue when the door shuts behind us. "Generally, feel like I've been run over by a truck."

"Sounds like a virus, alright," Jarrett says, already unpacking the groceries he brought. "Have you taken any meds?"

"Yeah."

His pointed look tells me he doesn't believe me, and when he tosses some cold medicine my way, I laugh.

"Why did you ask when you already knew the answer?"

"Wanted to see if you were still a shit liar."

We share a smile as he continues unpacking the groceries, and I open the medicine he brought, popping two of the nighttime pills.

Jarrett whistles as he looks around the condo. "This is a sweet pad. You live here by yourself?"

"Erin and Ashlei live here, too. They're both out tonight, though — Erin is with her study group, and Ashlei is at the pole studio working on her routine for competition. She said they'll probably all go out after..." I shake my head, taking a seat at one of the barstools at the kitchen island. "Must be nice to not be snotting involuntarily."

Jarrett laughs. "Honestly, I'm just surprised you posted about your situation. Last time I found out you were sick, it was a very different situation."

He cocks a brow as I hold up my hands. "Hey, I didn't want the dude I had major hots for seeing me all disgusting, okay?"

"You also didn't want to admit that you were falling for me."

"Shut up and make me soup."

The laugh that bubbles out of his chest is like music to my ears, a long-forgotten sound that warms my heart like a hot cup of tea. I swallow down the knot building in my throat as I watch him work.

And then like not a day has even passed, we slip into easy conversation.

It's the strangest thing, watching Jarrett Locke work in my kitchen like it's his own. He strips out of his leather jacket and takes the beanie off his head, and I try to ignore the way it makes my stomach tighten to see his biceps practically bulging out of the white thermal he's wearing as he slices and mixes and cooks. But he seems so relaxed and comfortable that before I know it, I feel the same way.

I ask him about his new tattoos, the ones lining his arms that weren't there the last time we were together, and smile when he tells me how he got the one of the American-style fish to remind him to go with the flow. He asks me how the job hunt is going, and I fill him in on my latest embarrassment, making him laugh so hard he has to pause his work in the kitchen to brace his hands on his knees.

Back and forth, question after question, we catch up like two old friends. We talk about school and work, I catch him up on the girls while he fills me in on his work at the Miami branch of the nonprofit so far. We even talk about me and Kade, and he tells me about his short stint dating a girl in Manhattan who turned out to be on the run from a grand theft she'd committed in Nebraska. He'd been in her apartment when they found and arrested her.

The later it gets, the more the cold medicine swims through my system like a tall glass of whiskey. I feel my eyelids getting heavier, my words harder to get out.

"Mmm," I say when we're finally sitting on the couch with a bowl of soup in each of our hands. "Seriously, this is the best soup recipe in the world."

"It's about the only thing I know how to cook well, so thank you."

I smile, sipping on the creamy potato broth. "It's your mom's recipe, right?"

Something passes over him, and he pauses where his spoon is lifted, taking a breath before he answers. "It is."

"I remember the first time you made it for me, and you told me the story..." I frown, stirring my spoon in the soup. "Why didn't you tell me back then that you had brothers?"

I can see it happening, as if in slow motion, all the warmth draining from him, the gates closing, walls going up. He shrugs. "Didn't think it was pertinent information at the time."

"Okay," I concede, because at that point, we hadn't even defined what we were. "But even after we were officially dating... you never told me... I always assumed you were an only child."

"My family life is complicated," he says, lifting his eyes to mine. "My dad is a piece of shit and an addict. My mom died when I was young. I don't have a good relationship with either one of my brothers." He sighs, staring down at the soup in his hands. "And if I'm being honest, I've tried my whole life to grow outside of who I was in that family, to leave that shit behind, and I didn't want it to be part of my story when it came to you."

My heart squeezes painfully in my chest. I know enough to know I'm fortunate to have grown up the way I did, with money and parents who gave a shit. College was the first time I woke up to the fact that not *everyone* has those luxuries. Hell, I used to give Skyler shit for playing poker all the time instead of partying with us, until I found out her situation.

I reach over and squeeze Jarrett's wrist, and when I do, a shiver rolls through me that I hope he can't see. "I get it," I say with an understanding smile. Then, I lean in to whisper, "You just wanted me to focus on the tattoos and general badassery, instead."

"Damn straight," he says, and I feel him lighten with the tease. "These tattoos are my armor."

I chuckle, but as Jarrett takes another bite of soup, a yawn rips through me, so long and strong it makes my eyes water and sends another shutter through me.

Jarrett smirks. "I think someone's ready for bed."

"No, no, I'm fine. Tell me what else you've been up to."

He chuckles, setting his soup aside and standing. He reaches his hand down for mine. "There will be plenty of time to catch up. Right now, you need rest."

I just stare at his hand for the longest time, like it's a wire that I'm not sure is safe to touch or will blow me to smithereens.

"Come on," he ushers, wiggling his fingers.

So, I set my nearly empty bowl aside, slipping my hand into his, and do my best to fend off the blush that heats my cheeks as he pulls me to stand.

Even though he's the one guiding me, I have to tell him which room is mine. He helps me get into bed, and then turns down all the lights, save for the lamp by my bed. I have the corner room, the one with the floor-to-ceiling windows lining two walls, so the city lights stream in even when Jarrett turns off the lamp.

He's sitting on the edge of my bed, helping me pull the comforter up to my chin, and he smiles when I'm settled. "I think those meds are knocking you out."

"I feel loopy," I say with another yawn.

"Good. Hopefully you'll get a good night's rest."

Maybe it's the medicine. Maybe it's the virus. Maybe it's the way the lights streaming in from the windows remind me of the way Jarrett looked every time we'd video chat when he lived in the city. Whatever the reason, there's no way to stop the question that tumbles from my lips.

"Jarrett," I whisper.

"Yes?"

"Why did you break up with me?"

The breath he inhales is stiff, and he looks away from me, out the window. I expect him to say we shouldn't talk about it, that I should get some sleep, but instead, he answers with brutal honesty.

"Because I was a fucking idiot."

The words slam into my chest like an anvil, and I roll my lips together, forcing a swallow and waiting for him to continue.

"I let other people get inside my head. I was just... I was so impressionable, this new fish in the big city, and I thought everyone else knew better than I did. When I told my team about how you were reacting to me working with Jenny, not a single person said you had a right to be upset, that long distance was hard, that I was doing a shit job of being a good boyfriend from afar." His eyes find mine. "Which I was, for the record."

I sigh. "No, you weren't, Jarrett. I was young and sus—"

"Normal," he finishes for me. "You were asking the exact questions I would have been asking in the reverse. But I was so fucking stressed out. We were working all the time, and I forgot I had a life outside of that office, outside of those people. So, when they started talking about how you were young and jealous, how I'd outgrown you... I listened. And they were with me the night I saw that post of you and Greg. They hyped me up, saying how childish it was, how you were playing games and I was above it all and I just... I don't know. Something inside me snapped."

"Nothing happened with Greg," I assure him. "At least... not that night. Not until well after we'd broken up. And even then, it was just a temporary... thing."

"You don't owe me an explanation. I know you didn't do anything with him that night. But I think, in a way, I also knew that I couldn't be what you needed. Not at that time in my life. So, I just..." He inhales another stiff breath. "I let you go."

God, I wish I hadn't taken that cold medicine, because I'm so fucking drowsy I can't even convince myself that I'm not dreaming all of this.

Jarrett brushes my hair off my forehead, his eyes searching mine in the low light coming in from the city. "Get some rest, Jess."

"Wait," I say, reaching for him. "Don't go. Not yet."

He smiles, and I don't miss the way his next swallow is strained. "I'll wait until you're asleep, okay?"

I nod, and then, even though I have a million questions racing through my mind, I succumb to the drowsiness slowly pulling me under.

And I feel him there beside me, staying just like he promised he would.

Maybe I'm dreaming. Maybe the medicine is still making me loopy. But I swear it's not long after sleep takes me that I feel Jarrett lower his lips to press a kiss to my forehead.

But I can't quite make out what he whispers in my ear before he goes.

Ashlei

I never knew numb could be felt so hard.

When you hear someone say they're numb, you think it's this state of nothingness, of insensitivity, of apathy.

But the numbness I feel when I take first place in my category at the pole competition I've been preparing for for months now is an all-encompassing heaviness.

I feel weighed down as I stand on the platform, smiling and thanking the organizers as they place a gold medal around my neck. My arms are too heavy, my head too slow, like I've been drugged or am existing in an underwater hell.

I should be light and airy and happy right now. I should be ecstatic that I hit every move just how I planned, that every trick was executed flawlessly, that my hair and makeup and outfit are on point, that the crowd went absolutely berzerk when I finished.

But I feel... nothing.

Other than a sick longing to call Brandon.

I hate that I can't enjoy this moment because my thoughts are on him, but ever since the launch party, he's been an all-consuming thought. His eyes haunt my dreams, and where I'd felt like I was finally moving on, I now feel like I've taken so many steps backward that I'm no better off than I was the second I left his condo and felt my heart break inside that elevator.

I want to be happy and celebrating my win.

But more than anything, I want to be celebrating *with him*.

I wish he was here. I wish he would have seen my routine. I wish I would have heard his cheers in the crowd. I wish I had his arms to run to right now, that his lips would be on mine as he congratulated me.

I wish he were still in my life.

Period.

"Holy fucking *shit*, Lei!" Jess says, she and the other girls sprinting to me once I'm off the platform. The entire room is buzzing now that the ceremony is done, the chatter loud even over the music the DJ is playing. "I knew you were talented, but I had no *idea* you were that strong."

"You made it look so easy!" Cassie says.

"That move where you were hanging by just your knee pit!" Skyler chimes in.

"No, no, when she hulked herself up and held her entire body to the side like a freaking Olympian! What even was that?!" Erin asks just as excitedly.

I chuckle. "Iron X."

"You literally defied gravity!"

The girls ramble on, hooking their arms through mine and dragging me out of the convention room into the hall. The hotel bar is already crawling with competitors and spectators alike, and even though Jess is still recovering from her cold, she promptly orders us each a shot of tequila.

"To my best friend, Ashlei Fucking Daniels, and her insane badassery that no one else can touch."

"Hear, hear!" the girls all chant in unison, and then we down our shots, grimacing and sucking on a lime to ease the burn.

"Okay, I've decided. We should all take a pole class," Jess declares once her shot is gone.

"Oh my God! Yes!" Cassie agrees.

They're already pulling out their phones to find a day on the calendar that works for all of them when I quietly excuse myself to the bathroom. When I'm in the stall, I finally find a breath, and as if on autopilot, I pull out my phone and tap away until I'm staring at Brandon's contact.

The picture I assigned his number in my phone is one of us on his yacht, the sunshine bright above us as we hold onto each other, swimsuit clad and laughing. I can still remember the day that photo was taken — how effortless it was, the two of us together.

We were meant to be.

Until I fucked it all up.

Tears prick my eyes as I hit the message button, and I type out a long text to him that would make even a middle school girl cringe. It says how much I miss him, how sorry I still am, how I wish on everything that I am that I could take back what happened. It says how I won first place and yet I can't even be happy without him. It says how much I wish he was here.

And as I flush the toilet, I stare at the text with my thumb hovering over the send button.

But I never let it drop.

Bear

Erin looks way too fucking beautiful when I pick her up on Saturday night.

She rushes out the doors of the skyrise building she, Jess, and Ashlei live in, her hair flying back behind her as the breeze hits her cheeks. She's smiling wide and bright as she jumps into the passenger side of my truck, and even with strands of hair sticking to her glossy lips when she turns to smile at me, she's an absolute vision.

It damn near kills me.

"Hi!" she greets, situating her purse by her feet. As soon as she does, she's rummaging inside it. "Before we go anywhere, I have something for you."

"For me?" I smirk, mostly at the fact that she's so goddamn oblivious to how gorgeous she is, and how her simply getting into my truck felt more like her stopping the record of my life mid-song with a dramatic scratch.

When she sits back up, it's with something hidden in her hands, and she bites back a smile as she looks at me. "Close your eyes."

"Okay," I oblige.

"Hold out your hand."

When I do, I feel her place something small and light into my palm.

"Okay. Open!"

I smile at the absolutely hideous crocheted bracelet in my hand. Not only is it made with the worst color combination — burnt orange and shit brown — but it looks worse than the ones elementary girls make.

"Um... thanks?"

Erin laughs. "It's our friendship bracelet, silly. See?" She holds up her wrist, and sure enough, she's wearing one identical to the one in my hand. "I know they're kind of... ugly. But I'm out of practice, and honestly, I think it gives them charm."

I smile, handing her the bracelet and holding out my wrist. "They're perfect."

Erin blushes a little as she ties the thread around my wrist, and then our eyes meet, and I hold her gaze for a long moment as I shove down everything I want to say.

"Alright," I finally declare, putting the truck in drive and tearing my eyes away from Erin and back to the road. "You ready to get your ass kicked in some skeeball?"

"You wish. I'll have you know, I'm the skeeball champion back home."

"Well, you're about to be dethroned."

It's kind of an awkward silence after that as we make our way closer to one of my favorite off-campus hangs. It's a newer bar with arcade games lining every wall and a giant dance floor that usually has a live band playing on the stage above it. When Erin said she wanted to get out of the house, I figured it was just the spot.

"It's kind of weird, isn't it?" Erin asks when I put the truck in park. "Me and you hanging out after all this time."

"It doesn't have to be."

She gives a sigh of a laugh at that. "I'm not sure how it couldn't be." Her little mouth pulls to the side when she looks back up at me. "Clinton, I know I've said it, but I'm sorry for—"

I cut her off by reaching over the center console and grabbing her hands in mine. I pull her to face me, lowering my gaze to meet hers with a smile.

"Stop apologizing. Okay? We've hashed out all of the shit in our past. Yes, we've both been assholes along the way, but I don't want to think about any of that anymore. I just want to hang out with you and catch up and beat your ass in every game inside that bar," I add, nodding toward the building.

Erin laughs, but I don't miss the way her eyes gloss over. "Yeah. I like that plan."

"Good," I say, and then I realize I'm smoothing my thumbs over her wrists where I hold them, and both our gazes fall to the point of contact.

We pull back like a jolt of electricity stung us, and before the awkwardness can seep back in, I hop out of the truck and jog around to open her door.

When we get inside, I head for the bar to get us a couple beers while Erin hits the token machine. We meet at skeeball first, and after a quick cheers, the games begin.

I've seen Erin in many situations — all dolled up for formal, looking hot as sin in a swimsuit on the top deck of a cruise ship, crying in my shower as I hold her together as much as I can, running a Kappa Kappa Beta chapter like a bad ass, pouring her heart out over a candlelit dinner.

But I've never seen her like this.

I've never seen this bright, unbreakable smile. I've never heard this carefree bubble of a laugh.

And yet, underneath it, I can sense something is off.

That's how it's always been with me and Erin. We're in tune in a way that no one else is. Sure, with Skyler, she's one of my best friends and I know when she's hurting. But Skyler is also open with me when it comes to what's going on in her life. I'm usually one of the first she runs to, and she's one of the first I go to, too.

But with Erin, it's like no matter how we try to hide the truth from each other, it's always there, buzzing under the surface like a live wire.

We can't ignore it.

We can't run from it.

We can't let each other go.

"So, how are things going with Gavin?" I ask as casually as I can after Erin absolutely wrecks me at a round of air hockey.

She's still a little out of breath when she plops down at one of the high-top tables in the center of the bar, and I take the seat across from her. "Really good," she says with a smile.

I wait for her to continue, but that's all I get.

I arch a brow, taking a sip of my beer and trying again. "He was busy tonight?"

"He's been busy a lot lately," she says with a sigh, and her eyes fall to where her hands are around her beer. "I think... I think I might have scared him a little."

"How in the world could you possibly scare anyone?"

She chuckles. "Well, in case you missed it over the years, I'm a hot mess with a pretty impressive load of baggage for a girl who's fresh out of college."

"You don't have baggage."

"Come on, Bear," she says. "I've had an abortion, been gang-raped, fucked over my closest friends under the guise of self-therapy, and I've lied to even those I love more than anyone in the world just to save myself the pain of telling the truth."

Her eyes find mine with those last words, and I feel the full weight of them — the full weight of everything that's happened between us.

"Sorry for putting it all so bluntly," she continues. "But therapy has really helped me see that running from my past, or hiding it, or lying to myself or anyone else about it doesn't do anything but hurt me. So, I'm embracing it. All of it. It's all led me here, and... all things considered?" I smile. "I'm pretty happy."

"I'm glad you're in therapy," I say earnestly. "And I'm glad it's helping. But... I still don't understand how you could scare Gavin. Isn't he in therapy, too?"

"I think everyone should be in therapy," she says with a laugh, and I have to chug half my beer to keep myself from boiling over at the memory of the fight Gavin and I had over this same topic at Friendsgiving.

Purely because I was pissed when I saw him there with Erin, if I were being honest with myself.

"I just... I might have rushed some things between us..." She bites her lip, shaking her head. "I feel weird talking about this with you."

"Why?" I reach over, grabbing her hand and giving it a squeeze. "Come on, Ex. It's me. You don't have to feel weird or sugarcoat anything."

"I know, but..."

"Just spill it."

She chuckles. "Alright... well, on Valentine's Day, I wanted to... um... to go all the way with him."

Her cheeks flush so furiously that I chuckle a bit despite the way my stomach bottoms out at her admission.

"But he stopped us. And really, he had good reason. He's being respectful to what I've been through, and he knows I haven't... um... you know... with anyone else... since..." She waves her hand around. "Anyway, so he stopped it, and we cuddled and everything, and I felt fine when I left the next morning. But ever since then, he's been distant. I mean, I haven't seen him for more than a mid-day lunch."

God, I want to punch him.

I want to literally find him and knock him the fuck out.

But then again, I kind of want to shake his hand and thank him.

Because although I don't like the thought of him so much as laying a finger on Erin, I respect the hell out of him for taking things slow. Even when Erin said she was ready, he knew she wasn't.

I still hate him, but I'm thankful to him at least for that much.

I force a breath, taking a sip of my beer before I say, "Well, I know it hurts to be rejected like that. Even if it was for good reason. And I don't like that he's being kind of distant, but it might be that he has something else going on, something entirely unrelated."

"He has been really busy with school," she admits. "It's his last semester in the graduate program."

"I'm sure that's very intense."

She sighs and nods, but I can see the hurt on her face as she takes a sip of her beer.

"Erin, look at me."

For the longest time, she keeps her eyes on her glass, but then those warm brown irises finally find mine.

"Gavin is a good guy," I say, even as my chest tightens with the words. "He cares about you. I could see that much after just one hour at Friendsgiving, and I saw it again when I ran into you downtown. And as much as I know it hurt, I'm glad he turned you down."

Erin laughs a little, though her eyebrows pinch together. "Well, that's kind of harsh."

"No, no," I say with a laugh of my own. I reach over to grab her hand, folding her fingers over mine. "I just mean that he's right. You have been through a lot, and I think taking it slow is the best move for both of you. The fact that he gives a shit about you enough to put your emotional well-being ahead of his hormones is pretty fucking impressive, honestly. Because he's a man, Erin, and being one myself, I can tell you it took a *lot* of willpower to stop in that moment." I pause, swallowing. "Especially because you are the most goddamn beautiful woman who has ever existed."

Erin's expression softens at that, and her eyes flick back and forth between mine. "You think I'm beautiful?"

"I do," I say, throat tight. "And the craziest thing is that as stunning as you are, your beauty is the least interesting thing about you."

Her eyes flood with tears, but they don't fall, not even when her hand squeezes mine.

"You're sensational, Erin. In every way. And Gavin knows that, too."

Erin blows out a long breath at that, and to my dismay, she pulls her hand from mine so she can use both to wipe her cheeks before the tears fall too far. "God, I'm crying in a bar."

"Don't worry, I'll tell anyone who asks that I just kicked your ass in air hockey."

"Except it was *me* doing the ass-kicking."

"Do you want a cover story or not?"

She chuckles, wiping the mascara from under her left eye before she smiles at me. "Thank you, Bear. I'm actually really glad we talked about this. I tried talking to Jess about it, but it wasn't the same. You… you know more about me than anyone else in this world, I think. You've been here through so much."

"And I'll always be here," I promise.

"Thank God for that."

Erin and I share a smile, and then I stand, grabbing our empty cups. "I'll refill these. And, hey, a word of advice?"

She nods.

"Tell the girls what happened to you. Tell them everything." I shrug. "I know it's hard, and I know you're afraid of them judging you. But I promise, they won't. They love you. And as much as I mean it that I'll *always* be here, there are going to be times when you need your girls. And they can't help you if they don't know the whole story."

Her eyes well up again, but she swallows back the emotion and gives me another smile. "Go get our refills so I can beat you at the next game."

"Ha! Don't bet on it, Ex. I don't lose twice."

I give her a wink, but before I can turn, she's up out of her chair and in my arms.

She wraps herself all around me, her arms around my neck, hair in my face and body flush against mine as I stand there stupidly holding our empty cups.

"Thank you, Bear. Really." She inhales a long breath and lets it go just as slowly, still holding me tight. "I love you."

I go rigid at her words, at how fiercely I want to throw these cups across the room, take her face in my palms, and kiss her breathless until she feels just how much I love her, too.

But she's not mine to kiss.

With a slow breath through my nose, I wrap her in a hug that's not as good as I'd like with the cups in my hands. Still, I hold her, and smell her hair, and close my eyes against the emotion building in my chest.

"I love you, too," I say.

And I do. More than she'll ever know.

When she pulls away with her bright smile back in place, I die a little inside.

Because there's a pit in my gut that tells me I've lost whatever small chance I ever had with this girl, and that I'll never have my chance again. It's likely that nights like tonight — where we hang out as just friends — is the most I'll ever have.

I hate that truth.

I can't stomach it.

I don't know if I can survive it.

But if there's one thing I know for sure, it's that even if it kills me, I'll never leave Erin alone. I can't.

So, I hold onto hope.

Because I'm a patient man.

And for her, I'll wait forever if I have to.

EPISODE 4

Erin

"You're mad."

"I'm not mad," I assure Gavin, hand too tight around my cell phone.

"You sound mad."

"Well, I'm not exactly thrilled that you're bailing on our date night... again..." I sigh. "But I'm not mad. I get it. School comes first. I would do the same if I were in your position."

There's a brief silence, and then Gavin says, "I really am sorry, Erin. I'll make it up to you."

I force a smile. "I know you will. But, for now, you better get going. Tell the group I said hey."

"Thank you for understanding."

"Mm-hmm." *That sounds like you're mad.* "Always. Have a good night."

"You, too."

The line goes dead instantly, and I sigh, letting the phone fall into my lap. I feel stupid now, all dolled up in my favorite faux-leather leggings and a top that shows more cleavage than I'm usually comfortable with. I even slapped on some red high heels and painted my lips to match.

And now, it's Friday night and I have nowhere to go.

My heart squeezes in my chest, the same warning bell that's been ringing ever since Valentine's Day. I know it's a busy semester for Gavin — that was the whole reason we did the trip over break. We knew I'd be busy with my first semester of law school and he'd be busy with his last semester of grad school.

Still, I can't shake the feeling that he's avoiding me after what happened.

Or rather, what *didn't* happen.

Another sigh finds me, and I think about what Bear said, how he assured me that Gavin had my best interests at heart when he turned me down. And while I want to believe that, the bigger part of me screams that there's something wrong with me, that he doesn't want me, that I'm not desirable.

I've been trying to process everything with my therapist, and she's told me it's a great time to throw effort into dating myself. She encouraged me to fill my time when I'm not with Gavin, and to not overanalyze anything he says to me.

Trust him. Take his words for what they are instead of trying to make them mean something else.

As if it's that easy.

I've been understanding, and I've been trying to let go of all the insecurities his rejection brought out in me. But it's hard — especially on nights like tonight, when he bails on our plans last minute.

I'm still sitting on the couch with my phone in my hand when Jess blows through the front door.

"Job interviews are the fucking *worst*," she huffs, slinging her purse over one of the hooks by the door before she promptly kicks off her heels. She plops down next to me with a groan. "I swear, if I have to answer one more question about my strengths and weaknesses, I'm going to pitch myself off our balcony."

I chuckle. "Please don't do that. Someone would have to clean up the mess and that's not fair."

That earns me a smile, and Jess sighs, letting her head loll to the side until she's looking at me. She opens her mouth to say something, but then snaps upright, brows furrowed as she takes in my appearance.

"Damn, Ex," she says with a low whistle. "Gavin is going to come on the spot when he sees your tits pushed up like that."

I laugh, looking down at my cleavage. "The girls do look nice, don't they?"

"I'll say. You've got me questioning my sexuality."

"Well, touch them if you want," I say, flopping back with a huff. "Because otherwise, this entire outfit is going to waste."

"What do you mean?"

I shrug. "Gavin had to cancel. Study group thing he forgot about."

"Ex..."

"I know, I know," I say, holding up my hands. "I don't want to talk about it, okay?"

Jess has to physically bite her lip to keep from asking me more questions, but then she claps her hands together and points a finger up at the sky. "That's it. Adult Spring Break."

I laugh. "What?"

"This is the perfect occasion. I've had a shit day of trying to convince people to hire me. You've been blown off by a stupid boy. And we haven't gone out on the town together in way too long. So, let me get changed, and then we're going to go fuck up downtown like we're on Spring Break."

"But you're not in college anymore. And I'm in law school. Spring Break isn't really a thing."

"Well, tonight it is." She pulls me up from the couch and smacks my ass. "Pack a flask in your purse and cancel any plans you have in the morning. Neither of us is sleeping tonight."

***

Not even three hours later, I'm dancing on a bar stage with a man dressed in lederhosen.

I'm not really sure how we got here. We started with tequila shots at a bar across the street from our condo building, and then we just started hopping from place to place. Every time we'd enter a new bar, Jess would scream, "SPRING BREAK!" at the top of her lungs and then we'd promptly take another shot.

I lost count after the fifth one.

And as silly as it is, two grown ass women bar hopping like we're still in college, it *does* feel reminiscent of Spring Break.

And it's fun as hell.

The bar we're at now has a live band playing German music, and there must be some sort of event because half the bar is dressed like it's Oktoberfest. When Jess screamed our Spring Break entrance and we slammed another shot, we instantly caught the attention of a group of what had to be frat boys.

All of them dressed in lederhosen.

I don't recognize any of them, so I assume they're not from PSU. It *is* Spring Break time, so for all we know, they could be on vacation from Ohio.

Regardless, they bought our next round of shots, and now we're on the stage next to the live band dancing like a bunch of hippies.

"This was the best idea ever!" Jess screams into my ear over the music. Then, she promptly grabs the man in the lederhosen behind her by the suspenders he's wearing and starts dancing like a loon. It would be one thing if she was bumping and grinding on him, but she's doing this weird humping motion with her hips, her tongue sticking out, and there's absolutely nothing sexy about it.

Which makes me love the whole situation even more.

I mimic her, turning to face the guy behind me — who looks no older than nineteen, if I'm being honest with myself. But I don't care. The tequila in my system makes it hard to care about anything, really.

He's wearing this ridiculous black fedora-like hat with a red feather in it, and I pull it off his head and slap it on my own. He tries to grab my hips to pull me in closer for our dance, but I back away with a moonwalk and then promptly start pretending like I'm shopping for groceries around him.

Pick the item off the shelf.

Put it in the cart.

Do a little shimmy.

Repeat.

Jess is laughing so hard at me, she can barely stand straight, and lederhosen man seems intrigued. He starts shopping next to me, and then pulls out the lawnmower dance.

Back and forth, we trade off every awful dance style we can think of. I'm almost out of ideas when I remember one my dad used to do at weddings where he'd grab his ankle with one hand and the back of his neck with the other, and then proceed to pull his knee toward his face on a hop, and then knee back on a hop, over and over. I think he called it the funky chicken? Mom always called it his aneurysm dance.

Regardless, now is the perfect time to whip it out.

I reach for my ankle and get my other hand in place behind my neck, and then in what has to be the worst timing ever, lederhosen boy turns toward me and reaches like he's going to pull me in for a kiss.

But with me mid-dance move, instead of a kiss, he gets a knee to the balls.

He stumbles back with a groan, but in the process, he's grabbed ahold of my hips and is taking me with him. I know he's in pain, which is likely why he doesn't hear his friend's warnings that he's dangerously close to the edge of the stage. There's a windmill of arms and a desperate attempt from me to try to keep us balanced, but it's no use.

We tumble off the stage to a chorus of *ooohhh!*

The first thing I realize is that I should be in more pain than I am after falling off a stage. The second thing I realize is that the reason I'm *not* in pain is because lederhosen boy broke my fall.

Jess gets to me first, and she's asking me if I'm okay through laughter so strong it's got her eyes all welled with tears. Once we're both standing, my lederhosen man groans, his buddies rushing over to make sure he's alright.

"I think that's our cue to get out of here," Jess says through another spout of laughter, and she's already tugging me toward the door.

"Oh wait, I still have his hat!"

"Keep it," she says, tapping the black fabric on my head. "Souvenir."

We link arms and sprint out of the bar and down the block, laughing the entire way. When we're a few doors down, Jess tugs me into the next bar, one much quieter and low key with far less patrons.

"I can't do another shot, Jess. I'll throw up," I tell her before she has the chance to scream Spring Break.

"I think we both need waters," Jess agrees with a smile. "I'll get a couple beers for us, too, just in case. Grab us that table in the corner?"

I nod, sliding into the high top and wiping the sweat off my forehead once I take off the German hat. My heart is still racing, and when Jess joins me with drinks in hand, she shakes her head.

"That poor kid is never going to forget dancing with you."

I laugh. "God, I hope he's okay."

"He'll be fine. Cheers," she says, holding up her water. I clink my plastic water cup to hers, and then we both sigh with relief after chugging nearly all of it.

For a while, we just sit there catching our breath and sipping on our water as we look around the bar. And I can't help but smile as I look at one of my best friends in the entire world and think of all we've been through.

I also can't help but think about what Bear said about telling her what happened to me.

It makes my stomach cramp thinking about it, but I know in my heart it's time.

"So, job hunt wasn't that fun today, huh?"

Jess makes a gagging notion. "It's the worst. But, really, I'm just keeping myself busy while I wait to hear from that wedding planner I interviewed with last week."

"Know when you'll hear back?"

"Probably never," she says on a laugh. "I was snotting all over them in the interview. But if they have a heart and can look past that, hopefully in the next couple of weeks. She said they had more candidates to interview."

"I bet you get the job."

"We'll see," she says with a shrug. Then, her eyes are sad. "I'm sorry Gavin bailed tonight, Ex."

"Don't be. He said he'd make it up to me and I believe it."

"You're a better woman than me."

I chuckle. "No, I just... I believe him. I trust him. Gavin has been nothing but an amazing guy to me since I met him. He's definitely different," I add. "But in a good way. I'm trying not to overthink it."

"Well, I like that plan."

"Me, too."

I pause for a moment, chewing the inside of my cheek.

"Jess... I need to tell you something."

"You feel like you're going to throw up?" she asks on a belch. "Because I kinda do, too."

I laugh. "No. I, uh... it's..." I sigh. "I don't even know where to start."

Jess frowns when she sees the serious expression on my face, and instantly she's leaning over the table. "What's going on? Are you okay?"

"I am. Now. But... I don't think anyone would be surprised to hear that I haven't been okay. Not for a long time."

Jess's brows pull together, and she reaches over the table to squeeze my hand.

I'm not sure why through the tequila haze that in that moment, I think of how Bear did the very same thing.

"I'm sorry for pulling away the way I did, and for being such a bitch to Skyler with the whole Kip thing."

"Babe, we've moved past that," Jess assures me.

"I know. I know. But... I never told you the real reason why I did what I did."

I take a deep breath and a long sip of water, and then in a flurry of slurred words, I tell Jess everything.

I tell her about how I actually had been pregnant, how the baby was Bear's, how I'd aborted our child without telling anyone about it. I told her about what happened to me that night at our formal, how Bear found me, how I swore him to secrecy and went home that summer to my mom. I told her how I just wanted to get my life back. I told her how Kip seemed like the key to getting back on track again, and how I couldn't see how badly I was hurting those around me as I tried to hold onto what was left of me.

And the entire time, Jess just listened.

She listened and nodded and squeezed my hand. When I started crying, she scooted her barstool over closer to me and hugged me tight. And when I was done, when all the words were said, she held me again.

"I am so fucking sorry you had to go through all that," she says, and when she pulls back from our hug, her eyes are glossy like mine. "It breaks my fucking heart that you had to do it alone."

"I wasn't alone," I assure her. "Bear knew."

She nods. "I'm glad you had him. But Ex, we love you. Me, Ashlei, Skyler, Cassie? We have your back no matter what. Don't ever feel like you have to hide from us."

"I don't," I say with a sniff. "At least, not anymore. But when this all happened, I was just... younger. I cared about what everyone thought of me. I wanted to be the strong, independent, boss bitch Erin Xander. I was president of our sorority. I was a future lawyer in training. I didn't want anyone to think any less of me." I laugh at that. "Turns out, I just made things worse."

Jess lets out a sigh and squeezes my arm. "I love you. Thank you for telling me." She pauses. "Did you ever tell the cops about..."

"No," I finish for her, shaking my head. "At this point, it's too late. I wish I did. Looking back, I really wish I would have just let Bear take me when he wanted to. But... I mean, how many times have we seen in the news that a girl comes forward about being raped, and all they talk about is how she's ruining this boy's life? She's painted as a liar and a bitch, and everyone feels sorry for the guy."

"Not everyone."

"You know what I mean."

Jess sighs. "I do. God, I'm so sorry, Erin. I want to fucking kill them all."

"Get in line."

She smiles, and after a sip of beer, she asks, "You and Bear must have gotten pretty close, huh?"

"Very," I say. "He was really all I had for a while. Until he found out about our baby. After that..." I sigh, running a hand back through my hair. "But we're on the mend. We decided to put everything behind us and be friends."

"That's good," Jess says, but she's watching me in a weird way.

"What?"

"Nothing. I just... I never pictured you and Bear together, but now... God, you guys really would make a hot couple."

She laughs. "Yeah, well, we hooked up one night, okay? We never dated. And besides... I have Gavin now."

Jess arches a brow. "I never said anything about dating him. I was just making an observation." Her gaze narrows. "Do you like Bear as *more* than a friend?"

"Don't be ridiculous." I wave her off.

"Oh, my God. You do. You *do*, don't you?!"

"No!" I stand. "We're friends. And barely that, thanks to me being a fuck up." I smooth my hands over my leggings. "I'm just trying to hold onto that."

Jess smirks. "Uh-huh."

"I'm going pee."

And with a laugh, Jess blessedly lets the topic go, even once I return from the bathroom.

We stumble home and curl up on the couch in our sweatpants, and for the first time in years, I feel at peace knowing that Jess knows everything I've hidden for so long. She makes me promise I'll tell the other girls soon, too, and I agree.

And what was shaping up to be a sad Friday night ends up being one of the best I've had in years.

It just goes to show that what they told us when we first rushed is true.

Kappa Kappa Beta isn't just for four years.

It's for life.

Ashlei

It's been a while since I've gone for a long run, and I forgot just how calming it can be. The constant movement, leg muscles engaged, core tight, arms pumping. The rhythm of sneakers hitting pavement. The steady inhale and exhale, my lungs contracting and filling, sweat dripping from my hairline.

Since the competition, I've been indulging myself in some different kinds of cardio and strength training — yoga, high-intensity interval training, kickboxing, and now, running. It's nice to switch it up, to give my body something new.

Besides, running gives me plenty of time to think.

I'm one of the weirdos who prefers not to run with headphones. With the running path winding along the beach and bayside park, it's nice to just listen to the waves, the conversation, the laughter, and even the distant sound of cars passing on A1A.

Work has been picking up ever since the launch event. Celeste wanted us to make our presence known, and boy did we do just that. Our phones have been ringing off the hooks with requests for potential client meetings, as well as collaborations with other agencies. Just like that, *Ball & Pen* went from new kid on the block to one of the most desired agencies in the city.

We showed what we could do.

And now, the clients are rolling in faster than we can take them.

Good business means I'm busy — not just with my own clients and events, but with hiring a bigger team to manage the new workload. We even had to buy out the office next to ours to expand. It's a good problem to have, but exhausting, nonetheless.

And to think, if I were still in college, I'd be getting ready for Spring Break right now.

I smile a little at that, remembering how fun it was to shop for new swimsuits with the girls, plan out our outfits, make custom mugs and t-shirts, and just be ridiculous whenever possible. Of course, I've had Spring Breaks that weren't so fun... like the one where Bo and I were caught having a threesome on tape. Even still, a big part of me misses it, that carefree time when my biggest concern was finding the perfect swimsuit and packing enough booze for the trip.

I'm lost in memory lane when I round an oak tree at the corner of the path, and when I do, I nearly slam into another runner.

"Oh, shit!" I exclaim, pressing my hands into the man's chest when we nearly collide. I'm not sure if I did it to keep him steady, me steady, or if it's just an automatic reaction. I'm already laughing when I look up at the almost-victim. "God, sorry. I wasn't paying att—"

My voice cuts off mid-sentence, because under the shadow of a damp gray hoodie, I find Brandon's dark, menacing eyes staring back at me.

I can feel how stupid I look standing there with my jaw all slack, hands still against his chest as I take in the sight of him. He's dressed in long, black basketball shorts, and a gray zipper hoodie. The zipper is halfway undone, revealing his slick, bare chest underneath and a cross hanging from a silver chain. I remember that necklace. It was a gift from Darnell, the young man who got him out of foster care. Brandon almost never takes it off.

I suddenly realize I still have my hands pressed against his chest, and I rip them away, putting a few feet between us and crossing my arms over my chest. "Uh, hi. Sorry about..." I wave my hand between us.

Brandon doesn't smile or say it's okay, he just nods, and then side steps around me, ready to continue on his jog.

"Wait!" I say before he can take more than a few steps.

He stops short, and I see it in the swell of his back that he has to take a deep breath before he turns to face me again.

"Is this really what it's going to be like?" I ask. "Awkwardly avoiding each other at work events, not even able to be friendly when we run into each other?"

Brandon sniffs, throwing his hood off his head and hanging his hands on his hips as his eyes wash over the beach. "I don't know what you want from me, Ashlei."

"Look at me," I almost whisper. "That's a start."

He presses his tongue into his cheek, but then slowly, he pulls his gaze to me.

I can still see it, the pain behind those dark eyes. But more so, I see the anger, the resentment, the disgust.

I shiver.

"Exchanging pleasantries is a waste of time," he says definitively. "I'll be cordial at work events, but past that? I don't see any reason for us to pretend like we're friends."

I scoff past the knife those words send right through my heart. "Cool. Got it." I make an *okay* sign with my fingers and click my tongue. "Thanks for clearing that up."

His nostrils flare, and it's in that moment that I can see it — the hunger in his eyes. I felt it that first time he touched me on his jet. I felt it every time after, when he'd watch me in the office and I knew he couldn't wait to get me alone, or when we'd go out for a night on the town, and I knew all he wanted was to get me back to his place.

My heart kicks up a notch.

He still wants me.

"I don't know why you're acting like you're so upset, anyway," he says after a moment, his brows bending together. "From what I saw at the *Ball & Pen* launch event, you've moved on just fine, haven't you?"

I cock my head to the side in confusion for just a moment before I remember the little show I put on, the hot guy at the bar whom I let guide me outside just because I knew Brandon was watching me. Of course, nothing happened with that guy, other than him giving me his card and me promising to call about working together.

But Brandon doesn't know that.

And he doesn't need to.

"Whether I've moved on or not is none of your business, since you so decidedly cut me out of your life."

Something of a laugh comes from Brandon's nose, and he looks out at the ocean again before his eyes are back on mine. "You're right."

With that, he pulls his hoodie back up and turns, jogging away from me as I stand there and watch him go.

I stay until he's completely out of sight.

Then, I jog another four miles and think about all the ways I can make him want me back.

Skyler

"Best. Spring. Break. *Ever*," Kip says on a long sigh as he slips into the hot tub. He groans more and more as the warm water envelops him, and I smile as I take in the view of his chest and abs, and the incredible Colorado sunset casting orange and pink rays over the snow-covered mountains behind him.

"Even better than last year?"

"Last year was a disaster," he says.

"Well, yes, in the sense that we had a huge fight. But," I add as I strip out of my robe and lay it over one of the nearby chairs. "We also had a lot of fun. And some pretty hot sex, if I remember right."

"Our sex has always been on fire."

"Okay, Kings of Leon."

Kip smiles, and then lets out a whistle as I climb the little steps up to the hot tub. "Damn, girl. Get your fine ass in here so I can hold you already."

I let out a groan of my own when the water climbs up my legs, over my hips and up to the middle of my chest as I sink all the way in. After a long day of learning how to ski, my body feels like I've been flatlined by a steamroller.

"God, I think I found muscles I didn't know existed today," I say, wincing against another wave of soreness as I sink down farther and sit next to Kip.

He tucks me under one arm with a kiss to my temple. "Yeah, skiing definitely makes you sore. But it's so fucking fun that it's worth it."

"Speak for yourself," I say, massaging my calves under the water. "I think Cassie and I are going to hang back in the village tomorrow and day drink."

"Over it already?"

"Let's just say I have no desire to tear my ACL or break my neck, and I don't have the grace to feel confident that either of those are off the table."

Kip laughs. "I grew up skiing. Every winter, Dad would load me and Mom up in the van and we'd drive to Salt Lake City." He pauses. "Well, every winter Dad was home, anyway. Never knew with the Army."

I smile, rubbing his hip under the water. "I bet that was fun."

"It was. Some of my favorite memories of us together as a family are from being on the slopes or playing board games back in our cabin."

"How's Mom doing?"

"She's good, holding up. Wants me to come home for the summer. But with the show..."

"Maybe we could go visit for a long weekend."

"I know she'd love to see you."

"Well, I'd love to see her. And besides, you'll want a break by then."

Kip laughs at that. "Highly doubtful. The more likely scenario is that you'll have to pack my bags for me and force me on a flight." He shakes his head with a lazy smile on his lips. "I'm already obsessed with the project. I can't stop thinking about it. I'm even *dreaming* about it."

I smile, but my stomach pinches in the same breath, because while I'm happy he's enjoying making the show, I know Natalia is a big part of it.

And I can't shake my distrust for her.

Ever since they started filming, and especially since the KKB date auction, Natalia has just been *around.* No matter where I meet up with Kip, and no matter what kind of day it is for the show, she's always there. Either she's filming or she's volunteering to help with something else. Even when it's not one of her scenes, she's on set, helping Kip or costume design or set design or whatever she can think of. She's not even above running to get coffee or food for the crew.

Which, of course, means everyone *loves* her.

How could they not? She's always there to help, never says no to a task, always dependable. She's funny and cute and smart. And since I've made it my mission to befriend her, I've been out with her and the rest of the crew a handful of times now.

And every time, she's been an absolute blast.

She can go with me shot for shot, loves to dance and party and stay up all night, and is always somehow just together enough to help someone else if they get too drunk.

I wish I didn't hate her.

If I didn't hate her, I bet we'd be *actual* friends and not just the fake friends I've made us so I can keep an eye on her. I bet we'd party and laugh and get into *way* too much trouble together.

But I can't shake that she's got the hots for Kip, and that she's waiting for her perfect time to strike.

I don't trust her.

And I hate that Kip does.

"I need to talk to you about something," I say, sliding into Kip's lap. I straddle him, lacing my arms around his neck as his hands find my hips.

"Mmm, well, whatever it is, this might not be the best position to talk in," he says with a grind of his pelvis against mine. "I can't think when your tits are in my face and you're riding me like this."

"You want to fuck me in this hot tub, don't you?"

Kip groans and bites his lip, gripping my hips even tighter. "God, do I."

"Even knowing the rest of the crew could come back at any second?"

"Even still."

I chuckle, kissing him as he wraps his arms around me. When we made the decision to do Breckenridge for Spring Break, we had no idea we'd be basically bringing all of Palm South with us. Of course, Omega Chi and Kappa Kappa Beta are here, but when Adam found out about our plans, he threw Alpha Sigma into the mix, too. And since they're now the hottest fraternity on campus, that meant the rest of Greek Row was right behind.

We quickly realized that getting one place for everyone wasn't possible, so we all split up, and Bear and I booked a sick cabin just outside of town that sleeps ten and has a deck with a hot tub. Our first night here was rowdy as hell, but right now, it's just me and Kip, since everyone else hasn't made it back from the slopes yet.

Kip's hands slide down my back, slipping under my swimsuit bottoms to cup my ass and drag me against him.

"Look," I say against his next kiss, threading my hands into his hair. "I know you're oblivious." *Kiss.* "Because you're focused on the show." *Ass squeeze. Kiss.* "But Natalia wants you."

At that, Kip breaks our kiss and pulls back with a confused expression. "What?"

I sigh. "I know I sound ridiculous, which is part of the reason I've held off on saying anything. But... I just worry and... Kip, that girl wants you. Bad. And she's just waiting for the right time to make a move."

"Babe," Kip says through a laugh. "All Natalia wants from me is a ticket to Los Angeles. She's buttering *all* of us up because she wants to be a movie star, and honestly, I think her dedication to the project is admirable, considering it's just a college web series."

I frown, shoulders slumping as I lean back, but Kip holds me in his lap. "Do you honestly not see the way she looks at you?"

Kip chuckles, threading his hands at the small of my back. "No. I don't see how *any* girl looks at me, because the one I have is too fucking gorgeous to see anyone else."

I smile, but my lip is still in a protruding pout.

Kip thumbs it with a grin. "I'm all yours, baby. You've got nothing to worry about."

"Just promise me you'll be aware when she's around, okay? Don't put yourself into any stupid situations."

"I promise," he says, and then he's pulling me in again, his next kiss greedy and deep. "It's kind of hot when you're jealous."

"I'm *not* jealous," I say, dragging my hand down his abdomen.

He sucks in a breath when my fingertips skate over his hard-on through his swim trunks. "Good. Because no one holds a candle to you."

With that, he's crushing me to him, his arms wrapped all the way around me as he devours me kiss for kiss. I nearly pass out from lack of oxygen before he releases my mouth and travels down my neck, over my collarbone, down to the swells of my breasts. He pulls his hands from around me just long enough to slip each triangle-shaped piece of fabric from my swimsuit to the side, leaving my tits exposed, nipples pebbling to a hard peak from the cold and his touch combined.

Kip groans and bites his lip, rolling his thumbs over each nipple as he takes in the view. Then, his blue eyes flick to mine before he's licking and biting and sucking each one, making me writhe in his lap.

"Seriously, they're going to be home any moment. Maybe we should take this inside."

"Or maybe we should just make this quick," Kip counters, and then his hands disappear under the water.

He's still kissing me as he moves, and he lifts me off his lap for just a moment before he lowers me back down. This time, though, his shorts are gone, somewhere in the water or around his ankles, I can't be sure.

Kip's hand slips between us, and I brace myself for him to press his fingers inside me next. But he doesn't. Instead, he pulls my swimsuit to the side, lines himself up with my entrance, and pulls me down onto him as he thrusts his hips up.

He fills me in one slick, all-consuming flex.

"Fuck," we both groan together, our foreheads meeting as we take a moment to revel in how it feels to be connected. Slowly, Kip grabs my hips and starts to move me — up and down, up and down — as his mouth travels the length of my neck, showering me in devastating kisses.

It's always like this when Kip touches me. It doesn't matter how long we've been together, how many times I've felt him inside me — it never gets old. It never feels boring. It's always this passionate fire with blue flames that lick at every inch of my skin every second that we're fucking.

I grip his shoulders, using my knees against the hot tub seat to bounce myself faster, to feel him deeper. Still, there's something off, something missing from our connection under the water.

"I need more," I pant, biting his bottom lip.

He thrusts deep, and I cry out with pleasure but hop off him in the next moment.

"I can't feel all of you with the water," I pant, and then I stand, slide my bikini bottoms down to my shins, and brace my hands on the edge of the hot tub. "I want it like this."

"Jesus Christ, Sky," Kip says, his eyes trailing a blaze over me. "You look so fucking hot bent over like that, with your pussy all wet and swollen and begging for me." He stands, stroking himself as he makes his way over. "The mountains behind you, the sunset over your hair and your eyes."

"Alright, alright, enough with the poetry," I tease, arching my back more. "Fuck me hard and tell me when you're close. I want you to finish in my mouth."

The groan that rips from Kip's throat next is guttural and raw, and then he's behind me, using one hand to press my back down even more and the other to pull my hips toward him. He lines us up, flexes into me, and there's barely time for me to adjust to the way it feels to have all of him — no water — before he's slamming it home.

Our wet skin slaps together with each thrust, my tits bouncing where they've been freed from my swimsuit, and if there's anyone hiking the trails below our cabin, they're getting one hell of a view right now.

I can feel every inch of him this way, though, and every time he pumps, I nearly pass out from my orgasm building quickly. It comes on so fast I almost fall over the hot tub before I grip harder and hold my balance. Kip reaches around me to rub my clit in just the right way when he realizes I'm coming undone, and with him circling and pumping, I fly apart into a million little stars.

And I moan loud enough for the entire town to hear.

"Fuck, Skyler," Kip says, removing his hand from my clit. He pumps twice more and then rips out of me. "I'm—"

He doesn't even have to say it before I'm flipped around, and I sink into the water far enough to take him in my mouth. I cup his balls and roll them as I take him in deep, and he curses, eyes rolling up to the skies before he empties inside my throat.

I look up at him with a wicked smile and swallow.

An all-over body shiver racks him in the next instant, and he hangs one hand on his hip as the other runs back through his hair. "Fucking *hell*, babe. That was ridiculously hot."

I bite my lip, and I'm just about to stand to kiss him when the sliding glass door opens and a loud whistle rings out.

"Nice ass, Jackson," Kade says, waggling his brows. He's still in his ski pants and jacket, his goggles pushed up in his hair. "Looks like we missed the party."

Kip immediately sinks down into the water to shield me, even though I'm already covered by the bubbles. I can't help but laugh hysterically, and after the shock wears off, Kip chuckles, too.

"What's going on out he—*ewwww*, Big! Did you two just contaminate our hot tub?!" Cassie asks, her eyes wide and nose wrinkled. Her hair is even wilder than usual, a frizzy, wind-blown mess from skiing all day.

"Don't worry, Little," I say with a wink. "I swallowed, and the chlorine will kill the rest."

Kade bends over in a fit of laughter as Cassie flushes such a deep red she looks sunburned. She shakes her head, leaving first, and then Kade wiggles his fingers at us as he closes the door again. "I'll let you two get dressed. Let me know if you need a cigarette or anything."

Kip laughs, and when the door is shut and we're alone again, he looks at me with an arched brow. "Round two, shower?"

I fix my suit and hop out, wrapping myself in my robe. "And then round three, bed."

"I'm not going to have energy left for the slopes tomorrow."

"Sorry, not sorry," I say, and Kip smacks my ass as he follows me inside.

Adam

My heart is more like a ravenous beast banging against the confines of my rib cage as Cassie and I stroll through Breckenridge hand in hand.

Spring Break has been incredible so far, days filled with skiing, and nights filled with hot tubs and partying our faces off only to get up and do it all over again. Skyler and Bear booked us all the perfect cabin on the edge of town, and where last Spring Break, Cassie and I had our breaking point, this year, everything is perfect.

It feels like all the drama we've gone through, all the other people, the misplaced timing, the hidden feelings and miscommunication… it's all led to this moment.

I'm about to lavalier Cassie.

And she has no idea.

In Greek world, lavaliering a girl is about as close to committing to her for life as you can get, other than proposing. When you get your fraternity's letters on a chain and put them around your girl's neck, you're letting her know she's as important to you as your brotherhood — if not more. You trust her. You love her. You'll fight for her.

And one day, when college is over and the timing is right, you'll marry her.

For me, that day can't come soon enough.

"I'm kind of hungry," Cassie says. "Wanna get tacos?"

"You know I will *never* say no to tacos."

She leans in close enough to whisper. "Or blowjobs."

I bark out a laugh. "Right, or those. Although, we've come a long way. I remember the first time you went down on me… you remember?"

"In the shower," she recalls with a smile. "You had your hand in my hair and you had to guide me and show me what to do."

My cock twitches under my snow pants when I think of how she looked on her knees staring up at me, and I clear my throat and aim for a subtle adjustment as we walk. "Alright, enough of that talk, otherwise I'm going to have to find a dark alley to drag you into, and I don't think there are many dark alleys in Breckenridge."

Cassie giggles, light and airy, her strawberry pink lips curling up into the prettiest smile. Her face is slightly pink from our days on the slopes, save for the outline of her ski goggles, and it's adorable how fresh and rejuvenated she looks. Her hair is unkempt, but her shoulders are relaxed, and the way she's smiling up at me makes me want to take out my phone and snap a picture.

Except, I don't *have* my phone. Right now, it's in Skyler's hands where she's hidden away ready to capture what's about to happen on camera.

"So, tacos," Cassie says, releasing my hand to loop her arm through mine, instead. The main street of Breckenridge is what you'd expect any western town to look like, except with mountains sprawling up all around and snow covering every inch. We walk carefully even in our snow boots to make sure we don't slip on the ice hidden in patches. "What about that place," she says, nodding toward a little Mexican restaurant at the end of the strip.

"Looks perfect," I say, and then I glance around, making sure everyone and everything is in place. "But first, you should come over here."

I drag her toward a staircase lined with fairy lights and flowers that leads up to the outlet mall on the main strip, smiling at her confusion the whole way.

"I don't really feel like shopping."

"We're not. Just stand here," I say, placing her in the middle of the staircase about halfway up. "It'll be a nice picture."

She chuckles at that, crossing her arms over her chest. "Since when have you been on the lookout for photo ops?"

I grin, kissing her forehead before I hop down the stairs two at a time. When I get to the bottom, I turn to face her again. "Since now."

Suddenly, the music coming from the speakers lining the main street goes dead, and four of my brothers scramble from where they'd been blending in at various outdoor dining tables along the street. They gather right in the middle of the road — one with a guitar, one with a cajón, and one with a tambourine — while the last of them starts singing into the wireless microphone now connected to the speakers.

Jason Mraz.

"I'm Yours."

Cassie's brows tug inward at first, and then she laughs, shaking her head and looking from the band to me and back again. "What in the wo—"

Before she can finish her sentence, a few more of my brothers jump up from where they'd been pretending to shop or eat, and start dancing. Then, a handful of Cassie's sisters do the same. It's a waterfall effect, and as the first verse is sweetly sung, dozens and dozens of Alpha Sigmas and Kappa Kappa Betas start filling the street below Cassie and dancing in a choreographed flash mob.

Cassie is laughing and clapping along, and every time her eyes find mine, she's looking at me like I've lost my mind. I can see the confusion in her eyes, and she mouths, "What is this?!"

When the first chorus finishes, my brother who was singing tosses me the mic, and I catch it with a spin just as everyone else freezes.

Suddenly, the jubilant affair is at a stand-still, and Cassie gasps, still smiling as she looks around at everyone frozen in various dance moves.

"Cassie McBee," I start, still standing at the foot of the stairs with the microphone in my hand. "You and I... we have put each other through the wringer. From other people stealing our attention to our own damn pride standing in the way, we have taken anything but the easy route to finally being together."

She chuckles at that, and already, I can see her eyes welling with tears.

"From the first moment I laid eyes on you, I knew you'd be mine. Even if I didn't realize at the time what the feeling was, I can look back now and say with confidence that the way the world tilted, the way my breath caught, the way everything before that moment seemed to fade away — it was my body and soul's recognition of forever standing right in front of me."

I start slowly walking up the stairs, one by one.

"It killed me to see you hurt by others while I fought my way to you. It killed me even more that I was so blind to see what we had from the start, that it took us both so long to finally make this official. But one thing I know without a single doubt is that I wouldn't change any of it. Because all the pain, all the heartache, all the frustration," I add with a chuckle. "It all led us right here, to this moment, to this incredible, one-of-a-kind love that no one else in this world has."

The first tears slip free when Cassie blinks as I step up to stand on the step right below her.

"You're my person, Cassie," I say, reaching into my pocket for the delicate silver chain with my fraternity's letters on it. When I withdraw it and let it dangle from my fingers, Cassie gasps, covering her mouth with both hands. The tears flow stronger. "You're my now. You're my forever. And though I may have a lot to figure out still, I know I can do anything with you by my side."

"Adam..."

I step up to meet her, tucking the microphone between my arm and ribs long enough to unclasp the necklace and hold it up.

"Cassie McBee, will you wear my letters? Will you take this lavalier as a promise that I am yours? Because if you will, one day, I'll put a ring on your finger so the whole world knows it, too."

She shakes her head as more tears slip free. "Of course, I will, you idiot."

That earns her a laugh from the frozen crowd, and once the necklace is around her neck, I toss the microphone behind me and back into the hands of my brother. The band launches into the next verse as everyone starts dancing again, and — yes, I went full-out cheese — Cassie's sisters launch confetti out of little cannons and cover every single one of us in a paper shower.

Cassie's arms are around my neck in the next instant, and she's crying and holding on tight as I spin her around while being careful not to take us both tumbling down the stairs. When I land her on her feet once more, she looks up at me with those glistening emerald eyes and says, "I love you more than anyone or anything in the world."

"I love you, too," I promise, and then we share a kiss so long and deep and passionate that it shouldn't be allowed in public, but I don't care.

I'm hers.

And she's mine.

And nothing in this world can ever keep us apart.

***

Later that evening, Cassie is tucked under my arm in the hot tub as we listen to Skyler and Kip telling a funny story about their summer in Kansas. My phone buzzes from the edge of the tub, and I glance at it, heart jumping into my throat when I see an email from the Alpha Sigma National Chapter.

I clear my throat, excusing myself inside to use the restroom, and only after I close the door and lock it behind me do I open the email.

Mr. Brooks, it is our pleasure to offer you a position as a Field Executive for the Alpha Sigma National Chapter.

The rest of the email is a blur, even though I read it several times, because it takes all my strength to keep myself standing upright as the meaning of what I'm reading sinks in.

"Holy shit," I murmur to myself, and with the phone still in my hands, I lift my gaze to lock eyes on my reflection. "I got it."

Bear

On the last night of Spring Break, I'm nostalgic as fuck.

As I get dressed for an evening out — *slowly* get dressed, thanks to how sore I am from skiing — I can't help but reflect on the past four years. I guess this isn't anything new. I guess most seniors in college go through this. When you first come to college, everything is fresh and new and exciting. Then, as the years go on, you're a veteran. You're experienced and know what to expect and can make the most of everything.

But when you're in your last semester and just a couple of months from graduation, it's hard not to experience every moment with a sense of longing and sadness.

This is my last semester living in the fraternity house. This is my last couple of months of classes — and no matter how many times I cut class or bitched about exams, a part of me knows I'll miss it. I'll miss having a house full of rowdy brothers who are always down to do something, go out, party, play video games, hit the gym, whatever. A part of me will miss learning something new every day, and that feeling of studying hard and seeing it pay off with a good grade.

And on the last night of my last Spring Break, all I can think is *did I take advantage of this the way I should have? Did I soak up every minute? Did I appreciate these responsibility-free vacations with my brothers?*

I'm still lost in my contemplation and fucking with my button up when my phone rings. It's sitting on top of the old wooden dresser with the mirror I'm currently staring at my reflection in, and when I glance down, I'm surprised to see Erin's face on the screen.

Requesting a video chat.

I smile, but my brows furrow in confusion as I slide my thumb over the screen to answer. "Well, hello there."

Erin whistles. "Damn, Bear. You're all dressed up!"

I hold the phone out more so she can get a better look of the full outfit. "You can't see, but my sneakers match the hat."

"I wouldn't expect anything less." After a chuckle, she narrows her eyes at the screen. "Where the hell *are* you?"

"The cabin. We're all about to go grab dinner and then hit the town for the night."

At that, her smile fades, and she shakes her head and drags a hand over her face. "Spring Break. God, why I did completely space on that?" She rolls her lips together and paints on another smile. "Breckenridge, right?"

"Indeed."

"Lots of skiing?"

"*Too* much," I say. "I haven't been this sore since I attempted ice hockey for Omega Chi."

Erin laughs, but I can hear the way the sound has changed just in the few minutes we've been on the phone. It's softer now, more dejected. I finally take a good look at her, her dark blonde hair pulled up into a high ponytail, her face makeup-free but beautiful, nonetheless. She looks cozy in her sweatpants and a t-shirt hanging off her shoulder.

"Well, I'll let you get to it!" she says. "I hope you have a great night."

"Wait."

Erin looks to the side, tongue in cheek, and though she's trying to hide it, I can tell she's not okay.

"What's going on, Ex?"

"Nothing," she says on a sigh.

"Okay. Let's pretend like I've asked you that a few times and now you're finally ready to tell me what's wrong."

She smiles at that, but when her eyes meet mine, the smile fades. "I'm good. Really, I promise. I just... I was kind of needing a friend night and was going to see if you wanted to..." She waves her hand in the air. "I don't know. Go somewhere. Do something." When her hand falls again, she shakes her head. "But, silly me, I forgot it's still Spring Break, so. Yeah. Anyway. I'll see you when you get back."

"Wait, Erin, don't hang up."

I sigh, resting my hand on top of my hat as I glance at the door to my room. I can already hear everyone gathering in the living room to head out, the sound of laughter and pregaming filling the air. And while I can feel that the part of me that was stressing earlier over it being my last night of Spring Break, the part reminding me to seize the day, there's a louder, more pressing voice inside me saying not to let this girl hang up the phone.

"Can you hold for just a sec?"

Erin nods, and I put my phone on mute and leave it facing the ceiling long enough to jog down the hall to the balcony that overlooks the lower-level living room. I spot Skyler easy enough and wave her up the stairs.

"Everything okay?"

"Yeah, I just... I think I'm going to hang back tonight."

Skyler frowns. "What? Why? It's the last night!"

"I know, I know, I'm just..." *Helplessly in love with your Big*. "Hungover. And sore. I just want to chill."

Skyler arches a brow. "Why do I feel like you're having a ski bunny come over and you don't plan on leaving your room?"

I plaster on my famous smirk and shrug in lieu of confirming or denying, which makes Skyler smile and shake her head.

"Use protection. And have fun. I'll cover for you."

"Thank you," I say, and after a quick hug, I'm back in the room and staring at Erin's beautiful face.

"I'm all yours."

"What?!" Her eyes go wide. "Bear, no! It's Spring Break. I'm fine, really, I'll just—"

"Look, I'm hungover and sore, anyway. I didn't even want to go out," I lie. "Besides, I'd much rather hang out with you. Even if it's just a FaceTime date."

My throat goes dry at my last word, but thankfully, Erin doesn't seem to read too much into it. She's too busy fighting back tears on a smile.

"You really don't mind?"

"I *want* to talk to you. I want to be here."

Erin sinks farther into the couch, and it's then that I see the glass of red wine in her hand. "You're too good for me, Bear. Too good for this world."

"Tell that to my ex-girlfriends."

That earns me my first real, head-thrown-back signature Erin laugh, all light and bubbly and sweet like champagne.

I make it my goal to tally up at least ten of those bad boys by the night's end.

***

Three hours later, I've got my phone plugged in and propped up on a mountain of luggage while I kick back against the bed frame, a half-empty bottle of whiskey at my side. Erin has already finished a bottle of red and opened a second, and both of us have got to have eight packs by now from the insane amount of laughter we've been doing.

So far, we've played five rounds of never have I ever, a couple rounds of charades, watched an episode of *Drunk History* together and Erin has given me a tour of her keepsakes box she keeps in her closet with old photos of her and other childhood memorabilia.

My favorite was a photo of her in eighth grade with braces and pigtails and overalls — the quintessential, adorable nerd.

"God, Bear," Erin says, wiping tears from the corner of her eyes after our latest fit of laughter. "I can't tell you how much I needed this."

"Well, I'm glad I could help," I reply. I take a sip of my whiskey, aiming for nonchalance when I ask, "You ever going to tell me what's going on that has you in your feels, or is that to remain a mystery?"

She sighs. "A half a bottle ago, I would have said let's change the subject. But..." She wiggles her almost-empty glass with a smile.

"Is it school?"

"Somewhat. I mean, I knew law school wouldn't be easy, but I guess I *did* wrongly assume that I was smarter than nearly everyone else." She smiles with the joke. "I spend so much time on campus, and when I'm not there, I'm studying. And speaking of studying, the people in my study group kind of suck," she adds with a laugh, but her eyes are sad.

"Why did the words *study group* just make you almost cry?"

She shakes her head. "You're going to think I'm stupid."

"I promise, that's not possible."

Another sigh. "I just... Gavin and I haven't seen each other much since... since... the whole..."

"Valentine's Day thing?" I finish for her.

She nods. "And we were supposed to have a date night last week, but he bailed for a study group thing. Which I totally understand. He's graduating with his master's degree in a couple months, and I know he's worked hard for this. But honestly? I'm worried about him."

I tilt my head, biting back the curse words I want to throw out for that idiot blowing her off for a fucking study group. "Why's that?"

"He hasn't been coming to therapy, not for about a month now. He says he's gotten what he needed out of it, that he needs to focus on school. And he has a part-time job helping out in the admissions office, too. And I get it, I do, but... I just don't know that he's *cured* or whatever. I don't think *any* of us really are. You know? And I just hate to see him pull away from therapy." She swallows, eyes on her glass. "Away from *me*."

"He feels distant?"

She snorts a laugh. "Very much so."

I inhale a deep breath, let it go, do it all again once more for good measure while I sort through my thoughts and what I want to say. That little voice inside me is screaming now for me to tell her he's an idiot and not good enough for her and that she should tell him not to let the doorknob hit him on the way out of her fucking life forever.

But, thankfully, even in my tipsiness, I know that's not the best move.

As much as it sours my gut, she cares about this guy. And this is the first guy she's *allowed* herself to care about since that horrendous night happened to her.

"I understand that school is important. I mean, I'm in my last semester, too, and you just graduated. We get that pressure."

Erin nods.

"But that being said, I can always find time for people who are important to me." I wave a hand at the phone. "Case in point, tonight. And I know that even though you're up to your neck in schoolwork, you still find time for the girls when they need you, and if Gavin called you right now and said to come over, you would be in your car in the next five minutes."

"Seven," she corrects. "I'd have to brush my teeth."

I smirk, taking a moment to think about my next words carefully. "What I'm saying is, maybe you should just remind him that if you're important to him, he needs to show it. And Erin, I hate to say it, but no one can read your mind. Least of all a man."

She laughs.

"I mean it. I think you're one of those girls who says yes to everything, helps everyone, while silently wishing that someone would see you and ask you what *you* need, too."

Her eyes well up at that, and she rolls her lips together. "I do. I really do."

"Well, sometimes you've just got to tell people what you need. Especially if he's got so much going on, he probably doesn't even know he's upsetting you. He just thinks you're cool with him bailing and rescheduling and not giving you his time." I shrug. "Tell him you need him. Tell him you want him at therapy and then you want him to take you out and spend the night with you."

"You make it sound so easy."

"It is. Do you want me to make you some cue cards?"

She chuckles. "If you were here, I'd glob you with a pillow."

I grab the one behind me and knock myself over the head, which makes her burst out into a full-belly laugh.

Number thirteen for the night, if my numbers are right.

"Ugh, okay. I'll just... tell him that I need to see him."

"Good girl."

She bites her lip. "What if he still bails, or makes an excuse?"

"I think you know the answer to that."

She nods, her eyes sad again as she sips the last of her wine.

"Hey, look at me." I wait until she does, and then I smile, hoping she can feel my sincerity when I say, "No matter what, you always have me."

Her warm brown eyes are still glossy under her thick lashes, but she smiles a little. "Promise?"

My heart thumps loud in my chest, so desperate to reach for her, hold her, touch her...

Kiss her.

I swallow, trying to assure myself that everything will be okay even though I can't be sure. All I *do* know is that as long as Erin wants me around, as long as she lets me be here for her, I'll be here.

Waiting.

Wanting.

Wishing.

I force a smile and hold my hand to the sky before covering my heart. "Swear."

Cassie

The airport scene after Spring Break is nothing short of tragic.

All around Denver International, you can see college students from around the nation dragging their asses to their gates with all the grace of a hungover zombie. There are kids slouched in chairs with hoodies pulled up over their faces, girls sprawled out in chairs with their head in their friends' lap, mascara-stained cheeks and red eyes on some, and *I just got lucky* victorious smiles on others.

The whole place reeks of sweat and tequila.

And yet, there's a bit of jubilance hanging around.

It's that feeling of knowing you just locked in some of the best memories of your life, ones you'll pull out in conversation with future friends and maybe even kids one day. It's that realization that you're still young and wild and free, and that even if only for a little while longer, you don't have to adult.

As for me, I'm sitting next to Skyler and a pile of bags belonging to the crew that was in our cabin, waiting for our plane to Miami to board. The rest of the gang went their separate ways for food or snacks or bathroom breaks while we stayed back.

Skyler is studying for an entrepreneurship exam she has when we get back, while I people-watch and absentmindedly smooth my fingers over the new silver letters hanging from my neck.

With a goofy smile on my face, of course.

Spring Break was nothing short of epic. And as weird as it seems, it doesn't bother me that it's my last one. Part of me longs for college forever, sure, but ever since Adam lavaliered me, my mind has been spinning with thoughts and wishes for the future.

I can see us moving in together after graduation, making a little house a home of our own.

I can see us grocery shopping together, having "our shows," and traveling the world.

I can see him at the end of the aisle, me dressed in white.

I can see him holding a bouncing baby boy…

Or girl.

"Ugh," Skyler huffs, slamming her laptop shut and scrubbing her hands over her face. "I'm going to vomit."

I chuckle. "From studying or from all those vodka shots last night?"

Skyler fights back a gag, covering her mouth with a fist as she looks at me. "Don't say that word."

"Vodka? Or shots?"

She flicks my arm as she stands, abandoning her laptop in her chair. "I'm going to grab some club soda and a few snacks for the flight. You want anything?"

I shake my head. "Adam's getting us stuff. But can I use your laptop? I want to check my email."

"Of course," she says with a wave, and then she's gone.

I pull her laptop into my lap and type in my mail host in the search bar. When it loads, I sign in and filter through all the unread messages from the past week.

My heart stops when I see one from Johns Hopkins.

"Oh my God," I whisper to myself, and I stare at the vague subject line for the longest time before I finally click inside the email.

Dear Ms. McBee,

Congratulations. It is with great pleasure that I write to inform you of your admission into the Johns Hopkins School of Medicine. Following this email, you can expect a full admissions packet to be delivered to the mailing address provided in your application. You have until April 30th to confirm your intention to attend and narrow your field of study. We understand your interest in...

The rest of the email goes fuzzy, as well as my brain as I scan the words over and over.

I got in.

I got in.

I. Got. *In!*

Even seeing the words in black and white, I don't believe it. I mean, I applied even though I knew I wouldn't be able to start until the spring term of *next* year, since I'll be graduating in the fall with Skyler. I expected them to write me with feedback and encourage me to apply for the following scholastic year.

I never expected an acceptance.

Especially not from my first school of choice.

My heart races faster as I focus on the email again, reading that they have read my request to start in the spring and have flexibility in their programs to accommodate the request. There's also links for housing, orientation, and more at the bottom.

"Alright, I got all the goods," Adam says, dropping two plastic sacks into the chair next to me. "We got Pringles, trail mix, Ore-*oh shit!*"

I don't warn him before I slide Skyler's laptop to the side and jump straight into his arms, but he catches me, nonetheless, laughing as I kiss all over his neck.

"I missed you, too, for the whole fifteen minutes I was gone, but maybe we should tone down the PDA a little."

"I got in!"

He freezes at that, and when he drops me back to my feet, I'm nodding so furiously with a smile so big I'm afraid I'll split my face.

"To Johns Hopkins medical school. I GOT IN!"

I jump into his arms again, and he catches me with a spin, though he seems more confused than anything at first. It's like it hits him slowly, and then he's kissing me and squeezing me and twirling me around.

"Baby! You got in!"

"I got in!"

We both laugh as he frames my face and kisses my nose, my cheeks, and finally my lips. When he pulls back, he shakes his head in disbelief.

"I had no doubts, but *wow,* this is amazing!"

"I think I'm in shock."

He chuckles, and then his smile slips, and he brushes my hair out of my face.

"What?" I ask. "What's wrong?"

"Nothing. Nothing's wrong," he assures me. "I just... I have news, too."

I arch a brow.

"I got the job."

"The job..." My eyes go wide when I realize what he means. "The Field Executive position? With Alpha Sigma?"

"The very one."

"ADAM!" I launch into his arms again, nearly crying with joy. "Oh, my God, why didn't you tell me?!"

"I just found out on the night I lavaliered you. I wanted to wait until we got back to break the news, but now seems like the perfect time."

"I'm so proud of you!" I say, but even as the words come out, I feel my stomach do a flip. "So... wait, where... uh... what does this mean?"

Adam swallows. "It means after graduation I'm going to Boston. And then... who knows. Wherever the chapter needs me."

I'm struck still for a moment before I smile, shaking my head. "Well, this is amazing! And hey, maybe you'll get assigned to a university in Baltimore, and then we can—"

"There's no Alpha Sigma chapter in Baltimore," he says, still holding me in his arms. "The closest one is University of Virginia."

"Oh," I say as my heart rate kicks up. "Well, that's not too far."

"It sure isn't. Just a few hours."

"We can make that drive."

"Of course," he says. "If that's where they send me."

And with those words I hear all the ones he *doesn't* say, like *or they could assign me to a school in Georgia or Illinois or freaking Alaska.*

Still, I keep my smile in place, and I wrap my arms around his neck to pull him in for a tight hug.

"No matter where they send you, we'll figure it out. I'll go to Boston with you for the summer and then come finish out my last semester here at Palm South and then..." I bite my lip, pulling back with a shrug. "And then, we're on a new adventure."

"Exactly. A new adventure. Together."

"Together," I repeat.

But when Adam pulls me back into his chest and presses a kiss to my hair, I can feel his heart beating even faster than mine.

Jess

Ralph's doesn't feel the same.

I can't figure out why. I'm no older than I was the last time I was here — which was only a few months ago. I haven't changed much since I graduated, unless you count living in a new place and becoming best friends with rejection, thanks to the never-ending job hunt. And not a single person here is looking at me like I'm too old or washed up to be at what once was my favorite college bar.

I still fit in.

I still look the same.

But the problem is that I feel so damn different that I can't even relax enough to have a good time.

It's actually kind of sad. I walked in here with the intention of pretending like I'm just like everyone else here, partying it up for the last couple nights of Spring Break before classes start back up on Monday. But when I got here, I found it wasn't the same without my girls, without Kade, without being a student.

Instead, I'm just a sad, jobless graduate here by herself.

And I've drank way too much sitting at this bar.

"Another?" one of the bartenders asks me as she flies by. It's a busy night, and I'm lucky she's even paying attention to me at all with all the college kids hanging on every inch of the bar with their hands up trying to get a drink.

"Please," I say, and then because I'm trying to at least be a *little* bit of an adult, I add, "And a water, too."

She nods, and once she's filled my order, she's off and fluttering to the next person.

I stare at my gin and tonic for a long time before taking my first sip, and at this point, I barely taste the alcohol at all. Knowing how dangerous that is, I chug half my water right behind the sip.

I should just do a shot and commit.

I should go find someone hot to dance with.

But whoever I find, they wouldn't be Kade.

I miss Kade...

Okay, I should go find a group of girls to hang with.

That would be weird...

There's got to be some KKB's here somewhere!

... Except they're all flying back from Denver tonight.

I sigh, running my finger over the rim of my plastic cup. Kade and I had amazing video chat sex last night, and we've been texting the whole time he's been away for his trip. I'm glad he's having fun. I *want* him to soak up every last drop of college that he has.

But I'd be lying if I said I didn't feel a little left out.

We're at different times in our lives, and the saddest thing is that I *wish* I was in his time. I want to be in Breckenridge with him. I want to be making a fool of myself learning how to snow board and then fucking him by the fire in a cabin every night.

I want to feel like the old me instead of this new me, the one who has no idea what she's doing next in life.

Another sigh leaves my chest, and I'm about ready to throw in the towel and call it a night when a familiar voice rasps behind me.

"Fancy meeting you here."

I look over my shoulder confused, but I'm already smiling when I ask Jarrett, "What the hell are *you* doing here?"

He laughs, sliding between me and a group of frat boys lining up shots on the bar. He angles himself so that his back is to them, and with how crowded it is, his thighs are pressed against my hips. It's one-hundred percent unfair how enticing he looks right now. It could be the booze, I realize distantly, or it could be the fact that he's wearing dark jeans that fit him just right and a Buck Mason t-shirt that hugs him in all the right places. It could be that I'm drunk, or it could be that this man has always been sex on a stick deep fried twice over.

His leg is so warm.

He smells so good.

I sink into those thoughts for about point two seconds before I snap out of it, sniffing and inching to the other side of my barstool until we're no longer touching.

"That is a great question that I wish I had the answer to," he says, grabbing the back of his neck. "I worked late at the office and it's been a long fucking week. I just wanted a drink, and for some reason I can't explain, I thought of this place."

"Well, Ralph's does leave a lasting impression."

Something dances in Jarrett's eyes then. "Indeed, it does."

My cheeks heat under his gaze, so much so that I tear my eyes away and take a big gulp from my gin and tonic. It's perfect timing, because the bartender stops by to take his order, and after he's fixed up with some Irish whiskey on the rocks, I find the courage to look at him again.

"What about you?" he asks after a sip. "Are you... are you here alone?"

I groan, burying my face in my hands. "Sadly, yes. And before you say it, I realize how pathetic that is."

He chuckles. "Hey, I'm here alone, too."

"So we can be pathetic together."

"Stop that."

I shrug. "What? You don't like my self-deprecating humor?"

"No, because you're too amazing to talk about yourself like that."

"Yeah, well, I don't feel amazing right now," I admit, and with that admission, I frown, trailing my fingers over the wet sides of my cup.

"What's going on?" Jarrett asks, and as the frat boys behind him take their shots and make their way back to the dance floor, he grabs a barstool they abandoned and pulls it up next to me.

"We don't need to talk about my sad life."

"We don't," he agrees, and he waits until I take my eyes off my cup and meet his gaze before he says. "But do you want to?"

I frown. "I'm just... *lost*, Jarrett. I'm stuck in this in-between state of being where I'm not a college student, but I don't feel like an adult either. I feel accomplished to have a degree, but also not prepared to actually have a job. And it's fitting, because no one will call me back after interviews. Ashlei is kicking ass at her new firm, Erin is working her ass off to be a lawyer, and then there's me." I hold up my drink. "Getting wasted by myself at a college bar."

Jarrett smiles sympathetically, and then his hand reaches over and squeezes my knee under the bar.

It's such a simple, friendly gesture. It's an *I hear you, I get it, it's going to be okay.* It's something I wouldn't think twice about if I was comforting a friend.

But when Jarrett touches me, when that warm, strong hand of his wraps around my leg and squeezes, a million tiny fireworks go off in every inch of my body, and I hum to life for the first time in weeks.

"You're not the first one to feel like this," he says. "And you're not alone. Trust me. This is completely normal."

I swallow, trying to listen to him and forget the fact that he's touching me for the first time in years.

Trying to ignore the fact that in my very drunken state, I want him to touch me more.

"When I graduated, I felt the same way. I was working at the beach bar and all my friends were moving on. I thought grad school was the answer, but even that felt hollow, like I was just doing it to avoid the fact that I didn't know what I wanted to do."

I frown. "You seemed so in love with your GA position when I met you."

"Oh, by then I was. But it took a while to get there."

He finally removes his hand from my leg, and I take a deep breath of much-needed oxygen.

"I think when we're in college, we don't realize that we sort of have this free pass while we're there, you know? No one expects anything of us past getting good grades. We're free to go out every night and sleep in all day, to party and travel and do whatever feels good, and as long as we're passing, all is right in the world. But then you graduate, and suddenly you're expected to have it all figured out. You should have a job right away — and not just *any* job, a professional job, one that uses your degree. And if you don't, then everyone starts to look at you like you're some sort of failure, like just because you don't have everything figured out at twenty-two, you're not okay."

My jaw goes slack. "Exactly! God, that's *exactly* how I've been feeling. I know they don't mean to, but I can sense the pitiful way Ashlei and Erin look at me when I talk about job hunting. And even Kade. I mean, he's got plans. He's going to be the next president of Alpha Sigma. And then there's me and—"

Suddenly, I realize I'm talking about Kade to his brother.

His brother who is my ex.

I shake my head, a sheepish smile slipping over my lips. "Sorry."

"Don't be," Jarrett insists. "Kade cares about you, Jess. He isn't judging you, I promise. If anything, he thinks the world revolves around you."

"Well, that's because it *does*, obviously," I joke, but it feels flat even as I say it.

"Jess, listen to me," Jarrett says, leaning down until I lift my eyes to his. "You're not behind. You're not a failure. You're exactly where you're meant to be. Just because you don't have a job yet doesn't mean you won't. It means the right opportunity hasn't come along yet. It means there's something better down the line. I know it's hard, but try to trust in the fact that every part of life, even the confusing, frustrating, low moments, have purpose. And one day, you'll look back at this period of time and realize that it all happened for a reason."

I smile. "You sound like a self-help book."

"Maybe I should write one."

"You could call it *Drunk Truth Bombs with Jarrett*."

"Do I have to be drunk when I write it, or does the person reading it have to be drunk?"

"Both for maximum effectiveness."

Jarrett chuckles, shaking his head as his eyes search mine. "I've missed you."

The words slip out so easily, like he doesn't realize how they feel akin to a ninja star to my chest. My next breath is shallow, burning, like the entire bar is on fire.

But Jarret just takes a sip of his whiskey and looks around with a smile, like what he said was the most casual, most natural thing in the world.

"So, working on a Saturday," I muse, opting for my water when I realize my words are slurring a bit. "Must be busy at the new office."

"Very much so. It's exciting to open a new branch here, but it's a lot of pressure, too."

I nod. "I'm sure. But you're the man for the job."

"You think so?" he asks, shaking his head. "Sometimes I'm not so sure."

"Jarrett, I've never met anyone so passionate about giving back to the community, about using their political knowledge for good instead of personal gain. I don't know if you know this, but most politicians are skeezy little assholes."

"I can be one of those, too."

I snort. "No, you can't."

"I was to you."

His words shock me silent, and I look down at the bar on a shrug. "I wasn't exactly girlfriend of the year either."

Neither of us have anything to say after that, and for a while, we just sit there and look around the bar, watching college students dance and party like they'll be forever young.

I'm smiling at a girl hustling a group of guys at the pool table when Jarrett laughs beside me.

I glance over, and he's still chuckling to himself, but his eyes are on where his hands are wrapped around his glass.

"What's so funny?"

"Nothing."

"Don't *nothing* me," I say, nudging his elbow. "What are you giggling like a schoolgirl about?"

He cracks his neck, glancing up and beyond the bar before he smirks again. "Just remembering."

"Remembering?"

He nods toward the back of the bar before arching a brow at me. "That closet, though..."

I frown at first, wondering if I missed something, but when I follow his gaze to the far side of the bar by the bathrooms, all the blood rushes to my face.

The closet.

Halloween.

I was playing games, and he dragged me in there and fucked me senseless to remind me just how much I belonged to him, even when we couldn't be together.

"Oh, God," I murmur, burying my face in my hands again as Jarrett lets out a bark of a laugh.

"You have to admit, that was fun."

"Oh, fun is one word for it," I say, smiling when my eyes find his.

And maybe it's the alcohol. Maybe it's the low lighting of the bar and the deep bass of the music thumping through me. But in that moment, looking up at Jarrett, I can remember exactly what that night felt like.

I can remember his hands gripping me with enough force to leave bruises.

I can remember his voice husking in my ear.

I can remember the long length of him sliding inside me, the pitch dark of the closet, the hot panting of our moans mixing together in the most sinful dance.

Kade's face flashes in my mind, and I clear my throat, shaking my head fiercely and closing my eyes tight against the guilt rolling my stomach.

"Uh, I think I should probably get going," I say.

"Feeling okay?"

"Not really," I admit.

"Let me drive you home."

"No," I say quickly, shaking my head as I stand and wave the bartender over to take my card. "No, no, really, it's okay."

"Jess, you shouldn't drive right now."

"I can get a cab."

Jarrett stands then, leveling his warm brown eyes with mine. "Jess, please. I don't want you getting into a cab by yourself like this. Just let me take you home."

I swallow, because the fact is, I really don't want to be in a cab by myself, but I also feel like spending any more time with Jarrett in the state I'm in is far more dangerous than anything a cab driver could do to me.

Still, I nod, conceding.

And after we pay our bills, we're out the door and in his truck.

***

I knew I was drunk, but I didn't realize just *how* drunk I was until the car ride back to my place.

The streetlights blurred as Jarrett drove us downtown, and I had to rest my head against the cool glass of his truck and close my eyes to keep from vomiting. Neither of us spoke a word the entire ride, and by the time he parks below my building, I'm certain throwing up is inevitable.

Jarrett hops out first, jogging around to open my door and help me out of the truck. He hoists my arm up around his neck and secures his around my waist, taking most of my weight as he guides me inside.

"I got you," he promises.

It feels like a dream, or a movie, or someone else living my life as Jarrett digs for my key fob in my purse and pushes my floor number on the elevator. I barely remember the ride up or us walking inside, but somehow, my eyelids flutter open and I'm in my bed in my bra and panties with my bathroom trashcan pulled up next to my bedside table.

I groan. "God, I'm such a mess. I'm so sorry."

"Don't be," Jarrett says from where he's sitting on the edge of the bed. When I peek up at him, he's smiling. "You've always been so cute when you're drunk."

"It's going to be real cute when I throw up."

"I'll hold your hair back if you need."

I smile, and then my eyes close again, and I'm not sure how long I lie there, how much time passes before I wake from an almost sleep to Jarrett brushing my hair off my face.

"Hey, can you lean up long enough to take these Advil and drink this glass of water?"

I nod with my eyes still closed, and though it takes all my energy, I manage to swallow the pills and chug almost all the water before I'm settling back down into my pillows.

"That should help in the morning," Jarrett says.

"Thank you. I already feel better."

He smiles. "Good."

Jarrett stands then, adjusting the trashcan closer to the bed just in case before he heads toward the door to see himself out.

Except when he gets there, he stops.

Even through my drunken haze, I can see how white his knuckles are where they grip the door handle, how labored his breathing is as he stands there at the precipice, but doesn't walk all the way out.

"Jarrett?"

"I got your text that night, you know," he says suddenly, turning to face me with his nostrils flaring. "When you said you'd always love me."

I swallow, eyes wide open now, and I scoot myself to sit upright in my bed, clothing the sheets to my chest.

Suddenly, I feel very, very sober.

"You did?"

He nods. "I texted you back, but I take it you had already blocked me, because I kept getting a notification that the text couldn't be delivered."

I breathe in.

I breathe out.

In the darkness of my room, the lights from the city are the only thing illuminating where Jarrett's silhouette is still framed in my doorway.

"What did you say?"

He swallows, crossing the room to sit on the edge of the bed again. I can see his eyes now, even if faintly, and I can see the pain in them when he whispers, "I said I'd always love you, too."

I bite my bottom lip to keep it from quivering, and I want to slap myself across the face for the way my heart jolts at his admission.

"And did you mean it?" I ask softly.

He blows out a long breath through his nose, shaking his head, and then he leans in, closer, closer, until his forehead is pressed against mine. His warm hand wraps around the back of my neck, fingers sliding into my hair.

I suck in a sip of air and hope it's enough to sustain me, because it's impossible to breathe now.

"I did," he whispers, his warm breath washing over my lips. "I still do."

I can't hold back the whimper that escapes me then, and I squeeze my eyes shut as Jarrett's hand squeezes the back of my neck.

"Jarrett, I—"

"I know," he says, pulling back so suddenly I nearly fall off the bed at the loss of his warmth. He stands just as quickly, shaking his head and clearing his throat. "It's too late. I know. I fucked up and I lost my chance, and now you're with Kade."

I open my mouth to say something, but find I have nothing more to say than what he just did, so I swallow and close my lips once more.

"And I'm happy for you," he says. "I am. My brother is one hell of a guy, and I know he'll treat you right."

Again, I'm speechless. Even with a million thoughts racing in my head, I have nothing to say.

"I'm sorry if I... I shouldn't have..." He shakes his head, and then with one last glance at me, he nods toward the door. "I'm going to head out. Goodnight, Jess."

But I just sit there with the sheets clutched to my heart, eyes dry from not blinking, stomach cramping for a completely different reason now.

I think he's already downstairs and in his truck by the time I finally respond.

"Goodnight."

EPISODE 5

Jess

"Mmm, that's nice," I murmur as Kade plants little kisses all down my stomach. My hands slip into his hair when he starts kissing along my panty line, and I bite my lip, thighs clenching together as my pussy tingles and longs for him again. This is now the fifth time this week that he's come over — the most since the semester started — and each and every time, we've spent nearly all our time together in my bed.

I'm not complaining.

Kade slides his fingers under the band of my panties, lifting up onto his knees long enough to drag them off my legs before he's settled back in. He props my thighs up on his shoulders, hands gripping where my leg meets my hip, and then he drags the flat of his hot, wet tongue along my swollen clit.

"Fuck," I hiss, arching into the touch.

"Goddamn, Jess, you taste so good."

Another moan leaves me as I twist my hands in the sheet, and I close my eyes, reveling in the way his expert mouth knows just how to lick and kiss and suck me.

The morning after Kade got back from Spring Break, he was at my door, and he spent the duration of the day showing me just how much he missed me. It was a welcome release, especially after the weird, drunken, hazy night I'd had with Jarrett.

Who hasn't talked to me since, thank God.

It's not that I'm not happy he's back, even if I never expected to see him again. I weirdly like that we've found a friendship. But *God*, that boy confuses me. And when he's around, it's like stepping into a time machine and going back to how we used to be.

Which is a very, very dangerous thing.

So when Kade came over and told me he missed me so much he wanted to ditch every fraternity event for the next week and spend all his free time with me, I didn't argue.

Well, okay, I argued a *little* bit, because I *do* want him to be the next president, and I know that takes a lot of work and dedication. But still, I've missed him, too.

And Alpha Sigma can survive a week without him.

All week long, we've been wrapped up in each other, lounging in bed and losing days on end.

It kind of makes me thankful that I'm not a working woman just yet.

I'm doing my best to keep my moans in check, since Ashlei is set to be home any second now, but the way Kade is sucking my clit, it's virtually impossible. And when he slips two fingers inside me, one and then the other, curling them in just the right way, I lose the fight completely.

Distantly, I hear my phone buzzing on the bedside table. I know it only sounds faint to me because I'm wrapped up in the pleasure Kade is wreaking on my body, but in reality, it's buzzing so loud and hard, it's moving itself across the wood.

It goes off, and I sigh, focusing on Kade's mouth again.

Until the phone starts ringing again.

"Goddammit!"

"Leave it," Kade says, kissing up my thighs, my stomach, until he's between my legs. He hikes one knee up, and with a swift removal of his boxers, he's lined up at my entrance when the phone stops buzzing again.

I press my heels into his ass, and the tip of him slips inside.

We both sigh, foreheads together, our bodies trembling at the feel of being connected.

And then my fucking phone goes off again.

Kade groans, dropping his head to my chest. "Maybe you should see who it is."

"Maybe I should kill whoever it is."

Kade chuckles as he grabs the phone and glances at the screen. He frowns, holding it to me. "It's Cassie."

"Cassie?" I ask with a frown of my own. And then sadly, Kade and I separate, and I scoot up against the headboard before answering the call. "Cassie, everything alright?"

"No," she answers immediately, and it's with a blubbery voice and a sniff.

"Oh, babe," I say, giving Kade an apologetic smile. "What happened?"

Kade kisses my forehead and mouths that he's going to get some water, and then he dresses and leaves me alone, closing the bedroom door behind him.

I can barely understand Cassie through her blubbering, but after listening for a few minutes, I gather the gist.

Adam got a job in another state. He's moving after graduation and she's staying here. Cassie is losing her shit about long distance. And she's scared.

She's practically out of breath when she finally stops, and she sniffs, waiting for my response.

"Well," I start on a breath. "I'll be honest, long distance is going to be tough."

Cassie whimpers.

"But," I continue. "It's not going to be anything you and Adam can't get through. Okay?"

"How can you be so sure?"

"Oh, I don't know, maybe it's because I've had a front-row seat to the shit show back and forth games you two have played for years."

Cassie laughs through her next sob.

"Seriously," I say. "Adam loves you more than anything. I mean, you're wearing his letters around your neck, are you not?"

A sniff. "I am."

"He wouldn't lavalier you if he wasn't serious."

"I know, I know," she says. "It's just that I had this whole picture in my mind of where our lives would go next, and now..."

I laugh a little. "If there's anything I've learned in the past few months, it's that life rarely goes as we think it will, or as planned. We just have to roll with the tides, babe. And look, yes, it's going to be different. But like you said, you'll have the whole summer together, and then you'll have school to distract you, and then you'll only be a few hours from him when you start at Johns Hopkins."

"*If* he stays in Boston," she reminds me.

"Right. And if he doesn't, he's still going to go see you as much as he can, and I know you'll do the same. And in the meantime, you call, and text, and video chat. It'll be hard, yes, but in the end, it'll only make you stronger."

Cassie is silent for a long pause before she asks, "What was the hardest part for you and Jarrett?"

I haven't heard those words together in so long, they steal my next breath.

You and Jarrett.

And suddenly, I understand why Cassie called me, why she wanted my advice.

I sigh. "Well, I don't think we were ready for long distance. I mean, we had barely gotten our shit together, and then he was just... gone. And for a while, we were fine but..." I swallow. "Honestly, Cassie? I was young. And jealous. I couldn't see the big picture. I was too obsessed with wanting my boyfriend here with me, partying, going to social events, whatever, to understand that what we had was special."

I chew my lip for a moment, remembering the good times with Jarrett, and the bad, too.

"In the end, for us, it was a communication breakdown. When he got busy, I took it personally. When he was with other girls, I got jealous. And instead of giving him his space and focusing on my own things, I became consumed with what I felt like we were lacking. I looked around at everyone else with their boyfriends *here* and I was mad I couldn't have the same."

"That had to be so hard."

"It was," I admit. "And it will be for you, too. But here's my advice — when you're feeling sad or lonely or jealous, talk to him. Open up to him and let him in. Don't let other people get between you."

"I think we've had our fair share of that."

I chuckle. "Yeah, I think you have, too. But you two are the real deal. I'm telling you, this will just be one chapter, and you and Adam have many more to write together."

Before Cassie can respond, my phone beeps in my ear to signal another call coming in. I glance at the screen, frowning when I don't recognize the number.

"Hey, I've got another call coming in. Hang on a sec."

"Actually, I've got to run, anyway. But thank you, J-Love. This helped me more than you know."

"Always here, babe. Talk to you soon."

We end the call when I switch over, and Kade comes back in the room with two full glasses of water and a bag of white cheddar popcorn just as I answer.

"Hello?"

"May I speak with Ms. Vonnegut?"

"This is she," I answer, and Kade makes a face at me like I sound ridiculous with the formality.

I throw a piece of popcorn at him.

"Oh, wonderful. Jess, this is Brittany Nova with *Celestial Weddings*."

I shoot up from where I'd been reclined on the bed, eyes wide as saucers.

Play it cool, Jess.

"Oh yes, hello! Nice to hear from you. How are you?"

"I'm doing very well, thank you," she answers on an airy laugh.

Brittany is the owner of *Celestial Weddings*, and one of the three I interviewed with when I was sick as a dog. Her event planning company is my top choice and has been ever since I graduated. She built everything from the ground up and has thrown some of the most lavish weddings in Miami over the past eight years.

My throat is suddenly very, very dry.

"I'm calling to thank you for coming in for your interview a couple weeks ago, especially since you clearly weren't feeling well."

I grimace. "Thank you for still *letting* me interview and not throwing me out at the first sight."

"Well, we appreciated that you wore a mask, at least," she says with a laugh.

I think I manage one in return, but I'm mostly trying not to die of embarrassment.

"We interviewed quite a few stellar candidates, all with considerably more experience than you have as a fresh graduate from Palm South University."

My chest deflates, along with the hope I had building in my chest.

"On paper, you were the least qualified of the bunch."

Okay, lady, you don't have to stick a dagger in my throat.

"But..."

I perk up again, and Kade pinches my leg mouthing *what...what...what?*

"If I've learned one thing in this business, it's to trust my gut. And there was just something about you when we interviewed you that really stuck with me. I appreciated your tenacity, your passion, and your willingness to do whatever it takes to get the job done. The fact that you had such a great interview even when you clearly felt like death is impressive, and an admirable trait."

"Thank you, Ms. Nova."

"Well, don't thank me yet. Here's what I'd like to offer you. I'd like to bring you on part time, just to start. I want to see what you can do. It'll be thirty hours a week, no benefits, no vacation until after ninety days and you get forty hours after that to use in your first year. At the end of that time, we can revisit your role and see if there's a permanent spot here for you on our team. What do you say?"

"I say hell fucking yeah!"

I slap a hand over my mouth, groaning at myself as Kade fights back a laugh.

"God, I'm sorry. I mean yes, absolutely, I'd be honored."

Brittany chuckles. "I think I liked your first response better."

I smile.

"My assistant will send an email with more information and some paperwork to fill out, but I want you to start as soon as possible. We have twelve weddings next month and I need all hands on deck."

"I can be there tomorrow morning."

"Well, since tomorrow's Saturday, how about we go for Monday, mm?"

I grimace again. "Yes. Of course. Monday."

"See you, then, Ms. Vonnegut. And welcome to the Celestial team."

"Thank you, see you," I say, and then the line goes dead, and I throw my phone and immediately jump up and down on my bed like a loon.

"What?! What happened?!" Kade screams over my celebrations.

"Jump with me!"

I pull him up from where he's reclining, and he laughs, taking my hands as we jump around and around. Kade is going easier than me — probably worried his beastly frame will break my bed — but I can't contain my excitement. I squeal and jump until I tackle Kade and we land in a flutter of sheets on the mattress.

"I got the job!"

"Oh, my God! With *Celestial Weddings*?!"

"Yes!"

"Babe!"

"I know!" I scream, and then I'm covering him in kisses until he captures my jaw in his hand and presses a good, long kiss to my lips.

"I'm so fucking proud of you!" he says. "We have to celebrate. I'm taking you out. Anywhere you want to go. Dinner. A movie. Dancing. To the beach. Hell, I'll even rent you a yacht if you want."

I pause, arching a brow. "Oh, you got money like that?"

"No, but I can find a way."

I laugh, shaking my head as he presses another kiss to my lips. "I fucking love you."

We both freeze instantly, our eyes shooting open wide, jaws slack.

"Uh..." I start, my cheeks hot, throat dry. "You know what I meant. Like, *I love you, buddy! You're super cool! You're really fun! I—"*

"I love you, too."

That shuts me up again, and for a long moment, I just stare at Kade, at his endless hazel eyes, at the stupid, sexy smirk he's wearing as he watches me trip all over myself.

"You do?"

He chuckles. "Yeah," he whispers. "I really do."

My heart flutters in my chest. "Holy shit."

At that, Kade barks out a laugh. "I know, right?"

"Now we *really* have to celebrate."

"Whatever you want," Kade says, and then he flips me onto my back, pressing me into the sheets. "But first, I think we have some unfinished business..."

And then he kisses his way down and picks up right where he left off.

I come in less than sixty seconds.

Erin

I'm trying real hard not to be a square right now.

I am quite aware of my square-ish tendencies. *Know thyself,* they say, and I know myself well enough to know that I'm not the most spontaneous or fun girl in the world. When I was in college, I put more emphasis on sisterhood and education than I did on partying or hooking up with guys. Still, the last year has changed me, opened me up, loosened my strings a little, and I really do feel like — for the most part — I'm a more laid-back version of the girl I used to be.

And yet, I really, *really* hate that Gavin is high as a kite right now, and that his whole place smells like marijuana.

I don't really have anything against the drug. Jess smokes all the time and I know Skyler dabbles in it, too. I've read articles on the medical benefits for many people, and I believe Gavin that it helps his anxiety and depression.

But I also feel like he's leaned on it instead of therapy.

And I *don't* like that.

I took Bear's advice to heart, and the next day, I called Gavin and told him that I needed him. I told him I really needed him to make time for therapy this week, and to spend a real evening with me.

And just like Bear said, he was quick to give me exactly what I asked for.

I don't know why it takes me so long to come out with what I want, what I need, but it's like I feel like the biggest burden in the world to ask for *anything* from *anyone*. But Gavin made it seem like the most natural thing in the world, and he went to therapy earlier this week and participated more than he ever has. And now, after a fun night out at the boardwalk and a nice dinner, we're back at his place, cuddled on the couch.

Maybe Bear was right.

Maybe everything with us is fine, and I just needed to speak up.

"You want a hit?" he asks me, offering the joint as smoke slips through his lips.

I smile but decline with a shake of my head. "Not really my thing, but thank you."

Gavin grins. "I had a feeling." Then, his eyes go wide. "Ah shit, I didn't even ask if you're okay with me doing it while you're here. Let me put this out."

"No, no," I say, stopping him before he can extinguish the joint. "It's okay. I... I'm trying *not* to mind it."

Gavin chuckles. "Yeah? How's that going?"

"I think I just don't understand it."

"Well, that's because you've never tried it."

"On contrary," I say, holding up one finger. "Last spring, I accidentally ate a whole pot brownie."

"Oh shit," Gavin says after another pull of the joint. "And?"

"*And* I vomited my brains out."

Gavin laughs, but my stomach bottoms out at the memory of that night, because I didn't just throw up literally. I also *word* vomited to Bear that I'd been pregnant with his child.

And that I'd aborted that child without even talking to him first.

I shake off the guilt before it can seep in, reminding myself what my therapist continues to. Bear and I have moved past what happened. He's forgiven me, and now I have to forgive myself.

Easier said than done.

"I can't believe it made you sick, that's never happened to me."

"Well, I *was* already wasted when I had the brownie, so..."

"Ah," he says. "You got the spins."

"Very much so."

"Well, if it bothers you at all, please tell me. I don't have to do it." He shrugs. "It's just nice every now and then, and it takes the edge off."

I frown. "I'm glad it helps. But..."

I stop, suddenly afraid I'll upset him if I say what I want to.

"But... you hate that I'm not going to therapy anymore?"

I grimace, but nod.

Gavin puts out what's left of the joint, and then he turns to face me, pulling me more into his lap. "Listen. I love that you care about me enough to even notice that I haven't gone as much, but I need you to trust me that I'm really okay. I've been focused on school, and I'm happier than I have been in a long time. I'm so close to graduation, to actually being able to *do* something with my degree..." He shakes his head on a smile. "I'm okay. Really."

"Even with the anniversary of Angelica's passing coming up?"

Gavin goes rigid at my words, but it's only for a split second before he nods. "Yeah. Even so. I know she's proud of me." He swallows, the motion emphasized by the bob of his Adam's apple. And then, for a long while, he's silent, just staring at where his hands are holding mine.

"We can—"

"I think it's time for a subject change," he says before I can even finish my sentence, and then in a swift motion, I'm yanked forward and over until I'm straddling him on the couch.

Gavin threads his hands into my hair and pulls my mouth to his in the next instant, kissing me long and deep, and I can taste the unfamiliar earthiness of the marijuana on his tongue. I relax into the kiss, feeling my body humming to life under his touch, and when I roll my hips against him, I feel him already hard and ready.

"Gavin," I gasp, reaching down to roll my hand over his hard-on through his sweatpants. "You're so hard."

"Fuck, Erin," he pants against my lips, pressing his forehead to mine long enough to catch his breath. He shakes his head. "I want you so fucking bad."

"So take me," I plead.

He swallows, groans, bites his lip and shakes his head again. "I want to. *God*, do I want to, Erin. But I..." He pauses. "I promised I wouldn't hurt you."

"You won't. I know you won't," I say, kissing him earnestly. "I trust you."

He grimaces at that, and suddenly, he unloops my hands from around his neck and puts space between us, dropping his head back against the couch cushion on a sigh.

"What?" I ask. "What did I do?"

"Nothing. You're perfect, Erin. It's me who..."

But he doesn't finish. He just sits there, breathing, eyes closed and hands holding my wrists so I don't reach back to touch him. It's not long before he's softening between my legs, and I bite back the urge to cry even as the tears well in my eyes.

When Gavin looks up and sees me, his face crumples. "Jesus. Erin, please, I'm sor—"

"It's fine," I say, the statement clipped as I climb off him. I sniff, adjusting my leggings and t-shirt before I reach down for my purse on the coffee table. "I think I should go."

Everything inside me wants Gavin to reach for me, pull me into him, finish his sentence. I want him to tell me he's sorry, that he's wrong, that he wants me and that's it, period, end of story, no buts. I want him to tell me not to go. I want him to ask me to stay.

Instead, he sighs, his eyes sad as he nods and says, "I'll walk you out."

Rejection seeps into my bones as he walks me to my car, but I manage to fight back the tears even as he gives me a long, sweet kiss goodnight and promises he'll call me tomorrow. He says he wants to see me again this weekend. He says to drive home safe. He says to text him when I get there, just so he doesn't worry.

I barely hear a thing.

My ears are ringing so loudly that by the time I pull away from his apartment, it's like I'm being chased by a train. I drive only a few blocks before I nearly pull out in front of someone, and after slamming on my brakes and flinching from the sound of their horn, all the noise clears.

I drive to the next block, pull over to the side of the road, and let myself cry.

Bear

"Holy shit, he is so fast!" Skyler says, her mouth hanging open as she watches my little brother sprint across the Palm South University practice field. He gets fifteen yards down before he cuts left, looking back just in time to catch the ball thrown in a perfect spiral right to his chest. He takes off toward the end zone, running the play all the way through before the coach blows his whistle.

"I'm telling you, he has more talent in his pinky finger than I ever had when I played," I muse with a proud smile.

It's family weekend at Palm South, and that means the campus is crawling with moms and dads and siblings who have come to check out the university. Family weekend is always filled with barbecues and field games, Greek Row presentations and fancy family dinners, and more. My personal favorite part is how the college bars that are usually crawling with students take on a completely new vibe once the parents are involved.

Sometimes, they party harder than the kids.

As for my family, this is the first time I've had them all here. Sure, Clayton has come out a few years now to visit, but other than when she showed up to ask for money, Mom has never been. Carleton, my older brother, and his wife and kids, are here, too.

It's a surreal experience, having them here, and knowing that in just a couple more months they'll be watching me walk across the stage, too.

"His coach talked to me after this past season ended," my mom chimes in from the other side of Skyler. "He said scouts are already asking to come watch as early as next season, even though he'll only be a junior."

"They want to snag him early so he doesn't even consider other options," I say. "But if he hasn't changed his mind, the last I heard, Palm South University was the *only* school he was considering."

"He wants to be like his big brother," Mom says, smiling at me. "Can't say I blame him."

When I found out the whole family was coming for family weekend, I set an appointment to talk to the head coach for Palm South University's football team. I told him about Clayton and showed him some of his tapes, pleading for him to carve some time out to run some drills with him. I was honestly flabbergasted that coach actually agreed.

And that was just further proof that Clayton has what it takes to play at the collegiate level.

So, for the last hour, coach and a few of his second- and third-string players have been running drills with Clayton while Mom, Skyler, and I watch from the sidelines. Carleton took his wife and the kids to the beach for the day, but they'll be meeting up with us later.

"I kind of wish we were closer in age," I say, watching as Clayton takes a giant swig of water from his bottle before jogging back out onto the field for the next drill. "It would be cool to be here with him."

"Ohhh no," Skyler says with a shake of her head. "There's no way this campus could handle two Penningtons at once."

"Touché."

"I'm actually thinking of moving down here with him," Mom says, and Skyler and I both snap our heads in her direction.

"Really?" Skyler asks.

Mom nods. "I know he'll be in a dorm or living in the fraternity house — since I know he wants to rush immediately." She winks at me with that. "But... I don't know. I missed so much of Clinton's experience, I don't want to do the same with Clayton. I want to be around to see his games and help him with schoolwork or whatever. If I get a little place not too far from campus, I can be there when he needs me."

Something pinches my stomach, something that feels a little like resentment and a lot like jealousy. But it's only there for a moment before genuine relief and joy wash over me.

"I think that's amazing, Mom," I say.

Her brown eyes glisten in the sun when she returns my smile. "And then you'd have a place to visit, if you ever wanted to come back to PSU."

Skyler whips her head in my direction then. "Come back? Are you leaving?"

I give Mom a *thanks a lot* look, because the truth is, I haven't really decided anything. But Pittsburgh is calling to me. I could be there for the last two years of high school for Clayton, and be closer to my nephews, and spend time with my mom. Besides, I miss the Burgh. I miss seasons. I miss not always sweating when I walk outside.

"I haven't decided anything," I tell Skyler. "But... I'm leaning toward going back to Pittsburgh. There are a lot of creative agencies up there, and I think it would be cool to start my graphic design career in my home city."

I can see how hard the next swallow is for Skyler, how her eyebrows furrow together, her bottom lip quivering. But she still manages a smile, and she reaches over to squeeze my arm. "You'll be amazing no matter where you go. And hey, gives me an excuse to visit. I like Pittsburgh, too."

"You're welcome anytime, honey," Mom says from her side.

Coach blows the whistle, and then he waves to where we are on the sideline, calling us to come onto the field where Clayton is jogging over.

"Great job, son," he says when we're all gathered, clapping Clayton on the back. My little brother is absolutely drenched in sweat, his hands hanging on his hips, chest heaving as he attempts to catch his breath.

"Thank you, sir."

"And you're not even done growing yet," one of the students who was running drills with Clayton says. "You're going to be one massive receiver."

"Big and fast," Clayton says with his megawatt smile. "I want to be untouchable."

Coach chuckles, squeezing his shoulders. "I think you're well on your way. Listen, you're a little too young to give a full-on offer to. It goes against scouting laws. Besides, we need to see how the next season goes, see what our team is looking like, too. But, as far as I'm concerned? You keep playing like this..." He nods toward where the drills were being run. "And I have full faith that come your senior year, I'll be in the stands at your first home game with a scholarship offer in hand."

Clayton's eyes nearly bug out of his head. "A scholarship?"

Coach grins. "With skills like that, kid? I won't be the only one offering. So I just hope your heart stays set on PSU."

"Oh, trust me, sir," he says, smiling at him first and then at me. "This is the only university for me."

"Atta boy," coach says, then he turns to my mother, extending his hand. "Ma'am, you've raised a fine young man. It was an honor to spend some time on the field with him."

"Well, thank you, but it's his older brother here who gets the credit for the way Clayton has turned out. He's always been his role model, and I haven't always been around."

Coach looks at me, then, and there's something in his eyes, a level of understanding, maybe, as he shakes my hand next. "Well done, son. And might I ask why I never saw you at try outs?" he adds, eyeing my size with a smirk.

I grin. "Too busy partying, I'm afraid."

"Can't win 'em all." Coach tips his hat at us. "I've got to get going, but it was a pleasure meeting all of you. Enjoy the rest of your weekend."

"You too," we all chime, and when he's gone, Clayton turns to face us with his hands laced on top of his head.

"DID YOU GUYS SEE THAT SHIT?!"

"Language, Clayton!" Mom says at the same time I high-five him and say, "Hell fucking yeah, I saw it!"

I throw my arm around his shoulder, steering all of us back to the Omega Chi house so he can shower before the Omega Chi family dinner.

We're all rambling as we walk through campus, and eventually, Mom and Clayton pull ahead a little, Mom smiling as Clayton excitedly tells her about everything coach said. Skyler falls in step beside me with a soft smile on her face.

"I can't believe how much he's grown."

"You're telling me. I can't stop seeing him as ten years old. I don't know why, but that's where he stopped growing in my eyes. I don't think I'll ever see him past that."

Skyler chuckles. "I'm glad they could all be here. You must be over the moon."

"It's weird," I admit. "But yeah, it's cool, too. Please tell me I get to see your parents this weekend?"

"Dad couldn't get off work, sadly, *but* they did promise they'd come for your graduation."

I frown. "They don't need to do that."

"Are you kidding?" Skyler nudges my arm. "You're my best friend, Bear, and practically my brother. They wouldn't miss it."

I smile, throwing my arm around her shoulders. "You'll be right behind me in the fall," I comment. "How are your entrepreneur classes going? Still think this is the right move?"

Skyler gives me a genuine smile at that. "Without a doubt. I've actually been thinking about telling Kip that I'll come out to Los Angeles with him and try my startup there."

"Wow. California. Really?"

She nods. "There are so many opportunities for events in that city, and if I build my company up the right way, I can get in with the elite crowd. Can you picture it? Charity casino events with Hollywood's rich and famous?"

"You'd better be careful. You're the kind of gorgeous that they'd be talking you into a movie role before you know it."

Skyler scoffs. "Yeah, I don't think that life is for me."

Her smile slips with the words, and I frown, squeezing her shoulder. "What's with the sad panda face?"

She shrugs. "I don't know. I've been all up in my lady feels lately."

"Do tell."

"It's just... I was so excited when Kip surprised me last semester and told me he was going to be back at PSU. After all the long distance, it was like a dream come true, you know? But he's been so caught up with his show that, other than Spring Break, I've barely seen him."

I pause, trying to think of how to say what I want to. "Well, Sky, this is important to him. I mean, this could be his ticket to a job after graduation."

"I know. I guess I just thought I'd be more of a priority to him."

"Think about it this way — what if it was you going out to L.A. with the opportunity to kickstart your casino company? Don't you think that would take up the majority of your time and energy? And don't you think you'd want Kip to understand and support that?"

Skyler frowns. "I hate when you're right."

"You must hate me most of the time, then."

She rolls her eyes. "It's just... oh God, how do I say this without sounding petty..." She rolls her lips together. "So, remember how I helped out a little with casting?"

"Yeah. I remember you saying the girl you picked to play you was perfect."

"Ha! Well, this is me eating my words."

"Uh-oh."

"Yeah," she says with a long sigh. "Let's just say the girl's got it bad for Kip, and since he's spending most of his time working on the show, they're together like... *all* the time. I tried telling him to keep his guard up, that she wants him, but of course he's oblivious."

I chuckle. "*Or* he's so obsessed with you that he wouldn't notice a girl flirting with him even if she had her naked titties hanging in his face."

"I'm surprised Natalia hasn't tried that yet, honestly."

I laugh. "Sky, I promise, you have nothing to worry about. Kip is yours. After all the shit you two went through, I can promise you that not even a hot-ass movie star could take your place in his heart."

Even as she nods, I can see the worry etched into my best friend's face, and I pull her to a stop on the sidewalk, telling Mom and Clayton to go on without us and we'll catch up.

"Talk to him," I say, framing her arms in my hands. "Okay? Tell him you miss him and you need some quality time. Tell him it's important to you. He may be caught up in filming and the excitement of the show, but if you level with him, if you *communicate*," I add, tickling her sides as she giggles and tries to break free. "He won't let you down."

Skyler sighs as I pull her into my chest for a long hug, and she squeezes my waist in return. "Thank you, Bear. I love you."

"Love you more."

Jess

I wake to the feeling of Kade's warm palm running down my back.

Like a cat, I arch into the touch, practically purring as he grabs my hip and pulls me into his chest. His hard-on is rock solid through his boxers, and I rub my ass against it, hissing in my next breath.

"Morning, baby," he husks into my ear, sucking the lobe between his teeth.

"Good morning, indeed."

He chuckles, kissing down my neck and already working my sleep shorts down my hips, my thighs, until they're restraining my knees. I kick them the rest of the way off, which is a feat through the heavy, drugged feeling of just waking up.

"God, you feel so good," he whispers, running his hand up to grab my tits under my sleep tank. He palms one and then the other, pebbling my nipples into peaks.

"I want you," I whisper back.

"What about me?"

I creak my eyes open and find Jarrett standing in the doorway.

My heart accelerates at the sight of him, naked as the day he was born, all those tattoos sprawling over his body, his beard freshly trimmed, eyes on fire as they watch me and Kade in the bed.

"Jarrett?"

He smirks, slowly stalking toward me like I'm his prey, his fist slowly pumping over his cock all the way. "Do you want me, too?"

I try to swallow, but my mouth is too dry.

"Answer him," Kade says from behind me, biting my shoulder.

"I..."

Before I can get another word out, Jarrett stops at the edge of the bed and reaches down to grip my chin in his hand, forcing me to look up at him over the valleys and ridges of his abdomen.

"Tell me, Jess," he commands. "Do you want me?"

"Yes."

The word is a whisper and a plea and a guilty admission all at once. I wait for Kade to stop, to tear away from me, to scream and demand answers, but instead, he only growls in my ear as he runs his hard-on against my ass again.

"You want my brother, huh?"

I swallow. "Yes."

Kade removes his boxers, lining himself up at my entrance from behind, his hands gripping my hips and pulling me back until I open for him.

"Well, now that we know the truth, that you want both of us," he says between licks and sucks of my neck. "The question is can you *handle* both of us?"

I gasp, my pussy so wet and swollen I nearly come just from his words in my ear.

"Only one way to find out," Jarrett says from where he towers over me.

And as his brother slides inside me, filling me from behind, I gasp.

And Jarrett slides his cock inside my wide-open mouth.

I moan around the fullness, both in my mouth and in my pussy, heart racing so fast I'm sure I'll pass out or have a heart attack at any moment.

I can barely breathe, all thought lost as Jarrett groans, his head falling back. "Fuck yes, Jess, suck my cock."

I moan again, taking him in deeper, and Kade groans behind me, kissing my shoulders. "She's so fucking tight, brother."

"Yeah?" Jarrett asks. "You should feel her mouth."

"Not until I make her come," Kade says, and as if on a mission, he wraps one hand around me to rub my clit.

"Oh, God," I mouth around Jarrett's cock, still as smooth and big as I remembered.

"You like that?" Jarrett asks. "You like when my brother rubs your clit?"

"Yes," I pant, taking Jarrett's cock in my hand as I let my head fall back. "I'm going to... Oh fuck... Oh *fuck!*"

My orgasm is a volcano, hot and all-consuming, erupting from the very core of me and covering every inch of my body in its wake. I writhe in my sheets with my eyes squeezed shut, heart racing, shallow breaths racking my chest as I fly apart.

And when I open my eyes, it's early dawn, the sun barely rising over the city.

And I'm alone in my bed.

I let out a long gasp when my orgasm recedes, my body trembling, and I lie there for just a split second before I rip my covers back and scurry up to sit against the headboard.

I blink, over and over, my chest still heaving as I let myself come down from the wet dream.

A dream.

That's all it was.

"Fuck me," I say, letting my head fall back to hit the headboard. It all felt so real...

And that's the fucking issue.

It felt real, and I *wanted* it. I wanted Kade. I wanted Jarrett.

I wanted them both at the same time.

"Jesus fucking Christ, Jess, what is *wrong* with you?!"

I run my hands back through my hair, still catching my breath. I stay there for a long while, until the sun starts shining directly into my room, and then I peel myself out of my damp sheets and waltz my still-swollen pussy into the shower.

The water is too hot, but I let it sear my skin as I stand under the showerhead. Then, I turn it all the way cold, sucking in a gasp and fighting the urge to jump out.

You deserve this, bitch.

I fall onto the tile floor, leaning my back against the corner and letting the water rain down over me.

I just told Kade I love him. And I *do*. I do love him. I love how caring he is, and how fucking goofy he is, and how he captured my heart when I didn't even think I still had a heart to give.

And of course, I still have feelings for Jarrett. With how we ended, how could I not?

But enough is enough.

I have to let go of this fantasy.

A threesome dream? Really, Jess?

I shake my head at myself, but don't make any moves to get off the shower floor.

No, I'm going to stay here, for as long as it takes to drop this fantasy of Jarrett. He was my past. What we had was real, that's true. And maybe we *would* always love each other, just like we texted when we broke up.

But he broke up with me.

And I moved on.

And Kade has my heart now.

That's all there is to it. Jarrett and I are done. We're over.

And when I shut the shower off, I let the last bit of him that I was holding onto wash down the drain with the icy cold water.

Ashlei

Every girl has this unique feeling when they *know* they look fine as hell.

Sure, there are days when I'm in my sweatpants and a t-shirt with my hair in a messy bun and I'm like *aww, I'm kind of cute right now*. And there are days when my business casual outfit at work is color coordinated and fresh. And sure, there are nights when I go out with the girls, hair curled and lashes on, when all the looks from guys — and girls — as we pass lets me know I nailed the outfit.

But then, there are nights like *this*.

It's the South Beach Agency Awards, which is about as close to the Grammys as it comes in our industry. Just like the event I went to with Brandon in Atlanta as his intern, only the best of the best are invited to the SBAA. This is where you learn who is at the top of the game, be it events, advertising, weddings, corporate conventions, or any other creative space.

And if you're invited, you better have enough sense to dress *all* the way up.

Since the *Ball & Pen* Miami branch just opened in the first quarter, we're not nominated for any of the awards tonight. But thanks to my memorable launch event, Celeste received two shiny gold tickets as an invitation to the festivities.

One for her, and one for me.

I would have dressed up regardless, but going through the nominees on the website and seeing that *Okay, Cool* was up for both Best Pop Up Event and Best Brand Engagement Event, I knew Brandon would be here.

With that in mind, I went all out.

My silky red dress is custom-made, floor-length, and strapless with a delicate loop of fabric draped across my left arm. It has a pearl-accented bust and a highly tapered waist that accentuates my figure and gives it even more of an hourglass shape, especially the way the fabric rouches around my hips and drapes down elegantly to the floor. Of course, there's a long slit, just enough for my freshly tanned legs to peek through as I walk. And each time, my pearl and Swarovski crystal-covered heels glimmer in the chandelier light.

My hair waterfalls over one shoulder in elegant curls, my highlights fresh and shiny, and my makeup is done to perfection. My lashes are black and thick, accented with falsies, my lips are painted a bright matte red to match my dress, and my eyes are smokey and sultry. Each accessory I picked out is tasteful, just enough to add to the outfit without detracting from it.

I felt it when I left the house, and I feel it even more now as Celeste and I walk through the crowd, stopping to say hello and chat every now and then.

All eyes are on me.

I feel like a siren, a vixen, a witch. I keep my eyes non-focused for the most part, trained on Celeste as we walk and talk, or perhaps on taking in the scenery. But the moment I drop my gaze to a man or woman staring at me, all the blood rushes to their cheeks, and they falter for a smile or a nod of their head or a quiet, subdued *hello*.

There are many ways for a woman to feel powerful, and I don't care what anyone says — wearing a badass dress and heels is one of them.

"We'll be here again next year," Celeste says softly to me as we walk, a smile on her face as she nods to groups as we pass. "Only next year, we'll have a dozen nominations. Mark my words."

"Oh, I don't doubt it."

"One of them will be Best Launch Event," she adds with a smirk. "You know I'm *still* getting calls requesting co-ops."

"The more the merrier, right?"

"You're going to be a very busy woman, Ashlei. I hope you're ready for it."

I smile, and not just at her insinuation, but at the pair of warm brown eyes I just caught staring at me from across the ballroom.

"Born ready."

Brandon is standing in a small group next to a cocktail table, a drink in his hand and the same woman at his side who was with him at our launch event. He looks absolutely delectable in his beige suit, tailored to perfection as always. I don't have to be close to him to know it's designer and expensive as fuck, that the shoes on his feet probably cost more than my entire outfit combined, and that he's wearing a Rolex watch worth more than any car I've ever owned.

I also don't have to be close to him to see that the sight of me knocked the breath from his chest.

It's in the way he's holding his glass — a little too tight, a little too close to his chest — and in the way his brows are furrowed, his jaw set, his eyes ablaze where they watch me move across the room.

"Excuse me, Celeste," I say. "I'm going to freshen up."

She nods, and we part ways — her joining one group while I slowly make my way toward Brandon. He watches me the entire way, and I think I even see him shake his head subtly, as if to warn me.

Don't do this.

Don't try me.

But it's all I want to do.

Someone else in the group notices as I approach, and his brow arches, his conversation cutting off right in the middle of whatever he was saying — which, of course, makes the rest of the group turn my way, too.

It doesn't make me quicken my steps.

I take my time, squeezing the arms of a few people I know as I pass them on the way. *Hello, lovely to see you, oh you look wonderful, too, yes let's get a drink, I'll be right back.*

I've got a confident smile painted on my lips when I finally reach Brandon, and I sidle up directly across from him, between two older gentlemen who are practically dripping drool on my arms.

"Hello, Mr. Church."

I see the flash of fire in his eyes, the flare of his nostrils, the ticking of his jaw as he tries to soothe his breath. "Ms. Daniels."

"I wanted to congratulate you on your nominations this evening," I say. "I have no doubt you'll take home the gold."

"That's the plan."

"We have stiff competition, though," the young woman next to him adds. "And once you've been in the game for a year, I imagine it'll be even more so."

I smile, reaching across the small circle to squeeze her wrist briefly. "You're too kind, Colleen."

Her eyes widen. "You remembered my name."

"Of course, I did," I say. "You work for my old agency, and for one of the best, in my opinion." I pause, then, locking my eyes on Brandon's. "*Okay, Cool* will always have a special place in my heart."

Colleen covers her chest with clasped hands. "That's so sweet. I will say, you're sorely missed. Most of all by MyKayla. She talks about you all the time."

"Ha! That reminds me, I need to get her check in the mail."

That earns me a chuckle from the group, and just as quickly as I came, I nod and smile to each of them before excusing myself.

I hold Brandon's gaze last, my eyes lingering, and when everyone else has turned away and back to their conversation, I take my shot.

Come and get me, I mouth.

Brandon frowns, his nose flaring again as he blinks several times like he's trying to convince himself he couldn't have possibly heard what he just did.

I just smile and bite my lower lip, turning slowly and making my way out of the ballroom to the hallway where the restrooms are.

When I get to the door, I look over my shoulder, my eyes catching his again.

Come on, I plead with my gaze. *I know you want this just as bad as I do.*

With that final bit of voodoo, I exit the ballroom, inhaling what feels like my first fresh breath now that I'm out of his fiery gaze. I keep my shoulders held back and my head high as I walk to the restrooms, but instead of going to the ladies' room, I duck around the corner and into the one and only family bathroom tucked away from the main hallway.

When I'm inside, I blow out a breath, planting my hands on the sink and staring at my reflection. Suddenly, a laugh bubbles out of me, and I shake my head, arching a brow at myself.

"This will never work," I say out loud, as if to hammer it home and diminish any hope I have left.

Still, I smooth my hands over my dress, touch up my hair, and stand against the wall directly across from where the door opens.

The bathroom is large, made for moms with kids, I'm sure. There's even an elegant changing table and a royal blue velvet chaise lounge. The counter has a basket with baby wipes and powder and even deodorant and a small first aid kit.

My eyes keep flicking to the chaise.

The longer I stand there, the more my heart rate recedes, and the excitement and adrenaline I had coursing through my veins starts to slowly drain.

It must be at least five minutes since I walked in here, and he didn't follow.

I sigh, letting my head drop back against the wall. What did I really expect? The last time I ran into him, he essentially reiterated that he hated me.

But the way he *looked* at me...

I swallow, shaking my head at myself as a soft laugh leaves my chest. "Stupid girl."

And just as I'm ready to give up, to check my appearance one last time and rejoin the event, the doorhandle jiggles.

My head pops off where I'd been resting it against the wall, and my breath hitches in my throat as the gold knob turns. The wide door slowly opens, just a sliver, just enough.

Brandon slips through the opening and locks the door behind him.

God, the way the air crackles to life when that lock clicks into place.

Brandon keeps his back to the door, his hand on the knob, as if he's one wrong look or word or move from bolting out again. His chest is already heaving, his eyes fiercely burning into mine.

But he's just standing there.

Waiting.

As if he can't believe he followed me, that he found me, that he knew from just one look where I was going and what I wanted.

But that's the way it is with us, the way it's *always* been.

We're connected on a chemical, molecular level.

And nothing can change it.

This is it, my heart whispers. *It's now or never*.

I still a breath, one that fills my lungs and helps me stand straighter as I push off where I was leaning against the wall. I take two steps toward Brandon, watching the way my approach makes his throat tighten, his grip on the doorknob increases.

"So," I say when I'm just a foot away from him. "Are we done with this *break* you wanted, or what? Because I want you, Brandon. I never *stopped* wanting you. And if you're done punishing me now, I'd like you to bend me over this chaise and remind me that I belong to you. To *only* you."

The growl that rips from Brandon's chest is primal, elemental, so animalistic that it makes me freeze up just like a gazelle threatened by a lion's roar. In the next breath, Brandon's hands are in my hair, yanking back as he shoves me back across the room until my spine hits the wall. My neck arches, my chin tilts, and with my next breath still lodged somewhere in my throat, Brandon crushes his mouth to mine.

The moment our lips meet, we both exhale on a greedy moan, Brandon's grip in my hair tightening even more as I reach around and grab his ass firmly in my palms. He kisses me so hard I taste the metallic tang of blood, but I push back just as hard, seeking him just as much.

"I fucking *hate* you," he seethes, grabbing both my wrists and pinning them over my head. When they're locked under one of his hands, the other trails down to hike the silky fabric of my dress up over my hips.

"No, you don't," I breathe back, dragging my tongue up his neck. "You could never hate something you own."

Another growl rips through him, and he skates his fingers under the band of my strap of a thong, slipping two fingers inside me without warning.

I cry out, arching my back off the wall as Brandon bites my neck like a fucking vampire. "You broke me," he pants, curling his fingers deep inside me.

"So break me back."

"*Fucking hell,*" he hisses, and then just like I asked, he spins me until I nearly fall flat on my face on the navy blue chaise. My hands fly out just in time to break my fall, but my hips are bent over the back of it, my palms on the plush cushions, ass up in the air.

I peek over my shoulder, batting my lashes as Brandon shakes his head and starts to undo his belt.

"Pull your dress up and drop your panties," he commands.

A shiver runs through me, and I do as he says, assuming the same position once my bare ass is exposed.

Brandon groans at the sight of me, dropping his pants to his knees and taking his full, heavy, heaving cock in his hand as he makes his way to me.

His other hand is holding his belt.

"Are you going to spank me?" I breathe.

"You're damn fucking right, I am."

Excitement and terror rip through me in equal measure. I've never been spanked before, not with anything more than a hand, and the way Brandon is glaring at me, I can't tell if I'm going to like this or not be able to sit for a week.

Maybe both.

"Safe word?" he asks, rubbing his palm over my ass before folding his belt in two.

"I trust you."

He shakes his head in warning, but then his focus is on my ass.

He rears back, just a little, and then lands the leather on my skin.

I hiss, arching away from the hit, but it only stings a little. I know he can hit harder, but he didn't.

"Don't ever fucking kiss anyone else again," he says, and he rears back a little more, slapping my ass with the leather enough to make me yelp.

"Yes, sir."

"That mouth of yours belongs to *me*."

Another whip.

Another welt, I imagine.

Another whispered, "Yes, sir."

"And for the love of God, Ashlei," he says, holding the belt up higher, his eyes locked on mine where I'm watching him over my shoulder. "If I give you my heart again, don't fucking break it. Don't..."

He swallows, and it's then that I see the pain in his eyes, the emotion he's been hiding. I push off the chaise, turning and wrapping my arms around him.

"I won't. I promise. I never will again." I kiss his lips, his jaw, his cheeks, his neck. "I'm sorry. I'm so fucking sorry."

Brandon holds the belt up even more, and then with a wince, he drops it.

And his arms are around me.

He crushes me to him so tight I can't breathe, kissing me senseless and winding his hands in my hair. Then, without warning, he spins me again, and I fall hands first onto the chaise with my ass up in the air.

My dress had fallen back down when I stood, but it takes Brandon only seconds to have it up over my hips again. And no sooner than he does do I feel the slick tip of him press inside me.

And with a flex, he fills me to the hilt.

"Oh, *fuck,* Brandon!" I cry out, and he grabs the back of my dress and rips me to stand so he can slap a hand over my mouth.

"Shhhh."

I stifle the laugh against his palm, and once I nod, he removes it, and I pant out my desire as he withdraws and presses into me once more.

"Goddammit, I've missed this," he curses, kissing the back of my neck. "I've missed *you.*"

His hands grip my hips so he can find a rhythm, and he pounds into me harder, faster, his release building.

With my palms gripping the edge of the chaise, I meet him pump for pump, my ass slapping against his thighs. When his hands reach around and rip the strapless top of my dress down to free my breasts, they swing wildly, his fingertips just barely touching my sensitive nipples and driving me insane.

"Brandon," I pant. "Oh, God."

"Fuck, I'm not going to last."

"Don't," I say, short and simple, and with that permission, I feel him empty his release inside me, his cock pulsing, and he reaches down to circle my clit and make me topple over the edge with him.

My legs tremble and quake with the orgasm, and it takes every ounce of willpower I have to keep myself quiet. I want to scream. I want to cry out his name. I want to declare myself this man's forever.

When we're both spent, Brandon carefully pulls out and falls directly down to the floor, his back sliding against the tile wall. I laugh as I do the same, and then we're side by side, his pants around his ankles and my dress no more than a heap of fabric, my naked breasts heaving under his gaze.

For the longest time, we just sit there, trying to catch our breaths, our eyes dancing between each other's.

After a while, a smile curls on Brandon's lips, and I laugh, letting my head fall back against the wall.

"Now what?"

Bear

"Are you sure I'm not imposing?" Erin asks, holding one elbow with the opposite hand. "We could hang out another day if—"

"Nonsense," Mom answers for me. "The more the merrier. We have an uneven number for games, anyway."

Erin smiles at Mom before her big eyes flick to mine.

"What she said," I echo, and then I throw my arm around Erin and start leading the group down Greek Row.

"Uncle Bear, can I ride on your shoulders?!" my youngest nephew, Camron, asks. He just turned four last month, and with his mom's golden eyes and my brother's dimples, he's become quite accustomed to getting whatever he asks for.

So, of course, I smile at Erin and remove my arm from around her shoulder so I can bend down and help Camron climb up.

My older nephew, Cole, is nine now. His eyes are the darker brown of my brothers, and where Camron is lean and lanky, Cole has started bulking out — thanks to working out with his dad ever since he came back. He's almost to that age where he's too cool for us, but hasn't quite made it yet.

My heart squeezes a little when he runs to catch up with me and grabs my hand.

"You good, buddy?" I ask him.

"Yeah," he answers simply. He's become a lot quieter over the last couple years, and I know a big part of that has to do with his dad disappearing and then coming back out of nowhere.

I know from experience how that can mess with your mind as a kid.

It's the last day of family weekend, and the Panhellenic Council put together a day of field events in the open half-acre between Zeta Rho Kappa and Zeta Pi Alpha. It's a chance for families to have a little friendly competition while also stopping by the booths hosted by each fraternity and sorority to learn a little more about the organizations.

Plus, food and booze, of course.

Lots of food and booze.

Mom, Clayton, Carleton, Carleton's wife Janae, and my nephews met up with me at the house about fifteen minutes ago so we could head down together.

But when we opened the door to leave, Erin was walking up the lawn to the Omega Chi house.

God, the way my chest tightened at the sight of her. Her dark blonde hair was straight and parted down the middle, falling just to her shoulders. She was wearing a yellow sundress that highlighted her smooth, tan skin, and the way the straps of it hung delicately on her shoulders made me want to slip a finger beneath the fabric and slide it off.

I don't know why she showed up here today, why she was at the house without even texting to see if I'd be around. Something tells me she showed up on a whim, that part of her was hoping she wouldn't find me at all.

But she did.

Along with my entire family.

"So, how are we breaking up these teams?" Clayton asks when we make it to the field. It's already bustling with Greeks and parents alike. "Because I think I want dibs on Erin."

He winks up at her, which makes her laugh and arch a brow at me.

"Hey, I'm not responsible," I claim, throwing my hands up.

"I like that idea," Mom says. "You and Erin, Carleton and Janae..." She pauses, then, her eyes a bit apprehensive when she smiles at me. "And me and you, Bear?"

I smile back. "Let's do it."

Mom's eyes water up a bit, but she smiles to clear the emotion, and once we drop my nephews off at the kids' area, we make our way to the first event.

It's a beautiful day in South Florida, warm but breezy with plenty of cloud cover. There's supposed to be a storm moving in later this evening, but right now, it's paradise.

We start with the long jump, which Carleton wins in a landslide, thanks to his beanstalk legs. We used to tease him and call him Daddy Long Legs when we were kids. He's always been a lanky sonofabitch, but this time, it came in handy for him.

Next is the tug of war, which Mom and I win, mostly thanks to the fact that I haven't missed a day at the gym since I was fourteen. Then there's the one-hundred-yard dash, which stuns us all when Janae pulls out some speed we had no idea she contained.

"First place relay team in high school, suckers," she teases after the victory, and she and Carleton high-five each other before kissing in a way that makes Clayton murmur, "Gross."

There's disc golf and relay races, an egg and spoon course, and a ping-pong ball race where you have to use a water gun to get the ball to move. There's a balloon pop and three-legged race, and of course, a Double Dutch jump rope competition which Mom dominates because she grew up on that game.

Course after course, race after race, we frolic around the field as a family.

And the longer we play, the more emotional I get.

I swear, I'm getting soft in my old age. Maybe it's that graduation is sneaking up on me, and all those same feelings that were haunting me over Spring Break are only getting stronger now. But I'm laughing harder than I have in years, and yet I also feel like I'm on the verge of tears.

This is the first time I think we've *ever* been like this as a family.

Sure, when we were younger, Mom would take us to the park on her day off sometimes, or let us play basketball at the courts while she watched. But we never took family vacations. Timing never seemed to work out, especially once we got older, once Carleton settled down and I went off to college. That limited time we'd managed to save for each other became less and less.

I think the last time we were even all together at the same time was the Christmas after Camron was born.

Four years ago.

It's something I never thought I'd see — Mom clean and healthy, Carleton being a good father and husband, my nephews carefree and living it up. It makes it all better to see how positively it's impacting Clayton, how he's able to recoup his relationship with our mother and have her around while he chases his football dreams and finishes high school.

What a stark contrast to where we all were just a few years ago, when Skyler was writing checks for my drugged-out mom and older brother, and my little brother had to move in with his best friend's family.

To top it all off, Erin is here.

And *fuck* if that doesn't wreck me, too.

Because I see her joking with my brothers, playing with my nephews, and talking with my mother, and I have this ridiculous pinch in my gut that she belongs here.

That *we* belong here.

I can also see that she's not okay.

I don't know what's going on, but the fact that she showed up to the O Chi house unannounced tells me something isn't right. Pair that with the fact that I know the difference between her real smiles and the ones she has to fake, and it's plain as day.

I make a mental note to ask later.

For now, I've got to beat her ass in this wheelbarrow race to break the tie between our team and hers.

"Alright, teams," Skyler says, blowing her whistle once to get our attention before she lets it dangle around her neck. As the president of KKB, she's one of the hosts of the field day, and she's got the suntan to prove it. "One of you assumes the position of the wheelbarrow, putting your hands on the ground and letting your other partner hold your legs around their waist. Then, you have to work together to get down around the cones and back first. If the wheelbarrow's feet touch the ground at any point, you have to start over."

"You're going down," Erin whispers to me.

"In your dreams, Ex."

She just smirks, and then when Skyler says to get ready, she effortlessly cartwheels into a handstand.

I gape at her while Clayton does the same, and then he sidles up to grab her legs and hoist them around his waist.

When he grins back at me, I kind of want to punch him.

"Alright, Bear," Mom says, planting her hands on the ground. "I'm not going to be as graceful, but we can win this. Let's focus on going slow and steady. That's what wins the race."

I don't know that I agree with her, but I don't have a chance to argue before Skyler blows the whistle and the race begins.

Erin and Clayton speed off instantly, Erin's hands moving fast as lightning as my little brother struggles to keep up behind her. Mom and I start a little slower, starting with me carefully hoisting her legs up before we talk each other through the movement.

Left, right, left, right.

Slow and steady.

I have to fight to keep from grinding my teeth together as Erin and Clayton expand their lead, and they're already rounding the cones and heading back our way when Mom and I have only made it to the half-way point. But then, something happens, and Clayton loses his footing, stumbling forward too fast for Erin to keep herself upright. They tumble to the ground, and then mutter a string of curses as they scramble up and back to the line to start again.

"We've got this!" Mom yells, and she picks up the pace while I use all my focus to keep her straight and steady.

We round the cones and make our way back, but Erin and Clayton are already hot on our heels. They round the cones behind us when we still have about halfway to go to get back to the finish line.

I can hear them panting and plodding in the grass behind us, so I hold onto Mom tighter and yell, "Double-time, Mom. Let's win this thing!"

We go as fast as we can, and even still, Clayton and Erin are gaining on us. In the end, we're so close when we all tumble over the finish line that I have no idea who actually won. We stare up at Skyler from where we're laid out in the grass now, and she blows her whistle, walking over to the four of us.

Then, she grabs my Mom's hand first and then my own, lifting them high in the air.

"Winners!"

Mom screams, jumping up first and launching herself at me as soon as I'm standing, too. Clayton is yelling something about *bullshit* while I throw Mom up for a piggyback and do a victory lap with her in tow.

When I round the cones and head back, Erin is standing with her arms crossed and a smirk on her face, shaking her head as she watches me.

***

Later that evening, we're all gathered around a giant table at the Mexican place right off campus, the ones with margaritas the size of your head and the best damn guacamole money can buy.

When we order our second round, Clayton complains that he's the only one other than our nephews who can't drink. Mom placates him with a pat on the head, but when she turns to continue telling her story, Erin slides her margarita over to Clayton so he can get a sip.

He grimaces, face contorting like he just bit into a lemon. "Ugh, why do you guys even *like* this stuff?"

"Just wait, baby brother," I tell him, swiping a chip through the guac and popping it into my mouth. "When you get to college, you'll not only be subjected to shitty tequila, but also the questionable lager they serve up for nickel beer at the college bars."

"Or," Erin says, holding up a finger. "You could be a trendsetter and not drink at all."

"Yeah, right," Clayton says. "And be a loser?"

"I didn't drink for a while," she tells him.

"Really?"

She nods. "I just..."

Her words falter a little, her eyes flicking to mine, because I know *exactly* why she stopped drinking. I reach under the table and squeeze her knee, reassuring her.

"I just got tired of it, you know? What's fun about blacking out and not remembering what you did the night before? Or waking up feeling sick and shitty for a whole day?" Erin shakes her head. "I took a break, and even now, I drink, but not to get wasted. I prefer to enjoy what I'm drinking and take it slow."

My little brother frowns, nodding. "I definitely don't want to feel shitty all day."

"Language," Mom chimes in even though she's locked into her own conversation. She shares a smile with Clayton before she goes back to talking to Janae.

"What if I have a football game the next day? Or practice?"

"Exactly," I say. "Maybe you try doing your first year sober, see what you think of it."

He nods, and already I can see the wheels turning in his head. "Yeah. Yeah, I think I just might."

Just then, Camron pops out of his seat and tugs on Erin's dress. "Miss Erin, will you come to the bubble gum machine with me?" He holds up a shiny quarter. "Dad gave me a quarter to get some!"

Erin smiles, folding her napkin and setting it on the table before she stands. "I'd be delighted to." Then, she pauses, looking at Cole. "You want to come, too?"

He shrugs, but I can see it in his eyes that he doesn't want to be left out.

"I saw a claw machine over there," Erin says. "Bet we can win one of those stuffed cars. Wanna try?"

Cole smiles, and then slides out of his chair and follows Erin and Camron over to the toy machines by the hostess stand.

The minute they're gone, all eyes are on me.

I blink. "What? Do I have something in my teeth?"

"More like you've got a giant black stamp mark on your forehead that reads *idiot*," Carleton says, which makes Janae chuckle.

I narrow my eyes. "Okay?"

"Why haven't you married that girl yet?" Clayton asks, and the blood drains from my face as I look at Erin over his shoulder.

"Who, Erin? We're just—"

"*Friends?*" Mom says on a laugh. "Sure. And I'm sober."

The words are punctuated with a hiccup that makes everyone chuckle.

I shake my head, running a hand over my fade as I sit back in my chair. "It's complicated, guys. And you're going to make it more so if you start acting weird, so don't."

"Well, my advice, son?" Mom says, leaning over the table to tap my hand. "Uncomplicate it. Tell her how you feel. The way she's been looking at you all day, my gut tells me your confession won't be one-sided."

I smile, but my stomach sinks at everything I can't tell them. To them, it's simple. Erin and I are young and attracted to each other, end of story.

But we have history.

Hell, we just started being cordial with each other again.

I know I have to tread lightly, or I won't just blow my chance with her romantically, but I'll lose her altogether.

My throat dries at the thought.

There's a sudden squeal from the hostess stand, and we all turn just in time to see Camron reach into the claw machine and pull out a stuffed car. He hoists it over his head victoriously and sprints toward us while Erin and Cole stay back. Erin holds up her hand, and Cole high-fives it, hanging his head shyly afterward.

But he's wearing a smile.

And when Erin lifts her eyes to mine, she's wearing one, too.

I hold her gaze the whole way as she and Cole walk back over to the table, her cheeks reddening more and more. And when she sits down next to me, a chip hits me in the neck from the other side.

I turn and find Clayton making big, expressive, *don't be an idiot* eyes at me.

Trust me, little brother.

I'm trying not to.

***

After dinner, I drop the family back off at their hotel, giving each of them a big hug. They fly out early tomorrow morning, but I'll see them all again soon for graduation.

"Take care of my boy," Mom tells Erin when they hug.

"I think it's him who takes care of me," she answers.

"As he should."

I take Erin home next, both of us silent the car ride to the condo she's sharing with Ashlei and Jess downtown. It isn't until I park in the twenty-minute parking in front of the building and put the truck in park that I realize she's been crying.

She thinks she's hiding it from me, the subtle swipe of her thumb across her cheekbone to catch the lone tear, but I see the remnants of it shining in the streetlight when I round the truck and open her door for her.

We walk up to the building in silence, stopping just outside the door.

She looks up at me with a pitiful smile.

And I just pull her into my chest.

Everything in her releases once she's in my arms, a heavy sigh and shake of her head letting go of the tension she's been holding. I just grip her tighter, running my hand through her hair.

"I know you're not okay," I say softly. "And we don't have to talk about it if you don't want to. But thank you for coming today, for putting up with my family," I add with a chuckle. "I hope it helped."

Erin pulls back, and though I long for her warmth as soon as it's gone, I step back, too, giving her space.

"It did, it really did. Your family..." She smiles, shaking her head. "They're wonderful."

"It hasn't always been this way."

"That makes it even more special."

I smile. "Yeah, I guess it does."

Another quiet pause falls over us, and I'm just about to wish her goodnight when she rolls her lips together, crossing her arms over her chest and looking at my truck instead of at me when she asks, "Bear, am I desirable?"

Fuuuuuck me.

The ability to inhale or exhale or do anything at all is stolen with her question, my chest burning with the need to reach for her, pull her into me, and show her just how desirable she is. If I had my chance to have a real night with her, not like the one we had where we were both too drunk to remember, but a *real* night, she'd never even think of asking that question.

She wouldn't have to.

She'd already know.

My throat is tight, nostrils flaring when I finally blow out a breath, and I slide my hands into my pockets to keep myself from reaching for her. "Erin, why would you even ask that?"

I mean for it to come off as *are you fucking kidding me? Obviously, you are and how do you not already know that?* But the way her bottom lip quivers, the way she tucks her chin and shakes her head before lifting her eyes to mine again and forcing a smile, I know I've said something wrong.

"No reason," she whispers. "It was silly to even ask."

"Erin..." I try, but she sniffs, leaning in to give me such a quick hug I don't even get my hands out of my pockets to hug her back.

"Goodnight, Bear."

And before I have the chance to get to the bottom of anything, she's gone.

Still, I stand there, and I watch her wave at the front desk clerk of the lobby, watch her disappear into the elevator, watch the doors shut and block my view of her sad, broken face.

And I know in my gut the person responsible.

Gavin.

I may not know much past that, but there's one thing I know for sure.

The sonofabitch is lucky I don't know where he lives.

EPISODE 6

Ashlei

Now what?

It was the question I asked Brandon after we *finally* stopped playing games and fucked at the South Beach Agency Awards. It was the question I asked myself the next morning, when I woke up tangled in his sheets, feeling like I never left them at all and yet like a complete stranger in a place that once felt like a second home.

And now, two weeks later, I'm left wondering the same thing.

I stretch my arms up over my head and point my toes, feeling the juicy twist as I lean my hips one way and then the other in Brandon's high-quality Egyptian sheets. When I creak my eyes open, the sun is splaying in through the windows, painting me in a ray of gold.

"I wish I was a painter," Brandon muses from the doorway.

I smile when I flip onto my side to face him, propping my head up on my palm. "I seem to remember you painting a masterpiece last night," I say, dragging the tip of my finger down the middle of my chest where he came after I gave him a long, slow blowjob.

Brandon chuckles and shakes his head, crossing the room and handing me one of the two cups of coffee in his hand. "How are you feeling?"

"Sore," I admit, and I wince a little as I sit up and take the coffee from him. We've fucked more than any two humans should naturally be able to in the past two weeks.

Not that I'm complaining.

I eye him with my first sip, taking in his khaki slacks, leather dress shoes, and olive-green button up. "I hate that you're already dressed."

"Well, it *is* Monday."

I sigh. "It is, isn't it?"

"I wish I could lie here in this bed with you all day, but we're both going to be late if we don't get a move on." Brandon checks the watch on his wrist, and then his warm eyes are on me again. "Come back for dinner after?"

I chuckle. "I should just pack a bag."

"Maybe you should pack all of them."

I pause with my coffee mug hovering below my lips, heart sluggish in my chest before it kicks to life with a *thud*. "What do you mean?"

"I mean," he says, taking both our coffees and setting them on the bedside table. He folds his hands over mine and leans in close, his breath sweet and warm. "Move in with me."

I blanch. "Move in?"

Brandon nods. "I know you have a place with Jess and Erin, and I know we just made up and there are a lot of things to discuss, but I—"

"Yes."

He pauses, frowning at me like he can't be sure he really heard me correctly. "Yes?"

I laugh, pulling my hands from his so I can loop my arms around his neck. "Yes, *sir*."

The corner of his mouth pulls up into a sexy smirk at that, and he bites his lower lip, shaking his head before he kisses me long and deep. "You're going to make me late for work if you keep talking like that."

"I don't think either of us would get fired," I whisper, licking the seam of his lips until he opens his mouth and lets my tongue sweep inside.

We both groan at the touch, and he pulls me into his lap until I'm straddling him and wishing he was in briefs rather than dress pants.

"I mean it," he says, breaking our kiss and holding my hips still so I don't keep dragging them along his slowly hardening length. "I want you here, every night, every morning, every weekend. I want to see you walk through that door sweaty after pole class, and I want your workday frustrations, and I want to watch you soak this beautiful body of yours in my giant bathtub that I don't use nearly enough."

I smile. "I mean it, too." Searching his eyes, I reach back to play with the short hair at the nape of his neck. "I don't think you understand. These last few months without you… I haven't known what to do. I was going to work, and I was going to pole, and I was hanging out with friends and going out and trying to move on, but I just felt… *stuck*. Numb. Like the world was still spinning but I was hovering right above it, unable to put my feet on the ground and walk forward."

Brandon heaves a sigh, letting his forehead rest against mine. "I know exactly what you mean. God, that day after I ran into you on my run…" He shakes his head. "I don't know what death feels like, but I imagine the way my chest was splitting open that I came pretty close."

"Stubborn asshole," I tease, kissing his nose. "You could have had me, right then and there."

"I was angry."

"And stubborn."

"That, too," he admits, pulling back to look me in the eyes. "But you kissed someone else."

"She kissed *me*."

Brandon levels his gaze with me, then, and I sigh, waving him off.

"Fine," I admit. "I wasn't innocent, I'll give you that. But that little bitch ambushed me!" I pout. "Am I going to have to defend myself forever?"

Brandon chuckles at that. "No. I've already forgiven you, and I'm ready for both of us to move on."

"Me, too."

"You are the most frustrating woman I have ever met, but you keep me on my toes. I can't predict you. And I like it."

I smirk. "Good, because that won't change once I move in."

"I hope it never changes. It's what I love about you."

I sigh, closing my eyes. "Say it again."

"What?"

"That you love me."

His hands squeeze my hips and I squeal when he effortlessly lifts me and presses me into the sheets, his hips separating my thighs.

"I love you, Ashlei Daniels," he whispers against my neck before kissing a line down to my collarbone.

"I love you, too, Mr. Church."

For a while, we just hold each other, kissing and touching and soaking in the morning rays. I haven't dressed after Brandon stripped me last night, so as he runs his fingertips over my skin, I break out into a waterfall of chills.

"This is a big step, you know," I say after a while. "With big implications."

"Implications, huh?"

"Mm-hmm," I say. "I mean, if I tell my parents that I'm moving in with a man, I imagine they'll want to know what comes next."

"And what do *you* want to come next?"

"I want to marry you and have twelve babies."

"*Twelve*?" He barks out a laugh. "We need a bigger penthouse."

"Or a *real* house. With a yard. Oh, and a dog!"

Brandon smiles, his eyes flicking between mine, and I expect him to laugh or call me crazy or tell me to slow down and hold my horses.

Instead, he just sweeps my hair out of my eyes and kisses me, soft and sweet. "Whatever you want."

"You're asking for trouble, not giving me any parameters."

"I only want one thing, and that's you. So as long as you're mine, the rest is your call."

I bite my lip, accepting his next kiss with my heart riding on the wings of a thousand butterflies.

"So," he says, already kissing his way down to the swells of my breasts. He sucks a nipple between his teeth and bites gently. "Should we make a plan?"

I moan, arching into his touch, and I already know without him touching me that I'm wet and aching between my legs.

"Step one, I ride you until we're both *very* late for work," I say, and with the words, I roll us so I'm sitting on top. "Step two, we go to work." I unfasten his belt, unzip his pants. "Step three, you meet me at my place and help me pack." I yank his pants and briefs down, both of us laughing as I struggle in the process. But once his cock is free, both of our laughter fades. "And step four," I breathe, running the smooth pad of my thumb over his glistening tip. "You bring me home."

"Home," he echoes, and then he groans as I roll my fist over his shaft. "I could get used to that."

"Me, too, Mr. Church."

And then my mouth is on his cock, and his hands are in my hair, and we're well on our way to step one.

Who knows.

Maybe one day I'll be *Mrs.* Church.

I rather like the sound of that.

Erin

Why have I been here so many times?

I know this feeling as if it's meant to be my perpetual state of being — the shaky hands, the shallow breaths, the racing heart, the dizziness and gut-wrenching sense of dread.

I'm not sure I even remember what it was like *before* I felt this for the first time, when I was staring down at that positive pregnancy test in my bathroom at the sorority house. Who was I, before that pivotal moment? That seems to be when it all changed, when I went from Erin Xanders, sorority girl living the dream, to Erin Xanders, magnet for eternal misery.

I thought it was finally turning around. I found a therapist who works well with me, and a therapy group that I feel comfortable sharing with. I feel like I've finally buried the demons of my past and stepped fully into the present. I graduated college. I started law school, just like I always said I would.

And I found an incredible guy.

Gavin has been everything I never thought a man could be — funny, mysterious, caring, and kind. From the moment he first laid eyes on me, I knew he saw deeper than even my closest friends ever did.

He knew my misery and pain, my scars, because he had them, too.

It feels like a dream, dizzying and foggy, how up and down my time with him has been. From him blowing off our first date to then pleasantly surprising me with an impromptu sushi dinner, from being a sarcastic little prick in group therapy to being the sweetest, most gentle and sensual partner on our spontaneous trip, and most recently, from being with me almost every night to only making time for lunch every other week.

He's like the spinning teacup ride at Disney World, full of joy and laughter, but one wrong turn of the wheel away from a nauseating disaster.

I haven't seen him since I left his apartment that night he rejected me.

For the first week after that, he was calling me every night, texting me throughout the day, checking in. But then the contact became less and less, the texts fewer and farther between. I asked him multiple times when I'd see him next, and he always found a clever way to avoid the question.

He didn't show up to group therapy like he said he would.

He didn't meet me for lunch or take me out for dinners or even stop by after work or school.

And eventually, he just stopped talking to me altogether.

It was a gut punch, one I didn't know how to sit with. I tried to convince myself that he was just busy, that he wouldn't just abandon me, that he wouldn't ghost me after all we'd been through. But the more calls that went unanswered, the more texts I sent without a reply, the more reality sank in.

I tried tracking him down through our group therapist, but she hadn't heard from him in weeks.

I tried showing up unannounced at his job, but they said he quit unexpectedly.

I even showed up at the Palm South campus and marched right into the building where I knew he had class that afternoon. But when the class let out, he wasn't among the students that flowed from the classroom, and his professor said he'd been absent the past three classes.

He didn't just ghost me.

He ghosted everyone.

Which is why I have that all-too-familiar sense of dread simmering low in my gut as I stare at the envelope with my name sprawled across the front.

It's his handwriting.

And it was delivered anonymously to the front desk downstairs, no stamp or return address.

Usually, I'd want to be alone for this. I don't like anyone around when I'm feeling this way. I want to be left alone to my misery so no one can talk me out of it.

But right now, I need a friend.

Ashlei is either with Brandon or at work, no telling these days, and Jess is in her second week now at her brand-new job. I can't just bombard her when she hasn't even learned the employee handbook.

And I definitely can't wait until after work.

I debate calling Skyler, but it's Wednesday, which means, as president, she's at the Panhellenic meeting. And though I *could* call Cassie, she's probably in class.

Even if she isn't, I'm not sure she's the one I want here right now.

"Looks like I'm on my own," I finally decide, letting a deep sigh flow from my chest before I slip my fingernail under the crease of the envelope and slide it along the top to tear it open. I pull out a neatly folded sheet of notebook paper, then with an internal pep talk, I convince myself I can handle whatever it says.

And I open it.

Erin,

I'm sorry to do this to you.

I swallow just at the first line, and tears already prick my eyes, because I know now that whatever follows that sentence is going to hurt me.

There are many things I wish for in this world, and I could write a five-page letter if I detailed all of them to you, but I'll save you the boredom. All you really need to know is that what I wish more than anything is that I would have met you in a different time in my life.

Whether it was before the car accident or ten years from now when, hopefully, I'll actually have my shit together, I just wish it was different.

As it is now, I'm no good for you.

I'm no good for anyone.

The tears blur my vision so much I have to look up at the ceiling and force a breath before I can keep reading.

I've never met anyone like you. You're an enigma, a light so strong I couldn't help but be drawn to you from the start. I knew I should have resisted, which was why I blew you off that first time I was supposed to take you out. But then I saw you again, and I just couldn't tell myself no.

I've been living in this fairytale with you, in this place where I pretend like I'm okay and that you're the answer to all my prayers and that we're good together. It's why I touched you that first night outside of the poetry bar. It's why I soaked up every minute of our trip together. But something happened on Valentine's Day that struck me back to reality.

You trusted me enough to give yourself fully to me, even after what happened to you.

And I realized that I didn't feel the same.

I've been so eager to take all your scars and mend them, to hold you and bring you peace, but I haven't been willing to let you in to do the same for me. I can barely talk about what happened with my sister, let alone the myriad of other things in my life that you have no idea about.

To be blunt, I'm fucked up, Erin.

And I can't be with you.

A sob racks my chest so violently that I slap a hand over my mouth to try to soothe it, my tears splotting the blue ink on the notebook paper when they fall. I squeeze my eyes shut and compose myself as best I can before reading further.

I know it won't make a difference, because even now, reading this far, I know I've hurt you. But I want you to know that it's not just you. It's everything — school, work, life.

I'm not okay, and I'm finally admitting it.

That's why I'm voluntarily checking myself into a treatment center.

I think about killing myself every single day, Erin. Sometimes multiple times a day. And as much as I care about you, I can't submit you to this. You don't deserve it. In fact, it's because *I care about you that I'm doing the right thing in letting you go.*

I'm a ticking time bomb just waiting to go off, and I won't let you get caught in the wreckage.

I know this is all hard to read. And I know I'm breaking your heart. I won't even ask you to forgive me for doing it. All I ask is that you keep that beautiful spirit of yours and that you go on and live your life to the fullest, because that's what you deserve.

Thank you for sharing your light with me.

I'm sorry I dimmed it.

Take care of yourself,

Gavin

"Take *care* of yourself?!" I repeat incredulously, staring at the letter in my hand. The longer I stare, the more I re-read, the angrier I become.

My chest starts to ache, and before I realize it, I'm breathing like a dragon, each pull of air thick and heavy before I blow it through my nose. And when I hit that last line again, I scream, letting everything out while I viciously tear at the paper until it's a shredded mess on the floor at my feet.

That fucker.

That *motherfucker.*

How selfish of him. How fucking *narcissistic* to try to make it seem like he's some hero, like he's doing me a favor.

I'm still seeing red when I grab my purse off the kitchen island and swing out of the condo, slamming the door behind me. I'm in the elevator and then in my car and peeling out of the garage before I even realize where I'm heading.

But as soon as I hit the highway, my anger dissolves into thin, smoky wisps.

And in its place, all I feel is devastation.

Tears well in my eyes so fast I can't stop them from falling, but I'm not crying, I'm not sobbing, I'm not breaking down. It's just a silent, heartbreaking release of emotion, my eyes still wide open and focused on the road as the tears shed themselves.

I pull up at the Omega Chi house twenty minutes later and park around back. I don't even know if Bear is here. I don't know why *I'm* here. But my body, my heart, my *soul* carried me here instinctively.

So, I'm listening.

I don't bother knocking on the front door of the house, just let myself inside and try to keep what I'm sure is a mascara-stained face out of sight of the brothers hanging out in the common room. There are four brothers shooting a game of pool in the corner, and a big group gathered around a video game match on the big sofa.

I get a few head nods and *heys*, but that's about it.

It's not until I round the corner into the hallway that leads to Bear's room that I realize what I'm doing, and my feet falter, breath hitching in my chest.

I stop in the middle of the hall and debate turning around, but the pause is so brief I almost question if I did it at all, because in the next second, I'm knocking on his door.

"Just a minute," I hear his voice call from inside, and then he's mumbling something like he's on the phone, silence, and then the turning of the door handle.

Clinton Pennington has a tendency to suck up all the air in a room.

Whenever I see him, whenever his cedar eyes lock on mine, whenever his beastly body fills a doorframe the way it is right now, I find it absolutely impossible to breathe.

He looks like he just got back from the gym, his white t-shirt with the sleeves cut off sticking to his still-damp chest. And even in the ratty shirt and red basketball shorts, he's so crushingly handsome.

I expect him to ask why I'm here, to furrow his brows and cock his head to the side, confused. But one look at me — one brief, understanding look — and his hand jets out for mine, tugging me inside, and the door shuts behind us, and then I'm wrapped in his arms.

A sob chokes my next breath, and Bear runs his hand into my hair, holding me to his chest as he softly whispers, "Shhh, shhh, it's alright, I'm here, it's okay."

Those words only make me cry harder, my fists twisting in his shirt like he's the last thing holding me to this earth.

I can't be sure how long we stay like that, Bear holding me while I soak the dry shoulder of his t-shirt, but eventually, my cries subside, and my breath evens out, and with a long inhale, I pull back to look up at him.

"I'm sorry."

He shakes his head, eyebrows bending together as he smooths his thumb over my cheek and takes a fresh tear with it. "Don't ever be sorry for coming to me." He pauses, his eyes searching mine. "What happened?"

I almost laugh, almost cry again, but finally manage to tell him the short version of Gavin's recent rejection, disappearance, and letter. By the time I finish, I'm all out of tears, my throat dry and voice hoarse.

Bear sucks in a deep breath when I'm done, chewing the inside of his cheek for a moment before he finally says, "There are a lot of things I want to say right now, but I don't want to upset you by talking shit about him, because I know you still care about him, even if you're angry now."

I nod, sniffing. "Maybe just *one* little insult won't hurt."

"He's a weak, idiotic coward who royally fucked up the best thing to ever happen to him and he's lucky I don't know what treatment center he checked himself into or I'd check *my*self in long enough to punch the fucker right in the balls."

It's terrible. It's an absolutely *awful* thing to say.

But it makes me chuckle.

"I'm sorry I always come to you with my mess," I say on a sigh.

"I'm glad you do."

I sniff, and Bear releases his grip on me long enough to get me a tissue before guiding us over to sit on the edge of his bed. I wipe my tears and blow my nose and then sit there with that tissue balled in my fist, eyes drying out as I stare down at my knees.

"I'm just so tired of this, Bear," I whisper, shaking my head and fighting the urge to cry even more. "For years now, I've gone through more than any human can take. It's been one dumpster fire after the other. And I finally thought I was on the track to being happy again." I sniff. "I *was* happy again. And now..."

Bear doesn't try to cheer me up or make me look at the bright side, he just sighs like he really gets it, like he understands, and then his warm palm reaches up to rub my back.

"Maybe I'm just delusional. Maybe everything I did to Skyler, to *all* my friends when I wasn't okay, maybe it's my karma now and I'm not done paying for it. You know? Maybe this is just my destiny."

Bear shakes his head. "It's not. I promise."

"I know I messed up. I know I'm not perfect. But I've been working so hard on making amends, on straightening myself out." My bottom lip quivers as I shake my head against more tears building in my eyes. "Don't I deserve more?" I ask Bear and the universe and God and whoever else. When I lift my eyes to meet Bear's, it's like I can see my own pain reflected in his warm brown irises. "Don't I deserve to be happy?"

He blows out a breath through his nose, nostrils flaring as his eyes search mine. His hand wraps around my back to my hip, squeezing, his thumb smoothing the bit of skin exposed between my jeans and blouse.

"You deserve *everything*, Erin," he whispers.

Suddenly, I'm very aware that we're alone. In his room. On his bed. I'm very aware of how warm his hand is, how good he smells, how sexy he looks even in his workout clothes.

I'm very aware of the way my thighs clench together when he shifts, just marginally, until he's facing me, his mouth so close to mine I can feel the heat of his breath.

"You asked me last weekend if you were desirable," he says, and then his Adam's apple bobs hard in his throat, his eyes flicking back and forth between mine. "And Erin, I didn't know how to answer you then. I *still* don't know how to answer, not with words."

His hand at the small of my back pulls me closer, and his free one slips up my arm, over my shoulder, along the length of my neck until he's cradling my head, his fingers wrapping into my hair, thumb brushing my jaw.

"But I can show you," he says, his voice rasping, another thick swallow lining the length of his throat.

Chills race down my spine, and every cell of my being seems to flutter to life when his lips drop to my mouth.

My lips part with an unspoken plea, and my heart stops beating altogether until the moment Bear slips his hands farther into my hair, pulls me into him, and kisses me.

Then, everything kicks back to life at once.

I gasp into his mouth, which only seems to fuel him more as he breathes me in, his hands gripping tighter, tongue sweeping in over mine. When I taste him, a jolt of electricity zips straight down between my thighs, and I moan, reaching for him with just as much urgency as he's holding me.

I snake my hands around his neck, pulling him in for more even though there's not so much as an inch of space between us. Flashes of that first night we were together hit me in little bursts of stars, the memory fuzzy and fleeting, but there all the same.

"Clinton," I whisper against his lips, and he shudders at the sound of his name.

His expert mouth is unlike anything I've ever felt before, even though I know I've technically had it once before. I was drunk, then, too drunk to remember, too drunk to appreciate his full lips massaging mine, his large hands caressing my hip, his fingers weaving in my hair and pulling me in like allowing even a centimeter of space between us would devastate the moment.

But when a flash of Gavin's smile hits me like a train out of nowhere, I gasp for a completely different reason, tearing myself away from Bear and scrambling off his bed until my back hits his door.

I pant hard, trying to catch my breath, my palms against the wood and my wide eyes fixed on Bear.

His go just as wide in the next instant.

"Shit, Erin, I'm sorry. I shouldn't have... not with you like..." He shakes his head, running a hand over his fade as he stands. "Please, can we just—"

"I have to go."

I fly out of his room with him still calling my name, but I don't stop or look back. I just haul ass to my car and slam the door behind me, peeling out of the parking lot like a thief on the run.

Oh, God.

What have we done?

Jess

Well, it might have taken me longer than expected, but *damn* does it feel good to have a big girl job.

My first two weeks with *Celestial Weddings* have been both crazy and amazing. I walked in the doors right in the middle of wedding season, hence the crazy part, but the work is so fulfilling and everything I've ever wanted to do.

Well, since changing my major, anyway.

Hence, the amazing.

I've been awake and dressed and out the door every morning by six-thirty, and haven't come back home until after eight most nights. The "part time" offer quickly turned full time with how busy the agency is. My weekends have been slammed with events, a crash-course introduction to what it's like to be an event planner for Miami's rich and famous. I've worked with brides who were absolute angels, and also had my fair share of bridezillas. And from what my boss says — I haven't seen *anything* yet.

But while I'm honored to have the job and excited to be a part of the team, I'm *exhausted*, and very, *very* thankful to have a Friday evening off. Between learning the ropes at the office, running around town to gather supplies and work with vendors, making and taking more phone calls in two weeks than I have my entire life, meeting family after family and herding bridal party after bridal party, organizing photographers and DJs and bands and caterers and the works, all while doing my damndest to knock my new boss' socks off and make a lasting first impression?

I'm not just tired.

I'm about two fake smiles and *no problem, I'll take care of it*'s away from collapsing and never being able to get back up again.

Fortunately, I have a very understanding boyfriend, who didn't give me even a little grief about not joining him for his formal tonight. I know how important fraternity formals are. They signal the end of a semester, the end of a *year*, the start of summer, and the transition of power. Kade is just a week away from finding out if he's going to be the next president of Alpha Sigma, and I know this event means a lot to him.

But he understood when I explained how tired I was, and also, how *weird* it made me feel to think about attending a fraternity event now that I've graduated. Hell, I already stayed an extra semester to finish off my commitment as the recruitment chair for Kappa Kappa Beta.

It was high time for me to leave Palm South, and now that I have a condo downtown and a salaried job to boot? I feel like I've taken a big step into adulthood, and there's no going back.

She says, as she eats a pizza Lunchable and drinks a bottle of wine.

Kade *did* send me a picture of him looking snazzy as fuck before the limo ride to the venue downtown, and just for fun, I snapped him a nude in return.

What kind of girlfriend would I be if I didn't give him a chub around all his fraternity brothers from time to time?

The only thing that would make this night even better is if my sisters joined me, but Ashlei has already moved half her shit out and into Brandon's, and I'm sure they're *very* busy on this Friday night. And Erin has been holed up in her room studying for her big exam all week, tonight included. She's promised me she'll join if she gets to a point where she feels comfortable enough to take a break tomorrow, but if I know her well enough, I'll be lucky to get a glimpse of her on a snack break.

Even so, I'm not mad at it being just me, my kid food, sweatpants, and a *Friends* marathon.

If anything, I'd say this is the best Friday night I've had in a while.

It finally feels like everything is falling into place, I think to myself as I pour up another glass of wine. It's crazy how just being offered a job boosted my self-confidence. And now that I've been kicking ass for two weeks, I feel like the baddest bitch in the world.

Look out, Miami.

The city's next hottest wedding planner just stepped on the scene.

As the night goes on, Erin does pop her head out from time to time to check on me, and I even manage to convince her to stay for half of the *The One Where They're Going to Party!* episode before she chains herself to her textbooks again. As for me, a full bottle of wine has me feeling pleasantly warm and relaxed.

So much so that I almost don't notice my phone buzzing under my butt on the couch.

I snap out of my haze around the fifth buzz, not even bothering to look at the number before I answer. "Hello?"

"Ms. Vonnegut, it's Herb down at the front desk. I've got a visitor here for you."

"Send him up," I say before he even finishes, because I know exactly who it is, and if he's even a little bit as tipsy as I am after his formal, then I'm *more* than happy to welcome him to a romp in my sheets to cap off our Friday nights.

Herb chuckles. "Will do, miss. Have a good evening."

I pop off the couch with a little squeal and a heel click once we end the call, and then fly down the hall to change into my cute sleep shorts and matching spaghetti strap tank. My hair is a mess, but I take it down just to throw it up in a slightly-better-looking messy bun. After a quick run of lip balm over my lips and a touch of mascara, I bound back down the hall just in time for two swift knocks to sound on the front door.

Smoothing my hands over my shorts, I adjust my tits in my sleep tank and roll my shoulders back before putting on my *come and get me* sex-kitten smirk and open the door.

As soon as I do, that sexy smirk is replaced with wide eyes and my jaw nearly hitting the floor.

Where I expected Kade to be waiting with a drunken glaze in his eyes, I instead find his brother, stone cold sober, his hands in tight fists at his sides. His chest is heaving like he just ran three miles uphill, and his nose flares as he lets his eyes crawl down the length of me, taking in what very little clothing I'm wearing now.

"Jarrett?" I ask, crossing my arms over myself, as if that will do *anything* to cover my legs or midriff or very hard nipples peeking through this silky top. "What are you—"

I stop short when Jarrett holds up one finger, his eyes hard on mine again. With that one gesture, my lips snap together, heart picking up its pace in my chest.

"You showed up on my doorstep like this once," he says, his voice ragged, and with the words I remember all too well the night I beat down his front door. "You made me listen. So now you have to do the same."

I swallow. "Okay, do you want to come in or—"

"I love you."

My next words die in a chokehold, as if Jarrett physically reached out and wrapped his hand around my neck. I let my mouth fall open, shut it, part my lips again, zip them back together. Before I realize it, I'm leaning a hip against the doorframe to keep from falling over. "You what?"

"I love you," he repeats, face contorting like it physically pains him to admit. "I never *stopped* loving you. I don't think I can."

I swallow, hating that my heart is thumping so loud in my ears, that hearing him say those words feels like wading into warm, tropical water.

"And I know it's fucked up and wrong for me to come here and tell you that," he says when I don't respond. "And I know I said I could just be your friend but goddammit, Jess, I lied. Okay?

I lied. I can't be your *friend*," he says, shaking his head at the audacity of it. "Because the truth is that I want you, all of you, everything that you have to give. And I don't want to share."

My weight sinks more into the doorframe, and I cover my shaking lips with fingertips trembling just as much. "Jarrett..."

"Wait," he says, holding his finger up again. "I'm not finished."

I swallow, waiting.

"I know my brother may potentially hate me for the rest of my life for saying this," he says, rolling his lips together as he looks off to the side. I don't miss the way tears prick his eyes then, as if the mere thought of Kade hating him is too much to bear. "But I want you to choose me."

"Oh, my God," I whisper, so low I'm not even sure he can hear me.

"Give me a chance," he pleads, his eyes finding me again, and this time, he takes two massive strides toward me, until he's so close I could reach out my hand and touch him without any effort if I really wanted to. "Don't throw away what we had. Because I can see it on your face when you're with me that you still feel it, too."

I close my eyes when he says that, freeing two tears that I didn't realize I'd been holding at bay with my eyes wide with shock. I let out a shaky breath, swallow down the emotion, and open my eyes again.

"How can you do this?" I ask, my voice barely a whisper. I shake my head, over and over, anger and confusion settling in in equal measure. "How can you show up here and say this after all this time? After everything that... and we didn't talk for *so long*... and then *Kade*..."

"I know it's inconvenient," Jarrett says, but he stands just as tall, staring down at me over the bridge of his nose. "I know my timing is shit. But I can't go back and undo what I did. I can't go back and make a different choice. All I have is right here, and right now, and I may not know much, but I know that I refuse to let you go without a fight."

I think I scoff, or maybe I gasp, or maybe I just let out a whimper of a breath with my jaw still hanging down on the ground.

"Don't answer me now. Think about it," he says, and then he backs away, giving me space to breathe again. "I'm not going anywhere. Not until you tell me all hope is gone."

"And if I do?"

He takes a long, slow breath, letting it out through his nose before he says, "Then, I'll wish you and my brother well, and I'll leave you alone. For good." He swallows. "Forever."

Those words spark more tears in my eyes, but I don't know what to say back. And after a moment's pause, Jarrett crosses the space between us, slides his hands to frame my face and tilts my head until his lips brush my hairline.

"Please," he pleads with the kiss. "Come back to me."

I can feel the tension in his arms, the bend of his brows even though I can't see them as he presses one final kiss and releases me like it kills him to do so. He turns and leaves me like that, not even looking back once, and in less than ten seconds, he's on the elevator again and out of sight.

I stumble back, hand flying up to press against the still-warm spot where his lips were.

Erin comes out of her room to refill her water, frowning at the sight of me. "Who was that?"

"Jarrett," I whisper.

"*Jarrett?!*" She shakes her head, leaning a hip against the kitchen island. "What did he want?"

When I look at her, I can't fight back the tears that gloss over my eyes, no matter how hard I try to. "Me." I shake my head. "He wants *me*."

Erin's face goes slack. "Oh, shit."

"Yeah," I say on a mix of a laugh and a scoff, and I look back down the hall to where he disappeared. "*Oh, shit* is right."

Bear

The Omega Chi formal always symbolized the end of an era to me.

It was the end of one semester and the beginning of the next, a send-off to spring and a welcome to summer, a turning of the tides to new leadership and new opportunity.

But that's because, in the past, I always had more yet to come.

I always had a next semester, a next year, a summer break, and then a welcome back to campus.

But this time?

It's the end.

The semester has zoomed by so fast I feel dizzy from it. And now, climbing onto the bus after partying all night with my brothers at our formal, it's really starting to hit me.

This is it.

I took my last tests this week, and my family is flying in for graduation in just a few days.

This was my last fraternity event.

Tomorrow, I'll start packing up my room at the house, only this time, I won't be coming back.

There's no more time to think about what comes next, because the future is here. It's been knocking on my door for months, and now that I'm looking it in the face, I can't push it off any longer.

What are you going to do, it's asking me.

And I have no choice but to answer.

Along with the flurry of events that mark the end of a semester, my mind has also been a tornado ever since Erin flew out of my room like it was on fire.

Ever since I kissed her.

Even still, I'm torn about how I feel regarding that day. Part of me is so angry, I could punch my own damn self in the balls. After all this time being patient and waiting for the right opportunity, being there for her while remembering she belonged to someone else, focusing on our friendship and trying to ignore my true feelings for her, and then I go and blow it, making my move on the day she's literally crying on my shoulder over another dude.

But the other part of me isn't sorry at all.

This feeling between us has been building for months. No, *years*. It's always been there, humming under the surface like a volcano waiting to erupt.

And I couldn't fight it anymore.

In that moment, with Erin sitting on my bed, her eyes puffy and red and tears staining her cheeks, all I wanted was to comfort her and show her how special she is, how much she means to me.

And I did just that.

The way she leaned into the kiss, too, tells me that she feels the same way I do.

But the way she ran away tells me I don't know shit.

She was supposed to be here tonight, at my last formal, at my last Omega Chi event ever. I invited her to come with me the day after my family left from family weekend, and she told me she'd be honored. She promised me she'd be here.

Of course, that was *before* the kiss.

I wonder if that's how I'll refer to my life now, before the kiss and after the kiss, BK and AK. Because in my gut, I know nothing will ever be the same again.

There's no going back.

That's why when the bus dumps me and the rest of my brothers off at the Omega Chi house, instead of joining all of them inside for the afterparty, I slip around back to my truck and fire up the engine.

It's time to shoot my final shot.

I speed across town with nothing but my thoughts to keep me company. I don't even bother turning on the radio. Instead, I play through every word in my head, everything I'll say to try to get her to open her eyes.

When I make it to her building downtown, the guy behind the desk in the lobby calls Jess to buzz me up. But the dude frowns after a moment, murmuring a *yes, miss* before handing me the phone.

"Bear? What are you doing here?"

I clear my throat. "I, um, I was looking for Erin. Is she around?"

"She's studying at the Grove library, got a big exam tomorrow morning." She pauses. "Is everything okay?"

"Uh, yeah, I just..." I grab the back of my neck, wondering how much I should lie here since no one really knows anything about me and Erin other than that we're casual friends. "She left her sweater at the restaurant when we were with my family, so I was just bringing it back."

"At midnight on a Saturday?" Jess challenges.

Shit.

After a moment, she sighs. "Look... I know what happened between you two."

I blanch. "You do?"

"She told me a while back... about how she was pregnant... and... well..."

Oh.

That.

"I just need to talk to her," I say.

Jess is quiet for a moment before she sighs again. "You know where the Grove campus is, right?"

"Yeah."

"Park by the Philips Building and follow the winding path through the park. The library is about a quarter mile into the center of campus, it's the big white building with the gold windows. I think she usually studies on the third floor with her study group, in one of the corner rooms."

"Thanks, Jess."

"You love her, don't you?"

I freeze, eyeing the guy behind the desk, who's impatiently waiting for me to give the phone back and get out of his lobby.

"Afraid so," I murmur.

Jess makes a noise that sounds like she laughed and clapped at the same time. "I fucking *knew* it."

"Doesn't mean she feels the same."

"Doesn't mean she doesn't, either. Give her hell, tiger."

I hand the phone back to the guy behind the desk, and then I'm back in my truck and headed across town to the Grove campus.

***

Jess's instructions are right on the money, and I find my way to the library easy enough. There's a student at the front desk scanning ID cards to let people in, but it's so late that she's got her nose buried in a book, so I open the door as quietly as I can and sneak through, ducking around the first corner before she spies me.

I have no idea where I'm going. I don't even know where the elevators or stairs are. But eventually, I find my way, and make it to the third floor. In the middle, there are long, wooden tables spanning the room that's not covered in bookshelves, and students pepper every other chair, laptops and textbooks open and headphones over their ears. Along the edges of the room are a dozen study group rooms.

I start with the first one.

It only takes me six times of bursting through the door and apologizing to confused groups of students before I find the one Erin is in.

Her eyes go wide when she sees me, and the rest of her group is already yelling at me that they have the room reserved for the night. I ignore them all, standing in the doorway with my heart beating so fast and hard it's all I hear in my ears.

My hands are cold and curled at my sides.

Every breath feels like my last.

And all I can focus on is Erin Xanders and the way I burn for her, a truth I can no longer hide.

"Bear?" she asks, looking around the table apologetically before she stands and folds her arms over her chest. "What are you doing here? The library is for students on—"

"I'm graduating, Erin."

She tucks her hair behind her ear, cheeks pink with embarrassment. "I'm well aware of that. And I know I was supposed to go to formal with you tonight, but—"

"But you didn't," I finish for her. "Because I kissed you earlier this week, and I scared you. I scared myself, too."

Her study group is suddenly very interested, every single one of them looking between me and Erin with intrigue.

"Bear, this isn't the place."

"Where is, hmm? Because isn't this the way it always is with us? It's not the right time. It's not the right place. There's someone else in the picture. There's always *something* standing between us." I shake my head. "I'm done with making excuses. This is it for me, Erin. I'm out of time."

Erin swallows, crossing her arms tighter, but she doesn't tell me to leave again.

I take it as my sign to say whatever I have to say.

With a deep breath, I step more into the room, ignoring the small group of students who have stopped studying in the main room to listen, too.

"Look, I know what happened between us the other day was crazy and unexpected. You came to me when you were hurting over Gavin, and I should have just listened and comforted you. It was what I intended to do. But sometimes, our hearts take over. Sometimes we do shit we don't understand. And in that moment, with you there crying over a guy who didn't deserve even a moment of your time, I was done waiting." I swallow. "I was done pretending that I don't love you, that I haven't loved you for years, and not as a friend, Erin."

Her nose flares, and she rolls her lips together against the tears building in her eyes.

Keep going.

Don't let up now.

"I get that it isn't perfect timing, but at the same time, you're either blind or in denial if you say there's nothing between us, that there hasn't *always* been something between us. And I think a part of you knows as well as I do that there always *will* be."

Erin sniffs, and now, we've gained the attention of practically the entire library.

I take another step toward her, my chest heaving as I do. "Erin, I graduate one week from today. And then I have to decide — do I leave? Go to Pittsburgh and start a career? Or do I stay?" I pause. "And if I'm being honest, you are the only thing tying me to this place."

I think a girl in the room says *awww* before someone shushes her.

"So, this is it. This is me coming to you with everything that I am, everything that I feel, no holds barred." I step right up to her, then, my eyes flicking between hers, begging her to see that I mean every word. "I love you, Erin Xanders. So, if there's even a tiny part of you who still wants me here, you have to tell me now. You have to." I swallow with how urgent and consuming those words feel in my throat. "Don't let me go if there's even an ounce of you that feels the same way I do."

Erin's face crumples, her brows bending together fiercely, tears bubbling in her eyes as she watches me, her chest heaving just the same as mine.

It feels like the longest day of my life happens in the span of the next several seconds, waiting for her response, seeing it in her eyes that whatever it is, it's killing her.

And finally, she says two words that ring out louder and clearer than anything I've said.

"I can't."

Her lips tremble with the confession, and I let out a long breath, taking a step back from her like I don't know her at all.

"I *can't* give you anything right now," she says, shaking her head. "I have nothing to give. What little I did have just got obliterated and now I..." She looks away from me, squeezing her eyes shut and freeing the tears that had been building. When she opens her eyes again and looks at me, she doesn't say another word.

I lick my lips, nodding, letting the meaning of what she's said settle in. "It's okay," I whisper, even though it's everything *but* okay. "I understand."

Everything inside me longs to reach for her, to have one last hug, one last kiss, one last moment of pretending like she'll ever be mine. But I know it will hurt more than it will help.

This is it.

I put my heart out there, I told her everything.

She doesn't feel the same.

The only thing left to do now is to go, so with another nod in her direction, I turn, ignoring the heavy silence of everyone watching us. The group that had gathered at the doorway clears quickly, making way for me to pass through with sympathetic looks reflected in their eyes.

When I push past the doorframe, Erin calls out behind me.

"Bear, wait!"

I pause, slapping the doorframe with one hand and waiting, just like she asked, but I can't turn around to face her again.

"I have nothing left to give," she repeats, her voice strangled. There's a long pause, so long I almost start walking again, but then she speaks again. "But whatever I do have, whatever is left of me... it's yours."

A flurry of gasps echoes in my ears as my head snaps back around, and Erin is standing there with her arms at her side, tears flooding her eyes and slipping down her cheeks. She smiles, and shrugs, and then her bottom lip wobbles again as she stands there and waits for my next move.

I shove off the doorframe and race across the room to her, and in a split second that feels like coming home, I sweep her into my arms and capture her next sob with my mouth on hers.

The library erupts in a thunderous roar of applause and cheers so loud I'm sure we'll all get kicked out, but I couldn't care less in this moment. Right now, all that matters is that Erin is in my arms, and she feels the same, and *finally*, after all these years, she's mine.

I finally break her kiss as she laughs and looks around the room embarrassed, burying her face in my chest.

"I know you think what's left of you isn't much," I whisper for only her to hear. "But I think it's the very best of you."

She shakes her head, looking up at me with glossy eyes. "I'm a mess, Bear. It's never going to be easy for us. I'm always going to be difficult. It's in my nature."

I smile, sweeping her hair back over her shoulder. "Good thing I don't like anything that's easy, then, huh?"

I'm not sure if she cries or laughs, but her lips spread into a smile the longer she watches me. "You're right. I have always felt this," she says, pressing her hands to my chest. "I just didn't know what to do about it."

"We'll figure it out together."

"This is really happening, isn't it?"

I smile, leaning down to press another kiss to her lips. "You bet your ass it is."

Then, I bend down and swing her over my shoulder caveman style, earning us another cheer from the crowd as I gather her stuff off the table and toss it haphazardly in her bag. Once I've got her *and* her belongings loaded up, I steer us toward the exit.

"Bear! Put me down! I need to study!"

"You can study when I'm done kissing you," I tell her, and then with a wink at the group as I pass through the doorway, I add, "Which probably won't be until the morning, so hopefully you're ready for that test of yours by now."

Everyone laughs and sends us off with a final set of cheers.

And then I carry that stubborn, impossibly frustrating, absolutely perfect girl into the next era.

I have a feeling it will be the best one yet.

Adam

"You looked so hot walking across that stage," Cassie says, drawing circles on my chest as we lie in my bed.

Or should I say *on* my bed, since it's just a mattress on a bed frame now that I've packed up my whole room.

"Oh, yeah? That oversized, shiny, black gown really does it for you, huh?"

"Mmm, I think it was more the funny hat on your head. And when you switched that tassel over to the other side?" She groans. "So sexy."

I chuckle, absentmindedly playing with the strands of her hair with one hand, the other propped under my head, both of us looking up at the ceiling.

"I've spent a lot of days and nights staring at this ceiling," I say on a sigh. Then, I pinch Cassie's side. "Most of them driving myself crazy over *you*."

"Hey!" She giggles, squirming away from my pinch until I hold her close again. "You drove me just as insane, thank you very much." She pauses, rubbing my chest again. "It's so weird, seeing this room empty, seeing all your stuff packed up in boxes. I mean, sure, we pack up at the end of every semester, but when I come back in the fall... you won't be here."

She swallows, and I can feel the motion against my chest at the same time my stomach does a somersault. I pull her close and kiss her hair. "I know. It's surreal. I think even though I knew college was only for four years, it's always felt like it would never end. I just thought I had all this time, you know? And now..."

"*Now* you're about to be a freaking Field Executive!" Cassie says, squeezing me.

I shake my head. "So crazy."

"And *I* will have to figure out how to survive this place without you." She sighs. "I met you so early on, my first day being a KKB sister. Remember? The slip and slide?"

"Like I could forget. Have you seen yourself in a bikini?"

"Have you seen *you* shirtless?" Cassie whistles. "Abs for days."

"One day, I'm going to be hairy and have a dad bod. You still going to love me, then?"

"Probably even more," she says, kissing my neck.

I smile, holding her close as we lie together with nowhere else to be. It was all I wanted tonight, after graduation — to be with Cassie. My aunt drove in for the ceremony, of course, but she's got a hotel on the beach and a new boyfriend keeping her company for the evening. The rest of the weekend will be filled with family celebration.

But tonight, it's just us.

"Remember the first time I climbed through that window?" Cassie asks, nodding to the window, which is open now, letting the breeze softly roll in the empty room.

"I remember *every* time."

"You were always there for me," she says, propping herself up on one elbow to look down at me. "Even when you were with Skyler, even when I was with Grayson. It's crazy, isn't it? How we were always more than friends, but *never* more than friends."

"At least, not until we both pulled our heads out of our asses."

"Mostly you, though."

"Yes," I agree with a laugh. "Mostly me."

Cassie chews her lip, drawing circles on my chest again with her eyes focused there. "I'm scared, Adam."

A painful zing hits me right in the middle of my chest, and I roll us over until I'm on top of Cassie, pressing a kiss to her lips. "Don't be. You and I have been through much worse than a little distance."

"What if you find some hot girl who's super cool and funny at one of these other universities?"

"She'd never hold a candle to you."

"I'm serious," Cassie insists. "You're a graduate now. You're about to go out in the real world."

"And you'll be right behind me. By the end of this year, we'll both be out there. Together," I remind her. "Don't you know by now that you're the only girl for me?"

She smiles at that. "And you're the only boy for me."

"Man," I say, furrowing my brows and puffing my chest.

Cassie pokes my stomach, making me let out all my air in an *oof.*

"Just promise me we won't mess everything up over this," she pleads, holding my gaze. "We have to communicate. We have to see each other as much as we can. And we have to have patience and understanding, even on the hard days."

"I promise," I whisper, and then I hold out my pinky, waiting until she wraps hers around mine before I kiss my thumb and press it to hers to seal the deal.

Even so, I can tell Cassie is still worried, and I can't blame her. We've seen our friends struggle through long-distance relationships — some of them successful, others not. I'm not naïve enough to think we won't have some rough patches to overcome.

But I'm also not stupid enough to ever let this girl go, no matter what we face.

I lean down and capture her lips with mine, hoping she can feel it in the way I kiss her, in the way I cradle her face in my hands, in the way my breaths don't begin until hers end. We're in sync. We always have been.

And I'd never do anything to mess that up.

The longer we kiss, the more my desire burns for her, and I slip myself between her legs, widening her thighs with my hips. She moans, arching off the bed and into the touch, her head falling back to allow me access as I kiss down her neck.

I'm not rough with her tonight. I don't toss her around or pin her arms or slam inside her with a wicked grin and a mission to make her come as fast as I can. I don't talk dirty or fuck her mouth or twist her up in one of the many positions we've discovered since we've been together.

No, tonight isn't about fucking.

It's about sealing the promise between us.

It's about reminding her that I put those letters around her neck with intent and purpose.

And that I meant every word I said.

As I strip her down and kiss every inch of her body, I take my time, touching and tasting, licking and sucking. I commit every moan to my memory, every touch, every curve and slope that makes up who she is.

I look longingly and deep into her eyes when I slide inside her, and I hold her gaze as we move together, breathing in tandem, our slick chests pressed together like a seam. When she comes, it's softly and sweetly, and she digs her nails into my back with the release. I'm right behind her, and the moment we both finish, tears flood Cassie's eyes until I roll over and tuck her into me, wrapping myself all around her so she feels safe.

"We're going to be okay," I whisper in her ear, kissing the sensitive skin right below it. "We're going to get through this."

Cassie nods, holding me tighter and wiping away the tears that have slipped free.

"Me and you forever," she whispers.

I nod, kissing her shoulder as my eyes softly close. "And even longer after that."

Skyler

"I still can't believe you *never* told me," I tell Bear through speakerphone, shaking my head as I apply a thin layer of gloss over my lips. "I mean, she's my *Big,* for Christ's sake. And you're my best friend. Like... how the hell did you keep me in the dark?"

Bear chuckles. "To be fair, it was a *very* messy situation, one that we just figured out ourselves."

"I know that feeling well," I mumble.

"Exactly. Which is part of the reason you never saw anything. You were too busy tied up in your own shit. As you should be," he adds.

I sigh, turning left and right to check my reflection in the mirror one last time. "To be fair, I *did* suspect something weird was going on when she showed up at your room last semester. Before she took me on a walk to apologize for everything that went down. You guys did this..." I scrunch my nose, waving my hand in the air even though Bear can't see me through the phone. "*Thing* where you just stared at each other all weird and didn't say a word."

Bear laughs. "Yeah. We've done a lot of that."

"It's weird," I admit. "You two. But at the same time..."

"It fits."

"Yeah," I breathe. "It really, really does."

"We still have a lot to figure out."

"Don't we all."

"I just wanted to make sure you were cool with it. Erin has been worried."

I smile. "Look at you, handling shit on behalf of your lady. What a gentleman."

"I'd do anything for her."

"Okay, okay, stop before I gag," I tease, but it's more like *stop before I cry because I'm so happy for two of my best friends.* "I gotta go, Kip should be here any second."

"Have fun tonight. And happy anniversary," Bear says. "I still think you should have cleaned that motherfucker out in Vegas, but then again, we all do crazy shit for love."

"You can say that again."

"Love you, Sky."

"I love you more. And hey," I say, pausing a moment. "I'm really proud of you, *graduate.*"

"Thanks," he says. "Now, the scary part."

"Dating Ex?"

"Job hunting."

I shiver. "I'm not sure which is more terrifying."

Bear snorts. "Alright, alright, go have fun. I'll see you at the barbecue tomorrow. My little brother will murder me if he doesn't get to see his favorite girl before he flies back to Pitt."

"I wouldn't miss it."

With a kiss, I end the call, and then I let myself primp for a couple minutes more before I grab my purse and phone and fly down the stairs. The Kappa Kappa Beta house is empty, thanks to the end of the semester, but since I'm president, I don't have to clean out my room, since I'll be occupying it again in the fall.

Perks of the job.

I skid to a stop at the bottom of the stairs, chest aching a bit at the sight of the common room empty, the sound of silence echoing through the house.

One more semester, and this place will be a part of my past.

One more semester, and I'll be on to the next chapter of my life.

Before I can get too wrapped up in the feels, I smile, walking outside and locking the door behind me. I wait on the front porch swing, enjoying the warm yet pleasant evening.

One year ago, Kip and I were head to head at the finals table in Las Vegas. That tournament seems so long ago now, and the girl who sat at that table is almost unrecognizable to me now. I learned a lot in the time Kip and I spent playing games with each other's heart, and since then, we've survived the passing of his father, a semester of long distance, *literally* being on opposite sides of the country, and this semester? The reality of being in a relationship while also still chasing our own dreams.

Other than Spring Break, we've barely been able to spend time together. Kip has been busy directing and producing his show, while I've been working on the casino boat, running the sorority, and keeping up with my classes in the midst of it all. Plus, knowing that Bear was graduating, I tried to spend as much time with him as I could.

It makes me kind of sad, really, because just five months ago when Kip told me he was going to be here for the spring and summer semester, all I could think about was how we'd have so much time together, and how great it would be to be at the same university.

And now, on the other side of it, I feel more distance between us than I did when he was in California.

I know this is part of being in a healthy relationship, that we're both going to have to do our own thing from time to time. And I *want* him focused on his show. Still, I can't deny that I've had nights I've been pretty butthurt that I have an evening free, but he doesn't. And it seemed like any time *he* was free, I wasn't.

We were constantly spinning around each other, rarely ever catching the other in the same place.

But nothing lasts forever, and now that we've gotten through the semester, we have the whole summer to be together. Sure, he'll still be working on the show and I'll have work, but it'll be a small break from the sorority, and hopefully there will be plenty of time for beach days and date nights and *us* time.

Bear talked some sense into me, too, during family weekend, and I told Kip I *needed* a no-distractions date night. He was more than happy to oblige, and he booked us a fancy dinner reservation and scored us two tickets to a musical at the theatre downtown to celebrate our one-year anniversary.

Yes, we consider the night of the tournament our *true* anniversary date.

So here I am, all dolled up and ready for a very adult night out. It sounds like a date my parents would have, dinner and a show, but I love the way it feels to put on a sparkly black dress and do my hair and makeup to perfection.

I *especially* love the way I feel on Kip's arm when I'm done up the way I am tonight.

I can already picture it, the way his eyes will pop open wide when he sees me, his jaw going slack. I can hear him whistling without him even being here yet, can feel his hands on my waist as he says something along the lines of *hot damn, woman, I can't believe you're mine.*

My cheeks heat at the thought, and I sigh, impatiently waiting for him to pull into the driveway.

Except he never does.

Ten minutes goes by, and then another ten, and then another, until it's been a half hour since the time he told me he was picking me up. I try texting a few times with no response, and when I call, I get his voicemail.

That's weird.

I know I shouldn't panic, but it's the first thing my traitorous body does, heart racing and chest tightening with thoughts of what could have gone wrong. Maybe he slipped and hit his head in the shower. Maybe he got in a car accident on the way over. Maybe he's laid out on a stretcher right now and I'm sitting here all impatient when he's fighting for his life.

The anxiety is too much to bear, so when it's been almost forty-five minutes without a response, I get in my car and drive straight to his apartment on the outskirts of campus.

It's the same building he was in last year when we first met, close to the beach and a little rundown but charming in its sixties glamour. It's a nice fit for the Hollywood posters that always decorate his walls. I slam the car into park and jog up the stairs two at a time, knocking on his door for a full minute without an answer.

"Okay, he's not here," I say out loud to myself, heart racing. "That doesn't mean anything. I didn't see any car accidents on the way over. Where else could he be?"

Jumping back in my car, I continue my search by checking the route it would take him to drive to the sorority house from here. I double back and check another when that route comes up empty, and both times, the sorority house is still without a sign of him.

I try calling again, and when I get his voicemail, I can't hide the worry in my voice. "Kip, please, it's been an hour and a half now. Where are you?"

My throat is thick with emotion as I drive around aimlessly, and in a last measure of desperation, I decide to swing by the auditorium. Kip and his crew have secured an office there for the show, a sort of home base, and I hope like hell he just fell asleep while working or something.

When I get to the office, I fly through the door and find a surprised Dina sitting at the long table with one of the producers. They each have their laptops open in front of them while dub-step music plays softly on the speaker next to them.

"Hey, Sky," Dina says, tilting her head. "You alright?"

"Is Kip here?" I ask, still out of breath from the chase. "We were supposed to go on a date tonight. He was supposed to pick me up almost two hours ago now and... and I can't... he never showed, and I can't find him and..."

I'm breathing so hard now I'm pretty sure I'm going to have a panic attack, and Dina jumps up out of her chair, the legs squeaking against the tile as she does.

"Hey, hey, it's okay, breathe," she says, grabbing my arms and leveling her gaze with mine. "Kip is just fine. He's with Natalia and Jameson filming a scene at my apartment."

My next breath is a little slower than the last, and the next slower still, until the dizziness starts to clear, and I comprehend what Dina's just said.

"He... *what*?"

Dina balks. "Shit. I'm sorry, Sky. I didn't know he had any plans tonight. Earlier today we were going over tape, and the shower scene just didn't come out right, so Kip wanted to refilm it. He called Natalia and Jameson right away and then he left, and I haven't..." She swallows the more my worry turns to anger right before her. "I haven't heard from any of them since."

I swallow, trying to calm myself even though everything inside me wants to throw a brick through a window. "Take me there. Now."

"Maybe we should call—"

"*Now*, Dina!"

"Yep, okay, let me get my keys," she says, releasing my arms, and as soon as she's got her belongings, we're back in my car and headed across campus.

They decided to use Dina's apartment for the scene because it has the best lighting and, let's be honest, she's able to keep it the cleanest, being that she's a girl. She also had no problem decorating her place the way Kip had his when we dated, and when I shove through the front door, it's almost like walking back in time.

There are muffled voices in the back, and though Dina tries to stop me, I shrug her off and storm back, flinging the bedroom door open.

Across the room is the entryway to the bathroom, and Jameson — the guy Kip cast to play him — is standing in the doorframe. His gaze snaps to mine immediately, but before he can ask questions, I storm across the room to stand where he is.

And that's when I find Natalia standing in the shower, naked.

And Kip is holding her hips.

"Are you fucking *kidding* me?!" I scream, and then before I can think better of it, before I can take a breath and be rational, I walk straight over to Kip and slap him hard across the face.

His head snaps with the force, his hand reaching up to hold his cheek as Natalia flies back and out of his grasp.

"Jesus, Skyler, what the fuck?!"

I point at her with a menacing glare. "Don't you fucking talk to me, you sneaky bitch."

She throws her hands up and arches a brow. "Whoa. What did I do?"

"You know *exactly* what you did."

"Alright, alright," Kip says, grabbing my arm and yanking me toward the door. "Take five, guys, I'll be right back."

"The hell you will," I say to him, and then I give Natalia another glare until I'm ripped out of the bathroom.

Kip keeps his grip on my arm, yanking me past a confused Jameson and Dina until we're all the way outside the apartment. He shuts the door behind us, and then turns on me with wild eyes. "What the hell is wrong with you, Skyler?"

"*Me*?" I laugh incredulously. "What is wrong with *you*?"

"I'm filming," he deadpans. "Which you've made abundantly clear is hard for you to cope with, but I have a lot riding on this project, okay?"

"Oh, and I assume you holding onto Natalia while she's naked is a *super* important part of making the show so great, huh?"

"I was trying to demonstrate how it happened in real life so Jameson could get the emotion right," he defends, throwing his hands up. "*God*, what is it with you and Natalia? She's a professional, Skyler. We work together and that's it. You're being insecure and jealous, and it's a really bad look if I'm being honest."

My head snaps back at his words, and I lick my lower lip, tearing my eyes from him and shaking my head with a million thoughts racing through my mind.

The first one being *who is this guy and what has he done with my boyfriend*?

"Look, I know it's hard to understand, but this is how it's always going to be with me. Work is going to be a huge part of my life. I'm going to have days when I'm busy, with filming or producing or whatever."

"Too busy to remember date nights, I guess, huh?" I ask, looking him in the eyes again. "Should I just get dressed up and be waiting for you to pick me up, and then when you don't show, laugh it off? *'Oh! Welp, guess Kip must be busy with his show. Oh well, I'll just got changed back into sweats now.'*"

Kip's brows furrow together in confusion. "What are you tal—" But he doesn't finish the question, because in the next moment, his eyes take a slow dive over the length of me, taking in my hair and makeup and dress, and then all the color drains from his face. "Shit. Our anniversary."

"Yeah, you asshole. Our anniversary."

He closes his eyes, pinching the bridge of his nose on a breath. "Skyler, I'm sorry. I completely spaced. We ran into an issue with this scene earlier today and I wanted to—"

"Re-film it, yeah, I heard," I finish for him, shaking my head. "Well, I hope you got the shot."

With that, I turn and storm down the stairs, ignoring him when he calls my name and attempts to jog after me. I rip off my heels at the bottom of the stairs and take off in a sprint toward the car. As soon as I'm inside, I roar the engine to life and peel out, leaving Kip in my rearview mirror.

And when I hit the highway, I finally break down, succumbing to the first sob that rips through me.

Cassie

"Well, last semester, I said if we ever needed each other that we had to promise to meet up right back here," I say, patting Skyler's bed. "Looks like we kept our promise."

Jess snorts. "Yeah. Except I think we all should have been piled together in this thing many other times before now." Jess, Erin, and Ashlei are leaned up against the headboard, while Skyler is sprawled out in the middle on her back. I'm at the foot of the bed, legs swinging off the edge.

"True," I agree. "But life gets in the way."

"I hate that," Erin says, her little mouth pulling to the side. "I mean, I get how it happens... law school, work, class, boys."

We all groan at that one.

"But I don't want us to ever pull too far away from each other."

"I don't either," Ashlei says. "I think in addition to our promise to meet here when things are a mess, we should also make a promise to meet up at least once a month for a girls' day. Beach, pool, night out on the town, or PJ party, I don't care."

"Deal," Jess says instantly. She nudges Skyler. "Hey, you alive over there?"

Skyler grunts in lieu of an answer, and the rest of us share concerned glances. It seems at the end of every semester, we all find ourselves in different stages of life. Where one of us might be flying high, another has just hit a new low, and this semester is no different.

I sigh, lying myself down over my Big and cuddling her. "It's going to be alright. Kip loves you. You love him. That's all that matters."

"I'm glad you're confident in that, because right now, I'm not sure of anything." Skyler rolls onto her side. "I'm so mad at him. I haven't been this mad at him since I found his laptop with that file of stuff his dad had gathered on me." She shakes her head. "I was blindsided then, and hurt. But this? This is another level."

"He's been caught up in the show, babe," Ashlei says. "He messed up. But he'll make it right."

Skyler swallows. "What if he can't?"

"You're just upset," Erin assures her. "Trust me, when the dust settles, it'll all straighten itself out."

Skyler nods, falling quiet again, and I know she's tired of talking about it — especially with everything still fresh and up in the air. So, I pat her butt and turn the conversation to Jess. "What about you? What are you going to do about this little family affair you've found yourself in?"

She huffs, reaching over for the fruit snacks on Skyler's bedside table. She pops three in her mouth before she answers. "I have no fucking idea. If I thought Jarrett showing up last semester was a shock, it's nothing compared to him beating down my door and confessing that he still loves me."

"What about Kade?" Ashlei asks.

"He's pissed," Jess says. "Reasonably so. But... I think more than anything, he's scared. He knows Jarrett and I have a history. And now that he's the new president of Alpha Sigma, he also knows he's going to be busy. I think a part of him worries he's already lost the fight."

"Or maybe he doesn't think he should have to fight at all," Skyler pipes up.

"True." Jess sighs. "I don't know, guys. This might be the most selfish thing I have ever admitted, but... I love them both."

"But you can't have them both," I remind her.

"I know." She shakes her head, popping another fruit snack in her mouth. "No matter what I decide, I'm going to hurt one of them. And I'm going to hurt myself in the process, too."

"What are you going to do now?" Erin asks.

"Cry," Jess answers on a laugh. "I told both of them I wanted to take the summer to be alone. I just started this job and I need to focus on that, especially with so many weddings coming up. My career means a lot to me, and I don't want to fuck it up because I'm caught up in a love triangle." She swallows. "Besides, maybe some room to clear my head and think is what I need."

"Think you'll have some sort of epiphany?" I ask.

"Or mental breakdown, both of which would be helpful, I think."

We all share sympathetic smiles before Ashlei reaches over and pats her leg. "I think it will work out. And for the record, I'm Team Whoever-Makes-Jess-Happiest."

"Me, too," Erin says. "And Lei, I'm really happy for you and Brandon. I'm so glad the breakup didn't last."

"God, so am I," she says, shaking her head. "I'm not sure how either of us survived. But I will admit, it was kind of thrilling to do the whole cat and mouse thing again."

I laugh. "You're a masochist."

She shrugs, but throws me a wink because she knows it, too.

"Now you're moving in with your boyfriend while mine moves across the country," I say with a sigh I know is nothing short of envious. "How the tides have turned."

"I'm not even a little worried about you and Adam," Erin says. "The two of you are more solid than anyone I know. And I saw the video Skyler took of you being lavaliered." She shakes her head. "That boy is yours forever, whether you like it or not."

"Long distance isn't so bad either," Jess chimes in. "The video sex is *hot*."

"True," Skyler chimes in again, still lying back looking up at the ceiling when she points a finger at Jess.

I chuckle. "I'm just excited for the summer together. It'll be fun exploring Boston." I tap Erin's foot, then. "And *ahem*, missy, I think you have some explaining to do. You and *Bear*?"

"Surprised, huh?" she asks on a laugh.

"Shocked," I answer, Ashlei and Skyler nodding in agreement.

"Not me," Jess says. "I had a feeling. He's always looked at you with this very specific stare."

"And what stare is that?" Erin asks.

Jess shrugs. "Like he's two seconds away from either strangling you or ripping your clothes off. Maybe both."

"Oh, my God, J-Love," Erin says, hitting Jess with a pillow.

Jess just hugs it to her chest and sticks her tongue out.

"We've been through a lot together," Erin says after the laughter dies down, and then she frowns, folding her hands together in her lap. "Bear has been there for me through some of the hardest times of my life. The way I feel about him... I always thought it was just this deep friendship, but I think I've loved him all along. Ever since he took me to semi-formal three years ago." She smiles. "Maybe even before that."

"You're lucky to be loved by him," Skyler says, leaning up on her palms to look at Erin when she says the words. "And if you hurt him, I'll hurt you. And don't worry, I gave him the same warning."

Erin chuckles. "I'll do my best." Then, she blows out a slow breath, everything in her demeanor changing as she sits up a little straighter. "I need to tell you all something. Actually, several somethings." She pauses. "But this is going to be really hard for me to say."

The girls and I share looks, but don't say a word, giving Erin the space she needs to process whatever it is.

"I know I've hurt you. All of you. In one way or another. And last semester, I told you I was getting better, that therapy was helping. And it is. I've come a long way." She swallows, picking the nail polish off her nails. "Part of my recovery is leaning on the people I love and trust and letting them in. So... here goes nothing."

She stills another breath, looks each of us in the eyes, and then pours out her heart.

For nearly a half hour, she tells us everything she's been hiding, everything she's been bearing the weight of all on her own for years now. She tells us about the one-night stand with Bear, the pregnancy, the clinic, the impossible choice. She tells us about how dark that time was for her, and then she was betrayed in the worst way, violated by a group of fraternity boys by way of a date-rape drug.

We all started crying, then.

The tears continued as she walked us through the horrors of recovering from that, the way her mother had told her to essentially suck it up and power on, and why she made the incredibly difficult choice not to report the assault.

And through it all, Bear was there for her.

Even after he found out about her aborting their baby, it didn't take him long to forgive her.

I'm not sure I could have done the same in his shoes.

When she finishes telling us everything, including what happened with her and Gavin, too, we all just cover her up in a massive group hug. It's a chorus of cries and sniffs as we hold her, each of us hurting because of how much *she* has been hurting.

"I can't believe you went through all of that alone," Skyler says. "I'm so sorry, Big."

"It's no one's fault. And I'm on the other side of it now. I just... I wanted to tell all of you. I wanted you to understand why I behaved the way I did. But more than anything, I wanted you all to know how much I love and trust you, and how important you are in my life."

"We love you, too, Ex," Ashlei says, squeezing tighter. "So, so much. And we're always here. Please, whatever happens in the future, don't ever shoulder it alone again. Lean on us. That's what we're here for."

"I will," Erin promises.

"Can we turn into a badass hit woman team and kill those douchebags who raped you, though? Because I've got some anger to work through and this just amplified it," Skyler says.

Erin smiles, but shakes her head. "I don't think killing them would be justice," she says, and then she heaves a deep breath. "But, maybe, reporting them would."

We all go still, then.

"Are you thinking of filing a report?" Skyler asks.

"I'm not thinking anymore. I'm doing it. I don't know all the laws with statutes of limitation, and everything in my gut still tells me that the system won't work in my favor. But... I owe it not only to myself, but to every other woman out there who has gone through this, too. Maybe I'll be laughed out of the court. Maybe I'll be called names. Maybe no one will believe me other than you guys and Bear. Maybe those guys will walk free and go on to live their lives without ever paying for what they did to me." She shrugs. "All I know is that I have to try. And I finally feel like I'm strong enough."

Ashlei's eyes well with big, watery tears, and they shed before she can do anything to stop them. "You're the strongest person I know, Erin. And we've all got your back. We'll be here every step of the way."

We hold each other just like that for what feels like hours, no one wanting to move, no one wanting to break the iron chain of support shielding us from the outside world. In the end, boys come and go, but through heartbreaks and breakthroughs, the highest highs and the lowest lows, it's these girls who are always here.

Who always will be.

As much as our lives shifted after Erin, Ashlei, and Jess graduated, I know there's even more change to come. We're all going our separate ways for the summer — some heartbroken, some happier than they've ever been — and in the fall, Skyler and I return as the final two of our entire group to finish out our college careers.

After that, Palm South University won't be our home anymore.

It will be a part of our past.

But one thing I know for sure, the women in this bed will never be. They'll always be my present and my future, too.

"You ladies are my soulmates," I whisper after a while.

Jess nods. "It's us against the world."

"Always," Skyler agrees. "No matter what."

"We'll never be alone," Ashlei echoes.

And finally, Erin lifts her head, looking at each of us before she whispers. "Kappa Kappa Beta forever."

Palm South
UNIVERSITY

GREEK

BOOK 7

EPISODE 1

Jess

If anyone were to look down upon this scene from an aerial view, they would likely remark that it's a lovely and serene sight to behold.

A stunning penthouse suite at a gorgeous Mexican resort, the sheer white curtains floating in the breeze, the expanded balcony with a private hot tub and plunge pool all so alluring and beautiful. The magical backdrop of a pristine white beach and turquoise water, currently reflecting the full moonlight overhead, and the distant sound of the waves washing ashore.

From the outside, it appears to be an absolutely extraordinary slice of paradise on Earth.

But inside?

It's a goddamn disaster.

"I... I... I'm a monster," Cassie cries to herself, snot and tears dripping down her face as she rocks herself back and forth on one of the daybeds. She sniffs, not even bothering to wipe away the mascara staining her cheeks. "How could I do that to Adam? How can I ever live with myself again?" She balked. "How do I tell him? Oh, God."

She covers her face and sobs even harder, and Skyler winces, rubbing her back and doing her best to comfort her Little as she falls apart.

Erin is pacing back and forth, arms folded hard over her chest as she shakes her head over and over, tossing between murmuring to herself and screaming curse words loud enough for the entire resort to hear. Something happened to her around the same time Cassie had her meltdown, about an hour ago amidst the thumping music of the beach club, but she has yet to tell us what, exactly.

All we know is she looked at her phone, screamed bloody murder, cried, and has been pacing ever since we all dragged Cassie back here to console her.

Ashlei disappeared into the bathroom as soon as we got back, and for how long she's been in there, I can only imagine she's ralphing up the fruity shots we've been knocking back all night.

And then there's me, swiping back and forth between two pictures on my phone, each depicting a different man I love.

Swipe.

Me on Kade's back, my arms wrapped around his shoulders, lips pressed to his cheek as my hair falls over us like a curtain. His warm brown eyes are bright with love and adoration, his smile megawatt in size as he snaps the selfie.

Swipe.

Me and Jarrett in bed, his beast of a body encompassing all of mine as I curl my back into his chest like a cat. The morning sunlight reflects on our soft, sated smiles, and his dark eyes smolder at the camera, promising he's nowhere near finished with the girl in his arms.

Swipe.

Kade.

Swipe.

Jarrett.

Swipe. Swipe. Swipe. Swipe.

Back and forth, over and over, I stare at those men — the men who own my heart — and feel it break at the realization that I will hurt one of them.

That I've *already* hurt them both.

I don't deserve the patience they've given me — the space, the time. And I definitely don't deserve their love.

But I have it, and though I love them both in return, I know there's no putting off the decision I have to make.

The decision I made long before I was ready to admit it to myself, if I was being honest.

In my daze, I don't realize Erin is screaming and Cassie is having a full-on panic attack until I snap out of the trance my phone has me in. I close the screen and drop it to the cushion beside me, popping up and running over to Erin first.

"It's not fucking fair! This whole system... this whole *world* is fucked!" she screams.

"Will you bitches shut up?!" Ashlei yells from inside the bathroom. "It's impossible for a girl to poop with all this racket going on!"

Skyler gives me a look that says she's got Cassie, so I grab Erin's hand and lead her to the edge of the balcony, letting the fresh sea breeze calm us both. I don't say anything, just hold her there and smooth my hand over her arm, letting her take a moment for whatever it is that's going on.

She opens her mouth to say something when my ringtone sounds from the chair I was sitting on, and Erin and I both look at the screen, stilling at the sight of Jarrett's name in bold above the new message.

My chest caves in on itself, and I close my eyes for a long moment before I open them to find Erin staring back at me.

"What are you going to do?" she asks, her voice just a whisper.

Before I can answer, Ashlei clears her throat from where she's now standing in the middle of the balcony between us all. Her hair is a mess tied loosely on top of her head, her arm still in a sling from the accident, and her face is ghostly pale.

She doesn't say a word.

But when I spot what she's holding in her hand, she doesn't have to.

Her eyes lock on mine, and I exhale, stomach roiling for a whole new reason. Skyler is the first to say what I know we're all thinking.

"Oh, shit."

THREE MONTHS EARLIER

Bear

Of all the classes they made me take during my time at Palm South, they never forced one on me called *Life After College*. And only three months removed from being a student, I'm seriously wondering why that isn't the number one required credit for every single one of us.

I had no idea how easy I had it, even when it was hard. I didn't realize how having classes and finals was a piece of cake compared to maneuvering the oversaturated job hunt, how partying on a school night is a hell of a lot easier than partying on a work night, or how that degree doesn't mean shit once you actually get a job — for your salary or for your day-to-day tasks.

If anything, there should have been a class during every kid's last semester called *Welcome to the Real World, Where You Have Student Loan Debt and a Shitty Salary and a Job You're Not Actually Prepared for and a Boss Who Expects You To Work Double the Hours Required.*

Good Luck!

These are the thoughts that trickle through my mind like a leaky faucet as I eat lunch out of a plastic container in the break room, staring at the calendar on my phone with the list of shit I still have to do when I go back to my cubicle.

It had taken me all damn summer to get a job. It turned out that while I had a degree, my lack of on-the-job experience made me less appealing than those who had internships out the ass. Luckily for me, Erin helped me spruce up my resume, and Ashlei hooked me up with an unpaid internship for a couple months at her firm, working on graphics for her clients.

With a professional portfolio finally under my belt, I landed my first paid gig — Junior Graphic Designer at *Sparrow Creative*, a young but hungry advertising agency downtown.

As much as the journey to get here sucked, and as much as I'm not thrilled with the salary — even though I was able to negotiate a little higher than they originally offered — I'm thankful to be working, to finally be applying what I learned in school.

But something is... missing.

I thought it was sports. After all, I played all through high school and college, and now I'm a quote, unquote, *adult* and not a professional athlete. So, I joined a CrossFit gym, thinking that would fill the gap.

And it has, for the most part.

In fact, I've become so competitive and so knowledgeable about the culture and the training that the owner at my gym has been whispering in my ear about possibly coming on as a personal trainer or class instructor.

For now, though, I'm content just to train and compete on my own.

And still...

Something's missing.

I could argue that it's sex, being that Erin and I have been taking it excruciatingly slow. But that's been *my* decision — mostly because I know what she's been through, what she's *going* through, and when I do take her, it's going to be with nothing but reverence and a cherished understanding of how lucky I am to be the one she trusts to give herself to.

Besides, we've been doing plenty of other things that satiate my sexual needs, including me coaching her through sucking my cock, which might be the most erotic thing I've ever done in my life — and I've had a finger up the asshole, so that's saying something.

If I'm being honest, that woman is so goddamn hot, all she has to do is kiss me and rub that tight little body against mine and I'm ready to come.

So it's not the sex, and it's not the job, and it's not the lack of physical output.

But still...

Something.

The slam of the microwave snaps me from my thoughts, and I look up just in time to see a longing smile spread on my co-worker's face.

"*God*," she says, shaking her head with her eyes on my food. "That looks so much better than the Lean Cuisine I have. Tell me what it tastes like." Her eyes flick to mine. "Slowly, so I can savor it."

I laugh, taking the bite of salmon and asparagus I have stacked on my fork before I set it down. "I won't submit you to such torture, Giselle."

She sighs. "I should probably thank you, but maybe I like a little torture from time to time."

She winks as I shake my head and stack up another bite. "It's just salmon. You could easily be eating this, too."

"Define *easily*," she says, grabbing her frozen meal from the microwave once it dings and sitting across from me. "Because someone had to cook that salmon and those veggies, and I can tell you that after a long day here?" She shakes her head, peeling the plastic wrapper back from her container. "It ain't me."

I cringe at the sight of the rubbery-looking pasta she's unveiled. "I think I'd stay up until two in the morning meal prepping if it meant I didn't have to eat *that*."

She sighs again, stabbing the noodles with her plastic fork and twirling until she has a bite prepped. "It's awful," she admits. "But it's worth every savory minute I had on my couch last night."

I chuckle, and we hold our forks up in a sort of *cheers* before both taking a bite.

Giselle is a few years older than me, and though she's joking about being lazy, I know for a fact that she's not. For one, she's too toned and slim to not be active and watching what she eats, and for two, I've seen her bust her ass day in and day out in this office since my first day three weeks ago.

She's the youngest account manager in the agency.

And it doesn't take more than three days of working with her to understand why.

As if her boldly colored skirt-suits and matching high — *high* — heels don't command enough of a presence when she walks into a room, her light brown skin, cat-lined eyes and painted lips certainly do the trick. I've never seen her onyx hair down, it's always pulled back in a slick, tight bun, and the way she holds her shoulders square and back straight told me long before I ever talked to her that she took no shit from anyone.

The first time I was in a meeting with her, she single-handedly saved us from losing a client the agency had been working with for three years. Not only that, but she ran through a list of reasons it was *their* fault that their content was under-performing, and by the end of the meeting, convinced the client to invest double what they were before in the advertising efforts.

All without breaking a sweat.

So, while I could understand why she might not have the energy to meal prep every night, I wasn't foolish enough to believe she didn't work just as hard outside of this office as she did inside it.

"How are you feeling now that you're a little more settled in?" she asks when she's done chewing.

"Great," I say with a smile I hope is more convincing than it feels. "I'm excited to be here. I just hope my work is up to standard for the agency."

"You know it is," she says instantly. "Don't fish for a compliment when you already know."

I gape. "I... I wasn't—"

"Confidence, Mr. Pennington. *That's* what turns me on. You walked in here with it on the day of your interview and every day since. I understand you wanting to taper that down a bit, be modest around someone in a higher position than you, but I'll tell you right now that you'll get farther here

— and everywhere in this field — by owning your talent and reminding every single person every single chance you get that they can't find that same talent anywhere else. If you're not demanding a raise in six months' time, you might as well quit and find a new job. Because unless you demand the respect and the pay you deserve in this career, you'll never get it."

I swallow, not sure if I should be flattered or scared.

But Giselle just lifts one eyebrow, nods, and continues eating. "Did I see you walking into Black-Sheep last night?"

I pause with my next bite mid-air at the mention of my CrossFit gym. "Yes..."

She chuckles. "I'm not stalking you. I go to the yoga studio two doors down." She pauses. "I've always been curious about CrossFit though. Think I would like it?"

I take a breath, thankful for the subject change and the way my balls relax a little now that she's not grilling me. "Depends. I think if you're athletic and like a challenge, absolutely. But it's a little harder on the body than yoga." I pause. "No offense. I just mean you'll bulk up a little more, and get callouses."

Giselle takes a sip of her water with a slick smile on those painted lips of hers. "Oh, I don't mind getting my hands dirty."

My phone pings on the table, the vibration of it loud enough that both our eyes slip to the screen where Erin's bright, beautiful smile reflects back — along with a text that asks how my day is going.

I smile, feeling more like a little boy with a crush than a grown man with a serious girlfriend. Even though I know Erin better than probably anyone, and she knows *me* better than anyone, everything between us feels fresh and new now. Every night I spend with her is a new discovery, every conversation one I want to commit to memory, every kiss one that leaves its own permanent brand.

I'm still wearing that goofy smile as I type back a response.

"Girlfriend?" Giselle asks.

"The best one on the planet."

When I finish the text and look at her, she's wearing a smile laced with a million things she won't say. "Glad you found her before you found this place," she decides on, popping another bite in her mouth. "Because you damn sure wouldn't have found the time or energy to date if you'd come here first."

I'm not sure if I should laugh or ask her if she needs someone to talk to, but I don't get the chance before there's a knock on the door panel of the break room, and my boss peeks his head in.

"Sorry to bother during lunch, but can I get your eyes on this website?"

I nod, gathering my things. "I'm finished, anyway."

"Great. See you in my office."

He ducks out, and once I've cleared the table, I nod to Giselle. "Nice talking to you. Enjoy the rest of your lunch."

She holds her fork up to me with a wink, and there's something in her eyes still, like she's assessing every move I make, every word I say.

I can still feel her watching me even when I'm down the hall and out of sight.

Cassie

"We are the girls of KKB,
We are the ones you came to see.
Looking for the life of the party?
Look no further than KKB!
Sisterhood through and through,
Scholarship and athletics, too.
If you want fun and sisters true,
KKB is the house for you!"

I scream the words to our door chant loud and proud with my sisters, and then to a roar of applause from the potential new members waiting outside the door, we all scurry to our spots in the hallway, lining up in perfect order to receive the girls.

I've done this three times before now — once on the outside and twice on the inside — and every time, my stomach fills with butterflies. But this time, those butterflies seem to be flying with wet wings, slow and sad.

Because it's my last rush week.

Ever.

A thick knot forms in my throat at the thought, the same kind that blocked my breath when I clung to Adam in the Boston airport two weeks ago. Saying goodbye to him after spending half the summer with our families, and the other half getting him set up in his new apartment, and with his new job which felt impossible.

Just like saying goodbye to Kappa Kappa Beta does now.

Change...

I'm no stranger to it, and yet I've never been hit with so much at once. It felt like a dream, getting my acceptance email from Johns Hopkins, and now here I am just four months from graduating and leaving this sorority and this university behind me.

Tears well in my eyes, and I look up at the ceiling and fan myself to keep them from falling. I'm about to match up with a girl I'm supposed to convince to rush KKB, not run away thinking we're all a bunch of emotional weirdos.

Hands grab my arms as I'm still staring at the ceiling, and when I drop my gaze, I find Skyler smiling at me with tears of her own.

"I want to hug you so fucking bad right now," she says. "But if I do, we'll both lose it and ruin our makeup and chase the poor new girls away."

I bark out a laugh, swiping the lone tear that escapes from my cheek before it can mar my makeup. "This is it," I whisper.

Skyler nods, her bottom lip trembling, but then she quickly shakes her head and blows out a breath as the Recruitment Chair hollers back that the doors are opening.

"We can cry later. For now, plaster on that smile I love so much and find us some new sisters."

I smile and nod, and with a kiss to my cheek, she releases me and makes her way to the front of the hall to greet the girls.

As the president.

My stomach roils a bit at the tradition I'm breaking, the one that has been around longer than I can even wrap my head around. Every girl in our line has been president for years and years, but that ends with Skyler.

Or maybe, it just skips a generation.

Maybe *I* won't be president, but with my sights set on finding a Little, I find myself smiling at the thought that maybe, one day, *she* could be.

When the doors finally open, it's pure madness. Music blasts from our speakers, all my sisters clapping in sync to the beat as we file toward the door. When we get there, we're matched up with a girl rushing, the line-up planned by our Exec Board. They review the girls each night before and select who they think would be the best match to talk to the potential new member. It's all a dance, a beautiful, coordinated dance of courting.

If only dating were so lovely.

When I'm a few girls away from picking up my own match, I spot a potential new member on the other side.

Chewing her fingernails down to the nubs.

Her slicked-black hair is styled in two adorable space buns, a pair of oversized glasses slipping down her nose before she pushes them up and goes right back to chewing her thumb nail. She's wearing the cutest romper I've ever seen, navy blue with a white and yellow floral design and a small gap showing the pale skin between her breasts and her belly button. It takes confidence to put on an outfit like that, and yet she looks like she's ready to bolt at any second.

She doesn't look up at me when it's our turn, not until I step halfway out of the house and extend my hand for hers.

"Hi!" I say cheerily. "I'm Cassie. Welcome to KKB. I know it's a little loud right now, let's go inside and find somewhere we can talk."

Her eyes are a cloudy river, blue and green swirling together inside an iris lined with a thick, navy blue rim. They stun me so much I have a hard time not gasping and commenting on them right away. Instead, I hold out my arm for her to link with mine, and she does so hesitantly before following me back down the hallway.

I'm *supposed* to lead her to a corner in the main dining room, where we'll scream over the rest of the conversations happening in the house and strain to hear one another. But I'm already hoarse from the day before, and I can tell just by looking at her that this girl would appreciate some quiet. So, I lead her upstairs and back to my room.

"Whew," I say when we're inside, leaving the door open so we can still hear everything going on downstairs. "It's a little crazy out there, huh?"

She nods emphatically, her eyes growing a bit wider as she folds her hands in front of her waist.

"Sorry, it's kind of a mess up here," I say, looking around at the rogue hair extensions and makeup and clothing tossed this way and that. "During Rush, we open up our rooms to everyone — even if they don't live in the house. And with seventy-six of us getting ready every morning, there's not much time to clean up after."

She smiles. "This is your room?"

I nod. "It is. I have a roommate, Lindsey, who rushed last semester. She's really sweet. And my Big is the president, the one who greeted you before you came in. Her room is right down the hall."

The girl's eyes go wide. "Wow. That's so cool."

I smile. "What's your name?"

"Tera," she says. "Tera Rosebaum."

"Nice to meet you, Tera. I'm Cassie, in case you couldn't hear me downstairs. How's Rush going so far?" I grab my desk chair and pull it over to Lindsey's, sliding that one out for Tera to have a seat.

She hesitates at first, but when she finally sits down, I don't miss the relief she feels to no longer be standing in her wedges. "It's... going."

I laugh. "Kind of overwhelming, isn't it?"

"That's an understatement," she says, wincing a little as she rolls her ankles. "To be honest... I kind of feel out of my element here. All the hair and makeup, the dresses, the heels, the screaming, the music... it's a lot."

I nod, remembering all too well how it felt to be on that side of it. "I had those same thoughts when I rushed. I remember thinking to myself that I was among a bunch of walking, talking Barbies."

"Oh, my God. That's exactly what it is!"

"Like how did all these girls learn how to do makeup like this?"

"I can barely keep up with mascara and lip gloss."

"You should see me try to contour. Hideous. Like a clown."

Tera giggles, relaxing a little more in her seat. "How did you get over that initial discomfort?"

I sigh, looking to the side as I try to recall who I'd been at that time in my life. It feels so long ago now that it takes a lot of effort.

"Well, for me, it took meeting the right girls. Some of the houses I went to, I could just tell I wouldn't fit in. It was nothing against them, I just didn't feel that connection, that spark, you know? But when I came to KKB, I met a girl named Erin." I smile at the memory. "I didn't know it then, but one day, she'd be my GrandBig."

"Your what?"

I chuckle. "It's kind of like your family within the family of the sisterhood as a whole. After you Rush, a girl in our sorority will pick you for her Little, and you have to pick her for your Big, in return. Then you're part of a line. So, Erin was *my* Big's Big."

"Makes my head spin."

Another laugh from me. "We can get into it later. But yeah, for me, meeting her, and then a few other girls in this sorority… I just felt like I was home. I was torn, actually, on the night before bid day, and I talked to a girl down by the reflection pond who helped me pick. Come to find out, she was a KKB sister, too." I paused. "And she became my Big."

Tera smiles, but then the light goes out in her eyes, gaze falling to her shoes. "What if you don't fit in anywhere?"

I tilt my head. "Is that how you feel?"

She nods. "Don't get me wrong, I'm not like the girl who has no friends. I have a lot, actually." She pauses. "Had. Back home. But I don't know, I'm… different. I like anime, and romance books, and video games and cosplay." She clears her throat, smoothing her hands over the shorts of her romper. "And *look* at me. I look like I ate three of your sisters before I came in here."

My heart lurches into my throat, and I instantly want to reach for her, to pet her arm and say she's gorgeous, and that her size was the *last* thing I noticed about her. But I can tell just from this small interaction that Tera doesn't trust easily, doesn't open easily, and I want her to feel safe with me — not like I pity her, especially since from what I can see, there's nothing to pity.

She's a badass. I can sense it.

"Cosplay, huh?" I decide on. "What exactly does that mean?"

She laughs uncomfortably, grabbing the back of her neck. "It's really nerdy."

"Stop that. I bet it's cool if you love it so much."

She shrugs. "I mean, *I* think it's cool."

"And you have a whole slew of friends who do, too, right?"

She nods. "We dress up like our favorite characters from movies, or books, or video games or shows."

"Wow! Like, costumes?"

"Yes, but *way* more intense. I mean, especially for conventions and stuff, we go all out. I'm talking chopping our hair off, or growing it out for years to get a specific look, spending thousands of dollars on fabric and supplies to make our costumes."

"So you're not just buying them online or something?"

"*God*, no," she says, brows furrowing with the offense.

I chuckle. "Sounds like I have a lot to learn. Do you have any pictures of you dressed up?"

Tera bites her lip, like she's deciding if she can trust me, but in the end, she pulls out her phone and taps until there's an image so striking it makes me gasp.

I grab the phone out of her hand, pulling it closer and zooming in to inspect the intricate design of the fire-engine red costume. It's skin-tight, leather-like and hugging every curve she has. Paired with the badass thigh-high boots and her bright red hair — which I can't tell if it's is a wig or her actual hair dyed that color — she looks like a completely different person.

"Bitch!" I say without thinking, but she laughs, so I take it as permission. "Get out of here with that *I can't do makeup* shit. Look at you! This is incredible!"

"I was Asuka Langley Soryu. She's an anime character."

"She's iconic," I correct, handing her phone back to her. "And so are you."

The smile she's wearing now is her most genuine once since she walked in the room, but with a shout from below and a music cue, I know it's time to start walking her out.

I sigh, standing. "There's never enough time during these things."

"It's time to go already?"

"Afraid so," I answer as she stands to join me. "But I really hope I'll see you back here tomorrow. I'd love to get to know you better."

She smiles, her mesmerizing eyes flicking back and forth between mine. "I'd like that, too."

We link arms and walk downstairs, chatting a little until the music is too loud to do much other than smile and wave goodbye.

And when the doors shut, my sisters excitedly filling into the kitchen for lunch, I run around the house until I find Skyler, nearly toppling into her once I finally do.

"Whoa, whoa!" she says, catching my arms as we both find our balance. She laughs. "Slow down there, killer."

"I think I just met my Little."

Her mouth pops open at that, and her eyes search mine for a moment before her lips meet again and spread into a knowing smile.

"Tell me everything."

Skyler

I'm used to the way lonely feels.

Growing up, I was an outcast, a nerd, the girl who hung out with her poor family and didn't have more than a handful of friends — if you could even call them that. When I wasn't playing poker with my parents, I was studying or coloring or listening to music in my room. Sometimes I would ride my bike around town by myself, just listening to the wind breezing through my hair.

When I came to Palm South, all that changed.

With a snap of my fingers, I altered that past and became a new me — the me I'd always felt like I was inside. I embraced my sass, my courage, my fearlessness and channeled it into being the girl I'd always known was simmering there under the surface.

With my sisters in Kappa Kappa Beta always around, and practically every boy on Greek Row begging for my time, I never had another lonely day.

Until this summer.

How I could have lived in such a blissful heaven for a full year only to tumble down from the clouds and slam into the dirt is beyond me.

Kip felt like the safest, most sure thing in the world.

Now, I don't know him at all.

The Kip I love wouldn't have forgotten our one-year anniversary, or the date *he'd* planned. The Kip I love wouldn't have had his hands on another girl's hips while she was naked in a shower, whether it was for work or not. The Kip I love would have listened to me, would have understood my anger and hurt.

And more than anything, the Kip I know would have found a way to make it right.

It wasn't that he didn't try, I suppose. He called. He texted. He came by the house. When I finally did decide I was ready to see him and hear him out, he apologized.

But not for what he did.

For how he'd made me feel.

It was a monstrous slap to the face. *"I'm sorry I made you feel that way,"* as if I was being irrational, as if he still stood firm in his delusion that he was right and I was wrong. I knew I wasn't a saint. I knew I could have handled that situation better than I did.

But he couldn't even see it, couldn't see Natalia for the games she played, couldn't see how him putting her and the show before our anniversary killed me.

The show about *our love.*

How ironic.

He went right back to filming, editing, producing — like everything was fine. It wasn't until he showed up one evening and tried to kiss me and I pulled away that I think he realized a simple apology wasn't going to be enough.

"I need some time," I'd told him. *"And some space."*

I could close my eyes now and still see the hurt in his eyes, the deflation of his shoulders, could still feel the way his lips pressed against my temple at the same time one lone tear slipped down my cheek.

That was the last time I saw him, almost two months ago.

I threw myself into recruitment, into my last semester as president, into making damn sure I leave this sorority in even better shape than I found it. Spending time with the girls helped, too, and now that we're in the thick of Rush week, I'm distracted.

Distracted, but lonely.

Even in a house full of my sisters.

Even at night when Cassie and I curl up in my bed and talk and laugh and reminisce.

Every minute I'm awake, every second I'm alive — I'm lonely.

Because my other half, that person who completed me and made me feel whole for the first time in my life is gone.

And I don't know if I'll ever have that piece of me again.

"Sky," a voice says, shaking me from my haze as I filter through the profile binders of the potential new members coming through the house tonight. It's the last night before we make our bids and hope they pick us for their top choice, in return.

I turn in my chair, finding Ava, our recruitment chair, with an apologetic grimace on her beautiful face.

"Sorry to bother," she says instantly. "But, um... you have a visitor."

I frown. "Is it one of the other presidents?"

"It's Kip."

All the blood drains from my face, my stomach roiling violently.

I clear my throat. "Be right down."

She nods, her eyes sympathetic as she closes the door and leaves me alone.

I take a moment to check my reflection in the mirror, smoothing my hands over my elegant, short black dress. It's a halter top with thin straps and a body that hugs all my slim curves. My favorite accent is the slit that accents my toned thigh, and the strappy high heels I paired with it. My hair is pulled back in a delicate braid, my makeup applied to perfection, natural and light, but with enough precision to stun.

Pref night is perhaps the most important of all of Rush week. It's our final chance to convince the girls we want that this should be their home for the next four years.

It's also the most emotional night for the seniors, as they realize *their* time here is coming to an end, and a new chapter is beginning.

Without them.

I blow out a soft breath, succumbing to numbness as my feet carry me blindly down the hall, the stairs, and out to the front porch where Kip is leaning against one of the tall columns, his hands in his pockets, eyes on the cement ground.

When he lifts those cerulean blue pools and locks his gaze on mine, my bones lock up, stopping me mid-stride a good four feet away from him.

My skin heats as he drags his gaze down the length of me, and he shakes his head slightly as he pushes off the banister to stand tall. "Sky... *Jesus*," he breathes, running a hand over his scruff. "You are so goddamn beautiful."

Everything in me wants to melt.

I want to swoon, to run to him, to fold myself into his arms and press my lips to his.

But my heart refuses, making me cross my arms and clear my throat, instead. "Thank you," I say flatly. "Do you need something? I'm kind of busy."

Kip doesn't wince, but I see the pain my words inflict regardless. He never was able to hide his emotions from me.

"We finished the show."

He waits for me to react, and when I don't, he presses his tongue into his cheek, steeling a breath before he continues.

"I mean, we finished filming. We still have some post-production to do, but it'll be done back at the school before we turn in the final product." He swallows. "I think the mini-series will be live on the web by the end of November."

"Congratulations."

I can't help how flat the word is when I release it, can't help that I'm already turning to leave, but Kip's hand shoots out to hook my elbow, stopping me in my tracks.

"Skyler, I'm leaving," he breathes against my neck, his body inching closer and closer. "I'm going back to California. Please," he pleads, his voice breaking. "Don't make me leave like this."

I close my eyes against the pain splitting my chest, against the urge to weep.

"What do you want from me, Kip?" I ask on a breath.

"Forgiveness."

I turn then, pulling from his grip on my arm. "Forgiveness for what, exactly?"

I need to hear him say it. I need to hear him say he was wrong, that he understands why I was upset — why I *still* am.

Kip rolls his lips together, pushing his glasses up the bridge of his nose before he hangs his hands on his hips and looks off in the distance down Greek Row.

I shake my head. "Kip, what happened that night... what happened all last semester... it killed me."

His nose flared, eyes watering, but he wouldn't look at me.

"Whether you realize it and want to admit it or not, you chose the show over me." I swallow. "You chose *her* over me."

"Natalia is a professional."

"Natalia is a bitch," I correct, not even a little sorry when he finally looks at me with a frown etched in his brows. "She's conniving and smarter than you give her credit for, and she knew what she was doing."

"Why are you attacking her? *You're* the one who picked her for the part!"

"And that was my mistake. Now, can you admit to yours?"

Kip pinches the bridge of his nose on a long breath. "Skyler, nothing happened. I was directing them through the shower scene so we could get it right. Natalia was there because I asked her to be, she wasn't trying to—"

"You forgot," I interrupted, and my bottom lip trembled as I waited for his eyes to meet mine once more. "You forgot to pick me up. For our date. For our *anniversary*. And then I walked in on you touching another woman, naked, in the shower. Let me ask you this, Kip. If it were me who forgot, who you had to track down, who you found holding another man in the shower — would you be okay with it?"

"Skyler, it's work. It's nothing—"

"Don't do that to me," I say curtly. "Don't make it seem like I don't support you, like I haven't *always* supported you. I understood when you needed to move across the country to go to the right school to get you where you want to be. I understood even when you came back here and you explained that I wouldn't see you much. I understood when your time was wrapped up in filming. I even understood why you didn't see it at first, the way Natalia looked at you, the things she was doing to make sure I felt threatened." I swallow. "But I have a right to be upset over what happened, and I deserve a proper apology."

"I'm sorry," Kip says quickly, reaching for my hands. He holds them up and presses his lips to the knuckles. "I'm sorry for hurting you."

I nod, biting my lip.

It still isn't enough.

"I have to go," I whisper, pulling my hands from his. "It's Pref Night and I have a lot to do."

"Skyler, please," Kip begs when I turn. "I don't want to leave like this. I... I don't even know what we are anymore."

I pause with my hand on the front doorknob, my breath hitched in my throat, tears swelling in my eyes until the wood panel blurs.

"That makes two of us."

I open the door, close it behind me, and press my back to the wood, smoothing my breaths as much as I can as I listen to Kip shuffle off the front porch.

Then, I lose it.

Jess

"We need to call the florist," my boss, Brittany, says in a slight panic through the phone. I just left the office not even an hour ago, and I hadn't even had the chance to put my leggings on before my phone was ringing.

But this is how it is working with Brittany Nova.

That bitch doesn't know how to *not* work.

"I called them this morning. The arrangements are all set, centerpieces complete, bouquets ready, they're just finishing up prepping for the arch, which they'll build on site," I say, grabbing a wine glass from the cabinet and a half-full bottle of Malbec from the fridge.

"Oh, good. Okay, next, we need to finalize the wedding cocktail."

"Already done. Bride and I decided on tequila, and the bartenders whipped up a few options for her this afternoon. She loved the one with grapefruit. We're calling it, *Rose in Love* and I already have the team making a sign for the bar."

"Rose in Love," she repeats. "I don't hate it as much as I thought I would. Okay, the seven-tier cheesecake — *God help us* — we need to—"

"Made to perfection. I stopped by the bakery on my way home. They made a smaller tier for me to taste and inspect. All the filling options are exactly as we asked, the colors are remarkable... although, I'll be honest, the poor team of bakers looked like they were ready to collapse from decorating it. They'll deliver it at four-thirty tomorrow evening, and I already made sure the venue has an entire fridge saved for it. They'll store each tier separately and assemble in the kitchen during dinner, rolling it out just in time to be cut."

"Brilliant," Brittany breathed, and I could hear the pen sliding across paper as she ticked that off the list. "The surfboard guest book."

"Set up with gold, silver, and black Sharpies right next to the Polaroid table."

"The lights—"

"Are all prepped and ready, along with speakers and mics, and the team will be bringing them over at ten tomorrow morning so we have plenty of time to get it all set up the way we need. The only thing I'm waiting to hear back on are whether the tree lanterns are too heavy for the limbs to support, but don't worry — we have gold bird feeder holders on stand-by if needed."

"Fireworks?"

"I'm pouring a glass of wine and am about to start tying the ribbons on the sparklers now. Buckets are already decorated. The team and I have a plan of attack for lighting all three-hundred-and-forty-five guests. And the pyrotechnics have forty-thousand dollars' worth of fireworks that will put Disney to shame and a boat to set them off of from the middle of the lake. We tested last night, and the lawn will be perfect for viewing."

There's a brief pause before Brittany lets out a dramatic exhale, and I can almost see her slumping back in her chair. "How did I get so lucky to find someone like you?"

"You say that now..."

She chuckles. "Okay, so I guess all that's left for me to do is—"

"Is to go to the rehearsal dinner and *have fun.*"

"That's never been a part of this job."

I snort. "Well, okay, maybe fun is the wrong term. But *relax*. Jenna and Howard will be there and they are well prepped to take care of everything. You just focus on making sure the bride is calm, and keep her mother away from the schnapps."

"That might be the hardest job of the evening."

"That's why we saved that one for you."

She lets out a puff of a laugh. "Thank you, Jess. For everything. Try to get some rest tonight, too."

"I plan on it, right after I put the final touches on the seating chart board."

"See you in the morning."

"Bright and early, boss."

When we hang up, I chuckle to myself and leave my phone on the counter, bringing my wine glass and the rest of the bottle over to the dining room table — which has been more of my craft table lately than anything. Since Ashlei moved out of our place and in with Brandon, and Erin spends most of her time at Bear's, there's never really any reason to clean it.

A ping of loneliness filters through me, but it's gone just as quickly as it appears.

If I'm being honest with myself, I've enjoyed the last couple of months on my own. I've been able to throw all my energy into the job I worked so hard to get, into making a name for myself with my boss and the rest of our team. Even though summer is the slowest season for weddings in Florida, we still had several weddings each month — all with affluent brides who expected the best from us.

I've been thankful to not have any distractions.

But just because Kade and Jarrett both respected my wishes and left me alone for the summer, doesn't mean I haven't been thinking of them every single day.

I don't know what I thought I was doing when I asked for the summer, as if them giving me some time and space would somehow give me clarity. Like I would have some sort of epiphany. Instead, I feel like I've sunk even deeper into thick, nasty mud that keeps seeping up, up, up. At this point, it's got to be at least chest-high and threatening to take me all the way under if I don't do something soon.

The issue is that I have *no* idea *what* to do.

I meant what I told the girls back in May — I love Kade and Jarrett both.

But just like the girls had so gently reminded me then, I also know I can't *have* them both.

And maybe that's the truth that's kept me latching onto this notion that somehow, space and time would help. Maybe, if I was being brutally honest with myself, I just didn't want to make the decision and was putting it off for as long as I could.

What a selfish, awful thing to do.

I'm halfway through my first glass of wine and first dozen sparklers when my phone buzzes loud on the counter, moving along the granite to the beat of my ringtone.

"Hey, Herb," I say when I see the front desk's number on the screen. "Another package?"

"Not this time, Miss Vonnegut. You have a visitor. A Mister Kade Brewer. Shall I send him up?"

Ice freezes my veins, and I pause for so long, Herb clears his throat to remind me to answer.

"Um, yes," I say weakly. "Yes."

I stare at the phone for too long after the call ends, unable to breathe, let alone fix my appearance or think about what the hell I'm going to say once Kade makes it up to our floor.

I'm still frozen in place when there's a soft knock on the front door, and I snap out of my daze, slamming back the last of my wine before I answer it.

The sight of Kade turns my knees to jelly.

His style has changed so much since I first met him. I've watched him grow from a boy into a man, from a silly flirt into someone who knows what they want and isn't afraid to go for it. Still, to see him standing here in fitted navy dress pants and a sleek white button down, a sports jacket folded over his left arm and mocha oxfords on his feet, it's enough to shock me silent.

His short hair is styled, his face clean-shaven, skin dark and smooth from the summer sun. I know as president of his fraternity, he's likely spent most of his days at the beach or the campus pool, and he has the tan to show for it.

And then there are his eyes, endless pools of honey gold and warm maple syrup brown swirling together.

And he's watching me like he's a sick dog and I'm the motherfucker with a gun about to put him out of his misery.

After a long pause and not a peep from either of us, he finally swallows, standing a little straighter as he says, "I know the last day of summer isn't technically until September, but school is starting back up next week, which signals fall to me." He shakes his head. "And honestly, I couldn't stand to be away from you. Not for one second more." His shoulders slump. "Please, Jess."

I close my eyes on a breath, and when I open them again, Kade's brows are bent together, his eyes searching mine for a response.

For permission.

So I simply take a step forward, and in the next breath, I'm swept into his arms.

Everything about him encompasses me — his big, muscular arms, his broad, warm chest, his hands splaying on my rib cage, his scent, earthy and strong. I feel like a little girl again in those arms, like I'm free.

Like I'm safe.

Kade exhales at the embrace, burying his face in my neck. "Fucking hell, I've missed you so much."

I squeeze him back. "I've missed you, too."

He doesn't release his hold on me for a long time, and when he finally does, he keeps his hands on my hips and just barely pulls back, watching me, waiting.

"Come inside," I say, grabbing his hand and tugging him out of the hallway. I close the door behind us and head for the couch, sitting down first and patting the cushion next to me so Kade does the same.

For a long pause, we just sit there, staring at each other, the silence somehow comfortable and awkward all at once.

"You look... weird," he finally comments, arching a brow as he takes in my attire.

I look down, realizing I'd only half-changed out of my work clothes, so I'm wearing an oversized Kappa Kappa Beta t-shirt and a bright orange pencil skirt.

"Shit," I say on a laugh, running a hand back through my hair that's no doubt just as much of a mess. "It's been a busy day. Busy *week*. We have a wedding at the Hennington Estate tomorrow."

Kade whistles. "Must be a fancy one if it's there."

"The budget was four-hundred-thousand dollars, if that tells you anything."

He balks. "That's a joke, right?"

"Not even a little bit." I slide a finger along the buttons on his shirt. "What are *you* so dressed up for?"

I didn't miss the way his Adam's apple bobbed in his throat at the touch, but his smile was quick and easy. "Had a meeting with the Director of Development and Chapter Operations for Alpha Sigma."

My eyebrows shoot up. "He came all the way from national headquarters? That doesn't sound good."

"It was very good, actually," he says, grabbing the back of his neck. "They're so impressed with how we've turned the fraternity around, they're giving us a sixty-thousand-dollar budget for house-expansion."

I gasp. "Kade! Oh, my God! That's amazing!"

"He said to put in a pool," he adds with a laugh. "The brothers are going to flip out."

"*I'm* flipping out. This is amazing!"

He nods. "Well, we mostly have Adam to thank."

"And Jeremy. And *you*," I say, pointing a finger into his chest. "You were a big part of it, too. Still are."

"Yeah."

I frown. "Why aren't you doing backflips from excitement right now?"

He blows out a laugh, shaking his head and looking out of the floor-to-ceiling windows behind me. "Jess, I haven't been capable of being happy for months."

My stomach sours. "Kade..."

"No, no, don't say you're sorry, okay?" He chews his lip. "I don't want to talk about the summer, or about *him*." His nose flares a bit with that word, and then his eyes are on me. "I just want to hear how you are, and talk to you, and fucking *hold* you in my arms. I just want to know I still have a fighting chance to make you mine. I have to know."

I was already nodding before he finished, and I climb into his lap, straddling his thighs and wrapping my arms around his neck as I press my mouth to his.

The moment our lips touch, we both shiver, gasping at the sensation of being connected again.

Kade folds his arms around me and pulls me even closer, swallowing my next breath and kissing me like it's the last time he'll ever get the chance to.

"I love you," I whisper, pulling back to look him in the eyes when I say the words.

He nods, brushing my hair from my face. "I love *you*."

"Consider the summer over," I add. "I don't want to stay away from you any longer."

"Oh, thank fuck."

I smile.

"I was actually hoping you would come to the A Sig karaoke event in a couple weeks. You know how big of a deal it is... I really want you there. I *need* you there."

"Then I'm there."

"Really?"

I nod, and when he pulls me in for another kiss, I wonder how I've stayed away from him this long.

Or how I could have ever walked away from him in the first place.

Cassie

"Wait, so the pledge *actually* streaked through class?" I ask Adam.

"Not only did he strip down naked in the middle of class — a class with almost a hundred students, I might add — but he ran up and down the stairs, his junk just bouncing everywhere."

"Oh, my God."

"The poor professor, she's seventy-four years old. She fainted."

"She fainted?!"

"His waving willy sent her right to the floor."

I snort, but cover the sound with my hands in shame. "That's awful," I say, but I can't stop laughing.

"She's alright, thankfully. But yeah... *that's* what I'm dealing with."

I shake my head. "Well, at least you're in a cool place. You'll have a fall! Unlike us here," I add with a sigh.

Adam chuckles. "I do love it here. But it reminds me of spring break last year." He pauses. "Makes me miss you even more."

"Thanksgiving," I remind him, pressing my fingertips to my laptop screen, right over where his lips are. "And I fully expect you to show me around. We were in the Rockies, but I've never been to Boulder. Or Denver, really, other than to fly in and out."

"I can't wait," he says, and his brows fold together with the sentiment.

It's only been a few weeks since we both left Boston — him to go to his first Alpha Sigma chapter assignment as a Field Executive, and me to come back to Florida for my last semester of college. But after having the whole summer together, it's like torture, being in different states, living different lives.

I finger the ΑΣ letters hanging from the white gold chain on my neck, remembering the day he lavaliered me like it was yesterday instead of six months ago. Any time I feel lonely or distraught over us being so far from each other, over not knowing the next time we'll be in the same place, I reach for that charm and let it ground me, let it remind me that what we have is far too strong for distance to destroy.

"What about you? How's it going over there?"

I sigh. "Well, I survived Rush Week, so that's always something to celebrate. Classes are already kicking my ass, but with it being my last semester, that's to be expected, I guess." I frown. "It's weird. Since I already got into Johns Hopkins, I feel... less motivated."

"Hey, maybe for the first time in your life, you just skate by for a semester. Take it easy."

I laugh. "Yeah, right. Do you know me?"

"I do," he says with a smile. "You'll be busting your ass for straight A's like always."

Adam kicks back in his bed — an unfamiliar bed so different from the one we set up for him in Boston. He gave me a tour of his little room in the Alpha Sigma house in Boulder when we first got on the call, and it made my stomach hurt that he was having new experiences at a new university without me.

It also makes me long to be there in bed with him, to be held by him, touched... kissed...

I shift against the little tingle that thought sends between my legs.

"Are you happy with the pledges you picked up?" Adam asks.

"Yeah," I say genuinely, smiling at the memory of that crazy week. "It's always a blur, but I tried to really take it all in this time. My *last* time. And... there's this girl I really like, I really feel a connection to." I bite my lip. "I think I might try to take her as my Little."

"Really? Who is she?"

"Her name is Tera. She's..." I laugh to myself. "Unique. Different in the best ways. She's got this amazing style, and all these fun hobbies and interests that are completely new to me. She does cosplay."

"Whoa," Adam remarks, brows shooting up. "What kind?"

"I don't really understand it all, but she said like anime characters. She showed me a picture and holy hell, it was hot."

"Who was she dressed as?"

I arch a brow at his earnest interest. "I can't remember... Asuka or something?"

"Asuka Langley Soryu?"

My jaw drops. "Yes. How the hell do you know that?"

Adam grimaces, grabbing the back of his neck. "I *may* or may not watch anime sometimes..."

"You never told me that!"

He laughs. "It's not exactly something to brag about, especially in a fraternity."

I shake my head, sitting back on the bed and folding my arms over my stomach. "Adam Brooks. I learn something new about you every day."

But Adam doesn't respond. In fact, he doesn't move at all. His eyes are glued on the screen, and after a moment, he lets out a long groan.

"Your tits look amazing right now."

I bark out a laugh, looking down at the simple tank top I'm wearing and the way my cleavage is on display with my arms crossed under the wire of my bra.

"You're such a perv."

"Can you blame me? It's been so long."

"Too long," I agree. "Seeing you in bed makes me wish I was there with you more than usual."

"Seeing your legs in those little sleep shorts makes *me* hard as a rock."

I flush, tucking my hair behind one ear as my eyes fall to my lap. "Adam..."

"When does Lindsey come back?"

I look at the door of our room, as if I expect him saying her name to have conjured my roommate. "I don't know. She's at the Omega Chi Beta house."

"Maybe we should take advantage of the alone time..."

I blush even harder, but just hearing him say the words has me clenching my thighs together. "I... I don't really know what to do."

Adam grins, a devilish smirk that tells me he knows *exactly* what to do.

"Lie back into your pillows," he says. "Let me see you."

I swallow, heat rushing from my neck to my toes as I do as he says. I use my hands to scoot back more toward the headboard, and then I lean back, posing like I'm on display for him and him only.

Adam bites his lip. "You're so beautiful," he murmurs, and then he repositions his own camera, and I can see his hard-on straining against his boxer briefs.

"Adam..." I breathe at the sight.

"I told you you make me hard," he says, and he runs his hands over the thick outline, moaning as he flexes into the touch. "Does this make you wet?"

My mouth parts. "Yes."

"Show me."

I roll my lips together, not sure if my face is hot from embarrassment, or from how insanely turned on I am.

"Come on, baby," Adam purrs. "Open your legs for me."

My heart pounds harder at the request, and I tuck my knees up to my chest before slowly letting them fall open, my feet spreading to opposite sides of the bed.

"Now pull your shorts to the side."

Adam strips off his shirt, and then lays back in bed, waiting for me to do what I was told.

Hesitantly, I run my fingers down the inside of my thigh, and then slip them under the thin, plaid fabric of my shorts, pulling them to the side just a half inch.

"More," Adam pants.

I can see my reflection on the screen, though it's small in the top corner and Adam takes up most of the space. But when I pull the fabric a little farther, there's no mistaking the pink glossy image I reveal.

"*Fuck*," Adam hisses, and he reaches into his boxer briefs, tugging them down just below his ass and freeing his length. It springs up, hard and ready, and he thumbs the bit of precum on the tip before rolling his fist over the tip, the shaft, all the way down to the base.

I don't realize I'm moaning at the sight until the sound is vibrating through me, and I snap my mouth shut as soon as it happens.

"Don't be quiet," Adam says.

"I have to. House full of sorority girls, remember?"

Adam bites his lip, and then he sinks down farther into his sheets, his back against the headboard, abs folding in on themselves. He kicks his briefs the rest of the way off, and now I have a perfect view of his hand around his shaft, his tight balls, and his face full of lust and wanting in the background.

"This is a really hot view," I comment.

"You're telling me. I want to tear those shorts off you and kiss my way down between your legs. I want to run my tongue along those wet lips and suck your perfect little clit between my teeth."

I gasp at the vision of it, as if I can feel it actually happening, and without him having to tell me to, I strip out of my shorts and my tank top, unlatching my bra and tossing it aside until I'm completely naked on the screen.

"Jesus, Cassie," he moans, stroking himself slowly as his eyes devour me. "What do you want to do to me?"

"I want to lie back on that bed and hang my head off the edge of it, and I want you to fuck my mouth the way you did in the tent that night at Boca Chita Key. I want to feel every inch of you sliding into my mouth, my throat, until I gag for you."

Adam stifles his groan, but he's already pumping faster, flexing into his hand time and time again. "I fucking love when you have me in your mouth."

"And then I want to ride you. I want you deep inside me."

"How deep?"

I don't even realize that I'm palming my breast, tweaking the nipple, that my back is arched and my fingertips are circling my clit softly. It's like watching him on screen transports me in time and space, like I'm there with him.

Like it's *him* touching me.

I slip my fingers inside myself, watching on the screen as they disappear. "So deep I see stars," I breathe, closing my eyes as I let the sensation of being filled take me under.

"Rub your clit for me, baby. I want you to come."

I do as he says, dragging my fingertips down from my breast until they're circling my tender clit. I'm still pulsing my other fingers in and out, but then I keep them as deep as I can reach, wiggling the tips back and forth to hit the right spot.

"You're so fucking sexy, Cassie," Adam says, picking up his pace. "I want to come on those perfect tits of yours."

"I want you to come in my mouth."

He groans his approval, pumping faster as I match his pace.

"I'm so tight, Adam," I find myself whispering, and I'm not even a little ashamed. In fact, I'm spreading my legs wider, arching my back, chasing my release.

"You're always so tight. Tight and wet and *mine*."

"Oh God... I think..."

But I don't finish the sentence before the spark I've been chasing catches fire, and a powerful orgasm rolls through me, pulsing and numbing and all-consuming. I have to hold my breath to keep from crying out, and as my climax starts to recede, Adam catches his, his face contorting as he tries not to be too loud. Watching him spill on his stomach makes me ready for round two, makes me want to be there to lick it up and beg for more.

Jesus, who am I?

Adam's entire body shivers when he's spent, and he lets out a long breath, shaking his head. "Fuck *me*, that was hot."

I giggle, my face heating as I grab my shorts and pull them back on, slipping the tank top over my bare breasts.

"Nooo," Adam whines. "Don't cover them up."

I laugh, but before I can even pop back with a reply, the door to my room flies open and Lindsey bounds through it.

"Oh, my God. The party is so fun, Cass! You have to come!" she says, ignoring the way I jump at her entrance.

Adam covers his mouth to keep from laughing, meanwhile looking around him for something to clean up.

"I just came back to change real quick. Some stupid freshman spilled her rum punch all over me." Lindsey rolls her eyes, strips off her shirt and quickly replaces it with another. Her eyes find me then. "You coming?"

I swallow, hoping like hell I don't have *I just had phone sex with my boyfriend* written all over my red face. "I'll catch up, just finishing up some studying."

Lindsey rolls her eyes. "You already got into your dream school, remember?" She checks the time on her phone. "If you're not there in twenty minutes, I'm coming back and dragging your ass out of that bed."

She doesn't wait for a response before she flies out the door, and Adam howls with laughter as soon as she's gone.

"That's not funny, Adam! What if she would have been even sixty seconds earlier!"

"She would have had *quite* the view, and would have understood why I'm so obsessed with you."

I narrow my eyes and flick him off, but then I'm laughing, too, relaxing back against the headboard again. My eyes soften, and Adam's smile turns sad, too.

"I miss you," I whisper.

"Miss you more."

Bear

Anyone who knows anything about me knows that I don't get nervous.

That word, that state of being? It doesn't exist for me. Put me in the game with thirty seconds left and an impossible play to make. I'm your guy. Put me in front of a room full of angry fraternity brothers with the mission to get us all on the same page again. I'm your guy. Put me in front of the most drop-dead gorgeous and unobtainable woman in the world and watch me woo the panties right off her.

I'm. Your. Guy.

Nothing phases me — there's no amount of pressure you could put on me that would make me feel anything but completely confident that I can do whatever the fuck I want to do or need to do to get the job done.

But they say when you graduate college, things change.

And boy, are they a changin'.

My palms are so slick I can barely hold onto the handle of the pan as I sauté the mushrooms for the recipe I picked out, and I can't count the times I've double-checked that every candle is lit, that the flowers are in the perfect place, that my tie is on correctly, that the music is just the right volume. I also may or may not have restarted the album three times now, because the song I want playing when Erin gets here keeps coming on before she's arrived.

There's no denying it, no faking like I'm calm, cool, and collected.

Because Erin wants to have sex tonight.

And I have absolutely zero fucking chill about it.

It's not like it will be our first time. No, our *first* time together consisted of entirely too much alcohol and a sorority formal that neither of us remembers. That night has a black ink smudge over it, and if you asked either of us what positions we were in or who came first, we'd have no answer.

All we know is we woke up naked in bed together, and not too long after, Erin found out she was pregnant.

So, clearly, we didn't use protection.

My hand pauses mid-stir over the mushrooms, heart thrumming in my ears as I remember the choice Erin had to make. I can't imagine what I would have done if I'd been in her shoes, and as much as it angered and upset me for a long time, now, all I have in my heart is respect for her.

And love.

God, I love that woman so much it burns me.

So no, it's not our first time, but it's the first time since mountains and mountains of shit piled up between us — pain and longing and miscommunication.

Plus, I'll be the first man inside her since the ones who violated her, who took something from her she'll never get back.

The memory of walking in on that scene, on seeing Erin with mascara marring her cheeks and her dress hiked up over her hips, those monsters prowling out of the room like they were kings instead of scum...

I nearly break the spatula in my hand, but shake off the thought before it can sweep me under, tapping the spatula on the edge of the pan. I set it to the side and mix in the heavy whipping cream and melty mozzarella cheese.

And then there's a knock at the door.

Wiping my hands on the kitchen towel hanging from the stove, I fidget with my hair and my tie one last time, and then I swing my front door open, losing my breath at the sight of Erin on the other side of it.

She's always beautiful. She's always poised and classy, always naturally glowing — even in her worst moments. But tonight, there's a sparkle behind that glow, a magnetic light in her eyes, a sensual smile on her soft pink lips that makes my rib cage squeeze tight around my lungs. Her hair is down and curled, the dark blonde tendrils flowing over her shoulders, and a pastel yellow sundress hugs her breasts, her waist, her hips, cutting off mid-thigh to reveal her tan legs and the nude heels strapped to her feet.

"I think this is the part where you invite me inside," she comments with an amused brow.

"Shit, sorry," I say instantly, opening the door wider and ushering her inside. "Ah, sorry for cursing, too."

She chuckles at that, hanging her purse on one of the hooks I adhered to the wall just beside the door. And then she's in my arms, pressing up on her toes, her lips on mine.

"Since *when* are you sorry for cursing?"

I breathe a laugh against her lips, my shoulders releasing a little now that I'm holding her. "I don't know. I just..." I pause, shaking my head. "You're radiant, Erin. As always."

"Thank you," she says with a little blush playing on her cheeks. "And *you*," she comments next, holding my arms as she pulls back and lets her eyes trail down the length of me. "Are wearing a suit." She looks at me again. "In your own house."

I didn't think it was funny until she said it, and now, I feel about as idiotic as any guy can.

I laugh, kissing her cheek before I release her. "Can't a guy dress up for his girlfriend for date night?"

"You can dress up for me any time you want," she says, looping her arm through mine. "But just so you know, you could have worn sweatpants and I'd have loved it just as much."

"Oh, I *know* why you love my sweatpants," I tease.

She giggles, hiding her blush as she presses her face into my chest. But then, she pulls back, sniffing at something in the air and frowning. "Um... is something burning?"

I balk, eyes nearly bulging out of my head as I rip from her grasp and jog across the entryway back to the kitchen.

"Ah, Christ," I curse when I make it back to the stove and see the burning, ruined sauce in the pan. I cut the burner and pull the pan over to a burner that's not on, sighing as I debate whether the sauce is salvageable.

It's not.

Erin chuckles when she comes up behind me, her arms wrapping around my waist, chin resting between the lower part of my shoulder blades. "Whoops."

I shake my head. "I'm so stupid."

"No, you're not."

"I am."

"You were distracted."

"Still, I knew I had it on, I should have turned the heat down or come back over or—"

Erin tugs on me until I turn and face her. "It's okay, Clinton."

The sound of my name on her lips has me closing my eyes and letting out a soft breath.

"We can order in," she continues. "I have to pee, but when I get out, I'll look on my phone and see what's around here. Okay? It's all good. We'll find something to eat, I promise."

I nod, but still don't open my eyes, not until she kisses my cheek and hurries off to the bathroom connected to my bedroom.

The house I found to rent after graduation is small, old, built sometime in the 1940s. It's a two-bedroom, one-and-a-half bath with a small fenced-in yard and a porch. The floors creak and the plumbing needs updating, but it has charm, and the landlord gave me a price that even Erin said was too good to be true for this close to downtown.

Scrubbing a hand over my face, I finally move from the spot where Erin left me, grabbing the pan like it's a poor bastard I'm about to pulverize in a street fight. I hastily scrub the charred contents into the trash can and then toss the pan in the sink, turning the water hot as I fill it and squeezing a healthy amount of soap in to soak.

Erin comes back into the kitchen silently, and when I turn and find her watching me with a soft smile and a red rose petal in her hand, all the blood drains from my face.

I completely forgot I had the room all set up — candles, rose petals, music. I thought if she used the restroom, she'd use the half bath in the living area.

"Shit..." I murmur mostly to myself, shoulders deflating as I pinch the bridge of my nose.

I just stay like that, unsure what to say, unsure whether I should try to explain myself or just pretend like I don't see her standing there. But with a chuckle, Erin crosses the room and sneaks her way into my arms, forcing me to release the hold on my nose so I can wrap her up, instead.

"Hey," she whispers, waiting until I meet her eyes. "Talk to me. What's going on?" She frowns then, grabbing ahold of my biceps. "You're shaking."

"Because I'm nervous as hell."

She barks out a laugh at that. "You? Nervous? I didn't think you were even capable of that emotion."

"That makes two of us."

Her brows fold together over her soft brown eyes as they search mine. "Talk to me."

I sigh, folding my hands behind the small of her back, but my eyes are across the room. "I just wanted everything to be perfect tonight."

I swallow, unsure what else to say. The right words don't exist for this moment, and I've already fucked it all to hell, so I don't even feel confident enough to try.

Erin slides her hands up my chest, over my shoulders, up still until she's cradling my face and angling it toward her. My nose flares as I drop my gaze to meet hers.

"I don't need a fancy dinner or rose petals or candles or you in a suit," she says, glancing at my tie as she does. "Although, you *do* look sexy as hell in it."

I smirk.

Her eyes find mine again, endlessly warm and inviting. She slides her fingertips back to hold my neck, her nails brushing the tender skin and setting off a wave of chills.

"I just need you," she whispers.

I nod, dropping my forehead down until it meets hers on a long inhale from both of us.

"Clinton?"

"Mm?"

"Take me to bed."

Fuck, the things those words do to me, the animalistic way my body responds — gripping her tighter, heart racing, cock already thickening in my slacks. It's like she owns me, like those four words were a snap of her fingers, and now I'm at her beck and call, ready to do whatever she wants.

Whatever she needs.

With something between a growl and an exhale, I bend down and swoop her into my arms, my lips on hers just in time to catch her giggle of surprise as I carry her down the short hall to my room.

This girl is my drug.

I realize it distantly as I carry her back, chasing her tongue with mine, savoring each little gasp and moan along with the little buzz they give me. I could never put into words what it is with her, what it's *always* been with her. All I know is that in the very depths of my existence, there's one thought that overcomes me any time I'm with her.

Mine.

Even when she wasn't.

Even when I wasn't sure she ever would be.

Neither of us had a choice in the matter.

She belongs to me and always has — just as I belong to her.

My bedroom is dimly lit from the candles and smells like teakwood and bourbon. I lie Erin gently down on top of my dark comforter, right on top of the rose petals, making a handful of them float up and back down like feathers on her skin and in her hair. She backs up until she's resting on her elbows against the pillows, her legs crossed, eyes big and soft as she watches me and waits for what I'll do next.

The night is completely in my hands.

I'm not fool enough to not realize how fucking lucky I am, and how much I must mean to her for her to trust me this way.

The soft, sexy sounds of the Tank album I put on filter around the space between us, and I turn the volume up a little more before I tug at my tie, releasing it first and then working every button on my suit jacket until I can shrug it over my shoulders.

Erin watches me with her bottom lip pinned between her teeth, her knees pulling up toward her chest.

I don't take my eyes off her as I strip off my dress shirt next, and then make quick work of my belt, shoes, and socks. When I unfasten the top button of my pants, Erin snaps up, sitting on the edge of the bed and placing her hands on top of mine to stop me.

"Let me," she pleads.

I let out a pained breath through my nose, because the way she looks up at me when she says those words, the flush on her cheeks, the way her fingers tremble as she struggles with the button and then the zipper and then helps me pull the slacks over my hips, my ass, down my thighs... it's the most erotic sight I've ever seen in my life.

I'm so fucking hard that I've pitched a tent in my briefs, and Erin gulps as she runs her palm along the length of me, the cotton fabric still between us.

I hiss, letting my head fall back, flexing my hips into the warm touch.

"Clinton," she whispers, and when I look back down at her, she doesn't have to say more. I can see it in her eyes.

She's the nervous one, now.

I nod in understanding, leaning down until my fists hit the bed on either side of her and my mouth captures hers. Then I'm backing her up into the pillows again, one arm swooping around her waist to hoist her up and set her back down.

"Look at me," I whisper when she's settled, when her trembling fingertips are digging into my shoulders. "You are safe. Okay? You're safe, and you're in control. You don't even have to say anything, I'm listening to your body."

Her eyes gloss with tears, but she nods, grabbing my neck and pulling me in for a long, hard kiss. I kiss her back just as earnestly, sealing my promise.

And then I trail those kisses down, down, down.

Over her chin, her neck, across every inch of her collarbone, I kiss. My lips leave little invisible marks across the petite swells of her breast over the fabric of her dress, and then on the lace covering her ribs, until I'm settled between her legs on my elbows.

I grab her ass firmly and lift her up just enough to free her dress, and then I push it up over her hips, hands gripping her thighs as I press a kiss sweetly over the thin, silky fabric of her beige thong.

She gasps, fisting the sheets and arching her back.

We've taken it slow over the summer, but if there's one thing I know about my girl, it's that she tastes just as sweet as she looks, and enough time with my tongue on her will have her open and panting and pleading for more.

Or coming, if I'm not careful.

I take my time stripping her panties off, kissing each part of her leg the fabric slides down before I discard them to the side. Then, I press my lips to the arch of her foot, her ankle, dragging my tongue along her calf and inner thigh until I'm settled in and ready to eat again.

Just the first lash of my tongue against her makes her writhe.

I smirk, teasing her mound before I run my tongue flat along the length of her, soaking up her taste and how much she wants me already.

"Oh, *Clinton*," she breathes, her hips grinding, seeking more friction when I do the same thing again.

I answer by pointing my tongue and circling the tip around her clit — once, twice, three times, quick and slick, before I lap her up long and slow.

I love that she calls out my name — my *real* name — not Bear, not God, not the myriad of things I've heard before. When she says my name, I'm like a dog snapping to attention for its master, the syllables of it from her lips a reminder of who I belong to.

Sliding my hands under her ass, I grip where her thighs meet her hips and tug her closer, feasting on her perfect, swollen, pink pussy as she squirms. She's twisting her hands in the covers and breathing so hard I almost wonder if she wants me to stop, if she's trying to get away, but any time I let up on the pressure, she mewls like a kitten, whimpering for more.

When her legs start really quaking around me, she snaps up suddenly, pressing her hand into my chest to break my contact. And when I bring my eyes to hers, sliding the back of my wrist across my damp lips, she flushes before calling me up to her with one *come here* wave of her finger.

I fist the front of her dress and yank, pulling her to sit so I can strip it up overhead in one fell swoop. I unclasp her bra next, sucking each perfect, pebbled mound between my teeth as soon as they're exposed. Erin clings to me, holding me to her, moaning and soaking up every touch.

When my lips are on hers again, I blindly reach into the drawer of my bedside table, fumbling a bit until I withdraw the golden foil packet. I bring it to my teeth and rip it open, making quick work of my briefs, and when I sit back on my knees, Erin's hand covers mine once more.

"Can I?" she asks, her eyes on the condom, and then on my length.

My answer is simply to give her the condom, and then we both watch as her shaking fingers bring it to my tip, stretching it over with a slow, rolling motion. She inches it down, and then wraps her hands around my shaft and the condom completely, rolling it the rest of the way until it covers me as close to the base as it can get.

I nearly come just at the sight of it, the feel of her hands squeezing and working me with her perfect little breasts heaving with each breath.

When the condom's in place, she swallows, sitting back a little and bringing her shy gaze to mine.

Leaning over until I can press my lips to hers once more, I sweep my arms around her and gently lift, sitting in her place as I hoist her up and over until she's straddling my lap. When she's there, I keep her up on her knees, holding her hips with my hands and kissing her long and soft.

"You're safe," I remind her when I break the kiss, trailing my lips over her jaw. "And you're in control."

She nods on an exhale, but before I can do anything else, she grabs my face in her hands, holding my gaze to hers.

"I love you."

The words slam into me, but not from surprise and not from fear — from relief. Because I've always known it, haven't I? I've always known Erin loved me, just as I've always known I love her.

I press my forehead to hers. "There is no measurement for how much I love you."

Even with our foreheads connected, I see the way her lips curve into a smile, the way a lone tear leaks from her eyes. When she pulls back, I thumb it away easily.

Then my hands are back on her hips, waiting, holding her steady and letting her decide what to do next.

Erin presses her hands against my chest, the tips of her fingers folding over each shoulder. I reach down between us just long enough to position me where she needs me, for the tip of me to glide into the shallow entrance of her.

We both stiffen and steel a breath at the feeling, the most sensitive part of me stretching her open just a centimeter, but enough that we both tremble and quake.

And then she sinks, just a half an inch, and we both moan in sync.

My hands wrap around her hips even more, encompassing her entire waist, and I hold onto her for dear life as she stretches a little more, letting me a little more inside her.

Stars. In my room and my head and swimming in every vein of my body is a galaxy of stars.

My cock pulses inside her, and she slips down a little more before she's grimacing and squeezing my shoulders tight.

"Are you okay?"

She nods, letting out a slow breath. "It hurts a little," she confesses. And then her sass makes an appearance, her brow popping into her hairline as she adds, "I've never had anyone this big before."

I can't help the cocky smirk that blooms on my face at that.

"You *technically* already had it once before," I remind her. "Remember? Oh, wait..."

She pinches my rib, and then we're both laughing, and kissing, and all the tension floats away on a nonexistent breeze.

Erin pushes up on her knees just a bit before she drops back down, sinking a little farther, another grimace warping her face.

"Go slow," I tell her, and I hold her hips to help, guiding her down so slowly I'm afraid by the time she sits all the way, I'm going to come twice over.

She's so fucking tight, so wet and slick and *mine.*

Slowly, Erin starts to take over again, picking up her pace. Up and down, sliding off my length just to sit back down and take more of me inside her.

Up, down, up, down.

A pant, a moan, a kiss, a sigh.

And then she sinks all the way, opening wide and gobbling me up so that I'm balls deep inside her.

We both still again at the sensation, holding onto each other with slick chests and shaking limbs.

It's like coming home after thinking we were dead, like finding the part of ourselves we never knew existed and yet always sensed was right under the surface.

Now it's my turn to take control.

I grip her hips tight, lifting her all the way up before gliding her back down, and we both moan again, louder, more urgent, Erin's fingernails digging into my skin. Again, all the way up, and all the way down, our climaxes building like a wildfire.

"Oh, my *God,* Clinton," Erin cries, her legs quaking violently. "This... I... it feels so *good.*"

I groan my agreement, and then I capture her next moan with my mouth, eagerly sucking it down and kissing her hard. My tongue swirls with hers as I help her ride me, faster and faster, but I refrain from slamming into her the way I desperately want to. And *God,* do I want to. Every feral part of me is begging me to lose control, to obliterate that pussy and make sure she doesn't walk a day in her life without remembering what I feel like inside her.

But tonight, I let her drive, let her call the shots for how deep and how fast and how hard. She wants me tame? I can do tame.

The beast inside me will live.

Something happens, and the walls of her tighten even more, squeezing every inch of my cock so hard I grunt and hold her tighter. One look at her face tells me what it was — she's on the brink of coming.

I kiss her harder, urging her on, and then I wrap my arms full around her and pull her closer, so that her hips open more, her back arched, body tilted.

And every new flex has her rubbing her clit against my pelvis.

Her moans are wild now, completely uninhibited, and she rocks faster and faster, keeping me inside her for the most part until that pussy clenches around me again and I know she's finding her release.

I give myself permission to follow, moving her hips the way I need them to move, but continuing that pressure on her clit so she can ride out her wave. And just like I saw when we first connected, stars blast me from every angle again, my climax a shocking, power-drunk punch to the gut that leaves me still and holding onto Erin for dear life as it shreds me apart.

For a long moment, I'm in outerspace — floating, numb and intoxicated by an all-consuming pleasure.

Slowly, the room comes back to me, starting with the soft sound of Erin's haggard breaths, the feeling of me growing soft inside her, of her slick chest against mine and her hands twisted in my short hair.

She drops her forehead to my shoulder, and then her shoulders begin to shake — softly at first, and then uncontrollably, sobs racking her body there in my arms.

I don't say a word.

I just hold her tighter, let her cry, and press my lips gently to her shoulder, her neck, her cheek. I don't rush her to talk or to look at me. I just wrap her up and pray that she knows she can feel whatever she needs to feel with me — good, bad, or in-between.

You're safe.

You're in control.

I seal those silent promises with every kiss.

EPISODE 2

Ashlei

My mom used to call me her little bird when I was a kid.

I had a knack for getting into trouble, for getting into precarious situations, and for getting hurt — mostly because I had such an appetite for challenge and a competitiveness like no other. Boy or girl, older or younger, it didn't matter. If someone challenged me to do something or said I *couldn't* do something, I'd prove them wrong.

I had more stitches than Barbie dolls by the time I was ten, but Mom always said I was her little bird, always flying from the nest without fear of falling.

I knew I would fly.

And right now, I feel like I've never soared higher in my life.

The last four years have taken me through some major ups and downs. From the drug escapade and getting caught up with the wrong people, to trying to turn my life around only to sleep with my boss, then fall in love with him, then lose him along with my job because I was stupid, then win him back and move in with him... you could say it's been a whirlwind.

But as it often does, the sea has been settling in my life, the storm gone, waters calming and breeze gently blowing through my hair. For the first time in a very long time, I feel completely at peace.

The summer only brought on more clients and more responsibility for me at *Ball & Pen*, and my boss, Celeste, became more and more comfortable handing me the more challenging events. She also gave me a bigger budget to hire more staff, including a *second* assistant for me in addition to Jeannie, who has become my right-hand woman.

Brandon had tried desperately to get me to come back to work at *Okay, Cool* when we'd made up, but as much as I love him *and* his company — *Ball & Pen* felt like the right place for me to be. It was a chance to build my name outside of Brandon, to not be seen as his previous intern-turned-employee-turned-girlfriend. Although we'd embraced our relationship head on and no one seemed to have a problem with it, I wasn't naïve enough to think the rumor mill didn't run behind both our backs.

Besides, Celeste sees my potential, and she trusts me with the responsibility I've always dreamed of having — ever since I decided event planning was a career I could see myself loving.

And *boy*, do I love it.

I work tirelessly every day and night, sometimes into the weekends — much to Brandon's dismay — and even on the most stressful days, I feel so alive, so *in love*, that I don't mind.

The only things that fuel me just as much as working are loving Brandon and pole dancing.

It amazes me still how easily the transition was with Brandon, from fighting and breaking up, to not talking for months, to fucking and dating like nothing had changed at all. The little games we played in the spring were maddening, but I'd go through them all again if that's what it took to have him. The truth is that Brandon's just as full of pride as I am, and it took playing those games to break him down and get him to realize he still loved me — even if he *was* mad at me.

And he had a right to be.

It isn't always easy. Even now, the pain I caused him surfaces and I have to smooth his worries about me possibly betraying his trust again. I never would, not in a million years, and I have no problem continually proving that to him.

But for the most part, the summer was pure magic for us — and I've never been happier or more in love.

And as much as I love work, and love *him*, there's a special kind of love I hold for this place — my pole studio — where I can get out of my head and fully into my body, where I can challenge *myself* and continually be humbled and find a way to rise again.

"That combo is fucking sick," Leona says when both my feet are on the hardwood floor again. She's a younger student, a perky, curvy little thing with pixie short hair and more tattoos on her pale skin than anyone I've ever known in my life.

I bend over and grab my knees, panting, chest heaving as I try to catch my breath. "Thanks," I say with a smile.

"Seriously, how the hell do you bend like that? And the Iron X... I'll never be able to do that." She shakes her head, wrapping both hands around her own pole and staring up at it like it's both the only thing she's ever loved, and her biggest enemy.

It kind of fits, to be honest.

"You will," I assure her. "Trust me. I've been doing this for four years now, off and on, and everything I can do now felt impossible to me at one point or another. Just keep working," I say. "I promise, you're stronger than you realize."

Leona smiles and nods at me in thanks, and then she's climbing up the pole again, working a layback combo I remember being a bitch to conquer myself when I was in my intermediate stage.

Leona is just one of the students I've come to love at the studio. From taking classes and attending almost every open pole practice, the girls here have become like family. Now that I've started to compete again, I've even roomed with some of them at competitions and conventions, and I've been both challenged and inspired by every single woman here.

"Has Karen convinced you to come on as a teacher yet?" one of the other girls chimes in from the back. "Because I'm dying to take a class with you."

I smirk, grabbing my water bottle from the cubbies on the far wall and taking a big swig. "Not yet, but she's getting close."

That earns a few gasps and excited claps from the room.

"Oh, my God, *please*, Lei!"

"I NEED to learn from you."

"Can you do a dance class? Your flow is insane!"

I laugh and hold up my hands to calm them all. "I'm still thinking on it. My big girl job is pretty demanding, and this is where I come to release. I don't want to lose that."

Silence falls over them before Leona says, "That's fair. But if you ever *do* decide to teach, I'll be the first one to sign up."

There's a chorus of agreement that makes me flush, and then the girls are all back to climbing and practicing their tricks.

I grab the bottle of Dry Hands out of my bag and squeeze a small amount in one palm, rubbing my hands together with my eyes on the pole as I debate what I want to work next. I'm nice and warm, and after nailing that last combo, all I can think about is that I'm ready to work my nemesis.

Bird of Paradise.

The twisty move is an absolute freak of nature, and one that my body hasn't particularly loved since I started training it over the summer.

It's an outside leg hang variation where you wrap your inside arm around the front of your inside leg, that's extended toward your face, by the way, and wrap your outside arm around the pole to grab that inside hand. Then, when you've got *that* bitch of a back breaking twist achieved, you release the outside leg and extend it back in a split, balancing everything while you hold on in this anatomy-defying pose.

All while upside down.

And spinning.

No big deal...

I first saw the move at a competition back when I competed for Leslie's studio, and I remember how loud the crowd cheered when the girl did it, how much my jaw dropped, how furious my little voice was in my head.

I have *to do that move!*

I didn't realize how much went into it, how flexibility and strength training had to combine for it to be achieved.

But I've been working tirelessly at it for almost a year now, and particularly hard over the summer.

Maybe today's the day...

I clap my hands together one last time, making sure the Dry Hands is sticky and ready to go, and then I launch myself at the pole.

Gripping tight, I power climb up, using only my hands and bicep muscles, legs swinging out behind me. When I'm up three climbs, I hold a pencil pose, body in line with the pole, and then tuck the chrome into my armpit and lift my legs up and over my head.

Chopper.

Leg hang.

For a while, I lie back and enjoy the brief rest. I remember a time when a leg hang was so painful, I thought my inner thigh was on fire. But now, it's a breather, a chance to let my body relax before I go for the next move.

Inhale.

Exhale.

Slowly, I grab for the pole and maneuver my shoulder into position — one that's extremely bendy and difficult, even with being warm. I take my time, and when I feel confident, I swing my inside leg around and grab hold with my inside hand.

This part is always sketchy, inching my shoulder under the pole more and more, centimeter by centimeter, my hands reaching for each other to lock behind my shin and hold me in place. I breathe through it, eyes closed so I won't get too dizzy.

And finally, my fingers touch.

A few more breaths and I've got my hands locked together, though my shoulders are screaming.

"You've got this, Lei!" someone shouts, and a few other girls cheer me on as I go for the last part to clench the move.

Squeeze everything tight.

Breathe.

Relax.

And when I feel ready, I unhook my outside leg and send it back behind me, straight and extended, toes pointed.

Bird of Paradise: unlocked.

The girls roar their approval, and for a moment, I'm smiling and internally freaking out that I actually fucking did it.

But the next, I slip, just an inch, just enough for all the joy to drain from my face, for my heart to race into my throat, and for me to realize I'm not secure.

Shit.

It's not easy to come out of this move, and I don't have enough time to think about how to do it properly, to save myself from slipping all the way down. I try to bring my outside leg back in to hook, but it's too late.

I can't squeeze hard enough.

I can't re-grip the pole.

And in the next second, I'm free falling — desperate hands grasping for chrome that I never quite find.

Cheers turn to gasps, and I hit the floor with a nasty *snap, rip, crack*. There's a brief shot of the most agonizing pain I've ever felt in my life.

And then everything goes dark.

Adam

The sun is high and blinding as I walk University Hill, taking in the crisp Colorado air with each breath. September at Palm South always meant pool parties and sweating every walk to class, but here? The days are pleasantly warm, the evenings cool, fall constantly whispering in your ear that it's well on its way.

I've got my hands tucked into the pockets of my light jacket, one branded with the Alpha Sigma letters and given to me when I joined the national staff as a Field Executive. The summer in Boston was a crash-course of learning — not necessarily the fraternity rituals or standards, which I already knew well — but rather how I would take my knowledge and experience from the last four years and apply them in my new role.

A role they did everything they could to prepare me for, but I'm not stupid enough to think it'll be so easy.

In their eyes, Field Executives are welcome with open arms, but if I know anything about fraternities, it's that having someone from nationals visit is hardly ever a good thing — and I wouldn't be anyone's favorite guest of honor.

Every chapter I visit, every group of guys I seek to mentor will need me for some reason, whether they want to admit it or not.

And the group here in Boulder *definitely* falls under the *not* category.

There are a few brothers sprawled on the grass when I reach the A Sig house, a monstrous Neo-classical beast that puts every house at Palm South to shame. Aspen University is older than Palm South, more prestigious, and has four times the amount of students. They also have more money, and their "Greek Row" is spread out all over The Hill, giant mansions with letters proudly fixed to the front like Easter eggs you can't help but hunt as you walk.

The brothers I pass by give me nods of hello, most of them friendly, most of them glad I'm there. The past two years of recruitment haven't gone so well, and though I was able to help them get a better turnout this year, my work had only just begun.

Through Rush Week, I'd become close with a lot of the brothers — the president and recruitment chair, the philanthropic chair, who I was most excited to work with, and a number of brothers of various ages. The new pledges knew me as if I was the House Director, and I intended to earn everyone's trust by the time I left — and to leave them in better shape than I found them.

Oddly enough, the current brothers aren't the issue.

It's the alumni presiding over the chapter that take the cake.

It's standard to have older brothers governing each Alpha Sigma chapter. After all, leaving a national organization in the hands of a bunch of rowdy college kids wouldn't work out in anyone's favor. Still, the goal of the alumni members is simply to ensure order. They may be present at chapter meetings to make sure everything is done correctly, may sign off on philanthropic or social events, and may step in to take care of punishment should one of the brothers, or all of them, need it.

But it's the current brothers who run exec, who make decisions, who hold their brothers accountable and make a name for the chapter on campus.

Or at least, it's *supposed* to be.

I pull my shoulders back as I walk through the front door of the house, preparing myself for the meeting ahead. I can't help but smile at the various pods of brothers as I pass through the house — some playing video games, some studying, some in the backyard playing beer pong. On the surface, everything looks right, looks in place, looks successful.

But this chapter has slowly gained the reputation for being dull and old school, for not performing in athletics, scholarship, *or* social activities, and for just being lackluster, in general.

And it didn't take me long to figure out that the alumni were the reason for most of it.

That's why I called this meeting, and though I know it won't be easy, I pray the guys will hear me out and make changes to better our presence on the Aspen University campus.

I take my time setting up the meeting room, setting the donuts I picked up from the popular spot on The Hill right in the center of the boardroom table. There are four alumni chapter advisors who preside over this particular chapter, and one by one, they all file in.

There aren't technically supposed to be titles among them, but when I met them the first time, they introduced themselves as Shawn, Secretary, Derek, Treasurer, Jared, Vice President, and Corey, President.

Corey was, so far, the biggest pain in my ass.

As they sit down and mutter among themselves, I find myself wishing Cassie were here. I would give anything to have had her in my arms before this meeting, to be kissing her senseless before running out the door, to know I had her just down the block when the meeting's over.

As it is, I'll have to settle for texts, phone calls, and the occasional video chat.

Memories of our *last* video chat bring a whole new slew of thoughts to mind, but I clear my throat and tamper them down, saving that energy for later.

"Gentlemen, thank you for joining me," I start, and that quiets the room.

Corey, the president, and Jared, the VP, both watch me with bored, suspicious glares, but the other two offer smiles and their full attention. I could tell after the first twenty minutes with them that they're divided, but with the two snarly ones being the oldest and regarded as the highest roles, they seem to make all the rules.

My plan is to change that.

"I'll try to make this as brief as possible, as I know you all have jobs and lives to get back to."

I make sure I say that last part firmly, because I want to remind them that they are *not*, in fact, frat brothers anymore.

"As you know, recruitment went well, all things considered, but having a great pledge class won't erase the hard work ahead of us. I have put together a plan that attacks three main categories of focus this semester: athletics, scholarship, and social activity," I explain, watching the room as the guys read over the binders I've put together in front of them. "I think we should focus on athletics and social activity first and foremost, with scholarship and philanthropy being introduced but more heavily focused on in the next semester."

"That doesn't make sense," Corey says instantly. "Why wouldn't it be scholarship and philanthropy first? What, are we trying to be the party boys now?"

"No," I assure him. "However, these are kids. Think back to when you were eighteen, nineteen, even twenty. Did you care about your grades or giving to the community as much as you did about partying with your brothers, making out with girls, and winning championships?"

Shawn snorts. "God, no."

Corey glares at him, then says, "Maybe this is how things were run in Florida, Adam, but we have more prestigious goals here."

"That may be," I say, not giving him the satisfaction of thinking I give a rat's ass about what he thinks of me or my chapter. "But these brothers need a win. They need to throw a great party, as weird as that sounds. A *safe* party, but a rager, nonetheless. And they need to feel like they're gaining popularity, like they stand a chance at being known on The Hill."

"I agree," Derek says. "But honestly, I don't see how these goals are achievable." He reads from the list. "Win the IM football championship, create a new annual Alpha Sigma event with high Greek Life attendance, host a social at a new and exciting venue?" He shakes his head. "We need actual athletes. And money."

"You've got more talent here than you give yourself credit for. I've been watching the guys, and I think if we talk to the Athletics Chair, we can get them to gather the new pledges as well as the older brothers together and get a good team going. We have two weeks until the sign-up date, three weeks until the first game."

"And what about this fancy new event?" Corey asks. "Who's going to come up with that?"

"The brothers, of course," I say without blinking. "This is their chapter. They're young and creative, give them a shot to come up with some ideas that we can sign off on. That's our role, after all," I remind them.

There's a pregnant pause before Jared sighs and drops his binder to the table. "I think this is a terrible idea."

"Listen, guys, I know it's hard to step out of the comfort zone, to throw all our eggs into baskets we can't even see yet. But I've been trained," I say, trying to earn their trust. "Give me a chance to prove I know what I'm doing. And if you still feel like I'm a nutcase by the end of the semester, I'll write to nationals myself and ask them to place me elsewhere."

"I don't know why they sent you in the first place," Corey mutters, which earns him an eye roll from Shawn that I smirk at.

"Let me talk with the Athletics Chair," I say calmly. "We became fast friends over Rush Week. And at our next chapter, I'll introduce the event, get the brothers excited and thinking."

"I guess we don't really have a choice," Jared says.

I smile and nod, letting them know the meeting is over.

Because no — they *don't* have a choice.

I saw Ricky, the Athletics Chair, playing beer pong in the backyard on my way up to the meeting, so I stop to talk to him on my way out the door. As I expected, he's pumped about the challenge, and a few brothers in the yard are already chomping at the bit to help him put the team together.

I clap him on the back and leave them to it, then check my watch, deciding I should head to the Student Union to fill out paperwork and get a date reserved for our on-campus event.

On the way, I text Cassie, and I'm so locked into our conversation that I don't notice the poor girl crossing my path until I run her over, literally knocking her over and leaving her sprawled out on the lawn below me.

"Shit, I'm so sorry," I say, hurriedly putting my phone away before I reach down a hand to help her up.

The girl has long, thick, messy black hair and tattoos lining both her arms. When she looks up at me, I'm knocked silent by shocking blue-green eyes outlined by dark charcoal and lashes. Her dusty-pink lips curve into a smile at the sight of me, and she lets me take her hand and pull her up.

She's wearing a tight, crop t-shirt with some band name I don't recognize, and I swear on my life her tits are bigger than any I've ever seen in person. Pair that with her slim waist, thick hips, and ripped-up black jeans, and she's in a whole league of her own. My eyes flick to her combat boots that I'm hoping she doesn't want to stomp me with, but she just dusts herself off with a chuckle once she's fully upright, arching a brow at me.

"It's all good. Maybe keep an eye on the road there, though, eh?"

I try to smile against the grimace coming to me naturally. "Sorry," I say again. Stupidly.

The girl just nods, and then with a curious smile, she leaves me and continues on her way.

Stitched into the pocket of her backpack are the letters ΔΒΓ, and I can't help but shake my head, because I would have bet money she was at least a grad student, if not older.

I think of when I met Cassie, how sweet and innocent she was, how she was naturally beautiful without a stitch of makeup on, how she looked so young and full of life. This girl was built like a woman, with eyes that told me she had stories and scars alike.

But times are changing, and young girls don't look as young to me as they should, I guess.

I shake my head, pulling out my phone again as I continue on my way to the Union.

But this time, I decide to call instead of text.

Erin

This room is too stuffy.

Brown and dark, wood and leather, shelves of boring books and even more boring documents proving their worth hanging on every wall. The windows are too small, not allowing enough light through for my tastes. This has been my most dreaded thought when it comes to the career I chose — finding a firm that doesn't make me want to crawl out of my skin with its architectural and interior design.

"Erin," my lawyer says — softly, tenderly. "I know this is hard."

I blink, tearing my blank stare from the law books on her shelf and meeting her eyes, instead. Candice is striking — tall and curvy, dark skin and even darker hair, long and filled with small braids that grow red in tint toward the ends. Her makeup is always flawless, red lips powerful, and every suit she has — pants or skirt — is tailored to fit her perfectly. Sometimes she's in kitten heels, sometimes flats, but no matter what's on her feet, her energy is tall and loud enough that she commands attention from everyone the second she enters the room.

Everyone but me, it seems, because I can't help but zone out during this meeting — mostly because I don't want to hear what she's telling me.

"And I also know hearing me say that doesn't make it any better," she adds, her brows bending together. "But look, this will all be worth it. Justice waits for these boys, and we might have to crawl through some muck to get it, but get it we will." She leans over the glossy mahogany table and folds her hand over mine. "I promise."

I swallow, nodding, which gives her permission to continue talking about the next steps.

Candice and I first met back in May, as soon as I told the girls what happened to me and decided I was ready to finally report the incident. Going to the police was the hardest part — detectives and bright rooms with questions being fired at me. I knew quickly that I needed a lawyer, and Candice stepped in ready for battle.

She showed me a long list of cases she'd fought — most of which she'd won — and promised me she would give me her all.

Of course, that was just the beginning of a hellish summer, and now, hearing what we have to do next, I realize the worst is yet to come.

"The detective they've assigned to your case is a hard ass," Candice says, filing through some paperwork before handing me a small profile on Gene Riley. His headshot smiles back at me as I fight down the bile rising in my throat. "But he's fair. I've seen him make the right call countless times. He's got a strong moral compass, which means if the evidence is there? He's got no problem pushing the case forward to court." She pauses. "But... it also means that if the evidence *isn't* there, he's not willing to send what could be an innocent man — or in this case, multiple innocent men — through the system."

"They're not innocent," I say, almost growl, my eyes hardening as I meet her gaze.

"I know," Candice insists. "And that's why we're going to cooperate with Mr. Riley on whatever he wants, so we can make sure he sees that, too."

I sigh, looking at the bio again, at the file of paperwork in front of me that I refuse to open because I know there are four other faces in there that I would like to never see again in my life.

"This step is crucial, Erin, and I need you to understand that before we move forward. He's going to question you, Clinton, your family, your friends — they need to know this is coming." She pauses. "He's also going to be questioning the defendants, and *their* family and friends."

"Who will lie," I say without hesitation. "They're never going to admit to it."

"Of course not, who would?"

I grit my teeth, biting down my urge to scream.

"That's why it's important that we tell Mr. Riley *everything*. Be as detailed as possible. We need to give any and every possible shred of evidence we have."

I close my eyes. Just thinking of reliving that nightmarish night makes me want to jump out of the window of this thirty-seven-story building.

"You can do this," Candice says earnestly, knocking her knuckles on the wood. "We *will* make those boys pay for what they did to you."

My next swallow is thick, tongue like sandpaper in my mouth, but I nod, trying my best to actually believe her and not just fake like I do.

A cheerful little melody from my phone breaks the tension, and I frown when I see Ashlei's name on the screen. She should be at work right now, and we almost never call each other — it's either text or in person.

"Mind if I take this?" I ask Candice.

She waves me on, picking up her own phone and tapping away on the screen as I slide a thumb across mine and answer the call.

"Hey, babe. Everything okay?"

There's a long pause of silence before she sniffs. And then, a whispered, "No."

My heart stops in my chest before kicking back to life, and I swivel in my leather seat, turning away from Candice altogether. "What's going on? Where are you? Are you hurt?"

That breaks Ashlei into full-on sobs, and I curse, grabbing my things off the table.

I cover the phone with my hand to mute it. "I'm sorry, I have to go. I'll call you," I tell Candice.

She nods, questions and concern in her eyes, but I don't have time to assure her things are fine — mostly because I don't know that they are.

"Where are you?" I repeat when I'm out of the room and dashing through the firm for the elevator.

"Palm Medical."

I stop short. "The hospital?"

"I was at the pole studio yesterday and..." She sniffs, another long pause breaking between us. "There was an accident."

I close my eyes, saying a silent prayer before I punch the down button to signal the elevator. "Hey, it's going to be okay. Alright? You hear me? I'm going to pick up the girls and we'll be right there."

"Hurry," is all Ashlei says, and then the line goes dead.

***

The girls are still in a tizzy when we blow through the doors of Palm Medical. It doesn't matter that I spent the entire drive here reminding them that we needed to be calm for Ashlei, that we don't even know what's happened yet. There *is* no calm when it comes to one of us being in trouble or hurt, hence the literal tornado of us entering the hospital, papers flying in our wake.

The poor nurse at the front desk doesn't know who to listen to as Cassie, Skyler, and mostly Jess talk over each other to try to get information. Finally, I hold up a hand to stop them all mid-sentence, and calmly explain to the woman who we're looking for.

As soon as we get the floor and room number, along with the clearance for visitation rights — which wasn't easy, considering there are four of us and our lame attempt at convincing her we were Ashlei's real sisters went over about as well as a lead balloon — we were in the elevator and on our way to the surgery wing.

"I'm going to remind you all one more time — *calm,*" I say on our ride up, and though I know it's hard, the girls all nod in agreement. And true to their word, we stroll at a softer pace in the surgery wing, speaking to the nurse at the desk there before being led back to Ashlei's room.

When we see her, we all stop dead.

She's laid up in the hospital bed in a gown that she somehow still makes look pretty, her hair greasy and piled on top of her head, dark circles under her eyes, and her arm in a massive sling that covers her entire shoulder and most of her chest. Brandon is in a chair beside her bed, his eyes glazed as he pretends to watch the TV.

"Well," Ashlei says when she sees us, attempting a smile. "Am I a beauty queen, or what?"

Cassie covers her mouth at the same time Jess curses, and Skyler and I just deflate, shoulders slumping.

"Oh, Lei," I say softly, and then wish I hadn't, because those words immediately bring tears to her eyes, her bottom lip quivering like a child.

We rush her in an instant, enveloping her in a group hug and holding on for dear life as she sobs. Cassie cries softly, too, but Sky, Jess, and I exchange understanding looks that say we need to hold our shit together.

"I'm going to get some coffee," Brandon says when we pull back, and he leans down to kiss Ashlei's forehead before leaving us alone.

"What happened?" Jess asks as soon as he's gone, taking his seat and pulling it close to the bed.

Ashlei wipes her nose on the back of her wrist. "I was doing a complicated leg hang move, and I just... I lost grip. I fell, landed awkwardly on my arm, banged my head pretty hard." She pauses, rolling her lips together. "Shredded my rotator cuff, broke my collarbone, gave myself a nasty concussion."

"Fuck," Jess says, shaking her head and instantly reaching for Ashlei's hand.

"When did this happen?" Skyler asks next.

"Day before yesterday."

"And you're just now telling us?" Cassie squeaks. It earns her a glare from me and Jess alike, but she just shrugs like *what, she should have told us sooner!*

"I was in and out of consciousness for a while," Ashlei admits. "And then after some X-rays and tests, monitoring me overnight, and measuring my pain... they decided I needed surgery. So I couldn't really call yesterday, either."

"How do you feel now?" I ask.

"Terrible," she admits, her eyes glossing again. "Everything hurts, and I'm stiff as hell. I keep getting dizzy, and I feel super nauseous. The best time is when I'm sleeping." She blinks. "Except for the nightmares."

A long pause falls over us, and Skyler sits on the edge of the bed, wrapping her hand around Ashlei's ankle. "So, talk to us. What does this mean?"

Ashlei sighs. "Well, short term, it means I miss some work and get to wear this lovely accessory for at least a couple months," she says, gesturing to the monstrosity of a sling fixed to her shoulder and holding her arm. "Long term?" She shrugs. "Physical therapy, I guess."

There's a relieved sigh from all of us, and Cassie leans against the bars of the bed, brushing Ashlei's hair from her face. "Well, that's all good. I'm so happy it's not worse."

Ashlei nods and tries to smile, but her lips quiver again, and then tears slip free and slide down her cheeks even though she hastily wipes them away.

"Lei?" I ask, frowning as I sit on the other edge of the bed opposite Skyler.

She shakes her head, more tears falling as she furiously wipes them away. "No, you're right. I'm lucky I'm alive. I'm lucky it wasn't worse. It's just..." Her face warps, and she looks at her lap instead of at any of us when she says, "I might not ever pole again."

A violent silence suffocates us all, and our eyes jump around the room, because we know there's nothing we could ever do or say to comfort her when that's a real possibility.

Finally, I lean forward and fold my hand over hers, waiting until her eyes meet mine. "We're here," I say.

Because if nothing else, I know that one thing for sure.

Jess

"Does it feel weird, being back on campus?" Skyler asks me as she delivers our drinks. She taps her clear plastic up against mine and then we both take a sip, grimacing in equal measure at the awful taste.

"Very," I admit. "And the drinks suck."

I make a gesture with my tongue and Skyler snort-laughs.

"We just make 'em stronger here. Plus, it's an Alpha Sig event. What do you expect?"

"I've become so spoiled by good martinis downtown."

"Poor baby," Skyler mocks with her bottom lip protruding.

I shove her on a laugh from both of us, and then we're watching the stage as the next sorority takes over, ready to karaoke and go for the gold.

It's been a hard couple of weeks. With work being bananas and finding out that my best friend is in the hospital, it's been hard to find anything worth smiling over. I debated bailing on Kade a million times before tonight, but he'd given me my space since showing up at the condo that evening, and this was all he'd asked of me — that I come to his first big event as president.

He needs me, and I don't want to let him down.

As if I've conjured him, Kade jogs up on stage, taking over the mic and introducing the sorority about to perform. He's looking fine as hell tonight, his tattooed muscles popping out under his tight Alpha Sig shirt — a royal blue one made especially for the event tonight. He's paired it with a light gray, flat-billed hat and matching Chubbies, and they're just short enough to show his thigh definition.

He looks like Frat Boy Royalty, and I hate that it makes me so hot for him I have to fan my neck to keep from sweating.

I'm smiling like a loon as he does his bit as the emcee, and when he jogs off the stage again and the girls start singing, Skyler leans into me with her shoulder, shaking her head.

"What?" I ask.

"You're so fucking smitten."

I blush, but don't deny it.

Skyler takes a sip of her drink before casually asking, "What about Jarrett?"

My smile slips like a sandal on a freshly mopped floor, and the joy I felt reverberating through me a moment before is doused instantly.

I sigh. "That *is* the question, isn't it?"

"I can't believe they both left you alone for the summer," Skyler remarks. "Does he know you're seeing Kade again?"

"No."

"Are you going to tell him?"

"I don't know."

"Are you going to *see* him?"

I sigh, turning to face her. "Sky, I don't know. Anything. Like, at all. I'm flying by the seat of my pants here and just trying to hold on. As soon as I know something… you'll know. Okay?"

She grimaces. "Sorry. I was just trying to be a good friend and ask the right questions."

"Don't be sorry," I tell her. "They *are* good questions," I confess, turning back to the stage and taking a long pull from my cup. "I'm just not ready to answer them yet. Just like I'm sure you're not ready to answer questions about Kip."

Skyler offers me a sympathetic smile and a *touché* before we're rocking along with the performance, and at least for the moment, the conversation is dropped.

The longer the night goes on, the better the show seems to get. Not only are the fraternities and sororities battling it out for the karaoke title, but Kade has planned game-show-like events in-between each act that keeps everyone engaged. Prizes are flying like crazy, drinks are flowing, and there's a massive foam pit dance floor keeping the party going.

It really is an incredible event — and pride for Kade swells in my chest.

When I'm teetering on the line between tipsy and drunk, I suddenly hear my name blast over the speakers, and I snap my gaze from the foam pit up to the stage to find Kade grinning wickedly and waving me up.

I instantly shake my head.

"Oh, come on now, J-Love. We all know you're not shy."

That earns some laughs and cheers from the crowd, along with a few whistles that make me laugh, too, before I flip them all off.

"Someone's playing shy. Come on, guys. Help me out. *J-Love, J-Love, J-Love,*" Kade starts chanting, and Skyler is the first one to join in before the rest of the crowd follows.

I pinch her ribs, but she just giggles and scurries away from me before snatching my drink and giving me a playful shove toward the stage.

I sigh, knowing the argument is pointless. So I throw my hands up and yell, "Alright, alright!"

The crowd cheers and parts for me to make my way through, and then a couple younger Alpha Sigma brothers I don't recognize help hoist me up onto the stage.

"There she is," Kade says with a wide, lazy smile. He pulls me into him for a kiss far too inappropriate to have thousands of people witness, which earns us a slew of cat calls, whistles, and *get a room!*'s before he pulls back with a grin. "Ready for our duet?"

I blanch. "I'm a terrible singer."

"Prove it."

Before I can save myself, the music starts, and someone is shoving a microphone into my hand as Kade takes his off the mic stand and starts snapping along.

To "Don't Go Breaking My Heart" by Elton John and Kiki Dee.

I burst out in a laugh as Kade jumps up, crosses his feet before he lands, and then does a full spin as the crowd goes wild. Then, he belts out the first line, and I don't have any choice but to follow with my part.

Back and forth, we sing the lyrics, my eyes drifting to the teleprompter more than his. After the first few, he grabs my hand and spins me into him like he's a professional dancer, somehow holding me steady when he twirls me back out. I'm laughing through my next line, and then he drops to his knees in front of me to belt out the pre-chorus bridge, which everyone else sings along with us.

The more the music goes on, the more I loosen up, letting my hips sway and playing into Kade's antics. Before I realize it, it's just me and him up there, the stars shining bright above us, the crowd and the music gone altogether. All I hear is my heartbeat in my ears. All I see are his warm eyes and playful smile. All I feel is his steady grip on my body, his muscles under my hands, the familiar, comfortable buzz of energy flowing between us.

And by the end of the song, I'm mesmerized by this man, wondering how the hell the douchebag, cocky sonofabitch I first met became this coolly confident sex pot that I'm so fucking obsessed with I can't stand it.

When the music finally cuts off, the crowd erupts, and Kade picks me up and throws me onto his shoulders. I toss my hands in the air, one still holding the microphone, as he takes us for a lap around the stage.

He starts running so fast I have to hold on for dear life, and then with a wave and a breathless, "We'll be right back with the announcement of tonight's champions. Until then, enjoy this special performance by Red Leather Chains!"

The crowd goes even more crazy at the announcement of an up-and-coming band that's been all over the music charts. I gasp, too, and try to scream over the noise to ask Kade how the hell he got them for this event, but I don't get the chance before he runs us backstage. Darkness hits like a train, along with a strange kind of quiet. We can still hear the music, the crowd, but it's slightly muted, like it's far, far away.

My ears ring as Kade carefully helps me off his shoulders and drops me to my toes on the ground in front of him, my body sliding down every inch of his along the way.

We're both panting, the music blasting from the stage, crowd cheering — but in the little pocket we've found ourselves in backstage, it feels like we're the only ones in the whole universe.

Kade's eyes flick between mine, and then he splays his palm across my heaving chest, running up the slick skin to wrap his hand around my throat. I gasp at the touch, letting my head fall back, and watching him through hooded eyes — eyes that dare him to keep going.

He squeezes a little harder, leaning in to hover over me as his gaze falls to my lips. "I know I promised you space," he husks. "But I lied."

His mouth crashes onto mine before I can tell him I don't give a fuck what I said and that space is the last thing I want right now, so I pull him into me, meeting his kiss with equal need. He grips my throat even tighter, cutting my oxygen short, but I fucking love it, so I drag my nails down his back and beg for more.

I yelp as Kade bites my lip hard enough to draw blood, and then I'm in his arms being carried backward in the blinding darkness until my back slams against something hard — a ledge or a shelf or a speaker case, I don't fucking care. All I know is my ass is half-propped on it, half hanging off, and I've got my legs wrapped around Kade like an anaconda.

"Do you know how mad you've driven me this summer?" he asks, snapping his hands over my wrists and clamping them to my sides, my fingers curling on the edge of whatever I'm sitting on. "How badly I've wanted to call you, see you, kiss you." He forces my mouth open with a demanding sweep of his tongue. "Taste you." His hard-on grinds against my core, sparking a trail of chills down the length of me. "*Fuck* you?"

"Show me how badly," I dare him, and then with a monstrous growl, he rips me off the ledge and whips me around, slamming my chest into the metal this time.

I have no idea if we're hidden from view, if we're safe back here, or if a pledge is going to walk through at any second and see us. But I couldn't care less — not when Kade grabs my skirt and rips it down my thighs like a beast, not when he bends down and grabs my ass, spreading my cheeks and making me arch more so he can eat me out from behind, and *definitely* not when he stands again and spanks me so hard I see stars.

"I'm not going to be easy with you tonight," he promises.

And I just spread my legs a little wider and look over my shoulder with a grin that says *promises, promises.*

Kade smirks, shaking his head as he makes quick work of his belt, his shorts, his briefs, pulling them all down far enough to whip out his thick, glorious cock. There's no time for a condom or foreplay or so much as a warning. He just roughly rubs his fingers between my lips, slicking his hand with my desire, and then coats himself with it before lining his tip up with my entrance and ramming it home.

Kade covers my yelp with another bruising kiss, and then he grabs my elbows in his hands, holding them behind me like handlebars as he rails me. When his mouth releases mine, my cheek pressed against the metal of whatever object we're fucking against is the only thing I have holding me upright — the rest is all him.

His hands grip my arms so hard I know they'll bruise, and every thrust is a punishment — a lashing I'm desperate to receive. I want it hard. I want it brutal.

I want him to fuck me *all* the way up.

I'm so turned on from the fact that we're in a public space, that one brush of my clit would send me over the edge, and as if he senses it, Kade slows his pace just enough to reach around with one hand and rub my sensitive bud.

My legs instantly tremble and shake, and the hand he freed flies up to slap against the metal and hold me upright as I chase my orgasm.

It comes on like a tsunami, the wave building savagely quick before it topples over and takes me under. Kade bites down on my shoulder to remind me not to be too loud, and holding in my screams only makes the orgasm that much more powerful. My face is fiery hot, body full of numbing stars.

And then, all at once, I fall limp, panting, a tremor shaking me from head to toe.

"We're not done yet, baby," Kade promises, and then he withdraws so quickly, I nearly fall from the sensation of losing his warmth. He spins me, grabs my cheeks between his thumb and fingers and kisses me forcefully.

Then, he guides me down to my knees.

"I can't make a mess back here," he explains with a wicked grin, swiping my hair out of my face. "So open that pretty mouth wide."

It shouldn't turn me on so much, the demanding arrogance in his voice, the degrading act of bending to my knees on a dirty floor for him.

But it does.

God, it does.

And as I take his cock in my mouth, I can feel my desire building again, and I'm literally dripping between my legs.

Kade groans as I swirl my tongue over every inch of him, teasing him a bit before I take him all the way inside. I don't waste time, coating him with saliva before I use both my hands, each of them rotating around his slick shaft while my tongue tortures his tip.

I know exactly what he likes, exactly what to do to get him to release.

His hand fists in my hair, and then he holds my head still, pumping his hips and fucking my mouth. I close my eyes and try to remember to breathe, to open my throat and relax.

And I don't gag until his cum shoots out and hits the back of my throat.

The groan that leaves him is guttural, hungry and wild as he holds me there, his cock deep in my throat, my tongue flat and splayed out so far I can nearly lick his balls. I open my eyes and watch him from below, which makes him curse under his breath, and then with a shudder, he finishes, slowly releasing me, slowly withdrawing.

After I swallow, I want to grin, wipe my lips, and spout something sassy at him, but I don't get the chance before he reaches down and grabs my arms, hauling me up to stand. He grips my cheeks in one hand again, and crashes his mouth to mine, kissing me senseless before he releases me.

"You're fucking *mine,*" he says, his dark eyes hooded, jaw set.

Then, he pulls up his shorts and like nothing happened at all, strolls right back out on the stage just in time for someone to hand him an envelope with what I assume is the winner information for the contest.

And I can't help it.

My jaw drops, and then I belt out the loudest laugh of my life.

That fucking asshole...

Goddamnit, I love him so much.

When I finally come to my senses and realize there's a breeze in a place where there shouldn't be, I grab my panties and skirt off the floor and hastily pull them on, smoothing my clothes and then doing my best to fix my hair with no mirror. I know it's going to be damn near impossible to make it look like I wasn't just thoroughly fucked, but part of me doesn't care at all.

Let them all wonder.

Let them all know *I'm* the bitch who gets to have him.

I make my way back through the crowd to Skyler in a daze, a stupid smile fixed to my face.

When she sees me, her mouth pops open and she folds her arms over her chest, shaking her head as she eyes me up and down. "You dirty skank, did you just pull a quickie backstage?"

"I'll never tell," I say, but my words are slurred, a little from the booze and a *lot* from being completely drained after that romp with Kade.

Skyler snickers, and then hands me my clutch and asks if I want another drink. With an affirmative, she leaves me at our spot to head to the bar, and I fish through my clutch for my phone.

When I pull it out, my heart stops in my chest at the text waiting for me on the screen.

From Jarrett.

I open it with a knot in my throat blocking my airway, and when I see a screenshot of a picture of me and Kade on stage from Skyler's social media post, I nearly pass out.

I guess summer is over.

When's my turn?

Ashlei

I punch the pillow that's supposed to be propping me up, huffing again when I lean back and still feel uncomfortable. I lean up again, shifting for another *punch, punch* as the ice I have balanced on my shoulder slides off me, the bed, and then onto the floor with a *thwack*.

"Ugh!" I growl, letting my hands flop down on the bed and rolling my eyes.

I nearly cry at the thought of having to get up, bend over to get the ice, and then get situated again. Thankfully, Brandon comes into the bedroom with a soft, knowing smile and picks the ice up for me, helping me get it in the right place on my shoulder as he sits on the edge of the bed.

"I hear a lot of grunting coming from in here," he comments.

"How the hell am I supposed to try to sleep like this?" I whine. "Have you ever tried to sleep propped up? It's awful. My mouth keeps falling open, and then I'm snoring and my throat is dry and I'm drooling on myself."

"You're sexy when you drool."

I glare at him, but he just chuckles, rubbing my thigh sweetly and leaning in to press a kiss to my lips — which I return with a half-hearted pucker of my own.

"Who needs wine?" Skyler purrs, coming in through the door right behind Brandon.

A little whimper is all the answer I give, but it's enough, and Skyler hands me a damn sippy cup full of Sauvignon blanc.

I begrudgingly take the first sip, but feel marginally better afterward.

"I figured the nap wasn't happening," she remarks, climbing into bed next to me. She snuggles in under the covers and leans her back against the headboard. "Are you sore?"

"Yes. And irritable."

"No, really?"

I give her a flat look.

Skyler smiles, patting my arm and sharing a glance with Brandon before she says, "You're sad, babe. And it's okay to be sad."

That permission nearly breaks me, and I sniff, looking down at my bright orange sippy cup. "I just can't stop thinking about my life without pole."

"You're going to pole again," Brandon says quickly. "You heard Doctor Long after your surgery. He said once you get through these two months of recovery, you can start up at PT, and there's no reason you can't eventually get back to pole."

"Except he also said my shoulder will never be the same again," I remind him. "And that I may never get the full strength I had back. And that I might injure myself further."

"Only if you don't take recovery and PT seriously," Brandon argues.

"Wait," Skyler chimes in, brows popping up. "You really had a Doctor *Long*?" She smirks, wag-gling her eyebrows.

I snicker, too, which earns us an eye roll from Brandon.

"I'm just saying, we will get you the best physical therapy money can buy," Brandon promises me, and he waits until I look at him, until I'm watching as he brings my knuckles to his lips and presses a soft kiss to them. "We will get you back to pole, okay? I promise."

I close my eyes on a long exhale when he leans up to kiss my forehead, and I wish I could rewind to even two weeks ago, to when we were coming off the most perfect summer of my life. I wish I could go back to coming home and being ravaged by him before I could even drop my purse, wish I could go back to events at work being my biggest concern, go back to knowing at the end of every day, the pole studio was waiting for me to decompress.

"I love you," Brandon whispers, and I don't miss how Skyler smiles shyly down at her lap at the words of affirmation.

"I love you, too," I say, but it comes out more of a whine that makes Brandon smile.

His phone buzzes from his pocket, and when he pulls it out, he frowns at the screen, standing. "Excuse me," he says simply, and then he's out the door and answering the call.

I turn to Skyler immediately with a dramatic sigh. "Tell me about your life so I can forget about mine," I beg, taking another sip from my cup.

"Hey, go easy on that," she says. "You can't have more than one glass with the pain meds you're on now."

I flick her off.

"My life is boring," she says with a shrug and a smile at my gesture, but the smile slips quickly. "Rounding out my final classes, recruitment is over. I've been focusing on new member events so we can get the pledges lined up with their new Bigs. Cassie has her eyes on this one girl, so I've been trying to get them in the same places as much as I can."

"Little matchmaker, huh?"

"Something like that," she muses. "I've been talking to my guidance counselor about what to do next, whether I should go for my MBA or start applying for jobs, or maybe formulate a business plan and try to get investors to get started."

"Don't you have enough money to do it on your own from winning second place in that tournament?"

Her face goes ashen, but she doesn't miss a beat. "Sure, but I think I'd like to have at least one other partner in on the project with me."

She doesn't have to say so for me to know she was originally planning on that partner being Kip.

"Have you talked to him?" I ask softly.

Again, no name needed. She shakes her head, eyes on her wine glass.

"Do you want to?"

"Of course, I do," she says, finally lifting her eyes to mine. "I miss him every second of every minute of every hour of every day."

Her eyes gloss with the words, and I frown, reaching over to grab her wrist. "So *call him*."

Skyler shakes her head, sniffing away the tears that hadn't quite formed yet. "No. I know it may not make sense to anyone else, and maybe it looks like stubborn pride." She pauses. "Hell, maybe it *is* stubborn pride. But he still doesn't see it. He still doesn't understand what he did wrong, how badly he hurt me. He apologized, sure, but he doesn't even know what to apologize for. He's blind to Natalia's true motives, blind to how he walked right into her trap, blind to how he put me behind everything else in his life and expected me to be fine with it." She shrugs. "He's sorry he lost me, but if he doesn't even understand why he did, then what would I be walking into if I just brushed this under the rug and said *okay*?"

My frown intensifies because she's got a point I can't really argue with.

I open my mouth to at least attempt to ramble through some sort of positivity speech when there's a soft rap of knuckles on the doorframe.

"Sorry to interrupt," Brandon says, and the look on his face makes me sit up a little straighter. "Um… you have a visitor."

If it was one of the girls, they would have just plowed right in by now. And if it was someone from the office, Brandon likely would have told them I'd see them next week when I came back. So I just answer with a confused frown, not sure what to say.

And when he moves to the side and Bo Hán walks under the arch, I drop my sippy cup, thankful for the child-proof lid as it hits my leg and bounces off to the floor.

"Holy shit," Skyler says, popping up first with a wide grin. "Bo?! Oh, my God!"

Skyler runs to Bo, who's smiling uncomfortably, her eyes flicking to me and then back to Skyler just in time to catch her crushing hug. I don't miss the relief that washes over her the longer Skyler squeezes her, and the way her shoulders relax, her smile widening.

"I haven't seen you in forever! How are you?" Skyler asks, pulling back to frame her arms. "You look amazing."

And she does. Her sleek, sable hair is short and edged at her chin, her warm brown eyes highlighted with gold, lashes long and sleek. She's as petite as I remember from college, only now she seems to stand taller, more confident, like she's not hiding a damn thing about herself anymore. The long-sleeve, white, lace top she's wearing buttons all the way from her chin to the hem of the little black flare skirt she's paired with it, and though the heels she's wearing are slight, they're strappy and bright red and just enough pop of color to tell you you're in the presence of a bad bitch.

"I'm good," Bo says, tucking her hair behind her ear. Her eyes dart to mine then, and she holds my gaze, a soft smile spreading on her smooth, peony pink lips.

Skyler looks between us, then at Brandon — who looks majorly confused and marginally concerned — before saying, "Brandon, can you come help me with something in the kitchen?"

She doesn't wait for his response before looping her arm through his and steering him down the hall. He gives me a questioning glance, but I smile and blow him a kiss, hoping it soothes whatever concerns he might have.

And then I'm alone with Bo Hán.

In the bedroom I share with my boyfriend.

Bo swallows, stepping inside a little bit as her eyes take in the length of me. "Do I want to know what happened to put you in that hardcore of an arm sling?"

"I fell off the pole," I say, a little breathlessly, a little too quickly. I just keep blinking over and over like she'll disappear with the next opening of my eyes.

Bo's face falls slack at that. "You're... you're doing that again?"

I shake my head. "Not like you think. I got out of that situation, and I never looked back. But, once I got my career on track, and found Brandon..." I shrug. "I found my heart missing that piece. So, I found a new studio. I've been dancing and competing... they even asked me to teach," I add with a small smile. Then, I nod down to my arm. "Until this, anyway."

"I'm sure they'll still want you," Bo offers quickly. "Especially if you're even half as amazing as you used to be."

I nod, trying to smile, but the frown etched in my brows overpowers it.

"I never thought I'd see you again," I finally whisper.

Bo's eyes well with tears, and she moves closer, letting out a long exhale as she leans down to retrieve the sippy cup of wine I dropped. She places it on the bedside table before sitting on the edge of the mattress, hands folding in her lap.

"I thought the same," she admitted, her eyes searching mine.

A long silence passes between us, no words necessary as we took each other in. I wonder if the memories are flashing in her mind the way they are in mine, but the way her eyes stay watery, the way her smile quivers a bit — I know I don't have to ask.

"I graduated in the spring," she explains. "My parents sent me to a tiny university in Montana, of all places. Can you believe it?" When my only answer is a deadpan look, she chuckles. "Yes, I suppose you can. But... strangely, I grew to love it. The mountains, the pastures, the quiet. I had space to think, and to grow, and to come into myself."

I nodded. "You seem happy."

"I am," she says earnestly. "I really am. And I... I finally got my parents to understand. I mean, I know it's still hard for them, but I brought someone home — someone I met in Montana who I love very, very much," she adds.

There's a strange cracking of my heart, a splintering of a piece of it I'd forgotten even existed. That piece will always belong to her, I realize — no matter what.

"I know it's not easy for them, but they love me, and I think they're beginning to realize that that matters more than anything else." She pauses, brows folding over her warm eyes. "I'm just so sorry you had to bear the brunt of their shock and confusion at the beginning of it all."

"Don't be," I tell her quickly, and without thinking, I reach out to cover her hand with mine.

We both still at the touch, eyes falling to the contact before we meet each other's gaze once more. But it's not a touch born of desire or lust, it's one of true, unyielding love and understanding.

Of sisterhood.

She squeezes my hand, and I close my eyes, a single tear breaking free and rolling down my cheek.

"I'm not here long," Bo says. "Just passing through, really. The company I'm with right now just secured a client in the Brickell Arch building, so we're here to court them a little and go over how our technology will integrate into their systems."

I arch a brow.

"Oh," she says with a chuckle. "Yeah, I changed my major. I'm a coding engineer."

"Not even a little bit surprised, you little baddie."

She laughs. "Anyway, I just... When I found out I was coming here, I knew I had to see you. I wanted to explain where I went, wanted you to know I didn't have a choice, and that I thought of you every day for quite some time." She pauses. "I *still* think of you. And I'm just so happy *you're* happy. You know — all things considered," she adds with a smirk at my sling.

I smile, too, and nod vigorously. "I'm happy you're happy, too. And thank you, for coming to see me, for... for caring enough to give me this closure I didn't realize I still needed."

"I needed it, too," she says. "And... hey, maybe instead of closure, it's a new chapter. I'd love to have a friend here in Miami. If you'll have me."

I pull her in for a long hug as my answer, closing my eyes at the way it feels to have her back in my life — even in this small way. "Always."

When we pull back, I shoo her off the bed so I can wiggle my way out and stand, too. Then, I loop my good arm through hers.

"Come on, I need you to get better acquainted with the man who swayed me to the more phallic side of my sexual desires."

She barks out a laugh at that. "I don't want to impose..."

"Nonsense. Stay for dinner. Stay the night, if you want to." I squeeze her. "We have a lot of catching up to do."

And with a smile from each of us, we venture down the hall to join Brandon and Skyler, and I find a bright gold lining on the dark cloud that had been hovering over me ever since the accident.

Adam

"I think we should do it."

I stifle a laugh at how serious Cassie's face is as she says it, how wide her bright green irises grow at the thought.

"Come on, aren't you even a little curious?" she asks.

"I've done it before."

"Oh..." She waves me off. "Well, you've never done it with *me*. And you know... I heard the sex when you're high is..." She makes a chef's kiss gesture with her fingers and lips, waggling her brows at me as I laugh again.

"Hey, no need to convince me. I'm in. Do you think you want to smoke it?"

She shakes her head. "Maybe a chocolate or gummy or something? And I want to just hang out in your dorm when we do it." She blinks. "Or maybe my hotel room. I'm sure they don't allow it on campus."

"They don't, but that's not a rule that's exactly strictly followed," I add with a smile. "But okay, it's a plan. When you come for Thanksgiving break, we'll get you high."

"And you. Oh! And we should load up on yummy Thanksgiving food and munchies for the occasion."

"I'll order from a restaurant, that way we don't have to cook. And get some Twizzlers."

Her eyes grow even wider. "My favorite."

"I know."

She sighs, leaning her chin on her hands as her eyes wash over me. "I miss you so much."

"I miss you, too," I say, and my chest aches with the truth of it. "Are you going out tonight?"

"Nah, I think Skyler and I are going to court that girl I was telling you about who I want as my Little. Skyler invited her to come hang out in the president's suite, and we're going to make her introduce us to anime."

My brows shoot up. "That should be... interesting."

"I'm actually really excited! The characters seem so cool."

"You're the biggest nerd."

"And *you're* obsessed with me."

I sigh. "Also true."

"What are you doing tonight? And where are you?" She looks at the scene behind me. "It looks gorgeous."

I tap the part of my screen that makes the camera switch from facing me to facing my view and show her around. "I'm just hanging out in this little park on The Hill. The sun is starting to set over the mountains," I say, showing her the orange glow in the distance. "See it?"

"It's beautiful."

"We'll get up for a sunrise hike when you're here," I tell her, putting the camera back on me. "It's even more breathtaking."

"You'll have to peel me out of bed."

"Oh, I can be *very* persuasive when I want to be."

She bites her lip against a smile. "I'm well aware of those particular talents of yours."

I chuckle, leaning back on the blanket I'm on and propping my phone up against my water bottle so I can relax. "How is Skyler, by the way? I haven't talked to her since..."

I don't finish the sentence, but Cassie frowns, a heavy sigh leaving her that tells me all I need to know.

"She's... I don't know. Numb, I think. She barely talks about it, about *him*. She's just been focusing on the pledges and her last semester as president, talking to the girls who want to run for office, finishing up classes and making her plan for after graduation." She pauses. "Have you talked to Kip at all?"

"I tried calling him, but no dice. He texted me a few days later apologizing, and just said things were crazy busy in California right now but that he'd get back to me when he could."

"Ugh! So he's just living it up," Cassie says, throwing her hands up. "Just being *busy* when he's left Sky back here with a broken heart."

"Babe," I say with a smile. "I know you love her, but if I have my facts correct, Kip *tried* to make things right with her, and Skyler essentially said too little too late."

"Well, he clearly didn't try hard enough, then."

I laugh, but before I can argue the other side of it again, I'm nearly run over by a frantic tornado of hair and arms and legs.

"I need your help."

I squint up at the silhouette of the girl I ran into on my way to the Student Union last week, frowning in confusion.

"Now. Please. I don't know what to do. She's... she's fucking wasted, and I think..." She swallows, running her hands back through her long hair, her chest heaving. "Please."

"Who is that?" Cassie asks.

"I'll call you back," I tell her, and I end the call, jumping to my feet to grab the girl's arms. "Okay, it's alright. Just take a breath here and tell me what's going on."

The girl looks so different than she did the first time I ran into her. Her tattoos are covered by a long-sleeve pink cardigan, a matching band in her hair, and she's wearing long, slim, cream dress pants with small brown kitten heels. Her makeup is subdued and natural, and the combination of it all is what made it so hard for me to recognize her at first.

"I'm an Educational Leadership Consultant for Delta Beta Gamma, and I've been here with the girls all summer and they've been working so hard. They wanted to have a party at the house today and I... I covered for them and let them and... there's a girl, a young girl — freshman — she's... she's really drunk." She swallows, her blue eyes wild and animated. "I have her propped up in the bed, but I'm worried she might need to go to the hospital."

"Let's go," I say instantly, and then in a flash, we're flying up The Hill to the Delta Beta Gamma house.

The party is still raging when we run through, but we bypass all the games and shot taking and dancing, running up the stairs where it's a little quieter. The girl guides me down a long hall, and then into a bedroom where the girl in question is propped up against the headboard.

Her head is lolled to the side, mouth hanging open, and there's vomit on her shirt.

I cringe, rushing over to her side and taking her hand in mine before sweeping the hair from her face.

"What's her name?" I ask.

"Martina."

I nod, then start saying her name softly, shaking her gently until her eyes peel open like it takes all her strength to do so.

I know that feeling.

"Hey, Martina," I say as soothingly as I can. "How are we feeling?"

"Mm...okay," she slurs.

I nod. The fact that she's responding is a good sign. "Just feeling a little drunk?"

She nods, making a horse sound with her lips before her head lolls back again.

"Stay with me for a moment, Martina," I tell her. "I know you're tired, but can you just talk to me for a bit?"

She sighs, but holds her head up, her eyes bouncing between mine.

"Good girl. Can you tell me how old you are?"

"Nineteen."

The ELC curses from where she's standing behind me, but I hold out my hand to calm her so I can focus on my task.

"What's your major?"

She makes a sticking sound with her tongue and the roof of her mouth. "Accounting. But, you-knowha?" she adds, holding up a finger. "I really wanna study litratrer."

I smile. "Literature, huh?"

"Mm-hmm," she says with an over-exaggerated nod. "I wanna edit booksh."

"Who's your favorite author?"

"I read romance," she says, shaking her head. "You wouldn't understand."

"I like romance."

Her eyes pop open. "Really?" Then she sighs, dropping her head back against the headboard. "I wish Josh liked romance."

She pouts, and I relax a little more. The fact that she can remember names, that she's talking to me, that her skin isn't cold or clammy and she's breathing normally are all very good signs that she's going to be okay.

"Do you like Josh?"

"Sadly," she admits. "But he's oblivion."

"Oblivious?"

"That," she says, pointing at my chest.

I chuckle again. "Well, any guy who has your attention is a lucky one."

She nods, but then I see her start to doze again, and I sit up from the edge of the bed, turning to the ELC who looks like she's just killed a puppy.

"She's going to be fine," I tell her.

"Oh, thank God," she says on a long breath. "What do we do? Should I get some Advil or water or?"

"No," I say, shaking my head. "We just need to get her lying on her side. Nothing but time can make her sober up — not food or water or a cold shower or any of that." I glance back down at Martina and her stained shirt. "If I step out of the room, do you think you could change her top? Just get her in something clean and maybe wipe her mouth a little?"

The girl nods, and then I step out for a few minutes until she calls me back in.

"Okay, let's get her on her side, just in case she gets sick again. We need to prop pillows and maybe bags or whatever we have around her so she can't really move without difficulty. And if you can, stay here with her and make sure she stays on her side. Check on her every now and then. As long as she's breathing normally, not too slow, and she's waking up and answering your questions... she's alright."

When we get Martina situated, the girl slumps down in one of the desk chairs in the room, and I grab the other, sitting on it backward with my forearms perched on the top. I extend a hand for hers. "I'm Adam, by the way. Adam Brooks. I'm a Field Executive for Alpha Sigma."

She takes my hand and shakes it gently before running a hand back through her hair again. It takes the pink band off when she does, and she looks at it begrudgingly before throwing it to the side and raking her nails over her scalp. "I'm Chandler. Chandler Simmons."

"Nice to meet you."

"I wish it was under better circumstances," she remarks.

"You mean like when I ran you over last week?"

That makes her smile. "Even that was better than this."

"Hey, I'm just glad I could help."

"I am, too. They didn't teach us this during training."

"Really? I'm shocked. We went over it several times in mine."

"Well, you're a guy," she shoots at me with pursed lips. "It's acceptable for fraternity guys to get hammered. But as a sorority girl, you're supposed to be a lady, to uphold a certain standard. They won't even talk about what to do if a girl gets too drunk because it's never supposed to happen."

"That's just naïve."

"Welcome to the patriarchy."

I frown. "I'm sorry. But consider me here to help however I can."

Chandler relaxes a bit, and then she smiles, her eyes running the length of me. When she finds my gaze again, there's nothing but true gratitude. "Thank you."

I nod, and then a slightly uncomfortable silence falls between us — mostly because I'm remembering the tattoos hiding under her sleeves, and the well-endowed breasts hiding under her cardigan.

"Well, I should get going," I say, standing. "Need to call my girlfriend back and explain what happened."

I think I see a flicker of disappointment in Chandler's eyes, but it's gone as quick as it came, and then she stands, too. "Apologize on my behalf for stealing you away. If she ever comes to visit, I'll take you both out to make up for it."

"It's all good." I clear my throat, heading for the door, but I pause at the exit and say, "See you around?"

Chandler nods on a smile, gives me a little wave of her hand, and then I'm out the door and pulling out my phone to call Cassie back.

Erin

"I don't wanna," I whine, sticking out my bottom lip as far as I can and batting my lashes for good measure.

Clinton chuckles, kissing my knuckles before he stands and tugs on my wrists to try to get me to stand. "I know you don't wanna, but that's exactly why we should."

"It's been such a long week. With the detective and school and tests and poor Lei being laid up and I just..." I sink farther into the couch, despite him holding my hands. "I really don't wanna."

He gives me a gentle tug until I finally groan and reluctantly stand, and then he sweeps me into his massive arms, encompassing me in his classic Bear Hug that instantly fills me with warmth. I sigh, leaning into the embrace, my head resting on his chest as I clasp my hands behind the small of his back.

"Tell you what. Give me one hour. If in one hour you still want to come back and get in these sweatpants, I'll cuddle you all night and deliver wine on demand."

"I want to cry just thinking about that."

He smiles, pulling back to search my gaze. "What if I told you wine is still involved?"

"I'm listening..."

"And food."

I tilt my head to the side, sighing. "Fine. But I'm not putting on makeup or doing my hair."

"Good because you look perfect without doing a damn thing," he says, kissing my nose, and then he releases me and practically skips into his kitchen, telling me to get dressed.

It still takes me a while to drag myself back to his room where my weekender bag is, and I dig through it, pulling out a pair of linen shorts and a loose, comfortable blouse to go with them. I tug on my Sperrys and put my hair in a ponytail, grimacing when I see my reflection in the mirror.

Perfect, my ass.

The long week of studying and tests and meeting with my lawyer is evident on every inch of my face — namely in the dark circles under my eyes. I debate putting on makeup despite what I said, but I don't have the chance before Clinton calls my name from down the hall and tells me to hurry up.

With one last sight, I flick the light off in the bathroom and let him lead me out into the sticky, humid night.

We're quiet on the drive to wherever he's taking me, but he's wearing a wide smile and singing along to the songs on the stereo, one hand on the steering wheel, and the other tucked possessively around my thigh.

I stare at that massive dark hand, the way the fingers curl easily around me, the way I know exactly what they feel like on every inch of my body and like clockwork, my neck heats, mouth watering a bit at the thought of what he might do to me tonight.

We took it *excruciatingly* slow over the summer — which was half my idea and half my own personal torture. But after Gavin, I wanted to be sure Bear and I were serious before I opened that part of me to him — especially since I hadn't been with anyone since the night I was raped.

A little shutter goes through me at the thought of the word, but I'm getting better at saying it, at accepting it, at remembering that it's something that happened to me — not something that defines me.

So the summer was slow, but we still played and touched and kissed and laughed. I still explored him under the covers just as he did with me. And then, a few weeks ago, we finally broke the barrier and went all the way.

And *God*, it was all I wanted to do nowadays.

It's hard for me to keep my hands off him, to not kiss him longer and deeper every time, knowing that if I kiss him just the right way, he'll grow hard without being able to control himself.

I love that I have that effect on him.

I love that he wants me so badly he can barely stand it.

After a slow, calm cruise through town with the windows down, we pull up to a small park by the beach. Clinton climbs out before I can even unbuckle, opening my door for me and helping me out before he grabs a big cooler and duffle bag out of the bed of his truck.

"Did you pack us a picnic?" I ask, eyeing the bag as he slings it over his shoulder and carries the cooler in that same hand so he can hold mine with his other.

"I did, indeed."

"Wow," I comment as he steers us toward the water's edge. "You've become such a romantic."

"I blame you."

I smile, but can't help but lean into him a little more as we walk, into this man who I always knew I loved, but never thought I'd actually ever be with. Thinking about all we've been through, the obstacles we've had to overcome... it's enough to make me want to cry and rejoice all at once.

Clinton picks a spot under a tree, spreading out a large blanket and unpacking the contents of the cooler and bag while I settle in. He pours me a plastic tumbler full of wine, and then one for him, and after we cheers and take a sip, he leans in to kiss me, long and sweet.

The sun is already setting, just ten minutes or so left before it will dip behind us and dusk will move in. We sip our wine and munch on the different cheeses and meats and fruits Bear packed for us as we watch the colors change in the sky over the beach and the water.

"Have you ever seen a sunset on the west coast?" I ask him.

"Of Florida? Or like California?"

"Both. Either."

He frowns, thinking. "You know... actually? I don't believe I have. I mean, we went to Tampa a couple times for Gasparilla, but that was mostly drinking — never really cared to watch the sunset."

"We should go."

He smiles. "We should. Where else?"

"Hmm..." I nibble on a piece of sharp cheddar, thinking. "I've always wanted to see the Red Woods."

"Sounds like we'll be seeing the sunset in California, too, then."

"Oh! What about Greece?"

He chuckles. "That's a big leap from California, but yes. Add Greece to the bucket list."

I instantly pull out my phone and start a new note, titling it *Erin and Bear's Epic List of Adventures*.

"Okay," I say after writing down what we've discussed so far. "Your turn. What do you want to add?"

He sighs, eyeing the cotton candy clouds that are now turning a deep shade of purple. "Well, first... I want to take you home."

I roll my eyes. "Okay, perv. Focus."

"No, I mean *home* home," he says, and when I look at him, his eyes are sincere. "To Pittsburgh."

Butterflies zip through my stomach so fiercely, I place a hand over my navel to soothe them. "You do?"

He nods. "I want to take you to all the spots I went to as a kid, show you where I grew up. You've already met my family and hung out with them, so I know you can survive the crazy."

I laugh at that. "I love their crazy."

"So, that's a yes?"

I smile, typing on my phone. "It's at the top of the list. And you know what? I want to take *you* home, too."

Bear frowns. "To Kansas?"

I laugh. "That's where my *grandparents* live," I correct him. "My parents live here in Florida. Jupiter Beach."

"Oh," he says, relieved. "Alright, then. Add it to the list."

We spend the evening drinking wine, snacking, and laughing while we add places to our list. We daydream about what we'll do, the things we'll see, the people we'll meet. And before I know it, it's been two hours, and I haven't thought about wanting to go back home once.

Except now, with the night heavy around us, and Clinton holding my back to his chest as he leans up against the tree, I can feel a certain part of him at the small of my back, and the urge to go back to his place is strong again.

I nuzzle into him, wrapping his arms even more around me. "So, I'm thinking it might be sweatpants time again," I say.

"Oh? Done with being out?"

I bite my lip, reaching behind me and down between us to rub him over his basketball shorts. He stiffens at the touch, and then stifles a groan as I rub the length of him, which grows hard instantly as if I've commanded him to do so.

"Very much so," I whisper.

I turn in his arms, finding his heated gaze just as yearning as mine. He pulls me into him, framing my face for a deep kiss before he stands, yanks me up, and smacks my ass. "Help me pack this shit."

I laugh at his haste, even more so when I see him adjust himself in his shorts with a shake of his head at me. With lightning speed, he tosses everything back in the cooler and the duffle bag, not the least bit concerned with whether things were packaged correctly or standing upright.

And then, we're back in the truck and speeding across town.

I can't help but watch him as he drives, his grip tight on the steering wheel, jaw clenched, and that bulge ever present under his shorts. When we hit a stoplight downtown, I tug on my seatbelt enough to loosen it so I can lean over the console, and I hesitantly smooth my hand over his abdomen, the band of his shorts, until my hand folds over his hard-on and squeezes.

"*Fuck*, Erin," he hisses, grinding his hips into me.

I lick my lips, eyes on his growing length as the light turns green and I squeeze him a little harder, rolling my palm over the slick fabric of his shorts. When we hit the next light, I tug on the string tying his shorts at the top, freeing the knot.

"Can you take these down a bit?"

Bear's head snaps in my direction, and he gapes for just a millisecond before he presses his foot into the brake and lifts his hips enough to slide his shorts and briefs down to mid-thigh, freeing his cock.

I moan at the sight, biting my lip again before I lean even farther over the console. Clinton adjusts, holding the steering wheel high with one hand so I have enough room to peek my head in, and his other hand is holding his pants out of the way.

Careful not to hit his arm, I run my fist over him — one pump, two — and then I cover his large tip with my lips, spreading them wide until at last my tongue tastes him, swirling and sucking and teasing.

He groans loud, but keeps his eyes on the road, his focus steady as I take him a little farther inside each time. I feel wild and free, sexual in a way I haven't in a long time — if ever. He makes me feel this way... comfortable, confident, desired.

Safe.

It's hard for me to take Bear all the way in my mouth even with the best positioning, so being at this awkward angle with his pants in the way, it's impossible. But I slick my tongue along the walls of his shaft, curling it over his tip and moving in time with my hands as best I can. I know I won't get him off this way, but I also know I've got him so hard, his balls so tight that he's ready to burst.

When we pull into the small driveway of his house, he slams the truck into park and instantly reaches over to unbuckle my seatbelt. In the next breath, he's pulling me on top of him, flipping the center console up and out of the way so my knees have more room to steady myself. I straddle him as he crashes his mouth to mine, hand at the back of my head and crushing me to him like that kiss is his lifeline.

"You are everything I've ever wanted," he breathes against my lips before bruising them with another kiss. "Everything I need."

I kiss back in earnest as my answer, frustrated that he's exposed but my shorts are between us. "Take me inside."

Blindly, he reaches for the handle and shoves the door open, holding me to him as he stumbles out of the truck. He doesn't even bother to pull his pants up, doesn't give a shit if anyone in the neighborhood is watching. He just holds tight, my legs wrapped around his waist, and shuffles up the few stairs to his porch, fumbling with his key in the door, and then we tumble inside.

My back slams against the wood the second the door closes, and Bear pins me there, kissing my neck, my collarbone before frantically tearing my shirt off and sucking the swells of my breasts where they heave above the shell of my white bra.

A growl seeps from his throat, and then he drops me to my feet long enough to yank my shorts down to my ankles. He reaches for my panties next, but they're just a thin scrap of a thong, and without meaning to, he shreds the threading, quite *literally* ripping them off me.

"Shit," he says, looking at the lace in his hands, his chest rising and falling in erratic huffs.

"Whatever, I have more," I say quickly, and I grab the lace from his hands and throw it across the room before leaping back into his arms.

Our lips fuse together, and we're on the move again, though I can't see where. Suddenly, my ass is placed on top of the cool countertop, and Bear tugs me forward until I'm hanging off the edge and leaning back on my hands to steady myself.

He doesn't even take the time to remove my bra, just tugs the cups down until my breasts pop out, and he devours both, sucking the nipples and swirling his expert tongue hard and fast. I let my head drop back, legs already quivering at the need to have him inside me.

Suddenly, he stills.

His forehead drops to my chest, and he shakes his head, meeting my gaze with an apologetic look in his eyes. "I'm sorry," he says, swallowing a gulp of air. "I... I want you so bad I..." He shakes his head. "I'll slow down, I'm sorry."

"No," I whine, and I press up until I'm kissing him just as hard and desperate as before. "Don't slow down, Clinton. Don't stop."

He curses, sucking my lip between his teeth before releasing it with a pop. "I want to fuck you right now, Erin. Hard. Brutally. Do you understand?"

My pussy clenches at the words.

"I want to slam into you. I want to feel you stretch open for me, and then I want to fuck you hard and fast. This is how animalistic you make me. So if I don't slow down now, I won't be able to."

"Don't," I whisper again, scooching closer, my ass hanging off the edge of the counter now. I reach down to stroke his long length, coating him with the pre-cum on his tip. "Condom."

In a flash, he's gone, reaching into his shorts that he'd abandoned by the door without me even realizing. He fishes out a condom from his wallet, slides it on, and rips his shirt overhead, stalking toward me like a hungry beast.

Yes, my body hums.

I don't want tender. I don't want gentle and careful. I don't want to be something everyone thinks will shatter in a moment's notice, some fragile, doll-like thing.

I want to be the powerful woman who drives him wild.

I want to be the source of his every desire.

I want to feel every ounce of his lust-driven madness.

He must see it in my eyes, too, because the second he reaches me, he runs his large hands back through my hair, tugging until my neck is arched, chin turned skyward, his mouth crushing down on top of mine. He steals a soul-shattering kiss, and then he holds my hair there in one fist so I'm watching his face as he reaches down and positions himself at my entrance.

Then, without warning, without care for gentleness — he impales me.

The burning sensation of stretching open makes me cry out, but it's gone in a flash, replaced by an all-consuming desire as Bear picks me up off the countertop and holds me in his arms as he rams into me again.

How the hell this man can hold me, balance me, *and* fuck me to the hilt is beyond me, but I know one thing — he's in control this time.

So I just hold on tight and let him take me for the ride.

"*Fuck*, you feel so good," he purrs, kissing me hard as he wraps himself all around me. One arm holds the small of my back, crushing me to him, and the other firmly grips my ass, helping me ride him as he bends into a bit of a squat. His hips thrust, in and out, slow at first but quickly picking up speed. "So fucking good."

I can't say anything in return.

It's all I can do to hold on, to moan, to cry out and keep breathing as he pummels me. He gives me exactly what I asked for — all of him, no holds barred.

Without me realizing it, he's walked us to the couch, and he lays me down into the cushions, dropping to his knees and pulling my ass to hang off the edge. He reaches up to palm my tits, and then he's pounding me again, harder, faster, relentless and menacing.

I come without warning.

There's no slow building, no little spark that catches and softly tingles through my limbs. No, one second I'm holding on for dear life, the next I'm screaming so loud I feel like a porn star as the unexpected waves topple over me.

My cries only fuel Clinton more, and he keeps his pace, growling something like *yes, baby* but I can't be sure because I've completely blacked out. Stars are in my veins, gravity doesn't exist, I'm floating and free-falling all at once.

With a grunt, he slams into me even deeper somehow, holding me there with him buried inside me. I feel his cock pulse between my walls, the emptying of himself inside the condom as a lion-like roar rips from his throat.

And then, as if we've been running for miles, we both collapse.

He falls into me, I sink farther into the couch, wrapping my legs around him and holding onto his slick shoulders with my still-trembling hands. We stay like that a long while, just breathing, existing.

Slowly, Bear starts planting soft kisses on my shoulder, my neck, until he tilts my chin with his knuckles and captures a long, slow, sensual kiss.

Safe.

I am so safe with him.

"Fucking *Christ*, Erin," he pants, smiling before he kisses me again. "That was... you are..." But he can't finish the sentence, just shakes his head and folds me in his arms, maneuvering us until we're lying on the couch — him on his back, me on my side with my head on his chest.

"I loved that," I admit, trailing my fingertips along his chest.

"I didn't hurt you?"

"God, no," I snort. "Can you not tell?"

A devilish smirk breaks on his lips. "You *were* screaming my name pretty loud."

"I think I screamed loud enough for the whole city to hear."

"Good. Let them hear," he says, twisting until he's facing me. "Let the whole damn world know you're mine."

My heart flutters.

"And you're mine?"

He shakes his head, one corner of his mouth lifting as if it's the most obvious answer in the world.

"Haven't I always been?"

And then he kisses me, his hand roaming down to trail the sensitive skin on my hip, and we slip easily into round two.

EPISODE 3

Cassie

"What about this?" I ask the girls, holding up a shiny, silver vest. "I could wear it over a lime green tube top!"

"Ooooh, yes!" Jess says with glee, grabbing the vest from me and holding it up over my chest. "If you button this top one, it'll push your titties up all nice and pretty."

I snort as Skyler adds, "We *have* to put LED lights on your cowboy hat."

"Duh," I say with a flip of my hair. "And star earrings. Every space cowboy has star earrings."

I grab the vest from Jess and toss it in our cart, and then we move along.

"I love thrift shopping," Erin says, dragging her fingertips along the rack of clothes as we walk. "Especially when it comes to planning for Halloween."

"What are you going to be again?" I ask.

"We're going to be a doctor and a nurse," she says with her cheeks shading red.

"*We*," Jess repeats with a cock of her eyebrow. "As in, you and Bear?"

Erin nods.

"God, I'm obsessed with you two," Jess says with a shake of her head. "I think I ship you more than any celebrity relationship I've ever followed."

"I think Bear just wants to see me in a little nurse uniform," Erin says.

"Obviously," I chime in. "But hey, that's half the fun of Halloween — get all dressed up just to have someone else strip it all off."

The girls laugh at that, but mine is cut short when I remember I *won't* have that part of the night this year.

This will be the first Halloween I haven't spent with Adam since... well, since coming to college.

Of course, half of those Halloweens, I was with another guy. The first time, Adam was with Skyler and I was with Clay. Then, there was Grayson. Truthfully, we've only really had one together.

And this year, we'll be on opposite sides of the country.

"What about you over there, mopey pants?" Jess asks Ashlei — who has been quiet all day long. She's just dragged along behind us, eyes dull, hands not even bothering to reach for a single article of clothing.

"A mummy," she deadpans, making a dramatic gesture to her slung-up arm.

Skyler chuckles, looping her arm through Ashlei's healthy one. "You know, we could probably make that hot. Just wrap a thin layer of gauze around your titties, a tiny skirt around your waist... show of that lean tummy of yours."

"It won't be lean for long with all this sitting around I'm doing."

The joke falls flat when Ashlei delivers it, because it doesn't have bite or any semblance of sarcasm. It's just... sad. Pitiful. The way she has been ever since the accident.

"I'm sorry, Lei," I say softly, reaching out to squeeze her wrist. "I hate this for you. Do you have any update when you start PT?"

"Not until I'm cleared from wearing this thing," she says, again gesturing to the sling. "And that won't be for another six weeks or so."

"It could be less," Skyler tries.

"I don't want to get my hopes up," Ashlei responds. "I can't afford to."

The girls and I share glances, knowing our friend is in a rough patch and there's not much we can do but just be there for her.

Sometimes, things are so dark and bleary, the last thing you need is someone telling you it'll be alright or to look on the bright side. Sometimes, you just need someone to lie down in the darkness with you and remind you you're not alone.

Jess wraps her up in a careful hug. "We'll make you the hottest mummy yet. And if you want to call off Halloween altogether and watch scary movies on the couch with some junk food and wine? I got you."

"Me, too," Skyler says. "Honestly, I don't have any plans other than make sure our new pledges don't get into too much trouble."

"I told Tera I'd take her to Ralph's, but I can totally cancel," I say.

"No, you can't," Skyler throws at me. "Big-Little Reveal is soon, and you're not the only one with eyes on Tera."

"Besides, every KKB sister *has* to experience Halloween at Ralph's," Jess chimes in.

I sigh. "I know, and I'm excited to take her and show her the ropes. Really, I am. It's just..."

"It's just that Adam won't be there," Ashlei finishes for me, and when our eyes meet, a soft nod is all I can give as a response.

"How has it been going with him gone?" Jess asks.

"Fine, I guess," I say, stopping at a rack with neon colors. I hold up a pair of hot pink fishnets, and before I can even ask, Skyler grabs them from my hands and throws them in our cart.

"*Fine* never actually means fine," Ashlei assesses.

"Well, it *was* fine. At first. I mean, we had the summer together, and then when he got sent to Boulder, we would text and call and video chat all the time. But lately... I don't know. He's been busier, and I keep seeing him tagged in pictures with all these girls. I know it's part of the job — he's helping the brothers throw events, working with other executive members in the fraternities and sororities, but..."

"But he has a whole life without you," Jess finishes, her eyes understanding. "That was the hardest part for me with Jarrett."

"Yes," I agree, rubbing a velvet jacket between my fingertips as my gaze loses focus. "He just feels... distant. He always has to go. He always has something to do. And there's this girl he keeps mentioning, Chandler. They met when he helped her with a girl in her sorority who was entirely too drunk, and now they're kind of like... I don't know, mentors for each other? He's been helping her out and she's returning the favor. It sounds friendly, but..."

"It's natural to feel jealous and intimidated and scared," Jess tells me, squeezing my arm. "But listen to me — Adam is all yours. I mean, you're wearing his letters. That might as well be an engagement ring around your neck."

I finger the necklace as she says the words, heart thrumming at the memory of the day he gave it to me.

"Don't make the mistake I did and make a bigger deal out of something than it is. Trust him. He loves you. Okay?"

I nod. "Thank you."

"Speaking of that... what's going on with the boys?" Ashlei asks Jess.

She sighs, throwing her hands up. "God if I know. Taking the summer away from both of them didn't help anything — I think I was just trying to avoid it. But Kade came over and we've been talking so much, and I had such an amazing time with him at the A Sig karaoke event."

"Oh, we know," Skyler says with a smirk.

Jess flicks her arm. "But now Jarett wants his turn."

"Are you going to give it to him?" I ask.

Jess stops at a rack and leans into it, the clothes and hangers groaning with the weight of her. "I know it sounds fucked up but... I *have* to. I have to see him. I have to talk to him and ask questions that have been eating me up. I have to see if what we had is still there." She pauses. "He was my first real love. He was my first real heartbreak, too. And I... I don't think I can let him go."

"Ever?" I ask.

She shrugs. "I don't know. All I know right now is that I have plans with him on Halloween, so we'll see what happens."

"Well, now I'm *definitely* not asking for a girls' night," Ashlei says.

"I'd bail on him for you," Jess promises.

Ashlei smiles, kissing her cheek. "I know. But this drama is too good for me to pass up on. It'd be like missing a week of my favorite TV show."

Jess flicks her off, and with a soft laugh, we all start perusing the clothes racks again.

Skyler avoids the Kip question when it comes up, and Ashlei falls back into her silent, glazed state of being.

The KKB girls aren't in the best shape right now.

But at least we have each other.

Bear

"I fucking *hate* you," Giselle says from the floor where I'm standing over her. Sweat covers her neck, her chest, drips off her hairline and into her eyes.

"Kick your legs up like you mean it," I challenge.

She grits her teeth, and then with a grunt, she sends her legs up, straight and together, her core firing up before I grab her sneakers and throw her legs back down toward the ground. It takes a focused breath from her not to let them hit the ground, and then she pushes them back up to me.

Again, and again, and again.

I finally call it, and she flops out like a fish, chest panting as I grab a towel and hand it to her. "Get some water," I say, doing the same. "I think we're done for today."

"You think?" she pants, groaning a bit as she sits up to grab her water bottle. She takes a long swig, shaking her head. "When I asked you to be my personal trainer, I imagined jumping jacks and high knees and some pushups. I *didn't* picture a full hour of unimaginable torture."

I chuckle. "You're already stronger than last week, and remember — you asked for this."

"Yeah, yeah," she says, extending a hand up for mine. "I only do it so I can stare at you without a shirt on."

I grab her hand and help her stand, laughing off the comment. When she's up, I don't miss the guys on the benches behind her letting their eyes wander every inch.

She's wearing tiny black workout shorts, similar to those a volleyball player might wear, and a matching black sports bra. It's strappy in the back, but otherwise plain. But it's not the outfit that draws everyone's attention — it's the body wearing it.

I knew Giselle was fit. I could tell even under her suits she wore in the office. But seeing her rippled midriff, her toned arms, her muscular legs with nothing covering them? There's no doubt in my mind that while I may be pushing her or challenging her with different exercises than she's used to, she's no stranger to hard work in the gym.

After toweling off her face, she lets the white cloth hang around her neck, squirting a healthy amount of water in her mouth. "You're really good at this, Clinton."

"Thank you."

"No, I mean it. *Really* good. I've worked with other trainers, and they're not like this. They don't check in, they don't offer nutrition guidance — at least, not past what I can easily research myself online. I feel so much stronger ever since you calculated my macros, since you taught me how to give my body the proper nutrition it needs."

"You were starving yourself before. It doesn't surprise me that you were tired all the time."

She shrugs. "I thought caloric and fat deficiency was the key. Thanks for teaching me otherwise." She pauses, assessing me. "How many other clients do you have?"

"Just a few. I can't take on too many — not right now, anyway. I need to stay focused on my real job."

"What if this *was* your real job?"

I blanch at her question, toweling off my neck before I take a seat on one of the benches. When I don't answer, Giselle crooks a smile and plops down next to me.

"Think about it. You understand fitness. You understand nutrition. You know how they work together. You get joy out of helping others, right?"

I nod a little more with each statement.

"And you have a degree in graphic design, with experience in client management and a little HTML knowledge, too. I mean, you could literally run your own business." She pauses. "If you wanted to."

I lift my brows, turning to face her. "I never thought of that."

"Well, now you have," she says with a smile. Her eyes are warm, almost playful as she watches me. She opens her mouth to say something else, but before she can, my phone rings, the sound making both of us jolt a little.

"Hey, babe," I answer. "Finishing up training with Giselle. Can I call you right back?"

"Of course. I've got about forty-five minutes before my next class."

"Give me ten."

When I hang up, I know there's a goofy grin on my face, and Giselle pokes her finger right where I know my cheek indents a bit when I smile like that.

"Whew, you are *smitten*, aren't you?" she teases.

I blow out a breath. "You have no idea."

"She must be something."

"She is," I say, showing Giselle the picture on my background. "And let's just say the road here wasn't an easy one."

Giselle whistles, taking my phone and studying Erin. "She's gorgeous. I'd say you're a lucky guy, but since I know you, I think the luck is mutual between you both."

"Thanks," I say with a shrug, taking my phone and tucking it away again. "But trust me — I'm *very* much the lucky one."

Giselle doesn't say anything but smiles and looks at her watch. "Alright, I guess I should get going. Dinner meeting with a client," she adds with an eye roll. "But let's touch base about the next month — because I'm officially hiring you as my trainer *and* nutritionist."

"You already paid me."

"Well, I'm going to pay you more."

I grab my neck. "Well, thank you, I guess. I'll make a plan for the next four weeks. Just so you know, I'm doing a little traveling at the beginning of November."

"Oh? Where to?"

"Just going home for the weekend. Pittsburgh," I clarify when I see her frown of confusion. "Erin's never been, and I want to show her around where I grew up."

"Erin is the girlfriend, I presume?"

I nod. "It's just for the weekend, though, so it shouldn't affect our training."

Giselle frowns, standing when I do. "You're flying all that way just for a weekend?"

"No paid time off yet," I say with a shrug.

Giselle's mouth tugs to the side, then she waves her hand in the air like she's batting away a fly. "Take a longer weekend, maybe a Wednesday to Sunday."

I frown. "But I—"

"Don't worry about it, I'll work it out with Henry."

Henry my *boss*, she means.

"You've been working your ass off and you deserve it."

My head is spinning a little — first from the idea she put in my head about my own company, and now from this. "Um... I guess if you're sure."

"I am. And remember what I said about the confidence thing?" She smacks my ass with her towel. It's playful, along with the grin on her face, but I admit it makes me a little uncomfortable. "Stop acting like you're surprised when I tell you how great you are. It's kind of annoying."

I smirk, but don't have anything to say in response.

"See you at the office," she says, and then she grabs her water bottle and struts away toward the locker rooms.

Every guy she walks by has to fight not to watch.

Ninety percent of them lose.

My thoughts are still whirring when I pack up my own gym bag and head out of the gym. I pull my phone out to call Erin back, and that's when I see the text from Skyler.

I know you have plans on Halloween, but are you free the night after?

I could really use a Bear Hug.

My chest aches. Skyler and I haven't had the chance to hang out much, what with her in her last semester as president and finishing up school, and me working and focusing on my new relationship with Erin.

I've got a big one with your name on it, I type back.

Her only response is a heart emoji, and I make a mental note to pick up burritos from her favorite spot off campus on my way to see her.

Once the text is sent, I call Erin back, and count down the hours until she's in my arms again.

Jess

This might be my most boring Halloween costume to date.

Blame it on the fact that it's my *first* Halloween out of college, or that I'm exhausted from work and didn't have time or creative energy to think of something better, or perhaps that I have no idea what I'm walking into tonight — or what I want to walk into — but this year, I'm a classic witch.

My long, blonde hair is curled and flowing over my shoulders, the highlights fresh and bright under the black pointy hat on my head. My makeup is dark and fierce — smokey eyeshadow, long, fake lashes, black glittery lips. The dress I picked for my witchy vibe is an old black sequin one that I wore on New Year's Eve one year. I shredded the bottom of it, ripping it in triangle strips of different shapes, sizes, and lengths, and I ripped holes in the midriff and chest area for good measure. Wide fishnet leggings and pointy-toed high-heeled boots finish the look — along with a broomstick I paid some kid two condo doors down to spray paint and glitterfy.

And while I didn't aim for sexy, as I usually do, I think I landed there, anyway.

It's classic and simple, but the darkness of it matches my mood completely.

I'm fixing my lipstick when my phone lights up with a text from Kade.

Have fun tonight.

My stomach tightens at the words because I know he's not saying them genuinely. I know there's a bit of jealousy underlining them, a bit of worry, a bit of unmanageable rage at the fact that he has to share.

I wonder how he doesn't already hate me — how they *both* don't. Ever since Jarrett confessed he still had feelings for me, the two of them haven't so much as talked, let alone been in the same room.

I've driven brothers apart, and what's worse are the head games I know I'm submitting them to.

I should just let them both go. I should tell them that they're better off without me, that they'll both move on and find someone better. Because I don't see a single way this can end where someone won't get hurt.

And yet, I can't let them go.

I groan, typing back a response before I slump down in the barstool at the kitchen island. "I'm the fucking worst," I mutter to myself.

My phone rings again, and this time, it's Herb downstairs.

Jarrett's here.

I tell Herb not to send him up, that I'll be right down, and then I stand as tall as I can in front of the full-length mirror by the front door.

"Okay, bitch. This is the night. You figure out what the hell you're doing and either choose Jarrett or cut him loose. No hanky-panky, okay?" I say to myself, making a peace sign and drawing a line between my eyes and the girl's in the mirror. "It hasn't even been a month since you fucked Kade. Don't be a whore."

I swear, I see the girl in the mirror wink before I turn for the door.

My palms are slick on the elevator ride down to the lobby, and when the doors slide open and I see Jarrett standing in the middle of the marble floor, my mouth goes dry.

His back is to me, lean and muscular, his hands sitting easily in his pockets. His head is smooth and freshly shaved, and he must sense me, because he turns — ever so slowly — until his dark eyes lock on mine.

He's wearing an all-black outfit, just like me.

And he looks like every sin I'm trying not to commit.

A black tunic is tapered at his waist with a belt, the chest of it ripped open to show the muscles and tattoos underneath. He's shoved the sleeves up to just below his elbows, showing off his tanned, toned forearms and the ink that covers them, too. His beard is neat and trimmed, salt and pepper gray touching the dark brown of it, and the leather pants he's wearing are something out of a *GQ* photoshoot — fitted, but that slouchy kind of casual that makes your mouth water on sight.

He smirks when my eyes make it back to his, no doubt loving the fact that I just ogled him and almost had the elevator doors shut on me in the process. I step fully out, standing tall as I stride over to him in my heels, and that's when I see the tastefully painted blood dripping from one side of his mouth.

"Vampire," I muse, arching a brow when I notice he's wearing blood-red contacts. "I'll be honest, I thought you'd show up as a beach bar bartender."

"Didn't want to turn you on too early in the night. Although, I *can* drive my truck instead of us catching a cab, if you'd like. Just in case."

He doesn't wink, doesn't make any facial expression with the tease other than to smirk just a fraction more. But the memory of that first time fucking in his truck makes my neck heat, my core tighten.

I flick him off and shove past him before he's on my heels, chuckling as he catches up.

"Where are we going?" I ask.

"Dancing."

And then as if it's the easiest thing in the world, as if I belong to him, as if he never left me or hurt me or pulverized my heart — he takes my hand in his and leads me to the waiting cab.

***

The Lemon Club is one known for its bustling nightlife, often hosting well-known DJs and never closing before four in the morning. It's already bumping when we finally get through the line outside, and in the doors, orange and purple lights thumping with the music and fog filling the floor. Above us, aerial artists hang from hoops and silks, and all around us, girls and boys alike dance in go-go cages, their bodies moving in time with the heavy bass.

The club is packed, people squeezed in at the bar and dancing on every inch of the dance floor. Jarrett pulls me into a dark little corner before looking around with a mixture of amusement and annoyance.

Then, he slips his hand around my waist, tugging me closer.

Again, as if it's the most natural thing in the world.

My breath hitches at the contact, at the way it feels to be held by him after all these years, to have his hands on me, that familiar energy buzzing through my veins just with that simple contact. My traitorous body hums to life, pussy throbbing, nipples pebbling and aching for more.

I really am the fucking worst.

"Sorry it's so loud in here," he yells over the music, leaning in close enough to my ear that his warm breath brushes my lobe.

I swallow. "It's okay!"

We stand there for a long moment, Jarrett dragging his gaze down the length of me, his jaw tight.

"You look incredible," he says, and though I know he had to scream it for me to be able to hear, it feels like a weighted whisper in my ear.

"So do you," I say, and it's almost a pout — enough so that Jarrett chuckles and lifts a brow.

"You say that like it's a bad thing."

I offer a slight smile in lieu of answering that *yes, it is a very bad thing.* Because taking the summer away from him numbed my brain to the power he exudes over me. I'd forgotten his rugged, earthy scent, his thick, muscular arms, his devilish smirk, his dark, hypnotizing eyes. I'd forgotten what it felt like to be pinned by his gaze, to know without him saying a word that he wants me — desperately.

But with him standing right in front of me, his hand possessively holding my half-bare waist, I'm all too aware of everything I'd tried so hard to forget.

Jarrett's expression is a little more solemn when he says, "It's been excruciating staying away from you."

I close my eyes, letting out a slow breath like it'll somehow save me.

"Did it help?" he asks, leaning in even closer, his breath on my neck. "Did you find the space you needed to think?"

A wave of chills runs over me at the feeling of him being so close, and *thinking* is about the last thing I can do.

"Let's dance," I say instead of answering, and I grab his hand, pulling him deep into the middle of the dance floor.

I know immediately that it was a mistake.

I didn't want to talk, didn't want to answer his questions, didn't want to look him in the eyes and admit that I'm more confused than ever. I didn't want to confess that I still love him, that just like he told me — I never stopped. Because I also love his brother, and it just doesn't seem fair or right or sane for both of those things to be true.

But now that we're on the dance floor, his hands snaking around my waist and pulling my back flush to his chest, I realize that talking or crying or literally *anything else* would be safer than this.

The music seems louder out here — thicker, heavier, like a physical presence pulling both of us in. Jarrett grabs my hip hard with one hand, the other splaying over my midriff, and then he's moving us, hips swaying slowly at first before finding the beat.

We haven't even had a drink yet. I can't blame it on the alcohol that the moment his body lines up flush with mine, I moan, biting my lip and letting my head fall back against his chest. I reach one hand up to hook behind his neck, the other covering his hand where it spreads across my stomach. Lights pulse overhead, blinding me from time to time as we dip and sway and move together.

It's intoxicating, that buzz of desire that shoots through me with every new touch. His hand moves from my hip to my thigh, and I gasp. His other hand slides up just an inch, his thumb pressing into the hollow space between my breasts, and I arch my back, grinding my ass against him.

He's hard as a fucking diamond, and the way he rolls that impressive length against me, I know he couldn't care less about me or anyone else in this club knowing it.

"Your costume is very fitting," he rumbles in my ear, sucking the lobe of it between his teeth. "My little witch, spinning her web, keeping me under her spell."

His words stroke me like expert fingertips, and I grind against him more, grabbing his hand and moving it up until it fully palms my breast. His moan is guttural, a menacing growl as he bites down on my neck like it's the only thing he can do to keep his composure now that he's touching me.

In front of everyone.

But who cares? Who's looking? And even if they are, maybe I want them to. Maybe I need to feel this connection again, to remember what we had, to let myself have everything I once took for granted like I never lost it at all.

It's selfish and fucked up, but I can't find it in me to care.

Before I can talk myself out of it, before the angel on my shoulder can get a peep out, I whip around in Jarrett's arms, crushing my mouth to his.

He catches the kiss with intention, one hand coming to the back of my head to hold me there. My witch hat flies off in the process, which only gives him permission to run his fingertips more through my hair, to grab the back of my skull and kiss me like it's his chance to mark me, to claim me for good.

His arm wraps around me like a boa, squeezing tight, holding me to him so I can feel every breath, every muscle, every inch of his rock-hard length. And the moment our lips meet, I feel every memory rush back in a furious wave.

I remember that first time in his truck, and that last time in the hotel — the time I didn't *realize* would be our last. I remember him caring for me when I was sick, remember him taking all my friends out for dinner, remember how every time his fingertips ran along my skin, my entire body came to life. I remember how fiercely I loved him.

And how utterly destroyed I was when he left me.

I wince against the pain that memory brings, and Jarrett seems to sense it, because he kisses me harder, slicking his tongue along my lips until I open up and let him inside. We both moan, and I press up on my toes to get more, Jarrett's hand sliding along my ass, my thigh until he hooks his hand behind my knee and hikes my leg up.

The kiss is deep and bruising, tied up with emotions of love and lust and pure fucking hatred. Slowly, we start to move again, grinding to the beat with his thigh between my legs and my dress hiked up over where he holds me in place. All of my weight is in his arms. I have no choice but to move the way he dictates, to sway the way his hands tell me to, to rub where he wants me to rub.

Holding me steadfast with one arm around the small of my back, he snakes the other one between us, sliding up my hiked leg along the tender skin of my inner thigh.

I shiver, barely breathing the words, "What are you doing?"

His only answer is a wicked grin, and then his fingertips slide up and up, higher and higher, dangerously close to where I know I'm slick for him.

Suddenly, the music is too loud. We're too close. The kiss is too hard. My heart pounds in my chest in a warning, reminding me how much this man hurt me, reminding me how dangerous it is to play with a fire that burns so fucking cruelly.

I snap back away from his mouth, shoving my hands into his chest and pushing with all my might until he has no choice but to let me go. I stumble backward once he no longer carries my weight, but I don't take more than a second to watch the stunned look on his face before I'm squeezing through the crowd, running over anyone who doesn't move at the first muttered *excuse me*.

I have to get out of here. I can't do this to Kade. I can't do this to *myself*.

I want him.

I want him so fucking bad it hurts.

And I love him.

I still fucking love him.

Tears sting my eyes, not just at the admission, but at the realization that the love I have for him burns just as hot as the love I have for Kade.

Someone will end up broken.

The someone who deserves it most is me.

I push and shove and tear through the thick crowd until I finally push outside, stumbling over my heels in the process. But I catch my footing, straighten my dress, fix my hair and strut on once I'm on the sidewalk. Sniffing, I keep my eyes focused forward.

I have no idea where I'm going, but I know I can't stay still.

I hear him calling my name after a moment — softly at first before he's jogging up and hooking my elbow to rip me around. I expect to find anger, to find a man who was cock-teased and is now pissed off about it.

What I find breaks me even more.

Jarrett must have removed the stupid red contacts he was wearing, because his natural dark brown ones are flicking between mine, brows furrowed over top of them as he searches me for where I'm hurt. There's nothing but care and concern and pure fucking love, and it instantly makes those tears I've been holding back build and rush over before I have the chance to stop them.

"What's wrong? Are you okay? Did I hurt you?"

I laugh at that last question, which makes him frown more. Slowly, tentatively, he pulls me into him, wrapping me in a soft, sincere hug. He holds me like that for a long while, and I just let the tears come, let them soak his tunic and the street we stand on.

"Yes," I finally breathe. "You did hurt me."

With my head on his chest, I see the way his throat hollows out, the way a thick swallow strains his neck. I pull back, breaking all contact and swiping at my face before I fold my arms over my middle and stand a few feet away from him. It's far from fall in Florida, no matter what the date on the calendar, but the nights are cooler than they were before, and the breeze chills me to the bone as I look around at the people laughing and talking as they walk by us — oblivious to the turmoil raging inside me.

"You hurt me worse than anyone ever has in my entire life," I continue. "I loved you, Jarrett. I trusted you. I gave you everything I had to give. I put up with the long distance and the lack of communication because I knew, at the end of the day, that I wanted you — no matter the cost."

I sniff, more tears building in my eyes that I refuse to let fall.

"And then you tossed me to the side."

Jarrett shakes his head, pain etched in his features as he reaches for me, but I pull away.

"You did. You let them get in your head, let other people convince you I was crazy. You left me like some silly part of your past."

"It was a mistake," he says quickly. "The worst fucking mistake I've ever made. I was stupid. I was *wrong*."

"All I wanted was for you to come back," I admit on a strained whisper, rolling my lips together and shaking my head. "And now that you have, I hate that I wished for it."

Jarrett tries reaching for me again, but I flinch away.

"I wish you'd have stayed gone. I wish you'd have never shown back up and turned my life upside down as soon as I figured out how to right it again."

"No, you don't."

I cry at his words, covering my face and forcing a breath to stop the tears as much as I can before crossing my arms and lifting my chin to face him again. I don't want to break, but goddamnit if he doesn't undo me.

"I never left you."

I laugh under my breath, but Jarrett moves in closer. I back away, but he doesn't relent. He just keeps closing the space until my back is against a brick wall and his chest is touching mine.

"You've always had me and you know it — just like I've always had you."

I swallow, staring at him through bleary eyes, but already I can feel it — my pulse quickening, thighs tightening, head pounding as every molecule of my body swirls at the way it feels to be watched by him.

"This?" he says, gesturing between us. "What we have? It's elemental. It's... *transcendental.* It doesn't matter what happens, what mistakes we make, how much time we have apart or who might come between us."

He shakes his head, stepping into me more, his entire body pressing against mine as his hands snake up my arms, over my neck, up my jaw to cradle my face between them.

"It's always going to be us, Jess." He licks his lips. "For me, it's *always* going to be you."

His mouth is on me in the next second, stealing any response I had.

And I let him take it.

Let him take *all* of me.

We're in a cab back to my place less than sixty seconds later.

***

Hands.

Hands *everywhere.*

Grabbing my hips, my thighs, my ass, my back, my neck. Gripping my hair. Shredding my clothes.

And lips.

Lips everywhere.

On my mouth, my breasts, my neck, the sensitive skin along my inner thighs.

I might as well be drunk, or high, or in a fucking meditative state for how time passes, how I lose track of everything as that man sweeps me away to a universe all his own.

It's all a sensory-overdrive blur until the moment he rips his briefs down.

He's already on the prowl for me, crawling his way up the bed where I wait for him propped against the pillows. Before he can reach me, I press my toes into his chest, pushing back until he's on his knees so I can get a good, long look.

A good, long, *hard* look.

A good, long, hard, perfectly shaped, perfectly thick, perfectly *mine* look.

Jarrett crooks a smile, tilting his head a bit. "Someone likes what they see."

"Someone hasn't seen it in far too long."

In a feat of movement my brain can't comprehend, Jarrett flips me onto my back, stands at the edge of the bed, and grabs me under the arms to drag me until my head hangs off the mattress.

"Maybe someone should taste it," he husks, carefully moving my hair from my face and gently, tenderly tilting my head until my throat is long and exposed, head hanging completely off the bed.

Jesus fucking Christ.

He doesn't wait for my smartass answer that I'm sure he knows I have on the tip of my tongue. Instead, he grabs his cock and presses it to my lips, arching a brow and slicking his tip along them until I grant him entrance.

The gentleness is gone.

He presses inside before I'm ready, slicking himself with my saliva as I force a breath and open my throat wide so as not to gag. He curses when he's fully inside me, and then he's palming my breasts, pulling out again only to slide back in nice and slow.

I kind of wish I had his view, kind of wish I could see his dick bulging in my throat, my tits under his hands, my thighs spread, body writhing with need.

This is what he does to me.

This is that elemental, carnal connection he was referring to.

It's the most powerful high.

"Goddamnit, Jess. Do you know how many nights I've laid awake thinking about this, about you?" he asks, withdrawing just to push inside my throat once more. "Do you know how badly you've ruined me for any other woman, how dull and lifeless their touch is compared to yours?"

I threaten with a little bit of teeth when he mentions other women, and it makes him yelp a little before he chuckles, pulling all the way out and yet again flipping me on the bed. He picks me up—

Picks. Me. *Up.*

And throws me into the pillows, dropping down on top of me before the mattress has even adjusted to the weight. He kisses me hard and long, our teeth clashing, and then he's trailing little bites and sucks of skin all the way down.

Before I can prepare for it, he drags the flat of his tongue along my slick pussy, groaning as he laps up my desire. "Fuck, I never forgot how much I loved breakfast in bed with you."

"It's nighttime," I remind him.

"It's after midnight, technically. And besides," he adds with a quirk of his brow. "Haven't you ever had breakfast for dinner?"

He steals my breath to answer with another lash of his tongue, and then his fingers are spreading me wide, creating better access for him to tease and suck my clit.

It's fire and ice, my body heating to unbearable temperatures before a chill shudders through me, over and over again.

He knows just how to lick me, suck me, touch me.

And I know before we even get there that he knows just how to fuck me, too.

For a split second, a flash of guilt surges in my stomach. It's so fierce I sit up and grab Jarrett, but then it's gone, replaced by the hunger raging through me as Jarrett takes that as his cue that I've had enough foreplay and am ready for him to be inside me.

He answers the plea by grabbing my ass and pulling me toward him, and then he pushes my feet toward my face, like I'm doing the fucking happy baby yoga pose.

"Hold on," he says, waiting until I grab my feet — *literally* the yoga pose.

Then, he presses up onto his knees, grabs the condom I didn't realize he'd slapped on the bedside table, and rolls it on.

"Spread," he commands, and I pull harder on my feet, opening myself completely. I mean, there is no more vulnerable position for me to be in. I'm spread with my vagina just waiting there, catching a draft, my legs restrained by my own strength like a good little girl.

I shiver as he lowers himself down once more, just long enough to slick his tongue over my asshole, my pussy, sucking my clit long and hard and releasing it with a yelp from my lips.

Then, he's at my entrance, one hand holding my thigh as the other presses the tip of his cock inside me.

And he nails it home.

I gasp at the sensation, at the fullness of him inside me, at the forbidden juiciness of not having him for so long, of him somehow being off-limits and yet never anyone else's but mine.

Jarrett groans when he withdraws and presses inside again, feeling every inch of me taking him in. "I hope you're as ready as I am," he breathes like he's in pain. "Because I'm not going to last long."

He slips out and back in, finding a rhythm — slow at first as he reaches down and strokes my clit with his thumb. He knows just how to circle, just where to apply the pressure so it builds my orgasm without hitting any too-sensitive spots.

It's like fucking magic, how fast I build for him, how fast my heart races and blood pumps right where I need it.

"Come on," is all he says, and as if that invitation was what I was waiting for, I explode, holding onto my feet even tighter and spreading my legs wide enough to know I'll be sore in the morning. My glutes clench as I ride the wave, reaching for more, *begging* for the orgasm not to recede too early.

Jarrett takes my moans as permission to find his own release, and I'm glad Erin is with Bear tonight when he comes, because his screams are as loud as mine, the deep baritone of his voice rumbling off the walls like a fucking lion's roar.

I don't have time to come down, to pant, to wrap my slick body around him and laugh at how fast we both came. As soon as he finishes, Jarrett pulls out, disposes of the condom in the trashcan by my bed, and rolls another one back on in its place.

I gape at the sight, and he just arches a brow, smirking at my dumbfounded expression.

"I know you didn't think one round would be enough," he says, shaking his head before descending on me like a predator. "It's been too long since I've touched you, kissed you," he says, pressing his lips to mine before he whispers, "*fucked* you. I'm nowhere near satiated."

My body heats to life again at his words, at how much this man desires me, how badly he craves my body. And with another bruising kiss and lust-drunk moan, Jarrett flips me, pulling me into his lap.

He grabs my hips and guides me down, my sore, wet pussy opening for him once again.

Round two.

Ding ding.

Skyler

A thousand Bear hugs wouldn't be enough.

I never thought I'd say the words, never thought there was *anything* a hug from my best friend couldn't fix. But even lying on his couch, my feet in his lap and a fetus-sized burrito in my belly, even with a half-bottle of wine swimming in my system, even with an entire evening of talking and laughing, and even with the dozens of hugs I've stolen tonight — I'm still on the verge of tears.

I've been feeling it for months, the constant knot in my throat, the pain and aching in my chest. Like at any moment, at any time, I could just burst into tears and then into flames.

Unstable.

Unsettled.

Unknown.

I've been keeping my shit together in front of everyone, working hard in my last semester as president of KKB, acing my classes as I prepare for graduation, being there for Ashlei through her injury, supporting Cassie in her long-distance relationship, and Jess in her difficult decision she knows she has to make soon. I've cheered Erin on in her case against the guys who violated her, and called home to check in on Mom and Dad, to promise them I'd be home for the holidays before going wherever post-graduation would take me.

I'm graduating.

The realization always makes those tears I've been holding at bay build a little stronger.

Because I've dreamed about this for so long, but I never dreamed I'd feel so fucking lost when the time actually came.

"You know," Bear says, rubbing my arches with his eyes still on the TV. "You could call him."

"And say what?"

He shrugs. "Whatever you're feeling."

"I don't know what I'm feeling," I say on a sigh. "That's the problem."

"You know exactly what you're feeling," Bear argues. He finally looks at me then. "You're sad. You miss him. You love him. You're hurt by what he did. You don't know if you can forgive him."

"Exactly," I say, pointing at his chest when he says that last part. "So, if I don't know if I can forgive him and move forward, why would I call him? What would it change?" I look at my chipped nail polish where I balance the half-empty wine glass in my hand. "Besides, he's apologized, yes, but... he doesn't even understand *why* he has to apologize."

"I'm sure that's not true."

"He doesn't see Natalia the way I do. And he feels like I should be understanding with the show, with his career. And I *am* it's just..."

"It's just that you want to know where you stand in his life," Bear finishes for me. "If you're less important than his career, on the same level, or more."

My stomach cramps. "Yes," I whisper.

We're quiet for a while, me sipping my wine while Bear pretends to watch the TV. I know he's just giving me space to process, to think.

"Maybe I am being too hard on him," I confess. "Maybe it wasn't as big of a deal as I'm making it."

"Don't do that," Bear says. "Don't make yourself feel crazy. I would have been upset, if it were me."

"You would have killed her," I said with a smirk at my best friend. "You would have grabbed her wet hair and slammed her head against the tile."

"Jesus, Sky," he says with a frown. "That's so violent." A pause, and then a tilt of his head. "But, not *entirely* far-fetched."

I chuckle. "I'm just saying, maybe his apology was more sincere than I'm giving him credit for. Maybe it's *me* being dramatic."

"You? Never."

I roll my eyes, but then my nails are tapping against the wine glass, and I suddenly shoot up to set it down and reach for Bear's phone.

"What are you doing?"

"I'm pulling up his Instagram."

Bear's eyes widen, and he snatches his phone out of my hand before I can even unlock it. "Um, first of all, why do you need my phone to do that?"

"Because I blocked him," I say with a shrug. "I had to. It made me physically ill every time he liked one of my photos, or any time I saw him post something."

Bear sighs. "Yeah. It would make me sick, too... which leads me to my second point of caution — I don't think this is a good idea."

"I just want to see what he's been up to. You were right," I confess. "I do miss him. And maybe this will help push me over the edge, help me get the lady balls to just call him."

Bear's mouth pulls to the side.

"Please."

He sighs, handing me his phone before kicking back on the couch again. "I still feel like this is a bad idea."

"Noted," I say, but I'm already typing *Kip Jackson* into the search bar on the app. He and Bear are friends, so Kip's profile pops up before I even finish typing the full name, and my heart squeezes at the sight of that familiar smile, those ocean blue eyes framed by thick black glasses.

I tap the little circle.

And then I freeze when I see the most recent post.

For a moment, my thumb just hovers over it. I don't want to see it blown up to full-screen. I can tell just from the small thumbnail what it is.

Kip, dressed to the nines, full suit and bow tie and dress shoes and a watch I bought him in Vegas.

And Natalia, in a short, silver, slinky dress with thin straps.

He has his arm around her waist, and she has hers around his, and when the picture was snapped, he was smiling at the camera.

She was smiling up at *him*.

I nearly vomit when I finally tap it and pull it full size — especially when I see all the likes and comments underneath it. The caption reads *That's a wrap on editing! Can't wait to bring* Black Number Four *to your laptop screens and home TVs, and for you all to see this amazing girl in action.*

The comments range from *congratulations!* and *can't wait!* to *cute couple!* and *wow, you're both glowing!*

The more I scroll, the more those tears I've been holding back threaten to break loose. I feel them blurring my vision, feel them tightening my throat, feel them suffocating me and demanding to be felt.

"Sky..." Bear says, leaning up to look at the screen with me. When he sees it, he mutters, "shit," and takes the phone from me, tossing it on the coffee table.

I look at him.

And then I break.

Covering my face with my hands, I do my best to breathe through the terrible sobs that wash over me like a thunderous, relentless wave. Bear pulls me into his chest and holds me close, whispering that it will be okay.

But I know it won't.

When we had our fight, I was angry. I was pissed off. I was so fucking hurt that I couldn't see him. Over the summer, I needed that space. And even when he left to go back to California, I was still upset, but I think...

I think deep down, through all that, I just always assumed it was a phase.

I always assumed it was just a fight, just a summer apart, just something we would have to work through.

I thought we'd make it through.

The realization that I was wrong strikes me like a fist to the gut, and I double over, surrendering to another massive attack of painful cries.

He's having the time of his life while my life falls apart.

And somehow, I can't help but feel like it's all my fault.

Jess

"Shit!" I curse as the contents carefully balanced on the top shelf of my closet tumble out and rain down on me, a shower of shoes and yoga equipment and long-forgotten hobbies.

Erin runs over from her room, makeup half-done and hair pinned back. "What was that? Are you okay?"

I grunt, looking at the mess on the floor. But spotting what I was looking for, I swipe it off the ground and plop onto my unmade bed. "Just peachy."

Erin offers a soft smile at that, her shoulders deflating a little. She strolls over to me and sits on the edge of the bed. "Is this your favorite pair of shoes or something?" she asks, tapping the lid of the old shoebox in front of me.

"It's my own personal form of torture that I like to succumb myself to from time to time."

Erin cocks a brow.

I sigh. "It's a memory box," I explain, flipping the lid off to reveal the contents inside. "Mostly of Jarrett. And then..."

"Kade," Erin finishes for me, fishing out a picture of us from that first formal we attended together.

"Yep."

Erin smiles at the picture, setting it aside before holding up a greasy pizza napkin. She wrinkles her nose. "Pictures, I understand. But this?"

"They're memories," I defend, swiping the napkin from her. I smile at the nasty thing. "This was from when Jarrett flew in to visit from New York. We had amazing sex when he first landed, and then knew we weren't leaving the room. So, I ordered pizza, and we stayed in." I bite my lip. "All. Night. Long."

"Okay," Erin says, holding up her hands and standing. "I think this memory box is a personal experience."

I chuckle. "You off to class?"

"Leaving in ten. Are you going to work?"

I shake my head. "We had three weddings this weekend — Friday, Saturday, *and* last night, so we all have today off to recover."

Erin nods. "I'll be back tonight. If you want to talk," she adds, her eyes falling to the box before they land on me again.

"You sure you're up for that crazy ride of me talking through my feelings right now?"

"Always."

She blows me a kiss, and then she's out the door, and I settle back into memory lane.

The last week has been a whirlwind.

After Jarrett left — which wasn't until very, *very* late the morning after Halloween — I nearly had a breakdown. All the memories of us had come rushing back, completely washing over the foundation I'd just rebuilt and fortified with Kade.

I thought after the karaoke event that I knew. I thought I would just call Jarrett up and tell him that while I did care about him, I couldn't see him.

But then stupid me *had* to see him.

And stupid me remembered why I'd loved him so fiercely, why he'd broken me so completely, why even when I tried — I could never forget him.

I pull a thin, lacy, hot pink bra out of the box, smirking when I remember Kade's face the time I wore it for him, the time I punished him for being a jerk to me over the summer, for blowing off the plan *he* had made for us. That was the closest I'd ever been to a Dom, and I loved it.

And God, I love *him.*

I love that he rose to every challenge I gave him, love that he wanted to learn, that he wanted to please me, that he wanted to be my every sexual desire. I love that it quickly became so much more than that, that he snuck into my heart and made me fall for him without so much as trying.

I love how effortless we are, tried and true.

A team.

My eyes catch on a box of matches with *Ralph's* in script on the front, and I pull them from the box, smiling again. I snatched them from the supply closet that night Jarrett railed me on Halloween, reminding me that playing the games of flaunting college boys in front of him wouldn't work.

And I love him, too.

I love how just one look from him can strip me utterly naked, how he knows me better than I know myself sometimes. I love that he's not afraid to push my buttons, that he calls me on my bullshit, and that he fucks me like a goddamn pro.

I love that toxic, completely addicted feeling of losing him and winning him back.

The most beautiful mess.

I close my eyes, sighing before I pull out more items, one by one, each little menu or picture or scrap of clothing or stolen tchotchke another memory pulling me this way or that.

It's a vicious tug of war, one where no one wins.

My phone buzzes in the sheets next to me, and I hitch a breath at the sight of Kade's name.

Can I see you?

I sigh, shaking my head and typing back a response before I can think on it more.

Not today.

Erin calls out a goodbye from down the hall, and then the condo door opens and shuts, and I'm alone.

Another ping of my phone.

Were you with him on Halloween?

Him. He doesn't even have to say who for me to know.

I didn't post anything on the holiday, not a single picture, which is unlike me — since everyone knows I love my costumes. I'm sure he put two and two together that I wasn't with Erin and Bear, nor was I with Ashlei — who posted a sad, albeit cute, picture of her dressed as a mummy on the couch with Brandon — and I certainly wasn't with Skyler and Cassie at Ralph's wooing Cassie's soon-to-be Little.

And still, I can't bring myself to answer him.

Suddenly, my phone rings, and I jolt, thinking it's Kade. But it's Herb at the front desk, and I answer surprised, "Herb?"

"Good morning, Miss Vonnegut. You have a visitor."

I swallow. Maybe Kade isn't taking my non-answer as an answer. "May I ask who?"

"The young man who picked you up for Halloween, Miss."

My heart jolts again, but this time, in a traitorous, excited way.

"Send him up, please."

I jump off the bed as soon as we end the call, fussing with my hair a bit and changing out of my giant sweatpants into a small, cute pair of sleep shorts. I'm wearing a tank top without a bra, and decide I shouldn't bother putting one on.

When I see the box and its contents on my bed, I curse, gathering everything and shoving it back inside before kicking the whole box under my bed. I close my closet door to hide that mess, too, and then scuttle down the hall.

My phone buzzes as I do.

Kade.

You're killing me, Jess.

When I open the door and see Jarrett smirking, holding two coffees in a carrier and a bag of what I assume are donuts from one of the best places downtown, my heart cracks.

"I'm on my way to the office," he explains, a beautiful smirk on that beautiful face of his. "But I had to see you first."

I bite my lip against the smile I feel building, opening the door more for him to come inside.

My phone feels like a bomb in my hand.

I read Kade's text again, and then I type back the most honest thing I can.

I'm killing me, too.

Before he can respond, I toss my phone on the kitchen counter face down, following Jarrett inside. I lead him back to my bedroom, snatching the bag of donuts from his hands.

"Mmmm," I say, inhaling the intoxicating scent as I pull out the first one. "Blueberry cake. How did you remember my favorite?"

"Come on, like I could ever forget. You ate *five* in one sitting the first time we went."

I laugh around the mouthful I've already started chewing on. "Hey, I never said I was a lady."

"I never said I wanted you to be one."

Jarrett takes a bite off the other end of the donut, and I swat away his victorious smile when he takes half the thing with him.

When we're done chewing, Jarrett sits on my bed, patting the seat next to him until I do, too.

"I feel like we didn't get to talk much," he says with a wry smile. "On Halloween, that is."

My cheeks heat. "I don't think either one of us had an issue with that."

"At the time, no," he agrees. "But... I don't want you to think that's all I want. That that's all you are to me."

I frown. "I didn't. But now..."

Jarrett laughs under his breath, opening his arm and pulling me under it. His lips press against my temple, and I melt at the touch, at how soft and sweet it is, at how good and lovely and *right* it feels when his hand rests on my waist.

"I want to take you on a date," he says, but already I can feel it — that magnetic field between us firing to life. His hand tightens where it holds me, eyes falling to my lips. "An actual date where we talk and catch up and maybe get to know something new about each other, too."

"Okay," I say breathlessly, and my fingers trail up the buttons of his shirt, hooking over the collar. "When?"

"As soon as you'll let me," he purrs, his free hand finding my knee. It trails up, slow and steady, leaving chills in its wake.

I unfasten the first button of his shirt, then the second. "This week is kind of busy at work... can I let you know?"

Jarrett's hand splays over my thigh, fingertips so long they brush the hem of my tiny shorts. "As long as you *actually* let me know, yes."

"I will," I promise, mouth parting, eyes flicking to his. "We could talk now, you know," I offer, but even as I say the words, I'm undoing the last of his shirt buttons and shoving the fabric back, over his shoulders, down to his elbows where it catches.

"We could," he muses with a smirk, helping me get his shirt the rest of the way off. As soon as he's topless, my eyes roaming the painted valleys and ridges of his abdomen, he grabs my hips and tosses me like a teddy bear back into my pillows. "*Or* you could take your shorts off, pull those perfect tits out of that thin little thank top they've been teasing me through, and let me make you come a couple times before I have to go to work."

My pussy tightens at the words, and without me having to answer, he's already slipping his fingers under the bands of my shorts and tugging. I lift my hips to allow him access to strip them off, and then he reaches for my tank top, roughly yanking until my tits pop up through the neckline.

He bites his lip on a moan, sucking my left nipple hard between his teeth before moving on to the right. When they're both puckered and I'm writhing beneath him, he kisses his way down, and then flips us so that I'm on top.

Straddling that beautiful face of his.

"You're always so hungry in the morning," I tease, but the words lose their bark at the end when he flicks his tongue against me, his hands grabbing my ass and pulling me into him.

"Insatiable, really," he growls.

My hands fly to the headboard to keep me steady when he licks me long and slow, seam to bud, and then sucks my clit with just enough pressure to make my legs quake around him.

And just like that, any attempt at talking is forgotten.

Jarrett's hands are steadfast on my ass as he helps me ride his face, sucking and licking and biting and kissing like eating pussy for breakfast is his favorite pastime. I lose myself completely with him, succumbing to not one, not two, but *three* orgasms. The first one comes from his tongue, the second from him taking me from behind, and the third time in the shower where we're both trying to be good and get clean.

But we're naked, and *wet*, and steamy... like we could keep our hands off each other.

By the time he forces me to let him go so he can get dressed and go to work, I'm sore and aching in all the best places, my eyes ready to close for a long nap when he kisses my forehead and lets himself out.

I surrender to sleep the second he's gone.

And somewhere in that strange state of not quite sleeping but not quite awake, I swear I can hear my phone buzzing on the kitchen counter down the hall.

Bear

"Go, go, go!" ERIN screams beside me, jumping up and down like a wild animal, and now that she's stripped off her beanie, her dark blonde hair is flying everywhere — including right in my face. She nearly steps on my toes before I grab her waist to hold her steady, laughing when she turns to face me with wide eyes. "What?"

"I love that you're excited," I tell her. "Just... watch for other people's feet. And faces."

She smiles — and *God*, the sight knocks my next breath from my chest. It's not a small smile or a soft, reserved one. It's full on, eyes crinkled, teeth dazzling and lips spread smiling.

My happy Erin.

How I've missed her.

She whips around again in time to see my little brother get tackled to the ground about five yards from the end zone, and she throws her hands up in victory, jumping up and down again before crushing me in a hug.

"He's amazing!" she says, stripping her scarf off. "And so *tall* and massive. He's going to kill it when he gets to college. I'm sure he'll have the ladies all over him, too." She pauses, then starts unzipping her jacket. "Do you think he'll go pro?!"

I laugh, stopping her before she can remove the puffy Patagonia. "Hey, don't take off too many layers. You're warm now because you're jumping around, but I don't want you catching a cold."

"I love this," she says breathlessly as the team lines up for the next play. "Football, cold weather, hot chocolate, fire pits, pumpkin everything... *this* is fall."

"I don't know how you do it in Florida," Mom chimes in from next to her, shaking her head. "Still eighty degrees in November? No, thank you."

"*Ninety* when we left for the airport," Erin corrects her.

"Maybe you'll end up here one day," Mom says, and I don't miss the mischievous look in her eyes when she says it. I also don't miss how bright *her* smile is, how full her cheeks are, how healthy and happy she looks compared to the woman who'd run off my freshman year of college.

Whatever happened in Mexico, it seems to have set her right. And I'm thankful, at least, Clayton gets to see this side of her, gets to grow up with a mom who's present and working and *sober*.

"Real subtle there, Mom," I tease.

She shrugs. "Hey, I'm just saying, Erin has only been here two days and she's fallen in love already."

"It's true. I mean, how could I not? Just driving through that tunnel, being in the country one second and then *bam*," Erin says, illustrating with her hands splaying wide like a panorama. "A whole city!" She looks at me and shrugs. "Who knows where life will take us after I graduate."

My heart flips in my stomach at the thought, at the way she's watching me, at the fact that she sees *me* in the picture after graduation, sees a future where we might possibly move to my home city.

The ball is snapped on the field, and we all turn in time to watch the quarterback throw a perfect spiral to Clayton, giving him the touchdown he almost had on the play before.

We go wild, along with the rest of the stadium, and Erin jumps into my arms, pressing a celebration kiss to my lips that makes me wish for my little brother to get at least a dozen more touchdowns just like that one.

After the game — which we win by a landslide — we all go to our favorite family-owned sports bar for a late-night dinner. Clayton might as well be a celebrity for how many people want to shake his hand or take a picture with him or get his autograph when we walk through the door. He gets interrupted the whole time we're there, but I don't mind at all.

I'm so fucking proud of him, my chest is the size of a hot air balloon.

"Stop looking at me like that," he teases, his voice a deep baritone I'm not used to. He's grown up so fast, in the blink of an eye it seems, and that stubborn, cocky teenage attitude I had is settling in on him just the same. He's got longer hair now, dreaded and styled, and when a few girls walk by giggling, I laugh at the lazy-eyed smile he gives them.

If Palm South thought *I* was trouble...

"Like I'm proud of you?" I shrug. "No can do, little brother. Going to have to get used to it."

Clayton throws a French fry at me.

"Did you see the scouts?" Mom asks him, eating a sweet potato tot from her own plate. "This is the third game that one from Alabama has been to."

Clayton shrugs. "He can come to as many as he wants. I'm going to PSU."

"I love that you love my alma mater so much," I tell him, clapping a hand on his shoulder. "But there's nothing wrong with exploring options. Alabama is a D1 school."

"Doesn't matter. I know where I'm going. I've known since I was twelve," he says, meeting my eye.

The admiration there, the respect... it's enough to make my throat squeeze tight like there's a fist around it.

Erin smiles, leaning her head on my shoulder as she says, "Well, I for one think you've got your head on straight. Palm South is the best university there is."

"And they're going to be the best *football* team there is when I'm there," Clayton says.

The two of them high five across me, and Mom and I shrug, knowing that — at least for now — we've been beat.

I'm on a high after dinner, and with Clayton going out to celebrate with his friends and Mom going to sleep, it leaves only Erin and me. Once I confirm she's as far from sleepy as I am, I bundle her up and pack a few blankets, taking her to my favorite rooftop.

"Wait, wait, wait," she says through a mixture of laughter and tears around midnight. The moon is hidden behind thick, navy-gray clouds tonight, but it somehow illuminates her just enough for me to see that beautiful smile. "You're telling me that *you*," she says, pointing at me. "And *Skyler*?"

She laughs again before she can even get the rest of the sentence out.

I nod. "Yep. Right here," I say, patting the rooftop under our blanket. "It was her first time coming to Pittsburgh with me. She was single at the time, and so was I, and we were very, *very* drunk." He shrugs. "Everyone always asked if we had ever had feelings, I think we just got curious."

"And did you?" Erin asks, her voice a little tinged with something akin to jealousy. "Have feelings for her, I mean?"

"God, no," I say instantly, shaking my head. "Not like that, anyway. We made out, got about as far as me taking her shirt off, and then we both burst into laughter."

"Sounds like you two."

"We're best friends," I explain. "We've been through a lot of shit together. I'd kill anyone who hurt her, and I know she'd do the same for me."

"So I should call Kip and warn him?"

I sigh. "Don't get me started on that fiasco."

Erin chuckles, then crawls over from where she was reclining on the blanket to cuddle with me. "Okay. *Now* I'm cold," she says.

"We can go back to the hotel," I say softly in her ear, dragging the tip of my nose up her neck. "I know many ways to warm you right up."

"Mmmm," she says. "Yes, please. But let's stay here a while. This view..."

We both sweep our gazes over the city lights, the way they dance over the river and twinkle like stars all around us.

"You really think we could end up here one day?" I ask her after a while.

"I think it's as possible as staying in Florida. I mean, it's not like you're super in love with your job, right? And I could go anywhere after graduation."

"You know," I say. "I've been thinking about that, actually. My job. You know the account manager I work with, the one who hired me as her personal trainer?"

"Giselle, yeah?"

I nod. "Well, she thinks I might be onto something with my training and nutrition. She thinks I could open my own business."

Erin goes stiff in my arms, then turns to face me, her eyes wide. "Oh, my God. I can't believe I didn't think of that first."

"You really think I could do it?"

"Are you *kidding* me?" she asks, knocking on my abs like a wooden door to illustrate.

I laugh.

"Look at you! You know more about fitness and nutrition than anyone I know. I'm in the best shape of my life since we started dating, and I didn't even have to hire you."

I shrug. "I don't know."

"I do. And you have the graphic design skills, the coding experience to do a website. You might need to hire some help eventually, but you could get started on your own. For sure."

"Giselle said the same thing."

"Well, she's a smart woman." Erin kisses my cheek. "I can help you with a business plan."

"Will you be my sexy little lawyer on call, too?" I tease, biting her neck when she turns back around and leans into me.

"I'll wear your favorite pencil skirt and everything."

That earns her a moan from me, and she chuckles, but then goes silent for a long while.

"They're questioning me this week," she says.

I swallow. I don't have to ask who. The case has been slow going, but the detectives and lawyers have already questioned me, the girls, and the fucking assholes who raped Erin, as well as their disgusting friends. Who would go to bat for them, I can't imagine — but they have to be pure scum.

"You're going to crush it," I whisper.

"It's going to crush *me*," she whispers back.

I hold her tighter, kissing her neck and wrapping her up as much as I can, letting her know I have her, that she's safe, that it will all be okay.

"I just... what if we go through all this, and they win anyway? What if we go to court and the judge rules in their favor?" She pauses. "What if it doesn't even *make* it to court?"

"They won't win," I tell her. I don't say anything further. Those three words are everything she needs to know, everything I firmly believe.

"I love you," she whispers into the night, those words sweeping up on a soft breeze to caress my ears.

"I love you," I tell her. "And I'm proud of you, for stepping forward, for speaking out against them."

"I hope I don't regret it."

"No matter what happens, you shouldn't," I tell her. "Win or lose, court or no court — you're an example for other victims, an inspiration for other women to tell their stories, too."

Erin nods softly, but I don't miss the single tear that wells up and rolls down her right cheek.

I thumb it away, tilting her chin until she's facing me, and seal my admiration for her with a long kiss.

"So," I ask her, knowing she needs a break in the subject. "Will we live in the city, or the outskirts?"

"City, of course," she says. "How about that building there?"

She points at one across the city that I know costs at least a half-a-million dollars for a two-bedroom condo, but I nod anyway.

"Looks perfect."

Erin turns, wrapping her arms around my neck. "Perfect is wherever I am with you."

Cassie

I can't tell if Skyler wants to wrap me up in the biggest hug ever...

Or strangle me.

On the one hand, I know her heart is full that I'm taking a Little, that our family is growing, that our legacy in Kappa Kappa Beta will live on after we're gone. Erin never took the news well that I didn't want a Little, but Skyler supported me no matter what. Still, I know deep down she's always wanted me to take a Little, too, and I know she was ecstatic to hear I'd changed my mind.

On the other hand, I made her dress up like Ron from *Harry Potter* for the reveal.

With a gold and garnet scarf around her neck, a long black robe down to her knees, an orange wig, a stuffed toy rat in one hand, and a wand in the other — she looks absolutely adorable.

And also ready to kill me.

"She should be here soon," I promise Skyler, checking the time on my watch. "If she followed all the clues and spells correctly — which I have no doubt she did — we've got maybe ten minutes."

"I'm fine, Little," Skyler says, and her smile tells me maybe she *is* closer to wanting to crush me in a hug rather than cut off my oxygen supply.

"You really do look great."

She chuckles. "Your hair is ridiculous."

I laugh at that, touching the frizzy curls I pulled off to complete my Hermione look — thanks to an overwhelming amount of teasing and hairspray.

"You're excited," she says after a minute, that small smile holding firm.

I nod. "I really am. Tera is awesome. If anyone is going to take on our family number and reputation, I couldn't have asked for anyone better than her."

"She's lucky to have you for her Big."

I frown. "For a couple more months. Then, we both leave her."

A light flashes in Skyler's eyes at something behind me, and her smile grows. "Something tells me she'll be *just* fine."

We're on one side of the reflection pond, the water backlist and spraying up into the night, and when I turn to look where Skyler's gaze has fallen, I can't help but burst into laughter.

I set up a scavenger hunt of sorts for Tera all across campus, giving her clues of where to find hidden mystery items to complete her Harry Potter costume — like his glasses, a gold lightning bolt tattoo for her forehead, her robe, her Gryffindor scarf, and even a stuffed Hedwig. Along with finding the objects, she had to perform "spells" to random people I had in on the event in order to get her next clue.

And the last task? Defeat the cardboard Voldemort I had printed out and staged in the middle of the pond.

It looks like a scene out of a movie, the way her hair is flying back behind her, scarf in the wind, her wand held high as she banshee screams and runs through the water toward the cardboard cutout. In dramatic fashion, she stops right in front of him, the most determined look in her eyes, and then she holds her wand right to his nose and screams, "*Avada Kedavra!*"

When nothing happens, she pauses, breathing heavy and looking around.

So, I take my cue, sprinting from our hiding spot and splashing into the pond, too.

Tera's eyes light up at the sight of me, and to match her energy, I land a kick right to the cardboard cutout Voldemort's chest, bending him in half before he falls into the water.

Then, Tera and I are screaming and laughing and hugging and crying and all the memories of when I found out Skyler was *my* Big rush back to me in the most vicious, most beautiful flood.

"I'm so glad it's you!" Tera says when we pull back, both of our eyes glossy.

I sniff. "Welcome to the family, Little."

Skyler joins us then, and when Tera sees her, she covers her laugh before wrapping Skyler in a hug.

"A fine Ron Weasley you make, President."

"You can call me G-Big now," Skyler says, and when they're done hugging, she holds up her wand and says, "Now, what's the spell to make a very strong cocktail appear?"

We all laugh, already making our way out of the pond and waving to the spectators who had watched the scene. Some of them are snapping pics, so we pose with our soggy Voldemort and take a few of our own.

"Are we changing before we go out?" Tera asks.

"Absolutely not," Skyler answers. "Fully committed to the *Harry Potter* theme tonight. We need to look up a recipe for spiked butter beer and order it at Ralph's."

I wrinkle my nose. "Something tells me we can't trust any bartender at Ralph's to even remotely know how to make a drink that isn't three parts whatever alcohol you want and one part soda."

"Fair," Skyler concedes. "But we should try anyway."

"Oh! Before we change, I told Adam we'd video chat him," I say, pulling out my phone.

Tera is all bright smiles and red cheeks, and she, Skyler, and I cuddle in close to make sure we're all in frame as the phone rings. Skyler touches up her hair while Tera fixes her glasses on her nose, and then the screen connects.

"Merlin's beard!" Adam answers, completely on theme. "Looks like we've got ourselves a new Gryffindor."

"Hi, Adam! Nice to finally meet you," Tera says. "Virtually, anyway. I've heard so much about you."

"Same here, Tera. Welcome to the family."

There's a voice somewhere near Adam — a female voice — that makes my heart stop.

It's then that I notice his surroundings, a candlelit restaurant with plush, deep red booth-like seats and chandeliers hanging above him. Mahogany wood trims everything in sight, and he's not in his normal Alpha Sig polo, or in any of his chill clothes.

He's got on a suit and tie.

"Yes, it is! Here, come say hi," he answers to the girl, patting the seat next to him. A second later, she scoots over next to him and waves at us on the screen.

Which means she couldn't have been that far away to begin with.

"Hi, Cassie! Oh, my gosh. You guys look amazing!"

Skyler and Tera do some silly movements with their wands to get the full effect, but I just stand there, trying to remember to breathe, trying to force a smile.

Because I know without looking at myself in the screen that I look crazy right now — wild, frizzy hair, baggy cloak, puffy scarf around my neck.

But *she* — the girl with Adam — is the one who looks amazing.

Her dark hair is pin straight and hanging over her shoulders, her eyes lined like a cat's, and tinged with smoky eyeliner. Her lips are painted a blood red, spread wide to reveal her perfect, straight white teeth. I can't see everything she's wearing, but I *can* see her quite impressive cleavage and the thin black straps straining to hold said bosom in place.

Skyler gives me a look, and it's enough to make me clear my throat and remember to speak.

"Hi!" I say.

Simply.

Stupidly.

"I'm Chandler," the girl says. "Adam has told me *so* much about you. I can't wait to meet you when you come visit!"

"Same here," I manage, and it's not a complete lie. Adam *has* told me a lot about her, too. The part about not being able to wait to meet her, though...

"Chandler scored a free dinner at one of the nicest restaurants in town," Adam explains.

"It was a gift since we booked our dinner before our semi-formal here," Chandler adds. "But I didn't want to come to this fancy-schmancy steakhouse by myself, so I dragged your boyfriend here with me and told him we could talk business."

I force the most pathetic laugh of my life.

"Where are you girls off to now?" Adam asks.

"Ralph's, of course," Skyler says. And she must sense that I'm uncomfortable, must know that Tera is about two seconds away from knowing the same, so she grabs the phone from my hands and smiles wide at the screen. "And we better get going. So much to drink, so little time."

Adam chuckles. "Take care of my girl. And hey, Tera," he says, waiting for Skyler to put her on the screen again. "Nice to meet you. You picked the best Big there is."

Tera beams at me. "I know. I'm the luckiest Little."

The smile I wear is a little less forced then, my heart caught between surging with love and happiness, and breaking from jealousy and insecurity.

"I love you, babe," he says to me next, blowing me a kiss. "Call me tomorrow."

Skyler ends the call before I can get out my answer, and then she immediately loops her arms through mine and Tera's, taking up the middle. "Alright, bitches — let's party!"

She and Tera give a little hoot of approval, and then we're making our way across campus. Skyler holds up the conversation as we try to find a cab once we hit Greek Row, and when Tera runs inside the KKB house real quick to meet up with some of the other pledges and take some pictures, Skyler pulls me to the side in the yard.

"Hey, she's just a friend. Adam loves you. She is not a threat."

I nod, but almost start crying.

"He loves *you*," Skyler says again, holding my arms and searching my eyes.

"I know," I say. "But people cheat on the ones they love all the time."

Skyler frowns, pulling me in for a long hug. "He's not cheating on you. Okay? I promise. I know Adam. *You* know Adam. He could never."

I nod, sighing when she releases me from the hug. "I'm just being crazy."

"No, you're being *normal*. Long distance is hard."

Skyler's attempt at being strong dies with that, as if she's just remembered the distance between her and Kip — both literally and metaphorically — at this very moment.

She clears her throat. "Let's go out and have fun with your new *Little* tonight, okay? You can talk to him in the morning. Tell him how you're feeling. Let him clear your worries."

I blow out a breath. "You're right. I want to make sure Tera has the best night."

And then like we've summoned her, Tera is bolting across the yard, waving her wand around and saying random spells as we laugh and watch.

A cab pulls up. We all pile in.

And then we celebrate the new addition to our legacy.

Skyler

I plop into bed with a sigh heavier than any I've ever released in my life, freshly showered and bleary-eyed after a long, but fun, night out with the girls. My legs are sore from dancing, my throat sore from screaming, and I already know that regardless of not drinking a crazy amount, I'll have a headache in the morning.

But it was worth it.

Seeing Cassie take a Little, getting to know Tera more, celebrating with all our sisters as our sorority gets bigger and stronger… it's the best feeling in the world. Perhaps what touches my heart most is knowing I'm a part of it, knowing these are friendships that will last a lifetime, values that will settle in and help young women grow into professionals, maybe mothers or wives, maybe country leaders.

The possibilities are endless, and I get giddy when I think about how something so seemingly small — a sorority at a tiny private university — can have such huge impacts on so many lives.

On the world, really.

I didn't even bother getting dressed after my shower, and now I'm wishing I would have thought to plug in my phone to charge and shut off the light before collapsing, because it's going to take every ounce of energy I have left just to roll over and do those things before I pass out.

Except when I make my move and reach for my phone to plug it in, it vibrates in my hand.

And Kip's face fills the screen.

I swallow down the knot that immediately builds in my throat, pressing my free hand to my chest to try to ease my racing heart. We haven't talked in so long, and the only time I've seen his face was when I stole Bear's phone to stalk his Instagram and immediately regretted it.

I let it ring for a long time, debating just letting him hit voicemail.

But at the last second, I answer.

"Hello?"

There's a brief pause on the other end, and then a half-shocked, half-relieved sigh. "You answered."

I bite my lip. "Don't make me regret it."

He blows out a breath, and even though I can't see him, I can imagine him — the way he pinches the bridge of his nose, moving his glasses up in the process, and the way he runs his hands back through his hair, the way his eyes look when he's sad or distraught, how they somehow morph into an even deeper blue.

"What are you doing?" he asks after a moment. "It's late there. I thought you'd be asleep."

"It was Big/Little reveal. I just got home from Ralph's."

"Oh." I hear the hesitancy in his voice, the questions he wants to ask but doesn't dare — like if I was there with another guy, if I danced with another guy, if I kissed another guy, if I'm with another guy in any capacity.

It would kill him.

Just like the thought of him and Natalia has been killing me.

"So, Cassie did take a Little, huh? I bet you're excited."

"I am. She's sweet." I pause. "What do you want, Kip? Why did you call?"

He lets out another long, slow breath. "I called to tell you I'm sorry."

My shoulders deflate at the words.

"But not like I did before."

I sit up a little straighter in bed, pulling the sheets to my chest and waiting.

"Skyler, I hope you believed me when I said I never meant to hurt you, and that I was sorry that I did." He sighs. "But… I didn't fully hear you out. I was stubborn and didn't want to believe I'd done anything wrong, because I'd been so far up my own ass that I didn't stop to consider how my actions might be affecting other people around me. It's a good excuse, right? To feel like you don't have to apologize if you didn't do it intentionally? But I was wrong. I was so, so wrong."

I close my eyes against the tears building there.

"Not only was I wrong for not seeing your side, for not agreeing with you because you were right — if it were me in your shoes, I would have felt the same way. Hell, I would have been even angrier, I wouldn't have been nearly as controlled as you." He pauses. "And you were right about Natalia."

My heart squeezes so painfully in my chest that I can't help the choked sob that rips free from me. To see the picture of them together was enough pain to last me a lifetime, but if he's called now to tell me they're together, to tell me I was right about them…

I'll fucking die.

I will *die*.

"The other night, we got together for a mini premiere night. It was for cast and crew to watch the series before it hits the small screen."

I can already feel it, my body breaking down, because I know he's about to tell me that something happened that made him realize his feelings for her.

Bile rises in my throat.

"The show is good, Sky," he whispers. "It's so fucking good."

I want to tell him I'm proud of him, that I'm happy for him, but every word — every *breath* is lodged in my throat.

"We were on such a high afterward, and we decided to go out. We were at this rooftop club. The music was going, we were all dancing and drinking and…"

My stomach turns again, and I double over on myself, squeezing my eyes shut against the burning urge to cry. Images of Natalia dancing with him, her ass grinding against his crotch, his hands on her waist…

I want to beg him to stop. I want to beg him to hang up and cut me out of his life and just leave me to rot without him.

I can't handle it.

I can't take this pain.

"She said she needed air, needed a break, and asked me to go with her. We went to this little corner garden with benches and a fountain, and we were just sitting there, talking, looking out over the skyline." He pauses. "And then… she kissed me."

I can't fight against it this time, the guttural cry that rips free from me, the tears that pour down, the ugly sobs that free themselves.

"Skyler, baby, don't cry," Kip pleads, and I swear he sounds like he's in just as much pain as I am, like hearing me cry is a dagger to his chest.

I can't even catch my breath long enough to tell him not to call me baby, not to coddle me as he breaks my heart.

"I saw it then," he says. "I saw everything you'd been telling me, everything I'd been ignoring, everything I'd said was innocent even when I knew deep down that it was suspicious, that it was maybe a hair too much."

"Kip, please," I finally manage to beg. "Please, stop. I can't breathe. I can't…" My next sentence is robbed by another painful squeeze of my chest.

"I know. I'm so fucking sorry, Sky. I didn't want to tell you, but I knew I had to. I wanted to be upfront and clear about everything. If I stand another chance at having you, at getting back into your heart, there can't be any secrets between us."

Those words make me pause, though my rib cage is still painfully tight around my lungs. "What?"

"I'm sorry," he says again. "I should have listened to you. I should have respected you. I should have sat Natalia down and had a conversation with her about professionalism, about drawing a clear, dark boundary so she understood. More than anything, I should have been there to pick you up." His voice catches. "I should have been there. And I'll live every day of my life regretting that I wasn't."

I sniff. "I don't understand. What happened between you two? After... after she kissed you?" My stomach knots.

Kip blows out a breath. "Well, I grabbed her arms and pushed her back to stop her. She basically said I was fighting it and she knew I wanted her too, which I immediately informed her was a gross misinterpretation."

My chest kicks in my chest, and I can't help but feel a small twinge of petty victory.

"I told her she'd been drinking and needed to sleep it off, then the next day, I sat her down and told her it was out of line. She was pissed," he adds. "But I was disappointed more than anything. Disappointed that I didn't see it, that I'd hurt you, that she was the star of my first show, that she plays the most amazing woman in the world, the woman I love, and I can't go back and change that now."

I swallow. "You can't go back and change it," I finally say. "And maybe it happened for a reason. You said it's good, right?"

"It is," he admits. "But now, it all just feels... tainted."

I nod, even though he can't see me, because I can only imagine how contrary those feelings must be — pride and shame all at once.

"I don't ever want to work with her again," he says after a while. "And I don't plan on it. I just wish I would have seen it sooner. I wish..." He curses. "God, I wish so many things. Most of all that I was with you, right now, holding you in my arms and looking into your eyes when I tell you that I love you, that I'm truly, *truly*, sorry, and that I'm begging you to give me another chance."

His words release another wave of tears, but they're silent, slipping down my tears like assassins in the night.

"Will you ever forgive me?"

I swallow down a sob, and it takes me a long while before I can answer.

"I want to," I admit, my voice raspy and strained. My heart is already breaking before I say the words. "But I don't know how."

My face warps with the admission, with the truth that Kip has hurt me so much — possibly past the point of fixing. But it's the truth.

And if there are no more secrets between us, then I won't keep one, either.

"You know more than anyone how hard it is for me to trust," I say. "How hard it was for me to trust *you* again, specifically, after what happened with your dad and Vegas and... just... *everything*."

"I know. I know," he says, and I wait for more, but he doesn't say anything else.

"I love you," I whisper. "But I've forgiven you once. I... I don't know if I can do it again."

I hear something on the other end, something that sounds like a restrained cry, like a grunt of a grown man trying to hold it together when he's on the verge of breaking down.

For a long while, we sit on the phone together. Sometimes it's just breathing, sometimes one of us is crying, sometimes it's more silent than a desert in the middle of the night.

After what feels like an eternity, Kip speaks.

"Hold onto us, Skyler," he pleads, his voice rough. "You know me. You know my love for you. Hold onto that. Hold on."

I close my eyes, sending one last set of hot tears rolling down my cheeks.

And though my heart surges in my chest with the urge to do what he's asking, and I can already feel every molecule of my being latching onto him, onto our memories, onto everything I know and love and trust in him, I end the call and force myself to make peace with the truth.

It's over.

EPISODE 4

Erin

There's something iniquely horrifying about reliving sexual abuse.

For years, I've blocked out that night — the shock of it, the pain, the embarrassment. I've blocked it out so hard, so fiercely, that it almost feels as if it never happened at all.

Did I imagine it, the way I'd felt more drunk than usual, the way the chandelier light spun and spun above me as we danced at semi-formal? Did I imagine the way Landon's warm eyes turned cold, the way he gripped my wrist when he pulled me back to that room, his brothers following us? Was it all a dream that I sensed something was off, that I got uncomfortable when his friends started touching me, kissing me... that I tried to fight... tried to leave?

Sometimes, it feels like it. It feels like it happened to someone else, or never happened at all.

But reliving it with a room full of lawyers and detectives, it was more real than it ever had been.

The questions they asked, the notes they took, the looks they gave me... it was the perfect combination to split open the carefully constructed cast I'd worn all this time. I relived it all — the feeling of being unknowingly drugged, the confusion of being dragged away from the ballroom, the fear when I felt them all moving in on me, their laughter and soft words of assurance that everything was fine like the most vivid nightmare.

Candice, my lawyer, begins to silently cry when I tell the room how Landon slapped me when I tried to run for the door, how he threw me on the pool table hard enough to knock the breath from me, how he wasn't the first to molest me — but rather, he held me down, his hands bruising my arms as one of his friends took the first turn.

No, not one of his friends. Not a nameless brother.

I list out their names in order of how they raped me — Nick Simmons, Daniel Cole, Landon Turner, and last, Aiden Harrison.

There is a young girl with the lawyers of the boys who raped me. From the way she's taking notes and listening intently to every move Landon's lawyers make, I gather that she must be an intern or a new employee.

Her eyes well with tears, too, when I tell the room how I cried through the first one, begging them to stop, but that when Daniel pushed inside me and I knew there was no stopping them, I fell silent. I numbed out. I grasped onto the only survival mechanism I could in that moment, which was to just hold onto that pool table and wait for them to be done, wait for them to finish.

And silently pray that they would leave me alive in the end.

I didn't know if they would, at the time. I wondered if they'd kill me, if those terrible moments of embarrassment and pain would be my last.

And in that moment, telling that room full of people what had happened to me, I knew every detail was true — down to the painting of a mermaid sitting on the edge of a sailboat, which I had stared at while they raped me, holding her gaze, letting the anchor she sat beside anchor me, too.

The room is quiet when I finish, and I hold my head high, looking each of them in the eye. I answer all their questions — clarifying timelines and terms, repeating names, explaining *again* why I didn't go to the police immediately, why I didn't get a rape kit, why none of my friends knew until very recently.

By the time we finish, I'm so tired I could pass out on the spot.

"Thank you, Erin," Candice says, her eyes still red as she leans over to squeeze my wrist.

My mind goes fuzzy after that, a blur of legal jargon as they explain to me that the process of arresting the offenders is complex, and this is only one step. They inform me that should Landon or any of the other offenders try to contact me, I should call the police immediately, and that they'll keep me informed on what happens next.

After a formal goodbye handshake with each of them, I excuse myself, and as soon as I'm out of the door, my legs begin to shake, all the adrenaline that had been coursing through me leaving my body at once.

I stare at the tile floor as my heels click along it, and in its natural fashion, my mind begins to erase the last couple of hours. I feel it almost like a black wall of steel slowly stretching toward the sky and blocking that part of my memory, as if to say *you don't need to see this, let's just leave it in the past where it belongs.*

When I make it to my car, I shut the door and stare at the steering wheel for a long time. I'm supposed to go to therapy, but all I want is to go home.

No, all I want is to go to Clinton.

But I know after such a traumatic event, therapy is the best place I can go. I know I can't just leave it all buried, can't ignore it, can't pretend like nothing is happening or never happened in the past. I have to face it, sit with it — no matter how uncomfortable it is.

So, I fire up the engine and make my way across town.

***

I'm about five minutes late to the meeting, thanks to South Florida traffic and a random thunderstorm. So I rush inside with my hair a frizzy mess, not bothering with an umbrella now that it's just a drizzle. I take my usual seat as quietly as I can, trying not to interrupt the person talking — a young boy, newer addition, talking about his addiction. I give him my full attention the moment I'm seated, even as I smooth out my damp clothes and try to fix my hair a bit.

When he finishes speaking, Jackie, our therapy leader, smiles and thanks him for sharing.

There's a brief moment of silence, some of the other attendees offering words of encouragement to the young man, and I take the opportunity to fully settle in, letting my gaze wander the room to see who's here tonight.

And that's when I see him.

How I walked in without sensing him, without feeling those brazen eyes on me, I don't understand. I could blame it on the afternoon I've had, I suppose, but even that shouldn't have kept me from noticing my ex sitting in the same chair he used to, right across the circle from me.

Smiling.

Smiling, as if he never left.

Smiling, as if he didn't leave me with nothing but a note to explain.

Smiling, his eyes heated, ankle crossed over his knee and leather-jacket-clad arms folded across his chest like he owns the place.

Like he still owns *me*.

Gavin's sky blue eyes watch me unabashedly as I gape back at him, and it's only when Jackie says my name that I snap out of what I convince myself *must* be a daydream.

"How are you this evening?" she asks.

"I..." I swallow. "I'm fine."

Jackie gives me a sympathetic smile. "Do you want to talk about what happened today? I believe you told us last week that you were meeting with the lawyers and detectives. How did it go?"

I open my mouth to answer, to do what I came here to do, but then my eyes snap back to Gavin, and I have to zip my lips closed again to keep them from trembling.

He's not smiling anymore.

I want to scream at him. I want to demand answers. I want to punch him in his stupid face and throw him out of *my* safe place and tell him to never come back.

I want to ask him why he left.

I want to tell him his letter wasn't enough.

I want to make him feel the way he broke me.

But more than anything, I want to get far, *far* away from him.

"I'm sorry," I say, shaking my head and immediately reaching down for my purse. I don't offer any other explanation before I'm heading for the door, and I don't take my next breath until I'm through it.

I know Jackie will tell the room that it's okay, that I'll be alright, that she'll check in on me – and she will. I know I'll have a call from her likely as soon as session is over. She'll move on and ask someone else to share because that's what has to be done.

She won't press me to stay.

That's what I love about her.

The rain has mostly stopped when I push out into the evening air, warm and humid, the sky quickly fading from gray to deep navy as night settles in. I fumble in my purse for my keys, the familiar *beep beep* of my car unlocking hitting my ears right before an even more familiar voice calls my name.

"Erin," Gavin repeats when I don't stop, and his footsteps splash through the puddles behind me as he jogs to catch up. "Hey, please, wait."

"You don't get to ask a damn thing of me," I say, whirling on him. I point my finger right in his face – his face that is far too close for my taste. "You don't get to show back up here, in *my* space, in my *life*. I don't know why you're here, why you're back, and I don't want to know. Okay? So just fuck off."

The words shock me more than him when they roll off my tongue with ease, but I hold my chin high as I turn on my heels and set for my car again.

"I'm sorry."

I stop at the sound of those words, but I don't turn. I just stand there with my hand on the smooth metal handle of my car door, waiting.

"I'm sorry I left like that. I'm sorry I did that to you. I'm sorry for..." He sighs. "For everything."

Tears burn my eyes.

"I can explain, if you'll give me the chance."

I shake my head. "No."

"Please," he begs, and I feel his hand warm on my shoulder before I shrug it off.

I turn on him then. "How dare you," I spit.

"Don't be like this. I care about you, Erin. I know you still care about me."

"That's where you're wrong."

Even as I say the words, they burn as only lies do. I *do* care about him. I *do* want him to be okay. But I also want him to leave me the hell alone.

"I know I hurt you, but if you just give me another chance—"

"No," I say, more firmly than the last time. "I'm sorry, Gavin, but I've moved on and you should, too."

I open my car door, slipping inside and slamming the door shut. Gavin stands there dumbfounded for a moment, the drizzle soaking his shirt and jacket before he taps on my window.

I grit my teeth but roll it down just an inch.

"Moved on, huh?" he asks, hurt evident in his voice. "It's Bear, isn't it?"

I don't answer.

Which is answer enough.

He laughs. "Well, that was fast."

"Goodbye, Gavin."

"Wait," he says, slipping his fingers in the gap my rolled-down window has made.

He must trust me an awful lot more than I trust myself to think I won't smash his fingers.

"It doesn't have to be romantic. It doesn't have to be anything more than..." He pauses, blowing out a breath. "Can I take you for a drink? Please."

I swallow, my chest tight and heavy with all the things left unsaid and unfinished between us.

"Maybe another time," I whisper, but when our eyes meet through the crack, I know he sees what I'm really saying.

Never going to happen.

His jaw is tight when he withdraws his fingers, and I roll up my window and peel out of the parking lot without a glance in my rearview mirror.

I don't even tell Clinton I'm coming, just burst through his front door when I finally make it to his house. He's on the couch watching a basketball game, a full plate of chicken and veggies in his lap.

One look at me, and the plate is tossed aside.

He runs to me, swooping me into his arms as the first sob chokes through me.

"It's okay," he promises. "I'm here."

And with that permission, I fully let go.

Adam

"This is fucking horse shit!" I bang my fists on the wooden table for emphasis, rattling the entire thing and causing half-a-dozen students to startle at the sound.

"Shhh!" the librarian immediately scolds, her brows folded hard as she shakes her head. She points her bony finger at me as one last warning — likely because this isn't my first outburst in the last four hours, but she's saying it'll be my last, or else.

I murmur an apology before letting my head fall into my hands again, digging my palms into my eyes enough that I see colors behind the lids. I suppress the urge to groan, to growl, to flip the fucking table and try to force a calming breath.

This is supposed to be the easy part.

It's November. I'm supposed to be coasting after fighting with the alums and the exec board, supposed to be watching all the fruits of our labor come together, supposed to be taking my hands off and letting these brothers ride their metaphorical bikes on their own, supposed to be more focused on planning what Cassie and I will do when she visits for Thanksgiving than anything Alpha Sigma related.

Instead, I'm nose deep in books far too thick with words far too big explaining policies far too complicated — all because the alumni brothers decided to be twats.

"Wow," a voice purrs over me. I look up to find Chandler smirking, her fingers toying with a few pages of one of the books spread out around me. "I haven't seen this much fun since senior year Spring Break."

I try to smile, but know it falls flat as I slump back in my chair.

Chandler chuckles, shrugging off her small backpack and tossing it on the table before taking the chair next to me. She peers over at the book currently splayed at the center. "Aspen University Student Organized Event Policies," she reads, arching a brow at me.

"Don't even ask."

"Too late."

I sigh, sitting up a little straighter as the back of my hand slaps against the open pages. "I've been working with the brothers on an event that will hopefully help put them back on the map — an Anything But Clothes Bubble Bonfire." I pause when Chandler has to fight back a smile. "Hey, they came up with it, alright? And honestly, as cheesy as it sounds, they've been working their asses off and it's going to be a kickass event. They got a popular band on campus to come play, have an epic set up for the bonfire, all these different seating areas and photo ops, plus a foam pit."

"Girls *do* love a foam pit."

"And the theme being Anything But Clothes? Can you even imagine?"

She laughs. "I know me and my sisters would have been *all* over that."

"Everyone on Greek Row is talking about it, and the guys are so stoked." I sigh. "They're going to be crushed when I tell them it can't happen."

Chandler frowns. "Why not?"

"Apparently, there's some policy that states that student-run events can't have any kind of open fire. I mean, I get it," I added. "It's Colorado. And even though we're out of fire season, I'm sure they don't want some fraternity event causing the next wildfire that runs rampant across the Rockies."

"Is it an open fire?"

"I guess," I say, waving my hand at the books. "That's what the asshole alumni guys I've been working with explained to me this morning. I've been digging through these books all afternoon trying to find the exact law, but so far, nothing. I figure there's got to be a loophole, or some way we can still have the event but be in line with the policy."

Chandler frowns even deeper, and then she scoots her chair in closer to the table and digs her laptop out of her bag. I watch as she types in the university website, fingers clicking away a lot faster than I can type.

"What are you doing?"

"Helping," she says easily.

"You don't have to do that. It's Friday, I'm sure—"

"I've got nothing to do," she says with a look that tells me she's not too happy about that fact. "Besides, you helped me once. Remember?"

Her eyes find mine, and the smile we share is one I imagine only kids caught between being in college and being an adult could really understand.

"You can leave at any time," I say as I turn back to the books.

"Shut up and keep digging."

Silence envelops the library again, other than the soft sounds of students whispering, typing, and flipping pages. Every now and then, Chandler will pause me to show me something, or I'll show her something, but we never quite find what we're looking for.

Until...

"Aha!" she says — loud enough that the new librarian on shift gives her a look. She apologizes before moving her laptop over closer to me and whispering, "Look at this."

I follow her cursor, reading to myself. When I finish, I sigh, pushing back in my chair again.

"So it *is* a real rule." I shake my head. "I mean, not that I doubted it, but I hoped there would be a way. Stones around the fire or... or... a number of fire extinguishers on hand, buckets of water, something."

"Adam, you didn't read it all."

I frown, looking at a smiling Chandler before I lean forward again. She lets me take the laptop from her, and I scroll down until I see the starred amendment at the bottom.

The amendment that says bonfire events may be approved by the Student Union so long as the following requirements are met and sufficient paperwork is provided.

The article goes on to list out the requirements — and just like I thought, it's all things we can manage.

"I fucking knew it!"

"Shhh!"

Chandler and I bite back our laughs as we apologize, yet again, to the librarian. Then, we huddle closer as we look through the website.

"Okay, so we just need to make sure the fire is contained within a permanently structured area — easy enough, we could have it be a new addition to the house — and have a hose hooked up to the house for emergency." I shake my head, and when I turn to Chandler, we're nearly nose to nose. "Holy shit, you figured it out."

"*We* figured it out," she says, and as if she realizes how close we are, she clears her throat and sits back in her chair. Her hand sweeps out over the screen. "So, once you get those things taken care of and provide the paperwork and proof? You'll be good to go."

"Thank God," I say, pushing her laptop back toward her. "Can you email that to me? I'll get started in the morning." I pause. "*After* a round of very stiff drinks tonight."

She chuckles. "You got it."

"Thank you," I say earnestly.

"No problem," she insists, her cheeks turning a soft shade of pink.

"Is there any way I can repay you?"

"Well, I kind of owed you, anyway," she reminds me. "But... if you insist, how about not letting me hang out alone on a Friday night?" Her eyes meet mine then. "I'm so sick and tired of being the old girl on campus with no real friends."

I bark out a laugh at that. "You are *far* from old."

"Tell that to these eighteen-year-old bitches."

Another laugh from me before I look at my phone, frowning at the time. "I'm supposed to have a video chat date night with Cassie in about an hour."

When I look up at Chandler again, it's just in time to see her playful smile slip, her eyes going back to her laptop as she sends off the email before closing the lid. "Oh," she says, forcing a smile again and waving me off. "Well, consider us even, then. I've got some shows to catch up on, anyway."

She's already packing her things away, but I sigh, because I know exactly how she's feeling. It *does* feel weird, to be too old to party and be a student, but too young to be an adult. It's the strangest in-between, and being in a new place with no friends...

Well, it's lonely.

"Wait," I tell her, stopping her before she can stand. "Let me just step out and call Cassie. We can reschedule."

Chandler shakes her head. "No, no, don't do that, I'm sure she's looking forward to it."

"We talk all the time," I assure her. "And I'm going to see her in just a couple weeks. She'll understand."

Chandler bites her lip. "You're sure?"

"Positive. Give me a sec."

We walk out of the library together after putting away all the books I'd strewn out, and then I excuse myself to the corner of the building, cursing against the biting cold as I find Cassie's contact and let my thumb drop on the screen.

"Hey, babe," she answers. "I thought we had another forty-five minutes."

"We did. Uh, *do*. Um..." I grab the back of my neck, casting a look at Chandler. "Hey, would you mind if we rescheduled?"

A pause on the other end was my only answer.

"I can explain later, but a friend just helped me out of a bind, and... well, again, I can explain later. But if you're cool with it, could we have our date tomorrow night instead?"

The silence is long before Cassie finally says, "Sure. I mean... Yeah, I don't see why not." She pauses again. "Who's the friend?"

"It's Chandler, the one you met when we video chatted after Big/Little reveal." I let out a breath of a laugh that fogs in the cold night air. "She literally just saved my ass. I owe her a drink."

"Oh."

I smirk, narrowing my eyes as I turn even more so Chandler can't read my lips or overhear. "Is someone *jealous*?"

"No!" A pause. "I just... you promise she's just a friend?"

I don't mean to laugh, and by the way Cassie screams my name when I do, I know it's an asshole mistake. "I'm sorry," I say, still laughing. "It's just, the fact that you think I've got eyes for literally any other woman but you is hysterical."

"You're a prick," she says, but I can tell by the way she says it that she's smiling, too. "I'm sorry. Of course, you should go have fun. I know you don't know anyone there, and I'm glad y'all have become friends. I just..."

"You miss me," I finish for her. "And I miss you, too. And if it'll ease your mind, I'll tell you a million times. She's just a friend. You are the love of my life. You have nothing to worry about."

She sighs. "That does help."

"I love you," I say softly. "Call you in the morning?"

"Text me later tonight," she says. "When you're home."

I chuckle. "Yes, ma'am."

"And Adam?"

"Yeah?"

"Have fun."

I blow her a kiss through the phone before we both hang up.

Ashlei

Balling up another Dove chocolate wrapper with my left hand, I close one eye and stick my tongue out, aiming for the ceramic decorative bowl on the coffee table.

"She lines up the shot," I say softly. "And... she shoots!"

With a flick of my wrist, the blue and silver foil wrapper goes flying.

And completely misses the coffee table altogether.

I blow out a breath through flat lips, looking at the empty bowl and the tiny foil balls littered all around it. Then, I look at the TV, at the rerun of *America's Top Model*, and then out the window at the palm trees swaying in the breeze along the beach.

Sighing, I grab another piece of chocolate.

I know without a mirror that I look as pathetic as I feel, and I wish with everything in me that I could snap out of my pity party and get back to the bad bitch I was before the accident. So far, I've only been able to pull myself together long enough to go to work, give it all the energy I had, and then come home and cry about the fact that I can't go to the pole studio.

Not that I haven't been invited.

Karen has called me almost every day, has even popped by unannounced a few times, saying the girls miss me and they'd love to have me back — even if just to coach from the sidelines until I'm well enough to get back on the pole.

But she doesn't understand how much even the thought of that scenario breaks me.

To be watching and unable to *do*, to coach without being able to *show*, to have this vital part of me ripped away... possibly forever...

It's been akin to losing a lung, each breath reminding me that I'm closer to death.

I'm close to being able to start PT — or so my doctor says. But I'm healing slower than he first anticipated, and every time I hear him tack another week on the end of my sentence, despair creeps in and grabs ahold of me tighter and tighter.

I thought I knew heartbreak, thought I knew depression.

I've never known any kind of pain quite like this.

A whistle shakes me from my thoughts, my unfocused eyes drifting from the TV screen to where Brandon is standing at the edge of the hallway. He's freshly showered after his long run this morning, his short hair damp and glistening, gray sweatpants hanging deliciously off his hips. Without a shirt on, I have a front row show to the phenomena that is his abdomen, with his pecs and biceps a solid opening act.

"I didn't know I was dating a basketball star," he muses with a grin, eyeing the wrappers all over the ground.

"Watch out, Lebron James."

He chuckles, arching a brow at the TV as he makes his way across the room to the couch. He plops down next to me, carefully pulling me into him while being mindful of my shoulder. "So, what was wrong with her?" he asks, nodding to the model now wrapped in a blanket and looking pale as hell at the judging ceremony.

"Food poisoning," I explained. "But look, she still showed up."

"Think it'll gain points with Tyra?"

"It should. She nearly died and still got her ass to work." My heart sinks, and then against every ounce of willpower I have, tears burn my eyes.

Brandon notices immediately, and he looses a breath, tucking me closer as he balances his chin on the crown of my head. "It's going to be okay."

"When?" I manage on a shaky whisper.

The question breaks me — even more so when Brandon just holds me tighter in answer.

He doesn't know.

No one does.

"Will you take a walk with me?" he asks after a while.

I groan, but before I can reject, he pulls back and meets my eyes with his.

"Please?"

I sigh. "That's not fair. I can't say no to you when you look like that."

"Then say yes."

I do a little temper tantrum flail, whine, and then concede, letting him help me up off the couch.

Once I'm dressed in shorts and a tank top, Brandon and I take the elevator down to the lobby and push out into the pleasantly warm morning. Fall in Florida may not be cold, but there's a break from the humidity, and the temperature hanging in the mid-seventies with little puffy white clouds and an otherwise blue sky make me smile in gratitude.

Brandon takes my hand as we cross the street to the park, a lush, green patch of land with running trails along the water and right to the beach. This was where we ran into each other in the spring, when he was trying to pretend like he didn't still want me.

The prick.

He smooths his thumb over my wrist as our hands swing gently between us. "I know it seems like your world has crashed down around you," he says, eyes on the water, then his shoes, then me before doing the circle all over again. "It's hard not to lose hope when something so important has been taken away from you."

"It is," I agree, but already just being outside has my soul feeling lighter, my heart a little less tight. "But thank you for being here for me. For *always* being here for me. I..." I swallow at the truth of what I'm about to say. "I honestly don't think I could do this without you. I think if I had lost pole in the spring when I'd just lost you, I... I..."

I couldn't finish the sentence.

Brandon squeezes my hand tighter, and then leads us to a little bench in the shade under a wide oak. Spanish moss hangs from the limbs, and I stare at the sun rays peeking through it as we listen to the waves, to the people, to the soft sounds of a Sunday morning.

"You'll never have to do anything without me," he promises after a moment. "I'll be by your side through PT, and when you go back to the studio and no doubt come home frustrated every night until you're doing the tricks you were before the accident."

I chuckle. "God, I will try my best *not* to be a nightmare, but..."

Brandon smiles, and it's then that I see it — the worry etched in his features, the way his hands are trembling slightly.

"What's wrong?" I ask him.

"Nothing," he lies.

"Brandon..."

"Nothing is wrong, Ashlei," he says, his eyes meeting mine. "And that's just the thing, isn't it? When I'm with you, when we're together, it doesn't matter what we're facing. Everything feels right. Everything feels... whole."

I smile, looping my arm through his and laying my head on his shoulder. "I love you."

He's silent for a long time, and again we sit and enjoy the sun's warmth, the ocean's breeze, the feeling of being together — even when things suck.

And then, out of nowhere, he says the absolute last thing I expected.

"Let's elope."

I balk, sitting up ramrod straight so I can look at him and make sure it isn't some sick joke. But when I meet his gaze, it's as serious and level as if he'd just made a business proposal.

"What?"

"Let's elope," he repeats, turning to fully face me and folding his hands in mine. "Ashlei, I know without a fragment of doubt that you're it for me. You're the one. You're *my* one. I want you and me, forever, and I want it right now. I want to put the biggest fucking diamond rock on your finger so everyone knows it, and I want to marry you somewhere far away where it's just the two of us, and I want to make love to you on a tropical shore, and I..." He swallows. "I want you to say yes. I want you to pack up what you need right now, today, and I want to be on a jet or my yacht by dinnertime."

"Why by dinnertime?"

"So I can marry you in the morning."

My heart is beating so furiously in my chest that I have to steal one of my hands from Brandon to press it against the bones, trying to soothe, trying to calm.

"Tell me what you're thinking," he begs.

I sniff against the tears welling in my eyes. "I'm thinking I can't say no to you when you look like that."

"So say yes."

I laugh, nodding as tears slip free. "Yes."

"Yes?"

Another laugh as I climb into his lap and kiss him all over, not even caring when he points out that I'm not supposed to lift my arm that high to rest around his neck. "Yes. Yes, right now. Yes, forever. What do I pack? When do we leave?"

He slams a kiss hard to my mouth, holding the back of my head in his palm as we breathe each other in.

The kiss grows deeper and more urgent the longer we sit there, until Brandon finally helps me up off the bench and we half walk, half run back to the condo. It doesn't take long to pick the place, and though I know we're forgetting things we'll need, we decide we don't care as we haphazardly pack our bags in twenty minutes' time.

And then we're boarding the yacht and sailing off into the horizon.

Jess

"Shit," I murmur to myself as I scurry along the side of the dance floor being built. Or should I say, the dance floor that *was* being built... before the entire crew we hired for the event decided to go on strike.

Literally.

"Everything okay?" Brittany asks when I pass her. She's looking over something on the iPad with our intern — likely the bride's instructions for centerpieces or the seating chart.

The smile I force comes too naturally, and it scares me a little how easy the lie spills. "Yep! Right on schedule. You good here? Need me?"

She waves me off. "No, just going to wrap this up and then we're both leaving. You should go, too. You'll need rest for tomorrow."

"I just have to check on a few more things and then I'm out."

She nods to excuse me, and when she's back in the works with the intern, I resume my cursing as I run back to the kitchen where the owner of the event company we hired is desperately trying to get her crew to stop packing up their things.

"We told you," one of the guys says when I push through the swinging doors. "Meet our demands, or we're out. You thought we were bluffing. Well, now you know we're not."

"Jeremiah, we can discuss this at the office on Monday," the owner tries to say — calmly, especially now that I've made myself present. "But right now, we have half a dance floor to assemble, chairs and tables to set up, lighting, and—"

"And you can do it yourself," one of the other guys says, which earns him some enthusiastic agreement from his comrades.

I watch in horror as this fight continues on, something about Christmas bonuses being canceled this year, as well as them having to work all through the holidays, plus some murmurings about what they're being paid. Whatever is going on, the crew isn't happy.

And no matter how hard the owner, Sammi, begs them, they don't go back into the ballroom I need turned into a glamorous wedding venue by the morning.

They all just leave.

Sammi sighs when it's just the two of us alone, pinching the bridge of her nose and muttering something that sounds like a prayer in a language I don't recognize under her breath before she turns to me with a dazzling smile.

"Well," she says, and I wait for the solution.

But instead, she just throws her hands up, let's them clap down on her thighs, and starts crying.

Another curse word finds my tongue.

"It's okay," I soothe her, running a hand along her back.

She blubbers something about being a failure and how her father is going to gut her like a fish, and as much as I feel for her, as much as I would comfort her even more if I was her friend, the fact of the matter is that I'm the woman who hired her.

And now I'm in a bind.

"Why don't you go home, talk to your dad, figure out what can be done to get your crew happy again, okay?"

She sniffs. "What about you? What about the wedding in the morning?"

I tongue my cheek, but force a smile against my urge to scream. "I'll handle it."

"Are you sure? I... I can stay to help, I can—"

"Go," I insist again, already shoving her toward the back hallway that her entire crew left through. "Just leave all your supplies and I'll... figure it out." *God help me.* "Can I call if I have questions?"

"Of course, but—"

"You're not going to be any help to me or anyone like this," I interrupt before she can argue again. "Go work through whatever needs to be worked through. It won't ruin our relationship with you, okay? We'll give you another chance, but you've *got* to get your crew happy."

She nods, nearly bursting into tears again when I tell her she'll have another chance. In this industry, a mishap like this can be the difference between a booming business booked every weekend, and a sad sap going door to door at event agencies begging for work.

I don't want to be the one to hang her up to dry.

But I also have to do *my* job.

As soon as Sammi leaves, Brittany pops her head into the kitchen. "Alright, we're heading out." She frowns, looking around the empty space. "I thought I saw the crew come back here. I was going to tell them they need to move the dance floor about seven inches to the left. It's not going to be center with the stage."

"They just took a quick break to eat," I explain. "Ran down to their favorite restaurant. Don't worry, I'll stick around until they get back."

She arches a brow. "You sure?"

"I got this," I assure her. "I want to take a second look at the cake, anyway, and you know how picky I am when it comes to table runners. I just want to make sure it's all in order, then I'm out the door. Promise," I added when she went to argue with me.

"Okay, but don't stay too late." She sighs, shaking her head. "A *morning* wedding. Who does that? I'm already crying thinking about setting my alarm for three AM."

My smile is tight. "You and me both."

With a salute, my boss leaves, and then I'm alone.

"Motherfucking shit balls!" I scream, grinding my teeth as I lean back against the countertop. I tap my fingers on the edge of the granite, thinking.

The wedding is huge — two-hundred-and-sixty guests, plus all the vendors. There's no way I can set up the tables, chairs, linens, centerpieces, and dance floor by myself. I'd be lucky to get even half done before Brittany showed back up in the morning.

I sigh, pulling out my phone and dialing the first person I can think of who might be able to help.

Which, coincidentally, happens to be the last person who was inside me.

The phone rings and rings, but Jarrett doesn't pick up. I debate just hanging up but decide I don't have time for pride right now.

"Hey, I need your help. I'm texting you an address now. Can you grab some of your coworkers or a couple buddies and help me with some event set up? I can pay. Long story but... I'm in a bind."

I don't know what else to say, so I hang up and text the address.

As soon as I do, Jarrett texts back with a line of question marks. Then, he texts *Is this where I should go when I'm ready to ravage you after the rally?*

The rally.

Shit.

I close my eyes and force a breath as I text back *Going to be honest, completely forgot about the rally. Disregard my voicemail and have a good time. Text me after.*

Jarrett asks if everything is okay next, to which I lie and say of course. His agency is running a rally downtown for the guy they want to support in the next election for mayor. I know how important it is for him, and how hard he's been working on it. I can't steal him away just because my vendor left me in hot water.

My stomach twists as I pull up my next option — who would have been the first person I called, if I'm being honest with myself, had I not been avoiding him for weeks.

I just don't know how to face him, now that I've spent time with Jarrett.

I don't know how to tell him that I still have really intense feelings for his brother.

I don't know how to tell him that I might...

No, I think to myself, shaking my head. *These thoughts can wait for another night.*

Before I can talk myself out of it by reminding myself just how shitty a person I am, I find Kade's contact in my phone — heart squeezing at the photo of me on his back, arms wrapped around his neck, both of us smiling.

"Jess?" he answers on the second ring.

"I need you."

And that's all I have to say.

***

It's an absolute masterpiece to watch, Kade and his brothers whipping a ballroom into immaculate event shape in under three hours. They're all so brawny and attentive that I just point and instruct and like little worker bees, they do exactly what I ask of them.

Of course, it's a *little* rowdy, too. After all, it's a Friday night and I've suckered them into working. But when Kade said he could come and he'd have a crew, I immediately ran to the store and grabbed provisions — meaning lots and lots of booze.

And pizza, of course.

Someone hooked their phone up to one of the giant speakers and has been blasting dubstep all night, and I've seen just as many shots being taken as I've seen tables being set up.

But I don't care.

Whatever gets the job done.

And as much as I'm running around and supervising everything, helping where I can, ensuring all the details are exactly as the bride described, I can't keep my eyes from wandering to Kade.

He was emotionless when he got here — no hug or kiss for a greeting, just a thin smile and a *What should we do first?*

I can't blame him. He knows I've been with Jarrett. He knows I *haven't* been with him.

I know it's killing him.

It's killing me, too.

He must be working his frustrations out in the gym, because his already-impressive physique is even more cut than I remember, and I watch every muscle ebb and flow as he unstacks chairs and places them around the room, helps his brothers rebuild the dance floor, and sets up the band's equipment on the stage.

It's almost midnight by the time we get everything where we need it, and Kade dismisses his brothers after I hug them all and pay them cash out of my own pocket.

What Brittany doesn't know won't hurt her, and they saved my ass tonight.

When they're gone, taking what's left of the bottles and the music with them, the ballroom door swings shut and an eerie silence falls over me and Kade.

My soul wants to jump out of my body, the way he's looking at me. His hands are in his pockets, eyes under folded brows, jaw tight. He still doesn't have a shirt on, and I can see the band of his briefs peeking out above his basketball shorts — a sight that makes me ache for him right between my thighs.

"Thank you," I finally manage. I open my mouth again to say that I would have been fucked without him, that he saved me, that I love him, that I've missed him.

But I close it just as quickly, because the menacing look in his eyes tells me he doesn't want to hear it.

He watches me for so long I can't bear to meet his gaze anymore, and I don't know why, but my eyes sting with tears when I look away.

Kade sighs, and then he slowly crosses the space between us, until he's just inches from me.

"Jess."

I close my eyes at the sound of my name on his lips, at the tender way he says it.

I don't deserve that tenderness.

"Look at me," he commands, and when I don't, his finger and thumb gently touch my chin, tilting it until I'm forced to meet his gaze.

And the way he's watching me now, it's like *he's* the one who's been a class A prick.

"I'm sorry," I whisper.

He nods, the gesture cutting me off before I can tell him all that I'm sorry for.

His eyes search mine, his tongue snaking out to wet his lips. "I never had to leave, you know."

I frown, tilting my head, but Kade just steps into me, his palm sliding along my cheek as I lean into it and close my eyes to soak in the touch.

I *have* missed him — it wasn't a lie.

And feeling that connection with him again, seeing him again, everything inside me swirls like a nasty storm. I want to vomit. I want to pitch myself off the nearest roof. I want to whip myself and lock myself up.

Because I still love him, with every cell in my body I love him.

And I've been fucking another man.

"I never had to lose you to know," he continues, his voice soft, just a rumble over my skin as I let my eyes flutter open to meet his gaze once more. "I've known since the moment I saw you, since you thought I was just some douchebag frat boy," he adds with a smirk that makes me smile, too — though the smile releases two hot tears down my cheeks. "And I was already so far gone, Jess. I was so far gone. There was no saving me, and there was no way I could ever live without having you."

"Kade..."

"I know you've been with him," he says, his jaw hardening, chest heaving with a deep breath. "And I meant it when I said it's fucking killing me to know that."

I roll my lips together as more silent tears slip free, but Kade wipes them away as quick as they come.

"As angry as it makes me, and as much as it fucking *wrecks* my heart," he says, beating his fist on his chest with a break in his voice that I feel in my own soul. "I understand. I understand why you have to give him another chance, why you have to see if there... if there's something still..."

He can't finish the sentence.

I wrap my arms around his waist, and he pulls me in closer, letting out a long, slow breath as he drops his forehead to mine.

"Please," he begs. "Give me my chance, too. Don't write me out of the story yet."

I shake my head because I haven't — I *can't* write him out.

But before I can answer, the ballroom door swings open.

And Jarrett flies into the room.

"Jess?" he calls, and then his head snaps in our direction, his eyes dilating when he sees us — Kade's hands still framing my face, my hands on his hips.

His hands curl into fists at his sides, and Kade releases me with his jaw so tight I think he might chip a tooth.

Fuck.

"I got your voicemail," Jarrett says, his eyes on his brother even though he's talking to me. He doesn't move an inch.

Kade blinks at that, a brief look of confusion washing over his face before he turns to me.

And the pain in his eyes makes my knees wobble.

"You called him first?" he asks me, but I can't answer. I just swallow, reaching for him, wishing I had the words to make everything right, to make this all go away.

For both of them.

For *all* of us.

But he rips his arm away before I can touch him, sniffing as he grabs his shirt off the back of one of the chairs and storms toward Jarrett.

"Kade, wait," I try, but he doesn't so much as give me another glance.

Jarrett tries to catch his arm as he storms past, but Kade rips away from him, too, turning on him with a menacing glare. "Don't you fucking *touch* me, you backstabbing bastard."

He doesn't react — not physically — but I see the way those words shred Jarrett, the way he knows he's hurting his little brother, but can't help himself.

Kade shakes his head, stepping right up to Jarrett's face, the two brothers chest to chest as he says, "You left."

Jarrett closes his eyes, a long blink before he opens them to face his brother again.

"You fucking *left* her. You *broke* her. And you know who loved her when she was in pieces, who helped her find herself again, who watched her build an even stronger version of herself with you out of the picture?" He jabbed a thumb into his chest. "*Me*. And now you have the fucking *nerve* to show up again, rip open her wounds, play with her like you always played with every fucking girl growing up? They didn't deserve that shit, and neither does she."

I frown, but don't have time to wonder what he's referring to before Kade shoves Jarrett — hard.

"Wake the fuck up and let her go, let her be happy," Kade says as Jarrett steps right back up into his space. "Because we all know you don't have any intentions past fucking her until you're bored again."

"You don't know shit," Jarrett seethes.

Kade just laughs, shaking his head and looking his brother up and down as he puts space between them. "I know everything about you. And I know even more about her. I *love* her, you piece of shit," he says.

My heart squeezes so violently I feel my ribs creak with the pressure.

"So do I," Jarret responds. "And I loved her first."

Kade's jaw clamps shut at that, but after a moment, he shakes his head and shoves through the ballroom door, letting it slam shut behind him.

I flinch at the sound, closing my eyes as my throat burns.

When I open them again, Jarrett is already on his way over to me, but I hold up my hands. "Stop."

He does.

I shake my head. "You should go, Jarrett."

"I'm sorry I didn't come sooner. I'm sorry I—"

"Jarrett, please," I beg, and my eyes shine with fresh tears that make his shoulders slump, make him nearly cry out that I won't let him come closer. "Please, I need to be alone. Please. *Please*."

I can't stop pleading, can't stop crying, and though I can tell it kills him, Jarrett scrubs a hand over his jaw and nods, backing up, giving me space.

"Okay," he says, holding up his hands. "Okay. Just... call me. Tomorrow. Please."

I nod, but it's a dismissive one, one that says I can't make any promises.

To anyone.

Not even myself.

He watches me for a long moment before he finally rips his gaze from mine and leaves through the same door Kade did.

And I collapse onto the floor and succumb to every heartbreaking sob my body lashes me with.

Erin

The holiday season always feels a little off in Florida.

While the rest of the country is bundled up, drinking hot spiced pumpkin drinks and reading by the fire, it's business as usual in South Florida — which is to say it's very, very hot.

My hair is already damp at my neck after talking outside with a few people from therapy, and a single bead of sweat slides down my back as I trek toward my car, a heavy sigh leaving my lips after a long day.

A long *week*, really.

Candice has been keeping me in the loop with the trial, but unfortunately, there won't be any news one way or another until after Thanksgiving. So for now, there's nothing more for me to do but try to forget about it all and enjoy myself.

Those were her words.

As if I could forget.

As if I could focus on school or on calling my mom to see if she wants me and Bear to come home for the holiday or *literally anything else* other than the fact that Landon and his brothers have been questioned, as have I, as have all other witnesses in question.

And a decision will be made.

A decision I have absolutely zero control over.

I'm so lost in thought — something that seems to be happening to me more and more lately — that I don't notice Gavin leaning against my car door until I'm about ten steps away. He straightens at the soft *beep* of me unlocking the vehicle, and while he offers a sheepish smile, I only give him a glare in return.

"What?" I clip, moving around him to toss my purse in the car before I stand — door still open — waiting for whatever he wants before I climb in and peel out of here.

"You shared a lot in therapy today," he said, tucking his hands in his pockets. "I... I didn't realize you were going to court for... for what happened."

"I might not be."

He frowns. "But you said—"

"We were all questioned, yes. I'm trying to press charges, yes. But nothing is certain. The detectives and lawyers have done their jobs for now, and it's up to the prosecutor what happens next."

"They're going to pay," he says, his jaw tense. "They will, Erin."

I shrug, mostly because I don't want to cry — nor do I want to get caught up in this conversation with the boy who broke my heart and left me behind because he couldn't handle me.

"I'm proud of you," he says after a quiet pause from me. "I know it couldn't have been easy, to come forward after all this time. But you're setting an example. You're doing the right thing. And I believe the justice system will do its job and make them pay for what they did."

I fight the urge to roll my eyes.

"Is that all?" I ask.

His shoulders deflate, and it's then that I see how though his eyes are red from what I assume is lack of sleep, he *does* look better than when I last saw him. He's filled out, his skin a bronze instead of that translucent gray, his cheekbones no longer hollow. Maybe he did get help. Maybe he meant what he said in his letter to me.

Regardless, I don't owe him anything — least of all this conversation.

"Erin, I truly am so sorry," he says, his voice just above a whisper. "For hurting you, for leaving the way I did. For… everything. I know it doesn't matter now, I know you're happy with Bear and I'm happy *for* you. But…" He shakes his head, running a hand back through his hair as he looks away from me. Sweat beads along his neck. "Goddamnit, Erin, you are so fucking important to me. To my life. You were instrumental in my recovery. And I don't know if I helped you the way you helped me," he says, his eyes meeting mine then. "But I meant what I said. I would really like to be friends. *Just* friends. Not the creepy kind of friend who says that's all they want and then tries to make a move."

I can't help how my nose stings, eyes pricking with tears that dry as soon as they appear. Because as he said those words, that I helped him, I know he helped me, too.

"I just don't want to lose you in my life," he pleads. "And with everything going on in yours… I want to be there."

I sigh, biting my lip as I mull over his words. To his credit, he *does* seem genuine.

And in so many ways, I feel the same as he does.

I never wanted him to leave the way he did. In fact, him breaking up with me because I'm not pretty enough would have been easier to handle than that letter he left me with.

But if he really did check himself into a treatment center, if he really was in that low of a place… and now he's back… and we can be friends?

I know how much it would mean to him.

Even more — I know how much it would mean to *me*.

He was there for me when no one else was — not because they wouldn't have been if I'd have told them, but because I didn't have the strength to own what had happened to me. He was the first to touch me, the first to make me desire after having something so viciously taken from me.

He was — *is* — part of my recovery.

And it seems I'm part of his.

After a long moment debating, I sigh again, extending my hand. "Friends," I say, pulling back a little when he goes for the shake. "*Just* friends. The second you try to cross a line, it's over."

Gavin throws his hands up. "Just friends. I swear. It's all I want."

I nod. "I'd like that, too."

His smile is one of relief, his shoulders sagging with the breath, and then we shake hands.

And on that touch, the first time touching him since he broke my heart, I feel an all-too-familiar aching pain radiate right to my heart.

"What are you doing now? Want to go grab a drink, catch up?" he asks. Then, he laughs, grabbing the back of his neck. "Or, well, maybe grab *you* a drink. I don't drink anymore."

"At all?"

"Nope."

I smile. "I think that's a good thing."

"I do, too."

"I have plans tonight," I lie. The only plans I have are with my bed, but this *friendship* is new, and I'm too tired to dive in deeper than just agreeing that it's okay. "Maybe next time."

Gavin's smile is a bit flat, but he nods. "Sure, next time."

He grabs my door to open it farther for me, waiting for me to climb in before he carefully shuts it and taps the top of my car.

Adam

"I just hope you're ready to barely leave the hotel room," I tell Cassie under my breath, looking around the bar to make sure no one's heard me. Of course, not that I really care — but I am *trying* to be polite to any innocent bystanders.

Cassie giggles into the phone. "I wish I could just talk to you all night."

"Me too," I tell her, my chest squeezing with the admission. "But we'll see each other in just over a week. That's not too long."

"I might die waiting."

"Better not. You've got your first cosplay convention to go to."

She squeals a little at that. "You really think I look okay? I'm excited to dive into Tera's world a little bit, but I don't want to embarrass her."

"Are you kidding? You make the absolute sexiest Daphne Blake I've ever seen..." I whistle. "I just wish I was there to be your Fred Jones."

"You'd need a very good wig to pull that off."

"And I'd wear it," I say. "For you."

A pause passes between us, and then Cassie sighs. "I really should get going. I'm picking Tera up from her dorm room across campus."

"Take lots of pictures and videos and tell me all the crazy things you see."

"I will," she promises. "Eight days."

"Eight days," I repeat on a sigh. "I love you."

"I love you."

When she hangs up, I hold the phone to my ear a while longer, heart heavy and aching with the need to hold her, see her, *be* with her. I finally set my phone down on the bar, signaling to the bartender to pour me another IPA as I polish off the last of the one in front of me.

It's been a long time since I've gone to a bar by myself — let alone on a Monday night. But with the Alpha Sigma bonfire behind me and the semester winding down as the brothers focus on holidays and finals, I'm in a pensive move.

And I'm lonely.

I miss my own brothers, miss how busy it always was this time of year back at Palm South. I miss having a purpose as president, and though I thought this position would fill that need, the simple fact is that it just doesn't.

I'm not in a fraternity anymore.

I'm not in *college* anymore.

Lost is the sad term that keeps coming to mind, and as the bartender slides a fresh beer in front of me, I sigh, drinking down the feelings that come with that admission.

My eyes find one of the big screens hanging above the bottles on the back wall, watching as the Cowboys and Steelers take the field. At least I have football to distract me.

"This seat taken?"

I blink, frowning at first when I turn to find Chandler beside me. But then a surprised smile curls on my lips. "Looks like it is now. What are you doing here?"

"Same as you, I'd imagine," she says with a sigh, propping her hands on the bar to help her up until she plops down onto the barstool next to me. "Drinking away Monday."

I laugh. "What are you having? I've got a tab open."

"What's that?" she asks, nodding to my glass.

"IPA."

"Perfect."

I get the bartender's attention, and once Chandler has a cold beer in front of her and has shrugged off her jacket and scarf, we clink our glasses together and take a long chug.

"Ah," she says, smacking her lips. "That's *exactly* what I needed." Her eyes find the television, and she wrinkles her nose. "Ugh. Football."

"Not a fan, I take it?"

"Not after growing up with a dad and three brothers who were obsessed with it, no." She shakes her head. "Constant screaming on Sundays, I tell you. No peace."

I laugh. "*Three* brothers? Your poor boyfriends."

"Very few made it past the *meet the family* stage," she says. "And as you can tell by my glorious single state of being now, no one lasts long after."

I smirk, not allowing myself the opportunity to take in her appearance any lower than her eyes. She knows as well as I do that she's a very attractive woman — unique, edgy, with a rack that you can see from outer space. "I doubt you stay single long. Unless you want to, that is."

She shrugs. "I don't know what I want."

"What a loaded statement," I say with a sigh of my own. "I've been feeling the same, actually."

Chandler takes a long drink. "Trouble in paradise?"

I frown, not understanding until I meet her gaze and then piece together that she thinks I mean Cassie.

"Oh, *God* no," I say quickly. "Cassie is the only thing *right* in my life." I pause. "Honestly, it's been that way for a while, I think."

"I don't know, it looks like you've done a lot of good here. My girls can't stop talking about Alpha Sigma's *transformation.*" She does a little move with her hands to illustrate the word, her voice going up a pitch.

I chuckle. "And I'm happy for them. It's been fun, it's just..."

"Not what you thought it would be."

"Not at all," I admit.

"You thought it would be like college 2.0, that you would get the same satisfaction as a Field Executive that you did as president."

"You're too good at this."

She smiles. "I know the feeling is all. It's not the same when you're not an active member. It makes you feel old, like an outsider. And fuck, it's lonely."

I nod in agreement. "I think I'm done after this year."

"They'll be sad to lose you."

"Maybe. But the bigger issue is that I have no idea what I want to do next, only that it has to be in Baltimore."

Chandler nearly chokes on her next sip of beer at that. "Jesus Christ, *why* Baltimore of all places?"

"That's where Cassie will be going to med school." I meet her gaze. "Johns Hopkins."

Chandler's brows shoot into her hairline. "Wow. Gorgeous *and* smart as hell... it's just not fair. Some girls get all the fun."

I smile. "She's had to work her ass off for it."

"I don't doubt it." Chandler taps the bar for a moment, watching me like she wants to say something. But she keeps biting her lip, her cheek, looking away just to look back again.

"What?" I ask.

"Nothing, it's just..." She shakes her head. "This is crazy, and I doubt you'd be interested but..." She stops. "Never mind."

"Chandler," I say, arching a brow to let her know I don't like playing these games.

"Okay, okay," she says, turning to face me more. "It's just... what a small fucking world. *I'm* from Baltimore."

I blanch. "You are?"

"I am. My whole family is. That whole football hate I was talking about earlier? Try being in a house full of Ravens fans."

I chuckle.

"Anyway, my dad's parents own a pretty big company based in Baltimore... Simmons Snacks."

It was my turn to choke on my beer. "Simmons Snacks? As in the potato chip company?"

"Potato chips, popcorn, salsa and queso, cookies, crackers..." She nods. "Yep."

I gape at her. "What the fuck, Chandler. You never told me you were the granddaughter of some of the wealthiest people in the world."

"It's not my wealth," she says quickly. "Anyway, they've been hounding me for about a month now to come work for them. They're in desperate need of someone to head their Public Relations and Events team." She pauses. "In Baltimore."

My ears heat.

"I have no interest," she adds quickly. "And they know that. They've wanted me to work for the family business since I was born, but I just... I don't want anything to do with it. Not because it isn't a great company," she clarifies. "Because it is. I just want to make a name for myself outside of it." She pauses. "Also, I don't want to live in Baltimore."

I laugh at that. "So, why are you telling me this?"

"Isn't it obvious?" She shrugs. "What if *you* lead their team?"

I blink.

"Don't look so surprised," she says with a smile. "You'd be great at it. I mean, that's essentially what you're doing here, what you did all through college — public relations and events. You'd get to do what you love professionally, outside of a fraternity organization. For a company you know and love. In the city where your girlfriend is." She cocks a brow. "Did I lose you?"

"I'm just trying to decide if you're a figment of my imagination," I say, playfully swinging at the air around her like she's a ghost.

She chuckles and swats my hand down. "Look. Come home to Baltimore with me for Thanksgiving. They're stubborn, but I know once my PopPop meets you, he'll jump at the opportunity to hire you. He probably won't wait for you to finish out your job as Field Executive," she adds with a cringe. "But as long as you're not opposed to leaving before Spring semester..."

"I'm not. I mean, that's when Cassie is going, so... it'd be perfect."

"Well, there you have it."

My smile is so big it nearly breaks my face. "I don't know what to say, Chandler."

"Well, it's not done yet. But you can start with a thank you."

"Thank you," I say hurriedly, but then my stomach sinks to my shoes. "Wait... *fuck*. Cassie is coming here for Thanksgiving."

Chandler frowns. "Can she come out a different time?"

"It's her last semester at PSU, and she's in a sorority. You know how that goes."

"I do." Chandler's mouth tugs to the side as she thinks. "I mean, I could try to talk my grandparents into coming out here to visit, but their schedule is so crazy... we're lucky to pull them away even for a single day for things like Thanksgiving and Christmas."

"Do you think they'd meet with me over the phone?"

"Possibly, but I'll be honest... PopPop doesn't sway lightly. I think charming him in person would be your best bet."

I curse again.

"Look, I know it would suck to call off the trip for Cassie to come, but on the heels of that disappointment would come the best news ever — that you both get to be in the same city again. You could *live* together." Chandler reaches over to squeeze my wrist. "A little sacrifice now could pay off in a big way later."

I nod. "Or Cassie could castrate me and break up with me for good measure."

"You really think she'd do that?"

I sigh. "No. But I don't want to tell her about this, just in case it doesn't happen. She'll get her hopes up and then... if I don't get the job..."

"You'll get the job," Chandler says quickly. "But whether you want to tell her about the meeting or not is up to you. For now, I'm going to tell my mom to have another setting at the table for dinner. And you need to figure out what to tell Cassie."

I frown, nodding. Then, I turn to face her. "What's in this for you?"

"Well, one, they'll get off *my* back about the damn job," she says. "Two, I'll have a friend to hang out with over the holidays instead of my insufferable brothers. And three?" She shrugs. "I think we've got a pretty good track record of helping each other out. I don't want to break it."

I smile. "Friends, huh? I didn't think I'd find one of those out here."

"That makes two of us. Now," she says, downing the last of her beer and holding the empty glass up to the bartender. "Let's get another round and you start taking notes. I'm going to tell you every single way to woo my grandfather."

I grin, chugging the last of mine to match her, and once we have new beers, we get to work.

The fire burning in my belly is unmatched, fueled by the thought that this might be it, this might be how I can do what I love but not be away from Cassie any longer.

No more long distance.

No more video chat dates or texts or calls.

Just me and her, in the same city, the same *house*, potentially.

My pulse races at the thought, at the surprised look on Cassie's face should I be able to land the job. It'd be the best Christmas gift I could ever give her — the news that we'd both be in Baltimore come spring.

So, with that as my motivation, I took detailed notes, and by the time we asked for the check, we were booking me a flight to Baltimore.

Ashlei

"You look absolutely radiant, Miss Daniels," Riel says, tucking a beautiful fuchsia flower into the crown she's been weaving into my hair. The electric blue water of St. John can be seen out of every window of Brandon's yacht, and it reflects off Riel's dark eyes as she puts the final touches on my updo.

She pulls back with a smile, clapping her hands together. "All done."

With her hands on my arms, Riel gently turns me to look in the full-length mirror in my cabin.

And I gasp.

I did my own makeup, wanting to be sure I still looked like *me* for such a special day, but I chose not to look in the mirror after I slipped my dress on, nor did I sneak a glance as Riel did my hair.

And now here it is, all at once.

Me, in a delicate, flowy, A-line wedding dress — the straps delicate around my collarbone, waist cinched, elaborate beading covering the bust and a weightless, silky, long skirt with four deep slits all the way to my upper thigh. I know with just a little turn that those slits will allow the fabric to flow all around me in the Caribbean wind.

My hair is woven into a thick braid, the most colorful flower crown playing with the warm pinks and oranges of my eyeshadow and bringing out the gold in my hazel eyes. Brilliant Swarovski crystals cover the straps of my high heels, highlighting my immaculate pedicure.

I touch my neck, the simple diamond hanging on the end of a slim gold chain.

And that makes me look at my ring finger — the one about to be covered with the perfect engagement ring Brandon picked out for me.

And a wedding band, too.

My eyes well, and I turn back around to wrap Riel in a hug. "Thank you," I whisper.

We met Riel when we first arrived in St. John, and she's been our wedding planner of sorts, helping us find everything we desired for our ceremony — which wasn't much, but what we *did* want, Brandon wanted top of the line.

She's been a saving grace to me, helping me with flowers, choosing a photographer, decorating the bow of the yacht, and ensuring we have the best local chef onboard for our wedding night dinner.

"One last thing," I tell her, turning around to face the mirror again. "Help me get this off."

I'm already fidgeting with the straps of my arm sling when Riel stops me. "I don't think that's a good idea."

"Riel, I am not wearing this monstrosity while I get married. I refuse."

I sigh when I see the worried look on her face.

"I'll put it on as soon as the vows are exchanged and that man gives me the kiss of my life, okay? Just... please. Don't make me wear this out there."

Riel smiles softly, and with a nod, she does as I ask.

When the arm brace is off, I chuckle a little at how that arm is slightly paler than my other, but nevertheless, I feel one-hundred times lighter.

I let myself take in the whole image one last time before my eyes wander to the bits of Cruz Bay I can see off in the distance through the magnificent windows in my cabin. The lush green mountains stretch up over the cerulean blue water, sailboats and yachts peppering the shoreline, and my heart leaps into my throat as I realize where I am.

Realize what I'm doing.

I close my eyes on a smile, thinking of how many times I've played through what this day would be like. From the time I was a little girl, I've dreamed of what I'd wear, the kind of cake I'd have, the party...

And now, it's just me and the man I love on an island far, far away.

It couldn't be more perfect.

"Okay," I breathe, opening my eyes and taking a long, slow breath. "I'm ready."

Riel nods, leading the way for me out of my cabin and carefully down the stairs to the main deck. She hides me in the back of the parlor, curtains pulled over the usually open airway that leads out to the bow. I haven't seen the decorations come all together yet, haven't seen the lilies and roses and baby's breath wreaths or arch that match my bouquet. I haven't seen the freshly polished teak deck, or the fairy lights hung in a zig zag fashion over the bow.

And I haven't seen my groom — not since dinner last night.

It was torture for both of us to sleep in separate cabins, but it was the one thing I wanted to keep old-fashioned.

And when Riel comes back in through the parlor bar entry, nodding to let me know that everything is ready, I step up to stand right at the edge of the curtain as two of Riel's friends pull open opposite ends of it back in sync.

And I see him.

And he sees me.

And all the wait, all the time apart was worth it.

I wish I can say I hear the music playing — the sweet, soft sounds of a violin from the musician we hired our first day on the island. I wish I could hear her playing our song, "Unchained Melody," as I slowly drift across the teak toward where Brandon waits for me at the bow. I wish I could take in the golden rays of sun on the island, the shockingly blue water, the waves softly lapping at the sides of the boat, the flowers and the lights and everything we'd set up for this very occasion.

But I can't see, can't hear, can't feel anything or anyone else but Brandon Church.

He stands tall and regal as ever at the bow, his cream suit casual yet sophisticated, highlighted by the Carolina blue dress shirt underneath. Diamond studs glisten in each earlobe, his hair in a neat, styled fade, facial hair trimmed to perfection. Every inch of the outfit is tapered to fit him, hugging and hanging off all the right places.

I take my time letting my eyes wander the length of him, feeling the pulse of his heartbeat even with the distance still between us. It's an energy, I realize — one I've been in tune with since the moment he stepped onto the same elevator with me at *Okay, Cool.*

When my eyes finally crawl up to meet his, he lets out a slow, steady breath. His jaw tightens, nose flares, and he shakes his head once, twice, before he tears his eyes away from me and bows his head down.

He pinches the bridge of his nose, one shake of his shoulders telling me he was moved to tears before he finds the strength to stand tall again.

And those warm brown eyes glistening in the sun, those slender wet streaks staining his cheeks, those lips rolling together as he tries to fight back his emotion — they're what undo me.

My own eyes water, and a single tear slips free before I can even think to stop it.

I don't make it all the way to him before he's meeting me halfway, pulling me into him for a soul-shattering, life-altering, *you're mine forever* kiss.

His lips are warm and commanding, his hands wrapping around the beaded bodice of my dress, and he still shakes with emotion as he holds me tighter and tighter.

When we finally pull away, our foreheads pressed together, I chuckle. "I think you were supposed to wait until the end to do that."

"I couldn't."

I smile, pulling back to look him in the eyes, and he shakes his head, his gaze one of absolute reverence.

"You are a masterpiece," he whispers.

My eyes gloss again, and I press up on my toes to kiss him again before Riel clears her throat and ushers us the rest of the way down the make-shift aisle.

The sea breeze is cool and lovely, the sun still warm on our skins as it slowly makes its descent over the island. Brandon holds my hands in his, our tear-filled eyes flicking back and forth between each other's as Riel's officiant reads the sweet but short ceremony we selected. He has us laughing and smiling all the way up until he says it's time for us to exchange our personal vows.

The entire time, all I can focus on is where Brandon's thumb smooths the top of my knuckles, a sensual promise of what's to come *after* the vows.

"Brandon Church," I say first, and his dazzling smile makes me smile, too. "I wish I could say I've known since the moment I met you that you'd be my husband one day, but the truth is, I was doing everything I could back then *not* to think of you as anything other than my boss."

That earns me a chuckle from Riel and the officiant, both.

"But I knew... something. From the moment you stepped into the elevator, from the first time our eyes met and I heard your voice, a part of my heart that had been dormant all my life came alive. I stirred beneath your gaze, and though I tried to deny it, tried to fight it, I think I knew even then that there was no way I'd be able to stay away from you."

"That makes two of us," Brandon chimes in.

I chuckle. "I don't think either of us can deny our chemistry, but it's our love that makes me happiest. I know at the end of the day, no matter what we go through — you have my back, and I have yours. There's no better feeling than that." I squeeze his hand. "There was a time when I didn't know if I'd walk life alone or with someone by my side, a time when I wondered if life was worth living at all. But then I found you. And you saved me."

"We saved each other," he amends.

I smile, nodding with tears glossing my eyes once more. "I love you. And I am yours, for today, tomorrow, and evermore."

Riel sniffs and wipes a tear from the corner of her eye before it can fall. I offer her a soft smile before Brandon clears his throat, pulling my attention back to him.

"Contrary to the many public events in which I have delivered speeches deserving of a standing ovation, I have to admit... I failed every time I tried to write down in words what you mean to me, Ashlei Daniels."

My heart throbs in my throat, and I swallow it down as my eyes blur.

"I never knew what it was to be truly hungry until I laid eyes on you and knew I couldn't have you. That desire, that wanting is something I will never forget. But as you said before, what started as something so carnal swiftly turned into something I couldn't place, couldn't name, because I'd never experienced it before in my life." He takes a breath. "*Love.* Love so pure and powerful and sweeping that I had no choice but to get caught up in the wave of it."

I bit my bottom lip.

"You are, without a doubt, the strongest, smartest, most incredible woman I have ever had the pleasure of knowing. You own every room you walk into. You command the attention of every man, woman, and child. You, my sweet wife—"

"*Almost* wife," I correct.

"Are going to take this whole damn world by storm," he finishes. "And I am just honored beyond measure to be the man who gets to stand by your side while you do it."

I smile, squeezing his hands, desperate to get to the kissing part now.

"Our love has been tested," Brandon says. "But if nothing else, we have proven that even when we hurt each other, we know at the end of the day that there is no one else. Your love was meant for me, and mine was meant for you. We are souls destined to find each other in this lifetime and every one after. I vow to treasure each moment with you as if it were my last, and to spend every moment away from you praying for your return to my arms. I will make you happy, Ashlei. I will care for you, protect you, and most of all, respect you." Brandon's eyes are sincere, heavy as they hold mine. "That is my promise."

My bottom lip trembles as I nod, accepting his vows, knowing their truth. And once again, everything fades into the background — the water, the breeze, the sunlight, the music, and even the officiant's voice as he declares us husband and wife and allows Brandon to kiss his bride.

In the next moment, I'm swept back in a dramatic dip, and all around us, sailboats and yachts and tourist ferries alike roar with applause.

But for me, it's just Brandon's arms around my waist, his lips on mine, his heart forever joined with the one beating in my chest.

And just like that.

I'm Mrs. Ashlei Church.

***

"Please don't make me."

I cross my arms and bat my lashes, hoping the wedding hair and makeup is still intact enough after our breezy sunset dinner for Brandon to show mercy on me.

He chuckles, crossing the space in the master bedroom to hold my elbows in his massive hands. "I'm not doing it to be mean, my love. You've gone all day without it. The doctor said—"

"I know what the doctor said," I growl, wrinkling my nose. "But it's so ugly, and bulky, and *not* sexy."

"You are sexy no matter what you wear."

"You say that now, but when that strap is smushing down my boob..."

Brandon plants a soft kiss to my lips. "First, let me help you out of this," he says, fingertips walking down my hips and slipping under the high slits of my dress. He tugs at the fabric as my breath catches. "And then, we put the brace on, and I fuck you as my *wife* should be properly fucked."

I pout. "But—"

Brandon catches my bottom lip with his teeth, biting hard enough for me to yelp before he releases me. "Stick that lip out one more time and I'll bend you over my knee."

This time it's *me* who bites my lip, my thighs clenching with the thought of being punished, of being spanked.

Yes, please.

Brandon's lips are on mine in the next breath, his kiss soft and slow and purposeful as he backs me up more and more until my spine hits the window. With the added support, he presses me into it, careful of my shoulder as he hikes one of my legs up and slides my dress skirt up over my hips.

"Every time the wind blew, I'd see your thigh, this little spot where your hip meets the muscle," he teases, running his fingertip along my hip flexor. "And it drove me mad, knowing I'd have to wait to kiss that spot, to have this pussy," he husks, his hand dipping between my legs without warning. His fingers skate under my panties and slide through my desire, a groan of approval on his lips when he adds, "*My* pussy."

"All this talk, but no action..." I tease, wrapping my arms around his shoulders. I want desperately for him to pin me against the window and let me hold on for dear life as he eats the pussy he was just raving about.

But the bastard is too worried about my safety.

He laughs against my lips, giving me a brief kiss before he pulls away. "Too much pressure on your shoulder to hold on like that," he says, reading my mind. "Tonight, you'll have to be content with me ravaging you the way I want to."

I'm tempted to pout again, but then Brandon holds my hand in his — the one connected to my good shoulder — and gives me a little spin, the skirt of my dress flaring as I turn to face the window.

His lips are warm, little kisses pressing against my neck and the top of my spine as he carefully undoes each button at the back of my dress. When it's loose enough, he slips one strap off my shoulder, and then the other, letting the fabric pool at my feet.

He moans when he sees what he no doubt suspected with the open back of the dress — that I'm not wearing a bra — and before I can prepare for it, his hands palm each breast, weighing them, massaging as he presses his hard-on against my ass.

"I can't believe I get to touch these for the rest of my life."

"Even when they're old and saggy."

He almost laughs, but the slight pressure change on my nipple has me gasping, moaning, arching back into him and begging for more contact.

"No more jokes," he whispers in my ear, and then his fingers slip under the bands of my lace panties, and he strips them down my thighs, too.

I want to protest again when he pulls out the brace, but I'm so desperate to have him inside me that I just let him help me into it. I catch a glimpse of how stupid I look in the mirror and make to tell him so, but he kisses me silent.

I'm swept into his arms in the next breath, his mouth still on mine as he carries me over to the master bed. It's lush on an average day, but with brand new sheets with a higher thread count than anything I've ever slept in, it feels like being laid down in a cloud of cool silk when he deposits me.

He stands then, his eyes drinking in every inch of me as he shrugs off his suit jacket, unbuttons his dress shirt, makes quick work of his belt and his dress slacks. Hunger grows in his gaze as much as I feel it burning in my soul at the sight of this powerful, sexy man stripping for me.

My man.

My *husband.*

Desire pools between my legs at the thought, at the ownership, and as soon as he's out of his dress shoes, I pull him onto the bed and down on top of me.

His mouth eagerly devours mine, swallowing my next breath as the hard length of him slips between my thighs. His shaft glides through my wetness and over my sensitive clit, making me shudder, making my nails dig into his flesh to beg for more.

"Easy," he teases, kissing my brace as I fight the urge to roll my eyes.

"I'm fine."

"I want to keep it that way."

Brandon balances on his elbows then, his eyes searching mine as he sweeps a bit of my fallen braid out of my face. His thumb drags down my nose, over my lips, tracing my jaw before he wraps my neck in a gentle but possessive embrace. "I meant every word I said," he whispers. "I am yours, Ashlei."

My brows tug together, and I nod, pulling him down to kiss me. I don't have to say it. I know he feels it without my words.

I'm yours, too.

I want him to fuck me against the window. I want to be bent over the railing so all of St. John can watch. I want him fast and hard and furious, desperate and needy — the way he was the first time he had me on his private jet.

But I know we'll have a lifetime for that.

Tonight, I'm limited, and perhaps more than that, it feels... *more.* It's not just his skin on mine, our mouths fused, our breaths labored between us as our bodies ache to be connected.

It's a union, a promise, a tender turn of the page that starts a new chapter in our story.

"I love you," Brandon whispers against my lips.

And then he hikes one leg up, kisses me with enough pressure to bruise, and fills me.

I cry out at the first thrust, the way it leaves me breathless as always. His long, hard, thick length stretches me, but the burn fades quickly, pleasure taking its place.

The waves rock the boat in time with him flexing inside of me, in and out, and I hold on with my good arm while letting my other rest.

Fire licks at my core quickly, with the way he brushes my sensitive clit with every thrust. Or maybe it's the wedding, the vows, the fact that this man is mine in every way there is to be.

Forever.

"Ashlei," he groans, kissing me hard as his pace intensifies. "Come with me, baby. Find it."

I reach down between us, and he presses up onto his palms to give me the space I need to rub my clit and find my release. It doesn't take long, not with him towering over me like that, not with the wicked grin he gives me as he watches me play with myself, watches himself sink inside me deeper and deeper with each thrust.

My legs spread wider, toes curling as I quicken my circles and find my release, panting and screaming out his name. And he comes undone with me, a grunt loud and feral ricocheting off the cabin walls as he spills inside me.

Yes.

Yes, yes, yes.

Even after he's done, he continues to move, in and out, feeling his slick release leaking out of me. And before we have the chance to come down, to breathe and prepare, he's already hardening again.

"Round two already, Mr. Church?" I ask, arching a brow.

"Followed very quickly by round three, *Mrs*. Church."

I bite my lip at that, and Brandon smirks, rolling until I'm on top.

And this time, I ride my husband until we both come again, and realize my wedding night might be the most sleepless of my life.

Jess

A week before Thanksgiving, I text the girls and call an emergency video chat call.

It takes more back and forth than I'd like for us to nail down a time for the call, given everyone's schedules, but somehow — miraculously — I get them all to agree on six p.m.

Erin comes over to my room for the call, her hair wet from her shower and a bottle of wine in hand — along with two glasses.

"I don't know what this is about," she says, shuffling in in her fuzzy slippers. "But something tells me we'll need this."

I motion for her to hand me the bottle as I connect my laptop to the video chat, and then I pour us two full glasses as the other girls click into frame one by one.

Cassie and Skyler are together, too, cuddled on Skyler's bed. Ashlei looks happier than I've seen her since the accident where she sits on her and Brandon's couch — and a little too tan for all the moping she's been doing.

I don't even let the small talk happen. I just take a long swig of wine and say, "I'm calling an emergency Friendsgiving."

Skyler frowns. "What's going on, J-Love?"

I shake my head, tears already forming in my eyes — and provided I cry about as much as Cassie skips class, all the girls instantly sit up straighter, Erin's hand smoothing over my back.

"I need you. All of you. I have no idea what to do. I feel lost and guilty and fucked up and *sad*. I'm so, so sad," I admit. "I don't care where we go, but I need us all to get away. Out of town, out of the vicinity of everything here. I just... please. I need you."

"I'm there," Erin says instantly. "I can't bail on my family for Thanksgiving. I'm bringing Bear home for the first time. But I don't have to be back at the office until Tuesday, so... long weekend?"

"That works for me," Skyler says.

"Same," Ashlei chimes in. "I can't take more time off work, but we have Black Friday and the following Monday off already."

I arch a brow. "What do you mean *more* time? Are they seriously punishing you for the whole two days you were out of the office for your surgery?"

"Um... not exactly."

She bites her lip, and the girls and I exchange glances, waiting.

"Instead of a Friendsgiving... how would y'all feel about a belated bachelorette?"

I blink.

Cassie tilts her head.

Skyler and Erin both frown so intensely I'm worried they might get wrinkles on the spot.

And then Ashlei bites back a smile and holds up her left hand.

Showcasing a very large, very shiny, very *new* diamond ring.

Chaos erupts. Skyler and Cassie are bouncing up and down on the bed, their video frame shaking wildly as they squeal and demand details. Erin claps and grabs my laptop from me to see the ring closer, to which I smack her hand and grab it back, pushing a shortcut on the keyboard to make the window go full-screen.

“Jesus Christ, Lei! It’s gorgeous!” I scream.

“It’s *huge*,” Erin adds.

“What the hell happened?” Skyler asks.

Ashlei holds up her hands to calm us with a giggle. “He proposed,” she says simply with a shrug. “And then… we eloped. We just packed a bag and got on the yacht and sailed away. We shopped for everything we needed when we got there.”

“Got *where*?” Cassie probes.

“St. John.”

A collective sigh from the group makes Ashlei chuckle.

“You better have pictures, bitch,” I warn, pointing my finger at the camera. And though I’m joking and smiling and joining in the celebration, I can’t deny the way my chest aches, the way I feel both happy for my best friend and still wholly gutted for me.

“I do. Video, too,” she promises.

“Alright, that settles it,” I say, clapping my hands together. “Bachelorette party, next weekend, Black Friday through Cyber Monday. I’ll take care of everything. All you bitches need to do is pack and show up at the airport. And also help me figure out my life once we get there.”

“Where are we going?” Skyler asks.

I wave her off, letting her know she can find out once I do.

“Um, small problem…” Cassie says, holding up her finger. She sighs. “I’m sorry, but I’m flying to see Adam. And I don’t want to miss this. *God*, I don’t want to miss this, Lei,” she says more pointedly at Ashlei. “But I haven’t seen him since July, and things have been so hard lately, so…”

Her voice fades, and Skyler gives her a sympathetic look before squeezing her arm. We all know how hard it’s been for her and Adam doing long distance.

Long distance is what killed me and Jarrett.

It’s what killed Skyler and Kip.

We don’t need another casualty.

“I’ll allow your absence,” I say. “Just this once. Only because I love Adam, and you, and the two of you together. But you’re sponsoring a round of shots.”

“Of course,” she says, but her smile isn’t one of relief. I know that look of FOMO, and I’d have it, too, if I were in her shoes.

“We’ll party when you’re back, too,” Ashlei promises. “Don’t worry.”

Cassie nods, and then I rub my hands together again.

“Don’t stuff yourselves too full of turkey and mashed potatoes, ladies,” I say with a wicked smile as I pull up my phone, already searching for resorts. “I’m thinking… *Mexico*.”

That earns me a group of squeals, and Skyler starts talking about which swimsuits to pack as Ashlei says she’s almost positive Brandon has a timeshare at a resort in Cabo.

Already, my heart feels lighter, my soul warmer knowing I’ll have my girls to help me sort through this mess I’m in — and that we can celebrate our girl finding the man of her dreams, too.

There’s a short round of catching up and happy holiday wishes before we end the call.

And when we hang up, I get to work planning the most epic bachelorette party ever.

EPISODE 5

Cassie

"Please say something."

Adam's voice pierces through the ringing in my ears, the fog clouding my vision as I grip my phone tighter than necessary. I blink, over and over, processing what he's said.

"Cassie..."

"I don't know what you want me to say, Adam," I finally whisper, sniffing back the urge to cry. I'm not sure if they would be sad or angry tears at this point.

"It's not ideal, I know."

"Not ideal?" I scoff, and Lindsey — my roommate — widens her eyes before closing her textbook and popping off her bed. She gives me a little wave to let me know she's giving me space, and closes the door on her way out.

I grit my teeth.

"Not only are you saying that the trip to Colorado to see you that I've been looking forward to since the day we said goodbye is now not happening, but you're also saying you're going to have Thanksgiving with *some other girl's family.*"

"In Baltimore," he adds for me. "In order to secure a job that would put me there permanently." There's a long pause before he says, "With you."

I shake my head. "Is there something going on with her? Are you..." Bile rises in my throat. "Are you cheating on me?"

My bottom lip wobbles with the question, and Adam curses. "Of course not. Baby, how could you even ask that?"

I don't answer.

"Hey, look down. You see that silver chain and those two letters hanging around your neck?" he asks.

And I do. I wrap my fingers around the charm, closing my eyes and freeing a silent tear.

"That was a promise to you. A promise that I love you, more than anyone, and that I will be true to you. Always. You're my person, Cassie."

"But things change. You've been away for a whole semester almost, and you've spent so much time with this girl." I sniff again. "I wouldn't blame you if you... if you found other interests. If you outgrew me. If you..."

"Stop. Stop right there," he says. "First of all, you would kill me if that were true, and you know it."

I almost smile at that.

"Secondly, I love you. I *miss* you — and that's exactly why this is important to me. I know it sucks in the short term. It breaks my fucking heart to have to make this call," he admits with a strained voice. "But what if this is the key to us being together come spring? What if we could not only be in the same city, but in the same house?" He pauses. "Or apartment, or whatever."

My heart squeezes at that. "You want to move in together?"

"If I get this job? Hell fucking yes, I do. I want to be able to kiss you every night before I go to sleep and kiss you as soon as my eyes open in the morning."

I clutch my necklace, slumping back against the headboard. “I hate this.”

“I know. I do, too. I tried to do it through just a phone call, but... I mean, this is Simmons Snacks, Cassie. They’re a big deal. They’re not going to be won over by a resume and some guy they don’t know on a phone call — if they would even take it. But to Chandler, they aren’t Fortune 100 business owners — they’re Nana and PopPop. It wouldn’t be an interview, it’d be a family meal, maybe a cigar and a glass with her grandfather. And *maybe,* a job offer.”

“This is a lot to give up for *maybe*.”

“It’s a sacrifice, yes,” he agrees. “And I hate asking you to make it. But I’m willing to, if it means I might have a chance to have a great job with a great company in the city where my amazing girlfriend is moving.”

My heart wars with my brain, logic and emotions clawing and hissing over who’s right and who’s wrong. In the end, it’s confusion who wins, and I slump even more.

“I’ll see you at Christmas,” he adds when I don’t respond. “That’s just one more month.”

My mouth tugs to the side. That *is* true, but it doesn’t change the fact that my Thanksgiving plans have been blown to smithereens.

And that he’s going to some other girl’s house for a holiday.

“Trust me,” he begs after another long silence, as if he can hear my thoughts shredding me apart. “I would never do anything to hurt you.”

And I know he’s right.

I know he’d never hurt me.

I nod even though he can’t see me, and then let out a long, slow sigh. “I trust you.”

We talk for a little while longer, and eventually, the tears dry up and I’m laughing and aching with how much I miss him. We end the call with a million *I love you*’s and I feel half-assured that everything really will be okay in the end.

The other half of me feels like a woman unhinged, like I’m teetering on the edge of a dangerous cliff.

I flop back on the bed, eyes losing focus as I stare up at the ceiling.

And then, I grab my phone and group text the girls.

Change of plans. Got room for one more?

Bear

My nails are dug so deep into my palms, I'm about to draw blood.

These balled-up fists are all that's saving me from trashing Erin's room and this whole damn condo as she calmly, casually packs her bag for her girls' trip.

I'm not mad about the girls' trip. No, I'm happy for her. I'm happy she's getting away. I'm happy she can take a break from the trial and school and therapy. I'm happy for Ashlei, too — for her and Brandon and the whole celebration.

What I'm *not* happy about is the text that came through Erin's phone on our way home from her parents this morning, having had a very pleasant Thanksgiving dinner last night.

Hey, any word from lawyer?

From Gavin.

My jaw clenches so tight it gives me a headache as I remember those words flittering on her phone screen in the console between us as she drove, his name in bold letters above it.

It'd been all I could do to wait until we got home to discuss it.

"I'm not hanging out with him outside of therapy," Erin repeats as she folds another swimsuit and tucks it into her bag. "He's asked, but I've said no every time."

"But he's back," I say as calmly as I can. "He's back and you didn't tell me. He's back and you're friendly with each other. He's back and he's *texting you.*"

Erin sighs, pausing with her hands in her bag as her eyes meet mine. "Are we really doing this?"

"Hell fucking yes, we're doing this. Why did you keep it from me?"

"I didn't keep it from you. I planned on telling you by inviting Gavin over for dinner. With *both* of us. So you could see that while he's back, he's nothing to me."

"If he's nothing to you, then why are you talking to him at all?"

She frowns. "Okay, maybe not *nothing*."

My blood boils, but before I can scream, Erin holds up her hands.

"He's nothing like *that* — romantic or anything past a friend. Okay? I just..." She bites her lip, eyes focusing on something across the room. "I don't expect you to understand this, but Gavin is important to me. He's important to my recovery." Her eyes meet mine then. "He's part of the closure I'm seeking, as well as a very important part of my entire healing process. He was there for me, Bear. He was there when no one else was."

That makes me growl, and Erin shakes her head.

"You can be upset if you want to, but you weren't talking to me. You were pissed off and dating someone else and," she adds, pointing at me. "I'm not mad at you for that. I don't blame you. You had every right to be upset with me, and to be in love with another woman. But similarly, I had the right to be with another man, and to lean on him when I had no one else."

I'm breathing like a bull now, nostrils flaring as I try to see her side, try to calm myself.

But I simply can't.

"This is all bullshit," I spit. "Gavin, therapy, all of it. He wasn't part of your healing, Erin. He was part of the problem."

I expect those words to hit her hard, but instead, her shoulders slump, brows folding together. "Therapy is bullshit?" she repeats, shaking her head. "We're back to this?"

"You know what I mean," I say flippantly.

"No, I don't think I do. And I don't think *you* understand how therapy didn't just help me — it *saved* me. And in a lot of ways, so did Gavin. I'm sorry you hate to hear that, but it's true."

I force a long inhale, folding my arms over my chest and shaking my head over and over as I stare out her floor-to-ceiling window at the Miami skyline.

"Look, I'm glad you're perfect and you've got everything figured out in your life," she says, tossing a pair of sandals into her bag with more force than necessary. "No trauma in your life. No feelings to sort through. Absolutely no family drama at all for you, right?"

I grit my teeth. "Don't bring my family into this."

"Oh, of course not. Why would I? We never talk about them, do we?"

Her words slam into me.

"That's how it always goes," she continues. "I'm the crazy one for going to therapy, but you're completely sane not talking about your mother's abandonment, her addiction, the way that addiction spread to your older brother, how she's back now, how Clayton's relationship with her is different – will forever *be* different from yours."

I swallow the knot in my throat, still too angry to admit she might be right.

"I have to get to the airport," she says, forcefully zipping up her bag.

Her declaration snaps me back to the present moment, to the whole reason I was angry in the first place.

"I don't want you seeing him."

"Well, that's just too damn bad."

I hook her elbow when she tries to swing past me. "What would you do if this were me? What if Shawna showed up and wanted to be my *friend*?"

Erin's brows pinch together, and she shakes her head. "Are you kidding?" She rests her hand on my forearm, giving it a gentle squeeze. "I would be *happy* for you. After what happened between you two, the way things went down? I would be ecstatic for that closure for you, for that opportunity to mend a relationship that meant so much to you — even if was just platonic now."

"I don't need a relationship with her. I don't ever want to talk to her again."

"And that's *your* choice. I respect it." She shakes her head, her doe eyes searching mine. "Why can't you do the same for me?"

My jaw muscles pop, and I look away from her, trying again to see through my fury and understand what she's saying.

But I just fucking *can't.*

Erin sighs, dropping her hold on me and moving for her door again. "You can let yourself out. Just lock up before you go."

"Erin," I say, catching her elbow again.

She pauses at the door, turning to look at me with eyes that tell me more than her words that she's not just sad we're fighting.

She's disappointed.

In me.

And I wish I could be level-headed, that I could see it from her point of view, but regardless of how pissed off I am, I don't want her to leave like this.

I gently tug until she lets me pull her into my arms, and I wrap her in a fierce hug, letting out a slow breath at the way she feels in my arms, her head against my chest, the scent of her hair in my nose.

"I love you," I remind her.

"I love you, too."

I swallow as she pulls away, waiting for me to say something else. But I don't have anything to say that wouldn't upset her more — or me.

So I say nothing at all.

She leaves.

And I punch a hole through her wall.

Skyler

"Shot ski! Shot ski! Shot ski! Shot ski!"

You would think it's Spring Break instead of a family holiday weekend by the amount of twenty-something year olds gathered around the pool at *La Rose Roja Resort*. The girls and I were all pleasantly surprised to find it so packed and happening when we arrived yesterday, the resort employees handing us our first fruity cocktails.

And the party has raged on ever since.

As to be expected, we nearly blacked out on our first night, not even bothering to get all dolled up to go out. We just got to our penthouse, freaked the fuck out over what Brandon had set up for us, and then promptly changed into our swimsuits and went down to the pool party.

After that, things got a little fuzzy.

A few things I remember...

One, Jess dancing on the bar during a wet t-shirt contest and winning easily when she decided the wet t-shirt was just getting in the way, so she stripped it up over her head.

Two, Cassie and Ashlei making a giant, teetering pyramid out of beer cans, stealing empties from every guy and girl alike to add to their masterpiece. They let out a victorious cheer when it finally got so big that it crashed to the ground and half of it ended up in the pool.

Three, Erin letting loose more than I'd seen her since *maybe* my freshman year of college. She took shots and danced in the pool, and even played along with some guy who's here for a bachelor party and needed to get a girl to ride around on his shoulders to knock an item off their scavenger hunt list.

And four — yet another text from Kip lighting up my phone, haunting me even through my buzzed haze.

Where are you?

Maybe it's self-preservation, how I've ignored every message from him since that night he called me to apologize. He told me to hold onto him, but inside, I know I have to do the opposite.

I have to let him go.

So I've been focusing on school, on Kappa Kappa Beta, on my new Grand Little, on my meetings with the guidance counselor to figure out where I'm going after graduation.

I've ignored every call, every *how are you, I miss you, are you okay, where are you, please call me* that he's sent.

Being out of the country with my best friends has made it easier to do so — well, as easy as letting Kip Jackson go can be, at least.

Which is to say, it's slightly less torturous.

Now, it's day two of our trip, and after a successful morning brunch, afternoon of relaxing by the pool, and evening of massages — we're back for round two, the sun setting over the resort, bass thumping from the DJ's booth perched over the pool.

Erin, Cassie, and Jess have a shot ski in their hands — an old wooden ski painted with the resort's colors and fitted with shot-glass-sized holes that now host a full mouthful of tequila. It takes precision to get the shots lined up with each of their mouths and to pour them down without spilling all over someone, but they pull it off — to the roaring approval of the crowd.

When they finish, Erin holds the ski over her head in victory, and then someone at the resort is taking it from her and carrying it to the back to wash it and no doubt line it up for the next victims.

"I'm drunk," Cassie slurs, slinging her arm around my neck.

"Easy, Little — it's only nine."

"Come dance with me," she says instead of acknowledging how young the night is, but I oblige her, letting her take my hand and drag me to the shallow end of the pool right in front of the DJ.

Everything is warped and blurry, not because I'm drunk, but because that's just the state of being I've existed in since Kip and I fought last semester. It's like being half-frozen, half-numb, like a dream where you're underwater and try to punch something but can't.

My hands are up in the air, hips swaying to the rhythm, eyes closed and lights coloring my eyelids green and blue and pink and purple as we dance.

But inside, I'm sitting alone in a dark room, staring at the ceiling.

Existing.

Cassie finally decides she needs water, and we make our way through the crowd and over to the VIP booth that comes with our penthouse rental. It's got three massive day beds and two dedicated servers to bring us alcohol or food — or water, which is very much needed in this moment.

Jess and Ashlei are kicked back on one of the day beds, lost in conversation, and Erin is somewhere still dancing in the pool when Cassie and I slip through the roped-off entryway.

I can't help but smile at the sight of Ashlei in her all-white bikini, the gold sash across her chest reading BRIDE-TO-BE — except *to be* is scratched out and ALREADY is written in Sharpie above it. Even with her arm in a sling, she's radiant, glowing only the way a new bride can.

Bride.

She's *married.*

As if the thought has just finally sunk in, I wrap her in a fierce hug as soon as I'm inside our little area, and she giggles, squeezing me in return.

"You're married," I whisper in her ear.

"I know. How crazy is this?"

"Insanely crazy. Also, insanely amazing."

She nods when I pull back, her eyes glossy. "I love that rich bastard."

I bark out a laugh. "I know."

"Oh, here," Jess says when I'm standing again. She tosses my phone to me before I'm prepared to catch it. It bobbles a little in my hand before I grip it tight. "That thing has been blowing up."

I frown, looking at the dozen missed call requests on the screen. They're from a number I don't recognize, an area code I've never seen before.

I chew my cheek, wondering if it's Kip trying any means necessary to get ahold of me. I can't think of anyone else it would be.

"Just call him back," Erin says from over my shoulder. I jump, not realizing she had joined us, and she gives me a knowing smile as she squeezes my arm. "Hear him out. Even if your choice is still the same and you think it's over, you at least owe it to him to put him out of his misery and make sure *he* knows that's your decision, too."

My mouth tugs to the side, stomach roiling at the thought of ever saying those words, at ever officially admitting that we're done. But I nod, letting her know I hear her.

And then I grab my bag and tell the girls I'll be back in a bit, disappearing through the hotel lobby doors.

It's a quiet ride up the elevator, though I can still hear the music thumping on when I make it to our suite. It's absolutely massive, three bedrooms and a huge sitting area finessed with the finest furniture and interior design. There's a fireplace and an infinity plunge pool that has the illusion of hanging off the deck and over the ocean below, as well as an expansive balcony, and a stacked minibar that we've more than taken advantage of.

I slip my bag off my shoulder, laying a towel out on one of the daybeds on the balcony before I pull up the missed call notifications on my phone. I almost regret setting up international calls and texts with my service provider for this trip, but I wanted to make sure I was available in case my parents needed me.

Or maybe, deep down, I *wanted* Kip to call.

I sigh at the absolute mess I am before tapping the number on the screen to call it back. I tap the button to put it on speakerphone next, leaning back against the plush pillows and waiting as it rings, my eyes on the last rays of sun touching the beach.

"Where the hell *are* you?"

The voice that answers is not what I expected. Female, angry, and... and... *familiar*.

"Who is this?"

"Natalia."

I snap upright, eyes narrowing. "You have a lot of fucking nerve to call me."

"Yeah, well, you can tell me how much you hate me later. Right now, I need you to tell me where you fucking are. Actually, I need you to answer Kip and tell *him* where you are."

"How about I hang up and you go fuck yourself?"

I'm about to do just that when she screams, "Wait!"

I pause with my finger over the red button that will end the call.

"Just... look. I know you hate me."

"I don't hate you. Hating you would require that I give a shit about you in some way, and I don't," I clarify.

"Fine. But just... please. *Please* call Kip and talk to him. He's worried sick about you."

I swallow. "And you would know this how?"

"Oh, don't worry — he's not talking to me anymore than he has to to wrap up the show," she says with a scoff. "So, you won. If that's what you're wondering."

"I never knew I was in a fight."

"That's a lie and you know it."

"And you're a *bitch* and you know it."

There's a pause, then a sigh. "Maybe. Or maybe I just know what I want and have learned in my short life that sometimes you've got to do some fucked-up things to get what you deserve."

I shake my head.

"Look, I didn't call to fight you. I called to... to... I don't know, try to talk some sense into you, or at least plead to whatever part of you still cares about Kip."

"Don't you dare question my feelings for him."

"Well, he's fucking sick over you. He's not eating, barely sleeping, and tonight is the premier and he's nowhere to be found."

I blink, my heart stopping dead before kicking back with a violent thump in my chest. "It's premier night?"

"Yes. And not just for the cast — for *everyone*. There's going to be a packed theater. Professors, students, even some well-known indie film producers. It's a big deal, Skyler, and this series is good enough that Kip should be entering it into film festivals. But he hates it. He hates *himself* for how he hurt you when he was making it. It's tainted."

"Not just by me," I seethe. "And you know damn well if it's anyone's fault, her name starts with an N."

"I'm just asking you to call him."

"And I'm telling you that I don't owe you a single damn thing. You say you did what you thought you needed to do to get what you want? Well, let me tell you this. I saw talent that day you auditioned. I saw a sweet, kind, humble girl who deserved success. But the more I got to know you, the more games you played, the more I realized you're nothing but a snot-nosed brat too big for her britches, an entitled little girl who thinks she's owed the world before having to work for it. You will burn more bridges than you can build if you keep this up. So, from one woman to another, drop the games and the manipulation and *work* for what's important to you." I pause. "You already had the gig. You didn't need to have the man."

"But the man was a tie to my dreams."

"Get your dreams on your own."

I hang up before she can answer, and nearly throw my phone but refrain. I do grip it so hard the screen protector cracks, though, and then I force a breath, dropping it to the side and flopping back on the daybed.

The sun has set now, the moon sliding in to take its place, and I stare up at the navy and purple sky with my heart racing.

Racing, and aching, and bleeding out.

I close my eyes, holding back the tears I feel burning behind my lids.

Slowly, I peel myself up again, reach for my phone, and pull up Kip's contact.

I'm okay. I'm in Mexico for Ashlei's bachelorette. Long story.

I pause, not yet sending it as I debate what to say next.

Go enjoy the premier — you've earned it.

Another pause, and then I add.

I'm so proud of you.

I send it before I can overthink it.

The little bubbles letting me know he's typing appear in an instant, then disappear, then appear again, then disappear.

His heart is just as much at war as mine.

Finally, one simple text comes through.

Thank you.

For texting him back, for telling him where I am, for saying that I'm proud of him? I don't know which.

I love you, I type out, the blinking cursor at the end of the sentence my only point of focus.

But I delete the words instead of sending them, and then I head back downstairs to the party, leaving my phone in the room for the rest of the night.

Bear

A low growl rips out of me as I thrust the barbell up again, chest puffing, lips flat as I force myself to keep breathing through the reps.

Seven.

Eight.

My muscles quake in protest, but I grit through the pain, willing my mental capability to be stronger than my physical as I thrust the bar up again.

Nine.

"Come on, one more," Giselle says, standing over me with her fingertips under the bar like she could actually help me if I needed it.

She's a buck thirty soaking wet, and I'm benching two-hundred-and-fifty pounds.

With all the effort I have left, I grunt and shove the bar away from my chest, hooking it on the rack as soon as I've extended my elbows to get the full lift.

A few guys around the gym murmur various encouragements to me as I sit up, mopping my forehead with my towel. They say *damn, bro* and *nice* and *yes, sir* as Giselle walks around the bench to face me, holding up her hand for a high five with a proud grin on her face.

I slap her hand. "Why are you looking at me like *you're* the trainer?"

"For that little show, I was."

I try to smile, but it comes up short. I haven't had a full smile since Thanksgiving, since before I found out Gavin was back in town and Erin was talking to him.

And that she didn't tell me.

The fact that she left town right after to go on Ashlei's bachelorette didn't help. She's texted me a few times checking in, but I know she's hanging with her sisters and I don't *want* her to be glued to her phone.

I just wish she hadn't left after a fight like that.

Planting weight onto my feet, I push off from where I'm seated on the bench and over to the barbell in front of the mirror. I start loading it up, preparing for a heavy deadlift when Giselle touches my shoulder.

"Hey, don't you think we've pushed it hard enough for today?"

I shake my head without looking at her. "I need the release."

"Well, what you *don't* need is an injury."

"I'm fine."

"Maybe so," she says, stepping in front of me to block me from putting more weight on the bar. "But as your boss, I'm calling it."

"You're not my boss," I say, arching a brow.

"Your superior, whatever." She waves her hand, and then when her arms fold over her chest again, she frowns. "Come on. Let's hit the sauna. You can sweat it out."

I hang my hands on my hips, body aching and so tired I know the possibility of injuring myself is actually higher than I want to admit.

"Sauna," Giselle says, snapping her fingers in front of my face. "Now."

I sigh, but relent, tossing my towel over my shoulder and cleaning up our space before I let her lead the way.

The gym is quiet for a Saturday evening, likely because most people are still spending time with their families. I'm thankful Giselle was down for a training session. I needed to get out of my house, out of my head.

We both sigh in relief when we take a seat on the warm wood in the sauna, the dark room already soothing us — body and soul. Hot rocks cook in the middle of the room, steam rising all around us, and we nod to the only other two people in with us — two girls who look fresh off a swim in the lap pool.

"God, I'm going to be so sore tomorrow," Giselle groans, leaning back to balance her elbows on the wood behind her. She rolls her shoulders, hissing. "I know leg day is the worst, but upper body day sucks, too."

The corner of my mouth lifts. "I loved it."

"Yeah, well, you're a masochist," she says, eyeing me for a second before her attention is back on the rocks. "Besides, sounds like you were blowing off some steam. There's always more energy when you're pissed off."

I clench my jaw, but don't reply.

"What's going on?" Giselle asks.

The swimmers must think we want privacy, because they give us a little nod and smile before they see themselves out, and then it's just the two of us.

I sigh. "I don't really want to talk about it."

"Come on. Maybe I can help. Besides, I'm nosy and the workplace drama has been unfortunately dry lately. Give me something."

I shake my head on another fake smile. "It's nothing, really. Just... Erin and I got into a little disagreement before she left for her trip."

"Uh-oh. What'd you do?"

I actually chuckle at that. "Overreact, most likely. I don't know. Her ex is back in town, and he goes to therapy with her, and they've been talking. I saw a text come through from him and I just... I lost it."

"She didn't tell you he was back?"

I shake my head, and Giselle whistles, massaging the side of her neck for a moment.

"Well, I'd be upset, too."

"They're just friends," I say with confidence — which is funny, considering I didn't want to hear it when Erin told me that same thing.

"Friends, with an ex?" She shakes her head. "I don't know if that's possible."

"With them, I think it is. They have a complicated relationship, one that's tied up in a lot more than just romance." I frown. "I think he's been an important part of her recovery."

"Recovery?"

That makes my throat go dry, and I shake my head. "It's not my story to tell. Just... I guess what I'm saying is that talking to you about it now, I realize I trust her, and I'm not threatened by him. But I certainly didn't act that way originally. And she said some things, some *true* things, but still... they stung."

"Like?"

"Like calling me out on the fact that I have a lot of family shit in my life that I've never properly dealt with, that I laugh at her going to therapy when in reality I probably need it, too."

"This is your therapy," Giselle says simply, and when I turn to look at her, it's with a gaze of wonder.

Because she just nailed what I have been trying to tell Erin forever, I just never knew how.

"I mean, you come here to be silent, to sit with your thoughts, to work through frustrations. And from what you've told me, it's always been this way, yeah?"

I nod. "Yes."

She shrugs. "Not everyone has to talk about what's happened to them. Sometimes, we handle trauma by working through it physically, overcoming it the same way we overcome a challenge in the gym."

I watch her for longer than appropriate.

"What?" she asks on a smile.

"I just... yes. That's exactly it."

She looks at her nails before polishing them on her sports bra. "I know. I'm good."

I smirk, relaxing a little bit and digesting her words as silence falls between us. After a long while, Giselle clears her throat, wiping at a bead of sweat rolling down her neck.

"You know," she says softly, tentatively. "There are other ways to find that release you need."

My heart halts in my chest.

"I could help," she continues, and to my absolute horror, she scoots a little closer, angles her body toward mine, and touches my knee with one hand. Her eyes find mine, and where I hope she can read the warning in my gaze, I find only heat and lust in hers as she slides her hand up my thigh, higher and higher. "No one would have to know."

"Giselle..."

Her smile turns wicked when I say her name, and unabashedly, she runs her hand up even more, wrapping around my cock before I can stop her.

I jerk away quickly, grabbing her wrist with more force than necessary and keeping hold of it as she giggles and bites her lip.

"You want to take control?" she asks. "I like that."

"Giselle," I say again, this time more firm. "This is inappropriate."

Her smile wanes, and she blinks a few times before ripping her arm out of my grasp. "Oh, *calm down*. It's not that serious." She rolls her eyes. "It's just a little fun. And trust me — you're in need of it."

"I have a girlfriend."

"And I went to bat for you so you could have an extra-long weekend to take said girlfriend home to Pittsburgh, remember?" she challenges, arching a brow at me. "Erin is out of town. She also doesn't know me and never has to find out." Her gaze falls to my lap. "And I don't know if you've noticed, but you're hard as fucking tungsten right now."

"I would never cheat on her," I clip. "I would never hurt her like that. And if you're implying that I somehow owe you for what you did for me, then you should have explained those terms before you assumed I'd agree to them."

Giselle scoffs, her little mouth falling open as she shakes her head and watches me with narrowing eyes. She closes her lips together, rolls them, and then, like she was under some sort of spell, all the anger disappears. She smiles, genuine and calm, and stands up.

"No worries, it was just a miscommunication." She throws her towel over her shoulder before grabbing her gym bag from the floor. "I'm going to shower and head out. See you Monday?"

She doesn't wait for me to answer before she leaves me alone in the sauna, and as soon as she does, I bark out a curse, elbows coming to my knees as I dig the heels of my hands into my eyeballs.

The heat soaks into my skin.

And along with it — the most severe doubt I've ever felt in my life.

Every ounce of trust I had for Giselle has been vanquished. What if she didn't mean what she said about me starting my own business, about me having the chops to have my own company? Was she just spitting that nonsense to try to get close to me?

To try to fuck me?

I grimace, cursing again as I kick back in my seat.

And Erin...

What if she meant what she said to me in the spring, that she didn't have anything to give me? Did I push her? Did I ask too much?

What if she rushed into this because she felt like she had to?

What if she's not ready?

I swallow, thinking of how I acted when I saw that text, the jealous rage that consumed me.

What if *I'm* not ready?

Thought after thought pummels me like fists to a speed bag, and I take every blow harder than the last until I can't take it any longer. My fists ball, legs quake, lungs seize up as they try to calm me with fresh air.

But it's no use.

I might be able to work out my physical frustrations, but there's no escaping this hell that lives inside my head.

I grab my duffle bag and sling it over my shoulder, shoving through the sauna doors and barreling out of the gym.

And I drive straight to the office.

Skyler

"Jesus said Sunday is the day of rest, y'all," Erin tries, popping a grape into her mouth while we lounge by our plunge pool.

"And we *are* resting. Until..." Jess looks at her watch. "About two hours from now, in which case we will be transitioning into pre-gaming and then full-on party mode."

Erin shakes her head. "My liver will never recover from this trip."

"How often is it that your best friend gets married?" Cassie remarks.

"It better only be once for this bestie," Ashlei says, holding up her finger. "Because if I lose a man this fine, just hang me up to dry, y'all, I'm done."

We all laugh and raise our water bottles in a cheers before chugging — which may very well be our most important chug of the day. If we're going to hit up the pool party again tonight, we'll need all the hydration we can get.

Electronic dance music softly thumps up to our room from the pool deck below, and we tap our feet along to the beat as we soak in the sun's rays. Ashlei has taken off her sling to avoid tan lines, and she and Cassie are reminiscing on the night before as Erin flips through a textbook — one we tried to get her to leave behind, but to no avail.

That girl is nothing if not serious about law school.

Jess and I are quiet for a while, just enjoying the breeze and the nice weather and the music, and then I notice her looking at her phone. She sighs, flipping between two photos. I lean in a little closer and chuckle when I see one is of her and Kade, and the other is her and Jarrett.

"Sadist," I tease.

She groans, closing her screen and throwing her phone onto the table face down. "I know, I know. I can't stop."

"I don't think swiping between pictures is going to make the answer come to you."

"No, probably not. But they *are* nice to look at."

I offer a sympathetic smile. "How are you feeling? After getting away and clearing your head a bit."

Jess is silent for a long pause. "Sick. Absolutely sick."

"Because you still don't know?"

"Because I think I *do* know, and somehow that makes it even worse."

I frown. "How so?"

Jess's maple eyes meet mine. "I have to hurt one of them, Skyler. I've already hurt them *both*." She shakes her head. "I don't deserve either of them after the way I've played them back and forth under the guise of needing time, needing space, needing... whatever. The truth is I fucked Kade and then fucked his brother two weeks later." Her eyes water. "I'm the most awful human to ever walk the face of the Earth."

"You love them," I say, sitting up. "And they both knew what they were getting into. If either of them was against it, *really* against it, they would have told you to kick rocks already."

"*That's* what I deserve."

"Well, love makes us do some crazy shit," I say with a laugh. "I mean, come on — this group is nothing if not proof of that."

Jess nods. "They really love me. And I really do love *them*." She swallows. "But like Cassie said — I can't have them both."

"No, you can't."

There's a knock at our suite door, and Cassie pops up, already jogging inside. "Room service is here!"

Jess closes her eyes and sinks down into her lounge even more, ignoring the call for food. "It's going to hurt him so bad. It's going to *kill* me."

"It's going to hurt *who* so bad?" I ask.

Jess sighs, opening her mouth to answer me, but then her eyes go wide as basketballs at something behind me.

I whip around, scared there's a bug or a monster or a fucking tsunami.

Instead, I find Kip.

My jaw drops as he walks onto the balcony with Cassie trailing behind him, her face just as shocked as mine. He looks like absolute shit — wearing what I can only assume is the tux he wore to the premier the night before, a five o'clock shadow on his jaw, his eyes red and puffy.

In his hand is a bouquet of flowers.

"What are you doing here?" I breathe.

Kip's eyes search mine, a thick swallow bobbing his Adam's apple before he shrugs. "I came to fight and win my girl back."

Jess rolls her lips together and smacks my arm as Cassie, Ashlei, and Erin all do a miserable job of hiding their collective sighs at his declaration.

"Actually," he clarifies. "I came to grovel, and plead, and put all my chips on the table, to pray like hell my measly pair of deuces is enough." He takes a confident step toward me. "Pray that *I* am enough."

My heart squeezes in my chest, tears pricking my eyes.

"I am sick without you, Skyler. I could say my entire world has been flipped upside down, but the truth is that *you* are my world. The show, school, whatever future career I might have — none of it matters without you." He swallows. "You are my dream. And without you, life is just... sleep deprivation. Punishment. Unrelenting torture."

"Kip..."

"I am so sorry for hurting you, for not listening to you, for having my head so far up my ass I couldn't see my mistakes. Please," he begs, his own eyes watering, nose flaring. "Please forgive me. Please tell me you'll give me another chance. I swear I won't waste it. I swear, if you let me, I'll spend the rest of my life making sure you know you are my everything."

"If you don't kiss him, I will!" Jess says, shoving me until I have no choice but to either tumble out of the daybed onto my face or stand. I choose the latter, and Kip smirks at Jess before his eyes are on mine again.

Sincere and more apologetic than I've ever seen.

And I hate myself for putting him through this, for making him so sick he thought he could ever truly lose me.

As if I haven't been his since the moment I laid eyes on his stupid glasses and his stupid perfect smile.

I inhale, exhale, and slowly make my way over to where he stands.

But I don't say a word.

I just nod.

In the next breath, I'm swept into his arms, and then I'm spinning, my hair flying behind me as the girls laugh and cheer. I don't have the chance to laugh, though — because Kip captures my mouth with his, holding me to him in a beautiful, long-overdue kiss.

"I will never hurt you again," he swears against my lips. "I'm so sorry, Skyler. I'm so fucking sorry."

"I'm sorry, too," I breathe into him.

"You have nothing to be sorry for."

"Sure, I do. I put you through more torture than you deserve. I didn't accept your apology."

"Well, I didn't apologize correctly. I was blinded... I couldn't see your point of view, and I'm sorry for that."

"Okay, okay," Jess says, making a gagging notion with her finger, tongue sticking out. "He's sorry, you're sorry, we all get it. Now, can you two get out of here and go fuck already?"

I cover my laugh by burying my face in Kip's chest, peeking up at him. "I... I love you, and I'm so happy you came all this way but... I'm here with the girls. It's Ashlei's bachelorette."

"I know, I know, and I don't want to take you from them. I just had to see you." He sweeps my hair from my face, and I lean into his palm as he says, "I had to know you were okay. That *we* were okay."

"We are," I promise.

"Skyler, I swear to God, if you don't have that man naked in the next ten minutes," Jess warns.

I spin in Kip's arms, throwing my hands up. "But we're going out!"

"*We* are going out," Ashlei corrects, pointing to the four of them and purposefully leaving me out. "*You* are getting railed." She pauses. "Sorry, Kip."

He throws his hands up with a smile.

"If you still have energy after, come join us," Erin says.

I bite my lip, looking at all of them. "Are you sure? I don't—"

"GO!" they all yell in unison.

And then I'm swept up again and carried out of the suite.

***

My feet don't hit the ground again until I'm halfway across the resort in Kip's room. It's much smaller than the penthouse suite Brandon booked us, but I couldn't care less as I immediately slip my hands under Kip's suit jacket and shove the fabric back over his wide shoulders.

"Help," I pant against his lips, trying unsuccessfully again to strip him.

Kip chuckles, shrugging out of his jacket and unfastening his tie. "Are you sure you don't want to talk for a while? We haven't—"

"Later."

I don't wait for him to unbutton his dress shirt. Instead, I grab at the collar with both hands and then rip them in opposite directions, sending the first two buttons skittering to the floor. Kip roars a laugh at that, and then helps me rip it the rest of the way because two buttons was all I got with all my might.

I laugh then, too, before Kip steals my breath with a passionate, demanding kiss — one that has me pressing up on my toes for more as he tugs at the string of my bikini top. It falls loose, dangling from the string wrapped around my neck, and Kip palms my breasts with a groan that makes me ache and clench and tingle.

"*Fuck*, it's been so long..." he husks, pressing his forehead to mine and looking down to appreciate the view of what his hands are doing to me.

I capture his mouth again just as my fingers start fumbling with the button and zipper of his pants, and in-between bruising kisses and lip biting, I manage to undo them, yanking as hard as I can to get them down over his ass.

Kip shoves them the rest of the way down, hopping a little as he frees one leg and then the other. I'm in his arms in the next instant, and then I'm falling into the lush comforter, pillows making a soft *whoosh* when I collapse into them.

It's a glorious sight to behold, Kip watching me from the foot of the bed as he slowly strips his boxer briefs down. His length springs free of them, making me bite my lip, and when he palms that impressive cock with his heated gaze on me, I spread my knees, leaning up on one elbow as I slowly slide my other hand down my exposed breast, my navel, and dive beneath the small triangle fabric of my bikini bottoms.

"Have you touched yourself thinking about me?" Kip asks, his eyes on where my fingers move under the swimsuit.

"Only every night."

He closes his eyes on a hot breath, stroking himself as his cock twitches at my words. "Me too. I've come so many nights thinking about you, about how fucking tight you are, how perfectly you fit around me."

"Why don't you remind me what that feels like?"

"Soon," he promises, and then he's prowling onto the bed, climbing between my legs.

His shoulder hits the bottom of one of my legs and then the other, until my knees are spread even farther, and he nips my fingers through the fabric of my bottoms.

"My turn," he says, and I remove my fingers just in time for him to pull at the string over my left hip, then the one over my right, the fabric falling away like silk and leaving my bare pussy right in his face.

Kip growls, carefully trailing his middle finger from my clit down through my slick lips as I tremble and quake.

"Perfect," he mutters, shaking his head and sliding his finger up again. He circles my clit in a swift motion that makes my legs convulse, and then that finger slides down again, entering me with a shock between pleasure and the pain that comes with having been empty for so long. I arch into the touch, and Kip smirks, kissing my inner thigh. "So goddamn perfect."

That featherlight kiss on my thigh turns into a tongue gliding along the seam where my leg meets my pelvis, and then he's sucking and biting and teasing his way to where I want him most, his finger slowly moving inside me and making me writhe.

It's like a dream and the most alert awakening of my life all at once. My head is fuzzy, focus distant, as if I'm both experiencing and watching it happen from above. At the same time, every nerve in my body is sensitive and buzzing, coming alive at the faintest touch from this man.

This man whom I've missed.

This man who traveled halfway across the world to get me back.

This man whom I love.

This man I can't live without.

Kip's mouth finally descends on my clit as he slips another finger inside me, and I cry out at the warmth, the pressure, the all-encompassing feeling of being connected again. When he groans and sweeps his tongue long, hot, and flat over my sensitive nerves, I buck into the touch, twisting my fists in the sheets and grinding my hips.

He knows just how to lick me, how to tease me, how to move his fingers inside me along with the rhythm of his tongue. He knows to move slow at first, exaggerating the movements, and then to pick up speed as my breath hitches, my hips moving of their own accord as I reach for my climax.

And he knows just where to press a third finger at the sensitive opening below where his other two are now, giving me a shock of forbidden pleasure. He glances up at me, his tongue still sweeping, eyes asking me for permission.

"Yes," I breathe, pleading, and he slicks his finger through my desire before gently, slowly, inching it inside my ass.

I cry out, seeing stars, and then he's sucking on my clit and moving his fingers inside me in a slow, hypnotizing rhythm that pushes me closer and closer to my release with every pump. The finger inside my ass is just barely in there, barely moving, but it's pushing all the sensitive, bundled-up nerves in just the right way.

And with his name barreling off my lips, I fly apart.

I know if anyone is in the rooms around us, they hear every moan as I find my release, tearing at the sheets with my nails and arching my back and riding out every blissful wave. Kip smirks against my clit before blowing a gentle *shhhh* on it that only makes me convulse harder.

I come for longer than possible — at least that's how it feels — and when I'm done, everything falls lax, my legs opening wide, arms flopping out, sweat-sheened skin sticking to the cool sheets.

Kip kisses my clit gently, but it still makes all my limbs shutter, and he slowly makes his way up to capture my mouth with his.

"That was fucking hot," he says, smirking.

"Your turn," is my only response before I'm flipping us over, pinning him to the sheets as I make my way down his body, kiss by kiss, on shaky, sated limbs.

"Wait," he says, halting me before I can reach the promise land.

I look up at him with a pout that makes him chuckle, but he pulls me back up until I'm straddling him, and he kisses me long and hard.

"I want these lips around my cock," he says, biting my bottom one to emphasize. "But not before I fill that beautiful pussy I just had the pleasure of tasting."

I moan when he kisses me hard again, our teeth clashing, but I don't have time to tell him how much I love his dirty talk before my hips are lifted, and he's situated at my entrance, and then he grabs my ass and guides me down over him, flexing his hips as I swallow him whole.

We both cry out at the sensation, at him stretching me and filling me so fast it steals both our breaths. I sit there for a long moment, him completely inside me, our breaths heavy and hot between us as we soak in the way it feels.

And then he spanks my ass, lifts me, and slams into me again.

A long curse leaves his lips, and he arches back, eyes squeezing closed as I press my hands into his chest and take control. I ride him slow at first, letting him hit deep and feel every inch of me opening for him. But after every thrust, I pick up the pace just a little, just enough to have him biting his lip and groaning and peeling his heavy eyelids open to watch my breasts swell above him or to look down at where his cock disappears inside me.

I know without him telling me that he's not going to last long — not after months of being apart, after just spending so much time going down on me, after being inside me again with my tits bouncing in his face.

I ride him a little faster, moving my hips just like I know he loves, tucking my pelvis anytime I sit fully down so I can take him as much inside me as possible. And when he groans loud and heavy, his hands gripping my hips hard enough to leave a mark, I know he's close enough.

I hop off him without warning, which makes his eyes shoot open wide, a desperate *no* almost flowing off his lips.

But before he can say it, I flip around, putting my pussy in his face again as I take his cock deep in my throat.

"Oh *fuck*, Sky," he curses, and I bob my head up and down, taking advantage of the angle that lets his cock curve into my throat just right.

I hold myself steady with one hand and slide the other down over his balls, rubbing them in time with my mouth. Then, I press my index finger just between his ball and his ass, finding that sensitive spot and massaging it as I deep throat him again.

And that does it.

With a curse, Kip holds my head down and spills into my throat, his body pulsing and trembling under me as he releases. I swallow every last drop, soaking in the way it feels to make this man fall apart from my touch alone.

Kip shutters when he's fully spent, and then just like I did, he falls lax, his breaths tickling my pussy as he comes down. I swirl my tongue around him one last time before I release, and then I carefully crawl off of him, sitting on one hip and looking back at him with a grin before wiping the corners of my mouth with my thumb.

He shakes his head. "You wicked little girl," he growls.

And then he pulls me back up the bed, his mouth finding mine, and we slip easily into round two.

***

We finally hit a point where we need water, and food, and rest.

Kip orders us far too much from room service, and when it arrives, we have a buffet in bed.

And I beg him to play the web series for me.

It's surreal, seeing our story brought to life on the screen, and past the gut reaction the first time Natalia's face shows, I don't even feel animosity toward her. It's like I slip in so easily that I feel like it's me, not her, and it's Kip, not the actor playing him. It's *our* story.

She'll never be able to taint that.

We're on episode three, me sucking on a chocolate milkshake while Kip draws lazy circles on my hip between pressing gentle kisses there, when my phone buzzes loud on the bedside table.

My breath hitches in my chest at the simple text on the screen.

S.O.S. Get down here. Now!

Jess.

Cassie

I slam back another shot of tequila.

I've lost count which one I'm on.

All I know is that I don't even need the salt or the lime anymore. It doesn't burn, it doesn't sting, it just makes me let out a victorious cheer and slam my hand on the bar, ready for another.

"Ooohkay," Ashlei says, peeling me away before I have the chance to get the bartender's attention. The girls I just took the shot with are high-fiving me as Ashlei steals me from them — they're a bachelorette party, too, from New York. "Maybe we hold off on another shot for a while."

"But I want another one," I pout.

"I know you do, but let's give that one time to set in first, mmkay?"

I wave her off, shrugging free of her grasp before I blow a breath through flat lips. "*Fine.* But then I'm going to dance."

"Dancing we can do," Ashlei says, and she leads me down into the pool, the water warm and pleasant as we join the other dancing bodies right in front of the DJ booth.

The music is loud and energetic, bass thumping through me as the lights sway above us and reflect off the water, too. I throw my hands up and move my hips, enjoying the buzz.

Or, at least, trying to.

Under that joy and fun is a thick layer of slimy anger holding on for dear life and refusing to let go.

Kip showing up to surprise Skyler was the sweetest thing I've ever seen. It reminded me of something out of a movie, and the way he looked at her, the way he flew hundreds of miles without sleeping because he was so sick at the thought of losing her...

It makes my stomach hurt.

Because it's beautiful.

And because I want it to be Adam who showed up like that.

I want it to be him who surprised me, who said he couldn't wait to leave Baltimore after the Thanksgiving meeting, couldn't stand to be away from me any longer. I want it to be the two of us holed up in a room somewhere in the resort, making love for hours. I want it to be me wrapped up in my guy's arms, smitten from the fact that he flew all the way here just to find me, just to have me and remind me that it's us against the world.

Instead, I've had a string of measly text messages that make my blood boil.

We barely talked on Thanksgiving, save for the early call he made to wish me a happy holiday. We watched part of the Macy's Day Parade together before he said he had to go, and my gut soured at the sound of Chandler's voice in the background of that call.

It shouldn't have upset me. He said all the right things, assured me everything was okay, and I *knew* he was doing it for us. He wanted a job in the same city where I would go to school so we wouldn't have to be apart any longer.

But he was willing to sacrifice being with me to do it.

And I hate that fact.

I hate that he didn't say no to Chandler, that he didn't say he could find a different job. As selfish as it sounds, because I *know* Simmons is an amazing company he'd be lucky to work for, I just don't want to have to share him.

Not even like this.

Perhaps what's driven me past sad to angry is how he hasn't called since then, nor has he been attentive over texts. Sure, I'm with my girls and want to be present to celebrate Ashlei, but when my texts go unanswered for hours only to get a *sorry, it's really busy over here, but I miss you so much and I think I've got this job in the bag!*

Well...

It just hurts.

And maybe it's the alcohol swimming in my body, the music thumping through my soul, and the hopeless romantic still swooning after what Kip did — but I'm sad and lonely and pissed off.

The more the night goes on, the more I fear that may be the most dangerous combination of emotions.

"I want another shot," I tell Ashlei, and I don't wait for her before I'm making a beeline through the crowd, back to the stairs that exit the pool.

She chases after me, catching my elbow just as I hit the bar.

"I don't think that's a good idea."

I shrug her off. "I'm fine. You want one?"

Ashlei frowns. "No. And I don't want *you* to take one, either."

"Come *on*, Lei. Loosen up! This is your bachelorette party and I feel like you've been the most tame of all of us."

Lei frowns, and then her eyes are scanning the crowd.

I have no doubt she's looking for Erin, or Jess, or both of them for backup, so I make my move before she can stop me.

"Two tequila shots," I tell the same bartender who has been helping me all night, and he smiles, shaking his head before he pours them up.

"Be careful, señorita," he warns.

I wink at him, taking the shots and fully preparing to take both, but then a warm hand wraps around me from behind.

"Looks like you could use some help with one of those."

The voice is deep and seductive, the words whispered into the shell of my ear as I'm pulled against a rock-hard body. For a moment, I let myself imagine it's Adam, that he's come to apologize, to tell me he hated being away from me so badly he couldn't stand another minute apart, to dance with his girl and take her back to his room and...

I sway my hips against the stranger in time with the music, letting my head drop back against his chest. I feel his lips smirk against my neck as his hands find my waist, and he moves with me, taking the weight of me as the alcohol sets in even more.

I'm dizzy, the world spinning, my legs barely holding me up anymore. But it feels so *good* to be touched, to be held, to have warm arms wrapped around me and warm breath touching my skin.

The stranger trails his hand down my arm, grabbing one of the shots from me before he carefully, slowly spins me around to face him. Or maybe he spun me quickly and I was just moving in slow motion, because some of my shot sloshes out of the glass, and he laughs, steadying me with a, "Whoa, there."

I smile, peering through the drunken haze to study his face.

He's absolutely gorgeous.

His dark blond hair is wet from the pool, sticking up this way and that, his skin a little red from being in the sun. He's got a goofy, charming sort of smile, a broad jaw, a little dent in his nose like he maybe got into a fight once and took a blow he never recovered from.

He's still holding my hip with one hand, his other wrapped around the shot glass, and he clinks it to mine before throwing his back.

I know I shouldn't do it.

I know I'm well past my limit.

But I throw mine back, anyway, this time grimacing and fighting down the roil of my stomach that immediately comes once I've swallowed.

The guy smirks at me, taking both our empty glasses and setting them on the counter.

Then his hands are on my hips again.

And his eyes are searching mine.

And I press up on my toes, launch myself into his arms, wrap my hands around his neck...

And kiss him.

He groans, sliding his hands around my hips to palm my ass and pull me more into him as I thread my hands through his hair. He smells like sunscreen and chlorine and tequila, his lips foreign, not moving the way they should with mine, his hands too aggressive, his hair not the right texture.

And when he slides one of his hands beneath my swimsuit to grab my bare ass and squeeze, my eyes shoot open and I realize what I've done.

I press my hands into his chest and shove him back, making him stumble into a group of girls who curse at him and shove him back toward me. His eyes are wild, hands up as he stares at me like I'm crazy.

"Oh, my God," I whisper, covering my mouth, shaking my head as my eyes blur with tears.

I whip around and find Jess staring at me as she makes her way through the crowd, and Erin is behind her, screaming into her phone, her face bent in anger.

When Jess finally reaches me, she wraps a hand around my wrist and tugs. "Let's go."

"I kissed him," I breathe, letting her pull me.

"I know."

"I kissed him."

She sighs, stopping her rampage through the crowd and turning to face me. She braces her hands on my arms, leveling her gaze with mine. "I know. It's okay. You're drunk. It didn't mean anything."

But I just shake my head, over and over, the fiercest chill of my life breaking across my skin as my stomach twists and turns, my throat burning.

And before Jess can pull me any farther through the crowd, I rip away from her hold and rush to the nearest bush, surrendering what little dinner I ate and every ounce of tequila I consumed.

Then, I drop to my knees and sob.

Jess

If anyone were to look down upon this scene from an aerial view, they would likely remark that it's a lovely and serene sight to behold.

A stunning penthouse suite at a gorgeous Mexican resort, the sheer white curtains floating in the breeze, the expanded balcony with a private hot tub and plunge pool all so alluring and beautiful. The magical backdrop of a pristine white beach and turquoise water, currently reflecting the full moonlight overhead, and the distant sound of the waves washing ashore.

From the outside, it appears to be an absolutely extraordinary slice of paradise on Earth.

But inside?

It's a goddamn disaster.

"I... I... I'm a monster," Cassie cries to herself, snot and tears dripping down her face as she rocks herself back and forth on one of the daybeds. She sniffs, not even bothering to wipe away the mascara staining her cheeks. "How could I do that to Adam? How can I ever live with myself again?" She balked. "How do I tell him? Oh, God."

She covers her face and sobs even harder, and Skyler winces, rubbing her back and doing her best to comfort her Little as she falls apart. She got down to the pool just in time to see Cassie vomit in the bushes after I sent her the S.O.S. text — and that was before I even knew about Cassie.

I sent it because of Erin.

Erin, who is now pacing back and forth, arms folded hard over her chest as she shakes her head over and over, tossing between murmuring to herself and screaming curse words loud enough for the entire resort to hear. Something happened to her around the same time Cassie had her meltdown, about an hour ago amidst the thumping music of the beach club, but she has yet to tell us what, exactly.

All we know is she looked at her phone, screamed bloody murder, cried, and has been pacing ever since we all dragged Cassie back here to console her.

Ashlei disappeared into the bathroom as soon as we got back, and for how long she's been in there, I can only imagine she's ralphing up the fruity shots we've been knocking back all night.

And then there's me, swiping back and forth between two pictures on my phone, each depicting a different man I love.

Swipe.

Me on Kade's back, my arms wrapped around his shoulders, lips pressed to his cheek as my hair falls over us like a curtain. His warm brown eyes are bright with love and adoration, his smile megawatt in size as he snaps the selfie.

Swipe.

Me and Jarrett in bed, his beast of a body encompassing all of mine as I curl my back into his chest like a cat. The morning sunlight reflects on our soft, sated smiles, and his dark eyes smolder at the camera, promising he's nowhere near finished with the girl in his arms.

Swipe.

Kade.

Swipe.

Jarrett.

Swipe. Swipe. Swipe. Swipe.

Back and forth, over and over, I stare at those men — the men who own my heart — and feel it break at the realization that I will hurt one of them.

That I've *already* hurt them both.

I don't deserve the patience they've given me — the space, the time. And I definitely don't deserve their love.

But I have it, and though I love them both in return, I know there's no putting off the decision I have to make.

The decision I made long before I was ready to admit it to myself, if I were being honest.

Talking to Skyler earlier was the first time I was ready to admit it out loud, and Erin took her place tonight, asking me all the hard questions and not letting me change the subject until I answered them.

I know what I have to do.

But I also know it will kill me to do it.

In my daze, I don't realize Erin is screaming and Cassie is having a full-on panic attack until I snap out of the trance my phone has me in. I close the screen and drop it to the cushion beside me, popping up and running over to Erin first.

"It's not fucking fair! This whole system... this whole *world* is fucked!" she screams.

"Will you bitches shut up?!" Ashlei yells from inside the bathroom. "It's impossible for a girl to poop with all this racket going on!"

Skyler gives me a look that says she's got Cassie, so I grab Erin's hand and lead her to the edge of the balcony, letting the fresh sea breeze calm us both. I don't say anything, just hold her there and smooth my hand over her arm, letting her take a moment for whatever it is that's going on.

She opens her mouth to say something when my ringtone sounds from the chair I was sitting on, and Erin and I both look at the screen, stilling at the sight of Jarrett's name in bold above the new message.

My chest caves in on itself, and I close my eyes for a long moment before I open them to find Erin staring back at me.

"What are you going to do?" she asks, her voice just a whisper.

Before I can answer, Ashlei clears her throat from where she's now standing in the middle of the balcony between us all. Her hair is a mess tied loosely on top of her head, her arm still slung up from the accident, and her face is ghostly pale.

She doesn't say a word.

But when I spot what she's holding in her hand, she doesn't have to.

Her eyes lock on mine, and I exhale, stomach roiling for a whole new reason. Skyler is the first to say what I know we're all thinking.

"Oh, shit."

And Ashlei smiles, *smiles* so wide her eyes water in the process. She shakes her head, staring at the stick before finding my eyes first. Everything is silent somehow, the music from below muted, the ocean waves quiet, the universe balancing in the wake and waiting along with the rest of us.

"I'm pregnant," she whispers.

And then she covers her mouth and cries.

EPISODE 6

Adam

"Please say something."

Cassie's voice is weak, hoarse, pained as if she's being tortured and I'm the one holding the whip.

All I can do is stare at the string of Christmas lights hanging above me in the Alpha Sigma courtyard, somehow immune to how freezing it is, and unable to hear the party raging inside. With finals next week, the brothers are letting loose and trying to have a little fun before they're chained to their textbooks.

I imagined this call so differently.

I've been anxious to talk to Cassie since Thanksgiving, since I hit it out of the park meeting Chandler's grandparents. Mr. Simmons was in a fraternity, too, when he was younger, and we bonded over our love of brotherhood. He had also been raised by his grandfather, so sharing stories about the lessons we learned and how we grew up only strengthened our easy friendship. Pair that with the fact that his wife, Mrs. Simmons, thought I was absolutely adorable and nearly fainted when I helped her clean up the kitchen and washed every dish instead of joining the other guys in the living room watching football?

It was a smash hit, a home run, an all-around win.

I had a job offer by the time we got on the plane to head home Sunday night.

I'd tried to call Cassie then, eager to share the news, but her service had been shoddy at the resort and I wasn't surprised when the call didn't go through. She was exhausted after her flight home yesterday, so our call had been short and sweet, and I told her I got the job with all the intention of filling her in on every single detail today.

This call was supposed to be excitement and celebration. It was supposed to be *let's shop for an apartment* and *oh, my God, we're going to live together*. It was supposed to be our Thanksgiving sacrifice paying off, and a new date marked on the calendar for when we'd be together again, and a moving truck rental and...

It was just supposed to be so *happy*.

Instead, it's a heavy, hard fist to the gut.

"Adam, please," she begs again when I don't answer.

My heart is in my throat, chest so tight there's little room for the breaths I'm trying to force. "I don't know what to say."

She whimpers, and we don't have to be on video chat for me to know how she looks right now, to know that beautiful face is blotchy and red and tear-stained.

It's sick that I want to hold her, to comfort her, when she's the one breaking *me*.

"I'm so sorry," she says again, a broken record at this point. "I... I was drunk, and upset, and *stupid* and I—"

"Didn't listen to me," I finish for her.

"What?"

"You didn't listen to me. Or, at least, if you did, you clearly didn't hear me when I said I was doing this *for us*. I gave up seeing you for the holiday so that I could find a way for us to be in the same city. *Together*. For us to *move in* together. For us to..."

I can't finish the sentence, tears stinging my eyes, nose flaring as I shake them off.

"But you didn't call me," she says through her tears. "We barely texted. This whole semester has felt like... like... like we aren't even a couple."

"We've had dates almost every weekend," I argue. "We talk *all* the time."

"It's not the same. It's not enough."

"I know!" I scream. "Which is exactly why I flew to fucking Baltimore to get a job near *your* future school. So we could be together. So we wouldn't have to do this anymore. And you..."

Again, my words are cut short, throat constricting with the effort to say them. I'm so sick I have to stand and pace for fear of actually vomiting.

Cassie is silent.

The longer she is, the more my mind races, the more I think about how many times I had the opportunity to do the same to her, but never would have even considered it.

I couldn't stomach the thought of kissing another woman.

And the thought of *her* kissing another man...

I close my eyes, jaw popping, chest tight with a mixture of rage and the fiercest despair I've ever known.

"How could you do this, Cassie?" I ask, voice just above a whisper. "How could you so much as *look* at another man that way, let alone act on it?"

"It meant nothing. I was drunk, I don't even remember what he looks like, I—"

"Well, that makes it better, doesn't it? That just makes it all forgivable. I guess if I get rip-roaring drunk tonight, I can kiss whoever I want and it's fine, right?"

Her silence is answer enough for me.

"Tell me what you would do, if it were you," I say. "If you were on this end of the call, and I told you I got drunk and kissed another woman. What would you feel?"

She sniffs. "You can't possibly hate me as much as I hate myself right now."

I let out a long exhale.

"Adam, I love you," Cassie whispers. "I'm so sorry I hurt you. I can't even look at myself in the mirror. I swear, it will never happen again. It was a mistake. A stupid mistake. Please," she begs. "Please forgive me."

My chest is on fire as I pinch the bridge of my nose and fight back the emotion threatening to strangle me.

"I have to go."

"No," she cries. "Please, Adam. Please."

"I can't talk to you right now, Cassie. You have to respect that. Just... I need some time."

"Adam—"

But I hang up before she can say another word.

My fist curls around my phone, desire to crush it surging through me. I shove through the back door and inside, instantly feeling suffocated by the heat coming from the fireplace. I jog upstairs before any of the guys can ask me what's wrong, but I don't miss the way they watch me, the concern in their eyes.

When I make it to my room, I slam the door shut, finally letting myself heave my phone across the room. It hits the wall and bounces off, the screen cracking when it hits the hardwood floor. And with the music loud enough to drown it out, I let out an animalistic scream, one loud and long enough to make my throat hurt when I finish.

I stand in the middle of the room, panting, and then the anger starts to fade, and my imagination turns even more cruel in its absence.

I can see it, another man's hand sliding in to caress her face, her neck, tilting her chin up, finding those big, innocent green eyes staring up at him, those light pink lips parted and waiting, those soft hands twisting in his shirt...

I barely make it to the trash can by my desk before I vomit, mostly stomach acid burning my throat and my nose as I release.

I stay there for a while, waiting, expecting more before I finally kick back and lean against my bed. I can't stop shaking my head, can't stop closing my eyes tight and opening them again only to discover I'm not stuck in a nightmare the way I wish I was.

I just want to wake up and this all be gone.

I want to wake up and laugh at the audacity, at the outrageousness of even thinking Cassie could hurt me like this.

Barbed wire shreds my guts as I crawl over to my desk, pulling the top drawer open and reaching my hand inside. I feel around until I find what I'm looking for, and then I sit back on my heels, staring at the box in my hand as the hardwood digs into my knees.

I pop it open, and the diamond ring glistens in the Christmas lights, sending another pang of torture through my chest.

I fall back against the bed again so hard it moves, banging into the wall a bit and scraping against the floor.

Then I clutch the ring to my chest.

And I break.

Jess

I can remember a time when walking this very same walk would fill me with power.

I remember the sound of my heels clacking on Greek Row, the Boss Bitch energy flowing through me with the knowledge that I wore nothing but lacy lingerie under my long coat. I remember storming inside the Alpha Sigma house like I owned it, like I owned Kade.

And I did.

I had him wrapped around my little finger, and he had me.

It doesn't seem possible that that moment was in this same lifetime, let alone just a little over a year ago. We were so new then, exploring each other, having fun — all under the premise that I was training him to be good in bed, to be good with girls, and he was just helping me medicate my broken heart.

How quickly that turned to love.

How easily he became one of my best friends.

How comfortably he fit into my life, and made me fit into his.

The thought makes me sick as I walk Greek Row now, feeling about as out of place as a bride wearing black. This wasn't my home anymore, these weren't my streets to rule, and this wasn't my man to own.

I don't even know what I'll find when I get to the Alpha Sigma house now, if the boy who first caught my attention on that cruise ship will shine through, or if the man I fell in love with will still be there, or if they've both been replaced by the shell of who he's become in the time it's taken me to damn near kill him.

It's an effort to hold my dinner down when I walk through the door — open, as per usual, the living room filled with brothers. Half of them are at the long dinner table in the back, textbooks and laptops spread out around them, and the other half are trying and failing to be quiet as they play video games on the big screen. I don't get more than a few glances when I walk in — and since I look like absolute shit, no one stares long enough to care who I am.

I walk slowly back to Kade's room, stomach in knots, but find it empty.

"He's outside hanging Christmas lights," one of the brothers says to me, and then he's texting away on his phone and walking back down the hall.

I blow out a breath, following him until I'm rounding the dining room and making my way to the courtyard.

I stop at the sliding glass door when I spy him, standing at the bottom of a tall ladder and pointing at something on the roof as he instructs the brother at the top of the ladder where to hang the next strand. His face is aglow, the light and shadow of the night playing against his muscles. It's pleasantly cool tonight, and he's wearing a long sleeve A Sig shirt and black sweatpants that make me want to curl up with him on the couch.

My eyes water, heart stinging in my chest.

And as if he senses the spirit of our past, too, he stops what he's doing, frowns, and turns to find me staring at him.

There's no confusion in this face when he finds me, no surprise or shock. It's a lifeless sort of stare, one laced with pain and accusation and something a lot like hope. He swallows after a moment, muttering something to the brother on the ladder before he makes his way to me.

I open the sliding glass door, meeting him halfway, and the brothers who were working outside with him give me a polite nod and hello as they squeeze past me and inside, shutting the door behind them.

An eerie quiet falls over us, brothers laughing and talking inside, but the sound muted by the soft hum of the night. The Christmas lights that have been successfully hung glow above us, the other strands curled at our feet, waiting for their turn.

Kade's eyes search mine for a long moment before his body ebbs toward me, like he wants to wrap me in a hug, but he stops himself, shoving his hands in the pockets of his sweats, instead.

"Can we go for a walk?" I ask, my voice cracking.

Kade closes his eyes, opens them again, his gaze on his shoes. He nods.

We don't say a word as we walk around the side of the house and back onto Greek Row, and I start the trek that leads into the heart of campus, listening to the sound of our sneakers on the sidewalk.

"How are you?" I ask when we're far enough from the house.

Kade glances at me like he's not sure he actually believes I asked him that before shaking his head a little.

You already know — that's what he says without words.

I tuck my hands in the back pockets of my jeans on a nod, my eyes watering. I don't know where to start other than the obvious place.

"I'm sorry, Kade," I whisper.

He blows out a breath — long, slow, and shaky.

"I don't have an excuse for how I've behaved. I don't have any words that will make any of it right, make it go away, or make it feel better. I just don't. All I have for you is honesty," I say, glancing at him before my eyes are on my shoes again. "I vow to give you that."

Kade doesn't say a word, but I know he's listening.

"When Jarrett came back," I start. "It blew up my entire world. Everything I thought I knew about him, about you, about *us*... it just became clouded behind this big, heavy fog. But when we finally talked, I got some clarity, some... closure, I guess, that I didn't realize I needed. I thought everything was going to be fine. And I meant it," I say, looking at him then. "I meant what I said to you last semester. That I love you."

"I know," Kade whispers. His voice is laced with such pain it feels like it's splitting my ribs in half.

"I never expected to ever see him again. I damn sure never expected for him to tell me he still had feelings for me." I bite my lip as tears blur my vision. "I have been the most atrocious person, all because I was confused, trying to hold onto what I have with you, while also reaching for what I had with him."

We make it to the reflection pond, the palm trees around it decked out in red and white lights, and I tug Kade's sleeve, guiding him over to one of the benches. When we take a seat, he scoots away from me, his back rigid, eyes on the pond.

"I am so sorry, for everything I have done, for everything I can't take back," I whisper.

I reach out for him, covering one of his hands with mine and heaving a sigh of relief when he doesn't jerk away.

"Please, look at me," I beg.

Kade closes his eyes on a burning exhale before he does as I asked, and the moment our eyes meet — *really* meet — both our lips tremble with emotion.

"Kade, I love you," I whisper, tears pooling in my eyes and falling over my cheeks, silently carving rivers down to my jaw. "I love you. And I want to be with you."

Kade cracks then, a brief moment of shock washing over his face before he crumples, pinching the bridge of his nose in one hand as his shoulders begin to shake. He can't fight back the emotion, and seeing him succumb to it makes my tears come even faster.

"I want to be with you," I repeat. "But..."

His eyes snap to mine.

"But I don't know if it's right to be."

"Jesus Christ, Jess," he says. "What are you saying?"

"I'm saying that I want you. I want *us*. But what I've done to you... I don't think I could ever forgive you, if it were me in the reverse. I don't deserve you, Kade. Or your love. I..."

My words choke off on a sob, and I cover my mouth with my hand, shaking my head as tears sting my cheeks.

Kade lets out a breath, something of a smile on his lips before his arms are around me, pulling me across the space between us on the bench and crushing me to him. He inhales my scent once I'm in his arms, and I do the same, crying harder at the way it feels to have him hold me, at the warmth of his body, at the familiar smell of his cologne.

"You deserve so much more than me," I sob into his chest. "So much better than what I have done to you."

"Shhh..."

"No," I say, shaking my head as I pull away from him. I look right into his eyes when I continue. "I can't ever forgive myself. I don't know how you could. I want to be with you, but how could I honestly ask that of you, after everything?"

Kade sighs, rubbing my arm with his hand as his eyes flick between mine. He doesn't say anything for a long while, and I know he's realizing it, too — I've hurt him too badly to ever repair it.

"I won't deny that I have been sick for the last four months," he says. "And I won't say you didn't hurt me, because you did. But, *fuck*, Jess, if I didn't think you were worth the pain, if I didn't think you were worth the wait, and if I didn't believe in us the way I do, do you honestly think I would have stuck around?"

I sniff. "But—"

"You say you wouldn't have been able to do the same, but I know that's a lie, too. Because if I would have asked you for time, for space, you would have given it to me. And if I would have asked you to wait for me to figure out what I needed, you would have done it. Tell me you wouldn't have."

I bite my bottom lip hard against the emotion building in my throat. Kade just lifts a brow, waiting.

"I would have," I whisper.

"And why?"

I close my eyes, then, releasing more tears. "Because I love you."

"Because you love me. And I love *you*, Jess. In case you haven't realized it yet, love isn't some beautiful painting hanging in a museum. It's scarred with pencil marks and eraser stains and layers of paint trying to hide the one underneath it and failing miserably. It's messy — perfectly so. Maybe you don't deserve me. Maybe I don't deserve *you*. But we love each other enough that none of that matters."

"I just don't know if I'm good for you..."

He smiles then, swiping away a fresh tear with his thumb before I lean into his touch.

"Why don't you let me be the one to decide that."

I don't get the chance to answer because he frames my face in his hands and pulls me into him, his lips warm and salty when they meet mine, and I taste our tears when I open my mouth and he slides his tongue inside.

Our hearts breathe a sigh of relief at the kiss, hands trembling where we hold each other, and suddenly it's far too cold to be comfortable. I climb into his lap, holding on tight as I soak in every kiss I've missed in the last four months, and he holds me just as tight, wrapping himself up in my warmth.

"Come on," he whispers, reluctantly breaking our kiss and pulling me to stand. "I don't want to fuck you in a public place this time. I want you all to myself."

I blush at the memory of the karaoke event, laughing a little as he tucks me under his arm and steers us back toward Greek Row.

Time seems to pass unnaturally on that walk, our hands intertwined, words no longer needed, our hearts beating soundly for the first time in months. When we make it back to the A Sig house, he quietly leads me inside and back to his room, locking the door behind him once we're inside.

It's pitch black, not a single light on, and his blackout curtains shielding the Christmas lights from the courtyard. I feel his hands on me before my eyes adjust, and even then, I can barely make him out, barely see more than an inch in front of my face.

But I feel him.

I feel his breath on my skin, his lips against my neck as he tugs me into him and presses his body flush against mine. He kisses blindly until he finds my mouth, his hands exploring in the dark, gliding the length of my ass before cupping and slipping between my legs.

I loose a breath at the feeling, at being touched, at knowing he'll be the *only* one touching me forever—

Or, at least, until he's sick of me.

Anxiety tries to fight its way through, but Kade's next kiss silences all attempts, and then I'm led backward, the back of my knees hitting the bed before we tumble into it.

"Everything that I am," he whispers against my stomach as he peels my sweatshirt off, my hair tumbling through the neck hole and over my breasts as he discards it. "Everything that I have," he says as he wrangles me out of my sports bra. "It all belongs to you."

I run my hands through his short hair, pulling him to me until I can find his mouth, and I kiss him with the promise that I feel the same.

Slowly, piece by piece, I strip him down as he does the same to me. We climb under the comforter and pull it up over our heads, our hot, needy breaths warming us as we explore every inch of each other in the dark.

I flip him onto his back, tasting his abs on my way down to his shaft, and he hisses a breath when I take him inside my mouth, swallowing him whole.

I don't even get to adequately tease him before it's me being flipped, my legs spread wide, Kade's fingers parting me at the seam before his tongue lashes the part of me aching for him most.

Gone is the urgency, the rush, the need to claim that we both felt surging through us that night at the concert. In its place is reverence and understanding, wonder and awe, disbelief and gratitude. I touch him like it's both the first and the last time, and he makes love to me like these hours here in this bed are the last we have on Earth.

Neither of us chase our orgasm. Neither of us speed up our pace or do the things we know will make the other unravel. We soak in every second, moaning and tasting and biting and licking. He fucks me from behind, and then I roll him over to ride. He straddles my face to fuck my mouth while he sucks on my clit, and then I'm spread underneath him, hooking one leg on his shoulder.

All night long, we exist in that dark room of a universe.

My soul is at peace. My heart is finally home.

But in the back of my mind, I know the worst part is still to come.

Because I've finally made my choice.

And there's still one person left to tell.

Bear

The rain pelts my jacket as I exit the parking garage and make a left, hands in my pockets and head down. I wish I had my umbrella, wish I would have been smart enough to check the weather before I left my house, but I'm a bundle of nerves, and it was all I could do to choke down breakfast with my stomach like this.

I thought I'd already tackled the hardest part earlier this morning, that walking into the agency and handing in my two weeks' notice would be the biggest challenge of the day. It wasn't easy — especially when my boss offered me a raise to try to keep me. Giselle glaring at me from her office didn't add to the comfort, either, but I ignored her altogether.

I made up my mind over the weekend.

And there was no amount of money that could change it.

I spent the morning making a list of the projects I'll need to finish before I leave, and listing out who I think will be the best to delegate my work to once I'm gone.

And now, on my lunch break, I'm checking the next thing off my list.

I thought this would be the easy part.

The way my ribs are closing in on my lungs suggests otherwise.

The last two weeks of my life have been spent preparing me for this exact moment. I've dedicated every waking hour not at work to researching, analyzing, planning out strategy, compiling the documents I need, and filing the necessary paperwork to get this lunch meeting in the first place.

I've been so focused that I haven't even seen Erin since she got back from her trip.

In all fairness, she told me she needed some space, too. I don't know what happened in Mexico, but I do know the way we left things couldn't have had her in that great of a mood. I wanted to see her the moment her plane landed, wanted to hold her and talk through everything that had happened.

But she said she needed to get sleep for school, that she had finals coming up, that she needed to focus. I think I've known in my gut that it's a lie, an excuse, but the truth is I've been busy, too.

Maybe this is what we both needed.

Space. Time. Distance.

The rain lets up a little as I make it to the high brass doors that lead into the Palm South University Credit Union, and I pause under the overhang to remove my jacket and shake off the water as best I can. Wiping my feet on the mat, I take a deep breath, pull my shoulders back, and push through the door.

The downtown branch is much nicer than the one on campus, mahogany wood desks lining the left side of the main space, while private offices span out to my right. There's a hall in the back that a group of women walk down as soon as I enter, and directly in front of me are seven teller windows, the brass and wood making up their stations playing well with the warm burgundy carpet.

"Good afternoon, sir," a young man greets me from his place by the door. "How can we help you today?"

Holding my soaked rain jacket away from me as much as I can, I pull the binder full of paperwork from inside my suit jacket, relieved to see it's still dry. "I have a meeting with Mrs. Jarwolowski."

"Inquiring about a small business loan?" he asks.

My stomach somersaults when I answer, "Yes, sir."

With a beaming smile, the young man leads me to the small waiting area stretched out in front of the glass-window offices, letting me know Mrs. Jarwolowski will be with me soon. He takes my jacket and hangs it on the rack near the door, and I take a seat, smoothing my clammy hands over my slacks.

I've never been more prepared for anything in my life, and yet I'm so nervous I think I might actually shit myself.

I barely studied for tests at Palm South, depending on my skill set and good luck to get me by most of the time. I never cared much about getting A's. I just wanted to pass and get my degree — which I did by the hair of my chin.

But this...

This loan is the difference between a pipe dream and a reality. It's the difference between being jobless and being an entrepreneur. It's the difference of being a struggling graphic designer with a major lack of experience and being the CEO and Owner of my own business.

This loan isn't just money.

It's everything.

When I left the gym after what happened with Giselle, I couldn't shake myself from the thoughts assaulting me — not just about Erin, but about what would come next for me. I wondered if what Giselle had said, what Erin had agreed with, could ever be true.

So, I started crunching numbers.

The more research I did, the more ideas started flowing. Before I knew it, I had Word doc after Word doc of a business plan — rough in nature, but fleshing out slowly and surely. I stayed up every night until well into the early morning, passion flowing out of me like sunlight. It was just after midnight about a week after the gym incident when the realization dawned on me.

I wanted it.

I wanted my own business.

I wanted it so bad I could taste it, see it, *feel* it.

What started as a *let's just see what this could be like* quickly turned into me making an exit plan from my job and a business plan for Pennington Personal Fitness, LLC.

And now, I couldn't stop until I had it.

The binder in my hand is heavy and weighted with dreams and numbers that I hope will add up to whatever this bank needs to trust me with their money, to trust I can pay them back and succeed. I tap my thumb against it, knee bouncing as I wait.

My phone vibrates in my pocket, and I fish it out, swallowing hard when I see Erin's name.

Erin: *Hi.*

I blow out a breath.

Hi I type back.

Erin: *I miss you.*

I close my eyes on another long sigh.

Me: *I miss you so much it hurts.*

Erin: *Come over tonight.*

My stomach ties up in knots, because as much as I want to see her — *need* to see her — I have no idea what shape I'll be in tonight. I might be high on life and celebrating, or I might be a depressed mess who realizes he quit his job before having a steady plan in place. I have savings to get me through for a while, but it's not much, and if I don't get this loan...

"Bear?"

I look up from the blinking cursor on my phone, still having not answered Erin, and find a young woman staring at me.

She's petite, slim, dressed in a creamy pink blouse and beige dress slacks that hug her long legs all the way down to her nude high heels. She looks familiar, and I tilt my head, trying to place her.

It isn't until she pushes the rose-gold framed glasses up her nose and smiles that I realize.

"Oh, my God, it *is* you, isn't it?" she asks, adjusting her purse on her shoulder. She takes a tentative step toward me as I stare at her in disbelief.

It can't be her...

It can't be the same bright green eyes I stared into so many nights, the same plump, rosy pink lips I kissed more times than I can count. That jet black hair, it can't be the same that was once shaded a shocking violet, that I once bunched in my fists between the sheets.

But when she takes another step, I know without a doubt that it is.

"It's me..." she says shyly, tucking a strand of hair behind her ear. "Shawna."

I nearly drop the binder of papers from my lap as I shuffle to stand, fumbling with the folder until I have it secured under my arm. Then I just stand there, looking at the girl I used to have such deep feelings for it nearly killed me.

Almost as much as the way we broke up.

Her brows fold together, bottom lip disappearing between her teeth as her eyes flick between mine. The last time we talked, she told me she couldn't stand up to her parents, that she couldn't claim me as her boyfriend because I was black and her parents were *old-fashioned*.

The memory makes my jaw clench.

"I... I'm sorry," she says, shaking her head and already turning to leave. "I shouldn't have said anything. I'm going."

"Wait."

She stops, turning over her shoulder.

I sigh, swallowing. "How are you?"

I see the relief swell through her, her shoulders releasing a bit of tension as she turns to face me again. "I'm well. I was just dropping off a deposit for my boss," she says, tapping her purse. "And I'm certainly happy I ran into you."

A tight smile is about all I have to give.

"Are you waiting to see someone?"

"I'm inquiring about a small business loan," I answer.

Her eyes light up at that, smile wide and glowing. "Really? What kind of business?"

"Personal training and nutrition."

"Wow," she breathes. "That's... that's actually quite perfect for you, isn't it?"

My heart surges with the assessment, because it does feel perfect. It feels right.

But I still can't move, can't do much other than answer her questions as I stare at the ghost I never thought I'd see again.

Shawna's mouth pulls to the side as she motions to the chair next to the one I was seated in. "Mind if I join you for just a few minutes? I'm not exactly in a rush to get back to the office."

I blink out of my daze, nodding and gesturing to the chair for her to sit. I wait until she does before I take the seat next to her, rigid and uncomfortable and yet I'm glad she stayed.

"So," she says, balancing her purse in her lap with a wide smile angled at me. "Starting your own business, huh?"

"Hopefully." I tap the binder. "We'll see if I make the cut."

"They'd be crazy not to offer you a loan. I've got to say, though, after hearing Skyler won second place in that tournament in Vegas, I'm kind of surprised you're not asking *her* for the loan."

I sigh. "Well, to be honest, she's my backup plan. But that's *her* money, you know? She's about to graduate, and I know she's got her own dreams to go after." I pause, sniffing. "I want to do this on my own."

"You will," Shawna assures me.

A silence falls between us, her looking at me and me looking at the binder in my hands.

"Clinton, I am so sorry for what I did to you."

I close my eyes on a breath. "It's—"

"Not okay," she finishes for me. "I could sit here and give you every excuse in the world, repeat all the ones I did when everything happened... tell you my family is old-fashioned, that they were my money source, that I was scared, that I needed time, but the truth is that what I did to you, the way I behaved, the way my *parents* behaved... it was racist. Plain and simple. And I'm sorry. I'm sorry I treated you that way, that I hurt you like that, that I was too blinded by what I thought was okay to see what was really right and what was so blatantly wrong."

I finally meet her gaze, and finding such sincerity there makes my chest ache. "Thank you."

She nods. "I know I can never go back and undo what happened, but running into you today... well, maybe it was the universe giving me one last chance to make amends. The right way."

"What if I would have cursed at you and spit on your shoes?"

"I would have gladly taken the lashing," she says with a smirk. "Although, I would have been pissed about the shoes. These are Michael Kors."

I smile, relaxing a little more in my seat.

"So, other than opening a business, how are you?" Shawna asks.

"Good," I lie. She must see right through it, because she arches a brow that makes me chuckle in surrender. "Or well, I *was* good... until about two weeks ago when everything blew to smithereens."

"What did you do?"

"How do you know it was me who did something?"

She just gives me a pointed look, which makes me laugh again.

I run a hand over my fade, but don't reply to her question. The truth is, I don't know Shawna Ballentine anymore. I don't trust her the way I once did. And while it was nice to hear her apologize, what's going on between me and Erin, between me and myself... it's not for her to be a part of.

My phone lights up where I dropped it on top of my folder, and Erin's name fills the screen. I curse, thumbing open the text I had yet to respond to. She sent through a question mark after the text asking me to come over, and I shake my head, knowing I probably gave her a heart attack by not responding right away.

See you at seven. I'll bring dinner.

She replies with a little heart emoji, and then I tuck my phone away again.

And find Shawna grinning at me.

"What?" I ask.

"You and Erin Xanders, huh?"

Though my skin is dark enough not to show it, I blush. "Yes."

She shakes her head, sitting back and folding her arms. "It's about damn time."

I arch a brow.

"I always knew it would be you two in the end," she says. "I'm so happy you finally figured it out."

I want to laugh, but the gesture gets cut short when her words hit me square in the chest with the force of a tow truck.

I always knew it would be you two in the end.

She's not the first to say it to me, not the first to see it, to know it.

And I knew it, too.

I knew it all along — from the first time I really talked to her on that bench on campus, when she saw what no one else saw and offered to help me when no one else even knew I needed a hand.

From the first time I danced with her, silly and uncoordinated.

From the first time I tasted her lips, even as drunk as I was.

From the first time I woke up next to her, even though she kicked me out in a panic.

I knew.

"Bear?" Shawna asks when I sit there for far too long, but I can't help it.

It's all hitting me.

It doesn't matter that she's friends with Gavin, that he's back, that he may have other intentions than the innocent ones he's painted for her. Who cares if he texts her, or if he even tries to make a move?

Because just like I did with Giselle, Erin would turn him down.

She loves me.

As unyieldingly as I love her.

I want to kick myself for being so stupid, for fighting with her, for letting my stubborn pride and jealousy threaten the one thing in this world that I truly love.

"Mr. Pennington?" a soft voice calls from one of the glass offices, and I blink, standing abruptly.

An older woman with long silver hair and a youthful smile strides over to me, shaking my hand as Shawna stands to join us.

"I'm Mrs. Jarwolowski," she says. "Sorry about the wait."

"It's no problem at all," I assure her, and then I turn back to Shawna, who watches me with a warm, genuine smile so different from the one she used to hold for me, but familiar all the same. "It was really nice running into you," I say. And I mean it.

"You, too. Take care of yourself, Bear."

I smile and nod, and then Shawna makes her way to the front door, and I follow Mrs. Jarwoloski back to her office where I plead my case for Pennington Personal Training, LLC.

All the while, I make an even more important plan for this evening.

Erin

You know when you say a word so many times, it stops making sense?

The first time you say fork, you think of the shiny metal instrument you eat with. You say it again, and the same happens. But say it out loud, over and over, twenty times in a row, and suddenly you're wondering if it's a real word, wondering what words even *are* and who decided what sounds and syllables equate to a definition. And what of a definition? Isn't it just more strange sounds forming strange words that we have somehow come to agree *mean* a certain something?

It's enough to make my head spin, and it has been — for two long weeks, I've done nothing but stew and steam and boil over thinking about one stupid word.

Dropped.

Dropped, like a football meant for a receiver, a touchdown opportunity lost. Dropped, like a slippery wine glass, crashing to the floor and shattering. Dropped, like a façade, someone finally admitting what they've truly desired all along.

Or dropped, like the charges against Landon Turner and the three other men who raped me.

I've been through enough trauma in my life to know how the grieving process goes. I fully expected the anger, the denial, the painful sadness and despair. I knew I'd cycle through it all, and I have been, every waking moment since Candice called to tell me the news.

I heard her voice replaying in my nightmares, little snippets of jargon and disappointing phrases nestled between sincere apologies.

Due to lack of evidence...

If we'd have had a rape kit...

Their word against yours...

They had multiple witness testimonials...

There were videos and pictures taken that night that dispute our claimed timeline...

Clinton was your only witness...

Without evidence we can't...

It's all blurry. All of it. Even after formally meeting with Candice upon my return and going over it more thoroughly in person, all the details are lost behind the one bold statement I can't fully process.

The charges against Landon and his brothers have been dropped.

They won't go to trial. They won't have to answer for what they did to me. They won't have so much as a pencil smudge on their permanent record.

They're free to go.

They're free to live their lives.

They're free to keep working at their jobs and dating their girlfriends — who likely don't even know what they've been accused of.

They're *free.*

It is the most jagged pill I have ever had to swallow.

I know I don't look much better than I feel when Herb calls from downstairs to let me know Clinton has arrived. I light a few candles and pull a fresh bottle of wine from the fridge, lining up two glasses on the counter and uncorking the bottle to let it breathe.

Jess is spending the evening with Ashlei — likely trying to convince her that it's time to tell Brandon what she discovered during our trip. The poor girl is so scared of his reaction that she's taken four more tests since we returned home, all with the same result.

With Jess out of the condo, I have it all to myself, and I'm finally ready to see Clinton and tell him what happened.

Three firm knocks signal that he's at the door, and when I open it, my tongue turns to sandpaper at what I see. He looks just as devastated as me, bags under his bloodshot eyes and shoulders sagging. Suddenly, all the fighting, all the silence after and the space I thought I needed from him to process feel like the most pointless, stupid waste of time.

My bottom lip wobbles, and that's all it takes for Bear to rush through the threshold and crush me into his arms.

"I'm here," he whispers into my hair, and I nod vigorously, clutching him tight as I reluctantly give in to emotion.

I don't want to cry over them, over what they did to me — not anymore.

But I can't deny that this hurts.

Clinton holds me until I give him the cue that I'm ready to go inside, and when I do, he takes my hand and guides me. Soft jazz plays from the small speaker in our kitchen, and that along with the candles set a soothing scene.

He drops the bag of food he brought on the kitchen counter, ignoring it as he pulls me over to the couch. He sinks down first, then guides me into his lap, holding me once more.

"I'm sorry," I breathe.

"Stop," he says, kissing my forehead. "It's me who should be sorry."

"I don't have to see him anymore if it's going to hurt you. Gavin," I clarify. "I care about him, but I care about you more."

"I'm not threatened by him."

I lean back at that, arching a brow.

"Contrary to how I acted," Bear adds with a sheepish smirk. "I was wrong. I trust you, and while I hate that Gavin ever got the pleasure of being with you, I know you're mine now, and I also know he's an important friend to you. I'm sorry I put you in that position and acted like a child."

My brows fold together, and I shake my head in wonder. "You've really grown a lot in the time I've known you, Clinton Pennington."

"Yeah, well, I've had a few badass women in my life to slap me into shape along the way."

I chuckle at that, and then with those apologies still dancing in our eyes, Clinton slides his palm along my cheek to frame my neck, and I lean into the touch on a content sigh.

Home.

The word flitters through me like a warm wind, and I blink my eyes open, smiling as I realize it's not being here in this condo that makes me feel this way.

It's being with him.

"I've missed you," Clinton croaks.

I nod, leaning in to kiss him, and he wraps his arms around me even tighter.

"I have some news," he says.

"I do, too."

"You first."

I shake my head. "I'd rather hear yours. Especially if it's good, because mine is not."

That makes him frown, but I smooth my thumb over the line between his brows.

"I'm okay. But you first," I say again.

He sighs, and I know he wants to argue, but he refrains. Sitting up a little straighter, he covers my hand with his, fingers trailing the skin of my palm. "I don't think there's any slow and easy way to say this, so I'll just get to the point." His eyes meet mine. "I quit my job."

My eyebrows shoot into my hairline.

"Well," I say. "That wasn't what I was expecting."

"Trust me — I didn't expect it either. But I had a sort of... I don't know. *Awakening*, maybe? While you were gone, and over the last couple of weeks that we've been apart. I've had a lot of time to think, and when I wasn't mulling over how stupid I was to pick a fight with you over Gavin—"

"You're not stupid."

"—I was thinking over what comes next. For me. For *us*," he adds, bringing my knuckles to his lips. A gentle kiss, and then he holds them there, his eyes on mine. "I went to the bank today and applied for a small business loan."

My jaw drops. "Oh, my God, Bear."

"And I got approved."

That makes me jump off the couch. "Oh, my God!" The smile that splits my face is so big, so wide that it hurts a little as I yank Clinton off the couch and make him jump around with me. He laughs and picks me up with a spin, and when my feet are on the ground again, I slug him in the arm.

"Ouch!" He pretends it actually hurt, rubbing his arm.

"Why didn't you tell me?! I would have gone with you!"

He chuckles, holding my arms in his hands. "I wanted to do it on my own. Besides... things have been strained between us. I thought maybe if I showed up with some good news, you'd forgive me easier."

"I forgave you before you even thought to apologize."

"And that's just one of the many reasons why I love you."

I blush, plopping back down on the couch and tugging Clinton to follow. "So, what does this mean?"

"It means..." He laughs, shaking his head. "It means I have my own business. Or, well, I have the *start* of it, anyway. I found a few small retail spaces that I could potentially rent out for the studio. Now that I have my loan, and my business plan, I just need to get my website up and running, plan out a marketing strategy, get the studio set up with everything it needs and then..."

"And then make a million fucking dollars in the first year," I finish for him.

He barks out a laugh at that. "I'm pretty sure that's impossible as a personal trainer, but I appreciate your enthusiasm."

"I'm going to help you. We'll make videos for social media, and everyone will fall in love with you and be clamoring to get your time. It doesn't have to be confined to *just* the studio, you know. You could have virtual clients."

He frowns. "Virtual clients... I hadn't even considered that."

"You're welcome."

"Want to be my VP?"

I scoff. "More like *you're* the VP. I've always been El Presidente, babe."

Bear smiles, his warm eyes searching mine as he leans in and presses a slow, soft kiss to my lips. "I can't tell you how much it means to have you in my corner. I have no idea what I'm doing, so I'm going to need you. As per usual."

"I'm here," I promise.

"There's one more thing I need to tell you," Bear says with a sigh. "Giselle hit on me."

I blanch. "*What*?"

"It was while you were gone. We were at the gym, went to the sauna after, and she started by asking why I was off. I thought she was just being there for me as a colleague, but then she had her hand on my thigh and was—"

"I'll kill her."

Clinton chuckles, squeezing my hand in his. "No need. I put her in her place. And then promptly quit."

"Is that *why* you quit?"

"Partly," he admits. "But not completely. I believe in this dream. Almost as much as I believe in us."

I smile, shoulders deflating. "Well... I still want to kill her, but I also feel all warm and fuzzy knowing you handled it."

Clinton leans in for a long kiss before he sits back, tapping my knee. "Your turn."

My stomach sours, then, smile instantly slipping.

I can't sit still while I talk about it, so I stand, pacing the living room for a moment before I finally say the words.

"The charges got dropped."

A pause.

A breath.

And then a roar.

"*What?!*"

Bear jumps to his feet, his chest puffed, fists clenched.

"What the fuck do you *mean,* the charges got dropped?"

"Exactly what I said. They got dropped." I wave my hand in the air. "Lack of evidence."

"Lack of—" Clinton's jaw drops, and then he smiles — a sadistic, twisted sort of smile as he shakes his head. He hangs his hands on his hips, tongue in cheek. "I'll kill them."

As if he's going to do it right in this very moment, he stomps toward the door, and because I don't trust that he's kidding, I hook him around the elbow and pull him to a stop.

"It's over, Bear."

"Like hell it is. It's not over until they're all behind bars or dead. And since the first apparently isn't happening..."

"Bear, please," I plead, and he looks at me then, seeing the hurt in my eyes. "I've been agonizing over this for two weeks now. I don't want to get angry again. I've finally come to accept it."

"Two *weeks*? Erin, why didn't you tell me sooner? Why wasn't I the first one you called?"

"Because just like you needed to get your loan on your own, I needed to process this first — *before* letting anyone else in. I needed to be alone."

He frowns. "I hate that."

"I know. But thank you for respecting it, anyway."

A ginormous sigh leaves his chest, and his eyes find the windows, the lights of the city reflected in his hazel irises. "So... that's just it? There's no fighting it, nothing else we can do?"

"That's it," I whisper.

He shakes his head. "I'm so sorry, Erin."

"Me, too."

Bear pulls me in for a hug, resting his chin on the crown of my head.

"I'm proud of you," he whispers. "It took a lot of guts to do what you did. I'm sorry the justice system failed you, but I hope you don't regret coming forward."

"I don't," I assure him, pulling back to look into his eyes. "In fact... I don't want to stop here."

He frowns. "I thought you said there was nothing else we could do."

"About Landon? No. There's not." I swallow. "But I want to help other victims. I want to be there when a woman is brave enough to come forward, and I want to fight for her, fight against the system set up to continue making this something to be ashamed of, something to be afraid to do."

Bear just rubs my arms, waiting.

"I'm shifting my focus into criminal law. I want to be a prosecutor."

He whistles. "Damn, girl. That's a tough career to get into."

"It'll take a lot of hard work, a lot of persistence, and likely a lot of luck. Everyone wants an internship at the prosecutor's office this summer. I just have to somehow find a way to make sure they pick me."

"How can I help?"

"I'll let you know when I figure it out. For now, I need to focus on finals and getting through the rest of this semester. I'm heartbroken over the prosecutor's decision in my case," I admit. "But if anything, it's lit a fire in me. I feel stronger now that I've faced those monsters head on — even if they never have to pay for what they did to me."

Bear's fists curl again at that.

"I may not be able to win every time, but I promise this," I say, pulling back to gaze up at Bear. "I will never stop fighting."

His chest swells again. "And I thought I was proud of you before."

I smirk, and then his lips are on mine, warm and comforting and safe.

"I have something for you," he says almost sheepishly when he pulls away.

"Okay..."

"I have to run down and get it from the lobby. Why don't you pour us a glass of wine and I'll heat up our food when I get back?"

I nod, and then he's gone, leaving my door cracked behind him as he jets into the hallway.

I take my time pouring us the wine, taking the first sip and sighing at the release it brings. I'm staring out the window with my thoughts running wild when the door creaks open again.

And when I turn, I nearly drop my wine glass.

There he is — my Bear, my man, my *everything* — smirking in that sexy way he does.

And cradled in his beastly arms is the tiniest, fluffiest puppy I've ever seen.

"Oh, my God! Bear! You got me a puppy?!" I set my wine glass down without caring that I spill a little in the process, and then I rush over, swooping the golden fluff ball out of Clinton's arms and holding it to my chest.

"I got *us* a puppy."

I giggle as the little thing licks my face. It has floppy auburn ears and fluffy golden fur, but its paws tell me that it won't be this little for long.

"Boy or girl?"

"Girl. I didn't name her yet. Wanted to let you have the honor."

"She's so cute," I whine — and it really is a whine, my voice three octaves higher than I realized it could even reach as I move us over to the couch and sit down.

I plop the puppy beside me, laughing when her little leg slips between the cushions and she sinks before rolling over and offering me her belly. I pet it as her tongue lolls out to the side.

When I look up at Clinton, he smiles down at the puppy before sitting on the other side of her, petting behind her ears as I rub her tummy. Then, his eyes find mine, a bit of fear mixed with adoration in those irises.

"Move in with me."

My hand stalls.

"Erin, I realized a lot of things in this time we've been apart — like that I drive myself absolutely insane thinking about the possibility of ever losing you."

I roll my lips together, eyes glossing.

"You were right. I do have a lot of things in my past that I haven't faced, haven't handled. And we *both* have a lot of hurdles ahead of us. But I want you there for all of it. I want you to know everything about me, to be there through the good and the bad, and I want to be there for yours, too."

"Bear..."

"I want forever with you, Erin Xanders."

My heart swells like a balloon, and I choke on something between a laugh and a sob as Clinton grabs my hands in his.

"And I don't care if it's in Pennsylvania or Florida or middle of nowhere Kansas," he says as I laugh, squeezing his hands. "I'm never going to be perfect. I'm *always* going to find new ways to frustrate you and piss you off."

"Ditto."

"None of that matters, though. As long as we have each other, I want it all." He slides a little closer as the puppy climbs on top of our laps, nipping at our shirts for attention. "Move in with me, Erin. Start a life with me. Because I can't live without you, and I never want to try."

Tears blur my vision as I nod, but I can't speak the word.

"Is that a yes?"

I laugh, setting the first rush of tears free. "Yes," I whisper.

I'm swept into his arms in the next instant, and the puppy takes it as a cue to play, nipping at us and letting out the cutest bark I've ever heard. We both pull back on a smile, and Clinton pulls a little toy from his pocket, offering it to the pup who eagerly chews on it.

"You had that the whole time?"

"Oh, you should see the supplies in my truck right now."

I laugh. "So... when do we do this?"

"Is now too soon?"

"Maybe," I say on a chuckle. "I need to pack. And Jess..."

"Will be just fine," he promises me. "How about you focus on getting through the rest of the semester, and I'll handle packing and moving. Deal?"

I nod. “Deal.” Then, I shake my head, covering my mouth with both hands. “We’re moving in together.”

“We are.”

“We need a Christmas tree.”

“That can be arranged.”

“And we have a *puppy!*”

He laughs. “We do. What do you want to name the little girl?”

He grabs one end of the toy, playing tug of war as the puppy presses weight into her haunches and fights against him. She loses her grip, plopping down on her butt and looking up at me with the cutest face before she’s up and going again.

Knocked down, but never defeated.

“Zelda,” I whisper, eyes flicking to Clinton.

“A little warrior, huh?” he muses, ruffling the fur behind Zelda’s neck. “Just like her mama.”

“Does that make you *daddy*?” I purr, arching a brow when Bear freezes, his eyes flashing to mine.

“Say that again, and I’ll show you just how *daddy* I can be.”

“Swear it?”

And with a wicked smile, he pulls me into him for a hot, promising kiss.

Ashlei

Everything is quiet under here.

Eyes closed, breath locked in my chest, hair floating all around me.

The bath water is warm, pleasant against my sore muscles after physical therapy. And while nothing has been able to calm my racing thoughts over the last couple of weeks, this is pretty close to peace.

Here, submerged, I can hear my heartbeat.

And I swear I can almost hear hers.

Or maybe it's *his*. I won't know for a while. But she feels like a girl. She feels like she's got my sass, my competitiveness, my will to never back down. I find myself wondering about her far too often already. Will she be athletic? Intelligent? Funny? Charming? Will she have her dad's eyes or mine? Whose smile? Whose temper — because either way, she's likely in trouble, and so are we.

My lungs start searing in my chest, and I come up for a breath, warm water dripping down my face as I blink my eyes open.

The bathroom is dark, save for the little bit of sunlight streaming in from the door I left open. It gets too hot in here when I take a bath, but the open door lets in a draft, and I relax as a gentle breeze wafts over my face.

Everything is loud up here.

Out of the water, anxiety attacks me, pressing me to tell Brandon while also warning me that when I do, I might not get the reaction I want. What reaction *do* I want? I don't even know. But fear has me gripped, has the microphone on the stage of my mind as it swears to me that he won't want our baby — or me once he finds out I slipped on my birth control and made this possible at all.

That anxiety leads straight into wondering if I could do it alone, if I could be strong enough to raise a child without him. How badly would I damage her if I did it on my own? How many times would I fail her in the process of trying to raise her right?

I suppose, partner or not, we all mess our kids up somehow.

Rich, poor, doting parents, or alcoholics — we can trace so much of our trauma back to the mother and father who bore us.

That sends another pang through my chest, and I sigh, sinking down under water once more to block out all the noise.

I think I knew even before I took the test. I think I knew the moment it happened, the very second I felt him spill inside me. It's like I sensed his little swimmers on their mission, felt my eggs drop and open up. I woke in the middle of the night that night, my back to Brandon's chest, his arms around my stomach, and I swore I felt it — that little connection inside me that would spark life.

It's why I didn't drink at my own bachelorette party.

I faked shots, putting the liquid in my mouth only to spit them into the drink I pretended to chase the shot with. When the girls ordered me a drink, I'd sip on it so lightly I barely tasted it at all until they weren't looking and I could ditch it. When I ordered my own, it was soda water and lime.

I knew.

I just *knew*, and the anxiety was too much to not see proof on a little stick.

I took my first pregnancy test before we left for the trip, but of course, it was too soon then. It hadn't even been a full week since Brandon and I had returned from St. John. But that last night of the bachelorette, when Cassie was wailing over kissing a stranger, and Erin was fuming over something she wouldn't tell us about, and Skyler was getting railed by Kip somewhere across the resort, and Jess was swiping between two photos of the men she loves… I felt it again.

That kick in my chest.

That stirring in my gut.

I just knew it was time to take the test again.

And when I did, the word *pregnant* showed up on the little screen just like I knew it would.

Since then, I've taken multiple tests, just to be sure — and it's been the same result every time. There's no denying it.

I have a little human growing inside me.

A smile spreads on my lips, warmth washing over my soul at the thought, and then I'm jerked out of the water and back to reality.

"Ashlei! Jesus Christ, are you okay? What are you doing?"

I wipe the water out of my eyes to find a worried Brandon holding me by the arms — careful of my still-healing shoulder — and searching my eyes like he's sure he just saved me from a suicide attempt.

"I'm taking a bath. Wanna join?"

"You were under water."

I shrug. "It's just quiet."

He sighs, releasing me and taking a seat on the edge of the tub. He pinches the bridge of his nose, laughing a little as he shakes his head. "God. Sorry. I just… I thought…"

"I hate physical therapy, but I don't hate it that bad," I tease.

He gives me a grim smile. "It's just… you've been different lately. You've been… distant."

I grimace. "I know."

"Did I do something? Did I… did we rush into getting married and now you're regretting it?"

I balk, sitting up so fast some of the water splashes onto the edge of the tub. "Oh, my God, no. Of course not." I squeeze his forearm. "Baby, I'm the happiest I've ever been now that I'm Mrs. Church."

His shoulders release again, and he covers my hand with his. "Is it your shoulder?"

I chew my lip, knowing I can't keep it from him any longer.

All I can do is pray this won't be the end of our fairy tale.

"My shoulder is sore," I confess. "PT is kicking my ass. But… there's something else. Something I need to tell you."

"Okay…" Brandon swallows. "Tell me. Anything."

I take a long breath, releasing it fully before I grab his hand in mine. Slowly, I sink it into the water, pulling him forward a little until he's touching my stomach.

He frowns at first, and then heat glosses his eyes, those dark irises flashing with want when he looks at me again. He smirks, just a little, and slides his hand down farther.

"Is this what you want, Mrs. Church?" he asks, his fingers brushing against my clit as he leans in for a kiss.

My pussy flutters at the touch, legs clenching, but I laugh in his face before pulling his hand back up. "No, pervert." I pause. "Well, at least, not right now. Hold that thought. First…" I hold his hand to my stomach again, pressing my palm over his and holding it there.

He looks down at the water, at where he's holding me, frowning when he finds my gaze again. "I don't understand."

I swallow, applying a little more pressure so that his palm is splayed flat against my belly. My eyes search his under lifted brows, waiting, not able to say the words.

And just like it did for me, I see the exact moment it hits him.

His frown disappears, the line between his eyebrows wiped clean as his eyes double in size. His lips part, gaze falling to my stomach before slowly crawling back up to my eyes.

"You're…"

"Pregnant," I finish for him, and my eyes water with the admission, with the weight of releasing the truth. I nod. "Yes."

He lets out a short breath through his gaping mouth, but it's slack, no emotion one way or another evident in his eyes or lips. He looks as if he's seen a ghost, or has just been told the meaning of life and finds it impossible to fathom.

His eyes slowly trail down again, sticking to the spot where his hand is pressed against my stomach. His fingers curl, just a centimeter, the tips of them indenting my skin softly.

Then his eyes snap to mine, brimming with tears, and he makes that same sound again — the short puff of air through his open mouth.

Only this time, it's a laugh.

"You're pregnant," he whispers, the first tear slipping free. It falls so quickly off the apple of his cheek that I don't even have time to reach for it.

"I'm pregnant," I repeat, and I blame the damn hormones for the way my eyes instantly water, too.

"We're having a baby."

My heart pinches to the size of a penny before exploding into a hot air balloon. "We are. I mean... if... if you want to."

All emotion leaves his face then, frown back in place. "Are you fucking kidding me?"

"I just... I understand if you don't want to be a part of this. We didn't plan it. I know you've been avid about me taking my birth control and being careful. We haven't even *talked* about kids and..." I rub my belly next to where his hand still rests. "I can do it on my own, if you—"

I'm swooped out of the tub in the next instant, the words stuck in my throat as water sloshes out of the tub and off of me, soaking the rug and the bathroom floor and all of Brandon's suit.

"You are fucking *mad* if you think you'll ever have to do it alone," he breathes against my lips before kissing me, punishing and promising all at once. "You're *mine*, Ashlei Church. And that little boy is *ours*."

"*Boy*?" I say on a laugh, the release of which seems to deflate my anxiety in one fell swoop. "How do you know if it's a boy?"

"I just know."

"Well, I think it's a girl," I say as he carries me out of the bathroom and plops me into our sheets, not a care in the world that we're both soaking wet.

Brandon takes a moment to appreciate my body splayed out on the bed before he lowers down over me, gently, carefully, and starts peppering my stomach with soft, slow kisses.

"Should we make a bet?" he asks between them.

"Only if you want to lose."

"I think I win either way," he argues, those kisses trailing up over my breasts, my neck, my jaw, until he's at my lips. "Because boy or girl, they have you as a mom. And I have you as my wife."

I can't help the visible swoon that rolls off me at his words, and he chuckles into my mouth as he kisses me, rolling over to the side a bit so his hand can splay on my stomach once more.

"Can I ask you something?"

"Anything," I whisper, arching a little into his touch as his hand inches down.

"Why does knowing you're carrying my baby make me want to fuck you so goddamn bad I can hardly breathe?"

My legs squeeze together of their own accord, but Brandon reaches down to grab my thigh and pulls it toward him, spreading me once again.

"Because you love to own me," I say, biting his lower lip. "In every. Single. Way."

A growl is affirmation that I'm right, and then Brandon squeezes my thigh before jumping off the bed. His eyes bore into mine as he unfastens his belt, shoves the button of his pants through the slip, and rips the zipper down. He tugs at his tie next, undoing the knot with expert hands as I spread my knees wider for him, one hand palming my breast as the other slips between my legs.

His breathing turns wild, erratic as he watches me, but he doesn't fumble with his clothes. He takes each layer off with precision and power radiating off him, just like always, until he's nude and hard and pulsing with need.

He descends on me like a wolf, his mouth crashing into mine before he sits back on his heels, admiring the view of me spread before him. He trails a finger down one of my legs, pulling my ankle to his lips before setting it on his shoulder. He does the same with the other leg, hiking it up high, until my back is flat in the sheets and both ankles are balanced on his shoulders.

I've seen Brandon lust for me — ever since that first day in the elevator at *Okay, Cool*, I've seen how badly he desires me. But this... the carnal way his hands grip me, the somehow careful yet relentless way he fills me as I stretch and arch and cry out his name?

This isn't just want, or need, or dominance.

It's love.

It's the kind of love that drives a man mad, that sends soldiers to war, that breaks up continents and rains down hellfire on earth.

It's the damning, redeeming, torturous and ecstasy-inducing rush he'll never get enough of, an always-present yearning that will never leave him sated.

But I'm the lucky woman who gets to watch him try.

Brandon makes love to me for the rest of the evening, and well into the night and early morning, until we're both so sore and weak we can barely move to give ourselves sustenance.

Turns out my fears were unfounded.

Turns out this man of mine is everything I knew he was and more.

Turns out I'm going to be a *mom*.

And boy or girl, my baby is going to have the best dad *ever*.

Jess

It's an unbearably hot night for December, sweat beading at the base of my neck and dripping down my spine as I walk through downtown. It doesn't help that work was chaotic today, holiday weddings being of a special kind of demanding nature all their own. I thought we would have a lull in the season until spring, but since Florida is about the only state not covered in snow right now, we're a hot spot for winter weddings.

In a way, I appreciate the workload. Because while my heart and soul feel at peace for the first time in months, keeping busy has helped me avoid one unfortunate fact.

I have to tell Jarrett my decision.

Kade assured me there was no rush when he saw how anxious I was after our night reunited. He even offered to do it for me, to take the brunt of his brother's pain so I wouldn't have to. But it's not his battle to fight.

I got myself into this mess.

I have to be the one to crawl out of the mud.

My heart beats loud and off rhythm in my ears as I approach the building where Jarrett's office is. The building itself is owned by a bank, the floors above it occupying small and large businesses alike, everything from tech companies and law firms to advertising agencies and nonprofits.

I take a seat in the lobby at five after five, crossing my legs and balancing my hands in my lap as I wait. I didn't have the lady balls to ask him to meet me. Hell, I didn't even know today was going to be the day I'd break the news. I just felt it. About halfway through the afternoon, my stomach flipped violently, chills breaking on my skin, and I knew it was time.

At five-thirty, I start to wonder if he's already gone for the day. The holiday season seems to be a weird one for anyone working in a nine-to-five. It's like the month of December allows permission to leave early, come in late, and take longer weekends without explanation.

But just as I'm thinking maybe I should text him, the elevator dings, and he walks off with a group of four other individuals.

Two of them are laughing at something on a phone screen while Jarrett and a middle-aged woman converse quietly, Jarrett speaking animatedly with his hands as she listens.

The first sight of him makes my stomach drop.

Dressed in relaxed navy slacks and a crisp cream button down, he looks every bit relaxed as he does business-ready. His head is freshly shaved, beard trimmed neat, and though he's smiling as he talks with the woman, I see the same evidence in him that I saw in Kade, that I've seen in myself, proof that sleep hasn't come easy.

Dark bags under his eyes.

Slumped shoulders.

Strained concentration as he tries to listen to the woman's response to whatever he's said.

Emotion tries to strangle me as I stand, tries to tear me from where I stand on that marble floor and steer me outside before he can see me.

But I'm tired of running.

I'm ready to face him — even if I know it will hurt like hell.

He almost blows past me, and I'm fully prepared to chase him out into the streets. But just as his colleagues sweep through the revolving door, he stops dead in his tracks, stilling like a deer spotted by a hunter before he slowly, carefully, cranks his neck to look at me.

A myriad of emotions wash over him in a split second, everything from shock and delight to pain and fear. I watch each of them show themselves in his eyes, his lips, his stature before he takes a tentative step toward me.

The woman he was speaking to pops her head back to check on him, and he tells her to go on, that he'll catch up. Her eyes skirt to me suspiciously before she leaves, and then it's just the two of us in the vast, echoing lobby.

His eyes warm the closer he gets, one hand holding a messenger bag, while the other slips into the pocket of his slacks. He takes his time trailing the length of me, no doubt noticing that while I wear the same pained expression as he does, I look better than I have since the day he showed back up at Palm South.

I think he knows already, before I can say a word.

"Hello," he says after a long pause.

I offer a small, apologetic smile in return. "Hi."

Jarrett sniffs, looking away from me and out the large windows before his gaze reluctantly travels back. "I think I need a drink for this."

He doesn't say another word before turning for the door, and I follow him outside, the two of us walking silently next to each other until we duck inside a small bar a block over.

It's already filling up with patrons in business-casual dress, each of them eager for happy hour after a hellish day. Jarrett orders himself a rye whiskey neat, and I opt for a glass of red wine, knowing I won't be drinking much of it so I can say what I need to with a clear head.

I wait until Jarrett takes the first sip of his drink, hissing through his teeth a bit when he does. And when he finally looks at me again, his dark eyes shielded under bent brows, he sighs.

"Well," he says. "You've been ignoring me. I guess I should have known this was coming."

"I'm sorry," I breathe. "I... I've been a coward."

He shakes his head once, frowning even more, but doesn't say anything else.

"I don't know where to start," I admit.

"How about by telling me you've made your choice," Jarrett says, and then his eyes hit mine again. "And that it's not me."

My nose stings. "I'm sorry," I whisper.

He nods, looking away again, his eyes on the bottles lining the back of the bar.

"I loved you," I start, not knowing where the right place is, just knowing I have to say *something*. "And... I love you still."

His eyes shoot to mine.

"Maybe that will never change," I confess. "I think... I think there's a part of me that will always belong to you."

He swallows, Adam's apple bobbing hard in this throat.

"But what we have," I continue, circling the rim of my glass with my fingertip. "At least, what we have *now*... it's purely physical. It's chemistry and carnal need," I say, meeting his gaze once more. "But it's not real love. I think we both know that."

"It could be."

"Maybe," I say. "But... I'm not sure what we have anymore, Jarrett — past that desire to fuck."

The words slap him across the face, the sting visible to anyone around us.

"I don't trust you," I admit on a cracked voice. "And I don't think you trust me, either. Do we want each other? Yes. But you broke me. And I broke you, too."

Jarrett nods, taking a long pull of his whiskey.

He doesn't say a word.

"I've done a lot of thinking in the past few months, a lot of self-reflection, a lot of thinking about why I feel the way I do, why this has been so hard for all of us." I tilt my head a bit. "It's the strangest thing, thinking back to that time when we were together. Because... *so much* of the time, we weren't *actually* together."

Jarrett opens his mouth to argue, but I continue.

"Think about it. The first time we met, we fucked in a parking lot. Then, we found out you were the graduate assistant for one of my professors." I wet my lips. "I became your mouse. You wanted me because you couldn't have me, because I was off-limits, and I loved to play that game, to make you want me, to parade other guys in front of you to drive you mad until you snapped. And it worked. You *did* snap, and then..."

"We dated."

"Kind of," I admit. "But think about it. For a long while, we played games. Mostly me, I admit that, but even when I showed up at your door and confessed that I had deeper feelings, I remember being so scared I nearly vomited on my way up to your place."

His brows fold in at that.

"You scared the shit out of me," I whisper. "Because I knew, even then, that you aren't the kind of man who is kept by any woman."

I know the look washing over him in this moment, that realization, that uncomfortable feeling of being viewed under a microscope and having someone peg you down in a way you didn't even know yourself.

"When we were *finally* official, you left. And I don't blame you for that," I say quickly when I see him growing on the defense. "You were going after your dream job, what you want in life, and you should. But that's what I'm saying. How much time did we *really* spend together, where it was truly us?" I pause. "How much do you really know about me, other than the way I moan your name?"

"Jess..."

"You wanted me so badly when you couldn't have me," I whisper, tears blurring my vision of him. "And then found me an annoyance as soon as you did. When you were in New York, I felt like a stain on your shirt that you couldn't get rid of, like a rash you so desperately wanted to hide."

"I came to visit you," he argues. "I took you and your friends out, I—"

"Once, Jarrett," I interrupt. "One time. And we fought even then."

Silence.

"The only reason you want me now is because you came back and I was taken. You get a rush over me being off-limits to you — especially when you can break those walls and prove that I still want you, despite the consequences."

He swallows hard.

"It's toxic — to *both* of us. And I won't do it. I refuse to participate any longer."

Jarrett's shoulders slump, and he shakes his head, an argument building on his lips.

"If you wouldn't have had to come back to Florida for work," I say, reaching over to squeeze his forearm and make him look at me. "You never would have thought of me again."

"I thought of you every day."

His words kick me in the chest.

"Maybe so," I say softly. "But you don't love me. You love the chase."

His jaw tics, and he shakes his head, but tears his gaze away from me, unable to stare the truth in the eyes.

"I want happiness for you," I say after a long while. "I do. You are such a—"

"If you say *great guy*, I swear to God, I'm pitching myself off the first rooftop I can find."

I swallow, picking at my nail polish with my eyes on my hands. "I'm sorry."

Jarrett sighs, deep and heavy, like all the hope he was holding onto left him with that breath. He holds his tumbler in his hand lightly, giving it a toss with his wrist, and then downs what whiskey is left before turning to face me.

"I hope my brother knows how lucky he is."

I try to smile, but it falls flat. Instead, the tears I've been holding at bay slip free, the realization that Jarrett and I will never be sinking in and tearing my soul to shreds.

"And if he ever fucks up," Jarrett warns.

"I know," I say before he can finish, reaching for his hand. He turns his palm up, letting me hold him, and I squeeze his hand tightly. "I know."

He nods, his eyes searching mine, and tears well in his eyes before he sniffs and jumps up without warning. His hand pulls from mine, digging into his pocket for his wallet. He slaps down a twenty to cover our drinks, and I slowly stand to mirror him.

"So, I guess this is it," he says.

"I guess so."

He bites the inside of his cheek, and then opens his arms, and without hesitation, I slip into them, both of us sighing when he wraps me in a tight embrace.

"You're wrong about one thing," he says against the shell of my ear. "I *do* love you."

I nod against his neck, squeezing him tight, and we hold that hug for just a second, or was it a lifetime, before finally letting go.

And we do.

We let go.

In that moment, with that final embrace, I feel the last bit of Jarrett that has always stuck to my heart washing away, the waves taking him out to the Sea of the Past. And when I look into his eyes, I know he feels it, too.

The cleanse.

"Goodbye, Jarrett," I whisper.

And then I leave him behind.

***

Later that night, Kade draws lines on my skin with his fingertips, my back to his chest, his chin on my shoulder as he holds me.

"So," I say after a while, rolling in his arms to face him. Every limb is sore from how much we've made up lately, but it's the delicious kind that I don't mind at all. "What now?"

"What now?" he repeats, kissing my nose before he looks up at the ceiling, thinking. "Hmm... well, I'm thinking we might need a little food, maybe a shower, and then I have this position I want to try where—"

I flick his forehead, laughing when he pins me down into the sheets and kisses me breathless. I finally push him away and hold my hands to his chest where he balances over me.

"I'm serious," I say. "With all this behind us... now what?"

Kade smiles, smoothing my hair out of my face. "Well, I've got a semester left of school," he says. "*You've* got a busy wedding season coming up in the spring. And then..." He shrugs. "The world is our oyster."

"What does that mean?"

He laughs, leaning down to press a brief kiss to the frown line between my brows. "It means we don't have to have it all figured out right now. We're young, Jess. Young and *madly* in love. I'm finishing up school, you're starting a new career, and we're building a future... together."

The corner of my mouth lifts. "We are, aren't we?"

"I don't know that I'm ready to dive in as head-first as your bestie has but..."

I snort laugh. "Oh no, I'm not ready for babies either. Although, I *do* plan to spoil the shit out of hers."

"Oh! Can we be the cool aunt and uncle who gives the kid ungodly amounts of sugar and loud toys and then send them home again at the end of the day?"

"Obviously. I also plan to buy them any and everything they want so that they know when they're old enough to need beer for a high school party, Aunt Jess has their back."

"That's illegal."

I snort. "Like that ever stops anyone."

Kade chuckles, settling more in-between my thighs, and when he nestles into my warmth, I feel him start growing hard again.

"Insatiable," I whisper against his lips as he kisses me.

"Only when it comes to you." He nibbles my lip before pushing up to balance on his elbows again. His eyes search mine, his smile warm and just... *happy*. So, so happy. "I don't have a ten-year plan for you, Jess. Or a five-year one or hell, even one for the next three-hundred-and-sixty-five days. But I can tell you this. One day, I will get on my knee, and I will ask you to spend your life with me — officially, because to be clear, you've already agreed to that whether you know it or not."

I laugh, but it's against the tears building at his words.

"And one day, I'll cry like a fucking baby when you walk down the aisle to me. And one day, I'll hold your hand when you give birth to the first of our twelve babies."

"*Twelve*?!" I laugh. "And what if I don't want any of those things? What if I said I never want to get married or have kids?"

Kade shrugs. "Then I would say whatever you want in this life, wherever it may take you — count me in. Traveling the world, joining the circus, partying until we're too old to take drugs," he says as I laugh. "Whatever you choose — I'm your co-pilot." He swallows. "For as long as you'll have me."

I curl my fingers in the hair at the nape of his neck, reaching up to press a kiss to his lips. "What if I want you longer than you want me?"

"Impossible."

"What if I drive you insane?"

"Oh, you *absolutely* will," he says, and I pinch his side. "But I wouldn't have it any other way."

I bite my lip when he rolls his hips against me, doing his best to distract me from this conversation — and it's working.

"So, no matter what comes next, it's me and you."

"Me and you," he echoes, kissing me deeply.

"I love the sound of that," I whisper, wrapping my ankles around his hips.

"And I love *you*."

With that promise, he captures my mouth with his, effectively silencing the conversation as he rolls against me once more.

And finally — *finally* — every jagged little piece of me falls into place.

Cassie

I should be getting ready for my last semi-formal.

I should be laughing with Skyler as she does my hair and I help her pick out the perfect accessories to go with the dynamite black dress she bought a few weeks ago for the occasion.

I should be taking Tera under my wing, showing her the ropes, passing the torch to her as Skyler and I leave and she starts the new line of our family.

Instead, I'm on a flight to Denver, my tail tucked firmly between my legs and what's left of my bleeding heart on my sleeve.

It's all I have to offer Adam. No apology will be enough. No amount of admitted regret can take back what I've done. Nothing I ever say or do will be able to atone for how I betrayed him in the most fundamental and hurtful way there is to betray someone you love.

In my heart, in the very pit of my gut, I know I'm walking into a losing battle. Like a soldier on the front line against an impossible force, I know I won't walk out a survivor. But I can't let him go without a fight. I can't let go of him without knowing I did everything I could to hold on.

A soft, quiet voice whispers in my ear that Adam loves me, that we can make it through anything, that it will all be okay — but I don't see how it ever could. Adam hasn't spoken to me even once in the three long weeks since I confessed what happened in Mexico.

I wouldn't speak to me, either.

For all I know, he's written me out of his life forever. For all I know, he's shacking up with any girl who looks his way and trying to fuck me out of his system. For all I know, he's moved past the grieving stage and right on to the *fuck her* stage where he firmly believes everything between us was a lie.

I cover my mouth against the bile burning my throat at the thought, closing my eyes and willing myself to calm down as the captain announces we're descending into Denver.

I was supposed to be on this flight three weeks ago, flying in to spend a long holiday weekend with the man I love.

Instead, he went to try to secure our future.

And I put my mouth on another man.

If I hadn't already cried out every bit of moisture left in my body, I know I'd be sobbing once again. None of the girls have been successful at pulling me out of my depression — no matter how they tried. It's taken all my energy just to drag myself to class and pass my last finals. I barely passed them, my long run with all A's slipping from my fingers. I'll still graduate just fine, and I'm already set for Johns Hopkins, but it doesn't change the fact that not only did I fail Adam, but I've failed myself, too.

Regret and longing sour in my gut as I grab my carry-on out of the top compartment once we land, wheeling it behind me. My mind races, trying to grasp words out of thin air, to string together the right declarations that will somehow prove to Adam that I'm still worthy of his love.

How can I convince him when I don't even know that I believe it myself?

My phone pings to life when I turn it off airplane mode, texts from both Tera and Skyler filling the screen. They send pictures of their outfits, of them doing our sorority hand sign in front of the house, and the latest is them piled into the back of the limo, loading up to go to dinner and then to the venue.

Fire burns my chest as I type back that I miss them and hope they have the best time. Skyler just types in all caps GO GET YOUR MAN while Tera sends a string of emojis.

I'm still staring at the pictures when I hear my name called.

"Cassie?"

My feet stop moving.

My heart stops beating.

My lungs cease to provide air as the familiarity of that voice sinks in.

Everything comes back to life in slow motion, and I turn just the same, finding Adam sitting in a chair by gate C45. His phone balances in his hand, brows furrowed together as he blinks over and over like it can't actually be me he's seeing.

When he realizes it is, he's off his feet in the next instant, his phone dropped on top of his duffle bag and left behind.

I immediately start to cry.

And then I'm swept into his arms.

I clutch him so tight my knuckles whiten, and he crushes me in return, soothing me as I sob and struggle to catch my breath.

"Cassie? What are you doing here?" he asks, but still, he holds me, kissing my hair before pulling back to search my eyes. "Why didn't you tell me you were coming?"

"I didn't want you to tell me not to."

My bottom lip quivers with the admission, and Adam sighs, shaking his head and pulling me into his chest again. "Oh, baby. I would never say that."

"Not even after the monster I've become?"

His laugh is soft, blowing up the tendrils of my messy hair. "You're not a monster."

"Sir," a stern voice interrupts behind us. "Please don't leave your bags unattended."

It's one of the flight attendants working the gate desk, and Adam nods, grabbing my hand and my bag before pulling us both over to where he was sitting. When we get there, he drops his hold on my bag, but keeps his hold on me.

"I'm supposed to be boarding a flight in twenty minutes," he says with a laugh. "To come see *you*."

I sniff, looking at the monitor behind him. Sure enough, Miami is written in big letters at the top.

"You were coming to see me?"

"I was going to crash semi-formal," he says on another laugh. "I mean, come on — you know it's my favorite thing to do when it comes to you."

"I seem to remember it being *me* who crashed through your bedroom window last year."

"True," he admits. "And then we went to semi in our pajamas."

The memory makes him smile, but it makes tears well in my eyes again, and I cover my mouth, shaking my head as they relentlessly fall free.

"Hey," Adam says softly, pulling me into his chest. "Shhh, it's okay, it's okay."

"No, it's not," I sob, wiping my nose with the back of my wrist as I press space between us. "Adam, why were *you* coming to *me*? I'm the one who messed up. I'm the one who... who..."

I can't even finish the words, and Adam frowns, rubbing my arms. "Have you been torturing yourself this whole time?"

"How could I not?"

I sob harder, and Adam sighs, looking pointedly at an older man staring at us before saying, "A little privacy, please?" The man looks away, and Adam grabs our stuff and leads us to the corner of the waiting area, tucked between a wall and a window.

I finally find the strength to look into his eyes, my hands clinging to his shirt. "I'm so sorry, Adam."

"I know," he says. "I already know. Okay? Trust me — I've been on that side plenty of times to know you didn't mean to hurt me, and even more that it meant nothing to you."

"It didn't," I swear. "I was so drunk I don't even remember it, which I hate admitting, but it's true."

Adam just smooths his hand up and down my arm for a long moment, letting me breathe, willing me to steady my racing heart. His touch alone is enough to do it, and slowly, my tears start to dry.

And then I hiccup.

Adam smiles. "There's my girl."

"I hate myself," I whisper on another hiccup.

"Don't. Look at me," he says, lowering his gaze to mine. "*I'm* sorry, too. I should have made you more of a priority this semester, should have listened to you when you told me you missed me and we weren't spending enough time together. I was so focused on the fraternity, on the drama with the exec board, and then my focus shifted completely to getting a job in Baltimore. When the opportunity came up with Chandler, I just... I couldn't see all the ways it might threaten you or upset you because I was too zeroed in on what it would mean if I landed the job. I promised you last year that I wouldn't mess things up over this, and I meant it. But I failed you. I just hope you see that it's always been us in my mind — even if I didn't do things the right way."

"You were doing it for us," I say. "I know that now. I see it. But in the moment, I was just..."

"I know. And you had every right to be. I'm sorry I didn't follow up on my word to you. I'm sorry I ever made you doubt that there's anything or anyone more important to me than you."

That makes my nose sting again, and I stifle the tears threatening to spill. "How can you say that after what I did?"

"You fucked up," he says — simply, casually, as if I left my purse in a restaurant rather than kissed another man. "And you know what, so did I. I have. Multiple times. I mean, have you forgotten the absolute ass I made of myself in the first two years I knew you?"

I laugh a little at that.

"I don't care about some loser in Mexico," he says, waving his hand. "He might have got one kiss. But I want the rest of them. I want them all, every kiss from here on out, from now until the end of time."

"So dramatic," I tease.

"Have I ever been any other way?"

I shake my head, tentatively leaning into him. "So, you forgive me?"

"I do. And I'm sorry it took me so long. I hate that I made you sick all this time. I know you've been sick, because I have been, too."

"It's been the worst three weeks of my life," I admit. "I thought I lost you. For *real*, this time."

"Silly girl," he says, lining my jaw with his thumb. "Were you not listening to me at Spring Break last year?"

I try to smile, but my chest is still so tight, it's impossible to hold in place.

"Cassie McBee," he says softly, tilting my chin until I look into his eyes. "What did I say?"

I swallow. "That I'm your now. And your forever."

"Yes," he says. "And that means you're my pain in the ass and no one else's."

A little laugh breaks free from me at that, and before it can turn to tears, Adam pulls me in for a sweet, slow kiss.

"You know, I had a whole plan for tonight," he confesses, and it's then that I notice his hands trembling, his breath a little shaky. "Semi-formal has always held such significance for us. I almost fought Clay at your first one, nearly killed Grayson after he broke your heart at the second one, and came pretty close to losing you forever last year, thanks to my pride. We don't have the best track record when it comes to them, so I was really hoping to set that straight tonight."

"Well, I beat you to the punch," I tease. "I just... I couldn't go. I couldn't get dressed up and dance and pretend I'm okay."

"I was flying in for your graduation, too," he adds. "Which is in three days. So we need to get you back home."

I nod.

Adam sighs, still thumbing my jaw.

I frown, covering his shaking knuckle with my hand. "Are you okay?"

"About to shit myself, actually, thanks for asking."

I laugh, searching his eyes, confused. "What? Why are you—*ohmygod.*"

My hands fly over my mouth, eyes bulging out of my head as Adam carefully lowers down onto one knee.

Distantly, I hear the collective gasp around us, traveling strangers as shocked as I am as they pull out their cell phones and watch Adam dig into his jacket pocket.

"Like I said," he starts, freeing the box. "I had a whole plan for this. But I guess if we've learned anything by now, it's that plans don't ever work out the way we think they will. Not for us. The world loves to throw us curveballs, to test us, to throw every hurdle at us it can just to see if we'll break." He smiles then. "But we don't. We *won't*. We never could. Because you and me, Cassie? We're indestructible." A pause. "Just like diamond."

He pops the lid open, a chorus of squeals and swoons echoing all around us. Nestled inside the cream cushion is a delicate gold band with a solitaire round diamond glimmering in the light.

"Adam," I whisper, shaking my head, eyes flicking from the ring to him and back again.

"No more games, Cassie McBee. No more letting other people get in the way, or cursing bad timing, or letting miles stretch between us. I want you — *all* of you — from this very moment until my last full breath. I want to follow you to Baltimore and then to wherever you may go next. I want to be the only man who has the pleasure of cuddling you in your sweatpants and feeding you mint chocolate chip ice cream," he says, and another round of laughters and *awww's* reverberate around us. "I want to wipe away your tears, even if I cause them. I want to be the first one to call you doctor when you get that white coat — and I know you will. But more than anything else," he breathes, taking the ring from the box and holding it in his shaking fingertips. "I want you to know with every beat of your heart that I am yours, that you are everything to me, and that we can face anything this crazy universe throws at us. Together."

He reaches for my hand then — my left hand — and I tremble as he takes me in his grasp.

"Marry me, Cassie," he says, his green eyes shining where they look up at me. "Marry me, and I promise, I will spend all my life infuriating you."

A laugh rips from my chest, but tears invade my vision all the same as I nod, vigorously and relentlessly. "Yes," I whisper for good measure.

And he slips the ring on my finger.

The crowd at the gate cheers, whistles and claps and hoots and hollers ringing in our ears as Adam rushes to his feet and pulls me into his arms. I kiss him in a way that is *far* from airport appropriate, but I don't care. No one else exists to me in this moment. It's just me and Adam floating on a cloud, his promise weighing down my finger, his love forever in my heart.

"Thank God you said yes," he breathes into my ear for just me to hear. "It would have been *really* embarrassing if you'd said no."

I laugh. "You knew my answer before you even thought to ask."

"You've been known to surprise me."

"That's true," I concede. When we pull back, I hold my hand up between us, moving my finger at the shiny, unfamiliar ring now occupying it. "Wow," I breathe.

"Do you like it?"

"I would have said yes to an onion ring."

He laughs, but I can't take my eyes off the rock.

"Damn, that would have been a lot more affordable. Why don't we return this one and just hit Burger King on the—"

I press my finger to his lips to shush him, and then kiss him to silence him even more, allowing him nothing but a satisfied chuckle against my mouth.

"Alright, before I lose myself completely and check us into the nearest airport hotel, we need to go beg that flight attendant to give us another ticket for this flight."

I frown. "Wait, we're still going?"

"Are you kidding? It's your last semi-formal. Besides," he says, kissing my hand. "We've got to get you graduated."

Graduated.

I've been so lost in my heartache that I haven't had time to let it sink in, that this is it, this is the end.

My time at Palm South University is almost up.

Adam collects my bag and then his, shrugging the duffle over his shoulder as he wheels mine behind him. Then, his blazing eyes find mine, and he crooks a smile.

“Ready?”

There he is. My fiancé. My future husband. The man who owns me, body and soul.

I slip my arm around his, the diamond on my finger catching the light. And I know that no matter what happens next, life will be the biggest adventure with him by my side.

“Ready.”

Skyler

"Okay, bitch," Jess says as soon as we're in my room. To call it *my room* at this point is kind of a stretch, seeing as how I have until tomorrow morning to have all my stuff moved out of the house. My sheets and comforter are the only thing still in place, everything else packed in boxes lining the walls. "Time to show me the money."

"You *really* don't believe me?" I ask.

"You *really* want her to prove it?" Cassie mirrors with a wrinkled nose.

Jess waves her off, popping one of the bottles of champagne we snuck into the house and covering the opening with her mouth to save any drops from spilling over. She snaps her fingers and points at me, then at the floor, telling me without words what she wants.

I laugh. "Alright, but remember you asked for it."

"Oh, God. *She* did but *we*—"

Erin doesn't have time to plead her case before I dramatically unzip my graduation gown, letting it fall to my feet in a puddle of polyester.

"Ow ow!" Ashlei screams as Cassie covers her eyes and Erin laughs uncontrollably.

Poor Tera, the newest edition to our room squad, is blushing so hard I could probably fry an egg on her cheek.

Jess just smirks, shaking her head and filling red Solo cups with champagne before divvying them out to everyone except Ashlei — who has a water bottle, instead. "I knew you weren't lying. I just wanted to see your tits."

"Well, take a long, hard look, baby," I say with a wink, jiggling them a little bit to further prove that I did, in fact, go commando under my gown.

"Does Kip know you did that?" Cassie asks, hands still over her eyes.

I pull a pair of sleep shorts and a tank top from one of my duffle bags and slip them on. "Please. He was the first to find out. Why do you think I was almost late?"

"I'm surprised you got him to let you come back here instead of straight to a hotel with him after that little fact," Ashlei muses.

"He's with the rest of the guys at Ralph's until we join them," Cassie answers for me. "Good thing we all picked smart men. They know sisters come first."

"Damn straight," Jess says, but eyes the glistening rock on Cassie's finger. "Although, is that still the case?"

"Always," Cassie promises, holding out her hand to admire the ring. "He's my future husband, yes. But you bitches are my soulmates." She wraps Tera in a hug next. "Yes, that includes you."

Tera squeezes her back. "I think I picked the best sorority on campus."

"Duh," Jess answers easily. "And you've got a legacy to uphold, so, allow me to bestow upon you three golden rules."

I roll my eyes as the rest of the girls groan in unison.

"Number one: sisters before misters, always. You've just been reminded of how long that one lasts. Rule two: always be the funnest bitch at Spring Break."

"Funnest, J-Love? Really? I think I need to see that degree you supposedly got..." Erin teases.

Jess waves her off. "And rule three: avoid dating brothers *at all costs*." She pauses. "But if you become an Eskimo sister? Well... whatever. It happens."

"A... what?" Tera asks.

"Listen, the only rule out of all of that is number one. And trust me," Cassie says, pulling her Little in closer. "It's not hard to follow."

"I'm going to miss you. It sucks I only had one semester with y'all here," Tera says to Cassie, her eyes finding me next.

"Don't worry. We won't be far," I promise her.

Erin gives Tera a sweet smile before wrapping her in a hug, too, and even Jess looks a little emotional before she covers it with declaring we all drink.

We clink our plastic cups together in the center, take a big gulp of champagne, and then climb into my bed.

Cassie is still in her gown, the other girls in beautiful dresses for the occasion, but we all flop onto the bed and cuddle up, not caring.

"This poor old bed," Erin says, patting the mattress. "She's seen more than she probably would have liked."

"She's definitely had her share of drama," I agree. "God, I can still remember us in here when you told us your master plan for Kip."

"Stop," Erin says, holding up her hand with a cringey smile. "That's a time in my life I would very much like to forget."

"I'm sure there are *many* things we'd classify in the *Happy to Leave That Shit Here* category," Ashlei says.

"Not me," Jess chimes in. "I don't have a single regret."

"Not one?" Cassie asks.

Jess frowns, thinking. "Nope. Not one. Well... except maybe when I was a dick to you and Bo, Lei," she amends. "I haven't quite forgiven myself for that."

Ashlei reaches over to squeeze Jess's ankle.

"I don't think I have any regrets, either," I say. "In fact, I don't think any of us should. We lived a lot of life in this house, on this campus."

"A lot of mistakes," Ashlei says.

"A lot of fun," Cassie adds.

"A lot of booze," Jess says with a tilt of her cup.

"A lot of sisterhood," Erin whispers, and when we turn to see her eyes welled with tears, we all smack her.

"Not yet!" Cassie warns. "Please, I've cried so much in the last month. Don't make me bawl again."

Erin laughs, wiping her face. "I can't help it. I mean, I've already graduated, you'd think it wouldn't be that emotional for me but... this is it. This is the last time we'll all be here, in this room, in this bed."

We all fall silent then, looking around the room, at each other, the words we can't say written all over our faces.

"Hey, maybe not the last time," Tera finally says. "Who knows? Maybe... Maybe I'll be president one day."

I swear, Erin beams so bright at her Great-Grand-Little that I'm surprised she doesn't steal all the wattage from every lightbulb in the house.

"You'd be an excellent president," Cassie says.

"Think the girls would be down with a cosplay themed social?" Tera asks with a smirk.

We all laugh, knowing that's answer enough.

"Well, you're all welcome into my bed in L.A. anytime," I say. "It's going to be a hell of a lot nicer than this one."

"I still can't believe you're moving across the country," Ashlei muses, absentmindedly rubbing her belly. "I mean, I *can*, because... well, because you're a badass. But, moving to Hollywood, starting a casino-event business..."

"Starting a *life* with Kip," Cassie adds.

"It's surreal," I say, smiling. "But... I'm ready. And with Kip entering his show into the film festival this upcoming summer? Who knows what life will bring us next."

"Riches," Jess says over a sip of champagne. "And I'm sure glad you bitches are taking care of our money, because the wedding planner life isn't one of fame and fortune, I'll tell you that."

"Yet," Ashlei says. "You just wait. You're already making a name for yourself, and you're only a year removed from college."

"Says the one who's likely to make partner at her agency before next year is up."

"I don't know," she says, looking down at her stomach with a serene smile. "I might take a little time off. Not a lot," she adds quickly, eyes wide when she looks at us again. "But... maybe a little."

"I don't blame you. I'd want to do the same thing," Cassie says.

"I can't wait to spoil the brat," Jess says. "Kade and I have already decided we're taking on the role of aunt and uncle for all of your little ones. So just be prepared for them to love us more than you."

"I feel like I should keep them far, *far* away from you once they're sixteen," Ashlei says with an arched brow.

Jess just gives her a mischievous smile in return.

"What about you, Little?" I ask Cassie, tapping her foot. "You ready to plan a wedding?"

"Not yet," she says with a laugh. "I need to get through medical school first."

Erin frowns. "Long engagement?"

"At least a few years."

"Okay, I'll allow that," Jess says, pointing her finger at Cassie. "But I will *not* allow you to elope like this bitch did." She points at Ashlei next. "I expect God-awful bridesmaid dresses and a proper bachelorette party and an open bar with a dance floor I can occupy all night long. Got it?"

"Yes, ma'am," Cassie says with a chuckle.

"I'm so envious of y'all who are *done* done with school," Erin says with a longing sigh. "Poor Cassie and I won't be free for years."

"But then she'll be a badass doctor and you'll be a badass prosecutor and Ashlei will be running the world from her and Brandon's yacht and Skyler will be throwing an illegal poker tournament *on* said yacht."

"And you'll be..." I prompt her.

She scoffs. "Probably banging Kade on the balcony."

"It *is* a rather fun place to canoodle," Ashlei says with a reminiscent sigh.

"Jess, seriously. What about you?" I ask. "Stop downplaying like you're not just as badass as all of us — if not all of us *combined*."

"Seriously — I don't know," she confesses. "And I think that's okay. I'm only twenty-three. I don't *need* to have everything figured out. All I know is, right now, I love my job, I love my boyfriend, I love my messy, no-direction life, and I *love* being here," she adds, grabbing us in a group hug. "Celebrating you bitches."

We're quiet for a moment, all of us lost in thought as we look around the room again, snuggling into each other's arms.

"We can't ever lose this," Cassie whispers. "No matter what happens, where life takes us... we always have to have each other."

"Come on, Grand Little," Erin says. "Didn't you know that when you rushed? Kappa Kappa Beta isn't just for four years." She shrugs. "It's for life."

Another silence falls over us, and my heart swells in my chest, tears pricking my eyes.

"Okay," I say, leaning up to face them all head on. "I don't want to get super mushy, but I have to say this, so you all just sit there and let me say it." I point at Jess. "Shut up," I tease before she can get the words out.

She smiles. "Fine. Two minutes only. Go."

I take a deep breath, looking at each of them. "I couldn't have survived the last four years without you. I mean it. I came into this university not knowing who I was or who I wanted to be, and while I still might be figuring that second part out, you girls loved me every step of the way. In the in-between," I whisper. "And I know if you loved me then, you'll love me always."

Ashlei squeezes my hand.

"Thank you for being my friends," I say, and then I can't help it — I start blubbering, which makes them all peg me with pillows before we're wrapped in a tight group hug, our heads resting on each other as we sigh and soak it all in.

"We shouldn't make the guys wait all night," Ashlei says. "Especially since I'm not sure I trust Brandon with a bunch of ex-frat boys."

"Technically, Kade still *is* one for another semester," Jess reminds her.

Ashlei taps her nose. "Even more reason to get to Ralph's."

"You're just being driven mad by your hormones and want to sneak off with Mr. Church," Erin teases.

Ashlei shrugs, not denying as we all start making moves.

"Wait!" Cassie cries out before we can get off the bed. She jumps off long enough to grab her phone before piling back in, and we all huddle in close so she can snap a selfie.

She flips to the camera roll to show it to us, and for a long time, we just stare at the picture, at our smiles, our red, puffy eyes.

"I love you," Jess whispers, wiping her tears before they can fall. "All of you. So much."

We wrap her up in another fierce hug and stay there, fighting back emotion for as long as we can before Jess claps her hands and hops up first.

"Alright! That's enough. Come on," she says with a wicked smile, yanking us up off the bed one by one. "Skyler, put on a dress. Cassie, ditch the gown. The rest of you, in the bathroom so we can fix our hair. And in ten minutes exactly, I'm calling a cab and we're going to Ralph's one last time."

"One last time," I echo.

"Guys," Cassie whines, about to cry again, but Ashlei smacks her arm.

"No," she warns with a laugh. She points at Tera next. "Get your Big in line, Tera."

"Aye-aye, captain," she salutes.

Once we're dressed and ready, we link our arms together as we walk across the yard to where the cab waits. But Erin pulls us to a stop at the street, making us all turn back toward the Kappa Kappa Beta house.

Memories flash like rave lights in my mind — socials and formals, sisterhood events and boys snuck into our rooms, Spring Breaks planned and Halloween costumes assembled, happy tears... and plenty of sad ones, too.

We stand there for a long while before Erin sighs, turning us toward the cab.

"Come on, girls," she says. "Let's make it a night we'll never forget."

And as we join our guys at the bar, I start to feel it — this unnamable spark.

It flickers to life when Bear wraps me in a hug, telling me for the hundredth time tonight how proud he is of me. It grows a little stronger when he then turns and takes my Big into his arms, his eyes on her like she's everything his world revolves around.

That spark burns brighter at the sight of Brandon's hand on Ashlei's stomach, her eyes wide and bright as she stares up at him before he leads her to the dance floor. It nearly blinds me when Adam takes Cassie's hand in his, kissing her ring, and then her lips.

Tera joins up with a group of our active sisters at the bar, taking pictures and laughing with young women I *know* will play a huge role in her life now and forever.

Jess and Kade order a round of shots, doing some awkward kind of hand dance at the bar that makes us all laugh and sets the spark into a full-blown fire.

But I can't name it — not until the exact moment Kip slides up behind me, wrapping his arms around my waist and setting his chin on my shoulder. He kisses the sensitive skin under my ear, and I sigh, warmth and light flooding through me.

And then I feel it in my bones, deep in my soul, the truth that anchors us all.

This isn't the end.

No, this is only just the beginning.

MORE FROM KANDI STEINER

The Kings of the Ice Series
Step into the high-stakes world of professional hockey, where passion burns as fiercely as the ice beneath their blades. The *Kings of the Ice* series is a collection of sizzling, emotional sports romances filled with raw tension, forbidden love, and heart-pounding action—on and off the ice. Whether it's a second chance at love, an enemies-to-lovers feud, or a slow burn that leaves you breathless, these stories will melt your heart while keeping you hooked until the final buzzer. Perfect for fans of angst, steam, and unforgettable happily-ever-afters.

The Red Zone Rivals Series
Welcome to the ruthless world of college football, where rivalries are fierce, emotions run high, and love is the ultimate endgame. **The** *Red Zone Rivals* series delivers unforgettable stories packed with forbidden romance, heart-stopping drama, and swoon-worthy heroes fighting for glory on and off the field. From delicious fake dating tension to second chances that will steal your breath, these angsty, steamy romances are perfect for readers who love a little heartbreak before the happily-ever-after.

The Becker Brothers Series
Four brothers finding love in a small Tennessee town that revolves around a whiskey distillery with a dark past — including the mysterious death of their father.

The Best Kept Secrets Series
Charlie's marriage is dying. She's perfectly content to go down in the flames, until her first love shows back up and reminds her the other way love can burn.

A Love Letter to Whiskey
An angsty, emotional romance between two lovers fighting the curse of bad timing.

Close Quarters
A summer yachting the Mediterranean sounded like heaven to Jasmine after finishing her undergrad degree. But her boyfriend's billionaire boss always gets what he wants. And this time, he wants her.

Make Me Hate You
Jasmine has been avoiding her best friend's brother for years, but when they're both in the same house for a wedding, she can't resist him — no matter how she tries.

The Wrong Game
Gemma's plan is simple: invite a new guy to each home game using her season tickets for the Chicago Bears. It's the perfect way to avoid getting emotionally attached and also get some action. But after Zach gets his chance to be her practice round, he decides one game just isn't enough. A sexy, fun sports romance.

The Right Player
She's avoiding love at all costs. He wants nothing more than to lock her down. Sexy, hilarious and swoon-worthy, The Right Player is the perfect read for sports romance lovers.

On the Way to You
It was only supposed to be a road trip, but when Cooper discovers the journal of the boy driving the getaway car, everything changes. An emotional, angsty road trip romance.

Weightless
Young Natalie finds self-love and romance with her personal trainer, along with a slew of secrets that tie them together in ways she never thought possible.

Revelry
Recently divorced, Wren searches for clarity in a summer cabin outside of Seattle, where she makes an unforgettable connection with the broody, small town recluse next door.

Say Yes
Harley is studying art abroad in Florence, Italy. Trying to break free of her perfectionism, she steps outside one night determined to Say Yes to anything that comes her way. Of course, she didn't expect to run into Liam Benson...

Washed Up
Gregory Weston, the boy I once knew as my son's best friend, now a man I don't know at all. No, not just a man. A doctor. And he wants me...

The Christmas Blanket
Stuck in a cabin with my ex-husband waiting out a blizzard? Not exactly what I had pictured when I planned a surprise visit home for the holidays...

Black Number Four
A college, Greek-life romance of a hot young poker star and the boy sent to take her down.

The Palm South University Series
#1 NYT Bestselling Author Rachel Van Dyken says, "If Gossip Girl and Riverdale had a love child, it would be PSU." This angsty college series will be your next guilty addiction.

Tag Chaser
She made a bet that she could stop chasing military men, which seemed easy — until her knight in shining armor and latest client at work showed up in Army ACUs.

Song Chaser
Tanner and Kellee are perfect for each other. They frequent the same bars, love the same music, and have the same desire to rip each other's clothes off. Only problem? Tanner is still in love with his best friend.

ABOUT THE AUTHOR

KANDI STEINER is a *USA Today* and #1 Amazon Bestselling Author living in Tennessee. Best known for writing "emotional rollercoaster" stories, she loves bringing flawed characters to life and writing about real, raw romance — in all its forms. No two Kandi Steiner books are the same, and if you're a lover of angsty, emotional, and inspirational reads, she's your gal.

An alumna of the University of Central Florida, Kandi graduated with a double major in Creative Writing and Advertising/PR with a minor in Women's Studies. Her love for writing started at the ripe age of 10, and in 6th grade, she wrote and edited her own newspaper and distributed to her classmates. Eventually, the principal caught on and the newspaper was quickly halted, though Kandi tried fighting for her "freedom of press."

She took particular interest in writing romance after college, as she has always been a hopeless romantic and found herself bursting at the seams with love stories she was eager to tell.

When Kandi isn't writing, you can find her reading books of all kinds, planning her next adventure, or pole dancing (yes, you read that right). She enjoys live music, traveling, hiking, yoga, spending quality time with her family (fur babies included) and soaking up the sweetness of life.

CONNECT WITH KANDI:

NEWSLETTER: kandisteiner.com/newsletter
FACEBOOK: @kandisteiner
FACEBOOK READER GROUP (Kandiland): facebook.com/groups/kandilandks
INSTAGRAM: @kandisteiner
TIKTOK: @authorkandisteiner
WEBSITE: kandisteiner.com

Kandi Steiner may be coming to a city near you! Check out her "events" tab on her website to see all the signings she's attending in the near future.